Classic Works
from
Women Writers

Classic Works from Women Writers

Introduction by A. J. Odasso

Canterbury Classics

San Diego

Canterbury Classics
An imprint of Printers Row Publishing Group
10350 Barnes Canyon Road, Suite 100, San Diego, CA 92121
www.canterburyclassicsbooks.com

Printers Row Publishing Group is a division of Readerlink Distribution Services, LLC. Canterbury Classics is a registered trademark of Readerlink Distribution Services, LLC.

All correspondence concerning the content of this book should be addressed to Canterbury Classics, Editorial Department, at the above address.

Publisher: Peter Norton
Associate Publisher: Ana Parker
Publishing/Editorial Team: April Farr, Kelly Larsen, Kathryn C. Dalby
Editorial Team: JoAnn Padgett, Melinda Allman, Dan Mansfield, Traci Douglas
Production Team: Jonathan Lopes, Rusty von Dyl

Cover and endpaper design by Ray Caramanna

Library of Congress Cataloging-in-Publication Data available on request.

ISBN: 978-1-68412-554-8

PRINTED IN CHINA

22 21 20 19 18 1 2 3 4 5

CONTENTS

INTRODUCTION

The women whose works are collected in this volume represent no less than a selection of the most distinct and artistically accomplished voices to emerge in Anglophone literature between the seventeenth and twentieth centuries. Doubtless, the reader will find a familiar entry point and touchstone in Agatha Christie, whose broad and brilliant appeal has earned her the undisputed title of best-selling writer of all time; likewise, Mary Wollstonecraft Shelley is now recognized as the founder of an entire genre. In previous centuries, the survival of women writers' work with their names attached—recognition beyond the finality of death—was relatively rare and therefore a luxury. Although such accomplished figures as Marie de France, Margery Kempe, and Julian of Norwich have survived from the Middle Ages with both their names and bodies of work startlingly intact, what sets the women in these pages apart is not only the prolific and accessible nature of their work but also our access to details about their lives.

In the course of this literary tour, you will encounter names both familiar and unfamiliar. What makes these women stand out is that their works were recognized for their exceptional merit and that they were published and circulated accordingly. Each of them led a diverse and active life beyond print, engaging with both their texts and their audiences in the public sphere. What's more, their triumphs and losses informed their work at every turn.

As with so many literary journeys, it is often most enlightening to begin at the end. In the case of this volume, starting at the end helps us to appreciate why an anthology of classic writing by women is both timely and crucial. At the back of this book, the reader will discover three short poems—"Barter," "There Will Come Soft Rains," and "Winter Stars"—from Sara Teasdale. Writing against the ominous, all-pervasive backdrop of World War I, Teasdale underscores, with dazzling and introspective precision, the imperative of finding transcendence in what fleeting beauties the world has to offer. In the final stanzas of "Winter Stars," which appeared in her 1920 collection *Flame and Shadow*, she writes:

> From windows in my father's house,
> Dreaming my dreams on winter nights,
> I watched Orion as a girl
> Above another city's lights.

Years go, dreams go, and youth goes too,
The world's heart breaks beneath its wars,
All things are changed, save in the east
The faithful beauty of the stars.

The intrinsic musicality of Teasdale's language was consistently praised by her contemporaries and critics, although she never attained what might be considered "major poet" status in her short lifetime. After a comfortable St. Louis childhood marked by solitary confinement due to illness, a divorce sought out of intense loneliness resulting from her husband Ernst Filsinger's constant business travel, and some years of wistful rekindled friendship in New York with former suitor and poet Vachel Lindsay, Teasdale committed suicide by overdosing on sleeping pills in 1933. She was forty-eight.

What is rarely emphasized—let alone celebrated—in classroom discussion of Teasdale's verse is that she was the recipient of the first Columbia Poetry Prize in 1918 (for her fourth collection, *Love Songs*, published the previous year). This award was later to be renamed the Pulitzer Prize for Poetry. It is both shameful and shocking how seldom Teasdale is recognized for having been not only the first woman to attain this coveted honor but also the first winner of the prize. Teasdale's verse at the end of this volume—when considered alongside the details of her brief, fraught life—demonstrate precisely why an anthology on the subject of women's writing remains more urgent than ever. It is imperative that we recognize the transcendence of these writers and their works.

Traversing backward through these pages from the precedent set by Teasdale's example, the reader will find still more work from women poets who, although their names will likely be recognizable from standard high school and university English syllabuses, are rarely given the depth of consideration they are due in comparison to the time spent analyzing their male counterparts. Gertrude Stein's 1914 experimental Modernist volume, *Tender Buttons*, is a prime example. A sequence of meditations on everyday objects, consumables, and places, its premise is deceptively simple. Thanks to Stein's playful, riddlelike, and highly unorthodox use of language, the words for her subjects take on as much sensory weight as the concrete things they signify.

Stein—not only a poet but also a playwright, novelist, and art collector—spent her seventy-two colorful years between Pennsylvania, California, and France. After making Paris her home in 1903, Stein and her partner, Alice B. Toklas, hosted an interdisciplinary arts salon frequented by such luminaries as Ernest Hemingway, F. Scott Fitzgerald, Ezra Pound, Henri Matisse, and Pablo Picasso. Stein authored more than fifty works across the genres in which she worked to staggering acclaim. Among them was her 1903 *Q.E.D. (Quod Erat Demonstrandum)*, one of the first coming-out narratives ever to be published.

Her longevity and literary successes stand as a testament to her immense talent and incisive wit, as well as to the groundbreaking contributions she made to the Modernist movement. Her forays into both prose and verse were highly experimental, frequently stream-of-consciousness in narrative style, and answered to such approaches in visual art as Cubism, symbolism, collage, and other nontraditional movements. As an avid collector of modern art, particularly works from Picasso, Stein sought to thoroughly document her process in the fabric of her text. The images she creates are inimitably vivid.

Stein, like her contemporary Teasdale, also frequently penned lyrical ruminations, as well as scathing criticism, upon the subject of war—as did Massachusetts poet Amy Lowell, who posthumously won the Pulitzer Prize for Poetry in 1926 (for *What's O'Clock*). Lowell's poem in this volume, "Patterns," begins as a bucolic, stiff-starched stroll through a garden filled with daffodils and lime trees. However, the lovers' tryst at the heart of this narrative spins off, ominously mazelike, into weary and scathingly satirical territory. Lowell's closing lines in particular are marked by her characteristic, refreshing bluntness. Known for being brash and outspoken even at school, Lowell went on to defy her wealthy family's disapproval of educated women. Although she never pursued a higher degree, she became an avid reader and book collector. Lowell's public image was larger than life. Short and rotund, she wore high-necked dark gowns, a pince-nez, and kept her hair in a tightly wound bun. She smoked cigars constantly, gave public readings of both her own work and that of other poets, and frequently butted heads with critics. An unstoppable force with frequent presence in the press, she even graced the cover of *Time* magazine on March 2, 1925. Lowell's work is a master class in observation—both in outward voyeurism and in keen self-awareness.

Where the poets of this volume tend to address the experiences of feminine identity and existence through intensely personal (and often linguistically and structurally elaborate) micro-narratives, the prose writers develop their arguments in far more outward-facing frameworks. While poems can and often do contain dialogue and plot structure, the short stories and novels included in these pages convey a number of the same aspirations, observations, and themes on a broader scale. They engage with, and memorably express, the writers' experiences of both womanhood and humanity. Each of these works, while crucial in a feminist context, transcends the experience of gendered existence. They ask and seek to answer universal questions.

Mary Wollestonecraft Shelley, the mother of modern science fiction, masterfully and scathingly critiques a world dominated by fatal hubris in *Frankenstein*. When the reanimated, so-called monster is abandoned by his neurotic and self-centered creator, he struggles to comprehend the cruelty he faces at every turn. Through Shelley's masterful use of suspense and satire, the monster's experience speaks to the experience of every marginalized population. Embedded in the monster's struggle for acceptance, legitimacy, and the recognition of his full humanity is the experience not of inherently lacking a voice, but of actively being denied one. Similarly, no female character in Shelley's seminal tour de force—from Elizabeth to Justine to the ill-fated female monster—has complete agency, let alone a say in her (inevitably tragic) fate. Shelley's parents were staunch feminist/humanist writers who encouraged her talents from childhood, which no doubt accounts for the success of her ambitious, impressive writing career.

Even a century later, Charlotte Perkins Gilman, whose famous "The Yellow Wallpaper" joins Shelley's novel as a masterpiece of both physical and psychological horror, struggled to define her sense of self and make herself heard. Raised in a poor but supportive extended family that included Harriet Beecher Stowe (one of Gilman's paternal aunts), as a child Gilman was constantly berated at school for being what her teachers considered a poor student. Eventually, Gilman's tenacity and broad scope of natural creative inclinations permitted her to enroll in the Rhode Island School of Design. A talented painter, she was able to support herself as an artist of trade cards (precursors to the modern business card), and she also supplemented her income by tutoring students in a range of subjects. Following her marriage to Charles Walter Stetson and the birth of her daughter, Katharine Beecher Stetson, Gilman suffered a severe bout of postpartum depression. From this experience, "The Yellow Wallpaper" emerged; the captivating follow-up essay in which Gilman explained her writing process is also included in this anthology. Gilman's unflinching explorations of paranoia, mental illness, and self-doubt speak of being cast as an unreliable narrator in her own existence.

The inclusion of Agatha Christie's *The Mysterious Affair at Styles* as an opener for this volume states an unapologetic and necessary agenda from the beginning. Responsible for sixty-six detective novels and fourteen short-story collections, as well as six romance novels and a play penned under the alias of Mary Westmacott, Christie is the undisputed best-selling author of all time—with over two billion sales to her name. Penned in 1916, *Styles* was Christie's first published novel. Without it, the mystery genre would never have acquired Hercule Poirot, the fictional detective whose reputation reaches the heights achieved by Arthur Conan Doyle's Sherlock Holmes and Edgar Allan Poe's C. Auguste Dupin. In comparison to many of the women whose works appear here, Christie seems to have enjoyed a relatively content and stable life. The one notable exception occurred after her husband, Archibald Christie, asked for a divorce, when the writer vanished without a trace for ten days. The discovery of her car, driver's license, and clothes at Newlands Corner (a remote picnic spot above a chalk cliff in Surrey, England) led to wild speculation, but the writer was eventually located safe and sound in a Yorkshire hotel. Christie's later life, marked by a happier second marriage and exotic travel, resulted in such masterpieces as *Murder on the Orient Express*. No woman's life is an open book, and Christie's was certainly not without episodes of heartache and a subplot of unsolved mystery.

It is worth remembering, too, that humor is as intrinsic to literary craft as the serious. Mary Anne Evans, who wrote in the nineteenth century under the pen name George Eliot, had ample reason to toe the line of levity. In addition to seven novels, the best known of which are *The Mill on the Floss* and *Middlemarch*, Evans also wrote plays, verse, and essays. An example of the latter included in this anthology, "Silly Novels by Lady Novelists," lampoons without mercy the subjects upon which women in her day were expected to write. She was a proponent of sincere and realistic storytelling, and this is reflected fiercely in her works of fiction. Dogged by scandal in both marriages and affairs, Evans defiantly excelled in her substantial career as a critic, editor, and writer until she died in 1880.

In another striking departure from fiction, Jane Austen is represented in this volume by a letter she wrote to Fanny Knight on November 30, 1814. Responding to Fanny's earnest desire for advice on marriage, Austen impressed upon her then twenty-one-year-old niece that no one's opinion should carry greater weight in such a decision than Fanny's own. "Impressed with the impossible evil that may arise to [Fanny] from engaging [herself] to him," Austen implores her niece to exercise caution and prudence and not to rush engagement to her paramour. Concerned about how little opportunity Fanny has had to meet other potential partners, Austen's heartfelt insights ring true to so many of the themes for which her subtle, witty, and eternally appealing social novels have endured as reader favorites.

More sobering, in some ways, than the presence of several of her contemporaries, Virginia Woolf lends incomparable gravitas with *The Voyage Out*. Written between 1910 and 1912 and not published until 1915, her debut novel was produced while Woolf was in an exceptionally vulnerable state. Enduring depressive episodes so intense that at one point she attempted suicide, Woolf fashioned the sea voyage of her protagonist, Rachel Vinrace, as a receptacle for exploration and intersection of such themes as femininity, sexuality, and mortality. It is in this particular work that Woolf seems to have developed her inimitably poetic and unsettling narrative style, which would eventually reach its peak in *Mrs. Dalloway*—and fittingly, given that *The Voyage Out* first introduced Clarissa Dalloway as a character. At the time of her death by drowning at the age of fifty-nine, Woolf had written nine novels, forty-six short stories across five collections, and more than twice as many works of creative nonfiction. Where freedom was not possible for her due to social constraints and the constant presence of mental illness, Woolf nonetheless demonstrated that writing offered space in which a marginalized person, with the talent and means to do so, might explore the scope of their identity.

In similar fashion, Elizabeth Gaskell's (1810–1865) *Cousin Phillis* demonstrates sterling character development set within an unadorned yet compelling plot. Its restless protagonist, the adolescent Paul Manning, moves to a rural setting in which he becomes acquainted with his mother's extended family. He learns that his second cousin, Phillis Holman, is struggling with similar anxiety and a sense of displacement as she comes of age. This popular novel was published in four parts, giving it the distinction of having been a wildly successful serial.

The remaining pieces included in this anthology—all works of short fiction—each continue in the vital work of contributing an inimitable style and invaluable perspective. Neither as constrained as verse, nor as sprawling as the average novel, the short story offers a compact framework in which writers, since the form's coming of age in the nineteenth century, have found freedom to construct self-contained narratives that are readable in a single sitting. As shown in the success of Gaskell's serialized novel, broadsheets and magazines were an innovative medium through which high-quality fiction was circulated to an increasingly literate public. The cultural elitism that had once acted as a barrier to such access began to disintegrate not only due to affordability and wide availability, but also thanks to the progressive themes frequently explored in the fiction of the day. Women writers were instrumental in addressing social inequalities—not just in the realm of gender, but also in those of race and class.

In "The Shadowy Third," Ellen Glasgow (1873–1945) offers a compassionate yet unsettling portrait of mental illness with an undercurrent of the supernatural. At the behest of Dr. Maradick, its first-person narrator, Miss Randolph, takes employment as the sickly Mrs. Maradick's nurse. Glasgow blurs the lines between internal and external causes of psychological trauma, exploring what it means to provide compassionate medical and pastoral care, as skillfully as she blurs the lines between mainstream literary fiction and the Gothic sensibility.

Meanwhile, "The Garden Party" by Katherine Mansfield (1888–1923) deftly examines issues of social class and mortality. Tensions within the well-to-do Sheridan family come to a head surrounding the planning of a garden party. Laura Sheridan, as the eldest daughter and the chief organizer of the soirée, feels torn between carrying out her mother's wishes and being respectful of the passing of Mr. Scott, their working-class neighbor. While Laura makes her decision and adheres to it, she must nonetheless face weighty (and rightly) self-imposed existential consequences. Questions of compassion, community, and decency abound.

Finally, Mary E. Wilkins Freeman (1852–1930), Grace MacGowan Cooke

(1863–1944), Willa Cather (1873–1947), and Edith Wharton (1862–1937) also contribute short stories whose shared defining feature is an earnest, determined, and innovative approach to the portrayal of impactful and thought-provoking perspectives. Freeman, who began writing as a teenager to support her struggling family, certainly understood the difference that a single determined voice could make in improving the lives of those around her. Cooke and her sister, Alice MacGowan, wrote collaboratively; their bodies of work, both joint and individually authored, frequently illustrated the plight and championed the cause of working women in the mills of Appalachia. In the same vein, Cather's well-loved novels offered a stark portrait of existence on the American frontier. Finally, Wharton's contribution to her time and place was no less revolutionary: she volunteered tirelessly during wartime and offered generous financial support to charitable organizations, with a particular focus on the displaced, injured, and unemployed. These women not only wrote boldly on provocative and necessary subjects but lived by courageous example.

Without the contributions of these brilliant writers, from a craft standpoint alone, the literary tradition of the English language would be indisputably poorer. From the standpoints of diversity and humanity, it would be irredeemable. Let us remember the imperative set by the anthologizing of these fine works—and, in reading them, transcend with these authors.

A. J. Odasso, MFA
Albuquerque, NM
April 6, 2018

THE MYSTERIOUS AFFAIR AT STYLES

Agatha Christie

Chapter I

I GO TO STYLES

The intense interest aroused in the public by what was known at the time as "The Styles Case" has now somewhat subsided. Nevertheless, in view of the world-wide notoriety which attended it, I have been asked, both by my friend Poirot and the family themselves, to write an account of the whole story. This, we trust, will effectually silence the sensational rumours which still persist.

I will therefore briefly set down the circumstances which led to my being connected with the affair.

I had been invalided home from the Front; and, after spending some months in a rather depressing Convalescent Home, was given a month's sick leave. Having no near relations or friends, I was trying to make up my mind what to do, when I ran across John Cavendish. I had seen very little of him for some years. Indeed, I had never known him particularly well. He was a good fifteen years my senior, for one thing, though he hardly looked his forty-five years. As a boy, though, I had often stayed at Styles, his mother's place in Essex.

We had a good yarn about old times, and it ended in his inviting me down to Styles to spend my leave there.

"The mater will be delighted to see you again—after all those years," he added.

"Your mother keeps well?" I asked.

"Oh, yes. I suppose you know that she has married again?"

I am afraid I showed my surprise rather plainly. Mrs. Cavendish, who had married John's father when he was a widower with two sons, had been a handsome woman of middle-age as I remembered her. She certainly could not be a day less than seventy now. I recalled her as an energetic, autocratic personality, somewhat inclined to charitable and social notoriety, with a fondness for opening bazaars and playing the Lady Bountiful. She was a most generous woman, and possessed a considerable fortune of her own.

Their country-place, Styles Court, had been purchased by Mr. Cavendish early in their married life. He had been completely under his wife's ascendancy, so much so that, on dying, he left the place to her for her lifetime, as well as the larger part of his income; an arrangement that was distinctly unfair to his two sons. Their step-mother, however, had always been most generous to them; indeed, they were so young at the time of their father's remarriage that they always thought of her as their own mother.

Lawrence, the younger, had been a delicate youth. He had qualified as a doctor but early relinquished the profession of medicine, and lived at home while pursuing literary ambitions; though his verses never had any marked success.

John practiced for some time as a barrister, but had finally settled down to the more congenial life of a country squire. He had married two years ago, and had taken his wife to live at Styles, though I entertained a shrewd suspicion that he would have preferred his mother to increase his allowance, which would have enabled him to have a home of his own. Mrs. Cavendish, however, was a lady who liked to make her own plans, and expected other people to fall in with them, and in this case she certainly had the whip hand, namely: the purse strings.

John noticed my surprise at the news of his mother's remarriage and smiled rather ruefully.

"Rotten little bounder too!" he said savagely. "I can tell you, Hastings, it's making life jolly difficult for us. As for Evie—you remember Evie?"

"No."

"Oh, I suppose she was after your time. She's the mater's factotum, companion, Jack of all trades! A great sport—old Evie! Not precisely young and beautiful, but as game as they make them."

"You were going to say—?"

"Oh, this fellow! He turned up from nowhere, on the pretext of being a second cousin or something of Evie's, though she didn't seem particularly keen to acknowledge the relationship. The fellow is an absolute outsider, anyone can see that. He's got a great black beard, and wears patent leather boots in all weathers! But the mater cottoned to him at once, took him on as secretary—you know how she's always running a hundred societies?"

I nodded.

"Well, of course the war has turned the hundreds into thousands. No doubt the fellow was very useful to her. But you could have knocked us all down with a feather when, three months ago, she suddenly announced that she and Alfred were engaged! The fellow must be at least twenty years younger than she is! It's simply bare-faced fortune hunting; but there you are—she is her own mistress, and she's married him."

"It must be a difficult situation for you all."

"Difficult! It's damnable!"

Thus it came about that, three days later, I descended from the train at Styles St. Mary, an absurd little station, with no apparent reason for existence, perched up in the midst of green fields and country lanes. John Cavendish was waiting on the platform, and piloted me out to the car.

"Got a drop or two of petrol still, you see," he remarked. "Mainly owing to the mater's activities."

The village of Styles St. Mary was situated about two miles from the little station, and Styles Court lay a mile the other side of it. It was a still, warm day in early July. As one looked out over the flat Essex country, lying so green and peaceful under the afternoon sun, it seemed almost impossible to believe that, not so very far away, a great war was running its appointed course. I felt I had suddenly strayed into another world. As we turned in at the lodge gates, John said:

"I'm afraid you'll find it very quiet down here, Hastings."

"My dear fellow, that's just what I want."

"Oh, it's pleasant enough if you want to lead the idle life. I drill with the volunteers twice a week, and lend a hand at the farms. My wife works regularly 'on the land.' She is up at five every morning to milk, and keeps at it steadily until lunchtime. It's a jolly good life taking it all round—if it weren't for that fellow Alfred Inglethorp!" He checked the car suddenly, and glanced at his watch. "I wonder if we've time to pick up Cynthia. No, she'll have started from the hospital by now."

"Cynthia! That's not your wife?"

"No, Cynthia is a protégée of my mother's, the daughter of an old schoolfellow of hers, who married a rascally solicitor. He came a cropper, and the girl was left an orphan and penniless. My mother came to the rescue, and Cynthia has been with us nearly two years now. She works in the Red Cross Hospital at Tadminster, seven miles away."

As he spoke the last words, we drew up in front of the fine old house. A lady in a stout tweed skirt, who was bending over a flower bed, straightened herself at our approach.

"Hullo, Evie, here's our wounded hero! Mr. Hastings—Miss Howard."

Miss Howard shook hands with a hearty, almost painful, grip. I had an impression of very blue eyes in a sunburnt face. She was a pleasant-looking woman of about forty, with a deep voice, almost manly in its stentorian tones, and had a large sensible square body, with feet to match—these last encased in good thick boots. Her conversation, I soon found, was couched in the telegraphic style.

"Weeds grow like house afire. Can't keep even with 'em. Shall press you in. Better be careful."

"I'm sure I shall be only too delighted to make myself useful," I responded.

"Don't say it. Never does. Wish you hadn't later."

"You're a cynic, Evie," said John, laughing. "Where's tea today—inside or out?"

"Out. Too fine a day to be cooped up in the house."

"Come on then, you've done enough gardening for today. 'The labourer is worthy of his hire,' you know. Come and be refreshed."

"Well," said Miss Howard, drawing off her gardening gloves, "I'm inclined to agree with you."

She led the way round the house to where tea was spread under the shade of a large sycamore.

A figure rose from one of the basket chairs, and came a few steps to meet us.

"My wife, Hastings," said John.

I shall never forget my first sight of Mary Cavendish. Her tall, slender form, outlined against the bright light; the vivid sense of slumbering fire that seemed to find expression only in those wonderful tawny eyes of hers, remarkable eyes, different from any other woman's that I have ever known; the intense power of stillness she possessed, which nevertheless conveyed the impression of a wild untamed spirit in an exquisitely civilised body—all these things are burnt into my memory. I shall never forget them.

She greeted me with a few words of pleasant welcome in a low clear voice, and I sank into a basket chair feeling distinctly glad that I had accepted John's invitation. Mrs. Cavendish gave me some tea, and her few quiet remarks heightened my first impression of her as a thoroughly fascinating woman. An appreciative listener is always stimulating, and I described, in a humorous manner, certain incidents of my Convalescent Home, in a way which, I flatter myself, greatly amused my hostess. John, of course, good fellow though he is, could hardly be called a brilliant conversationalist.

At that moment a well remembered voice floated through the open French window near at hand:

"Then you'll write to the Princess after tea, Alfred? I'll write to Lady Tadminster for the second day, myself. Or shall we wait until we hear from the Princess? In case of a refusal, Lady Tadminster might open it the first day, and Mrs. Crosbie the second. Then there's the Duchess—about the school fête."

There was the murmur of a man's voice, and then Mrs. Inglethorp's rose in reply:

"Yes, certainly. After tea will do quite well. You are so thoughtful, Alfred dear."

The French window swung open a little wider, and a handsome white-haired old lady, with a somewhat masterful cast of features, stepped out of it on to the lawn. A man followed her, a suggestion of deference in his manner.

Mrs. Inglethorp greeted me with effusion.

"Why, if it isn't too delightful to see you again, Mr. Hastings, after all these years. Alfred, darling, Mr. Hastings—my husband."

I looked with some curiosity at "Alfred darling." He certainly struck a rather alien note. I did not wonder at John objecting to his beard. It was one of the longest and blackest I have ever seen. He wore gold-rimmed pince-nez, and had a curious impassivity of feature. It struck me that he might look natural on a stage, but was strangely out of place in real life. His voice was rather deep and unctuous. He placed a wooden hand in mine and said:

"This is a pleasure, Mr. Hastings." Then, turning to his wife: "Emily dearest, I think that cushion is a little damp."

She beamed fondly on him, as he substituted another with every demonstration of the tenderest care. Strange infatuation of an otherwise sensible woman!

With the presence of Mr. Inglethorp, a sense of constraint and veiled hostility seemed to settle down upon the company. Miss Howard, in particular, took no pains to conceal her feelings. Mrs. Inglethorp, however, seemed to notice nothing unusual. Her volubility, which I remembered of old, had lost nothing in the intervening years, and she poured out a steady flood of conversation, mainly on the subject of the forthcoming bazaar which she was organizing and which was to take place shortly. Occasionally she referred to her husband over a question of days or dates. His watchful and attentive manner never varied. From the very first I took a firm and rooted dislike to him, and I flatter myself that my first judgments are usually fairly shrewd.

Presently Mrs. Inglethorp turned to give some instructions about letters to Evelyn Howard, and her husband addressed me in his painstaking voice:

"Is soldiering your regular profession, Mr. Hastings?"

"No, before the war I was in Lloyd's."

"And you will return there after it is over?"

"Perhaps. Either that or a fresh start altogether."

Mary Cavendish leant forward.

"What would you really choose as a profession, if you could just consult your inclination?"

"Well, that depends."

"No secret hobby?" she asked. "Tell me—you're drawn to something? Every one is—usually something absurd."

"You'll laugh at me."

She smiled.

"Perhaps."

"Well, I've always had a secret hankering to be a detective!"

"The real thing—Scotland Yard? Or Sherlock Holmes?"

"Oh, Sherlock Holmes by all means. But really, seriously, I am awfully drawn to it. I came across a man in Belgium once, a very famous detective, and he quite inflamed me. He was a marvellous little fellow. He used to say that all good detective work was a mere matter of method. My system is based on his—though of course I have progressed rather further. He was a funny little man, a great dandy, but wonderfully clever."

"Like a good detective story myself," remarked Miss Howard. "Lots of nonsense written, though. Criminal discovered in last chapter. Every one dumbfounded. Real crime—you'd know at once."

"There have been a great number of undiscovered crimes," I argued.

"Don't mean the police, but the people that are right in it. The family. You couldn't really hoodwink them. They'd know."

"Then," I said, much amused, "you think that if you were mixed up in a crime, say a murder, you'd be able to spot the murderer right off?"

"Of course I should. Mightn't be able to prove it to a pack of lawyers. But I'm certain I'd know. I'd feel it in my fingertips if he came near me."

"It might be a 'she,'" I suggested.

"Might. But murder's a violent crime. Associate it more with a man."

"Not in a case of poisoning." Mrs. Cavendish's clear voice startled me. "Dr. Bauerstein was saying yesterday that, owing to the general ignorance of the more uncommon poisons among the medical profession, there were probably countless cases of poisoning quite unsuspected."

"Why, Mary, what a gruesome conversation!" cried Mrs. Inglethorp. "It makes me feel as if a goose were walking over my grave. Oh, there's Cynthia!"

A young girl in V. A. D. uniform ran lightly across the lawn.

"Why, Cynthia, you are late today. This is Mr. Hastings—Miss Murdoch."

Cynthia Murdoch was a fresh-looking young creature, full of life and vigour. She tossed off her little V. A. D. cap, and I admired the great loose waves of her auburn hair, and the smallness and whiteness of the hand she held out to claim her tea. With dark eyes and eyelashes she would have been a beauty.

She flung herself down on the ground beside John, and as I handed her a plate of sandwiches she smiled up at me.

"Sit down here on the grass, do. It's ever so much nicer."

I dropped down obediently.

"You work at Tadminster, don't you, Miss Murdoch?"

She nodded.

"For my sins."

"Do they bully you, then?" I asked, smiling.

"I should like to see them!" cried Cynthia with dignity.

"I have got a cousin who is nursing," I remarked. "And she is terrified of 'Sisters.'"

"I don't wonder. Sisters *are*, you know, Mr. Hastings. They simp-ly *are*! You've no idea! But I'm not a nurse, thank heaven, I work in the dispensary."

"How many people do you poison?" I asked, smiling.

Cynthia smiled too.

"Oh, hundreds!" she said.

"Cynthia," called Mrs. Inglethorp, "do you think you could write a few notes for me?"

"Certainly, Aunt Emily."

She jumped up promptly, and something in her manner reminded me that her position was a dependent one, and that Mrs. Inglethorp, kind as she might be in the main, did not allow her to forget it.

My hostess turned to me.

"John will show you your room. Supper is at half-past seven. We have given up late dinner for some time now. Lady Tadminster, our Member's wife—she was the late Lord Abbotsbury's daughter—does the same. She agrees with me that one must set an example of economy. We are quite a war household; nothing is wasted here—every scrap of waste paper, even, is saved and sent away in sacks."

I expressed my appreciation, and John took me into the house and up the broad staircase, which forked right and left half-way to different wings of the building. My room was in the left wing, and looked out over the park.

John left me, and a few minutes later I saw him from my window walking slowly across the grass arm in arm with Cynthia Murdoch. I heard Mrs. Inglethorp call "Cynthia" impatiently, and the girl started and ran back to the house. At the same moment, a man stepped out from the shadow of a tree and walked slowly in the same direction. He looked about forty, very dark with a melancholy clean-shaven face. Some violent emotion seemed to be mastering him. He looked up at my window as he passed, and I recognized him, though he had changed much in the fifteen years that had elapsed since we last met. It was John's younger brother, Lawrence Cavendish. I wondered what it was that had brought that singular expression to his face.

Then I dismissed him from my mind, and returned to the contemplation of my own affairs.

The evening passed pleasantly enough; and I dreamed that night of that enigmatical woman, Mary Cavendish.

The next morning dawned bright and sunny, and I was full of the anticipation of a delightful visit.

I did not see Mrs. Cavendish until lunch-time, when she volunteered to take me for a walk, and we spent a charming afternoon roaming in the woods, returning to the house about five.

As we entered the large hall, John beckoned us both into the smoking-room. I saw at once by his face that something disturbing had occurred. We followed him in, and he shut the door after us.

"Look here, Mary, there's the deuce of a mess. Evie's had a row with Alfred Inglethorp, and she's off."

"Evie? Off?"

John nodded gloomily.

"Yes; you see she went to the mater, and—Oh, here's Evie herself."

Miss Howard entered. Her lips were set grimly together, and she carried a small suit-case. She looked excited and determined, and slightly on the defensive.

"At any rate," she burst out, "I've spoken my mind!"

"My dear Evelyn," cried Mrs. Cavendish, "this can't be true!"

Miss Howard nodded grimly.

"True enough! Afraid I said some things to Emily she won't forget or forgive in a hurry. Don't mind if they've only sunk in a bit. Probably water off a duck's back, though. I said right out: 'You're an old woman, Emily, and there's no fool like an old fool. The man's twenty years younger than you, and don't you fool yourself as to what he married you for. Money! Well, don't let him have too much of it. Farmer Raikes has got a very pretty young wife. Just ask your Alfred how much time he spends over there.' She was very angry. Natural! I went on, 'I'm going to warn you, whether you like it or not. That man would as soon murder you in your bed as look at you. He's a bad lot. You can say what you like to me, but remember what I've told you. He's a bad lot!'"

"What did she say?"

Miss Howard made an extremely expressive grimace.

"'Darling Alfred'—'dearest Alfred'—'wicked calumnies'—'wicked lies'—'wicked woman'—to accuse her 'dear husband'! The sooner I left her house the better. So I'm off."

"But not now?"

"This minute!"

For a moment we sat and stared at her. Finally John Cavendish, finding his persuasions of no avail, went off to look up the trains. His wife followed him, murmuring something about persuading Mrs. Inglethorp to think better of it.

As she left the room, Miss Howard's face changed. She leant towards me eagerly.

"Mr. Hastings, you're honest. I can trust you?"

I was a little startled. She laid her hand on my arm, and sank her voice to a whisper.

"Look after her, Mr. Hastings. My poor Emily. They're a lot of sharks—all of them. Oh, I know what I'm talking about. There isn't one of them that's not hard up and trying to get money out of her. I've protected her as much as I could. Now I'm out of the way, they'll impose upon her."

"Of course, Miss Howard," I said, "I'll do everything I can, but I'm sure you're excited and overwrought."

She interrupted me by slowly shaking her forefinger.

"Young man, trust me. I've lived in the world rather longer than you have. All I ask you is to keep your eyes open. You'll see what I mean."

The throb of the motor came through the open window, and Miss Howard rose and moved to the door. John's voice sounded outside. With her hand on the handle, she turned her head over her shoulder, and beckoned to me.

"Above all, Mr. Hastings, watch that devil—her husband!"

There was no time for more. Miss Howard was swallowed up in an eager chorus of protests and good-byes. The Inglethorps did not appear.

As the motor drove away, Mrs. Cavendish suddenly detached herself from the group, and moved across the drive to the lawn to meet a tall bearded man who had been evidently making for the house. The colour rose in her cheeks as she held out her hand to him.

"Who is that?" I asked sharply, for instinctively I distrusted the man.

"That's Dr. Bauerstein," said John shortly.

"And who is Dr. Bauerstein?"

"He's staying in the village doing a rest cure, after a bad nervous breakdown. He's a London specialist; a very clever man—one of the greatest living experts on poisons, I believe."

"And he's a great friend of Mary's," put in Cynthia, the irrepressible.

John Cavendish frowned and changed the subject.

"Come for a stroll, Hastings. This has been a most rotten business. She always had a rough tongue, but there is no stauncher friend in England than Evelyn Howard."

He took the path through the plantation, and we walked down to the village through the woods which bordered one side of the estate.

As we passed through one of the gates on our way home again, a pretty young woman of gipsy type coming in the opposite direction bowed and smiled.

"That's a pretty girl," I remarked appreciatively.

John's face hardened.

"That is Mrs. Raikes."

"The one that Miss Howard—"

"Exactly," said John, with rather unnecessary abruptness.

I thought of the white-haired old lady in the big house, and that vivid wicked little face that had just smiled into ours, and a vague chill of foreboding crept over me. I brushed it aside.

"Styles is really a glorious old place," I said to John.

He nodded rather gloomily.

"Yes, it's a fine property. It'll be mine some day—should be mine now by rights, if my father had only made a decent will. And then I shouldn't be so damned hard up as I am now."

"Hard up, are you?"

"My dear Hastings, I don't mind telling you that I'm at my wits' end for money."

"Couldn't your brother help you?"

"Lawrence? He's gone through every penny he ever had, publishing rotten verses in fancy bindings. No, we're an impecunious lot. My mother's always been awfully good to us, I must say. That is, up to now. Since her marriage, of course—" he broke off, frowning.

For the first time I felt that, with Evelyn Howard, something indefinable had gone from the atmosphere. Her presence had spelt security. Now that security was removed—and the air seemed rife with suspicion. The sinister face of Dr. Bauerstein recurred to me unpleasantly. A vague suspicion of every one and everything filled my mind. Just for a moment I had a premonition of approaching evil.

Chapter II

THE 16TH AND 17TH OF JULY

I had arrived at Styles on the 5th of July. I come now to the events of the 16th and 17th of that month. For the convenience of the reader I will recapitulate the incidents of those days in as exact a manner as possible. They were elicited subsequently at the trial by a process of long and tedious cross-examinations.

I received a letter from Evelyn Howard a couple of days after her departure, telling me she was working as a nurse at the big hospital in Middlingham, a manufacturing town some fifteen miles away, and begging me to let her know if Mrs. Inglethorp should show any wish to be reconciled.

The only fly in the ointment of my peaceful days was Mrs. Cavendish's extraordinary, and, for my part, unaccountable preference for the society of Dr. Bauerstein. What she saw in the man I cannot imagine, but she was always asking him up to the house, and often went off for long expeditions with him. I must confess that I was quite unable to see his attraction.

The 16th of July fell on a Monday. It was a day of turmoil. The famous bazaar had taken place on Saturday, and an entertainment, in connection with the same charity, at which Mrs. Inglethorp was to recite a War poem, was to be held that night. We were all busy during the morning arranging and decorating the Hall in the village where it was to take place. We had a late luncheon and spent the afternoon resting in the garden. I noticed that John's manner was somewhat unusual. He seemed very excited and restless.

After tea, Mrs. Inglethorp went to lie down to rest before her efforts in the evening and I challenged Mary Cavendish to a single at tennis.

About a quarter to seven, Mrs. Inglethorp called us that we should be late as supper was early that night. We had rather a scramble to get ready in time; and before the meal was over the motor was waiting at the door.

The entertainment was a great success, Mrs. Inglethorp's recitation receiving tremendous applause. There were also some tableaux in which Cynthia took part. She did not return with us, having been asked to a supper party, and to remain the night with some friends who had been acting with her in the tableaux.

The following morning, Mrs. Inglethorp stayed in bed to breakfast, as she was rather overtired; but she appeared in her briskest mood about 12.30, and swept Lawrence and myself off to a luncheon party.

"Such a charming invitation from Mrs. Rolleston. Lady Tadminster's sister, you know. The Rollestons came over with the Conqueror—one of our oldest families."

Mary had excused herself on the plea of an engagement with Dr. Bauerstein.

We had a pleasant luncheon, and as we drove away Lawrence suggested that we should return by Tadminster, which was barely a mile out of our way, and pay a visit to Cynthia in her dispensary. Mrs. Inglethorp replied that this was an excellent idea, but as she had several letters to write she would drop us there, and we could come back with Cynthia in the pony-trap.

We were detained under suspicion by the hospital porter, until Cynthia appeared to vouch for us, looking very cool and sweet in her long white overall. She took us up to her sanctum, and introduced us to her fellow dispenser, a rather awe-inspiring individual, whom Cynthia cheerily addressed as "Nibs."

"What a lot of bottles!" I exclaimed, as my eye travelled round the small room. "Do you really know what's in them all?"

"Say something original," groaned Cynthia. "Every single person who comes up here says that. We are really thinking of bestowing a prize on the first individual who does not say: 'What a lot of bottles!' And I know the next thing you're going to say is: 'How many people have you poisoned?'"

I pleaded guilty with a laugh.

"If you people only knew how fatally easy it is to poison someone by mistake, you wouldn't joke about it. Come on, let's have tea. We've got all sorts of secret stories in that cupboard. No, Lawrence—that's the poison cupboard. The big cupboard—that's right."

We had a very cheery tea, and assisted Cynthia to wash up afterwards. We had just put away the last teaspoon when a knock came at the door. The countenances of Cynthia and Nibs were suddenly petrified into a stern and forbidding expression.

"Come in," said Cynthia, in a sharp professional tone.

A young and rather scared looking nurse appeared with a bottle which she proffered to Nibs, who waved her towards Cynthia with the somewhat enigmatical remark:

"I'm not really here today."

Cynthia took the bottle and examined it with the severity of a judge.

"This should have been sent up this morning."

"Sister is very sorry. She forgot."

"Sister should read the rules outside the door."

I gathered from the little nurse's expression that there was not the least likelihood of her having the hardihood to retail this message to the dreaded "Sister."

"So now it can't be done until tomorrow," finished Cynthia.

"Don't you think you could possibly let us have it tonight?"

"Well," said Cynthia graciously, "we are very busy, but if we have time it shall be done."

The little nurse withdrew, and Cynthia promptly took a jar from the shelf, refilled the bottle, and placed it on the table outside the door.

I laughed.

"Discipline must be maintained?"

"Exactly. Come out on our little balcony. You can see all the outside wards there."

I followed Cynthia and her friend and they pointed out the different wards to me. Lawrence remained behind, but after a few moments Cynthia called to him over her shoulder to come and join us. Then she looked at her watch.

"Nothing more to do, Nibs?"

"No."

"All right. Then we can lock up and go."

I had seen Lawrence in quite a different light that afternoon. Compared to John, he was an astoundingly difficult person to get to know. He was the opposite of his brother in almost every respect, being unusually shy and reserved. Yet he had a certain charm of manner, and I fancied that, if one really knew him well, one could have a deep affection for him. I had always fancied that his manner to Cynthia was rather constrained, and that she on her side was inclined to be shy of him. But they were both gay enough this afternoon, and chatted together like a couple of children.

As we drove through the village, I remembered that I wanted some stamps, so accordingly we pulled up at the post office.

As I came out again, I cannoned into a little man who was just entering. I drew aside and apologised, when suddenly, with a loud exclamation, he clasped me in his arms and kissed me warmly.

"*Mon ami* Hastings!" he cried. "It is indeed *mon ami* Hastings!"

"Poirot!" I exclaimed.

I turned to the pony-trap.

"This is a very pleasant meeting for me, Miss Cynthia. This is my old friend, Monsieur Poirot, whom I have not seen for years."

"Oh, we know Monsieur Poirot," said Cynthia gaily. "But I had no idea he was a friend of yours."

"Yes, indeed," said Poirot seriously. "I know Mademoiselle Cynthia. It is by the charity of that good Mrs. Inglethorp that I am here." Then, as I looked at him inquiringly: "Yes, my friend, she had kindly extended hospitality to seven of my countrypeople who, alas, are refugees from their native land. We Belgians will always remember her with gratitude."

Poirot was an extraordinary looking little man. He was hardly more than five feet, four inches, but carried himself with great dignity. His head was exactly the shape of an egg, and he always perched it a little on one side. His moustache was very stiff and military. The neatness of his attire was almost incredible. I believe a speck of dust would have caused him more pain than a bullet wound. Yet this quaint dandified little man who, I was sorry to see, now limped badly, had been in his time one of the most celebrated members of the Belgian police. As a detective, his flair had been extraordinary, and he had achieved triumphs by unravelling some of the most baffling cases of the day.

He pointed out to me the little house inhabited by him and his fellow Belgians, and I promised to go and see him at an early date. Then he raised his hat with a flourish to Cynthia, and we drove away.

"He's a dear little man," said Cynthia. "I'd no idea you knew him."

"You've been entertaining a celebrity unawares," I replied.

And, for the rest of the way home, I recited to them the various exploits and triumphs of Hercule Poirot.

We arrived back in a very cheerful mood. As we entered the hall, Mrs. Inglethorp came out of her boudoir. She looked flushed and upset.

"Oh, it's you," she said.

"Is there anything the matter, Aunt Emily?" asked Cynthia.

"Certainly not," said Mrs. Inglethorp sharply. "What should there be?"

Then catching sight of Dorcas, the parlourmaid, going into the dining-room, she called to her to bring some stamps into the boudoir.

"Yes, m'm." The old servant hesitated, then added diffidently: "Don't you think, m'm, you'd better get to bed? You're looking very tired."

"Perhaps you're right, Dorcas—yes—no—not now. I've some letters I must finish by post-time. Have you lighted the fire in my room as I told you?"

"Yes, m'm."

"Then I'll go to bed directly after supper."

She went into the boudoir again, and Cynthia stared after her.

"Goodness gracious! I wonder what's up?" she said to Lawrence.

He did not seem to have heard her, for without a word he turned on his heel and went out of the house.

I suggested a quick game of tennis before supper and, Cynthia agreeing, I ran upstairs to fetch my racquet.

Mrs. Cavendish was coming down the stairs. It may have been my fancy, but she, too, was looking odd and disturbed.

"Had a good walk with Dr. Bauerstein?" I asked, trying to appear as indifferent as I could.

"I didn't go," she replied abruptly. "Where is Mrs. Inglethorp?"

"In the boudoir."

Her hand clenched itself on the banisters, then she seemed to nerve herself for some encounter, and went rapidly past me down the stairs across the hall to the boudoir, the door of which she shut behind her.

As I ran out to the tennis court a few moments later, I had to pass the open boudoir window, and was unable to help overhearing the following scrap of dialogue. Mary Cavendish was saying in the voice of a woman desperately controlling herself:

"Then you won't show it to me?"

To which Mrs. Inglethorp replied:

"My dear Mary, it has nothing to do with that matter."

"Then show it to me."

"I tell you it is not what you imagine. It does not concern you in the least."

To which Mary Cavendish replied, with a rising bitterness:

"Of course, I might have known you would shield him."

Cynthia was waiting for me, and greeted me eagerly with:

"I say! There's been the most awful row! I've got it all out of Dorcas."

"What kind of a row?"

"Between Aunt Emily and him. I do hope she's found him out at last!"

"Was Dorcas there, then?"

"Of course not. She 'happened to be near the door.' It was a real old bust-up. I do wish I knew what it was all about."

I thought of Mrs. Raikes's gipsy face, and Evelyn Howard's warnings, but wisely decided to hold my peace, whilst Cynthia exhausted every possible hypothesis, and cheerfully hoped, "Aunt Emily will send him away, and will never speak to him again."

I was anxious to get hold of John, but he was nowhere to be seen. Evidently something very momentous had occurred that afternoon. I tried to forget the few words I had overheard; but, do what I would, I could not dismiss them altogether from my mind. What was Mary Cavendish's concern in the matter?

Mr. Inglethorp was in the drawing-room when I came down to supper. His face was impassive as ever, and the strange unreality of the man struck me afresh.

Mrs. Inglethorp came down last. She still looked agitated, and during the meal there was a somewhat constrained silence. Inglethorp was unusually quiet. As a rule, he surrounded his wife with little attentions, placing a cushion at her back, and altogether playing the part of the devoted husband. Immediately after supper, Mrs. Inglethorp retired to her boudoir again.

"Send my coffee in here, Mary," she called. "I've just five minutes to catch the post."

Cynthia and I went and sat by the open window in the drawing-room. Mary Cavendish brought our coffee to us. She seemed excited.

"Do you young people want lights, or do you enjoy the twilight?" she asked. "Will you take Mrs. Inglethorp her coffee, Cynthia? I will pour it out."

"Do not trouble, Mary," said Inglethorp. "I will take it to Emily." He poured it out, and went out of the room carrying it carefully.

Lawrence followed him, and Mrs. Cavendish sat down by us.

We three sat for some time in silence. It was a glorious night, hot and still. Mrs. Cavendish fanned herself gently with a palm leaf.

"It's almost too hot," she murmured. "We shall have a thunderstorm."

Alas, that these harmonious moments can never endure! My paradise was rudely shattered by the sound of a well known, and heartily disliked, voice in the hall.

"Dr. Bauerstein!" exclaimed Cynthia. "What a funny time to come."

I glanced jealously at Mary Cavendish, but she seemed quite undisturbed, the delicate pallor of her cheeks did not vary.

In a few moments, Alfred Inglethorp had ushered the doctor in, the latter laughing, and protesting that he was in no fit state for a drawing-room. In truth, he presented a sorry spectacle, being literally plastered with mud.

"What have you been doing, doctor?" cried Mrs. Cavendish.

"I must make my apologies," said the doctor. "I did not really mean to come in, but Mr. Inglethorp insisted."

"Well, Bauerstein, you are in a plight," said John, strolling in from the hall. "Have some coffee, and tell us what you have been up to."

"Thank you, I will." He laughed rather ruefully, as he described how he had discovered a very rare species of fern in an inaccessible place, and in his efforts to obtain it had lost his footing, and slipped ignominiously into a neighbouring pond.

"The sun soon dried me off," he added, "but I'm afraid my appearance is very disreputable."

At this juncture, Mrs. Inglethorp called to Cynthia from the hall, and the girl ran out.

"Just carry up my despatch-case, will you, dear? I'm going to bed."

The door into the hall was a wide one. I had risen when Cynthia did, John was close by me. There were therefore three witnesses who could swear that Mrs. Inglethorp was carrying her coffee, as yet untasted, in her hand.

My evening was utterly and entirely spoilt by the presence of Dr. Bauerstein. It seemed to me the man would never go. He rose at last, however, and I breathed a sigh of relief.

"I'll walk down to the village with you," said Mr. Inglethorp. "I must see our agent over those estate accounts." He turned to John. "No one need sit up. I will take the latch-key."

Chapter III

THE NIGHT OF THE TRAGEDY

To make this part of my story clear, I append the following plan of the first floor of Styles.

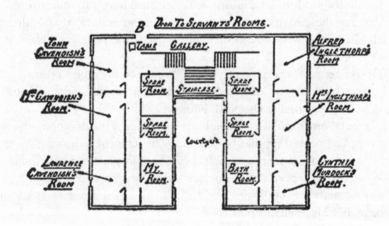

The servants' rooms are reached through the door B. They have no communication with the right wing, where the Inglethorps' rooms were situated.

It seemed to be the middle of the night when I was awakened by Lawrence Cavendish. He had a candle in his hand, and the agitation of his face told me at once that something was seriously wrong.

"What's the matter?" I asked, sitting up in bed, and trying to collect my scattered thoughts.

"We are afraid my mother is very ill. She seems to be having some kind of fit. Unfortunately she has locked herself in."

"I'll come at once."

I sprang out of bed; and, pulling on a dressing-gown, followed Lawrence along the passage and the gallery to the right wing of the house.

John Cavendish joined us, and one or two of the servants were standing round in a state of awe-stricken excitement. Lawrence turned to his brother.

"What do you think we had better do?"

Never, I thought, had his indecision of character been more apparent.

John rattled the handle of Mrs. Inglethorp's door violently, but with no effect. It was obviously locked or bolted on the inside. The whole household was aroused by now. The most alarming sounds were audible from the interior of the room. Clearly something must be done.

"Try going through Mr. Inglethorp's room, sir," cried Dorcas. "Oh, the poor mistress!"

Suddenly I realized that Alfred Inglethorp was not with us—that he alone had given no sign of his presence. John opened the door of his room. It was pitch dark, but Lawrence was following with the candle, and by its feeble light we saw that the bed had not been slept in, and that there was no sign of the room having been occupied.

We went straight to the connecting door. That, too, was locked or bolted on the inside. What was to be done?

"Oh, dear, sir," cried Dorcas, wringing her hands, "what ever shall we do?"

"We must try and break the door in, I suppose. It'll be a tough job, though. Here, let one of the maids go down and wake Baily and tell him to go for Dr. Wilkins at once. Now then, we'll have a try at the door. Half a moment, though, isn't there a door into Miss Cynthia's rooms?"

"Yes, sir, but that's always bolted. It's never been undone."

"Well, we might just see."

He ran rapidly down the corridor to Cynthia's room. Mary Cavendish was there, shaking the girl—who must have been an unusually sound sleeper—and trying to wake her.

In a moment or two he was back.

"No good. That's bolted too. We must break in the door. I think this one is a shade less solid than the one in the passage."

We strained and heaved together. The framework of the door was solid, and for a long time it resisted our efforts, but at last we felt it give beneath our weight, and finally, with a resounding crash, it was burst open.

We stumbled in together, Lawrence still holding his candle. Mrs. Inglethorp was lying on the bed, her whole form agitated by violent convulsions, in one of which she must have overturned the table beside her. As we entered, however, her limbs relaxed, and she fell back upon the pillows.

John strode across the room, and lit the gas. Turning to Annie, one of the housemaids, he sent her downstairs to the dining-room for brandy. Then he went across to his mother whilst I unbolted the door that gave on the corridor.

I turned to Lawrence, to suggest that I had better leave them now that there was no further need of my services, but the words were frozen on my lips. Never have I seen such a ghastly look on any man's face. He was white as chalk, the candle he held in his shaking hand was sputtering onto the carpet, and his eyes, petrified with terror, or some such kindred emotion, stared fixedly over my head at a point on the further wall. It was as though he had seen something that turned him to stone. I instinctively followed the direction of his eyes, but I could see nothing unusual. The still feebly flickering ashes in the grate, and the row of prim ornaments on the mantelpiece, were surely harmless enough.

The violence of Mrs. Inglethorp's attack seemed to be passing. She was able to speak in short gasps.

"Better now—very sudden—stupid of me—to lock myself in."

A shadow fell on the bed and, looking up, I saw Mary Cavendish standing near the door with her arm around Cynthia. She seemed to be supporting the girl, who looked utterly dazed and unlike herself. Her face was heavily flushed, and she yawned repeatedly.

"Poor Cynthia is quite frightened," said Mrs. Cavendish in a low clear voice. She herself, I noticed, was dressed in her white land smock. Then it must be later than I thought. I saw that a faint streak of daylight was showing through the curtains of the windows, and that the clock on the mantelpiece pointed to close upon five o'clock.

A strangled cry from the bed startled me. A fresh access of pain seized the unfortunate old lady. The convulsions were of a violence terrible to behold. Everything was confusion. We thronged round her, powerless to help or alleviate. A final convulsion lifted her from the bed, until she appeared to rest upon her head and her heels, with her body arched in an extraordinary manner. In vain Mary and John tried to administer more brandy. The moments flew. Again the body arched itself in that peculiar fashion.

At that moment, Dr. Bauerstein pushed his way authoritatively into the room. For one instant he stopped dead, staring at the figure on the bed, and, at the same instant, Mrs. Inglethorp cried out in a strangled voice, her eyes fixed on the doctor:

"Alfred—Alfred—" Then she fell back motionless on the pillows.

With a stride, the doctor reached the bed, and seizing her arms worked them energetically, applying what I knew to be artificial respiration. He issued a few short sharp orders to the servants. An imperious wave of his hand drove us all to the door. We watched him, fascinated, though I think we all knew in our hearts that it was too late, and that nothing could be done now. I could see by the expression on his face that he himself had little hope.

Finally he abandoned his task, shaking his head gravely. At that moment, we heard footsteps outside, and Dr. Wilkins, Mrs. Inglethorp's own doctor, a portly, fussy little man, came bustling in.

In a few words Dr. Bauerstein explained how he had happened to be passing the lodge gates as the car came out, and had run up to the house as fast as he could, whilst the car went on to fetch Dr. Wilkins. With a faint gesture of the hand, he indicated the figure on the bed.

"Ve—ry sad. Ve—ry sad," murmured Dr. Wilkins. "Poor dear lady. Always did far too much—far too much—against my advice. I warned her. Her heart was far from strong. 'Take it easy,' I said to her, 'Take—it—easy.' But no—her zeal for good works was too great. Nature rebelled. Na—ture—re—belled."

Dr. Bauerstein, I noticed, was watching the local doctor narrowly. He still kept his eyes fixed on him as he spoke.

"The convulsions were of a peculiar violence, Dr. Wilkins. I am sorry you were not here in time to witness them. They were quite—tetanic in character."

"Ah!" said Dr. Wilkins wisely.

"I should like to speak to you in private," said Dr. Bauerstein. He turned to John. "You do not object?"

"Certainly not."

We all trooped out into the corridor, leaving the two doctors alone, and I heard the key turned in the lock behind us.

We went slowly down the stairs. I was violently excited. I have a certain talent for deduction, and Dr. Bauerstein's manner had started a flock of wild surmises in my mind. Mary Cavendish laid her hand upon my arm.

"What is it? Why did Dr. Bauerstein seem so—peculiar?"

I looked at her.

"Do you know what I think?"

"What?"

"Listen!" I looked round, the others were out of earshot. I lowered my voice to a whisper. "I believe she has been poisoned! I'm certain Dr. Bauerstein suspects it."

"What?" She shrank against the wall, the pupils of her eyes dilating wildly. Then, with a sudden cry that startled me, she cried out: "No, no—not that—not that!" And breaking from me, fled up the stairs. I followed her, afraid that she was going to faint. I found her leaning against the bannisters, deadly pale. She waved me away impatiently.

"No, no—leave me. I'd rather be alone. Let me just be quiet for a minute or two. Go down to the others."

I obeyed her reluctantly. John and Lawrence were in the dining-room. I joined them. We were all silent, but I suppose I voiced the thoughts of us all when I at last broke it by saying:

"Where is Mr. Inglethorp?"

John shook his head.

"He's not in the house."

Our eyes met. Where *was* Alfred Inglethorp? His absence was strange and inexplicable. I remembered Mrs. Inglethorp's dying words. What lay beneath them? What more could she have told us, if she had had time?

At last we heard the doctors descending the stairs. Dr. Wilkins was looking important and excited, and trying to conceal an inward exultation under a manner of decorous calm. Dr. Bauerstein remained in the background, his grave bearded face unchanged. Dr. Wilkins was the spokesman for the two. He addressed himself to John:

"Mr. Cavendish, I should like your consent to a postmortem."

"Is that necessary?" asked John gravely. A spasm of pain crossed his face.

"Absolutely," said Dr. Bauerstein.

"You mean by that—?"

"That neither Dr. Wilkins nor myself could give a death certificate under the circumstances."

John bent his head.

"In that case, I have no alternative but to agree."

"Thank you," said Dr. Wilkins briskly. "We propose that it should take place tomorrow night—or rather tonight." And he glanced at the daylight. "Under the circumstances, I am afraid an inquest can hardly be avoided—these formalities are necessary, but I beg that you won't distress yourselves."

There was a pause, and then Dr. Bauerstein drew two keys from his pocket, and handed them to John.

"These are the keys of the two rooms. I have locked them and, in my opinion, they would be better kept locked for the present."

The doctors then departed.

I had been turning over an idea in my head, and I felt that the moment had now come to broach it. Yet I was a little chary of doing so. John, I knew, had a horror of any kind of publicity, and was an easygoing optimist, who preferred never to meet trouble half-way. It might be difficult to convince him of the soundness of my plan. Lawrence, on the other hand, being less conventional, and having more imagination, I felt I might count upon as an ally. There was no doubt that the moment had come for me to take the lead.

"John," I said, "I am going to ask you something."

"Well?"

"You remember my speaking of my friend Poirot? The Belgian who is here? He has been a most famous detective."

"Yes."

"I want you to let me call him in—to investigate this matter."

"What—now? Before the post-mortem?"

"Yes, time is an advantage if—if—there has been foul play."

"Rubbish!" cried Lawrence angrily. "In my opinion the whole thing is a mare's nest of Bauerstein's! Wilkins hadn't an idea of such a thing, until Bauerstein put it into his head. But, like all specialists, Bauerstein's got a bee in his bonnet. Poisons are his hobby, so of course he sees them everywhere."

I confess that I was surprised by Lawrence's attitude. He was so seldom vehement about anything.

John hesitated.

"I can't feel as you do, Lawrence," he said at last. "I'm inclined to give Hastings a free hand, though I should prefer to wait a bit. We don't want any unnecessary scandal."

"No, no," I cried eagerly, "you need have no fear of that. Poirot is discretion itself."

"Very well, then, have it your own way. I leave it in your hands. Though, if it is as we suspect, it seems a clear enough case. God forgive me if I am wronging him!"

I looked at my watch. It was six o'clock. I determined to lose no time.

Five minutes' delay, however, I allowed myself. I spent it in ransacking the library until I discovered a medical book which gave a description of strychnine poisoning.

Chapter IV

POIROT INVESTIGATES

The house which the Belgians occupied in the village was quite close to the park gates. One could save time by taking a narrow path through the long grass, which cut off the detours of the winding drive. So I, accordingly, went that way. I had nearly reached the lodge, when my attention was arrested by the running figure of a man approaching me. It was Mr. Inglethorp. Where had he been? How did he intend to explain his absence?

He accosted me eagerly.

"My God! This is terrible! My poor wife! I have only just heard."

"Where have you been?" I asked.

"Denby kept me late last night. It was one o'clock before we'd finished. Then I found that I'd forgotten the latch-key after all. I didn't want to arouse the household, so Denby gave me a bed."

"How did you hear the news?" I asked.

"Wilkins knocked Denby up to tell him. My poor Emily! She was so self-sacrificing—such a noble character. She over-taxed her strength."

A wave of revulsion swept over me. What a consummate hypocrite the man was!

"I must hurry on," I said, thankful that he did not ask me whither I was bound.

In a few minutes I was knocking at the door of Leastways Cottage.

Getting no answer, I repeated my summons impatiently. A window above me was cautiously opened, and Poirot himself looked out.

He gave an exclamation of surprise at seeing me. In a few brief words, I explained the tragedy that had occurred, and that I wanted his help.

"Wait, my friend, I will let you in, and you shall recount to me the affair whilst I dress."

In a few moments he had unbarred the door, and I followed him up to his room. There he installed me in a chair, and I related the whole story, keeping back nothing, and omitting no circumstance, however insignificant, whilst he himself made a careful and deliberate toilet.

I told him of my awakening, of Mrs. Inglethorp's dying words, of her husband's absence, of the quarrel the day before, of the scrap of conversation between Mary and her mother-in-law that I had overheard, of the former quarrel between Mrs. Inglethorp and Evelyn Howard, and of the latter's innuendoes.

I was hardly as clear as I could wish. I repeated myself several times, and occasionally had to go back to some detail that I had forgotten. Poirot smiled kindly on me.

"The mind is confused? Is it not so? Take time, *mon ami*. You are agitated; you are excited—it is but natural. Presently, when we are calmer, we will arrange the facts, neatly, each in his proper place. We will examine—and reject. Those of importance we will put on one side; those of no importance, pouf!"—he screwed up his cherub-like face, and puffed comically enough—"blow them away!"

"That's all very well," I objected, "but how are you going to decide what is important, and what isn't? That always seems the difficulty to me."

Poirot shook his head energetically. He was now arranging his moustache with exquisite care.

"Not so. *Voyons!* One fact leads to another—so we continue. Does the next fit in with that? *À merveille!* Good! We can proceed. This next little fact—no! Ah, that is curious! There is something missing—a link in the chain that is not there. We examine. We search. And that little curious fact, that possibly paltry little detail that will not tally, we put it here!" He made an extravagant gesture with his hand. "It is significant! It is tremendous!"

"Y—es—"

"Ah!" Poirot shook his forefinger so fiercely at me that I quailed before it. "Beware! Peril to the detective who says: 'It is so small—it does not matter. It will not agree. I will forget it.' That way lies confusion! Everything matters."

"I know. You always told me that. That's why I have gone into all the details of this thing whether they seemed to me relevant or not."

"And I am pleased with you. You have a good memory, and you have given me the facts faithfully. Of the order in which you present them, I say nothing—truly, it is deplorable! But I make allowances—you are upset. To that I attribute the circumstance that you have omitted one fact of paramount importance."

"What is that?" I asked.

"You have not told me if Mrs. Inglethorp ate well last night."

I stared at him. Surely the war had affected the little man's brain. He was carefully engaged in brushing his coat before putting it on, and seemed wholly engrossed in the task.

"I don't remember," I said. "And, anyway, I don't see—"

"You do not see? But it is of the first importance."

"I can't see why," I said, rather nettled. "As far as I can remember, she didn't eat much. She was obviously upset, and it had taken her appetite away. That was only natural."

"Yes," said Poirot thoughtfully, "it was only natural."

He opened a drawer, and took out a small despatch-case, then turned to me.

"Now I am ready. We will proceed to the château, and study matters on the spot. Excuse me, *mon ami*, you dressed in haste, and your tie is on one side. Permit me." With a deft gesture, he rearranged it.

"*Ça y est!* Now, shall we start?"

We hurried up the village, and turned in at the lodge gates. Poirot stopped for a moment, and gazed sorrowfully over the beautiful expanse of park, still glittering with morning dew.

"So beautiful, so beautiful, and yet, the poor family, plunged in sorrow, prostrated with grief."

He looked at me keenly as he spoke, and I was aware that I reddened under his prolonged gaze.

Was the family prostrated by grief? Was the sorrow at Mrs. Inglethorp's death so great? I realized that there was an emotional lack in the atmosphere. The dead woman had not the gift of commanding love. Her death was a shock and a distress, but she would not be passionately regretted.

Poirot seemed to follow my thoughts. He nodded his head gravely.

"No, you are right," he said, "it is not as though there was a blood tie. She has been kind and generous to these Cavendishes, but she was not their own mother. Blood tells—always remember that—blood tells."

"Poirot," I said, "I wish you would tell me why you wanted to know if Mrs. Inglethorp ate well last night? I have been turning it over in my mind, but I can't see how it has anything to do with the matter?"

He was silent for a minute or two as we walked along, but finally he said:

"I do not mind telling you—though, as you know, it is not my habit to explain until the end is reached. The present contention is that Mrs. Inglethorp died of strychnine poisoning, presumably administered in her coffee."

"Yes?"

"Well, what time was the coffee served?"

"About eight o'clock."

"Therefore she drank it between then and half-past eight—certainly not much later. Well, strychnine is a fairly rapid poison. Its effects would be felt very soon, probably in about an hour. Yet, in Mrs. Inglethorp's case, the symptoms do not manifest themselves until five o'clock the next morning: nine hours! But a heavy meal, taken at about the same time as the poison, might retard its effects, though hardly to that extent. Still, it is a possibility to be taken into account. But, according to you, she ate very little for supper, and yet the symptoms do not develop until early the next morning! Now that is a curious circumstance, my friend. Something may arise at the autopsy to explain it. In the meantime, remember it."

As we neared the house, John came out and met us. His face looked weary and haggard.

"This is a very dreadful business, Monsieur Poirot," he said. "Hastings has explained to you that we are anxious for no publicity?"

"I comprehend perfectly."

"You see, it is only suspicion so far. We have nothing to go upon."

"Precisely. It is a matter of precaution only."

John turned to me, taking out his cigarette-case, and lighting a cigarette as he did so.

"You know that fellow Inglethorp is back?"

"Yes. I met him."

John flung the match into an adjacent flower bed, a proceeding which was too much for Poirot's feelings. He retrieved it, and buried it neatly.

"It's jolly difficult to know how to treat him."

"That difficulty will not exist long," pronounced Poirot quietly.

John looked puzzled, not quite understanding the portent of this cryptic saying. He handed the two keys which Dr. Bauerstein had given him to me.

"Show Monsieur Poirot everything he wants to see."

"The rooms are locked?" asked Poirot.

"Dr. Bauerstein considered it advisable."

Poirot nodded thoughtfully.

"Then he is very sure. Well, that simplifies matters for us."

We went up together to the room of the tragedy. For convenience I append a plan of the room and the principal articles of furniture in it.

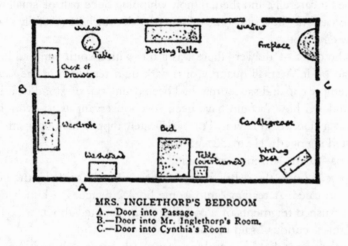

MRS. INGLETHORP'S BEDROOM
A.—Door into Passage
B.—Door into Mr. Inglethorp's Room.
C.—Door into Cynthia's Room

Poirot locked the door on the inside, and proceeded to a minute inspection of the room. He darted from one object to the other with the agility of a grasshopper. I remained by the door, fearing to obliterate any clues. Poirot, however, did not seem grateful to me for my forbearance.

"What have you, my friend," he cried, "that you remain there like—how do you say it?—ah, yes, the stuck pig?"

I explained that I was afraid of obliterating any foot-marks.

"Foot-marks? But what an idea! There has already been practically an army in the room! What foot-marks are we likely to find? No, come here and aid me in my search. I will put down my little case until I need it."

He did so, on the round table by the window, but it was an ill-advised proceeding; for, the top of it being loose, it tilted up, and precipitated the despatch-case on the floor.

"*Eh voilà une table!*" cried Poirot. "Ah, my friend, one may live in a big house and yet have no comfort."

After which piece of moralizing, he resumed his search.

A small purple despatch-case, with a key in the lock, on the writing-table, engaged his attention for some time. He took out the key from the lock, and passed it to me to inspect. I saw nothing peculiar, however. It was an ordinary key of the Yale type, with a bit of twisted wire through the handle.

Next, he examined the framework of the door we had broken in, assuring himself that the bolt had really been shot. Then he went to the door opposite leading into Cynthia's room. That door was also bolted, as I had stated. However, he went to the length of unbolting it, and opening and shutting it several times; this he did with the utmost precaution against making any noise. Suddenly something in the bolt itself seemed to rivet his attention. He examined it carefully, and then, nimbly whipping out a pair of small forceps from his case, he drew out some minute particle which he carefully sealed up in a tiny envelope.

On the chest of drawers there was a tray with a spirit lamp and a small saucepan on it. A small quantity of a dark fluid remained in the saucepan, and an empty cup and saucer that had been drunk out of stood near it.

I wondered how I could have been so unobservant as to overlook this. Here was a clue worth having. Poirot delicately dipped his finger into liquid, and tasted it gingerly. He made a grimace.

"Cocoa—with—I think—rum in it."

He passed on to the debris on the floor, where the table by the bed had been overturned. A reading-lamp, some books, matches, a bunch of keys, and the crushed fragments of a coffee-cup lay scattered about.

"Ah, this is curious," said Poirot.

"I must confess that I see nothing particularly curious about it."

"You do not? Observe the lamp—the chimney is broken in two places; they lie there as they fell. But see, the coffee-cup is absolutely smashed to powder."

"Well," I said wearily, "I suppose someone must have stepped on it."

"Exactly," said Poirot, in an odd voice. "Someone stepped on it."

He rose from his knees, and walked slowly across to the mantelpiece, where he stood abstractedly fingering the ornaments, and straightening them—a trick of his when he was agitated.

"Mon ami," he said, turning to me, "somebody stepped on that cup, grinding it to powder, and the reason they did so was either because it contained strychnine or—which is far more serious—because it did not contain strychnine!"

I made no reply. I was bewildered, but I knew that it was no good asking him to explain. In a moment or two he roused himself, and went on with his investigations. He picked up the bunch of keys from the floor, and twirling them round in his fingers finally selected one, very bright and shining, which he tried in the lock of the purple despatch-case. It fitted, and he opened the box, but after a moment's hesitation, closed and relocked it, and slipped the bunch of keys, as well as the key that had originally stood in the lock, into his own pocket.

"I have no authority to go through these papers. But it should be done—at once!"

He then made a very careful examination of the drawers of the wash-stand. Crossing the room to the left-hand window, a round stain, hardly visible on the dark brown carpet, seemed to interest him particularly. He went down on his knees, examining it minutely—even going so far as to smell it.

Finally, he poured a few drops of the cocoa into a test tube, sealing it up carefully. His next proceeding was to take out a little notebook.

"We have found in this room," he said, writing busily, "six points of interest. Shall I enumerate them, or will you?"

"Oh, you," I replied hastily.

"Very well, then. One, a coffee-cup that has been ground into powder; two, a despatch-case with a key in the lock; three, a stain on the floor."

"That may have been done some time ago," I interrupted.

"No, for it is still perceptibly damp and smells of coffee. Four, a fragment of some dark green fabric—only a thread or two, but recognizable."

"Ah!" I cried. "That was what you sealed up in the envelope."

"Yes. It may turn out to be a piece of one of Mrs. Inglethorp's own dresses, and quite unimportant. We shall see. Five, *this*!" With a dramatic gesture, he pointed to a large splash of candle grease on the floor by the writing-table. "It must have been done since yesterday, otherwise a good housemaid would have at once removed it with blotting-paper and a hot iron. One of my best hats once—but that is not to the point."

"It was very likely done last night. We were very agitated. Or perhaps Mrs. Inglethorp herself dropped her candle."

"You brought only one candle into the room?"

"Yes. Lawrence Cavendish was carrying it. But he was very upset. He seemed to see something over here"—I indicated the mantelpiece—"that absolutely paralysed him."

"That is interesting," said Poirot quickly. "Yes, it is suggestive"—his eye sweeping the whole length of the wall—"but it was not his candle that made this great patch, for you perceive that this is white grease; whereas Monsieur Lawrence's candle, which is still on the dressing-table, is pink. On the other hand, Mrs. Inglethorp had no candlestick in the room, only a reading-lamp."

"Then," I said, "what do you deduce?"

To which my friend only made a rather irritating reply, urging me to use my own natural faculties.

"And the sixth point?" I asked. "I suppose it is the sample of cocoa."

"No," said Poirot thoughtfully. "I might have included that in the six, but I did not. No, the sixth point I will keep to myself for the present."

He looked quickly round the room. "There is nothing more to be done here, I think, unless"—he stared earnestly and long at the dead ashes in the grate. "The fire burns—and it destroys. But by chance—there might be—let us see!"

Deftly, on hands and knees, he began to sort the ashes from the grate into the fender, handling them with the greatest caution. Suddenly, he gave a faint exclamation.

"The forceps, Hastings!"

I quickly handed them to him, and with skill he extracted a small piece of half charred paper.

"There, *mon ami*!" he cried. "What do you think of that?"

I scrutinized the fragment. This is an exact reproduction of it:

I was puzzled. It was unusually thick, quite unlike ordinary notepaper.

Suddenly an idea struck me.

"Poirot!" I cried. "This is a fragment of a will!"

"Exactly."

I looked up at him sharply.

"You are not surprised?"

"No," he said gravely, "I expected it."

I relinquished the piece of paper, and watched him put it away in his case, with the same methodical care that he bestowed on everything. My brain was in a whirl. What was this complication of a will? Who had destroyed it? The person who had left the candle grease on the floor? Obviously. But how had anyone gained admission? All the doors had been bolted on the inside.

"Now, my friend," said Poirot briskly, "we will go. I should like to ask a few questions of the parlourmaid—Dorcas, her name is, is it not?"

We passed through Alfred Inglethorp's room, and Poirot delayed long enough to make a brief but fairly comprehensive examination of it. We went out through that door, locking both it and that of Mrs. Inglethorp's room as before.

I took him down to the boudoir which he had expressed a wish to see, and went myself in search of Dorcas.

When I returned with her, however, the boudoir was empty.

"Poirot," I cried, "where are you?"

"I am here, my friend."

He had stepped outside the French window, and was standing, apparently lost in admiration, before the various shaped flower beds.

"Admirable!" he murmured. "Admirable! What symmetry! Observe that crescent; and those diamonds—their neatness rejoices the eye. The spacing of the plants, also, is perfect. It has been recently done; is it not so?"

"Yes, I believe they were at it yesterday afternoon. But come in—Dorcas is here."

"*Eh bien, eh bien*! Do not grudge me a moment's satisfaction of the eye."

"Yes, but this affair is more important."

"And how do you know that these fine begonias are not of equal importance?"

I shrugged my shoulders. There was really no arguing with him if he chose to take that line.

"You do not agree? But such things have been. Well, we will come in and interview the brave Dorcas."

Dorcas was standing in the boudoir, her hands folded in front of her, and her grey hair rose in stiff waves under her white cap. She was the very model and picture of a good old-fashioned servant.

In her attitude towards Poirot, she was inclined to be suspicious, but he soon broke down her defences. He drew forward a chair.

"Pray be seated, mademoiselle."

"Thank you, sir."

"You have been with your mistress many years, is it not so?"

"Ten years, sir."

"That is a long time, and very faithful service. You were much attached to her, were you not?"

"She was a very good mistress to me, sir."

"Then you will not object to answering a few questions. I put them to you with Mr. Cavendish's full approval."

"Oh, certainly, sir."

"Then I will begin by asking you about the events of yesterday afternoon. Your mistress had a quarrel?"

"Yes, sir. But I don't know that I ought—" Dorcas hesitated. Poirot looked at her keenly.

"My good Dorcas, it is necessary that I should know every detail of that quarrel as fully as possible. Do not think that you are betraying your mistress's secrets. Your mistress lies dead, and it is necessary that we should know all—if we are to avenge her. Nothing can bring her back to life, but we do hope, if there has been foul play, to bring the murderer to justice."

"Amen to that," said Dorcas fiercely. "And, naming no names, there's *one* in this house that none of us could ever abide! And an ill day it was when first *he* darkened the threshold."

Poirot waited for her indignation to subside, and then, resuming his business-like tone, he asked:

"Now, as to this quarrel? What is the first you heard of it?"

"Well, sir, I happened to be going along the hall outside yesterday—"

"What time was that?"

"I couldn't say exactly, sir, but it wasn't tea-time by a long way. Perhaps four o'clock—or it may have been a bit later. Well, sir, as I said, I happened to be passing along, when I heard voices very loud and angry in here. I didn't exactly mean to listen, but—well, there it is. I stopped. The door was shut, but the mistress was speaking very sharp and clear, and I heard what she said quite plainly. 'You have lied to me, and deceived me,' she said. I didn't hear what Mr. Inglethorp replied. He spoke a good bit lower than she did—but she answered: 'How dare you? I have kept you and clothed you and fed you! You owe everything to me! And this is how you repay me! By bringing disgrace upon our name!' Again I didn't hear what he said, but she went on: 'Nothing that you can say will make any difference. I see my duty clearly. My mind is made up. You need not think that any fear of publicity, or scandal between husband and wife will deter me.' Then I thought I heard them coming out, so I went off quickly."

"You are sure it was Mr. Inglethorp's voice you heard?"

"Oh, yes, sir, whose else's could it be?"

"Well, what happened next?"

"Later, I came back to the hall; but it was all quiet. At five o'clock, Mrs. Inglethorp rang the bell and told me to bring her a cup of tea—nothing to eat—to the boudoir. She was looking dreadful—so white and upset. 'Dorcas,' she says, 'I've had a great shock.' 'I'm sorry for that, m'm,' I says. 'You'll feel better after a nice hot cup of tea, m'm.' She had something in her hand. I don't know if it was a letter, or just a piece of paper, but it had writing on it, and she kept staring at it, almost as if she couldn't believe what was written there. She whispered to herself, as though she had forgotten I was there: 'These few words—and everything's changed.' And then she says to me: 'Never trust a man, Dorcas, they're not worth it!' I hurried off, and got her a good strong cup of tea, and she thanked me, and said she'd feel better when she'd drunk it. 'I don't know what to do,' she says. 'Scandal between husband and wife is a dreadful thing, Dorcas. I'd rather hush it up if I could.' Mrs. Cavendish came in just then, so she didn't say any more."

"She still had the letter, or whatever it was, in her hand?"

"Yes, sir."

"What would she be likely to do with it afterwards?"

"Well, I don't know, sir, I expect she would lock it up in that purple case of hers."

"Is that where she usually kept important papers?"

"Yes, sir. She brought it down with her every morning, and took it up every night."

"When did she lose the key of it?"

"She missed it yesterday at lunch-time, sir, and told me to look carefully for it. She was very much put out about it."

"But she had a duplicate key?"

"Oh, yes, sir."

Dorcas was looking very curiously at him and, to tell the truth, so was I. What was all this about a lost key? Poirot smiled.

"Never mind, Dorcas, it is my business to know things. Is this the key that was lost?" He drew from his pocket the key that he had found in the lock of the despatch-case upstairs.

Dorcas's eyes looked as though they would pop out of her head.

"That's it, sir, right enough. But where did you find it? I looked everywhere for it."

"Ah, but you see it was not in the same place yesterday as it was today. Now, to pass to another subject, had your mistress a dark green dress in her wardrobe?"

Dorcas was rather startled by the unexpected question.

"No, sir."

"Are you quite sure?"

"Oh, yes, sir."

"Has anyone else in the house got a green dress?"

Dorcas reflected.

"Miss Cynthia has a green evening dress."

"Light or dark green?"

"A light green, sir; a sort of chiffon, they call it."

"Ah, that is not what I want. And nobody else has anything green?"

"No, sir—not that I know of."

Poirot's face did not betray a trace of whether he was disappointed or otherwise. He merely remarked:

"Good, we will leave that and pass on. Have you any reason to believe that your mistress was likely to take a sleeping powder last night?"

"Not *last* night, sir, I know she didn't."

"Why do you know so positively?"

"Because the box was empty. She took the last one two days ago, and she didn't have any more made up."

"You are quite sure of that?"

"Positive, sir."

"Then that is cleared up! By the way, your mistress didn't ask you to sign any paper yesterday?"

"To sign a paper? No, sir."

"When Mr. Hastings and Mr. Lawrence came in yesterday evening, they found your mistress busy writing letters. I suppose you can give me no idea to whom these letters were addressed?"

"I'm afraid I couldn't, sir. I was out in the evening. Perhaps Annie could tell you, though she's a careless girl. Never cleared the coffee-cups away last night. That's what happens when I'm not here to look after things."

Poirot lifted his hand.

"Since they have been left, Dorcas, leave them a little longer, I pray you. I should like to examine them."

"Very well, sir."

"What time did you go out last evening?"

"About six o'clock, sir."

"Thank you, Dorcas, that is all I have to ask you." He rose and strolled to the window. "I have been admiring these flower beds. How many gardeners are employed here, by the way?"

"Only three now, sir. Five, we had, before the war, when it was kept as a gentleman's place should be. I wish you could have seen it then, sir. A fair sight it was. But now there's only old Manning, and young William, and a new-fashioned woman gardener in breeches and such-like. Ah, these are dreadful times!"

"The good times will come again, Dorcas. At least, we hope so. Now, will you send Annie to me here?"

"Yes, sir. Thank you, sir."

"How did you know that Mrs. Inglethorp took sleeping powders?" I asked, in lively curiosity, as Dorcas left the room. "And about the lost key and the duplicate?"

"One thing at a time. As to the sleeping powders, I knew by this."

He suddenly produced a small cardboard box, such as chemists use for powders.

"Where did you find it?"

"In the wash-stand drawer in Mrs. Inglethorp's bedroom. It was Number Six of my catalogue."

"But I suppose, as the last powder was taken two days ago, it is not of much importance?"

"Probably not, but do you notice anything that strikes you as peculiar about this box?"

I examined it closely.

"No, I can't say that I do."

"Look at the label."

I read the label carefully: "'One powder to be taken at bedtime, if required. Mrs. Inglethorp.' No, I see nothing unusual."

"Not the fact that there is no chemist's name?"

"Ah!" I exclaimed. "To be sure, that is odd!"

"Have you ever known a chemist to send out a box like that, without his printed name?"

"No, I can't say that I have."

I was becoming quite excited, but Poirot damped my ardour by remarking:

"Yet the explanation is quite simple. So do not intrigue yourself, my friend."

An audible creaking proclaimed the approach of Annie, so I had no time to reply.

Annie was a fine, strapping girl, and was evidently labouring under intense excitement, mingled with a certain ghoulish enjoyment of the tragedy.

Poirot came to the point at once, with a business-like briskness.

"I sent for you, Annie, because I thought you might be able to tell me something about the letters Mrs. Inglethorp wrote last night. How many were there? And can you tell me any of the names and addresses?"

Annie considered.

"There were four letters, sir. One was to Miss Howard, and one was to Mr. Wells, the lawyer, and the other two I don't think I remember, sir—oh, yes, one was to Ross's, the caterers in Tadminster. The other one, I don't remember."

"Think," urged Poirot.

Annie racked her brains in vain.

"I'm sorry, sir, but it's clean gone. I don't think I can have noticed it."

"It does not matter," said Poirot, not betraying any sign of disappointment. "Now I want to ask you about something else. There is a saucepan in Mrs. Inglethorp's room with some cocoa in it. Did she have that every night?"

"Yes, sir, it was put in her room every evening, and she warmed it up in the night—whenever she fancied it."

"What was it? Plain cocoa?"

"Yes, sir, made with milk, with a teaspoonful of sugar, and two teaspoonfuls of rum in it."

"Who took it to her room?"

"I did, sir."

"Always?"

"Yes, sir."

"At what time?"

"When I went to draw the curtains, as a rule, sir."

"Did you bring it straight up from the kitchen then?"

"No, sir, you see there's not much room on the gas stove, so Cook used to make it early, before putting the vegetables on for supper. Then I used to bring it up, and put it on the table by the swing door, and take it into her room later."

"The swing door is in the left wing, is it not?"

"Yes, sir."

"And the table, is it on this side of the door, or on the farther—servants' side?"

"It's this side, sir."

"What time did you bring it up last night?"

"About quarter-past seven, I should say, sir."

"And when did you take it into Mrs. Inglethorp's room?"

"When I went to shut up, sir. About eight o'clock. Mrs. Inglethorp came up to bed before I'd finished."

"Then, between 7:15 and 8 o'clock, the cocoa was standing on the table in the left wing?"

"Yes, sir." Annie had been growing redder and redder in the face, and now she blurted out unexpectedly:

"And if there *was* salt in it, sir, it wasn't me. I never took the salt near it."

"What makes you think there was salt in it?" asked Poirot.

"Seeing it on the tray, sir."

"You saw some salt on the tray?"

"Yes. Coarse kitchen salt, it looked. I never noticed it when I took the tray up, but when I came to take it into the mistress's room I saw it at once, and I suppose I ought to have taken it down again, and asked Cook to make some fresh. But I was in a hurry, because Dorcas was out, and I thought maybe the cocoa itself was all right, and the salt had only gone on the tray. So I dusted it off with my apron, and took it in."

I had the utmost difficulty in controlling my excitement. Unknown to herself, Annie had provided us with an important piece of evidence. How she would have gaped if she had realized that her "coarse kitchen salt" was strychnine, one of the most deadly poisons known to mankind. I marvelled at Poirot's calm. His self-control was astonishing. I awaited his next question with impatience, but it disappointed me.

"When you went into Mrs. Inglethorp's room, was the door leading into Miss Cynthia's room bolted?"

"Oh! Yes, sir; it always was. It had never been opened."

"And the door into Mr. Inglethorp's room? Did you notice if that was bolted too?"

Annie hesitated.

"I couldn't rightly say, sir; it was shut but I couldn't say whether it was bolted or not."

"When you finally left the room, did Mrs. Inglethorp bolt the door after you?"

"No, sir, not then, but I expect she did later. She usually did lock it at night. The door into the passage, that is."

"Did you notice any candle grease on the floor when you did the room yesterday?"

"Candle grease? Oh, no, sir. Mrs. Inglethorp didn't have a candle, only a reading-lamp."

"Then, if there had been a large patch of candle grease on the floor, you think you would have been sure to have seen it?"

"Yes, sir, and I would have taken it out with a piece of blotting-paper and a hot iron."

Then Poirot repeated the question he had put to Dorcas:

"Did your mistress ever have a green dress?"

"No, sir."

"Nor a mantle, nor a cape, nor a—how do you call it?—a sports coat?"

"Not green, sir."

"Nor anyone else in the house?"

Annie reflected.

"No, sir."

"You are sure of that?"

"Quite sure."

"*Bien*! That is all I want to know. Thank you very much."

With a nervous giggle, Annie took herself creakingly out of the room. My pent-up excitement burst forth.

"Poirot," I cried, "I congratulate you! This is a great discovery."

"What is a great discovery?"

"Why, that it was the cocoa and not the coffee that was poisoned. That explains everything! Of course it did not take effect until the early morning, since the cocoa was only drunk in the middle of the night."

"So you think that the cocoa—mark well what I say, Hastings, the *cocoa*—contained strychnine?"

"Of course! That salt on the tray, what else could it have been?"

"It might have been salt," replied Poirot placidly.

I shrugged my shoulders. If he was going to take the matter that way, it was no good arguing with him. The idea crossed my mind, not for the first time, that poor old Poirot was growing old. Privately I thought it lucky that he had associated with him someone of a more receptive type of mind.

Poirot was surveying me with quietly twinkling eyes.

"You are not pleased with me, *mon ami*?"

"My dear Poirot," I said coldly, "it is not for me to dictate to you. You have a right to your own opinion, just as I have to mine."

"A most admirable sentiment," remarked Poirot, rising briskly to his feet. "Now I have finished with this room. By the way, whose is the smaller desk in the corner?"

"Mr. Inglethorp's."

"Ah!" He tried the roll top tentatively. "Locked. But perhaps one of Mrs. Inglethorp's keys would open it." He tried several, twisting and turning them with a practiced hand, and finally uttering an ejaculation of satisfaction. "*Voilà*! It is not the key, but it will open it at a pinch." He slid back the roll top, and ran a rapid eye over the neatly filed papers. To my surprise, he did not examine them, merely remarking approvingly as he relocked the desk: "Decidedly, he is a man of method, this Mr. Inglethorp!"

A "man of method" was, in Poirot's estimation, the highest praise that could be bestowed on any individual.

I felt that my friend was not what he had been as he rambled on disconnectedly:

"There were no stamps in his desk, but there might have been, eh, *mon ami*? There might have been? Yes"—his eyes wandered round the room—"this boudoir has nothing more to tell us. It did not yield much. Only this."

He pulled a crumpled envelope out of his pocket, and tossed it over to me. It was rather a curious document. A plain, dirty looking old envelope with a few words scrawled across it, apparently at random. The following is a facsimile of it.

possessed

I am possessed

He is possessed.

I am possessed

possessed

Chapter V

"IT ISN'T STRYCHNINE, IS IT?"

Where did you find this?" I asked Poirot, in lively curiosity.

"In the waste-paper basket. You recognise the handwriting?"

"Yes, it is Mrs. Inglethorp's. But what does it mean?"

Poirot shrugged his shoulders.

"I cannot say—but it is suggestive."

A wild idea flashed across me. Was it possible that Mrs. Inglethorp's mind was deranged? Had she some fantastic idea of demoniacal possession? And, if that were so, was it not also possible that she might have taken her own life?

I was about to expound these theories to Poirot, when his own words distracted me.

"Come," he said, "now to examine the coffee-cups!"

"My dear Poirot! What on earth is the good of that, now that we know about the cocoa?"

"*Oh, là là!* That miserable cocoa!" cried Poirot flippantly.

He laughed with apparent enjoyment, raising his arms to heaven in mock despair, in what I could not but consider the worst possible taste.

"And, anyway," I said, with increasing coldness, "as Mrs. Inglethorp took her coffee upstairs with her, I do not see what you expect to find, unless you consider it likely that we shall discover a packet of strychnine on the coffee tray!"

Poirot was sobered at once.

"Come, come, my friend," he said, slipping his arms through mine. "*Ne vous fâchez pas!* Allow me to interest myself in my coffee-cups, and I will respect your cocoa. There! Is it a bargain?"

He was so quaintly humorous that I was forced to laugh; and we went together to the drawing-room, where the coffee-cups and tray remained undisturbed as we had left them.

Poirot made me recapitulate the scene of the night before, listening very carefully, and verifying the position of the various cups.

"So Mrs. Cavendish stood by the tray—and poured out. Yes. Then she came across to the window where you sat with Mademoiselle Cynthia. Yes. Here are the three cups. And the cup on the mantel-piece, half drunk, that would be Mr. Lawrence Cavendish's. And the one on the tray?"

"John Cavendish's. I saw him put it down there."

"Good. One, two, three, four, five—but where, then, is the cup of Mr. Inglethorp?"

"He does not take coffee."

"Then all are accounted for. One moment, my friend."

With infinite care, he took a drop or two from the grounds in each cup, sealing them up in separate test tubes, tasting each in turn as he did so. His physiognomy underwent a curious change. An expression gathered there that I can only describe as half puzzled, and half relieved.

"*Bien!*" he said at last. "It is evident! I had an idea—but clearly I was mistaken. Yes, altogether I was mistaken. Yet it is strange. But no matter!"

And, with a characteristic shrug, he dismissed whatever it was that was worrying him from his mind. I could have told him from the beginning that this obsession of his over the coffee was bound to end in a blind alley, but I restrained my tongue. After all, though he was old, Poirot had been a great man in his day.

"Breakfast is ready," said John Cavendish, coming in from the hall. "You will breakfast with us, Monsieur Poirot?"

Poirot acquiesced. I observed John. Already he was almost restored to his normal self. The shock of the events of the last night had upset him temporarily, but his equable poise soon swung back to the normal. He was a man of very little imagination, in sharp contrast with his brother, who had, perhaps, too much.

Ever since the early hours of the morning, John had been hard at work, sending telegrams—one of the first had gone to Evelyn Howard—writing notices for the papers, and generally occupying himself with the melancholy duties that a death entails.

"May I ask how things are proceeding?" he said. "Do your investigations point to my mother having died a natural death—or—or must we prepare ourselves for the worst?"

"I think, Mr. Cavendish," said Poirot gravely, "that you would do well not to buoy yourself up with any false hopes. Can you tell me the views of the other members of the family?"

"My brother Lawrence is convinced that we are making a fuss over nothing. He says that everything points to its being a simple case of heart failure."

"He does, does he? That is very interesting—very interesting," murmured Poirot softly. "And Mrs. Cavendish?"

A faint cloud passed over John's face.

"I have not the least idea what my wife's views on the subject are."

The answer brought a momentary stiffness in its train. John broke the rather awkward silence by saying with a slight effort:

"I told you, didn't I, that Mr. Inglethorp has returned?"

Poirot bent his head.

"It's an awkward position for all of us. Of course one has to treat him as usual—but, hang it all, one's gorge does rise at sitting down to eat with a possible murderer!"

Poirot nodded sympathetically.

"I quite understand. It is a very difficult situation for you, Mr. Cavendish. I would like to ask you one question. Mr. Inglethorp's reason for not returning last night was, I believe, that he had forgotten the latch-key. Is not that so?"

"Yes."

"I suppose you are quite sure that the latch-key was forgotten—that he did not take it after all?"

"I have no idea. I never thought of looking. We always keep it in the hall drawer. I'll go and see if it's there now."

Poirot held up his hand with a faint smile.

"No, no, Mr. Cavendish, it is too late now. I am certain that you would find it. If Mr. Inglethorp did take it, he has had ample time to replace it by now."

"But do you think—"

"I think nothing. If anyone had chanced to look this morning before his return, and seen it there, it would have been a valuable point in his favour. That is all."

John looked perplexed.

"Do not worry," said Poirot smoothly. "I assure you that you need not let it trouble you. Since you are so kind, let us go and have some breakfast."

Every one was assembled in the dining-room. Under the circumstances, we were naturally not a cheerful party. The reaction after a shock is always trying, and I think we were all suffering from it. Decorum and good breeding naturally enjoined that our demeanour should be much as usual, yet I could not help wondering if this self-control were really a matter of great difficulty. There were no red eyes, no signs of secretly indulged grief. I felt that I was right in my opinion that Dorcas was the person most affected by the personal side of the tragedy.

I pass over Alfred Inglethorp, who acted the bereaved widower in a manner that I felt to be disgusting in its hypocrisy. Did he know that we suspected him, I wondered. Surely he could not be unaware of the fact, conceal it as we would. Did he feel some secret stirring of fear, or was he confident that his crime would go unpunished? Surely the suspicion in the atmosphere must warn him that he was already a marked man.

But did every one suspect him? What about Mrs. Cavendish? I watched her as she sat at the head of the table, graceful, composed, enigmatic. In her soft grey frock, with white ruffles at the wrists falling over her slender hands, she looked very beautiful. When she chose, however, her face could be sphinx-like in its inscrutability. She was very silent, hardly opening her lips, and yet in some queer way I felt that the great strength of her personality was dominating us all.

And little Cynthia? Did she suspect? She looked very tired and ill, I thought. The heaviness and languor of her manner were very marked. I asked her if she were feeling ill, and she answered frankly:

"Yes, I've got the most beastly headache."

"Have another cup of coffee, mademoiselle?" said Poirot solicitously. "It will revive you. It is unparalleled for the *mal de tête*." He jumped up and took her cup.

"No sugar," said Cynthia, watching him, as he picked up the sugar-tongs.

"No sugar? You abandon it in the war-time, eh?"

"No, I never take it in coffee."

"*Sacré!*" murmured Poirot to himself, as he brought back the replenished cup.

Only I heard him, and glancing up curiously at the little man I saw that his face was working with suppressed excitement, and his eyes were as green as a cat's. He had heard or seen something that had affected him strongly—but what was it? I do not usually label myself as dense, but I must confess that nothing out of the ordinary had attracted my attention.

In another moment, the door opened and Dorcas appeared.

"Mr. Wells to see you, sir," she said to John.

I remembered the name as being that of the lawyer to whom Mrs. Inglethorp had written the night before.

John rose immediately.

"Show him into my study." Then he turned to us. "My mother's lawyer," he explained. And in a lower voice: "He is also Coroner—you understand. Perhaps you would like to come with me?"

We acquiesced and followed him out of the room. John strode on ahead and I took the opportunity of whispering to Poirot:

"There will be an inquest then?"

Poirot nodded absently. He seemed absorbed in thought; so much so that my curiosity was aroused.

"What is it? You are not attending to what I say."

"It is true, my friend. I am much worried."

"Why?"

"Because Mademoiselle Cynthia does not take sugar in her coffee."

"What? You cannot be serious?"

"But I am most serious. Ah, there is something there that I do not understand. My instinct was right."

"What instinct?"

"The instinct that led me to insist on examining those coffee-cups. *Chut!* no more now!"

We followed John into his study, and he closed the door behind us.

Mr. Wells was a pleasant man of middle-age, with keen eyes, and the typical lawyer's mouth. John introduced us both, and explained the reason of our presence.

"You will understand, Wells," he added, "that this is all strictly private. We are still hoping that there will turn out to be no need for investigation of any kind."

"Quite so, quite so," said Mr. Wells soothingly. "I wish we could have spared you the pain and publicity of an inquest, but of course it's quite unavoidable in the absence of a doctor's certificate."

"Yes, I suppose so."

"Clever man, Bauerstein. Great authority on toxicology, I believe."

"Indeed," said John with a certain stiffness in his manner. Then he added rather hesitatingly: "Shall we have to appear as witnesses—all of us, I mean?"

"You, of course—and ah—er—Mr.—er—Inglethorp."

A slight pause ensued before the lawyer went on in his soothing manner:

"Any other evidence will be simply confirmatory, a mere matter of form."

"I see."

A faint expression of relief swept over John's face. It puzzled me, for I saw no occasion for it.

"If you know of nothing to the contrary," pursued Mr. Wells, "I had thought of Friday. That will give us plenty of time for the doctor's report. The post-mortem is to take place tonight, I believe?"

"Yes."

"Then that arrangement will suit you?"

"Perfectly."

"I need not tell you, my dear Cavendish, how distressed I am at this most tragic affair."

"Can you give us no help in solving it, monsieur?" interposed Poirot, speaking for the first time since we had entered the room.

"I?"

"Yes, we heard that Mrs. Inglethorp wrote to you last night. You should have received the letter this morning."

"I did, but it contains no information. It is merely a note asking me to call upon her this morning, as she wanted my advice on a matter of great importance."

"She gave you no hint as to what that matter might be?"

"Unfortunately, no."

"That is a pity," said John.

"A great pity," agreed Poirot gravely.

There was silence. Poirot remained lost in thought for a few minutes. Finally he turned to the lawyer again.

"Mr. Wells, there is one thing I should like to ask you—that is, if it is not against professional etiquette. In the event of Mrs. Inglethorp's death, who would inherit her money?"

The lawyer hesitated a moment, and then replied:

"The knowledge will be public property very soon, so if Mr. Cavendish does not object—"

"Not at all," interpolated John.

"I do not see any reason why I should not answer your question. By her last will, dated August of last year, after various unimportant legacies to servants, etc., she gave her entire fortune to her stepson, Mr. John Cavendish."

"Was not that—pardon the question, Mr. Cavendish—rather unfair to her other stepson, Mr. Lawrence Cavendish?"

"No, I do not think so. You see, under the terms of their father's will, while John inherited the property, Lawrence, at his stepmother's death, would come into a considerable sum of money. Mrs. Inglethorp left her money to her elder stepson, knowing that he would have to keep up Styles. It was, to my mind, a very fair and equitable distribution."

Poirot nodded thoughtfully.

"I see. But I am right in saying, am I not, that by your English law that will was automatically revoked when Mrs. Inglethorp remarried?"

Mr. Wells bowed his head.

"As I was about to proceed, Monsieur Poirot, that document is now null and void."

"*Hein!*" said Poirot. He reflected for a moment, and then asked: "Was Mrs. Inglethorp herself aware of that fact?"

"I do not know. She may have been."

"She was," said John unexpectedly. "We were discussing the matter of wills being revoked by marriage only yesterday."

"Ah! One more question, Mr. Wells. You say 'her last will.' Had Mrs. Inglethorp, then, made several former wills?"

"On an average, she made a new will at least once a year," said Mr. Wells imperturbably. "She was given to changing her mind as to her testamentary dispositions, now benefiting one, now another member of her family."

"Suppose," suggested Poirot, "that, unknown to you, she had made a new will in favour of someone who was not, in any sense of the word, a member of the family—we will say Miss Howard, for instance—would you be surprised?"

"Not in the least."

"Ah!" Poirot seemed to have exhausted his questions.

I drew close to him, while John and the lawyer were debating the question of going through Mrs. Inglethorp's papers.

"Do you think Mrs. Inglethorp made a will leaving all her money to Miss Howard?" I asked in a low voice, with some curiosity.

Poirot smiled.

"No."

"Then why did you ask?"

"Hush!"

John Cavendish had turned to Poirot.

"Will you come with us, Monsieur Poirot? We are going through my mother's papers. Mr. Inglethorp is quite willing to leave it entirely to Mr. Wells and myself."

"Which simplifies matters very much," murmured the lawyer. "As technically, of course, he was entitled—" He did not finish the sentence.

"We will look through the desk in the boudoir first," explained John, "and go up to her bedroom afterwards. She kept her most important papers in a purple despatch-case, which we must look through carefully."

"Yes," said the lawyer, "it is quite possible that there may be a later will than the one in my possession."

"There is a later will." It was Poirot who spoke.

"What?" John and the lawyer looked at him startled.

"Or, rather," pursued my friend imperturbably, "there was one."

"What do you mean—there was one? Where is it now?"

"Burnt!"

"Burnt?"

"Yes. See here." He took out the charred fragment we had found in the grate in Mrs. Inglethorp's room, and handed it to the lawyer with a brief explanation of when and where he had found it.

"But possibly this is an old will?"

"I do not think so. In fact I am almost certain that it was made no earlier than yesterday afternoon."

"What?" "Impossible!" broke simultaneously from both men.

Poirot turned to John.

"If you will allow me to send for your gardener, I will prove it to you."

"Oh, of course—but I don't see—"

Poirot raised his hand.

"Do as I ask you. Afterwards you shall question as much as you please."

"Very well." He rang the bell.

Dorcas answered it in due course.

"Dorcas, will you tell Manning to come round and speak to me here."

"Yes, sir."

Dorcas withdrew.

We waited in a tense silence. Poirot alone seemed perfectly at his ease, and dusted a forgotten corner of the bookcase.

The clumping of hobnailed boots on the gravel outside proclaimed the approach of Manning. John looked questioningly at Poirot. The latter nodded.

"Come inside, Manning," said John, "I want to speak to you."

Manning came slowly and hesitatingly through the French window, and stood as near it as he could. He held his cap in his hands, twisting it very carefully round and round. His back was much bent, though he was probably not as old as he looked, but his eyes were sharp and intelligent, and belied his slow and rather cautious speech.

"Manning," said John, "this gentleman will put some questions to you which I want you to answer."

"Yes sir," mumbled Manning.

Poirot stepped forward briskly. Manning's eye swept over him with a faint contempt.

"You were planting a bed of begonias round by the south side of the house yesterday afternoon, were you not, Manning?"

"Yes, sir, me and Willum."

"And Mrs. Inglethorp came to the window and called you, did she not?"

"Yes, sir, she did."

"Tell me in your own words exactly what happened after that."

"Well, sir, nothing much. She just told Willum to go on his bicycle down to the village, and bring back a form of will, or such-like—I don't know what exactly—she wrote it down for him."

"Well?"

"Well, he did, sir."

"And what happened next?"

"We went on with the begonias, sir."

"Did not Mrs. Inglethorp call you again?"

"Yes, sir, both me and Willum, she called."

"And then?"

"She made us come right in, and sign our names at the bottom of a long paper—under where she'd signed."

"Did you see anything of what was written above her signature?" asked Poirot sharply.

"No, sir, there was a bit of blotting paper over that part."

"And you signed where she told you?"

"Yes, sir, first me and then Willum."

"What did she do with it afterwards?"

"Well, sir, she slipped it into a long envelope, and put it inside a sort of purple box that was standing on the desk."

"What time was it when she first called you?"

"About four, I should say, sir."

"Not earlier? Couldn't it have been about half-past three?"

"No, I shouldn't say so, sir. It would be more likely to be a bit after four—not before it."

"Thank you, Manning, that will do," said Poirot pleasantly.

The gardener glanced at his master, who nodded, whereupon Manning lifted a finger to his forehead with a low mumble, and backed cautiously out of the window.

We all looked at each other.

"Good heavens!" murmured John. "What an extraordinary coincidence."

"How—a coincidence?"

"That my mother should have made a will on the very day of her death!"

Mr. Wells cleared his throat and remarked drily:

"Are you so sure it is a coincidence, Cavendish?"

"What do you mean?"

"Your mother, you tell me, had a violent quarrel with—someone yesterday afternoon—"

"What do you mean?" cried John again. There was a tremor in his voice, and he had gone very pale.

"In consequence of that quarrel, your mother very suddenly and hurriedly makes a new will. The contents of that will we shall never know. She told no one of its provisions. This morning, no doubt, she would have consulted me on the subject—but she had no chance. The will disappears, and she takes its secret with her to her grave. Cavendish, I much fear there is no coincidence there. Monsieur Poirot, I am sure you agree with me that the facts are very suggestive."

"Suggestive, or not," interrupted John, "we are most grateful to Monsieur Poirot for elucidating the matter. But for him, we should never have known of this will. I suppose, I may not ask you, monsieur, what first led you to suspect the fact?"

Poirot smiled and answered:

"A scribbled over old envelope, and a freshly planted bed of begonias."

John, I think, would have pressed his questions further, but at that moment the loud purr of a motor was audible, and we all turned to the window as it swept past.

"Evie!" cried John. "Excuse me, Wells." He went hurriedly out into the hall.

Poirot looked inquiringly at me.

"Miss Howard," I explained.

"Ah, I am glad she has come. There is a woman with a head and a heart too, Hastings. Though the good God gave her no beauty!"

I followed John's example, and went out into the hall, where Miss Howard was endeavouring to extricate herself from the voluminous mass of veils that enveloped her head. As her eyes fell on me, a sudden pang of guilt shot through me. This was the woman who had warned me so earnestly, and to whose warning I had, alas, paid no heed! How soon, and how contemptuously, I had dismissed it from my mind. Now that she had been proved justified in so tragic a manner, I felt ashamed. She had known Alfred Inglethorp only too well. I wondered whether, if she had remained at Styles, the tragedy would have taken place, or would the man have feared her watchful eyes?

I was relieved when she shook me by the hand, with her well remembered painful grip. The eyes that met mine were sad, but not reproachful; that she had been crying bitterly, I could tell by the redness of her eyelids, but her manner was unchanged from its old gruffness.

"Started the moment I got the wire. Just come off night duty. Hired car. Quickest way to get here."

"Have you had anything to eat this morning, Evie?" asked John.

"No."

"I thought not. Come along, breakfast's not cleared away yet, and they'll make you some fresh tea." He turned to me. "Look after her, Hastings, will you? Wells is waiting for me. Oh, here's Monsieur Poirot. He's helping us, you know, Evie."

Miss Howard shook hands with Poirot, but glanced suspiciously over her shoulder at John.

"What do you mean—helping us?"

"Helping us to investigate."

"Nothing to investigate. Have they taken him to prison yet?"

"Taken who to prison?"

"Who? Alfred Inglethorp, of course!"

"My dear Evie, do be careful. Lawrence is of the opinion that my mother died from heart seizure."

"More fool, Lawrence!" retorted Miss Howard. "Of course Alfred Inglethorp murdered poor Emily—as I always told you he would."

"My dear Evie, don't shout so. Whatever we may think or suspect, it is better to say as little as possible for the present. The inquest isn't until Friday."

"Not until fiddlesticks!" The snort Miss Howard gave was truly magnificent. "You're all off your heads. The man will be out of the country by then. If he's any sense, he won't stay here tamely and wait to be hanged."

John Cavendish looked at her helplessly.

"I know what it is," she accused him, "you've been listening to the doctors. Never should. What do they know? Nothing at all—or just enough to make them dangerous. I ought to know—my own father was a doctor. That little Wilkins is about the greatest fool that even I have ever seen. Heart seizure!

Sort of thing he would say. Anyone with any sense could see at once that her husband had poisoned her. I always said he'd murder her in her bed, poor soul. Now he's done it. And all you can do is to murmur silly things about 'heart seizure' and 'inquest on Friday.' You ought to be ashamed of yourself, John Cavendish."

"What do you want me to do?" asked John, unable to help a faint smile. "Dash it all, Evie, I can't haul him down to the local police station by the scruff of his neck."

"Well, you might do something. Find out how he did it. He's a crafty beggar. Dare say he soaked fly papers. Ask Cook if she's missed any."

It occurred to me very forcibly at that moment that to harbour Miss Howard and Alfred Inglethorp under the same roof, and keep the peace between them, was likely to prove a Herculean task, and I did not envy John. I could see by the expression of his face that he fully appreciated the difficulty of the position. For the moment, he sought refuge in retreat, and left the room precipitately.

Dorcas brought in fresh tea. As she left the room, Poirot came over from the window where he had been standing, and sat down facing Miss Howard.

"Mademoiselle," he said gravely, "I want to ask you something."

"Ask away," said the lady, eyeing him with some disfavour.

"I want to be able to count upon your help."

"I'll help you to hang Alfred with pleasure," she replied gruffly. "Hanging's too good for him. Ought to be drawn and quartered, like in good old times."

"We are at one then," said Poirot, "for I, too, want to hang the criminal."

"Alfred Inglethorp?"

"Him, or another."

"No question of another. Poor Emily was never murdered until he came along. I don't say she wasn't surrounded by sharks—she was. But it was only her purse they were after. Her life was safe enough. But along comes Mr. Alfred Inglethorp—and within two months—hey presto!"

"Believe me, Miss Howard," said Poirot very earnestly, "if Mr. Inglethorp is the man, he shall not escape me. On my honour, I will hang him as high as Haman!"

"That's better," said Miss Howard more enthusiastically.

"But I must ask you to trust me. Now your help may be very valuable to me. I will tell you why. Because, in all this house of mourning, yours are the only eyes that have wept."

Miss Howard blinked, and a new note crept into the gruffness of her voice.

"If you mean that I was fond of her—yes, I was. You know, Emily was a selfish old woman in her way. She was very generous, but she always wanted a return. She never let people forget what she had done for them—and, that way she missed love. Don't think she ever realized it, though, or felt the lack of it. Hope not, anyway. I was on a different footing. I took my stand from the first. 'So many pounds a year I'm worth to you. Well and good. But not a penny piece besides—not a pair of gloves, nor a theatre ticket.' She didn't understand—was very offended sometimes. Said I was foolishly proud. It wasn't that—but I couldn't explain. Anyway, I kept my self-respect. And so, out of the whole bunch, I was the only one who could allow myself to be fond of her. I watched over her. I guarded her from the lot of them, and then a glib-tongued scoundrel comes along, and pooh! all my years of devotion go for nothing."

Poirot nodded sympathetically.

"I understand, mademoiselle, I understand all you feel. It is most natural. You think that we are lukewarm—that we lack fire and energy—but trust me, it is not so."

John stuck his head in at this juncture, and invited us both to come up to Mrs. Inglethorp's room, as he and Mr. Wells had finished looking through the desk in the boudoir.

As we went up the stairs, John looked back to the dining-room door, and lowered his voice confidentially:

"Look here, what's going to happen when these two meet?"

I shook my head helplessly.

"I've told Mary to keep them apart if she can."

"Will she be able to do so?"

"The Lord only knows. There's one thing, Inglethorp himself won't be too keen on meeting her."

"You've got the keys still, haven't you, Poirot?" I asked, as we reached the door of the locked room.

Taking the keys from Poirot, John unlocked it, and we all passed in. The lawyer went straight to the desk, and John followed him.

"My mother kept most of her important papers in this despatch-case, I believe," he said.

Poirot drew out the small bunch of keys.

"Permit me. I locked it, out of precaution, this morning."

"But it's not locked now."

"Impossible!"

"See." And John lifted the lid as he spoke.

"*Milles tonnerres!*" cried Poirot, dumbfounded. "And I—who have both the keys in my pocket!" He flung himself upon the case. Suddenly he stiffened. "*Eh voilà une affaire!* This lock has been forced."

"What?"

Poirot laid down the case again.

"But who forced it? Why should they? When? But the door was locked?" These exclamations burst from us disjointedly.

Poirot answered them categorically—almost mechanically.

"Who? That is the question. Why? Ah, if I only knew. When? Since I was here an hour ago. As to the door being locked, it is a very ordinary lock. Probably any other of the doorkeys in this passage would fit it."

We stared at one another blankly. Poirot had walked over to the mantel-piece. He was outwardly calm, but I noticed his hands, which from long force of habit were mechanically straightening the spill vases on the mantel-piece, were shaking violently.

"See here, it was like this," he said at last. "There was something in that case—some piece of evidence, slight in itself perhaps, but still enough of a clue to connect the murderer with the crime. It was vital to him that it should be destroyed before it was discovered and its significance appreciated. Therefore, he took the risk, the great risk, of coming in here. Finding the case locked, he was obliged to force it, thus betraying his presence. For him to take that risk, it must have been something of great importance."

"But what was it?"

"Ah!" cried Poirot, with a gesture of anger. "That, I do not know! A document of some kind, without doubt, possibly the scrap of paper Dorcas saw in her hand yesterday afternoon. And I—" his anger burst forth freely— "miserable animal that I am! I guessed nothing! I have behaved like an imbecile! I should never have left that case here. I should have carried it away with me. Ah, triple pig! And now it is gone. It is destroyed—but is it destroyed? Is there not yet a chance—we must leave no stone unturned—"

He rushed like a madman from the room, and I followed him as soon as I had sufficiently recovered my wits. But, by the time I had reached the top of the stairs, he was out of sight.

Mary Cavendish was standing where the staircase branched, staring down into the hall in the direction in which he had disappeared.

"What has happened to your extraordinary little friend, Mr. Hastings? He has just rushed past me like a mad bull."

"He's rather upset about something," I remarked feebly. I really did not know how much Poirot would wish me to disclose. As I saw a faint smile gather on Mrs. Cavendish's expressive mouth, I endeavoured to try and turn the conversation by saying: "They haven't met yet, have they?"

"Who?"

"Mr. Inglethorp and Miss Howard."

She looked at me in rather a disconcerting manner.

"Do you think it would be such a disaster if they did meet?"

"Well, don't you?" I said, rather taken aback.

"No." She was smiling in her quiet way. "I should like to see a good flare up. It would clear the air. At present we are all thinking so much, and saying so little."

"John doesn't think so," I remarked. "He's anxious to keep them apart."

"Oh, John!"

Something in her tone fired me, and I blurted out:

"Old John's an awfully good sort."

She studied me curiously for a minute or two, and then said, to my great surprise:

"You are loyal to your friend. I like you for that."

"Aren't you my friend too?"

"I am a very bad friend."

"Why do you say that?"

"Because it is true. I am charming to my friends one day, and forget all about them the next."

I don't know what impelled me, but I was nettled, and I said foolishly and not in the best of taste:

"Yet you seem to be invariably charming to Dr. Bauerstein!"

Instantly I regretted my words. Her face stiffened. I had the impression of a steel curtain coming down and blotting out the real woman. Without a word, she turned and went swiftly up the stairs, whilst I stood like an idiot gaping after her.

I was recalled to other matters by a frightful row going on below. I could hear Poirot shouting and expounding. I was vexed to think that my diplomacy had been in vain. The little man appeared to be taking the whole house into his confidence, a proceeding of which I, for one, doubted the wisdom. Once again I could not help regretting that my friend was so prone to lose his head in moments of excitement. I stepped briskly down the stairs. The sight of me calmed Poirot almost immediately. I drew him aside.

"My dear fellow," I said, "is this wise? Surely you don't want the whole house to know of this occurrence? You are actually playing into the criminal's hands."

"You think so, Hastings?"

"I am sure of it."

"Well, well, my friend, I will be guided by you."

"Good. Although, unfortunately, it is a little too late now."

"Sure."

He looked so crestfallen and abashed that I felt quite sorry, though I still thought my rebuke a just and wise one.

"Well," he said at last, "let us go, *mon ami*."

"You have finished here?"

"For the moment, yes. You will walk back with me to the village?"

"Willingly."

He picked up his little suit-case, and we went out through the open window in the drawing-room. Cynthia Murdoch was just coming in, and Poirot stood aside to let her pass.

"Excuse me, mademoiselle, one minute."

"Yes?" she turned inquiringly.

"Did you ever make up Mrs. Inglethorp's medicines?"

A slight flush rose in her face, as she answered rather constrainedly: "No."

"Only her powders?"

The flush deepened as Cynthia replied:

"Oh, yes, I did make up some sleeping powders for her once."

"These?"

Poirot produced the empty box which had contained powders.

She nodded.

"Can you tell me what they were? Sulphonal? Veronal?"

"No, they were bromide powders."

"Ah! Thank you, mademoiselle; good morning."

As we walked briskly away from the house, I glanced at him more than once. I had often before noticed that, if anything excited him, his eyes turned green like a cat's. They were shining like emeralds now.

"My friend," he broke out at last, "I have a little idea, a very strange, and probably utterly impossible idea. And yet—it fits in."

I shrugged my shoulders. I privately thought that Poirot was rather too much given to these fantastic ideas. In this case, surely, the truth was only too plain and apparent.

"So that is the explanation of the blank label on the box," I remarked. "Very simple, as you said. I really wonder that I did not think of it myself."

Poirot did not appear to be listening to me.

"They have made one more discovery, *là-bas*," he observed, jerking his thumb over his shoulder in the direction of Styles. "Mr. Wells told me as we were going upstairs."

"What was it?"

"Locked up in the desk in the boudoir, they found a will of Mrs. Inglethorp's, dated before her marriage, leaving her fortune to Alfred Inglethorp. It must have been made just at the time they were engaged. It came quite as a surprise to Wells—and to John Cavendish also. It was written on one of those printed will forms, and witnessed by two of the servants—not Dorcas."

"Did Mr. Inglethorp know of it?"

"He says not."

"One might take that with a grain of salt," I remarked sceptically. "All these wills are very confusing. Tell me, how did those scribbled words on the envelope help you to discover that a will was made yesterday afternoon?"

Poirot smiled.

"*Mon ami*, have you ever, when writing a letter, been arrested by the fact that you did not know how to spell a certain word?"

"Yes, often. I suppose every one has."

"Exactly. And have you not, in such a case, tried the word once or twice on the edge of the blotting-paper, or a spare scrap of paper, to see if it looked right? Well, that is what Mrs. Inglethorp did. You will notice that the word 'possessed' is spelt first with one 's' and subsequently with two—correctly. To make sure, she had further tried it in a sentence, thus: 'I am possessed.' Now, what did that tell me? It told me that Mrs. Inglethorp had been writing the word 'possessed' that afternoon, and, having the fragment of paper found in the grate fresh in my mind, the possibility of a will—(a document almost certain to contain that word)—occurred to me at once. This possibility was confirmed by a further circumstance. In the general confusion, the boudoir had not been swept that morning, and near the desk were several traces of brown mould and earth. The weather had been perfectly fine for some days, and no ordinary boots would have left such a heavy deposit.

"I strolled to the window, and saw at once that the begonia beds had been newly planted. The mould in the beds was exactly similar to that on the floor of the boudoir, and also I learnt from you that they *had* been planted yesterday afternoon. I was now sure that one, or possibly both of the gardeners—for there were two sets of footprints in the bed—had entered the boudoir, for if Mrs. Inglethorp had merely wished to speak to them she would in all probability have stood at the window, and they would not have come into the room at all. I was now quite convinced that she had made a fresh will, and had called the two gardeners in to witness her signature. Events proved that I was right in my supposition."

"That was very ingenious," I could not help admitting. "I must confess that the conclusions I drew from those few scribbled words were quite erroneous."

He smiled.

"You gave too much rein to your imagination. Imagination is a good servant, and a bad master. The simplest explanation is always the most likely."

"Another point—how did you know that the key of the despatch-case had been lost?"

"I did not know it. It was a guess that turned out to be correct. You observed that it had a piece of twisted wire through the handle. That suggested to me at once that it had possibly been wrenched off a flimsy key-ring. Now, if it had been lost and recovered, Mrs. Inglethorp would at once have replaced it on her bunch; but on her bunch I found what was obviously the duplicate key, very new and bright, which led me to the hypothesis that somebody else had inserted the original key in the lock of the despatch-case."

"Yes," I said, "Alfred Inglethorp, without doubt."

Poirot looked at me curiously.

"You are very sure of his guilt?"

"Well, naturally. Every fresh circumstance seems to establish it more clearly."

"On the contrary," said Poirot quietly, "there are several points in his favour."

"Oh, come now!"

"Yes."

"I see only one."

"And that?"

"That he was not in the house last night."

"'Bad shot!' as you English say! You have chosen the one point that to my mind tells against him."

"How is that?"

"Because if Mr. Inglethorp knew that his wife would be poisoned last night, he would certainly have arranged to be away from the house. His excuse was an obviously trumped up one. That leaves us two possibilities: either he knew what was going to happen or he had a reason of his own for his absence."

"And that reason?" I asked sceptically.

Poirot shrugged his shoulders.

"How should I know? Discreditable, without doubt. This Mr. Inglethorp, I should say, is somewhat of a scoundrel—but that does not of necessity make him a murderer."

I shook my head, unconvinced.

"We do not agree, eh?" said Poirot. "Well, let us leave it. Time will show which of us is right. Now let us turn to other aspects of the case. What do you make of the fact that all the doors of the bedroom were bolted on the inside?"

"Well—" I considered. "One must look at it logically."

"True."

"I should put it this way. The doors *were* bolted—our own eyes have told us that—yet the presence of the candle grease on the floor, and the destruction of the will, prove that during the night someone entered the room. You agree so far?"

"Perfectly. Put with admirable clearness. Proceed."

"Well," I said, encouraged, "as the person who entered did not do so by the window, nor by miraculous means, it follows that the door must have been opened from inside by Mrs. Inglethorp herself. That strengthens the conviction that the person in question was her husband. She would naturally open the door to her own husband."

Poirot shook his head.

"Why should she? She had bolted the door leading into his room—a most unusual proceeding on her part—she had had a most violent quarrel with him that very afternoon. No, he was the last person she would admit."

"But you agree with me that the door must have been opened by Mrs. Inglethorp herself?"

"There is another possibility. She may have forgotten to bolt the door into the passage when she went to bed, and have got up later, towards morning, and bolted it then."

"Poirot, is that seriously your opinion?"

"No, I do not say it is so, but it might be. Now, to turn to another feature, what do you make of the scrap of conversation you overheard between Mrs. Cavendish and her mother-in-law?"

"I had forgotten that," I said thoughtfully. "That is as enigmatical as ever. It seems incredible that a woman like Mrs. Cavendish, proud and reticent to the last degree, should interfere so violently in what was certainly not her affair."

"Precisely. It was an astonishing thing for a woman of her breeding to do."

"It is certainly curious," I agreed. "Still, it is unimportant, and need not be taken into account."

A groan burst from Poirot.

"What have I always told you? Everything must be taken into account. If the fact will not fit the theory—let the theory go."

"Well, we shall see," I said, nettled.

"Yes, we shall see."

We had reached Leastways Cottage, and Poirot ushered me upstairs to his own room. He offered me one of the tiny Russian cigarettes he himself occasionally smoked. I was amused to notice that he stowed away the used matches most carefully in a little china pot. My momentary annoyance vanished.

Poirot had placed our two chairs in front of the open window which commanded a view of the village street. The fresh air blew in warm and pleasant. It was going to be a hot day.

Suddenly my attention was arrested by a weedy looking young man rushing down the street at a great pace. It was the expression on his face that was extraordinary—a curious mingling of terror and agitation.

"Look, Poirot!" I said.

He leant forward.

"*Tiens!*" he said. "It is Mr. Mace, from the chemist's shop. He is coming here."

The young man came to a halt before Leastways Cottage, and, after hesitating a moment, pounded vigorously at the door.

"A little minute," cried Poirot from the window. "I come."

Motioning to me to follow him, he ran swiftly down the stairs and opened the door. Mr. Mace began at once.

"Oh, Mr. Poirot, I'm sorry for the inconvenience, but I heard that you'd just come back from the Hall?"

"Yes, we have."

The young man moistened his dry lips. His face was working curiously.

"It's all over the village about old Mrs. Inglethorp dying so suddenly. They do say—" he lowered his voice cautiously—"that it's poison?"

Poirot's face remained quite impassive.

"Only the doctors can tell us that, Mr. Mace."

"Yes, exactly—of course—" The young man hesitated, and then his agitation was too much for him. He clutched Poirot by the arm, and sank his voice to a whisper: "Just tell me this, Mr. Poirot, it isn't—it isn't strychnine, is it?"

I hardly heard what Poirot replied. Something evidently of a non-committal nature. The young man departed, and as he closed the door Poirot's eyes met mine.

"Yes," he said, nodding gravely. "He will have evidence to give at the inquest."

We went slowly upstairs again. I was opening my lips, when Poirot stopped me with a gesture of his hand.

"Not now, not now, *mon ami.* I have need of reflection. My mind is in some disorder—which is not well."

For about ten minutes he sat in dead silence, perfectly still, except for several expressive motions of his eyebrows, and all the time his eyes grew steadily greener. At last he heaved a deep sigh.

"It is well. The bad moment has passed. Now all is arranged and classified. One must never permit confusion. The case is not clear yet—no. For it is of the most complicated! It puzzles me. Me, Hercule Poirot! There are two facts of significance."

"And what are they?"

"The first is the state of the weather yesterday. That is very important."

"But it was a glorious day!" I interrupted. "Poirot, you're pulling my leg!"

"Not at all. The thermometer registered 80 degrees in the shade. Do not forget that, my friend. It is the key to the whole riddle!"

"And the second point?" I asked.

"The important fact that Monsieur Inglethorp wears very peculiar clothes, has a black beard, and uses glasses."

"Poirot, I cannot believe you are serious."

"I am absolutely serious, my friend."

"But this is childish!"

"No, it is very momentous."

"And supposing the Coroner's jury returns a verdict of Wilful Murder against Alfred Inglethorp. What becomes of your theories, then?"

"They would not be shaken because twelve stupid men had happened to make a mistake! But that will not occur. For one thing, a country jury is not anxious to take responsibility upon itself, and Mr. Inglethorp stands practically in the position of local squire. Also," he added placidly, "*I* should not allow it!"

"*You* would not allow it?"

"No."

I looked at the extraordinary little man, divided between annoyance and amusement. He was so tremendously sure of himself. As though he read my thoughts, he nodded gently.

"Oh, yes, *mon ami*, I would do what I say." He got up and laid his hand on my shoulder. His physiognomy underwent a complete change. Tears came into his eyes. "In all this, you see, I think of that poor Mrs. Inglethorp who is dead. She was not extravagantly loved—no. But she was very good to us Belgians—I owe her a debt."

I endeavoured to interrupt, but Poirot swept on.

"Let me tell you this, Hastings. She would never forgive me if I let Alfred Inglethorp, her husband, be arrested *now*—when a word from me could save him!"

Chapter VI

THE INQUEST

In the interval before the inquest, Poirot was unfailing in his activity. Twice he was closeted with Mr. Wells. He also took long walks into the country. I rather resented his not taking me into his confidence, the more so as I could not in the least guess what he was driving at.

It occurred to me that he might have been making inquiries at Raikes's farm; so, finding him out when I called at Leastways Cottage on Wednesday evening, I walked over there by the fields, hoping to meet him. But there was no sign of him, and I hesitated to go right up to the farm itself. As I walked away, I met an aged rustic, who leered at me cunningly.

"You'm from the Hall, bain't you?" he asked.

"Yes. I'm looking for a friend of mine whom I thought might have walked this way."

"A little chap? As waves his hands when he talks? One of them Belgies from the village?"

"Yes," I said eagerly. "He has been here, then?"

"Oh, ay, he's been here, right enough. More'n once too. Friend of yours, is he? Ah, you gentlemen from the Hall—you'n a pretty lot!" And he leered more jocosely than ever.

"Why, do the gentlemen from the Hall come here often?" I asked, as carelessly as I could.

He winked at me knowingly.

"One does, mister. Naming no names, mind. And a very liberal gentleman too! Oh, thank you, sir, I'm sure."

I walked on sharply. Evelyn Howard had been right then, and I experienced a sharp twinge of disgust, as I thought of Alfred Inglethorp's liberality with another woman's money. Had that piquant gipsy face been at the bottom of the crime, or was it the baser mainspring of money? Probably a judicious mixture of both.

On one point, Poirot seemed to have a curious obsession. He once or twice observed to me that he thought Dorcas must have made an error in fixing the time of the quarrel. He suggested to her repeatedly that it was 4.30, and not 4 o'clock when she had heard the voices.

But Dorcas was unshaken. Quite an hour, or even more, had elapsed between the time when she had heard the voices and 5 o'clock, when she had taken tea to her mistress.

The inquest was held on Friday at the Stylites Arms in the village. Poirot and I sat together, not being required to give evidence.

The preliminaries were gone through. The jury viewed the body, and John Cavendish gave evidence of identification.

Further questioned, he described his awakening in the early hours of the morning, and the circumstances of his mother's death.

The medical evidence was next taken. There was a breathless hush, and every eye was fixed on the famous London specialist, who was known to be one of the greatest authorities of the day on the subject of toxicology.

In a few brief words, he summed up the result of the post-mortem. Shorn of its medical phraseology and technicalities, it amounted to the fact that Mrs. Inglethorp had met her death as the result of strychnine poisoning. Judging from the quantity recovered, she must have taken not less than three-quarters of a grain of strychnine, but probably one grain or slightly over.

"Is it possible that she could have swallowed the poison by accident?" asked the Coroner.

"I should consider it very unlikely. Strychnine is not used for domestic purposes, as some poisons are, and there are restrictions placed on its sale."

"Does anything in your examination lead you to determine how the poison was administered?"

"No."

"You arrived at Styles before Dr. Wilkins, I believe?"

"That is so. The motor met me just outside the lodge gates, and I hurried there as fast as I could."

"Will you relate to us exactly what happened next?"

"I entered Mrs. Inglethorp's room. She was at that moment in a typical tetanic convulsion. She turned towards me, and gasped out: 'Alfred— Alfred—' "

"Could the strychnine have been administered in Mrs. Inglethorp's after-dinner coffee which was taken to her by her husband?"

"Possibly, but strychnine is a fairly rapid drug in its action. The symptoms appear from one to two hours after it has been swallowed. It is retarded under certain conditions, none of which, however, appear to have been present in this case. I presume Mrs. Inglethorp took the coffee after dinner about eight o'clock, whereas the symptoms did not manifest themselves until the early hours of the morning, which, on the face of it, points to the drug having been taken much later in the evening."

"Mrs. Inglethorp was in the habit of drinking a cup of cocoa in the middle of the night. Could the strychnine have been administered in that?"

"No, I myself took a sample of the cocoa remaining in the saucepan and had it analysed. There was no strychnine present."

I heard Poirot chuckle softly beside me.

"How did you know?" I whispered.

"Listen."

"I should say"—the doctor was continuing—"that I would have been considerably surprised at any other result."

"Why?"

"Simply because strychnine has an unusually bitter taste. It can be detected in a solution of 1 in 70,000, and can only be disguised by some strongly flavoured substance. Cocoa would be quite powerless to mask it."

One of the jury wanted to know if the same objection applied to coffee.

"No. Coffee has a bitter taste of its own which would probably cover the taste of strychnine."

"Then you consider it more likely that the drug was administered in the coffee, but that for some unknown reason its action was delayed."

"Yes, but, the cup being completely smashed, there is no possibility of analyzing its contents."

This concluded Dr. Bauerstein's evidence. Dr. Wilkins corroborated it on all points. Sounded as to the possibility of suicide, he repudiated it utterly. The deceased, he said, suffered from a weak heart, but otherwise enjoyed perfect health, and was of a cheerful and well-balanced disposition. She would be one of the last people to take her own life.

Lawrence Cavendish was next called. His evidence was quite unimportant, being a mere repetition of that of his brother. Just as he was about to step down, he paused, and said rather hesitatingly:

"I should like to make a suggestion if I may?"

He glanced deprecatingly at the Coroner, who replied briskly:

"Certainly, Mr. Cavendish, we are here to arrive at the truth of this matter, and welcome anything that may lead to further elucidation."

"It is just an idea of mine," explained Lawrence. "Of course I may be quite wrong, but it still seems to me that my mother's death might be accounted for by natural means."

"How do you make that out, Mr. Cavendish?"

"My mother, at the time of her death, and for some time before it, was taking a tonic containing strychnine."

"Ah!" said the Coroner.

The jury looked up, interested.

"I believe," continued Lawrence, "that there have been cases where the cumulative effect of a drug, administered for some time, has ended by causing death. Also, is it not possible that she may have taken an overdose of her medicine by accident?"

"This is the first we have heard of the deceased taking strychnine at the time of her death. We are much obliged to you, Mr. Cavendish."

Dr. Wilkins was recalled and ridiculed the idea.

"What Mr. Cavendish suggests is quite impossible. Any doctor would tell you the same. Strychnine is, in a certain sense, a cumulative poison, but it would be quite impossible for it to result in sudden death in this way. There would have to be a long period of chronic symptoms which would at once have attracted my attention. The whole thing is absurd."

"And the second suggestion? That Mrs. Inglethorp may have inadvertently taken an overdose?"

"Three, or even four doses, would not have resulted in death. Mrs. Inglethorp always had an extra large amount of medicine made up at a time, as she dealt with Coot's, the Cash Chemists in Tadminster. She would have had to take very nearly the whole bottle to account for the amount of strychnine found at the post-mortem."

"Then you consider that we may dismiss the tonic as not being in any way instrumental in causing her death?"

"Certainly. The supposition is ridiculous."

The same juryman who had interrupted before here suggested that the chemist who made up the medicine might have committed an error.

"That, of course, is always possible," replied the doctor.

But Dorcas, who was the next witness called, dispelled even that possibility. The medicine had not been newly made up. On the contrary, Mrs. Inglethorp had taken the last dose on the day of her death.

So the question of the tonic was finally abandoned, and the Coroner proceeded with his task. Having elicited from Dorcas how she had been awakened by the violent ringing of her mistress's bell, and had subsequently roused the household, he passed to the subject of the quarrel on the preceding afternoon.

Dorcas's evidence on this point was substantially what Poirot and I had already heard, so I will not repeat it here.

The next witness was Mary Cavendish. She stood very upright, and spoke in a low, clear, and perfectly composed voice. In answer to the Coroner's question, she told how, her alarm clock having aroused her at 4.30 as usual, she was dressing, when she was startled by the sound of something heavy falling.

"That would have been the table by the bed?" commented the Coroner.

"I opened my door," continued Mary, "and listened. In a few minutes a bell rang violently. Dorcas came running down and woke my husband, and we all went to my mother-in-law's room, but it was locked—"

The Coroner interrupted her.

"I really do not think we need trouble you further on that point. We know all that can be known of the subsequent happenings. But I should be obliged if you would tell us all you overheard of the quarrel the day before."

"I?"

There was a faint insolence in her voice. She raised her hand and adjusted the ruffle of lace at her neck, turning her head a little as she did so. And quite spontaneously the thought flashed across my mind: "She is gaining time!"

"Yes. I understand," continued the Coroner deliberately, "that you were sitting reading on the bench just outside the long window of the boudoir. That is so, is it not?"

This was news to me and glancing sideways at Poirot, I fancied that it was news to him as well.

There was the faintest pause, the mere hesitation of a moment, before she answered:

"Yes, that is so."

"And the boudoir window was open, was it not?"

Surely her face grew a little paler as she answered:

"Yes."

"Then you cannot have failed to hear the voices inside, especially as they were raised in anger. In fact, they would be more audible where you were than in the hall."

"Possibly."

"Will you repeat to us what you overheard of the quarrel?"

"I really do not remember hearing anything."

"Do you mean to say you did not hear voices?"

"Oh, yes, I heard the voices, but I did not hear what they said." A faint spot of colour came into her cheek. "I am not in the habit of listening to private conversations."

The Coroner persisted.

"And you remember nothing at all? *Nothing*, Mrs. Cavendish? Not one stray word or phrase to make you realize that it *was* a private conversation?"

She paused, and seemed to reflect, still outwardly as calm as ever.

"Yes; I remember. Mrs. Inglethorp said something—I do not remember exactly what—about causing scandal between husband and wife."

"Ah!" the Coroner leant back satisfied. "That corresponds with what Dorcas heard. But excuse me, Mrs. Cavendish, although you realized it was a private conversation, you did not move away? You remained where you were?"

I caught the momentary gleam of her tawny eyes as she raised them. I felt certain that at that moment she would willingly have torn the little lawyer, with his insinuations, into pieces, but she replied quietly enough:

"No. I was very comfortable where I was. I fixed my mind on my book."

"And that is all you can tell us?"

"That is all."

The examination was over, though I doubted if the Coroner was entirely satisfied with it. I think he suspected that Mary Cavendish could tell more if she chose.

Amy Hill, shop assistant, was next called, and deposed to having sold a will form on the afternoon of the 17th to William Earl, under-gardener at Styles.

William Earl and Manning succeeded her, and testified to witnessing a document. Manning fixed the time at about 4.30, William was of the opinion that it was rather earlier.

Cynthia Murdoch came next. She had, however, little to tell. She had known nothing of the tragedy, until awakened by Mrs. Cavendish.

"You did not hear the table fall?"

"No. I was fast asleep."

The Coroner smiled.

"A good conscience makes a sound sleeper," he observed. "Thank you, Miss Murdoch, that is all."

"Miss Howard."

Miss Howard produced the letter written to her by Mrs. Inglethorp on the evening of the 17th. Poirot and I had, of course already seen it. It added nothing to our knowledge of the tragedy. The following is a facsimile:

July 17th

My dear Evelyn
Can we not bury the hatchet? I have found it hard to forgive the things you said against my dear husband but I am an old woman + very fond of you
Yours affectionately,
Emily Inglethorp

It was handed to the jury who scrutinized it attentively.

"I fear it does not help us much," said the Coroner, with a sigh. "There is no mention of any of the events of that afternoon."

"Plain as a pikestaff to me," said Miss Howard shortly. "It shows clearly enough that my poor old friend had just found out she'd been made a fool of!"

"It says nothing of the kind in the letter," the Coroner pointed out.

"No, because Emily never could bear to put herself in the wrong. But *I* know her. She wanted me back. But she wasn't going to own that I'd been right. She went round about. Most people do. Don't believe in it myself."

Mr. Wells smiled faintly. So, I noticed, did several of the jury. Miss Howard was obviously quite a public character.

"Anyway, all this tomfoolery is a great waste of time," continued the lady, glancing up and down the jury disparagingly. "Talk—talk—talk! When all the time we know perfectly well—"

The Coroner interrupted her in an agony of apprehension:

"Thank you, Miss Howard, that is all."

I fancy he breathed a sigh of relief when she complied.

Then came the sensation of the day. The Coroner called Albert Mace, chemist's assistant.

It was our agitated young man of the pale face. In answer to the Coroner's questions, he explained that he was a qualified pharmacist, but had only recently come to this particular shop, as the assistant formerly there had just been called up for the army.

These preliminaries completed, the Coroner proceeded to business.

"Mr. Mace, have you lately sold strychnine to any unauthorized person?"

"Yes, sir."

"When was this?"

"Last Monday night."

"Monday? Not Tuesday?"

"No, sir, Monday, the 16th."

"Will you tell us to whom you sold it?"

You could have heard a pin drop.

"Yes, sir. It was to Mr. Inglethorp."

Every eye turned simultaneously to where Alfred Inglethorp was sitting, impassive and wooden. He started slightly, as the damning words fell from the young man's lips. I half thought he was going to rise from his chair, but he remained seated, although a remarkably well acted expression of astonishment rose on his face.

"You are sure of what you say?" asked the Coroner sternly.

"Quite sure, sir."

"Are you in the habit of selling strychnine indiscriminately over the counter?"

The wretched young man wilted visibly under the Coroner's frown.

"Oh, no, sir—of course not. But, seeing it was Mr. Inglethorp of the Hall, I thought there was no harm in it. He said it was to poison a dog."

Inwardly I sympathized. It was only human nature to endeavour to please "The Hall"—especially when it might result in custom being transferred from Coot's to the local establishment.

"Is it not customary for anyone purchasing poison to sign a book?"

"Yes, sir, Mr. Inglethorp did so."

"Have you got the book here?"

"Yes, sir."

It was produced; and, with a few words of stern censure, the Coroner dismissed the wretched Mr. Mace.

Then, amidst a breathless silence, Alfred Inglethorp was called. Did he realize, I wondered, how closely the halter was being drawn around his neck?

The Coroner went straight to the point.

"On Monday evening last, did you purchase strychnine for the purpose of poisoning a dog?"

Inglethorp replied with perfect calmness:

"No, I did not. There is no dog at Styles, except an outdoor sheepdog, which is in perfect health."

"You deny absolutely having purchased strychnine from Albert Mace on Monday last?"

"I do."

"Do you also deny *this*?"

The Coroner handed him the register in which his signature was inscribed.

"Certainly I do. The hand-writing is quite different from mine. I will show you."

He took an old envelope out of his pocket, and wrote his name on it, handing it to the jury. It was certainly utterly dissimilar.

"Then what is your explanation of Mr. Mace's statement?"

Alfred Inglethorp replied imperturbably:

"Mr. Mace must have been mistaken."

The Coroner hesitated for a moment, and then said:

"Mr. Inglethorp, as a mere matter of form, would you mind telling us where you were on the evening of Monday, July 16th?"

"Really—I can't remember."

"That is absurd, Mr. Inglethorp," said the Coroner sharply. "Think again."

Inglethorp shook his head.

"I cannot tell you. I have an idea that I was out walking."

"In what direction?"

"I really can't remember."

The Coroner's face grew graver.

"Were you in company with anyone?"

"No."

"Did you meet anyone on your walk?"

"No."

"That is a pity," said the Coroner dryly. "I am to take it then that you decline to say where you were at the time that Mr. Mace positively recognized you as entering the shop to purchase strychnine?"

"If you like to take it that way, yes."

"Be careful, Mr. Inglethorp."

Poirot was fidgeting nervously.

"*Sacré*!" he murmured. "Does this imbecile of a man *want* to be arrested?"

Inglethorp was indeed creating a bad impression. His futile denials would not have convinced a child. The Coroner, however, passed briskly to the next point, and Poirot drew a deep breath of relief.

"You had a discussion with your wife on Tuesday afternoon?"

"Pardon me," interrupted Alfred Inglethorp, "you have been misinformed. I had no quarrel with my dear wife. The whole story is absolutely untrue. I was absent from the house the entire afternoon."

"Have you anyone who can testify to that?"

"You have my word," said Inglethorp haughtily.

The Coroner did not trouble to reply.

"There are two witnesses who will swear to having heard your disagreement with Mrs. Inglethorp."

"Those witnesses were mistaken."

I was puzzled. The man spoke with such quiet assurance that I was staggered. I looked at Poirot. There was an expression of exultation on his face which I could not understand. Was he at last convinced of Alfred Inglethorp's guilt?

"Mr. Inglethorp," said the Coroner, "you have heard your wife's dying words repeated here. Can you explain them in any way?"

"Certainly I can."

"You can?"

"It seems to me very simple. The room was dimly lighted. Dr. Bauerstein is much of my height and build, and, like me, wears a beard. In the dim light, and suffering as she was, my poor wife mistook him for me."

"Ah!" murmured Poirot to himself. "But it is an idea, that!"

"You think it is true?" I whispered.

"I do not say that. But it is truly an ingenious supposition."

"You read my wife's last words as an accusation"—Inglethorp was continuing—"they were, on the contrary, an appeal to me."

The Coroner reflected a moment, then he said:

"I believe, Mr. Inglethorp, that you yourself poured out the coffee, and took it to your wife that evening?"

"I poured it out, yes. But I did not take it to her. I meant to do so, but I was told that a friend was at the hall door, so I laid down the coffee on the hall table. When I came through the hall again a few minutes later, it was gone."

This statement might, or might not, be true, but it did not seem to me to improve matters much for Inglethorp. In any case, he had had ample time to introduce the poison.

At that point, Poirot nudged me gently, indicating two men who were sitting together near the door. One was a little, sharp, dark, ferret-faced man, the other was tall and fair.

I questioned Poirot mutely. He put his lips to my ear.

"Do you know who that little man is?"

I shook my head.

"That is Detective Inspector James Japp of Scotland Yard—Jimmy Japp. The other man is from Scotland Yard too. Things are moving quickly, my friend."

I stared at the two men intently. There was certainly nothing of the policeman about them. I should never have suspected them of being official personages.

I was still staring, when I was startled and recalled by the verdict being given:

"Wilful Murder against some person or persons unknown."

Chapter VII

POIROT PAYS HIS DEBTS

As we came out of the Stylites Arms, Poirot drew me aside by a gentle pressure of the arm. I understood his object. He was waiting for the Scotland Yard men.

In a few moments, they emerged, and Poirot at once stepped forward, and accosted the shorter of the two.

"I fear you do not remember me, Inspector Japp."

"Why, if it isn't Mr. Poirot!" cried the Inspector. He turned to the other man. "You've heard me speak of Mr. Poirot? It was in 1904 he and I worked together—the Abercrombie forgery case—you remember, he was run down in Brussels. Ah, those were great days, moosier. Then, do you remember 'Baron' Altara? There was a pretty rogue for you! He eluded the clutches of half the police in Europe. But we nailed him in Antwerp—thanks to Mr. Poirot here."

As these friendly reminiscences were being indulged in, I drew nearer, and was introduced to Detective-Inspector Japp, who, in his turn, introduced us both to his companion, Superintendent Summerhaye.

"I need hardly ask what you are doing here, gentlemen," remarked Poirot.

Japp closed one eye knowingly.

"No, indeed. Pretty clear case I should say."

But Poirot answered gravely:

"There I differ from you."

"Oh, come!" said Summerhaye, opening his lips for the first time. "Surely the whole thing is clear as daylight. The man's caught red-handed. How he could be such a fool beats me!"

But Japp was looking attentively at Poirot.

"Hold your fire, Summerhaye," he remarked jocularly. "Me and Moosier here have met before—and there's no man's judgment I'd sooner take than his. If I'm not greatly mistaken, he's got something up his sleeve. Isn't that so, moosier?"

Poirot smiled.

"I have drawn certain conclusions—yes."

Summerhaye was still looking rather sceptical, but Japp continued his scrutiny of Poirot.

"It's this way," he said, "so far, we've only seen the case from the outside. That's where the Yard's at a disadvantage in a case of this kind, where the murder's only out, so to speak, after the inquest. A lot depends on being on the spot first thing, and that's where Mr. Poirot's had the start of us. We shouldn't have been here as soon as this even, if it hadn't been for the fact that there was a smart doctor on the spot, who gave us the tip through the Coroner. But you've been on the spot from the first, and you may have picked up some little hints. From the evidence at the inquest, Mr. Inglethorp murdered his wife as sure as I stand here, and if anyone but you hinted the contrary I'd laugh in his face. I must say I was surprised the jury didn't bring it in Wilful Murder against him right off. I think they would have, if it hadn't been for the Coroner—he seemed to be holding them back."

"Perhaps, though, you have a warrant for his arrest in your pocket now," suggested Poirot.

A kind of wooden shutter of officialdom came down from Japp's expressive countenance.

"Perhaps I have, and perhaps I haven't," he remarked dryly.

Poirot looked at him thoughtfully.

"I am very anxious, Messieurs, that he should not be arrested."

"I dare say," observed Summerhaye sarcastically.

Japp was regarding Poirot with comical perplexity.

"Can't you go a little further, Mr. Poirot? A wink's as good as a nod—from you. You've been on the spot—and the Yard doesn't want to make any mistakes, you know."

Poirot nodded gravely.

"That is exactly what I thought. Well, I will tell you this. Use your warrant: Arrest Mr. Inglethorp. But it will bring you no kudos—the case against him will be dismissed at once! *Comme ça!*" And he snapped his fingers expressively.

Japp's face grew grave, though Summerhaye gave an incredulous snort.

As for me, I was literally dumb with astonishment. I could only conclude that Poirot was mad.

Japp had taken out a handkerchief, and was gently dabbing his brow.

"I daren't do it, Mr. Poirot. I'd take your word, but there's others over me who'll be asking what the devil I mean by it. Can't you give me a little more to go on?"

Poirot reflected a moment.

"It can be done," he said at last. "I admit I do not wish it. It forces my hand. I would have preferred to work in the dark just for the present, but what you say is very just—the word of a Belgian policeman, whose day is past, is not enough! And Alfred Inglethorp must not be arrested. That I have sworn, as my friend Hastings here knows. See, then, my good Japp, you go at once to Styles?"

"Well, in about half an hour. We're seeing the Coroner and the doctor first."

"Good. Call for me in passing—the last house in the village. I will go with you. At Styles, Mr. Inglethorp will give you, or if he refuses—as is probable—I will give you such proofs that shall satisfy you that the case against him could not possibly be sustained. Is that a bargain?"

"That's a bargain," said Japp heartily. "And, on behalf of the Yard, I'm much obliged to you, though I'm bound to confess I can't at present see the faintest possible loop-hole in the evidence, but you always were a marvel! So long, then, moosier."

The two detectives strode away, Summerhaye with an incredulous grin on his face.

"Well, my friend," cried Poirot, before I could get in a word, "what do you think? *Mon Dieu*! I had some warm moments in that court; I did not figure to myself that the man would be so pig-headed as to refuse to say anything at all. Decidedly, it was the policy of an imbecile."

"H'm! There are other explanations besides that of imbecility," I remarked. "For, if the case against him is true, how could he defend himself except by silence?"

"Why, in a thousand ingenious ways," cried Poirot. "See; say that it is I who have committed this murder, I can think of seven most plausible stories! Far more convincing than Mr. Inglethorp's stony denials!"

I could not help laughing.

"My dear Poirot, I am sure you are capable of thinking of seventy! But, seriously, in spite of what I heard you say to the detectives, you surely cannot still believe in the possibility of Alfred Inglethorp's innocence?"

"Why not now as much as before? Nothing has changed."

"But the evidence is so conclusive."

"Yes, too conclusive."

We turned in at the gate of Leastways Cottage, and proceeded up the now familiar stairs.

"Yes, yes, too conclusive," continued Poirot, almost to himself. "Real evidence is usually vague and unsatisfactory. It has to be examined—sifted.

But here the whole thing is cut and dried. No, my friend, this evidence has been very cleverly manufactured—so cleverly that it has defeated its own ends."

"How do you make that out?"

"Because, so long as the evidence against him was vague and intangible, it was very hard to disprove. But, in his anxiety, the criminal has drawn the net so closely that one cut will set Inglethorp free."

I was silent. And in a minute or two, Poirot continued:

"Let us look at the matter like this. Here is a man, let us say, who sets out to poison his wife. He has lived by his wits as the saying goes. Presumably, therefore, he has some wits. He is not altogether a fool. Well, how does he set about it? He goes boldly to the village chemist's and purchases strychnine under his own name, with a trumped up story about a dog which is bound to be proved absurd. He does not employ the poison that night. No, he waits until he has had a violent quarrel with her, of which the whole household is cognisant, and which naturally directs their suspicions upon him. He prepares no defence—no shadow of an alibi, yet he knows the chemist's assistant must necessarily come forward with the facts. Bah! Do not ask me to believe that any man could be so idiotic! Only a lunatic, who wished to commit suicide by causing himself to be hanged, would act so!"

"Still—I do not see—" I began.

"Neither do I see. I tell you, *mon ami*, it puzzles me. *Me*—Hercule Poirot!"

"But if you believe him innocent, how do you explain his buying the strychnine?"

"Very simply. He did not buy it."

"But Mace recognized him!"

"I beg your pardon, he saw a man with a black beard like Mr. Inglethorp's, and wearing glasses like Mr. Inglethorp, and dressed in Mr. Inglethorp's rather noticeable clothes. He could not recognize a man whom he had probably only seen in the distance, since, you remember, he himself had only been in the village a fortnight, and Mrs. Inglethorp dealt principally with Coot's in Tadminster."

"Then you think—"

"*Mon ami*, do you remember the two points I laid stress upon? Leave the first one for the moment, what was the second?"

"The important fact that Alfred Inglethorp wears peculiar clothes, has a black beard, and uses glasses," I quoted.

"Exactly. Now suppose anyone wished to pass himself off as John or Lawrence Cavendish. Would it be easy?"

"No," I said thoughtfully. "Of course an actor—"

But Poirot cut me short ruthlessly.

"And why would it not be easy? I will tell you, my friend: Because they are both clean-shaven men. To make up successfully as one of these two in broad daylight, it would need an actor of genius, and a certain initial facial resemblance. But in the case of Alfred Inglethorp, all that is changed. His clothes, his beard, the glasses which hide his eyes—those are the salient points about his personal appearance. Now, what is the first instinct of the criminal? To divert suspicion from himself, is it not so? And how can he best do that? By throwing it on someone else. In this instance, there was a man ready to his hand. Everybody was predisposed to believe in Mr. Inglethorp's guilt. It was a foregone conclusion that he would be suspected; but, to make it a sure thing there must be tangible proof—such as the actual buying of the poison, and that, with a man of the peculiar appearance of Mr. Inglethorp, was not difficult. Remember, this young Mace had never actually spoken to Mr. Inglethorp. How should he doubt that the man in his clothes, with his beard and his glasses, was not Alfred Inglethorp?"

"It may be so," I said, fascinated by Poirot's eloquence. "But, if that was the case, why does he not say where he was at six o'clock on Monday evening?"

"Ah, why indeed?" said Poirot, calming down. "If he were arrested, he probably would speak, but I do not want it to come to that. I must make him see the gravity of his position. There is, of course, something discreditable behind his silence. If he did not murder his wife, he is, nevertheless, a scoundrel, and has something of his own to conceal, quite apart from the murder."

"What can it be?" I mused, won over to Poirot's views for the moment, although still retaining a faint conviction that the obvious deduction was the correct one.

"Can you not guess?" asked Poirot, smiling.

"No, can you?"

"Oh, yes, I had a little idea sometime ago—and it has turned out to be correct."

"You never told me," I said reproachfully.

Poirot spread out his hands apologetically.

"Pardon me, *mon ami*, you were not precisely *sympathique*." He turned to me earnestly. "Tell me—you see now that he must not be arrested?"

"Perhaps," I said doubtfully, for I was really quite indifferent to the fate of Alfred Inglethorp, and thought that a good fright would do him no harm.

Poirot, who was watching me intently, gave a sigh.

"Come, my friend," he said, changing the subject, "apart from Mr. Inglethorp, how did the evidence at the inquest strike you?"

"Oh, pretty much what I expected."

"Did nothing strike you as peculiar about it?"

My thoughts flew to Mary Cavendish, and I hedged:

"In what way?"

"Well, Mr. Lawrence Cavendish's evidence for instance?"

I was relieved.

"Oh, Lawrence! No, I don't think so. He's always a nervous chap."

"His suggestion that his mother might have been poisoned accidentally by means of the tonic she was taking, that did not strike you as strange—*hein?*"

"No, I can't say it did. The doctors ridiculed it of course. But it was quite a natural suggestion for a layman to make."

"But Monsieur Lawrence is not a layman. You told me yourself that he had started by studying medicine, and that he had taken his degree."

"Yes, that's true. I never thought of that." I was rather startled. "It is odd."

Poirot nodded.

"From the first, his behaviour has been peculiar. Of all the household, he alone would be likely to recognize the symptoms of strychnine poisoning, and yet we find him the only member of the family to uphold strenuously the theory of death from natural causes. If it had been Monsieur John, I could have understood it. He has no technical knowledge, and is by nature unimaginative. But Monsieur Lawrence—no! And now, today, he puts forward a suggestion that he himself must have known was ridiculous. There is food for thought in this, *mon ami!*"

"It's very confusing," I agreed.

"Then there is Mrs. Cavendish," continued Poirot. "That's another who is not telling all she knows! What do you make of her attitude?"

"I don't know what to make of it. It seems inconceivable that she should be shielding Alfred Inglethorp. Yet that is what it looks like."

Poirot nodded reflectively.

"Yes, it is queer. One thing is certain, she overheard a good deal more of that 'private conversation' than she was willing to admit."

"And yet she is the last person one would accuse of stooping to eavesdrop!"

"Exactly. One thing her evidence *has* shown me. I made a mistake. Dorcas was quite right. The quarrel did take place earlier in the afternoon, about four o'clock, as she said."

I looked at him curiously. I had never understood his insistence on that point.

"Yes, a good deal that was peculiar came out today," continued Poirot. "Dr. Bauerstein, now, what was he doing up and dressed at that hour in the morning? It is astonishing to me that no one commented on the fact."

"He has insomnia, I believe," I said doubtfully.

"Which is a very good, or a very bad explanation," remarked Poirot. "It covers everything, and explains nothing. I shall keep my eye on our clever Dr. Bauerstein."

"Any more faults to find with the evidence?" I inquired satirically.

"*Mon ami*," replied Poirot gravely, "when you find that people are not telling you the truth—look out! Now, unless I am much mistaken, at the inquest today only one—at most, two persons were speaking the truth without reservation or subterfuge."

"Oh, come now, Poirot! I won't cite Lawrence, or Mrs. Cavendish. But there's John—and Miss Howard, surely they were speaking the truth?"

"Both of them, my friend? One, I grant you, but both—!"

His words gave me an unpleasant shock. Miss Howard's evidence, unimportant as it was, had been given in such a downright straightforward manner that it had never occurred to me to doubt her sincerity. Still, I had a great respect for Poirot's sagacity—except on the occasions when he was what I described to myself as "foolishly pig-headed."

"Do you really think so?" I asked. "Miss Howard had always seemed to me so essentially honest—almost uncomfortably so."

Poirot gave me a curious look, which I could not quite fathom. He seemed to speak, and then checked himself.

"Miss Murdoch too," I continued, "there's nothing untruthful about *her*."

"No. But it was strange that she never heard a sound, sleeping next door; whereas Mrs. Cavendish, in the other wing of the building, distinctly heard the table fall."

"Well, she's young. And she sleeps soundly."

"Ah, yes, indeed! She must be a famous sleeper, that one!"

I did not quite like the tone of his voice, but at that moment a smart knock reached our ears, and looking out of the window we perceived the two detectives waiting for us below.

Poirot seized his hat, gave a ferocious twist to his moustache, and, carefully brushing an imaginary speck of dust from his sleeve, motioned me to precede him down the stairs; there we joined the detectives and set out for Styles.

I think the appearance of the two Scotland Yard men was rather a shock—especially to John, though of course after the verdict, he had realized that it was only a matter of time. Still, the presence of the detectives brought the truth home to him more than anything else could have done.

Poirot had conferred with Japp in a low tone on the way up, and it was the latter functionary who requested that the household, with the exception of the servants, should be assembled together in the drawing-room. I realized the significance of this. It was up to Poirot to make his boast good.

Personally, I was not sanguine. Poirot might have excellent reasons for his belief in Inglethorp's innocence, but a man of the type of Summerhaye would require tangible proofs, and these I doubted if Poirot could supply.

Before very long we had all trooped into the drawing-room, the door of which Japp closed. Poirot politely set chairs for every one. The Scotland Yard men were the cynosure of all eyes. I think that for the first time we realized that the thing was not a bad dream, but a tangible reality. We had read of such things—now we ourselves were actors in the drama. Tomorrow the daily papers, all over England, would blazon out the news in staring headlines:

"MYSTERIOUS TRAGEDY IN ESSEX"

"WEALTHY LADY POISONED"

There would be pictures of Styles, snap-shots of "The family leaving the Inquest"—the village photographer had not been idle! All the things that one had read a hundred times—things that happen to other people, not to oneself. And now, in this house, a murder had been committed. In front of us were "the detectives in charge of the case." The well-known glib phraseology passed rapidly through my mind in the interval before Poirot opened the proceedings.

I think every one was a little surprised that it should be he and not one of the official detectives who took the initiative.

"*Mesdames* and *messieurs*," said Poirot, bowing as though he were a celebrity about to deliver a lecture, "I have asked you to come here all together, for a certain object. That object, it concerns Mr. Alfred Inglethorp."

Inglethorp was sitting a little by himself—I think, unconsciously, every one had drawn his chair slightly away from him—and he gave a faint start as Poirot pronounced his name.

"Mr. Inglethorp," said Poirot, addressing him directly, "a very dark shadow is resting on this house—the shadow of murder."

Inglethorp shook his head sadly.

"My poor wife," he murmured. "Poor Emily! It is terrible."

"I do not think, monsieur," said Poirot pointedly, "that you quite realize how terrible it may be—for you." And as Inglethorp did not appear to understand, he added: "Mr. Inglethorp, you are standing in very grave danger."

The two detectives fidgeted. I saw the official caution "Anything you say will be used in evidence against you," actually hovering on Summerhaye's lips. Poirot went on.

"Do you understand now, monsieur?"

"No; What do you mean?"

"I mean," said Poirot deliberately, "that you are suspected of poisoning your wife."

A little gasp ran round the circle at this plain speaking.

"Good heavens!" cried Inglethorp, starting up. "What a monstrous idea! I—poison my dearest Emily!"

"I do not think"—Poirot watched him narrowly—"that you quite realize the unfavourable nature of your evidence at the inquest. Mr. Inglethorp, knowing what I have now told you, do you still refuse to say where you were at six o'clock on Monday afternoon?"

With a groan, Alfred Inglethorp sank down again and buried his face in his hands. Poirot approached and stood over him.

"Speak!" he cried menacingly.

With an effort, Inglethorp raised his face from his hands. Then, slowly and deliberately, he shook his head.

"You will not speak?"

"No. I do not believe that anyone could be so monstrous as to accuse me of what you say."

Poirot nodded thoughtfully, like a man whose mind is made up.

"*Soit!*" he said. "Then I must speak for you."

Alfred Inglethorp sprang up again.

"You? How can you speak? You do not know—" he broke off abruptly.

Poirot turned to face us. "*Mesdames* and *messieurs*! I speak! Listen! I, Hercule Poirot, affirm that the man who entered the chemist's shop, and purchased strychnine at six o'clock on Monday last was not Mr. Inglethorp, for at six o'clock on that day Mr. Inglethorp was escorting Mrs. Raikes back to her home from a neighbouring farm. I can produce no less than five witnesses to swear to having seen them together, either at six or just after and, as you may know, the Abbey Farm, Mrs. Raikes's home, is at least two and a half miles distant from the village. There is absolutely no question as to the alibi!"

Chapter VIII

FRESH SUSPICIONS

There was a moment's stupefied silence. Japp, who was the least surprised of any of us, was the first to speak.

"My word," he cried, "you're the goods! And no mistake, Mr. Poirot! These witnesses of yours are all right, I suppose?"

"*Voilà!* I have prepared a list of them—names and addresses. You must see them, of course. But you will find it all right."

"I'm sure of that." Japp lowered his voice. "I'm much obliged to you. A pretty mare's nest arresting him would have been." He turned to Inglethorp. "But, if you'll excuse me, sir, why couldn't you say all this at the inquest?"

"I will tell you why," interrupted Poirot. "There was a certain rumour—"

"A most malicious and utterly untrue one," interrupted Alfred Inglethorp in an agitated voice.

"And Mr. Inglethorp was anxious to have no scandal revived just at present. Am I right?"

"Quite right." Inglethorp nodded. "With my poor Emily not yet buried, can you wonder I was anxious that no more lying rumours should be started."

"Between you and me, sir," remarked Japp, "I'd sooner have any amount of rumours than be arrested for murder. And I venture to think your poor lady would have felt the same. And, if it hadn't been for Mr. Poirot here, arrested you would have been, as sure as eggs is eggs!"

"I was foolish, no doubt," murmured Inglethorp. "But you do not know, inspector, how I have been persecuted and maligned." And he shot a baleful glance at Evelyn Howard.

"Now, sir," said Japp, turning briskly to John, "I should like to see the lady's bedroom, please, and after that I'll have a little chat with the servants. Don't you bother about anything. Mr. Poirot, here, will show me the way."

As they all went out of the room, Poirot turned and made me a sign to follow him upstairs. There he caught me by the arm, and drew me aside.

"Quick, go to the other wing. Stand there—just this side of the baize door. Do not move till I come." Then, turning rapidly, he rejoined the two detectives.

I followed his instructions, taking up my position by the baize door, and wondering what on earth lay behind the request. Why was I to stand in this particular spot on guard? I looked thoughtfully down the corridor in front of me. An idea struck me. With the exception of Cynthia Murdoch's, every one's room was in this left wing. Had that anything to do with it? Was I to report who came or went? I stood faithfully at my post. The minutes passed. Nobody came. Nothing happened.

It must have been quite twenty minutes before Poirot rejoined me.

"You have not stirred?"

"No, I've stuck here like a rock. Nothing's happened."

"Ah!" Was he pleased, or disappointed? "You've seen nothing at all?"

"No."

"But you have probably heard something? A big bump—eh, mon *ami*?"

"No."

"Is it possible? Ah, but I am vexed with myself! I am not usually clumsy. I made but a slight gesture"—I know Poirot's gestures—"with the left hand, and over went the table by the bed!"

He looked so childishly vexed and crest-fallen that I hastened to console him.

"Never mind, old chap. What does it matter? Your triumph downstairs excited you. I can tell you, that was a surprise to us all. There must be more in this affair of Inglethorp's with Mrs. Raikes than we thought, to make him hold his tongue so persistently. What are you going to do now? Where are the Scotland Yard fellows?"

"Gone down to interview the servants. I showed them all our exhibits. I am disappointed in Japp. He has no method!"

"Hullo!" I said, looking out of the window. "Here's Dr. Bauerstein. I believe you're right about that man, Poirot. I don't like him."

"He is clever," observed Poirot meditatively.

"Oh, clever as the devil! I must say I was overjoyed to see him in the plight he was in on Tuesday. You never saw such a spectacle!" And I described the doctor's adventure. "He looked a regular scarecrow! Plastered with mud from head to foot."

"You saw him, then?"

"Yes. Of course, he didn't want to come in—it was just after dinner—but Mr. Inglethorp insisted."

"What?" Poirot caught me violently by the shoulders. "Was Dr. Bauerstein here on Tuesday evening? Here? And you never told me? Why did you not tell me? Why? Why?"

He appeared to be in an absolute frenzy.

"My dear Poirot," I expostulated, "I never thought it would interest you. I didn't know it was of any importance."

"Importance? It is of the first importance! So Dr. Bauerstein was here on Tuesday night—the night of the murder. Hastings, do you not see? That alters everything—everything!"

I had never seen him so upset. Loosening his hold of me, he mechanically straightened a pair of candlesticks, still murmuring to himself: "Yes, that alters everything—everything."

Suddenly he seemed to come to a decision.

"*Allons!*" he said. "We must act at once. Where is Mr. Cavendish?"

John was in the smoking-room. Poirot went straight to him.

"Mr. Cavendish, I have some important business in Tadminster. A new clue. May I take your motor?"

"Why, of course. Do you mean at once?"

"If you please."

John rang the bell, and ordered round the car. In another ten minutes, we were racing down the park and along the high road to Tadminster.

"Now, Poirot," I remarked resignedly, "perhaps you will tell me what all this is about?"

"Well, *mon ami*, a good deal you can guess for yourself. Of course you realize that, now Mr. Inglethorp is out of it, the whole position is greatly changed. We are face to face with an entirely new problem. We know now that there is one person who did not buy the poison. We have cleared away the manufactured clues. Now for the real ones. I have ascertained that anyone in the household, with the exception of Mrs. Cavendish, who was playing tennis with you, could have personated Mr. Inglethorp on Monday evening. In the same way, we have his statement that he put the coffee down in the hall. No one took much notice of that at the inquest—but now it has a very different significance. We must find out who did take that coffee to Mrs. Inglethorp eventually, or who passed through the hall whilst it was standing there. From your account, there are only two people whom we can positively say did not go near the coffee—Mrs. Cavendish, and Mademoiselle Cynthia."

"Yes, that is so." I felt an inexpressible lightening of the heart. Mary Cavendish could certainly not rest under suspicion.

"In clearing Alfred Inglethorp," continued Poirot, "I have been obliged to show my hand sooner than I intended. As long as I might be thought to be pursuing him, the criminal would be off his guard. Now, he will be doubly careful. Yes—doubly careful." He turned to me abruptly. "Tell me, Hastings, you yourself—have you no suspicions of anybody?"

I hesitated. To tell the truth, an idea, wild and extravagant in itself, had once or twice that morning flashed through my brain. I had rejected it as absurd, nevertheless it persisted.

"You couldn't call it a suspicion," I murmured. "It's so utterly foolish."

"Come now," urged Poirot encouragingly. "Do not fear. Speak your mind. You should always pay attention to your instincts."

"Well then," I blurted out, "it's absurd—but I suspect Miss Howard of not telling all she knows!"

"Miss Howard?"

"Yes—you'll laugh at me—"

"Not at all. Why should I?"

"I can't help feeling," I continued blunderingly; "that we've rather left her out of the possible suspects, simply on the strength of her having been away from the place. But, after all, she was only fifteen miles away. A car would do it in half an hour. Can we say positively that she was away from Styles on the night of the murder?"

"Yes, my friend," said Poirot unexpectedly, "we can. One of my first actions was to ring up the hospital where she was working."

"Well?"

"Well, I learnt that Miss Howard had been on afternoon duty on Tuesday, and that—a convoy coming in unexpectedly—she had kindly offered to remain on night duty, which offer was gratefully accepted. That disposes of that."

"Oh!" I said, rather nonplussed. "Really," I continued, "it's her extraordinary vehemence against Inglethorp that started me off suspecting her. I can't help feeling she'd do anything against him. And I had an idea she might know something about the destroying of the will. She might have burnt the new one, mistaking it for the earlier one in his favour. She is so terribly bitter against him."

"You consider her vehemence unnatural?"

"Y—es. She is so very violent. I wondered really whether she is quite sane on that point."

Poirot shook his head energetically.

"No, no, you are on a wrong tack there. There is nothing weak-minded or degenerate about Miss Howard. She is an excellent specimen of well-balanced English beef and brawn. She is sanity itself."

"Yet her hatred of Inglethorp seems almost a mania. My idea was—a very ridiculous one, no doubt—that she had intended to poison him—and that, in some way, Mrs. Inglethorp got hold of it by mistake. But I don't at all see how it could have been done. The whole thing is absurd and ridiculous to the last degree."

"Still you are right in one thing. It is always wise to suspect everybody until you can prove logically, and to your own satisfaction, that they are innocent. Now, what reasons are there against Miss Howard's having deliberately poisoned Mrs. Inglethorp?"

"Why, she was devoted to her!" I exclaimed.

"Tcha! Tcha!" cried Poirot irritably. "You argue like a child. If Miss Howard were capable of poisoning the old lady, she would be quite equally capable of simulating devotion. No, we must look elsewhere. You are perfectly correct in your assumption that her vehemence against Alfred Inglethorp is too violent to be natural; but you are quite wrong in the deduction you draw from it. I have drawn my own deductions, which I believe to be correct, but I will not speak of them at present." He paused a minute, then went on. "Now, to my way of thinking, there is one insuperable objection to Miss Howard's being the murderess."

"And that is?"

"That in no possible way could Mrs. Inglethorp's death benefit Miss Howard. Now there is no murder without a motive."

I reflected.

"Could not Mrs. Inglethorp have made a will in her favour?" Poirot shook his head.

"But you yourself suggested that possibility to Mr. Wells?"

Poirot smiled.

"That was for a reason. I did not want to mention the name of the person who was actually in my mind. Miss Howard occupied very much the same position, so I used her name instead."

"Still, Mrs. Inglethorp might have done so. Why, that will, made on the afternoon of her death may—"

But Poirot's shake of the head was so energetic that I stopped.

"No, my friend. I have certain little ideas of my own about that will. But I can tell you this much—it was not in Miss Howard's favour."

I accepted his assurance, though I did not really see how he could be so positive about the matter.

"Well," I said, with a sigh, "we will acquit Miss Howard, then. It is partly your fault that I ever came to suspect her. It was what you said about her evidence at the inquest that set me off."

Poirot looked puzzled.

"What did I say about her evidence at the inquest?"

"Don't you remember? When I cited her and John Cavendish as being above suspicion?"

"Oh—ah—yes." He seemed a little confused, but recovered himself. "By the way, Hastings, there is something I want you to do for me."

"Certainly. What is it?"

"Next time you happen to be alone with Lawrence Cavendish, I want you to say this to him. 'I have a message for you, from Poirot. He says: "Find the extra coffee-cup, and you can rest in peace!"' Nothing more. Nothing less."

"'Find the extra coffee-cup, and you can rest in peace.' Is that right?" I asked, much mystified.

"Excellent."

"But what does it mean?"

"Ah, that I will leave you to find out. You have access to the facts. Just say that to him, and see what he says."

"Very well—but it's all extremely mysterious."

We were running into Tadminster now, and Poirot directed the car to the "Analytical Chemist."

Poirot hopped down briskly, and went inside. In a few minutes he was back again.

"There," he said. "That is all my business."

"What were you doing there?" I asked, in lively curiosity.

"I left something to be analysed."

"Yes, but what?"

"The sample of cocoa I took from the saucepan in the bedroom."

"But that has already been tested!" I cried, stupefied. "Dr. Bauerstein had it tested, and you yourself laughed at the possibility of there being strychnine in it."

"I know Dr. Bauerstein had it tested," replied Poirot quietly.

"Well, then?"

"Well, I have a fancy for having it analysed again, that is all."

And not another word on the subject could I drag out of him.

This proceeding of Poirot's, in respect of the cocoa, puzzled me intensely. I could see neither rhyme nor reason in it. However, my confidence in him, which at one time had rather waned, was fully restored since his belief in Alfred Inglethorp's innocence had been so triumphantly vindicated.

The funeral of Mrs. Inglethorp took place the following day, and on Monday, as I came down to a late breakfast, John drew me aside, and informed me that Mr. Inglethorp was leaving that morning, to take up his quarters at the Stylites Arms until he should have completed his plans.

"And really it's a great relief to think he's going, Hastings," continued my honest friend. "It was bad enough before, when we thought he'd done it, but I'm hanged if it isn't worse now, when we all feel guilty for having been so down on the fellow. The fact is, we've treated him abominably. Of course, things did look black against him. I don't see how anyone could blame us for jumping to the conclusions we did. Still, there it is, we were in the wrong, and now there's a beastly feeling that one ought to make amends; which is difficult, when one doesn't like the fellow a bit better than one did before. The whole thing's damned awkward! And I'm thankful he's had the tact to take himself off. It's a good thing Styles wasn't the mater's to leave to him. Couldn't bear to think of the fellow lording it here. He's welcome to her money."

"You'll be able to keep up the place all right?" I asked.

"Oh, yes. There are the death duties, of course, but half my father's money goes with the place, and Lawrence will stay with us for the present, so there is his share as well. We shall be pinched at first, of course, because, as I once told you, I am in a bit of a hole financially myself. Still, the Johnnies will wait now."

In the general relief at Inglethorp's approaching departure, we had the most genial breakfast we had experienced since the tragedy. Cynthia, whose young spirits were naturally buoyant, was looking quite her pretty self again, and we all, with the exception of Lawrence, who seemed unalterably gloomy and nervous, were quietly cheerful, at the opening of a new and hopeful future.

The papers, of course, had been full of the tragedy. Glaring headlines, sandwiched biographies of every member of the household, subtle innuendoes, the usual familiar tag about the police having a clue. Nothing was spared us. It was a slack time. The war was momentarily inactive, and the newspapers seized with avidity on this crime in fashionable life: "The Mysterious Affair at Styles" was the topic of the moment.

Naturally it was very annoying for the Cavendishes. The house was constantly besieged by reporters, who were consistently denied admission, but who continued to haunt the village and the grounds, where they lay in wait with cameras, for any unwary members of the household. We all lived in a blast of publicity. The Scotland Yard men came and went, examining, questioning, lynx-eyed and reserved of tongue. Towards what end they were working, we did not know. Had they any clue, or would the whole thing remain in the category of undiscovered crimes?

After breakfast, Dorcas came up to me rather mysteriously, and asked if she might have a few words with me.

"Certainly. What is it, Dorcas?"

"Well, it's just this, sir. You'll be seeing the Belgian gentleman today perhaps?" I nodded. "Well, sir, you know how he asked me so particular if the mistress, or anyone else, had a green dress?"

"Yes, yes. You have found one?" My interest was aroused.

"No, not that, sir. But since then I've remembered what the young gentlemen"—John and Lawrence were still the "young gentlemen" to Dorcas—"call the 'dressing-up box.' It's up in the front attic, sir. A great chest, full of old clothes and fancy dresses, and what not. And it came to me sudden like that there might be a green dress amongst them. So, if you'd tell the Belgian gentleman—"

"I will tell him, Dorcas," I promised.

"Thank you very much, sir. A very nice gentleman he is, sir. And quite a different class from them two detectives from London, what goes prying about, and asking questions. I don't hold with foreigners as a rule, but from what the newspapers say I make out as how these brave Belges isn't the ordinary run of foreigners, and certainly he's a most polite spoken gentleman."

Dear old Dorcas! As she stood there, with her honest face upturned to mine, I thought what a fine specimen she was of the old-fashioned servant that is so fast dying out.

I thought I might as well go down to the village at once, and look up Poirot; but I met him half-way, coming up to the house, and at once gave him Dorcas's message.

"Ah, the brave Dorcas! We will look at the chest, although—but no matter—we will examine it all the same."

We entered the house by one of the windows. There was no one in the hall, and we went straight up to the attic.

Sure enough, there was the chest, a fine old piece, all studded with brass nails, and full to overflowing with every imaginable type of garment.

Poirot bundled everything out on the floor with scant ceremony. There were one or two green fabrics of varying shades; but Poirot shook his head over them all. He seemed somewhat apathetic in the search, as though he expected no great results from it. Suddenly he gave an exclamation.

"What is it?"

"Look!"

The chest was nearly empty, and there, reposing right at the bottom, was a magnificent black beard.

"Ohó!" said Poirot. "Ohó!" He turned it over in his hands, examining it closely. "New," he remarked. "Yes, quite new."

After a moment's hesitation, he replaced it in the chest, heaped all the other things on top of it as before, and made his way briskly downstairs. He went straight to the pantry, where we found Dorcas busily polishing her silver.

Poirot wished her good morning with Gallic politeness, and went on:

"We have been looking through that chest, Dorcas. I am much obliged to you for mentioning it. There is, indeed, a fine collection there. Are they often used, may I ask?"

"Well, sir, not very often nowadays, though from time to time we do have what the young gentlemen call 'a dress-up night.' And very funny it is sometimes, sir. Mr. Lawrence, he's wonderful. Most comic! I shall never forget the night he came down as the Char of Persia, I think he called it—a sort of Eastern King it was. He had the big paper knife in his hand, and 'Mind, Dorcas,' he says, 'you'll have to be very respectful. This is my specially sharpened scimitar, and it's off with your head if I'm at all displeased with you!' Miss Cynthia, she was what they call an Apache, or some such name—a Frenchified sort of cut-throat, I take it to be. A real sight she looked. You'd never have believed a pretty young lady like that could have made herself into such a ruffian. Nobody would have known her."

"These evenings must have been great fun," said Poirot genially. "I suppose Mr. Lawrence wore that fine black beard in the chest upstairs, when he was Shah of Persia?"

"He did have a beard, sir," replied Dorcas, smiling. "And well I know it, for he borrowed two skeins of my black wool to make it with! And I'm sure it looked wonderfully natural at a distance. I didn't know as there was a beard up there at all. It must have been got quite lately, I think. There was a red wig, I know, but nothing else in the way of hair. Burnt corks they use mostly—though 'tis messy getting it off again. Miss Cynthia was a nigger once, and, oh, the trouble she had."

"So Dorcas knows nothing about that black beard," said Poirot thoughtfully, as we walked out into the hall again.

"Do you think it is the one?" I whispered eagerly.

Poirot nodded.

"I do. You notice it had been trimmed?"

"No."

"Yes. It was cut exactly the shape of Mr. Inglethorp's, and I found one or two snipped hairs. Hastings, this affair is very deep."

"Who put it in the chest, I wonder?"

"Someone with a good deal of intelligence," remarked Poirot dryly. "You realize that he chose the one place in the house to hide it where its presence would not be remarked? Yes, he is intelligent. But we must be more intelligent. We must be so intelligent that he does not suspect us of being intelligent at all."

I acquiesced.

"There, *mon ami*, you will be of great assistance to me."

I was pleased with the compliment. There had been times when I hardly thought that Poirot appreciated me at my true worth.

"Yes," he continued, staring at me thoughtfully, "you will be invaluable."

This was naturally gratifying, but Poirot's next words were not so welcome.

"I must have an ally in the house," he observed reflectively.

"You have me," I protested.

"True, but you are not sufficient."

I was hurt, and showed it. Poirot hurried to explain himself.

"You do not quite take my meaning. You are known to be working with me. I want somebody who is not associated with us in any way."

"Oh, I see. How about John?"

"No, I think not."

"The dear fellow isn't perhaps very bright," I said thoughtfully.

"Here comes Miss Howard," said Poirot suddenly. "She is the very person. But I am in her black books, since I cleared Mr. Inglethorp. Still, we can but try."

With a nod that was barely civil, Miss Howard assented to Poirot's request for a few minutes' conversation.

We went into the little morning-room, and Poirot closed the door.

"Well, Monsieur Poirot," said Miss Howard impatiently, "what is it? Out with it. I'm busy."

"Do you remember, mademoiselle, that I once asked you to help me?"

"Yes, I do." The lady nodded. "And I told you I'd help you with pleasure— to hang Alfred Inglethorp."

"Ah!" Poirot studied her seriously. "Miss Howard, I will ask you one question. I beg of you to reply to it truthfully."

"Never tell lies," replied Miss Howard.

"It is this. Do you still believe that Mrs. Inglethorp was poisoned by her husband?"

"What do you mean?" she asked sharply. "You needn't think your pretty explanations influence me in the slightest. I'll admit that it wasn't he who bought strychnine at the chemist's shop. What of that? I dare say he soaked fly paper, as I told you at the beginning."

"That is arsenic—not strychnine," said Poirot mildly.

"What does that matter? Arsenic would put poor Emily out of the way just as well as strychnine. If I'm convinced he did it, it doesn't matter a jot to me *how* he did it."

"Exactly. *If* you are convinced he did it," said Poirot quietly. "I will put my question in another form. Did you ever in your heart of hearts believe that Mrs. Inglethorp was poisoned by her husband?"

"Good heavens!" cried Miss Howard. "Haven't I always told you the man is a villain? Haven't I always told you he would murder her in her bed? Haven't I always hated him like poison?"

"Exactly," said Poirot. "That bears out my little idea entirely."

"What little idea?"

"Miss Howard, do you remember a conversation that took place on the day of my friend's arrival here? He repeated it to me, and there is a sentence of yours that has impressed me very much. Do you remember affirming that if a crime had been committed, and anyone you loved had been murdered, you felt certain that you would know by instinct who the criminal was, even if you were quite unable to prove it?"

"Yes, I remember saying that. I believe it too. I suppose you think it nonsense?"

"Not at all."

"And yet you will pay no attention to my instinct against Alfred Inglethorp."

"No," said Poirot curtly. "Because your instinct is not against Mr. Inglethorp."

"What?"

"No. You wish to believe he committed the crime. You believe him capable of committing it. But your instinct tells you he did not commit it. It tells you more—shall I go on?"

She was staring at him, fascinated, and made a slight affirmative movement of the hand.

"Shall I tell you why you have been so vehement against Mr. Inglethorp? It is because you have been trying to believe what you wish to believe. It is because you are trying to drown and stifle your instinct, which tells you another name—"

"No, no, no!" cried Miss Howard wildly, flinging up her hands. "Don't say it! Oh, don't say it! It isn't true! It can't be true. I don't know what put such a wild—such a dreadful—idea into my head!"

"I am right, am I not?" asked Poirot.

"Yes, yes; you must be a wizard to have guessed. But it can't be so—it's too monstrous, too impossible. It must be Alfred Inglethorp."

Poirot shook his head gravely.

"Don't ask me about it," continued Miss Howard, "because I shan't tell you. I won't admit it, even to myself. I must be mad to think of such a thing."

Poirot nodded, as if satisfied.

"I will ask you nothing. It is enough for me that it is as I thought. And I—I, too, have an instinct. We are working together towards a common end."

"Don't ask me to help you, because I won't. I wouldn't lift a finger to—to—" She faltered.

"You will help me in spite of yourself. I ask you nothing—but you will be my ally. You will not be able to help yourself. You will do the only thing that I want of you."

"And that is?"

"You will watch!"

Evelyn Howard bowed her head.

"Yes, I can't help doing that. I am always watching—always hoping I shall be proved wrong."

"If we are wrong, well and good," said Poirot. "No one will be more pleased than I shall. But, if we are right? If we are right, Miss Howard, on whose side are you then?"

"I don't know, I don't know—"

"Come now."

"It could be hushed up."

"There must be no hushing up."

"But Emily herself—" She broke off.

"Miss Howard," said Poirot gravely, "this is unworthy of you."

Suddenly she took her face from her hands.

"Yes," she said quietly, "that was not Evelyn Howard who spoke!" She flung her head up proudly. "*This* is Evelyn Howard! And she is on the side of Justice! Let the cost be what it may." And with these words, she walked firmly out of the room.

"There," said Poirot, looking after her, "goes a very valuable ally. That woman, Hastings, has got brains as well a heart."

I did not reply.

"Instinct is a marvellous thing," mused Poirot. "It can neither be explained nor ignored."

"You and Miss Howard seem to know what you are talking about," I observed coldly. "Perhaps you don't realize that I am still in the dark."

"Really? Is that so, *mon ami?*"

"Yes. Enlighten me, will you?"

Poirot studied me attentively for a moment or two. Then, to my intense surprise, he shook his head decidedly.

"No, my friend."

"Oh, look here, why not?"

"Two is enough for a secret."

"Well, I think it is very unfair to keep back facts from me."

"I am not keeping back facts. Every fact that I know is in your possession. You can draw your own deductions from them. This time it is a question of ideas."

"Still, it would be interesting to know."

Poirot looked at me very earnestly, and again shook his head.

"You see," he said sadly, "*you* have no instincts."

"It was intelligence you were requiring just now," I pointed out.

"The two often go together," said Poirot enigmatically.

The remark seemed so utterly irrelevant that I did not even take the trouble to answer it. But I decided that if I made any interesting and important discoveries—as no doubt I should—I would keep them to myself, and surprise Poirot with the ultimate result.

There are times when it is one's duty to assert oneself.

Chapter IX

DR. BAUERSTEIN

I had had no opportunity as yet of passing on Poirot's message to Lawrence. But now, as I strolled out on the lawn, still nursing a grudge against my friend's high-handedness, I saw Lawrence on the croquet lawn, aimlessly knocking a couple of very ancient balls about, with a still more ancient mallet.

It struck me that it would be a good opportunity to deliver my message. Otherwise, Poirot himself might relieve me of it. It was true that I did not quite gather its purport, but I flattered myself that by Lawrence's reply, and perhaps a little skillful cross-examination on my part, I should soon perceive its significance. Accordingly I accosted him.

"I've been looking for you," I remarked untruthfully.

"Have you?"

"Yes. The truth is, I've got a message for you—from Poirot."

"Yes?"

"He told me to wait until I was alone with you," I said, dropping my voice significantly, and watching him intently out of the corner of my eye. I have always been rather good at what is called, I believe, creating an atmosphere.

"Well?"

There was no change of expression in the dark melancholic face. Had he any idea of what I was about to say?

"This is the message." I dropped my voice still lower. "'Find the extra coffee-cup, and you can rest in peace.'"

"What on earth does he mean?" Lawrence stared at me in quite unaffected astonishment.

"Don't you know?"

"Not in the least. Do you?"

I was compelled to shake my head.

"What extra coffee-cup?"

"I don't know."

"He'd better ask Dorcas, or one of the maids, if he wants to know about coffee-cups. It's their business, not mine. I don't know anything about the coffee-cups, except that we've got some that are never used, which are a perfect dream! Old Worcester. You're not a connoisseur, are you, Hastings?"

I shook my head.

"You miss a lot. A really perfect bit of old china—it's pure delight to handle it, or even to look at it."

"Well, what am I to tell Poirot?"

"Tell him I don't know what he's talking about. It's double Dutch to me."

"All right."

I was moving off towards the house again when he suddenly called me back.

"I say, what was the end of that message? Say it over again, will you?"

"'Find the extra coffee-cup, and you can rest in peace.' Are you sure you don't know what it means?" I asked him earnestly.

He shook his head.

"No," he said musingly, "I don't. I—I wish I did."

The boom of the gong sounded from the house, and we went in together. Poirot had been asked by John to remain to lunch, and was already seated at the table.

By tacit consent, all mention of the tragedy was barred. We conversed on the war, and other outside topics. But after the cheese and biscuits had been handed round, and Dorcas had left the room, Poirot suddenly leant forward to Mrs. Cavendish.

"Pardon me, madame, for recalling unpleasant memories, but I have a little idea"—Poirot's "little ideas" were becoming a perfect byword—"and would like to ask one or two questions."

"Of me? Certainly."

"You are too amiable, madame. What I want to ask is this: the door leading into Mrs. Inglethorp's room from that of Mademoiselle Cynthia, it was bolted, you say?"

"Certainly it was bolted," replied Mary Cavendish, rather surprised. "I said so at the inquest."

"Bolted?"

"Yes." She looked perplexed.

"I mean," explained Poirot, "you are sure it was bolted, and not merely locked?"

"Oh, I see what you mean. No, I don't know. I said bolted, meaning that it was fastened, and I could not open it, but I believe all the doors were found bolted on the inside."

"Still, as far as you are concerned, the door might equally well have been locked?"

"Oh, yes."

"You yourself did not happen to notice, madame, when you entered Mrs. Inglethorp's room, whether that door was bolted or not?"

"I—I believe it was."

"But you did not see it?"

"No. I—never looked."

"But I did," interrupted Lawrence suddenly. "I happened to notice that it *was* bolted."

"Ah, that settles it." And Poirot looked crestfallen.

I could not help rejoicing that, for once, one of his "little ideas" had come to naught.

After lunch Poirot begged me to accompany him home. I consented rather stiffly.

"You are annoyed, is it not so?" he asked anxiously, as we walked through the park.

"Not at all," I said coldly.

"That is well. That lifts a great load from my mind."

This was not quite what I had intended. I had hoped that he would have observed the stiffness of my manner. Still, the fervour of his words went towards the appeasing of my just displeasure. I thawed.

"I gave Lawrence your message," I said.

"And what did he say? He was entirely puzzled?"

"Yes. I am quite sure he had no idea of what you meant."

I had expected Poirot to be disappointed; but, to my surprise, he replied that that was as he had thought, and that he was very glad. My pride forbade me to ask any questions.

Poirot switched off on another tack.

"Mademoiselle Cynthia was not at lunch today? How was that?"

"She is at the hospital again. She resumed work today."

"Ah, she is an industrious little demoiselle. And pretty too. She is like pictures I have seen in Italy. I would rather like to see that dispensary of hers. Do you think she would show it to me?"

"I am sure she would be delighted. It's an interesting little place."

"Does she go there every day?"

"She has all Wednesdays off, and comes back to lunch on Saturdays. Those are her only times off."

"I will remember. Women are doing great work nowadays, and Mademoiselle Cynthia is clever—oh, yes, she has brains, that little one."

"Yes. I believe she has passed quite a stiff exam."

"Without doubt. After all, it is very responsible work. I suppose they have very strong poisons there?"

"Yes, she showed them to us. They are kept locked up in a little cupboard. I believe they have to be very careful. They always take out the key before leaving the room."

"Indeed. It is near the window, this cupboard?"

"No, right the other side of the room. Why?"

Poirot shrugged his shoulders.

"I wondered. That is all. Will you come in?"

We had reached the cottage.

"No. I think I'll be getting back. I shall go round the long way through the woods."

The woods round Styles were very beautiful. After the walk across the open park, it was pleasant to saunter lazily through the cool glades. There was hardly a breath of wind, the very chirp of the birds was faint and subdued. I strolled on a little way, and finally flung myself down at the foot of a grand old beech-tree. My thoughts of mankind were kindly and charitable. I even forgave Poirot for his absurd secrecy. In fact, I was at peace with the world. Then I yawned.

I thought about the crime, and it struck me as being very unreal and far off.

I yawned again.

Probably, I thought, it really never happened. Of course, it was all a bad dream. The truth of the matter was that it was Lawrence who had murdered Alfred Inglethorp with a croquet mallet. But it was absurd of John to make such a fuss about it, and to go shouting out: "I tell you I won't have it!"

I woke up with a start.

At once I realized that I was in a very awkward predicament. For, about twelve feet away from me, John and Mary Cavendish were standing facing each other, and they were evidently quarrelling. And, quite as evidently, they were unaware of my vicinity, for before I could move or speak John repeated the words which had aroused me from my dream.

"I tell you, Mary, I won't have it."

Mary's voice came, cool and liquid:

"Have *you* any right to criticize my actions?"

"It will be the talk of the village! My mother was only buried on Saturday, and here you are gadding about with the fellow."

"Oh," she shrugged her shoulders, "if it is only village gossip that you mind!"

"But it isn't. I've had enough of the fellow hanging about. He's a Polish Jew, anyway."

"A tinge of Jewish blood is not a bad thing. It leavens the"—she looked at him—"stolid stupidity of the ordinary Englishman."

Fire in her eyes, ice in her voice. I did not wonder that the blood rose to John's face in a crimson tide.

"Mary!"

"Well?" Her tone did not change.

The pleading died out of his voice.

"Am I to understand that you will continue to see Bauerstein against my express wishes?"

"If I choose."

"You defy me?"

"No, but I deny your right to criticize my actions. Have *you* no friends of whom I should disapprove?"

John fell back a pace. The colour ebbed slowly from his face.

"What do you mean?" he said, in an unsteady voice.

"You see!" said Mary quietly. "You *do* see, don't you, that *you* have no right to dictate to *me* as to the choice of my friends?"

John glanced at her pleadingly, a stricken look on his face.

"No right? Have I *no* right, Mary?" he said unsteadily. He stretched out his hands. "Mary—"

For a moment, I thought she wavered. A softer expression came over her face, then suddenly she turned almost fiercely away.

"None!"

She was walking away when John sprang after her, and caught her by the arm.

"Mary"—his voice was very quiet now—"are you in love with this fellow Bauerstein?"

She hesitated, and suddenly there swept across her face a strange expression, old as the hills, yet with something eternally young about it. So might some Egyptian sphinx have smiled.

She freed herself quietly from his arm, and spoke over her shoulder.

"Perhaps," she said; and then swiftly passed out of the little glade, leaving John standing there as though he had been turned to stone.

Rather ostentatiously, I stepped forward, crackling some dead branches with my feet as I did so. John turned. Luckily, he took it for granted that I had only just come upon the scene.

"Hullo, Hastings. Have you seen the little fellow safely back to his cottage? Quaint little chap! Is he any good, though, really?"

"He was considered one of the finest detectives of his day."

"Oh, well, I suppose there must be something in it, then. What a rotten world it is, though!"

"You find it so?" I asked.

"Good Lord, yes! There's this terrible business to start with. Scotland Yard men in and out of the house like a jack-in-the-box! Never know where they won't turn up next. Screaming headlines in every paper in the country—damn all journalists, I say! Do you know there was a whole crowd staring in at the lodge gates this morning. Sort of Madame Tussaud's chamber of horrors business that can be seen for nothing. Pretty thick, isn't it?"

"Cheer up, John!" I said soothingly. "It can't last for ever."

"Can't it, though? It can last long enough for us never to be able to hold up our heads again."

"No, no, you're getting morbid on the subject."

"Enough to make a man morbid, to be stalked by beastly journalists and stared at by gaping moon-faced idiots, wherever he goes! But there's worse than that."

"What?"

John lowered his voice:

"Have you ever thought, Hastings—it's a nightmare to me—who did it? I can't help feeling sometimes it must have been an accident. Because—because—who could have done it? Now Inglethorp's out of the way, there's no one else; no one, I mean, except—one of us."

Yes, indeed, that was nightmare enough for any man! One of us? Yes, surely it must be so, unless—

A new idea suggested itself to my mind. Rapidly, I considered it. The light increased. Poirot's mysterious doings, his hints—they all fitted in. Fool that I was not to have thought of this possibility before, and what a relief for us all.

"No, John," I said, "it isn't one of us. How could it be?"

"I know, but, still, who else is there?"

"Can't you guess?"

"No."

I looked cautiously round, and lowered my voice.

"Dr. Bauerstein!" I whispered.

"Impossible!"

"Not at all."

"But what earthly interest could he have in my mother's death?"

"That I don't see," I confessed, "but I'll tell you this: Poirot thinks so."

"Poirot? Does he? How do you know?"

I told him of Poirot's intense excitement on hearing that Dr. Bauerstein had been at Styles on the fatal night, and added:

"He said twice: 'That alters everything.' And I've been thinking. You know Inglethorp said he had put down the coffee in the hall? Well, it was just then that Bauerstein arrived. Isn't it possible that, as Inglethorp brought him through the hall, the doctor dropped something into the coffee in passing?"

"H'm," said John. "It would have been very risky."

"Yes, but it was possible."

"And then, how could he know it was her coffee? No, old fellow, I don't think that will wash."

But I had remembered something else.

"You're quite right. That wasn't how it was done. Listen." And I then told him of the cocoa sample which Poirot had taken to be analysed.

John interrupted just as I had done.

"But, look here, Bauerstein had had it analysed already?"

"Yes, yes, that's the point. I didn't see it either until now. Don't you understand? Bauerstein had it analysed—that's just it! If Bauerstein's the murderer, nothing could be simpler than for him to substitute some ordinary cocoa for his sample, and send that to be tested. And of course they would find no strychnine! But no one would dream of suspecting Bauerstein, or think of taking another sample—except Poirot," I added, with belated recognition.

"Yes, but what about the bitter taste that cocoa won't disguise?"

"Well, we've only his word for that. And there are other possibilities. He's admittedly one of the world's greatest toxicologists—"

"One of the world's greatest what? Say it again."

"He knows more about poisons than almost anybody," I explained. "Well, my idea is, that perhaps he's found some way of making strychnine tasteless. Or it may not have been strychnine at all, but some obscure drug no one has ever heard of, which produces much the same symptoms."

"H'm, yes, that might be," said John. "But look here, how could he have got at the cocoa? That wasn't downstairs?"

"No, it wasn't," I admitted reluctantly.

And then, suddenly, a dreadful possibility flashed through my mind. I hoped and prayed it would not occur to John also. I glanced sideways at him. He was frowning perplexedly, and I drew a deep breath of relief, for the terrible thought that had flashed across my mind was this: that Dr. Bauerstein might have had an accomplice.

Yet surely it could not be! Surely no woman as beautiful as Mary Cavendish could be a murderess. Yet beautiful women had been known to poison.

And suddenly I remembered that first conversation at tea on the day of my arrival, and the gleam in her eyes as she had said that poison was a woman's weapon. How agitated she had been on that fatal Tuesday evening! Had Mrs. Inglethorp discovered something between her and Bauerstein, and threatened to tell her husband? Was it to stop that denunciation that the crime had been committed?

Then I remembered that enigmatical conversation between Poirot and Evelyn Howard. Was this what they had meant? Was this the monstrous possibility that Evelyn had tried not to believe?

Yes, it all fitted in.

No wonder Miss Howard had suggested "hushing it up." Now I understood that unfinished sentence of hers: "Emily herself—" And in my heart I agreed with her. Would not Mrs. Inglethorp have preferred to go unavenged rather than have such terrible dishonour fall upon the name of Cavendish.

"There's another thing," said John suddenly, and the unexpected sound of his voice made me start guiltily. "Something which makes me doubt if what you say can be true."

"What's that?" I asked, thankful that he had gone away from the subject of how the poison could have been introduced into the cocoa.

"Why, the fact that Bauerstein demanded a post-mortem. He needn't have done so. Little Wilkins would have been quite content to let it go at heart disease."

"Yes," I said doubtfully. "But we don't know. Perhaps he thought it safer in the long run. Someone might have talked afterwards. Then the Home Office might have ordered exhumation. The whole thing would have come out, then, and he would have been in an awkward position, for no one would have believed that a man of his reputation could have been deceived into calling it heart disease."

"Yes, that's possible," admitted John. "Still," he added, "I'm blest if I can see what his motive could have been."

I trembled.

"Look here," I said, "I may be altogether wrong. And, remember, all this is in confidence."

"Oh, of course—that goes without saying."

We had walked, as we talked, and now we passed through the little gate into the garden. Voices rose near at hand, for tea was spread out under the sycamore-tree, as it had been on the day of my arrival.

Cynthia was back from the hospital, and I placed my chair beside her, and told her of Poirot's wish to visit the dispensary.

"Of course! I'd love him to see it. He'd better come to tea there one day. I must fix it up with him. He's such a dear little man! But he is funny. He made me take the brooch out of my tie the other day, and put it in again, because he said it wasn't straight."

I laughed.

"It's quite a mania with him."

"Yes, isn't it?"

We were silent for a minute or two, and then, glancing in the direction of Mary Cavendish, and dropping her voice, Cynthia said:

"Mr. Hastings."

"Yes?"

"After tea, I want to talk to you."

Her glance at Mary had set me thinking. I fancied that between these two there existed very little sympathy. For the first time, it occurred to me to wonder about the girl's future. Mrs. Inglethorp had made no provisions of any kind for her, but I imagined that John and Mary would probably insist on her making her home with them—at any rate until the end of the war. John, I knew, was very fond of her, and would be sorry to let her go.

John, who had gone into the house, now reappeared. His good-natured face wore an unaccustomed frown of anger.

"Confound those detectives! I can't think what they're after! They've been in every room in the house—turning things inside out, and upside down. It really is too bad! I suppose they took advantage of our all being out. I shall go for that fellow Japp, when I next see him!"

"Lot of Paul Prys," grunted Miss Howard.

Lawrence opined that they had to make a show of doing something.

Mary Cavendish said nothing.

After tea, I invited Cynthia to come for a walk, and we sauntered off into the woods together.

"Well?" I inquired, as soon as we were protected from prying eyes by the leafy screen.

With a sigh, Cynthia flung herself down, and tossed off her hat. The sunlight, piercing through the branches, turned the auburn of her hair to quivering gold.

"Mr. Hastings—you are always so kind, and you know such a lot."

It struck me at this moment that Cynthia was really a very charming girl! Much more charming than Mary, who never said things of that kind.

"Well?" I asked benignantly, as she hesitated.

"I want to ask your advice. What shall I do?"

"Do?"

"Yes. You see, Aunt Emily always told me I should be provided for. I suppose she forgot, or didn't think she was likely to die—anyway, I am not provided for! And I don't know what to do. Do you think I ought to go away from here at once?"

"Good heavens, no! They don't want to part with you, I'm sure."

Cynthia hesitated a moment, plucking up the grass with her tiny hands. Then she said: "Mrs. Cavendish does. She hates me."

"Hates you?" I cried, astonished.

Cynthia nodded.

"Yes. I don't know why, but she can't bear me; and he can't, either."

"There I know you're wrong," I said warmly. "On the contrary, John is very fond of you."

"Oh, yes—*John*. I meant Lawrence. Not, of course, that I care whether Lawrence hates me or not. Still, it's rather horrid when no one loves you, isn't it?"

"But they do, Cynthia dear," I said earnestly. "I'm sure you are mistaken. Look, there is John—and Miss Howard—"

Cynthia nodded rather gloomily. "Yes, John likes me, I think, and of course Evie, for all her gruff ways, wouldn't be unkind to a fly. But Lawrence never speaks to me if he can help it, and Mary can hardly bring herself to be civil to me. She wants Evie to stay on, is begging her to, but she doesn't want me, and—and—I don't know what to do." Suddenly the poor child burst out crying.

I don't know what possessed me. Her beauty, perhaps, as she sat there, with the sunlight glinting down on her head; perhaps the sense of relief at encountering someone who so obviously could have no connection with the tragedy; perhaps honest pity for her youth and loneliness. Anyway, I leant forward, and taking her little hand, I said awkwardly:

"Marry me, Cynthia."

Unwittingly, I had hit upon a sovereign remedy for her tears. She sat up at once, drew her hand away, and said, with some asperity:

"Don't be silly!"

I was a little annoyed.

"I'm not being silly. I am asking you to do me the honour of becoming my wife."

To my intense surprise, Cynthia burst out laughing, and called me a "funny dear."

"It's perfectly sweet of you," she said, "but you know you don't want to!"

"Yes, I do. I've got—"

"Never mind what you've got. You don't really want to—and I don't either."

"Well, of course, that settles it," I said stiffly. "But I don't see anything to laugh at. There's nothing funny about a proposal."

"No, indeed," said Cynthia. "Somebody might accept you next time. Good-bye, you've cheered me up *very* much."

And, with a final uncontrollable burst of merriment, she vanished through the trees.

Thinking over the interview, it struck me as being profoundly unsatisfactory.

It occurred to me suddenly that I would go down to the village, and look up Bauerstein. Somebody ought to be keeping an eye on the fellow. At the same time, it would be wise to allay any suspicions he might have as to his being suspected. I remembered how Poirot had relied on my diplomacy. Accordingly, I went to the little house with the "Apartments" card inserted in the window, where I knew he lodged, and tapped on the door.

An old woman came and opened it.

"Good afternoon," I said pleasantly. "Is Dr. Bauerstein in?"

She stared at me.

"Haven't you heard?"

"Heard what?"

"About him."

"What about him?"

"He's took."

"Took? Dead?"

"No, took by the perlice."

"By the police!" I gasped. "Do you mean they've arrested him?"

"Yes, that's it, and—"

I waited to hear no more, but tore up the village to find Poirot.

Chapter X

THE ARREST

To my extreme annoyance, Poirot was not in, and the old Belgian who answered my knock informed me that he believed he had gone to London.

I was dumbfounded. What on earth could Poirot be doing in London! Was it a sudden decision on his part, or had he already made up his mind when he parted from me a few hours earlier?

I retraced my steps to Styles in some annoyance. With Poirot away, I was uncertain how to act. Had he foreseen this arrest? Had he not, in all probability, been the cause of it? Those questions I could not resolve. But in the meantime what was I to do? Should I announce the arrest openly at Styles, or not? Though I did not acknowledge it to myself, the thought of Mary Cavendish was weighing on me. Would it not be a terrible shock to her? For the moment, I set aside utterly any suspicions of her. She could not be implicated—otherwise I should have heard some hint of it.

Of course, there was no possibility of being able permanently to conceal Dr. Bauerstein's arrest from her. It would be announced in every newspaper on the morrow. Still, I shrank from blurting it out. If only Poirot had been accessible, I could have asked his advice. What possessed him to go posting off to London in this unaccountable way?

In spite of myself, my opinion of his sagacity was immeasurably heightened. I would never have dreamt of suspecting the doctor, had not Poirot put it into my head. Yes, decidedly, the little man was clever.

After some reflecting, I decided to take John into my confidence, and leave him to make the matter public or not, as he thought fit.

He gave vent to a prodigious whistle, as I imparted the news.

"Great Scot! You were right, then. I couldn't believe it at the time."

"No, it is astonishing until you get used to the idea, and see how it makes everything fit in. Now, what are we to do? Of course, it will be generally known tomorrow."

John reflected.

"Never mind," he said at last, "we won't say anything at present. There is no need. As you say, it will be known soon enough."

But to my intense surprise, on getting down early the next morning, and eagerly opening the newspapers, there was not a word about the arrest! There was a column of mere padding about "The Styles Poisoning Case," but nothing further. It was rather inexplicable, but I supposed that, for some reason or other, Japp wished to keep it out of the papers. It worried me just a little, for it suggested the possibility that there might be further arrests to come.

After breakfast, I decided to go down to the village, and see if Poirot had returned yet; but, before I could start, a well-known face blocked one of the windows, and the well-known voice said:

"*Bonjour, mon ami!*"

"Poirot," I exclaimed, with relief, and seizing him by both hands, I dragged him into the room. "I was never so glad to see anyone. Listen, I have said nothing to anybody but John. Is that right?"

"My friend," replied Poirot, "I do not know what you are talking about."

"Dr. Bauerstein's arrest, of course," I answered impatiently.

"Is Bauerstein arrested, then?"

"Did you not know it?"

"Not the least in the world." But, pausing a moment, he added: "Still, it does not surprise me. After all, we are only four miles from the coast."

"The coast?" I asked, puzzled. "What has that got to do with it?"

Poirot shrugged his shoulders.

"Surely, it is obvious!"

"Not to me. No doubt I am very dense, but I cannot see what the proximity of the coast has got to do with the murder of Mrs. Inglethorp."

"Nothing at all, of course," replied Poirot, smiling. "But we were speaking of the arrest of Dr. Bauerstein."

"Well, he is arrested for the murder of Mrs. Inglethorp—"

"What?" cried Poirot, in apparently lively astonishment. "Dr. Bauerstein arrested for the murder of Mrs. Inglethorp?"

"Yes."

"Impossible! That would be too good a farce! Who told you that, my friend?"

"Well, no one exactly told me," I confessed. "But he is arrested."

"Oh, yes, very likely. But for espionage, *mon ami.*"

"Espionage?" I gasped.

"Precisely."

"Not for poisoning Mrs. Inglethorp?"

"Not unless our friend Japp has taken leave of his senses," replied Poirot placidly.

"But—but I thought you thought so too?"

Poirot gave me one look, which conveyed a wondering pity, and his full sense of the utter absurdity of such an idea.

"Do you mean to say," I asked, slowly adapting myself to the new idea, "that Dr. Bauerstein is a spy?"

Poirot nodded.

"Have you never suspected it?"

"It never entered my head."

"It did not strike you as peculiar that a famous London doctor should bury himself in a little village like this, and should be in the habit of walking about at all hours of the night, fully dressed?"

"No," I confessed, "I never thought of such a thing."

"He is, of course, a German by birth," said Poirot thoughtfully, "though he has practiced so long in this country that nobody thinks of him as anything but an Englishman. He was naturalized about fifteen years ago. A very clever man—a Jew, of course."

"The blackguard!" I cried indignantly.

"Not at all. He is, on the contrary, a patriot. Think what he stands to lose. I admire the man myself."

But I could not look at it in Poirot's philosophical way.

"And this is the man with whom Mrs. Cavendish has been wandering about all over the country!" I cried indignantly.

"Yes. I should fancy he had found her very useful," remarked Poirot. "So long as gossip busied itself in coupling their names together, any other vagaries of the doctor's passed unobserved."

"Then you think he never really cared for her?" I asked eagerly—rather too eagerly, perhaps, under the circumstances.

"That, of course, I cannot say, but—shall I tell you my own private opinion, Hastings?"

"Yes."

"Well, it is this: that Mrs. Cavendish does not care, and never has cared one little jot about Dr. Bauerstein!"

"Do you really think so?" I could not disguise my pleasure.

"I am quite sure of it. And I will tell you why."

"Yes?"

"Because she cares for someone else, *mon ami*."

"Oh!" What did he mean? In spite of myself, an agreeable warmth spread over me. I am not a vain man where women are concerned, but I remembered certain evidences, too lightly thought of at the time, perhaps, but which certainly seemed to indicate—

My pleasing thoughts were interrupted by the sudden entrance of Miss Howard. She glanced round hastily to make sure there was no one else in the room, and quickly produced an old sheet of brown paper. This she handed to Poirot, murmuring as she did so the cryptic words:

"On top of the wardrobe." Then she hurriedly left the room.

Poirot unfolded the sheet of paper eagerly, and uttered an exclamation of satisfaction. He spread it out on the table.

"Come here, Hastings. Now tell me, what is that initial—J. or L.?"

It was a medium sized sheet of paper, rather dusty, as though it had lain by for some time. But it was the label that was attracting Poirot's attention. At the top, it bore the printed stamp of Messrs. Parkson's, the well-known theatrical costumiers, and it was addressed to "— (the debatable initial) Cavendish, Esq., Styles Court, Styles St. Mary, Essex."

"It might be T., or it might be L.," I said, after studying the thing for a minute or two. "It certainly isn't a J."

"Good," replied Poirot, folding up the paper again. "I, also, am of your way of thinking. It is an L., depend upon it!"

"Where did it come from?" I asked curiously. "Is it important?"

"Moderately so. It confirms a surmise of mine. Having deduced its existence, I set Miss Howard to search for it, and, as you see, she has been successful."

"What did she mean by 'On the top of the wardrobe'?"

"She meant," replied Poirot promptly, "that she found it on top of a wardrobe."

"A funny place for a piece of brown paper," I mused.

"Not at all. The top of a wardrobe is an excellent place for brown paper and cardboard boxes. I have kept them there myself. Neatly arranged, there is nothing to offend the eye."

"Poirot," I asked earnestly, "have you made up your mind about this crime?"

"Yes—that is to say, I believe I know how it was committed."

"Ah!"

"Unfortunately, I have no proof beyond my surmise, unless—" With sudden energy, he caught me by the arm, and whirled me down the hall, calling out in French in his excitement: "Mademoiselle Dorcas, Mademoiselle Dorcas, *un moment, s'il vous plaît!*"

Dorcas, quite flurried by the noise, came hurrying out of the pantry.

"My good Dorcas, I have an idea—a little idea—if it should prove justified, what magnificent chance! Tell me, on Monday, not Tuesday, Dorcas, but Monday, the day before the tragedy, did anything go wrong with Mrs. Inglethorp's bell?"

Dorcas looked very surprised.

"Yes, sir, now you mention it, it did; though I don't know how you came to hear of it. A mouse, or some such, must have nibbled the wire through. The man came and put it right on Tuesday morning."

With a long drawn exclamation of ecstasy, Poirot led the way back to the morning-room.

"See you, one should not ask for outside proof—no, reason should be enough. But the flesh is weak, it is consolation to find that one is on the right track. Ah, my friend, I am like a giant refreshed. I run! I leap!"

And, in very truth, run and leap he did, gambolling wildly down the stretch of lawn outside the long window.

"What is your remarkable little friend doing?" asked a voice behind me, and I turned to find Mary Cavendish at my elbow. She smiled, and so did I. "What is it all about?"

"Really, I can't tell you. He asked Dorcas some question about a bell, and appeared so delighted with her answer that he is capering about as you see!"

Mary laughed.

"How ridiculous! He's going out of the gate. Isn't he coming back today?"

"I don't know. I've given up trying to guess what he'll do next."

"Is he quite mad, Mr. Hastings?"

"I honestly don't know. Sometimes, I feel sure he is as mad as a hatter; and then, just as he is at his maddest, I find there is method in his madness."

"I see."

In spite of her laugh, Mary was looking thoughtful this morning. She seemed grave, almost sad.

It occurred to me that it would be a good opportunity to tackle her on the subject of Cynthia. I began rather tactfully, I thought, but I had not gone far before she stopped me authoritatively.

"You are an excellent advocate, I have no doubt, Mr. Hastings, but in this case your talents are quite thrown away. Cynthia will run no risk of encountering any unkindness from me."

I began to stammer feebly that I hoped she hadn't thought—But again she stopped me, and her words were so unexpected that they quite drove Cynthia, and her troubles, out of my mind.

"Mr. Hastings," she said, "do you think I and my husband are happy together?"

I was considerably taken aback, and murmured something about it's not being my business to think anything of the sort.

"Well," she said quietly, "whether it is your business or not, I will tell you that we are *not* happy."

I said nothing, for I saw that she had not finished.

She began slowly, walking up and down the room, her head a little bent, and that slim, supple figure of hers swaying gently as she walked. She stopped suddenly, and looked up at me.

"You don't know anything about me, do you?" she asked. "Where I come from, who I was before I married John—anything, in fact? Well, I will tell you. I will make a father confessor of you. You are kind, I think—yes, I am sure you are kind."

Somehow, I was not quite as elated as I might have been. I remembered that Cynthia had begun her confidences in much the same way. Besides, a father confessor should be elderly, it is not at all the role for a young man.

"My father was English," said Mrs. Cavendish, "but my mother was a Russian."

"Ah," I said, "now I understand—"

"Understand what?"

"A hint of something foreign—different—that there has always been about you."

"My mother was very beautiful, I believe. I don't know, because I never saw her. She died when I was quite a little child. I believe there was some tragedy connected with her death—she took an overdose of some sleeping draught by mistake. However that may be, my father was broken-hearted. Shortly afterwards, he went into the Consular Service. Everywhere he went, I went with him. When I was twenty-three, I had been nearly all over the world. It was a splendid life—I loved it."

There was a smile on her face, and her head was thrown back. She seemed living in the memory of those old glad days.

"Then my father died. He left me very badly off. I had to go and live with some old aunts in Yorkshire." She shuddered. "You will understand me when I say that it was a deadly life for a girl brought up as I had been.

The narrowness, the deadly monotony of it, almost drove me mad." She paused a minute, and added in a different tone: "And then I met John Cavendish."

"Yes?"

"You can imagine that, from my aunts' point of view, it was a very good match for me. But I can honestly say it was not this fact which weighed with me. No, he was simply a way of escape from the insufferable monotony of my life."

I said nothing, and after a moment, she went on:

"Don't misunderstand me. I was quite honest with him. I told him, what was true, that I liked him very much, that I hoped to come to like him more, but that I was not in any way what the world calls 'in love' with him. He declared that that satisfied him, and so—we were married."

She waited a long time, a little frown had gathered on her forehead. She seemed to be looking back earnestly into those past days.

"I think—I am sure—he cared for me at first. But I suppose we were not well matched. Almost at once, we drifted apart. He—it is not a pleasing thing for my pride, but it is the truth—tired of me very soon." I must have made some murmur of dissent, for she went on quickly: "Oh, yes, he did! Not that it matters now—now that we've come to the parting of the ways."

"What do you mean?"

She answered quietly:

"I mean that I am not going to remain at Styles."

"You and John are not going to live here?"

"John may live here, but I shall not."

"You are going to leave him?"

"Yes."

"But why?"

She paused a long time, and said at last:

"Perhaps—because I want to be—free!"

And, as she spoke, I had a sudden vision of broad spaces, virgin tracts of forests, untrodden lands—and a realization of what freedom would mean to such a nature as Mary Cavendish. I seemed to see her for a moment as she was, a proud wild creature, as untamed by civilization as some shy bird of the hills. A little cry broke from her lips:

"You don't know, you don't know, how this hateful place has been prison to me!"

"I understand," I said, "but—but don't do anything rash."

"Oh, rash!" Her voice mocked at my prudence.

Then suddenly I said a thing I could have bitten out my tongue for:

"You know that Dr. Bauerstein has been arrested?"

An instant coldness passed like a mask over her face, blotting out all expression.

"John was so kind as to break that to me this morning."

"Well, what do you think?" I asked feebly.

"Of what?"

"Of the arrest?"

"What should I think? Apparently he is a German spy; so the gardener had told John."

Her face and voice were absolutely cold and expressionless. Did she care, or did she not?

She moved away a step or two, and fingered one of the flower vases.

"These are quite dead. I must do them again. Would you mind moving—thank you, Mr. Hastings." And she walked quietly past me out of the window, with a cool little nod of dismissal.

No, surely she could not care for Bauerstein. No woman could act her part with that icy unconcern.

Poirot did not make his appearance the following morning, and there was no sign of the Scotland Yard men.

But, at lunch-time, there arrived a new piece of evidence—or rather lack of evidence. We had vainly tried to trace the fourth letter, which Mrs. Inglethorp had written on the evening preceding her death. Our efforts having been in vain, we had abandoned the matter, hoping that it might turn up of itself one day. And this is just what did happen, in the shape of a communication, which arrived by the second post from a firm of French music publishers, acknowledging Mrs. Inglethorp's cheque, and regretting they had been unable to trace a certain series of Russian folksongs. So the last hope of solving the mystery, by means of Mrs. Inglethorp's correspondence on the fatal evening, had to be abandoned.

Just before tea, I strolled down to tell Poirot of the new disappointment, but found, to my annoyance, that he was once more out.

"Gone to London again?"

"Oh, no, monsieur, he has but taken the train to Tadminster. 'To see a young lady's dispensary,' he said."

"Silly ass!" I ejaculated. "I told him Wednesday was the one day she wasn't there! Well, tell him to look us up tomorrow morning, will you?"

"Certainly, monsieur."

But, on the following day, no sign of Poirot. I was getting angry. He was really treating us in the most cavalier fashion.

After lunch, Lawrence drew me aside, and asked if I was going down to see him.

"No, I don't think I shall. He can come up here if he wants to see us."

"Oh!" Lawrence looked indeterminate. Something unusually nervous and excited in his manner roused my curiosity.

"What is it?" I asked. "I could go if there's anything special."

"It's nothing much, but—well, if you are going, will you tell him—" he dropped his voice to a whisper—"I think I've found the extra coffee-cup!"

I had almost forgotten that enigmatical message of Poirot's, but now my curiosity was aroused afresh.

Lawrence would say no more, so I decided that I would descend from my high horse, and once more seek out Poirot at Leastways Cottage.

This time I was received with a smile. Monsieur Poirot was within. Would I mount? I mounted accordingly.

Poirot was sitting by the table, his head buried in his hands. He sprang up at my entrance.

"What is it?" I asked solicitously. "You are not ill, I trust?"

"No, no, not ill. But I decide an affair of great moment."

"Whether to catch the criminal or not?" I asked facetiously.

But, to my great surprise, Poirot nodded gravely.

"'To speak or not to speak,' as your so great Shakespeare says, 'that is the question.'"

I did not trouble to correct the quotation.

"You are not serious, Poirot?"

"I am of the most serious. For the most serious of all things hangs in the balance."

"And that is?"

"A woman's happiness, *mon ami*," he said gravely.

I did not quite know what to say.

"The moment has come," said Poirot thoughtfully, "and I do not know what to do. For, see you, it is a big stake for which I play. No one but I, Hercule Poirot, would attempt it!" And he tapped himself proudly on the breast.

After pausing a few minutes respectfully, so as not to spoil his effect, I gave him Lawrence's message.

"Aha!" he cried. "So he has found the extra coffee-cup. That is good. He has more intelligence than would appear, this long-faced Monsieur Lawrence of yours!"

I did not myself think very highly of Lawrence's intelligence; but I forebore to contradict Poirot, and gently took him to task for forgetting my instructions as to which were Cynthia's days off.

"It is true. I have the head of a sieve. However, the other young lady was most kind. She was sorry for my disappointment, and showed me everything in the kindest way."

"Oh, well, that's all right, then, and you must go to tea with Cynthia another day."

I told him about the letter.

"I am sorry for that," he said. "I always had hopes of that letter. But no, it was not to be. This affair must all be unravelled from within." He tapped his forehead. "These little grey cells. It is 'up to them'—as you say over here." Then, suddenly, he asked: "Are you a judge of finger-marks, my friend?"

"No," I said, rather surprised, "I know that there are no two finger-marks alike, but that's as far as my science goes."

"Exactly."

He unlocked a little drawer, and took out some photographs which he laid on the table.

"I have numbered them, 1, 2, 3. Will you describe them to me?"

I studied the proofs attentively.

"All greatly magnified, I see. No. 1, I should say, are a man's finger-prints; thumb and first finger. No. 2 are a lady's; they are much smaller, and quite different in every way. No. 3"—I paused for some time—"there seem to be a lot of confused finger-marks, but here, very distinctly, are No. 1's."

"Overlapping the others?"

"Yes."

"You recognize them beyond fail?"

"Oh, yes; they are identical."

Poirot nodded, and gently taking the photographs from me locked them up again.

"I suppose," I said, "that as usual, you are not going to explain?"

"On the contrary. No. 1 were the finger-prints of Monsieur Lawrence. No. 2 were those of Mademoiselle Cynthia. They are not important. I merely obtained them for comparison. No. 3 is a little more complicated."

"Yes?"

"It is, as you see, highly magnified. You may have noticed a sort of blur extending all across the picture. I will not describe to you the special apparatus, dusting powder, etc., which I used. It is a well-known process to the police, and by means of it you can obtain a photograph of the finger-prints of any object in a very short space of time. Well, my friend, you have seen the finger-marks—it remains to tell you the particular object on which they had been left."

"Go on—I am really excited."

"*Eh bien*! Photo No. 3 represents the highly magnified surface of a tiny bottle in the top poison cupboard of the dispensary in the Red Cross Hospital at Tadminster—which sounds like the house that Jack built!"

"Good heavens!" I exclaimed. "But what were Lawrence Cavendish's finger-marks doing on it? He never went near the poison cupboard the day we were there!"

"Oh, yes, he did!"

"Impossible! We were all together the whole time."

Poirot shook his head.

"No, my friend, there was a moment when you were not all together. There was a moment when you could not have been all together, or it would not have been necessary to call to Monsieur Lawrence to come and join you on the balcony."

"I'd forgotten that," I admitted. "But it was only for a moment."

"Long enough."

"Long enough for what?"

Poirot's smile became rather enigmatical.

"Long enough for a gentleman who had once studied medicine to gratify a very natural interest and curiosity."

Our eyes met. Poirot's were pleasantly vague. He got up and hummed a little tune. I watched him suspiciously.

"Poirot," I said, "what was in this particular little bottle?"

Poirot looked out of the window.

"Hydro-chloride of strychnine," he said, over his shoulder, continuing to hum.

"Good heavens!" I said it quite quietly. I was not surprised. I had expected that answer.

"They use the pure hydro-chloride of strychnine very little—only occasionally for pills. It is the official solution, Liq. Strychnine Hydro-clor. that is used in most medicines. That is why the finger-marks have remained undisturbed since then."

"How did you manage to take this photograph?"

"I dropped my hat from the balcony," explained Poirot simply. "Visitors were not permitted below at that hour, so, in spite of my many apologies, Mademoiselle Cynthia's colleague had to go down and fetch it for me."

"Then you knew what you were going to find?"

"No, not at all. I merely realized that it was possible, from your story, for Monsieur Lawrence to go to the poison cupboard. The possibility had to be confirmed, or eliminated."

"Poirot," I said, "your gaiety does not deceive me. This is a very important discovery."

"I do not know," said Poirot. "But one thing does strike me. No doubt it has struck you too."

"What is that?"

"Why, that there is altogether too much strychnine about this case. This is the third time we run up against it. There was strychnine in Mrs. Inglethorp's tonic. There is the strychnine sold across the counter at Styles St. Mary by Mace. Now we have more strychnine, handled by one of the household. It is confusing; and, as you know, I do not like confusion."

Before I could reply, one of the other Belgians opened the door and stuck his head in.

"There is a lady below, asking for Mr Hastings."

"A lady?"

I jumped up. Poirot followed me down the narrow stairs. Mary Cavendish was standing in the doorway.

"I have been visiting an old woman in the village," she explained, "and as Lawrence told me you were with Monsieur Poirot I thought I would call for you."

"Alas, madame," said Poirot, "I thought you had come to honour me with a visit!"

"I will some day, if you ask me," she promised him, smiling.

"That is well. If you should need a father confessor, madame" —she started ever so slightly—"remember, Papa Poirot is always at your service."

She stared at him for a few minutes, as though seeking to read some deeper meaning into his words. Then she turned abruptly away.

"Come, will you not walk back with us too, Monsieur Poirot?"

"Enchanted, madame."

All the way to Styles, Mary talked fast and feverishly. It struck me that in some way she was nervous of Poirot's eyes.

The weather had broken, and the sharp wind was almost autumnal in its shrewishness. Mary shivered a little, and buttoned her black sports coat closer. The wind through the trees made a mournful noise, like some great giant sighing.

We walked up to the great door of Styles, and at once the knowledge came to us that something was wrong.

Dorcas came running out to meet us. She was crying and wringing her hands. I was aware of other servants huddled together in the background, all eyes and ears.

"Oh, m'am! Oh, m'am! I don't know how to tell you—"

"What is it, Dorcas?" I asked impatiently. "Tell us at once."

"It's those wicked detectives. They've arrested him—they've arrested Mr. Cavendish!"

"Arrested Lawrence?" I gasped.

I saw a strange look come into Dorcas's eyes.

"No, sir. Not Mr. Lawrence—Mr. John."

Behind me, with a wild cry, Mary Cavendish fell heavily against me, and as I turned to catch her I met the quiet triumph in Poirot's eyes.

Chapter XI

THE CASE FOR THE PROSECUTION

The trial of John Cavendish for the murder of his stepmother took place two months later.

Of the intervening weeks I will say little, but my admiration and sympathy went out unfeignedly to Mary Cavendish. She ranged herself passionately on her husband's side, scorning the mere idea of his guilt, and fought for him tooth and nail.

I expressed my admiration to Poirot, and he nodded thoughtfully.

"Yes, she is of those women who show at their best in adversity. It brings out all that is sweetest and truest in them. Her pride and her jealousy have—"

"Jealousy?" I queried.

"Yes. Have you not realized that she is an unusually jealous woman? As I was saying, her pride and jealousy have been laid aside. She thinks of nothing but her husband, and the terrible fate that is hanging over him."

He spoke very feelingly, and I looked at him earnestly, remembering that last afternoon, when he had been deliberating whether or not to speak. With his tenderness for "a woman's happiness," I felt glad that the decision had been taken out of his hands.

"Even now," I said, "I can hardly believe it. You see, up to the very last minute, I thought it was Lawrence!"

Poirot grinned.

"I know you did."

"But John! My old friend John!"

"Every murderer is probably somebody's old friend," observed Poirot philosophically. "You cannot mix up sentiment and reason."

"I must say I think you might have given me a hint."

"Perhaps, *mon ami*, I did not do so, just because he *was* your old friend."

I was rather disconcerted by this, remembering how I had busily passed on to John what I believed to be Poirot's views concerning Bauerstein. He, by the way, had been acquitted of the charge brought against him. Nevertheless, although he had been too clever for them this time, and the charge of espionage could not be brought home to him, his wings were pretty well clipped for the future.

I asked Poirot whether he thought John would be condemned. To my intense surprise, he replied that, on the contrary, he was extremely likely to be acquitted.

"But, Poirot—" I protested.

"Oh, my friend, have I not said to you all along that I have no proofs. It is one thing to know that a man is guilty, it is quite another matter to prove him so. And, in this case, there is terribly little evidence. That is the whole trouble. I, Hercule Poirot, know, but I lack the last link in my chain. And unless I can find that missing link—" He shook his head gravely.

"When did you first suspect John Cavendish?" I asked, after a minute or two.

"Did you not suspect him at all?"

"No, indeed."

"Not after that fragment of conversation you overheard between Mrs. Cavendish and her mother-in-law, and her subsequent lack of frankness at the inquest?"

"No."

"Did you not put two and two together, and reflect that if it was not Alfred Inglethorp who was quarrelling with his wife—and you remember, he strenuously denied it at the inquest—it must be either Lawrence or John. Now, if it was Lawrence, Mary Cavendish's conduct was just as inexplicable. But if, on the other hand, it was John, the whole thing was explained quite naturally."

"So," I cried, a light breaking in upon me, "it was John who quarrelled with his mother that afternoon?"

"Exactly."

"And you have known this all along?"

"Certainly. Mrs. Cavendish's behaviour could only be explained that way."

"And yet you say he may be acquitted?"

Poirot shrugged his shoulders.

"Certainly I do. At the police court proceedings, we shall hear the case for the prosecution, but in all probability his solicitors will advise him to reserve his defence. That will be sprung upon us at the trial. And—ah, by the way, I have a word of caution to give you, my friend. I must not appear in the case."

"What?"

"No. Officially, I have nothing to do with it. Until I have found that last link in my chain, I must remain behind the scenes. Mrs. Cavendish must think I am working for her husband, not against him."

"I say, that's playing it a bit low down," I protested.

"Not at all. We have to deal with a most clever and unscrupulous man, and we must use any means in our power—otherwise he will slip through our fingers. That is why I have been careful to remain in the background. All the discoveries have been made by Japp, and Japp will take all the credit. If I am called upon to give evidence at all"—he smiled broadly—"it will probably be as a witness for the defence."

I could hardly believe my ears.

"It is quite *en règle*," continued Poirot. "Strangely enough, I can give evidence that will demolish one contention of the prosecution."

"Which one?"

"The one that relates to the destruction of the will. John Cavendish did not destroy that will."

Poirot was a true prophet. I will not go into the details of the police court proceedings, as it involves many tiresome repetitions. I will merely state baldly that John Cavendish reserved his defence, and was duly committed for trial.

September found us all in London. Mary took a house in Kensington, Poirot being included in the family party.

I myself had been given a job at the War Office, so was able to see them continually.

As the weeks went by, the state of Poirot's nerves grew worse and worse. That "last link" he talked about was still lacking. Privately, I hoped it might remain so, for what happiness could there be for Mary, if John were not acquitted?

On September 15th John Cavendish appeared in the dock at the Old Bailey, charged with "The Wilful Murder of Emily Agnes Inglethorp," and pleaded "Not Guilty."

Sir Ernest Heavywether, the famous K. C., had been engaged to defend him.

Mr. Philips, K. C., opened the case for the Crown.

The murder, he said, was a most premeditated and cold-blooded one. It was neither more nor less than the deliberate poisoning of a fond and trusting woman by the stepson to whom she had been more than a mother. Ever since his boyhood, she had supported him. He and his wife had lived at Styles Court in every luxury, surrounded by her care and attention. She had been their kind and generous benefactress.

He proposed to call witnesses to show how the prisoner, a profligate and spendthrift, had been at the end of his financial tether, and had also been carrying on an intrigue with a certain Mrs. Raikes, a neighbouring farmer's wife. This having come to his stepmother's ears, she taxed him with it on the afternoon before her death, and a quarrel ensued, part of which was overheard. On the previous day, the prisoner had purchased strychnine at the village chemist's shop, wearing a disguise by means of which he hoped to throw the onus of the crime upon another man—to wit, Mrs. Inglethorp's husband, of whom he had been bitterly jealous. Luckily for Mr. Inglethorp, he had been able to produce an unimpeachable alibi.

On the afternoon of July 17th, continued Counsel, immediately after the quarrel with her son, Mrs. Inglethorp made a new will. This will was found destroyed in the grate of her bedroom the following morning, but evidence had come to light which showed that it had been drawn up in favour of her husband. Deceased had already made a will in his favour before her marriage, but—and Mr. Philips wagged an expressive forefinger—the prisoner was not aware of that. What had induced the deceased to make a fresh will, with the old one still extant, he could not say. She was an old lady, and might possibly have forgotten the former one; or—this seemed to him more likely—she may have had an idea that it was revoked by her marriage, as there had been some conversation on the subject. Ladies were not always very well versed in legal knowledge. She had, about a year before, executed a will in favour of the prisoner. He would call evidence to show that it was the prisoner who ultimately handed his stepmother her coffee on the fatal night. Later in the evening, he had sought admission to her room, on which occasion, no doubt, he found an opportunity of destroying the will which, as far as he knew, would render the one in his favour valid.

The prisoner had been arrested in consequence of the discovery, in his room, by Detective Inspector Japp—a most brilliant officer—of the identical phial of strychnine which had been sold at the village chemist's to the supposed Mr. Inglethorp on the day before the murder. It would be for the jury to decide whether or not these damning facts constituted an overwhelming proof of the prisoner's guilt.

And, subtly implying that a jury which did not so decide, was quite unthinkable, Mr. Philips sat down and wiped his forehead.

The first witnesses for the prosecution were mostly those who had been called at the inquest, the medical evidence being again taken first.

Sir Ernest Heavywether, who was famous all over England for the unscrupulous manner in which he bullied witnesses, only asked two questions.

"I take it, Dr. Bauerstein, that strychnine, as a drug, acts quickly?"

"Yes."

"And that you are unable to account for the delay in this case?"

"Yes."

"Thank you."

Mr. Mace identified the phial handed him by Counsel as that sold by him to "Mr. Inglethorp." Pressed, he admitted that he only knew Mr. Inglethorp by sight. He had never spoken to him. The witness was not cross-examined.

Alfred Inglethorp was called, and denied having purchased the poison. He also denied having quarrelled with his wife. Various witnesses testified to the accuracy of these statements.

The gardeners' evidence, as to the witnessing of the will was taken, and then Dorcas was called.

Dorcas, faithful to her "young gentlemen," denied strenuously that it could have been John's voice she heard, and resolutely declared, in the teeth of everything, that it was Mr. Inglethorp who had been in the boudoir with her mistress. A rather wistful smile passed across the face of the prisoner in the dock. He knew only too well how useless her gallant defiance was, since it was not the object of the defence to deny this point. Mrs. Cavendish, of course, could not be called upon to give evidence against her husband.

After various questions on other matters, Mr. Philips asked:

"In the month of June last, do you remember a parcel arriving for Mr. Lawrence Cavendish from Parkson's?"

Dorcas shook her head.

"I don't remember, sir. It may have done, but Mr. Lawrence was away from home part of June."

"In the event of a parcel arriving for him whilst he was away, what would be done with it?"

"It would either be put in his room or sent on after him."

"By you?"

"No, sir, I should leave it on the hall table. It would be Miss Howard who would attend to anything like that."

Evelyn Howard was called and, after being examined on other points, was questioned as to the parcel.

"Don't remember. Lots of parcels come. Can't remember one special one."

"You do not know if it was sent after Mr. Lawrence Cavendish to Wales, or whether it was put in his room?"

"Don't think it was sent after him. Should have remembered it if it was."

"Supposing a parcel arrived addressed to Mr. Lawrence Cavendish, and afterwards it disappeared, should you remark its absence?"

"No, don't think so. I should think someone had taken charge of it."

"I believe, Miss Howard, that it was you who found this sheet of brown paper?" He held up the same dusty piece which Poirot and I had examined in the morning-room at Styles.

"Yes, I did."

"How did you come to look for it?"

"The Belgian detective who was employed on the case asked me to search for it."

"Where did you eventually discover it?"

"On the top of—of—a wardrobe."

"On top of the prisoner's wardrobe?"

"I—I believe so."

"Did you not find it yourself?"

"Yes."

"Then you must know where you found it?"

"Yes, it was on the prisoner's wardrobe."

"That is better."

An assistant from Parkson's, Theatrical Costumiers, testified that on June

29th, they had supplied a black beard to Mr. L. Cavendish, as requested. It was ordered by letter, and a postal order was enclosed. No, they had not kept the letter. All transactions were entered in their books. They had sent the beard, as directed, to "L. Cavendish, Esq., Styles Court."

Sir Ernest Heavywether rose ponderously.

"Where was the letter written from?"

"From Styles Court."

"The same address to which you sent the parcel?"

"Yes."

"And the letter came from there?"

"Yes."

Like a beast of prey, Heavywether fell upon him:

"How do you know?"

"I—I don't understand."

"How do you know that letter came from Styles? Did you notice the postmark?"

"No—but—"

"Ah, you did *not* notice the postmark! And yet you affirm so confidently that it came from Styles. It might, in fact, have been any postmark?"

"Y—es."

"In fact, the letter, though written on stamped notepaper, might have been posted from anywhere? From Wales, for instance?"

The witness admitted that such might be the case, and Sir Ernest signified that he was satisfied.

Elizabeth Wells, second housemaid at Styles, stated that after she had gone to bed she remembered that she had bolted the front door, instead of leaving it on the latch as Mr. Inglethorp had requested. She had accordingly gone downstairs again to rectify her error. Hearing a slight noise in the West wing, she had peeped along the passage, and had seen Mr. John Cavendish knocking at Mrs. Inglethorp's door.

Sir Ernest Heavywether made short work of her, and under his unmerciful bullying she contradicted herself hopelessly, and Sir Ernest sat down again with a satisfied smile on his face.

With the evidence of Annie, as to the candle grease on the floor, and as to seeing the prisoner take the coffee into the boudoir, the proceedings were adjourned until the following day.

As we went home, Mary Cavendish spoke bitterly against the prosecuting counsel.

"That hateful man! What a net he has drawn around my poor John! How he twisted every little fact until he made it seem what it wasn't!"

"Well," I said consolingly, "it will be the other way about tomorrow."

"Yes," she said meditatively; then suddenly dropped her voice. "Mr. Hastings, you do not think—surely it could not have been Lawrence—Oh, no, that could not be!"

But I myself was puzzled, and as soon as I was alone with Poirot I asked him what he thought Sir Ernest was driving at.

"Ah!" said Poirot appreciatively. "He is a clever man, that Sir Ernest."

"Do you think he believes Lawrence guilty?"

"I do not think he believes or cares anything! No, what he is trying for is to create such confusion in the minds of the jury that they are divided in their opinion as to which brother did it. He is endeavouring to make out that there is quite as much evidence against Lawrence as against John—and I am not at all sure that he will not succeed."

Detective-inspector Japp was the first witness called when the trial was reopened, and gave his evidence succinctly and briefly. After relating the earlier events, he proceeded:

"Acting on information received, Superintendent Summerhaye and myself searched the prisoner's room, during his temporary absence from the house. In his chest of drawers, hidden beneath some underclothing, we found: first, a pair of gold-rimmed pince-nez similar to those worn by Mr. Inglethorp"—these were exhibited—"secondly, this phial."

The phial was that already recognized by the chemist's assistant, a tiny bottle of blue glass, containing a few grains of a white crystalline powder, and labelled: "Strychnine Hydrochloride. POISON."

A fresh piece of evidence discovered by the detectives since the police court proceedings was a long, almost new piece of blotting-paper. It had been found in Mrs. Inglethorp's cheque book, and on being reversed at a mirror, showed clearly the words: ." . . erything of which I die possessed I leave to my beloved husband Alfred Ing..." This placed beyond question the fact that the destroyed will had been in favour of the deceased lady's husband. Japp then produced the charred fragment of paper recovered from the grate, and this, with the discovery of the beard in the attic, completed his evidence.

But Sir Ernest's cross-examination was yet to come.

"What day was it when you searched the prisoner's room?"

"Tuesday, the 24th of July."

"Exactly a week after the tragedy?"

"Yes."

"You found these two objects, you say, in the chest of drawers. Was the drawer unlocked?"

"Yes."

"Does it not strike you as unlikely that a man who had committed a crime should keep the evidence of it in an unlocked drawer for anyone to find?"

"He might have stowed them there in a hurry."

"But you have just said it was a whole week since the crime. He would have had ample time to remove them and destroy them."

"Perhaps."

"There is no perhaps about it. Would he, or would he not have had plenty of time to remove and destroy them?"

"Yes."

"Was the pile of underclothes under which the things were hidden heavy or light?"

"Heavyish."

"In other words, it was winter underclothing. Obviously, the prisoner would not be likely to go to that drawer?"

"Perhaps not."

"Kindly answer my question. Would the prisoner, in the hottest week of a hot summer, be likely to go to a drawer containing winter underclothing. Yes, or no?"

"No."

"In that case, is it not possible that the articles in question might have been put there by a third person, and that the prisoner was quite unaware of their presence?"

"I should not think it likely."

"But it is possible?"

"Yes."

"That is all."

More evidence followed. Evidence as to the financial difficulties in which the prisoner had found himself at the end of July. Evidence as to his intrigue with Mrs. Raikes—poor Mary, that must have been bitter hearing for a woman of her pride. Evelyn Howard had been right in her facts, though her animosity against Alfred Inglethorp had caused her to jump to the conclusion that he was the person concerned.

Lawrence Cavendish was then put into the box. In a low voice, in answer to Mr. Philips' questions, he denied having ordered anything from Parkson's in June. In fact, on June 29th, he had been staying away, in Wales.

Instantly, Sir Ernest's chin was shooting pugnaciously forward.

"You deny having ordered a black beard from Parkson's on June 29th?"

"I do."

"Ah! In the event of anything happening to your brother, who will inherit Styles Court?"

The brutality of the question called a flush to Lawrence's pale face. The judge gave vent to a faint murmur of disapprobation, and the prisoner in the dock leant forward angrily.

Heavywether cared nothing for his client's anger.

"Answer my question, if you please."

"I suppose," said Lawrence quietly, "that I should."

"What do you mean by you 'suppose'? Your brother has no children. You would inherit it, wouldn't you?"

"Yes."

"Ah, that's better," said Heavywether, with ferocious geniality. "And you'd inherit a good slice of money too, wouldn't you?"

"Really, Sir Ernest," protested the judge, "these questions are not relevant."

Sir Ernest bowed, and having shot his arrow proceeded.

"On Tuesday, the 17th July, you went, I believe, with another guest, to visit the dispensary at the Red Cross Hospital in Tadminster?"

"Yes."

"Did you—while you happened to be alone for a few seconds—unlock the poison cupboard, and examine some of the bottles?"

"I—I—may have done so."

"I put it to you that you did do so?"

"Yes."

Sir Ernest fairly shot the next question at him.

"Did you examine one bottle in particular?"

"No, I do not think so."

"Be careful, Mr. Cavendish. I am referring to a little bottle of Hydrochloride of Strychnine."

Lawrence was turning a sickly greenish colour.

"N—o—I am sure I didn't."

"Then how do you account for the fact that you left the unmistakable impress of your finger-prints on it?"

The bullying manner was highly efficacious with a nervous disposition.

"I—I suppose I must have taken up the bottle."

"I suppose so too! Did you abstract any of the contents of the bottle?"

"Certainly not."

"Then why did you take it up?"

"I once studied to be a doctor. Such things naturally interest me."

"Ah! So poisons 'naturally interest' you, do they? Still, you waited to be alone before gratifying that 'interest' of yours?"

"That was pure chance. If the others had been there, I should have done just the same."

"Still, as it happens, the others were not there?"

"No, but—"

"In fact, during the whole afternoon, you were only alone for a couple of minutes, and it happened—I say, it happened—to be during those two minutes that you displayed your 'natural interest' in Hydro-chloride of Strychnine?"

Lawrence stammered pitiably.

"I—I—"

With a satisfied and expressive countenance, Sir Ernest observed:

"I have nothing more to ask you, Mr. Cavendish."

This bit of cross-examination had caused great excitement in court. The heads of the many fashionably attired women present were busily laid together, and their whispers became so loud that the judge angrily threatened to have the court cleared if there was not immediate silence.

There was little more evidence. The hand-writing experts were called upon for their opinion of the signature of "Alfred Inglethorp" in the chemist's poison register. They all declared unanimously that it was certainly not his hand-writing, and gave it as their view that it might be that of the prisoner disguised. Cross-examined, they admitted that it might be the prisoner's hand-writing cleverly counterfeited.

Sir Ernest Heavywether's speech in opening the case for the defence was not a long one, but it was backed by the full force of his emphatic manner. Never, he said, in the course of his long experience, had he known a charge of murder rest on slighter evidence. Not only was it entirely circumstantial, but the greater part of it was practically unproved. Let them take the testimony they had heard and sift it impartially. The strychnine had been found in a drawer in the prisoner's room. That drawer was an unlocked one, as he had pointed out, and he submitted that there was no evidence to prove that it was the prisoner who had concealed the poison there. It was, in fact, a wicked and malicious attempt on the part of some third person to fix the crime on the prisoner. The prosecution had been unable to produce a shred of evidence in support of their contention that it was the prisoner who ordered the black beard from Parkson's. The quarrel which had taken place between prisoner and his stepmother was freely admitted, but both it and his financial embarrassments had been grossly exaggerated.

His learned friend—Sir Ernest nodded carelessly at Mr. Philips—had stated that if the prisoner were an innocent man, he would have come forward at the inquest to explain that it was he, and not Mr. Inglethorp, who had been the participator in the quarrel. He thought the facts had been misrepresented. What had actually occurred was this. The prisoner, returning to the house on Tuesday evening, had been authoritatively told that there had been a violent quarrel between Mr. and Mrs. Inglethorp. No suspicion had entered the prisoner's head that anyone could possibly have mistaken his voice for that of Mr. Inglethorp. He naturally concluded that his stepmother had had two quarrels.

The prosecution averred that on Monday, July 16th, the prisoner had entered the chemist's shop in the village, disguised as Mr. Inglethorp. The prisoner, on the contrary, was at that time at a lonely spot called Marston's Spinney, where he had been summoned by an anonymous note, couched in blackmailing terms, and threatening to reveal certain matters to his wife unless he complied with its demands. The prisoner had, accordingly, gone to the appointed spot, and after waiting there vainly for half an hour had returned home. Unfortunately, he had met with no one on the way there or back who could vouch for the truth of his story, but luckily he had kept the note, and it would be produced as evidence.

As for the statement relating to the destruction of the will, the prisoner had formerly practiced at the Bar, and was perfectly well aware that the will made in his favour a year before was automatically revoked by his stepmother's remarriage. He would call evidence to show who did destroy the will, and it was possible that that might open up quite a new view of the case.

Finally, he would point out to the jury that there was evidence against other people besides John Cavendish. He would direct their attention to the fact that the evidence against Mr. Lawrence Cavendish was quite as strong, if not stronger than that against his brother.

He would now call the prisoner.

John acquitted himself well in the witness-box. Under Sir Ernest's skilful handling, he told his tale credibly and well. The anonymous note received by him was produced, and handed to the jury to examine. The readiness with which he admitted his financial difficulties, and the disagreement with his stepmother, lent value to his denials.

At the close of his examination, he paused, and said:

"I should like to make one thing clear. I utterly reject and disapprove of Sir Ernest Heavywether's insinuations against my brother. My brother, I am convinced, had no more to do with the crime than I have."

Sir Ernest merely smiled, and noted with a sharp eye that John's protest had produced a very favourable impression on the jury.

Then the cross-examination began.

"I understand you to say that it never entered your head that the witnesses at the inquest could possibly have mistaken your voice for that of Mr. Inglethorp. Is not that very surprising?"

"No, I don't think so. I was told there had been a quarrel between my mother and Mr. Inglethorp, and it never occurred to me that such was not really the case."

"Not when the servant Dorcas repeated certain fragments of the conversation—fragments which you must have recognized?"

"I did not recognize them."

"Your memory must be unusually short!"

"No, but we were both angry, and, I think, said more than we meant. I paid very little attention to my mother's actual words."

Mr. Philips' incredulous sniff was a triumph of forensic skill. He passed on to the subject of the note.

"You have produced this note very opportunely. Tell me, is there nothing familiar about the hand-writing of it?"

"Not that I know of."

"Do you not think that it bears a marked resemblance to your own hand-writing—carelessly disguised?"

"No, I do not think so."

"I put it to you that it is your own hand-writing!"

"No."

"I put it to you that, anxious to prove an alibi, you conceived the idea of a fictitious and rather incredible appointment, and wrote this note yourself in order to bear out your statement!"

"No."

"Is it not a fact that, at the time you claim to have been waiting about at a solitary and unfrequented spot, you were really in the chemist's shop in Styles St. Mary, where you purchased strychnine in the name of Alfred Inglethorp?"

"No, that is a lie."

"I put it to you that, wearing a suit of Mr. Inglethorp's clothes, with a black beard trimmed to resemble his, you were there—and signed the register in his name!"

"That is absolutely untrue."

"Then I will leave the remarkable similarity of hand-writing between the note, the register, and your own, to the consideration of the jury," said Mr. Philips, and sat down with the air of a man who has done his duty, but who was nevertheless horrified by such deliberate perjury.

After this, as it was growing late, the case was adjourned till Monday.

Poirot, I noticed, was looking profoundly discouraged. He had that little frown between the eyes that I knew so well.

"What is it, Poirot?" I inquired.

"Ah, *mon ami*, things are going badly, badly."

In spite of myself, my heart gave a leap of relief. Evidently there was a likelihood of John Cavendish being acquitted.

When we reached the house, my little friend waved aside Mary's offer of tea.

"No, I thank you, madame. I will mount to my room."

I followed him. Still frowning, he went across to the desk and took out a small pack of patience cards. Then he drew up a chair to the table, and, to my utter amazement, began solemnly to build card houses!

My jaw dropped involuntarily, and he said at once:

"No, *mon ami*, I am not in my second childhood! I steady my nerves, that is all. This employment requires precision of the fingers. With precision of the fingers goes precision of the brain. And never have I needed that more than now!"

"What is the trouble?" I asked.

With a great thump on the table, Poirot demolished his carefully built up edifice.

"It is this, *mon ami*! That I can build card houses seven stories high, but I cannot"—thump—"find"—thump—"that last link of which I spoke to you."

I could not quite tell what to say, so I held my peace, and he began slowly building up the cards again, speaking in jerks as he did so.

"It is done—so! By placing—one card—on another—with mathematical—precision!"

I watched the card house rising under his hands, story by story. He never hesitated or faltered. It was really almost like a conjuring trick.

"What a steady hand you've got," I remarked. "I believe I've only seen your hand shake once."

"On an occasion when I was enraged, without doubt," observed Poirot, with great placidity.

"Yes indeed! You were in a towering rage. Do you remember? It was when you discovered that the lock of the despatch-case in Mrs. Inglethorp's bedroom had been forced. You stood by the mantel-piece, twiddling the things on it in your usual fashion, and your hand shook like a leaf! I must say—"

But I stopped suddenly. For Poirot, uttering a hoarse and inarticulate cry, again annihilated his masterpiece of cards, and putting his hands over his eyes swayed backwards and forwards, apparently suffering the keenest agony.

"Good heavens, Poirot!" I cried. "What is the matter? Are you taken ill?"

"No, no," he gasped. "It is—it is—that I have an idea!"

"Oh!" I exclaimed, much relieved. "One of your 'little ideas'?"

"Ah, *ma foi*, no!" replied Poirot frankly. "This time it is an idea gigantic! Stupendous! And you—*you*, my friend, have given it to me!"

Suddenly clasping me in his arms, he kissed me warmly on both cheeks, and before I had recovered from my surprise ran headlong from the room.

Mary Cavendish entered at that moment.

"What is the matter with Monsieur Poirot? He rushed past me crying out: 'A garage! For the love of Heaven, direct me to a garage, madame!' And, before I could answer, he had dashed out into the street."

I hurried to the window. True enough, there he was, tearing down the street, hatless, and gesticulating as he went. I turned to Mary with a gesture of despair.

"He'll be stopped by a policeman in another minute. There he goes, round the corner!"

Our eyes met, and we stared helplessly at one another.

"What can be the matter?"

I shook my head.

"I don't know. He was building card houses, when suddenly he said he had an idea, and rushed off as you saw."

"Well," said Mary, "I expect he will be back before dinner."

But night fell, and Poirot had not returned.

Chapter XII

THE LAST LINK

Poirot's abrupt departure had intrigued us all greatly. Sunday morning wore away, and still he did not reappear. But about three o'clock a ferocious and prolonged hooting outside drove us to the window, to see Poirot alighting from a car, accompanied by Japp and Summerhaye. The little man was transformed. He radiated an absurd complacency. He bowed with exaggerated respect to Mary Cavendish.

"Madame, I have your permission to hold a little *réunion* in the *salon*? It is necessary for every one to attend."

Mary smiled sadly.

"You know, Monsieur Poirot, that you have *carte blanche* in every way."

"You are too amiable, madame."

Still beaming, Poirot marshalled us all into the drawing-room, bringing forward chairs as he did so.

"Miss Howard—here. Mademoiselle Cynthia. Monsieur Lawrence. The good Dorcas. And Annie. *Bien!* We must delay our proceedings a few minutes until Mr. Inglethorp arrives. I have sent him a note."

Miss Howard rose immediately from her seat.

"If that man comes into the house, I leave it!"

"No, no!" Poirot went up to her and pleaded in a low voice.

Finally Miss Howard consented to return to her chair. A few minutes later Alfred Inglethorp entered the room.

The company once assembled, Poirot rose from his seat with the air of a popular lecturer, and bowed politely to his audience.

"*Messieurs, mesdames,* as you all know, I was called in by Monsieur John Cavendish to investigate this case. I at once examined the bedroom of the deceased which, by the advice of the doctors, had been kept locked, and was consequently exactly as it had been when the tragedy occurred. I found: first, a fragment of green material; second, a stain on the carpet near the window, still damp; thirdly, an empty box of bromide powders.

"To take the fragment of green material first, I found it caught in the bolt of the communicating door between that room and the adjoining one occupied by Mademoiselle Cynthia. I handed the fragment over to the police who did not consider it of much importance. Nor did they recognize it for what it was—a piece torn from a green land armlet."

There was a little stir of excitement.

"Now there was only one person at Styles who worked on the land—Mrs. Cavendish. Therefore it must have been Mrs. Cavendish who entered the deceased's room through the door communicating with Mademoiselle Cynthia's room."

"But that door was bolted on the inside!" I cried.

"When I examined the room, yes. But in the first place we have only her word for it, since it was she who tried that particular door and reported it fastened. In the ensuing confusion she would have had ample opportunity to shoot the bolt across. I took an early opportunity of verifying my conjectures. To begin with, the fragment corresponds exactly with a tear in Mrs. Cavendish's armlet. Also, at the inquest, Mrs. Cavendish declared that she had heard, from her own room, the fall of the table by the bed. I took an early opportunity of testing that statement by stationing my friend Monsieur Hastings in the left wing of the building, just outside Mrs. Cavendish's door. I myself, in company with the police, went to the deceased's room, and whilst there I, apparently accidentally, knocked over the table in question, but found that, as I had expected, Monsieur Hastings had heard no sound at all. This confirmed my belief that Mrs. Cavendish was not speaking the truth when she declared that she had been dressing in her room at the time of the tragedy. In fact, I was convinced that, far from having been in her own room, Mrs. Cavendish was actually in the deceased's room when the alarm was given."

I shot a quick glance at Mary. She was very pale, but smiling.

"I proceeded to reason on that assumption. Mrs. Cavendish is in her mother-in-law's room. We will say that she is seeking for something and has not yet found it. Suddenly Mrs. Inglethorp awakens and is seized with an alarming paroxysm. She flings out her arm, overturning the bed table, and then pulls desperately at the bell. Mrs. Cavendish, startled, drops her candle, scattering the grease on the carpet. She picks it up, and retreats quickly to Mademoiselle Cynthia's room, closing the door behind her. She hurries out into the passage, for the servants must not find her where she is. But it is too late! Already footsteps are echoing along the gallery which connects the two wings. What can she do? Quick as thought, she hurries back to the young girl's room, and starts shaking her awake. The hastily aroused household come trooping down the passage. They are all busily battering at Mrs. Inglethorp's door. It occurs to nobody that Mrs. Cavendish has not arrived with the rest, but—and this is significant—I can find no one who saw her come from the other wing." He looked at Mary Cavendish. "Am I right, madame?"

She bowed her head.

"Quite right, monsieur. You understand that, if I had thought I would do my husband any good by revealing these facts, I would have done so. But it did not seem to me to bear upon the question of his guilt or innocence."

"In a sense, that is correct, madame. But it cleared my mind of many misconceptions, and left me free to see other facts in their true significance."

"The will!" cried Lawrence. "Then it was you, Mary, who destroyed the will?"

She shook her head, and Poirot shook his also.

"No," he said quietly. "There is only one person who could possibly have destroyed that will—Mrs. Inglethorp herself!"

"Impossible!" I exclaimed. "She had only made it out that very afternoon!"

"Nevertheless, *mon ami*, it was Mrs. Inglethorp. Because, in no other way can you account for the fact that, on one of the hottest days of the year, Mrs. Inglethorp ordered a fire to be lighted in her room."

I gave a gasp. What idiots we had been never to think of that fire as being incongruous! Poirot was continuing:

"The temperature on that day, messieurs, was 80 degrees in the shade. Yet Mrs. Inglethorp ordered a fire! Why? Because she wished to destroy something, and could think of no other way. You will remember that, in consequence of the War economics practiced at Styles, no waste paper was thrown away. There was therefore no means of destroying a thick document such as a will. The moment I heard of a fire being lighted in Mrs. Inglethorp's room, I leaped to the conclusion that it was to destroy some important document— possibly a will. So the discovery of the charred fragment in the grate was no surprise to me. I did not, of course, know at the time that the will in question had only been made this afternoon, and I will admit that, when I learnt that fact, I fell into a grievous error. I came to the conclusion that Mrs. Inglethorp's determination to destroy her will arose as a direct consequence of the quarrel she had that afternoon, and that therefore the quarrel took place after, and not before the making of the will.

"Here, as we know, I was wrong, and I was forced to abandon that idea. I faced the problem from a new standpoint. Now, at 4 o'clock, Dorcas overheard her mistress saying angrily: 'You need not think that any fear of publicity, or scandal between husband and wife will deter me." I conjectured, and conjectured rightly, that these words were addressed, not to her husband, but to Mr. John Cavendish. At 5 o'clock, an hour later, she uses almost the same words, but the standpoint is different. She admits to Dorcas, 'I don't know what to do; scandal between husband and wife is a dreadful thing.' At 4 o'clock she has been angry, but completely mistress of herself. At 5 o'clock she is in violent distress, and speaks of having had a great shock.

"Looking at the matter psychologically, I drew one deduction which I was convinced was correct. The second 'scandal' she spoke of was not the same as the first—and it concerned herself!

"Let us reconstruct. At 4 o'clock, Mrs. Inglethorp quarrels with her son, and threatens to denounce him to his wife—who, by the way, overheard the greater part of the conversation. At 4.30, Mrs. Inglethorp, in consequence of a conversation on the validity of wills, makes a will in favour of her husband, which the two gardeners witness. At 5 o'clock, Dorcas finds her mistress in a state of considerable agitation, with a slip of paper—'a letter,' Dorcas thinks—in her hand, and it is then that she orders the fire in her room to be lighted. Presumably, then, between 4.30 and 5 o'clock, something has occurred to occasion a complete revolution of feeling, since she is now as anxious to destroy the will, as she was before to make it. What was that something?

"As far as we know, she was quite alone during that half-hour. Nobody entered or left that boudoir. What then occasioned this sudden change of sentiment?

"One can only guess, but I believe my guess to be correct. Mrs. Inglethorp had no stamps in her desk. We know this, because later she asked Dorcas to bring her some. Now in the opposite corner of the room stood her husband's desk—locked. She was anxious to find some stamps, and, according to my theory, she tried her own keys in the desk. That one of them fitted I know. She therefore opened the desk, and in searching for the stamps she came across something else—that slip of paper which Dorcas saw in her hand, and which assuredly was never meant for Mrs. Inglethorp's eyes. On the other hand, Mrs. Cavendish believed that the slip of paper to which her mother-in-law clung so tenaciously was a written proof of her own husband's infidelity. She demanded it from Mrs. Inglethorp who assured her, quite truly, that it had nothing to do with that matter. Mrs. Cavendish did not believe her. She thought that Mrs. Inglethorp was shielding her stepson. Now Mrs. Cavendish is a very resolute woman, and, behind her mask of reserve, she was madly jealous of her husband. She determined to get hold of that paper at all costs, and in this resolution chance came to her aid. She happened to pick up the key of Mrs. Inglethorp's despatch-case, which had been lost that morning.

She knew that her mother-in-law invariably kept all important papers in this particular case.

"Mrs. Cavendish, therefore, made her plans as only a woman driven desperate through jealousy could have done. Some time in the evening she unbolted the door leading into Mademoiselle Cynthia's room. Possibly she applied oil to the hinges, for I found that it opened quite noiselessly when I tried it. She put off her project until the early hours of the morning as being safer, since the servants were accustomed to hearing her move about her room at that time. She dressed completely in her land kit, and made her way quietly through Mademoiselle Cynthia's room into that of Mrs. Inglethorp."

He paused a moment, and Cynthia interrupted:

"But I should have woken up if anyone had come through my room?"

"Not if you were drugged, mademoiselle."

"Drugged?"

"*Mais, oui!*"

"You remember"—he addressed us collectively again—"that through all the tumult and noise next door Mademoiselle Cynthia slept. That admitted of two possibilities. Either her sleep was feigned—which I did not believe— or her unconsciousness was indeed by artificial means.

"With this latter idea in my mind, I examined all the coffee-cups most carefully, remembering that it was Mrs. Cavendish who had brought Mademoiselle Cynthia her coffee the night before. I took a sample from each cup, and had them analysed—with no result. I had counted the cups carefully, in the event of one having been removed. Six persons had taken coffee, and six cups were duly found. I had to confess myself mistaken.

"Then I discovered that I had been guilty of a very grave oversight. Coffee had been brought in for seven persons, not six, for Dr. Bauerstein had been there that evening. This changed the face of the whole affair, for there was now one cup missing. The servants noticed nothing, since Annie, the housemaid, who took in the coffee, brought in seven cups, not knowing that Mr. Inglethorp never drank it, whereas Dorcas, who cleared them away the following morning, found six as usual—or strictly speaking she found five, the sixth being the one found broken in Mrs. Inglethorp's room.

"I was confident that the missing cup was that of Mademoiselle Cynthia. I had an additional reason for that belief in the fact that all the cups found contained sugar, which Mademoiselle Cynthia never took in her coffee. My attention was attracted by the story of Annie about some 'salt' on the tray of cocoa which she took every night to Mrs. Inglethorp's room. I accordingly secured a sample of that cocoa, and sent it to be analysed."

"But that had already been done by Dr. Bauerstein," said Lawrence quickly.

"Not exactly. The analyst was asked by him to report whether strychnine was, or was not, present. He did not have it tested, as I did, for a narcotic."

"For a narcotic?"

"Yes. Here is the analyst's report. Mrs. Cavendish administered a safe, but effectual, narcotic to both Mrs. Inglethorp and Mademoiselle Cynthia. And it is possible that she had a *mauvais quart d'heure* in consequence! Imagine her feelings when her mother-in-law is suddenly taken ill and dies, and immediately after she hears the word 'Poison'! She has believed that the sleeping draught she administered was perfectly harmless, but there is no doubt that for one terrible moment she must have feared that Mrs. Inglethorp's death lay at her door. She is seized with panic, and under its influence she hurries downstairs, and quickly drops the coffee-cup and saucer used by Mademoiselle Cynthia into a large brass vase, where it is discovered later by Monsieur Lawrence. The remains of the cocoa she dare not touch. Too many eyes are upon her. Guess at her relief when strychnine is mentioned, and she discovers that after all the tragedy is not her doing.

"We are now able to account for the symptoms of strychnine poisoning being so long in making their appearance. A narcotic taken with strychnine will delay the action of the poison for some hours."

Poirot paused. Mary looked up at him, the colour slowly rising in her face.

"All you have said is quite true, Monsieur Poirot. It was the most awful hour of my life. I shall never forget it. But you are wonderful. I understand now—"

"What I meant when I told you that you could safely confess to Papa Poirot, eh? But you would not trust me."

"I see everything now," said Lawrence. "The drugged cocoa, taken on top of the poisoned coffee, amply accounts for the delay."

"Exactly. But was the coffee poisoned, or was it not? We come to a little difficulty here, since Mrs. Inglethorp never drank it."

"What?" The cry of surprise was universal.

"No. You will remember my speaking of a stain on the carpet in Mrs. Inglethorp's room? There were some peculiar points about that stain. It was still damp, it exhaled a strong odour of coffee, and imbedded in the nap of the carpet I found some little splinters of china. What had happened was plain to me, for not two minutes before I had placed my little case on the table near the window, and the table, tilting up, had deposited it upon the floor on precisely the identical spot. In exactly the same way, Mrs. Inglethorp had laid down her cup of coffee on reaching her room the night before, and the treacherous table had played her the same trick.

"What happened next is mere guess work on my part, but I should say that Mrs. Inglethorp picked up the broken cup and placed it on the table by the bed. Feeling in need of a stimulant of some kind, she heated up her cocoa, and drank it off then and there. Now we are faced with a new problem. We know the cocoa contained no strychnine. The coffee was never drunk. Yet the strychnine must have been administered between seven and nine o'clock that evening. What third medium was there—a medium so suitable for disguising the taste of strychnine that it is extraordinary no one has thought of it?" Poirot looked round the room, and then answered himself impressively. "Her medicine!"

"Do you mean that the murderer introduced the strychnine into her tonic?" I cried.

"There was no need to introduce it. It was already there—in the mixture. The strychnine that killed Mrs. Inglethorp was the identical strychnine prescribed by Dr. Wilkins. To make that clear to you, I will read you an extract from a book on dispensing which I found in the Dispensary of the Red Cross Hospital at Tadminster:

The following prescription has become famous in text books:

> Strychninae Sulph. . . . . . gr.I
> Potass Bromide 3vi
> Aqua ad. 3viii
> Fiat Mistura

This solution deposits in a few hours the greater part of the strychnine salt as an insoluble bromide in transparent crystals. A lady in England lost her life by taking a similar mixture: the precipitated strychnine collected at the bottom, and in taking the last dose she swallowed nearly all of it!

"Now there was, of course, no bromide in Dr. Wilkins' prescription, but you will remember that I mentioned an empty box of bromide powders. One or two of those powders introduced into the full bottle of medicine would effectually precipitate the strychnine, as the book describes, and cause it to be taken in the last dose. You will learn later that the person who usually poured out Mrs. Inglethorp's medicine was always extremely careful not to shake the bottle, but to leave the sediment at the bottom of it undisturbed.

"Throughout the case, there have been evidences that the tragedy was intended to take place on Monday evening. On that day, Mrs. Inglethorp's bell wire was neatly cut, and on Monday evening Mademoiselle Cynthia was spending the night with friends, so that Mrs. Inglethorp would have been quite alone in the right wing, completely shut off from help of any kind, and would have died, in all probability, before medical aid could have been summoned. But in her hurry to be in time for the village entertainment Mrs. Inglethorp forgot to take her medicine, and the next day she lunched away from home, so that the last—and fatal—dose was actually taken twenty-four hours later than had been anticipated by the murderer; and it is owing to that delay that the final proof—the last link of the chain—is now in my hands."

Amid breathless excitement, he held out three thin strips of paper.

"A letter in the murderer's own hand-writing, *mes amis*! Had it been a little clearer in its terms, it is possible that Mrs. Inglethorp, warned in time, would have escaped. As it was, she realized her danger, but not the manner of it."

In the deathly silence, Poirot pieced together the slips of paper and, clearing his throat, read:

"'Dearest Evelyn:

'You will be anxious at hearing nothing. It is all right—only it will be tonight instead of last night. You understand. There's a good time coming once the old woman is dead and out of the way. No one can possibly bring home the crime to me. That idea of yours about the bromides was a stroke of genius! But we must be very circumspect. A false step—'

"Here, my friends, the letter breaks off. Doubtless the writer was interrupted; but there can be no question as to his identity. We all know this hand-writing and—"

A howl that was almost a scream broke the silence.

"You devil! How did you get it?"

A chair was overturned. Poirot skipped nimbly aside. A quick movement on his part, and his assailant fell with a crash.

"*Messieurs, mesdames*," said Poirot, with a flourish, "let me introduce you to the murderer, Mr. Alfred Inglethorp!"

Chapter XIII

POIROT EXPLAINS

Poirot, you old villain," I said, "I've half a mind to strangle you! What do you mean by deceiving me as you have done?"

We were sitting in the library. Several hectic days lay behind us. In the room below, John and Mary were together once more, while Alfred Inglethorp and Miss Howard were in custody. Now at last, I had Poirot to myself, and could relieve my still burning curiosity.

Poirot did not answer me for a moment, but at last he said:

"I did not deceive you, *mon ami*. At most, I permitted you to deceive yourself."

"Yes, but why?"

"Well, it is difficult to explain. You see, my friend, you have a nature so honest, and a countenance so transparent, that—*enfin*, to conceal your feelings is impossible! If I had told you my ideas, the very first time you saw Mr. Alfred Inglethorp that astute gentleman would have—in your so expressive idiom—'smelt a rat'! And then, *bon jour* to our chances of catching him!"

"I think that I have more diplomacy than you give me credit for."

"My friend," besought Poirot, "I implore you, do not enrage yourself! Your help has been of the most invaluable. It is but the extremely beautiful nature that you have, which made me pause."

"Well," I grumbled, a little mollified. "I still think you might have given me a hint."

"But I did, my friend. Several hints. You would not take them. Think now, did I ever say to you that I believed John Cavendish guilty? Did I not, on the contrary, tell you that he would almost certainly be acquitted?"

"Yes, but—"

"And did I not immediately afterwards speak of the difficulty of bringing the murderer to justice? Was it not plain to you that I was speaking of two entirely different persons?"

"No," I said, "it was not plain to me!"

"Then again," continued Poirot, "at the beginning, did I not repeat to you several times that I didn't want Mr. Inglethorp arrested *now*? That should have conveyed something to you."

"Do you mean to say you suspected him as long ago as that?"

"Yes. To begin with, whoever else might benefit by Mrs. Inglethorp's death, her husband would benefit the most. There was no getting away from that. When I went up to Styles with you that first day, I had no idea as to how the crime had been committed, but from what I knew of Mr. Inglethorp I fancied that it would be very hard to find anything to connect him with it. When I arrived at the *château*, I realized at once that it was Mrs. Inglethorp who had burnt the will; and there, by the way, you cannot complain, my friend, for I tried my best to force on you the significance of that bedroom fire in midsummer."

"Yes, yes," I said impatiently. "Go on."

"Well, my friend, as I say, my views as to Mr. Inglethorp's guilt were very much shaken. There was, in fact, so much evidence against him that I was inclined to believe that he had not done it."

"When did you change your mind?"

"When I found that the more efforts I made to clear him, the more efforts he made to get himself arrested. Then, when I discovered that Inglethorp had nothing to do with Mrs. Raikes and that in fact it was John Cavendish who was interested in that quarter, I was quite sure."

"But why?"

"Simply this. If it had been Inglethorp who was carrying on an intrigue with Mrs. Raikes, his silence was perfectly comprehensible. But, when I discovered that it was known all over the village that it was John who was attracted by the farmer's pretty wife, his silence bore quite a different interpretation. It was nonsense to pretend that he was afraid of the scandal, as no possible scandal could attach to him. This attitude of his gave me furiously to think, and I was slowly forced to the conclusion that Alfred Inglethorp wanted to be arrested. *Eh bien*! from that moment, I was equally determined that he should not be arrested."

"Wait a minute. I don't see why he wished to be arrested?"

"Because, *mon ami*, it is the law of your country that a man once acquitted can never be tried again for the same offence. Aha! but it was clever—his idea! Assuredly, he is a man of method. See here, he knew that in his position he was bound to be suspected, so he conceived the exceedingly clever idea of preparing a lot of manufactured evidence against himself. He wished to be arrested. He would then produce his irreproachable alibi—and, hey presto, he was safe for life!"

"But I still don't see how he managed to prove his alibi, and yet go to the chemist's shop?"

Poirot stared at me in surprise.

"Is it possible? My poor friend! You have not yet realized that it was Miss Howard who went to the chemist's shop?"

"Miss Howard?"

"But, certainly. Who else? It was most easy for her. She is of a good height, her voice is deep and manly; moreover, remember, she and Inglethorp are cousins, and there is a distinct resemblance between them, especially in their gait and bearing. It was simplicity itself. They are a clever pair!"

"I am still a little fogged as to how exactly the bromide business was done," I remarked.

"*Bon*! I will reconstruct for you as far as possible. I am inclined to think that Miss Howard was the master mind in that affair. You remember her once mentioning that her father was a doctor? Possibly she dispensed his medicines for him, or she may have taken the idea from one of the many books lying about when Mademoiselle Cynthia was studying for her exam. Anyway, she was familiar with the fact that the addition of a bromide to a mixture containing strychnine would cause the precipitation of the latter. Probably the idea came to her quite suddenly. Mrs. Inglethorp had a box of bromide powders, which she occasionally took at night. What could be easier than quietly to dissolve one or more of those powders in Mrs. Inglethorp's large sized bottle of medicine when it came from Coot's? The risk is practically nil. The tragedy will not take place until nearly a fortnight later. If anyone has seen either of them touching the medicine, they will have forgotten it by that time. Miss Howard will have engineered her quarrel, and departed from the house. The lapse of time, and her absence, will defeat all suspicion. Yes, it was a clever idea! If they had left it alone, it is possible the crime might never have been brought home to them. But they were not satisfied. They tried to be too clever—and that was their undoing."

Poirot puffed at his tiny cigarette, his eyes fixed on the ceiling.

"They arranged a plan to throw suspicion on John Cavendish, by buying strychnine at the village chemist's, and signing the register in his hand-writing.

"On Monday Mrs. Inglethorp will take the last dose of her medicine. On Monday, therefore, at six o'clock, Alfred Inglethorp arranges to be seen by a number of people at a spot far removed from the village. Miss Howard has previously made up a cock and bull story about him and Mrs. Raikes to account for his holding his tongue afterwards. At six o'clock, Miss Howard, disguised as Alfred Inglethorp, enters the chemist's shop, with her story about a dog, obtains the strychnine, and writes the name of Alfred Inglethorp in John's handwriting, which she had previously studied carefully.

"But, as it will never do if John, too, can prove an alibi, she writes him an anonymous note—still copying his hand-writing—which takes him to a remote spot where it is exceedingly unlikely that anyone will see him.

"So far, all goes well. Miss Howard goes back to Middlingham. Alfred Inglethorp returns to Styles. There is nothing that can compromise him in any way, since it is Miss Howard who has the strychnine, which, after all, is only wanted as a blind to throw suspicion on John Cavendish.

"But now a hitch occurs. Mrs. Inglethorp does not take her medicine that night. The broken bell, Cynthia's absence—arranged by Inglethorp through his wife—all these are wasted. And then—he makes his slip.

"Mrs. Inglethorp is out, and he sits down to write to his accomplice, who, he fears, may be in a panic at the nonsuccess of their plan. It is probable that Mrs. Inglethorp returned earlier than he expected. Caught in the act, and somewhat flurried he hastily shuts and locks his desk. He fears that if he remains in the room he may have to open it again, and that Mrs. Inglethorp might catch sight of the letter before he could snatch it up. So he goes out and walks in the woods, little dreaming that Mrs. Inglethorp will open his desk, and discover the incriminating document.

"But this, as we know, is what happened. Mrs. Inglethorp reads it, and becomes aware of the perfidy of her husband and Evelyn Howard, though, unfortunately, the sentence about the bromides conveys no warning to her mind. She knows that she is in danger—but is ignorant of where the danger lies. She decides to say nothing to her husband, but sits down and writes to her solicitor, asking him to come on the morrow, and she also determines to destroy immediately the will which she has just made. She keeps the fatal letter."

"It was to discover that letter, then, that her husband forced the lock of the despatch-case?"

"Yes, and from the enormous risk he ran we can see how fully he realized its importance. That letter excepted, there was absolutely nothing to connect him with the crime."

"There's only one thing I can't make out, why didn't he destroy it at once when he got hold of it?"

"Because he did not dare take the biggest risk of all—that of keeping it on his own person."

"I don't understand."

"Look at it from his point of view. I have discovered that there were only five short minutes in which he could have taken it—the five minutes immediately before our own arrival on the scene, for before that time Annie was brushing the stairs, and would have seen anyone who passed going to the right wing. Figure to yourself the scene! He enters the room, unlocking the door by means of one of the other doorkeys—they were all much alike. He hurries to the despatch-case—it is locked, and the keys are nowhere to be seen. That is a terrible blow to him, for it means that his presence in the room cannot be concealed as he had hoped. But he sees clearly that everything must be risked for the sake of that damning piece of evidence. Quickly, he forces the lock with a penknife, and turns over the papers until he finds what he is looking for.

"But now a fresh dilemma arises: he dare not keep that piece of paper on him. He may be seen leaving the room—he may be searched. If the paper is found on him, it is certain doom. Probably, at this minute, too, he hears the sounds below of Mr. Wells and John leaving the boudoir. He must act quickly. Where can he hide this terrible slip of paper? The contents of the waste-paper-basket are kept and in any case, are sure to be examined. There are no means of destroying it; and he dare not keep it. He looks round, and he sees—what do you think, *mon ami*?"

I shook my head.

"In a moment, he has torn the letter into long thin strips, and rolling them up into spills he thrusts them hurriedly in amongst the other spills in the vase on the mantle-piece."

I uttered an exclamation.

"No one would think of looking there," Poirot continued. "And he will be able, at his leisure, to come back and destroy this solitary piece of evidence against him."

"Then, all the time, it was in the spill vase in Mrs. Inglethorp's bedroom, under our very noses?" I cried.

Poirot nodded.

"Yes, my friend. That is where I discovered my 'last link,' and I owe that very fortunate discovery to you."

"To me?"

"Yes. Do you remember telling me that my hand shook as I was straightening the ornaments on the mantel-piece?"

"Yes, but I don't see—"

"No, but I saw. Do you know, my friend, I remembered that earlier in the morning, when we had been there together, I had straightened all the objects on the mantel-piece. And, if they were already straightened, there would be no need to straighten them again, unless, in the meantime, someone else had touched them."

"Dear me," I murmured, "so that is the explanation of your extraordinary behaviour. You rushed down to Styles, and found it still there?"

"Yes, and it was a race for time."

"But I still can't understand why Inglethorp was such a fool as to leave it there when he had plenty of opportunity to destroy it."

"Ah, but he had no opportunity. I saw to that."

"You?"

"Yes. Do you remember reproving me for taking the household into my confidence on the subject?"

"Yes."

"Well, my friend, I saw there was just one chance. I was not sure then if Inglethorp was the criminal or not, but if he was I reasoned that he would not have the paper on him, but would have hidden it somewhere, and by enlisting the sympathy of the household I could effectually prevent his destroying it. He was already under suspicion, and by making the matter public I secured the services of about ten amateur detectives, who would be watching him unceasingly, and being himself aware of their watchfulness he would not dare seek further to destroy the document. He was therefore forced to depart from the house, leaving it in the spill vase."

"But surely Miss Howard had ample opportunities of aiding him."

"Yes, but Miss Howard did not know of the paper's existence. In accordance with their prearranged plan, she never spoke to Alfred Inglethorp. They were supposed to be deadly enemies, and until John Cavendish was safely convicted they neither of them dared risk a meeting. Of course I had a watch kept on Mr. Inglethorp, hoping that sooner or later he would lead me to the hiding-place. But he was too clever to take any chances. The paper was safe where it was; since no one had thought of looking there in the first week, it was not likely they would do so afterwards. But for your lucky remark, we might never have been able to bring him to justice."

"I understand that now; but when did you first begin to suspect Miss Howard?"

"When I discovered that she had told a lie at the inquest about the letter she had received from Mrs. Inglethorp."

"Why, what was there to lie about?"

"You saw that letter? Do you recall its general appearance?"

"Yes—more or less."

"You will recollect, then, that Mrs. Inglethorp wrote a very distinctive hand, and left large clear spaces between her words. But if you look at the date at the top of the letter you will notice that 'July 17th' is quite different in this respect. Do you see what I mean?"

"No," I confessed, "I don't."

"You do not see that that letter was not written on the 17th, but on the 7th—the day after Miss Howard's departure? The '1' was written in before the '7' to turn it into the '17th.' "

"But why?"

"That is exactly what I asked myself. Why does Miss Howard suppress the letter written on the 17th, and produce this faked one instead? Because she did not wish to show the letter of the 17th. Why, again? And at once a suspicion dawned in my mind. You will remember my saying that it was wise to beware of people who were not telling you the truth."

"And yet," I cried indignantly, "after that, you gave me two reasons why Miss Howard could not have committed the crime!"

"And very good reasons too," replied Poirot. "For a long time they were a stumbling-block to me until I remembered a very significant fact: that she and Alfred Inglethorp were cousins. She could not have committed the crime single-handed, but the reasons against that did not debar her from being an accomplice. And, then, there was that rather over-vehement hatred of hers! It concealed a very opposite emotion. There was, undoubtedly, a tie of passion between them long before he came to Styles. They had already arranged their infamous plot—that he should marry this rich, but rather foolish old lady, induce her to make a will leaving her money to him, and then gain their ends by a very cleverly conceived crime. If all had gone as they planned, they would probably have left England, and lived together on their poor victim's money.

"They are a very astute and unscrupulous pair. While suspicion was to be directed against him, she would be making quiet preparations for a very different *dénouement*. She arrives from Middlingham with all the compromising items in her possession. No suspicion attaches to her. No notice is paid to her coming and going in the house. She hides the strychnine and glasses in John's room. She puts the beard in the attic. She will see to it that sooner or later they are duly discovered."

"I don't quite see why they tried to fix the blame on John," I remarked. "It would have been much easier for them to bring the crime home to Lawrence."

"Yes, but that was mere chance. All the evidence against him arose out of pure accident. It must, in fact, have been distinctly annoying to the pair of schemers."

"His manner was unfortunate," I observed thoughtfully.

"Yes. You realize, of course, what was at the back of that?"

"No."

"You did not understand that he believed Mademoiselle Cynthia guilty of the crime?"

"No," I exclaimed, astonished. "Impossible!"

"Not at all. I myself nearly had the same idea. It was in my mind when I asked Mr. Wells that first question about the will. Then there were the bromide powders which she had made up, and her clever male impersonations, as Dorcas recounted them to us. There was really more evidence against her than anyone else."

"You are joking, Poirot!"

"No. Shall I tell you what made Monsieur Lawrence turn so pale when he first entered his mother's room on the fatal night? It was because, whilst his mother lay there, obviously poisoned, he saw, over your shoulder, that the door into Mademoiselle Cynthia's room was unbolted."

"But he declared that he saw it bolted!" I cried.

"Exactly," said Poirot dryly. "And that was just what confirmed my suspicion that it was not. He was shielding Mademoiselle Cynthia."

"But why should he shield her?"

"Because he is in love with her."

I laughed.

"There, Poirot, you are quite wrong! I happen to know for a fact that, far from being in love with her, he positively dislikes her."

"Who told you that, *mon ami*?"

"Cynthia herself."

"*La pauvre petite*! And she was concerned?"

"She said that she did not mind at all."

"Then she certainly did mind very much," remarked Poirot. "They are like that—*les femmes*!"

"What you say about Lawrence is a great surprise to me," I said.

"But why? It was most obvious. Did not Monsieur Lawrence make the sour face every time Mademoiselle Cynthia spoke and laughed with his brother? He had taken it into his long head that Mademoiselle Cynthia was in love with Monsieur John. When he entered his mother's room, and saw her obviously poisoned, he jumped to the conclusion that Mademoiselle Cynthia knew something about the matter. He was nearly driven desperate. First he crushed the coffee-cup to powder under his feet, remembering that she had gone up with his mother the night before, and he determined that there should be no chance of testing its contents. Thenceforward, he strenuously, and quite uselessly, upheld the theory of 'Death from natural causes.' "

"And what about the 'extra coffee-cup'?"

"I was fairly certain that it was Mrs. Cavendish who had hidden it, but I had to make sure. Monsieur Lawrence did not know at all what I meant; but, on reflection, he came to the conclusion that if he could find an extra coffee-cup anywhere his lady love would be cleared of suspicion. And he was perfectly right."

"One thing more. What did Mrs. Inglethorp mean by her dying words?"

"They were, of course, an accusation against her husband."

"Dear me, Poirot," I said with a sigh, "I think you have explained everything. I am glad it has all ended so happily. Even John and his wife are reconciled."

"Thanks to me."

"How do you mean—thanks to you?"

"My dear friend, do you not realize that it was simply and solely the trial which has brought them together again? That John Cavendish still loved his wife, I was convinced. Also, that she was equally in love with him. But they had drifted very far apart. It all arose from a misunderstanding. She married him without love. He knew it. He is a sensitive man in his way, he would not force himself upon her if she did not want him. And, as he withdrew, her love awoke. But they are both unusually proud, and their pride held them inexorably apart. He drifted into an entanglement with Mrs. Raikes, and she deliberately cultivated the friendship of Dr. Bauerstein. Do you remember the day of John Cavendish's arrest, when you found me deliberating over a big decision?"

"Yes, I quite understood your distress."

"Pardon me, *mon ami*, but you did not understand it in the least. I was trying to decide whether or not I would clear John Cavendish at once. I could have cleared him—though it might have meant a failure to convict the real criminals. They were entirely in the dark as to my real attitude up to the very last moment—which partly accounts for my success."

"Do you mean that you could have saved John Cavendish from being brought to trial?"

"Yes, my friend. But I eventually decided in favour of 'a woman's happiness.' Nothing but the great danger through which they have passed could have brought these two proud souls together again."

I looked at Poirot in silent amazement. The colossal cheek of the little man! Who on earth but Poirot would have thought of a trial for murder as a restorer of conjugal happiness!

"I perceive your thoughts, *mon ami*," said Poirot, smiling at me. "No one but Hercule Poirot would have attempted such a thing! And you are wrong in condemning it. The happiness of one man and one woman is the greatest thing in all the world."

His words took me back to earlier events. I remembered Mary as she lay white and exhausted on the sofa, listening, listening. There had come the sound of the bell below. She had started up. Poirot had opened the door, and meeting her agonized eyes had nodded gently. "Yes, madame," he said. "I have brought him back to you." He had stood aside, and as I went out I had seen the look in Mary's eyes, as John Cavendish had caught his wife in his arms.

"Perhaps you are right, Poirot," I said gently. "Yes, it is the greatest thing in the world."

Suddenly, there was a tap at the door, and Cynthia peeped in.

"I—I only—"

"Come in," I said, springing up.

She came in, but did not sit down.

"I—only wanted to tell you something—"

"Yes?"

Cynthia fidgeted with a little tassel for some moments, then, suddenly exclaiming: "You dears!" kissed first me and then Poirot, and rushed out of the room again.

"What on earth does this mean?" I asked, surprised.

It was very nice to be kissed by Cynthia, but the publicity of the salute rather impaired the pleasure.

"It means that she has discovered Monsieur Lawrence does not dislike her as much as she thought," replied Poirot philosophically.

"But—"

"Here he is."

Lawrence at that moment passed the door.

"Eh! Monsieur Lawrence," called Poirot. "We must congratulate you, is it not so?"

Lawrence blushed, and then smiled awkwardly. A man in love is a sorry spectacle. Now Cynthia had looked charming.

I sighed.

"What is it, *mon ami*?"

"Nothing," I said sadly. "They are two delightful women!"

"And neither of them is for you?" finished Poirot. "Never mind. Console yourself, my friend. We may hunt together again, who knows? And then—"

THE YELLOW WALLPAPER

Charlotte Perkins Gilman

It is very seldom that mere ordinary people like John and myself secure ancestral halls for the summer.

A colonial mansion, a hereditary estate, I would say a haunted house, and reach the height of romantic felicity—but that would be asking too much of fate!

Still I will proudly declare that there is something queer about it.

Else, why should it be let so cheaply? And why have stood so long untenanted?

John laughs at me, of course, but one expects that in marriage.

John is practical in the extreme. He has no patience with faith, an intense horror of superstition, and he scoffs openly at any talk of things not to be felt and seen and put down in figures.

John is a physician, and *perhaps*—(I would not say it to a living soul, of course, but this is dead paper and a great relief to my mind)—*perhaps* that is one reason I do not get well faster.

You see he does not believe I am sick!

And what can one do?

If a physician of high standing, and one's own husband, assures friends and relatives that there is really nothing the matter with one but temporary nervous depression—a slight hysterical tendency—what is one to do?

My brother is also a physician, and also of high standing, and he says the same thing.

So I take phosphates or phosphites—whichever it is, and tonics, and journeys, and air, and exercise, and am absolutely forbidden to "work" until I am well again.

Personally, I disagree with their ideas.

Personally, I believe that congenial work, with excitement and change, would do me good.

But what is one to do?

I did write for a while in spite of them; but it does exhaust me a good deal—having to be so sly about it, or else meet with heavy opposition.

I sometimes fancy that in my condition if I had less opposition and more society and stimulus—but John says the very worst thing I can do is to think about my condition, and I confess it always makes me feel bad.

So I will let it alone and talk about the house.

The most beautiful place! It is quite alone, standing well back from the road, quite three miles from the village. It makes me think of English places that you read about, for there are hedges and walls and gates that lock, and lots of separate little houses for the gardeners and people.

There is a *delicious* garden! I never saw such a garden—large and shady, full of box-bordered paths, and lined with long grape-covered arbors with seats under them.

There were greenhouses, too, but they are all broken now.

There was some legal trouble, I believe, something about the heirs and coheirs; anyhow, the place has been empty for years.

That spoils my ghostliness, I am afraid, but I don't care—there is something strange about the house—I can feel it.

I even said so to John one moonlight evening, but he said what I felt was a *draught*, and shut the window.

I get unreasonably angry with John sometimes. I'm sure I never used to be so sensitive. I think it is due to this nervous condition.

But John says if I feel so, I shall neglect proper self-control; so I take pains to control myself—before him, at least, and that makes me very tired.

I don't like our room a bit. I wanted one downstairs that opened on the piazza and had roses all over the window, and such pretty old-fashioned chintz hangings! but John would not hear of it.

He said there was only one window and not room for two beds, and no near room for him if he took another.

He is very careful and loving, and hardly lets me stir without special direction.

I have a schedule prescription for each hour in the day; he takes all care from me, and so I feel basely ungrateful not to value it more.

He said we came here solely on my account, that I was to have perfect rest and all the air I could get. "Your exercise depends on your strength, my dear," said he, "and your food somewhat on your appetite; but air you can absorb all the time." So we took the nursery at the top of the house.

It is a big, airy room, the whole floor nearly, with windows that look all ways, and air and sunshine galore. It was nursery first and then playroom and gymnasium, I should judge; for the windows are barred for little children, and there are rings and things in the walls.

The paint and paper look as if a boys' school had used it. It is stripped off—the paper—in great patches all around the head of my bed, about as far as I can reach, and in a great place on the other side of the room low down. I never saw a worse paper in my life.

One of those sprawling flamboyant patterns committing every artistic sin.

It is dull enough to confuse the eye in following, pronounced enough to constantly irritate and provoke study, and when you follow the lame uncertain curves for a little distance they suddenly commit suicide—plunge off at outrageous angles, destroy themselves in unheard of contradictions.

The color is repellent, almost revolting; a smouldering unclean yellow, strangely faded by the slow-turning sunlight.

It is a dull yet lurid orange in some places, a sickly sulphur tint in others.

No wonder the children hated it! I should hate it myself if I had to live in this room long.

There comes John, and I must put this away—he hates to have me write a word.

* * * * *

We have been here two weeks, and I haven't felt like writing before, since that first day.

I am sitting by the window now, up in this atrocious nursery, and there is nothing to hinder my writing as much as I please, save lack of strength.

John is away all day, and even some nights when his cases are serious.

I am glad my case is not serious!

But these nervous troubles are dreadfully depressing.

John does not know how much I really suffer. He knows there is no reason to suffer, and that satisfies him.

Of course it is only nervousness. It does weigh on me so not to do my duty in any way!

I meant to be such a help to John, such a real rest and comfort, and here I am a comparative burden already!

Nobody would believe what an effort it is to do what little I am able,—to dress and entertain, and order things.

It is fortunate Mary is so good with the baby. Such a dear baby!

And yet I *cannot* be with him, it makes me so nervous.

I suppose John never was nervous in his life. He laughs at me so about this wallpaper!

At first he meant to repaper the room, but afterwards he said that I was letting it get the better of me, and that nothing was worse for a nervous patient than to give way to such fancies.

He said that after the wallpaper was changed it would be the heavy bedstead, and then the barred windows, and then that gate at the head of the stairs, and so on.

"You know the place is doing you good," he said, "and really, dear, I don't care to renovate the house just for a three months' rental."

"Then do let us go downstairs," I said, "there are such pretty rooms there."

Then he took me in his arms and called me a blessed little goose, and said he would go down to the cellar, if I wished, and have it whitewashed into the bargain.

But he is right enough about the beds and windows and things.

It is an airy and comfortable room as any one need wish, and, of course, I would not be so silly as to make him uncomfortable just for a whim.

I'm really getting quite fond of the big room, all but that horrid paper.

Out of one window I can see the garden, those mysterious deep-shaded arbors, the riotous old-fashioned flowers, and bushes and gnarly trees.

Out of another I get a lovely view of the bay and a little private wharf belonging to the estate. There is a beautiful shaded lane that runs down there from the house. I always fancy I see people walking in these numerous paths and arbors, but John has cautioned me not to give way to fancy in the least. He says that with my imaginative power and habit of story-making, a nervous weakness like mine is sure to lead to all manner of excited fancies, and that I ought to use my will and good sense to check the tendency. So I try.

I think sometimes that if I were only well enough to write a little it would relieve the press of ideas and rest me.

But I find I get pretty tired when I try.

It is so discouraging not to have any advice and companionship about my work. When I get really well, John says we will ask Cousin Henry and Julia down for a long visit; but he says he would as soon put fireworks in my pillow-case as to let me have those stimulating people about now.

I wish I could get well faster.

But I must not think about that. This paper looks to me as if it *knew* what a vicious influence it had!

There is a recurrent spot where the pattern lolls like a broken neck and two bulbous eyes stare at you upside down.

I get positively angry with the impertinence of it and the everlastingness. Up and down and sideways they crawl, and those absurd, unblinking eyes are everywhere. There is one place where two breadths didn't match, and the eyes go all up and down the line, one a little higher than the other.

I never saw so much expression in an inanimate thing before, and we all know how much expression they have! I used to lie awake as a child and get more entertainment and terror out of blank walls and plain furniture than most children could find in a toy store.

I remember what a kindly wink the knobs of our big, old bureau used to have, and there was one chair that always seemed like a strong friend.

I used to feel that if any of the other things looked too fierce I could always hop into that chair and be safe.

The furniture in this room is no worse than inharmonious, however, for we had to bring it all from downstairs. I suppose when this was used as a playroom they had to take the nursery things out, and no wonder! I never saw such ravages as the children have made here.

The wallpaper, as I said before, is torn off in spots, and it sticketh closer than a brother—they must have had perseverance as well as hatred.

Then the floor is scratched and gouged and splintered, the plaster itself is dug out here and there, and this great heavy bed which is all we found in the room, looks as if it had been through the wars.

But I don't mind it a bit—only the paper.

There comes John's sister. Such a dear girl as she is, and so careful of me! I must not let her find me writing.

She is a perfect and enthusiastic housekeeper, and hopes for no better profession. I verily believe she thinks it is the writing which made me sick!

But I can write when she is out, and see her a long way off from these windows.

There is one that commands the road, a lovely shaded winding road, and one that just looks off over the country. A lovely country, too, full of great elms and velvet meadows.

This wallpaper has a kind of sub-pattern in a different shade, a particularly irritating one, for you can only see it in certain lights, and not clearly then.

But in the places where it isn't faded and where the sun is just so—I can see a strange, provoking, formless sort of figure, that seems to skulk about behind that silly and conspicuous front design.

There's sister on the stairs!

* * * * *

Well, the Fourth of July is over! The people are all gone and I am tired out. John thought it might do me good to see a little company, so we just had mother and Nellie and the children down for a week.

Of course I didn't do a thing. Jennie sees to everything now.

But it tired me all the same.

John says if I don't pick up faster he shall send me to Weir Mitchell in the fall.

But I don't want to go there at all. I had a friend who was in his hands once, and she says he is just like John and my brother, only more so!

Besides, it is such an undertaking to go so far.

I don't feel as if it was worth while to turn my hand over for anything, and I'm getting dreadfully fretful and querulous.

I cry at nothing, and cry most of the time.

Of course I don't when John is here, or anybody else, but when I am alone.

And I am alone a good deal just now. John is kept in town very often by serious cases, and Jennie is good and lets me alone when I want her to.

So I walk a little in the garden or down that lovely lane, sit on the porch under the roses, and lie down up here a good deal.

I'm getting really fond of the room in spite of the wallpaper. Perhaps *because* of the wallpaper.

It dwells in my mind so!

I lie here on this great immovable bed—it is nailed down, I believe—and follow that pattern about by the hour. It is as good as gymnastics, I assure you. I start, we'll say, at the bottom, down in the corner over there where it has not been touched, and I determine for the thousandth time that I *will* follow that pointless pattern to some sort of a conclusion.

I know a little of the principle of design, and I know this thing was not arranged on any laws of radiation, or alternation, or repetition, or symmetry, or anything else that I ever heard of.

It is repeated, of course, by the breadths, but not otherwise.

Looked at in one way each breadth stands alone, the bloated curves and flourishes—a kind of "debased Romanesque" with *delirium tremens*—go waddling up and down in isolated columns of fatuity.

But, on the other hand, they connect diagonally, and the sprawling outlines run off in great slanting waves of optic horror, like a lot of wallowing seaweeds in full chase.

The whole thing goes horizontally, too, at least it seems so, and I exhaust myself in trying to distinguish the order of its going in that direction.

They have used a horizontal breadth for a frieze, and that adds wonderfully to the confusion.

There is one end of the room where it is almost intact, and there, when the crosslights fade and the low sun shines directly upon it, I can almost fancy radiation after all—the interminable grotesques seem to form around a common centre and rush off in headlong plunges of equal distraction.

It makes me tired to follow it. I will take a nap I guess.

* * * * *

I don't know why I should write this.

I don't want to.

I don't feel able.

And I know John would think it absurd. But I must say what I feel and think in some way—it is such a relief!

But the effort is getting to be greater than the relief.

Half the time now I am awfully lazy, and lie down ever so much.

John says I musn't lose my strength, and has me take cod liver oil and lots of tonics and things, to say nothing of ale and wine and rare meat.

Dear John! He loves me very dearly, and hates to have me sick. I tried to have a real earnest reasonable talk with him the other day, and tell him how I wish he would let me go and make a visit to Cousin Henry and Julia.

But he said I wasn't able to go, nor able to stand it after I got there; and I did not make out a very good case for myself, for I was crying before I had finished.

It is getting to be a great effort for me to think straight. Just this nervous weakness I suppose.

And dear John gathered me up in his arms, and just carried me upstairs and laid me on the bed, and sat by me and read to me till it tired my head.

He said I was his darling and his comfort and all he had, and that I must take care of myself for his sake, and keep well.

He says no one but myself can help me out of it, that I must use my will and self-control and not let any silly fancies run away with me.

There's one comfort, the baby is well and happy, and does not have to occupy this nursery with the horrid wallpaper.

If we had not used it, that blessed child would have! What a fortunate escape! Why, I wouldn't have a child of mine, an impressionable little thing, live in such a room for worlds.

I never thought of it before, but it is lucky that John kept me here after all, I can stand it so much easier than a baby, you see.

Of course I never mention it to them any more—I am too wise—but I keep watch of it all the same.

There are things in that paper that nobody knows but me, or ever will.

Behind that outside pattern the dim shapes get clearer every day.

It is always the same shape, only very numerous.

And it is like a woman stooping down and creeping about behind that pattern. I don't like it a bit. I wonder—I begin to think—I wish John would take me away from here!

It is so hard to talk with John about my case, because he is so wise, and because he loves me so.

But I tried it last night.

It was moonlight. The moon shines in all around just as the sun does.

I hate to see it sometimes, it creeps so slowly, and always comes in by one window or another.

John was asleep and I hated to waken him, so I kept still and watched the moonlight on that undulating wallpaper till I felt creepy.

The faint figure behind seemed to shake the pattern, just as if she wanted to get out.

I got up softly and went to feel and see if the paper *did* move, and when I came back John was awake.

"What is it, little girl?" he said. "Don't go walking about like that—you'll get cold."

I thought it was a good time to talk, so I told him that I really was not gaining here, and that I wished he would take me away.

"Why darling!" said he, "our lease will be up in three weeks, and I can't see how to leave before.

"The repairs are not done at home, and I cannot possibly leave town just now. Of course if you were in any danger, I could and would, but you really are better, dear, whether you can see it or not. I am a doctor, dear, and I know. You are gaining flesh and color, your appetite is better, I feel really much easier about you."

"I don't weigh a bit more," said I, "nor as much; and my appetite may be better in the evening when you are here, but it is worse in the morning when you are away!"

"Bless her little heart!" said he with a big hug, "she shall be as sick as she pleases! But now let's improve the shining hours by going to sleep, and talk about it in the morning!"

"And you won't go away?" I asked gloomily.

"Why, how can I, dear? It is only three weeks more and then we will take a nice little trip of a few days while Jennie is getting the house ready. Really dear you are better!"

"Better in body perhaps—" I began, and stopped short, for he sat up straight and looked at me with such a stern, reproachful look that I could not say another word.

"My darling," said he, "I beg of you, for my sake and for our child's sake, as well as for your own, that you will never for one instant let that idea enter your mind! There is nothing so dangerous, so fascinating, to a temperament like yours. It is a false and foolish fancy. Can you not trust me as a physician when I tell you so?"

So of course I said no more on that score, and we went to sleep before long. He thought I was asleep first, but I wasn't, and lay there for hours trying to decide whether that front pattern and the back pattern really did move together or separately.

* * * * *

On a pattern like this, by daylight, there is a lack of sequence, a defiance of law, that is a constant irritant to a normal mind.

The color is hideous enough, and unreliable enough, and infuriating enough, but the pattern is torturing.

You think you have mastered it, but just as you get well underway in following, it turns a back-somersault and there you are. It slaps you in the face, knocks you down, and tramples upon you. It is like a bad dream.

The outside pattern is a florid arabesque, reminding one of a fungus. If you can imagine a toadstool in joints, an interminable string of toadstools, budding and sprouting in endless convolutions—why, that is something like it.

That is, sometimes!

There is one marked peculiarity about this paper, a thing nobody seems to notice but myself, and that is that it changes as the light changes.

When the sun shoots in through the east window—I always watch for that first long, straight ray—it changes so quickly that I never can quite believe it.

That is why I watch it always.

By moonlight—the moon shines in all night when there is a moon—I wouldn't know it was the same paper.

At night in any kind of light, in twilight, candle light, lamplight, and worst of all by moonlight, it becomes bars! The outside pattern I mean, and the woman behind it is as plain as can be.

I didn't realize for a long time what the thing was that showed behind, that dim sub-pattern, but now I am quite sure it is a woman.

By daylight she is subdued, quiet. I fancy it is the pattern that keeps her so still. It is so puzzling. It keeps me quiet by the hour.

I lie down ever so much now. John says it is good for me, and to sleep all I can.

Indeed he started the habit by making me lie down for an hour after each meal.

It is a very bad habit I am convinced, for you see I don't sleep.

And that cultivates deceit, for I don't tell them I'm awake—O no!

The fact is I am getting a little afraid of John.

He seems very queer sometimes, and even Jennie has an inexplicable look.

It strikes me occasionally, just as a scientific hypothesis,—that perhaps it is the paper!

I have watched John when he did not know I was looking, and come into the room suddenly on the most innocent excuses, and I've caught him several times *looking at the paper*! And Jennie too. I caught Jennie with her hand on it once.

She didn't know I was in the room, and when I asked her in a quiet, a very quiet voice, with the most restrained manner possible, what she was doing with the paper—she turned around as if she had been caught stealing, and looked quite angry—asked me why I should frighten her so!

Then she said that the paper stained everything it touched, that she had found yellow smooches on all my clothes and John's, and she wished we would be more careful!

Did not that sound innocent? But I know she was studying that pattern, and I am determined that nobody shall find it out but myself!

* * * * *

Life is very much more exciting now than it used to be. You see I have something more to expect, to look forward to, to watch. I really do eat better, and am more quiet than I was.

John is so pleased to see me improve! He laughed a little the other day, and said I seemed to be flourishing in spite of my wallpaper.

I turned it off with a laugh. I had no intention of telling him it was *because* of the wallpaper—he would make fun of me. He might even want to take me away.

I don't want to leave now until I have found it out. There is a week more, and I think that will be enough.

* * * * *

I'm feeling ever so much better! I don't sleep much at night, for it is so interesting to watch developments; but I sleep a good deal in the daytime.

In the daytime it is tiresome and perplexing.

There are always new shoots on the fungus, and new shades of yellow all over it. I cannot keep count of them, though I have tried conscientiously.

It is the strangest yellow, that wallpaper! It makes me think of all the yellow things I ever saw—not beautiful ones like buttercups, but old foul, bad yellow things.

But there is something else about that paper—the smell! I noticed it the moment we came into the room, but with so much air and sun it was not bad. Now we have had a week of fog and rain, and whether the windows are open or not, the smell is here.

It creeps all over the house.

I find it hovering in the dining-room, skulking in the parlor, hiding in the hall, lying in wait for me on the stairs.

It gets into my hair.

Even when I go to ride, if I turn my head suddenly and surprise it—there is that smell!

Such a peculiar odor, too! I have spent hours in trying to analyze it, to find what it smelled like.

It is not bad—at first, and very gentle, but quite the subtlest, most enduring odor I ever met.

In this damp weather it is awful, I wake up in the night and find it hanging over me.

It used to disturb me at first. I thought seriously of burning the house—to reach the smell.

But now I am used to it. The only thing I can think of that it is like is the *color* of the paper! A yellow smell.

There is a very funny mark on this wall, low down, near the mop-board. A streak that runs round the room. It goes behind every piece of furniture, except the bed, a long, straight, even *smooch*, as if it had been rubbed over and over.

I wonder how it was done and who did it, and what they did it for. Round and round and round—round and round and round—it makes me dizzy!

* * * * *

I really have discovered something at last.

Through watching so much at night, when it changes so, I have finally found out.

The front pattern *does* move—and no wonder! The woman behind shakes it!

Sometimes I think there are a great many women behind, and sometimes only one, and she crawls around fast, and her crawling shakes it all over.

Then in the very bright spots she keeps still, and in the very shady spots she just takes hold of the bars and shakes them hard.

And she is all the time trying to climb through. But nobody could climb through that pattern—it strangles so; I think that is why it has so many heads.

They get through, and then the pattern strangles them off and turns them upside down, and makes their eyes white!

If those heads were covered or taken off it would not be half so bad.

* * * * *

I think that woman gets out in the daytime!

And I'll tell you why—privately—I've seen her!

I can see her out of every one of my windows!

It is the same woman, I know, for she is always creeping, and most women do not creep by daylight.

I see her in that long shaded lane, creeping up and down. I see her in those dark grape arbors, creeping all around the garden.

I see her on that long road under the trees, creeping along, and when a carriage comes she hides under the blackberry vines.

I don't blame her a bit. It must be very humiliating to be caught creeping by daylight!

I always lock the door when I creep by daylight. I can't do it at night, for I know John would suspect something at once.

And John is so queer now, that I don't want to irritate him. I wish he would take another room! Besides, I don't want anybody to get that woman out at night but myself.

I often wonder if I could see her out of all the windows at once.

But, turn as fast as I can, I can only see out of one at one time.

And though I always see her, she *may* be able to creep faster than I can turn!

I have watched her sometimes away off in the open country, creeping as fast as a cloud shadow in a high wind.

* * * * *

If only that top pattern could be gotten off from the under one! I mean to try it, little by little.

I have found out another funny thing, but I shan't tell it this time! It does not do to trust people too much.

There are only two more days to get this paper off, and I believe John is beginning to notice. I don't like the look in his eyes.

And I heard him ask Jennie a lot of professional questions about me. She had a very good report to give.

She said I slept a good deal in the daytime.

John knows I don't sleep very well at night, for all I'm so quiet!

He asked me all sorts of questions, too, and pretended to be very loving and kind.

As if I couldn't see through him!

Still, I don't wonder he acts so, sleeping under this paper for three months.

It only interests me, but I feel sure John and Jennie are secretly affected by it.

* * * * *

Hurrah! This is the last day, but it is enough. John is to stay in town over night, and won't be out until this evening.

Jennie wanted to sleep with me—the sly thing! but I told her I should undoubtedly rest better for a night all alone.

That was clever, for really I wasn't alone a bit! As soon as it was moonlight and that poor thing began to crawl and shake the pattern, I got up and ran to help her.

I pulled and she shook, I shook and she pulled, and before morning we had peeled off yards of that paper.

A strip about as high as my head and half around the room.

And then when the sun came and that awful pattern began to laugh at me, I declared I would finish it to-day!

We go away tomorrow, and they are moving all my furniture down again to leave things as they were before.

Jennie looked at the wall in amazement, but I told her merrily that I did it out of pure spite at the vicious thing.

She laughed and said she wouldn't mind doing it herself, but I must not get tired.

How she betrayed herself that time!

But I am here, and no person touches this paper but me—not *alive*!

She tried to get me out of the room—it was too patent! But I said it was so quiet and empty and clean now that I believed I would lie down again and sleep all I could; and not to wake me even for dinner—I would call when I woke.

So now she is gone, and the servants are gone, and the things are gone, and there is nothing left but that great bedstead nailed down, with the canvas mattress we found on it.

We shall sleep downstairs to-night, and take the boat home to-morrow.

I quite enjoy the room, now it is bare again.

How those children did tear about here!

This bedstead is fairly gnawed!

But I must get to work.

I have locked the door and thrown the key down into the front path.

I don't want to go out, and I don't want to have anybody come in, till John comes.

I want to astonish him.

I've got a rope up here that even Jennie did not find. If that woman does get out, and tries to get away, I can tie her!

But I forgot I could not reach far without anything to stand on!

This bed will not move!

I tried to lift and push it until I was lame, and then I got so angry I bit off a little piece at one corner—but it hurt my teeth.

Then I peeled off all the paper I could reach standing on the floor. It sticks horribly and the pattern just enjoys it! All those strangled heads and bulbous eyes and waddling fungus growths just shriek with derision!

I am getting angry enough to do something desperate. To jump out of the window would be admirable exercise, but the bars are too strong even to try.

Besides I wouldn't do it. Of course not. I know well enough that a step like that is improper and might be misconstrued.

I don't like to *look* out of the windows even—there are so many of those creeping women, and they creep so fast.

I wonder if they all come out of that wallpaper as I did?

But I am securely fastened now by my well-hidden rope—you don't get *me* out in the road there!

I suppose I shall have to get back behind the pattern when it comes night, and that is hard!

It is so pleasant to be out in this great room and creep around as I please!

I don't want to go outside. I won't, even if Jennie asks me to.

For outside you have to creep on the ground, and everything is green instead of yellow.

But here I can creep smoothly on the floor, and my shoulder just fits in that long smooch around the wall, so I cannot lose my way.

Why there's John at the door!

It is no use, young man, you can't open it!

How he does call and pound!

Now he's crying for an axe.

It would be a shame to break down that beautiful door!

"John dear!" said I in the gentlest voice, "the key is down by the front steps, under a plantain leaf!"

That silenced him for a few moments.

Then he said—very quietly indeed, "Open the door, my darling!"

"I can't," said I. "The key is down by the front door under a plantain leaf!"

And then I said it again, several times, very gently and slowly, and said it so often that he had to go and see, and he got it of course, and came in. He stopped short by the door.

"What is the matter?" he cried. "For God's sake, what are you doing!"

I kept on creeping just the same, but I looked at him over my shoulder.

"I've got out at last," said I, "in spite of you and Jane. And I've pulled off most of the paper, so you can't put me back!"

Now why should that man have fainted? But he did, and right across my path by the wall, so that I had to creep over him every time!

WHY I WROTE
"THE YELLOW WALLPAPER"

Charlotte Perkins Gilman

This article first appeared in the October 1913 issue of the Forerunner—*a montnly magazine owned and edited by Gilman—more than twenty years after the initial publication of "The Yellow Wallpaper."*

Many and many a reader has asked that. When the story first came out, in the *New England Magazine* about 1891, a Boston physician made protest in *The Transcript*. Such a story ought not to be written, he said; it was enough to drive anyone mad to read it.

Another physician, in Kansas I think, wrote to say that it was the best description of incipient insanity he had ever seen, and—begging my pardon—had I been there?

Now the story of the story is this:

For many years I suffered from a severe and continuous nervous breakdown tending to melancholia—and beyond. During about the third year of this trouble I went, in devout faith and some faint stir of hope, to a noted specialist in nervous diseases, the best known in the country. This wise man put me to bed and applied the rest cure, to which a still-good physique responded so promptly that he concluded there was nothing much the matter with me, and sent me home with solemn advice to "live as domestic a life as far as possible," to "have but two hours' intellectual life a day," and "never to touch pen, brush, or pencil again" as long as I lived. This was in 1887.

I went home and obeyed those directions for some three months, and came so near the borderline of utter mental ruin that I could see over.

Then, using the remnants of intelligence that remained, and helped by a wise friend, I cast the noted specialist's advice to the winds and went to work again—work, the normal life of every human being; work, in which is joy and growth and service, without which one is a pauper and a parasite—ultimately recovering some measure of power.

Being naturally moved to rejoicing by this narrow escape, I wrote "The Yellow Wallpaper," with its embellishments and additions, to carry out the ideal (I never had hallucinations or objections to my mural decorations) and sent a copy to the physician who so nearly drove me mad. He never acknowledged it.

The little book is valued by alienists and as a good specimen of one kind of literature. It has, to my knowledge, saved one woman from a similar fate— so terrifying her family that they let her out into normal activity and she recovered.

But the best result is this. Many years later I was told that the great specialist had admitted to friends of his that he had altered his treatment of neurasthenia since reading "The Yellow Wallpaper."

It was not intended to drive people crazy, but to save people from being driven crazy, and it worked.

Letter to Fanny Knight

Jane Austen

By late 1814, Jane Austen had anonymously published her first three novels, but she earned little fame as an author during her lifetime. In this letter to her twenty-one-year-old niece Fanny Knight, Austen dispenses advice on love and marriage—subjects that are found throughout her novels.

23 Hans Place, Wednesday (Nov. 30, 1814).

I am very much obliged to you, my dear Fanny, for your letter, and I hope you will write again soon, that I may know you to be all safe and happy at home.

Our visit to Hendon will interest you, I am sure; but I need not enter into the particulars of it, as your papa will be able to answer *almost* every question. I certainly *could* describe her bedroom and her drawers and her closet, better than he can, but I do not feel that I can stop to do it. I was rather sorry to hear that she *is* to have an instrument; it seems throwing money away. They will wish the twenty-four guineas in the shape of sheets and towels six months hence; and as to her playing, it never can be anything.

Her purple pelisse rather surprised me. I thought we had known all paraphernalia of that sort. I do not mean to blame her; it looked very well, and I dare say she wanted it. I suspect nothing worse than its being got in secret, and not owned to anybody. I received a very kind note from her yesterday, to ask me to come again and stay a night with them. I cannot do it, but I was pleased to find that she had the *power* of doing so right a thing. My going was to give them *both* pleasure very properly.

I just saw Mr. Hayter at the play, and think his face would please me on acquaintance. I was sorry he did not dine here. It seemed rather odd to me to be in the theatre with nobody to *watch* for. I was quite composed myself, at leisure for all the agitated Isabella could raise.

Now, my dearest Fanny, I will begin a subject which comes in very naturally. You frighten me out of my wits by your reference. Your affection gives me the highest pleasure, but indeed you must not let anything depend on my opinion; your own feelings, and none but your own, should determine such an important point. So far, however, as answering your question, I have no scruple. I am perfectly convinced that your present feelings, supposing that you were to marry *now*, would be sufficient for his happiness; but when I think how very, very far it is from a "*now*," and take everything that *may be* into consideration, I dare not say, "Determine to accept him"; the risk is too great for *you*, unless your own sentiments prompt it.

You will think me perverse, perhaps; in my last letter I was urging everything in his favor, and now I am inclining the other way, but I cannot help it; I am at present more impressed with the possible evil that may arise to *you* from engaging yourself to him—in word or mind—than with anything else. When I consider how few young men you have yet seen much of, how capable you are (yes, I do still think you *very* capable) of being really in love, and how full of temptation the next six or seven years of your life will probably be (it is the very period of life for the *strongest* attachments to be formed),—I cannot wish you, with your present very cool feelings, to devote yourself in honor to him. It is very true that you never may attach another man his equal altogether; but if that other man has the power of attaching you *more*, he will be in your eyes the most perfect.

I shall be glad if you *can* revive past feelings, and from your unbiassed self resolve to go on as you have done, but this I do not expect; and without it I cannot wish you to be fettered. I should not be afraid of your *marrying* him; with all his worth you would soon love him enough for the happiness of both; but I should dread the continuance of this sort of tacit engagement, with such an uncertainty as there is of *when* it may be completed. Years may pass before he is independent; you like him well enough to marry, but not well enough to wait; the unpleasantness of appearing fickle is certainly great; but if you think you want punishment for past illusions, there it is, and nothing can be compared to the misery of being bound *without* love,—bound to one, and preferring another; *that* is a punishment which you do *not* deserve.

I know you did not meet, or rather will not meet, to-day, as he called here yesterday; and I am glad of it. It does not seem very likely, at least, that he should be in time for a dinner visit sixty miles off. We did not see him, only found his card when we came home at four. Your Uncle H. merely observed that he was a day *after "the fair."* We asked your brother on Monday (when Mr. Hayter was talked of) why he did not invite *him* too; saying, "I know he is in town, for I met him the other day in Bond St." Edward answered that he did not know where he was to be found. "Don't you know his chambers?" "No."

I shall be most glad to hear from you again, my dearest Fanny, but it must not be later than Saturday, as we shall be off on Monday long before the letters are delivered; and write *something* that may do to be read or told. I am to take the Miss Moores back on Saturday, and when I return I shall hope to find your pleasant little flowing scrawl on the table. It will be a relief to me after playing at ma'ams, for though I like Miss H. M. as much as one can at my time of life after a day's acquaintance, it is uphill work to be talking to those whom one knows so little.

Only *one* comes back with me to-morrow, probably Miss Eliza, and I rather dread it. We shall not have two ideas in common. She is young, pretty, chattering, and thinking chiefly, I presume, of dress, company, and admiration. Mr. Sanford is to join us at dinner, which will be a comfort, and in the evening, while your uncle and Miss Eliza play chess, he shall tell me comical things and I will laugh at them, which will be a pleasure to both.

I called in Keppel Street and saw them all, including dear Uncle Charles, who is to come and dine with us quietly to-day. Little Harriot sat in my lap, and seemed as gentle and affectionate as ever, and as pretty, except not being quite well. Fanny is a fine stout girl, talking incessantly, with an interesting degree of lisp and indistinctness, and very likely may be the handsomest in time. That puss Cassy did not show more pleasure in seeing me than her sisters, but I expected no better. She does not shine in the tender feelings. She will never be a Miss O'Neil, more in the Mrs. Siddons line.

Thank you, but it is not settled yet whether I *do* hazard a second edition. We are to see Egerton to-day, when it will probably be determined. People are more ready to borrow and praise than to buy, which I cannot wonder at; but though I like praise as well as anybody, I like what Edward calls *"Pewter,"* too. I hope he continues careful of his eyes, and finds the good effect of it. I cannot suppose we differ in our ideas of the Christian religion. You have given an excellent description of it. We only affix a different meaning to the word *evangelical*.

Yours most affectionately,

J. AUSTEN.

MISS KNIGHT,
Godmersham Park,
Faversham, Kent.

COUSIN PHILLIS

Elizabeth Gaskell

PART I

It is a great thing for a lad when he is first turned into the independence of lodgings. I do not think I ever was so satisfied and proud in my life as when, at seventeen, I sate down in a little three-cornered room above a pastry-cook's shop in the county town of Eltham. My father had left me that afternoon, after delivering himself of a few plain precepts, strongly expressed, for my guidance in the new course of life on which I was entering. I was to be a clerk under the engineer who had undertaken to make the little branch line from Eltham to Hornby. My father had got me this situation, which was in a position rather above his own in life; or perhaps I should say, above the station in which he was born and bred; for he was raising himself every year in men's consideration and respect. He was a mechanic by trade, but he had some inventive genius, and a great deal of perseverance, and had devised several valuable improvements in railway machinery. He did not do this for profit, though, as was reasonable, what came in the natural course of things was acceptable; he worked out his ideas, because, as he said, "until he could put them into shape, they plagued him by night and by day." But this is enough about my dear father; it is a good thing for a country where there are many like him. He was a sturdy Independent by descent and conviction; and this it was, I believe, which made him place me in the lodgings at the pastry-cook's. The shop was kept by the two sisters of our minister at home; and this was considered as a sort of safeguard to my morals, when I was turned loose upon the temptations of the county town, with a salary of thirty pounds a year.

My father had given up two precious days, and put on his Sunday clothes, in order to bring me to Eltham, and accompany me first to the office, to introduce me to my new master (who was under some obligations to my father for a suggestion), and next to take me to call on the Independent minister of the little congregation at Eltham. And then he left me; and though sorry to part with him, I now began to taste with relish the pleasure of being my own master. I unpacked the hamper that my mother had provided me with, and smelt the pots of preserve with all the delight of a possessor who might break into their contents at any time he pleased. I handled and weighed in my fancy the home-cured ham, which seemed to promise me interminable feasts; and, above all, there was the fine savour of knowing that I might eat of these dainties when I liked, at my sole will, not dependent on the pleasure of any one else, however indulgent. I stowed my eatables away in the little corner cupboard—that room was all corners, and everything was placed in a corner, the fire-place, the window, the cupboard; I myself seemed to be the only thing in the middle, and there was hardly room for me. The table was made of a folding leaf under the window, and the window looked out upon the market-place; so the studies for the prosecution of which my father had brought himself to pay extra for a sitting-room for me, ran a considerable chance of being diverted from books to men and women. I was to have my meals with the two elderly Miss Dawsons in the little parlour behind the three-cornered shop downstairs; my breakfasts and dinners at least, for, as my hours in an evening were likely to be uncertain, my tea or supper was to be an independent meal.

Then, after this pride and satisfaction, came a sense of desolation. I had never been from home before, and I was an only child; and though my father's spoken maxim had been, "Spare the rod, and spoil the child," yet, unconsciously, his heart had yearned after me, and his ways towards me were more tender than he knew, or would have approved of in himself could he have known. My mother, who never professed sternness, was far more severe than my father: perhaps my boyish faults annoyed her more; for I remember, now that I have written the above words, how she pleaded for me once in my riper years, when I had really offended against my father's sense of right.

But I have nothing to do with that now. It is about cousin Phillis that I am going to write, and as yet I am far enough from even saying who cousin Phillis was.

For some months after I was settled in Eltham, the new employment in which I was engaged—the new independence of my life—occupied all my thoughts. I was at my desk by eight o'clock, home to dinner at one, back at the office by two. The afternoon work was more uncertain than the morning's; it might be the same, or it might be that I had to accompany Mr. Holdsworth, the managing engineer, to some point on the line between Eltham and Hornby. This I always enjoyed, because of the variety, and because of the country we traversed (which was very wild and pretty), and because I was thrown into companionship with Mr. Holdsworth, who held the position of hero in my boyish mind. He was a young man of five-and-twenty or so, and was in a station above mine, both by birth and education; and he had travelled on the Continent, and wore mustachios and whiskers of a somewhat foreign fashion. I was proud of being seen with him. He was really a fine fellow in a good number of ways, and I might have fallen into much worse hands.

Every Saturday I wrote home, telling of my weekly doings—my father had insisted upon this; but there was so little variety in my life that I often found it hard work to fill a letter. On Sundays I went twice to chapel, up a dark narrow entry, to hear droning hymns, and long prayers, and a still longer sermon, preached to a small congregation, of which I was, by nearly a score of years, the youngest member. Occasionally, Mr. Peters, the minister, would ask me home to tea after the second service. I dreaded the honour, for I usually sate on the edge of my chair all the evening, and answered solemn questions, put in a deep bass voice, until household prayer-time came, at eight o'clock, when Mrs. Peters came in, smoothing down her apron, and the maid-of-all-work followed, and first a sermon, and then a chapter was read, and a long impromptu prayer followed, till some instinct told Mr. Peters that supper-time had come, and we rose from our knees with hunger for our predominant feeling. Over supper the minister did unbend a little into one or two ponderous jokes, as if to show me that ministers were men, after all. And then at ten o'clock I went home, and enjoyed my long-repressed yawns in the three-cornered room before going to bed. Dinah and Hannah Dawson, so their names were put on the board above the shop-door—I always called them Miss Dawson and Miss Hannah—considered these visits of mine to Mr. Peters as the greatest honour a young man could have; and evidently thought that if after such privileges, I did not work out my salvation, I was a sort of modern Judas Iscariot. On the contrary, they shook their heads over my intercourse with Mr. Holdsworth. He had been so kind to me in many ways, that when I cut into my ham, I hovered over the thought of asking him to tea in my room, more especially as the annual fair was being held in Eltham market-place, and the sight of the booths, the merry-go-rounds, the wild-beast shows, and such country pomps, was (as I thought at seventeen) very attractive. But when I ventured to allude to my wish in even distant terms, Miss Hannah caught me up, and spoke of the sinfulness of such sights, and something about wallowing in the mire, and then vaulted into France, and spoke evil of the nation, and all who had ever set foot therein, till, seeing that her anger was concentrating itself into a point, and that that point was Mr. Holdsworth, I thought it would be better to finish my breakfast, and make what haste I could out of the sound of her voice. I rather wondered afterwards to hear her and Miss Dawson counting up their weekly profits with glee, and saying that a pastry-cook's shop in the corner of the market-place, in Eltham fair week, was no such bad thing. However, I never ventured to ask Mr. Holdsworth to my lodgings.

There is not much to tell about this first year of mine at Eltham. But when I was nearly nineteen, and beginning to think of whiskers on my own account, I came to know cousin Phillis, whose very existence had been unknown to me till then. Mr. Holdsworth and I had been out to Heathbridge for a day, working hard. Heathbridge was near Hornby, for our line of railway was above half finished. Of course, a day's outing was a great thing to tell about in my weekly letters; and I fell to describing the country—a fault I was not often guilty of. I told my father of the bogs, all over wild myrtle and soft moss, and shaking ground over which we had to carry our line; and how Mr. Holdsworth and I had gone for our mid-day meals—for we had to stay here for two days and a night—to a pretty village hard by, Heathbridge proper; and how I hoped we should often have to go there, for the shaking, uncertain ground was puzzling our engineers—one end of the line going up as soon as the other was weighted down. (I had no thought for the shareholders' interests, as may be seen; we had to make a new line on firmer ground before the junction railway was completed.) I told all this at great length, thankful to fill up my paper. By return letter, I heard that a second-cousin of my mother's was married to the Independent minister of Hornby, Ebenezer Holman by name, and lived at Heathbridge proper; the very Heathbridge I had described, or so my mother believed, for she had never seen her cousin Phillis Green, who was something of an heiress (my father believed), being her father's only child, and old Thomas Green had owned an estate of near upon fifty acres, which must have come to his daughter. My mother's feeling of kinship seemed to have been strongly stirred by the mention of Heathbridge; for my father said she desired me, if ever I went thither again, to make inquiry for the Reverend Ebenezer Holman; and if indeed he lived there, I was further to ask if he had not married one Phillis Green; and if both these questions were answered in the affirmative, I was to go and introduce myself as the only child of Margaret Manning, born Moneypenny. I was enraged at myself for having named Heathbridge at all, when I found what it was drawing down upon me. One Independent minister, as I said to myself, was enough for any man; and here I knew (that is to say, I had been catechized on Sabbath mornings by) Mr. Dawson, our minister at home; and I had had to be civil to old Peters at Eltham, and behave myself for five hours running whenever he asked me to tea at his house; and now, just as I felt the free air blowing about me up at Heathbridge, I was to ferret out another minister, and I should perhaps have to be catechized by him, or else asked to tea at his house. Besides, I did not like pushing myself upon strangers, who perhaps had never heard of my mother's name, and such an odd name as it was—Moneypenny; and if they had, had never cared more for her than she had for them, apparently, until this unlucky mention of Heathbridge. Still, I would not disobey my parents in such a trifle, however irksome it might be. So the next time our business took me to Heathbridge, and we were dining in the little sanded inn-parlour, I took the opportunity of Mr. Holdsworth's being out of the room, and asked the questions which I was bidden to ask of the rosy-cheeked maid. I was either unintelligible or she was stupid; for she said she did not know, but would ask master; and of course the landlord came in to understand what it was I wanted to know; and I had to bring out all my stammering inquiries before Mr. Holdsworth, who would never have attended to them, I dare say, if I had not blushed, and blundered, and made such a fool of myself.

"Yes," the landlord said, "the Hope Farm was in Heathbridge proper, and the owner's name was Holman, and he was an Independent minister, and, as far as the landlord could tell, his wife's Christian name was Phillis, anyhow her maiden name was Green."

"Relations of yours?" asked Mr. Holdsworth.

"No, sir—only my mother's second-cousins. Yes, I suppose they are relations. But I never saw them in my life."

"The Hope Farm is not a stone's throw from here," said the officious landlord, going to the window. "If you carry your eye over yon bed of hollyhocks, over the damson-trees in the orchard yonder, you may see a stack of queer-like stone chimneys. Them is the Hope Farm chimneys; it's an old place, though Holman keeps it in good order."

Mr. Holdsworth had risen from the table with more promptitude than I had, and was standing by the window, looking. At the landlord's last words, he turned round, smiling—"It is not often that parsons know how to keep land in order, is it?"

"Beg pardon, sir, but I must speak as I find; and Minister Holman—we call the Church clergyman here 'parson,' sir; he would be a bit jealous if he heard a Dissenter called parson—Minister Holman knows what he's about as well as e'er a farmer in the neighbourhood. He gives up five days a week to his own work, and two to the Lord's; and it is difficult to say which he works hardest at. He spends Saturday and Sunday a-writing sermons and a-visiting his flock at Hornby; and at five o'clock on Monday morning he'll be guiding his plough in the Hope Farm yonder just as well as if he could neither read nor write. But your dinner will be getting cold, gentlemen."

So we went back to table. After a while, Mr. Holdsworth broke the silence: "If I were you, Manning, I'd look up these relations of yours. You can go and see what they're like while we're waiting for Dobson's estimates, and I'll smoke a cigar in the garden meanwhile."

"Thank you, sir. But I don't know them, and I don't think I want to know them."

"What did you ask all those questions for, then?" said he, looking quickly up at me. He had no notion of doing or saying things without a purpose. I did not answer, so he continued, "Make up your mind, and go off and see what this farmer-minister is like, and come back and tell me—I should like to hear."

I was so in the habit of yielding to his authority, or influence, that I never thought of resisting, but went on my errand, though I remember feeling as if I would rather have had my head cut off. The landlord, who had evidently taken an interest in the event of our discussion in a way that country landlords have, accompanied me to the house-door, and gave me repeated directions, as if I was likely to miss my way in two hundred yards. But I listened to him, for I was glad of the delay, to screw up my courage for the effort of facing unknown people and introducing myself. I went along the lane, I recollect, switching at all the taller roadside weeds, till, after a turn or two, I found myself close in front of the Hope Farm. There was a garden between the house and the shady, grassy lane; I afterwards found that this garden was called the court; perhaps because there was a low wall round it, with an iron railing on the top of the wall, and two great gates between pillars crowned with stone balls for a state entrance to the flagged path leading up to the front door. It was not the habit of the place to go in either by these great gates or by the front door; the gates, indeed, were locked, as I found, though the door stood wide open. I had to go round by a side-path lightly worn on a broad grassy way, which led past the court-wall, past a horse-mount, half covered with stone-crop and the little wild yellow fumitory, to another door—"the curate," as I found it was termed by the master of the house, while the front door, "handsome and all for show," was termed the "rector." I knocked with my hand upon the "curate" door; a tall girl, about my own age, as I thought, came and opened it, and stood there silent, waiting to know my errand. I see her now—cousin Phillis. The westering sun shone full upon her, and made a slanting stream of light into the room within. She was dressed in dark blue cotton of some kind; up to her throat, down to her wrists, with a little frill of the same wherever it touched her white skin. And such a white skin as it was! I have never seen the like. She had light hair, nearer yellow than any other colour. She looked me steadily in the face with large, quiet eyes, wondering, but untroubled by the sight of a stranger. I thought it odd that so old, so full-grown as she was, she should wear a pinafore over her gown.

Before I had quite made up my mind what to say in reply to her mute inquiry of what I wanted there, a woman's voice called out, "Who is it, Phillis? If it is any one for butter-milk send them round to the back door."

I thought I could rather speak to the owner of that voice than to the girl before me; so I passed her, and stood at the entrance of a room hat in hand, for this side-door opened straight into the hall or house-place where the family sate when work was done. There was a brisk little woman of forty or so ironing some huge muslin cravats under the light of a long vine-shaded casement window. She looked at me distrustfully till I began to speak. "My name is Paul Manning," said I; but I saw she did not know the name. "My mother's name was Moneypenny," said I, "Margaret Moneypenny."

"And she married one John Manning, of Birmingham," said Mrs. Holman, eagerly.

"And you'll be her son. Sit down! I am right glad to see you. To think of your being Margaret's son! Why, she was almost a child not so long ago. Well, to be sure, it is five-and-twenty years ago. And what brings you into these parts?"

She sate down herself, as if oppressed by her curiosity as to all the five-and-twenty years that had passed by since she had seen my mother. Her daughter Phillis took up her knitting—a long grey worsted man's stocking, I remember—and knitted away without looking at her work. I felt that the steady gaze of those deep grey eyes was upon me, though once, when I stealthily raised mine to hers, she was examining something on the wall above my head.

When I had answered all my cousin Holman's questions, she heaved a long breath, and said, "To think of Margaret Moneypenny's boy being in our house! I wish the minister was here. Phillis, in what field is thy father today?"

"In the five-acre; they are beginning to cut the corn."

"He'll not like being sent for, then, else I should have liked you to have seen the minister. But the five-acre is a good step off. You shall have a glass of wine and a bit of cake before you stir from this house, though. You're bound to go, you say, or else the minister comes in mostly when the men have their four o'clock."

"I must go—I ought to have been off before now."

"Here, then, Phillis, take the keys." She gave her daughter some whispered directions, and Phillis left the room.

"She is my cousin, is she not?" I asked. I knew she was, but somehow I wanted to talk of her, and did not know how to begin.

"Yes—Phillis Holman. She is our only child—now."

Either from that "now," or from a strange momentary wistfulness in her eyes, I knew that there had been more children, who were now dead.

"How old is cousin Phillis?" said I, scarcely venturing on the new name, it seemed too prettily familiar for me to call her by it; but cousin Holman took no notice of it, answering straight to the purpose.

"Seventeen last May-day; but the minister does not like to hear me calling it May-day," said she, checking herself with a little awe. "Phillis was seventeen on the first day of May last," she repeated in an emended edition.

"And I am nineteen in another month," thought I, to myself; I don't know why. Then Phillis came in, carrying a tray with wine and cake upon it.

"We keep a house-servant," said cousin Holman, "but it is churning day, and she is busy." It was meant as a little proud apology for her daughter's being the handmaiden.

"I like doing it, mother," said Phillis, in her grave, full voice.

I felt as if I were somebody in the Old Testament—who, I could not recollect—being served and waited upon by the daughter of the host. Was I like Abraham's servant, when Rebekah gave him to drink at the well? I thought Isaac had not gone the pleasantest way to work in winning him a wife. But Phillis never thought about such things. She was a stately, gracious young woman, in the dress and with the simplicity of a child.

As I had been taught, I drank to the health of my newfound cousin and her husband; and then I ventured to name my cousin Phillis with a little bow of my head towards her; but I was too awkward to look and see how she took my compliment. "I must go now," said I, rising.

Neither of the women had thought of sharing in the wine; cousin Holman had broken a bit of cake for form's sake.

"I wish the minister had been within," said his wife, rising too. Secretly I was very glad he was not. I did not take kindly to ministers in those days, and I thought he must be a particular kind of man, by his objecting to the term May-day. But before I went, cousin Holman made me promise that I would come back on the Saturday following and spend Sunday with them; when I should see something of "the minister."

"Come on Friday, if you can," were her last words as she stood at the curate-door, shading her eyes from the sinking sun with her hand. Inside the house sate cousin Phillis, her golden hair, her dazzling complexion, lighting up the corner of the vine-shadowed room. She had not risen when I bade her good-by; she had looked at me straight as she said her tranquil words of farewell.

I found Mr. Holdsworth down at the line, hard at work superintending. As soon as he had a pause, he said, "Well, Manning, what are the new cousins like? How do preaching and farming seem to get on together? If the minister turns out to be practical as well as reverend, I shall begin to respect him."

But he hardly attended to my answer, he was so much more occupied with directing his work-people. Indeed, my answer did not come very readily; and the most distinct part of it was the mention of the invitation that had been given me.

"Oh, of course you can go—and on Friday, too, if you like; there is no reason why not this week; and you've done a long spell of work this time, old fellow." I thought that I did not want to go on Friday; but when the day came, I found that I should prefer going to staying away, so I availed myself of Mr. Holdsworth's permission, and went over to Hope Farm some time in the afternoon, a little later than my last visit. I found the "curate" open to admit the soft September air, so tempered by the warmth of the sun, that it was warmer out of doors than in, although the wooden log lay smouldering in front of a heap of hot ashes on the hearth. The vine-leaves over the window had a tinge more yellow, their edges were here and there scorched and browned; there was no ironing about, and cousin Holman sate just outside the house, mending a shirt. Phillis was at her knitting indoors: it seemed as if she had been at it all the week. The manyspeckled fowls were pecking about in the farmyard beyond, and the milk-cans glittered with brightness, hung out to sweeten. The court was so full of flowers that they crept out upon the low-covered wall and horse-mount, and were even to be found self-sown upon the turf that bordered the path to the back of the house. I fancied that my Sunday coat was scented for days afterwards by the bushes of sweetbriar and the fraxinella that perfumed the air. From time to time cousin Holman put her hand into a covered basket at her feet, and threw handsful of corn down for the pigeons that cooed and fluttered in the air around, in expectation of this treat.

I had a thorough welcome as soon as she saw me. "Now this is kind— this is right down friendly," shaking my hand warmly. "Phillis, your cousin Manning is come!"

"Call me Paul, will you?" said I; "they call me so at home, and Manning in the office."

"Well, Paul, then. Your room is all ready for you, Paul, for, as I said to the minister, 'I'll have it ready whether he comes on Friday or not.'" And the minister said he must go up to the Ashfield whether you were to come or not; but he would come home betimes to see if you were here. I'll show you to your room, and you can wash the dust off a bit."

After I came down, I think she did not quite know what to do with me; or she might think that I was dull; or she might have work to do in which I hindered her; for she called Phillis, and bade her put on her bonnet, and go with me to the Ashfield, and find father. So we set off, I in a little flutter of a desire to make myself agreeable, but wishing that my companion were not quite so tall; for she was above me in height. While I was wondering how to begin our conversation, she took up the words.

"I suppose, cousin Paul, you have to be very busy at your work all day long in general."

"Yes, we have to be in the office at half-past eight; and we have an hour for dinner, and then we go at it again till eight or nine."

"Then you have not much time for reading."

"No," said I, with a sudden consciousness that I did not make the most of what leisure I had.

"No more have I. Father always gets an hour before going a-field in the mornings, but mother does not like me to get up so early."

"My mother is always wanting me to get up earlier when I am at home."

"What time do you get up?"

"Oh!—ah!—sometimes half-past six: not often though"; for I remembered only twice that I had done so during the past summer.

She turned her head and looked at me.

"Father is up at three; and so was mother till she was ill. I should like to be up at four."

"Your father up at three! Why, what has he to do at that hour?"

"What has he not to do? He has his private exercise in his own room; he always rings the great bell which calls the men to milking; he rouses up Betty, our maid; as often as not he gives the horses their feed before the man is up—for Jem, who takes care of the horses, is an old man; and father is always loth to disturb him; he looks at the calves, and the shoulders, heels, traces, chaff, and corn before the horses go a-field; he has often to whip-cord the plough-whips; he sees the hogs fed; he looks into the swill-tubs, and writes his orders for what is wanted for food for man and beast; yes, and for fuel, too. And then, if he has a bit of time to spare, he comes in and reads with me—but only English; we keep Latin for the evenings, that we may have time to enjoy it; and then he calls in the men to breakfast, and cuts the boys' bread and cheese; and sees their wooden bottles filled, and sends them off to their work;—and by this time it is half-past six, and we have our breakfast. There is father," she exclaimed, pointing out to me a man in his shirt-sleeves, taller by the head than the other two with whom he was working. We only saw him through the leaves of the ash-trees growing in the hedge, and I thought I must be confusing the figures, or mistaken: that man still looked like a very powerful labourer, and had none of the precise demureness of appearance which I had always imagined was the characteristic of a minister. It was the Reverend Ebenezer Holman, however. He gave us a nod as we entered the stubble-field; and I think he would have come to meet us but that he was in the middle of giving some directions to his men. I could see that Phillis was built more after his type than her mother's. He, like his daughter, was largely made, and of a fair, ruddy complexion, whereas hers was brilliant and delicate. His hair had been yellow or sandy, but now was grizzled. Yet his grey hairs betokened no failure in strength. I never saw a more powerful man—deep chest, lean flanks, well-planted head. By this time we were nearly up to him; and he interrupted himself and stepped forwards; holding out his hand to me, but addressing Phillis.

"Well, my lass, this is cousin Manning, I suppose. Wait a minute, young man, and I'll put on my coat, and give you a decorous and formal welcome. But—Ned Hall, there ought to be a water-furrow across this land: it's a nasty, stiff, clayey, dauby bit of ground, and thou and I must fall to, come next Monday—I beg your pardon, cousin Manning—and there's old Jem's cottage wants a bit of thatch; you can do that job tomorrow while I am busy." Then, suddenly changing the tone of his deep bass voice to an odd suggestion of chapels and preachers, he added. "Now, I will give out the psalm, 'Come all harmonious tongues,' to be sung to 'Mount Ephraim' tune."

He lifted his spade in his hand, and began to beat time with it; the two labourers seemed to know both words and music, though I did not; and so did Phillis: her rich voice followed her father's as he set the tune; and the men came in with more uncertainty, but still harmoniously. Phillis looked at me once or twice with a little surprise at my silence; but I did not know the words. There we five stood, bareheaded, excepting Phillis, in the tawny stubble-field, from which all the shocks of corn had not yet been carried—a dark wood on one side, where the woodpigeons were cooing; blue distance seen through the ash-trees on the other. Somehow, I think that if I had known the words, and could have sung, my throat would have been choked up by the feeling of the unaccustomed scene.

The hymn was ended, and the men had drawn off before I could stir. I saw the minister beginning to put on his coat, and looking at me with friendly inspection in his gaze, before I could rouse myself.

"I dare say you railway gentlemen don't wind up the day with singing a psalm together," said he; "but it is not a bad practice—not a bad practice. We have had it a bit earlier today for hospitality's sake—that's all."

I had nothing particular to say to this, though I was thinking a great deal. From time to time I stole a look at my companion. His coat was black, and so was his waistcoat; neckcloth he had none, his strong full throat being bare above the snow-white shirt. He wore drab-coloured knee-breeches, grey worsted stockings (I thought I knew the maker), and strong-nailed shoes. He carried his hat in his hand, as if he liked to feel the coming breeze lifting his hair. After a while, I saw that the father took hold of the daughter's hand, and so, they holding each other, went along towards home. We had to cross a lane. In it were two little children, one lying prone on the grass in a passion of crying, the other standing stock still, with its finger in its mouth, the large tears slowly rolling down its cheeks for sympathy. The cause of their distress was evident; there was a broken brown pitcher, and a little pool of spilt milk on the road.

"Hollo! Hollo! What's all this?" said the minister. "Why, what have you been about, Tommy," lifting the little petticoated lad, who was lying sobbing, with one vigorous arm. Tommy looked at him with surprise in his round eyes, but no affright—they were evidently old acquaintants.

"Mammy's jug!" said he, at last, beginning to cry afresh.

"Well! and will crying piece mammy's jug, or pick up spilt milk? How did you manage it, Tommy?"

"He" (jerking his head at the other) "and me was running races."

"Tommy said he could beat me," put in the other.

"Now, I wonder what will make you two silly lads mind, and not run races again with a pitcher of milk between you," said the minister, as if musing. "I might flog you, and so save mammy the trouble; for I dare say she'll do it if I don't." The fresh burst of whimpering from both showed the probability of this.

"Or I might take you to the Hope Farm, and give you some more milk; but then you'd be running races again, and my milk would follow that to the ground, and make another white pool. I think the flogging would be best— don't you?"

"We would never run races no more," said the elder of the two.

"Then you'd not be boys; you'd be angels."

"No, we shouldn't."

"Why not?"

They looked into each other's eyes for an answer to this puzzling question. At length, one said, "Angels is dead folk."

"Come; we'll not get too deep into theology. What do you think of my lending you a tin can with a lid to carry the milk home in? That would not break, at any rate; though I would not answer for the milk not spilling if you ran races. That's it!"

He had dropped his daughter's hand, and now held out each of his to the little fellows. Phillis and I followed, and listened to the prattle which the minister's companions now poured out to him, and which he was evidently enjoying. At a certain point, there was a sudden burst of the tawny, ruddy-evening landscape. The minister turned round and quoted a line or two of Latin.

"It's wonderful," said he, "how exactly Virgil has hit the enduring epithets, nearly two thousand years ago, and in Italy; and yet how it describes to a T what is now lying before us in the parish of Heathbridge, county ———, England."

"I dare say it does," said I, all aglow with shame, for I had forgotten the little Latin I ever knew.

The minister shifted his eyes to Phillis's face; it mutely gave him back the sympathetic appreciation that I, in my ignorance, could not bestow.

"Oh! this is worse than the catechism," thought I; "that was only remembering words."

"Phillis, lass, thou must go home with these lads, and tell their mother all about the race and the milk. Mammy must always know the truth," now speaking to the children. "And tell her, too, from me that I have got the best birch rod in the parish; and that if she ever thinks her children want a flogging she must bring them to me, and, if I think they deserve it, I'll give it them better than she can." So Phillis led the children towards the dairy, somewhere in the back yard, and I followed the minister in through the "curate" into the house-place. "Their mother," said he, "is a bit of a vixen, and apt to punish her children without rhyme or reason. I try to keep the parish rod as well as the parish bull."

He sate down in the three-cornered chair by the fire-side, and looked around the empty room.

"Where's the missus?" said he to himself. But she was there in a minute; it was her regular plan to give him his welcome home—by a look, by a touch, nothing more—as soon as she could after his return, and he had missed her now. Regardless of my presence, he went over the day's doings to her; and then, getting up, he said he must go and make himself "reverend," and that then we would have a cup of tea in the parlour. The parlour was a large room with two casemented windows on the other side of the broad flagged passage leading from the rector-door to the wide staircase, with its shallow, polished oaken steps, on which no carpet was ever laid. The parlour-floor was covered in the middle by a home-made carpeting of needlework and list. One or two quaint family pictures of the Holman family hung round the walls; the fire-grate and irons were much ornamented with brass; and on a table against the wall between the windows, a great beau-pot of flowers was placed upon the folio volumes of Matthew Henry's Bible. It was a compliment to me to use this room, and I tried to be grateful for it; but we never had our meals there after that first day, and I was glad of it; for the large house-place, living room, dining-room, whichever you might like to call it, was twice as comfortable and cheerful. There was a rug in front of the great large fire-place, and an oven by the grate, and a crook, with the kettle hanging from it, over the bright wood-fire; everything that ought to be black and polished in that room was black and Polished; and the flags, and window-curtains, and such things as were to be white and clean, were just spotless in their purity. Opposite to the fire-place, extending the whole length of the room, was an oaken shovel-board, with the right incline for a skilful player to send the weights into the prescribed space. There were baskets of white work about, and a small shelf of books hung against the wall, books used for reading, and not for propping up a beau-pot of flowers. I took down one or two of those books once when I was left alone in the house-place on the first evening—Virgil, Caesar, a Greek grammar—oh, dear! ah, me! and Phillis Holman's name in each of them! I shut them up, and put them back in their places, and walked as far away from the bookshelf as I could. Yes, and I gave my cousin Phillis a wide berth, as though she was sitting at her work quietly enough, and her hair was looking more golden, her dark eyelashes longer, her round pillar of a throat whiter than ever. We had done tea, and we had returned into the house-place that the minister might smoke his pipe without fear of contaminating the drab damask window-curtains of the parlour. He had made himself "reverend" by putting on one of the voluminous white muslin neckcloths that I had seen cousin Holman ironing that first visit I had paid to the Hope Farm, and by making one or two other unimportant changes in his dress. He sate looking steadily at me, but whether he saw me or not I cannot tell. At the time I fancied that he did, and was gauging me in some unknown fashion in his secret mind. Every now and then he took his pipe out of his mouth, knocked out the ashes, and asked me some fresh question. As long as these related to my acquirements or my reading, I shuffled uneasily and did not know what to answer. By-and-by he got round to the more practical subject of railroads, and on this I was more at home. I really had taken an interest in my work; nor would Mr. Holdsworth, indeed, have kept me in his employment if I had not given my mind as well as my time to it; and I was, besides, full of the difficulties which beset us just then, owing to our not being able to find a steady bottom on the Heathbridge moss, over which we wished to carry our line. In the midst of all my eagerness in speaking about this, I could not help being struck with the extreme pertinence of his questions. I do not mean that he did not show ignorance of many of the details of engineering: that was to have been expected; but on the premises he had got hold of; he thought clearly and reasoned logically. Phillis—so like him as she was both in body and mind—kept stopping at her work and looking at me, trying to fully understand all that I said. I felt she did; and perhaps it made me take more pains in using clear expressions, and arranging my words, than I otherwise should.

"She shall see I know something worth knowing, though it mayn't be her dead-and-gone languages," thought I.

"I see," said the minister, at length. "I understand it all. You've a clear, good head of your own, my lad—choose how you came by it."

"From my father," said I, proudly. "Have you not heard of his discovery of a new method of shunting? It was in the Gazette. It was patented. I thought every one had heard of Manning's patent winch."

"We don't know who invented the alphabet," said he, half smiling, and taking up his pipe.

"No, I dare say not, sir," replied I, half offended; "that's so long ago." Puff—puff—puff.

"But your father must be a notable man. I heard of him once before; and it is not many a one fifty miles away whose fame reaches Heathbridge."

"My father is a notable man, sir. It is not me that says so; it is Mr. Holdsworth, and—and everybody."

"He is right to stand up for his father," said cousin Holman, as if she were pleading for me.

I chafed inwardly, thinking that my father needed no one to stand up for him. He was man sufficient for himself.

"Yes—he is right," said the minister, placidly. "Right, because it comes from his heart—right, too, as I believe, in point of fact. Else there is many a young cockerel that will stand upon a dunghill and crow about his father, by way of making his own plumage to shine. I should like to know thy father," he went on, turning straight to me, with a kindly, frank look in his eyes.

But I was vexed, and would take no notice. Presently, having finished his pipe, he got up and left the room. Phillis put her work hastily down, and went after him. In a minute or two she returned, and sate down again. Not long after, and before I had quite recovered my good temper, he opened the door out of which he had passed, and called to me to come to him. I went across a narrow stone passage into a strange, many-cornered room, not ten feet in area, part study, part counting house, looking into the farm-yard; with a desk to sit at, a desk to stand at, a Spittoon, a set of shelves with old divinity books upon them; another, smaller, filled with books on farriery, farming, manures, and such subjects, with pieces of paper containing memoranda stuck against the whitewashed walls with wafers, nails, pins, anything that came readiest to hand; a box of carpenter's tools on the floor, and some manuscripts in short-hand on the desk.

He turned round, half laughing. "That foolish girl of mine thinks I have vexed you"—putting his large, powerful hand on my shoulder. "'Nay,' says I, 'kindly meant is kindly taken'—is it not so?"

"It was not quite, sir," replied I, vanquished by his manner; "but it shall be in future."

"Come, that's right. You and I shall be friends. Indeed, it's not many a one I would bring in here. But I was reading a book this morning, and I could not make it out; it is a book that was left here by mistake one day; I had subscribed to Brother Robinson's sermons; and I was glad to see this instead of them, for sermons though they be, they're . . . well, never mind! I took 'em both, and made my old coat do a bit longer; but all's fish that comes to my net. I have fewer books than leisure to read them, and I have a prodigious big appetite. Here it is."

It was a volume of stiff mechanics, involving many technical terms, and some rather deep mathematics. These last, which would have puzzled me, seemed easy enough to him; all that he wanted was the explanations of the technical words, which I could easily give.

While he was looking through the book to find the places where he had been puzzled, my wandering eye caught on some of the papers on the wall, and I could not help reading one, which has stuck by me ever since. At first, it seemed a kind of weekly diary; but then I saw that the seven days were portioned out for special prayers and intercessions: Monday for his family, Tuesday for enemies, Wednesday for the Independent churches, Thursday for all other churches, Friday for persons afflicted, Saturday for his own soul, Sunday for all wanderers and sinners, that they might be brought home to the fold.

We were called back into the house-place to have supper. A door opening into the kitchen was opened; and all stood up in both rooms, while the minister, tall, large, one hand resting on the spread table, the other lifted up, said, in the deep voice that would have been loud had it not been so full and rich, but without the peculiar accent or twang that I believe is considered devout by some people, "Whether we eat or drink, or whatsoever we do, let us do all to the glory of God."

The supper was an immense meat-pie. We of the house-place were helped first; then the minister hit the handle of his buck-horn carving-knife on the table once, and said—

"Now or never," which meant, did any of us want any more; and when we had all declined, either by silence or by words, he knocked twice with his knife on the table, and Betty came in through the open door, and carried off the great dish to the kitchen, where an old man and a young one, and a help-girl, were awaiting their meal.

"Shut the door, if you will," said the minister to Betty.

"That's in honour of you," said cousin Holman, in a tone of satisfaction, as the door was shut. "When we've no stranger with us, the minister is so fond of keeping the door open, and talking to the men and maids, just as much as to Phillis and me.

"It brings us all together like a household just before we meet as a household in prayer," said he, in explanation. "But to go back to what we were talking about—can you tell me of any simple book on dynamics that I could put in my pocket, and study a little at leisure times in the day?"

"Leisure times, father?" said Phillis, with a nearer approach to a smile than I had yet seen on her face.

"Yes; leisure times, daughter. There is many an odd minute lost in waiting for other folk; and now that railroads are coming so near us, it behoves us to know something about them."

I thought of his own description of his "prodigious big appetite" for learning. And he had a good appetite of his own for the more material victual before him. But I saw, or fancied I saw, that he had some rule for himself in the matter both of food and drink.

As soon as supper was done the household assembled for prayer. It was a long impromptu evening prayer; and it would have seemed desultory enough had I not had a glimpse of the kind of day that preceded it, and so been able to find a clue to the thoughts that preceded the disjointed utterances; for he kept there kneeling down in the centre of a circle, his eyes shut, his outstretched hands pressed palm to palm—sometimes with a long pause of silence was anything else he wished to "lay before the Lord!" (to use his own expression)—before he concluded with the blessing. He prayed for the cattle and live creatures, rather to my surprise; for my attention had begun to wander, till it was recalled by the familiar words.

And here I must not forget to name an odd incident at the conclusion of the prayer, and before we had risen from our knees (indeed before Betty was well awake, for she made a practice of having a sound nap, her weary head lying on her stalwart arms); the minister, still kneeling in our midst, but with his eyes wide open, and his arms dropped by his side, spoke to the elder man, who turned round on his knees to attend. "John, didst see that Daisy had her warm mash tonight; for we must not neglect the means, John—two quarts of gruel, a spoonful of ginger, and a gill of beer—the poor beast needs it, and I fear it slipped out of my mind to tell thee; and here was I asking a blessing and neglecting the means, which is a mockery," said he, dropping his voice.

Before we went to bed he told me he should see little or nothing more of me during my visit, which was to end on Sunday evening, as he always gave up both Saturday and Sabbath to his work in the ministry. I remembered that the landlord at the inn had told me this on the day when I first inquired about these new relations of mine; and I did not dislike the opportunity which I saw would be afforded me of becoming more acquainted with cousin Holman and Phillis, though I earnestly hoped that the latter would not attack me on the subject of the dead languages.

I went to bed, and dreamed that I was as tall as cousin Phillis, and had a sudden and miraculous growth of whisker, and a still more miraculous acquaintance with Latin and Greek. Alas! I wakened up still a short, beardless lad, with "tempus fugit" for my sole remembrance of the little Latin I had once learnt. While I was dressing, a bright thought came over me: I could question cousin Phillis, instead of her questioning me, and so manage to keep the choice of the subjects of conversation in my own power.

Early as it was, every one had breakfasted, and my basin of bread and milk was put on the oven-top to await my coming down. Every one was gone about their work. The first to come into the house-place was Phillis with a basket of eggs. Faithful to my resolution, I asked—

"What are those?"

She looked at me for a moment, and then said gravely—

"Potatoes!"

"No! they are not," said I. "They are eggs. What do you mean by saying they are potatoes?"

"What do you mean by asking me what they were, when they were plain to be seen?" retorted she.

We were both getting a little angry with each other.

"I don't know. I wanted to begin to talk to you; and I was afraid you would talk to me about books as you did yesterday. I have not read much; and you and the minister have read so much."

"I have not," said she. "But you are our guest; and mother says I must make it pleasant to you. We won't talk of books. What must we talk about?"

"I don't know. How old are you?"

"Seventeen last May. How old are you?"

"I am nineteen. Older than you by nearly two years," said I, drawing myself up to my full height.

"I should not have thought you were above sixteen," she replied, as quietly as if she were not saying the most provoking thing she possibly could. Then came a pause.

"What are you going to do now?" asked I.

"I should be dusting the bed-chambers; but mother said I had better stay and make it pleasant to you," said she, a little plaintively, as if dusting rooms was far the easiest task.

"Will you take me to see the live-stock? I like animals, though I don't know much about them."

"Oh, do you? I am so glad! I was afraid you would not like animals, as you did not like books."

I wondered why she said this. I think it was because she had begun to fancy all our tastes must be dissimilar. We went together all through the farm-yard; we fed the poultry, she kneeling down with her pinafore full of corn and meal, and tempting the little timid, downy chickens upon it, much to the anxiety of the fussy ruffled hen, their mother. She called to the pigeons, who fluttered down at the sound of her voice. She and I examined the great sleek cart-horses; sympathized in our dislike of pigs; fed the calves; coaxed the sick cow, Daisy; and admired the others out at pasture; and came back tired and hungry and dirty at dinner-time, having quite forgotten that there were such things as dead languages, and consequently capital friends.

PART II

Cousin Holman gave me the weekly county newspaper to read aloud to her, while she mended stockings out of a high piled-up basket, Phillis helping her mother. I read and read, unregardful of the words I was uttering, thinking of all manner of other things; of the bright colour of Phillis's hair, as the afternoon sun fell on her bending head; of the silence of the house, which enabled me to hear the double tick of the old clock which stood half-way up the stairs; of the variety of inarticulate noises which cousin Holman made while I read, to show her sympathy, wonder, or horror at the newspaper intelligence. The tranquil monotony of that hour made me feel as if I had lived for ever, and should live for ever droning out paragraphs in that warm sunny room, with my two quiet hearers, and the curled-up pussy cat sleeping on the hearth-rug, and the clock on the house-stairs perpetually clicking out the passage of the moments. By-and-by Betty the servant came to the door into the kitchen, and made a sign to Phillis, who put her half-mended stocking down, and went away to the kitchen without a word. Looking at cousin Holman a minute or two afterwards, I saw that she had dropped her chin upon her breast, and had fallen fast asleep. I put the newspaper down, and was nearly following her example, when a waft of air from some unseen source, slightly opened the door of communication with the kitchen, that Phillis must have left unfastened; and I saw part of her figure as she sate by the dresser, peeling apples with quick dexterity of finger, but with repeated turnings of her head towards some book lying on the dresser by her. I softly rose, and as softly went into the kitchen, and looked over her shoulder; before she was aware of my neighbourhood, I had seen that the book was in a language unknown to me, and the running title was *L'Inferno*. Just as I was making out the relationship of this word to "infernal," she started and turned round, and, as if continuing her thought as she spoke, she sighed out—

"Oh! it is so difficult! Can you help me?" putting her finger below a line.

"Me! I! I don't even know what language it is in!"

"Don't you see it is Dante?" she replied, almost petulantly; she did so want help.

"Italian, then?" said I, dubiously; for I was not quite sure.

"Yes. And I do so want to make it out. Father can help me a little, for he knows Latin; but then he has so little time."

"You have not much, I should think, if you have often to try and do two things at once, as you are doing now."

"Oh! that's nothing! Father bought a heap of old books cheap. And I knew something about Dante before; and I have always liked Virgil so much. Paring apples is nothing, if I could only make out this old Italian. I wish you knew it."

"I wish I did," said I, moved by her impetuosity of tone. "If, now, only Mr. Holdsworth were here; he can speak Italian like anything, I believe."

"Who is Mr. Holdsworth?" said Phillis, looking up.

"Oh, he's our head engineer. He's a regular first-rate fellow! He can do anything;" my hero-worship and my pride in my chief all coming into play.

Besides, if I was not clever and book-learned myself, it was something to belong to some one who was.

"How is it that he speaks Italian?" asked Phillis.

"He had to make a railway through Piedmont, which is in Italy, I believe; and he had to talk to all the workmen in Italian; and I have heard him say that for nearly two years he had only Italian books to read in the queer outlandish places he was in."

"Oh, dear!" said Phillis; "I wish—" and then she stopped. I was not quite sure whether to say the next thing that came into my mind; but I said it.

"Could I ask him anything about your book, or your difficulties?"

She was silent for a minute or so, and then she made reply—

"No! I think not. Thank you very much, though. I can generally puzzle a thing out in time. And then, perhaps, I remember it better than if some one had helped me. I'll put it away now, and you must move off, for I've got to make the paste for the pies; we always have a cold dinner on Sabbaths."

"But I may stay and help you, mayn't I?"

"Oh, yes; not that you can help at all, but I like to have you with me." I was both flattered and annoyed at this straightforward avowal. I was pleased that she liked me; but I was young coxcomb enough to have wished to play the lover, and I was quite wise enough to perceive that if she had any idea of the kind in her head she would never have spoken out so frankly. I comforted myself immediately, however, by finding out that the grapes were sour. A great tall girl in a pinafore, half a head taller than I was, reading books that I had never heard of, and talking about them too, as of far more interest than any mere personal subjects; that was the last day on which I ever thought of my dear cousin Phillis as the possible mistress of my heart and life. But we were all the greater friends for this idea being utterly put away and buried out of sight.

Late in the evening the minister came home from Hornby. He had been calling on the different members of his flock; and unsatisfactory work it had proved to him, it seemed from the fragments that dropped out of his thoughts into his talk.

"I don't see the men; they are all at their business, their shops, or their warehouses; they ought to be there. I have no fault to find with them; only if a pastor's teaching or words of admonition are good for anything, they are needed by the men as much as by the women."

"Cannot you go and see them in their places of business, and remind them of their Christian privileges and duties, minister?" asked cousin Holman, who evidently thought that her husband's words could never be out of place.

"No!" said he, shaking his head. "I judge them by myself. If there are clouds in the sky, and I am getting in the hay just ready for loading, and rain sure to come in the night, I should look ill upon brother Robinson if he came into the field to speak about serious things."

"But, at any rate, father, you do good to the women, and perhaps they repeat what you have said to them to their husbands and children?"

"It is to be hoped they do, for I cannot reach the men directly; but the women are apt to tarry before coming to me, to put on ribbons and gauds; as if they could hear the message I bear to them best in their smart clothes. Mrs. Dobson today—Phillis, I am thankful thou dost not care for the vanities of dress!" Phillis reddened a little as she said, in a low humble voice—

"But I do, father, I'm afraid. I often wish I could wear pretty-coloured ribbons round my throat like the squire's daughters."

"It's but natural, minister!" said his wife; "I'm not above liking a silk gown better than a cotton one myself!"

"The love of dress is a temptation and a snare," said he, gravely. "The true adornment is a meek and quiet spirit. And, wife," said he, as a sudden thought crossed his mind, "in that matter I, too, have sinned. I wanted to ask you, could we not sleep in the grey room, instead of our own?"

"Sleep in the grey room?—change our room at this time o' day?" cousin Holman asked, in dismay.

"Yes," said he. "It would save me from a daily temptation to anger. Look at my chin!" he continued; "I cut it this morning—I cut it on Wednesday when I was shaving; I do not know how many times I have cut it of late, and all from impatience at seeing Timothy Cooper at his work in the yard."

"He's a downright lazy tyke!" said cousin Holman. "He's not worth his wage. There's but little he can do, and what he can do, he does badly."

"True," said the minister. "He is but, so to speak, a half-wit; and yet he has got a wife and children."

"More shame for him!"

"But that is past change. And if I turn him off; no one else will take him on. Yet I cannot help watching him of a morning as he goes sauntering about his work in the yard; and I watch, and I watch, till the old Adam rises strong within me at his lazy ways, and some day, I am afraid, I shall go down and send him about his business—let alone the way in which he makes me cut myself while I am shaving—and then his wife and children will starve. I wish we could move to the grey room."

I do not remember much more of my first visit to the Hope Farm. We went to chapel in Heathbridge, slowly and decorously walking along the lanes, ruddy and tawny with the colouring of the coming autumn. The minister walked a little before us, his hands behind his back, his head bent down, thinking about the discourse to be delivered to his people, cousin Holman said; and we spoke low and quietly, in order not to interrupt his thoughts.

But I could not help noticing the respectful greetings which he received from both rich and poor as we went along; greetings which he acknowledged with a kindly wave of his hand, but with no words of reply. As we drew near the town, I could see some of the young fellows we met cast admiring looks on Phillis; and that made me look too. She had on a white gown, and a short black silk cloak, according to the fashion of the day. A straw bonnet with brown ribbon strings; that was all. But what her dress wanted in colour, her sweet bonny face had. The walk made her cheeks bloom like the rose; the very whites of her eyes had a blue tinge in them, and her dark eyelashes brought out the depth of the blue eyes themselves. Her yellow hair was put away as straight as its natural curliness would allow. If she did not perceive the admiration she excited, I am sure cousin Holman did; for she looked as fierce and as proud as ever her quiet face could look, guarding her treasure, and yet glad to perceive that others could see that it was a treasure. That afternoon I had to return to Eltham to be ready for the next day's work. I found out afterwards that the minister and his family were all "exercised in spirit," as to whether they did well in asking me to repeat my visits at the Hope Farm, seeing that of necessity I must return to Eltham on the Sabbath-day. However, they did go on asking me, and I went on visiting them, whenever my other engagements permitted me, Mr. Holdsworth being in this case, as in all, a kind and indulgent friend. Nor did my new acquaintances oust him from my strong regard and admiration. I had room in my heart for all, I am happy to say, and as far as I can remember, I kept praising each to the other in a manner which, if I had been an older man, living more amongst people of the world, I should have thought unwise, as well as a little ridiculous. It was unwise, certainly, as it was almost sure to cause disappointment if ever they did become acquainted; and perhaps it was ridiculous, though I do not think we any of us thought it so at the time. The minister used to listen to my accounts of Mr. Holdsworth's many accomplishments and various adventures in travel with the truest interest, and most kindly good faith; and Mr. Holdsworth in return liked to hear about my visits to the farm, and description of my cousin's life there—liked it, I mean, as much as he liked anything that was merely narrative, without leading to action.

So I went to the farm certainly, on an average, once a month during that autumn; the course of life there was so peaceful and quiet, that I can only remember one small event, and that was one that I think I took more notice of than any one else: Phillis left off wearing the pinafores that had always been so obnoxious to me; I do not know why they were banished, but on one of my visits I found them replaced by pretty linen aprons in the morning, and a black silk one in the afternoon. And the blue cotton gown became a brown stuff one as winter drew on; this sounds like some book I once read, in which a migration from the blue bed to the brown was spoken of as a great family event.

Towards Christmas my dear father came to see me, and to consult Mr. Holdsworth about the improvement which has since been known as "Manning's driving wheel." Mr. Holdsworth, as I think I have before said, had a very great regard for my father, who had been employed in the same great machine-shop in which Mr. Holdsworth had served his apprenticeship; and he and my father had many mutual jokes about one of these gentlemen-apprentices who used to set about his smith's work in white wash-leather gloves, for fear of spoiling his hands. Mr. Holdsworth often spoke to me about my father as having the same kind of genius for mechanical invention as that of George Stephenson, and my father had come over now to consult him about several improvements, as well as an offer of partnership. It was a great pleasure to me to see the mutual regard of these two men. Mr. Holdsworth, young, handsome, keen, well-dressed, an object of admiration to all the youth of Eltham; my father, in his decent but unfashionable Sunday clothes, his plain, sensible face full of hard lines, the marks of toil and thought—his hands, blackened beyond the power of soap and water by years of labour in the foundry; speaking a strong Northern dialect, while Mr. Holdsworth had a long soft drawl in his voice, as many of the Southerners have, and was reckoned in Eltham to give himself airs.

Although most of my father's leisure time was occupied with conversations about the business I have mentioned, he felt that he ought not to leave Eltham without going to pay his respects to the relations who had been so kind to his son. So he and I ran up on an engine along the incomplete line as far as Heathbridge, and went, by invitation, to spend a day at the farm.

It was odd and yet pleasant to me to perceive how these two men, each having led up to this point such totally dissimilar lives, seemed to come together by instinct, after one quiet straight look into each other's faces. My father was a thin, wiry man of five foot seven; the minister was a broad-shouldered, fresh-coloured man of six foot one; they were neither of them great talkers in general—perhaps the minister the most so—but they spoke much to each other. My father went into the fields with the minister; I think I see him now, with his hands behind his back, listening intently to all explanations of tillage, and the different processes of farming; occasionally taking up an implement, as if unconsciously, and examining it with a critical eye, and now and then asking a question, which I could see was considered as pertinent by his companion. Then we returned to look at the cattle, housed and bedded in expectation of the snow-storm hanging black on the western horizon, and my father learned the points of a cow with as much attention as if he meant to turn farmer. He had his little book that he used for mechanical memoranda and measurements in his pocket, and he took it out to write down "straight back," small muzzle," "deep barrel," and I know not what else, under the head "cow." He was very critical on a turnip-cutting machine, the clumsiness of which first incited him to talk; and when we went into the house he sate thinking and quiet for a bit, while Phillis and her mother made the last preparations for tea, with a little unheeded apology from cousin Holman, because we were not sitting in the best parlour, which she thought might be chilly on so cold a night. I wanted nothing better than the blazing, crackling fire that sent a glow over all the house-place, and warmed the snowy flags under our feet till they seemed to have more heat than the crimson rug right in front of the fire. After tea, as Phillis and I were talking together very happily, I heard an irrepressible exclamation from cousin Holman—

"Whatever is the man about!"

And on looking round, I saw my father taking a straight burning stick out of the fire, and, after waiting for a minute, and examining the charred end to see if it was fitted for his purpose, he went to the hard-wood dresser, scoured to the last pitch of whiteness and cleanliness, and began drawing with the stick; the best substitute for chalk or charcoal within his reach, for his pocket-book pencil was not strong or bold enough for his purpose. When he had done, he began to explain his new model of a turnip-cutting machine to the minister, who had been watching him in silence all the time. Cousin Holman had, in the meantime, taken a duster out of a drawer, and, under pretence of being as much interested as her husband in the drawing, was secretly trying on an outside mark how easily it would come off, and whether it would leave her dresser as white as before. Then Phillis was sent for the book on dynamics about which I had been consulted during my first visit, and my father had to explain many difficulties, which he did in language as clear as his mind, making drawings with his stick wherever they were needed as illustrations, the minister sitting with his massive head resting on his hands, his elbows on the table, almost unconscious of Phillis, leaning over and listening greedily, with her hand on his shoulder, sucking in information like her father's own daughter. I was rather sorry for cousin Holman; I had been so once or twice before; for do what she would, she was completely unable even to understand the pleasure her husband and daughter took in intellectual pursuits, much less to care in the least herself for the pursuits themselves, and was thus unavoidably thrown out of some of their interests. I had once or twice thought she was a little jealous of her own child, as a fitter companion for her husband than she was herself; and I fancied the minister himself was aware of this feeling, for I had noticed an occasional sudden change of subject, and a tenderness of appeal in his voice as he spoke to her, which always made her look contented and peaceful again. I do not think that Phillis ever perceived these little shadows; in the first place, she had such complete reverence for her parents that she listened to them both as if they had been St Peter and St Paul; and besides, she was always too much engrossed with any matter in hand to think about other people's manners and looks.

This night I could see, though she did not, how much she was winning on my father. She asked a few questions which showed that she had followed his explanations up to that point; possibly, too, her unusual beauty might have something to do with his favourable impression of her; but he made no scruple of expressing his admiration of her to her father and mother in her absence from the room; and from that evening I date a project of his which came out to me a day or two afterwards, as we sate in my little three-cornered room in Eltham. "Paul," he began, "I never thought to be a rich man; but I think it's coming upon me. Some folk are making a deal of my new machine (calling it by its technical name), and Ellison, of the Borough Green Works, has gone so far as to ask me to be his partner."

"Mr. Ellison the Justice!—who lives in King Street? why, he drives his carriage!" said I, doubting, yet exultant.

"Ay, lad, John Ellison. But that's no sign that I shall drive my carriage. Though I should like to save thy mother walking, for she's not so young as she was. But that's a long way off; anyhow. I reckon I should start with a third profit. It might be seven hundred, or it might be more. I should like to have the power to work out some fancies o' mine. I care for that much more than for th' brass. And Ellison has no lads; and by nature the business would come to thee in course o' time. Ellison's lasses are but bits o' things, and are not like to come by husbands just yet; and when they do, maybe they'll not be in the mechanical line. It will be an opening for thee, lad, if thou art steady. Thou'rt not great shakes, I know, in th' inventing line; but many a one gets on better without having fancies for something he does not see and never has seen. I'm right down glad to see that mother's cousins are such uncommon folk for sense and goodness. I have taken the minister to my heart like a brother; and she is a womanly quiet sort of a body. And I'll tell you frank, Paul, it will be a happy day for me if ever you can come and tell me that Phillis Holman is like to be my daughter. I think if that lass had not a penny, she would be the making of a man; and she'll have yon house and lands, and you may be her match yet in fortune if all goes well."

I was growing as red as fire; I did not know what to say, and yet I wanted to say something; but the idea of having a wife of my own at some future day, though it had often floated about in my own head, sounded so strange when it was thus first spoken about by my father. He saw my confusion, and half smiling said—

"Well, lad, what dost say to the old father's plans? Thou art but young, to be sure; but when I was thy age, I would ha' given my right hand if I might ha' thought of the chance of wedding the lass I cared for—"

"My mother?" asked I, a little struck by the change of his tone of voice.

"No! not thy mother. Thy mother is a very good woman—none better. No! the lass I cared for at nineteen ne'er knew how I loved her, and a year or two after and she was dead, and ne'er knew. I think she would ha' been glad to ha' known it, poor Molly; but I had to leave the place where we lived for to try to earn my bread and I meant to come back but before ever I did, she was dead and gone: I ha' never gone there since. But if you fancy Phillis Holman, and can get her to fancy you, my lad, it shall go different with you, Paul, to what it did with your father."

I took counsel with myself very rapidly, and I came to a clear conclusion. "Father," said I, "if I fancied Phillis ever so much, she would never fancy me. I like her as much as I could like a sister; and she likes me as if I were her brother—her younger brother."

I could see my father's countenance fall a little.

"You see she's so clever she's more like a man than a woman—she knows Latin and Greek."

"She'd forget 'em, if she'd a houseful of children," was my father's comment on this.

"But she knows many a thing besides, and is wise as well as learned; she has been so much with her father. She would never think much of me, and I should like my wife to think a deal of her husband."

"It is not just book-learning or the want of it as makes a wife think much or little of her husband," replied my father, evidently unwilling to give up a project which had taken deep root in his mind. "It's a something I don't rightly know how to call it—if he's manly, and sensible, and straightforward; and I reckon you're that, my boy."

"I don't think I should like to have a wife taller than I am, father," said I, smiling; he smiled too, but not heartily.

"Well," said he, after a pause. "It's but a few days I've been thinking of it, but I'd got as fond of my notion as if it had been a new engine as I'd been planning out. Here's our Paul, thinks I to myself, a good sensible breed o' lad, as has never vexed or troubled his mother or me; with a good business opening out before him, age nineteen, not so bad-looking, though perhaps not to call handsome, and here's his cousin, not too near cousin, but just nice, as one may say; aged seventeen, good and true, and well brought up to work with her hands as well as her head; a scholar—but that can't be helped, and is more her misfortune than her fault, seeing she is the only child of scholar—and as I said afore, once she's a wife and a she'll forget it all, I'll be bound—with a good fortune in land and house when it shall please the Lord to take her parents to himself; with eyes like poor Molly's for beauty, a colour that comes and goes on a milk-white skin, and as pretty a mouth—,

"Why, Mr. Manning, what fair lady are you describing?" asked Mr. Holdsworth, who had come quickly and suddenly upon our tete-a-tete, and had caught my father's last words as he entered the room. Both my father and I felt rather abashed; it was such an odd subject for us to be talking about; but my father, like a straightforward simple man as he was, spoke out the truth.

"I've been telling Paul of Ellison's offer, and saying how good an opening it made for him—"

"I wish I'd as good," said Mr. Holdsworth. "But has the business a 'pretty mouth'?"

"You're always so full of your joking, Mr. Holdsworth," said my father. "I was going to say that if he and his cousin Phillis Holman liked to make it up between them, I would put no spoke in the wheel."

"Phillis Holman!" said Mr. Holdsworth. "Is she the daughter of the minister-farmer out at Heathbridge? Have I been helping on the course of true love by letting you go there so often? I knew nothing of it."

"There is nothing to know," said I, more annoyed than I chose to show. "There is no more true love in the case than may be between the first brother and sister you may choose to meet. I have been telling father she would never think of me; she's a great deal taller and cleverer; and I'd rather be taller and more learned than my wife when I have one."

"And it is she, then, that has the pretty mouth your father spoke about? I should think that would be an antidote to the cleverness and learning. But I ought to apologize for breaking in upon your last night; I came upon business to your father."

And then he and my father began to talk about many things that had no interest for me just then, and I began to go over again my conversation with my father. The more I thought about it, the more I felt that I had spoken truly about my feelings towards Phillis Holman. I loved her dearly as a sister, but I could never fancy her as my wife. Still less could I think of her ever—yes, condescending, that is the word—condescending to marry me. I was roused from a reverie on what I should like my possible wife to be, by hearing my father's warm praise of the minister, as a most unusual character; how they had got back from the diameter of driving-wheels to the subject of the Holmans I could never tell; but I saw that my father's weighty praises were exciting some curiosity in Mr. Holdsworth's mind; indeed, he said, almost in a voice of reproach—

"Why, Paul, you never told me what kind of a fellow this minister-cousin of yours was!"

"I don't know that I found out, sir," said I. "But if I had, I don't think you'd have listened to me, as you have done to my father."

"No! most likely not, old fellow," replied Mr. Holdsworth, laughing. And again and afresh I saw what a handsome pleasant clear face his was; and though this evening I had been a bit put out with him—through his sudden coming, and his having heard my father's open-hearted confidence—my hero resumed all his empire over me by his bright merry laugh.

And if he had not resumed his old place that night, he would have done so the next day, when, after my father's departure, Mr. Holdsworth spoke about him with such just respect for his character, such ungrudging admiration of his great mechanical genius, that I was compelled to say, almost unawares—

"Thank you, sir. I am very much obliged to you."

"Oh, you're not at all. I am only speaking the truth. Here's a Birmingham workman, self-educated, one may say—having never associated with stimulating minds, or had what advantages travel and contact with the world may be supposed to afford—working out his own thoughts into steel and iron, making a scientific name for himself—a fortune, if it pleases him to work for money—and keeping his singleness of heart, his perfect simplicity of manner; it puts me out of patience to think of my expensive schooling, my travels hither and thither, my heaps of scientific books, and I have done nothing to speak of. But it's evidently good blood; there's that Mr. Holman, that cousin of yours, made of the same stuff."

"But he's only cousin because he married my mother's second cousin," said I.

"That knocks a pretty theory on the head, and twice over, too. I should like to make Holman's acquaintance."

"I am sure they would be so glad to see you at Hope Farm," said I, eagerly. "In fact, they've asked me to bring you several times: only I thought you would find it dull."

"Not at all. I can't go yet though, even if you do get me an invitation; for the —— Company want me to go to the —— Valley, and look over the ground a bit for them, to see if it would do for a branch line; it's a job which may take me away for some time; but I shall be backwards and forwards, and you're quite up to doing what is needed in my absence; the only work that may be beyond you is keeping old Jevons from drinking." He went on giving me directions about the management of the men employed on the line, and no more was said then, or for several months, about his going to Hope Farm. He went off into —— Valley, a dark overshadowed dale, where the sun seemed to set behind the hills before four o'clock on midsummer afternoon. Perhaps it was this that brought on the attack of low fever which he had soon after the beginning of the new year; he was very ill for many weeks, almost many months; a married sister—his only relation, I think—came down from

London to nurse him, and I went over to him when I could, to see him, and give him "masculine news," as he called it; reports of the progress of the line, which, I am glad to say, I was able to carry on in his absence, in the slow gradual way which suited the company best, while trade was in a languid state, and money dear in the market. Of course, with this occupation for my scanty leisure, I did not often go over to Hope Farm. Whenever I did go, I met with a thorough welcome; and many inquiries were made as to Holdsworth's illness, and the progress of his recovery.

At length, in June I think it was, he was sufficiently recovered to come back to his lodgings at Eltham, and resume part at least of his work. His sister, Mrs. Robinson, had been obliged to leave him some weeks before, owing to some epidemic amongst her own children. As long as I had seen Mr. Holdsworth in the rooms at the little inn at Hensleydale, where I had been accustomed to look upon him as an invalid, I had not been aware of the visible shake his fever had given to his health. But, once back in the old lodgings, where I had always seen him so buoyant, eloquent, decided, and vigorous in former days, my spirits sank at the change in one whom I had always regarded with a strong feeling of admiring affection. He sank into silence and despondency after the least exertion; he seemed as if he could not make up his mind to any action, or else that, when it was made up, he lacked strength to carry out his purpose. Of course, it was but the natural state of slow convalescence, after so sharp an illness; but, at the time, I did not know this, and perhaps I represented his state as more serious than it was to my kind relations at Hope Farm; who, in their grave, simple, eager way, immediately thought of the only help they could give.

"Bring him out here," said the minister. "Our air here is good to a proverb; the June days are fine; he may loiter away his time in the hay-field, and the sweet smells will be a balm in themselves—better than physic."

"And," said cousin Holman, scarcely waiting for her husband to finish his sentence, "tell him there is new milk and fresh eggs to be had for the asking; it's lucky Daisy has just calved, for her milk is always as good as other cows' cream; and there is the plaid room with the morning sun all streaming in." Phillis said nothing, but looked as much interested in the project as any one. I took it upon myself. I wanted them to see him; him to know them. I proposed it to him when I got home. He was too languid after the day's fatigue, to be willing to make the little exertion of going amongst strangers; and disappointed me by almost declining to accept the invitation I brought. The next morning it was different; he apologized for his ungraciousness of the night before; and told me that he would get all things in train, so as to be ready to go out with me to Hope Farm on the following Saturday.

"For you must go with me, Manning," said he; "I used to be as impudent a fellow as need be, and rather liked going amongst strangers, and making my way; but since my illness I am almost like a girl, and turn hot and cold with shyness, as they do, I fancy."

So it was fixed. We were to go out to Hope Farm on Saturday afternoon; and it was also understood that if the air and the life suited Mr. Holdsworth, he was to remain there for a week or ten days, doing what work he could at that end of the line, while I took his place at Eltham to the best of my ability. I grew a little nervous, as the time drew near, and wondered how the brilliant Holdsworth would agree with the quiet quaint family of the minister; how they would like him, and many of his half-foreign ways. I tried to prepare him, by telling him from time to time little things about the goings-on at Hope Farm.

"Manning," said he, "I see you don't think I am half good enough for your friends. Out with it, man."

"No," I replied, boldly. "I think you are good; but I don't know if you are quite of their kind of goodness."

"And you've found out already that there is greater chance of disagreement between two 'kinds of goodness,' each having its own idea of right, than between a given goodness and a moderate degree of naughtiness—which last often arises from an indifference to right?"

"I don't know. I think you're talking metaphysics, and I am sure that is bad for you."

" 'When a man talks to you in a way that you don't understand about a thing which he does not understand, them's metaphysics.' You remember the clown's definition, don't you, Manning?"

"No, I don't," said I. "But what I do understand is, that you must go to bed; and tell me at what time we must start tomorrow, that I may go to Hepworth, and get those letters written we were talking about this morning."

"Wait till tomorrow, and let us see what the day is like," he answered, with such languid indecision as showed me he was over-fatigued. So I went my way. The morrow was blue and sunny, and beautiful; the very perfection of an early summer's day. Mr. Holdsworth was all impatience to be off into the country; morning had brought back his freshness and strength, and consequent eagerness to be doing. I was afraid we were going to my cousin's farm rather too early, before they would expect us; but what could I do with such a restless vehement man as Holdsworth was that morning? We came down upon the Hope Farm before the dew was off the grass on the shady side of the lane; the great house-dog was loose, basking in the sun, near the closed side door. I was surprised at this door being shut, for all summer long it was open from morning to night; but it was only on latch. I opened it, Rover watching me with half-suspicious, half-trustful eyes. The room was empty.

"I don't know where they can be," said I. "But come in and sit down while I go and look for them. You must be tired."

"Not I. This sweet balmy air is like a thousand tonics. Besides, this room is hot, and smells of those pungent wood-ashes. What are we to do?"

"Go round to the kitchen. Betty will tell us where they are." So we went round into the farmyard, Rover accompanying us out of a grave sense of duty. Betty was washing out her milk-pans in the cold bubbling spring-water that constantly trickled in and out of a stone trough. In such weather as this most of her kitchen-work was done out of doors.

"Eh, dear!" said she, "the minister and missus is away at Hornby! They ne'er thought of your coming so betimes! The missus had some errands to do, and she thought as she'd walk with the minister and be back by dinner-time."

"Did not they expect us to dinner?" said I.

"Well, they did, and they did not, as I may say. Missus said to me the cold lamb would do well enough if you did not come; and if you did I was to put on a chicken and some bacon to boil; and I'll go do it now, for it is hard to boil bacon enough."

"And is Phillis gone, too?" Mr. Holdsworth was making friends with Rover.

"No! She's just somewhere about. I reckon you'll find her in the kitchen-garden, getting peas.

"Let us go there," said Holdsworth, suddenly leaving off his play with the dog. So I led the way into the kitchen-garden. It was in the first promise of a summer profuse in vegetables and fruits. Perhaps it was not so much cared for as other parts of the property; but it was more attended to than most kitchen-gardens belonging to farm-houses. There were borders of flowers along each side of the gravel walks; and there was an old sheltering wall on the north side covered with tolerably choice fruit-trees; there was a slope down to the fish-pond at the end, where there were great strawberry-beds; and raspberry-bushes and rose-bushes grew wherever there was a space; it seemed a chance which had been planted. Long rows of peas stretched at right angles from the main walk, and I saw Phillis stooping down among them, before she saw us. As soon as she heard our cranching steps on the gravel, she stood up, and shading her eyes from the sun, recognized us. She was quite still for a moment, and then came slowly towards us, blushing a little from evident shyness. I had never seen Phillis shy before.

"This is Mr. Holdsworth, Phillis," said I, as soon as I had shaken hands with her. She glanced up at him, and then looked down, more flushed than ever at his grand formality of taking his hat off and bowing; such manners had never been seen at Hope Farm before.

"Father and mother are out. They will be so sorry; you did not write, Paul, as you said you would."

"It was my fault," said Holdsworth, understanding what she meant as well as if she had put it more fully into words. "I have not yet given up all the privileges of an invalid; one of which is indecision. Last night, when your cousin asked me at what time we were to start, I really could not make up my mind."

Phillis seemed as if she could not make up her mind as to what to do with us. I tried to help her—

"Have you finished getting peas?" taking hold of the half-filled basket she was unconsciously holding in her hand; "or may we stay and help you?"

"If you would. But perhaps it will tire you, sir?" added she, speaking now to Holdsworth.

"Not a bit," said he. "It will carry me back twenty years in my life, when I used to gather peas in my grandfather's garden. I suppose I may eat a few as I go along?"

"Certainly, sir. But if you went to the strawberry-beds you would find some strawberries ripe, and Paul can show you where they are."

"I am afraid you distrust me. I can assure you I know the exact fulness at which peas should be gathered. I take great care not to pluck them when they are unripe. I will not be turned off, as unfit for my work." This was a style of half-joking talk that Phillis was not accustomed to. She looked for a moment as if she would have liked to defend herself from the playful charge of distrust made against her, but she ended by not saying a word. We all plucked our peas in busy silence for the next five minutes. Then Holdsworth lifted himself up from between the rows, and said, a little wearily,

"I am afraid I must strike work. I am not as strong as I fancied myself." Phillis was full of penitence immediately. He did, indeed, look pale; and she blamed herself for having allowed him to help her.

"It was very thoughtless of me. I did not know—I thought, perhaps, you really liked it. I ought to have offered you something to eat, sir! Oh, Paul, we have gathered quite enough; how stupid I was to forget that Mr. Holdsworth had been ill!" And in a blushing hurry she led the way towards the house. We went in, and she moved a heavy cushioned chair forwards, into which Holdsworth was only too glad to sink. Then with deft and quiet speed she brought in a little tray, wine, water, cake, home-made bread, and newly-churned butter. She stood by in some anxiety till, after bite and sup, the colour returned to Mr. Holdsworth's face, and he would fain have made us some laughing apologies for the fright he had given us. But then Phillis drew back from her innocent show of care and interest, and relapsed into the cold shyness habitual to her when she was first thrown into the company of strangers. She brought out the last week's county paper (which Mr. Holdsworth had read five days ago), and then quietly withdrew; and then he subsided into languor, leaning back and shutting his eyes as if he would go to sleep. I stole into the kitchen after Phillis; but she had made the round of the corner of the house outside, and I found her sitting on the horse-mount, with her basket of peas, and a basin into which she was shelling them. Rover lay at her feet, snapping now and then at the flies. I went to her, and tried to help her, but somehow the sweet crisp young peas found their way more frequently into my mouth than into the basket, while we talked together in a low tone, fearful of being overheard through the open casements of the house-place in which Holdsworth was resting.

"Don't you think him handsome?" asked I.

"Perhaps—yes—I have hardly looked at him," she replied "But is not he very like a foreigner?"

"Yes, he cuts his hair foreign fashion," said I.

"I like an Englishman to look like an Englishman."

"I don't think he thinks about it. He says he began that way when he was in Italy, because everybody wore it so, and it is natural to keep it on in England."

"Not if he began it in Italy because everybody there wore it so. Everybody here wears it differently."

I was a little offended with Phillis's logical fault-finding with my friend; and I determined to change the subject.

"When is your mother coming home?"

"I should think she might come any time now; but she had to go and see Mrs. Morton, who was ill, and she might be kept, and not be home till dinner. Don't you think you ought to go and see how Mr. Holdsworth is going on, Paul? He may be faint again."

I went at her bidding; but there was no need for it. Mr. Holdsworth was up, standing by the window, his hands in his pockets; he had evidently been watching us. He turned away as I entered.

"So that is the girl I found your good father planning for your wife, Paul, that evening when I interrupted you! Are you of the same coy mind still? It did not look like it a minute ago."

"Phillis and I understand each other," I replied, sturdily. "We are like brother and sister. She would not have me as a husband if there was not another man in the world; and it would take a deal to make me think of her—as my father wishes" (somehow I did not like to say "as a wife"), "but we love each other dearly."

"Well, I am rather surprised at it—not at your loving each other in a brother-and-sister kind of way—but at your finding it so impossible to fall in love with such a beautiful woman." Woman! beautiful woman! I had thought of Phillis as a comely but awkward girl; and I could not banish the pinafore from my mind's eye when I tried to picture her to myself. Now I turned, as Mr. Holdsworth had done, to look at her again out of the window: she had just finished her task, and was standing up, her back to us, holding the basket, and the basin in it, high in air, out of Rover's reach, who was giving vent to his delight at the probability of a change of place by glad leaps and barks, and snatches at what he imagined to be a withheld prize. At length she grew tired of their mutual play, and with a feint of striking him, and a "Down, Rover! do hush!" she looked towards the window where we were standing, as if to reassure herself that no one had been disturbed by the noise, and seeing us, she coloured all over, and hurried away, with Rover still curving in sinuous lines about her as she walked.

"I should like to have sketched her," said Mr. Holdsworth, as he turned away. He went back to his chair, and rested in silence for a minute or two. Then he was up again.

"I would give a good deal for a book," he said. "It would keep me quiet." He began to look round; there were a few volumes at one end of the shovel-board. "Fifth volume of Matthew Henry's Commentary," said he, reading their titles aloud. "Housewife's complete Manual; Berridge on Prayer; L'Inferno—Dante!" in great surprise. "Why, who reads this?"

"I told you Phillis read it. Don't you remember? She knows Latin and Greek, too."

"To be sure! I remember! But somehow I never put two and two together. That quiet girl, full of household work, is the wonderful scholar, then, that put you to rout with her questions when you first began to come here. To be sure, "Cousin Phillis!" What's here: a paper with the hard, obsolete words written out. I wonder what sort of a dictionary she has got. Baretti won't tell her all these words. Stay! I have got a pencil here. I'll write down the most accepted meanings, and save her a little trouble."

So he took her book and the paper back to the little round table, and employed himself in writing explanations and definitions of the words which had troubled her. I was not sure if he was not taking a liberty: it did not quite please me, and yet I did not know why. He had only just done, and replaced the paper in the book, and put the latter back in its place, when I heard the sound of wheels stopping in the lane, and looking out, I saw cousin Holman getting out of a neighbour's gig, making her little curtsey of acknowledgment, and then coming towards the house. I went to meet her.

"Oh, Paul!" said she, "I am so sorry I was kept; and then Thomas Dobson said if I would wait a quarter of an hour he would—But where's your friend Mr. Holdsworth? I hope he is come?"

Just then he came out, and with his pleasant cordial manner took her hand, and thanked her for asking him to come out here to get strong.

"I'm sure I am very glad to see you, sir. It was the minister's thought. I took it into my head you would be dull in our quiet house, for Paul says you've been such a great traveller; but the minister said that dulness would perhaps suit you while you were but ailing, and that I was to ask Paul to be here as much as he could. I hope you'll find yourself happy with us, I'm sure, sir. Has Phillis given you something to eat and drink, I wonder? there's a deal in eating a little often, if one has to get strong after an illness." And then she began to question him as to the details of his indisposition in her simple, motherly way. He seemed at once to understand her, and to enter into friendly relations with her. It was not quite the same in the evening when the minister came home. Men have always a little natural antipathy to get over when they first meet as strangers. But in this case each was disposed to make an effort to like the other; only each was to each a specimen of an unknown class. I had to leave the Hope Farm on Sunday afternoon, as I had Mr. Holdsworth's work as well as my own to look to in Eltham; and I was not at all sure how things would go on during the week that Holdsworth was to remain on his visit; I had been once or twice in hot water already at the near clash of opinions between the minister and my much-vaunted friend. On the Wednesday I received a short note from Holdsworth; he was going to stay on, and return with me on the following Sunday, and he wanted me to send him a certain list of books, his theodolite, and other surveying instruments, all of which could easily be conveyed down the line to Heathbridge. I went to his lodgings and picked out the books. Italian, Latin, trigonometry; a pretty considerable parcel they made, besides the implements. I began to be curious as to the general progress of affairs at Hope Farm, but I could not go over till the Saturday. At Heathbridge I found Holdsworth, come to meet me. He was looking quite a different man to what I had left him; embrowned, sparkles in his eyes, so languid before. I told him how much stronger he looked.

"Yes!" said he. "I am fidging fain to be at work again. Last week I dreaded the thoughts of my employment: now I am full of desire to begin. This week in the country has done wonders for me."

"You have enjoyed yourself, then?"

"Oh! it has been perfect in its way. Such a thorough country life! and yet removed from the dulness which I always used to fancy accompanied country life, by the extraordinary intelligence of the minister. I have fallen into calling him 'the minister,' like everyone else."

"You get on with him, then?" said I. "I was a little afraid."

"I was on the verge of displeasing him once or twice, I fear, with random assertions and exaggerated expressions, such as one always uses with other people, and thinks nothing of; but I tried to check myself when I saw how it shocked the good man; and really it is very wholesome exercise, this trying to make one's words represent one's thoughts, instead of merely looking to their effect on others."

"Then you are quite friends now?" I asked.

"Yes, thoroughly; at any rate as far as I go. I never met with a man with such a desire for knowledge. In information, as far as it can be gained from books, he far exceeds me on most subjects; but then I have travelled and seen—Were not you surprised at the list of things I sent for?"

"Yes; I thought it did not promise much rest."

"Oh! some of the books were for the minister, and some for his daughter. (I call her Phillis to myself, but I use euphuisms in speaking about her to others. I don't like to seem familiar, and yet Miss Holman is a term I have never heard used.)"

"I thought the Italian books were for her."

"Yes! Fancy her trying at Dante for her first book in Italian! I had a capital novel by Manzoni, I Promessi Sposi, just the thing for a beginner; and if she must still puzzle out Dante, my dictionary is far better than hers."

"Then she found out you had written those definitions on her list of words?"

"Oh! yes"—with a smile of amusement and pleasure. He was going to tell me what had taken place, but checked himself.

"But I don't think the minister will like your having given her a novel to read?"

"Pooh! What can be more harmless? Why make a bugbear of a word? It is as pretty and innocent a tale as can be met with. You don't suppose they take Virgil for gospel?"

By this time we were at the farm. I think Phillis gave me a warmer welcome than usual, and cousin Holman was kindness itself. Yet somehow I felt as if I had lost my place, and that Holdsworth had taken it. He knew all the ways of the house; he was full of little filial attentions to cousin Holman; he treated Phillis with the affectionate condescension of an elder brother; not a bit more; not in any way different. He questioned me about the progress of affairs in Eltham with eager interest.

"Ah!" said cousin Holman, "you'll be spending a different kind of time next week to what you have done this! I can see how busy you'll make yourself! But if you don't take care you'll be ill again, and have to come back to our quiet ways of going on.

"Do you suppose I shall need to be ill to wish to come back here?" he answered, warmly. "I am only afraid you have treated me so kindly that I shall always be turning up on your hands."

"That's right," she replied. "Only don't go and make yourself ill by over-work. I hope you'll go on with a cup of new milk every morning, for I am sure that is the best medicine; and put a teaspoonful of rum in it, if you like; many a one speaks highly of that, only we had no rum in the house." I brought with me an atmosphere of active life which I think he had begun to miss; and it was natural that he should seek my company, after his week of retirement. Once I saw Phillis looking at us as we talked together with a kind of wistful curiosity; but as soon as she caught my eye, she turned away, blushing deeply.

That evening I had a little talk with the minister. I strolled along the Hornby road to meet him; for Holdsworth was giving Phillis an Italian lesson, and cousin Holman had fallen asleep over her work. Somehow, and not unwillingly on my part, our talk fell on the friend whom I had introduced to the Hope Farm.

"Yes! I like him!" said the minister, weighing his words a little as he spoke. "I like him. I hope I am justified in doing it, but he takes hold of me, as it were; and I have almost been afraid lest he carries me away, in spite of my judgment."

"He is a good fellow; indeed he is," said I. "My father thinks well of him; and I have seen a deal of him. I would not have had him come here if I did not know that you would approve of him."

"Yes," (once more hesitating,) "I like him, and I think he is an upright man; there is a want of seriousness in his talk at times, but, at the same time, it is wonderful to listen to him! He makes Horace and Virgil living, instead of dead, by the stories he tells me of his sojourn in the very countries where they lived, and where to this day, he says—But it is like dram-drinking. I listen to him till I forget my duties, and am carried off my feet. Last Sabbath evening he led us away into talk on profane subjects ill befitting the day." By this time we were at the house, and our conversation stopped. But before the day was out, I saw the unconscious hold that my friend had got over all the family. And no wonder: he had seen so much and done so much as compared to them, and he told about it all so easily and naturally, and yet as I never heard any one else do; and his ready pencil was out in an instant to draw on scraps of paper all sorts of illustrations—modes of drawing up water in Northern Italy, wine-carts, buffaloes, stone-pines, I know not what. After we had all looked at these drawings, Phillis gathered them together, and took them. It is many years since I have seen thee, Edward Holdsworth, but thou wast a delightful fellow! Ay, and a good one too; though much sorrow was caused by thee!

PART III

Just after this I went home for a week's holiday. Everything was prospering there; my father's new partnership gave evident satisfaction to both parties. There was no display of increased wealth in our modest household; but my mother had a few extra comforts provided for her by her husband. I made acquaintance with Mr. and Mrs. Ellison, and first saw pretty Margaret Ellison, who is now my wife. When I returned to Eltham, I found that a step was decided upon, which had been in contemplation for some time; that Holdsworth and I should remove our quarters to Hornby; our daily presence, and as much of our time as possible, being required for the completion of the line at that end.

Of course this led to greater facility of intercourse with the Hope Farm people. We could easily walk out there after our day's work was done, and spend a balmy evening hour or two, and yet return before the summer's twilight had quite faded away. Many a time, indeed, we would fain have stayed longer—the open air, the fresh and pleasant country, made so agreeable a contrast to the close, hot town lodgings which I shared with Mr. Holdsworth; but early hours, both at eve and morn, were an imperative necessity with the minister, and he made no scruple at turning either or both of us out of the house directly after evening prayer, or "exercise," as he called it. The remembrance of many a happy day, and of several little scenes, comes back upon me as I think of that summer. They rise like pictures to my memory, and in this way I can date their succession; for I know that corn harvest must have come after hay-making, apple-gathering after corn-harvest.

The removal to Hornby took up some time, during which we had neither of us any leisure to go out to the Hope Farm. Mr. Holdsworth had been out there once during my absence at home. One sultry evening, when work was done, he proposed our walking out and paying the Holmans a visit. It so happened that I had omitted to write my usual weekly letter home in our press of business, and I wished to finish that before going out. Then he said that he would go, and that I could follow him if I liked. This I did in about an hour; the weather was so oppressive, I remember, that I took off my coat as I walked, and hung it over my arm. All the doors and windows at the farm were open when I arrived there, and every tiny leaf on the trees was still. The silence of the place was profound; at first I thought that it was entirely deserted; but just as I drew near the door I heard a weak sweet voice begin to sing; it was cousin Holman, all by herself in the house-place, piping up a hymn, as she knitted away in the clouded light. She gave me a kindly welcome, and poured out all the small domestic news of the fortnight past upon me, and, in return, I told her about my own people and my visit at home.

"Where were the rest?" at length I asked.

Betty and the men were in the field helping with the last load of hay, for the minister said there would be rain before the morning. Yes, and the minister himself, and Phillis, and Mr. Holdsworth, were all there helping. She thought that she herself could have done something; but perhaps she was the least fit

for hay-making of any one; and somebody must stay at home and take care
of the house, there were so many tramps about; if I had not had something
to do with the railroad she would have called them navvies. I asked her if she
minded being left alone, as I should like to go and help; and having her full
and glad permission to leave her alone, I went off, following her directions:
through the farmyard, past the cattle-pond, into the ashfield, beyond into the
higher field with two holly-bushes in the middle. I arrived there: there was
Betty with all the farming men, and a cleared field, and a heavily laden cart;
one man at the top of the great pile ready to catch the fragrant hay which the
others threw up to him with their pitchforks; a little heap of cast-off clothes
in a corner of the field (for the heat, even at seven o'clock, was insufferable),
a few cans and baskets, and Rover lying by them panting, and keeping watch.
Plenty of loud, hearty, cheerful talking; but no minister, no Phillis, no Mr.
Holdsworth. Betty saw me first, and understanding who it was that I was in
search of, she came towards me.

"They're out yonder—agait wi' them things o' Measter Holdsworth's."
So "out yonder" I went; out on to a broad upland common, full of red
sand-banks, and sweeps and hollows; bordered by dark firs, purple in the
coming shadows, but near at hand all ablaze with flowering gorse, or, as we
call it in the south, furze-bushes, which, seen against the belt of distant trees,
appeared brilliantly golden. On this heath, a little way from the field-gate, I
saw the three. I counted their heads, joined together in an eager group over
Holdsworth's theodolite. He was teaching the minister the practical art of
surveying and taking a level. I was wanted to assist, and was quickly set to
work to hold the chain. Phillis was as intent as her father; she had hardly time
to greet me, so desirous was she to hear some answer to her father's question.
So we went on, the dark clouds still gathering, for perhaps five minutes after
my arrival. Then came the blinding lightning and the rumble and quick-
following rattling peal of thunder right over our heads. It came sooner than
I expected, sooner than they had looked for: the rain delayed not; it came
pouring down; and what were we to do for shelter? Phillis had nothing on
but her indoor things—no bonnet, no shawl. Quick as the darting lightning
around us, Holdsworth took off his coat and wrapped it round her neck and
shoulders, and, almost without a word, hurried us all into such poor shelter
as one of the overhanging sand-banks could give. There we were, cowered
down, close together, Phillis innermost, almost too tightly packed to free her
arms enough to divest herself of the coat, which she, in her turn, tried to put
lightly over Holdsworth's shoulders. In doing so she touched his shirt.

"Oh, how wet you are!" she cried, in pitying dismay; "and you've hardly got
over your fever! Oh, Mr. Holdsworth, I am so sorry!" He turned his head a
little, smiling at her.

"If I do catch cold, it is all my fault for having deluded you into staying out here!" but she only murmured again, "I am so sorry." The minister spoke now. "It is a regular downpour. Please God that the hay is saved! But there is no likelihood of its ceasing, and I had better go home at once, and send you all some wraps; umbrellas will not be safe with yonder thunder and lightning."

Both Holdsworth and I offered to go instead of him; but he was resolved, although perhaps it would have been wiser if Holdsworth, wet as he already was, had kept himself in exercise. As he moved off, Phillis crept out, and could see on to the storm-swept heath. Part of Holdsworth's apparatus still remained exposed to all the rain. Before we could have any warning, she had rushed out of the shelter and collected the various things, and brought them back in triumph to where we crouched. Holdsworth had stood up, uncertain whether to go to her assistance or not. She came running back, her long lovely hair floating and dripping, her eyes glad and bright, and her colour freshened to a glow of health by the exercise and the rain.

"Now, Miss Holman, that's what I call wilful," said Holdsworth, as she gave them to him. "No, I won't thank you" (his looks were thanking her all the time). "My little bit of dampness annoyed you, because you thought I had got wet in your service; so you were determined to make me as uncomfortable as you were yourself. It was an unchristian piece of revenge!"

His tone of badinage (as the French call it) would have been palpable enough to any one accustomed to the world; but Phillis was not, and it distressed or rather bewildered her. "Unchristian" had to her a very serious meaning; it was not a word to be used lightly; and though she did not exactly understand what wrong it was that she was accused of doing, she was evidently desirous to throw off the imputation. At first her earnestness to disclaim unkind motives amused Holdsworth; while his light continuance of the joke perplexed her still more; but at last he said something gravely, and in too low a tone for me to hear, which made her all at once become silent, and called out her blushes. After a while, the minister came back, a moving mass of shawls, cloaks, and umbrellas. Phillis kept very close to her father's side on our return to the farm. She appeared to me to be shrinking away from Holdsworth, while he had not the slightest variation in his manner from what it usually was in his graver moods; kind, protecting, and thoughtful towards her. Of course, there was a great commotion about our wet clothes; but I name the little events of that evening now because I wondered at the time what he had said in that low voice to silence Phillis so effectually, and because, in thinking of their intercourse by the light of future events, that evening stands out with some prominence. I have said that after our removal to Hornby our communications with the farm became almost of daily occurrence. Cousin Holman and I were the two who had least to do with this intimacy. After

Mr. Holdsworth regained his health, he too often talked above her head in intellectual matters, and too often in his light bantering tone for her to feel quite at her ease with him. I really believe that he adopted this latter tone in speaking to her because he did not know what to talk about to a purely motherly woman, whose intellect had never been cultivated, and whose loving heart was entirely occupied with her husband, her child, her household affairs and, perhaps, a little with the concerns of the members of her husband's congregation, because they, in a way, belonged to her husband. I had noticed before that she had fleeting shadows of jealousy even of Phillis, when her daughter and her husband appeared to have strong interests and sympathies in things which were quite beyond her comprehension. I had noticed it in my first acquaintance with them, I say, and had admired the delicate tact which made the minister, on such occasions, bring the conversation back to such subjects as those on which his wife, with her practical experience of every-day life, was an authority; while Phillis, devoted to her father, unconsciously followed his lead, totally unaware, in her filial reverence, of his motive for doing so.

To return to Holdsworth. The minister had at more than one time spoken of him to me with slight distrust, principally occasioned by the suspicion that his careless words were not always those of soberness and truth. But it was more as a protest against the fascination which the younger man evidently exercised over the elder one more as it were to strengthen himself against yielding to this fascination—that the minister spoke out to me about this failing of Holdsworth's, as it appeared to him. In return Holdsworth was subdued by the minister's uprightness and goodness, and delighted with his clear intellect—his strong healthy craving after further knowledge. I never met two men who took more thorough pleasure and relish in each other's society. To Phillis his relation continued that of an elder brother: he directed her studies into new paths, he patiently drew out the expression of many of her thoughts, and perplexities, and unformed theories—scarcely ever now falling into the vein of banter which she was so slow to understand.

One day—harvest-time—he had been drawing on a loose piece of paper—sketching ears of corn, sketching carts drawn by bullocks and laden with grapes—all time talking with Phillis and me, cousin Holman putting in her not pertinent remarks, when suddenly he said to Phillis—

"Keep your head still; I see a sketch! I have often tried to draw your head from memory, and failed; but I think I can do it now. If I succeed I will give it to your mother. You would like a portrait of your daughter as Ceres, would you not, ma'am?"

"I should like a picture of her; yes, very much, thank you, Mr. Holdsworth; but if you put that straw in her hair," (he was holding some wheat ears above her passive head, looking at the effect with an artistic eye,) "you'll ruffle her hair. Phillis, my dear, if you're to have your picture taken, go up-stairs, and brush your hair smooth."

"Not on any account. I beg your pardon, but I want hair loosely flowing." He began to draw, looking intently at Phillis; I could see this stare of his discomposed her—her colour came and went, her breath quickened with the consciousness of his regard; at last, when he said, "Please look at me for a minute or two, I want to get in the eyes," she looked up at him, quivered, and suddenly got up and left the room. He did not say a word, but went on with some other part of the drawing; his silence was unnatural, and his dark cheek blanched a little. Cousin Holman looked up from her work, and put her spectacles down.

"What's the matter? Where is she gone?"

Holdsworth never uttered a word, but went on drawing. I felt obliged to say something; it was stupid enough, but stupidity was better than silence just then.

"I'll go and call her," said I. So I went into the hall, and to the bottom of the stairs; but just as I was going to call Phillis, she came down swiftly with her bonnet on, and saying, "I'm going to father in the five-acre," passed out by the open "rector," right in front of the house-place windows, and out at the little white side-gate. She had been seen by her mother and Holdsworth, as she passed; so there was no need for explanation, only cousin Holman and I had a long discussion as to whether she could have found the room too hot, or what had occasioned her sudden departure. Holdsworth was very quiet during all the rest of that day; nor did he resume the portrait-taking by his own desire, only at my cousin Holman's request the next time that he came; and then he said he should not require any more formal sittings for only such a slight sketch as he felt himself capable of making. Phillis was just the same as ever the next time I saw her after her abrupt passing me in the hall. She never gave any explanation of her rush out of the room.

So all things went on, at least as far as my observation reached at the time, or memory can recall now, till the great apple-gathering of the year. The nights were frosty, the mornings and evenings were misty, but at mid-day all was sunny and bright, and it was one mid-day that both of us being on the line near Heathbridge, and knowing that they were gathering apples at the farm, we resolved to spend the men's dinner-hour in going over there. We found the great clothes-baskets full of apples, scenting the house, and stopping up the way; and an universal air of merry contentment with this the final produce of the year. The yellow leaves hung on the trees ready to flutter down at the slightest puff of air; the great bushes of Michaelmas daisies in the kitchen-garden were making their last show of flowers. We must needs taste the fruit off the different trees, and pass our judgment as to their flavour; and we went away with our pockets stuffed with those that we liked best. As we had passed to the orchard, Holdsworth had admired and spoken about some flower which he saw; it so happened he had never seen this old-fashioned kind since the days of his boyhood. I do not know whether he had thought anything more about this chance speech of his, but I know I had not—when Phillis, who had been missing just at the last moment of our hurried visit, re-appeared with a little nosegay of this same flower, which she was tying up with a blade of grass. She offered it to Holdsworth as he stood with her father on the point of departure. I saw their faces. I saw for the first time an unmistakable look of love in his black eyes; it was more than gratitude for the little attention; it was tender and beseeching—passionate. She shrank from it in confusion, her glance fell on me; and, partly to hide her emotion, partly out of real kindness at what might appear ungracious neglect of an older friend, she flew off to gather me a few late-blooming China roses. But it was the first time she had ever done anything of the kind for me.

We had to walk fast to be back on the line before the men's return, so we spoke but little to each other, and of course the afternoon was too much occupied for us to have any talk. In the evening we went back to our joint lodgings in Hornby. There, on the table, lay a letter for Holdsworth, which had been forwarded to him from Eltham. As our tea was ready, and I had had nothing to eat since morning, I fell to directly without paying much attention to my companion as he opened and read his letter. He was very silent for a few minutes; at length he said,

"Old fellow! I'm going to leave you!"

"Leave me!" said I. "How? When?"

"This letter ought to have come to hand sooner. It is from Greathed the engineer" (Greathed was well known in those days; he is dead now, and his name half-forgotten); "he wants to see me about some business; in fact, I may as well tell you, Paul, this letter contains a very advantageous proposal for me to go out to Canada, and superintend the making of a line there."

I was in utter dismay.

"But what will our company say to that?"

"Oh, Greathed has the superintendence of this line, you know; and he is going to be engineer in chief to this Canadian line; many of the Shareholders in this company are going in for the other, so I fancy they will make no difficulty in following Greathed's lead. He says he has a young man ready to put in my place."

"I hate him," said I.

"Thank you," said Holdsworth, laughing.

"But you must not," he resumed; "for this is a very good thing for me, and, of course, if no one can be found to take my inferior work, I can't be spared to take the superior. I only wish I had received this letter a day sooner. Every hour is of consequence, for Greathed says they are threatening a rival line. Do you know, Paul, I almost fancy I must go up tonight? I can take an engine back to Eltham, and catch the night train. I should not like Greathed to think me luke-warm."

"But you'll come back?" I asked, distressed at the thought of this sudden parting.

"Oh, yes! At least I hope so. They may want me to go out by the next steamer, that will be on Saturday." He began to eat and drink standing, but I think he was quite unconscious of the nature of either his food or his drink.

"I will go tonight. Activity and readiness go a long way in our profession. Remember that, my boy! I hope I shall come back, but if I don't, be sure and recollect all the words of wisdom that have fallen from my lips. Now where's the portmanteau? If I can gain half an hour for a gathering up of my things in Eltham, so much the better. I'm clear of debt anyhow; and what I owe for my lodgings you can pay for me out of my quarter's salary, due November 4th."

"Then you don't think you will come back?" I said, despondingly.

"I will come back some time, never fear," said he, kindly. "I may be back in a couple of days, having been found in-competent for the Canadian work; or I may not be wanted to go out so soon as I now anticipate. Anyhow you don't suppose I am going to forget you, Paul this work out there ought not to take me above two years, and, perhaps, after that, we may be employed together again." Perhaps! I had very little hope. The same kind of happy days never returns. However, I did all I could in helping him: clothes, papers, books, instruments; how we pushed and struggled—how I stuffed. All was done in a much shorter time than we had calculated upon, when I had run down to the sheds to order the engine. I was going to drive him to Eltham. We sate ready for a summons. Holdsworth took up the little nosegay that he had brought away from the Hope Farm, and had laid on the mantel-piece on first coming into the room. He smelt at it, and caressed it with his lips.

"What grieves me is that I did not know—that I have not said good-bye to—to them."

He spoke in a grave tone, the shadow of the coming separation falling upon him at last.

"I will tell them," said I. "I am sure they will be very sorry." Then we were silent.

"I never liked any family so much."

"I knew you would like them."

"How one's thoughts change—this morning I was full of a hope, Paul." He paused, and then he said—

"You put that sketch in carefully?"

"That outline of a head?" asked I. But I knew he meant an abortive sketch of Phillis, which had not been successful enough for him to complete it with shading or colouring.

"Yes. What a sweet innocent face it is! and yet so—Oh, dear!" He sighed and got up, his hands in his pockets, to walk up and down the room in evident disturbance of mind. He suddenly stopped opposite to me.

"You'll tell them how it all was. Be sure and tell the good minister that I was so sorry not to wish him good-bye, and to thank him and his wife for all their kindness. As for Phillis—please God in two years I'll be back and tell her myself all in my heart."

"You love Phillis, then?" said I.

"Love her! Yes, that I do. Who could help it, seeing her as I have done? Her character as unusual and rare as her beauty! God bless her! God keep her in her high tranquillity, her pure innocence.—Two years! It is a long time.—But she lives in such seclusion, almost like the sleeping beauty, Paul"—(he was smiling now, though a minute before I had thought him on the verge of tears)—"but I shall come back like a prince from Canada, and waken her to my love. I can't help hoping that it won't be difficult, eh, Paul?"

This touch of coxcombry displeased me a little, and I made no answer. He went on, half apologetically—

"You see, the salary they offer me is large; and beside that, this experience will give me a name which will entitle me to expect a still larger in any future undertaking."

"That won't influence Phillis."

"No! but it will make me more eligible in the eyes of her father and mother." I made no answer.

"You give me your best wishes, Paul," said he, almost pleading. "You would like me for a cousin?"

I heard the scream and whistle of the engine ready down at the sheds.

"Ay, that I should," I replied, suddenly softened towards my friend now that he was going away. "I wish you were to be married tomorrow, and I were to be best man."

"Thank you, lad. Now for this cursed portmanteau (how the minister would be shocked); but it is heavy!" and off we sped into the darkness. He only just caught the night train at Eltham, and I slept, desolately enough, at my old lodgings at Miss Dawsons," for that night. Of course the next few days I was busier than ever, doing both his work and my own. Then came a letter from him, very short and affectionate. He was going out in the Saturday steamer, as he had more than half expected; and by the following Monday the man who was to succeed him would be down at Eltham. There was a P.S., with only these words: "My nosegay goes with me to Canada, but I do not need it to remind me of Hope Farm."

Saturday came; but it was very late before I could go out to the farm. It was a frosty night, the stars shone clear above me, and the road was crisping beneath my feet. They must have heard my footsteps before I got up to the house. They were sitting at their usual employments in the house-place when I went in. Phillis's eyes went beyond me in their look of welcome, and then fell in quiet disappointment on her work.

"And where's Mr. Holdsworth?" asked cousin Holman, in a minute or two. "I hope his cold is not worse—I did not like his short cough."

I laughed awkwardly; for I felt that I was the bearer of unpleasant news.

"His cold had need be better—for he's gone—gone away to Canada!"

I purposely looked away from Phillis, as I thus abruptly told my news.

"To Canada!" said the minister.

"Gone away!" said his wife. But no word from Phillis.

"Yes!" said I. "He found a letter at Hornby when we got home the other night—when we got home from here; he ought to have got it sooner; he was ordered to go up to London directly, and to see some people about a new line in Canada, and he's gone to lay it down; he has sailed today. He was sadly grieved not to have time to come out and wish you all good-by; but he started for London within two hours after he got that letter. He bade me thank you most gratefully for all your kindnesses; he was very sorry not to come here once again." Phillis got up and left the room with noiseless steps.

"I am very sorry," said the minister.

"I am sure so am I!" said cousin Holman. "I was real fond of that lad ever since I nursed him last June after that bad fever."

The minister went on asking me questions respecting Holdsworth's future plans; and brought out a large old-fashioned atlas, that he might find out the exact places between which the new railroad was to run. Then supper was ready; it was always on the table as soon as the clock on the stairs struck eight, and down came Phillis—her face white and set, her dry eyes looking defiance to me, for I am afraid I hurt her maidenly pride by my glance of sympathetic interest as she entered the room. Never a word did she say—never a question did she ask about the absent friend, yet she forced herself to talk.

And so it was all the next day. She was as pale as could be, like one who has received some shock; but she would not let me talk to her, and she tried hard to behave as usual. Two or three times I repeated, in public, the various affectionate messages to the family with which I was charged by Holdsworth; but she took no more notice of them than if my words had been empty air. And in this mood I left her on the Sabbath evening.

My new master was not half so indulgent as my old one. He kept up strict discipline as to hours, so that it was some time before I could again go out, even to pay a call at the Hope Farm.

It was a cold misty evening in November. The air, even indoors, seemed full of haze; yet there was a great log burning on the hearth, which ought to have made the room cheerful. Cousin Holman and Phillis were sitting at the little round table before the fire, working away in silence. The minister had his books out on the dresser, seemingly deep in study, by the light of his solitary candle; perhaps the fear of disturbing him made the unusual stillness of the room. But a welcome was ready for me from all; not noisy, not demonstrative—that it never was; my damp wrappers were taken off; the next meal was hastened, and a chair placed for me on one side of the fire, so that I pretty much commanded a view of the room. My eye caught on Phillis, looking so pale and weary, and with a sort of aching tone (if I may call it so) in her voice. She was doing all the accustomed things—fulfilling small household duties, but somehow differently—I can't tell you how, for she was just as deft and quick in her movements, only the light spring was gone out of them. Cousin Holman began to question me; even the minister put aside his books, and came and stood on the opposite side of the fireplace, to hear what waft of intelligence I brought. I had first to tell them why I had not been to see them for so long—more than five weeks. The answer was simple enough; business and the necessity of attending strictly to the orders of a new superintendent, who had not yet learned trust, much less indulgence. The minister nodded his approval of my conduct, and said, "Right, Paul! 'Servants, obey in all things your master according to the flesh.' I have had my fears lest you had too much licence under Edward Holdsworth."

"Ah," said cousin Holman, "poor Mr. Holdsworth, he'll be on the salt seas by this time!"

"No, indeed," said I, "he's landed. I have had a letter from him from Halifax." Immediately a shower of questions fell thick upon me. When? How? What was he doing? How did he like it? What sort of a voyage? &c.

"Many is the time we have thought of him when the wind was blowing so hard; the old quince-tree is blown down, Paul, that on the right-hand of the great pear-tree; it was blown down last Monday week, and it was that night that I asked the minister to pray in an especial manner for all them that went down in ships upon the great deep, and he said then, that Mr. Holdsworth might be already landed; but I said, even if the prayer did not fit him, it was sure to be fitting somebody out at sea, who would need the Lord's care. Both Phillis and I thought he would be a month on the seas." Phillis began to speak, but her voice did not come rightly at first. It was a little higher pitched than usual, when she said—

"We thought he would be a month if he went in a sailing-vessel, or perhaps longer. I suppose he went in a steamer?"

"Old Obadiah Grimshaw was more than six weeks in getting to America," observed cousin Holman.

"I presume he cannot as yet tell how he likes his new work?" asked the minister.

"No! he is but just landed; it is but one page long. I'll read it to you, shall I?

" 'Dear Paul— We are safe on shore, after a rough passage. Thought you would like to hear this, but homeward-bound steamer is making signals for letters. Will write again soon. It seems a year since I left Hornby. Longer since I was at the farm. I have got my nosegay safe. Remember me to the Holmans. —Yours, E. H.' "

"That's not much, certainly," said the minister. "But it's a comfort to know he's on land these blowy nights."

Phillis said nothing. She kept her head bent down over her work; but I don't think she put a stitch in, while I was reading the letter. I wondered if she understood what nosegay was meant; but I could not tell. When next she lifted up her face, there were two spots of brilliant colour on the cheeks that had been so pale before. After I had spent an hour or two there, I was bound to return back to Hornby. I told them I did not know when I could come again, as we—by which I mean the company—had undertaken the Hensleydale line; that branch for which poor Holdsworth was surveying when he caught his fever.

"But you'll have a holiday at Christmas," said my cousin. "Surely they'll not be such heathens as to work you then?"

"Perhaps the lad will be going home," said the minister, as if to mitigate his wife's urgency; but for all that, I believe he wanted me to come. Phillis fixed her eyes on me with a wistful expression, hard to resist. But, indeed, I had no thought of resisting. Under my new master I had no hope of a holiday long enough to enable me to go to Birmingham and see my parents with any comfort; and nothing could be pleasanter to me than to find myself at home at my cousins' for a day or two, then. So it was fixed that we were to meet in Hornby Chapel on Christmas Day, and that I was to accompany them home after service, and if possible to stay over the next day.

I was not able to get to chapel till late on the appointed day, and so I took a seat near the door in considerable shame, although it really was not my fault. When the service was ended, I went and stood in the porch to await the coming out of my cousins. Some worthy people belonging to the congregation clustered into a group just where I stood, and exchanged the good wishes of the season. It had just begun to snow, and this occasioned a little delay, and they fell into further conversation. I was not attending to what was not meant for me to hear, till I caught the name of Phillis Holman. And then I listened; where was the harm?

"I never saw anyone so changed!"

"I asked Mrs. Holman," quoth another, "'Is Phillis well?' and she just said she had been having a cold which had pulled her down; she did not seem to think anything of it."

"They had best take care of her," said one of the oldest of the good ladies; "Phillis comes of a family as is not long-lived. Her mother's sister, Lydia Green, her own aunt as was, died of a decline just when she was about this lass's age."

This ill-omened talk was broken in upon by the coming out of the minister, his wife and daughter, and the consequent interchange of Christmas compliments. I had had a shock, and felt heavy-hearted and anxious, and hardly up to making the appropriate replies to the kind greetings of my relations. I looked askance at Phillis. She had certainly grown taller and slighter, and was thinner; but there was a flush of colour on her face which deceived me for a time, and made me think she was looking as well as ever. I only saw her paleness after we had returned to the farm, and she had subsided into silence and quiet. Her grey eyes looked hollow and sad; her complexion was of a dead white. But she went about just as usual; at least, just as she had done the last time I was there, and seemed to have no ailment; and I was inclined to think that my cousin was right when she had answered the inquiries of the good-natured gossips, and told them that Phillis was suffering from the consequences of a bad cold, nothing more. I have said that I was to stay over the next day; a great deal of snow had come down, but not all, they said, though the ground was covered deep with the white fall. The minister was anxiously housing his cattle, and preparing all things for a long continuance of the same kind of weather. The men were chopping wood, sending wheat to the mill to be ground before the road should become impassable for a cart and horse. My cousin and Phillis had gone up-stairs to the apple-room to cover up the fruit from the frost. I had been out the greater part of the morning, and came in about an hour before dinner. To my surprise, knowing how she had planned to be engaged, I found Phillis sitting at the dresser, resting her head on her two hands and reading, or seeming to read. She did not look up when I came in, but murmured something about her mother having sent her down out of the cold. It flashed across me that she was crying, but I put it down to some little spirt of temper; I might have known better than to suspect the gentle, serene Phillis of crossness, poor girl; I stooped down, and began to stir and build up the fire, which appeared to have been neglected. While my head was down I heard a noise which made me pause and listen—a sob, an unmistakable, irrepressible sob. I started up.

"Phillis!" I cried, going towards her, with my hand out, to take hers for sympathy with her sorrow, whatever it was. But she was too quick for me, she held her hand out of my grasp, for fear of my detaining her; as she quickly passed out of the house, she said—

"Don't, Paul! I cannot bear it!" and passed me, still sobbing, and went out into the keen, open air.

I stood still and wondered. What could have come to Phillis? The most perfect harmony prevailed in the family, and Phillis especially, good and gentle as she was, was so beloved that if they had found out that her finger ached, it would have cast a shadow over their hearts. Had I done anything to vex her? No: she was crying before I came in. I went to look at her book— one of those unintelligible Italian books. I could make neither head nor tail of it. I saw some pencil-notes on the margin, in Holdsworth's handwriting.

Could that be it? Could that be the cause of her white looks, her weary eyes, her wasted figure, her struggling sobs? This idea came upon me like a flash of lightning on a dark night, making all things so clear we cannot forget them afterwards when the gloomy obscurity returns. I was still standing with the book in my hand when I heard cousin Holman's footsteps on the stairs, and as I did not wish to speak to her just then, I followed Phillis's example, and rushed out of the house. The snow was lying on the ground; I could track her feet by the marks they had made; I could see where Rover had joined her. I followed on till I came to a great stack of wood in the orchard— it was built up against the back wall of the outbuildings—and I recollected then how Phillis had told me, that first day when we strolled about together, that underneath this stack had been her hermitage, her sanctuary, when she was a child; how she used to bring her book to study there, or her work, when she was not wanted in the house; and she had now evidently gone back to this quiet retreat of her childhood, forgetful of the clue given me by her footmarks on the new-fallen snow. The stack was built up very high; but through the interstices of the sticks I could see her figure, although I did not all at once perceive how I could get to her. She was sitting on a log of wood, Rover by her. She had laid her cheek on Rover's head, and had her arm round his neck, partly for a pillow, partly from an instinctive craving for warmth on that bitter cold day. She was making a low moan, like an animal in pain, or perhaps more like the sobbing of the wind. Rover, highly flattered by her caress, and also, perhaps, touched by sympathy, was flapping his heavy tail against the ground, but not otherwise moving a hair, until he heard my approach with his quick erected ears. Then, with a short, abrupt bark of distrust, he sprang up as if to leave his mistress. Both he and I were immovably still for a moment. I was not sure if what I longed to do was wise: and yet I could not bear to see the sweet serenity of my dear cousin's life so disturbed by a suffering which I thought I could assuage. But Rover's ears were sharper than my breathing was noiseless: he heard me, and sprang out from under Phillis's restraining hand.

"Oh, Rover, don't you leave me, too," she plained out.

"Phillis!" said I, seeing by Rover's exit that the entrance to where she sate was to be found on the other side of the stack. "Phillis, come out! You have got a cold already; and it is not fit for you to sit there on such a day as this. You know how displeased and anxious it would make them all."

She sighed, but obeyed; stooping a little, she came out, and stood upright, opposite to me in the lonely, leafless orchard. Her face looked so meek and so sad that I felt as if I ought to beg her pardon for my necessarily authoritative words.

"Sometimes I feel the house so close," she said; "and I used to sit under the wood-stack when I was a child. It was very kind of you, but there was no need to come after me. I don't catch cold easily."

"Come with me into this cow-house, Phillis. I have got something to say to you; and I can't stand this cold, if you can."

I think she would have fain run away again; but her fit of energy was all spent. She followed me unwillingly enough that I could see. The place to which I took her was full of the fragrant breath of the cows, and was a little warmer than the outer air. I put her inside, and stood myself in the doorway, thinking how I could best begin. At last I plunged into it.

"I must see that you don't get cold for more reasons than one; if you are ill, Holdsworth will be so anxious and miserable out there" (by which I meant Canada)—

She shot one penetrating look at me, and then turned her face away with a slightly impatient movement. If she could have run away then she would, but I held the means of exit in my own power. "In for a penny, in for a pound," thought I, and I went on rapidly, anyhow.

"He talked so much about you, just before he left—that night after he had been here, you know—and you had given him those flowers." She put her hands up to hide her face, but she was listening now—listening with all her ears. "He had never spoken much about you before, but the sudden going away unlocked his heart, and he told me how he loved you, and how he hoped on his return that you might be his wife."

"Don't," said she, almost gasping out the word, which she had tried once or twice before to speak; but her voice had been choked. Now she put her hand backwards; she had quite turned away from me, and felt for mine. She gave it a soft lingering pressure; and then she put her arms down on the wooden division, and laid her head on it, and cried quiet tears. I did not understand her at once, and feared lest I had mistaken the whole case, and only annoyed her. I went up to her. "Oh, Phillis! I am so sorry—I thought you would, perhaps, have cared to hear it; he did talk so feelingly, as if he did love you so much, and somehow I thought it would give you pleasure."

She lifted up her head and looked at me. Such a look! Her eyes, glittering with tears as they were, expressed an almost heavenly happiness; her tender mouth was curved with rapture—her colour vivid and blushing; but as if she was afraid her face expressed too much, more than the thankfulness to me she was essaying to speak, she hid it again almost immediately. So it was all right then, and my conjecture was well-founded! I tried to remember something more to tell her of what he had said, but again she stopped me.

"Don't," she said. She still kept her face covered and hidden. In half a minute she added, in a very low voice, "Please, Paul, I think I would rather not hear any more I don't mean but what I have—but what I am very much obliged—Only—only, I think I would rather hear the rest from himself when he comes back."

And then she cried a little more, in quite a different way. I did not say any more, I waited for her. By-and-by she turned towards me—not meeting my eyes, however; and putting her hand in mine just as if we were two children, she said—

"We had best go back now—I don't look as if I had been crying, do I?"

"You look as if you had a bad cold," was all the answer I made.

"Oh! but I am quite well, only cold; and a good run will warm me. Come along, Paul."

So we ran, hand in hand, till, just as we were on the threshold of the house, she stopped—

"Paul, please, we won't speak about that again."

PART IV

When I went over on Easter Day I heard the chapel-gossips complimenting cousin Holman on her daughter's blooming looks, quite forgetful of their sinister prophecies three months before. And I looked at Phillis, and did not wonder at their words. I had not seen her since the day after Christmas Day. I had left the Hope Farm only a few hours after I had told her the news which had quickened her heart into renewed life and vigour. The remembrance of our conversation in the cow-house was vividly in my mind as I looked at her when her bright healthy appearance was remarked upon. As her eyes met mine our mutual recollections flashed intelligence from one to the other. She turned away, her colour heightening as she did so. She seemed to be shy of me for the first few hours after our meeting, and I felt rather vexed with her for her conscious avoidance of me after my long absence. I had stepped a little out of my usual line in telling her what I did; not that I had received any charge of secrecy, or given even the slightest promise to Holdsworth that I would not repeat his words. But I had an uneasy feeling sometimes when I thought of what I had done in the excitement of seeing Phillis so ill and in so much trouble. I meant to have told Holdsworth when I wrote next to him; but when I had my half-finished letter before me I sate with my pen in my hand hesitating. I had more scruple in revealing what I had found out or guessed at of Phillis's secret than in repeating to her his spoken words. I did not think I had any right to say out to him what I believed—namely, that she loved him dearly, and had felt his absence even to the injury of her health. Yet to explain what I had done in telling her how he had spoken about her that last night, it would be necessary to give my reasons, so I had settled within myself to leave it alone. As she had told me she should like to hear all the details and fuller particulars and more explicit declarations first from him, so he should have the pleasure of extracting the delicious tender secret from her maidenly lips. I would not betray my guesses, my surmises, my all but certain knowledge of the state of her heart. I had received two letters from him after he had settled to his business; they were full of life and energy; but in each there had been a message to the family at the Hope Farm of more than common regard; and a slight but distinct mention of Phillis herself, showing that she stood single and alone in his memory. These letters I had sent on to the minister, for he was sure to care for them, even supposing he had been unacquainted with their writer, because they were so clever and so picturesquely worded that they brought, as it were, a whiff of foreign atmosphere into his circumscribed life. I used to wonder what was the trade or business in which the minister would not have thriven, mentally I mean, if it had so happened that he had been called into that state. He would have made a capital engineer, that I know; and he had a fancy for the sea, like many other land-locked men to whom the great deep is a mystery and a fascination. He read law-books with relish; and, once happening to borrow De Lolme on the British Constitution (or some such title), he talked about jurisprudence till he was far beyond my depth. But to return to Holdsworth's letters. When the minister sent them back he also wrote out a list of questions suggested by their perusal, which I was to pass on in my answers to Holdsworth, until I thought of suggesting direct correspondence between the two. That was the state of things as regarded the absent one when I went to the farm for my Easter visit, and when I found Phillis in that state of shy reserve towards me which I have named before. I thought she was ungrateful; for I was not quite sure if I had done wisely in having told her what I did. I had committed a fault, or a folly, perhaps, and all for her sake; and here was she, less friends with me than she had even been before. This little estrangement only lasted a few hours. I think that as soon as she felt pretty sure of there being no recurrence, either by word, look, or allusion, to the one subject that was predominant in her mind, she came back to her old sisterly ways with me. She had much to tell me of her own familiar interests; how Rover had been ill, and how anxious they had all of them been, and how, after some little discussion between her father and her, both equally grieved by the sufferings of the old dog, he had been remembered in the household prayers," and how he had begun to get better only the very next day, and then she would have led me into a conversation on the right ends of prayer, and on special providences, and I know not what; only I "jibbed" like their old cart-horse, and refused to stir a step in that direction. Then we talked about the different broods of chickens, and she showed me the hens that were good mothers, and told me the characters of all the poultry with the utmost good faith; and in all good faith I listened, for I believe there was a good deal of truth in all she said. And then we strolled on into the wood beyond the ash-meadow, and both of us sought for early primroses, and the fresh green crinkled leaves. She was not afraid of being alone with me after the first day. I never saw her so lovely, or so happy. I think she hardly knew why she was so happy all the time. I can see her now, standing under the budding branches of the grey trees, over which a tinge of green seemed to be deepening day after day, her sun-bonnet fallen back on her neck, her hands full of delicate wood-flowers, quite unconscious of my gaze, but intent on sweet mockery of some bird in neighbouring bush or tree. She had the art of warbling, and replying to the notes of different birds, and knew their song, their habits and ways, more accurately than any one else I ever knew. She had often done it at my request the spring before; but this year she really gurgled, and whistled, and warbled just as they did, out of the very fulness and joy of her heart. She was more than ever the very apple of her father's eye; her mother gave her both her own share of love, and that of the dead child who had died in infancy. I have heard cousin Holman murmur, after a long dreamy look at Phillis, and tell herself how like she was growing to Johnnie, and soothe herself with plaintive inarticulate sounds, and many gentle shakes of the head, for the aching sense of loss she would never get over in this world. The old servants about the place had the dumb loyal attachment to the child of the land, common to most agricultural labourers; not often stirred into activity or expression. My cousin Phillis was like a rose that had come to full bloom on the sunny side of a lonely house, sheltered from storms. I have read in some book of poetry—

A maid whom there were none to praise, And very few to love.

And somehow those lines always reminded me of Phillis; yet they were not true of her either. I never heard her praised; and out of her own household there were very few to love her; but though no one spoke out their approbation, she always did right in her parents' eyes out of her natural simple goodness and wisdom. Holdsworth's name was never mentioned between us when we were alone; but I had sent on his letters to the minister, as I have said; and more than once he began to talk about our absent friend, when he was smoking his pipe after the day's work was done. Then Phillis hung her head a little over her work, and listened in silence.

"I miss him more than I thought for; no offence to you, Paul. I said once his company was like dram-drinking; that was before I knew him; and perhaps I spoke in a spirit of judgment. To some men's minds everything presents itself strongly, and they speak accordingly; and so did he. And I thought in my vanity of censorship that his were not true and sober words; they would not have been if I had used them, but they were so to a man of his class of perceptions. I thought of the measure with which I had been meting to him when Brother Robinson was here last Thursday, and told me that a poor little quotation I was making from the Georgics savoured of vain babbling and profane heathenism. He went so far as to say that by learning other languages than our own, we were flying in the face of the Lord's purpose when He had said, at the building of the Tower of Babel, that He would confound their languages so that they should not understand each other's speech. As Brother Robinson was to me, so was I to the quick wits, bright senses, and ready words of Holdsworth."

The first little cloud upon my peace came in the shape of a letter from Canada, in which there were two or three sentences that troubled me more than they ought to have done, to judge merely from the words employed. It was this: "I should feel dreary enough in this out-of-the-way place if it were not for a friendship I have formed with a French Canadian of the name of Ventadour. He and his family are a great resource to me in the long evenings. I never heard such delicious vocal music as the voices of these Ventadour boys and girls in their part songs; and the foreign element retained in their characters and manner of living reminds me of some of the happiest days of my life. Lucille, the second daughter, is curiously like Phillis Holman." In vain I said to myself that it was probably this likeness that made him take pleasure in the society of the Ventadour family. In vain I told my anxious fancy that nothing could be more natural than this intimacy, and that there was no sign of its leading to any consequence that ought to disturb me. I had a presentiment, and I was disturbed; and I could not reason it away. I dare say my presentiment was rendered more persistent and keen by the doubts which would force themselves into my mind, as to whether I had done well in repeating Holdsworth's words to Phillis. Her state of vivid happiness this summer was markedly different to the peaceful serenity of former days. If in my thoughtfulness at noticing this I caught her eye, she blushed and sparkled all over, guessing that I was remembering our joint secret. Her eyes fell before mine, as if she could hardly bear me to see the revelation of their bright glances. And yet I considered again, and comforted myself by the reflection that, if this change had been anything more than my silly fancy, her father or her mother would have perceived it. But they went on in tranquil unconsciousness and undisturbed peace.

A change in my own life was quickly approaching. In the July of this year my occupation on the —— railway and its branches came to an end. The lines were completed, and I was to leave ——shire, to return to Birmingham, where there was a niche already provided for me in my father's prosperous business. But before I left the north it was an understood thing amongst us all that I was to go and pay a visit of some weeks at the Hope Farm. My father was as much pleased at this plan as I was; and the dear family of cousins often spoke of things to be done, and sights to be shown me, during this visit. My want of wisdom in having told "that thing" (under such ambiguous words I concealed the injudicious confidence I had made to Phillis) was the only drawback to my anticipations of pleasure.

The ways of life were too simple at the Hope Farm for my coming to them to make the slightest disturbance. I knew my room, like a son of the house. I knew the regular course of their days, and that I was expected to fall into it, like one of the family. Deep summer peace brooded over the place; the warm golden air was filled with the murmur of insects near at hand, the more distant sound of voices out in the fields, the clear faraway rumble of carts over the stone-paved lanes miles away. The heat was too great for the birds to be singing; only now and then one might hear the wood-pigeons in the trees beyond the Ashfield. The cattle stood knee-deep in the pond, flicking their tails about to keep off the flies. The minister stood in the hay-field, without hat or cravat, coat or waistcoat, panting and smiling. Phillis had been leading the row of farm-servants, turning the swathes of fragrant hay with measured movement. She went to the end—to the hedge, and then, throwing down her rake, she came to me with her free sisterly welcome. "Go, Paul!" said the minister. "We need all hands to make use of the sunshine today. 'Whatsoever thine hand findeth to do, do it with all thy might.' It will be a healthy change of work for thee, lad; and I find best rest in change of work." So off I went, a willing labourer, following Phillis's lead; it was the primitive distinction of rank; the boy who frightened the sparrows off the fruit was the last in our rear. We did not leave off till the red sun was gone down behind the fir-trees bordering the common. Then we went home to supper—prayers—to bed; some bird singing far into the night, as I heard it through my open window, and the poultry beginning their clatter and cackle in the earliest morning. I had carried what luggage I immediately needed with me from my lodgings and the rest was to be sent by the carrier. He brought it to the farm betimes that morning, and along with it he brought a letter or two that had arrived since I had left. I was talking to cousin Holman—about my mother's ways of making bread, I remember; cousin Holman was questioning me, and had got me far beyond my depth—in the house-place, when the letters were brought in by one of the men, and I had to pay the carrier for his trouble before I could look at them. A bill—a Canadian letter! What instinct made me so thankful that I was alone with my dear unobservant cousin? What made me hurry them away into my coat-pocket? I do not know. I felt strange and sick, and made irrelevant answers, I am afraid. Then I went to my room, ostensibly to carry up my boxes. I sate on the side of my bed and opened my letter from Holdsworth. It seemed to me as if I had read its contents before, and knew exactly what he had got to say. I knew he was going to be married to Lucille Ventadour; nay, that he was married; for this was the 5th of July, and he wrote word that his marriage was fixed to take place on the 29th of June. I knew all the reasons he gave, all the raptures he went into. I held the letter loosely in my hands, and looked into vacancy, yet I saw the chaffinch's nest on the lichen-covered trunk of an old apple-tree opposite my window, and saw the mother-bird come fluttering in to feed her brood—and yet I did not see it, although it seemed to me afterwards as if I could have drawn every fibre, every feather. I was stirred up to action by the merry sound of voices and the clamp of rustic feet coming home for the mid-day meal. I knew I must go down to dinner; I knew, too, I must tell Phillis; for in his happy egotism, his new-fangled foppery, Holdsworth had put in a P.S., saying that he should send wedding-cards to me and some other Hornby and Eltham acquaintances, and "to his kind friends at Hope Farm." Phillis had faded away to one among several "kind friends." I don't know how I got through dinner that day. I remember forcing myself to eat, and talking hard; but I also recollect the wondering look in the minister's eyes. He was not one to think evil without cause; but many a one would have taken me for drunk. As soon as I decently could I left the table, saying I would go out for a walk. At first I must have tried to stun reflection by rapid walking, for I had lost myself on the high moorlands far beyond the familiar gorse-covered common, before I was obliged for very weariness to slacken my pace. I kept wishing—oh! how fervently wishing I had never committed that blunder; that the one little half-hour's indiscretion could be blotted out. Alternating with this was anger against Holdsworth; unjust enough, I dare say. I suppose I stayed in that solitary place for a good hour or more, and then I turned homewards, resolving to get over the telling Phillis at the first opportunity, but shrinking from the fulfilment of my resolution so much that when I came into the house and saw Phillis (doors and windows open wide in the sultry weather) alone in the kitchen, I became quite sick with apprehension. She was standing by the dresser, cutting up a great household loaf into hunches of bread for the hungry labourers who might come in any minute, for the heavy thunder-clouds were overspreading the sky. She looked round as she heard my step.

"You should have been in the field, helping with the hay," said she, in her calm, pleasant voice. I had heard her as I came near the house softly chanting some hymn-tune, and the peacefulness of that seemed to be brooding over her now.

"Perhaps I should. It looks as if it was going to rain."

"Yes; there is thunder about. Mother has had to go to bed with one of her bad headaches. Now you are come in—

"Phillis," said I, rushing at my subject and interrupting her, "I went a long walk to think over a letter I had this morning—a letter from Canada. You don't know how it has grieved me." I held it out to her as I spoke. Her colour changed a little, but it was more the reflection of my face, I think, than because she formed any definite idea from my words. Still she did not take the letter. I had to bid her to read it, before she quite understood what I wished. She sate down rather suddenly as she received it into her hands; and, spreading it on the dresser before her, she rested her forehead on the palms of her hands, her arms supported on the table, her figure a little averted, and her countenance thus shaded. I looked out of the open window; my heart was very heavy. How peaceful it all seemed in the farmyard! Peace and plenty. How still and deep was the silence of the house! Tick-tick went the unseen clock on the wide staircase. I had heard the rustle once, when she turned over the page of thin paper. She must have read to the end. Yet she did not move, or say a word, or even sigh. I kept on looking out of the window, my hands in my pockets. I wonder how long that time really was? It seemed to me interminable—unbearable. At length I looked round at her. She must have felt my look, for she changed her attitude with a quick sharp movement, and caught my eyes.

"Don't look so sorry, Paul," she said. "Don't, please. I can't bear it. There is nothing to be sorry for. I think not, at least. You have not done wrong, at any rate." I felt that I groaned, but I don't think she heard me. "And he—there's no wrong in his marrying, is there? I'm sure I hope he'll be happy. Oh! how I hope it!" These last words were like a wail; but I believe she was afraid of breaking down, for she changed the key in which she spoke, and hurried on.

"Lucille—that's our English Lucy, I suppose? Lucille Holdsworth! It's a pretty name; and I hope—I forget what I was going to say. Oh! it was this. Paul, I think we need never speak about this again; only remember you are not to be sorry. You have not done wrong; you have been very, very kind; and if I see you looking grieved I don't know what I might do;—I might breakdown, you know." I think she was on the point of doing so then, but the dark storm came dashing down, and the thunder-cloud broke right above the house, as it seemed. Her mother, roused from sleep, called out for Phillis; the men and women from the hay-field came running into shelter, drenched through. The minister followed, smiling, and not unpleasantly excited by the war of elements; for, by dint of hard work through the long summer's day, the greater part of the hay was safely housed in the barn in the field. Once or twice in the succeeding bustle I came across Phillis, always busy, and, as it seemed to me, always doing the right thing. When I was alone in my own room at night I allowed myself to feel relieved; and to believe that the worst was over, and was not so very bad after all. But the succeeding days were very miserable. Sometimes I thought it must be my fancy that falsely represented Phillis to me as strangely changed, for surely, if this idea of mine was well-founded, her parents—her father and mother—her own flesh and blood—would have been the first to perceive it. Yet they went on in their household peace and content; if anything, a little more cheerfully than usual, for the "harvest of the first-fruits," as the minister called it, had been more bounteous than usual, and there was plenty all around in which the humblest labourer was made to share. After the one thunderstorm, came one or two lovely serene summer days, during which the hay was all carried; and then succeeded long soft rains filling the ears of corn, and causing the mown grass to spring afresh. The minister allowed himself a few more hours of relaxation and home enjoyment than usual during this wet spell: hard earth-bound frost was his winter holiday; these wet days, after the hay harvest, his summer holiday. We sate with open windows, the fragrance and the freshness called out by the soft-falling rain filling the house-place; while the quiet ceaseless patter among the leaves outside ought to have had the same lulling effect as all other gentle perpetual sounds, such as mill-wheels and bubbling springs, have on the nerves of happy people. But two of us were not happy. I was sure enough of myself, for one. I was worse than sure—I was wretchedly anxious about Phillis. Ever since that day of the thunderstorm there had been a new, sharp, discordant sound to me in her voice, a sort of jangle in her tone; and her restless eyes had no quietness in them; and her colour came and went without a cause that I could find out. The minister, happy in ignorance of what most concerned him, brought out his books; his learned volumes and classics. Whether he read and talked to Phillis, or to me, I do not know; but feeling by instinct that she was not, could not be, attending to the peaceful details, so strange and foreign to the turmoil in her heart, I forced myself to listen, and if possible to understand.

"Look here!" said the minister, tapping the old vellum-bound book he held; "in the first Georgic he speaks of rolling and irrigation, a little further on he insists on choice of the best seed, and advises us to keep the drains clear. Again, no Scotch farmer could give shrewder advice than to cut light meadows while the dew is on, even though it involve night-work. It is all living truth in these days." He began beating time with a ruler upon his knee, to some Latin lines he read aloud just then. I suppose the monotonous chant irritated Phillis to some irregular energy, for I remember the quick knotting and breaking of the thread with which she was sewing. I never hear that snap repeated now, without suspecting some sting or stab troubling the heart of the worker. Cousin Holman, at her peaceful knitting, noticed the reason why Phillis had so constantly to interrupt the progress of her seam.

"It is bad thread, I'm afraid," she said, in a gentle sympathetic voice. But it was too much for Phillis.

"The thread is bad—everything is bad—I am so tired of it all!" And she put down her work, and hastily left the room. I do not suppose that in all her life Phillis had ever shown so much temper before. In many a family the tone, the manner, would not have been noticed; but here it fell with a sharp surprise upon the sweet, calm atmosphere of home. The minister put down ruler and book, and pushed his spectacles up to his forehead. The mother looked distressed for a moment, and then smoothed her features and said in an explanatory tone, "It's the weather, I think. Some people feel it different to others. It always brings on a headache with me." She got up to follow her daughter, but half-way to the door she thought better of it, and came back to her seat. Good mother! she hoped the better to conceal the unusual spirt of temper, by pretending not to take much notice of it. "Go on, minister," she said; "it is very interesting what you are reading about, and when I don't quite understand it, I like the sound of your voice." So he went on, but languidly and irregularly, and beat no more time with his ruler to any Latin lines. When the dusk came on, early that July night because of the cloudy sky, Phillis came softly back, making as though nothing had happened. She took up her work, but it was too dark to do many stitches; and she dropped it soon. Then I saw how her hand stole into her mother's, and how this latter fondled it with quiet little caresses, while the minister, as fully aware as I was of this tender pantomime, went on talking in a happier tone of voice about things as uninteresting to him, at the time, I very believe, as they were to me; and that is saying a good deal, and shows how much more real what was passing before him was, even to a farmer, than the agricultural customs of the ancients.

I remember one thing more—an attack which Betty the servant made upon me one day as I came in through the kitchen where she was churning, and stopped to ask her for a drink of buttermilk.

"I say, cousin Paul," (she had adopted the family habit of addressing me generally as cousin Paul, and always speaking of me in that form,) "something's amiss with our Phillis, and I reckon you've a good guess what it is. She's not one to take up wi' such as you," (not complimentary, but that Betty never was, even to those for whom she felt the highest respect,) "but I'd as lief yon Holdsworth had never come near us. So there you've a bit o' my mind." And a very unsatisfactory bit it was. I did not know what to answer to the glimpse at the real state of the case implied in the shrewd woman's speech; so I tried to put her off by assuming surprise at her first assertion.

"Amiss with Phillis! I should like to know why you think anything is wrong with her. She looks as blooming as any one can do."

"Poor lad! you're but a big child after all; and you've likely never heared of a fever-flush. But you know better nor that, my fine fellow! so don't think for to put me off wi' blooms and blossoms and such-like talk. What makes her walk about for hours and hours o' nights when she used to be abed and asleep? I sleep next room to her, and hear her plain as can be. What makes her come in panting and ready to drop into that chair"—nodding to one close to the door—"and it's 'Oh! Betty, some water, please'? That's the way she comes in now, when she used to come back as fresh and bright as she went out. If yon friend o' yours has played her false, he's a deal for t' answer for; she's a lass who's as sweet and as sound as a nut, and the very apple of her father's eye, and of her mother's too, only wi' her she ranks second to th' minister. You'll have to look after yon chap, for I, for one, will stand no wrong to our Phillis."

What was I to do, or to say? I wanted to justify Holdsworth, to keep Phillis's secret, and to pacify the woman all in the same breath. I did not take the best course, I'm afraid.

"I don't believe Holdsworth ever spoke a word of—of love to her in all his life. I'm sure he didn't."

"Ay. Ay! but there's eyes, and there's hands, as well as tongues; and a man has two o' th' one and but one o' t'other."

"And she's so young; do you suppose her parents would not have seen it?"

"Well! if you axe me that, I'll say out boldly, 'No.' They've called her 'the child' so long— the child' is always their name for her when they talk on her between themselves, as if never anybody else had a ewe-lamb before them— that she's grown up to be a woman under their very eyes, and they look on her still as if she were in her long clothes. And you ne'er heard on a man falling in love wi' a babby in long clothes!"

"No!" said I, half laughing. But she went on as grave as a judge.

"Ay! you see you'll laugh at the bare thought on it—and I'll be bound th' minister, though he's not a laughing man, would ha' sniggled at th' notion of falling in love wi' the child. Where's Holdsworth off to?"

"Canada," said I, shortly.

"Canada here, Canada there," she replied, testily. "Tell me how far he's off, instead of giving me your gibberish. Is he a two days' journey away? or a three? or a week?"

"He's ever so far off—three weeks at the least," cried I in despair. "And he's either married, or just going to be. So there." I expected a fresh burst of anger. But no; the matter was too serious. Betty sate down, and kept silence for a minute or two. She looked so miserable and downcast, that I could not help going on, and taking her a little into my confidence.

"It is quite true what I said. I know he never spoke a word to her. I think he liked her, but it's all over now. The best thing we can do—the best and kindest for her—and I know you love her, Betty—"

"I nursed her in my arms; I gave her little brother his last taste o' earthly food," said Betty, putting her apron up to her eyes.

"Well! don't let us show her we guess that she is grieving; she'll get over it the sooner. Her father and mother don't even guess at it, and we must make as if we didn't. It's too late now to do anything else."

"I'll never let on; I know nought. I've known true love mysel', in my day. But I wish he'd been farred before he ever came near this house, with his 'Please Betty' this, and 'Please Betty' that, and drinking up our new milk as if he'd been a cat. I hate such beguiling ways."

I thought it was as well to let her exhaust herself in abusing the absent Holdsworth; if it was shabby and treacherous in me, I came in for my punishment directly.

"It's a caution to a man how he goes about beguiling. Some men do it as easy and innocent as cooing doves. Don't you be none of 'em, my lad. Not that you've got the gifts to do it, either; you're no great shakes to look at, neither for figure, nor yet for face, and it would need be a deaf adder to be taken in wi' your words, though there may be no great harm in 'em. A lad of nineteen or twenty is not flattered by such an out-spoken opinion even from the oldest and ugliest of her sex; and I was only too glad to change the subject by my repeated injunctions to keep Phillis's secret. The end of our conversation was this speech of hers—

"You great gaupus, for all you're called cousin o' th' minister—many a one is cursed wi' fools for cousins—d'ye think I can't see sense except through your spectacles? I give you leave to cut out my tongue, and nail it up on th' barn-door for a caution to magpies, if I let out on that poor wench, either to herself, or any one that is hers, as the Bible says. Now you've heard me speak Scripture language, perhaps you'll be content, and leave me my kitchen to myself."

During all these days, from the 5th of July to the 17th, I must have forgotten what Holdsworth had said about cards. And yet I think I could not have quite forgotten; but, once having told Phillis about his marriage, I must have looked upon the after consequence of cards as of no importance. At any rate they came upon me as a surprise at last. The penny-post reform, as people call it, had come into operation a short time before; but the never-ending stream of notes and letters which seem now to flow in upon most households had not yet begun its course; at least in those remote parts. There was a post-office at Hornby; and an old fellow, who stowed away the few letters in any or all his pockets, as it best suited him, was the letter-carrier to Heathbridge and the neighbourhood. I have often met him in the lanes thereabouts, and asked him for letters. Sometimes I have come upon him, sitting on the hedge-bank resting; and he has begged me to read him an address, too illegible for his spectacled eyes to decipher. When I used to inquire if he had anything for me, or for Holdsworth (he was not particular to whom he gave up the letters, so that he got rid of them somehow, and could set off homewards), he would say he thought that he had, for such was his invariable safe form of answer; and would fumble in breast-pockets, waistcoat-pockets, breeches-pockets, and, as a last resource, in coat-tail pockets; and at length try to comfort me, if I looked disappointed, by telling me, "Hoo had missed this toime, but was sure to write tomorrow;" "Hoo" representing an imaginary sweetheart.

Sometimes I had seen the minister bring home a letter which he had found lying for him at the little shop that was the post-office at Heathbridge, or from the grander establishment at Hornby. Once or twice Josiah, the carter, remembered that the old letter-carrier had trusted him with an epistle to "Measter," as they had met in the lanes. I think it must have been about ten days after my arrival at the farm, and my talk to Phillis cutting bread-and-butter at the kitchen dresser, before the day on which the minister suddenly spoke at the dinner-table, and said—

"By-the-by, I've got a letter in my pocket. Reach me my coat here, Phillis." The weather was still sultry, and for coolness and ease the minister was sitting in his shirt-sleeves. "I went to Heathbridge about the paper they had sent me, which spoils all the pens—and I called at the post-office, and found a letter for me, unpaid—and they did not like to trust it to old Zekiel. Ay! here it is! Now we shall hear news of Holdsworth—I thought I'd keep it till we were all together." My heart seemed to stop beating, and I hung my head over my plate, not daring to look up. What would come of it now? What was Phillis doing? How was she looking? A moment of suspense—and then he spoke again. "Why! what's this? Here are two visiting tickets with his name on, no writing at all. No! it's not his name on both. Mrs. Holdsworth! The young man has gone and got married." I lifted my head at these words; I could not help looking just for one instant at Phillis. It seemed to me as if she had been keeping watch over my face and ways. Her face was brilliantly flushed; her eyes were dry and glittering; but she did not speak; her lips were set together almost as if she was pinching them tight to prevent words or sounds coming out. Cousin Holman's face expressed surprise and interest.

"Well!" said she, "who'd ha' thought it! He's made quick work of his wooing and wedding. I'm sure I wish him happy. Let me see"—counting on her fingers—"October, November, December, January, February, March, April, May, June, July—at least we're at the 28th—it is nearly ten months after all, and reckon a month each way off—"

"Did you know of this news before?" said the minister, turning sharp round on me, surprised, I suppose, at my silence—hardly suspicious, as yet.

"I knew—I had heard—something. It is to a French Canadian young lady," I went on, forcing myself to talk. "Her name is Ventadour."

"Lucille Ventadour!" said Phillis, in a sharp voice, out of tune.

"Then you knew too!" exclaimed the minister. We both spoke at once. I said, "I heard of the probability of—and told Phillis." She said, "He is married to Lucille Ventadour, of French descent; one of a large family near St. Meurice; am not I right?" I nodded "Paul told me—that is all we know, is not it? Did you see the Howsons, father, in Heathbridge?" and she forced herself to talk more than she had done for several days, asking many questions, trying, as I could see, to keep the conversation off the one raw surface, on which to touch was agony. I had less self-command; but I followed her lead. I was not so much absorbed in the conversation but what I could see that the minister was puzzled and uneasy; though he seconded Phillis's efforts to prevent her mother from recurring to the great piece of news, and uttering continual exclamations of wonder and surprise. But with that one exception we were all disturbed out of our natural equanimity, more or less. Every day, every hour, I was reproaching myself more and more for my blundering officiousness. If only I had held my foolish tongue for that one half-hour; if only I had not been in such impatient haste to do something to relieve pain! I could have knocked my stupid head against the wall in my remorse. Yet all I could do now was to second the brave girl in her efforts to conceal her disappointment and keep her maidenly secret. But I thought that dinner would never, never come to an end. I suffered for her, even more than for myself. Until now everything which I had heard spoken in that happy household were simple words of true meaning. If we had aught to say, we said it; and if any one preferred silence, nay if all did so, there would have been no spasmodic, forced efforts to talk for the sake of talking, or to keep off intrusive thoughts or suspicions.

At length we got up from our places, and prepared to disperse; but two or three of us had lost our zest and interest in the daily labour. The minister stood looking out of the window in silence, and when he roused himself to go out to the fields where his labourers were working, it was with a sigh; and he tried to avert his troubled face as he passed us on his way to the door. When he had left us, I caught sight of Phillis's face, as, thinking herself unobserved, her countenance relaxed for a moment or two into sad, woeful weariness. She started into briskness again when her mother spoke, and hurried away to do some little errand at her bidding. When we two were alone, cousin Holman recurred to Holdsworth's marriage. She was one of those people who like to view an event from every side of probability, or even possibility; and she had been cut short from indulging herself in this way during dinner.

"To think of Mr. Holdsworth's being married! I can't get over it, Paul. Not but what he was a very nice young man! I don't like her name, though; it sounds foreign. Say it again, my dear. I hope she'll know how to take care of him, English fashion. He is not strong, and if she does not see that his things are well aired, I should be afraid of the old cough."

"He always said he was stronger than he had ever been before, after that fever."

"He might think so, but I have my doubts. He was a very pleasant young man, but he did not stand nursing very well. He got tired of being coddled, as he called it. I hope they'll soon come back to England, and then he'll have a chance for his health. I wonder now, if she speaks English; but, to be sure, he can speak foreign tongues like anything, as I've heard the minister say." And so we went on for some time, till she became drowsy over her knitting, on the sultry summer afternoon; and I stole away for a walk, for I wanted some solitude in which to think over things, and, alas! to blame myself with poignant stabs of remorse.

I lounged lazily as soon as I got to the wood. Here and there the bubbling, brawling brook circled round a great stone, or a root of an old tree, and made a pool; otherwise it coursed brightly over the gravel and stones. I stood by one of these for more than half an hour, or, indeed, longer, throwing bits of wood or pebbles into the water, and wondering what I could do to remedy the present state of things. Of course all my meditation was of no use; and at length the distant sound of the horn employed to tell the men far afield to leave off work, warned me that it was six o'clock, and time for me to go home. Then I caught wafts of the loud-voiced singing of the evening psalm. As I was crossing the Ashfield, I saw the minister at some distance talking to a man. I could not hear what they were saying, but I saw an impatient or dissentient (I could not tell which) gesture on the part of the former, who walked quickly away, and was apparently absorbed in his thoughts, for though he passed within twenty yards of me, as both our paths converged towards home, he took no notice of me. We passed the evening in a way which was even worse than dinner-time. The minister was silent, depressed, even irritable. Poor cousin Holman was utterly perplexed by this unusual frame of mind and temper in her husband; she was not well herself, and was suffering from the extreme and sultry heat, which made her less talkative than usual. Phillis, usually so reverently tender to her parents, so soft, so gentle, seemed now to take no notice of the unusual state of things, but talked to me—to any one, on indifferent subjects, regardless of her father's gravity, of her mother's piteous looks of bewilderment. But once my eyes fell upon her hands, concealed under the table, and I could see the passionate, convulsive manner in which she laced and interlaced her fingers perpetually, wringing them together from time to time, wringing till the compressed flesh became perfectly white. What could I do? I talked with her, as I saw she wished; her grey eyes had dark circles round them and a strange kind of dark light in them; her cheeks were flushed, but her lips were white and wan. I wondered that others did not read these signs as clearly as I did. But perhaps they did; I think, from what came afterwards, the minister did. Poor cousin Holman! she worshipped her husband; and the outward signs of his uneasiness were more patent to her simple heart than were her daughter's. After a while she could bear it no longer. She got up, and, softly laying her hand on his broad stooping shoulder, she said—

"What is the matter, minister? Has anything gone wrong?"

He started as if from a dream. Phillis hung her head, and caught her breath in terror at the answer she feared. But he, looking round with a sweeping glance, turned his broad, wise face up to his anxious wife, and forced a smile, and took her hand in a reassuring manner.

"I am blaming myself, dear. I have been overcome with anger this afternoon. I scarcely knew what I was doing, but I turned away Timothy Cooper. He has killed the Ribstone pippin at the corner of the orchard; gone and piled the quicklime for the mortar for the new stable wall against the trunk of the tree—stupid fellow! killed the tree outright—and it loaded with apples!"

"And Ribstone pippins are so scarce," said sympathetic cousin Holman.

"Ay! But Timothy is but a half-wit; and he has a wife and children. He had often put me to it sore, with his slothful ways, but I had laid it before the Lord, and striven to bear with him. But I will not stand it any longer, it's past my patience. And he has notice to find another place. Wife, we won't talk more about it." He took her hand gently off his shoulder, touched it with his lips; but relapsed into a silence as profound, if not quite so morose in appearance, as before. I could not tell why, but this bit of talk between her father and mother seemed to take all the factitious spirits out of Phillis. She did not speak now, but looked out of the open casement at the calm large moon, slowly moving through the twilight sky. Once I thought her eyes were filling with tears; but, if so, she shook them off, and arose with alacrity when her mother, tired and dispirited, proposed to go to bed immediately after prayers. We all said good-night in our separate ways to the minister, who still sate at the table with the great Bible open before him, not much looking up at any of our salutations, but returning them kindly. But when I, last of all, was on the point of leaving the room, he said, still scarcely looking up—

"Paul, you will oblige me by staying here a few minutes. I would fain have some talk with you."

I knew what was coming, all in a moment. I carefully shut-to the door, put out my candle, and sate down to my fate. He seemed to find some difficulty in beginning, for, if I had not heard that he wanted to speak to me, I should never have guessed it, he seemed so much absorbed in reading a chapter to the end. Suddenly he lifted his head up and said—

"It is about that friend of yours, Holdsworth! Paul, have you any reason for thinking he has played tricks upon Phillis?" I saw that his eyes were blazing with such a fire of anger at the bare idea, that I lost all my presence of mind, and only repeated—

"Played tricks on Phillis!"

"Ay! you know what I mean: made love to her, courted her, made her think that he loved her, and then gone away and left her. Put it as you will, only give me an answer of some kind or another—a true answer, I mean—and don't repeat my words, Paul."

He was shaking all over as he said this. I did not delay a moment in answering him—

"I do not believe that Edward Holdsworth ever played tricks on Phillis, ever made love to her; he never, to my knowledge, made her believe that he loved her."

I stopped; I wanted to nerve up my courage for a confession, yet I wished to save the secret of Phillis's love for Holdsworth as much as I could; that secret which she had so striven to keep sacred and safe; and I had need of some reflection before I went on with what I had to say.

He began again before I had quite arranged my manner of speech. It was almost as if to himself—"She is my only child; my little daughter! She is hardly out of childhood; I have thought to gather her under my wings for years to come her mother and I would lay down our lives to keep her from harm and grief." Then, raising his voice, and looking at me, he said, "Something has gone wrong with the child; and it seemed to me to date from the time she heard of that marriage. It is hard to think that you may know more of her secret cares and sorrows than I do—but perhaps you do, Paul, perhaps you do—only, if it be not a sin, tell me what I can do to make her happy again; tell me."

"It will not do much good, I am afraid," said I, "but I will own how wrong I did; I don't mean wrong in the way of sin, but in the way of judgment.

Holdsworth told me just before he went that he loved Phillis, and hoped to make her his wife, and I told her."

There! it was out; all my part in it, at least; and I set my lips tight together, and waited for the words to come. I did not see his face; I looked straight at the wall opposite; but I heard him once begin to speak, and then turn over the leaves in the book before him. How awfully still that room was! The air outside, how still it was! The open windows let in no rustle of leaves, no twitter or movement of birds—no sound whatever. The clock on the stairs— the minister's hard breathing—was it to go on for ever? Impatient beyond bearing at the deep quiet, I spoke again—

"I did it for the best, as I thought."

The minister shut the book to hastily, and stood up. Then I saw how angry he was.

"For the best, do you say? It was best, was it, to go and tell a young girl what you never told a word of to her parents, who trusted you like a son of their own?"

He began walking about, up and down the room close under the open windows, churning up his bitter thoughts of me.

"To put such thoughts into the child's head," continued he; "to spoil her peaceful maidenhood with talk about another man's love; and such love, too," he spoke scornfully now—"a love that is ready for any young woman. Oh, the misery in my poor little daughter's face today at dinner—the misery, Paul! I thought you were one to be trusted—your father's son too, to go and put such thoughts into the child's mind; you two talking together about that man wishing to marry her."

I could not help remembering the pinafore, the childish garment which Phillis wore so long, as if her parents were unaware of her progress towards womanhood. Just in the same way the minister spoke and thought of her now, as a child, whose innocent peace I had spoiled by vain and foolish talk. I knew that the truth was different, though I could hardly have told it now; but, indeed, I never thought of trying to tell; it was far from my mind to add one iota to the sorrow which I had caused. The minister went on walking, occasionally stopping to move things on the table, or articles of furniture, in a sharp, impatient, meaningless way, then he began again—

"So young, so pure from the world! how could you go and talk to such a child, raising hopes, exciting feelings—all to end thus; and best so, even though I saw her poor piteous face look as it did. I can't forgive you, Paul; it was more than wrong—it was wicked—to go and repeat that man's words."

His back was now to the door, and, in listening to his low angry tones, he did not hear it slowly open, nor did he see Phillis, standing just within the room, until he turned round; then he stood still. She must have been half undressed; but she had covered herself with a dark winter cloak, which fell in long folds to her white, naked, noiseless feet. Her face was strangely pale: her eyes heavy in the black circles round them. She came up to the table very slowly, and leant her hand upon it, saying mournfully—

"Father, you must not blame Paul. I could not help hearing a great deal of what you were saying. He did tell me, and perhaps it would have been wiser not, dear Paul! But—oh, dear! oh, dear! I am so sick with shame! He told me out of his kind heart, because he saw—that I was so very unhappy at his going away." She hung her head, and leant more heavily than before on her supporting hand.

"I don't understand," said her father; but he was beginning to understand. Phillis did not answer till he asked her again. I could have struck him now for his cruelty; but then I knew all.

"I loved him, father!" she said at length, raising her eyes to the minister's face. "Had he ever spoken of love to you? Paul says not!"

"Never." She let fall her eyes, and drooped more than ever. I almost thought she would fall.

"I could not have believed it," said he, in a hard voice, yet sighing the moment he had spoken. A dead silence for a moment. "Paul! I was unjust to you. You deserved blame, but not all that I said." Then again a silence. I thought I saw Phillis's white lips moving, but it might have been the flickering of the candlelight—a moth had flown in through the open casement, and was fluttering round the flame; I might have saved it, but I did not care to do so, my heart was too full of other things. At any rate, no sound was heard for long endless minutes. Then he said—"Phillis! did we not make you happy here? Have we not loved you enough?"

She did not seem to understand the drift of this question; she looked up as if bewildered, and her beautiful eyes dilated with a painful, tortured expression. He went on, without noticing the look on her face; he did not see it, I am sure.

"And yet you would have left us, left your home, left your father and your mother, and gone away with this stranger, wandering over the world." He suffered, too; there were tones of pain in the voice in which he uttered this reproach. Probably the father and daughter were never so far apart in their lives, so unsympathetic. Yet some new terror came over her, and it was to him she turned for help. A shadow came over her face, and she tottered towards her father; falling down, her arms across his knees, and moaning out—

"Father, my head! my head!" and then slipped through his quick-enfolding arms, and lay on the ground at his feet.

I shall never forget his sudden look of agony while I live; never! We raised her up; her colour had strangely darkened; she was insensible. I ran through the back-kitchen to the yard pump, and brought back water. The minister had her on his knees, her head against his breast, almost as though she were a sleeping child. He was trying to rise up with his poor precious burden, but the momentary terror had robbed the strong man of his strength, and he sank back in his chair with sobbing breath.

"She is not dead, Paul! is she?" he whispered, hoarse, as I came near him. I, too, could not speak, but I pointed to the quivering of the muscles round her mouth. Just then cousin Holman, attracted by some unwonted sound, came down. I remember I was surprised at the time at her presence of mind, she seemed to know so much better what to do than the minister, in the midst of the sick affright which blanched her countenance, and made her tremble all over. I think now that it was the recollection of what had gone before; the miserable thought that possibly his words had brought on this attack, whatever it might be, that so unmanned the minister. We carried her upstairs, and while the women were putting her to bed, still unconscious, still slightly convulsed, I slipped out, and saddled one of the horses, and rode as fast as the heavy-trotting beast could go, to Hornby, to find the doctor there, and bring him back. He was out, might be detained the whole night. I remember saying, "God help us all!" as I sate on my horse, under the window, through which the apprentice's head had appeared to answer my furious tugs at the night-bell. He was a good-natured fellow. He said—

"He may be home in half an hour, there's no knowing; but I daresay he will. I'll send him out to the Hope Farm directly he comes in. It's that good-looking young woman, Holman's daughter, that's ill, isn't it?"

"Yes."

"It would be a pity if she was to go. She's an only child, isn't she? I'll get up, and smoke a pipe in the surgery, ready for the governor's coming home. I might go to sleep if I went to bed again."

"Thank you, you're a good fellow!" and I rode back almost as quickly as I came. It was a brain fever. The doctor said so, when he came in the early summer morning. I believe we had come to know the nature of the illness in the night-watches that had gone before. As to hope of ultimate recovery, or even evil prophecy of the probable end, the cautious doctor would be entrapped into neither. He gave his directions, and promised to come again; so soon, that this one thing showed his opinion of the gravity of the case.

By God's mercy she recovered, but it was a long, weary time first. According to previously made plans, I was to have gone home at the beginning of August. But all such ideas were put aside now, without a word being spoken. I really think that I was necessary in the house, and especially necessary to the minister at this time; my father was the last man in the world, under such circumstances, to expect me home.

I say, I think I was necessary in the house. Every person (1 had almost said every creature, for all the dumb beasts seemed to know and love Phillis) about the place went grieving and sad, as though a cloud was over the sun. They did their work, each striving to steer clear of the temptation to eye-service, in fulfilment of the trust reposed in them by the minister. For the day after Phillis had been taken ill, he had called all the men employed on the farm into the empty barn; and there he had entreated their prayers for his only child; and then and there he had told them of his present incapacity for thought about any other thing in this world but his little daughter, lying nigh unto death, and he had asked them to go on with their daily labours as best they could, without his direction. So, as I say, these honest men did their work to the best of their ability, but they slouched along with sad and careful faces, coming one by one in the dim mornings to ask news of the sorrow that overshadowed the house; and receiving Betty's intelligence, always rather darkened by passing through her mind, with slow shakes of the head, and a dull wistfulness of sympathy. But, poor fellows, they were hardly fit to be trusted with hasty messages, and here my poor services came in. One time I was to ride hard to Sir William Bentinck's, and petition for ice out of his ice-house, to put on Phillis's head. Another it was to Eltham I must go, by train, horse, anyhow, and bid the doctor there come for a consultation, for fresh symptoms had appeared, which Mr. Brown, of Hornby, considered unfavourable. Many an hour have I sate on the window-seat, half-way up the stairs, close by the old clock, listening in the hot stillness of the house for the sounds in the sick-room. The minister and I met often, but spoke together seldom. He looked so old—so old! He shared the nursing with his wife; the strength that was needed seemed to be given to them both in that day. They required no one else about their child. Every office about her was sacred to them; even Betty only went into the room for the most necessary purposes. Once I saw Phillis through the open door; her pretty golden hair had been cut off long before; her head was covered with wet cloths, and she was moving it backwards and forwards on the pillow, with weary, never-ending motion, her poor eyes shut, trying in the old accustomed way to croon out a hymn tune, but perpetually breaking it up into moans of pain. Her mother sate by her, tearless, changing the cloths upon her head with patient solicitude. I did not see the minister at first, but there he was in a dark corner, down upon his knees, his hands clasped together in passionate prayer. Then the door shut, and I saw no more. One day he was wanted; and I had to summon him. Brother Robinson and another minister, hearing of his "trial," had come to see him. I told him this upon the stair-landing in a whisper. He was strangely troubled.

"They will want me to lay bare my heart. I cannot do it. Paul, stay with me.

They mean well; but as for spiritual help at such a time—it is God only, God only, who can give it.

So I went in with him. They were two ministers from the neighbourhood; both older than Ebenezer Holman; but evidently inferior to him in education and worldly position. I thought they looked at me as if I were an intruder, but remembering the minister's words I held my ground, and took up one of poor Phillis's books (of which I could not read a word) to have an ostensible occupation. Presently I was asked to "engage in prayer," and we all knelt down; Brother Robinson "leading," and quoting largely as I remember from the Book of Job. He seemed to take for his text, if texts are ever taken for prayers,

"Behold thou hast instructed many; but now it is come upon thee, and thou faintest, it toucheth thee and thou art troubled." When we others rose up, the minister continued for some minutes on his knees. Then he too got up, and stood facing us, for a moment, before we all sate down in conclave. After a pause Robinson began—

"We grieve for you, Brother Holman, for your trouble is great. But we would fain have you remember you are as a light set on a hill; and the congregations are looking at you with watchful eyes. We have been talking as we came along on the two duties required of you in this strait; Brother Hodgson and me. And we have resolved to exhort you on these two points. First, God has given you the opportunity of showing forth an example of resignation." Poor Mr. Holman visibly winced at this word. I could fancy how he had tossed aside such brotherly preachings in his happier moments; but now his whole system was unstrung, and "resignation" seemed a term which presupposed that the dreaded misery of losing Phillis was inevitable. But good stupid Mr. Robinson went on. "We hear on all sides that there are scarce any hopes of your child's recovery; and it may be well to bring you to mind of Abraham; and how he was willing to kill his only child when the Lord commanded. Take example by him, Brother Holman. Let us hear you say, 'The Lord giveth and the Lord taketh away. Blessed be the name of the Lord!'"

There was a pause of expectancy. I verily believe the minister tried to feel it; but he could not. Heart of flesh was too strong. Heart of stone he had not.

"I will say it to my God, when He gives me strength—when the day comes," he spoke at last.

The other two looked at each other, and shook their heads. I think the reluctance to answer as they wished was not quite unexpected. The minister went on "There are yet" he said, as if to himself. "God has given me a great heart for hoping, and I will not look forward beyond the hour." Then turning more to them—and speaking louder, he added: "Brethren, God will strengthen me when the time comes, when such resignation as you speak of is needed. Till then I cannot feel it; and what I do not feel I will not express;

using words as if they were a charm." He was getting chafed, I could see. He had rather put them out by these speeches of his; but after a short time and some more shakes of the head, Robinson began again—

"Secondly, we would have you listen to the voice of the rod, and ask yourself for what sins this trial has been laid upon you; whether you may not have been too much given up to your farm and your cattle; whether this world's learning has not puffed you up to vain conceit and neglect of the things of God; whether you have not made an idol of your daughter?"

"I cannot answer—I will not answer," exclaimed the minister. "My sins I confess to God. But if they were scarlet (and they are so in His sight)," he added, humbly, "I hold with Christ that afflictions are not sent by God in wrath as penalties for sin."

"Is that orthodox, Brother Robinson?" asked the third minister, in a deferential tone of inquiry.

Despite the minister's injunction not to leave him, I thought matters were getting so serious that a little homely interruption would be more to the purpose than my continued presence, and I went round to the kitchen to ask for Betty's help.

"'Od rot 'em!" said she; "they're always a-coming at ill-convenient times; and they have such hearty appetites, they'll make nothing of what would have served master and you since our poor lass has been ill. I've but a bit of cold beef in th' house; but I'll do some ham and eggs, and that'll rout 'em from worrying the minister. They're a deal quieter after they've had their victual. Last time as old Robinson came, he was very reprehensible upon master's learning, which he couldn't compass to save his life, so he needn't have been afeard of that temptation, and used words long enough to have knocked a body down; but after me and missus had given him his fill of victual, and he'd had some good ale and a pipe, he spoke just like any other man, and could crack a joke with me."

Their visit was the only break in the long weary days and nights. I do not mean that no other inquiries were made. I believe that all the neighbours hung about the place daily till they could learn from some out-comer how Phillis Holman was. But they knew better than to come up to the house, for the August weather was so hot that every door and window was kept constantly open, and the least sound outside penetrated all through. I am sure the cocks and hens had a sad time of it; for Betty drove them all into an empty barn, and kept them fastened up in the dark for several days, with very little effect as regarded their crowing and clacking. At length came a sleep which was the crisis, and from which she wakened up with a new faint life. Her slumber had lasted many, many hours. We scarcely dared to breathe or move during the time; we had striven to hope so long, that we were sick at heart, and durst not trust in the favourable signs: the even breathing, the moistened skin, the slight return of delicate colour into the pale, wan lips. I recollect stealing out that evening in the dusk, and wandering down the grassy lane, under the shadow of the over-arching elms to the little bridge at the foot of the hill, where the lane to the Hope Farm joined another road to Hornby. On the low parapet of that bridge I found Timothy Cooper, the stupid, half-witted labourer, sitting, idly throwing bits of mortar into the brook below. He just looked up at me as I came near, but gave me no greeting either by word or gesture. He had generally made some sign of recognition to me, but this time I thought he was sullen at being dismissed. Nevertheless I felt as if it would be a relief to talk a little to some one, and I sate down by him. While I was thinking how to begin, he yawned weariedly.

"You are tired, Tim?" said I.

"Ay," said he. "But I reckon I may go home now."

"Have you been sitting here long?"

"Welly all day long. Leastways sin' seven i' th' morning."

"Why, what in the world have you been doing?"

"Nought."

"Why have you been sitting here, then?"

"T' keep carts off." He was up now, stretching himself, and shaking his lubberly limbs.

"Carts! what carts?"

"Carts as might ha' wakened yon wench! It's Hornby market day. I reckon yo're no better nor a half-wit yoursel'." He cocked his eye at me as if he were gauging my intellect.

"And have you been sitting here all day to keep the lane quiet?"

"Ay. I've nought else to do. Th' minister has turned me adrift. Have yo' heard how th' lass is faring tonight?"

"They hope she'll waken better for this long sleep. Good night to you, and God bless you, Timothy," said I.

He scarcely took any notice of my words, as he lumbered across a Stile that led to his cottage. Presently I went home to the farm. Phillis had stirred, had spoken two or three faint words. Her mother was with her, dropping nourishment into her scarce conscious mouth. The rest of the household were summoned to evening prayer for the first time for many days. It was a return to the daily habits of happiness and health. But in these silent days our very lives had been an unspoken prayer. Now we met in the house-place, and looked at each other with strange recognition of the thankfulness on all our faces. We knelt down; we waited for the minister's voice. He did not begin as usual. He could not; he was choking. Presently we heard the strong man's sob. Then old John turned round on his knees, and said—

"Minister, I reckon we have blessed the Lord wi' all our souls, though we've ne'er talked about it; and maybe He'll not need spoken words this night. God bless us all, and keep our Phillis safe from harm! Amen." Old John's impromptu prayer was all we had that night.

"Our Phillis," as he called her, grew better day by day from that time. Not quickly; I sometimes grew desponding, and feared that she would never be what she had been before; no more she has, in some ways.

I seized an early opportunity to tell the minister about Timothy Cooper's unsolicited watch on the bridge during the long summer's day.

"God forgive me!" said the minister. "I have been too proud in my own conceit. The first steps I take out of this house shall be to Cooper's cottage."

I need hardly say Timothy was reinstated in his place on the farm; and I have often since admired the patience with which his master tried to teach him how to do the easy work which was henceforward carefully adjusted to his capacity. Phillis was carried down-stairs, and lay for hour after hour quite silent on the great sofa, drawn up under the windows of the house-place. She seemed always the same, gentle, quiet, and sad. Her energy did not return with her bodily strength. It was sometimes pitiful to see her parents' vain endeavours to rouse her to interest. One day the minister brought her a set of blue ribbons, reminding her with a tender smile of a former conversation in which she had owned to a love of such feminine vanities. She spoke gratefully to him, but when he was gone she laid them on one side, and languidly shut her eyes. Another time I saw her mother bring her the Latin and Italian books that she had been so fond of before her illness—or, rather, before Holdsworth had gone away. That was worst of all. She turned her face to the wall, and cried as soon as her mother's back was turned. Betty was laying the cloth for the early dinner. Her sharp eyes saw the state of the case.

"Now, Phillis!" said she, coming up to the sofa; "we ha' done a' we can for you, and th' doctors has done a' they can for you, and I think the Lord has done a' He can for you, and more than you deserve, too, if you don't do something for yourself. If I were you, I'd rise up and snuff the moon, sooner than break your father's and your mother's hearts wi' watching and waiting till it pleases you to fight your own way back to cheerfulness. There, I never favoured long preachings, and I've said my say."

A day or two after Phillis asked me, when we were alone, if I thought my father and mother would allow her to go and stay with them for a couple of months. She blushed a little as she faltered out her wish for change of thought and scene.

"Only for a short time, Paul. Then—we will go back to the peace of the old days. I know we shall; I can, and I will!"

LUELLA MILLER

Mary E. Wilkins Freeman

Close to the village street stood the one-story house in which Luella Miller, who had an evil name in the village, had dwelt. She had been dead for years, yet there were those in the village who, in spite of the clearer light which comes on a vantage-point from a long-past danger, half believed in the tale which they had heard from their childhood. In their hearts, although they scarcely would have owned it, was a survival of the wild horror and frenzied fear of their ancestors who had dwelt in the same age with Luella Miller. Young people even would stare with a shudder at the old house as they passed, and children never played around it as was their wont around an untenanted building. Not a window in the old Miller house was broken: the panes reflected the morning sunlight in patches of emerald and blue, and the latch of the sagging front door was never lifted, although no bolt secured it. Since Luella Miller had been carried out of it, the house had had no tenant except one friendless old soul who had no choice between that and the far-off shelter of the open sky. This old woman, who had survived her kindred and friends, lived in the house one week, then one morning no smoke came out of the chimney, and a body of neighbours, a score strong, entered and found her dead in her bed. There were dark whispers as to the cause of her death, and there were those who testified to an expression of fear so exalted that it showed forth the state of the departing soul upon the dead face. The old woman had been hale and hearty when she entered the house, and in seven days she was dead; it seemed that she had fallen a victim to some uncanny power. The minister talked in the pulpit with covert severity against the sin of superstition; still the belief prevailed. Not a soul in the village but would have chosen the almshouse rather than that dwelling. No vagrant, if he heard the tale, would seek shelter beneath that old roof, unhallowed by nearly half a century of superstitious fear.

There was only one person in the village who had actually known Luella Miller. That person was a woman well over eighty, but a marvel of vitality and unextinct youth. Straight as an arrow, with the spring of one recently let loose from the bow of life, she moved about the streets, and she always went to church, rain or shine. She had never married, and had lived alone for years in a house across the road from Luella Miller's.

This woman had none of the garrulousness of age, but never in all her life had she ever held her tongue for any will save her own, and she never spared the truth when she essayed to present it. She it was who bore testimony to the life, evil, though possibly wittingly or designedly so, of Luella Miller, and to her personal appearance. When this old woman spoke—and she had the gift of description, although her thoughts were clothed in the rude vernacular of her native village—one could seem to see Luella Miller as she had really looked. According to this woman, Lydia Anderson by name, Luella Miller had been a beauty of a type rather unusual in New England. She had been a slight, pliant sort of creature, as ready with a strong yielding to fate and as unbreakable as a willow. She had glimmering lengths of straight, fair hair, which she wore softly looped round a long, lovely face. She had blue eyes full of soft pleading, little slender, clinging hands, and a wonderful grace of motion and attitude.

"Luella Miller used to sit in a way nobody else could if they sat up and studied a week of Sundays," said Lydia Anderson, "and it was a sight to see her walk. If one of them willows over there on the edge of the brook could start up and get its roots free of the ground, and move off, it would go just the way Luella Miller used to. She had a green shot silk she used to wear, too, and a hat with green ribbon streamers, and a lace veil blowing across her face and out sideways, and a green ribbon flyin' from her waist. That was what she came out bride in when she married Erastus Miller. Her name before she was married was Hill. There was always a sight of "l's" in her name, married or single. Erastus Miller was good lookin', too, better lookin' than Luella. Sometimes I used to think that Luella wa'n't so handsome after all. Erastus just about worshiped her. I used to know him pretty well. He lived next door to me, and we went to school together. Folks used to say he was waitin' on me, but he wa'n't. I never thought he was except once or twice when he said things that some girls might have suspected meant somethin'. That was before Luella came here to teach the district school. It was funny how she came to get it, for folks said she hadn't any education, and that one of the big girls, Lottie Henderson, used to do all the teachin' for her, while she sat back and did embroidery work on a cambric pocket-handkerchief. Lottie Henderson was a real smart girl, a splendid scholar, and she just set her eyes by Luella, as all the girls did. Lottie would have made a real smart woman, but she died when Luella had been here about a year—just faded away and died: nobody knew what ailed her. She dragged herself to that schoolhouse and helped Luella teach till the very last minute. The committee all knew how Luella didn't do much of the work herself, but they winked at it. It wa'n't long after Lottie died that Erastus married her. I always thought he hurried it up because she wa'n't fit to teach. One of the big boys used to help her after Lottie died, but he hadn't much government, and the school didn't do very well, and Luella might have had to give it up, for the committee couldn't have shut their eyes to things much longer. The boy that helped her was a real honest, innocent sort of fellow, and he was a good scholar, too. Folks said he overstudied, and that was the reason he was took crazy the year after Luella married, but I don't know. And I don't know what made Erastus Miller go into consumption of the blood the year after he was married: consumption wa'n't in his family. He just grew weaker and weaker, and went almost bent double when he tried to wait on Luella, and he spoke feeble, like an old man. He worked terrible hard till the last trying to save up a little to leave Luella. I've seen him out in the worst storms on a wood-sled—he used to cut and sell wood—and he was hunched up on top lookin' more dead than alive. Once I couldn't stand it: I went over and helped him pitch some wood on the cart—I was always strong in my arms. I wouldn't stop for all he told me to, and I guess he was glad enough for the help. That was only a week before he died. He fell on the kitchen floor while he was gettin' breakfast. He always got the breakfast and let Luella lay abed. He did all the sweepin' and the washin' and the ironin' and most of the cookin'. He couldn't bear to have Luella lift her finger, and she let him do for her. She lived like a queen for all the work she did. She didn't even do her sewin'. She said it made her shoulder ache to sew, and poor Erastus's sister Lily used to do all her sewin'. She wa'n't able to, either; she was never strong in her back, but she did it beautifully. She had to, to suit Luella, she was so dreadful particular. I never saw anythin' like the fagottin' and hemstitchin' that Lily Miller did for Luella. She made all Luella's weddin' outfit, and that green silk dress, after Maria Babbit cut it. Maria she cut it for nothin', and she did a lot more cuttin' and fittin' for nothin' for Luella, too. Lily Miller went to live with Luella after Erastus died. She gave up her home, though she was real attached to it and wa'n't a mite afraid to stay alone. She rented it and she went to live with Luella right away after the funeral."

Then this old woman, Lydia Anderson, who remembered Luella Miller, would go on to relate the story of Lily Miller. It seemed that on the removal of Lily Miller to the house of her dead brother, to live with his widow, the village people first began to talk. This Lily Miller had been hardly past her first youth, and a most robust and blooming woman, rosy-cheeked, with curls of strong, black hair overshadowing round, candid temples and bright dark eyes. It was not six months after she had taken up her residence with her sister-in-law that her rosy colour faded and her pretty curves became wan hollows. White shadows began to show in the black rings of her hair, and the light died out of her eyes, her features sharpened, and there were pathetic lines at her mouth, which yet wore always an expression of utter sweetness and even happiness. She was devoted to her sister; there was no doubt that she loved her with her whole heart, and was perfectly content in her service. It was her sole anxiety lest she should die and leave her alone.

"The way Lily Miller used to talk about Luella was enough to make you mad and enough to make you cry," said Lydia Anderson. "I've been in there sometimes toward the last when she was too feeble to cook and carried her some blanc-mange or custard—somethin' I thought she might relish, and she'd thank me, and when I asked her how she was, say she felt better than she did yesterday, and asked me if I didn't think she looked better, dreadful pitiful, and say poor Luella had an awful time takin' care of her and doin' the work—she wa'n't strong enough to do anythin'—when all the time Luella wa'n't liftin' her finger and poor Lily didn't get any care except what the neighbours gave her, and Luella eat up everythin' that was carried in for Lily. I had it real straight that she did. Luella used to just sit and cry and do nothin'. She did act real fond of Lily, and she pined away considerable, too. There was those that thought she'd go into a decline herself. But after Lily died, her Aunt Abby Mixter came, and then Luella picked up and grew as fat and rosy as ever. But poor Aunt Abby begun to droop just the way Lily had, and I guess somebody wrote to her married daughter, Mrs. Sam Abbot, who lived in Barre, for she wrote her mother that she must leave right away and come and make her a visit, but Aunt Abby wouldn't go. I can see her now. She was a real good-lookin' woman, tall and large, with a big, square face and a high forehead that looked of itself kind of benevolent and good. She just tended out on Luella as if she had been a baby, and when her married daughter sent for her she wouldn't stir one inch. She'd always thought a lot of her daughter, too, but she said Luella needed her and her married daughter didn't. Her daughter kept writin' and writin', but it didn't do any good. Finally she came, and when she saw how bad her mother looked, she broke down and cried and all but went on her knees to have her come away. She spoke her mind out to Luella, too. She told her that she'd killed her husband and everybody that had anythin' to do with her, and she'd thank her to leave her mother alone. Luella went into hysterics, and Aunt Abby was so frightened that she called me after her daughter went. Mrs. Sam Abbot she went away fairly cryin' out loud in the buggy, the neighbours heard her, and well she might, for she never saw her mother again alive. I went in that night when Aunt Abby called for me, standin' in the door with her little green-checked shawl over her head. I can see her now. 'Do come over here, Miss Anderson,' she sung out, kind of gasping for breath. I didn't stop for anythin'. I put over as fast as I could, and when I got there, there was Luella laughin' and cryin' all together, and Aunt Abby trying to hush her, and all the time she herself was white as a sheet and shakin' so she could hardly stand. 'For the land sakes, Mrs. Mixter,' says I, 'you look worse than she does. You ain't fit to be up out of your bed.'

"'Oh, there ain't anythin' the matter with me,' says she. Then she went on talkin' to Luella. 'There, there, don't, don't, poor little lamb,' says she. 'Aunt Abby is here. She ain't goin' away and leave you. Don't, poor little lamb.'

"'Do leave her with me, Mrs. Mixter, and you get back to bed,' says I, for Aunt Abby had been layin' down considerable lately, though somehow she contrived to do the work.

"'I'm well enough,' says she. 'Don't you think she had better have the doctor, Miss Anderson?'

"'The doctor,' says I, 'I think *you* had better have the doctor. I think you need him much worse than some folks I could mention.' And I looked right straight at Luella Miller laughin' and cryin' and goin' on as if she was the centre of all creation. All the time she was actin' so—seemed as if she was too sick to sense anythin'—she was keepin' a sharp lookout as to how we took it out of the corner of one eye. I see her. You could never cheat me about Luella Miller. Finally I got real mad and I run home and I got a bottle of valerian I had, and I poured some boilin' hot water on a handful of catnip, and I mixed up that catnip tea with most half a wineglass of valerian, and I went with it over to Luella's. I marched right up to Luella, a-holdin' out of that cup, all smokin'. 'Now,' says I, 'Luella Miller, *you swaller this!*'

"'What is—what is it, oh, what is it?' she sort of screeches out. Then she goes off a-laughin' enough to kill.

"'Poor lamb, poor little lamb,' says Aunt Abby, standin' over her, all kind of tottery, and tryin' to bathe her head with camphor.

"'*You swaller this right down,*' says I. And I didn't waste any ceremony. I just took hold of Luella Miller's chin and I tipped her head back, and I caught her mouth open with laughin', and I clapped that cup to her lips, and I fairly hollered at her: 'Swaller, swaller, swaller!' and she gulped it right down. She had to, and I guess it did her good. Anyhow, she stopped cryin' and laughin' and let me put her to bed, and she went to sleep like a baby inside of half an hour. That was more than poor Aunt Abby did. She lay awake all that night and I stayed with her, though she tried not to have me; said she wa'n't sick enough for watchers. But I stayed, and I made some good cornmeal gruel and I fed her a teaspoon every little while all night long. It seemed to me as if she was jest dyin' from bein' all wore out. In the mornin' as soon as it was light I run over to the Bisbees and sent Johnny Bisbee for the doctor. I told him to tell the doctor to hurry, and he come pretty quick. Poor Aunt Abby didn't seem to know much of anythin' when he got there. You couldn't hardly tell she breathed, she was so used up. When the doctor had gone, Luella came into the room lookin' like a baby in her ruffled nightgown. I can see her now. Her eyes were as blue and her face all pink and white like a blossom, and she looked at Aunt Abby in the bed sort of innocent and surprised. 'Why,' says she, 'Aunt Abby ain't got up yet?'

" 'No, she ain't,' says I, pretty short.

" 'I thought I didn't smell the coffee,' says Luella.

" 'Coffee,' says I. 'I guess if you have coffee this mornin' you'll make it yourself.'

" 'I never made the coffee in all my life,' says she, dreadful astonished. 'Erastus always made the coffee as long as he lived, and then Lily she made it, and then Aunt Abby made it. I don't believe I *can* make the coffee, Miss Anderson.'

" 'You can make it or go without, jest as you please,' says I.

" 'Ain't Aunt Abby goin' to get up?' says she.

" 'I guess she won't get up,' says I, 'sick as she is.' I was gettin' madder and madder. There was somethin' about that little pink-and-white thing standin' there and talkin' about coffee, when she had killed so many better folks than she was, and had jest killed another, that made me feel 'most as if I wished somebody would up and kill her before she had a chance to do any more harm.

" 'Is Aunt Abby sick?' says Luella, as if she was sort of aggrieved and injured.

" 'Yes,' says I, 'she's sick, and she's goin' to die, and then you'll be left alone, and you'll have to do for yourself and wait on yourself, or do without things.' I don't know but I was sort of hard, but it was the truth, and if I was any harder than Luella Miller had been I'll give up. I ain't never been sorry that I said it. Well, Luella, she up and had hysterics again at that, and I jest let her have 'em. All I did was to bundle her into the room on the other side of the entry where Aunt Abby couldn't hear her, if she wa'n't past it—I don't know but she was—and set her down hard in a chair and told her not to come back into the other room, and she minded. She had her hysterics in there till she got tired. When she found out that nobody was comin' to coddle her and do for her she stopped. At least I suppose she did. I had all I could do with poor Aunt Abby tryin' to keep the breath of life in her. The doctor had told me that she was dreadful low, and give me some very strong medicine to give to her in drops real often, and told me real particular about the nourishment. Well, I did as he told me real faithful till she wa'n't able to swaller any longer. Then I had her daughter sent for. I had begun to realize that she wouldn't last any time at all. I hadn't realized it before, though I spoke to Luella the way I did. The doctor he came, and Mrs. Sam Abbot, but when she got there it was too late; her mother was dead. Aunt Abby's daughter just give one look at her mother layin' there, then she turned sort of sharp and sudden and looked at me.

" 'Where is she?' says she, and I knew she meant Luella.

" 'She's out in the kitchen,' says I. 'She's too nervous to see folks die. She's afraid it will make her sick.'

"The Doctor he speaks up then. He was a young man. Old Doctor Park had died the year before, and this was a young fellow just out of college. 'Mrs. Miller is not strong,' says he, kind of severe, 'and she is quite right in not agitating herself.'

"'You are another, young man; she's got her pretty claw on you,' thinks I, but I didn't say anythin' to him. I just said over to Mrs. Sam Abbot that Luella was in the kitchen, and Mrs. Sam Abbot she went out there, and I went, too, and I never heard anythin' like the way she talked to Luella Miller. I felt pretty hard to Luella myself, but this was more than I ever would have dared to say. Luella she was too scared to go into hysterics. She jest flopped. She seemed to jest shrink away to nothin' in that kitchen chair, with Mrs. Sam Abbot standin' over her and talkin' and tellin' her the truth. I guess the truth was most too much for her and no mistake, because Luella presently actually did faint away, and there wa'n't any sham about it, the way I always suspected there was about them hysterics. She fainted dead away and we had to lay her flat on the floor, and the Doctor he came runnin' out and he said somethin' about a weak heart dreadful fierce to Mrs. Sam Abbot, but she wa'n't a mite scared. She faced him jest as white as even Luella was layin' there lookin' like death and the Doctor feelin' of her pulse.

"'Weak heart,' says she, 'weak heart; weak fiddlesticks! There ain't nothin' weak about that woman. She's got strength enough to hang onto other folks till she kills 'em. Weak? It was my poor mother that was weak: this woman killed her as sure as if she had taken a knife to her.'

"But the Doctor he didn't pay much attention. He was bendin' over Luella layin' there with her yellow hair all streamin' and her pretty pink-and-white face all pale, and her blue eyes like stars gone out, and he was holdin' onto her hand and smoothin' her forehead, and tellin' me to get the brandy in Aunt Abby's room, and I was sure as I wanted to be that Luella had got somebody else to hang onto, now Aunt Abby was gone, and I thought of poor Erastus Miller, and I sort of pitied the poor young Doctor, led away by a pretty face, and I made up my mind I'd see what I could do.

"I waited till Aunt Abby had been dead and buried about a month, and the Doctor was goin' to see Luella steady and folks were beginnin' to talk; then one evenin', when I knew the Doctor had been called out of town and wouldn't be round, I went over to Luella's. I found her all dressed up in a blue muslin with white polka dots on it, and her hair curled jest as pretty, and there wa'n't a young girl in the place could compare with her. There was somethin' about Luella Miller seemed to draw the heart right out of you, but she didn't draw it out of *me*. She was settin' rocking in the chair by her sittin'-room window, and Maria Brown had gone home. Maria Brown had been in to help her, or rather to do the work, for Luella wa'n't helped when she didn't do anythin'. Maria Brown was real capable and she didn't have any ties; she wa'n't married, and lived alone, so she'd offered. I couldn't see why she should do the work any more than Luella; she wa'n't any too strong; but she seemed to think she could and Luella seemed to think so, too, so she went over and did all the work—washed, and ironed, and baked, while Luella sat and rocked. Maria didn't live long afterward. She began to fade away just the same fashion the others had. Well, she was warned, but she acted real mad when folks said anythin': said Luella was a poor, abused woman, too delicate to help herself, and they'd ought to be ashamed, and if she died helpin' them that couldn't help themselves she would—and she did.

"'I s'pose Maria has gone home,' says I to Luella, when I had gone in and sat down opposite her.

"'Yes, Maria went half an hour ago, after she had got supper and washed the dishes,' says Luella, in her pretty way.

"'I suppose she has got a lot of work to do in her own house to-night,' says I, kind of bitter, but that was all thrown away on Luella Miller. It seemed to her right that other folks that wa'n't any better able than she was herself should wait on her, and she couldn't get it through her head that anybody should think it *wa'n't* right.

"'Yes,' says Luella, real sweet and pretty, 'yes, she said she had to do her washin' to-night. She has let it go for a fortnight along of comin' over here.'

"'Why don't she stay home and do her washin' instead of comin' over here and doin' *your* work, when you are just as well able, and enough sight more so, than she is to do it?' says I.

"Then Luella she looked at me like a baby who has a rattle shook at it. She sort of laughed as innocent as you please. 'Oh, I can't do the work myself, Miss Anderson,' says she. 'I never did. Maria *has* to do it.'

"Then I spoke out: 'Has to do it I' says I. 'Has to do it!' She don't have to do it, either. Maria Brown has her own home and enough to live on. She ain't beholden to you to come over here and slave for you and kill herself.'

"Luella she jest set and stared at me for all the world like a doll-baby that was so abused that it was comin' to life.

"'Yes,' says I, 'she's killin' herself. She's goin' to die just the way Erastus did, and Lily, and your Aunt Abby. You're killin' her jest as you did them. I don't know what there is about you, but you seem to bring a curse,' says I. 'You kill everybody that is fool enough to care anythin' about you and do for you.'

"She stared at me and she was pretty pale.

"'And Maria ain't the only one you're goin' to kill,' says I. 'You're goin' to kill Doctor Malcom before you're done with him.'

"Then a red colour came flamin' all over her face. 'I ain't goin' to kill him, either,' says she, and she begun to cry.

"'Yes, you *be*!' says I. Then I spoke as I had never spoke before. You see, I felt it on account of Erastus. I told her that she hadn't any business to think of another man after she'd been married to one that had died for her: that she was a dreadful woman; and she was, that's true enough, but sometimes I have wondered lately if she knew it—if she wa'n't like a baby with scissors in its hand cuttin' everybody without knowin' what it was doin'.

"Luella she kept gettin' paler and paler, and she never took her eyes off my face. There was somethin' awful about the way she looked at me and never spoke one word. After awhile I quit talkin' and I went home. I watched that night, but her lamp went out before nine o'clock, and when Doctor Malcom came drivin' past and sort of slowed up he see there wa'n't any light and he drove along. I saw her sort of shy out of meetin' the next Sunday, too, so he shouldn't go home with her, and I begun to think mebbe she did have some conscience after all. It was only a week after that that Maria Brown died—sort of sudden at the last, though everybody had seen it was comin'. Well, then there was a good deal of feelin' and pretty dark whispers. Folks said the days of witchcraft had come again, and they were pretty shy of Luella. She acted sort of offish to the Doctor and he didn't go there, and there wa'n't anybody to do anythin' for her. I don't know how she *did* get along. I wouldn't go in there and offer to help her—not because I was afraid of dyin' like the rest, but I thought she was just as well able to do her own work as I was to do it for her, and I thought it was about time that she did it and stopped killin' other folks. But it wa'n't very long before folks began to say that Luella herself was goin' into a decline jest the way her husband, and Lily, and Aunt Abby and the others had, and I saw myself that she looked pretty bad. I used to see her goin' past from the store with a bundle as if she could hardly crawl, but I remembered how Erastus used to wait and 'tend when he couldn't hardly put one foot before the other, and I didn't go out to help her.

"But at last one afternoon I saw the Doctor come drivin' up like mad with his medicine chest, and Mrs. Babbit came in after supper and said that Luella was real sick.

"'I'd offer to go in and nurse her,' says she, 'but I've got my children to consider, and mebbe it ain't true what they say, but it's queer how many folks that have done for her have died.'

"I didn't say anythin', but I considered how she had been Erastus's wife and how he had set his eyes by her, and I made up my mind to go in the next mornin', unless she was better, and see what I could do; but the next mornin' I see her at the window, and pretty soon she came steppin' out as spry as you please, and a little while afterward Mrs. Babbit came in and told me that the Doctor had got a girl from out of town, a Sarah Jones, to come there, and she said she was pretty sure that the Doctor was goin' to marry Luella.

"I saw him kiss her in the door that night myself, and I knew it was true. The woman came that afternoon, and the way she flew around was a caution. I don't believe Luella had swept since Maria died. She swept and dusted, and washed and ironed; wet clothes and dusters and carpets were flyin' over there all day, and every time Luella set her foot out when the Doctor wa'n't there there was that Sarah Jones helpin' of her up and down the steps, as if she hadn't learned to walk.

"Well, everybody knew that Luella and the Doctor were goin' to be married, but it wa'n't long before they began to talk about his lookin' so poorly, jest as they had about the others; and they talked about Sarah Jones, too.

"Well, the Doctor did die, and he wanted to be married first, so as to leave what little he had to Luella, but he died before the minister could get there, and Sarah Jones died a week afterward.

"Well, that wound up everything for Luella Miller. Not another soul in the whole town would lift a finger for her. There got to be a sort of panic. Then she began to droop in good earnest. She used to have to go to the store herself, for Mrs. Babbit was afraid to let Tommy go for her, and I've seen her goin' past and stoppin' every two or three steps to rest. Well, I stood it as long as I could, but one day I see her comin' with her arms full and stoppin' to lean against the Babbit fence, and I run out and took her bundles and carried them to her house. Then I went home and never spoke one word to her though she called after me dreadful kind of pitiful. Well, that night I was taken sick with a chill, and I was sick as I wanted to be for two weeks. Mrs. Babbit had seen me run out to help Luella and she came in and told me I was goin' to die on account of it. I didn't know whether I was or not, but I considered I had done right by Erastus's wife.

"That last two weeks Luella she had a dreadful hard time, I guess. She was pretty sick, and as near as I could make out nobody dared go near her. I don't know as she was really needin' anythin' very much, for there was enough to eat in her house and it was warm weather, and she made out to cook a little flour gruel every day, I know, but I guess she had a hard time, she that had been so petted and done for all her life.

"When I got so I could go out, I went over there one morning. Mrs. Babbit had just come in to say she hadn't seen any smoke and she didn't know but it was somebody's duty to go in, but she couldn't help thinkin' of her children, and I got right up, though I hadn't been out of the house for two weeks, and I went in there, and Luella she was layin' on the bed, and she was dyin'.

"She lasted all that day and into the night. But I sat there after the new doctor had gone away. Nobody else dared to go there. It was about midnight that I left her for a minute to run home and get some medicine I had been takin', for I begun to feel rather bad.

"It was a full moon that night, and just as I started out of my door to cross the street back to Luella's, I stopped short, for I saw something."

Lydia Anderson at this juncture always said with a certain defiance that she did not expect to be believed, and then proceeded in a hushed voice:

"I saw what I saw, and I know I saw it, and I will swear on my death bed that I saw it. I saw Luella Miller and Erastus Miller, and Lily, and Aunt Abby, and Maria, and the Doctor, and Sarah, all goin' out of her door, and all but Luella shone white in the moonlight, and they were all helpin' her along till she seemed to fairly fly in the midst of them. Then it all disappeared. I stood a minute with my heart poundin', then I went over there. I thought of goin' for Mrs. Babbit, but I thought she'd be afraid. So I went alone, though I knew what had happened. Luella was layin' real peaceful, dead on her bed."

This was the story that the old woman, Lydia Anderson, told, but the sequel was told by the people who survived her, and this is the tale which has become folklore in the village.

Lydia Anderson died when she was eighty-seven. She had continued wonderfully hale and hearty for one of her years until about two weeks before her death.

One bright moonlight evening she was sitting beside a window in her parlour when she made a sudden exclamation, and was out of the house and across the street before the neighbour who was taking care of her could stop her. She followed as fast as possible and found Lydia Anderson stretched on the ground before the door of Luella Miller's deserted house, and she was quite dead.

The next night there was a red gleam of fire athwart the moonlight and the old house of Luella Miller was burned to the ground. Nothing is now left of it except a few old cellar stones and a lilac bush, and in summer a helpless trail of morning glories among the weeds, which might be considered emblematic of Luella herself.

LIFE

Charlotte Brontë

Life, believe, is not a dream
So dark as sages say;
Oft a little morning rain
Foretells a pleasant day.
Sometimes there are clouds of gloom,
But these are transient all;
If the shower will make the roses bloom,
O why lament its fall?
Rapidly, merrily,
Life's sunny hours flit by,
Gratefully, cheerily
Enjoy them as they fly!
What though Death at times steps in,
And calls our Best away?
What though sorrow seems to win,
O'er hope, a heavy sway?
Yet Hope again elastic springs,
Unconquered, though she fell;
Still buoyant are her golden wings,
Still strong to bear us well.
Manfully, fearlessly,
The day of trial bear,
For gloriously, victoriously,
Can courage quell despair!

STARS

Emily Brontë

Ah! why, because the dazzling sun
Restored our Earth to joy,
Have you departed, every one,
And left a desert sky?

All through the night, your glorious eyes
Were gazing down in mine,
And, with a full heart's thankful sighs,
I blessed that watch divine.

I was at peace, and drank your beams
As they were life to me;
And revelled in my changeful dreams,
Like petrel on the sea.

Thought followed thought, star followed star
Through boundless regions on;
While one sweet influence, near and far,
Thrilled through, and proved us one!

Why did the morning dawn to break
So great, so pure a spell;
And scorch with fire the tranquil cheek,
Where your cool radiance fell?

Blood-red, he rose, and, arrow-straight,
His fierce beams struck my brow;
The soul of nature sprang, elate,
But mine sank sad and low.

My lids closed down, yet through their veil
I saw him, blazing, still,
And steep in gold the misty dale,
And flash upon the hill.

I turned me to the pillow, then,
To call back night, and see
Your worlds of solemn light, again,
Throb with my heart, and me!

It would not do——the pillow glowed,
And glowed both roof and floor;
And birds sang loudly in the wood,
And fresh winds shook the door.

The curtains waved, the wakened flies
Were murmuring round my room,
Imprisoned there, till I should rise,
And give them leave to roam.

O stars, and dreams, and gentle night;
O night and stars, return!
And hide me from the hostile light
That does not warm, but burn;

That drains the blood of suffering men;
Drinks tears, instead of dew;
Let me sleep through his blinding reign,
And only wake with you!

DREAMS

Anne Brontë

While on my lonely couch I lie,
I seldom feel myself alone,
For fancy fills my dreaming eye
With scenes and pleasures of its own.

Then I may cherish at my breast
An infant's form beloved and fair,
May smile and soothe it into rest
With all a Mother's fondest care.

How sweet to feel its helpless form
Depending thus on me alone!
And while I hold it safe and warm
What bliss to think it is my own!

And glances then may meet my eyes
That daylight never showed to me;
What raptures in my bosom rise,
Those earnest looks of love to see,

To feel my hand so kindly prest,
To know myself beloved at last,
To think my heart has found a rest,
My life of solitude is past!

But then to wake and find it flown,
The dream of happiness destroyed,
To find myself unloved, alone,
What tongue can speak the dreary void?

A heart whence warm affections flow,
Creator, thou hast given to me,
And am I only thus to know
How sweet the joys of love would be?

SILLY NOVELS BY LADY NOVELISTS

George Eliot

*This article was published anonymously in the October 1856 issue of
the* Westminster Review, *three years before Eliot published
her first novel,* Adam Bede.

Silly Novels by Lady Novelists are a genus with many species, determined by the particular quality of silliness that predominates in them—the frothy, the prosy, the pious, or the pedantic. But it is a mixture of all these—a composite order of feminine fatuity—that produces the largest class of such novels, which we shall distinguish as the *mind-and-millinery* species. The heroine is usually an heiress, probably a peeress in her own right, with perhaps a vicious baronet, an amiable duke, and an irresistible younger son of a marquis as lovers in the foreground, a clergyman and a poet sighing for her in the middle distance, and a crowd of undefined adorers dimly indicated beyond. Her eyes and her wit are both dazzling; her nose and her morals are alike free from any tendency to irregularity; she has a superb *contralto* and a superb intellect; she is perfectly well dressed and perfectly religious; she dances like a sylph, and reads the Bible in the original tongues. Or it may be that the heroine is not an heiress—that rank and wealth are the only things in which she is deficient; but she infallibly gets into high society, she has the triumph of refusing many matches and securing the best, and she wears some family jewels or other as a sort of crown of righteousness at the end. Rakish men either bite their lips in impotent confusion at her repartees, or are touched to penitence by her reproofs, which, on appropriate occasions, rise to a lofty strain of rhetoric; indeed, there is a general propensity in her to make speeches, and to rhapsodize at some length when she retires to her bedroom. In her recorded conversations she is amazingly eloquent, and in her unrecorded conversations amazingly witty. She is understood to have a depth of insight that looks through and through the shallow theories of philosophers, and her superior instincts are a sort of dial by which men have only to set their clocks and watches, and all will go well. The men play a very subordinate part by her side. You are consoled now and then by a hint that they have affairs, which keeps you in mind that the working-day business of the world is somehow being carried on, but ostensibly the final cause of their existence is that they may accompany the heroine on her "starring" expedition through life. They see her at a ball, and they are dazzled; at a flower-show, and they are fascinated; on a riding excursion, and they are witched by her noble horsemanship; at church, and they are awed by the sweet solemnity of her demeanor. She is the ideal woman in feelings, faculties, and flounces. For all this she as often as not marries the wrong person to begin with, and she suffers terribly from the plots and intrigues of the vicious baronet; but even death has a soft place in his heart for such a paragon, and remedies all mistakes for her just at the right moment. The vicious baronet is sure to be killed in a duel, and the tedious husband dies in his bed requesting his wife, as a particular favor to him, to marry the man she loves best, and having already dispatched a note to the lover informing him of the comfortable arrangement. Before matters arrive at this desirable issue our feelings are tried by seeing the noble, lovely, and gifted heroine pass through many *mauvais moments*, but we have the satisfaction of knowing that her sorrows are wept into embroidered pocket-handkerchiefs, that her fainting form reclines on the very best upholstery, and that whatever vicissitudes she may undergo, from being dashed out of her carriage to having her head shaved in a fever, she comes out of them all with a complexion more blooming and locks more redundant than ever.

We may remark, by the way, that we have been relieved from a serious scruple by discovering that silly novels by lady novelists rarely introduce us into any other than very lofty and fashionable society. We had imagined that destitute women turned novelists, as they turned governesses, because they had no other "lady-like" means of getting their bread. On this supposition, vacillating syntax, and improbable incident had a certain pathos for us, like the extremely supererogatory pincushions and ill-devised nightcaps that are offered for sale by a blind man. We felt the commodity to be a nuisance, but we were glad to think that the money went to relieve the necessitous, and we pictured to ourselves lonely women struggling for a maintenance, or wives and daughters devoting themselves to the production of "copy" out of pure heroism—perhaps to pay their husband's debts or to purchase luxuries for a sick father. Under these impressions we shrank from criticising a lady's novel: her English might be faulty, but we said to ourselves her motives are irreproachable; her imagination may be uninventive, but her patience is untiring. Empty writing was excused by an empty stomach, and twaddle was consecrated by tears. But no! This theory of ours, like many other pretty theories, has had to give way before observation. Women's silly novels, we are now convinced, are written under totally different circumstances. The fair writers have evidently never talked to a tradesman except from a carriage window; they have no notion of the working-classes except as "dependents"; they think £500 a year a miserable pittance; Belgravia and "baronial halls" are their primary truths; and they have no idea of feeling interest in any man who is not at least a great landed proprietor, if not a prime minister. It is clear that they write in elegant boudoirs, with violet-colored ink and a ruby pen; that they must be entirely indifferent to publishers' accounts, and inexperienced in every form of poverty except poverty of brains. It is true that we are constantly struck with the want of verisimilitude in their representations of the high society in which they seem to live; but then they betray no closer acquaintance with any other form of life. If their peers and peeresses are improbable, their literary men, tradespeople, and cottagers are impossible; and their intellect seems to have the peculiar impartiality of reproducing both what they *have* seen and heard, and what they have *not* seen and heard, with equal unfaithfulness.

There are few women, we suppose, who have not seen something of children under five years of age, yet in "Compensation," a recent novel of the mind-and-millinery species, which calls itself a "story of real life," we have a child of four and a half years old talking in this Ossianic fashion:

> "Oh, I am so happy, dear grand mamma;—I have seen—I have seen such a delightful person; he is like everything beautiful—like the smell of sweet flowers, and the view from Ben Lemond;—or no, *better than that*—he is like what I think of and see when I am very, very happy; and he is really like mamma, too, when she sings; and his forehead is like *that distant sea*," she continued, pointing to the blue Mediterranean; "there seems no end—no end; or like the clusters of stars I like best to look at on a warm fine night . . . Don't look so . . . your forehead is like Loch Lomond, when the wind is blowing and the sun is gone in; I like the sunshine best when the lake is smooth . . . So now—I like it better than ever . . . It is more beautiful still from the dark cloud that has gone over it, *when the sun suddenly lights up all the colors of the forests and shining purple rocks, and it is all reflected in the waters below.*"

We are not surprised to learn that the mother of this infant phenomenon, who exhibits symptoms so alarmingly like those of adolescence repressed by gin, is herself a phoenix. We are assured, again and again, that she had a remarkably original in mind, that she was a genius, and "conscious of her originality," and she was fortunate enough to have a lover who was also a genius and a man of "most original mind."

This lover, we read, though "wonderfully similar" to her "in powers and capacity," was "infinitely superior to her in faith and development," and she saw in him "'Agape'—so rare to find—of which she had read and admired the meaning in her Greek Testament; having, *from her great facility in learning languages*, read the Scriptures in their original *tongues.*" Of course! Greek and

Hebrew are mere play to a heroine; Sanscrit is no more than *a b c* to her; and she can talk with perfect correctness in any language, except English. She is a polking polyglot, a Creuzer in crinoline. Poor men. There are so few of you who know even Hebrew; you think it something to boast of if, like Bolingbroke, you only "understand that sort of learning and what is writ about it"; and you are perhaps adoring women who can think slightingly of you in all the Semitic languages successively. But, then, as we are almost invariably told that a heroine has a "beautifully small head," and as her intellect has probably been early invigorated by an attention to costume and deportment, we may conclude that she can pick up the Oriental tongues, to say nothing of their dialects, with the same aërial facility that the butterfly sips nectar. Besides, there can be no difficulty in conceiving the depth of the heroine's erudition when that of the authoress is so evident.

In "Laura Gay," another novel of the same school, the heroine seems less at home in Greek and Hebrew but she makes up for the deficiency by a quite playful familiarity with the Latin classics—with the "dear old Virgil," "the graceful Horace, the humane Cicero, and the pleasant Livy"; indeed, it is such a matter of course with her to quote Latin that she does it at a picnic in a very mixed company of ladies and gentlemen, having, we are told, "no conception that the nobler sex were capable of jealousy on this subject. And if, indeed," continues the biographer of Laura Gray, "the wisest and noblest portion of that sex were in the majority, no such sentiment would exist; but while Miss Wyndhams and Mr. Redfords abound, great sacrifices must be made to their existence." Such sacrifices, we presume, as abstaining from Latin quotations, of extremely moderate interest and applicability, which the wise and noble minority of the other sex would be quite as willing to dispense with as the foolish and ignoble majority. It is as little the custom of well-bred men as of well-bred women to quote Latin in mixed parties; they can contain their familiarity with "the humane Cicero" without allowing it to boil over in ordinary conversation, and even references to "the pleasant Livy" are not absolutely irrepressible. But Ciceronian Latin is the mildest form of Miss Gay's conversational power. Being on the Palatine with a party of sight-seers, she falls into the following vein of well-rounded remark:

> "Truth can only be pure objectively, for even in the creeds where it
> predominates, being subjective, and parcelled out into portions, each
> of these necessarily receives a hue of idiosyncrasy, that is, a taint of
> superstition more or less strong; while in such creeds as the Roman
> Catholic, ignorance, interest, the basis of ancient idolatries, and the
> force of authority, have gradually accumulated on the pure truth, and
> transformed it, at last, into a mass of superstition for the majority

of its votaries; and how few are there, alas! whose zeal, courage, and intellectual energy are equal to the analysis of this accumulation, and to the discovery of the pearl of great price which lies hidden beneath this heap of rubbish."

We have often met with women much more novel and profound in their observations than Laura Gay, but rarely with any so inopportunely long-winded. A clerical lord, who is half in love with her, is alarmed by the daring remarks just quoted, and begins to suspect that she is inclined to free-thinking. But he is mistaken; when in a moment of sorrow he delicately begs leave to "recall to her memory, a *dépôt* of strength and consolation under affliction, which, until we are hard pressed by the trials of life, we are too apt to forget," we learn that she really has "recurrence to that sacred *dépôt*," together with the tea-pot. There is a certain flavor of orthodoxy mixed with the parade of fortunes and fine carriages in "Laura Gay," but it is an orthodoxy mitigated by study of "the humane Cicero," and by an "intellectual disposition to analyze."

"Compensation" is much more heavily dosed with doctrine, but then it has a treble amount of snobbish worldliness and absurd incident to tickle the palate of pious frivolity. Linda, the heroine, is still more speculative and spiritual than Laura Gay, but she has been "presented," and has more and far grander lovers; very wicked and fascinating women are introduced—even a French *lionne*; and no expense is spared to get up as exciting a story as you will find in the most immoral novels. In fact, it is a wonderful *pot pourri* of Almack's, Scotch second-sight, Mr. Rogers's breakfasts, Italian brigands, death-bed conversions, superior authoresses, Italian mistresses, and attempts at poisoning old ladies, the whole served up with a garnish of talk about "faith and development" and "most original minds." Even Miss Susan Barton, the superior authoress, whose pen moves in a "quick, decided manner when she is composing," declines the finest opportunities of marriage; and though old enough to be Linda's mother (since we are told that she refused Linda's father), has her hand sought by a young earl, the heroine's rejected lover. Of course, genius and morality must be backed by eligible offers, or they would seem rather a dull affair; and piety, like other things, in order to be *comme il faut*, must be in "society," and have admittance to the best circles.

"Rank and Beauty" is a more frothy and less religious variety of the mind-and-millinery species. The heroine, we are told, "if she inherited her father's pride of birth and her mother's beauty of person, had in herself a tone of enthusiastic feeling that, perhaps, belongs to her age even in the lowly born, but which is refined into the high spirit of wild romance only in the far descended, who feel that it is their best inheritance." This enthusiastic young lady, by dint of reading the newspaper to her father, falls in love with the *prime minister*, who, through the medium of leading articles and "the *resumé* of the debates," shines upon her imagination as a bright particular star, which has no parallax for her living in the country as simple Miss Wyndham. But she forthwith becomes Baroness Umfraville in her own right, astonishes the world with her beauty and accomplishments when she bursts upon it from her mansion in Spring Gardens, and, as you foresee, will presently come into contact with the unseen *objet aimé*. Perhaps the words "prime minister" suggest to you a wrinkled or obese sexagenarian; but pray dismiss the image. Lord Rupert Conway has been "called while still almost a youth to the first situation which a subject can hold in the *universe*," and even leading articles and a *resumé* of the debates have not conjured up a dream that surpasses the fact.

> The door opened again, and Lord Rupert Conway entered. Evelyn gave one glance. It was enough; she was not disappointed. It seemed as if a picture on which she had long gazed was suddenly instinct with life, and had stepped from its frame before her. His tall figure, the distinguished simplicity of his air—it was a living Vandyke, a cavalier, one of his noble cavalier ancestors, or one to whom her fancy had always likened him, who long of yore had with an Umfraville fought the Paynim far beyond the sea. Was this reality?

Very little like it, certainly.

By and by it becomes evident that the ministerial heart is touched. Lady Umfraville is on a visit to the Queen at Windsor, and—

> The last evening of her stay, when they returned from riding, Mr. Wyndham took her and a large party to the top of the Keep, to see the view. She was leaning on the battlements, gazing from that "stately height" at the prospect beneath her, when Lord Rupert was by her side. "What an unrivalled view!" exclaimed she.
>
> "Yes, it would have been wrong to go without having been up here. You are pleased with your visit?"
>
> "Enchanted! 'A Queen to live and die under,' to live and die for!"
>
> "Ha!" cried he, with sudden emotion, and with a *eureka* expression of countenance, as if he had *indeed found a heart in unison with his own*.

The "*eureka* expression of countenance" you see at once to be prophetic of marriage at the end of the third volume; but before that desirable consummation there are very complicated misunderstandings, arising chiefly from the vindictive plotting of Sir Luttrel Wycherley, who is a genius, a poet, and in every way a most remarkable character indeed. He is not only a romantic poet, but a hardened rake and a cynical wit; yet his deep passion for Lady Umfraville has so impoverished his epigrammatic talent that he cuts an extremely poor figure in conversation. When she rejects him, he rushes into the shrubbery and rolls himself in the dirt; and on recovering, devotes himself to the most diabolical and laborious schemes of vengeance, in the course of which he disguises himself as a quack physician and enters into general practice, foreseeing that Evelyn will fall ill, and that he shall be called in to attend her. At last, when all his schemes are frustrated, he takes leave of her in a long letter, written, as you will perceive from the following passage, entirely in the style of an eminent literary man:

"Oh, lady, nursed in pomp and pleasure, will you ever cast one thought upon the miserable being who addresses you? Will you ever, as your gilded galley is floating down the unruffled stream of prosperity, will you ever, while lulled by the sweetest music—thine own praises— hear the far-off sigh from that world to which I am going?"

On the whole, however, frothy as it is, we rather prefer "Rank and Beauty" to the two other novels we have mentioned. The dialogue is more natural and spirited; there is some frank ignorance and no pedantry; and you are allowed to take the heroine's astounding intellect upon trust, without being called on to read her conversational refutations of sceptics and philosophers, or her rhetorical solutions of the mysteries of the universe.

Writers of the mind-and-millinery school are remarkably unanimous in their choice of diction. In their novels there is usually a lady or gentleman who is more or less of a upas tree; the lover has a manly breast; minds are redolent of various things; hearts are hollow; events are utilized; friends are consigned to the tomb; infancy is an engaging period; the sun is a luminary that goes to his western couch, or gathers the rain-drops into his refulgent bosom; life is a melancholy boon; Albion and Scotia are conversational epithets. There is a striking resemblance, too, in the character of their moral comments, such, for instance, as that "It is a fact, no less true than melancholy, that all people, more or less, richer or poorer, are swayed by bad example"; that "Books, however trivial, contain some subjects from which useful information may be drawn"; that "Vice can too often borrow the language of virtue"; that "Merit and nobility of nature must exist, to be accepted, for clamor and pretension cannot impose upon those too well read in human nature to be easily deceived"; and that "In order to forgive, we must have been injured." There is doubtless a class of readers to whom these remarks appear peculiarly pointed and pungent; for we often find them doubly and trebly scored with the pencil, and delicate hands giving in their determined adhesion to these hardy novelties by a distinct *très vrai*, emphasized by many notes of exclamation. The colloquial style of these novels is often marked by much ingenious inversion, and a careful avoidance of such cheap phraseology as can be heard every day. Angry young gentlemen exclaim, "'Tis ever thus, methinks"; and in the half hour before dinner a young lady informs her next neighbor that the first day she read Shakespeare she "stole away into the park, and beneath the shadow of the greenwood tree, devoured with rapture the inspired page of the great magician." But the most remarkable efforts of the mind-and-millinery writers lie in their philosophic reflections. The authoress of "Laura Gay," for example, having married her hero and heroine, improves the event by observing that "if those sceptics, whose eyes have so long gazed on matter that they can no longer see aught else in man, could once enter with heart and soul, into such bliss as this, they would come to say that the soul of man and the polypus are not of common origin, or of the same texture." Lady novelists, it appears, can see something else besides matter; they are not limited to phenomena, but can relieve their eyesight by occasional glimpses of the *noumenon*, and are, therefore, naturally better able than any one else to confound sceptics, even of that remarkable but to us unknown school which maintains that the soul of man is of the same texture as the polypus.

The most pitiable of all silly novels by lady novelists are what we may call the *oracular* species—novels intended to expound the writer's religious, philosophical, or moral theories. There seems to be a notion abroad among women, rather akin to the superstition that the speech and actions of idiots are inspired, and that the human being most entirely exhausted of common sense is the fittest vehicle of revelation. To judge from their writings, there are certain ladies who think that an amazing ignorance, both of science and of life, is the best possible qualification for forming an opinion on the knottiest moral and speculative questions. Apparently, their recipe for solving all such difficulties is something like this: Take a woman's head, stuff it with a smattering of philosophy and literature chopped small, and with false notions of society baked hard, let it hang over a desk a few hours every day, and serve up hot in feeble English when not required. You will rarely meet with a lady novelist of the oracular class who is diffident of her ability to decide on theological questions—who has any suspicion that she is not capable of discriminating with the nicest accuracy between the good and evil in all church parties—who does not see precisely how it is that men have gone wrong hitherto—and pity philosophers in general that they have not had the opportunity of consulting her. Great writers, who have modestly contented themselves with putting their experience into fiction, and have thought it quite a sufficient task to exhibit men and things as they are, she sighs over as deplorably deficient in the application of their powers. "They have solved no great questions"—and she is ready to remedy their omission by setting before you a complete theory of life and manual of divinity in a love story, where ladies and gentlemen of good family go through genteel vicissitudes, to the utter confusion of Deists, Puseyites, and ultra-Protestants, and to the perfect establishment of that peculiar view of Christianity which either condenses itself into a sentence of small caps, or explodes into a cluster of stars on the three hundred and thirtieth page. It is true, the ladies and gentlemen will probably seem to you remarkably little like any you have had the fortune or misfortune to meet with, for, as a general rule, the ability of a lady novelist to describe actual life and her fellow-men is in inverse proportion to her confident eloquence about God and the other world, and the means by which she usually chooses to conduct you to true ideas of the invisible is a totally false picture of the visible.

As typical a novel of the oracular kind as we can hope to meet with, is "The Enigma: a Leaf from the Chronicles of the Wolchorley House." The "enigma" which this novel is to solve is certainly one that demands powers no less gigantic than those of a lady novelist, being neither more nor less than the existence of evil. The problem is stated and the answer dimly foreshadowed on the very first page. The spirited young lady, with raven hair, says, "All life is an inextricable confusion"; and the meek young lady, with auburn hair, looks at the picture of the Madonna which she is copying, and—"*There* seemed the solution of that mighty enigma." The style of this novel is quite as lofty as its purpose; indeed, some passages on which we have spent much patient study are quite beyond our reach, in spite of the illustrative aid of italics and small caps; and we must await further "development" in order to understand them. Of Ernest, the model young clergyman, who sets every one right on all occasions, we read that "he held not of marriage in the marketable kind, after a social desecration"; that, on one eventful night, "sleep had not visited his divided heart, where tumultuated, in varied type and combination, the aggregate feelings of grief and joy"; and that, "for the *marketable* human article he had no toleration, be it of what sort, or set for what value it might, whether for worship or class, his upright soul abhorred it, whose ultimatum, the self-deceiver, was to him THE *great spiritual lie*, 'living in a vain show, deceiving and being deceived;' since he did not suppose the phylactery and enlarged border on the garment to be *merely* a social trick." (The italics and small caps are the author's, and we hope they assist the reader's comprehension.) Of Sir Lionel, the model old gentleman, we are told that "the simple ideal of the middle age, apart from its anarchy and decadence, in him most truly seemed to live again, when the ties which knit men together were of heroic cast. The first-born colours of pristine faith and truth engraven on the common soul of man, and blent into the wide arch of brotherhood, where the primæval law of *order* grew and multiplied each perfect after his kind, and mutually interdependent." You see clearly, of course, how colours are first engraven on the soul, and then blent into a wide arch, on which arch of colours—apparently a rainbow—the law of order grew and multiplied, each—apparently the arch and the law—perfect after his kind? If, after this, you can possibly want any further aid toward knowing what Sir Lionel was, we can tell you that in his soul "the scientific combinations of thought could educe no fuller harmonies of the good and the true than lay in the primæval pulses which floated as an atmosphere around it!" and that, when he was sealing a letter, "Lo! the responsive throb in that good man's bosom echoed back in simple truth the honest witness of a heart that condemned him not, as his eye, bedewed with love, rested, too, with something of ancestral pride, on the undimmed motto of the family—LOUIAUTÉ."

The slightest matters have their vulgarity fumigated out of them by the same elevated style. Commonplace people would say that a copy of Shakespeare lay on a drawing-room table; but the authoress of "The Enigma," bent on edifying periphrasis, tells you that there lay on the table, "that fund of human thought and feeling, which teaches the heart through the little name, 'Shakespeare.'" A watchman sees a light burning in an upper window rather longer than usual, and thinks that people are foolish to sit up late when they have an opportunity of going to bed; but, lest this fact should seem too low and common, it is presented to us in the following striking and metaphysical manner: "He marvelled—as a man *will* think for others in a necessarily separate personality, consequently (though disallowing it) in false mental premise—how differently *he* should act, how gladly *he* should prize the rest so lightly held of within." A footman—an ordinary Jeames, with large calves and aspirated vowels—answers the door-bell, and the opportunity is seized to tell you that he was a "type of the large class of pampered menials, who follow the curse of Cain—'vagabonds' on the face of the earth, and whose estimate of the human class varies in the graduated scale of money and expenditure. . . . These, and such as these, O England, be the false lights of thy morbid civilization!" We have heard of various "false lights," from Dr. Cumming to Robert Owen, from Dr. Pusey to the Spirit-rappers, but we never before heard of the false light that emanates from plush and powder.

In the same way very ordinary events of civilized life are exalted into the most awful crises, and ladies in full skirts and *manches à la chinoise*, conduct themselves not unlike the heroines of sanguinary melodramas. Mrs. Percy, a shallow woman of the world, wishes her son Horace to marry the auburn-haired Grace, she being an heiress; but he, after the manner of sons, falls in love with the raven-haired Kate, the heiress's portionless cousin; and, moreover, Grace herself shows every symptom of perfect indifference to Horace. In such cases sons are often sulky or fiery, mothers are alternately manœuvring and waspish, and the portionless young lady often lies awake at night and cries a good deal. We are getting used to these things now, just as we are used to eclipses of the moon, which no longer set us howling and beating tin kettles. We never heard of a lady in a fashionable "front" behaving like Mrs. Percy under these circumstances. Happening one day to see Horace talking to Grace at a window, without in the least knowing what they are talking about, or having the least reason to believe that Grace, who is mistress of the house and a person of dignity, would accept her son if he were to offer himself, she suddenly rushes up to them and clasps them both, saying, "with a flushed countenance and in an excited manner"—"This is indeed happiness; for, may I not call you so, Grace?—my Grace—my Horace's Grace!—my dear children!" Her son tells her she is mistaken, and that he is engaged to Kate, whereupon we have the following scene and tableau:

Gathering herself up to an unprecedented height (!) her eyes lightening forth the fire of her anger:

"Wretched boy!" she said, hoarsely and scornfully, and clenching her hand, "Take then the doom of your own choice! Bow down your miserable head and let a mother's—"

"Curse not!" spake a deep low voice from behind, and Mrs. Percy started, scared, as though she had seen a heavenly visitant appear, to break upon her in the midst of her sin.

Meantime Horace had fallen on his knees, at her feet, and hid his face in his hands.

Who then, is she—who! Truly his "guardian spirit" hath stepped between him and the fearful words, which, however unmerited, must have hung as a pall over his future existence;—a spell which could not be unbound—which could not be unsaid.

Of an earthly paleness, but calm with the still, iron-bound calmness of death—the only calm one there—Katherine stood; and her words smote on the ear in tones whose appallingly slow and separate intonation rung on the heart like a chill, isolated tolling of some fatal knell.

"He would have plighted me his faith, but I did not accept it; you cannot, therefore—you *dare* not curse him. And here," she continued, raising her hand to heaven, whither her large dark eyes also rose with a chastened glow, which, for the first time, *suffering* had lighted in those passionate orbs—"here I promise, come weal, come woe, that

Horace Wolchorley and I do never interchange vows without his mother's sanction—without his mother's blessing!"

Here, and throughout the story, we see that confusion of purpose which is so characteristic of silly novels written by women. It is a story of quite modern drawing-room society—a society in which polkas are played and Puseyism discussed; yet we have characters, and incidents, and traits of manner introduced, which are mere shreds from the most heterogeneous romances. We have a blind Irish harper, "relic of the picturesque bards of yore," startling us at a Sunday-school festival of tea and cake in an English village; we have a crazy gypsy, in a scarlet cloak, singing snatches of romantic song, and revealing a secret on her death-bed which, with the testimony of a dwarfish miserly merchant, who salutes strangers with a curse and a devilish laugh, goes to prove that Ernest, the model young clergyman, is Kate's brother; and we have an ultra-virtuous Irish Barney, discovering that a document is forged, by comparing the date of the paper with the date of the alleged signature, although the same document has passed through a court of law and occasioned a fatal decision. The "Hall" in which Sir Lionel lives is the venerable country-seat of an old family, and this, we suppose, sets the imagination of the authoress flying to donjons and battlements, where "lo! the warder blows his horn"; for, as the inhabitants are in their bedrooms on a night certainly within the recollection of Pleaceman X. and a breeze springs up, which we are at first told was faint, and then that it made the old cedars bow their branches to the greensward, she falls into this mediæval vein of description (the italics are ours):

> The banner *unfurled it* at the sound, and shook its guardian wing above, while the startled owl *flapped her* in the ivy; the firmament looking down through her "argus eyes"—
> "Ministers of heaven's mute melodies."
> And lo! two strokes tolled from out the warder tower, and "Two o'clock" re-echoed its interpreter below.

Such stories as this of "The Enigma" remind us of the pictures clever children sometimes draw "out of their own head," where you will see a modern villa on the right, two knights in helmets fighting in the foreground, and a tiger grinning in a jungle on the left, the several objects being brought together because the artist thinks each pretty, and perhaps still more because he remembers seeing them in other pictures.

But we like the authoress much better on her mediæval stilts than on her oracular ones—when she talks of the *Ich* and of "subjective" and "objective," and lays down the exact line of Christian verity, between "right-hand excesses and left-hand declensions." Persons who deviate from this line are introduced with a patronizing air of charity. Of a certain Miss Inshquine she informs us, with all the lucidity of italics and small caps, that "*function*, not *form*, as THE INEVITABLE OUTER EXPRESSION OF THE SPIRIT IN THIS TABERNACLE AGE, weakly engrossed her." And *à propos* of Miss Mayjar, an evangelical lady who is a little too apt to talk of her visits to sick women and the state of their souls, we are told that the model clergyman is "not one to disallow, through the *super* crust, the undercurrent toward good in the *subject*, or the positive benefits, nevertheless, to the *object*." We imagine the double-refined accent and protrusion of chin which are feebly represented by the italics in this lady's sentences! We abstain from quoting any of her oracular doctrinal passages, because they refer to matters too serious for our pages just now.

The epithet "silly" may seem impertinent, applied to a novel which indicates so much reading and intellectual activity as "The Enigma," but we use this epithet advisedly. If, as the world has long agreed, a very great amount of instruction will not make a wise man, still less will a very mediocre amount of instruction make a wise woman. And the most mischievous form of feminine silliness is the literary form, because it tends to confirm the popular prejudice against the more solid education of women.

When men see girls wasting their time in consultations about bonnets and ball dresses, and in giggling or sentimental love-confidences, or middle-aged women mismanaging their children, and solacing themselves with acrid gossip, they can hardly help saying, "For Heaven's sake, let girls be better educated; let them have some better objects of thought—some more solid occupations." But after a few hours' conversation with an oracular literary woman, or a few hours' reading of her books, they are likely enough to say, "After all, when a woman gets some knowledge, see what use she makes of it! Her knowledge remains acquisition instead of passing into culture; instead of being subdued into modesty and simplicity by a larger acquaintance with thought and fact, she has a feverish consciousness of her attainments; she keeps a sort of mental pocket-mirror, and is continually looking in it at her own 'intellectuality;' she spoils the taste of one's muffin by questions of metaphysics; 'puts down' men at a dinner-table with her superior information; and seizes the opportunity of a *soirée* to catechise us on the vital question of the relation between mind and matter. And then, look at her writings! She mistakes vagueness for depth, bombast for eloquence, and affectation for originality; she struts on one page, rolls her eyes on another, grimaces in a third, and is hysterical in a fourth. She may have read many writings of great men, and a few writings of great women; but she is as unable to discern the difference between her own style and theirs as a Yorkshireman is to discern the difference between his own English and a Londoner's: rhodomontade is the native accent of her intellect. No—the average nature of women is too shallow and feeble a soil to bear much tillage; it is only fit for the very lightest crops."

It is true that the men who come to such a decision on such very superficial and imperfect observation may not be among the wisest in the world; but we have not now to contest their opinion—we are only pointing out how it is unconsciously encouraged by many women who have volunteered themselves as representatives of the feminine intellect. We do not believe that a man was ever strengthened in such an opinion by associating with a woman of true culture, whose mind had absorbed her knowledge instead of being absorbed by it. A really cultured woman, like a really cultured man, is all the simpler and the less obtrusive for her knowledge; it has made her see herself and her opinions in something like just proportions; she does not make it a pedestal from which she flatters herself that she commands a complete view of men and things, but makes it a point of observation from which to form a right estimate of herself. She neither spouts poetry nor quotes Cicero on slight provocation; not because she thinks that a sacrifice must be made to the prejudices of men, but because that mode of exhibiting her memory and Latinity does not present itself to her as edifying or graceful. She does not write books to confound philosophers, perhaps because she is able to write books that delight them. In conversation she is the least formidable of women, because she understands you, without wanting to make you aware that you *can't* understand her. She does not give you information, which is the raw material of culture—she gives you sympathy, which is its subtlest essence.

A more numerous class of silly novels than the oracular (which are generally inspired by some form of High Church or transcendental Christianity) is what we may call the *white neck-cloth* species, which represent the tone of thought and feeling in the Evangelical party. This species is a kind of genteel tract on a large scale, intended as a sort of medicinal sweetmeat for Low Church young ladies; an Evangelical substitute for the fashionable novel, as the May Meetings are a substitute for the Opera. Even Quaker children, one would think, can hardly have been denied the indulgence of a doll; but it must be a doll dressed in a drab gown and a coal-scuttle-bonnet—not a worldly doll, in gauze and spangles. And there are no young ladies, we imagine—unless they belong to the Church of the United Brethren, in which people are married without any love-making—who can dispense with love stories. Thus, for Evangelical young ladies there are Evangelical love stories, in which the vicissitudes of the tender passion are sanctified by saving views of Regeneration and the Atonement. These novels differ from the oracular ones, as a Low Churchwoman often differs from a High Churchwoman: they are a little less supercilious and a great deal more ignorant, a little less correct in their syntax and a great deal more vulgar.

The Orlando of Evangelical literature is the young curate, looked at from the point of view of the middle class, where cambric bands are understood to have as thrilling an effect on the hearts of young ladies as epaulettes have in the classes above and below it. In the ordinary type of these novels the hero is almost sure to be a young curate, frowned upon, perhaps by worldly mammas, but carrying captive the hearts of their daughters, who can "never forget *that* sermon"; tender glances are seized from the pulpit stairs instead of the opera-box; *tête-à-têtes* are seasoned with quotations from Scripture instead of quotations from the poets; and questions as to the state of the heroine's affections are mingled with anxieties as to the state of her soul. The young curate always has a background of well-dressed and wealthy if not fashionable society—for Evangelical silliness is as snobbish as any other kind of silliness—and the Evangelical lady novelist, while she explains to you the type of the scapegoat on one page, is ambitious on another to represent the manners and conversations of aristocratic people. Her pictures of fashionable society are often curious studies, considered as efforts of the Evangelical imagination; but in one particular the novels of the White Neck-cloth School are meritoriously realistic—their favorite hero, the Evangelical young curate, is always rather an insipid personage.

The most recent novel of this species that we happen to have before us is "The Old Grey Church." It is utterly tame and feeble; there is no one set of objects on which the writer seems to have a stronger grasp than on any other; and we should be entirely at a loss to conjecture among what phases of life her experience has been gained, but for certain vulgarisms of style which sufficiently indicate that she has had the advantage, though she has been unable to use it, of mingling chiefly with men and women whose manners and characters have not had all their bosses and angles rubbed down by refined conventionalism. It is less excusable in an Evangelical novelist than in any other, gratuitously to seek her subjects among titles and carriages. The real drama of Evangelicalism—and it has abundance of fine drama for any one who has genius enough to discern and reproduce it—lies among the middle and lower classes; and are not Evangelical opinions understood to give an especial interest in the weak things of the earth, rather than in the mighty? Why, then, cannot our Evangelical lady novelists show us the operation of their religious views among people (there really are many such in the world) who keep no carriage, "not so much as a brass-bound gig," who even manage to eat their dinner without a silver fork, and in whose mouths the authoress's questionable English would be strictly consistent? Why can we not have pictures of religious life among the industrial classes in England, as interesting as Mrs. Stowe's pictures of religious life among the negroes? Instead of this, pious ladies nauseate us with novels which remind us of what we sometimes see in a worldly woman recently "converted";—she is as fond of a fine dinner-table as before, but she invites clergymen instead of beaux; she thinks as much of her dress as before, but she adopts a more sober choice of colors and patterns; her conversation is as trivial as before, but the triviality is flavored with Gospel instead of gossip. In "The Old Grey Church" we have the same sort of Evangelical travesty of the fashionable novel, and of course the vicious, intriguing baronet is not wanting. It is worth while to give a sample of the style of conversation attributed to this high-born rake—a style that, in its profuse italics and palpable innuendoes, is worthy of Miss Squeers. In an evening visit to the ruins of the Colosseum, Eustace, the young clergyman, has been withdrawing the heroine, Miss Lushington, from the rest of the party, for the sake of a *tête-à-tête*. The baronet is jealous, and vents his pique in this way:

> There they are, and Miss Lushington, no doubt, quite safe; for she is under the holy guidance of Pope Eustace the First, who has, of course, been delivering to her an edifying homily on the wickedness of the heathens of yore, who, as tradition tells us, in this very place let loose the wild *beasties* on poor Saint Paul!—Oh, no! by the bye, I believe I am wrong, and betraying my want of clergy, and that it was not at all Saint Paul, nor was it here. But no matter, it would equally serve as a text to preach from, and from which to diverge to the degenerate *heathen* Christians of the present day, and all their naughty practices, and so end with an exhortation to "come but from among them, and be separate"—and I am sure, Miss Lushington, you have most scrupulously conformed to that injunction this evening, for we have seen nothing of you since our arrival. But every one seems agreed it has been a *charming party of pleasure*, and I am sure we all feel *much indebted* to Mr. Gray for having *suggested* it; and as he seems so capital a cicerone, I hope he will think of something else equally agreeable to *all*.

This drivelling kind of dialogue, and equally drivelling narrative, which, like a bad drawing, represents nothing, and barely indicates what is meant to be represented, runs through the book; and we have no doubt is considered by the amiable authoress to constitute an improving novel, which Christian mothers will do well to put into the hands of their daughters. But everything is relative; we have met with American vegetarians whose normal diet was dry meal, and who, when their appetite wanted stimulating, tickled it with *wet* meal; and so, we can imagine that there are Evangelical circles in which "The Old Grey Church" is devoured as a powerful and interesting fiction.

But perhaps the least readable of silly women's novels are the *modern-antique* species, which unfold to us the domestic life of Jannes and Jambres, the private love affairs of Sennacherib, or the mental struggles and ultimate conversion of Demetrius the silversmith. From most silly novels we can at least extract a laugh; but those of the modern-antique school have a ponderous, a leaden kind of fatuity, under which we groan. What can be more demonstrative of the inability of literary women to measure their own powers than their frequent assumption of a task which can only be justified by the rarest concurrence of acquirement with genius? The finest effort to reanimate the past is of course only approximative—is always more or less an infusion of the modern spirit into the ancient form—

> Was ihr den Geist der Zeiten heisst,
> Das ist im Grund der Herren eigner Geist,
> In dem die Zeiten sich bespiegeln.

Admitting that genius which has familiarized itself with all the relics of an ancient period can sometimes, by the force of its sympathetic divination, restore the missing notes in the "music of humanity," and reconstruct the fragments into a whole which will really bring the remote past nearer to us, and interpret it to our duller apprehension—this form of imaginative power must always be among the very rarest, because it demands as much accurate and minute knowledge as creative vigor. Yet we find ladies constantly choosing to make their mental mediocrity more conspicuous by clothing it in a masquerade of ancient names; by putting their feeble sentimentality into the mouths of Roman vestals or Egyptian princesses, and attributing their rhetorical arguments to Jewish high-priests and Greek philosophers. A recent example of this heavy imbecility is "Adonijah, a Tale of the Jewish Dispersion," which forms part of a series, "uniting," we are told, "taste, humor, and sound principles." "Adonijah," we presume, exemplifies the tale of "sound principles"; the taste and humor are to be found in other members of the series. We are told on the cover that the incidents of this tale are "fraught with unusual interest," and the preface winds up thus: "To those who feel interested in the dispersed of Israel and Judea, these pages may afford, perhaps, information on an important subject, as well as amusement." Since the "important subject" on which this book is to afford information is not specified, it may possibly lie in some esoteric meaning to which we have no key; but if it has relation to the dispersed of Israel and Judea at any period of their history, we believe a tolerably well-informed school-girl already knows much more of it than she will find in this "Tale of the Jewish Dispersion." "Adonijah" is simply the feeblest kind of love story, supposed to be instructive, we presume, because the hero is a Jewish captive and the heroine a Roman vestal; because they and their friends are converted to Christianity after the shortest and easiest method approved by the "Society for Promoting the Conversion of the Jews"; and because, instead of being written in plain language, it is adorned with that peculiar style of grandiloquence which is held by some lady novelists to give an antique coloring, and which we recognize at once in such phrases as these:—"the splendid regnal talents undoubtedly possessed by the Emperor Nero"—"the expiring scion of a lofty stem"—"the virtuous partner of his couch"—"ah, by Vesta!"—and "I tell thee, Roman." Among the quotations which serve at once for instruction and ornament on the cover of this volume, there is one from Miss Sinclair, which informs us that "Works of imagination are *avowedly* read by men of science, wisdom, and piety"; from which we suppose the reader is to gather the cheering inference that Dr. Daubeny, Mr. Mill, or Mr. Maurice may openly indulge himself with the perusal of "Adonijah," without being obliged to secrete it among the sofa cushions, or read it by snatches under the dinner-table.

* * * * *

"Be not a baker if your head be made of butter," says a homely proverb, which, being interpreted, may mean, let no woman rush into print who is not prepared for the consequences. We are aware that our remarks are in a very different tone from that of the reviewers who, with perennial recurrence of precisely similar emotions, only paralleled, we imagine, in the experience of monthly nurses, tell one lady novelist after another that they "hail" her productions "with delight." We are aware that the ladies at whom our criticism is pointed are accustomed to be told, in the choicest phraseology of puffery, that their pictures of life are brilliant, their characters well drawn, their style fascinating, and their sentiments lofty. But if they are inclined to resent our plainness of speech, we ask them to reflect for a moment on the chary praise, and often captious blame, which their panegyrists give to writers whose works are on the way to become classics. No sooner does a woman show that she has genius or effective talent, than she receives the tribute of being moderately praised and severely criticised. By a peculiar thermometric adjustment, when a woman's talent is at zero, journalistic approbation is at the boiling pitch; when she attains mediocrity, it is already at no more than summer heat; and if ever she reaches excellence, critical enthusiasm drops to the freezing point. Harriet Martineau, Currer Bell, and Mrs. Gaskell have been treated as cavalierly as if they had been men. And every critic who forms a high estimate of the share women may ultimately take in literature, will, on principle, abstain from any exceptional indulgence toward the productions of literary women. For it must be plain to every one who looks impartially and extensively into feminine literature that its greatest deficiencies are due hardly more to the want of intellectual power than to the want of those moral qualities that contribute to literary excellence—patient diligence, a sense of the responsibility involved in publication, and an appreciation of the sacredness of the writer's art. In the majority of women's books you see that kind of facility which springs from the absence of any high standard; that fertility in imbecile combination or feeble imitation which a little self-criticism would check and reduce to barrenness; just as with a total want of musical ear people will sing out of tune, while a degree more melodic sensibility would suffice to render them silent. The foolish vanity of wishing to appear in print, instead of being counterbalanced by any consciousness of the intellectual or moral derogation implied in futile authorship, seems to be encouraged by the extremely false impression that to write *at all* is a proof of superiority in a woman. On this ground we believe that the average intellect of women is unfairly represented by the mass of feminine literature, and that while the few women who write well are very far above the ordinary intellectual level of their sex, the many women who write ill are very far below it. So that, after all, the severer critics are fulfilling a chivalrous duty in depriving the mere fact of feminine authorship of any false prestige which may give it a delusive attraction, and in recommending women of mediocre faculties—as at least a negative service they can render their sex—to abstain from writing.

The standing apology for women who become writers without any special qualification is that society shuts them out from other spheres of occupation. Society is a very culpable entity, and has to answer for the manufacture of many unwholesome commodities, from bad pickles to bad poetry. But society, like "matter," and Her Majesty's Government, and other lofty abstractions, has its share of excessive blame as well as excessive praise. Where there is one woman who writes from necessity, we believe there are three women who write from vanity; and besides, there is something so antispetic in the mere healthy fact of working for one's bread, that the most trashy and rotten kind of feminine literature is not likely to have been produced under such circumstances. "In all labor there is profit"; but ladies' silly novels, we imagine, are less the result of labor than of busy idleness.

Happily, we are not dependent on argument to prove that Fiction is a department of literature in which women can, after their kind, fully equal men. A cluster of great names, both living and dead, rush to our memories in evidence that women can produce novels not only fine, but among the very finest—novels, too, that have a precious speciality, lying quite apart from masculine aptitudes and experience. No educational restrictions can shut women out from the materials of fiction, and there is no species of art which is so free from rigid requirements. Like crystalline masses, it may take any form, and yet be beautiful; we have only to pour in the right elements— genuine observation, humor, and passion. But it is precisely this absence of rigid requirement which constitutes the fatal seduction of novel-writing to incompetent women. Ladies are not wont to be very grossly deceived as to their power of playing on the piano; here certain positive difficulties of execution have to be conquered, and incompetence inevitably breaks down. Every art which had its absolute *technique* is, to a certain extent, guarded from the intrusions of mere left-handed imbecility. But in novel-writing there are no barriers for incapacity to stumble against, no external criteria to prevent a writer from mistaking foolish facility for mastery. And so we have again and again the old story of La Fontaine's ass, who pats his nose to the flute, and, finding that he elicits some sound, exclaims, "Moi, aussie, je joue de la flute"—a fable which we commend, at parting, to the consideration of any feminine reader who is in danger of adding to the number of "silly novels by lady novelists."

FROM *THE ROMANCE OF THE FOREST*

Ann Radcliffe

TO THE VISIONS OF FANCY

Dear, wild illusions of creative mind!
  Whose varying hues arise to Fancy's art,
And by her magic force are swift combin'd
  In forms that please, and scenes that touch the heart:
Oh! whether at her voice ye soft assume
  The pensive grace of sorrow drooping low;
Or rise sublime on terror's lofty plume,
  And shake the soul with wildly thrilling woe;
Or, sweetly bright, your gayer tints ye spread,
  Bid scenes of pleasure steal upon my view,
Love wave his purple pinions o'er my head,
  And wake the tender thought to passion true;

O! still—ye shadowy forms! attend my lonely hours,
Still chase my real cares with your illusive powers!

SONG

Life's a varied, bright illusion,
  Joy and sorrow—light and shade;
Turn from sorrow's dark suffusion,
  Catch the pleasures ere they fade.

Fancy paints with hues unreal,
  Smile of bliss, and sorrow's mood;
If they both are but ideal,
  Why reject the seeming good?

Hence! no more! 'tis Wisdom calls ye,
  Bids ye court Time's present aid;
The future trust not—Hope enthrals ye,
  "Catch the pleasures ere they fade."

AIR

Now, at Moonlight's fairy hour,
  When faintly gleams each dewy steep,
And vale and Mountain, lake and bow'r,
  In solitary grandeur sleep;

When slowly sinks the evening breeze,
  That lulls the mind in pensive care,
And Fancy loftier visions sees,
  Bid Music wake the silent air.

Bid the merry, merry tabor sound,
  And with the Fays of lawn or glade,
In tripping circlet beat the ground,
  Under the high trees' trembling shade.

"Now, at Moonlight's fairy hour,"
  Shall Music breathe her dulcet voice,
And o'er the waves, with magic pow'r,
  Call on Echo to rejoice.

FRANKENSTEIN

Mary Shelley

Volume One

LETTER I

To Mrs. Saville, England.
St. Petersburgh, December 11th, 17—.

You will rejoice to hear that no disaster has accompanied the commencement of an enterprise which you have regarded with such evil forebodings. I arrived here yesterday, and my first task is to assure my dear sister of my welfare and increasing confidence in the success of my undertaking.

I am already far north of London, and as I walk in the streets of Petersburgh, I feel a cold northern breeze play upon my cheeks, which braces my nerves and fills me with delight. Do you understand this feeling? This breeze, which has travelled from the regions towards which I am advancing, gives me a foretaste of those icy climes. Inspirited by this wind of promise, my daydreams become more fervent and vivid. I try in vain to be persuaded that the pole is the seat of frost and desolation; it ever presents itself to my imagination as the region of beauty and delight. There, Margaret, the sun is forever visible, its broad disk just skirting the horizon and diffusing a perpetual splendour. There—for with your leave, my sister, I will put some trust in preceding navigators—there snow and frost are banished; and, sailing over a calm sea, we may be wafted to a land surpassing in wonders and in beauty every region hitherto discovered on the habitable globe. Its productions and features may be without example, as the phenomena of the heavenly bodies undoubtedly are in those undiscovered solitudes. What may not be expected in a country of eternal light? I may there discover the wondrous power which attracts the needle and may regulate a thousand celestial observations that require only this voyage to render their seeming eccentricities consistent forever. I shall satiate my ardent curiosity with the sight of a part of the world never before visited, and may tread a land never before imprinted by the foot of man. These are my enticements, and they are sufficient to conquer all fear of danger or death and to induce me to commence this laborious voyage with the joy a child feels when he embarks in a little boat, with his holiday mates, on an expedition of discovery up his native river. But supposing all these conjectures to be false, you cannot contest the inestimable benefit which I shall confer on all mankind, to the last generation, by discovering a passage near the pole to those countries, to reach which at present so many months are requisite; or by ascertaining the secret of the magnet, which, if at all possible, can only be effected by an undertaking such as mine.

These reflections have dispelled the agitation with which I began my letter, and I feel my heart glow with an enthusiasm which elevates me to heaven, for nothing contributes so much to tranquillize the mind as a steady purpose—a point on which the soul may fix its intellectual eye. This expedition has been the favourite dream of my early years. I have read with ardour the accounts of the various voyages which have been made in the prospect of arriving at the North Pacific Ocean through the seas which surround the pole. You may remember that a history of all the voyages made for purposes of discovery composed the whole of our good Uncle Thomas's library. My education was neglected, yet I was passionately fond of reading. These volumes were my study day and night, and my familiarity with them increased that regret which I had felt, as a child, on learning that my father's dying injunction had forbidden my uncle to allow me to embark in a seafaring life.

These visions faded when I perused, for the first time, those poets whose effusions entranced my soul and lifted it to heaven. I also became a poet and for one year lived in a paradise of my own creation; I imagined that I also might obtain a niche in the temple where the names of Homer and Shakespeare are consecrated. You are well acquainted with my failure and how heavily I bore the disappointment. But just at that time I inherited the fortune of my cousin, and my thoughts were turned into the channel of their earlier bent.

Six years have passed since I resolved on my present undertaking. I can, even now, remember the hour from which I dedicated myself to this great enterprise. I commenced by inuring my body to hardship. I accompanied the whale-fishers on several expeditions to the North Sea; I voluntarily endured cold, famine, thirst, and want of sleep; I often worked harder than the common sailors during the day and devoted my nights to the study of mathematics, the theory of medicine, and those branches of physical science from which a naval adventurer might derive the greatest practical advantage. Twice I actually hired myself as an under-mate in a Greenland whaler, and acquitted myself to admiration. I must own I felt a little proud when my captain offered me the second dignity in the vessel and entreated me to remain with the greatest earnestness, so valuable did he consider my services.

And now, dear Margaret, do I not deserve to accomplish some great purpose? My life might have been passed in ease and luxury, but I preferred glory to every enticement that wealth placed in my path. Oh, that some encouraging voice would answer in the affirmative! My courage and my resolution is firm; but my hopes fluctuate, and my spirits are often depressed. I am about to proceed on a long and difficult voyage, the emergencies of which will demand all my fortitude: I am required not only to raise the spirits of others, but sometimes to sustain my own, when theirs are failing.

This is the most favourable period for travelling in Russia. They fly quickly over the snow in their sledges; the motion is pleasant, and, in my opinion, far more agreeable than that of an English stagecoach. The cold is not excessive, if you are wrapped in furs—a dress which I have already adopted, for there is a great difference between walking the deck and remaining seated motionless for hours, when no exercise prevents the blood from actually freezing in your veins. I have no ambition to lose my life on the post-road between St. Petersburgh and Archangel.

I shall depart for the latter town in a fortnight or three weeks; and my intention is to hire a ship there, which can easily be done by paying the insurance for the owner, and to engage as many sailors as I think necessary among those who are accustomed to the whale-fishing. I do not intend to sail until the month of June; and when shall I return? Ah, dear sister, how can I answer this question? If I succeed, many, many months, perhaps years, will pass before you and I may meet. If I fail, you will see me again soon, or never.

Farewell, my dear, excellent Margaret. Heaven shower down blessings on you, and save me, that I may again and again testify my gratitude for all your love and kindness.

Your affectionate brother,
R. WALTON

LETTER II

To Mrs. Saville, England.
Archangel, March 28th, 17—.

How slowly the time passes here, encompassed as I am by frost and snow! Yet a second step is taken towards my enterprise. I have hired a vessel and am occupied in collecting my sailors; those whom I have already engaged appear to be men on whom I can depend and are certainly possessed of dauntless courage.

But I have one want which I have never yet been able to satisfy, and the absence of the object of which I now feel as a most severe evil. I have no friend, Margaret: when I am glowing with the enthusiasm of success, there will be none to participate my joy; if I am assailed by disappointment, no one will endeavour to sustain me in dejection. I shall commit my thoughts to paper, it is true; but that is a poor medium for the communication of feeling. I desire the company of a man who could sympathise with me, whose eyes would reply to mine. You may deem me romantic, my dear sister, but I bitterly feel the want of a friend. I have no one near me, gentle yet courageous, possessed of a cultivated as well as of a capacious mind, whose tastes are like my own, to approve or amend my plans. How would such a friend repair the faults of your poor brother! I am too ardent in execution and too impatient of difficulties. But it is a still greater evil to me that I am self-educated: for the first fourteen years of my life I ran wild on a common and read nothing but our Uncle Thomas's books of voyages. At that age I became acquainted with the celebrated poets of our own country; but it was only when it had ceased to be in my power to derive its most important benefits from such a conviction that I perceived the necessity of becoming acquainted with more languages than that of my native country. Now I am twenty-eight and am in reality more illiterate than many schoolboys of fifteen. It is true that I have thought more and that my daydreams are more extended and magnificent, but they want (as the painters call it) *keeping*; and I greatly need a friend who would have sense enough not to despise me as romantic, and affection enough for me to endeavour to regulate my mind.

Well, these are useless complaints; I shall certainly find no friend on the wide ocean, nor even here in Archangel, among merchants and seamen. Yet some feelings, unallied to the dross of human nature, beat even in these rugged bosoms. My lieutenant, for instance, is a man of wonderful courage and enterprise; he is madly desirous of glory, or rather, to word my phrase more characteristically, of advancement in his profession. He is an Englishman, and in the midst of national and professional prejudices, unsoftened by cultivation, retains some of the noblest endowments of humanity. I first became acquainted with him on board a whale vessel; finding that he was unemployed in this city, I easily engaged him to assist in my enterprise.

The master is a person of an excellent disposition and is remarkable in the ship for his gentleness and the mildness of his discipline. This circumstance, added to his well-known integrity and dauntless courage, made me very desirous to engage him. A youth passed in solitude, my best years spent under your gentle and feminine fosterage, has so refined the groundwork of my character that I cannot overcome an intense distaste to the usual brutality exercised on board ship: I have never believed it to be necessary, and when I heard of a mariner equally noted for his kindliness of heart and the respect and obedience paid to him by his crew, I felt myself peculiarly fortunate in being able to secure his services. I heard of him first in rather a romantic manner, from a lady who owes to him the happiness of her life. This, briefly, is his story. Some years ago he loved a young Russian lady of moderate fortune, and having amassed a considerable sum in prize-money, the father of the girl consented to the match. He saw his mistress once before the destined ceremony; but she was bathed in tears, and throwing herself at his feet, entreated him to spare her, confessing at the same time that she loved another, but that he was poor, and that her father would never consent to the union. My generous friend reassured the suppliant, and on being informed of the name of her lover, instantly abandoned his pursuit. He had already bought a farm with his money, on which he had designed to pass the remainder of his life; but he bestowed the whole on his rival, together with the remains of his prize-money to purchase stock, and then himself solicited the young woman's father to consent to her marriage with her lover. But the old man decidedly refused, thinking himself bound in honour to my friend, who, when he found the father inexorable, quitted his country, nor returned until he heard that his former mistress was married according to her inclinations. "What a noble fellow!" you will exclaim. He is so; but then he is wholly uneducated: he is as silent as a Turk, and a kind of ignorant carelessness attends him, which, while it renders his conduct the more astonishing, detracts from the interest and sympathy which otherwise he would command.

Yet do not suppose, because I complain a little or because I can conceive a consolation for my toils which I may never know, that I am wavering in my resolutions. Those are as fixed as fate, and my voyage is only now delayed until the weather shall permit my embarkation. The winter has been dreadfully severe, but the spring promises well, and it is considered as a remarkably early season, so that perhaps I may sail sooner than I expected. I shall do nothing rashly: you know me sufficiently to confide in my prudence and considerateness whenever the safety of others is committed to my care.

I cannot describe to you my sensations on the near prospect of my undertaking. It is impossible to communicate to you a conception of the trembling sensation, half pleasurable and half fearful, with which I am preparing to depart. I am going to unexplored regions, to "the land of mist and snow," but I shall kill no albatross; therefore do not be alarmed for my safety or if I should come back to you as worn and woeful as the "Ancient Mariner." You will smile at my allusion, but I will disclose a secret. I have often attributed my attachment to, my passionate enthusiasm for, the dangerous mysteries of ocean to that production of the most imaginative of modern poets. There is something at work in my soul which I do not understand. I am practically industrious—painstaking, a workman to execute with perseverance and labour—but besides this there is a love for the marvellous, a belief in the marvellous, intertwined in all my projects, which hurries me out of the common pathways of men, even to the wild sea and unvisited regions I am about to explore.

But to return to dearer considerations. Shall I meet you again, after having traversed immense seas, and returned by the most southern cape of Africa or America? I dare not expect such success, yet I cannot bear to look on the reverse of the picture. Continue for the present to write to me by every opportunity: I may receive your letters on some occasions when I need them most to support my spirits. I love you very tenderly. Remember me with affection, should you never hear from me again.

Your affectionate brother,
ROBERT WALTON

LETTER III

To Mrs. Saville, England.
July 7th, 17——.

My dear Sister,
I write a few lines in haste to say that I am safe—and well advanced on my voyage. This letter will reach England by a merchantman now on its homeward voyage from Archangel; more fortunate than I, who may not see my native land, perhaps, for many years. I am, however, in good spirits: my men are bold and apparently firm of purpose, nor do the floating sheets of ice that continually pass us, indicating the dangers of the region towards which we are advancing, appear to dismay them. We have already reached a very high latitude; but it is the height of summer, and although not so warm as in England, the southern gales, which blow us speedily towards those shores which I so ardently desire to attain, breathe a degree of renovating warmth which I had not expected.

No incidents have hitherto befallen us that would make a figure in a letter. One or two stiff gales and the springing of a leak are accidents which experienced navigators scarcely remember to record, and I shall be well content if nothing worse happen to us during our voyage.

Adieu, my dear Margaret. Be assured that for my own sake, as well as yours, I will not rashly encounter danger. I will be cool, persevering, and prudent.

But success shall crown my endeavours. Wherefore not? Thus far I have gone, tracing a secure way over the pathless seas, the very stars themselves being witnesses and testimonies of my triumph. Why not still proceed over the untamed yet obedient element? What can stop the determined heart and resolved will of man?

My swelling heart involuntarily pours itself out thus. But I must finish. Heaven bless my beloved sister!

R.W.

LETTER IV

To Mrs. Saville, England.
August 5th, 17—.

So strange an accident has happened to us that I cannot forbear recording it, although it is very probable that you will see me before these papers can come into your possession.

Last Monday (July 31st) we were nearly surrounded by ice, which closed in the ship on all sides, scarcely leaving her the searoom in which she floated. Our situation was somewhat dangerous, especially as we were compassed round by a very thick fog. We accordingly lay to, hoping that some change would take place in the atmosphere and weather.

About two o'clock the mist cleared away, and we beheld, stretched out in every direction, vast and irregular plains of ice, which seemed to have no end. Some of my comrades groaned, and my own mind began to grow watchful with anxious thoughts, when a strange sight suddenly attracted our attention and diverted our solicitude from our own situation. We perceived a low carriage, fixed on a sledge and drawn by dogs, pass on towards the north, at the distance of half a mile; a being which had the shape of a man, but apparently of gigantic stature, sat in the sledge and guided the dogs. We watched the rapid progress of the traveller with our telescopes until he was lost among the distant inequalities of the ice.

This appearance excited our unqualified wonder. We were, as we believed, many hundred miles from any land; but this apparition seemed to denote that it was not, in reality, so distant as we had supposed. Shut in, however, by ice, it was impossible to follow his track, which we had observed with the greatest attention.

About two hours after this occurrence we heard the ground sea, and before night the ice broke and freed our ship. We, however, lay to until the morning, fearing to encounter in the dark those large loose masses which float about after the breaking up of the ice. I profited of this time to rest for a few hours.

In the morning, however, as soon as it was light, I went upon deck and found all the sailors busy on one side of the vessel, apparently talking to someone in the sea. It was, in fact, a sledge, like that we had seen before, which had drifted towards us in the night on a large fragment of ice. Only one dog remained alive; but there was a human being within it whom the sailors were persuading to enter the vessel. He was not, as the other traveller seemed to be, a savage inhabitant of some undiscovered island, but a European. When I appeared on deck the master said, "Here is our captain, and he will not allow you to perish on the open sea."

On perceiving me, the stranger addressed me in English, although with a foreign accent. "Before I come on board your vessel," said he, "will you have the kindness to inform me whither you are bound?"

You may conceive my astonishment on hearing such a question addressed to me from a man on the brink of destruction and to whom I should have supposed that my vessel would have been a resource which he would not have exchanged for the most precious wealth the earth can afford. I replied, however, that we were on a voyage of discovery towards the northern pole.

Upon hearing this he appeared satisfied and consented to come on board. Good God! Margaret, if you had seen the man who thus capitulated for his safety, your surprise would have been boundless. His limbs were nearly frozen, and his body dreadfully emaciated by fatigue and suffering. I never saw a man in so wretched a condition. We attempted to carry him into the cabin, but as soon as he had quitted the fresh air he fainted. We accordingly brought him back to the deck and restored him to animation by rubbing him with brandy and forcing him to swallow a small quantity. As soon as he showed signs of life we wrapped him up in blankets and placed him near the chimney of the kitchen stove. By slow degrees he recovered and ate a little soup, which restored him wonderfully.

Two days passed in this manner before he was able to speak, and I often feared that his sufferings had deprived him of understanding. When he had in some measure recovered, I removed him to my own cabin and attended on him as much as my duty would permit. I never saw a more interesting creature: his eyes have generally an expression of wildness, and even madness, but there are moments when, if anyone performs an act of kindness towards him or does him any the most trifling service, his whole countenance is lighted up, as it were, with a beam of benevolence and sweetness that I never saw equalled. But he is generally melancholy and despairing, and sometimes he gnashes his teeth, as if impatient of the weight of woes that oppresses him.

When my guest was a little recovered I had great trouble to keep off the men, who wished to ask him a thousand questions; but I would not allow him to be tormented by their idle curiosity, in a state of body and mind whose restoration evidently depended upon entire repose. Once, however, the lieutenant asked why he had come so far upon the ice in so strange a vehicle.

His countenance instantly assumed an aspect of the deepest gloom, and he replied, "To seek one who fled from me."

"And did the man whom you pursued travel in the same fashion?"

"Yes."

"Then I fancy we have seen him, for the day before we picked you up we saw some dogs drawing a sledge, with a man in it, across the ice."

This aroused the stranger's attention, and he asked a multitude of questions concerning the route which the daemon, as he called him, had pursued. Soon after, when he was alone with me, he said, "I have, doubtless, excited your curiosity, as well as that of these good people; but you are too considerate to make enquiries."

"Certainly; it would indeed be very impertinent and inhuman in me to trouble you with any inquisitiveness of mine."

"And yet you rescued me from a strange and perilous situation; you have benevolently restored me to life."

Soon after this he enquired if I thought that the breaking up of the ice had destroyed the other sledge. I replied that I could not answer with any degree of certainty, for the ice had not broken until near midnight, and the traveller might have arrived at a place of safety before that time; but of this I could not judge.

From this time a new spirit of life animated the decaying frame of the stranger. He manifested the greatest eagerness to be upon deck to watch for the sledge which had before appeared; but I have persuaded him to remain in the cabin, for he is far too weak to sustain the rawness of the atmosphere. I have promised that someone should watch for him and give him instant notice if any new object should appear in sight.

Such is my journal of what relates to this strange occurrence up to the present day. The stranger has gradually improved in health but is very silent and appears uneasy when anyone except myself enters his cabin. Yet his manners are so conciliating and gentle that the sailors are all interested in him, although they have had very little communication with him. For my own part, I begin to love him as a brother, and his constant and deep grief fills me with sympathy and compassion. He must have been a noble creature in his better days, being even now in wreck so attractive and amiable.

I said in one of my letters, my dear Margaret, that I should find no friend on the wide ocean; yet I have found a man who, before his spirit had been broken by misery, I should have been happy to have possessed as the brother of my heart.

I shall continue my journal concerning the stranger at intervals, should I have any fresh incidents to record.

August 13th, 17——.

My affection for my guest increases every day. He excites at once my admiration and my pity to an astonishing degree. How can I see so noble a creature destroyed by misery without feeling the most poignant grief? He is so gentle, yet so wise; his mind is so cultivated, and when he speaks, although his words are culled with the choicest art, yet they flow with rapidity and unparalleled eloquence.

He is now much recovered from his illness and is continually on the deck, apparently watching for the sledge that preceded his own. Yet, although unhappy, he is not so utterly occupied by his own misery but that he interests himself deeply in the projects of others. He has frequently conversed with me on mine, which I have communicated to him without disguise. He entered attentively into all my arguments in favour of my eventual success and into every minute detail of the measures I had taken to secure it. I was easily led by the sympathy which he evinced to use the language of my heart, to give utterance to the burning ardour of my soul and to say, with all the fervour that warmed me, how gladly I would sacrifice my fortune, my existence, my every hope, to the furtherance of my enterprise. One man's life or death were but a small price to pay for the acquirement of the knowledge which I sought, for the dominion I should acquire and transmit over the elemental foes of our race. As I spoke, a dark gloom spread over my listener's countenance. At first I perceived that he tried to suppress his emotion; he placed his hands before his eyes, and my voice quivered and failed me as I beheld tears trickle fast from between his fingers; a groan burst from his heaving breast. I paused; at length he spoke, in broken accents: "Unhappy man! Do you share my madness? Have you drunk also of the intoxicating draught? Hear me; let me reveal my tale, and you will dash the cup from your lips!"

Such words, you may imagine, strongly excited my curiosity; but the paroxysm of grief that had seized the stranger overcame his weakened powers, and many hours of repose and tranquil conversation were necessary to restore his composure.

Having conquered the violence of his feelings, he appeared to despise himself for being the slave of passion; and quelling the dark tyranny of despair, he led me again to converse concerning myself personally. He asked me the history of my earlier years. The tale was quickly told, but it awakened various trains of reflection. I spoke of my desire of finding a friend, of my thirst for a more intimate sympathy with a fellow mind than had ever fallen to my lot, and expressed my conviction that a man could boast of little happiness who did not enjoy this blessing.

"I agree with you," replied the stranger; "we are unfashioned creatures, but half made up, if one wiser, better, dearer than ourselves—such a friend ought to be—do not lend his aid to perfectionate our weak and faulty natures. I once had a friend, the most noble of human creatures, and am entitled, therefore, to judge respecting friendship. You have hope, and the world before you, and have no cause for despair. But I—I have lost everything and cannot begin life anew."

As he said this his countenance became expressive of a calm, settled grief that touched me to the heart. But he was silent and presently retired to his cabin.

Even broken in spirit as he is, no one can feel more deeply than he does the beauties of nature. The starry sky, the sea, and every sight afforded by these wonderful regions seem still to have the power of elevating his soul from earth. Such a man has a double existence: he may suffer misery and be overwhelmed by disappointments, yet when he has retired into himself, he will be like a celestial spirit that has a halo around him, within whose circle no grief or folly ventures.

Will you smile at the enthusiasm I express concerning this divine wanderer? You would not if you saw him. You have been tutored and refined by books and retirement from the world, and you are therefore somewhat fastidious; but this only renders you the more fit to appreciate the extraordinary merits of this wonderful man. Sometimes I have endeavoured to discover what quality it is which he possesses that elevates him so immeasurably above any other person I ever knew. I believe it to be an intuitive discernment, a quick but never-failing power of judgement, a penetration into the causes of things, unequalled for clearness and precision; add to this a facility of expression and a voice whose varied intonations are soul-subduing music.

August 19th, 17—.

Yesterday the stranger said to me, "You may easily perceive, Captain Walton, that I have suffered great and unparalleled misfortunes. I had determined at one time that the memory of these evils should die with me, but you have won me to alter my determination. You seek for knowledge and wisdom, as I once did; and I ardently hope that the gratification of your wishes may not be a serpent to sting you, as mine has been. I do not know that the relation of my disasters will be useful to you; yet, when I reflect that you are pursuing the same course, exposing yourself to the same dangers which have rendered me what I am, I imagine that you may deduce an apt moral from my tale, one that may direct you if you succeed in your undertaking and console you in case of failure. Prepare to hear of occurrences which are usually deemed marvellous. Were we among the tamer scenes of nature I might fear to encounter your unbelief, perhaps your ridicule; but many things will appear possible in these wild and mysterious regions which would provoke the laughter of those unacquainted with the ever-varied powers of nature; nor can I doubt but that my tale conveys in its series internal evidence of the truth of the events of which it is composed."

You may easily imagine that I was much gratified by the offered communication, yet I could not endure that he should renew his grief by a recital of his misfortunes. I felt the greatest eagerness to hear the promised narrative, partly from curiosity and partly from a strong desire to ameliorate his fate if it were in my power. I expressed these feelings in my answer.

"I thank you," he replied, "for your sympathy, but it is useless; my fate is nearly fulfilled. I wait but for one event, and then I shall repose in peace. I understand your feeling," continued he, perceiving that I wished to interrupt him; "but you are mistaken, my friend, if thus you will allow me to name you; nothing can alter my destiny; listen to my history, and you will perceive how irrevocably it is determined."

He then told me that he would commence his narrative the next day when I should be at leisure. This promise drew from me the warmest thanks. I have resolved every night, when I am not imperatively occupied by my duties, to record, as nearly as possible in his own words, what he has related during the day. If I should be engaged, I will at least make notes. This manuscript will doubtless afford you the greatest pleasure; but to me, who know him, and who hear it from his own lips—with what interest and sympathy shall I read it in some future day! Even now, as I commence my task, his full-toned voice swells in my ears; his lustrous eyes dwell on me with all their melancholy sweetness; I see his thin hand raised in animation, while the lineaments of his face are irradiated by the soul within. Strange and harrowing must be his story, frightful the storm which embraced the gallant vessel on its course and wrecked it—thus!

CHAPTER I

I am by birth a Genevese, and my family is one of the most distinguished of that republic. My ancestors had been for many years counsellors and syndics, and my father had filled several public situations with honour and reputation. He was respected by all who knew him for his integrity and indefatigable attention to public business. He passed his younger days perpetually occupied by the affairs of his country; a variety of circumstances had prevented his marrying early, nor was it until the decline of life that he became a husband and the father of a family.

As the circumstances of his marriage illustrate his character, I cannot refrain from relating them. One of his most intimate friends was a merchant who, from a flourishing state, fell, through numerous mischances, into poverty. This man, whose name was Beaufort, was of a proud and unbending disposition and could not bear to live in poverty and oblivion in the same country where he had formerly been distinguished for his rank and magnificence. Having paid his debts, therefore, in the most honourable manner, he retreated with his daughter to the town of Lucerne, where he lived unknown and in wretchedness. My father loved Beaufort with the truest friendship and was deeply grieved by his retreat in these unfortunate circumstances. He bitterly deplored the false pride which led his friend to a conduct so little worthy of the affection that united them. He lost no time in endeavouring to seek him out, with the hope of persuading him to begin the world again through his credit and assistance.

Beaufort had taken effectual measures to conceal himself, and it was ten months before my father discovered his abode. Overjoyed at this discovery, he hastened to the house, which was situated in a mean street near the Reuss. But when he entered, misery and despair alone welcomed him. Beaufort had saved but a very small sum of money from the wreck of his fortunes, but it was sufficient to provide him with sustenance for some months, and in the meantime he hoped to procure some respectable employment in a merchant's house. The interval was, consequently, spent in inaction; his grief only became more deep and rankling when he had leisure for reflection, and at length it took so fast hold of his mind that at the end of three months he lay on a bed of sickness, incapable of any exertion.

His daughter attended him with the greatest tenderness, but she saw with despair that their little fund was rapidly decreasing and that there was no other prospect of support. But Caroline Beaufort possessed a mind of an uncommon mould, and her courage rose to support her in her adversity. She procured plain work; she plaited straw and by various means contrived to earn a pittance scarcely sufficient to support life.

Several months passed in this manner. Her father grew worse; her time was more entirely occupied in attending him; her means of subsistence decreased; and in the tenth month her father died in her arms, leaving her an orphan and a beggar. This last blow overcame her, and she knelt by Beaufort's coffin weeping bitterly, when my father entered the chamber. He came like a protecting spirit to the poor girl, who committed herself to his care; and after the interment of his friend he conducted her to Geneva and placed her under the protection of a relation. Two years after this event Caroline became his wife.

There was a considerable difference between the ages of my parents, but this circumstance seemed to unite them only closer in bonds of devoted affection. There was a sense of justice in my father's upright mind which rendered it necessary that he should approve highly to love strongly. Perhaps during former years he had suffered from the late-discovered unworthiness of one beloved and so was disposed to set a greater value on tried worth. There was a show of gratitude and worship in his attachment to my mother, differing wholly from the doting fondness of age, for it was inspired by reverence for her virtues and a desire to be the means of, in some degree, recompensing her for the sorrows she had endured, but which gave inexpressible grace to his behaviour to her. Everything was made to yield to her wishes and her convenience. He strove to shelter her, as a fair exotic is sheltered by the gardener, from every rougher wind and to surround her with all that could tend to excite pleasurable emotion in her soft and benevolent mind. Her health, and even the tranquillity of her hitherto constant spirit, had been shaken by what she had gone through. During the two years that had elapsed previous to their marriage my father had gradually relinquished all his public functions; and immediately after their union they sought the pleasant climate of Italy, and the change of scene and interest attendant on a tour through that land of wonders, as a restorative for her weakened frame.

From Italy they visited Germany and France. I, their eldest child, was born at Naples, and as an infant accompanied them in their rambles. I remained for several years their only child. Much as they were attached to each other, they seemed to draw inexhaustible stores of affection from a very mine of love to bestow them upon me. My mother's tender caresses and my father's smile of benevolent pleasure while regarding me are my first recollections. I was their plaything and their idol, and something better—their child, the innocent and helpless creature bestowed on them by heaven, whom to bring up to good, and whose future lot it was in their hands to direct to happiness or misery, according as they fulfilled their duties towards me. With this deep consciousness of what they owed towards the being to which they had given life, added to the active spirit of tenderness that animated both, it may be imagined that while during every hour of my infant life I received a lesson of patience, of charity, and of self-control, I was so guided by a silken cord that all seemed but one train of enjoyment to me.

For a long time I was their only care. My mother had much desired to have a daughter, but I continued their single offspring. When I was about five years old, while making an excursion beyond the frontiers of Italy, they passed a week on the shores of the Lake of Como. Their benevolent disposition often made them enter the cottages of the poor. This, to my mother, was more than a duty; it was a necessity, a passion—remembering what she had suffered, and how she had been relieved—for her to act in her turn the guardian angel to the afflicted. During one of their walks a poor cot in the foldings of a vale attracted their notice as being singularly disconsolate, while the number of half-clothed children gathered about it spoke of penury in its worst shape. One day, when my father had gone by himself to Milan, my mother, accompanied by me, visited this abode. She found a peasant and his wife, hard working, bent down by care and labour, distributing a scanty meal to five hungry babes. Among these there was one which attracted my mother far above all the rest. She appeared of a different stock. The four others were dark-eyed, hardy little vagrants; this child was thin and very fair. Her hair was the brightest living gold, and despite the poverty of her clothing, seemed to set a crown of distinction on her head. Her brow was clear and ample, her blue eyes cloudless, and her lips and the moulding of her face so expressive of sensibility and sweetness that none could behold her without looking on her as of a distinct species, a being heaven-sent, and bearing a celestial stamp in all her features.

The peasant woman, perceiving that my mother fixed eyes of wonder and admiration on this lovely girl, eagerly communicated her history. She was not her child, but the daughter of a Milanese nobleman. Her mother was a German and had died on giving her birth. The infant had been placed with these good people to nurse: they were better off then. They had not been long married, and their eldest child was but just born. The father of their charge was one of those Italians nursed in the memory of the antique glory of Italy—one among the *schiavi ognor frementi*, who exerted himself to obtain the liberty of his country. He became the victim of its weakness. Whether he had died or still lingered in the dungeons of Austria was not known. His property was confiscated; his child became an orphan and a beggar. She continued with her foster parents and bloomed in their rude abode, fairer than a garden rose among dark-leaved brambles.

When my father returned from Milan, he found playing with me in the hall of our villa a child fairer than a pictured cherub—a creature who seemed to shed radiance from her looks and whose form and motions were lighter than the chamois of the hills. The apparition was soon explained. With his permission my mother prevailed on her rustic guardians to yield their charge to her. They were fond of the sweet orphan. Her presence had seemed a blessing to them, but it would be unfair to her to keep her in poverty and want when Providence afforded her such powerful protection. They consulted their village priest, and the result was that Elizabeth Lavenza became the inmate of my parents' house—my more than sister—the beautiful and adored companion of all my occupations and my pleasures.

Everyone loved Elizabeth. The passionate and almost reverential attachment with which all regarded her became, while I shared it, my pride and my delight. On the evening previous to her being brought to my home, my mother had said playfully, "I have a pretty present for my Victor—tomorrow he shall have it." And when, on the morrow, she presented Elizabeth to me as her promised gift, I, with childish seriousness, interpreted her words literally and looked upon Elizabeth as mine—mine to protect, love, and cherish. All praises bestowed on her I received as made to a possession of my own. We called each other familiarly by the name of cousin. No word, no expression could body forth the kind of relation in which she stood to me—my more than sister, since till death she was to be mine only.

CHAPTER II

We were brought up together; there was not quite a year difference in our ages. I need not say that we were strangers to any species of disunion or dispute. Harmony was the soul of our companionship, and the diversity and contrast that subsisted in our characters drew us nearer together. Elizabeth was of a calmer and more concentrated disposition; but, with all my ardour, I was capable of a more intense application and was more deeply smitten with the thirst for knowledge. She busied herself with following the aerial creations of the poets; and in the majestic and wondrous scenes which surrounded our Swiss home—the sublime shapes of the mountains, the changes of the seasons, tempest and calm, the silence of winter, and the life and turbulence of our Alpine summers—she found ample scope for admiration and delight. While my companion contemplated with a serious and satisfied spirit the magnificent appearances of things, I delighted in investigating their causes. The world was to me a secret which I desired to divine. Curiosity, earnest research to learn the hidden laws of nature, gladness akin to rapture, as they were unfolded to me, are among the earliest sensations I can remember.

On the birth of a second son, my junior by seven years, my parents gave up entirely their wandering life and fixed themselves in their native country. We possessed a house in Geneva, and a *campagne* on Belrive, the eastern shore of the lake, at the distance of rather more than a league from the city. We resided principally in the latter, and the lives of my parents were passed in considerable seclusion. It was my temper to avoid a crowd and to attach myself fervently to a few. I was indifferent, therefore, to my school-fellows in general; but I united myself in the bonds of the closest friendship to one among them. Henry Clerval was the son of a merchant of Geneva. He was a boy of singular talent and fancy. He loved enterprise, hardship, and even danger for its own sake. He was deeply read in books of chivalry and romance. He composed heroic songs and began to write many a tale of enchantment and knightly adventure. He tried to make us act plays and to enter into masquerades, in which the characters were drawn from the heroes of Roncesvalles, of the Round Table of King Arthur, and the chivalrous train who shed their blood to redeem the holy sepulchre from the hands of the infidels.

No human being could have passed a happier childhood than myself. My parents were possessed by the very spirit of kindness and indulgence. We felt that they were not the tyrants to rule our lot according to their caprice, but the agents and creators of all the many delights which we enjoyed. When I mingled with other families I distinctly discerned how peculiarly fortunate my lot was, and gratitude assisted the development of filial love.

My temper was sometimes violent, and my passions vehement; but by some law in my temperature they were turned not towards childish pursuits but to an eager desire to learn, and not to learn all things indiscriminately. I confess that neither the structure of languages, nor the code of governments, nor the politics of various states possessed attractions for me. It was the secrets of heaven and earth that I desired to learn; and whether it was the outward substance of things or the inner spirit of nature and the mysterious soul of man that occupied me, still my enquiries were directed to the metaphysical, or in its highest sense, the physical secrets of the world.

Meanwhile Clerval occupied himself, so to speak, with the moral relations of things. The busy stage of life, the virtues of heroes, and the actions of men were his theme; and his hope and his dream was to become one among those whose names are recorded in story as the gallant and adventurous benefactors of our species. The saintly soul of Elizabeth shone like a shrine-dedicated lamp in our peaceful home. Her sympathy was ours; her smile, her soft voice, the sweet glance of her celestial eyes, were ever there to bless and animate us. She was the living spirit of love to soften and attract; I might have become sullen in my study, rough through the ardour of my nature, but that she was there to subdue me to a semblance of her own gentleness. And Clerval—could aught ill entrench on the noble spirit of Clerval? Yet he might not have been so perfectly humane, so thoughtful in his generosity, so full of kindness and tenderness amidst his passion for adventurous exploit, had she not unfolded to him the real loveliness of beneficence and made the doing good the end and aim of his soaring ambition.

I feel exquisite pleasure in dwelling on the recollections of childhood, before misfortune had tainted my mind and changed its bright visions of extensive usefulness into gloomy and narrow reflections upon self. Besides, in drawing the picture of my early days, I also record those events which led, by insensible steps, to my after tale of misery, for when I would account to myself for the birth of that passion which afterwards ruled my destiny I find it arise, like a mountain river, from ignoble and almost forgotten sources; but, swelling as it proceeded, it became the torrent which, in its course, has swept away all my hopes and joys.

Natural philosophy is the genius that has regulated my fate; I desire, therefore, in this narration, to state those facts which led to my predilection for that science. When I was thirteen years of age we all went on a party of pleasure to the baths near Thonon; the inclemency of the weather obliged us to remain a day confined to the inn. In this house I chanced to find a volume of the works of Cornelius Agrippa. I opened it with apathy; the theory which he attempts to demonstrate and the wonderful facts which he relates soon changed this feeling into enthusiasm. A new light seemed to dawn upon my mind, and bounding with joy, I communicated my discovery to my father. My father looked carelessly at the title page of my book and said, "Ah! Cornelius Agrippa! My dear Victor, do not waste your time upon this; it is sad trash."

If, instead of this remark, my father had taken the pains to explain to me that the principles of Agrippa had been entirely exploded and that a modern system of science had been introduced which possessed much greater powers than the ancient, because the powers of the latter were chimerical, while those of the former were real and practical, under such circumstances I should certainly have thrown Agrippa aside and have contented my imagination, warmed as it was, by returning with greater ardour to my former studies. It is even possible that the train of my ideas would never have received the fatal impulse that led to my ruin. But the cursory glance my father had taken of my volume by no means assured me that he was acquainted with its contents, and I continued to read with the greatest avidity.

When I returned home my first care was to procure the whole works of this author, and afterwards of Paracelsus and Albertus Magnus. I read and studied the wild fancies of these writers with delight; they appeared to me treasures known to few besides myself. I have described myself as always having been imbued with a fervent longing to penetrate the secrets of nature. In spite of the intense labour and wonderful discoveries of modern philosophers, I always came from my studies discontented and unsatisfied. Sir Isaac Newton is said to have avowed that he felt like a child picking up shells beside the great and unexplored ocean of truth. Those of his successors in each branch of natural philosophy with whom I was acquainted appeared even to my boy's apprehensions as tyros engaged in the same pursuit.

The untaught peasant beheld the elements around him and was acquainted with their practical uses. The most learned philosopher knew little more. He had partially unveiled the face of Nature, but her immortal lineaments were still a wonder and a mystery. He might dissect, anatomize, and give names; but, not to speak of a final cause, causes in their secondary and tertiary grades were utterly unknown to him. I had gazed upon the fortifications and impediments that seemed to keep human beings from entering the citadel of nature, and rashly and ignorantly I had repined.

But here were books, and here were men who had penetrated deeper and knew more. I took their word for all that they averred, and I became their disciple. It may appear strange that such should arise in the eighteenth century; but while I followed the routine of education in the schools of Geneva, I was, to a great degree, self-taught with regard to my favourite studies. My father was not scientific, and I was left to struggle with a child's blindness, added to a student's thirst for knowledge. Under the guidance of my new preceptors I entered with the greatest diligence into the search of the philosopher's stone and the elixir of life; but the latter soon obtained my undivided attention. Wealth was an inferior object, but what glory would attend the discovery if I could banish disease from the human frame and render man invulnerable to any but a violent death!

Nor were these my only visions. The raising of ghosts or devils was a promise liberally accorded by my favourite authors, the fulfilment of which I most eagerly sought; and if my incantations were always unsuccessful, I attributed the failure rather to my own inexperience and mistake than to a want of skill or fidelity in my instructors. And thus for a time I was occupied by exploded systems, mingling, like an unadept, a thousand contradictory theories, and floundering desperately in a very slough of multifarious knowledge, guided by an ardent imagination and childish reasoning, till an accident again changed the current of my ideas.

When I was about fifteen years old we had retired to our house near Belrive, when we witnessed a most violent and terrible thunderstorm. It advanced from behind the mountains of Jura, and the thunder burst at once with frightful loudness from various quarters of the heavens. I remained, while the storm lasted, watching its progress with curiosity and delight. As I stood at the door, on a sudden I beheld a stream of fire issue from an old and beautiful oak which stood about twenty yards from our house; and so soon as the dazzling light vanished, the oak had disappeared, and nothing remained but a blasted stump. When we visited it the next morning, we found the tree shattered in a singular manner. It was not splintered by the shock, but entirely reduced to thin ribbons of wood. I never beheld anything so utterly destroyed.

Before this I was not unacquainted with the more obvious laws of electricity. On this occasion a man of great research in natural philosophy was with us, and excited by this catastrophe, he entered on the explanation of a theory which he had formed on the subject of electricity and galvanism, which was at once new and astonishing to me. All that he said threw greatly into the shade Cornelius Agrippa, Albertus Magnus, and Paracelsus, the lords of my imagination; but by some fatality the overthrow of these men disinclined me to pursue my accustomed studies. It seemed to me as if nothing would or could ever be known. All that had so long engaged my attention suddenly grew despicable. By one of those caprices of the mind which we are perhaps most subject to in early youth, I at once gave up my former occupations, set down natural history and all its progeny as a deformed and abortive creation, and entertained the greatest disdain for a would-be science which could never even step within the threshold of real knowledge. In this mood of mind I betook myself to the mathematics and the branches of study appertaining to that science as being built upon secure foundations, and so worthy of my consideration.

Thus strangely are our souls constructed, and by such slight ligaments are we bound to prosperity or ruin. When I look back, it seems to me as if this almost miraculous change of inclination and will was the immediate suggestion of the guardian angel of my life—the last effort made by the spirit of preservation to avert the storm that was even then hanging in the stars and ready to envelop me. Her victory was announced by an unusual tranquillity and gladness of soul which followed the relinquishing of my ancient and latterly tormenting studies. It was thus that I was to be taught to associate evil with their prosecution, happiness with their disregard.

It was a strong effort of the spirit of good, but it was ineffectual. Destiny was too potent, and her immutable laws had decreed my utter and terrible destruction.

CHAPTER III

When I had attained the age of seventeen, my parents resolved that I should become a student at the university of Ingolstadt. I had hitherto attended the schools of Geneva, but my father thought it necessary for the completion of my education that I should be made acquainted with other customs than those of my native country. My departure was therefore fixed at an early date, but before the day resolved upon could arrive, the first misfortune of my life occurred—an omen, as it were, of my future misery.

Elizabeth had caught the scarlet fever; her illness was severe, and she was in the greatest danger. During her illness many arguments had been urged to persuade my mother to refrain from attending upon her. She had at first yielded to our entreaties, but when she heard that the life of her favourite was menaced, she could no longer control her anxiety. She attended her sickbed; her watchful attentions triumphed over the malignity of the distemper—Elizabeth was saved, but the consequences of this imprudence were fatal to her preserver. On the third day my mother sickened; her fever was accompanied by the most alarming symptoms, and the looks of her medical attendants prognosticated the worst event. On her deathbed the fortitude and benignity of this best of women did not desert her. She joined the hands of Elizabeth and myself. "My children," she said, "my firmest hopes of future happiness were placed on the prospect of your union. This expectation will now be the consolation of your father. Elizabeth, my love, you must supply my place to my younger children. Alas! I regret that I am taken from you; and, happy and beloved as I have been, is it not hard to quit you all? But these are not thoughts befitting me; I will endeavour to resign myself cheerfully to death and will indulge a hope of meeting you in another world."

She died calmly, and her countenance expressed affection even in death. I need not describe the feelings of those whose dearest ties are rent by that most irreparable evil, the void that presents itself to the soul, and the despair that is exhibited on the countenance. It is so long before the mind can persuade itself that she whom we saw every day and whose very existence appeared a part of our own can have departed forever—that the brightness of a beloved eye can have been extinguished and the sound of a voice so familiar and dear to the ear can be hushed, never more to be heard. These are the reflections of the first days; but when the lapse of time proves the reality of the evil, then the actual bitterness of grief commences. Yet from whom has not that rude hand rent away some dear connection? And why should I describe a sorrow which all have felt, and must feel? The time at length arrives when grief is rather an indulgence than a necessity; and the smile that plays upon the lips, although it may be deemed a sacrilege, is not banished. My mother was dead, but we had still duties which we ought to perform; we must continue our course with the rest and learn to think ourselves fortunate whilst one remains whom the spoiler has not seized.

My departure for Ingolstadt, which had been deferred by these events, was now again determined upon. I obtained from my father a respite of some weeks. It appeared to me sacrilege so soon to leave the repose, akin to death, of the house of mourning and to rush into the thick of life. I was new to sorrow, but it did not the less alarm me. I was unwilling to quit the sight of those that remained to me, and above all, I desired to see my sweet Elizabeth in some degree consoled.

She indeed veiled her grief and strove to act the comforter to us all. She looked steadily on life and assumed its duties with courage and zeal. She devoted herself to those whom she had been taught to call her uncle and cousins. Never was she so enchanting as at this time, when she recalled the sunshine of her smiles and spent them upon us. She forgot even her own regret in her endeavours to make us forget.

The day of my departure at length arrived. Clerval spent the last evening with us. He had endeavoured to persuade his father to permit him to accompany me and to become my fellow student, but in vain. His father was a narrow-minded trader and saw idleness and ruin in the aspirations and ambition of his son. Henry deeply felt the misfortune of being debarred from a liberal education. He said little, but when he spoke I read in his kindling eye and in his animated glance a restrained but firm resolve not to be chained to the miserable details of commerce.

We sat late. We could not tear ourselves away from each other nor persuade ourselves to say the word "Farewell!" It was said, and we retired under the pretence of seeking repose, each fancying that the other was deceived; but when at morning's dawn I descended to the carriage which was to convey me away, they were all there—my father again to bless me, Clerval to press my hand once more, my Elizabeth to renew her entreaties that I would write often and to bestow the last feminine attentions on her playmate and friend.

I threw myself into the chaise that was to convey me away and indulged in the most melancholy reflections. I, who had ever been surrounded by amiable companions, continually engaged in endeavouring to bestow mutual pleasure—I was now alone. In the university whither I was going I must form my own friends and be my own protector. My life had hitherto been remarkably secluded and domestic, and this had given me invincible repugnance to new countenances. I loved my brothers, Elizabeth, and Clerval; these were "old familiar faces," but I believed myself totally unfitted for the company of strangers. Such were my reflections as I commenced my journey; but as I proceeded, my spirits and hopes rose. I ardently desired the acquisition of knowledge. I had often, when at home, thought it hard to remain during my youth cooped up in one place and had longed to enter the world and take my station among other human beings. Now my desires were complied with, and it would, indeed, have been folly to repent.

I had sufficient leisure for these and many other reflections during my journey to Ingolstadt, which was long and fatiguing. At length the high white steeple of the town met my eyes. I alighted and was conducted to my solitary apartment to spend the evening as I pleased.

The next morning I delivered my letters of introduction and paid a visit to some of the principal professors. Chance—or rather the evil influence, the Angel of Destruction, which asserted omnipotent sway over me from the moment I turned my reluctant steps from my father's door—led me first to M. Krempe, professor of natural philosophy. He was an uncouth man, but deeply imbued in the secrets of his science. He asked me several questions concerning my progress in the different branches of science appertaining to natural philosophy. I replied carelessly, and partly in contempt, mentioned the names of my alchemists as the principal authors I had studied. The professor stared. "Have you," he said, "really spent your time in studying such nonsense?"

I replied in the affirmative. "Every minute," continued M. Krempe with warmth, "every instant that you have wasted on those books is utterly and entirely lost. You have burdened your memory with exploded systems and useless names. Good God! In what desert land have you lived, where no one was kind enough to inform you that these fancies which you have so greedily imbibed are a thousand years old and as musty as they are ancient? I little expected, in this enlightened and scientific age, to find a disciple of Albertus Magnus and Paracelsus. My dear sir, you must begin your studies entirely anew."

So saying, he stepped aside and wrote down a list of several books treating of natural philosophy which he desired me to procure, and dismissed me after mentioning that in the beginning of the following week he intended to commence a course of lectures upon natural philosophy in its general relations, and that M. Waldman, a fellow professor, would lecture upon chemistry the alternate days that he omitted.

I returned home, not disappointed, for I have said that I had long considered those authors useless whom the professor reprobated; but I returned not at all the more inclined to recur to these studies in any shape. M. Krempe was a little squat man with a gruff voice and a repulsive countenance; the teacher, therefore, did not prepossess me in favour of his pursuits. In rather a too philosophical and connected a strain, perhaps, I have given an account of the conclusions I had come to concerning them in my early years. As a child I had not been content with the results promised by the modern professors of natural science. With a confusion of ideas only to be accounted for by my extreme youth and my want of a guide on such matters, I had retrod the steps of knowledge along the paths of time and exchanged the discoveries of recent enquirers for the dreams of forgotten alchemists. Besides, I had a contempt for the uses of modern natural philosophy. It was very different when the masters of the science sought immortality and power; such views, although futile, were grand; but now the scene was changed. The ambition of the enquirer seemed to limit itself to the annihilation of those visions on which my interest in science was chiefly founded. I was required to exchange chimeras of boundless grandeur for realities of little worth.

Such were my reflections during the first two or three days of my residence at Ingolstadt, which were chiefly spent in becoming acquainted with the localities and the principal residents in my new abode. But as the ensuing week commenced, I thought of the information which M. Krempe had given me concerning the lectures. And although I could not consent to go and hear that little conceited fellow deliver sentences out of a pulpit, I recollected what he had said of M. Waldman, whom I had never seen, as he had hitherto been out of town.

Partly from curiosity and partly from idleness, I went into the lecturing room, which M. Waldman entered shortly after. This professor was very unlike his colleague. He appeared about fifty years of age, but with an aspect expressive of the greatest benevolence; a few grey hairs covered his temples, but those at the back of his head were nearly black. His person was short but remarkably erect and his voice the sweetest I had ever heard. He began his lecture by a recapitulation of the history of chemistry and the various improvements made by different men of learning, pronouncing with fervour the names of the most distinguished discoverers. He then took a cursory view of the present state of the science and explained many of its elementary terms. After having made a few preparatory experiments, he concluded with a panegyric upon modern chemistry, the terms of which I shall never forget:

"The ancient teachers of this science," said he, "promised impossibilities and performed nothing. The modern masters promise very little; they know that metals cannot be transmuted and that the elixir of life is a chimera. But these philosophers, whose hands seem only made to dabble in dirt, and their eyes to pore over the microscope or crucible, have indeed performed miracles. They penetrate into the recesses of nature and show how she works in her hiding-places. They ascend into the heavens; they have discovered how the blood circulates, and the nature of the air we breathe. They have acquired new and almost unlimited powers; they can command the thunders of heaven, mimic the earthquake, and even mock the invisible world with its own shadows."

Such were the professor's words—rather let me say such the words of the fate—enounced to destroy me. As he went on I felt as if my soul were grappling with a palpable enemy; one by one the various keys were touched which formed the mechanism of my being; chord after chord was sounded, and soon my mind was filled with one thought, one conception, one purpose. So much has been done, exclaimed the soul of Frankenstein—more, far more, will I achieve; treading in the steps already marked, I will pioneer a new way, explore unknown powers, and unfold to the world the deepest mysteries of creation.

I closed not my eyes that night. My internal being was in a state of insurrection and turmoil; I felt that order would thence arise, but I had no power to produce it. By degrees, after the morning's dawn, sleep came. I awoke, and my yesternight's thoughts were as a dream. There only remained a resolution to return to my ancient studies and to devote myself to a science for which I believed myself to possess a natural talent. On the same day, I paid M. Waldman a visit. His manners in private were even more mild and attractive than in public, for there was a certain dignity in his mien during his lecture which in his own house was replaced by the greatest affability and kindness. I gave him pretty nearly the same account of my former pursuits as I had given to his fellow professor. He heard with attention the little narration concerning my studies and smiled at the names of Cornelius Agrippa and Paracelsus, but without the contempt that M. Krempe had exhibited. He said that "these were men to whose indefatigable zeal modern philosophers were indebted for most of the foundations of their knowledge. They had left to us, as an easier task, to give new names and arrange in connected classifications the facts which they in a great degree had been the instruments of bringing to light. The labours of men of genius, however erroneously directed, scarcely ever fail in ultimately turning to the solid advantage of mankind." I listened to his statement, which was delivered without any presumption or affectation, and then added that his lecture had removed my prejudices against modern chemists; I expressed myself in measured terms, with the modesty and deference due from a youth to his instructor, without letting escape (inexperience in life would have made me ashamed) any of the enthusiasm which stimulated my intended labours. I requested his advice concerning the books I ought to procure.

"I am happy," said M. Waldman, "to have gained a disciple; and if your application equals your ability, I have no doubt of your success. Chemistry is that branch of natural philosophy in which the greatest improvements have been and may be made; it is on that account that I have made it my peculiar study; but at the same time, I have not neglected the other branches of science. A man would make but a very sorry chemist if he attended to that department of human knowledge alone. If your wish is to become really a man of science and not merely a petty experimentalist, I should advise you to apply to every branch of natural philosophy, including mathematics."

He then took me into his laboratory and explained to me the uses of his various machines, instructing me as to what I ought to procure and promising me the use of his own when I should have advanced far enough in the science not to derange their mechanism. He also gave me the list of books which I had requested, and I took my leave.

Thus ended a day memorable to me: it decided my future destiny.

CHAPTER IV

From this day natural philosophy, and particularly chemistry, in the most comprehensive sense of the term, became nearly my sole occupation. I read with ardour those works, so full of genius and discrimination, which modern enquirers have written on these subjects. I attended the lectures and cultivated the acquaintance of the men of science of the university, and I found even in M. Krempe a great deal of sound sense and real information, combined, it is true, with a repulsive physiognomy and manners, but not on that account the less valuable. In M. Waldman I found a true friend. His gentleness was never tinged by dogmatism, and his instructions were given with an air of frankness and good nature that banished every idea of pedantry. In a thousand ways he smoothed for me the path of knowledge and made the most abstruse enquiries clear and facile to my apprehension. My application was at first fluctuating and uncertain; it gained strength as I proceeded and soon became so ardent and eager that the stars often disappeared in the light of morning whilst I was yet engaged in my laboratory.

As I applied so closely, it may be easily conceived that my progress was rapid. My ardour was indeed the astonishment of the students, and my proficiency that of the masters. Professor Krempe often asked me, with a sly smile, how Cornelius Agrippa went on, whilst M. Waldman expressed the most heartfelt exultation in my progress. Two years passed in this manner, during which I paid no visit to Geneva, but was engaged, heart and soul, in the pursuit of some discoveries which I hoped to make. None but those who have experienced them can conceive of the enticements of science. In other studies you go as far as others have gone before you, and there is nothing more to know; but in a scientific pursuit there is continual food for discovery and wonder. A mind of moderate capacity which closely pursues one study must infallibly arrive at great proficiency in that study; and I, who continually sought the attainment of one object of pursuit and was solely wrapped up in this, improved so rapidly that at the end of two years I made some discoveries in the improvement of some chemical instruments, which procured me great esteem and admiration at the university. When I had arrived at this point and had become as well acquainted with the theory and practice of natural philosophy as depended on the lessons of any of the professors at Ingolstadt, my residence there being no longer conducive to my improvements, I thought of returning to my friends and my native town, when an incident happened that protracted my stay.

One of the phenomena which had peculiarly attracted my attention was the structure of the human frame, and, indeed, any animal endued with life. Whence, I often asked myself, did the principle of life proceed? It was a bold question, and one which has ever been considered as a mystery; yet with how many things are we upon the brink of becoming acquainted, if cowardice or carelessness did not restrain our enquiries. I revolved these circumstances in my mind and determined thenceforth to apply myself more particularly to those branches of natural philosophy which relate to physiology. Unless I had been animated by an almost supernatural enthusiasm, my application to this study would have been irksome and almost intolerable. To examine the causes of life, we must first have recourse to death. I became acquainted with the science of anatomy, but this was not sufficient; I must also observe the natural decay and corruption of the human body. In my education my father had taken the greatest precautions that my mind should be impressed with no supernatural horrors. I do not ever remember to have trembled at a tale of superstition or to have feared the apparition of a spirit. Darkness had no effect upon my fancy, and a churchyard was to me merely the receptacle of bodies deprived of life, which, from being the seat of beauty and strength, had become food for the worm. Now I was led to examine the cause and progress of this decay and forced to spend days and nights in vaults and charnel-houses. My attention was fixed upon every object the most insupportable to the delicacy of the human feelings. I saw how the fine form of man was degraded and wasted; I beheld the corruption of death succeed to the blooming cheek of life; I saw how the worm inherited the wonders of the eye and brain. I paused, examining and analysing all the minutiae of causation, as exemplified in the change from life to death, and death to life, until from the midst of this darkness a sudden light broke in upon me—a light so brilliant and wondrous, yet so simple, that while I became dizzy with the immensity of the prospect which it illustrated, I was surprised that among so many men of genius who had directed their enquiries towards the same science, that I alone should be reserved to discover so astonishing a secret.

Remember, I am not recording the vision of a madman. The sun does not more certainly shine in the heavens than that which I now affirm is true. Some miracle might have produced it, yet the stages of the discovery were distinct and probable. After days and nights of incredible labour and fatigue, I succeeded in discovering the cause of generation and life; nay, more, I became myself capable of bestowing animation upon lifeless matter.

The astonishment which I had at first experienced on this discovery soon gave place to delight and rapture. After so much time spent in painful labour, to arrive at once at the summit of my desires was the most gratifying consummation of my toils. But this discovery was so great and overwhelming that all the steps by which I had been progressively led to it were obliterated, and I beheld only the result. What had been the study and desire of the wisest men since the creation of the world was now within my grasp. Not that, like a magic scene, it all opened upon me at once: the information I had obtained was of a nature rather to direct my endeavours so soon as I should point them towards the object of my search than to exhibit that object already accomplished. I was like the Arabian who had been buried with the dead and found a passage to life, aided only by one glimmering and seemingly ineffectual light.

I see by your eagerness and the wonder and hope which your eyes express, my friend, that you expect to be informed of the secret with which I am acquainted; that cannot be; listen patiently until the end of my story, and you will easily perceive why I am reserved upon that subject. I will not lead you on, unguarded and ardent as I then was, to your destruction and infallible misery. Learn from me, if not by my precepts, at least by my example, how dangerous is the acquirement of knowledge and how much happier that man is who believes his native town to be the world, than he who aspires to become greater than his nature will allow.

When I found so astonishing a power placed within my hands, I hesitated a long time concerning the manner in which I should employ it. Although I possessed the capacity of bestowing animation, yet to prepare a frame for the reception of it, with all its intricacies of fibres, muscles, and veins, still remained a work of inconceivable difficulty and labour. I doubted at first whether I should attempt the creation of a being like myself, or one of simpler organization; but my imagination was too much exalted by my first success to permit me to doubt of my ability to give life to an animal as complex and wonderful as man. The materials at present within my command hardly appeared adequate to so arduous an undertaking, but I doubted not that I should ultimately succeed. I prepared myself for a multitude of reverses; my operations might be incessantly baffled, and at last my work be imperfect, yet when I considered the improvement which every day takes place in science and mechanics, I was encouraged to hope my present attempts would at least lay the foundations of future success. Nor could I consider the magnitude and complexity of my plan as any argument of its impracticability. It was with these feelings that I began the creation of a human being. As the minuteness of the parts formed a great hindrance to my speed, I resolved, contrary to my first intention, to make the being of a gigantic stature, that is to say, about eight feet in height, and proportionably large. After having formed this determination and having spent some months in successfully collecting and arranging my materials, I began.

No one can conceive the variety of feelings which bore me onwards, like a hurricane, in the first enthusiasm of success. Life and death appeared to me ideal bounds, which I should first break through, and pour a torrent of light into our dark world. A new species would bless me as its creator and source; many happy and excellent natures would owe their being to me. No father could claim the gratitude of his child so completely as I should deserve theirs. Pursuing these reflections, I thought that if I could bestow animation upon lifeless matter, I might in process of time (although I now found it impossible) renew life where death had apparently devoted the body to corruption.

These thoughts supported my spirits, while I pursued my undertaking with unremitting ardour. My cheek had grown pale with study, and my person had become emaciated with confinement. Sometimes, on the very brink of certainty, I failed; yet still I clung to the hope which the next day or the next hour might realize. One secret which I alone possessed was the hope to which I had dedicated myself; and the moon gazed on my midnight labours, while, with unrelaxed and breathless eagerness, I pursued nature to her hiding-places. Who shall conceive the horrors of my secret toil as I dabbled among the unhallowed damps of the grave or tortured the living animal to animate the lifeless clay? My limbs now tremble, and my eyes swim with the remembrance; but then a resistless and almost frantic impulse urged me forward; I seemed to have lost all soul or sensation but for this one pursuit. It was indeed but a passing trance, that only made me feel with renewed acuteness so soon as, the unnatural stimulus ceasing to operate, I had returned to my old habits. I collected bones from charnel-houses and disturbed, with profane fingers, the tremendous secrets of the human frame. In a solitary chamber, or rather cell, at the top of the house, and separated from all the other apartments by a gallery and staircase, I kept my workshop of filthy creation; my eyeballs were starting from their sockets in attending to the details of my employment. The dissecting room and the slaughter-house furnished many of my materials; and often did my human nature turn with loathing from my occupation, whilst, still urged on by an eagerness which perpetually increased, I brought my work near to a conclusion.

The summer months passed while I was thus engaged, heart and soul, in one pursuit. It was a most beautiful season; never did the fields bestow a more plentiful harvest or the vines yield a more luxuriant vintage, but my eyes were insensible to the charms of nature. And the same feelings which made me neglect the scenes around me caused me also to forget those friends who were so many miles absent, and whom I had not seen for so long a time. I knew my silence disquieted them, and I well remembered the words of my father: "I know that while you are pleased with yourself you will think of us with affection, and we shall hear regularly from you. You must pardon me if I regard any interruption in your correspondence as a proof that your other duties are equally neglected."

I knew well therefore what would be my father's feelings, but I could not tear my thoughts from my employment, loathsome in itself, but which had taken an irresistible hold of my imagination. I wished, as it were, to procrastinate all that related to my feelings of affection until the great object, which swallowed up every habit of my nature, should be completed.

I then thought that my father would be unjust if he ascribed my neglect to vice or faultiness on my part, but I am now convinced that he was justified in conceiving that I should not be altogether free from blame. A human being in perfection ought always to preserve a calm and peaceful mind and never to allow passion or a transitory desire to disturb his tranquillity. I do not think that the pursuit of knowledge is an exception to this rule. If the study to which you apply yourself has a tendency to weaken your affections and to destroy your taste for those simple pleasures in which no alloy can possibly mix, then that study is certainly unlawful, that is to say, not befitting the human mind. If this rule were always observed; if no man allowed any pursuit whatsoever to interfere with the tranquillity of his domestic affections, Greece had not been enslaved, Caesar would have spared his country, America would have been discovered more gradually, and the empires of Mexico and Peru had not been destroyed.

But I forget that I am moralizing in the most interesting part of my tale, and your looks remind me to proceed.

My father made no reproach in his letters and only took notice of my silence by enquiring into my occupations more particularly than before. Winter, spring, and summer passed away during my labours; but I did not watch the blossom or the expanding leaves—sights which before always yielded me supreme delight—so deeply was I engrossed in my occupation. The leaves of that year had withered before my work drew near to a close, and now every day showed me more plainly how well I had succeeded. But my enthusiasm was checked by my anxiety, and I appeared rather like one doomed by slavery to toil in the mines, or any other unwholesome trade than an artist occupied by his favourite employment. Every night I was oppressed by a slow fever, and I became nervous to a most painful degree; the fall of a leaf startled me, and I shunned my fellow creatures as if I had been guilty of a crime. Sometimes I grew alarmed at the wreck I perceived that I had become; the energy of my purpose alone sustained me: my labours would soon end, and I believed that exercise and amusement would then drive away incipient disease; and I promised myself both of these when my creation should be complete.

CHAPTER V

It was on a dreary night of November that I beheld the accomplishment of my toils. With an anxiety that almost amounted to agony, I collected the instruments of life around me, that I might infuse a spark of being into the lifeless thing that lay at my feet. It was already one in the morning; the rain pattered dismally against the panes, and my candle was nearly burnt out, when, by the glimmer of the half-extinguished light, I saw the dull yellow eye of the creature open; it breathed hard, and a convulsive motion agitated its limbs.

How can I describe my emotions at this catastrophe, or how delineate the wretch whom with such infinite pains and care I had endeavoured to form? His limbs were in proportion, and I had selected his features as beautiful. Beautiful! Great God! His yellow skin scarcely covered the work of muscles and arteries beneath; his hair was of a lustrous black, and flowing; his teeth of a pearly whiteness; but these luxuriances only formed a more horrid contrast with his watery eyes, that seemed almost of the same colour as the dun-white sockets in which they were set, his shrivelled complexion and straight black lips.

The different accidents of life are not so changeable as the feelings of human nature. I had worked hard for nearly two years, for the sole purpose of infusing life into an inanimate body. For this I had deprived myself of rest and health. I had desired it with an ardour that far exceeded moderation; but now that I had finished, the beauty of the dream vanished, and breathless horror and disgust filled my heart. Unable to endure the aspect of the being I had created, I rushed out of the room and continued a long time traversing my bedchamber, unable to compose my mind to sleep. At length lassitude succeeded to the tumult I had before endured, and I threw myself on the bed in my clothes, endeavouring to seek a few moments of forgetfulness. But it was in vain; I slept, indeed, but I was disturbed by the wildest dreams. I thought I saw Elizabeth, in the bloom of health, walking in the streets of Ingolstadt. Delighted and surprised, I embraced her, but as I imprinted the first kiss on her lips, they became livid with the hue of death; her features appeared to change, and I thought that I held the corpse of my dead mother in my arms; a shroud enveloped her form, and I saw the grave-worms crawling in the folds of the flannel. I started from my sleep with horror; a cold dew covered my forehead, my teeth chattered, and every limb became convulsed; when, by the dim and yellow light of the moon, as it forced its way through the window shutters, I beheld the wretch—the miserable monster whom I had created. He held up the curtain of the bed; and his eyes, if eyes they may be called, were fixed on me. His jaws opened, and he muttered some inarticulate sounds, while a grin wrinkled his cheeks. He might have spoken, but I did not hear; one hand was stretched out, seemingly to detain me, but I escaped and rushed downstairs. I took refuge in the courtyard belonging to the house which I inhabited, where I remained during the rest of the night, walking up and down in the greatest agitation, listening attentively, catching and fearing each sound as if it were to announce the approach of the demoniacal corpse to which I had so miserably given life.

Oh! No mortal could support the horror of that countenance. A mummy again endued with animation could not be so hideous as that wretch. I had gazed on him while unfinished; he was ugly then, but when those muscles and joints were rendered capable of motion, it became a thing such as even Dante could not have conceived.

I passed the night wretchedly. Sometimes my pulse beat so quickly and hardly that I felt the palpitation of every artery; at others, I nearly sank to the ground through languor and extreme weakness. Mingled with this horror, I felt the bitterness of disappointment; dreams that had been my food and pleasant rest for so long a space were now become a hell to me; and the change was so rapid, the overthrow so complete!

Morning, dismal and wet, at length dawned and discovered to my sleepless and aching eyes the church of Ingolstadt, its white steeple and clock, which indicated the sixth hour. The porter opened the gates of the court, which had that night been my asylum, and I issued into the streets, pacing them with quick steps, as if I sought to avoid the wretch whom I feared every turning of the street would present to my view. I did not dare return to the apartment which I inhabited, but felt impelled to hurry on, although drenched by the rain which poured from a black and comfortless sky.

I continued walking in this manner for some time, endeavouring by bodily exercise to ease the load that weighed upon my mind. I traversed the streets without any clear conception of where I was or what I was doing. My heart palpitated in the sickness of fear, and I hurried on with irregular steps, not daring to look about me:

Like one who, on a lonely road,
Doth walk in fear and dread,
And, having once turned round, walks on,
And turns no more his head;
Because he knows a frightful fiend
Doth close behind him tread.*

Continuing thus, I came at length opposite to the inn at which the various diligences and carriages usually stopped. Here I paused, I knew not why; but

* Coleridge's *Ancient Mariner*

I remained some minutes with my eyes fixed on a coach that was coming towards me from the other end of the street. As it drew nearer I observed that it was the Swiss diligence; it stopped just where I was standing, and on the door being opened, I perceived Henry Clerval, who, on seeing me, instantly sprung out. "My dear Frankenstein," exclaimed he, "how glad I am to see you! How fortunate that you should be here at the very moment of my alighting!"

Nothing could equal my delight on seeing Clerval; his presence brought back to my thoughts my father, Elizabeth, and all those scenes of home so dear to my recollection. I grasped his hand, and in a moment forgot my horror and misfortune; I felt suddenly, and for the first time during many months, calm and serene joy. I welcomed my friend, therefore, in the most cordial manner, and we walked towards my college. Clerval continued talking for some time about our mutual friends and his own good fortune in being permitted to come to Ingolstadt. "You may easily believe," said he, "how great was the difficulty to persuade my father that all necessary knowledge was not comprised in the noble art of book-keeping; and, indeed, I believe I left him incredulous to the last, for his constant answer to my unwearied entreaties was the same as that of the Dutch schoolmaster in *The Vicar of Wakefield*: 'I have ten thousand florins a year without Greek, I eat heartily without Greek.' But his affection for me at length overcame his dislike of learning, and he has permitted me to undertake a voyage of discovery to the land of knowledge."

"It gives me the greatest delight to see you; but tell me how you left my father, brothers, and Elizabeth."

"Very well, and very happy, only a little uneasy that they hear from you so seldom. By the by, I mean to lecture you a little upon their account myself. But, my dear Frankenstein," continued he, stopping short and gazing full in my face, "I did not before remark how very ill you appear; so thin and pale; you look as if you had been watching for several nights."

"You have guessed right; I have lately been so deeply engaged in one occupation that I have not allowed myself sufficient rest, as you see; but I hope, I sincerely hope, that all these employments are now at an end and that I am at length free."

I trembled excessively; I could not endure to think of, and far less to allude to, the occurrences of the preceding night. I walked with a quick pace, and we soon arrived at my college. I then reflected, and the thought made me shiver, that the creature whom I had left in my apartment might still be there, alive and walking about. I dreaded to behold this monster, but I feared still more that Henry should see him. Entreating him, therefore, to remain a few minutes at the bottom of the stairs, I darted up towards my own room. My hand was already on the lock of the door before I recollected myself. I then paused, and a cold shivering came over me. I threw the door forcibly open, as children are accustomed to do when they expect a spectre to stand in waiting for them on the other side; but nothing appeared. I stepped fearfully in: the apartment was empty, and my bedroom was also freed from its hideous guest. I could hardly believe that so great a good fortune could have befallen me, but when I became assured that my enemy had indeed fled, I clapped my hands for joy and ran down to Clerval.

We ascended into my room, and the servant presently brought breakfast; but I was unable to contain myself. It was not joy only that possessed me; I felt my flesh tingle with excess of sensitiveness, and my pulse beat rapidly. I was unable to remain for a single instant in the same place; I jumped over the chairs, clapped my hands, and laughed aloud. Clerval at first attributed my unusual spirits to joy on his arrival, but when he observed me more attentively, he saw a wildness in my eyes for which he could not account, and my loud, unrestrained, heartless laughter frightened and astonished him.

"My dear Victor," cried he, "what, for God's sake, is the matter? Do not laugh in that manner. How ill you are! What is the cause of all this?"

"Do not ask me," cried I, putting my hands before my eyes, for I thought I saw the dreaded spectre glide into the room; "he can tell. Oh, save me! Save me!" I imagined that the monster seized me; I struggled furiously and fell down in a fit.

Poor Clerval! What must have been his feelings? A meeting, which he anticipated with such joy, so strangely turned to bitterness. But I was not the witness of his grief, for I was lifeless and did not recover my senses for a long, long time.

This was the commencement of a nervous fever, which confined me for several months. During all that time Henry was my only nurse. I afterwards learned that, knowing my father's advanced age and unfitness for so long a journey, and how wretched my sickness would make Elizabeth, he spared them this grief by concealing the extent of my disorder. He knew that I could not have a more kind and attentive nurse than himself; and, firm in the hope he felt of my recovery, he did not doubt that, instead of doing harm, he performed the kindest action that he could towards them.

But I was in reality very ill, and surely nothing but the unbounded and unremitting attentions of my friend could have restored me to life. The form of the monster on whom I had bestowed existence was forever before my eyes, and I raved incessantly concerning him. Doubtless my words surprised Henry; he at first believed them to be the wanderings of my disturbed imagination, but the pertinacity with which I continually recurred to the same subject persuaded him that my disorder indeed owed its origin to some uncommon and terrible event.

By very slow degrees, and with frequent relapses that alarmed and grieved my friend, I recovered. I remember the first time I became capable of observing outward objects with any kind of pleasure, I perceived that the fallen leaves had disappeared and that the young buds were shooting forth from the trees that shaded my window. It was a divine spring, and the season contributed greatly to my convalescence. I felt also sentiments of joy and affection revive in my bosom; my gloom disappeared, and in a short time I became as cheerful as before I was attacked by the fatal passion.

"Dearest Clerval," exclaimed I, "how kind, how very good you are to me. This whole winter, instead of being spent in study, as you promised yourself, has been consumed in my sick room. How shall I ever repay you? I feel the greatest remorse for the disappointment of which I have been the occasion, but you will forgive me."

"You will repay me entirely if you do not discompose yourself, but get well as fast as you can; and since you appear in such good spirits, I may speak to you on one subject, may I not?"

I trembled. One subject! What could it be? Could he allude to an object on whom I dared not even think?

"Compose yourself," said Clerval, who observed my change of colour, "I will not mention it if it agitates you; but your father and cousin would be very happy if they received a letter from you in your own handwriting. They hardly know how ill you have been and are uneasy at your long silence."

"Is that all, my dear Henry? How could you suppose that my first thought would not fly towards those dear, dear friends whom I love and who are so deserving of my love?"

"If this is your present temper, my friend, you will perhaps be glad to see a letter that has been lying here some days for you; it is from your cousin, I believe."

CHAPTER VI

Clerval then put the following letter into my hands. It was from my own Elizabeth:

MY DEAREST COUSIN,

You have been ill, very ill, and even the constant letters of dear kind Henry are not sufficient to reassure me on your account. You are forbidden to write—to hold a pen; yet one word from you, dear Victor, is necessary to calm our apprehensions. For a long time I have thought that each post would bring this line, and my persuasions have restrained my uncle from undertaking a journey to Ingolstadt.

I have prevented his encountering the inconveniences and perhaps dangers of so long a journey, yet how often have I regretted not being able to perform it myself! I figure to myself that the task of attending on your sickbed has devolved on some mercenary old nurse, who could never guess your wishes nor minister to them with the care and affection of your poor cousin. Yet that is over now: Clerval writes that indeed you are getting better. I eagerly hope that you will confirm this intelligence soon in your own handwriting.

Get well—and return to us. You will find a happy, cheerful home and friends who love you dearly. Your father's health is vigorous, and he asks but to see you, but to be assured that you are well; and not a care will ever cloud his benevolent countenance. How pleased you would be to remark the improvement of our Ernest! He is now sixteen and full of activity and spirit. He is desirous to be a true Swiss and to enter into foreign service, but we cannot part with him, at least until his elder brother returns to us. My uncle is not pleased with the idea of a military career in a distant country, but Ernest never had your powers of application. He looks upon study as an odious fetter; his time is spent in the open air, climbing the hills or rowing on the lake. I fear that he will become an idler unless we yield the point and permit him to enter on the profession which he has selected.

Little alteration, except the growth of our dear children, has taken place since you left us. The blue lake and snow-clad mountains—they never change; and I think our placid home and our contented hearts are regulated by the same immutable laws. My trifling occupations take up my time and amuse me, and I am rewarded for any exertions by seeing none but happy, kind faces around me. Since you left us, but one change has taken place in our little household. Do you remember on what occasion Justine Moritz entered our family? Probably you do not; I will relate her history, therefore in a few words. Madame Moritz, her mother, was a widow with four children, of whom Justine was the third. This girl had always been the favourite of her father, but through a strange perversity, her mother could not endure her, and after the death of M. Moritz, treated her very ill. My aunt observed this, and when Justine was twelve years of age, prevailed on her mother to allow her to live at our house. The republican institutions of our country have produced simpler and happier manners than those which prevail in the great monarchies that surround it. Hence there is less distinction between the several classes of its inhabitants; and the lower orders, being neither so poor nor so despised, their manners are more refined and moral.

A servant in Geneva does not mean the same thing as a servant in France and England. Justine, thus received in our family, learned the duties of a servant, a condition which, in our fortunate country, does not include the idea of ignorance and a sacrifice of the dignity of a human being.

Justine, you may remember, was a great favourite of yours; and I recollect you once remarked that if you were in an ill humour, one glance from Justine could dissipate it, for the same reason that Ariosto gives concerning the beauty of Angelica—she looked so frank-hearted and happy. My aunt conceived a great attachment for her, by which she was induced to give her an education superior to that which she had at first intended. This benefit was fully repaid; Justine was the most grateful little creature in the world: I do not mean that she made any professions; I never heard one pass her lips, but you could see by her eyes that she almost adored her protectress. Although her disposition was gay and in many respects inconsiderate, yet she paid the greatest attention to every gesture of my aunt. She thought her the model of all excellence and endeavoured to imitate her phraseology and manners, so that even now she often reminds me of her.

When my dearest aunt died, everyone was too much occupied in their own grief to notice poor Justine, who had attended her during her illness with the most anxious affection. Poor Justine was very ill; but other trials were reserved for her.

One by one, her brothers and sister died; and her mother, with the exception of her neglected daughter, was left childless. The conscience of the woman was troubled; she began to think that the deaths of her favourites was a judgement from heaven to chastise her partiality. She was a Roman Catholic; and I believe her confessor confirmed the idea which she had conceived. Accordingly, a few months after your departure for Ingolstadt, Justine was called home by her repentant mother. Poor girl! She wept when she quitted our house; she was much altered since the death of my aunt; grief had given softness and a winning mildness to her manners, which had before been remarkable for vivacity. Nor was her residence at her mother's house of a nature to restore her gaiety. The poor woman was very vacillating in her repentance. She sometimes begged Justine to forgive her unkindness, but much oftener accused her of having caused the deaths of her brothers and sister. Perpetual fretting at length threw Madame Moritz into a decline, which at first increased her irritability, but she is now at peace forever. She died on the first approach of cold weather, at the beginning of this last winter. Justine has just returned to us; and I assure you I love her tenderly. She is very clever and gentle, and extremely pretty; as I mentioned before, her mien and her expression continually remind me of my dear aunt.

I must say also a few words to you, my dear cousin, of little darling William. I wish you could see him; he is very tall of his age, with sweet laughing blue eyes, dark eyelashes, and curling hair. When he smiles, two little dimples appear on each cheek, which are rosy with health. He has already had one or two little wives, but Louisa Biron is his favourite, a pretty little girl of five years of age.

Now, dear Victor, I dare say you wish to be indulged in a little gossip concerning the good people of Geneva. The pretty Miss Mansfield has already received the congratulatory visits on her approaching marriage with a young Englishman, John Melbourne, Esq. Her ugly sister, Manon, married M. Duvillard, the rich banker, last autumn. Your favourite school-fellow, Louis Manoir, has suffered several misfortunes since the departure of Clerval from Geneva. But he has already recovered his spirits, and is reported to be on the point of marrying a lively pretty Frenchwoman, Madame Tavernier. She is a widow, and much older than Manoir; but she is very much admired, and a favourite with everybody.

I have written myself into better spirits, dear cousin; but my anxiety returns upon me as I conclude. Write, dearest Victor—one line—one word will be a blessing to us. Ten thousand thanks to Henry for his kindness, his affection, and his many letters; we are sincerely grateful. Adieu, my cousin! Take care of yourself; and, I entreat you, write!

Elizabeth Lavenza.
Geneva, March 18th, 17—.

"Dear, dear Elizabeth!" I exclaimed, when I had read her letter: "I will write instantly and relieve them from the anxiety they must feel." I wrote, and this exertion greatly fatigued me; but my convalescence had commenced, and proceeded regularly. In another fortnight I was able to leave my chamber.

One of my first duties on my recovery was to introduce Clerval to the several professors of the university. In doing this, I underwent a kind of rough usage, ill befitting the wounds that my mind had sustained. Ever since the fatal night, the end of my labours, and the beginning of my misfortunes, I had conceived a violent antipathy even to the name of natural philosophy. When I was otherwise quite restored to health, the sight of a chemical instrument would renew all the agony of my nervous symptoms. Henry saw this, and had removed all my apparatus from my view. He had also changed my apartment; for he perceived that I had acquired a dislike for the room which had previously been my laboratory. But these cares of Clerval were made of no avail when I visited the professors. M. Waldman inflicted torture when he praised, with kindness and warmth, the astonishing progress I had made in the sciences. He soon perceived that I disliked the subject; but not guessing the real cause, he attributed my feelings to modesty, and changed the subject from my improvement to the science itself, with a desire, as I evidently saw, of drawing me out. What could I do? He meant to please, and he tormented me. I felt as if he had placed carefully, one by one, in my view those instruments which were to be afterwards used in putting me to a slow and cruel death. I writhed under his words, yet dared not exhibit the pain I felt. Clerval, whose eyes and feelings were always quick in discerning the sensations of others, declined the subject, alleging, in excuse, his total ignorance; and the conversation took a more general turn. I thanked my friend from my heart, but I did not speak. I saw plainly that he was surprised, but he never attempted to draw my secret from me; and although I loved him with a mixture of affection and reverence that knew no bounds, yet I could never persuade myself to confide in him that event which was so often present to my recollection, but which I feared the detail to another would only impress more deeply.

M. Krempe was not equally docile; and in my condition at that time, of almost insupportable sensitiveness, his harsh blunt encomiums gave me even more pain than the benevolent approbation of M. Waldman. "D——n the fellow!" cried he. "Why, M. Clerval, I assure you he has outstript us all. Ay, stare if you please; but it is nevertheless true. A youngster who, but a few years ago, believed in Cornelius Agrippa as firmly as in the gospel, has now set himself at the head of the university; and if he is not soon pulled down, we shall all be out of countenance. Ay, ay," continued he, observing my face expressive of suffering, "M. Frankenstein is modest; an excellent quality in a young man. Young men should be diffident of themselves, you know, M. Clerval: I was myself when young, but that wears out in a very short time."

M. Krempe had now commenced an eulogy on himself, which happily turned the conversation from a subject that was so annoying to me.

Clerval had never sympathised in my tastes for natural science; and his literary pursuits differed wholly from those which had occupied me. He came to the university with the design of making himself complete master of the Oriental languages, and thus he should open a field for the plan of life he had marked out for himself. Resolved to pursue no inglorious career, he turned his eyes toward the East, as affording scope for his spirit of enterprise. The Persian, Arabic, and Sanskrit languages engaged his attention, and I was easily induced to enter on the same studies. Idleness had ever been irksome to me, and now that I wished to fly from reflection, and hated my former studies, I felt great relief in being the fellow-pupil with my friend, and found not only instruction but consolation in the works of the Orientalists. I did not, like him, attempt a critical knowledge of their dialects, for I did not contemplate making any other use of them than temporary amusement. I read merely to understand their meaning, and they well repaid my labours. Their melancholy is soothing, and their joy elevating, to a degree I never experienced in studying the authors of any other country. When you read their writings, life appears to consist in a warm sun and a garden of roses, in the smiles and frowns of a fair enemy, and the fire that consumes your own heart. How different from the manly and heroical poetry of Greece and Rome!

Summer passed away in these occupations, and my return to Geneva was fixed for the latter end of autumn; but being delayed by several accidents, winter and snow arrived, the roads were deemed impassable, and my journey was retarded until the ensuing spring. I felt this delay very bitterly; for I longed to see my native town and my beloved friends. My return had only been delayed so long from an unwillingness to leave Clerval in a strange place, before he had become acquainted with any of its inhabitants. The winter, however, was spent cheerfully; and although the spring was uncommonly late, when it came its beauty compensated for its dilatoriness.

The month of May had already commenced, and I expected the letter daily which was to fix the date of my departure, when Henry proposed a pedestrian tour in the environs of Ingolstadt, that I might bid a personal farewell to the country I had so long inhabited. I acceded with pleasure to this proposition: I was fond of exercise, and Clerval had always been my favourite companion in the ramble of this nature that I had taken among the scenes of my native country.

We passed a fortnight in these perambulations: my health and spirits had long been restored, and they gained additional strength from the salubrious air I breathed, the natural incidents of our progress, and the conversation of my friend. Study had before secluded me from the intercourse of my fellow-creatures, and rendered me unsocial; but Clerval called forth the better feelings of my heart; he again taught me to love the aspect of nature, and the cheerful faces of children. Excellent friend! How sincerely you did love me, and endeavour to elevate my mind until it was on a level with your own. A selfish pursuit had cramped and narrowed me, until your gentleness and affection warmed and opened my senses; I became the same happy creature who, a few years ago, loved and beloved by all, had no sorrow or care. When happy, inanimate nature had the power of bestowing on me the most delightful sensations. A serene sky and verdant fields filled me with ecstasy. The present season was indeed divine; the flowers of spring bloomed in the hedges, while those of summer were already in bud. I was undisturbed by thoughts which during the preceding year had pressed upon me, notwithstanding my endeavours to throw them off, with an invincible burden.

Henry rejoiced in my gaiety, and sincerely sympathised in my feelings: he exerted himself to amuse me, while he expressed the sensations that filled his soul. The resources of his mind on this occasion were truly astonishing: his conversation was full of imagination; and very often, in imitation of the Persian and Arabic writers, he invented tales of wonderful fancy and passion. At other times he repeated my favourite poems, or drew me out into arguments, which he supported with great ingenuity.

We returned to our college on a Sunday afternoon: the peasants were dancing, and everyone we met appeared gay and happy. My own spirits were high, and I bounded along with feelings of unbridled joy and hilarity.

CHAPTER VII

On my return, I found the following letter from my father:

My dear Victor,

You have probably waited impatiently for a letter to fix the date of your return to us; and I was at first tempted to write only a few lines, merely mentioning the day on which I should expect you. But that would be a cruel kindness, and I dare not do it. What would be your surprise, my son, when you expected a happy and glad welcome, to behold, on the contrary, tears and wretchedness? And how, Victor, can I relate our misfortune? Absence cannot have rendered you callous to our joys and griefs; and how shall I inflict pain on my long-absent son? I wish to prepare you for the woeful news, but I know it is impossible; even now your eye skims over the page to seek the words which are to convey to you the horrible tidings.

William is dead! That sweet child, whose smiles delighted and warmed my heart, who was so gentle, yet so gay! Victor, he is murdered!

I will not attempt to console you; but will simply relate the circumstances of the transaction.

Last Thursday (May 7th), I, my niece, and your two brothers went to walk in Plainpalais. The evening was warm and serene, and we prolonged our walk farther than usual. It was already dusk before we thought of returning; and then we discovered that William and Ernest, who had gone on before, were not to be found. We accordingly rested on a seat until they should return. Presently

Ernest came, and enquired if we had seen his brother; he said that he had been playing with him, that William had run away to hide himself, and that he vainly sought for him, and afterwards waited for a long time, but that he did not return.

This account rather alarmed us, and we continued to search for him until night fell, when Elizabeth conjectured that he might have returned to the house. He was not there. We returned again, with torches; for I could not rest when I thought that my sweet boy had lost himself, and was exposed to all the damps and dews of night; Elizabeth also suffered extreme anguish. About five in the morning I discovered my lovely boy, whom the night before I had seen blooming and active in health, stretched on the grass livid and motionless; the print of the murderer's finger was on his neck.

He was conveyed home, and the anguish that was visible in my countenance betrayed the secret to Elizabeth. She was very earnest to see the corpse. At first I attempted to prevent her but she persisted, and entering the room where it lay, hastily examined the neck of the victim, and clasping her hands exclaimed, "O God! I have murdered my darling child!"

She fainted, and was restored with extreme difficulty. When she again lived, it was only to weep and sigh. She told me that that same evening William had teased her to let him wear a very valuable miniature that she possessed of your mother. This picture is gone, and was doubtless the temptation which urged the murderer to the deed. We have no trace of him at present, although our exertions to discover him are unremitted; but they will not restore my beloved William!

Come, dearest Victor; you alone can console Elizabeth. She weeps continually, and accuses herself unjustly as the cause of his death; her words pierce my heart. We are all unhappy; but will not that be an additional motive for you, my son, to return and be our comforter? Your dear mother! Alas, Victor! I now say, Thank God she did not live to witness the cruel, miserable death of her youngest darling!

Come, Victor; not brooding thoughts of vengeance against the assassin, but with feelings of peace and gentleness that will heal, instead of festering, the wounds of our minds. Enter the house of mourning, my friend, but with kindness and affection for those who love you, and not with hatred for your enemies.

Your affectionate and afflicted father,
ALPHONSE FRANKENSTEIN.
Geneva, May 12th, 17—.

Clerval, who had watched my countenance as I read this letter, was surprised to observe the despair that succeeded the joy I at first expressed on receiving news from my friends. I threw the letter on the table, and covered my face with my hands.

"My dear Frankenstein," exclaimed Henry, when he perceived me weep with bitterness, "are you always to be unhappy? My dear friend, what has happened?"

I motioned him to take up the letter, while I walked up and down the room in the extremest agitation. Tears also gushed from the eyes of Clerval, as he read the account of my misfortune.

"I can offer you no consolation, my friend," said he; "your disaster is irreparable. What do you intend to do?"

"To go instantly to Geneva: come with me, Henry, to order the horses."

During our walk, Clerval endeavoured to say a few words of consolation; he could only express his heartfelt sympathy. "Poor William!" said he. "Dear lovely child, he now sleeps with his angel mother! Who that had seen him bright and joyous in his young beauty, but must weep over his untimely loss! To die so miserably; to feel the murderer's grasp! How much more a murderer that could destroy radiant innocence! Poor little fellow! One only consolation have we; his friends mourn and weep, but he is at rest. The pang is over, his sufferings are at an end forever. A sod covers his gentle form, and he knows no pain. He can no longer be a subject for pity; we must reserve that for his miserable survivors."

Clerval spoke thus as we hurried through the streets; the words impressed themselves on my mind and I remembered them afterwards in solitude. But now, as soon as the horses arrived, I hurried into a cabriolet, and bade farewell to my friend.

My journey was very melancholy. At first I wished to hurry on, for I longed to console and sympathise with my loved and sorrowing friends; but when I drew near my native town, I slackened my progress. I could hardly sustain the multitude of feelings that crowded into my mind. I passed through scenes familiar to my youth, but which I had not seen for nearly six years. How altered everything might be during that time! One sudden and desolating change had taken place; but a thousand little circumstances might have by degrees worked other alterations, which, although they were done more tranquilly, might not be the less decisive. Fear overcame me; I dared no advance, dreading a thousand nameless evils that made me tremble, although I was unable to define them.

I remained two days at Lausanne, in this painful state of mind. I contemplated the lake: the waters were placid; all around was calm; and the snowy mountains, "the palaces of nature," were not changed. By degrees the calm and heavenly scene restored me, and I continued my journey towards Geneva.

The road ran by the side of the lake, which became narrower as I approached my native town. I discovered more distinctly the black sides of Jura, and the bright summit of Mont Blanc. I wept like a child. "Dear mountains! My own beautiful lake! How do you welcome your wanderer? Your summits are clear; the sky and lake are blue and placid. Is this to prognosticate peace, or to mock at my unhappiness?"

I fear, my friend, that I shall render myself tedious by dwelling on these preliminary circumstances; but they were days of comparative happiness, and I think of them with pleasure. My country, my beloved country! Who but a native can tell the delight I took in again beholding thy streams, thy mountains, and, more than all, thy lovely lake!

Yet, as I drew nearer home, grief and fear again overcame me. Night also closed around; and when I could hardly see the dark mountains, I felt still more gloomily. The picture appeared a vast and dim scene of evil, and I foresaw obscurely that I was destined to become the most wretched of human beings. Alas! I prophesied truly, and failed only in one single circumstance, that in all the misery I imagined and dreaded, I did not conceive the hundredth part of the anguish I was destined to endure.

It was completely dark when I arrived in the environs of Geneva; the gates of the town were already shut; and I was obliged to pass the night at Secheron, a village at the distance of half a league from the city. The sky was serene; and, as I was unable to rest, I resolved to visit the spot where my poor William had been murdered. As I could not pass through the town, I was obliged to cross the lake in a boat to arrive at Plainpalais. During this short voyage I saw the lightning playing on the summit of Mont Blanc in the most beautiful figures. The storm appeared to approach rapidly, and, on landing, I ascended a low hill, that I might observe its progress. It advanced; the heavens were clouded, and I soon felt the rain coming slowly in large drops, but its violence quickly increased.

I quitted my seat and walked on, although the darkness and storm increased every minute, and the thunder burst with a terrific crash over my head. It was echoed from Salêve, the Juras, and the Alps of Savoy; vivid flashes of lightning dazzled my eyes, illuminating the lake, making it appear like a vast sheet of fire; then for an instant everything seemed of a pitchy darkness, until the eye recovered itself from the preceding flash. The storm, as is often the case in Switzerland, appeared at once in various parts of the heavens. The most violent storm hung exactly north of the town, over the part of the lake which lies between the promontory of Belrive and the village of Copêt. Another storm enlightened Jura with faint flashes; and another darkened and sometimes disclosed the Môle, a peaked mountain to the east of the lake.

While I watched the tempest, so beautiful yet terrific, I wandered on with a hasty step. This noble war in the sky elevated my spirits; I clasped my hands and exclaimed aloud, "William, dear angel! This is thy funeral, this thy dirge!" As I said these words, I perceived in the gloom a figure which stole from behind a clump of trees near me; I stood fixed, gazing intently: I could not be mistaken. A flash of lightning illuminated the object, and discovered its shape plainly to me; its gigantic stature, and the deformity of its aspect more hideous than belongs to humanity, instantly informed me that it was the wretch, the filthy daemon, to whom I had given life. What did he there? Could he be (I shuddered at the conception) the murderer of my brother? No sooner did that idea cross my imagination, than I became convinced of its truth; my teeth chattered, and I was forced to lean against a tree for support. The figure passed me quickly, and I lost it in the gloom. Nothing in human shape could have destroyed the fair child. He was the murderer! I could not doubt it. The mere presence of the idea was an irresistible proof of the fact. I thought of pursuing the devil; but it would have been in vain, for another flash discovered him to me hanging among the rocks of the nearly perpendicular ascent of Mont Salêve, a hill that bounds Plainpalais on the south. He soon reached the summit, and disappeared.

I remained motionless. The thunder ceased, but the rain still continued, and the scene was enveloped in an impenetrable darkness. I revolved in my mind the events which I had until now sought to forget: the whole train of my progress toward the creation; the appearance of the work of my own hands at my bedside; its departure. Two years had now nearly elapsed since the night on which he first received life; and was this his first crime? Alas! I had turned loose into the world a depraved wretch, whose delight was in carnage and misery; had he not murdered my brother?

No one can conceive the anguish I suffered during the remainder of the night, which I spent, cold and wet, in the open air. But I did not feel the inconvenience of the weather; my imagination was busy in scenes of evil and despair. I considered the being whom I had cast among mankind, and endowed with the will and power to effect purposes of horror, such as the deed which he had now done, nearly in the light of my own vampire, my own spirit let loose from the grave, and forced to destroy all that was dear to me.

Day dawned; and I directed my steps towards the town. The gates were open, and I hastened to my father's house. My first thought was to discover what I knew of the murderer, and cause instant pursuit to be made. But I paused when I reflected on the story that I had to tell. A being whom I myself had formed, and endued with life, had met me at midnight among the precipices of an inaccessible mountain. I remembered also the nervous fever with which I had been seized just at the time that I dated my creation, and which would give an air of delirium to a tale otherwise so utterly improbable. I well knew that if any other had communicated such a relation to me, I should have looked upon it as the ravings of insanity. Besides, the strange nature of the animal would elude all pursuit, even if I were so far credited as to persuade my relatives to commence it. And then of what use would be pursuit? Who could arrest a creature capable of scaling the overhanging sides of Mont Salêve? These reflections determined me, and I resolved to remain silent.

It was about five in the morning when I entered my father's house. I told the servants not to disturb the family, and went into the library to attend their usual hour of rising.

Six years had elapsed, passed in a dream but for one indelible trace, and I stood in the same place where I had last embraced my father before my departure for Ingolstadt. Beloved and venerable parent! He still remained to me. I gazed on the picture of my mother, which stood over the mantel-piece. It was an historical subject, painted at my father's desire, and represented Caroline Beaufort in an agony of despair, kneeling by the coffin of her dead father. Her garb was rustic, and her cheek pale; but there was an air of dignity and beauty, that hardly permitted the sentiment of pity. Below this picture was a miniature of William; and my tears flowed when I looked upon it. While I was thus engaged, Ernest entered: he had heard me arrive, and hastened to welcome me. "Welcome, my dearest Victor," said he. "Ah! I wish you had come three months ago, and then you would have found us all joyous and delighted. You come to us now to share a misery which nothing can alleviate; yet your presence will, I hope, revive our father, who seems sinking under his misfortune; and your persuasions will induce poor Elizabeth to cease her vain and tormenting self-accusations. Poor William! He was our darling and our pride!"

Tears, unrestrained, fell from my brother's eyes; a sense of mortal agony crept over my frame. Before, I had only imagined the wretchedness of my desolated home; the reality came on me as a new, and a not less terrible, disaster. I tried to calm Ernest; I enquired more minutely concerning my father, and her I named my cousin.

"She most of all," said Ernest, "requires consolation; she accused herself of having caused the death of my brother, and that made her very wretched. But since the murderer has been discovered—"

"The murderer discovered! Good God! How can that be? Who could attempt to pursue him? It is impossible; one might as well try to overtake the winds, or confine a mountain-stream with a straw. I saw him too; he was free last night!"

"I do not know what you mean," replied my brother, in accents of wonder, "but to us the discovery we have made completes our misery. No one would believe it at first; and even now Elizabeth will not be convinced, notwithstanding all the evidence. Indeed, who would credit that Justine Moritz, who was so amiable, and fond of all the family, could suddenly become so capable of so frightful, so appalling a crime?"

"Justine Moritz! Poor, poor girl, is she the accused? But it is wrongfully; everyone knows that; no one believes it, surely, Ernest?"

"No one did at first; but several circumstances came out that have almost forced conviction upon us; and her own behaviour has been so confused as to add to the evidence of facts a weight that, I fear, leaves no hope for doubt. But she will be tried today, and you will then hear all."

He then related that, the morning on which the murder of poor William had been discovered, Justine had been taken ill, and confined to her bed for several days. During this interval, one of the servants, happening to examine the apparel she had worn on the night of the murder, had discovered in her pocket the picture of my mother, which had been judged to be the temptation of the murderer. The servant instantly showed it to one of the others, who, without saying a word to any of the family, went to a magistrate; and, upon their deposition, Justine was apprehended. On being charged with the fact, the poor girl confirmed the suspicion in a great measure by her extreme confusion of manner.

This was a strange tale, but it did not shake my faith; and I replied earnestly, "You are all mistaken; I know the murderer. Justine, poor, good Justine, is innocent."

At that instant my father entered. I saw unhappiness deeply impressed on his countenance, but he endeavoured to welcome me cheerfully; and, after we had exchanged our mournful greeting, would have introduced some other topic than that of our disaster, had not Ernest exclaimed, "Good God, Papa! Victor says that he knows who was the murderer of poor William."

"We do also, unfortunately," replied my father, "for indeed I had rather have been forever ignorant than have discovered so much depravity and ingratitude in one I valued so highly."

"My dear father, you are mistaken; Justine is innocent."

"If she is, God forbid that she should suffer as guilty. She is to be tried today, and I hope, I sincerely hope, that she will be acquitted."

This speech calmed me. I was firmly convinced in my own mind that Justine, and indeed every human being, was guiltless of this murder. I had no fear, therefore, that any circumstantial evidence could be brought forward strong enough to convict her. My tale was not one to announce publicly; its astounding horror would be looked upon as madness by the vulgar. Did anyone indeed exist, except I, the creator, who would believe, unless his senses convinced him, in the existence of the living monument of presumption and rash ignorance which I had let loose upon the world?

We were soon joined by Elizabeth. Time had altered her since I last beheld her; it had endowed her with loveliness surpassing the beauty of her childish years. There was the same candour, the same vivacity, but it was allied to an expression more full of sensibility and intellect. She welcomed me with the greatest affection. "Your arrival, my dear cousin," said she, "fills me with hope. You perhaps will find some means to justify my poor guiltless Justine. Alas! Who is safe, if she be convicted of crime? I rely on her innocence as certainly as I do upon my own. Our misfortune is doubly hard to us; we have not only lost that lovely darling boy, but this poor girl, whom I sincerely love, is to be torn away by even a worse fate. If she is condemned, I never shall know joy more. But she will not, I am sure she will not; and then I shall be happy again, even after the sad death of my little William."

"She is innocent, my Elizabeth," said I, "and that shall be proved; fear nothing, but let your spirits be cheered by the assurance of her acquittal."

"How kind and generous you are! Everyone else believes in her guilt, and that made me wretched, for I knew that it was impossible: and to see everyone else prejudiced in so deadly a manner rendered me hopeless and despairing." She wept.

"Dearest niece," said my father, "dry your tears. If she is, as you believe, innocent, rely on the justice of our laws, and the activity with which I shall prevent the slightest shadow of partiality."

CHAPTER VIII

We passed a few sad hours until eleven o'clock, when the trial was to commence. My father and the rest of the family being obliged to attend as witnesses, I accompanied them to the court. During the whole of this wretched mockery of justice I suffered living torture. It was to be decided whether the result of my curiosity and lawless devices would cause the death of two of my fellow beings: one a smiling babe full of innocence and joy, the other far more dreadfully murdered, with every aggravation of infamy that could make the murder memorable in horror. Justine also was a girl of merit and possessed qualities which promised to render her life happy; now all was to be obliterated in an ignominious grave, and I the cause! A thousand times rather would I have confessed myself guilty of the crime ascribed to Justine, but I was absent when it was committed, and such a declaration would have been considered as the ravings of a madman and would not have exculpated her who suffered through me.

The appearance of Justine was calm. She was dressed in mourning, and her countenance, always engaging, was rendered, by the solemnity of her feelings, exquisitely beautiful. Yet she appeared confident in innocence and did not tremble, although gazed on and execrated by thousands, for all the kindness which her beauty might otherwise have excited was obliterated in the minds of the spectators by the imagination of the enormity she was supposed to have committed. She was tranquil, yet her tranquillity was evidently constrained; and as her confusion had before been adduced as a proof of her guilt, she worked up her mind to an appearance of courage. When she entered the court she threw her eyes round it and quickly discovered where we were seated. A tear seemed to dim her eye when she saw us, but she quickly recovered herself, and a look of sorrowful affection seemed to attest her utter guiltlessness.

The trial began, and after the advocate against her had stated the charge, several witnesses were called. Several strange facts combined against her, which might have staggered anyone who had not such proof of her innocence as I had. She had been out the whole of the night on which the murder had been committed and towards morning had been perceived by a market-woman not far from the spot where the body of the murdered child had been afterwards found. The woman asked her what she did there, but she looked very strangely and only returned a confused and unintelligible answer. She returned to the house about eight o'clock, and when one enquired where she had passed the night, she replied that she had been looking for the child and demanded earnestly if anything had been heard concerning him. When shown the body, she fell into violent hysterics and kept her bed for several days. The picture was then produced which the servant had found in her pocket; and when Elizabeth, in a faltering voice, proved that it was the same which, an hour before the child had been missed, she had placed round his neck, a murmur of horror and indignation filled the court.

Justine was called on for her defence. As the trial had proceeded, her countenance had altered. Surprise, horror, and misery were strongly expressed. Sometimes she struggled with her tears, but when she was desired to plead, she collected her powers and spoke in an audible although variable voice.

"God knows," she said, "how entirely I am innocent. But I do not pretend that my protestations should acquit me; I rest my innocence on a plain and simple explanation of the facts which have been adduced against me, and I hope the character I have always borne will incline my judges to a favourable interpretation where any circumstance appears doubtful or suspicious."

She then related that, by the permission of Elizabeth, she had passed the evening of the night on which the murder had been committed at the house of an aunt at Chêne, a village situated at about a league from Geneva. On her return, at about nine o'clock, she met a man who asked her if she had seen anything of the child who was lost. She was alarmed by this account and passed several hours in looking for him, when the gates of Geneva were shut, and she was forced to remain several hours of the night in a barn belonging to a cottage, being unwilling to call up the inhabitants, to whom she was well known. Most of the night she spent here watching; towards morning she believed that she slept for a few minutes; some steps disturbed her, and she awoke. It was dawn, and she quitted her asylum, that she might again endeavour to find my brother. If she had gone near the spot where his body lay, it was without her knowledge. That she had been bewildered when questioned by the market-woman was not surprising, since she had passed a sleepless night and the fate of poor William was yet uncertain. Concerning the picture she could give no account.

"I know," continued the unhappy victim, "how heavily and fatally this one circumstance weighs against me, but I have no power of explaining it; and when I have expressed my utter ignorance, I am only left to conjecture concerning the probabilities by which it might have been placed in my pocket. But here also I am checked. I believe that I have no enemy on earth, and none surely would have been so wicked as to destroy me wantonly. Did the murderer place it there? I know of no opportunity afforded him for so doing; or, if I had, why should he have stolen the jewel, to part with it again so soon?

"I commit my cause to the justice of my judges, yet I see no room for hope. I beg permission to have a few witnesses examined concerning my character, and if their testimony shall not overweigh my supposed guilt, I must be condemned, although I would pledge my salvation on my innocence."

Several witnesses were called who had known her for many years, and they spoke well of her; but fear and hatred of the crime of which they supposed her guilty rendered them timorous and unwilling to come forward. Elizabeth saw even this last resource, her excellent dispositions and irreproachable conduct, about to fail the accused, when, although violently agitated, she desired permission to address the court.

"I am," said she, "the cousin of the unhappy child who was murdered, or rather his sister, for I was educated by and have lived with his parents ever since and even long before his birth. It may therefore be judged indecent in me to come forward on this occasion, but when I see a fellow creature about to perish through the cowardice of her pretended friends, I wish to be allowed to speak, that I may say what I know of her character. I am well acquainted with the accused. I have lived in the same house with her, at one time for five and at another for nearly two years. During all that period she appeared to me the most amiable and benevolent of human creatures. She nursed Madame Frankenstein, my aunt, in her last illness, with the greatest affection and care and afterwards attended her own mother during a tedious illness, in a manner that excited the admiration of all who knew her, after which she again lived in my uncle's house, where she was beloved by all the family. She was warmly attached to the child who is now dead and acted towards him like a most affectionate mother. For my own part, I do not hesitate to say that, notwithstanding all the evidence produced against her, I believe and rely on her perfect innocence. She had no temptation for such an action; as to the bauble on which the chief proof rests, if she had earnestly desired it, I should have willingly given it to her, so much do I esteem and value her."

A murmur of approbation followed Elizabeth's simple and powerful appeal, but it was excited by her generous interference, and not in favour of poor Justine, on whom the public indignation was turned with renewed violence, charging her with the blackest ingratitude. She herself wept as Elizabeth spoke, but she did not answer. My own agitation and anguish was extreme during the whole trial. I believed in her innocence; I knew it. Could the daemon who had (I did not for a minute doubt) murdered my brother also in his hellish sport have betrayed the innocent to death and ignominy? I could not sustain the horror of my situation, and when I perceived that the popular voice and the countenances of the judges had already condemned my unhappy victim, I rushed out of the court in agony. The tortures of the accused did not equal mine; she was sustained by innocence, but the fangs of remorse tore my bosom and would not forego their hold.

I passed a night of unmingled wretchedness. In the morning I went to the court; my lips and throat were parched. I dared not ask the fatal question, but I was known, and the officer guessed the cause of my visit. The ballots had been thrown; they were all black, and Justine was condemned.

I cannot pretend to describe what I then felt. I had before experienced sensations of horror, and I have endeavoured to bestow upon them adequate expressions, but words cannot convey an idea of the heart-sickening despair that I then endured. The person to whom I addressed myself added that Justine had already confessed her guilt. "That evidence," he observed, "was hardly required in so glaring a case, but I am glad of it, and, indeed, none of our judges like to condemn a criminal upon circumstantial evidence, be it ever so decisive."

This was strange and unexpected intelligence; what could it mean? Had my eyes deceived me? And was I really as mad as the whole world would believe me to be if I disclosed the object of my suspicions? I hastened to return home, and Elizabeth eagerly demanded the result.

"My cousin," replied I, "it is decided as you may have expected; all judges had rather that ten innocent should suffer than that one guilty should escape. But she has confessed."

This was a dire blow to poor Elizabeth, who had relied with firmness upon Justine's innocence. "Alas!" said she. "How shall I ever again believe in human goodness? Justine, whom I loved and esteemed as my sister, how could she put on those smiles of innocence only to betray? Her mild eyes seemed incapable of any severity or guile, and yet she has committed a murder."

Soon after we heard that the poor victim had expressed a desire to see my cousin. My father wished her not to go but said that he left it to her own judgement and feelings to decide. "Yes," said Elizabeth, "I will go, although she is guilty; and you, Victor, shall accompany me; I cannot go alone." The idea of this visit was torture to me, yet I could not refuse.

We entered the gloomy prison chamber and beheld Justine sitting on some straw at the farther end; her hands were manacled, and her head rested on her knees. She rose on seeing us enter, and when we were left alone with her, she threw herself at the feet of Elizabeth, weeping bitterly. My cousin wept also.

"Oh, Justine!" said she. "Why did you rob me of my last consolation? I relied on your innocence, and although I was then very wretched, I was not so miserable as I am now."

"And do you also believe that I am so very, very wicked? Do you also join with my enemies to crush me, to condemn me as a murderer?" Her voice was suffocated with sobs.

"Rise, my poor girl," said Elizabeth; "why do you kneel, if you are innocent? I am not one of your enemies; I believed you guiltless, notwithstanding every evidence, until I heard that you had yourself declared your guilt. That report, you say, is false; and be assured, dear Justine, that nothing can shake my confidence in you for a moment, but your own confession."

"I did confess, but I confessed a lie. I confessed, that I might obtain absolution; but now that falsehood lies heavier at my heart than all my other sins. The God of heaven forgive me! Ever since I was condemned, my confessor has besieged me; he threatened and menaced, until I almost began to think that I was the monster that he said I was. He threatened excommunication and hell fire in my last moments if I continued obdurate. Dear lady, I had none to support me; all looked on me as a wretch doomed to ignominy and perdition. What could I do? In an evil hour I subscribed to a lie; and now only am I truly miserable."

She paused, weeping, and then continued: "I thought with horror, my sweet lady, that you should believe your Justine, whom your blessed aunt had so highly honoured, and whom you loved, was a creature capable of a crime which none but the devil himself could have perpetrated. Dear William! Dearest blessed child! I soon shall see you again in heaven, where we shall all be happy; and that consoles me, going as I am to suffer ignominy and death."

"Oh, Justine! Forgive me for having for one moment distrusted you. Why did you confess? But do not mourn, dear girl. Do not fear. I will proclaim, I will prove your innocence. I will melt the stony hearts of your enemies by my tears and prayers. You shall not die! You, my playfellow, my companion, my sister, perish on the scaffold! No! No! I never could survive so horrible a misfortune."

Justine shook her head mournfully. "I do not fear to die," she said; "that pang is past. God raises my weakness and gives me courage to endure the worst. I leave a sad and bitter world; and if you remember me and think of me as of one unjustly condemned, I am resigned to the fate awaiting me. Learn from me, dear lady, to submit in patience to the will of heaven!"

During this conversation I had retired to a corner of the prison room, where I could conceal the horrid anguish that possessed me. Despair! Who dared talk of that? The poor victim, who on the morrow was to pass the awful boundary between life and death, felt not, as I did, such deep and bitter agony. I gnashed my teeth and ground them together, uttering a groan that came from my inmost soul. Justine started. When she saw who it was, she approached me and said, "Dear sir, you are very kind to visit me; you, I hope, do not believe that I am guilty?"

I could not answer. "No, Justine," said Elizabeth; "he is more convinced of your innocence than I was, for even when he heard that you had confessed, he did not credit it."

"I truly thank him. In these last moments I feel the sincerest gratitude towards those who think of me with kindness. How sweet is the affection of others to such a wretch as I am! It removes more than half my misfortune, and I feel as if I could die in peace now that my innocence is acknowledged by you, dear lady, and your cousin."

Thus the poor sufferer tried to comfort others and herself. She indeed gained the resignation she desired. But I, the true murderer, felt the never-dying worm alive in my bosom, which allowed of no hope or consolation. Elizabeth also wept and was unhappy, but hers also was the misery of innocence, which, like a cloud that passes over the fair moon, for a while hides but cannot tarnish its brightness. Anguish and despair had penetrated into the core of my heart; I bore a hell within me which nothing could extinguish. We stayed several hours with Justine, and it was with great difficulty that Elizabeth could tear herself away. "I wish," cried she, "that I were to die with you; I cannot live in this world of misery."

Justine assumed an air of cheerfulness, while she with difficulty repressed her bitter tears. She embraced Elizabeth and said in a voice of half-suppressed emotion, "Farewell, sweet lady, dearest Elizabeth, my beloved and only friend; may heaven, in its bounty, bless and preserve you; may this be the last misfortune that you will ever suffer! Live, and be happy, and make others so."

And on the morrow Justine died. Elizabeth's heart-rending eloquence failed to move the judges from their settled conviction in the criminality of the saintly sufferer. My passionate and indignant appeals were lost upon them. And when I received their cold answers and heard the harsh, unfeeling reasoning of these men, my purposed avowal died away on my lips. Thus I might proclaim myself a madman, but not revoke the sentence passed upon my wretched victim. She perished on the scaffold as a murderess!

From the tortures of my own heart, I turned to contemplate the deep and voiceless grief of my Elizabeth. This also was my doing! And my father's woe, and the desolation of that late so smiling home—all was the work of my thrice-accursed hands! Ye weep, unhappy ones, but these are not your last tears! Again shall you raise the funeral wail, and the sound of your lamentations shall again and again be heard! Frankenstein, your son, your kinsman, your early, much-loved friend; he who would spend each vital drop of blood for your sakes, who has no thought nor sense of joy except as it is mirrored also in your dear countenances, who would fill the air with blessings and spend his life in serving you—he bids you weep, to shed countless tears; happy beyond his hopes, if thus inexorable fate be satisfied, and if the destruction pause before the peace of the grave have succeeded to your sad torments!

Thus spoke my prophetic soul, as, torn by remorse, horror, and despair, I beheld those I loved spend vain sorrow upon the graves of William and Justine, the first hapless victims to my unhallowed arts.

Volume Two

CHAPTER I

Nothing is more painful to the human mind than, after the feelings have been worked up by a quick succession of events, the dead calmness of inaction and certainty which follows and deprives the soul both of hope and fear. Justine died, she rested, and I was alive. The blood flowed freely in my veins, but a weight of despair and remorse pressed on my heart which nothing could remove. Sleep fled from my eyes; I wandered like an evil spirit, for I had committed deeds of mischief beyond description horrible, and more, much more (I persuaded myself) was yet behind. Yet my heart overflowed with kindness and the love of virtue. I had begun life with benevolent intentions and thirsted for the moment when I should put them in practice and make myself useful to my fellow beings. Now all was blasted; instead of that serenity of conscience which allowed me to look back upon the past with self-satisfaction, and from thence to gather promise of new hopes, I was seized by remorse and the sense of guilt, which hurried me away to a hell of intense tortures such as no language can describe.

This state of mind preyed upon my health, which had perhaps never entirely recovered from the first shock it had sustained. I shunned the face of man; all sound of joy or complacency was torture to me; solitude was my only consolation—deep, dark, deathlike solitude.

My father observed with pain the alteration perceptible in my disposition and habits and endeavoured by arguments deduced from the feelings of his serene conscience and guiltless life to inspire me with fortitude and awaken in me the courage to dispel the dark cloud which brooded over me. "Do you think, Victor," said he, "that I do not suffer also? No one could love a child more than I loved your brother"—tears came into his eyes as he spoke—"but is it not a duty to the survivors that we should refrain from augmenting their unhappiness by an appearance of immoderate grief? It is also a duty owed to yourself, for excessive sorrow prevents improvement or enjoyment, or even the discharge of daily usefulness, without which no man is fit for society."

This advice, although good, was totally inapplicable to my case; I should have been the first to hide my grief and console my friends if remorse had not mingled its bitterness, and terror its alarm, with my other sensations. Now I could only answer my father with a look of despair and endeavour to hide myself from his view.

About this time we retired to our house at Belrive. This change was particularly agreeable to me. The shutting of the gates regularly at ten o'clock and the impossibility of remaining on the lake after that hour had rendered our residence within the walls of Geneva very irksome to me. I was now free. Often, after the rest of the family had retired for the night, I took the boat and passed many hours upon the water. Sometimes, with my sails set, I was carried by the wind; and sometimes, after rowing into the middle of the lake, I left the boat to pursue its own course and gave way to my own miserable reflections. I was often tempted, when all was at peace around me, and I the only unquiet thing that wandered restless in a scene so beautiful and heavenly—if I except some bat, or the frogs, whose harsh and interrupted croaking was heard only when I approached the shore—often, I say, I was tempted to plunge into the silent lake, that the waters might close over me and my calamities forever. But I was restrained, when I thought of the heroic and suffering Elizabeth, whom I tenderly loved, and whose existence was bound up in mine. I thought also of my father and surviving brother; should I by my base desertion leave them exposed and unprotected to the malice of the fiend whom I had let loose among them?

At these moments I wept bitterly and wished that peace would revisit my mind only that I might afford them consolation and happiness. But that could not be. Remorse extinguished every hope. I had been the author of unalterable evils, and I lived in daily fear lest the monster whom I had created should perpetrate some new wickedness. I had an obscure feeling that all was not over and that he would still commit some signal crime, which by its enormity should almost efface the recollection of the past. There was always scope for fear so long as anything I loved remained behind. My abhorrence of this fiend cannot be conceived. When I thought of him I gnashed my teeth, my eyes became inflamed, and I ardently wished to extinguish that life which I had so thoughtlessly bestowed. When I reflected on his crimes and malice, my hatred and revenge burst all bounds of moderation. I would have made a pilgrimage to the highest peak of the Andes, could I, when there, have precipitated him to their base. I wished to see him again, that I might wreak the utmost extent of abhorrence on his head and avenge the deaths of William and Justine.

Our house was the house of mourning. My father's health was deeply shaken by the horror of the recent events. Elizabeth was sad and desponding; she no longer took delight in her ordinary occupations; all pleasure seemed to her sacrilege toward the dead; eternal woe and tears she then thought was the just tribute she should pay to innocence so blasted and destroyed. She was no longer that happy creature who in earlier youth wandered with me on the banks of the lake and talked with ecstasy of our future prospects. The first of those sorrows which are sent to wean us from the earth had visited her, and its dimming influence quenched her dearest smiles.

"When I reflect, my dear cousin," said she, "on the miserable death of Justine Moritz, I no longer see the world and its works as they before appeared to me. Before, I looked upon the accounts of vice and injustice that I read in books or heard from others as tales of ancient days or imaginary evils; at least they were remote and more familiar to reason than to the imagination; but now misery has come home, and men appear to me as monsters thirsting for each other's blood. Yet I am certainly unjust. Everybody believed that poor girl to be guilty; and if she could have committed the crime for which she suffered, assuredly she would have been the most depraved of human creatures. For the sake of a few jewels, to have murdered the son of her benefactor and friend, a child whom she had nursed from its birth, and appeared to love as if it had been her own! I could not consent to the death of any human being, but certainly I should have thought such a creature unfit to remain in the society of men. But she was innocent. I know, I feel she was innocent; you are of the same opinion, and that confirms me. Alas! Victor, when falsehood can look so like the truth, who can assure themselves of certain happiness? I feel as if I were walking on the edge of a precipice, towards which thousands are crowding and endeavouring to plunge me into the abyss. William and Justine were assassinated, and the murderer escapes; he walks about the world free, and perhaps respected. But even if I were condemned to suffer on the scaffold for the same crimes, I would not change places with such a wretch."

I listened to this discourse with the extremest agony. I, not in deed, but in effect, was the true murderer. Elizabeth read my anguish in my countenance, and kindly taking my hand, said, "My dearest friend, you must calm yourself. These events have affected me, God knows how deeply; but I am not so wretched as you are. There is an expression of despair, and sometimes of revenge, in your countenance that makes me tremble. Dear Victor, banish these dark passions. Remember the friends around you, who centre all their hopes in you. Have we lost the power of rendering you happy? Ah! While we love, while we are true to each other, here in this land of peace and beauty, your native country, we may reap every tranquil blessing—what can disturb our peace?"

And could not such words from her whom I fondly prized before every other gift of fortune suffice to chase away the fiend that lurked in my heart? Even as she spoke I drew near to her, as if in terror, lest at that very moment the destroyer had been near to rob me of her.

Thus not the tenderness of friendship, nor the beauty of earth, nor of heaven, could redeem my soul from woe; the very accents of love were ineffectual. I was encompassed by a cloud which no beneficial influence could penetrate. The wounded deer dragging its fainting limbs to some untrodden brake, there to gaze upon the arrow which had pierced it, and to die, was but a type of me.

Sometimes I could cope with the sullen despair that overwhelmed me, but sometimes the whirlwind passions of my soul drove me to seek, by bodily exercise and by change of place, some relief from my intolerable sensations. It was during an access of this kind that I suddenly left my home, and bending my steps towards the near Alpine valleys, sought in the magnificence, the eternity of such scenes, to forget myself and my ephemeral, because human, sorrows. My wanderings were directed towards the valley of Chamounix. I had visited it frequently during my boyhood. Six years had passed since then: I was a wreck, but nought had changed in those savage and enduring scenes.

I performed the first part of my journey on horseback. I afterwards hired a mule, as the more sure-footed and least liable to receive injury on these rugged roads. The weather was fine; it was about the middle of the month of August, nearly two months after the death of Justine, that miserable epoch from which I dated all my woe. The weight upon my spirit was sensibly lightened as I plunged yet deeper in the ravine of Arve. The immense mountains and precipices that overhung me on every side—the sound of the river raging among the rocks, and the dashing of the waterfalls around spoke of a power mighty as Omnipotence—and I ceased to fear or to bend before any being less almighty than that which had created and ruled the elements, here displayed in their most terrific guise. Still, as I ascended higher, the valley assumed a more magnificent and astonishing character. Ruined castles hanging on the precipices of piny mountains, the impetuous Arve, and cottages every here and there peeping forth from among the trees formed a scene of singular beauty. But it was augmented and rendered sublime by the mighty Alps, whose white and shining pyramids and domes towered above all, as belonging to another earth, the habitations of another race of beings.

I passed the bridge of Pélissier, where the ravine, which the river forms, opened before me, and I began to ascend the mountain that overhangs it. Soon after, I entered the valley of Chamounix. This valley is more wonderful and sublime, but not so beautiful and picturesque as that of Servox, through which I had just passed. The high and snowy mountains were its immediate boundaries, but I saw no more ruined castles and fertile fields. Immense glaciers approached the road; I heard the rumbling thunder of the falling avalanche and marked the smoke of its passage. Mont Blanc, the supreme and magnificent Mont Blanc, raised itself from the surrounding *aiguilles*, and its tremendous *dôme* overlooked the valley.

A tingling long-lost sense of pleasure often came across me during this journey. Some turn in the road, some new object suddenly perceived and recognised, reminded me of days gone by, and were associated with the light-hearted gaiety of boyhood. The very winds whispered in soothing accents, and maternal nature bade me weep no more. Then again the kindly influence ceased to act—I found myself fettered again to grief and indulging in all the misery of reflection. Then I spurred on my animal, striving so to forget the world, my fears, and more than all, myself—or, in a more desperate fashion, I alighted and threw myself on the grass, weighed down by horror and despair.

At length I arrived at the village of Chamounix. Exhaustion succeeded to the extreme fatigue both of body and of mind which I had endured. For a short space of time I remained at the window watching the pallid lightnings that played above Mont Blanc and listening to the rushing of the Arve, which pursued its noisy way beneath. The same lulling sounds acted as a lullaby to my too keen sensations; when I placed my head upon my pillow, sleep crept over me; I felt it as it came and blessed the giver of oblivion.

CHAPTER II

I spent the following day roaming through the valley. I stood beside the sources of the Arveiron, which take their rise in a glacier that with slow pace is advancing down from the summit of the hills to barricade the valley. The abrupt sides of vast mountains were before me; the icy wall of the glacier overhung me; a few shattered pines were scattered around; and the solemn silence of this glorious presence-chamber of imperial nature was broken only by the brawling waves or the fall of some vast fragment, the thunder sound of the avalanche or the cracking, reverberated along the mountains, of the accumulated ice, which, through the silent working of immutable laws, was ever and anon rent and torn, as if it had been but a plaything in their hands. These sublime and magnificent scenes afforded me the greatest consolation that I was capable of receiving. They elevated me from all littleness of feeling, and although they did not remove my grief, they subdued and tranquillized it. In some degree, also, they diverted my mind from the thoughts over which it had brooded for the last month. I retired to rest at night; my slumbers, as it were, waited on and ministered to by the assemblance of grand shapes which I had contemplated during the day. They congregated round me; the unstained snowy mountain-top, the glittering pinnacle, the pine woods, and ragged bare ravine, the eagle, soaring amidst the clouds—they all gathered round me and bade me be at peace.

Where had they fled when the next morning I awoke? All of soul-inspiriting fled with sleep, and dark melancholy clouded every thought. The rain was pouring in torrents, and thick mists hid the summits of the mountains, so that I even saw not the faces of those mighty friends. Still I would penetrate their misty veil and seek them in their cloudy retreats. What were rain and storm to me? My mule was brought to the door, and I resolved to ascend to the summit of Montanvert. I remembered the effect that the view of the tremendous and ever-moving glacier had produced upon my mind when I first saw it. It had then filled me with a sublime ecstasy that gave wings to the soul and allowed it to soar from the obscure world to light and joy. The sight of the awful and majestic in nature had indeed always the effect of solemnizing my mind and causing me to forget the passing cares of life. I determined to go without a guide, for I was well acquainted with the path, and the presence of another would destroy the solitary grandeur of the scene.

The ascent is precipitous, but the path is cut into continual and short windings, which enable you to surmount the perpendicularity of the mountain. It is a scene terrifically desolate. In a thousand spots the traces of the winter avalanche may be perceived, where trees lie broken and strewed on the ground, some entirely destroyed, others bent, leaning upon the jutting rocks of the mountain or transversely upon other trees. The path, as you ascend higher, is intersected by ravines of snow, down which stones continually roll from above; one of them is particularly dangerous, as the slightest sound, such as even speaking in a loud voice, produces a concussion of air sufficient to draw destruction upon the head of the speaker. The pines are not tall or luxuriant, but they are sombre and add an air of severity to the scene. I looked on the valley beneath; vast mists were rising from the rivers which ran through it and curling in thick wreaths around the opposite mountains, whose summits were hid in the uniform clouds, while rain poured from the dark sky and added to the melancholy impression I received from the objects around me. Alas! Why does man boast of sensibilities superior to those apparent in the brute; it only renders them more necessary beings. If our impulses were confined to hunger, thirst, and desire, we might be nearly free; but now we are moved by every wind that blows and a chance word or scene that that word may convey to us.

> We rest; a dream has power to poison sleep.
> We rise; one wand'ring thought pollutes the day.
> We feel, conceive, or reason; laugh or weep,
> Embrace fond woe, or cast our cares away;
> It is the same: for, be it joy or sorrow,
> The path of its departure still is free.
> Man's yesterday may ne'er be like his morrow;
> Nought may endure but mutability!

It was nearly noon when I arrived at the top of the ascent. For some time I sat upon the rock that overlooks the sea of ice. A mist covered both that and the surrounding mountains. Presently a breeze dissipated the cloud, and I descended upon the glacier. The surface is very uneven, rising like the waves of a troubled sea, descending low, and interspersed by rifts that sink deep. The field of ice is almost a league in width, but I spent nearly two hours in crossing it. The opposite mountain is a bare perpendicular rock. From the side where I now stood Montanvert was exactly opposite, at the distance of a league; and above it rose Mont Blanc, in awful majesty. I remained in a recess of the rock, gazing on this wonderful and stupendous scene. The sea, or rather the vast river of ice, wound among its dependent mountains, whose aerial summits hung over its recesses. Their icy and glittering peaks shone in the sunlight over the clouds. My heart, which was before sorrowful, now swelled with something like joy; I exclaimed, "Wandering spirits, if indeed ye wander, and do not rest in your narrow beds, allow me this faint happiness, or take me, as your companion, away from the joys of life."

As I said this I suddenly beheld the figure of a man, at some distance, advancing towards me with superhuman speed. He bounded over the crevices in the ice, among which I had walked with caution; his stature, also, as he approached, seemed to exceed that of man. I was troubled; a mist came over my eyes, and I felt a faintness seize me, but I was quickly restored by the cold gale of the mountains. I perceived, as the shape came nearer (sight tremendous and abhorred!) that it was the wretch whom I had created. I trembled with rage and horror, resolving to wait his approach and then close with him in mortal combat. He approached; his countenance bespoke bitter anguish, combined with disdain and malignity, while its unearthly ugliness rendered it almost too horrible for human eyes. But I scarcely observed this; rage and hatred had at first deprived me of utterance, and I recovered only to overwhelm him with words expressive of furious detestation and contempt.

"Devil," I exclaimed, "do you dare approach me? And do not you fear the fierce vengeance of my arm wreaked on your miserable head? Begone, vile insect! Or rather, stay, that I may trample you to dust! And, oh, that I could, with the extinction of your miserable existence, restore those victims whom you have so diabolically murdered!"

"I expected this reception," said the daemon. "All men hate the wretched; how, then, must I be hated, who am miserable beyond all living things! Yet you, my creator, detest and spurn me, thy creature, to whom thou art bound by ties only dissoluble by the annihilation of one of us. You purpose to kill me. How dare you sport thus with life? Do your duty towards me, and I will do mine towards you and the rest of mankind. If you will comply with my conditions, I will leave them and you at peace; but if you refuse, I will glut the maw of death, until it be satiated with the blood of your remaining friends."

"Abhorred monster! Fiend that thou art! The tortures of hell are too mild a vengeance for thy crimes. Wretched devil! You reproach me with your creation; come on, then, that I may extinguish the spark which I so negligently bestowed."

My rage was without bounds; I sprang on him, impelled by all the feelings which can arm one being against the existence of another.

He easily eluded me, and said:

"Be calm! I entreat you to hear me before you give vent to your hatred on my devoted head. Have I not suffered enough, that you seek to increase my misery? Life, although it may only be an accumulation of anguish, is dear to me, and I will defend it. Remember, thou hast made me more powerful than thyself; my height is superior to thine, my joints more supple. But I will not be tempted to set myself in opposition to thee. I am thy creature, and I will be even mild and docile to my natural lord and king if thou wilt also perform thy part, the which thou owest me. Oh, Frankenstein, be not equitable to every other and trample upon me alone, to whom thy justice, and even thy clemency and affection, is most due. Remember that I am thy creature; I ought to be thy Adam, but I am rather the fallen angel, whom thou drivest from joy for no misdeed. Everywhere I see bliss, from which I alone am irrevocably excluded. I was benevolent and good; misery made me a fiend. Make me happy, and I shall again be virtuous."

"Begone! I will not hear you. There can be no community between you and me; we are enemies. Begone, or let us try our strength in a fight, in which one must fall."

"How can I move thee? Will no entreaties cause thee to turn a favourable eye upon thy creature, who implores thy goodness and compassion? Believe me, Frankenstein, I was benevolent; my soul glowed with love and humanity; but am I not alone, miserably alone? You, my creator, abhor me; what hope can I gather from your fellow creatures, who owe me nothing? They spurn and hate me. The desert mountains and dreary glaciers are my refuge. I have wandered here many days; the caves of ice, which I only do not fear, are a dwelling to me, and the only one which man does not grudge. These bleak skies I hail, for they are kinder to me than your fellow beings. If the multitude of mankind knew of my existence, they would do as you do, and arm themselves for my destruction. Shall I not then hate them who abhor me? I will keep no terms with my enemies. I am miserable, and they shall share my wretchedness. Yet it is in your power to recompense me, and deliver them from an evil which it only remains for you to make so great, that not only you and your family, but thousands of others, shall be swallowed up in the whirlwinds of its rage. Let your compassion be moved, and do not disdain me. Listen to my tale; when you have heard that, abandon or commiserate me, as you shall judge that I deserve. But hear me. The guilty are allowed, by human laws, bloody as they are, to speak in their own defence before they are condemned. Listen to me, Frankenstein. You accuse me of murder, and yet you would, with a satisfied conscience, destroy your own creature. Oh, praise the eternal justice of man! Yet I ask you not to spare me; listen to me, and then, if you can, and if you will, destroy the work of your hands."

"Why do you call to my remembrance," I rejoined, "circumstances of which I shudder to reflect, that I have been the miserable origin and author? Cursed be the day, abhorred devil, in which you first saw light! Cursed (although I curse myself) be the hands that formed you! You have made me wretched beyond expression. You have left me no power to consider whether I am just to you or not. Begone! Relieve me from the sight of your detested form."

"Thus I relieve thee, my creator," he said, and placed his hated hands before my eyes, which I flung from me with violence; "thus I take from thee a sight which you abhor. Still thou canst listen to me and grant me thy compassion. By the virtues that I once possessed, I demand this from you. Hear my tale; it is long and strange, and the temperature of this place is not fitting to your fine sensations; come to the hut upon the mountain. The sun is yet high in the heavens; before it descends to hide itself behind your snowy precipices and illuminate another world, you will have heard my story and can decide. On you it rests, whether I quit forever the neighbourhood of man and lead a harmless life, or become the scourge of your fellow creatures and the author of your own speedy ruin."

As he said this, he led the way across the ice; I followed. My heart was full, and I did not answer him, but as I proceeded, I weighed the various arguments that he had used and determined at least to listen to his tale. I was partly urged by curiosity, and compassion confirmed my resolution. I had hitherto supposed him to be the murderer of my brother, and I eagerly sought a confirmation or denial of this opinion. For the first time, also, I felt what the duties of a creator towards his creature were, and that I ought to render him happy before I complained of his wickedness. These motives urged me to comply with his demand. We crossed the ice, therefore, and ascended the opposite rock. The air was cold, and the rain again began to descend; we entered the hut, the fiend with an air of exultation, I with a heavy heart and depressed spirits. But I consented to listen, and seating myself by the fire which my odious companion had lighted, he thus began his tale.

CHAPTER III

It is with considerable difficulty that I remember the original era of my being; all the events of that period appear confused and indistinct. A strange multiplicity of sensations seized me, and I saw, felt, heard, and smelt at the same time; and it was, indeed, a long time before I learned to distinguish between the operations of my various senses. By degrees, I remember, a stronger light pressed upon my nerves, so that I was obliged to shut my eyes. Darkness then came over me and troubled me, but hardly had I felt this when, by opening my eyes, as I now suppose, the light poured in upon me again. I walked and, I believe, descended, but I presently found a great alteration in my sensations. Before, dark and opaque bodies had surrounded me, impervious to my touch or sight; but I now found that I could wander on at liberty, with no obstacles which I could not either surmount or avoid. The light became more and more oppressive to me, and the heat wearying me as I walked, I sought a place where I could receive shade. This was the forest near Ingolstadt; and here I lay by the side of a brook resting from my fatigue, until I felt tormented by hunger and thirst. This roused me from my nearly dormant state, and I ate some berries which I found hanging on the trees or lying on the ground. I slaked my thirst at the brook, and then lying down, was overcome by sleep.

"It was dark when I awoke; I felt cold also, and half frightened, as it were, instinctively, finding myself so desolate. Before I had quitted your apartment, on a sensation of cold, I had covered myself with some clothes, but these were insufficient to secure me from the dews of night. I was a poor, helpless, miserable wretch; I knew, and could distinguish, nothing; but feeling pain invade me on all sides, I sat down and wept.

"Soon a gentle light stole over the heavens and gave me a sensation of pleasure. I started up and beheld a radiant form rise from among the trees.* I gazed with a kind of wonder. It moved slowly, but it enlightened my path, and I again went out in search of berries. I was still cold when under one of the trees I found a huge cloak, with which I covered myself, and sat down upon the ground. No distinct ideas occupied my mind; all was confused. I felt light, and hunger, and thirst, and darkness; innumerable sounds rang in my ears, and on all sides various scents saluted me; the only object that I could distinguish was the bright moon, and I fixed my eyes on that with pleasure.

"Several changes of day and night passed, and the orb of night had greatly lessened, when I began to distinguish my sensations from each other. I gradually saw plainly the clear stream that supplied me with drink and the trees that shaded me with their foliage. I was delighted when I first discovered that a pleasant sound, which often saluted my ears, proceeded from the throats of the little winged animals who had often intercepted the light from my eyes. I began also to observe, with greater accuracy, the forms that surrounded me and to perceive the boundaries of the radiant roof of light which canopied me. Sometimes I tried to imitate the pleasant songs of the birds but was unable. Sometimes I wished to express my sensations in my own mode, but the uncouth and inarticulate sounds which broke from me frightened me into silence again.

"The moon had disappeared from the night, and again, with a lessened form, showed itself, while I still remained in the forest. My sensations had by this time become distinct, and my mind received every day additional ideas. My eyes became accustomed to the light and to perceive objects in their right forms; I distinguished the insect from the herb, and by degrees, one herb from another. I found that the sparrow uttered none but harsh notes, whilst those of the blackbird and thrush were sweet and enticing.

"One day, when I was oppressed by cold, I found a fire which had been left by some wandering beggars, and was overcome with delight at the warmth I experienced from it. In my joy I thrust my hand into the live embers, but quickly drew it out again with a cry of pain. How strange, I thought, that the same cause should produce such opposite effects! I examined the materials of the fire, and to my joy found it to be composed of wood. I quickly collected some branches, but they were wet and would not burn. I was pained at this and sat still watching the operation of the fire. The wet wood which I had placed near the heat dried and itself became inflamed. I reflected on this, and

* The moon (author's footnote)

by touching the various branches, I discovered the cause and busied myself in collecting a great quantity of wood, that I might dry it and have a plentiful supply of fire. When night came on and brought sleep with it, I was in the greatest fear lest my fire should be extinguished. I covered it carefully with dry wood and leaves and placed wet branches upon it; and then, spreading my cloak, I lay on the ground and sank into sleep.

"It was morning when I awoke, and my first care was to visit the fire. I uncovered it, and a gentle breeze quickly fanned it into a flame. I observed this also and contrived a fan of branches, which roused the embers when they were nearly extinguished. When night came again I found, with pleasure, that the fire gave light as well as heat and that the discovery of this element was useful to me in my food, for I found some of the offals that the travellers had left had been roasted, and tasted much more savoury than the berries I gathered from the trees. I tried, therefore, to dress my food in the same manner, placing it on the live embers. I found that the berries were spoiled by this operation, and the nuts and roots much improved.

"Food, however, became scarce, and I often spent the whole day searching in vain for a few acorns to assuage the pangs of hunger. When I found this, I resolved to quit the place that I had hitherto inhabited, to seek for one where the few wants I experienced would be more easily satisfied. In this emigration I exceedingly lamented the loss of the fire which I had obtained through accident and knew not how to reproduce it. I gave several hours to the serious consideration of this difficulty, but I was obliged to relinquish all attempt to supply it, and wrapping myself up in my cloak, I struck across the wood towards the setting sun. I passed three days in these rambles and at length discovered the open country. A great fall of snow had taken place the night before, and the fields were of one uniform white; the appearance was disconsolate, and I found my feet chilled by the cold damp substance that covered the ground.

"It was about seven in the morning, and I longed to obtain food and shelter; at length I perceived a small hut, on a rising ground, which had doubtless been built for the convenience of some shepherd. This was a new sight to me, and I examined the structure with great curiosity. Finding the door open, I entered. An old man sat in it, near a fire, over which he was preparing his breakfast. He turned on hearing a noise, and perceiving me, shrieked loudly, and quitting the hut, ran across the fields with a speed of which his debilitated form hardly appeared capable. His appearance, different from any I had ever before seen, and his flight somewhat surprised me. But I was enchanted by the appearance of the hut; here the snow and rain could not penetrate; the ground was dry; and it presented to me then as exquisite and divine a retreat as Pandemonium appeared to the daemons of hell after their sufferings in the lake of fire. I greedily devoured the remnants of the shepherd's breakfast, which consisted of bread, cheese, milk, and wine; the latter, however, I did not like. Then, overcome by fatigue, I lay down among some straw and fell asleep.

"It was noon when I awoke, and allured by the warmth of the sun, which shone brightly on the white ground, I determined to recommence my travels; and, depositing the remains of the peasant's breakfast in a wallet I found, I proceeded across the fields for several hours, until at sunset I arrived at a village. How miraculous did this appear! The huts, the neater cottages, and stately houses engaged my admiration by turns. The vegetables in the gardens, the milk and cheese that I saw placed at the windows of some of the cottages, allured my appetite. One of the best of these I entered, but I had hardly placed my foot within the door before the children shrieked, and one of the women fainted. The whole village was roused; some fled, some attacked me, until, grievously bruised by stones and many other kinds of missile weapons, I escaped to the open country and fearfully took refuge in a low hovel, quite bare, and making a wretched appearance after the palaces I had beheld in the village. This hovel, however, joined a cottage of a neat and pleasant appearance; but after my late dearly bought experience, I dared not enter it. My place of refuge was constructed of wood, but so low that I could with difficulty sit upright in it. No wood, however, was placed on the earth, which formed the floor, but it was dry; and although the wind entered it by innumerable chinks, I found it an agreeable asylum from the snow and rain.

"Here, then, I retreated and lay down happy to have found a shelter, however miserable, from the inclemency of the season, and still more from the barbarity of man.

"As soon as morning dawned I crept from my kennel, that I might view the adjacent cottage and discover if I could remain in the habitation I had found. It was situated against the back of the cottage and surrounded on the sides which were exposed by a pig sty and a clear pool of water. One part was open, and by that I had crept in; but now I covered every crevice by which I might be perceived with stones and wood, yet in such a manner that I might move them on occasion to pass out; all the light I enjoyed came through the sty, and that was sufficient for me.

"Having thus arranged my dwelling and carpeted it with clean straw, I retired, for I saw the figure of a man at a distance, and I remembered too well my treatment the night before to trust myself in his power. I had first, however, provided for my sustenance for that day by a loaf of coarse bread, which I purloined, and a cup with which I could drink more conveniently than from my hand of the pure water which flowed by my retreat. The floor was a little raised, so that it was kept perfectly dry, and by its vicinity to the chimney of the cottage it was tolerably warm.

"Being thus provided, I resolved to reside in this hovel until something should occur which might alter my determination. It was indeed a paradise compared to the bleak forest, my former residence, the rain-dropping branches, and dank earth. I ate my breakfast with pleasure and was about to remove a plank to procure myself a little water when I heard a step, and looking through a small chink, I beheld a young creature, with a pail on her head, passing before my hovel. The girl was young and of gentle demeanour, unlike what I have since found cottagers and farmhouse servants to be. Yet she was meanly dressed, a coarse blue petticoat and a linen jacket being her only garb; her fair hair was plaited but not adorned: she looked patient yet sad. I lost sight of her, and in about a quarter of an hour she returned bearing the pail, which was now partly filled with milk. As she walked along, seemingly incommoded by the burden, a young man met her, whose countenance expressed a deeper despondence. Uttering a few sounds with an air of melancholy, he took the pail from her head and bore it to the cottage himself. She followed, and they disappeared. Presently I saw the young man again, with some tools in his hand, cross the field behind the cottage; and the girl was also busied, sometimes in the house and sometimes in the yard.

"On examining my dwelling, I found that one of the windows of the cottage had formerly occupied a part of it, but the panes had been filled up with wood. In one of these was a small and almost imperceptible chink through which the eye could just penetrate. Through this crevice a small room was visible, whitewashed and clean but very bare of furniture. In one corner, near a small fire, sat an old man, leaning his head on his hands in a disconsolate attitude. The young girl was occupied in arranging the cottage; but presently she took something out of a drawer, which employed her hands, and she sat down beside the old man, who, taking up an instrument, began to play and to produce sounds sweeter than the voice of the thrush or the nightingale. It was a lovely sight, even to me, poor wretch who had never beheld aught beautiful before. The silver hair and benevolent countenance of the aged cottager won my reverence, while the gentle manners of the girl enticed my love. He played a sweet mournful air which I perceived drew tears from the eyes of his amiable companion, of which the old man took no notice, until she sobbed audibly; he then pronounced a few sounds, and the fair creature, leaving her work, knelt at his feet. He raised her and smiled with such kindness and affection that I felt sensations of a peculiar and overpowering nature; they were a mixture of pain and pleasure, such as I had never before experienced, either from hunger or cold, warmth or food; and I withdrew from the window, unable to bear these emotions.

"Soon after this the young man returned, bearing on his shoulders a load of wood. The girl met him at the door, helped to relieve him of his burden, and taking some of the fuel into the cottage, placed it on the fire; then she and the youth went apart into a nook of the cottage, and he showed her a large loaf and a piece of cheese. She seemed pleased and went into the garden for some roots and plants, which she placed in water, and then upon the fire. She afterwards continued her work, whilst the young man went into the garden and appeared busily employed in digging and pulling up roots. After he had been employed thus about an hour, the young woman joined him and they entered the cottage together.

"The old man had, in the meantime, been pensive, but on the appearance of his companions he assumed a more cheerful air, and they sat down to eat. The meal was quickly dispatched. The young woman was again occupied in arranging the cottage, the old man walked before the cottage in the sun for a few minutes, leaning on the arm of the youth. Nothing could exceed in beauty the contrast between these two excellent creatures. One was old, with silver hairs and a countenance beaming with benevolence and love; the younger was slight and graceful in his figure, and his features were moulded with the finest symmetry, yet his eyes and attitude expressed the utmost sadness and despondency. The old man returned to the cottage, and the youth, with tools different from those he had used in the morning, directed his steps across the fields.

"Night quickly shut in, but to my extreme wonder, I found that the cottagers had a means of prolonging light by the use of tapers, and was delighted to find that the setting of the sun did not put an end to the pleasure I experienced in watching my human neighbours. In the evening the young girl and her companion were employed in various occupations which I did not understand; and the old man again took up the instrument which produced the divine sounds that had enchanted me in the morning. So soon as he had finished, the youth began, not to play, but to utter sounds that were monotonous, and neither resembling the harmony of the old man's instrument nor the songs of the birds; I since found that he read aloud, but at that time I knew nothing of the science of words or letters.

"The family, after having been thus occupied for a short time, extinguished their lights and retired, as I conjectured, to rest."

CHAPTER IV

I lay on my straw, but I could not sleep. I thought of the occurrences of the day. What chiefly struck me was the gentle manners of these people, and I longed to join them, but dared not. I remembered too well the treatment I had suffered the night before from the barbarous villagers, and resolved, whatever course of conduct I might hereafter think it right to pursue, that for the present I would remain quietly in my hovel, watching and endeavouring to discover the motives which influenced their actions.

"The cottagers arose the next morning before the sun. The young woman arranged the cottage and prepared the food, and the youth departed after the first meal.

"This day was passed in the same routine as that which preceded it. The young man was constantly employed out of doors, and the girl in various laborious occupations within. The old man, whom I soon perceived to be blind, employed his leisure hours on his instrument or in contemplation. Nothing could exceed the love and respect which the younger cottagers exhibited towards their venerable companion. They performed towards him every little office of affection and duty with gentleness, and he rewarded them by his benevolent smiles.

"They were not entirely happy. The young man and his companion often went apart and appeared to weep. I saw no cause for their unhappiness, but I was deeply affected by it. If such lovely creatures were miserable, it was less strange that I, an imperfect and solitary being, should be wretched. Yet why were these gentle beings unhappy? They possessed a delightful house (for such it was in my eyes) and every luxury; they had a fire to warm them when chill and delicious viands when hungry; they were dressed in excellent clothes; and, still more, they enjoyed one another's company and speech, interchanging each day looks of affection and kindness. What did their tears imply? Did they really express pain? I was at first unable to solve these questions, but perpetual attention and time explained to me many appearances which were at first enigmatic.

"A considerable period elapsed before I discovered one of the causes of the uneasiness of this amiable family: it was poverty, and they suffered that evil in a very distressing degree. Their nourishment consisted entirely of the vegetables of their garden and the milk of one cow, which gave very little during the winter, when its masters could scarcely procure food to support it. They often, I believe, suffered the pangs of hunger very poignantly, especially the two younger cottagers, for several times they placed food before the old man when they reserved none for themselves.

"This trait of kindness moved me sensibly. I had been accustomed, during the night, to steal a part of their store for my own consumption, but when I found that in doing this I inflicted pain on the cottagers, I abstained and satisfied myself with berries, nuts, and roots which I gathered from a neighbouring wood.

"I discovered also another means through which I was enabled to assist their labours. I found that the youth spent a great part of each day in collecting wood for the family fire, and during the night I often took his tools, the use of which I quickly discovered, and brought home firing sufficient for the consumption of several days.

"I remember, the first time that I did this, the young woman, when she opened the door in the morning, appeared greatly astonished on seeing a great pile of wood on the outside. She uttered some words in a loud voice, and the youth joined her, who also expressed surprise. I observed, with pleasure, that he did not go to the forest that day, but spent it in repairing the cottage and cultivating the garden.

"By degrees I made a discovery of still greater moment. I found that these people possessed a method of communicating their experience and feelings to one another by articulate sounds. I perceived that the words they spoke sometimes produced pleasure or pain, smiles or sadness, in the minds and countenances of the hearers. This was indeed a godlike science, and I ardently desired to become acquainted with it. But I was baffled in every attempt I made for this purpose. Their pronunciation was quick, and the words they uttered, not having any apparent connection with visible objects, I was unable to discover any clue by which I could unravel the mystery of their reference. By great application, however, and after having remained during the space of several revolutions of the moon in my hovel, I discovered the names that were given to some of the most familiar objects of discourse; I learned and applied the words, 'fire,' 'milk,' 'bread,' and 'wood.' I learned also the names of the cottagers themselves. The youth and his companion had each of them several names, but the old man had only one, which was 'father.' The girl was called 'sister' or 'Agatha,' and the youth 'Felix,' 'brother,' or 'son.' I cannot describe the delight I felt when I learned the ideas appropriated to each of these sounds and was able to pronounce them. I distinguished several other words without being able as yet to understand or apply them, such as 'good,' 'dearest,' 'unhappy.'

"I spent the winter in this manner. The gentle manners and beauty of the cottagers greatly endeared them to me; when they were unhappy, I felt depressed; when they rejoiced, I sympathised in their joys. I saw few human beings besides them, and if any other happened to enter the cottage, their harsh manners and rude gait only enhanced to me the superior accomplishments of my friends. The old man, I could perceive, often endeavoured to encourage his children, as sometimes I found that he called them, to cast off their melancholy. He would talk in a cheerful accent, with an expression of goodness that bestowed pleasure even upon me. Agatha listened with respect, her eyes sometimes filled with tears, which she endeavoured to wipe away unperceived; but I generally found that her countenance and tone were more cheerful after having listened to the exhortations of her father. It was not thus with Felix. He was always the saddest of the group, and even to my unpractised senses, he appeared to have suffered more deeply than his friends. But if his countenance was more sorrowful, his voice was more cheerful than that of his sister, especially when he addressed the old man.

"I could mention innumerable instances which, although slight, marked the dispositions of these amiable cottagers. In the midst of poverty and want, Felix carried with pleasure to his sister the first little white flower that peeped out from beneath the snowy ground. Early in the morning, before she had risen, he cleared away the snow that obstructed her path to the milk-house, drew water from the well, and brought the wood from the outhouse, where, to his perpetual astonishment, he found his store always replenished by an invisible hand. In the day, I believe, he worked sometimes for a neighbouring farmer, because he often went forth and did not return until dinner, yet brought no wood with him. At other times he worked in the garden, but as there was little to do in the frosty season, he read to the old man and Agatha.

"This reading had puzzled me extremely at first, but by degrees I discovered that he uttered many of the same sounds when he read as when he talked. I conjectured, therefore, that he found on the paper signs for speech which he understood, and I ardently longed to comprehend these also; but how was that possible when I did not even understand the sounds for which they stood as signs? I improved, however, sensibly in this science, but not sufficiently to follow up any kind of conversation, although I applied my whole mind to the endeavour: for I easily perceived that, although I eagerly longed to discover myself to the cottagers, I ought not to make the attempt until I had first become master of their language, which knowledge might enable me to make them overlook the deformity of my figure, for with this also the contrast perpetually presented to my eyes had made me acquainted.

"I had admired the perfect forms of my cottagers—their grace, beauty, and delicate complexions; but how was I terrified when I viewed myself in a transparent pool! At first I started back, unable to believe that it was indeed I who was reflected in the mirror; and when I became fully convinced that I was in reality the monster that I am, I was filled with the bitterest sensations of despondence and mortification. Alas! I did not yet entirely know the fatal effects of this miserable deformity.

"As the sun became warmer and the light of day longer, the snow vanished, and I beheld the bare trees and the black earth. From this time Felix was more employed, and the heart-moving indications of impending famine disappeared. Their food, as I afterwards found, was coarse, but it was wholesome; and they procured a sufficiency of it. Several new kinds of plants sprang up in the garden, which they dressed; and these signs of comfort increased daily as the season advanced.

"The old man, leaning on his son, walked each day at noon, when it did not rain, as I found it was called when the heavens poured forth its waters. This frequently took place, but a high wind quickly dried the earth, and the season became far more pleasant than it had been.

"My mode of life in my hovel was uniform. During the morning I attended the motions of the cottagers, and when they were dispersed in various occupations, I slept; the remainder of the day was spent in observing my friends. When they had retired to rest, if there was any moon or the night was star-light, I went into the woods and collected my own food and fuel for the cottage. When I returned, as often as it was necessary, I cleared their path from the snow and performed those offices that I had seen done by Felix. I afterwards found that these labours, performed by an invisible hand, greatly astonished them; and once or twice I heard them, on these occasions, utter the words 'good spirit,' 'wonderful'; but I did not then understand the signification of these terms.

"My thoughts now became more active, and I longed to discover the motives and feelings of these lovely creatures; I was inquisitive to know why Felix appeared so miserable and Agatha so sad. I thought (foolish wretch!) that it might be in my power to restore happiness to these deserving people. When I slept or was absent, the forms of the venerable blind father, the gentle Agatha, and the excellent Felix flitted before me. I looked upon them as superior beings who would be the arbiters of my future destiny. I formed in my imagination a thousand pictures of presenting myself to them, and their reception of me. I imagined that they would be disgusted, until, by my gentle demeanour and conciliating words, I should first win their favour and afterwards their love.

"These thoughts exhilarated me and led me to apply with fresh ardour to the acquiring the art of language. My organs were indeed harsh, but supple; and although my voice was very unlike the soft music of their tones, yet I pronounced such words as I understood with tolerable ease. It was as the ass and the lap-dog; yet surely the gentle ass whose intentions were affectionate, although his manners were rude, deserved better treatment than blows and execration.

"The pleasant showers and genial warmth of spring greatly altered the aspect of the earth. Men who before this change seemed to have been hid in caves dispersed themselves and were employed in various arts of cultivation. The birds sang in more cheerful notes, and the leaves began to bud forth on the trees. Happy, happy earth! Fit habitation for gods, which, so short a time before, was bleak, damp, and unwholesome. My spirits were elevated by the enchanting appearance of nature; the past was blotted from my memory, the present was tranquil, and the future gilded by bright rays of hope and anticipations of joy."

CHAPTER V

I now hasten to the more moving part of my story. I shall relate events that impressed me with feelings which, from what I had been, have made me what I am.

"Spring advanced rapidly; the weather became fine and the skies cloudless. It surprised me that what before was desert and gloomy should now bloom with the most beautiful flowers and verdure. My senses were gratified and refreshed by a thousand scents of delight and a thousand sights of beauty.

"It was on one of these days, when my cottagers periodically rested from labour—the old man played on his guitar, and the children listened to him—that I observed the countenance of Felix was melancholy beyond expression; he sighed frequently, and once his father paused in his music, and I conjectured by his manner that he enquired the cause of his son's sorrow. Felix replied in a cheerful accent, and the old man was recommencing his music when someone tapped at the door.

"It was a lady on horseback, accompanied by a countryman as a guide. The lady was dressed in a dark suit and covered with a thick black veil. Agatha asked a question, to which the stranger only replied by pronouncing, in a sweet accent, the name of Felix. Her voice was musical but unlike that of either of my friends. On hearing this word, Felix came up hastily to the lady, who, when she saw him, threw up her veil, and I beheld a countenance of angelic beauty and expression. Her hair of a shining raven black, and curiously braided; her eyes were dark, but gentle, although animated; her features of a regular proportion, and her complexion wondrously fair, each cheek tinged with a lovely pink.

"Felix seemed ravished with delight when he saw her, every trait of sorrow vanished from his face, and it instantly expressed a degree of ecstatic joy, of which I could hardly have believed it capable; his eyes sparkled, as his cheek flushed with pleasure; and at that moment I thought him as beautiful as the stranger. She appeared affected by different feelings; wiping a few tears from her lovely eyes, she held out her hand to Felix, who kissed it rapturously and called her, as well as I could distinguish, his sweet Arabian. She did not appear to understand him, but smiled. He assisted her to dismount, and dismissing her guide, conducted her into the cottage. Some conversation took place between him and his father, and the young stranger knelt at the old man's feet and would have kissed his hand, but he raised her and embraced her affectionately.

"I soon perceived that although the stranger uttered articulate sounds and appeared to have a language of her own, she was neither understood by nor herself understood the cottagers. They made many signs which I did not comprehend, but I saw that her presence diffused gladness through the cottage, dispelling their sorrow as the sun dissipates the morning mists. Felix seemed peculiarly happy and with smiles of delight welcomed his Arabian. Agatha, the ever-gentle Agatha, kissed the hands of the lovely stranger, and pointing to her brother, made signs which appeared to me to mean that he had been sorrowful until she came. Some hours passed thus, while they, by their countenances, expressed joy, the cause of which I did not comprehend. Presently I found, by the frequent recurrence of some sound which the stranger repeated after them, that she was endeavouring to learn their language; and the idea instantly occurred to me that I should make use of the same instructions to the same end. The stranger learned about twenty words at the first lesson; most of them, indeed, were those which I had before understood, but I profited by the others.

"As night came on, Agatha and the Arabian retired early. When they separated, Felix kissed the hand of the stranger and said, 'Good night, sweet Safie.' He sat up much longer, conversing with his father, and by the frequent repetition of her name I conjectured that their lovely guest was the subject of their conversation. I ardently desired to understand them, and bent every faculty towards that purpose, but found it utterly impossible.

"The next morning Felix went out to his work, and after the usual occupations of Agatha were finished, the Arabian sat at the feet of the old man, and taking his guitar, played some airs so entrancingly beautiful that they at once drew tears of sorrow and delight from my eyes. She sang, and her voice flowed in a rich cadence, swelling or dying away like a nightingale of the woods.

"When she had finished, she gave the guitar to Agatha, who at first declined it. She played a simple air, and her voice accompanied it in sweet accents, but unlike the wondrous strain of the stranger. The old man appeared enraptured and said some words which Agatha endeavoured to explain to Safie, and by which he appeared to wish to express that she bestowed on him the greatest delight by her music.

"The days now passed as peaceably as before, with the sole alteration that joy had taken place of sadness in the countenances of my friends. Safie was always gay and happy; she and I improved rapidly in the knowledge of language, so that in two months I began to comprehend most of the words uttered by my protectors.

"In the meanwhile also the black ground was covered with herbage, and the green banks interspersed with innumerable flowers, sweet to the scent and the eyes, stars of pale radiance among the moonlight woods; the sun became warmer, the nights clear and balmy; and my nocturnal rambles were an extreme pleasure to me, although they were considerably shortened by the late setting and early rising of the sun, for I never ventured abroad during daylight, fearful of meeting with the same treatment I had formerly endured in the first village which I entered.

"My days were spent in close attention, that I might more speedily master the language; and I may boast that I improved more rapidly than the Arabian, who understood very little and conversed in broken accents, whilst I comprehended and could imitate almost every word that was spoken.

"While I improved in speech, I also learned the science of letters as it was taught to the stranger, and this opened before me a wide field for wonder and delight.

"The book from which Felix instructed Safie was Volney's *Ruins of Empires*. I should not have understood the purport of this book had not Felix, in reading it, given very minute explanations. He had chosen this work, he said, because the declamatory style was framed in imitation of the Eastern authors. Through this work I obtained a cursory knowledge of history and a view of the several empires at present existing in the world; it gave me an insight into the manners, governments, and religions of the different nations of the earth. I heard of the slothful Asiatics, of the stupendous genius and mental activity of the Grecians, of the wars and wonderful virtue of the early Romans—of their subsequent degenerating—of the decline of that mighty empire, of chivalry, Christianity, and kings. I heard of the discovery of the American hemisphere and wept with Safie over the hapless fate of its original inhabitants.

"These wonderful narrations inspired me with strange feelings. Was man, indeed, at once so powerful, so virtuous and magnificent, yet so vicious and base? He appeared at one time a mere scion of the evil principle and at another as all that can be conceived of noble and godlike. To be a great and virtuous man appeared the highest honour that can befall a sensitive being; to be base and vicious, as many on record have been, appeared the lowest degradation, a condition more abject than that of the blind mole or harmless worm. For a long time I could not conceive how one man could go forth to murder his fellow, or even why there were laws and governments; but when I heard details of vice and bloodshed, my wonder ceased and I turned away with disgust and loathing.

"Every conversation of the cottagers now opened new wonders to me. While I listened to the instructions which Felix bestowed upon the Arabian, the strange system of human society was explained to me. I heard of the division of property, of immense wealth and squalid poverty, of rank, descent, and noble blood.

"The words induced me to turn towards myself. I learned that the possessions most esteemed by your fellow creatures were high and unsullied descent united with riches. A man might be respected with only one of these advantages, but without either he was considered, except in very rare instances, as a vagabond and a slave, doomed to waste his powers for the profits of the chosen few! And what was I? Of my creation and creator I was absolutely ignorant, but I knew that I possessed no money, no friends, no kind of property. I was, besides, endued with a figure hideously deformed and loathsome; I was not even of the same nature as man. I was more agile than they and could subsist upon coarser diet; I bore the extremes of heat and cold with less injury to my frame; my stature far exceeded theirs. When I looked around I saw and heard of none like me. Was I, then, a monster, a blot upon the earth, from which all men fled and whom all men disowned?

"I cannot describe to you the agony that these reflections inflicted upon me; I tried to dispel them, but sorrow only increased with knowledge. Oh, that I had forever remained in my native wood, nor known nor felt beyond the sensations of hunger, thirst, and heat!

"Of what a strange nature is knowledge! It clings to the mind when it has once seized on it like a lichen on the rock. I wished sometimes to shake off all thought and feeling, but I learned that there was but one means to overcome the sensation of pain, and that was death—a state which I feared yet did not understand. I admired virtue and good feelings and loved the gentle manners and amiable qualities of my cottagers, but I was shut out from intercourse with them, except through means which I obtained by stealth, when I was unseen and unknown, and which rather increased than satisfied the desire I had of becoming one among my fellows. The gentle words of Agatha and the animated smiles of the charming Arabian were not for me. The mild exhortations of the old man and the lively conversation of the loved Felix were not for me. Miserable, unhappy wretch!

"Other lessons were impressed upon me even more deeply. I heard of the difference of sexes, and the birth and growth of children, how the father doted on the smiles of the infant, and the lively sallies of the older child, how all the life and cares of the mother were wrapped up in the precious charge, how the mind of youth expanded and gained knowledge, of brother, sister, and all the various relationships which bind one human being to another in mutual bonds.

"But where were my friends and relations? No father had watched my infant days, no mother had blessed me with smiles and caresses; or if they had, all my past life was now a blot, a blind vacancy in which I distinguished nothing. From my earliest remembrance I had been as I then was in height and proportion. I had never yet seen a being resembling me or who claimed any intercourse with me. What was I? The question again recurred, to be answered only with groans.

"I will soon explain to what these feelings tended, but allow me now to return to the cottagers, whose story excited in me such various feelings of indignation, delight, and wonder, but which all terminated in additional love and reverence for my protectors (for so I loved, in an innocent, half-painful self-deceit, to call them)."

CHAPTER VI

Some time elapsed before I learned the history of my friends. It was one which could not fail to impress itself deeply on my mind, unfolding as it did a number of circumstances, each interesting and wonderful to one so utterly inexperienced as I was.

"The name of the old man was De Lacey. He was descended from a good family in France, where he had lived for many years in affluence, respected by his superiors and beloved by his equals. His son was bred in the service of his country, and Agatha had ranked with ladies of the highest distinction. A few months before my arrival they had lived in a large and luxurious city called Paris, surrounded by friends and possessed of every enjoyment which virtue, refinement of intellect, or taste, accompanied by a moderate fortune, could afford.

"The father of Safie had been the cause of their ruin. He was a Turkish merchant and had inhabited Paris for many years, when, for some reason which I could not learn, he became obnoxious to the government. He was seized and cast into prison the very day that Safie arrived from Constantinople to join him. He was tried and condemned to death. The injustice of his sentence was very flagrant; all Paris was indignant; and it was judged that his religion and wealth rather than the crime alleged against him had been the cause of his condemnation.

"Felix had accidentally been present at the trial; his horror and indignation were uncontrollable when he heard the decision of the court. He made, at that moment, a solemn vow to deliver him and then looked around for the means. After many fruitless attempts to gain admittance to the prison, he found a strongly grated window in an unguarded part of the building, which lighted the dungeon of the unfortunate Muhammadan, who, loaded with chains, waited in despair the execution of the barbarous sentence. Felix visited the grate at night and made known to the prisoner his intentions in his favour. The Turk, amazed and delighted, endeavoured to kindle the zeal of his deliverer by promises of reward and wealth. Felix rejected his offers with contempt, yet when he saw the lovely Safie, who was allowed to visit her father and who by her gestures expressed her lively gratitude, the youth could not help owning to his own mind that the captive possessed a treasure which would fully reward his toil and hazard.

"The Turk quickly perceived the impression that his daughter had made on the heart of Felix and endeavoured to secure him more entirely in his interests by the promise of her hand in marriage so soon as he should be conveyed to a place of safety. Felix was too delicate to accept this offer, yet he looked forward to the probability of the event as to the consummation of his happiness.

"During the ensuing days, while the preparations were going forward for the escape of the merchant, the zeal of Felix was warmed by several letters that he received from this lovely girl, who found means to express her thoughts in the language of her lover by the aid of an old man, a servant of her father who understood French. She thanked him in the most ardent terms for his intended services towards her parent, and at the same time she gently deplored her own fate.

"I have copies of these letters, for I found means, during my residence in the hovel, to procure the implements of writing; and the letters were often in the hands of Felix or Agatha. Before I depart I will give them to you; they will prove the truth of my tale; but at present, as the sun is already far declined, I shall only have time to repeat the substance of them to you.

"Safie related that her mother was a Christian Arab, seized and made a slave by the Turks; recommended by her beauty, she had won the heart of the father of Safie, who married her. The young girl spoke in high and enthusiastic terms of her mother, who, born in freedom, spurned the bondage to which she was now reduced. She instructed her daughter in the tenets of her religion and taught her to aspire to higher powers of intellect and an independence of spirit forbidden to the female followers of Muhammad. This lady died, but her lessons were indelibly impressed on the mind of Safie, who sickened at the prospect of again returning to Asia and being immured within the walls of a harem, allowed only to occupy herself with infantile amusements, ill-suited to the temper of her soul, now accustomed to grand ideas and a noble emulation for virtue. The prospect of marrying a Christian and remaining in a country where women were allowed to take a rank in society was enchanting to her.

"The day for the execution of the Turk was fixed, but on the night previous to it he quitted his prison and before morning was distant many leagues from Paris. Felix had procured passports in the name of his father, sister, and himself. He had previously communicated his plan to the former, who aided the deceit by quitting his house, under the pretence of a journey and concealed himself, with his daughter, in an obscure part of Paris.

"Felix conducted the fugitives through France to Lyons and across Mont Cenis to Leghorn, where the merchant had decided to wait a favourable opportunity of passing into some part of the Turkish dominions.

"Safie resolved to remain with her father until the moment of his departure, before which time the Turk renewed his promise that she should be united to his deliverer; and Felix remained with them in expectation of that event; and in the meantime he enjoyed the society of the Arabian, who exhibited towards him the simplest and tenderest affection. They conversed with one another through the means of an interpreter, and sometimes with the interpretation of looks; and Safie sang to him the divine airs of her native country.

"The Turk allowed this intimacy to take place and encouraged the hopes of the youthful lovers, while in his heart he had formed far other plans. He loathed the idea that his daughter should be united to a Christian, but he feared the resentment of Felix if he should appear lukewarm, for he knew that he was still in the power of his deliverer if he should choose to betray him to the Italian state which they inhabited. He revolved a thousand plans by which he should be enabled to prolong the deceit until it might be no longer necessary, and secretly to take his daughter with him when he departed. His plans were facilitated by the news which arrived from Paris.

"The government of France were greatly enraged at the escape of their victim and spared no pains to detect and punish his deliverer. The plot of Felix was quickly discovered, and De Lacey and Agatha were thrown into prison. The news reached Felix and roused him from his dream of pleasure. His blind and aged father and his gentle sister lay in a noisome dungeon while he enjoyed the free air and the society of her whom he loved. This idea was torture to him. He quickly arranged with the Turk that if the latter should find a favourable opportunity for escape before Felix could return to Italy, Safie should remain as a boarder at a convent at Leghorn; and then, quitting the lovely Arabian, he hastened to Paris and delivered himself up to the vengeance of the law, hoping to free De Lacey and Agatha by this proceeding.

"He did not succeed. They remained confined for five months before the trial took place, the result of which deprived them of their fortune and condemned them to a perpetual exile from their native country.

"They found a miserable asylum in the cottage in Germany, where I discovered them. Felix soon learned that the treacherous Turk, for whom he and his family endured such unheard-of oppression, on discovering that his deliverer was thus reduced to poverty and ruin, became a traitor to good feeling and honour and had quitted Italy with his daughter, insultingly sending Felix a pittance of money to aid him, as he said, in some plan of future maintenance.

"Such were the events that preyed on the heart of Felix and rendered him, when I first saw him, the most miserable of his family. He could have endured poverty, and while this distress had been the meed of his virtue, he gloried in it; but the ingratitude of the Turk and the loss of his beloved Safie were misfortunes more bitter and irreparable. The arrival of the Arabian now infused new life into his soul.

"When the news reached Leghorn that Felix was deprived of his wealth and rank, the merchant commanded his daughter to think no more of her lover, but to prepare to return to her native country. The generous nature of Safie was outraged by this command; she attempted to expostulate with her father, but he left her angrily, reiterating his tyrannical mandate.

"A few days after, the Turk entered his daughter's apartment and told her hastily that he had reason to believe that his residence at Leghorn had been divulged and that he should speedily be delivered up to the French government; he had consequently hired a vessel to convey him to Constantinople, for which city he should sail in a few hours. He intended to leave his daughter under the care of a confidential servant, to follow at her leisure with the greater part of his property, which had not yet arrived at Leghorn.

"When alone, Safie resolved in her own mind the plan of conduct that it would become her to pursue in this emergency. A residence in Turkey was abhorrent to her; her religion and her feelings were alike averse to it. By some papers of her father which fell into her hands she heard of the exile of her lover and learnt the name of the spot where he then resided. She hesitated some time, but at length she formed her determination. Taking with her some jewels that belonged to her and a sum of money, she quitted Italy with an attendant, a native of Leghorn, but who understood the common language of Turkey, and departed for Germany.

"She arrived in safety at a town about twenty leagues from the cottage of De Lacey, when her attendant fell dangerously ill. Safie nursed her with the most devoted affection, but the poor girl died, and the Arabian was left alone, unacquainted with the language of the country and utterly ignorant of the customs of the world. She fell, however, into good hands. The Italian had mentioned the name of the spot for which they were bound, and after her death the woman of the house in which they had lived took care that Safie should arrive in safety at the cottage of her lover."

CHAPTER VII

Such was the history of my beloved cottagers. It impressed me deeply. I learned, from the views of social life which it developed, to admire their virtues and to deprecate the vices of mankind.

"As yet I looked upon crime as a distant evil, benevolence and generosity were ever present before me, inciting within me a desire to become an actor in the busy scene where so many admirable qualities were called forth and displayed. But in giving an account of the progress of my intellect, I must not omit a circumstance which occurred in the beginning of the month of August of the same year.

"One night during my accustomed visit to the neighbouring wood where I collected my own food and brought home firing for my protectors, I found on the ground a leathern portmanteau containing several articles of dress and some books. I eagerly seized the prize and returned with it to my hovel. Fortunately the books were written in the language, the elements of which I had acquired at the cottage; they consisted of *Paradise Lost*, a volume of Plutarch's *Lives*, and the *Sorrows of Werter*. The possession of these treasures gave me extreme delight; I now continually studied and exercised my mind upon these histories, whilst my friends were employed in their ordinary occupations.

"I can hardly describe to you the effect of these books. They produced in me an infinity of new images and feelings, that sometimes raised me to ecstasy, but more frequently sunk me into the lowest dejection. In the *Sorrows of Werter*, besides the interest of its simple and affecting story, so many opinions are canvassed and so many lights thrown upon what had hitherto been to me obscure subjects that I found in it a never-ending source of speculation and astonishment. The gentle and domestic manners it described, combined with lofty sentiments and feelings, which had for their object something out of self, accorded well with my experience among my protectors and with the wants which were forever alive in my own bosom. But I thought Werter himself a more divine being than I had ever beheld or imagined; his character contained no pretension, but it sank deep. The disquisitions upon death and suicide were calculated to fill me with wonder. I did not pretend to enter into the merits of the case, yet I inclined towards the opinions of the hero, whose extinction I wept, without precisely understanding it.

"As I read, however, I applied much personally to my own feelings and condition. I found myself similar yet at the same time strangely unlike to the beings concerning whom I read and to whose conversation I was a listener. I sympathised with and partly understood them, but I was unformed in mind; I was dependent on none and related to none. 'The path of my departure was free,' and there was none to lament my annihilation. My person was hideous and my stature gigantic. What did this mean? Who was I? What was I? Whence did I come? What was my destination? These questions continually recurred, but I was unable to solve them.

"The volume of Plutarch's *Lives* which I possessed contained the histories of the first founders of the ancient republics. This book had a far different effect upon me from the *Sorrows of Werter*. I learned from Werter's imaginations despondency and gloom, but Plutarch taught me high thoughts; he elevated me above the wretched sphere of my own reflections, to admire and love the heroes of past ages. Many things I read surpassed my understanding and experience. I had a very confused knowledge of kingdoms, wide extents of country, mighty rivers, and boundless seas. But I was perfectly unacquainted with towns and large assemblages of men. The cottage of my protectors had been the only school in which I had studied human nature, but this book developed new and mightier scenes of action. I read of men concerned in public affairs, governing or massacring their species. I felt the greatest ardour for virtue rise within me, and abhorrence for vice, as far as I understood the signification of those terms, relative as they were, as I applied them, to pleasure and pain alone. Induced by these feelings, I was of course led to admire peaceable lawgivers, Numa, Solon, and Lycurgus, in preference to Romulus and Theseus. The patriarchal lives of my protectors caused these impressions to take a firm hold on my mind; perhaps, if my first introduction to humanity had been made by a young soldier, burning for glory and slaughter, I should have been imbued with different sensations.

"But *Paradise Lost* excited different and far deeper emotions. I read it, as I had read the other volumes which had fallen into my hands, as a true history. It moved every feeling of wonder and awe that the picture of an omnipotent God warring with his creatures was capable of exciting. I often referred the several situations, as their similarity struck me, to my own. Like Adam, I was apparently united by no link to any other being in existence; but his state was far different from mine in every other respect. He had come forth from the hands of God a perfect creature, happy and prosperous, guarded by the especial care of his Creator; he was allowed to converse with and acquire knowledge from beings of a superior nature, but I was wretched, helpless, and alone. Many times I considered Satan as the fitter emblem of my condition, for often, like him, when I viewed the bliss of my protectors, the bitter gall of envy rose within me.

"Another circumstance strengthened and confirmed these feelings. Soon after my arrival in the hovel I discovered some papers in the pocket of the dress which I had taken from your laboratory. At first I had neglected them, but now that I was able to decipher the characters in which they were written, I began to study them with diligence. It was your journal of the four months that preceded my creation. You minutely described in these papers every step you took in the progress of your work; this history was mingled with accounts of domestic occurrences. You doubtless recollect these papers. Here they are. Everything is related in them which bears reference to my accursed origin; the whole detail of that series of disgusting circumstances which produced it is set in view; the minutest description of my odious and loathsome person is given, in language which painted your own horrors and rendered mine indelible. I sickened as I read. 'Hateful day when I received life!' I exclaimed in agony. 'Accursed creator! Why did you form a monster so hideous that even you turned from me in disgust? God, in pity, made man beautiful and alluring, after his own image; but my form is a filthy type of yours, more horrid even from the very resemblance. Satan had his companions, fellow devils, to admire and encourage him, but I am solitary and abhorred.'

"These were the reflections of my hours of despondency and solitude; but when I contemplated the virtues of the cottagers, their amiable and benevolent dispositions, I persuaded myself that when they should become acquainted with my admiration of their virtues they would compassionate me and overlook my personal deformity. Could they turn from their door one, however monstrous, who solicited their compassion and friendship? I resolved, at least, not to despair, but in every way to fit myself for an interview with them which would decide my fate. I postponed this attempt for some months longer, for the importance attached to its success inspired me with a dread lest I should fail. Besides, I found that my understanding improved so much with every day's experience that I was unwilling to commence this undertaking until a few more months should have added to my sagacity.

"Several changes, in the meantime, took place in the cottage. The presence of Safie diffused happiness among its inhabitants, and I also found that a greater degree of plenty reigned there. Felix and Agatha spent more time in amusement and conversation, and were assisted in their labours by servants. They did not appear rich, but they were contented and happy; their feelings were serene and peaceful, while mine became every day more tumultuous. Increase of knowledge only discovered to me more clearly what a wretched outcast I was. I cherished hope, it is true, but it vanished when I beheld my person reflected in water or my shadow in the moonshine, even as that frail image and that inconstant shade.

"I endeavoured to crush these fears and to fortify myself for the trial which in a few months I resolved to undergo; and sometimes I allowed my thoughts, unchecked by reason, to ramble in the fields of Paradise, and dared to fancy amiable and lovely creatures sympathising with my feelings and cheering my gloom; their angelic countenances breathed smiles of consolation. But it was all a dream; no Eve soothed my sorrows nor shared my thoughts; I was alone. I remembered Adam's supplication to his Creator. But where was mine? He had abandoned me, and in the bitterness of my heart I cursed him.

"Autumn passed thus. I saw, with surprise and grief, the leaves decay and fall, and nature again assume the barren and bleak appearance it had worn when I first beheld the woods and the lovely moon. Yet I did not heed the bleakness of the weather; I was better fitted by my conformation for the endurance of cold than heat. But my chief delights were the sight of the flowers, the birds, and all the gay apparel of summer; when those deserted me,

I turned with more attention towards the cottagers. Their happiness was not decreased by the absence of summer. They loved and sympathised with one another; and their joys, depending on each other, were not interrupted by the casualties that took place around them. The more I saw of them, the greater became my desire to claim their protection and kindness; my heart yearned to be known and loved by these amiable creatures; to see their sweet looks directed towards me with affection was the utmost limit of my ambition. I dared not think that they would turn them from me with disdain and horror. The poor that stopped at their door were never driven away. I asked, it is true, for greater treasures than a little food or rest: I required kindness and sympathy; but I did not believe myself utterly unworthy of it.

"The winter advanced, and an entire revolution of the seasons had taken place since I awoke into life. My attention at this time was solely directed towards my plan of introducing myself into the cottage of my protectors. I revolved many projects, but that on which I finally fixed was to enter the dwelling when the blind old man should be alone. I had sagacity enough to discover that the unnatural hideousness of my person was the chief object of horror with those who had formerly beheld me. My voice, although harsh, had nothing terrible in it; I thought, therefore, that if in the absence of his children I could gain the good will and mediation of the old De Lacey, I might by his means be tolerated by my younger protectors.

"One day, when the sun shone on the red leaves that strewed the ground and diffused cheerfulness, although it denied warmth, Safie, Agatha, and Felix departed on a long country walk, and the old man, at his own desire, was left alone in the cottage. When his children had departed, he took up his guitar and played several mournful but sweet airs, more sweet and mournful than I had ever heard him play before. At first his countenance was illuminated with pleasure, but as he continued, thoughtfulness and sadness succeeded; at length, laying aside the instrument, he sat absorbed in reflection.

"My heart beat quick; this was the hour and moment of trial, which would decide my hopes or realize my fears. The servants were gone to a neighbouring fair. All was silent in and around the cottage; it was an excellent opportunity; yet, when I proceeded to execute my plan, my limbs failed me and I sank to the ground. Again I rose, and exerting all the firmness of which I was master, removed the planks which I had placed before my hovel to conceal my retreat. The fresh air revived me, and with renewed determination I approached the door of their cottage.

"I knocked. 'Who is there?' said the old man. 'Come in.'

"I entered. 'Pardon this intrusion,' said I; 'I am a traveller in want of a little rest; you would greatly oblige me if you would allow me to remain a few minutes before the fire.'

"'Enter,' said De Lacey, 'and I will try in what manner I can to relieve your wants; but, unfortunately, my children are from home, and as I am blind, I am afraid I shall find it difficult to procure food for you.'

"'Do not trouble yourself, my kind host; I have food; it is warmth and rest only that I need.'

"I sat down, and a silence ensued. I knew that every minute was precious to me, yet I remained irresolute in what manner to commence the interview, when the old man addressed me. 'By your language, stranger, I suppose you are my countryman; are you French?'

"'No; but I was educated by a French family and understand that language only. I am now going to claim the protection of some friends, whom I sincerely love, and of whose favour I have some hopes.'

"'Are they Germans?'

"'No, they are French. But let us change the subject. I am an unfortunate and deserted creature; I look around and I have no relation or friend upon earth. These amiable people to whom I go have never seen me and know little of me. I am full of fears, for if I fail there, I am an outcast in the world forever.'

"'Do not despair. To be friendless is indeed to be unfortunate, but the hearts of men, when unprejudiced by any obvious self-interest, are full of brotherly love and charity. Rely, therefore, on your hopes; and if these friends are good and amiable, do not despair.'

"'They are kind—they are the most excellent creatures in the world; but, unfortunately, they are prejudiced against me. I have good dispositions; my life has been hitherto harmless and in some degree beneficial; but a fatal prejudice clouds their eyes, and where they ought to see a feeling and kind friend, they behold only a detestable monster.'

"'That is indeed unfortunate; but if you are really blameless, cannot you undeceive them?'

"'I am about to undertake that task; and it is on that account that I feel so many overwhelming terrors. I tenderly love these friends; I have, unknown to them, been for many months in the habits of daily kindness towards them; but they believe that I wish to injure them, and it is that prejudice which I wish to overcome.'

"'Where do these friends reside?'

"'Near this spot.'

"The old man paused and then continued, 'If you will unreservedly confide to me the particulars of your tale, I perhaps may be of use in undeceiving them. I am blind and cannot judge of your countenance, but there is something in your words which persuades me that you are sincere. I am poor and an exile, but it will afford me true pleasure to be in any way serviceable to a human creature.'

"'Excellent man! I thank you and accept your generous offer. You raise me from the dust by this kindness; and I trust that, by your aid, I shall not be driven from the society and sympathy of your fellow creatures.'

"'Heaven forbid! Even if you were really criminal, for that can only drive you to desperation, and not instigate you to virtue. I also am unfortunate; I and my family have been condemned, although innocent; judge, therefore, if I do not feel for your misfortunes.'

"'How can I thank you, my best and only benefactor? From your lips first have I heard the voice of kindness directed towards me; I shall be forever grateful; and your present humanity assures me of success with those friends whom I am on the point of meeting.'

"'May I know the names and residence of those friends?'

"I paused. This, I thought, was the moment of decision, which was to rob me of or bestow happiness on me forever. I struggled vainly for firmness sufficient to answer him, but the effort destroyed all my remaining strength; I sank on the chair and sobbed aloud. At that moment I heard the steps of my younger protectors. I had not a moment to lose, but seizing the hand of the old man, I cried, 'Now is the time! Save and protect me! You and your family are the friends whom I seek. Do not you desert me in the hour of trial!'

"'Great God!' exclaimed the old man. 'Who are you?'

"At that instant the cottage door was opened, and Felix, Safie, and Agatha entered. Who can describe their horror and consternation on beholding me? Agatha fainted, and Safie, unable to attend to her friend, rushed out of the cottage. Felix darted forward, and with supernatural force tore me from his father, to whose knees I clung: in a transport of fury, he dashed me to the ground and struck me violently with a stick. I could have torn him limb from limb, as the lion rends the antelope. But my heart sank within me as with bitter sickness, and I refrained. I saw him on the point of repeating his blow, when, overcome by pain and anguish, I quitted the cottage, and in the general tumult escaped unperceived to my hovel."

CHAPTER VIII

Cursed, cursed creator! Why did I live? Why, in that instant, did I not extinguish the spark of existence which you had so wantonly bestowed? I know not; despair had not yet taken possession of me; my feelings were those of rage and revenge. I could with pleasure have destroyed the cottage and its inhabitants and have glutted myself with their shrieks and misery.

"When night came I quitted my retreat and wandered in the wood; and now, no longer restrained by the fear of discovery, I gave vent to my anguish in fearful howlings. I was like a wild beast that had broken the toils, destroying the objects that obstructed me and ranging through the wood with a staglike swiftness. Oh! What a miserable night I passed! The cold stars shone in mockery, and the bare trees waved their branches above me; now and then the sweet voice of a bird burst forth amidst the universal stillness. All, save I, were at rest or in enjoyment; I, like the archfiend, bore a hell within me, and finding myself unsympathised with, wished to tear up the trees, spread havoc and destruction around me, and then to have sat down and enjoyed the ruin.

"But this was a luxury of sensation that could not endure; I became fatigued with excess of bodily exertion and sank on the damp grass in the sick impotence of despair. There was none among the myriads of men that existed who would pity or assist me; and should I feel kindness towards my enemies? No; from that moment I declared everlasting war against the species, and more than all, against him who had formed me and sent me forth to this insupportable misery.

"The sun rose; I heard the voices of men and knew that it was impossible to return to my retreat during that day. Accordingly I hid myself in some thick underwood, determining to devote the ensuing hours to reflection on my situation.

"The pleasant sunshine and the pure air of day restored me to some degree of tranquillity; and when I considered what had passed at the cottage, I could not help believing that I had been too hasty in my conclusions. I had certainly acted imprudently. It was apparent that my conversation had interested the father in my behalf, and I was a fool in having exposed my person to the horror of his children. I ought to have familiarized the old De Lacey to me, and by degrees to have discovered myself to the rest of his family, when they should have been prepared for my approach. But I did not believe my errors to be irretrievable, and after much consideration I resolved to return to the cottage, seek the old man, and by my representations win him to my party.

"These thoughts calmed me, and in the afternoon I sank into a profound sleep; but the fever of my blood did not allow me to be visited by peaceful dreams. The horrible scene of the preceding day was forever acting before my eyes; the females were flying and the enraged Felix tearing me from his father's feet. I awoke exhausted, and finding that it was already night, I crept forth from my hiding-place, and went in search of food.

"When my hunger was appeased, I directed my steps towards the well-known path that conducted to the cottage. All there was at peace. I crept into my hovel and remained in silent expectation of the accustomed hour when the family arose. That hour passed, the sun mounted high in the heavens, but the cottagers did not appear. I trembled violently, apprehending some dreadful misfortune. The inside of the cottage was dark, and I heard no motion; I cannot describe the agony of this suspense.

"Presently two countrymen passed by, but pausing near the cottage, they entered into conversation, using violent gesticulations; but I did not understand what they said, as they spoke the language of the country, which differed from that of my protectors. Soon after, however, Felix approached with another man; I was surprised, as I knew that he had not quitted the cottage that morning, and waited anxiously to discover from his discourse the meaning of these unusual appearances.

"'Do you consider,' said his companion to him, 'that you will be obliged to pay three months' rent and to lose the produce of your garden? I do not wish to take any unfair advantage, and I beg therefore that you will take some days to consider of your determination.'

"'It is utterly useless,' replied Felix; 'we can never again inhabit your cottage. The life of my father is in the greatest danger, owing to the dreadful circumstance that I have related. My wife and my sister will never recover from their horror. I entreat you not to reason with me any more. Take possession of your tenement and let me fly from this place.'

"Felix trembled violently as he said this. He and his companion entered the cottage, in which they remained for a few minutes, and then departed. I never saw any of the family of De Lacey more.

"I continued for the remainder of the day in my hovel in a state of utter and stupid despair. My protectors had departed and had broken the only link that held me to the world. For the first time the feelings of revenge and hatred filled my bosom, and I did not strive to control them, but allowing myself to be borne away by the stream, I bent my mind towards injury and death. When I thought of my friends, of the mild voice of De Lacey, the gentle eyes of Agatha, and the exquisite beauty of the Arabian, these thoughts vanished and a gush of tears somewhat soothed me. But again when I reflected that they had spurned and deserted me, anger returned, a rage of anger, and unable to injure anything human, I turned my fury towards inanimate objects. As night advanced I placed a variety of combustibles around the cottage, and after having destroyed every vestige of cultivation in the garden, I waited with forced impatience until the moon had sunk to commence my operations.

"As the night advanced, a fierce wind arose from the woods and quickly dispersed the clouds that had loitered in the heavens; the blast tore along like a mighty avalanche and produced a kind of insanity in my spirits that burst all bounds of reason and reflection. I lighted the dry branch of a tree and danced with fury around the devoted cottage, my eyes still fixed on the western horizon, the edge of which the moon nearly touched. A part of its orb was at length hid, and I waved my brand; it sank, and with a loud scream I fired the straw, and heath, and bushes, which I had collected. The wind fanned the fire, and the cottage was quickly enveloped by the flames, which clung to it and licked it with their forked and destroying tongues.

"As soon as I was convinced that no assistance could save any part of the habitation, I quitted the scene and sought for refuge in the woods.

"And now, with the world before me, whither should I bend my steps? I resolved to fly far from the scene of my misfortunes; but to me, hated and despised, every country must be equally horrible. At length the thought of you crossed my mind. I learned from your papers that you were my father, my creator; and to whom could I apply with more fitness than to him who had given me life? Among the lessons that Felix had bestowed upon Safie, geography had not been omitted; I had learned from these the relative situations of the different countries of the earth. You had mentioned Geneva as the name of your native town, and towards this place I resolved to proceed.

"But how was I to direct myself? I knew that I must travel in a southwesterly direction to reach my destination, but the sun was my only guide. I did not know the names of the towns that I was to pass through, nor could I ask information from a single human being; but I did not despair. From you only could I hope for succour, although towards you I felt no sentiment but that of hatred. Unfeeling, heartless creator! You had endowed me with perceptions and passions and then cast me abroad an object for the scorn and horror of mankind. But on you only had I any claim for pity and redress, and from you I determined to seek that justice which I vainly attempted to gain from any other being that wore the human form.

"My travels were long and the sufferings I endured intense. It was late in autumn when I quitted the district where I had so long resided. I travelled only at night, fearful of encountering the visage of a human being. Nature decayed around me, and the sun became heatless; rain and snow poured around me; mighty rivers were frozen; the surface of the earth was hard and chill, and bare, and I found no shelter. Oh, earth! How often did I imprecate curses on the cause of my being! The mildness of my nature had fled, and all within me was turned to gall and bitterness. The nearer I approached to your habitation, the more deeply did I feel the spirit of revenge enkindled in my heart. Snow fell, and the waters were hardened, but I rested not. A few incidents now and then directed me, and I possessed a map of the country; but I often wandered wide from my path. The agony of my feelings allowed me no respite; no incident occurred from which my rage and misery could not extract its food; but a circumstance that happened when I arrived on the confines of Switzerland, when the sun had recovered its warmth and the earth again began to look green, confirmed in an especial manner the bitterness and horror of my feelings.

"I generally rested during the day and travelled only when I was secured by night from the view of man. One morning, however, finding that my path lay through a deep wood, I ventured to continue my journey after the sun had risen; the day, which was one of the first of spring, cheered even me by the loveliness of its sunshine and the balminess of the air. I felt emotions of gentleness and pleasure, that had long appeared dead, revive within me. Half surprised by the novelty of these sensations, I allowed myself to be borne away by them, and forgetting my solitude and deformity, dared to be happy. Soft tears again bedewed my cheeks, and I even raised my humid eyes with thankfulness towards the blessed sun, which bestowed such joy upon me.

"I continued to wind among the paths of the wood, until I came to its boundary, which was skirted by a deep and rapid river, into which many of the trees bent their branches, now budding with the fresh spring. Here I paused, not exactly knowing what path to pursue, when I heard the sound of voices, that induced me to conceal myself under the shade of a cypress. I was scarcely hid when a young girl came running towards the spot where I was concealed, laughing, as if she ran from someone in sport. She continued her course along the precipitous sides of the river, when suddenly her foot slipped, and she fell into the rapid stream. I rushed from my hiding-place and with extreme labour, from the force of the current, saved her and dragged her to shore. She was senseless, and I endeavoured by every means in my power to restore animation, when I was suddenly interrupted by the approach of a rustic, who was probably the person from whom she had playfully fled. On seeing me, he darted towards me, and tearing the girl from my arms, hastened towards the deeper parts of the wood. I followed speedily, I hardly knew why; but when the man saw me draw near, he aimed a gun, which he carried, at my body and fired. I sank to the ground, and my injurer, with increased swiftness, escaped into the wood.

"This was then the reward of my benevolence! I had saved a human being from destruction, and as a recompense I now writhed under the miserable pain of a wound which shattered the flesh and bone. The feelings of kindness and gentleness which I had entertained but a few moments before gave place to hellish rage and gnashing of teeth. Inflamed by pain, I vowed eternal hatred and vengeance to all mankind. But the agony of my wound overcame me; my pulses paused, and I fainted.

"For some weeks I led a miserable life in the woods, endeavouring to cure the wound which I had received. The ball had entered my shoulder, and I knew not whether it had remained there or passed through; at any rate I had no means of extracting it. My sufferings were augmented also by the oppressive sense of the injustice and ingratitude of their infliction. My daily vows rose for revenge—a deep and deadly revenge, such as would alone compensate for the outrages and anguish I had endured.

"After some weeks my wound healed, and I continued my journey. The labours I endured were no longer to be alleviated by the bright sun or gentle breezes of spring; all joy was but a mockery which insulted my desolate state and made me feel more painfully that I was not made for the enjoyment of pleasure.

"But my toils now drew near a close, and in two months from this time I reached the environs of Geneva.

"It was evening when I arrived, and I retired to a hiding-place among the fields that surround it to meditate in what manner I should apply to you. I was oppressed by fatigue and hunger and far too unhappy to enjoy the gentle breezes of evening or the prospect of the sun setting behind the stupendous mountains of Jura.

"At this time a slight sleep relieved me from the pain of reflection, which was disturbed by the approach of a beautiful child, who came running into the recess I had chosen, with all the sportiveness of infancy. Suddenly, as I gazed on him, an idea seized me that this little creature was unprejudiced and had lived too short a time to have imbibed a horror of deformity. If, therefore, I could seize him and educate him as my companion and friend, I should not be so desolate in this peopled earth.

"Urged by this impulse, I seized on the boy as he passed and drew him towards me. As soon as he beheld my form, he placed his hands before his eyes and uttered a shrill scream; I drew his hand forcibly from his face and said, 'Child, what is the meaning of this? I do not intend to hurt you; listen to me.'

"He struggled violently. 'Let me go,' he cried. 'Monster! Ugly wretch! You wish to eat me and tear me to pieces. You are an ogre. Let me go, or I will tell my papa.'

" 'Boy, you will never see your father again; you must come with me.'

" 'Hideous monster! Let me go. My papa is a syndic—he is M. Frankenstein— he will punish you. You dare not keep me.'

" 'Frankenstein! You belong then to my enemy—to him towards whom I have sworn eternal revenge; you shall be my first victim.'

"The child still struggled, and loaded me with epithets which carried despair to my heart; I grasped his throat to silence him, and in a moment he lay dead at my feet.

"I gazed on my victim, and my heart swelled with exultation and hellish triumph; clapping my hands, I exclaimed, 'I too can create desolation; my enemy is not invulnerable; this death will carry despair to him, and a thousand other miseries shall torment and destroy him.'

"As I fixed my eyes on the child, I saw something glittering on his breast. I took it; it was a portrait of a most lovely woman. In spite of my malignity, it softened and attracted me. For a few moments I gazed with delight on her dark eyes, fringed by deep lashes, and her lovely lips; but presently my rage returned; I remembered that I was forever deprived of the delights that such beautiful creatures could bestow and that she whose resemblance I contemplated would, in regarding me, have changed that air of divine benignity to one expressive of disgust and affright.

"Can you wonder that such thoughts transported me with rage? I only wonder that at that moment, instead of venting my sensations in exclamations and agony, I did not rush among mankind and perish in the attempt to destroy them.

"While I was overcome by these feelings, I left the spot where I had committed the murder, and seeking a more secluded hiding-place, I entered a barn which had appeared to me to be empty. A woman was sleeping on some straw; she was young, not indeed so beautiful as her whose portrait I held, but of an agreeable aspect and blooming in the loveliness of youth and health. Here, I thought, is one of those whose joy-imparting smiles are bestowed on all but me. And then I bent over her and whispered, 'Awake, fairest, thy lover is near—he who would give his life but to obtain one look of affection from thine eyes; my beloved, awake!'

"The sleeper stirred; a thrill of terror ran through me. Should she indeed awake, and see me, and curse me, and denounce the murderer? Thus would she assuredly act if her darkened eyes opened and she beheld me. The thought was madness; it stirred the fiend within me—not I, but she, shall suffer; the murder I have committed because I am forever robbed of all that she could give me, she shall atone. The crime had its source in her; be hers the punishment! Thanks to the lessons of Felix and the sanguinary laws of man, I had learned now to work mischief. I bent over her and placed the portrait securely in one of the folds of her dress. She moved again, and I fled.

"For some days I haunted the spot where these scenes had taken place, sometimes wishing to see you, sometimes resolved to quit the world and its miseries forever. At length I wandered towards these mountains, and have ranged through their immense recesses, consumed by a burning passion which you alone can gratify. We may not part until you have promised to comply with my requisition. I am alone and miserable; man will not associate with me; but one as deformed and horrible as myself would not deny herself to me. My companion must be of the same species and have the same defects. This being you must create."

CHAPTER IX

The being finished speaking, and fixed his looks upon me in the expectation of a reply. But I was bewildered, perplexed, and unable to arrange my ideas sufficiently to understand the full extent of his proposition. He continued.

"You must create a female for me, with whom I can live in the interchange of those sympathies necessary for my being. This you alone can do, and I demand it of you as a right which you must not refuse to concede."

The latter part of his tale had kindled anew in me the anger that had died away while he narrated his peaceful life among the cottagers, and as he said this I could no longer suppress the rage that burned within me.

"I do refuse it," I replied; "and no torture shall ever extort a consent from me. You may render me the most miserable of men, but you shall never make me base in my own eyes. Shall I create another like yourself, whose joint wickedness might desolate the world? Begone! I have answered you; you may torture me, but I will never consent."

"You are in the wrong," replied the fiend; "and instead of threatening, I am content to reason with you. I am malicious because I am miserable. Am I not shunned and hated by all mankind? You, my creator, would tear me to pieces and triumph; remember that, and tell me why I should pity man more than he pities me? You would not call it murder if you could precipitate me into one of those ice-rifts and destroy my frame, the work of your own hands. Shall I respect man when he condemns me? Let him live with me in the interchange of kindness, and instead of injury I would bestow every benefit upon him with tears of gratitude at his acceptance. But that cannot be; the human senses are insurmountable barriers to our union. Yet mine shall not be the submission of abject slavery. I will revenge my injuries; if I cannot inspire love, I will cause fear, and chiefly towards you my archenemy, because my creator, do I swear inextinguishable hatred. Have a care; I will work at your destruction, nor finish until I desolate your heart, so that you shall curse the hour of your birth."

A fiendish rage animated him as he said this; his face was wrinkled into contortions too horrible for human eyes to behold; but presently he calmed himself and proceeded.

"I intended to reason. This passion is detrimental to me, for you do not reflect that you are the cause of its excess. If any being felt emotions of benevolence towards me, I should return them a hundred and a hundredfold; for that one creature's sake I would make peace with the whole kind! But I now indulge in dreams of bliss that cannot be realized. What I ask of you is reasonable and moderate; I demand a creature of another sex, but as hideous as myself; the gratification is small, but it is all that I can receive, and it shall content me. It is true, we shall be monsters, cut off from all the world; but on that account we shall be more attached to one another. Our lives will not be happy, but they will be harmless and free from the misery I now feel. Oh! My creator, make me happy; let me feel gratitude towards you for one benefit! Let me see that I excite the sympathy of some existing thing; do not deny me my request!"

I was moved. I shuddered when I thought of the possible consequences of my consent, but I felt that there was some justice in his argument. His tale and the feelings he now expressed proved him to be a creature of fine sensations, and did I not as his maker owe him all the portion of happiness that it was in my power to bestow? He saw my change of feeling and continued.

"If you consent, neither you nor any other human being shall ever see us again; I will go to the vast wilds of South America. My food is not that of man; I do not destroy the lamb and the kid to glut my appetite; acorns and berries afford me sufficient nourishment. My companion will be of the same nature as myself and will be content with the same fare. We shall make our bed of dried leaves; the sun will shine on us as on man and will ripen our food. The picture I present to you is peaceful and human, and you must feel that you could deny it only in the wantonness of power and cruelty. Pitiless as you have been towards me, I now see compassion in your eyes; let me seize the favourable moment and persuade you to promise what I so ardently desire."

"You propose," replied I, "to fly from the habitations of man, to dwell in those wilds where the beasts of the field will be your only companions. How can you, who long for the love and sympathy of man, persevere in this exile? You will return and again seek their kindness, and you will meet with their detestation; your evil passions will be renewed, and you will then have a companion to aid you in the task of destruction. This may not be; cease to argue the point, for I cannot consent."

"How inconstant are your feelings! But a moment ago you were moved by my representations, and why do you again harden yourself to my complaints? I swear to you, by the earth which I inhabit, and by you that made me, that with the companion you bestow I will quit the neighbourhood of man and dwell, as it may chance, in the most savage of places. My evil passions will have fled, for I shall meet with sympathy! My life will flow quietly away, and in my dying moments I shall not curse my maker."

His words had a strange effect upon me. I compassionated him and sometimes felt a wish to console him, but when I looked upon him, when I saw the filthy mass that moved and talked, my heart sickened and my feelings were altered to those of horror and hatred. I tried to stifle these sensations; I thought that as I could not sympathise with him, I had no right to withhold from him the small portion of happiness which was yet in my power to bestow.

"You swear," I said, "to be harmless; but have you not already shown a degree of malice that should reasonably make me distrust you? May not even this be a feint that will increase your triumph by affording a wider scope for your revenge?"

"How is this? I must not be trifled with, and I demand an answer. If I have no ties and no affections, hatred and vice must be my portion; the love of another will destroy the cause of my crimes, and I shall become a thing of whose existence everyone will be ignorant. My vices are the children of a forced solitude that I abhor, and my virtues will necessarily arise when I live in communion with an equal. I shall feel the affections of a sensitive being and become linked to the chain of existence and events from which I am now excluded."

I paused some time to reflect on all he had related and the various arguments which he had employed. I thought of the promise of virtues which he had displayed on the opening of his existence and the subsequent blight of all kindly feeling by the loathing and scorn which his protectors had manifested towards him. His power and threats were not omitted in my calculations; a creature who could exist in the ice caves of the glaciers and hide himself from pursuit among the ridges of inaccessible precipices was a being possessing faculties it would be vain to cope with. After a long pause of reflection I concluded that the justice due both to him and my fellow creatures demanded of me that I should comply with his request. Turning to him, therefore, I said:

"I consent to your demand, on your solemn oath to quit Europe forever, and every other place in the neighbourhood of man, as soon as I shall deliver into your hands a female who will accompany you in your exile."

"I swear," he cried, "by the sun, and by the blue sky of heaven, and by the fire of love that burns my heart, that if you grant my prayer, while they exist you shall never behold me again. Depart to your home and commence your labours; I shall watch their progress with unutterable anxiety; and fear not but that when you are ready I shall appear."

Saying this, he suddenly quitted me, fearful, perhaps, of any change in my sentiments. I saw him descend the mountain with greater speed than the flight of an eagle, and quickly lost among the undulations of the sea of ice.

His tale had occupied the whole day, and the sun was upon the verge of the horizon when he departed. I knew that I ought to hasten my descent towards the valley, as I should soon be encompassed in darkness; but my heart was heavy, and my steps slow. The labour of winding among the little paths of the mountain and fixing my feet firmly as I advanced perplexed me, occupied as I was by the emotions which the occurrences of the day had produced. Night was far advanced when I came to the halfway resting-place and seated myself beside the fountain. The stars shone at intervals as the clouds passed from over them; the dark pines rose before me, and every here and there a broken tree lay on the ground; it was a scene of wonderful solemnity and stirred strange thoughts within me. I wept bitterly, and clasping my hands in agony, I exclaimed, "Oh! Stars and clouds and winds, ye are all about to mock me; if ye really pity me, crush sensation and memory; let me become as nought; but if not, depart, depart, and leave me in darkness."

These were wild and miserable thoughts, but I cannot describe to you how the eternal twinkling of the stars weighed upon me and how I listened to every blast of wind as if it were a dull ugly siroc on its way to consume me.

Morning dawned before I arrived at the village of Chamounix; I took no rest, but returned immediately to Geneva. Even in my own heart I could give no expression to my sensations—they weighed on me with a mountain's weight and their excess destroyed my agony beneath them. Thus I returned home, and entering the house, presented myself to the family. My haggard and wild appearance awoke intense alarm, but I answered no question, scarcely did I speak. I felt as if I were placed under a ban—as if I had no right to claim their sympathies—as if never more might I enjoy companionship with them. Yet even thus I loved them to adoration; and to save them, I resolved to dedicate myself to my most abhorred task. The prospect of such an occupation made every other circumstance of existence pass before me like a dream, and that thought only had to me the reality of life.

Volume Three

CHAPTER I

Day after day, week after week, passed away on my return to Geneva; and I could not collect the courage to recommence my work. I feared the vengeance of the disappointed fiend, yet I was unable to overcome my repugnance to the task which was enjoined me. I found that I could not compose a female without again devoting several months to profound study and laborious disquisition. I had heard of some discoveries having been made by an English philosopher, the knowledge of which was material to my success, and I sometimes thought of obtaining my father's consent to visit England for this purpose; but I clung to every pretence of delay and shrank from taking the first step in an undertaking whose immediate necessity began to appear less absolute to me. A change indeed had taken place in me; my health, which had hitherto declined, was now much restored; and my spirits, when unchecked by the memory of my unhappy promise, rose proportionably. My father saw this change with pleasure, and he turned his thoughts towards the best method of eradicating the remains of my melancholy, which every now and then would return by fits, and with a devouring blackness overcast the approaching sunshine. At these moments I took refuge in the most perfect solitude. I passed whole days on the lake alone in a little boat, watching the clouds and listening to the rippling of the waves, silent and listless. But the fresh air and bright sun seldom failed to restore me to some degree of composure, and on my return I met the salutations of my friends with a readier smile and a more cheerful heart.

It was after my return from one of these rambles that my father, calling me aside, thus addressed me:

"I am happy to remark, my dear son, that you have resumed your former pleasures and seem to be returning to yourself. And yet you are still unhappy and still avoid our society. For some time I was lost in conjecture as to the cause of this, but yesterday an idea struck me, and if it is well founded, I conjure you to avow it. Reserve on such a point would be not only useless, but draw down treble misery on us all."

I trembled violently at his exordium, and my father continued:

"I confess, my son, that I have always looked forward to your marriage with our dear Elizabeth as the tie of our domestic comfort and the stay of my declining years. You were attached to each other from your earliest infancy; you studied together, and appeared, in dispositions and tastes, entirely suited to one another. But so blind is the experience of man that what I conceived to be the best assistants to my plan may have entirely destroyed it. You, perhaps, regard her as your sister, without any wish that she might become your wife. Nay, you may have met with another whom you may love; and considering yourself as bound in honour to Elizabeth, this struggle may occasion the poignant misery which you appear to feel."

"My dear father, reassure yourself. I love my cousin tenderly and sincerely. I never saw any woman who excited, as Elizabeth does, my warmest admiration and affection. My future hopes and prospects are entirely bound up in the expectation of our union."

"The expression of your sentiments of this subject, my dear Victor, gives me more pleasure than I have for some time experienced. If you feel thus, we shall assuredly be happy, however present events may cast a gloom over us. But it is this gloom which appears to have taken so strong a hold of your mind that I wish to dissipate. Tell me, therefore, whether you object to an immediate solemnization of the marriage. We have been unfortunate, and recent events have drawn us from that everyday tranquillity befitting my years and infirmities. You are younger; yet I do not suppose, possessed as you are of a competent fortune, that an early marriage would at all interfere with any future plans of honour and utility that you may have formed. Do not suppose, however, that I wish to dictate happiness to you or that a delay on your part would cause me any serious uneasiness. Interpret my words with candour and answer me, I conjure you, with confidence and sincerity."

I listened to my father in silence and remained for some time incapable of offering any reply. I revolved rapidly in my mind a multitude of thoughts and endeavoured to arrive at some conclusion. Alas! To me the idea of an immediate union with my Elizabeth was one of horror and dismay. I was bound by a solemn promise which I had not yet fulfilled and dared not break, or if I did, what manifold miseries might not impend over me and my devoted family! Could I enter into a festival with this deadly weight yet hanging round my neck and bowing me to the ground? I must perform my engagement and let the monster depart with his mate before I allowed myself to enjoy the delight of a union from which I expected peace.

I remembered also the necessity imposed upon me of either journeying to England or entering into a long correspondence with those philosophers of that country whose knowledge and discoveries were of indispensable use to me in my present undertaking. The latter method of obtaining the desired intelligence was dilatory and unsatisfactory; besides, I had an insurmountable aversion to the idea of engaging myself in my loathsome task in my father's house while in habits of familiar intercourse with those I loved. I knew that a thousand fearful accidents might occur, the slightest of which would disclose a tale to thrill all connected with me with horror. I was aware also that I should often lose all self-command, all capacity of hiding the harrowing sensations that would possess me during the progress of my unearthly occupation. I must absent myself from all I loved while thus employed. Once commenced, it would quickly be achieved, and I might be restored to my family in peace and happiness. My promise fulfilled, the monster would depart forever. Or (so my fond fancy imaged) some accident might meanwhile occur to destroy him and put an end to my slavery forever.

These feelings dictated my answer to my father. I expressed a wish to visit England, but concealing the true reasons of this request, I clothed my desires under a guise which excited no suspicion, while I urged my desire with an earnestness that easily induced my father to comply. After so long a period of an absorbing melancholy that resembled madness in its intensity and effects, he was glad to find that I was capable of taking pleasure in the idea of such a journey, and he hoped that change of scene and varied amusement would, before my return, have restored me entirely to myself.

The duration of my absence was left to my own choice; a few months, or at most a year, was the period contemplated. One paternal kind precaution he had taken to ensure my having a companion. Without previously communicating with me, he had, in concert with Elizabeth, arranged that

Clerval should join me at Strasbourg. This interfered with the solitude I coveted for the prosecution of my task; yet at the commencement of my journey the presence of my friend could in no way be an impediment, and truly I rejoiced that thus I should be saved many hours of lonely, maddening reflection. Nay, Henry might stand between me and the intrusion of my foe. If I were alone, would he not at times force his abhorred presence on me to remind me of my task or to contemplate its progress?

To England, therefore, I was bound, and it was understood that my union with Elizabeth should take place immediately on my return. My father's age rendered him extremely averse to delay. For myself, there was one reward I promised myself from my detested toils—one consolation for my unparalleled sufferings; it was the prospect of that day when, enfranchised from my miserable slavery, I might claim Elizabeth and forget the past in my union with her.

I now made arrangements for my journey, but one feeling haunted me which filled me with fear and agitation. During my absence I should leave my friends unconscious of the existence of their enemy and unprotected from his attacks, exasperated as he might be by my departure. But he had promised to follow me wherever I might go, and would he not accompany me to England? This imagination was dreadful in itself, but soothing inasmuch as it supposed the safety of my friends. I was agonised with the idea of the possibility that the reverse of this might happen. But through the whole period during which I was the slave of my creature I allowed myself to be governed by the impulses of the moment; and my present sensations strongly intimated that the fiend would follow me and exempt my family from the danger of his machinations.

It was in the latter end of August that I again quitted my native country. My journey had been my own suggestion, and Elizabeth therefore acquiesced, but she was filled with disquiet at the idea of my suffering, away from her, the inroads of misery and grief. It had been her care which provided me a companion in Clerval—and yet a man is blind to a thousand minute circumstances which call forth a woman's sedulous attention. She longed to bid me hasten my return; a thousand conflicting emotions rendered her mute as she bade me a tearful, silent farewell.

I threw myself into the carriage that was to convey me away, hardly knowing whither I was going, and careless of what was passing around. I remembered only, and it was with a bitter anguish that I reflected on it, to order that my chemical instruments should be packed to go with me. Filled with dreary imaginations, I passed through many beautiful and majestic scenes, but my eyes were fixed and unobserving. I could only think of the bourne of my travels and the work which was to occupy me whilst they endured.

After some days spent in listless indolence, during which I traversed many leagues, I arrived at Strasbourg, where I waited two days for Clerval. He came. Alas, how great was the contrast between us! He was alive to every new scene, joyful when he saw the beauties of the setting sun, and more happy when he beheld it rise and recommence a new day. He pointed out to me the shifting colours of the landscape and the appearances of the sky. "This is what it is to live," he cried; "how I enjoy existence! But you, my dear Frankenstein, wherefore are you desponding and sorrowful?" In truth, I was occupied by gloomy thoughts and neither saw the descent of the evening star nor the golden sunrise reflected in the Rhine. And you, my friend, would be far more amused with the journal of Clerval, who observed the scenery with an eye of feeling and delight, than in listening to my reflections. I, a miserable wretch, haunted by a curse that shut up every avenue to enjoyment.

We had agreed to descend the Rhine in a boat from Strasbourg to Rotterdam, whence we might take shipping for London. During this voyage we passed many willowy islands and saw several beautiful towns. We stayed a day at Mannheim, and on the fifth from our departure from Strasbourg, arrived at Mainz. The course of the Rhine below Mainz becomes much more picturesque. The river descends rapidly and winds between hills, not high, but steep, and of beautiful forms. We saw many ruined castles standing on the edges of precipices, surrounded by black woods, high and inaccessible. This part of the Rhine, indeed, presents a singularly variegated landscape. In one spot you view rugged hills, ruined castles overlooking tremendous precipices, with the dark Rhine rushing beneath; and on the sudden turn of a promontory, flourishing vineyards with green sloping banks and a meandering river and populous towns occupy the scene.

We travelled at the time of the vintage and heard the song of the labourers as we glided down the stream. Even I, depressed in mind, and my spirits continually agitated by gloomy feelings, even I was pleased. I lay at the bottom of the boat, and as I gazed on the cloudless blue sky, I seemed to drink in a tranquillity to which I had long been a stranger. And if these were my sensations, who can describe those of Henry? He felt as if he had been transported to Fairy-land and enjoyed a happiness seldom tasted by man. "I have seen," he said, "the most beautiful scenes of my own country; I have visited the lakes of Lucerne and Uri, where the snowy mountains descend almost perpendicularly to the water, casting black and impenetrable shades, which would cause a gloomy and mournful appearance were it not for the most verdant islands that relieve the eye by their gay appearance; I have seen this lake agitated by a tempest, when the wind tore up whirlwinds of water and gave you an idea of what the waterspout must be on the great ocean; and the waves dash with fury the base of the mountain, where the priest and his mistress were overwhelmed by an avalanche and where their dying voices are still said to be heard amid the pauses of the nightly wind; I have seen the mountains of La Valais, and the Pays de Vaud; but this country, Victor, pleases me more than all those wonders. The mountains of Switzerland are more majestic and strange, but there is a charm in the banks of this divine river that I never before saw equalled. Look at that castle which overhangs yon precipice; and that also on the island, almost concealed amongst the foliage of those lovely trees; and now that group of labourers coming from among their vines; and that village half hid in the recess of the mountain. Oh, surely the spirit that inhabits and guards this place has a soul more in harmony with man than those who pile the glacier or retire to the inaccessible peaks of the mountains of our own country."

Clerval! Beloved friend! Even now it delights me to record your words and to dwell on the praise of which you are so eminently deserving. He was a being formed in the "very poetry of nature." His wild and enthusiastic imagination was chastened by the sensibility of his heart. His soul overflowed with ardent affections, and his friendship was of that devoted and wondrous nature that the worldly-minded teach us to look for only in the imagination. But even human sympathies were not sufficient to satisfy his eager mind. The scenery of external nature, which others regard only with admiration, he loved with ardour:

> The sounding cataract
> Haunted him like a passion: the tall rock,
> The mountain, and the deep and gloomy wood,
> Their colours and their forms, were then to him
> An appetite; a feeling, and a love,
> That had no need of a remoter charm,
> By thought supplied, or any interest
> Unborrow'd from the eye.

And where does he now exist? Is this gentle and lovely being lost forever? Has this mind, so replete with ideas, imaginations fanciful and magnificent, which formed a world, whose existence depended on the life of its creator— has this mind perished? Does it now only exist in my memory? No, it is not thus; your form so divinely wrought, and beaming with beauty, has decayed, but your spirit still visits and consoles your unhappy friend.

Pardon this gush of sorrow; these ineffectual words are but a slight tribute to the unexampled worth of Henry, but they soothe my heart, overflowing with the anguish which his remembrance creates. I will proceed with my tale.

Beyond Cologne we descended to the plains of Holland; and we resolved to post the remainder of our way, for the wind was contrary and the stream of the river was too gentle to aid us.

Our journey here lost the interest arising from beautiful scenery, but we arrived in a few days at Rotterdam, whence we proceeded by sea to England. It was on a clear morning, in the latter days of September, that I first saw the white cliffs of Britain. The banks of the Thames presented a new scene; they were flat but fertile, and almost every town was marked by the remembrance of some story. We saw Tilbury Fort and remembered the Spanish Armada; Gravesend, Woolwich, and Greenwich—places which I had heard of even in my country.

At length we saw the numerous steeples of London, St. Paul's towering above all, and the Tower, famed in English history.

CHAPTER II

London was our present point of rest; we determined to remain several months in this wonderful and celebrated city. Clerval desired the intercourse of the men of genius and talent who flourished at this time, but this was with me a secondary object; I was principally occupied with the means of obtaining the information necessary for the completion of my promise and quickly availed myself of the letters of introduction that I had brought with me, addressed to the most distinguished natural philosophers.

If this journey had taken place during my days of study and happiness, it would have afforded me inexpressible pleasure. But a blight had come over my existence, and I only visited these people for the sake of the information they might give me on the subject in which my interest was so terribly profound. Company was irksome to me; when alone, I could fill my mind with the sights of heaven and earth; the voice of Henry soothed me, and I could thus cheat myself into a transitory peace. But busy, uninteresting, joyous faces brought back despair to my heart. I saw an insurmountable barrier placed between me and my fellow men; this barrier was sealed with the blood of William and Justine, and to reflect on the events connected with those names filled my soul with anguish.

But in Clerval I saw the image of my former self; he was inquisitive and anxious to gain experience and instruction. The difference of manners which he observed was to him an inexhaustible source of instruction and amusement. He was also pursuing an object he had long had in view. His design was to visit India, in the belief that he had in his knowledge of its various languages, and in the views he had taken of its society, the means of materially assisting the progress of European colonization and trade. In Britain only could he further the execution of his plan. He was forever busy, and the only check to his enjoyments was my sorrowful and dejected mind. I tried to conceal this as much as possible, that I might not debar him from the pleasures natural to one who was entering on a new scene of life, undisturbed by any care or bitter recollection. I often refused to accompany him, alleging another engagement, that I might remain alone. I now also began to collect the materials necessary for my new creation, and this was to me like the torture of single drops of water continually falling on the head. Every thought that was devoted to it was an extreme anguish, and every word that I spoke in allusion to it caused my lips to quiver, and my heart to palpitate.

After passing some months in London, we received a letter from a person in Scotland who had formerly been our visitor at Geneva. He mentioned the beauties of his native country and asked us if those were not sufficient allurements to induce us to prolong our journey as far north as Perth, where he resided. Clerval eagerly desired to accept this invitation, and I, although I abhorred society, wished to view again mountains and streams and all the wondrous works with which Nature adorns her chosen dwelling-places.

We had arrived in England at the beginning of October, and it was now February. We accordingly determined to commence our journey towards the north at the expiration of another month. In this expedition we did not intend to follow the great road to Edinburgh, but to visit Windsor, Oxford, Matlock, and the Cumberland lakes, resolving to arrive at the completion of this tour about the end of July. I packed up my chemical instruments and the materials I had collected, resolving to finish my labours in some obscure nook in the northern highlands of Scotland.

We quitted London on the 27th of March and remained a few days at Windsor, rambling in its beautiful forest. This was a new scene to us mountaineers; the majestic oaks, the quantity of game, and the herds of stately deer were all novelties to us.

From thence we proceeded to Oxford. As we entered this city our minds were filled with the remembrance of the events that had been transacted there more than a century and a half before. It was here that Charles I had collected his forces. This city had remained faithful to him, after the whole nation had forsaken his cause to join the standard of Parliament and liberty. The memory of that unfortunate king and his companions, the amiable Falkland, the insolent Goring, his queen, and son, gave a peculiar interest to every part of the city which they might be supposed to have inhabited. The spirit of elder days found a dwelling here, and we delighted to trace its footsteps. If these feelings had not found an imaginary gratification, the appearance of the city had yet in itself sufficient beauty to obtain our admiration. The colleges are ancient and picturesque; the streets are almost magnificent; and the lovely Isis, which flows beside it through meadows of exquisite verdure, is spread forth into a placid expanse of waters, which reflects its majestic assemblage of towers, and spires, and domes, embosomed among aged trees.

I enjoyed this scene, and yet my enjoyment was embittered both by the memory of the past and the anticipation of the future. I was formed for peaceful happiness. During my youthful days discontent never visited my mind, and if I was ever overcome by ennui, the sight of what is beautiful in nature or the study of what is excellent and sublime in the productions of man could always interest my heart and communicate elasticity to my spirits. But I am a blasted tree; the bolt has entered my soul; and I felt then that I should survive to exhibit what I shall soon cease to be—a miserable spectacle of wrecked humanity, pitiable to others and intolerable to myself.

We passed a considerable period at Oxford, rambling among its environs and endeavouring to identify every spot which might relate to the most animating epoch of English history. Our little voyages of discovery were often prolonged by the successive objects that presented themselves. We visited the tomb of the illustrious Hampden and the field on which that patriot fell. For a moment my soul was elevated from its debasing and miserable fears to contemplate the divine ideas of liberty and self-sacrifice of which these sights were the monuments and the remembrancers. For an instant I dared to shake off my chains and look around me with a free and lofty spirit, but the iron had eaten into my flesh, and I sank again, trembling and hopeless, into my miserable self.

We left Oxford with regret and proceeded to Matlock, which was our next place of rest. The country in the neighbourhood of this village resembled, to a greater degree, the scenery of Switzerland; but everything is on a lower scale, and the green hills want the crown of distant white Alps which always attend on the piny mountains of my native country. We visited the wondrous cave and the little cabinets of natural history, where the curiosities are disposed in the same manner as in the collections at Servox and Chamounix. The latter name made me tremble when pronounced by Henry, and I hastened to quit Matlock, with which that terrible scene was thus associated.

From Derby, still journeying northwards, we passed two months in Cumberland and Westmorland. I could now almost fancy myself among the Swiss mountains. The little patches of snow which yet lingered on the northern sides of the mountains, the lakes, and the dashing of the rocky streams were all familiar and dear sights to me. Here also we made some acquaintances, who almost contrived to cheat me into happiness. The delight of Clerval was proportionably greater than mine; his mind expanded in the company of men of talent, and he found in his own nature greater capacities and resources than he could have imagined himself to have possessed while he associated with his inferiors. "I could pass my life here," said he to me;

"and among these mountains I should scarcely regret Switzerland and the Rhine."

But he found that a traveller's life is one that includes much pain amidst its enjoyments. His feelings are forever on the stretch; and when he begins to sink into repose, he finds himself obliged to quit that on which he rests in pleasure for something new, which again engages his attention, and which also he forsakes for other novelties.

We had scarcely visited the various lakes of Cumberland and Westmorland and conceived an affection for some of the inhabitants when the period of our appointment with our Scotch friend approached, and we left them to travel on. For my own part I was not sorry. I had now neglected my promise for some time, and I feared the effects of the daemon's disappointment. He might remain in Switzerland and wreak his vengeance on my relatives. This idea pursued me and tormented me at every moment from which I might otherwise have snatched repose and peace. I waited for my letters with feverish impatience; if they were delayed I was miserable and overcome by a thousand fears; and when they arrived and I saw the superscription of Elizabeth or my father, I hardly dared to read and ascertain my fate. Sometimes I thought that the fiend followed me and might expedite my remissness by murdering my companion. When these thoughts possessed me, I would not quit Henry for a moment, but followed him as his shadow, to protect him from the fancied rage of his destroyer. I felt as if I had committed some great crime, the consciousness of which haunted me. I was guiltless, but I had indeed drawn down a horrible curse upon my head, as mortal as that of crime.

I visited Edinburgh with languid eyes and mind; and yet that city might have interested the most unfortunate being. Clerval did not like it so well as Oxford, for the antiquity of the latter city was more pleasing to him. But the beauty and regularity of the new town of Edinburgh, its romantic castle and its environs, the most delightful in the world, Arthur's Seat, St. Bernard's Well, and the Pentland Hills compensated him for the change and filled him with cheerfulness and admiration. But I was impatient to arrive at the termination of my journey.

We left Edinburgh in a week, passing through Coupar, St. Andrew's, and along the banks of the Tay, to Perth, where our friend expected us. But I was in no mood to laugh and talk with strangers or enter into their feelings or plans with the good humour expected from a guest; and accordingly I told Clerval that I wished to make the tour of Scotland alone. "Do you," said I, "enjoy yourself, and let this be our rendezvous. I may be absent a month or two; but do not interfere with my motions, I entreat you; leave me to peace and solitude for a short time; and when I return, I hope it will be with a lighter heart, more congenial to your own temper."

Henry wished to dissuade me, but seeing me bent on this plan, ceased to remonstrate. He entreated me to write often. "I had rather be with you," he said, "in your solitary rambles, than with these Scotch people, whom I do not know; hasten, then, my dear friend, to return, that I may again feel myself somewhat at home, which I cannot do in your absence."

Having parted from my friend, I determined to visit some remote spot of Scotland and finish my work in solitude. I did not doubt but that the monster followed me and would discover himself to me when I should have finished, that he might receive his companion.

With this resolution I traversed the northern highlands and fixed on one of the remotest of the Orkneys as the scene of my labours. It was a place fitted for such a work, being hardly more than a rock whose high sides were continually beaten upon by the waves. The soil was barren, scarcely affording pasture for a few miserable cows, and oatmeal for its inhabitants, which consisted of five persons, whose gaunt and scraggy limbs gave tokens of their miserable fare. Vegetables and bread, when they indulged in such luxuries, and even fresh water, was to be procured from the mainland, which was about five miles distant.

On the whole island there were but three miserable huts, and one of these was vacant when I arrived. This I hired. It contained but two rooms, and these exhibited all the squalidness of the most miserable penury. The thatch had fallen in, the walls were unplastered, and the door was off its hinges. I ordered it to be repaired, bought some furniture, and took possession, an incident which would doubtless have occasioned some surprise had not all the senses of the cottagers been benumbed by want and squalid poverty. As it was, I lived ungazed at and unmolested, hardly thanked for the pittance of food and clothes which I gave, so much does suffering blunt even the coarsest sensations of men.

In this retreat I devoted the morning to labour; but in the evening, when the weather permitted, I walked on the stony beach of the sea to listen to the waves as they roared and dashed at my feet. It was a monotonous yet ever-changing scene. I thought of Switzerland; it was far different from this desolate and appalling landscape. Its hills are covered with vines, and its cottages are scattered thickly in the plains. Its fair lakes reflect a blue and gentle sky, and when troubled by the winds, their tumult is but as the play of a lively infant when compared to the roarings of the giant ocean.

In this manner I distributed my occupations when I first arrived, but as I proceeded in my labour, it became every day more horrible and irksome to me. Sometimes I could not prevail on myself to enter my laboratory for several days, and at other times I toiled day and night in order to complete my work. It was, indeed, a filthy process in which I was engaged. During my first experiment, a kind of enthusiastic frenzy had blinded me to the horror of my employment; my mind was intently fixed on the consummation of my labour, and my eyes were shut to the horror of my proceedings. But now I went to it in cold blood, and my heart often sickened at the work of my hands.

Thus situated, employed in the most detestable occupation, immersed in a solitude where nothing could for an instant call my attention from the actual scene in which I was engaged, my spirits became unequal; I grew restless and nervous. Every moment I feared to meet my persecutor. Sometimes I sat with my eyes fixed on the ground, fearing to raise them lest they should encounter the object which I so much dreaded to behold. I feared to wander from the sight of my fellow creatures lest when alone he should come to claim his companion.

In the meantime I worked on, and my labour was already considerably advanced. I looked towards its completion with a tremulous and eager hope, which I dared not trust myself to question but which was intermixed with obscure forebodings of evil that made my heart sicken in my bosom.

CHAPTER III

I sat one evening in my laboratory; the sun had set, and the moon was just rising from the sea; I had not sufficient light for my employment, and I remained idle, in a pause of consideration of whether I should leave my labour for the night or hasten its conclusion by an unremitting attention to it. As I sat, a train of reflection occurred to me which led me to consider the effects of what I was now doing. Three years before, I was engaged in the same manner and had created a fiend whose unparalleled barbarity had desolated my heart and filled it forever with the bitterest remorse. I was now about to form another being of whose dispositions I was alike ignorant; she might become ten thousand times more malignant than her mate and delight, for its own sake, in murder and wretchedness. He had sworn to quit the neighbourhood of man and hide himself in deserts, but she had not; and she, who in all probability was to become a thinking and reasoning animal, might refuse to comply with a compact made before her creation. They might even hate each other; the creature who already lived loathed his own deformity, and might he not conceive a greater abhorrence for it when it came before his eyes in the female form? She also might turn with disgust from him to the superior beauty of man; she might quit him, and he be again alone, exasperated by the fresh provocation of being deserted by one of his own species.

Even if they were to leave Europe and inhabit the deserts of the new world, yet one of the first results of those sympathies for which the daemon thirsted would be children, and a race of devils would be propagated upon the earth who might make the very existence of the species of man a condition precarious and full of terror. Had I right, for my own benefit, to inflict this curse upon everlasting generations? I had before been moved by the sophisms of the being I had created; I had been struck senseless by his fiendish threats; but now, for the first time, the wickedness of my promise burst upon me; I shuddered to think that future ages might curse me as their pest, whose selfishness had not hesitated to buy its own peace at the price, perhaps, of the existence of the whole human race.

I trembled, and my heart failed within me, when, on looking up, I saw by the light of the moon the daemon at the casement. A ghastly grin wrinkled his lips as he gazed on me, where I sat fulfilling the task which he had allotted to me. Yes, he had followed me in my travels; he had loitered in forests, hid himself in caves, or taken refuge in wide and desert heaths; and he now came to mark my progress and claim the fulfilment of my promise.

As I looked on him, his countenance expressed the utmost extent of malice and treachery. I thought with a sensation of madness on my promise of creating another like to him, and trembling with passion, tore to pieces the thing on which I was engaged. The wretch saw me destroy the creature on whose future existence he depended for happiness, and with a howl of devilish despair and revenge, withdrew.

I left the room, and locking the door, made a solemn vow in my own heart never to resume my labours; and then, with trembling steps, I sought my own apartment. I was alone; none were near me to dissipate the gloom and relieve me from the sickening oppression of the most terrible reveries.

Several hours passed, and I remained near my window gazing on the sea; it was almost motionless, for the winds were hushed, and all nature reposed under the eye of the quiet moon. A few fishing vessels alone specked the water, and now and then the gentle breeze wafted the sound of voices as the fishermen called to one another. I felt the silence, although I was hardly conscious of its extreme profundity, until my ear was suddenly arrested by the paddling of oars near the shore, and a person landed close to my house.

In a few minutes after, I heard the creaking of my door, as if someone endeavoured to open it softly. I trembled from head to foot; I felt a presentiment of who it was and wished to rouse one of the peasants who dwelt in a cottage not far from mine; but I was overcome by the sensation of helplessness, so often felt in frightful dreams, when you in vain endeavour to fly from an impending danger, and was rooted to the spot.

Presently I heard the sound of footsteps along the passage; the door opened, and the wretch whom I dreaded appeared. Shutting the door, he approached me and said in a smothered voice:

"You have destroyed the work which you began; what is it that you intend? Do you dare to break your promise? I have endured toil and misery; I left Switzerland with you; I crept along the shores of the Rhine, among its willow islands and over the summits of its hills. I have dwelt many months in the heaths of England and among the deserts of Scotland. I have endured incalculable fatigue, and cold, and hunger; do you dare destroy my hopes?"

"Begone! I do break my promise; never will I create another like yourself, equal in deformity and wickedness."

"Slave, I before reasoned with you, but you have proved yourself unworthy of my condescension. Remember that I have power; you believe yourself miserable, but I can make you so wretched that the light of day will be hateful to you. You are my creator, but I am your master—obey!"

"The hour of my irresolution is past, and the period of your power is arrived. Your threats cannot move me to do an act of wickedness; but they confirm me in a determination of not creating you a companion in vice. Shall I, in cool blood, set loose upon the earth a daemon whose delight is in death and wretchedness? Begone! I am firm, and your words will only exasperate my rage."

The monster saw my determination in my face and gnashed his teeth in the impotence of anger. "Shall each man," cried he, "find a wife for his bosom, and each beast have his mate, and I be alone? I had feelings of affection, and they were requited by detestation and scorn. Man! You may hate, but beware! Your hours will pass in dread and misery, and soon the bolt will fall which must ravish from you your happiness forever. Are you to be happy while I grovel in the intensity of my wretchedness? You can blast my other passions, but revenge remains—revenge, henceforth dearer than light or food! I may die, but first you, my tyrant and tormentor, shall curse the sun that gazes on your misery. Beware, for I am fearless and therefore powerful. I will watch with the wiliness of a snake, that I may sting with its venom. Man, you shall repent of the injuries you inflict."

"Devil, cease; and do not poison the air with these sounds of malice. I have declared my resolution to you, and I am no coward to bend beneath words. Leave me; I am inexorable."

"It is well. I go; but remember, I shall be with you on your wedding-night."

I started forward and exclaimed, "Villain! Before you sign my death-warrant, be sure that you are yourself safe."

I would have seized him, but he eluded me and quitted the house with precipitation. In a few moments I saw him in his boat, which shot across the waters with an arrowy swiftness and was soon lost amidst the waves.

All was again silent, but his words rang in my ears. I burned with rage to pursue the murderer of my peace and precipitate him into the ocean. I walked up and down my room hastily and perturbed, while my imagination conjured up a thousand images to torment and sting me. Why had I not followed him and closed with him in mortal strife? But I had suffered him to depart, and he had directed his course towards the mainland. I shuddered to think who might be the next victim sacrificed to his insatiate revenge. And then I thought again of his words—"I will be with you on your wedding-night." That, then, was the period fixed for the fulfilment of my destiny. In that hour I should die and at once satisfy and extinguish his malice. The prospect did not move me to fear; yet when I thought of my beloved Elizabeth, of her tears and endless sorrow, when she should find her lover so barbarously snatched from her, tears, the first I had shed for many months, streamed from my eyes, and I resolved not to fall before my enemy without a bitter struggle.

The night passed away, and the sun rose from the ocean; my feelings became calmer, if it may be called calmness when the violence of rage sinks into the depths of despair. I left the house, the horrid scene of the last night's contention, and walked on the beach of the sea, which I almost regarded as an insuperable barrier between me and my fellow creatures; nay, a wish that such should prove the fact stole across me. I desired that I might pass my life on that barren rock, wearily, it is true, but uninterrupted by any sudden shock of misery. If I returned, it was to be sacrificed or to see those whom I most loved die under the grasp of a daemon whom I had myself created.

I walked about the isle like a restless spectre, separated from all it loved and miserable in the separation. When it became noon, and the sun rose higher, I lay down on the grass and was overpowered by a deep sleep. I had been awake the whole of the preceding night, my nerves were agitated, and my eyes inflamed by watching and misery. The sleep into which I now sank refreshed me; and when I awoke, I again felt as if I belonged to a race of human beings like myself, and I began to reflect upon what had passed with greater composure; yet still the words of the fiend rang in my ears like a death-knell; they appeared like a dream, yet distinct and oppressive as a reality.

The sun had far descended, and I still sat on the shore, satisfying my appetite, which had become ravenous, with an oaten cake, when I saw a fishing-boat land close to me, and one of the men brought me a packet; it contained letters from Geneva, and one from Clerval entreating me to join him. He said that he was wearing away his time fruitlessly where he was, that letters from the friends he had formed in London desired his return to complete the negotiation they had entered into for his Indian enterprise. He could not any longer delay his departure; but as his journey to London might be followed, even sooner than he now conjectured, by his longer voyage, he entreated me to bestow as much of my society on him as I could spare. He besought me, therefore, to leave my solitary isle and to meet him at Perth, that we might proceed southwards together. This letter in a degree recalled me to life, and I determined to quit my island at the expiration of two days.

Yet, before I departed, there was a task to perform, on which I shuddered to reflect: I must pack up my chemical instruments, and for that purpose I must enter the room which had been the scene of my odious work, and I must handle those utensils the sight of which was sickening to me. The next morning, at daybreak, I summoned sufficient courage and unlocked the door of my laboratory. The remains of the half-finished creature, whom I had destroyed, lay scattered on the floor, and I almost felt as if I had mangled the living flesh of a human being. I paused to collect myself and then entered the chamber. With trembling hand I conveyed the instruments out of the room, but I reflected that I ought not to leave the relics of my work to excite the horror and suspicion of the peasants; and I accordingly put them into a basket, with a great quantity of stones, and laying them up, determined to throw them into the sea that very night; and in the meantime I sat upon the beach, employed in cleaning and arranging my chemical apparatus.

Nothing could be more complete than the alteration that had taken place in my feelings since the night of the appearance of the daemon. I had before regarded my promise with a gloomy despair as a thing that, with whatever consequences, must be fulfilled; but I now felt as if a film had been taken from before my eyes and that I for the first time saw clearly. The idea of renewing my labours did not for one instant occur to me; the threat I had heard weighed on my thoughts, but I did not reflect that a voluntary act of mine could avert it. I had resolved in my own mind that to create another like the fiend I had first made would be an act of the basest and most atrocious selfishness, and I banished from my mind every thought that could lead to a different conclusion.

Between two and three in the morning the moon rose; and I then, putting my basket aboard a little skiff, sailed out about four miles from the shore. The scene was perfectly solitary; a few boats were returning towards land, but I sailed away from them. I felt as if I was about the commission of a dreadful crime and avoided with shuddering anxiety any encounter with my fellow-creatures. At one time the moon, which had before been clear, was suddenly overspread by a thick cloud, and I took advantage of the moment of darkness and cast my basket into the sea; I listened to the gurgling sound as it sank and then sailed away from the spot. The sky became clouded, but the air was pure, although chilled by the northeast breeze that was then rising. But it refreshed me and filled me with such agreeable sensations that I resolved to prolong my stay on the water, and fixing the rudder in a direct position, stretched myself at the bottom of the boat. Clouds hid the moon, everything was obscure, and I heard only the sound of the boat as its keel cut through the waves; the murmur lulled me, and in a short time I slept soundly.

I do not know how long I remained in this situation, but when I awoke I found that the sun had already mounted considerably. The wind was high, and the waves continually threatened the safety of my little skiff. I found that the wind was northeast and must have driven me far from the coast from which I had embarked. I endeavoured to change my course but quickly found that if I again made the attempt the boat would be instantly filled with water.

Thus situated, my only resource was to drive before the wind. I confess that I felt a few sensations of terror. I had no compass with me and was so slenderly acquainted with the geography of this part of the world that the sun was of little benefit to me. I might be driven into the wide Atlantic and feel all the tortures of starvation or be swallowed up in the immeasurable waters that roared and buffeted around me. I had already been out many hours and felt the torment of a burning thirst, a prelude to my other sufferings. I looked on the heavens, which were covered by clouds that flew before the wind, only to be replaced by others; I looked upon the sea; it was to be my grave. "Fiend," I exclaimed, "your task is already fulfilled!" I thought of Elizabeth, of my father, and of Clerval—all left behind, on whom the monster might satisfy his sanguinary and merciless passions. This idea plunged me into a reverie so despairing and frightful that even now, when the scene is on the point of closing before me forever, I shudder to reflect on it.

Some hours passed thus; but by degrees, as the sun declined towards the horizon, the wind died away into a gentle breeze and the sea became free from breakers. But these gave place to a heavy swell; I felt sick and hardly able to hold the rudder, when suddenly I saw a line of high land towards the south.

Almost spent, as I was, by fatigue and the dreadful suspense I endured for several hours, this sudden certainty of life rushed like a flood of warm joy to my heart, and tears gushed from my eyes.

How mutable are our feelings, and how strange is that clinging love we have of life even in the excess of misery! I constructed another sail with a part of my dress and eagerly steered my course towards the land. It had a wild and rocky appearance, but as I approached nearer I easily perceived the traces of cultivation. I saw vessels near the shore and found myself suddenly transported back to the neighbourhood of civilised man. I carefully traced the windings of the land and hailed a steeple which I at length saw issuing from behind a small promontory. As I was in a state of extreme debility, I resolved to sail directly towards the town, as a place where I could most easily procure nourishment. Fortunately I had money with me. As I turned the promontory I perceived a small neat town and a good harbour, which I entered, my heart bounding with joy at my unexpected escape.

As I was occupied in fixing the boat and arranging the sails, several people crowded towards the spot. They seemed much surprised at my appearance, but instead of offering me any assistance, whispered together with gestures that at any other time might have produced in me a slight sensation of alarm. As it was, I merely remarked that they spoke English, and I therefore addressed them in that language. "My good friends," said I, "will you be so kind as to tell me the name of this town and inform me where I am?"

"You will know that soon enough," replied a man with a hoarse voice. "Maybe you are come to a place that will not prove much to your taste, but you will not be consulted as to your quarters, I promise you."

I was exceedingly surprised on receiving so rude an answer from a stranger, and I was also disconcerted on perceiving the frowning and angry countenances of his companions. "Why do you answer me so roughly?" I replied. "Surely it is not the custom of Englishmen to receive strangers so inhospitably."

"I do not know," said the man, "what the custom of the English may be, but it is the custom of the Irish to hate villains."

While this strange dialogue continued, I perceived the crowd rapidly increase. Their faces expressed a mixture of curiosity and anger, which annoyed and in some degree alarmed me. I enquired the way to the inn, but no one replied. I then moved forward, and a murmuring sound arose from the crowd as they followed and surrounded me, when an ill-looking man approaching tapped me on the shoulder and said, "Come, sir, you must follow me to Mr. Kirwin's, to give an account of yourself."

"Who is Mr. Kirwin? Why am I to give an account of myself? Is not this a free country?"

"Ay, sir, free enough for honest folks. Mr. Kirwin is a magistrate, and you are to give an account of the death of a gentleman who was found murdered here last night."

This answer startled me, but I presently recovered myself. I was innocent; that could easily be proved; accordingly I followed my conductor in silence and was led to one of the best houses in the town. I was ready to sink from fatigue and hunger, but being surrounded by a crowd, I thought it politic to rouse all my strength, that no physical debility might be construed into apprehension or conscious guilt. Little did I then expect the calamity that was in a few moments to overwhelm me and extinguish in horror and despair all fear of ignominy or death.

I must pause here, for it requires all my fortitude to recall the memory of the frightful events which I am about to relate, in proper detail, to my recollection.

CHAPTER IV

I was soon introduced into the presence of the magistrate, an old benevolent man with calm and mild manners. He looked upon me, however, with some degree of severity, and then, turning towards my conductors, he asked who appeared as witnesses on this occasion.

About half a dozen men came forward; and, one being selected by the magistrate, he deposed that he had been out fishing the night before with his son and brother-in-law, Daniel Nugent, when, about ten o'clock, they observed a strong northerly blast rising, and they accordingly put in for port. It was a very dark night, as the moon had not yet risen; they did not land at the harbour, but, as they had been accustomed, at a creek about two miles below. He walked on first, carrying a part of the fishing tackle, and his companions followed him at some distance. As he was proceeding along the sands, he struck his foot against something and fell at his length on the ground. His companions came up to assist him, and by the light of their lantern they found that he had fallen on the body of a man, who was to all appearance dead. Their first supposition was that it was the corpse of some person who had been drowned and was thrown on shore by the waves, but on examination they found that the clothes were not wet and even that the body was not then cold. They instantly carried it to the cottage of an old woman near the spot and endeavoured, but in vain, to restore it to life. It appeared to be a handsome young man, about five and twenty years of age. He had apparently been strangled, for there was no sign of any violence except the black mark of fingers on his neck.

The first part of this deposition did not in the least interest me, but when the mark of the fingers was mentioned I remembered the murder of my brother and felt myself extremely agitated; my limbs trembled, and a mist came over my eyes, which obliged me to lean on a chair for support. The magistrate observed me with a keen eye and of course drew an unfavourable augury from my manner.

The son confirmed his father's account, but when Daniel Nugent was called he swore positively that just before the fall of his companion, he saw a boat, with a single man in it, at a short distance from the shore; and as far as he could judge by the light of a few stars, it was the same boat in which I had just landed.

A woman deposed that she lived near the beach and was standing at the door of her cottage, waiting for the return of the fishermen, about an hour before she heard of the discovery of the body, when she saw a boat with only one man in it push off from that part of the shore where the corpse was afterwards found.

Another woman confirmed the account of the fishermen having brought the body into her house; it was not cold. They put it into a bed and rubbed it, and Daniel went to the town for an apothecary, but life was quite gone.

Several other men were examined concerning my landing, and they agreed that, with the strong north wind that had arisen during the night, it was very probable that I had beaten about for many hours and had been obliged to return nearly to the same spot from which I had departed. Besides, they observed that it appeared that I had brought the body from another place, and it was likely that as I did not appear to know the shore, I might have put into the harbour ignorant of the distance of the town of —— from the place where I had deposited the corpse.

Mr. Kirwin, on hearing this evidence, desired that I should be taken into the room where the body lay for interment, that it might be observed what effect the sight of it would produce upon me. This idea was probably suggested by the extreme agitation I had exhibited when the mode of the murder had been described. I was accordingly conducted, by the magistrate and several other persons, to the inn. I could not help being struck by the strange coincidences that had taken place during this eventful night; but, knowing that I had been conversing with several persons in the island I had inhabited about the time that the body had been found, I was perfectly tranquil as to the consequences of the affair.

I entered the room where the corpse lay, and was led up to the coffin. How can I describe my sensations on beholding it? I feel yet parched with horror, nor can I reflect on that terrible moment without shuddering and agony. The examination, the presence of the magistrate and witnesses, passed like a dream from my memory when I saw the lifeless form of Henry Clerval stretched before me. I gasped for breath, and throwing myself on the body, I exclaimed, "Have my murderous machinations deprived you also, my dearest Henry, of life? Two I have already destroyed; other victims await their destiny; but you, Clerval, my friend, my benefactor—"

The human frame could no longer support the agonies that I endured, and I was carried out of the room in strong convulsions.

A fever succeeded to this. I lay for two months on the point of death; my ravings, as I afterwards heard, were frightful; I called myself the murderer of William, of Justine, and of Clerval. Sometimes I entreated my attendants to assist me in the destruction of the fiend by whom I was tormented; and at others I felt the fingers of the monster already grasping my neck, and screamed aloud with agony and terror. Fortunately, as I spoke my native language, Mr. Kirwin alone understood me; but my gestures and bitter cries were sufficient to affright the other witnesses.

Why did I not die? More miserable than man ever was before, why did I not sink into forgetfulness and rest? Death snatches away many blooming children, the only hopes of their doting parents; how many brides and youthful lovers have been one day in the bloom of health and hope, and the next a prey for worms and the decay of the tomb! Of what materials was I made that I could thus resist so many shocks, which, like the turning of the wheel, continually renewed the torture?

But I was doomed to live, and in two months found myself as awaking from a dream, in a prison, stretched on a wretched bed, surrounded by jailers, turnkeys, bolts, and all the miserable apparatus of a dungeon. It was morning, I remember, when I thus awoke to understanding; I had forgotten the particulars of what had happened and only felt as if some great misfortune had suddenly overwhelmed me; but when I looked around and saw the barred windows and the squalidness of the room in which I was, all flashed across my memory and I groaned bitterly.

This sound disturbed an old woman who was sleeping in a chair beside me. She was a hired nurse, the wife of one of the turnkeys, and her countenance expressed all those bad qualities which often characterize that class. The lines of her face were hard and rude, like that of persons accustomed to see without sympathising in sights of misery. Her tone expressed her entire indifference; she addressed me in English, and the voice struck me as one that I had heard during my sufferings:

"Are you better now, sir?" said she.

I replied in the same language, with a feeble voice, "I believe I am; but if it be all true, if indeed I did not dream, I am sorry that I am still alive to feel this misery and horror."

"For that matter," replied the old woman, "if you mean about the gentleman you murdered, I believe that it were better for you if you were dead, for I fancy it will go hard with you! However, that's none of my business; I am sent to nurse you and get you well; I do my duty with a safe conscience; it were well if everybody did the same."

I turned with loathing from the woman who could utter so unfeeling a speech to a person just saved, on the very edge of death; but I felt languid and unable to reflect on all that had passed. The whole series of my life appeared to me as a dream; I sometimes doubted if indeed it were all true, for it never presented itself to my mind with the force of reality.

As the images that floated before me became more distinct, I grew feverish; a darkness pressed around me; no one was near me who soothed me with the gentle voice of love; no dear hand supported me. The physician came and prescribed medicines, and the old woman prepared them for me; but utter carelessness was visible in the first, and the expression of brutality was strongly marked in the visage of the second. Who could be interested in the fate of a murderer but the hangman who would gain his fee?

These were my first reflections, but I soon learned that Mr. Kirwin had shown me extreme kindness. He had caused the best room in the prison to be prepared for me (wretched indeed was the best); and it was he who had provided a physician and a nurse. It is true, he seldom came to see me, for although he ardently desired to relieve the sufferings of every human creature, he did not wish to be present at the agonies and miserable ravings of a murderer. He came, therefore, sometimes to see that I was not neglected, but his visits were short and with long intervals.

One day, while I was gradually recovering, I was seated in a chair, my eyes half open and my cheeks livid like those in death. I was overcome by gloom and misery and often reflected I had better seek death than desire to remain in a world which to me was replete with wretchedness. At one time I considered whether I should not declare myself guilty and suffer the penalty of the law, less innocent than poor Justine had been. Such were my thoughts when the door of my apartment was opened and Mr. Kirwin entered. His countenance expressed sympathy and compassion; he drew a chair close to mine and addressed me in French:

"I fear that this place is very shocking to you; can I do anything to make you more comfortable?"

"I thank you, but all that you mention is nothing to me; on the whole earth there is no comfort which I am capable of receiving."

"I know that the sympathy of a stranger can be but of little relief to one borne down as you are by so strange a misfortune. But you will, I hope, soon quit this melancholy abode, for doubtless evidence can easily be brought to free you from the criminal charge."

"That is my least concern; I am, by a course of strange events, become the most miserable of mortals. Persecuted and tortured as I am and have been, can death be any evil to me?"

"Nothing indeed could be more unfortunate and agonising than the strange chances that have lately occurred. You were thrown, by some surprising accident, on this shore, renowned for its hospitality, seized immediately, and charged with murder. The first sight that was presented to your eyes was the body of your friend, murdered in so unaccountable a manner and placed, as it were, by some fiend across your path."

As Mr. Kirwin said this, notwithstanding the agitation I endured on this retrospect of my sufferings, I also felt considerable surprise at the knowledge he seemed to possess concerning me. I suppose some astonishment was exhibited in my countenance, for Mr. Kirwin hastened to say:

"Immediately upon your being taken ill, all the papers that were on your person were brought me, and I examined them that I might discover some trace by which I could send to your relations an account of your misfortune and illness. I found several letters, and, among others, one which I discovered from its commencement to be from your father. I instantly wrote to Geneva; nearly two months have elapsed since the departure of my letter. But you are ill; even now you tremble; you are unfit for agitation of any kind."

"This suspense is a thousand times worse than the most horrible event; tell me what new scene of death has been acted, and whose murder I am now to lament?"

"Your family is perfectly well," said Mr. Kirwin with gentleness; "and someone, a friend, is come to visit you."

I know not by what chain of thought the idea presented itself, but it instantly darted into my mind that the murderer had come to mock at my misery and taunt me with the death of Clerval, as a new incitement for me to comply with his hellish desires. I put my hand before my eyes, and cried out in agony, "Oh! Take him away! I cannot see him; for God's sake, do not let him enter!"

Mr. Kirwin regarded me with a troubled countenance. He could not help regarding my exclamation as a presumption of my guilt and said in rather a severe tone:

"I should have thought, young man, that the presence of your father would have been welcome instead of inspiring such violent repugnance."

"My father!" cried I, while every feature and every muscle was relaxed from anguish to pleasure. "Is my father indeed come? How kind, how very kind! But where is he, why does he not hasten to me?"

My change of manner surprised and pleased the magistrate; perhaps he thought that my former exclamation was a momentary return of delirium, and now he instantly resumed his former benevolence. He rose and quitted the room with my nurse, and in a moment my father entered it.

Nothing, at this moment, could have given me greater pleasure than the arrival of my father. I stretched out my hand to him and cried:

"Are you, then, safe—and Elizabeth—and Ernest?"

My father calmed me with assurances of their welfare and endeavoured, by dwelling on these subjects so interesting to my heart, to raise my desponding spirits; but he soon felt that a prison cannot be the abode of cheerfulness. "What a place is this that you inhabit, my son!" said he, looking mournfully at the barred windows and wretched appearance of the room. "You travelled to seek happiness, but a fatality seems to pursue you. And poor Clerval—"

The name of my unfortunate and murdered friend was an agitation too great to be endured in my weak state; I shed tears.

"Alas! Yes, my father," replied I; "some destiny of the most horrible kind hangs over me, and I must live to fulfil it, or surely I should have died on the coffin of Henry."

We were not allowed to converse for any length of time, for the precarious state of my health rendered every precaution necessary that could ensure tranquillity. Mr. Kirwin came in and insisted that my strength should not be exhausted by too much exertion. But the appearance of my father was to me like that of my good angel, and I gradually recovered my health.

As my sickness quitted me, I was absorbed by a gloomy and black melancholy that nothing could dissipate. The image of Clerval was forever before me, ghastly and murdered. More than once the agitation into which these reflections threw me made my friends dread a dangerous relapse. Alas! Why did they preserve so miserable and detested a life? It was surely that I might fulfil my destiny, which is now drawing to a close. Soon, oh, very soon, will death extinguish these throbbings and relieve me from the mighty weight of anguish that bears me to the dust; and, in executing the award of justice, I shall also sink to rest. Then the appearance of death was distant, although the wish was ever present to my thoughts; and I often sat for hours motionless and speechless, wishing for some mighty revolution that might bury me and my destroyer in its ruins.

The season of the assizes approached. I had already been three months in prison, and although I was still weak and in continual danger of a relapse, I was obliged to travel nearly a hundred miles to the country town where the court was held. Mr. Kirwin charged himself with every care of collecting witnesses and arranging my defence. I was spared the disgrace of appearing publicly as a criminal, as the case was not brought before the court that decides on life and death. The grand jury rejected the bill, on its being proved that I was on the Orkney Islands at the hour the body of my friend was found; and a fortnight after my removal I was liberated from prison.

My father was enraptured on finding me freed from the vexations of a criminal charge, that I was again allowed to breathe the fresh atmosphere and permitted to return to my native country. I did not participate in these feelings, for to me the walls of a dungeon or a palace were alike hateful. The cup of life was poisoned forever, and although the sun shone upon me, as upon the happy and gay of heart, I saw around me nothing but a dense and frightful darkness, penetrated by no light but the glimmer of two eyes that glared upon me. Sometimes they were the expressive eyes of Henry, languishing in death, the dark orbs nearly covered by the lids and the long black lashes that fringed them; sometimes it was the watery, clouded eyes of the monster, as I first saw them in my chamber at Ingolstadt.

My father tried to awaken in me the feelings of affection. He talked of Geneva, which I should soon visit, of Elizabeth and Ernest; but these words only drew deep groans from me. Sometimes, indeed, I felt a wish for happiness and thought with melancholy delight of my beloved cousin or longed, with a devouring *maladie du pays*, to see once more the blue lake and rapid Rhône, that had been so dear to me in early childhood; but my general state of feeling was a torpor in which a prison was as welcome a residence as the divinest scene in nature; and these fits were seldom interrupted but by paroxysms of anguish and despair. At these moments I often endeavoured to put an end to the existence I loathed, and it required unceasing attendance and vigilance to restrain me from committing some dreadful act of violence.

Yet one duty remained to me, the recollection of which finally triumphed over my selfish despair. It was necessary that I should return without delay to Geneva, there to watch over the lives of those I so fondly loved and to lie in wait for the murderer, that if any chance led me to the place of his concealment, or if he dared again to blast me by his presence, I might, with unfailing aim, put an end to the existence of the monstrous image which I had endued with the mockery of a soul still more monstrous. My father still desired to delay our departure, fearful that I could not sustain the fatigues of a journey, for I was a shattered wreck—the shadow of a human being. My strength was gone. I was a mere skeleton, and fever night and day preyed upon my wasted frame.

Still, as I urged our leaving Ireland with such inquietude and impatience, my father thought it best to yield. We took our passage on board a vessel bound for Havre-de-Grâce and sailed with a fair wind from the Irish shores. It was midnight. I lay on the deck looking at the stars and listening to the dashing of the waves. I hailed the darkness that shut Ireland from my sight, and my pulse beat with a feverish joy when I reflected that I should soon see Geneva. The past appeared to me in the light of a frightful dream; yet the vessel in which I was, the wind that blew me from the detested shore of Ireland, and the sea which surrounded me told me too forcibly that I was deceived by no vision and that Clerval, my friend and dearest companion, had fallen a victim to me and the monster of my creation. I repassed, in my memory, my whole life—my quiet happiness while residing with my family in Geneva, the death of my mother, and my departure for Ingolstadt. I remembered, shuddering, the mad enthusiasm that hurried me on to the creation of my hideous enemy, and I called to mind the night in which he first lived. I was unable to pursue the train of thought; a thousand feelings pressed upon me, and I wept bitterly.

Ever since my recovery from the fever I had been in the custom of taking every night a small quantity of laudanum, for it was by means of this drug only that I was enabled to gain the rest necessary for the preservation of life. Oppressed by the recollection of my various misfortunes, I now swallowed double my usual quantity and soon slept profoundly. But sleep did not afford me respite from thought and misery; my dreams presented a thousand objects that scared me. Towards morning I was possessed by a kind of nightmare; I felt the fiend's grasp in my neck and could not free myself from it; groans and cries rang in my ears. My father, who was watching over me, perceiving my restlessness, awoke me; the dashing waves were around, the cloudy sky above; the fiend was not here: a sense of security, a feeling that a truce was established between the present hour and the irresistible, disastrous future imparted to me a kind of calm forgetfulness, of which the human mind is by its structure peculiarly susceptible.

CHAPTER V

The voyage came to an end. We landed, and proceeded to Paris. I soon found that I had overtaxed my strength and that I must repose before I could continue my journey. My father's care and attentions were indefatigable, but he did not know the origin of my sufferings and sought erroneous methods to remedy the incurable ill. He wished me to seek amusement in society. I abhorred the face of man. Oh, not abhorred! They were my brethren, my fellow beings, and I felt attracted even to the most repulsive among them, as to creatures of an angelic nature and celestial mechanism. But I felt that I had no right to share their intercourse. I had unchained an enemy among them whose joy it was to shed their blood and to revel in their groans. How they would, each and all, abhor me and hunt me from the world did they know my unhallowed acts and the crimes which had their source in me!

My father yielded at length to my desire to avoid society and strove by various arguments to banish my despair. Sometimes he thought that I felt deeply the degradation of being obliged to answer a charge of murder, and he endeavoured to prove to me the futility of pride.

"Alas! My father," said I, "how little do you know me. Human beings, their feelings and passions, would indeed be degraded if such a wretch as I felt pride. Justine, poor unhappy Justine, was as innocent as I, and she suffered the same charge; she died for it; and I am the cause of this—I murdered her. William, Justine, and Henry—they all died by my hands."

My father had often, during my imprisonment, heard me make the same assertion; when I thus accused myself, he sometimes seemed to desire an explanation, and at others he appeared to consider it as the offspring of delirium, and that, during my illness, some idea of this kind had presented itself to my imagination, the remembrance of which I preserved in my convalescence. I avoided explanation and maintained a continual silence concerning the wretch I had created. I had a persuasion that I should be supposed mad, and this in itself would forever have chained my tongue. But, besides, I could not bring myself to disclose a secret which would fill my hearer with consternation and make fear and unnatural horror the inmates of his breast. I checked, therefore, my impatient thirst for sympathy and was silent when I would have given the world to have confided the fatal secret. Yet, still, words like those I have recorded would burst uncontrollably from me. I could offer no explanation of them, but their truth in part relieved the burden of my mysterious woe.

Upon this occasion my father said, with an expression of unbounded wonder, "My dearest Victor, what infatuation is this? My dear son, I entreat you never to make such an assertion again."

"I am not mad," I cried energetically; "the sun and the heavens, who have viewed my operations, can bear witness of my truth. I am the assassin of those most innocent victims; they died by my machinations. A thousand times would I have shed my own blood, drop by drop, to have saved their lives; but I could not, my father, indeed I could not sacrifice the whole human race."

The conclusion of this speech convinced my father that my ideas were deranged, and he instantly changed the subject of our conversation and endeavoured to alter the course of my thoughts. He wished as much as possible to obliterate the memory of the scenes that had taken place in Ireland and never alluded to them or suffered me to speak of my misfortunes.

As time passed away I became more calm; misery had her dwelling in my heart, but I no longer talked in the same incoherent manner of my own crimes; sufficient for me was the consciousness of them. By the utmost self-violence I curbed the imperious voice of wretchedness, which sometimes desired to declare itself to the whole world, and my manners were calmer and more composed than they had ever been since my journey to the sea of ice. A few days before we left Paris on our way to Switzerland, I received the following letter from Elizabeth:

MY DEAR FRIEND,

It gave me the greatest pleasure to receive a letter from my uncle dated at Paris; you are no longer at a formidable distance, and I may hope to see you in less than a fortnight. My poor cousin, how much you must have suffered! I expect to see you looking even more ill than when you quitted Geneva. This winter has been passed most miserably, tortured as I have been by anxious suspense; yet I hope to see peace in your countenance and to find that your heart is not totally void of comfort and tranquillity.

Yet I fear that the same feelings now exist that made you so miserable a year ago, even perhaps augmented by time. I would not disturb you at this period, when so many misfortunes weigh upon you, but a conversation that I had with my uncle previous to his departure renders some explanation necessary before we meet.

Explanation! You may possibly say, What can Elizabeth have to explain? If you really say this, my questions are answered and all my doubts satisfied. But you are distant from me, and it is possible that you may dread and yet be pleased with this explanation; and in a probability of this being the case, I dare not any longer postpone writing what, during your absence, I have often wished to express to you but have never had the courage to begin.

You well know, Victor, that our union had been the favourite plan of your parents ever since our infancy. We were told this when young, and taught to look forward to it as an event that would certainly take place. We were affectionate playfellows during childhood, and, I believe, dear and valued friends to one another as we grew older. But as brother and sister often entertain a lively affection towards each other without desiring a more intimate union, may not such also be our case? Tell me, dearest Victor. Answer me, I conjure you by our mutual happiness, with simple truth—Do you not love another?

You have travelled; you have spent several years of your life at Ingolstadt; and I confess to you, my friend, that when I saw you last autumn so unhappy, flying to solitude from the society of every creature, I could not help supposing that you might regret our connection and believe yourself bound in honour to fulfil the wishes of your parents, although they opposed themselves to your inclinations. But this is false reasoning. I confess to you, my friend, that I love you and that in my airy dreams of futurity you have been my constant friend and companion. But it is your happiness I desire as well as my own when I declare to you that our marriage would render me eternally miserable unless it were the dictate of your own free choice. Even now I weep to think that, borne down as you are by the cruellest misfortunes, you may stifle, by the word 'honour,' all hope of that love and happiness which would alone restore you to yourself. I, who have so disinterested an affection for you, may increase your miseries tenfold by being an obstacle to your wishes. Ah! Victor, be assured that your cousin and playmate has too sincere a love for you not to be made miserable by this supposition. Be happy, my friend; and if you obey me in this one request, remain satisfied that nothing on earth will have the power to interrupt my tranquillity.

Do not let this letter disturb you; do not answer tomorrow, or the next day, or even until you come, if it will give you pain. My uncle will send me news of your health, and if I see but one smile on your lips when we meet, occasioned by this or any other exertion of mine, I shall need no other happiness.

ELIZABETH LAVENZA
Geneva, May 18th, 17—.

This letter revived in my memory what I had before forgotten, the threat of the fiend—"*I will be with you on your wedding-night!*" Such was my sentence, and on that night would the daemon employ every art to destroy me and tear me from the glimpse of happiness which promised partly to console my sufferings. On that night he had determined to consummate his crimes by my death. Well, be it so; a deadly struggle would then assuredly take place, in which if he were victorious I should be at peace and his power over me be at an end. If he were vanquished, I should be a free man. Alas! What freedom? Such as the peasant enjoys when his family have been massacred before his eyes, his cottage burnt, his lands laid waste, and he is turned adrift, homeless, penniless, and alone, but free. Such would be my liberty except that in my Elizabeth I possessed a treasure, alas, balanced by those horrors of remorse and guilt which would pursue me until death.

Sweet and beloved Elizabeth! I read and reread her letter, and some softened feelings stole into my heart and dared to whisper paradisiacal dreams of love and joy; but the apple was already eaten, and the angel's arm bared to drive me from all hope. Yet I would die to make her happy. If the monster executed his threat, death was inevitable; yet, again, I considered whether my marriage would hasten my fate. My destruction might indeed arrive a few months sooner, but if my torturer should suspect that I postponed it, influenced by his menaces, he would surely find other and perhaps more dreadful means of revenge.

He had vowed *to be with me on my wedding-night*, yet he did not consider that threat as binding him to peace in the meantime, for as if to show me that he was not yet satiated with blood, he had murdered Clerval immediately after the enunciation of his threats. I resolved, therefore, that if my immediate union with my cousin would conduce either to hers or my father's happiness, my adversary's designs against my life should not retard it a single hour.

In this state of mind I wrote to Elizabeth. My letter was calm and affectionate. "I fear, my beloved girl," I said, "little happiness remains for us on earth; yet all that I may one day enjoy is centred in you. Chase away your idle fears; to you alone do I consecrate my life and my endeavours for contentment. I have one secret, Elizabeth, a dreadful one; when revealed to you, it will chill your frame with horror, and then, far from being surprised at my misery, you will only wonder that I survive what I have endured. I will confide this tale of misery and terror to you the day after our marriage shall take place, for, my sweet cousin, there must be perfect confidence between us. But until then, I conjure you, do not mention or allude to it. This I most earnestly entreat, and I know you will comply."

In about a week after the arrival of Elizabeth's letter, we returned to Geneva. The sweet girl welcomed me with warm affection, yet tears were in her eyes as she beheld my emaciated frame and feverish cheeks. I saw a change in her also. She was thinner and had lost much of that heavenly vivacity that had before charmed me; but her gentleness and soft looks of compassion made her a more fit companion for one blasted and miserable as I was.

The tranquillity which I now enjoyed did not endure. Memory brought madness with it, and when I thought of what had passed, a real insanity possessed me; sometimes I was furious and burnt with rage, sometimes low and despondent. I neither spoke nor looked at anyone, but sat motionless, bewildered by the multitude of miseries that overcame me.

Elizabeth alone had the power to draw me from these fits; her gentle voice would soothe me when transported by passion and inspire me with human feelings when sunk in torpor. She wept with me and for me. When reason returned, she would remonstrate and endeavour to inspire me with resignation. Ah! It is well for the unfortunate to be resigned, but for the guilty there is no peace. The agonies of remorse poison the luxury there is otherwise sometimes found in indulging the excess of grief.

Soon after my arrival my father spoke of my immediate marriage with Elizabeth. I remained silent.

"Have you, then, some other attachment?"

"None on earth. I love Elizabeth and look forward to our union with delight. Let the day therefore be fixed; and on it I will consecrate myself, in life or death, to the happiness of my cousin."

"My dear Victor, do not speak thus. Heavy misfortunes have befallen us, but let us only cling closer to what remains and transfer our love for those whom we have lost to those who yet live. Our circle will be small but bound close by the ties of affection and mutual misfortune. And when time shall have softened your despair, new and dear objects of care will be born to replace those of whom we have been so cruelly deprived."

Such were the lessons of my father. But to me the remembrance of the threat returned; nor can you wonder that, omnipotent as the fiend had yet been in his deeds of blood, I should almost regard him as invincible, and that when he had pronounced the words "*I shall be with you on your wedding-night*," I should regard the threatened fate as unavoidable. But death was no evil to me if the loss of Elizabeth were balanced with it, and I therefore, with a contented and even cheerful countenance, agreed with my father that if my cousin would consent, the ceremony should take place in ten days, and thus put, as I imagined, the seal to my fate.

Great God! If for one instant I had thought what might be the hellish intention of my fiendish adversary, I would rather have banished myself forever from my native country and wandered a friendless outcast over the earth than have consented to this miserable marriage. But, as if possessed of magic powers, the monster had blinded me to his real intentions; and when I thought that I had prepared only my own death, I hastened that of a far dearer victim.

As the period fixed for our marriage drew nearer, whether from cowardice or a prophetic feeling, I felt my heart sink within me. But I concealed my feelings by an appearance of hilarity that brought smiles and joy to the countenance of my father, but hardly deceived the ever-watchful and nicer eye of Elizabeth. She looked forward to our union with placid contentment, not unmingled with a little fear, which past misfortunes had impressed, that what now appeared certain and tangible happiness might soon dissipate into an airy dream and leave no trace but deep and everlasting regret.

Preparations were made for the event, congratulatory visits were received, and all wore a smiling appearance. I shut up, as well as I could, in my own heart the anxiety that preyed there and entered with seeming earnestness into the plans of my father, although they might only serve as the decorations of my tragedy. Through my father's exertions a part of the inheritance of Elizabeth had been restored to her by the Austrian government. A small possession on the shores of Como belonged to her. It was agreed that, immediately after our union, we should proceed to Villa Lavenza and spend our first days of happiness beside the beautiful lake near which it stood.

In the meantime I took every precaution to defend my person in case the fiend should openly attack me. I carried pistols and a dagger constantly about me and was ever on the watch to prevent artifice, and by these means gained a greater degree of tranquillity. Indeed, as the period approached, the threat appeared more as a delusion, not to be regarded as worthy to disturb my peace, while the happiness I hoped for in my marriage wore a greater appearance of certainty as the day fixed for its solemnization drew nearer and I heard it continually spoken of as an occurrence which no accident could possibly prevent.

Elizabeth seemed happy; my tranquil demeanour contributed greatly to calm her mind. But on the day that was to fulfil my wishes and my destiny, she was melancholy, and a presentiment of evil pervaded her; and perhaps also she thought of the dreadful secret which I had promised to reveal to her on the following day. My father was in the meantime overjoyed and in the bustle of preparation only recognized in the melancholy of his niece the diffidence of a bride.

After the ceremony was performed a large party assembled at my father's, but it was agreed that Elizabeth and I should commence our journey by water, sleeping that night at Evian and continuing our voyage on the following day. The day was fair, the wind favourable; all smiled on our nuptial embarkation.

Those were the last moments of my life during which I enjoyed the feeling of happiness. We passed rapidly along; the sun was hot, but we were sheltered from its rays by a kind of canopy while we enjoyed the beauty of the scene, sometimes on one side of the lake, where we saw Mont Salève, the pleasant banks of Montalègre, and at a distance, surmounting all, the beautiful Mont Blanc and the assemblage of snowy mountains that in vain endeavour to emulate her; sometimes coasting the opposite banks, we saw the mighty Jura opposing its dark side to the ambition that would quit its native country, and an almost insurmountable barrier to the invader who should wish to enslave it.

I took the hand of Elizabeth. "You are sorrowful, my love. Ah! If you knew what I have suffered and what I may yet endure, you would endeavour to let me taste the quiet and freedom from despair that this one day at least permits me to enjoy."

"Be happy, my dear Victor," replied Elizabeth; "there is, I hope, nothing to distress you; and be assured that if a lively joy is not painted in my face, my heart is contented. Something whispers to me not to depend too much on the prospect that is opened before us, but I will not listen to such a sinister voice. Observe how fast we move along and how the clouds, which sometimes obscure and sometimes rise above the dome of Mont Blanc, render this scene of beauty still more interesting. Look also at the innumerable fish that are swimming in the clear waters, where we can distinguish every pebble that lies at the bottom. What a divine day! How happy and serene all nature appears!"

Thus Elizabeth endeavoured to divert her thoughts and mine from all reflection upon melancholy subjects. But her temper was fluctuating; joy for a few instants shone in her eyes, but it continually gave place to distraction and reverie.

The sun sank lower in the heavens; we passed the river Drance and observed its path through the chasms of the higher and the glens of the lower hills. The Alps here come closer to the lake, and we approached the amphitheatre of mountains which forms its eastern boundary. The spire of Evian shone under the woods that surrounded it and the range of mountain above mountain by which it was overhung.

The wind, which had hitherto carried us along with amazing rapidity, sank at sunset to a light breeze; the soft air just ruffled the water and caused a pleasant motion among the trees as we approached the shore, from which it wafted the most delightful scent of flowers and hay. The sun sank beneath the horizon as we landed, and as I touched the shore I felt those cares and fears revive which soon were to clasp me and cling to me forever.

CHAPTER VI

It was eight o'clock when we landed; we walked for a short time on the shore, enjoying the transitory light, and then retired to the inn and contemplated the lovely scene of waters, woods, and mountains, obscured in darkness, yet still displaying their black outlines.

The wind, which had fallen in the south, now rose with great violence in the west. The moon had reached her summit in the heavens and was beginning to descend; the clouds swept across it swifter than the flight of the vulture and dimmed her rays, while the lake reflected the scene of the busy heavens, rendered still busier by the restless waves that were beginning to rise. Suddenly a heavy storm of rain descended.

I had been calm during the day, but so soon as night obscured the shapes of objects, a thousand fears arose in my mind. I was anxious and watchful, while my right hand grasped a pistol which was hidden in my bosom; every sound terrified me, but I resolved that I would sell my life dearly and not shrink from the conflict until my own life or that of my adversary was extinguished.

Elizabeth observed my agitation for some time in timid and fearful silence, but there was something in my glance which communicated terror to her, and trembling, she asked, "What is it that agitates you, my dear Victor? What is it you fear?"

"Oh! Peace, peace, my love," replied I; "this night, and all will be safe; but this night is dreadful, very dreadful."

I passed an hour in this state of mind, when suddenly I reflected how fearful the combat which I momentarily expected would be to my wife, and I earnestly entreated her to retire, resolving not to join her until I had obtained some knowledge as to the situation of my enemy.

She left me, and I continued some time walking up and down the passages of the house and inspecting every corner that might afford a retreat to my adversary. But I discovered no trace of him and was beginning to conjecture that some fortunate chance had intervened to prevent the execution of his menaces when suddenly I heard a shrill and dreadful scream. It came from the room into which Elizabeth had retired. As I heard it, the whole truth rushed into my mind, my arms dropped, the motion of every muscle and fibre was suspended; I could feel the blood trickling in my veins and tingling in the extremities of my limbs. This state lasted but for an instant; the scream was repeated, and I rushed into the room.

Great God! Why did I not then expire! Why am I here to relate the destruction of the best hope and the purest creature on earth? She was there, lifeless and inanimate, thrown across the bed, her head hanging down and her pale and distorted features half covered by her hair. Everywhere I turn I see the same figure—her bloodless arms and relaxed form flung by the murderer on its bridal bier. Could I behold this and live? Alas! Life is obstinate and clings closest where it is most hated. For a moment only did I lose recollection; I fell senseless on the ground.

When I recovered, I found myself surrounded by the people of the inn; their countenances expressed a breathless terror, but the horror of others appeared only as a mockery, a shadow of the feelings that oppressed me. I escaped from them to the room where lay the body of Elizabeth, my love, my wife, so lately living, so dear, so worthy. She had been moved from the posture in which I had first beheld her, and now, as she lay, her head upon her arm and a handkerchief thrown across her face and neck, I might have supposed her asleep. I rushed towards her and embraced her with ardour, but the deadly languor and coldness of the limbs told me that what I now held in my arms had ceased to be the Elizabeth whom I had loved and cherished. The murderous mark of the fiend's grasp was on her neck, and the breath had ceased to issue from her lips.

While I still hung over her in the agony of despair, I happened to look up. The windows of the room had before been darkened, and I felt a kind of panic on seeing the pale yellow light of the moon illuminate the chamber. The shutters had been thrown back, and with a sensation of horror not to be described, I saw at the open window a figure the most hideous and abhorred. A grin was on the face of the monster; he seemed to jeer, as with his fiendish finger he pointed towards the corpse of my wife. I rushed towards the window, and drawing a pistol from my bosom, fired; but he eluded me, leaped from his station, and running with the swiftness of lightning, plunged into the lake.

The report of the pistol brought a crowd into the room. I pointed to the spot where he had disappeared, and we followed the track with boats; nets were cast, but in vain. After passing several hours, we returned hopeless, most of my companions believing it to have been a form conjured up by my fancy. After having landed, they proceeded to search the country, parties going in different directions among the woods and vines.

I attempted to accompany them, and proceeded a short distance from the house, but my head whirled round, my steps were like those of a drunken man, I fell at last in a state of utter exhaustion; a film covered my eyes, and my skin was parched with the heat of fever. In this state I was carried back and placed on a bed, hardly conscious of what had happened; my eyes wandered round the room as if to seek something that I had lost.

After an interval I arose, and as if by instinct, crawled into the room where the corpse of my beloved lay. There were women weeping around; I hung over it and joined my sad tears to theirs; all this time no distinct idea presented itself to my mind, but my thoughts rambled to various subjects, reflecting confusedly on my misfortunes and their cause. I was bewildered, in a cloud of wonder and horror. The death of William, the execution of Justine, the murder of Clerval, and lastly of my wife; even at that moment I knew not that my only remaining friends were safe from the malignity of the fiend; my father even now might be writhing under his grasp, and Ernest might be dead at his feet. This idea made me shudder and recalled me to action. I started up and resolved to return to Geneva with all possible speed.

There were no horses to be procured, and I must return by the lake; but the wind was unfavourable, and the rain fell in torrents. However, it was hardly morning, and I might reasonably hope to arrive by night. I hired men to row and took an oar myself, for I had always experienced relief from mental torment in bodily exercise. But the overflowing misery I now felt, and the excess of agitation that I endured rendered me incapable of any exertion. I threw down the oar, and leaning my head upon my hands, gave way to every gloomy idea that arose. If I looked up, I saw scenes which were familiar to me in my happier time and which I had contemplated but the day before in the company of her who was now but a shadow and a recollection. Tears streamed from my eyes. The rain had ceased for a moment, and I saw the fish play in the waters as they had done a few hours before; they had then been observed by Elizabeth. Nothing is so painful to the human mind as a great and sudden change. The sun might shine or the clouds might lower, but nothing could appear to me as it had done the day before. A fiend had snatched from me every hope of future happiness; no creature had ever been so miserable as I was; so frightful an event is single in the history of man.

But why should I dwell upon the incidents that followed this last overwhelming event? Mine has been a tale of horrors; I have reached their acme, and what I must now relate can but be tedious to you. Know that, one by one, my friends were snatched away; I was left desolate. My own strength is exhausted, and I must tell, in a few words, what remains of my hideous narration.

I arrived at Geneva. My father and Ernest yet lived, but the former sunk under the tidings that I bore. I see him now, excellent and venerable old man! His eyes wandered in vacancy, for they had lost their charm and their delight—his Elizabeth, his more than daughter, whom he doted on with all that affection which a man feels, who in the decline of life, having few affections, clings more earnestly to those that remain. Cursed, cursed be the fiend that brought misery on his grey hairs and doomed him to waste in wretchedness! He could not live under the horrors that were accumulated around him; the springs of existence suddenly gave way; he was unable to rise from his bed, and in a few days he died in my arms.

What then became of me? I know not; I lost sensation, and chains and darkness were the only objects that pressed upon me. Sometimes, indeed, I dreamt that I wandered in flowery meadows and pleasant vales with the friends of my youth, but I awoke and found myself in a dungeon. Melancholy followed, but by degrees I gained a clear conception of my miseries and situation and was then released from my prison. For they had called me mad, and during many months, as I understood, a solitary cell had been my habitation.

Liberty, however, had been a useless gift to me, had I not, as I awakened to reason, at the same time awakened to revenge. As the memory of past misfortunes pressed upon me, I began to reflect on their cause—the monster whom I had created, the miserable daemon whom I had sent abroad into the world for my destruction. I was possessed by a maddening rage when I thought of him, and desired and ardently prayed that I might have him within my grasp to wreak a great and signal revenge on his cursed head.

Nor did my hate long confine itself to useless wishes; I began to reflect on the best means of securing him; and for this purpose, about a month after my release, I repaired to a criminal judge in the town and told him that I had an accusation to make, that I knew the destroyer of my family, and that I required him to exert his whole authority for the apprehension of the murderer.

The magistrate listened to me with attention and kindness. "Be assured, sir," said he, "no pains or exertions on my part shall be spared to discover the villain."

"I thank you," replied I; "listen, therefore, to the deposition that I have to make. It is indeed a tale so strange that I should fear you would not credit it were there not something in truth which, however wonderful, forces conviction. The story is too connected to be mistaken for a dream, and I have no motive for falsehood." My manner as I thus addressed him was impressive but calm; I had formed in my own heart a resolution to pursue my destroyer to death, and this purpose quieted my agony and for an interval reconciled me to life. I now related my history briefly but with firmness and precision, marking the dates with accuracy and never deviating into invective or exclamation.

The magistrate appeared at first perfectly incredulous, but as I continued he became more attentive and interested; I saw him sometimes shudder with horror; at others a lively surprise, unmingled with disbelief, was painted on his countenance.

When I had concluded my narration I said, "This is the being whom I accuse and for whose seizure and punishment I call upon you to exert your whole power. It is your duty as a magistrate, and I believe and hope that your feelings as a man will not revolt from the execution of those functions on this occasion."

This address caused a considerable change in the physiognomy of my own auditor. He had heard my story with that half kind of belief that is given to a tale of spirits and supernatural events; but when he was called upon to act officially in consequence, the whole tide of his incredulity returned. He, however, answered mildly, "I would willingly afford you every aid in your pursuit, but the creature of whom you speak appears to have powers which would put all my exertions to defiance. Who can follow an animal which can traverse the sea of ice and inhabit caves and dens where no man would venture to intrude? Besides, some months have elapsed since the commission of his crimes, and no one can conjecture to what place he has wandered or what region he may now inhabit."

"I do not doubt that he hovers near the spot which I inhabit, and if he has indeed taken refuge in the Alps, he may be hunted like the chamois and destroyed as a beast of prey. But I perceive your thoughts; you do not credit my narrative and do not intend to pursue my enemy with the punishment which is his desert."

As I spoke, rage sparkled in my eyes; the magistrate was intimidated. "You are mistaken," said he. "I will exert myself, and if it is in my power to seize the monster, be assured that he shall suffer punishment proportionate to his crimes. But I fear, from what you have yourself described to be his properties, that this will prove impracticable; and thus, while every proper measure is pursued, you should make up your mind to disappointment."

"That cannot be; but all that I can say will be of little avail. My revenge is of no moment to you; yet, while I allow it to be a vice, I confess that it is the devouring and only passion of my soul. My rage is unspeakable when I reflect that the murderer, whom I have turned loose upon society, still exists. You refuse my just demand; I have but one resource, and I devote myself, either in my life or death, to his destruction."

I trembled with excess of agitation as I said this; there was a frenzy in my manner, and something, I doubt not, of that haughty fierceness which the martyrs of old are said to have possessed. But to a Genevan magistrate, whose mind was occupied by far other ideas than those of devotion and heroism, this elevation of mind had much the appearance of madness. He endeavoured to soothe me as a nurse does a child and reverted to my tale as the effects of delirium.

"Man," I cried, "how ignorant art thou in thy pride of wisdom! Cease; you know not what it is you say."

I broke from the house angry and disturbed and retired to meditate on some other mode of action.

CHAPTER VII

My present situation was one in which all voluntary thought was swallowed up and lost. I was hurried away by fury; revenge alone endowed me with strength and composure; it moulded my feelings and allowed me to be calculating and calm at periods when otherwise delirium or death would have been my portion.

My first resolution was to quit Geneva forever; my country, which, when I was happy and beloved, was dear to me, now, in my adversity, became hateful. I provided myself with a sum of money, together with a few jewels which had belonged to my mother, and departed.

And now my wanderings began which are to cease but with life. I have traversed a vast portion of the earth and have endured all the hardships which travellers in deserts and barbarous countries are wont to meet. How I have lived I hardly know; many times have I stretched my failing limbs upon the sandy plain and prayed for death. But revenge kept me alive; I dared not die and leave my adversary in being.

When I quitted Geneva my first labour was to gain some clue by which I might trace the steps of my fiendish enemy. But my plan was unsettled, and I wandered many hours round the confines of the town, uncertain what path I should pursue. As night approached I found myself at the entrance of the cemetery where William, Elizabeth, and my father reposed. I entered it and approached the tomb which marked their graves. Everything was silent except the leaves of the trees, which were gently agitated by the wind; the night was nearly dark, and the scene would have been solemn and affecting even to an uninterested observer. The spirits of the departed seemed to flit around and to cast a shadow, which was felt but not seen, around the head of the mourner.

The deep grief which this scene had at first excited quickly gave way to rage and despair. They were dead, and I lived; their murderer also lived, and to destroy him I must drag out my weary existence. I knelt on the grass and kissed the earth and with quivering lips exclaimed, "By the sacred earth on which I kneel, by the shades that wander near me, by the deep and eternal grief that I feel, I swear; and by thee, O Night, and the spirits that preside over thee, to pursue the daemon who caused this misery, until he or I shall perish in mortal conflict. For this purpose I will preserve my life; to execute this dear revenge will I again behold the sun and tread the green herbage of earth, which otherwise should vanish from my eyes forever. And I call on you, spirits of the dead, and on you, wandering ministers of vengeance, to aid and conduct me in my work. Let the cursed and hellish monster drink deep of agony; let him feel the despair that now torments me."

I had begun my adjuration with solemnity and an awe which almost assured me that the shades of my murdered friends heard and approved my devotion, but the furies possessed me as I concluded, and rage choked my utterance.

I was answered through the stillness of night by a loud and fiendish laugh. It rang on my ears long and heavily; the mountains re-echoed it, and I felt as if all hell surrounded me with mockery and laughter. Surely in that moment I should have been possessed by frenzy and have destroyed my miserable existence but that my vow was heard and that I was reserved for vengeance. The laughter died away, when a well-known and abhorred voice, apparently close to my ear, addressed me in an audible whisper, "I am satisfied, miserable wretch! You have determined to live, and I am satisfied."

I darted towards the spot from which the sound proceeded, but the devil eluded my grasp. Suddenly the broad disk of the moon arose and shone full upon his ghastly and distorted shape as he fled with more than mortal speed.

I pursued him, and for many months this has been my task. Guided by a slight clue, I followed the windings of the Rhône, but vainly. The blue Mediterranean appeared, and by a strange chance, I saw the fiend enter by night and hide himself in a vessel bound for the Black Sea. I took my passage in the same ship, but he escaped, I know not how.

Amidst the wilds of Tartary and Russia, although he still evaded me, I have ever followed in his track. Sometimes the peasants, scared by this horrid apparition, informed me of his path; sometimes he himself, who feared that if I lost all trace of him I should despair and die, left some mark to guide me. The snows descended on my head, and I saw the print of his huge step on the white plain. To you first entering on life, to whom care is new and agony unknown, how can you understand what I have felt and still feel? Cold, want, and fatigue were the least pains which I was destined to endure; I was cursed by some devil and carried about with me my eternal hell; yet still a spirit of good followed and directed my steps and when I most murmured would suddenly extricate me from seemingly insurmountable difficulties. Sometimes, when nature, overcome by hunger, sank under the exhaustion, a repast was prepared for me in the desert that restored and inspired me. The fare was, indeed, coarse, such as the peasants of the country ate, but I will not doubt that it was set there by the spirits that I had invoked to aid me. Often, when all was dry, the heavens cloudless, and I was parched by thirst, a slight cloud would bedim the sky, shed the few drops that revived me, and vanish.

I followed, when I could, the courses of the rivers; but the daemon generally avoided these, as it was here that the population of the country chiefly collected. In other places human beings were seldom seen, and I generally subsisted on the wild animals that crossed my path. I had money with me and gained the friendship of the villagers by distributing it; or I brought with me some food that I had killed, which, after taking a small part, I always presented to those who had provided me with fire and utensils for cooking.

My life, as it passed thus, was indeed hateful to me, and it was during sleep alone that I could taste joy. O blessed sleep! Often, when most miserable, I sank to repose, and my dreams lulled me even to rapture. The spirits that guarded me had provided these moments, or rather hours, of happiness that I might retain strength to fulfil my pilgrimage. Deprived of this respite, I should have sunk under my hardships. During the day I was sustained and inspirited by the hope of night, for in sleep I saw my friends, my wife, and my beloved country; again I saw the benevolent countenance of my father, heard the silver tones of my Elizabeth's voice, and beheld Clerval enjoying health and youth. Often, when wearied by a toilsome march, I persuaded myself that I was dreaming until night should come and that I should then enjoy reality in the arms of my dearest friends. What agonising fondness did I feel for them! How did I cling to their dear forms, as sometimes they haunted even my waking hours, and persuade myself that they still lived! At such moments vengeance, that burned within me, died in my heart, and I pursued my path towards the destruction of the daemon more as a task enjoined by heaven, as the mechanical impulse of some power of which I was unconscious, than as the ardent desire of my soul.

What his feelings were whom I pursued I cannot know. Sometimes, indeed, he left marks in writing on the barks of the trees or cut in stone that guided me and instigated my fury. "My reign is not yet over"—these words were legible in one of these inscriptions—"you live, and my power is complete. Follow me; I seek the everlasting ices of the north, where you will feel the misery of cold and frost, to which I am impassive. You will find near this place, if you follow not too tardily, a dead hare; eat and be refreshed. Come on, my enemy; we have yet to wrestle for our lives, but many hard and miserable hours must you endure until that period shall arrive."

Scoffing devil! Again do I vow vengeance; again do I devote thee, miserable fiend, to torture and death. Never will I give up my search until he or I perish; and then with what ecstasy shall I join my Elizabeth and my departed friends, who even now prepare for me the reward of my tedious toil and horrible pilgrimage!

As I still pursued my journey to the northward, the snows thickened and the cold increased in a degree almost too severe to support. The peasants were shut up in their hovels, and only a few of the most hardy ventured forth to seize the animals whom starvation had forced from their hiding-places to seek for prey. The rivers were covered with ice, and no fish could be procured; and thus I was cut off from my chief article of maintenance.

The triumph of my enemy increased with the difficulty of my labours. One inscription that he left was in these words: "Prepare! Your toils only begin; wrap yourself in furs and provide food, for we shall soon enter upon a journey where your sufferings will satisfy my everlasting hatred."

My courage and perseverance were invigorated by these scoffing words; I resolved not to fail in my purpose, and calling on heaven to support me, I continued with unabated fervour to traverse immense deserts, until the ocean appeared at a distance and formed the utmost boundary of the horizon. Oh! How unlike it was to the blue seasons of the south! Covered with ice, it was only to be distinguished from land by its superior wildness and ruggedness. The Greeks wept for joy when they beheld the Mediterranean from the hills of Asia, and hailed with rapture the boundary of their toils. I did not weep, but I knelt down and with a full heart thanked my guiding spirit for conducting me in safety to the place where I hoped, notwithstanding my adversary's gibe, to meet and grapple with him.

Some weeks before this period I had procured a sledge and dogs and thus traversed the snows with inconceivable speed. I know not whether the fiend possessed the same advantages, but I found that, as before I had daily lost ground in the pursuit, I now gained on him, so much so that when I first saw the ocean he was but one day's journey in advance, and I hoped to intercept him before he should reach the beach. With new courage, therefore, I pressed on, and in two days arrived at a wretched hamlet on the seashore. I enquired of the inhabitants concerning the fiend and gained accurate information. A gigantic monster, they said, had arrived the night before, armed with a gun and many pistols, putting to flight the inhabitants of a solitary cottage through fear of his terrific appearance. He had carried off their store of winter food, and placing it in a sledge, to draw which he had seized on a numerous drove of trained dogs, he had harnessed them, and the same night, to the joy of the horror-struck villagers, had pursued his journey across the sea in a direction that led to no land; and they conjectured that he must speedily be destroyed by the breaking of the ice or frozen by the eternal frosts.

On hearing this information, I suffered a temporary access of despair. He had escaped me, and I must commence a destructive and almost endless journey across the mountainous ices of the ocean, amidst cold that few of the inhabitants could long endure and which I, the native of a genial and sunny climate, could not hope to survive. Yet at the idea that the fiend should live and be triumphant, my rage and vengeance returned, and like a mighty tide, overwhelmed every other feeling. After a slight repose, during which the spirits of the dead hovered round and instigated me to toil and revenge, I prepared for my journey.

I exchanged my land-sledge for one fashioned for the inequalities of the frozen ocean, and purchasing a plentiful stock of provisions, I departed from land.

I cannot guess how many days have passed since then, but I have endured misery which nothing but the eternal sentiment of a just retribution burning within my heart could have enabled me to support. Immense and rugged mountains of ice often barred up my passage, and I often heard the thunder of the ground sea, which threatened my destruction. But again the frost came and made the paths of the sea secure.

By the quantity of provision which I had consumed, I should guess that I had passed three weeks in this journey; and the continual protraction of hope, returning back upon the heart, often wrung bitter drops of despondency and grief from my eyes. Despair had indeed almost secured her prey, and I should soon have sunk beneath this misery. Once, after the poor animals that conveyed me had with incredible toil gained the summit of a sloping ice mountain, and one, sinking under his fatigue, died, I viewed the expanse before me with anguish, when suddenly my eye caught a dark speck upon the dusky plain. I strained my sight to discover what it could be and uttered a wild cry of ecstasy when I distinguished a sledge and the distorted proportions of a well-known form within. Oh! With what a burning gush did hope revisit my heart! Warm tears filled my eyes, which I hastily wiped away, that they might not intercept the view I had of the daemon; but still my sight was dimmed by the burning drops, until, giving way to the emotions that oppressed me, I wept aloud.

But this was not the time for delay: I disencumbered the dogs of their dead companion, gave them a plentiful portion of food, and after an hour's rest, which was absolutely necessary, and yet which was bitterly irksome to me, I continued my route. The sledge was still visible, nor did I again lose sight of it except at the moments when for a short time some ice-rock concealed it with its intervening crags. I indeed perceptibly gained on it, and when, after nearly two days' journey, I beheld my enemy at no more than a mile distant, my heart bounded within me.

But now, when I appeared almost within grasp of my foe, my hopes were suddenly extinguished, and I lost all trace of him more utterly than I had ever done before. A ground sea was heard; the thunder of its progress, as the waters rolled and swelled beneath me, became every moment more ominous and terrific. I pressed on, but in vain. The wind arose; the sea roared; and, as with the mighty shock of an earthquake, it split and cracked with a tremendous and overwhelming sound. The work was soon finished; in a few minutes a tumultuous sea rolled between me and my enemy, and I was left drifting on a scattered piece of ice that was continually lessening and thus preparing for me a hideous death. In this manner many appalling hours passed; several of my dogs died, and I myself was about to sink under the accumulation of distress when I saw your vessel riding at anchor and holding forth to me hopes of succour and life. I had no conception that vessels ever came so far north and was astounded at the sight. I quickly destroyed part of my sledge to construct oars, and by these means was enabled, with infinite fatigue, to move my ice raft in the direction of your ship. I had determined, if you were going southwards, still to trust myself to the mercy of the seas rather than abandon my purpose. I hoped to induce you to grant me a boat with which I could pursue my enemy. But your direction was northwards. You took me on board when my vigour was exhausted, and I should soon have sunk under my multiplied hardships into a death which I still dread—for my task is unfulfilled.

Oh! When will my guiding spirit, in conducting me to the daemon, allow me the rest I so much desire; or must I die, and he yet live? If I do, swear to me, Walton, that he shall not escape, that you will seek him and satisfy my vengeance in his death. And do I dare to ask of you to undertake my pilgrimage, to endure the hardships that I have undergone? No; I am not so selfish. Yet, when I am dead, if he should appear, if the ministers of vengeance should conduct him to you, swear that he shall not live—swear that he shall not triumph over my accumulated woes and survive to add to the list of his dark crimes. He is eloquent and persuasive, and once his words had even power over my heart; but trust him not. His soul is as hellish as his form, full of treachery and fiend-like malice. Hear him not; call on the names of William, Justine, Clerval, Elizabeth, my father, and of the wretched Victor, and thrust your sword into his heart. I will hover near and direct the steel aright.

WALTON, IN CONTINUATION.
August 26th, 17—.

You have read this strange and terrific story, Margaret; and do you not feel your blood congeal with horror, like that which even now curdles mine? Sometimes, seized with sudden agony, he could not continue his tale; at others, his voice broken, yet piercing, uttered with difficulty the words so replete with anguish. His fine and lovely eyes were now lighted up with indignation, now subdued to downcast sorrow and quenched in infinite wretchedness. Sometimes he commanded his countenance and tones and related the most horrible incidents with a tranquil voice, suppressing every mark of agitation; then, like a volcano bursting forth, his face would suddenly change to an expression of the wildest rage as he shrieked out imprecations on his persecutor.

His tale is connected and told with an appearance of the simplest truth, yet I own to you that the letters of Felix and Safie, which he showed me, and the apparition of the monster seen from our ship, brought to me a greater conviction of the truth of his narrative than his asseverations, however earnest and connected. Such a monster has, then, really existence! I cannot doubt it, yet I am lost in surprise and admiration. Sometimes I endeavoured to gain from Frankenstein the particulars of his creature's formation, but on this point he was impenetrable.

"Are you mad, my friend?" said he. "Or whither does your senseless curiosity lead you? Would you also create for yourself and the world a demoniacal enemy? Peace, peace! Learn my miseries and do not seek to increase your own."

Frankenstein discovered that I made notes concerning his history; he asked to see them and then himself corrected and augmented them in many places, but principally in giving the life and spirit to the conversations he held with his enemy. "Since you have preserved my narration," said he, "I would not that a mutilated one should go down to posterity."

Thus has a week passed away, while I have listened to the strangest tale that ever imagination formed. My thoughts and every feeling of my soul have been drunk up by the interest for my guest which this tale and his own elevated and gentle manners have created. I wish to soothe him, yet can I counsel one so infinitely miserable, so destitute of every hope of consolation, to live? Oh, no! The only joy that he can now know will be when he composes his shattered spirit to peace and death. Yet he enjoys one comfort, the offspring of solitude and delirium; he believes that when in dreams he holds converse with his friends and derives from that communion consolation for his miseries or excitements to his vengeance, that they are not the creations of his fancy, but the beings themselves who visit him from the regions of a remote world. This faith gives a solemnity to his reveries that render them to me almost as imposing and interesting as truth.

Our conversations are not always confined to his own history and misfortunes. On every point of general literature he displays unbounded knowledge and a quick and piercing apprehension. His eloquence is forcible and touching; nor can I hear him, when he relates a pathetic incident or endeavours to move the passions of pity or love, without tears. What a glorious creature must he have been in the days of his prosperity, when he is thus noble and godlike in ruin! He seems to feel his own worth and the greatness of his fall.

"When younger," said he, "I believed myself destined for some great enterprise. My feelings are profound, but I possessed a coolness of judgement that fitted me for illustrious achievements. This sentiment of the worth of my nature supported me when others would have been oppressed, for I deemed it criminal to throw away in useless grief those talents that might be useful to my fellow creatures. When I reflected on the work I had completed, no less a one than the creation of a sensitive and rational animal, I could not rank myself with the herd of common projectors. But this thought, which supported me in the commencement of my career, now serves only to plunge me lower in the dust. All my speculations and hopes are as nothing, and like the archangel who aspired to omnipotence, I am chained in an eternal hell. My imagination was vivid, yet my powers of analysis and application were intense; by the union of these qualities I conceived the idea and executed the creation of a man. Even now I cannot recollect without passion my reveries while the work was incomplete. I trod heaven in my thoughts, now exulting in my powers, now burning with the idea of their effects. From my infancy I was imbued with high hopes and a lofty ambition; but how am I sunk! Oh! My friend, if you had known me as I once was, you would not recognize me in this state of degradation. Despondency rarely visited my heart; a high destiny seemed to bear me on, until I fell, never, never again to rise."

Must I then lose this admirable being? I have longed for a friend; I have sought one who would sympathise with and love me. Behold, on these desert seas I have found such a one, but I fear I have gained him only to know his value and lose him. I would reconcile him to life, but he repulses the idea.

"I thank you, Walton," he said, "for your kind intentions towards so miserable a wretch; but when you speak of new ties and fresh affections, think you that any can replace those who are gone? Can any man be to me as Clerval was, or any woman another Elizabeth? Even where the affections are not strongly moved by any superior excellence, the companions of our childhood always possess a certain power over our minds which hardly any later friend can obtain. They know our infantine dispositions, which, however they may be afterwards modified, are never eradicated; and they can judge of our actions with more certain conclusions as to the integrity of our motives. A sister or a brother can never, unless indeed such symptoms have been shown early, suspect the other of fraud or false dealing, when another friend, however strongly he may be attached, may, in spite of himself, be contemplated with suspicion. But I enjoyed friends, dear not only through habit and association, but from their own merits; and wherever I am, the soothing voice of my Elizabeth and the conversation of Clerval will be ever whispered in my ear. They are dead, and but one feeling in such a solitude can persuade me to preserve my life. If I were engaged in any high undertaking or design, fraught with extensive utility to my fellow creatures, then could I live to fulfil it. But such is not my destiny; I must pursue and destroy the being to whom I gave existence; then my lot on earth will be fulfilled, and I may die."

September 2nd.

MY BELOVED SISTER,

I write to you, encompassed by peril and ignorant whether I am ever doomed to see again dear England and the dearer friends that inhabit it. I am surrounded by mountains of ice which admit of no escape and threaten every moment to crush my vessel. The brave fellows whom I have persuaded to be my companions look towards me for aid, but I have none to bestow. There is something terribly appalling in our situation, yet my courage and hopes do not desert me. Yet it is terrible to reflect that the lives of all these men are endangered through me. If we are lost, my mad schemes are the cause.

And what, Margaret, will be the state of your mind? You will not hear of my destruction, and you will anxiously await my return. Years will pass, and you will have visitings of despair and yet be tortured by hope. Oh! My beloved sister, the sickening failing of your heartfelt expectations is, in prospect, more terrible to me than my own death. But you have a husband and lovely children; you may be happy. Heaven bless you and make you so!

My unfortunate guest regards me with the tenderest compassion. He endeavours to fill me with hope and talks as if life were a possession which he valued. He reminds me how often the same accidents have happened to other navigators who have attempted this sea, and in spite of myself, he fills me with cheerful auguries.

Even the sailors feel the power of his eloquence; when he speaks, they no longer despair; he rouses their energies, and while they hear his voice they believe these vast mountains of ice are molehills which will vanish before the resolutions of man. These feelings are transitory; each day of expectation delayed fills them with fear, and I almost dread a mutiny caused by this despair.

September 5th.

A scene has just passed of such uncommon interest that, although it is highly probable that these papers may never reach you, yet I cannot forbear recording it.

We are still surrounded by mountains of ice, still in imminent danger of being crushed in their conflict. The cold is excessive, and many of my unfortunate comrades have already found a grave amidst this scene of desolation. Frankenstein has daily declined in health; a feverish fire still glimmers in his eyes, but he is exhausted, and when suddenly roused to any exertion, he speedily sinks again into apparent lifelessness.

I mentioned in my last letter the fears I entertained of a mutiny. This morning, as I sat watching the wan countenance of my friend— his eyes half closed and his limbs hanging listlessly—I was roused by half a dozen of the sailors, who demanded admission into the cabin. They entered, and their leader addressed me. He told me that he and his companions had been chosen by the other sailors to come in deputation to me to make me a requisition which, in justice, I could not refuse. We were immured in ice and should probably never escape, but they feared that if, as was possible, the ice should dissipate and a free passage be opened, I should be rash enough to continue my voyage and lead them into fresh dangers, after they might happily have surmounted this. They insisted, therefore, that I should engage with a solemn promise that if the vessel should be freed I would instantly direct my course southwards.

This speech troubled me. I had not despaired, nor had I yet conceived the idea of returning if set free. Yet could I, in justice, or even in possibility, refuse this demand? I hesitated before I answered, when Frankenstein, who had at first been silent, and indeed appeared hardly to have force enough to attend, now roused himself; his eyes sparkled, and his cheeks flushed with momentary vigour. Turning towards the men, he said:

"What do you mean? What do you demand of your captain? Are you, then, so easily turned from your design? Did you not call this a glorious expedition? And wherefore was it glorious? Not because the way was smooth and placid as a southern sea, but because it was full of dangers and terror, because at every new incident your fortitude was to be called forth and your courage exhibited, because danger and death surrounded it, and these you were to brave and overcome. For this was it a glorious, for this was it an honourable undertaking. You were hereafter to be hailed as the benefactors of your species, your names adored as belonging to brave men who encountered death for honour and the benefit of mankind. And now, behold, with the first imagination of danger, or, if you will, the first mighty and terrific trial of your courage, you shrink away and are content to be handed down as men who had not strength enough to endure cold and peril; and so, poor souls, they were chilly and returned to their warm firesides. Why, that requires not this preparation; ye need not have come thus far and dragged your captain to the shame of a defeat merely to prove yourselves cowards. Oh! Be men, or be more than men. Be steady to your purposes and firm as a rock. This ice is not made of such stuff as your hearts may be; it is mutable and cannot withstand you if you say that it shall not. Do not return to your families with the stigma of disgrace marked on your brows. Return as heroes who have fought and conquered and who know not what it is to turn their backs on the foe."

He spoke this with a voice so modulated to the different feelings expressed in his speech, with an eye so full of lofty design and heroism, that can you wonder that these men were moved? They looked at one another and were unable to reply. I spoke; I told them to retire and consider of what had been said, that I would not lead them farther north if they strenuously desired the contrary, but that I hoped that, with reflection, their courage would return.

They retired, and I turned towards my friend, but he was sunk in languor and almost deprived of life.

How all this will terminate, I know not, but I had rather die than return shamefully, my purpose unfulfilled. Yet I fear such will be my fate; the men, unsupported by ideas of glory and honour, can never willingly continue to endure their present hardships.

September 7th.
The die is cast; I have consented to return if we are not destroyed. Thus are my hopes blasted by cowardice and indecision; I come back ignorant and disappointed. It requires more philosophy than I possess to bear this injustice with patience.

September 12th.

It is past; I am returning to England. I have lost my hopes of utility and glory; I have lost my friend. But I will endeavour to detail these bitter circumstances to you, my dear sister; and while I am wafted towards England and towards you, I will not despond.

September 9th, the ice began to move, and roarings like thunder were heard at a distance as the islands split and cracked in every direction. We were in the most imminent peril, but as we could only remain passive, my chief attention was occupied by my unfortunate guest whose illness increased in such a degree that he was entirely confined to his bed. The ice cracked behind us and was driven with force towards the north; a breeze sprang from the west, and on the 11th the passage towards the south became perfectly free. When the sailors saw this and that their return to their native country was apparently assured, a shout of tumultuous joy broke from them, loud and long-continued. Frankenstein, who was dozing, awoke and asked the cause of the tumult. "They shout," I said, "because they will soon return to England."

"Do you, then, really return?"

"Alas! Yes; I cannot withstand their demands. I cannot lead them unwillingly to danger, and I must return."

"Do so, if you will; but I will not. You may give up your purpose, but mine is assigned to me by heaven, and I dare not. I am weak, but surely the spirits who assist my vengeance will endow me with sufficient strength." Saying this, he endeavoured to spring from the bed, but the exertion was too great for him; he fell back and fainted.

It was long before he was restored, and I often thought that life was entirely extinct. At length he opened his eyes; he breathed with difficulty and was unable to speak. The surgeon gave him a composing draught and ordered us to leave him undisturbed. In the meantime he told me that my friend had certainly not many hours to live.

His sentence was pronounced, and I could only grieve and be patient. I sat by his bed, watching him; his eyes were closed, and I thought he slept; but presently he called to me in a feeble voice, and bidding me come near, said:

"Alas! The strength I relied on is gone; I feel that I shall soon die, and he, my enemy and persecutor, may still be in being. Think not, Walton, that in the last moments of my existence I feel that burning hatred and ardent desire of revenge I once expressed; but I feel myself justified in desiring the death of my adversary. During these last days I have been occupied in examining my past conduct; nor do

I find it blamable. In a fit of enthusiastic madness I created a rational creature and was bound towards him to assure, as far as was in my power, his happiness and well-being. This was my duty, but there was another still paramount to that. My duties towards the beings of my own species had greater claims to my attention because they included a greater proportion of happiness or misery. Urged by this view, I refused, and I did right in refusing, to create a companion for the first creature. He showed unparalleled malignity and selfishness in evil; he destroyed my friends; he devoted to destruction beings who possessed exquisite sensations, happiness, and wisdom; nor do I know where this thirst for vengeance may end. Miserable himself that he may render no other wretched, he ought to die. The task of his destruction was mine, but I have failed. When actuated by selfish and vicious motives, I asked you to undertake my unfinished work, and I renew this request now, when I am only induced by reason and virtue.

"Yet I cannot ask you to renounce your country and friends to fulfil this task; and now that you are returning to England, you will have little chance of meeting with him. But the consideration of these points, and the well balancing of what you may esteem your duties, I leave to you; my judgement and ideas are already disturbed by the near approach of death. I dare not ask you to do what I think right, for I may still be misled by passion.

"That he should live to be an instrument of mischief disturbs me; in other respects, this hour, when I momentarily expect my release, is the only happy one which I have enjoyed for several years. The forms of the beloved dead flit before me, and I hasten to their arms. Farewell, Walton! Seek happiness in tranquillity and avoid ambition, even if it be only the apparently innocent one of distinguishing yourself in science and discoveries. Yet why do I say this? I have myself been blasted in these hopes, yet another may succeed."

His voice became faint as he spoke, and at length, exhausted by his effort, he sank into silence. About half an hour afterwards he attempted again to speak but was unable; he pressed my hand feebly, and his eyes closed forever, while the irradiation of a gentle smile passed away from his lips.

Margaret, what comment can I make on the untimely extinction of this glorious spirit? What can I say that will enable you to understand the depth of my sorrow? All that I should express would be inadequate and feeble. My tears flow; my mind is overshadowed by a cloud of disappointment. But I journey towards England, and I may there find consolation.

I am interrupted. What do these sounds portend? It is midnight; the breeze blows fairly, and the watch on deck scarcely stir. Again there is a sound as of a human voice, but hoarser; it comes from the cabin where the remains of Frankenstein still lie. I must arise and examine. Good night, my sister.

Great God! What a scene has just taken place! I am yet dizzy with the remembrance of it. I hardly know whether I shall have the power to detail it; yet the tale which I have recorded would be incomplete without this final and wonderful catastrophe.

I entered the cabin where lay the remains of my ill-fated and admirable friend. Over him hung a form which I cannot find words to describe—gigantic in stature, yet uncouth and distorted in its proportions. As he hung over the coffin, his face was concealed by long locks of ragged hair; but one vast hand was extended, in colour and apparent texture like that of a mummy. When he heard the sound of my approach, he ceased to utter exclamations of grief and horror and sprung towards the window. Never did I behold a vision so horrible as his face, of such loathsome yet appalling hideousness. I shut my eyes involuntarily and endeavoured to recollect what were my duties with regard to this destroyer. I called on him to stay.

He paused, looking on me with wonder, and again turning towards the lifeless form of his creator, he seemed to forget my presence, and every feature and gesture seemed instigated by the wildest rage of some uncontrollable passion.

"That is also my victim!" he exclaimed. "In his murder my crimes are consummated; the miserable series of my being is wound to its close! Oh, Frankenstein! Generous and self-devoted being! What does it avail that I now ask thee to pardon me? I, who irretrievably destroyed thee by destroying all thou lovedst. Alas! He is cold, he cannot answer me."

His voice seemed suffocated, and my first impulses, which had suggested to me the duty of obeying the dying request of my friend in destroying his enemy, were now suspended by a mixture of curiosity and compassion. I approached this tremendous being; I dared not again raise my eyes to his face, there was something so scaring and unearthly in his ugliness. I attempted to speak, but the words died away on my lips. The monster continued to utter wild and incoherent self-reproaches. At length I gathered resolution to address him in a pause of the tempest of his passion. "Your repentance," I said, "is now superfluous. If you had listened to the voice of conscience and heeded the stings of remorse before you had urged your diabolical vengeance to this extremity, Frankenstein would yet have lived."

"And do you dream?" said the daemon. "Do you think that I was then dead to agony and remorse? He," he continued, pointing to the corpse, "he suffered not in the consummation of the deed. Oh! Not the ten-thousandth portion of the anguish that was mine during the lingering detail of its execution. A frightful selfishness hurried me on, while my heart was poisoned with remorse. Think you that the groans of Clerval were music to my ears? My heart was fashioned to be susceptible of love and sympathy, and when wrenched by misery to vice and hatred, it did not endure the violence of the change without torture such as you cannot even imagine.

"After the murder of Clerval, I returned to Switzerland, heartbroken and overcome. I pitied Frankenstein; my pity amounted to horror; I abhorred myself. But when I discovered that he, the author at once of my existence and of its unspeakable torments, dared to hope for happiness, that while he accumulated wretchedness and despair upon me he sought his own enjoyment in feelings and passions from the indulgence of which I was forever barred, then impotent envy and bitter indignation filled me with an insatiable thirst for vengeance. I recollected my threat and resolved that it should be accomplished. I knew that I was preparing for myself a deadly torture, but I was the slave, not the master, of an impulse which I detested yet could not disobey. Yet when she died! Nay, then I was not miserable. I had cast off all feeling, subdued all anguish, to riot in the excess of my despair. Evil thenceforth became my good. Urged thus far, I had no choice but to adapt my nature to an element which I had willingly chosen. The completion of my demoniacal design became an insatiable passion. And now it is ended; there is my last victim!"

I was at first touched by the expressions of his misery; yet, when I called to mind what Frankenstein had said of his powers of eloquence and persuasion, and when I again cast my eyes on the lifeless form of my friend, indignation was rekindled within me. "Wretch!" I said. "It is well that you come here to whine over the desolation that you have made. You throw a torch into a pile of buildings, and when they are consumed, you sit among the ruins and lament the fall. Hypocritical fiend! If he whom you mourn still lived, still would he be the object, again would he become the prey, of your accursed vengeance. It is not pity that you feel; you lament only because the victim of your malignity is withdrawn from your power."

"Oh, it is not thus—not thus," interrupted the being. "Yet such must be the impression conveyed to you by what appears to be the purport of my actions. Yet I seek not a fellow feeling in my misery. No sympathy may I ever find. When I first sought it, it was the love of virtue, the feelings of happiness and affection with which my whole being overflowed, that I wished to be participated. But now that virtue has become to me a shadow, and that happiness and affection are turned into bitter and loathing despair, in what should I seek for sympathy? I am content to suffer alone while my sufferings shall endure; when I die, I am well satisfied that abhorrence and opprobrium should load my memory. Once my fancy was soothed with dreams of virtue, of fame, and of enjoyment. Once I falsely hoped to meet with beings who, pardoning my outward form, would love me for the excellent qualities which I was capable of unfolding. I was nourished with high thoughts of honour and devotion. But now crime has degraded me beneath the meanest animal. No guilt, no mischief, no malignity, no misery, can be found comparable to mine. When I run over the frightful catalogue of my sins, I cannot believe that I am the same creature whose thoughts were once filled with sublime and transcendent visions of the beauty and the majesty of goodness. But it is even so; the fallen angel becomes a malignant devil. Yet even that enemy of God and man had friends and associates in his desolation; I am alone.

"You, who call Frankenstein your friend, seem to have a knowledge of my crimes and his misfortunes. But in the detail which he gave you of them he could not sum up the hours and months of misery which I endured wasting in impotent passions. For while I destroyed his hopes, I did not satisfy my own desires. They were forever ardent and craving; still I desired love and fellowship, and I was still spurned. Was there no injustice in this? Am I to be thought the only criminal, when all humankind sinned against me? Why do you not hate Felix, who drove his friend from his door with contumely? Why do you not execrate the rustic who sought to destroy the saviour of his child? Nay, these are virtuous and immaculate beings! I, the miserable and the abandoned, am an abortion, to be spurned at, and kicked, and trampled on. Even now my blood boils at the recollection of this injustice.

"But it is true that I am a wretch. I have murdered the lovely and the helpless; I have strangled the innocent as they slept and grasped to death his throat who never injured me or any other living thing. I have devoted my creator, the select specimen of all that is worthy of love and admiration among men, to misery; I have pursued him even to that irremediable ruin. There he lies, white and cold in death. You hate me, but your abhorrence cannot equal that with which I regard myself. I look on the hands which executed the deed; I think on the heart in which the imagination of it was conceived and long for the moment when these hands will meet my eyes, when that imagination will haunt my thoughts no more.

"Fear not that I shall be the instrument of future mischief. My work is nearly complete. Neither yours nor any man's death is needed to consummate the series of my being and accomplish that which must be done, but it requires my own. Do not think that I shall be slow to perform this sacrifice. I shall quit your vessel on the ice raft which brought me thither and shall seek the most northern extremity of the globe; I shall collect my funeral pile and consume to ashes this miserable frame, that its remains may afford no light to any curious and unhallowed wretch who would create such another as I have been. I shall die. I shall no longer feel the agonies which now consume me or be the prey of feelings unsatisfied, yet unquenched. He is dead who called me into being; and when I shall be no more, the very remembrance of us both will speedily vanish. I shall no longer see the sun or stars or feel the winds play on my cheeks. Light, feeling, and sense will pass away; and in this condition must I find my happiness. Some years ago, when the images which this world affords first opened upon me, when I felt the cheering warmth of summer and heard the rustling of the leaves and the warbling of the birds, and these were all to me, I should have wept to die; now it is my only consolation. Polluted by crimes and torn by the bitterest remorse, where can I find rest but in death?

"Farewell! I leave you, and in you the last of humankind whom these eyes will ever behold. Farewell, Frankenstein! If thou wert yet alive and yet cherished a desire of revenge against me, it would be better satiated in my life than in my destruction. But it was not so; thou didst seek my extinction, that I might not cause greater wretchedness; and if yet, in some mode unknown to me, thou hadst not ceased to think and feel, thou wouldst not desire against me a vengeance greater than that which I feel. Blasted as thou wert, my agony was still superior to thine, for the bitter sting of remorse will not cease to rankle in my wounds until death shall close them forever.

"But soon," he cried with sad and solemn enthusiasm, "I shall die, and what I now feel be no longer felt. Soon these burning miseries will be extinct. I shall ascend my funeral pile triumphantly and exult in the agony of the torturing flames. The light of that conflagration will fade away; my ashes will be swept into the sea by the winds. My spirit will sleep in peace, or if it thinks, it will not surely think thus. Farewell."

He sprang from the cabin window as he said this, upon the ice raft which lay close to the vessel. He was soon borne away by the waves and lost in darkness and distance.

CONTEMPLATIONS

Anne Bradstreet

1

Sometime now past in the Autumnal Tide,
When Phoebus wanted but one hour to bed,
The trees all richly clad, yet void of pride,
Were gilded o'er by his rich golden head.
Their leaves and fruits seem'd painted but was true
Of green, of red, of yellow, mixed hew,
Rapt were my senses at this delectable view.

2

I wist not what to wish, yet sure thought I,
If so much excellence abide below,
How excellent is he that dwells on high?
Whose power and beauty by his works we know.
Sure he is goodness, wisdom, glory, light,
That hath this under world so richly dight.
More Heaven than Earth was here, no winter and
        no night.

3

Then on a stately Oak I cast mine Eye,
Whose ruffling top the Clouds seem'd to aspire;
How long since thou wast in thine Infancy?
Thy strength and stature, more thy years admire,
Hath hundred winters past since thou wast born?
Or thousand since thou brakest thy shell of horn,
If so, all these as nought, Eternity doth scorn.

4

Then higher on the glistering Sun I gaz'd,
Whose beams was shaded by the leafy Tree.

The more I look'd, the more I grew amaz'd
And softly said, what glory's like to thee?
Soul of this world, this Universe's Eye,
No wonder some made thee a Deity:
Had I not better known (alas) the same had I.

5

Thou as a Bridegroom from thy Chamber rushes
And as a strong man joys to run a race.
The morn doth usher thee with smiles and blushes.
The Earth reflects her glances in thy face.
Birds, insects, Animals with Vegative,
Thy heat from death and dullness doth revive:
And in the darksome womb of fruitful nature dive.

6

Thy swift Annual and diurnal Course,
Thy daily straight and yearly oblique path,
Thy pleasing fervour, and thy scorching force,
All mortals here the feeling knowledge hath.
Thy presence makes it day, thy absence night,
Quaternal seasons caused by thy might:
Hail Creature, full of sweetness, beauty, and delight.

7

Art thou so full of glory that no Eye
Hath strength thy shining Rays once to behold?
And is thy splendid Throne erect so high?
As, to approach it, can no earthly mould.
How full of glory then must thy Creator be?
Who gave this bright light luster unto thee:
Admir'd, ador'd for ever be that Majesty.

8

Silent alone where none or saw, or heard,
In pathless paths I lead my wand'ring feet.
My humble Eyes to lofty Skies I rear'd

To sing some Song my mazed Muse thought meet.
My great Creator I would magnifie,
That nature had thus decked liberally:
But Ah and Ah again, my imbecility!

9

I heard the merry grasshopper then sing,
The black clad Cricket bear a second part.
They kept one tune and played on the same string,
Seeming to glory in their little Art.
Shall creatures abject thus their voices raise?
And in their kind resound their maker's praise:
Whilst I, as mute, can warble forth no higher layes.

10

When present times look back to Ages past
And men in being fancy those are dead,
It makes things gone perpetually to last
And calls back months and years that long since fled
It makes a man more aged in conceit,
Than was Methuselah or's grand-sire great:
While of their persons and their acts his mind doth treat.

11

Sometimes in Eden fair he seems to be,
See glorious Adam there made Lord of all,
Fancies the Apple, dangle on the Tree,
That turn'd his Sovereign to a naked thrall,
Who like a miscreant's driven from that place
To get his bread with pain and sweat of face:
A penalty impos'd on his backsliding Race.

12

Here sits our Grandame in retired place,
And in her lap her bloody Cain new born,
The weeping Imp oft looks her in the face,
Bewails his unknown hap and fate forlorn;

His Mother sighs to think of Paradise,
And how she lost her bliss, to be more wise,
Believing him that was, and is, Father of lyes.

13

Here Cain and Abel come to sacrifice,
Fruits of the Earth and Fatlings each do bring,
On Abels gift the fire descends from Skies,
But no such sign on false Cain's offering;
With sullen hateful looks he goes his wayes.
Hath thousand thoughts to end his brothers dayes,
Upon whose blood his future good he hopes to raise.

14

There Abel keeps his sheep, no ill he thinks,
His brother comes, then acts his fratricide.
The Virgin Earth of blood her first draught drinks,
But since that time she often hath been cloy'd;
The wretch with ghastly face and dreadful mind,
Thinks each he sees will serve him in his kind,
Though none on Earth but kindred near then could he find.

15

Who fancies not his looks now at the Barr,
His face like death, his heart with horror fraught,
Nor Male-factor ever felt like warr,
When deep despair with wish of life hath fought,
Branded with guilt, and crusht with treble woes,
A Vagabond to Land of Nod he goes.
A City builds, that wals might him secure from foes.

16

Who thinks not oft upon the Fathers ages.
Their long descent, how nephews sons they saw,
The starry observations of those Sages,
And how their precepts to their sons were law,
How Adam sigh'd to see his Progeny,

Cloath'd all in his black, sinful Livery,
Who neither guilt not yet the punishment could fly.

17

Our Life compare we with their length of dayes
Who to the tenth of theirs doth now arrive?
And though thus short, we shorten many wayes,
Living so little while we are alive;
In eating, drinking, sleeping, vain delight
So unawares comes on perpetual night,
And puts all pleasures vain unto eternal flight.

18

When I behold the heavens as in their prime,
And then the earth (though old) still clad in green,
The stones and trees, insensible of time,
Nor age nor wrinkle on their front are seen;
If winter come, and greenness then do fade,
A Spring returns, and they more youthfull made;
But Man grows old, lies down, remains where once
       he's laid.

19

By birth more noble than those creatures all,
Yet seems by nature and by custom curs'd,
No sooner born, but grief and care makes fall
That state obliterate he had at first:
Nor youth, nor strength, nor wisdom spring again
Nor habitations long their names retain,
But in oblivion to the final day remain.

20

Shall I then praise the heavens, the trees, the earth
Because their beauty and their strength last longer
Shall I wish there, or never to had birth,
Because they're bigger and their bodyes stronger?
Nay, they shall darken, perish, fade and dye,

And when unmade, so ever shall they lye,
But man was made for endless immortality.

21

Under the cooling shadow of a stately Elm
Close sate I by a goodly Rivers side,
Where gliding streams the Rocks did overwhelm;
A lonely place, with pleasures dignifi'd.
I once that lov'd the shady woods so well,
Now thought the rivers did the trees excel,
And if the sun would ever shine, there would I
     dwell.

22

While on the stealing stream I fixt mine eye,
Which to the long'd-for Ocean held its course,
I markt, nor crooks, nor rubs that there did lye
Could hinder ought but still augment its force:
O happy Flood, quoth I, that holds thy race
Till thou arrive at thy beloved place,
Nor is it rocks or shoals that can obstruct thy pace.

23

Nor is't enough that thou alone may'st slide,
But hundred brooks in thy cleer waves do meet,
So hand in hand along with thee they glide
To Thetis house, where all imbrace and greet:
Thou Emblem true of what I count the best,
O could I lead my Rivolets to rest,
So may we press to that vast mansion, ever blest.

24

Ye Fish which in this liquid Region 'bide
That for each season have your habitation,
Now salt, now fresh where you think best to glide
To unknown coasts to give a visitation,
In Lakes and ponds, you leave your numerous fry,

So Nature taught, and yet you know not why,
You watry folk that know not your felicity.

25

Look how the wantons frisk to tast the air,
Then to the colder bottome streight they dive,
Eftsoon to Neptun's glassy Hall repair
To see what trade they, great ones, there do drive,
Who forrage o're the spacious sea-green field,
And take the trembling prey before it yield,
Whose armour is their scales, their spreading fins
       their shield.

26

While musing thus with contemplation fed,
And thousand fancies buzzing in my brain,
The sweet-tongu'd Philomel percht ore my head,
And chanted forth a most melodious strain
Which rapt me so with wonder and delight,
I judg'd my hearing better than my sight,
And wisht me wings with her a while to take my flight.

27

O merry Bird (said I) that fears no snares,
That neither toyles nor hoards up in thy barn,
Feels no sad thoughts, nor cruciating cares
To gain more good, or shun what might thee harm
Thy clothes ne'er wear, thy meat is every where,
Thy bed a bough, thy drink the water cleer,
Reminds not what is past, nor whats to come dost fear.

28

The dawning morn with songs thou dost prevent,
Sets hundred notes unto thy feathered crew,
So each one tunes his pretty instrument,
And warbling out the old, begin anew,
And thus they pass their youth in summer season,

Then follow thee into a better Region,
Where winter's never felt by that sweet airy legion.

29

Man at the best a creature frail and vain,
In knowledge ignorant, in strength but weak,
Subject to sorrows, losses, sickness, pain,
Each storm his state, his mind, his body break,
From some of these he never finds cessation,
But day or night, within, without, vexation,
Troubles from foes, from friends, from dearest, near'st
    Relation.

30

And yet this sinfull creature, frail and vain,
This lump of wretchedness, of sin and sorrow,
This weather-beaten vessel wrackt with pain,
Joys not in hope of an eternal morrow;
Nor all his losses, crosses and vexation,
In weight, in frequency and long duration
Can make him deeply groan for that divine Translation.

31

The Mariner that on smooth waves doth glide,
Sings merrily and steers his Barque with ease,
As if he had command of wind and tide,
And now becomes great Master of the seas;
But suddenly a storm spoils all the sport,
And makes him long for a more quiet port,
Which 'gainst all adverse winds may serve for fort.

32

So he that faileth in this world of pleasure,
Feeding on sweets, that never bit of th' sowre,
That's full of friends, of honour and of treasure,
Fond fool, he takes this earth ev'n for heav'ns bower,
But sad affliction comes and makes him see

Here's neither honour, wealth, nor safety;
Only above is found all with security.

33

O Time the fatal wrack of mortal things,
That draws oblivions curtains over kings,
Their sumptuous monuments, men know them not,
Their names without a Record are forgot,
Their parts, their ports, their pomp's all laid in th' dust.
Nor wit, nor gold, nor buildings scape times rust;
But he whose name is grav'd in the white stone
Shall last and shine when all of these are gone.

A Call

Grace MacGowan Cooke

A boy in an unnaturally clean, country-laundered collar walked down a long white road. He scuffed the dust up wantonly, for he wished to veil the all-too-brilliant polish of his cowhide shoes. Also the memory of the whiteness and slipperiness of his collar oppressed him. He was fain to look like one accustomed to social diversions, a man hurried from hall to hall of pleasure, without time between to change collar or polish boot. He stooped and rubbed a crumb of earth on his overfresh neck-linen.

This did not long sustain his drooping spirit. He was mentally adrift upon the "Hints and Helps to Young Men in Business and Social Relations," which had suggested to him his present enterprise, when the appearance of a second youth, taller and broader than himself, with a shock of light curling hair and a crop of freckles that advertised a rich soil, threw him a lifeline. He put his thumbs to his lips and whistled in a peculiarly ear-splitting way. The two boys had sat on the same bench at Sunday-school not three hours before; yet what a change had come over the world for one of them since then!

"Hello! Where you goin', Ab?" asked the newcomer, gruffly.

"Callin'," replied the boy in the collar, laconically, but with carefully averted gaze.

"On the girls?" inquired the other, awestruck. In Mount Pisgah you saw the girls home from night church, socials, or parties; you could hang over the gate; and you might walk with a girl in the cemetery of a Sunday afternoon; but to ring a front-door bell and ask for Miss Heart's Desire one must have been in long trousers at least three years—and the two boys confronted in the dusty road had worn these dignifying garments barely six months.

"Girls," said Abner, loftily; "I don't know about girls—I'm just going to call on one girl—Champe Claiborne." He marched on as though the conversation was at an end; but Ross hung upon his flank. Ross and Champe were neighbors, comrades in all sorts of mischief; he was in doubt whether to halt Abner and pummel him, or propose to enlist under his banner.

"Do you reckon you could?" he debated, trotting along by the irresponsive Jilton boy.

"Run home to your mother," growled the originator of the plan, savagely. "You ain't old enough to call on girls; anybody can see that; but I am, and I'm going to call on Champe Claiborne."

Again the name acted as a spur on Ross. "With your collar and boots all dirty?" he jeered. "They won't know you're callin'."

The boy in the road stopped short in his dusty tracks. He was an intense creature, and he whitened at the tragic insinuation, longing for the wholesome stay and companionship of freckle-faced Ross. "I put the dirt on o' purpose so's to look kind of careless," he half whispered, in an agony of doubt. "S'pose I'd better go into your house and try to wash it off? Reckon your mother would let me?"

"I've got two clean collars," announced the other boy, proudly generous. "I'll lend you one. You can put it on while I'm getting ready. I'll tell mother that we're just stepping out to do a little calling on the girls."

Here was an ally worthy of the cause. Abner welcomed him, in spite of certain jealous twinges. He reflected with satisfaction that there were two Claiborne girls, and though Alicia was so stiff and prim that no boy would ever think of calling on her, there was still the hope that she might draw Ross's fire, and leave him, Abner, to make the numerous remarks he had stored up in his mind from "Hints and Helps to Young Men in Social and Business Relations" to Champe alone.

Mrs. Pryor received them with the easy-going kindness of the mother of one son. She followed them into the dining-room to kiss and feed him, with an absent "Howdy, Abner; how's your mother?"

Abner, big with the importance of their mutual intention, inclined his head stiffly and looked toward Ross for explanation. He trembled a little, but it was with delight, as he anticipated the effect of the speech Ross had outlined. But it did not come.

"I'm not hungry, mother," was the revised edition which the freckle-faced boy offered to the maternal ear. "I—we are going over to Mr. Claiborne's—on—er—on an errand for Abner's father."

The black-eyed boy looked reproach as they clattered up the stairs to Ross's room, where the clean collar was produced and a small stock of ties.

"You'd wear a necktie—wouldn't you?" Ross asked, spreading them upon the bureau-top.

"Yes. But make it fall carelessly over your shirt-front," advised the student of Hints and Helps. "Your collar is miles too big for me. Say! I've got a wad of white chewing-gum; would you flat it out and stick it over the collar button? Maybe that would fill up some. You kick my foot if you see me turning my head so's to knock it off."

"Better button up your vest," cautioned Ross, laboring with the "careless" fall of his tie.

"Huh-uh! I want 'that easy air which presupposes familiarity with society'—that's what it says in my book," objected Abner.

"Sure!" Ross returned to his more familiar jeering attitude. "Loosen up all your clothes, then. Why don't you untie your shoes? Flop a sock down over one of 'em—that looks 'easy' all right."

Abner buttoned his vest. "It gives a man lots of confidence to know he's good-looking," he remarked, taking all the room in front of the mirror.

Ross, at the wash-stand soaking his hair to get the curl out of it, grumbled some unintelligible response. The two boys went down the stairs with tremulous hearts.

"Why, you've put on another clean shirt, Rossie!" Mrs. Pryor called from her chair—mothers' eyes can see so far! "Well—don't get into any dirty play and soil it." The boys walked in silence—but it was a pregnant silence; for as the roof of the Claiborne house began to peer above the crest of the hill, Ross plumped down on a stone and announced, "I ain't goin'."

"Come on," urged the black-eyed boy. "It'll be fun—and everybody will respect us more. Champe won't throw rocks at us in recess-time, after we've called on her. She couldn't."

"Called!" grunted Ross. "I couldn't make a call any more than a cow. What'd I say? What'd I do? I can behave all right when you just go to people's houses—but a call!"

Abner hesitated. Should he give away his brilliant inside information, drawn from the "Hints and Helps" book, and be rivalled in the glory of his manners and bearing? Why should he not pass on alone, perfectly composed, and reap the field of glory unsupported? His knees gave way and he sat down without intending it.

"Don't you tell anybody and I'll put you on to exactly what grown-up gentlemen say and do when they go calling on the girls," he began.

"Fire away," retorted Ross, gloomily. "Nobody will find out from me. Dead men tell no tales. If I'm fool enough to go, I don't expect to come out of it alive."

Abner rose, white and shaking, and thrusting three fingers into the buttoning of his vest, extending the other hand like an orator, proceeded to instruct the freckled, perspiring disciple at his feet.

"'Hang your hat on the rack, or give it to a servant.'" Ross nodded intelligently. He could do that.

"'Let your legs be gracefully disposed, one hand on the knee, the other—'"

Abner came to an unhappy pause. "I forget what a fellow does with the other hand. Might stick it in your pocket, loudly, or expectorate on the carpet. Indulge in little frivolity. Let a rich stream of conversation flow."

Ross mentally dug within himself for sources of rich streams of conversation. He found a dry soil. "What you goin' to talk about?" he demanded, fretfully. "I won't go a step farther till I know what I'm goin' to say when I get there."

Abner began to repeat paragraphs from "Hints and Helps." "'It is best to remark,'" he opened, in an unnatural voice, "'How well you are looking!' although fulsome compliments should be avoided. When seated ask the young lady who her favorite composer is.'"

"What's a composer?" inquired Ross, with visions of soothing-syrup in his mind.

"A man that makes up music. Don't butt in that way; you put me all out— 'composer is. Name yours. Ask her what piece of music she likes best. Name yours. If the lady is musical, here ask her to play or sing.'"

This chanted recitation seemed to have a hypnotic effect on the freckled boy; his big pupils contracted each time Abner came to the repetend, "Name yours."

"I'm tired already," he grumbled; but some spell made him rise and fare farther.

When they had entered the Claiborne gate, they leaned toward each other like young saplings weakened at the root and locking branches to keep what shallow foothold on earth remained.

"You're goin' in first," asserted Ross, but without conviction. It was his custom to tear up to this house a dozen times a week, on his father's old horse or afoot; he was wont to yell for Champe as he approached, and quarrel joyously with her while he performed such errand as he had come upon; but he was gagged and hamstrung now by the hypnotism of Abner's scheme.

"'Walk quietly up the steps; ring the bell and lay your card on the servant,'" quoted Abner, who had never heard of a server.

"'Lay your card on the servant!'" echoed Ross. "Cady'd dodge. There's a porch to cross after you go up the steps—does it say anything about that?"

"It says that the card should be placed on the servant," Abner reiterated, doggedly. "If Cady dodges, it ain't any business of mine. There are no porches in my book. Just walk across it like anybody. We'll ask for Miss Champe Claiborne."

"We haven't got any cards," discovered Ross, with hope.

"I have," announced Abner, pompously. "I had some struck off in Chicago. I ordered 'em by mail. They got my name Pillow, but there's a scalloped gilt border around it. You can write your name on my card. Got a pencil?" He produced the bit of cardboard; Ross fished up a chewed stump of lead pencil, took it in cold, stiff fingers, and disfigured the square with eccentric scribblings.

"They'll know who it's meant for," he said, apologetically, "because I'm here. What's likely to happen after we get rid of the card?"

"I told you about hanging your hat on the rack and disposing your legs."

"I remember now," sighed Ross. They had been going slower and slower. The angle of inclination toward each other became more and more pronounced.

"We must stand by each other," whispered Abner.

"I will—if I can stand at all," murmured the other boy, huskily.

"Oh, Lord!" They had rounded the big clump of evergreens and found Aunt Missouri Claiborne placidly rocking on the front porch! Directed to mount steps and ring bell, to lay cards upon the servant, how should one deal with a rosy-faced, plump lady of uncertain years in a rocking-chair. What should a caller lay upon her? A lion in the way could not have been more terrifying. Even retreat was cut off. Aunt Missouri had seen them. "Howdy, boys; how are you?" she said, rocking peacefully. The two stood before her like detected criminals.

Then, to Ross's dismay, Abner sank down on the lowest step of the porch, the westering sun full in his hopeless eyes. He sat on his cap. It was characteristic that the freckled boy remained standing. He would walk up those steps according to plan and agreement, if at all. He accepted no compromise. Folding his straw hat into a battered cone, he watched anxiously for the delivery of the card. He was not sure what Aunt Missouri's attitude might be if it were laid on her. He bent down to his companion. "Go ahead," he whispered. "Lay the card."

Abner raised appealing eyes. "In a minute. Give me time," he pleaded.

"Mars' Ross—Mars' Ross! Head 'em off!" sounded a yell, and Babe, the house-boy, came around the porch in pursuit of two half-grown chickens.

"Help him, Rossie," prompted Aunt Missouri, sharply. "You boys can stay to supper and have some of the chicken if you help catch them."

Had Ross taken time to think, he might have reflected that gentlemen making formal calls seldom join in a chase after the main dish of the family supper. But the needs of Babe were instant. The lad flung himself sidewise, caught one chicken in his hat, while Babe fell upon the other in the manner of a football player. Ross handed the pullet to the house-boy, fearing that he had done something very much out of character, then pulled the reluctant negro toward to the steps.

"Babe's a servant," he whispered to Abner, who had sat rigid through the entire performance. "I helped him with the chickens, and he's got to stand gentle while you lay the card on."

Confronted by the act itself, Abner was suddenly aware that he knew not how to begin. He took refuge in dissimulation.

"Hush!" he whispered back. "Don't you see Mr. Claiborne's come out? He's going to read something to us."

Ross plumped down beside him. "Never mind the card; tell 'em," he urged.

"Tell 'em yourself."

"No—let's cut and run."

"I—I think the worst of it is over. When Champe sees us she'll?"

Mention of Champe stiffened Ross's spine. If it had been glorious to call upon her, how very terrible she would make it should they attempt calling, fail, and the failure come to her knowledge! Some things were easier to endure than others; he resolved to stay till the call was made.

For half an hour the boys sat with drooping heads, and the old gentleman read aloud, presumably to Aunt Missouri and themselves. Finally their restless eyes discerned the two Claiborne girls walking serene in Sunday trim under the trees at the edge of the lawn. Arms entwined, they were whispering together and giggling a little. A caller, Ross dared not use his voice to shout nor his legs to run toward them.

"Why don't you go and talk to the girls, Rossie?" Aunt Missouri asked, in the kindness of her heart. "Don't be noisy—it's Sunday, you know—and don't get to playing anything that'll dirty up your good clothes."

Ross pressed his lips hard together; his heart swelled with the rage of the misunderstood. Had the card been in his possession, he would, at that instant, have laid it on Aunt Missouri without a qualm.

"What is it?" demanded the old gentleman, a bit testily.

"The girls want to hear you read, father," said Aunt Missouri, shrewdly; and she got up and trotted on short, fat ankles to the girls in the arbor. The three returned together, Alicia casting curious glances at the uncomfortable youths, Champe threatening to burst into giggles with every breath.

Abner sat hard on his cap and blushed silently. Ross twisted his hat into a three-cornered wreck.

The two girls settled themselves noisily on the upper step. The old man read on and on. The sun sank lower. The hills were red in the west as though a brush fire flamed behind their crests. Abner stole a furtive glance at his companion in misery, and the dolor of Ross's countenance somewhat assuaged his anguish. The freckle-faced boy was thinking of the village over the hill, a certain pleasant white house set back in a green yard, past whose gate, the two-plank sidewalk ran. He knew lamps were beginning to wink in the windows of the neighbors about, as though the houses said, "Our boys are all at home—but Ross Pryor's out trying to call on the girls, and can't get anybody to understand it." Oh, that he were walking down those two planks, drawing a stick across the pickets, lifting high happy feet which could turn in at that gate! He wouldn't care what the lamps said then. He wouldn't even mind if the whole Claiborne family died laughing at him—if only some power would raise him up from this paralyzing spot and put him behind the safe barriers of his own home!

The old man's voice lapsed into silence; the light was becoming too dim for his reading. Aunt Missouri turned and called over her shoulder into the shadows of the big hall: "You Babe! Go put two extra plates on the supper-table."

The boys grew red from the tips of their ears, and as far as any one could see under their wilting collars. Abner felt the lump of gum come loose and slip down a cold spine. Had their intentions but been known, this inferential invitation would have been most welcome. It was but to rise up and thunder out, "We came to call on the young ladies."

They did not rise. They did not thunder out anything. Babe brought a lamp and set it inside the window, and Mr. Claiborne resumed his reading. Champe giggled and said that Alicia made her. Alcia drew her skirts about her, sniffed, and looked virtuous, and said she didn't see anything funny to laugh at. The supper-bell rang. The family, evidently taking it for granted that the boys would follow, went in.

Alone for the first time, Abner gave up. "This ain't any use," he complained. "We ain't calling on anybody."

"Why didn't you lay on the card?" demanded Ross, fiercely. "Why didn't you say: 'We've-just-dropped-into-call-on-Miss-Champe. It's-a -pleasant-evening. We-feel-we-must-be-going,' like you said you would? Then we could have lifted our hats and got away decently."

Abner showed no resentment.

"Oh, if it's so easy, why didn't you do it yourself?" he groaned.

"Somebody's coming," Ross muttered, hoarsely. "Say it now. Say it quick."

The somebody proved to be Aunt Missouri, who advanced only as far as the end of the hall and shouted cheerfully: "The idea of a growing boy not coming to meals when the bell rings! I thought you two would be in there ahead of us. Come on." And clinging to their head-coverings as though these contained some charm whereby the owners might be rescued, the unhappy callers were herded into the dining-room. There were many things on the table that boys like. Both were becoming fairly cheerful, when Aunt Missouri checked the biscuit-plate with: "I treat my neighbors' children just like I'd want children of my own treated. If your mothers let you eat all you want, say so, and I don't care; but if either of them is a little bit particular, why, I'd stop at six!"

Still reeling from this blow, the boys finally rose from the table and passed out with the family, their hats clutched to their bosoms, and clinging together for mutual aid and comfort. During the usual Sunday-evening singing Champe laughed till Aunt Missouri threatened to send her to bed. Abner's card slipped from his hand and dropped face up on the floor. He fell upon it and tore it into infinitesimal pieces.

"That must have been a love-letter," said Aunt Missouri, in a pause of the music. "You boys are getting 'most old enough to think about beginning to call on the girls." Her eyes twinkled.

Ross growled like a stoned cur. Abner took a sudden dive into "Hints and Helps," and came up with, "You flatter us, Miss Claiborne," whereat Ross snickered out like a human boy. They all stared at him.

"It sounds so funny to call Aunt Missouri 'Mis' Claiborne,'" the lad of the freckles explained.

"Funny?" Aunt Missouri reddened. "I don't see any particular joke in my having my maiden name."

Abner, who instantly guessed at what was in Ross's mind, turned white at the thought of what they had escaped. Suppose he had laid on the card and asked for Miss Claiborne!

"What's the matter, Champe?" inquired Ross, in a fairly natural tone. The air he had drawn into his lungs when he laughed at Abner seemed to relieve him from the numbing gentility which had bound his powers since he joined Abner's ranks.

"Nothing. I laughed because you laughed," said the girl.

The singing went forward fitfully. Servants traipsed through the darkened yard, going home for Sunday night. Aunt Missouri went out and held some low-toned parley with them. Champe yawned with insulting enthusiasm. Presently both girls quietly disappeared. Aunt Missouri never returned to the parlor—evidently thinking that the girls would attend to the final amenities with their callers. They were left alone with old Mr. Claiborne. They sat as though bound in their chairs, while the old man read in silence for a while. Finally he closed his book, glanced about him, and observed absently:

"So you boys were to spend the night?" Then, as he looked at their startled faces: "I'm right, am I not? You are to spent the night?"

Oh, for courage to say: "Thank you, no. We'll be going now. We just came over to call on Miss Champe." But thought of how this would sound in face of the facts, the painful realization that they dared not say it because they had not said it, locked their lips. Their feet were lead; their tongues stiff and too large for their mouths. Like creatures in a nightmare, they moved stiffly, one might have said creakingly, up the stairs and received each—a bedroom candle!

"Good night, children," said the absent-minded old man. The two gurgled out some sounds which were intended for words and doged behind the bedroom door.

"They've put us to bed!" Abner's black eyes flashed fire. His nervous hands clutched at the collar Ross had lent him. "That's what I get for coming here with you, Ross Pryor!" And tears of humiliation stood in his eyes.

In his turn Ross showed no resentment. "What I'm worried about is my mother," he confessed. "She's so sharp about finding out things. She wouldn't tease me—she'd just be sorry for me. But she'll think I went home with you."

"I'd like to see my mother make a fuss about my calling on the girls!" growled Abner, glad to let his rage take a safe direction.

"Calling on the girls! Have we called on any girls?" demanded clear-headed, honest Ross.

"Not exactly—yet," admitted Abner, reluctantly. "Come on—let's go to bed. Mr. Claiborne asked us, and he's the head of this household. It isn't anybody's business what we came for."

"I'll slip off my shoes and lie down till Babe ties up the dog in the morning," said Ross. "Then we can get away before any of the family is up."

Oh, youth—youth—youth, with its rash promises! Worn out with misery the boys slept heavily. The first sound that either heard in the morning was Babe hammering upon their bedroom door. They crouched guiltily and looked into each other's eyes. "Let pretend we ain't here and he'll go away," breathed Abner.

But Babe was made of sterner stuff. He rattled the knob. He turned it. He put in a black face with a grin which divided it from ear to ear. "Cady say I mus' call dem fool boys to breakfus'," he announced. "I never named you-all dat. Cady, she say dat."

"Breakfast!" echoed Ross, in a daze.

"Yessuh, breakfus'," reasserted Babe, coming entirely into the room and looking curiously about him. "Ain't you-all done been to bed at all?" wrapping his arms about his shoulders and shaking with silent ecstasies of mirth. The boys threw themselves upon him and ejected him.

"Sent up a servant to call us to breakfast," snarled Abner. "If they'd only sent their old servant to the door in the first place, all this wouldn't 'a' happened. I'm just that way when I get thrown off the track. You know how it was when I tried to repeat those things to you—I had to go clear back to the beginning when I got interrupted."

"Does that mean that you're still hanging around here to begin over and make a call?" asked Ross, darkly. "I won't go down to breakfast if you are."

Abner brightened a little as he saw Ross becoming wordy in his rage. "I dare you to walk downstairs and say, 'We-just-dropped-in-to-call-on-Miss-Champe'!" he said. "I—oh—I—darn it all! there goes the second bell. We may as well trot down."

"Don't leave me, Ross," pleaded the Jilton boy. "I can't stay here—and I can't go down."

The tone was hysterical. The boy with freckles took his companion by the arm without another word and marched him down the stairs. "We may get a chance yet to call on Champe all by herself out on the porch or in the arbor before she goes to school," he suggested, by way of putting some spine into the black-eyed boy.

An emphatic bell rang when they were half-way down the stairs. Clutching their hats, they slunk into the dining-room. Even Mr. Claiborne seemed to notice something unusual in their bearing as they settled into the chairs assigned to them, and asked them kindly if they had slept well.

It was plain that Aunt Missouri had been posting him as to her understanding of the intentions of these young men. The state of affairs gave an electric hilarity to the atmosphere. Babe travelled from the sideboard to the table, trembling like chocolate pudding. Cady insisted on bringing in the cakes herself, and grinned as she whisked her starched blue skirts in and out of the dining-room. A dimple even showed itself at the corners of pretty Alicia's prim little mouth. Champe giggled, till Ross heard Cady whisper:

"Now you got one dem snickerin' spells agin. You gwine bust yo' dress buttons off in the back ef you don't mind."

As the spirits of those about them mounted, the hearts of the two youths sank—if it was like this among the Claibornes, what would it be at school and in the world at large when their failure to connect intention with result became village talk? Ross bit fiercely upon an unoffending batter-cake, and resolved to make a call single-handed before he left the house.

They went out of the dining-room, their hats as ever pressed to their breasts. With no volition of their own, their uncertain young legs carried them to the porch. The Claiborne family and household followed like small boys after a circus procession. When the two turned, at bay, yet with nothing between them and liberty but a hypnotism of their own suggestion, they saw the black faces of the servants peering over the family shoulders.

Ross was the boy to have drawn courage from the desperation of their case, and made some decent if not glorious ending. But at the psychological moment there came around the corner of the house that most contemptible figure known to the Southern plantation, a shirt-boy—a creature who may be described, for the benefit of those not informed, as a pickaninny clad only in a long, coarse cotton shirt. While all eyes were fastened upon him this inglorious ambassador bolted forth his message:

"Yo' ma say"—his eyes were fixed upon Abner—"ef yo' don' come home, she gwine come after yo'—an' cut yo' into inch pieces wid a rawhide when she git yo'. Dat jest what Miss Hortense say."

As though such a book as "Hints and Helps" had never existed, Abner shot for the gate—he was but a hobbledehoy fascinated with the idea of playing gentleman. But in Ross there were the makings of a man. For a few half-hearted paces, under the first impulse of horror, he followed his deserting chief, the laughter of the family, the unrestrainable guffaws of the negroes, sounding in the rear. But when Champe's high, offensive giggle, topping all the others, insulted his ears, he stopped dead, wheeled, and ran to the porch faster than he had fled from it. White as paper, shaking with inexpressible rage, he caught and kissed the tittering girl, violently, noisily, before them all.

The negroes fled—they dared not trust their feelings; even Alicia sniggered unobtrusively; Grandfather Claiborne chuckled, and Aunt Missouri frankly collapsed into her rocking-chair, bubbling with mirth, crying out:

"Good for you, Ross! Seems you did know how to call on the girls, after all."

But Ross, paying no attention, walked swiftly toward the gate. He had served his novitiate. He would never be afraid again. With cheerful alacrity he dodged the stones flung after him with friendly, erratic aim by the girl upon whom, yesterday afternoon, he had come to make a social call.

Goblin Market

Christina Rossetti

Morning and evening
Maids heard the goblins cry:
"Come buy our orchard fruits,
Come buy, come buy:
Apples and quinces,
Lemons and oranges,
Plump unpecked cherries,
Melons and raspberries,
Bloom-down-cheeked peaches,
Swart-headed mulberries,
Wild free-born cranberries,
Crab-apples, dewberries,
Pine-apples, blackberries,
Apricots, strawberries;—
All ripe together
In summer weather,—
Morns that pass by,
Fair eves that fly;
Come buy, come buy:
Our grapes fresh from the vine,
Pomegranates full and fine,
Dates and sharp bullaces,
Rare pears and greengages,
Damsons and bilberries,
Taste them and try:
Currants and gooseberries,
Bright-fire-like barberries,
Figs to fill your mouth,
Citrons from the South,
Sweet to tongue and sound to eye;
Come buy, come buy."

Evening by evening
Among the brookside rushes,
Laura bowed her head to hear,

Lizzie veiled her blushes:
Crouching close together
In the cooling weather,
With clasping arms and cautioning lips,
With tingling cheeks and finger tips.
"Lie close," Laura said,
Pricking up her golden head:
"We must not look at goblin men,
We must not buy their fruits:
Who knows upon what soil they fed
Their hungry thirsty roots?"
"Come buy," call the goblins
Hobbling down the glen.
"Oh," cried Lizzie, "Laura, Laura,
You should not peep at goblin men."
Lizzie covered up her eyes,
Covered close lest they should look;
Laura reared her glossy head,
And whispered like the restless brook:
"Look, Lizzie, look, Lizzie,
Down the glen tramp little men.
One hauls a basket,
One bears a plate,
One lugs a golden dish
Of many pounds weight.
How fair the vine must grow
Whose grapes are so luscious;
How warm the wind must blow
Through those fruit bushes."
"No," said Lizzie, "No, no, no;
Their offers should not charm us,
Their evil gifts would harm us."
She thrust a dimpled finger
In each ear, shut eyes and ran:
Curious Laura chose to linger
Wondering at each merchant man.
One had a cat's face,
One whisked a tail,
One tramped at a rat's pace,
One crawled like a snail,
One like a wombat prowled obtuse and furry,

One like a ratel tumbled hurry skurry.
She heard a voice like voice of doves
Cooing all together:
They sounded kind and full of loves
In the pleasant weather.

    Laura stretched her gleaming neck
Like a rush-imbedded swan,
Like a lily from the beck,
Like a moonlit poplar branch,
Like a vessel at the launch
When its last restraint is gone.

    Backwards up the mossy glen
Turned and trooped the goblin men,
With their shrill repeated cry,
"Come buy, come buy."
When they reached where Laura was
They stood stock still upon the moss,
Leering at each other,
Brother with queer brother;
Signalling each other,
Brother with sly brother.
One set his basket down,
One reared his plate;
One began to weave a crown
Of tendrils, leaves, and rough nuts brown
(Men sell not such in any town);
One heaved the golden weight
Of dish and fruit to offer her:
"Come buy, come buy," was still their cry.
Laura stared but did not stir,
Longed but had no money:
The whisk-tailed merchant bade her taste
In tones as smooth as honey,
The cat-faced purr'd,
The rat-faced spoke a word
Of welcome, and the snail-paced even was heard;
One parrot-voiced and jolly
Cried "Pretty Goblin" still for "Pretty Polly";—
One whistled like a bird.

But sweet-tooth Laura spoke in haste:
"Good folk, I have no coin;
To take were to purloin:
I have no copper in my purse,
I have no silver either,
And all my gold is on the furze
That shakes in windy weather
Above the rusty heather."
"You have much gold upon your head,"
They answered all together:
"Buy from us with a golden curl."
She clipped a precious golden lock,
She dropped a tear more rare than pearl,
Then sucked their fruit globes fair or red:
Sweeter than honey from the rock,
Stronger than man-rejoicing wine,
Clearer than water flowed that juice;
She never tasted such before,
How should it cloy with length of use?
She sucked and sucked and sucked the more
Fruits which that unknown orchard bore;
She sucked until her lips were sore;
Then flung the emptied rinds away
But gathered up one kernel stone,
And knew not was it night or day
As she turned home alone.

    Lizzie met her at the gate
Full of wise upbraidings:
"Dear, you should not stay so late,
Twilight is not good for maidens;
Should not loiter in the glen
In the haunts of goblin men.
Do you not remember Jeanie,
How she met them in the moonlight,
Took their gifts both choice and many,
Ate their fruits and wore their flowers
Plucked from bowers
Where summer ripens at all hours?
But ever in the noonlight
She pined and pined away;

Sought them by night and day,
Found them no more, but dwindled and grew grey;
Then fell with the first snow,
While to this day no grass will grow
Where she lies low:
I planted daisies there a year ago
That never blow.
You should not loiter so."
"Nay, hush," said Laura:
"Nay, hush, my sister:
I ate and ate my fill,
Yet my mouth waters still;
To-morrow night I will
Buy more": and kissed her:
"Have done with sorrow;
I'll bring you plums to-morrow
Fresh on their mother twigs,
 Cherries worth getting;
You cannot think what figs
My teeth have met in,
What melons icy-cold
Piled on a dish of gold
Too huge for me to hold,
What peaches with a velvet nap,
Pellucid grapes without one seed:
Odorous indeed must be the mead
Whereon they grow, and pure the wave they drink
With lilies at the brink,
And sugar-sweet their sap."

 Golden head by golden head,
Like two pigeons in one nest
Folded in each other's wings,
They lay down in their curtained bed:
Like two blossoms on one stem,
Like two flakes of new-fall'n snow,
Like two wands of ivory
Tipped with gold for awful kings.
Moon and stars gazed in at them,
Wind sang to them lullaby,
Lumbering owls forbore to fly,

Not a bat flapped to and fro
Round their rest:
Cheek to cheek and breast to breast
Locked together in one nest.

Early in the morning
When the first cock crowed his warning,
Neat like bees, as sweet and busy,
Laura rose with Lizzie:
Fetched in honey, milked the cows,
Aired and set to rights the house,
Kneaded cakes of whitest wheat,
Cakes for dainty mouths to eat,
Next churned butter, whipped up cream,
Fed their poultry, sat and sewed;
Talked as modest maidens should:
Lizzie with an open heart,
Laura in an absent dream,
One content, one sick in part;
One warbling for the mere bright day's delight,
One longing for the night.

At length slow evening came:
They went with pitchers to the reedy brook;
Lizzie most placid in her look,
Laura most like a leaping flame.
They drew the gurgling water from its deep;
Lizzie plucked purple and rich golden flags,
Then turning homeward said: "The sunset flushes
Those furthest loftiest crags;
Come, Laura, not another maiden lags,
No wilful squirrel wags,
The beasts and birds are fast asleep."
But Laura loitered still among the rushes
And said the bank was steep.

And said the hour was early still
The dew not fall'n, the wind not chill:
Listening ever, but not catching
The customary cry,
"Come buy, come buy,"

With its iterated jingle
Of sugar-baited words:
Not for all her watching
Once discerning even one goblin
Racing, whisking, tumbling, hobbling;
Let alone the herds
That used to tramp along the glen,
In groups or single,
Of brisk fruit-merchant men.

Till Lizzie urged, "O Laura, come;
I hear the fruit-call but I dare not look:
You should not loiter longer at this brook:
Come with me home.
The stars rise, the moon bends her arc,
Each glowworm winks her spark,
Let us get home before the night grows dark:
For clouds may gather
Though this is summer weather,
Put out the lights and drench us through;
Then if we lost our way what should we do?"

Laura turned cold as stone
To find her sister heard that cry alone,
That goblin cry,
"Come buy our fruits, come buy."
Must she then buy no more such dainty fruit?
Must she no more such succous pasture find,
Gone deaf and blind?
Her tree of life drooped from the root:
She said not one word in her heart's sore ache;
But peering thro' the dimness, nought discerning,
Trudged home, her pitcher dripping all the way;
So crept to bed, and lay
Silent till Lizzie slept;
Then sat up in a passionate yearning,
And gnashed her teeth for baulked desire, and wept
As if her heart would break.

Day after day, night after night,
Laura kept watch in vain

In sullen silence of exceeding pain.
She never caught again the goblin cry:
"Come buy, come buy";—
She never spied the goblin men
Hawking their fruits along the glen:
But when the noon waxed bright
Her hair grew thin and grey;
She dwindled, as the fair full moon doth turn
To swift decay and burn
Her fire away.

One day remembering her kernel-stone
She set it by a wall that faced the south;
Dewed it with tears, hoped for a root,
Watched for a waxing shoot,
But there came none;
It never saw the sun,
It never felt the trickling moisture run:
While with sunk eyes and faded mouth
She dreamed of melons, as a traveller sees
False waves in desert drouth
With shade of leaf-crowned trees,
And burns the thirstier in the sandful breeze.
She no more swept the house,
Tended the fowls or cows,
Fetched honey, kneaded cakes of wheat,
Brought water from the brook:
But sat down listless in the chimney-nook
And would not eat.

Tender Lizzie could not bear
To watch her sister's cankerous care
Yet not to share.
She night and morning
Caught the goblins' cry:
"Come buy our orchard fruits,
Come buy, come buy";—
Beside the brook, along the glen,
She heard the tramp of goblin men,
The voice and stir
Poor Laura could not hear;

Longed to buy fruit to comfort her,
But feared to pay too dear.
She thought of Jeanie in her grave,
Who should have been a bride;
But who for joys brides hope to have
Fell sick and died
In her gay prime,
In earliest Winter time
With the first glazing rime,
With the first snow-fall of crisp Winter time.

Till Laura dwindling
Seemed knocking at Death's door:
Then Lizzie weighed no more
Better and worse;
But put a silver penny in her purse,
Kissed Laura, crossed the heath with clumps of furze
At twilight, halted by the brook:
And for the first time in her life
Began to listen and look.

Laughed every goblin
When they spied her peeping:
Came towards her hobbling,
Flying, running, leaping,
Puffing and blowing,
Chuckling, clapping, crowing,
Clucking and gobbling,
Mopping and mowing,
Full of airs and graces,
Pulling wry faces,
Demure grimaces,
Cat-like and rat-like,
Ratel- and wombat-like,
Snail-paced in a hurry,
Parrot-voiced and whistler,
Helter skelter, hurry skurry,
Chattering like magpies,
Fluttering like pigeons,
Gliding like fishes,—
Hugged her and kissed her:

Squeezed and caressed her:
Stretched up their dishes,
Panniers, and plates:
"Look at our apples
Russet and dun,
Bob at our cherries,
Bite at our peaches,
Citrons and dates,
Grapes for the asking,
Pears red with basking
Out in the sun,
Plums on their twigs;
Pluck them and suck them,
Pomegranates, figs."—

  "Good folk," said Lizzie,
Mindful of Jeanie:
"Give me much and many":—
Held out her apron,
Tossed them her penny.
"Nay, take a seat with us,
Honour and eat with us,"
They answered grinning:
"Our feast is but beginning.
Night yet is early,
Warm and dew-pearly,
Wakeful and starry:
Such fruits as these
No man can carry;
Half their bloom would fly,
Half their dew would dry,
Half their flavour would pass by.
Sit down and feast with us,
Be welcome guest with us,
Cheer you and rest with us."—
"Thank you," said Lizzie: "But one waits
At home alone for me:
So without further parleying,
If you will not sell me any
Of your fruits though much and many,
Give me back my silver penny

I tossed you for a fee."—
They began to scratch their pates,
No longer wagging, purring,
But visibly demurring,
Grunting and snarling.
One called her proud,
Cross-grained, uncivil;
Their tones waxed loud,
Their looks were evil.
Lashing their tails
They trod and hustled her,
Elbowed and jostled her,
Clawed with their nails,
Barking, mewing, hissing, mocking,
Tore her gown and soiled her stocking,
Twitched her hair out by the roots,
Stamped upon her tender feet,
Held her hands and squeezed their fruits
Against her mouth to make her eat.

White and golden Lizzie stood,
Like a lily in a flood,—
Like a rock of blue-veined stone
Lashed by tides obstreperously,—
Like a beacon left alone
In a hoary roaring sea,
Sending up a golden fire,—
Like a fruit-crowned orange-tree
White with blossoms honey-sweet
Sore beset by wasp and bee,—
Like a royal virgin town
Topped with gilded dome and spire
Close beleaguered by a fleet
Mad to tug her standard down.

One may lead a horse to water,
Twenty cannot make him drink.
Though the goblins cuffed and caught her,
Coaxed and fought her,
Bullied and besought her,
Scratched her, pinched her black as ink,

Kicked and knocked her,
Mauled and mocked her,
Lizzie uttered not a word;
Would not open lip from lip
Lest they should cram a mouthful in:
But laughed in heart to feel the drip
Of juice that syrupped all her face,
And lodged in dimples of her chin,
And streaked her neck which quaked like curd.
At last the evil people,
Worn out by her resistance,
Flung back her penny, kicked their fruit
Along whichever road they took,
Not leaving root or stone or shoot;
Some writhed into the ground,
Some dived into the brook
With ring and ripple,
Some scudded on the gale without a sound,
Some vanished in the distance.

In a smart, ache, tingle,
Lizzie went her way;
Knew not was it night or day;
Sprang up the bank, tore thro' the furze,
Threaded copse and dingle,
And heard her penny jingle
Bouncing in her purse,—
Its bounce was music to her ear.
She ran and ran
As if she feared some goblin man
Dogged her with gibe or curse
Or something worse:
But not one goblin skurried after,
Nor was she pricked by fear;
The kind heart made her windy-paced
That urged her home quite out of breath with haste
And inward laughter.

She cried "Laura," up the garden,
"Did you miss me?

Come and kiss me.
Never mind my bruises,
Hug me, kiss me, suck my juices
Squeezed from goblin fruits for you,
Goblin pulp and goblin dew.
Eat me, drink me, love me;
Laura, make much of me:
For your sake I have braved the glen
And had to do with goblin merchant men."

Laura started from her chair,
Flung her arms up in the air,
Clutched her hair:
"Lizzie, Lizzie, have you tasted
For my sake the fruit forbidden?
Must your light like mine be hidden,
Your young life like mine be wasted,
Undone in mine undoing,
And ruined in my ruin,
Thirsty, cankered, goblin-ridden?"—
She clung about her sister,
Kissed and kissed and kissed her:
Tears once again
Refreshed her shrunken eyes,
Dropping like rain
After long sultry drouth;
Shaking with aguish fear, and pain,
She kissed and kissed her with a hungry mouth.

Her lips began to scorch,
That juice was wormwood to her tongue,
She loathed the feast:
Writhing as one possessed she leaped and sung,
Rent all her robe, and wrung
Her hands in lamentable haste,
And beat her breast.
Her locks streamed like the torch
Borne by a racer at full speed,
Or like the mane of horses in their flight,
Or like an eagle when she stems the light

Straight toward the sun,
Or like a caged thing freed,
Or like a flying flag when armies run.

   Swift fire spread through her veins, knocked at her heart,
Met the fire smouldering there
And overbore its lesser flame;
She gorged on bitterness without a name:
Ah! fool, to choose such part
Of soul-consuming care!
Sense failed in the mortal strife:
Like the watch-tower of a town
Which an earthquake shatters down,
Like a lightning-stricken mast,
Like a wind-uprooted tree
Spun about,
Like a foam-topped waterspout
Cast down headlong in the sea,
She fell at last;
Pleasure past and anguish past,
Is it death or is it life?

   Life out of death.
That night long Lizzie watched by her,
Counted her pulse's flagging stir,
Felt for her breath,
Held water to her lips, and cooled her face
With tears and fanning leaves:
But when the first birds chirped about their eaves,
And early reapers plodded to the place
Of golden sheaves,
And dew-wet grass
Bowed in the morning winds so brisk to pass,
And new buds with new day
Opened of cup-like lilies on the stream,
Laura awoke as from a dream,
Laughed in the innocent old way,
Hugged Lizzie but not twice or thrice;
Her gleaming locks showed not one thread of grey,
Her breath was sweet as May
And light danced in her eyes.

Days, weeks, months, years
Afterwards, when both were wives
With children of their own;
Their mother-hearts beset with fears,
Their lives bound up in tender lives;
Laura would call the little ones
And tell them of her early prime,
Those pleasant days long gone
Of not-returning time:
Would talk about the haunted glen,
The wicked, quaint fruit-merchant men,
Their fruits like honey to the throat
But poison in the blood;
(Men sell not such in any town:)
Would tell them how her sister stood
In deadly peril to do her good,
And win the fiery antidote:
Then joining hands to little hands
Would bid them cling together,
"For there is no friend like a sister
In calm or stormy weather;
To cheer one on the tedious way,
To fetch one if one goes astray,
To lift one if one totters down,
To strengthen whilst one stands."

On the Gulls' Road

Willa Cather

The Ambassador's Story

It often happens that one or another of my friends stops before a red chalk drawing in my study and asks me where I ever found so lovely a creature. I have never told the story of that picture to any one, and the beautiful woman on the wall, until yesterday, in all these twenty years has spoken to no one but me. Yesterday a young painter, a countryman of mine, came to consult me on a matter of business, and upon seeing my drawing of Alexandra Ebbling, straightway forgot his errand. He examined the date upon the sketch and asked me, very earnestly, if I could tell him whether the lady were still living. When I answered him, he stepped back from the picture and said slowly:

"So long ago? She must have been very young. She was happy?"

"As to that, who can say—about any one of us?" I replied. "Out of all that is supposed to make for happiness, she had very little."

He shrugged his shoulders and turned away to the window, saying as he did so: "Well, there is very little use in troubling about anything, when we can stand here and look at her, and you can tell me that she has been dead all these years, and that she had very little."

We returned to the object of his visit, but when he bade me goodbye at the door his troubled gaze again went back to the drawing, and it was only by turning sharply about that he took his eyes away from her.

I went back to my study fire, and as the rain kept away less impetuous visitors, I had a long time in which to think of Mrs. Ebbling. I even got out the little box she gave me, which I had not opened for years, and when Mrs. Hemway brought my tea I had barely time to close the lid and defeat her disapproving gaze.

My young countryman's perplexity, as he looked at Mrs. Ebbling, had recalled to me the delight and pain she gave me when I was of his years. I sat looking at her face and trying to see it through his eyes—freshly, as I saw it first upon the deck of the *Germania*, twenty years ago. Was it her loveliness, I often ask myself, or her loneliness, or her simplicity, or was it merely my own youth? Was her mystery only that of the mysterious North out of which she came? I still feel that she was very different from all the beautiful and brilliant women I have known; as the night is different from the day, or as the sea is different from the land. But this is our story, as it comes back to me.

For two years I had been studying Italian and working in the capacity of clerk to the American legation at Rome, and I was going home to secure my first consular appointment. Upon boarding my steamer at Genoa, I saw my luggage into my cabin and then started for a rapid circuit of the deck. Everything promised well. The boat was thinly peopled, even for a July crossing; the decks were roomy; the day was fine; the sea was blue; I was sure of my appointment, and, best of all, I was coming back to Italy. All these things were in my mind when I stopped sharply before a *chaise longue* placed sidewise near the stern. Its occupant was a woman, apparently ill, who lay with her eyes closed, and in her open arm was a chubby little red-haired girl, asleep. I can still remember that first glance at Mrs. Ebbling, and how I stopped as a wheel does when the band slips. Her splendid, vigorous body lay still and relaxed under the loose folds of her clothing, her white throat and arms and red-gold hair were drenched with sunlight. Such hair as it was: wayward as some kind of gleaming seaweed that curls and undulates with the tide. A moment gave me her face; the high cheekbones, the thin cheeks, the gentle chin, arching back to a girlish throat, and singular loveliness of the mouth. Even then it flashed through me that the mouth gave the whole face its peculiar beauty and distinction. It was proud and sad and tender, and strangely calm. The curve of the lips could not have been cut more cleanly with the most delicate instrument, and whatever shade of feeling passed over them seemed to partake of their exquisiteness.

But I am anticipating. While I stood stupidly staring (as if, at twenty-five, I had never before beheld a beautiful woman) the whistles broke into a hoarse scream, and the deck under us began to vibrate. The woman opened her eyes, and the little girl struggled into a sitting position, rolled out of her mother's arm, and ran to the deck rail. After putting my chair near the stern, I went forward to see the gang-plank up and did not return until we were dragging out to sea at the end of a long tow-line.

The woman in the *chaise longue* was still alone. She lay there all day, looking at the sea. The little girl, Carin, played noisily about the deck. Occasionally she returned and struggled up into the chair, plunged her head, round and red as a little pumpkin, against her mother's shoulder in an impetuous embrace, and then struggled down again with a lively flourishing of arms and legs. Her mother took such opportunities to pull up the child's socks or to smooth the fiery little braids; her beautiful hands, rather large and very white, played about the riotous little girl with a quieting tenderness. Carin chattered away in Italian and kept asking for her father, only to be told that he was busy.

When any of the ship's officers passed, they stopped for a word with my neighbor, and I heard the first mate address her as Mrs. Ebbling. When they spoke to her, she smiled appreciatively and answered in low, faltering Italian, but I fancied that she was glad when they passed on and left her to her fixed contemplation of the sea. Her eyes seemed to drink the color of it all day long, and after every interruption they went back to it. There was a kind of pleasure in watching her satisfaction, a kind of excitement in wondering what the water made her remember or forget. She seemed not to wish to talk to any one, but I knew I should like to hear whatever she might be thinking. One could catch some hint of her thoughts, I imagined, from the shadows that came and went across her lips, like the reflection of light clouds. She had a pile of books beside her, but she did not read, and neither could I. I gave up trying at last, and watched the sea, very conscious of her presence, almost of her thoughts. When the sun dropped low and shone in her face, I rose and asked if she would like me to move her chair. She smiled and thanked me, but said the sun was good for her. Her yellow-hazel eyes followed me for a moment and then went back to the sea.

After the first bugle sounded for dinner, a heavy man in uniform came up the deck and stood beside the *chaise longue*, looking down at its two occupants with a smile of satisfied possession. The breast of his trim coat was hidden by waves of soft blond beard, as long and heavy as a woman's hair, which blew about his face in glittering profusion. He wore a large turquoise ring upon the thick hand that he rubbed good-humoredly over the little girl's head. To her he spoke Italian, but he and his wife conversed in some Scandinavian tongue. He stood stroking his fine beard until the second bugle blew, then bent stiffly from his hips, like a soldier, and patted his wife's hand as it lay on the arm of her chair. He hurried down the deck, taking stock of the passengers as he went, and stopped before a thin girl with frizzed hair and a lace coat, asking her a facetious question in thick English. They began to talk about Chicago and went below. Later I saw him at the head of his table in the dining room, the befrizzed Chicago lady on his left. They must have got a famous start at luncheon, for by the end of the dinner Ebbling was peeling figs for her and presenting them on the end of a fork.

The Doctor confided to me that Ebbling was the chief engineer and the dandy of the boat; but this time he would have to behave himself, for he had brought his sick wife along for the voyage. She had a bad heart valve, he added, and was in a serious way.

After dinner Ebbling disappeared, presumably to his engines, and at ten o'clock, when the stewardess came to put Mrs. Ebbling to bed, I helped her to rise from her chair, and the second mate ran up and supported her down to her cabin. About midnight I found the engineer in the card room, playing with the Doctor, an Italian naval officer, and the commodore of a Long

Island yacht club. His face was even pinker than it had been at dinner, and his fine beard was full of smoke. I thought a long while about Ebbling and his wife before I went to sleep.

The next morning we tied up at Naples to take on our cargo, and I went on shore for the day. I did not, however, entirely escape the ubiquitous engineer, whom I saw lunching with the Long Island commodore at a hotel in the Santa Lucia. When I returned to the boat in the early evening, the passengers had gone down to dinner, and I found Mrs. Ebbling quite alone upon the deserted deck. I approached her and asked whether she had had a dull day. She looked up smiling and shook her head, as if her Italian had quite failed her. I saw that she was flushed with excitement, and her yellow eyes were shining like two clear topazes.

"Dull? Oh, no! I love to watch Naples from the sea, in this white heat. She has just lain there on her hillside among the vines and laughed for me all day long. I have been able to pick out many of the places I like best."

I felt that she was really going to talk to me at last. She had turned to me frankly, as to an old acquaintance, and seemed not to be hiding from me anything of what she felt. I sat down in a glow of pleasure and excitement and asked her if she knew Naples well.

"Oh, yes! I lived there for a year after I was first married. My husband has a great many friends in Naples. But he was at sea most of the time, so I went about alone. Nothing helps one to know a city like that. I came first by sea, like this. Directly to Naples from Finmark, and I had never been South before." Mrs. Ebbling stopped and looked over my shoulder. Then, with a quick, eager glance at me, she said abruptly: "It was like a baptism of fire. Nothing has ever been quite the same since. Imagine how this bay looked to a Finmark girl. It seemed like the overture to Italy."

I laughed. "And then one goes up the country—song by song and wine by wine."

Mrs. Ebbling sighed. "Ah, yes. It must be fine to follow it. I have never been away from the seaports myself. We live now in Genoa."

The deck steward brought her tray, and I moved forward a little and stood by the rail. When I looked back, she smiled and nodded to let me know that she was not missing anything. I could feel her intentness as keenly as if she were standing beside me.

The sun had disappeared over the high ridge behind the city, and the stone pines stood black and flat against the fires of the afterglow. The lilac haze that hung over the long, lazy slopes of Vesuvius warmed with golden light, and films of blue vapor began to float down toward Baiæ. The sky, the sea, and the city between them turned a shimmering violet, fading grayer as the lights began to glow like luminous pearls along the water-front—the necklace of an irreclaimable queen. Behind me I heard a low exclamation; a slight, stifled sound, but it seemed the perfect vocalization of that weariness with which we at last let go of beauty, after we have held it until the senses are darkened. When I turned to her again, she seemed to have fallen asleep.

That night, as we were moving out to sea and the tail lights of Naples were winking across the widening stretch of black water, I helped Mrs. Ebbling to the foot of the stairway. She drew herself up from her chair with effort and leaned on me wearily. I could have carried her all night without fatigue.

"May I come and talk to you tomorrow?" I asked. She did not reply at once. "Like an old friend?" I added. She gave me her languid hand, and her mouth, set with the exertion of walking, softened altogether. "Grazia," she murmured.

I returned to the deck and joined a group of my countrywomen, who, primed with inexhaustible information, were discussing the baseness of Renaissance art. They were intelligent and alert, and as they leaned forward in their deck chairs under the circle of light, their faces recalled to me Rembrandt's picture of a clinical lecture. I heard them through, against my will, and then went to the stern to smoke and to see the last of the island lights. The sky had clouded over, and a soft, melancholy wind was rushing over the sea. I could not help thinking how disappointed I would be if rain should keep Mrs. Ebbling in her cabin tomorrow. My mind played constantly with her image. At one moment she was very clear and directly in front of me; the next she was far away. Whatever else I thought about, some part of my consciousness was busy with Mrs. Ebbling; hunting for her, finding her, losing her, then groping again. How was it that I was so conscious of whatever she might be feeling? that when she sat still behind me and watched the evening sky, I had had a sense of speed and change, almost of danger; and when she was tired and sighed, I had wished for night and loneliness.

II

Though when we are young we seldom think much about it, there is now and again a golden day when we feel a sudden, arrogant pride in our youth; in the lightness of our feet and the strength of our arms, in the warm fluid that courses so surely within us; when we are conscious of something powerful and mercurial in our breasts, which comes up wave after wave and leaves us irresponsible and free. All the next morning I felt this flow of life, which continually impelled me toward Mrs. Ebbling. After the merest greeting, however, I kept away. I found it pleasant to thwart myself, to measure myself against a current that was sure to carry me with it in the end. I was content to let her watch the sea—the sea that seemed now to have come into me, warm and soft, still and strong. I played shuffleboard with the Commodore, who was anxious to keep down his figure, and ran about the deck with the stout legs of the little pumpkin-colored Carin about my neck. It was not until the child was having her afternoon nap below that I at last came up and stood beside her mother.

"You are better today," I exclaimed, looking down at her white gown. She colored unreasonably, and I laughed with a familiarity which she must have accepted as the mere foolish noise of happiness, or it would have seemed impertinent.

We talked at first of a hundred trivial things, and we watched the sea. The coast of Sardinia had lain to our port for some hours and would lie there for hours to come, now advancing in rocky promontories, now retreating behind blue bays. It was the naked south coast of the island, and though our course held very near the shore, not a village or habitation was visible; there was not even a goatherd's hut hidden away among the low pinkish sand hills. Pinkish sand hills and yellow headlands; with dull-colored scrubby bushes massed about their bases and following the dried watercourses. A narrow strip of beach glistened like white paint between the purple sea and the umber rocks, and the whole island lay gleaming in the yellow sunshine and translucent air. Not a wave broke on that fringe of white sand, not the shadow of a cloud played across the bare hills. In the air about us there was no sound but that of a vessel moving rapidly through absolutely still water. She seemed like some great sea-animal, swimming silently, her head well up. The sea before us was so rich and heavy and opaque that it might have been lapis lazuli. It was the blue of legend, simply; the color that satisfies the soul like sleep.

And it was of the sea we talked, for it was the substance of Mrs. Ebbling's story. She seemed always to have been swept along by ocean streams, warm or cold, and to have hovered about the edge of great waters. She was born and had grown up in a little fishing town on the Arctic Ocean. Her father was a doctor, a widower, who lived with his daughter and who divided his time between his books and his fishing rod. Her uncle was skipper on a coasting vessel, and with him she had made many trips along the Norwegian coast. But she was always reading and thinking about the blue seas of the South.

"There was a curious old woman in our village, Dame Ericson, who had been in Italy in her youth. She had gone to Rome to study art, and had copied a great many pictures there. She was well connected, but had little money, and as she grew older and poorer she sold her pictures one by one, until there was scarcely a well-to-do family in our district that did not own one of Dame Ericson's paintings. But she brought home many other strange things; a little orange-tree which she cherished until the day of her death, and bits of colored marble, and sea shells and pieces of coral, and a thin flask full of water from the Mediterranean. When I was a little girl she used to show me her things and tell me about the South; about the coral fishers, and the pink islands, and the smoking mountains, and the old, underground Naples. I suppose the water in her flask was like any other, but it never seemed so to me. It looked so elastic and alive, that I used to think if one unsealed the bottle something penetrating and fruitful might leap out and work an enchantment over Finmark."

Lars Ebbling, I learned, was one of her father's friends. She could remember him from the time when she was a little girl and he a dashing young man who used to come home from the sea and make a stir in the village. After he got his promotion to an Atlantic liner and went South, she did not see him until the summer she was twenty, when he came home to marry her. That was five years ago. The little girl, Carin, was three. From her talk, one might have supposed that Ebbling was proprietor of the Mediterranean and its adjacent lands, and could have kept her away at his pleasure. Her own rights in him she seemed not to consider.

But we wasted very little time on Lars Ebbling. We talked, like two very young persons, of arms and men, of the sea beneath us and the shores it washed. We were carried a little beyond ourselves, for we were in the presence of the things of youth that never change; fleeing past them. To-morrow they would be gone, and no effort of will or memory could bring them back again. All about us was the sea of great adventure, and below us, caught somewhere in its gleaming meshes, were the bones of nations and navies . . . nations and navies that gave youth its hope and made life something more than a hunger of the bowels. The unpeopled Sardinian coast unfolded gently before us, like something left over out of a world that was gone; a place that might well have had no later news since the corn ships brought the tidings of Actium.

"I shall never go to Sardinia," said Mrs. Ebbling. "It could not possibly be as beautiful as this."

"Neither shall I," I replied.

As I was going down to dinner that evening, I was stopped by Lars Ebbling, freshly brushed and scented, wearing a white uniform, and polished and glistening as one of his own engines. He smiled at me with his own kind of geniality. "You have been very kind to talk to my wife," he explained. "It is very bad for her this trip that she speaks no English. I am indebted to you."

I told him curtly that he was mistaken, but my acrimony made no impression upon his blandness. I felt that I should certainly strike the fellow if he stood there much longer, running his blue ring up and down his beard. I should probably have hated any man who was Mrs. Ebbling's husband, but Ebbling made me sick.

III

The next day I began my drawing of Mrs. Ebbing. She seemed pleased and a little puzzled when I asked her to sit for me. It occurred to me that she had always been among dull people who took her looks as a matter of course, and that she was not at all sure that she was really beautiful. I can see now her quick, confused look of pleasure. I thought very little about the drawing then, except that the making of it gave me an opportunity to study her face; to look as long as I pleased into her yellow eyes, at the noble lines of her mouth, at her splendid, vigorous hair.

"We have a yellow vine at home," I told her, "that is very like your hair. It seems to be growing while one looks at it, and it twines and tangles about itself and throws out little tendrils in the wind."

"Has it any name?"

"We call it love vine."

How little a thing could disconcert her!

As for me, nothing disconcerted me. I awoke every morning with a sense of speed and joy. At night I loved to hear the swish of the water rushing by. As fast as the pistons could carry us, as fast as the water could bear us, we were going forward to something delightful; to something together. When Mrs. Ebbling told me that she and her husband would be five days in the docks in New York and then return to Genoa, I was not disturbed, for I did not believe her. I came and went, and she sat still all day, watching the water. I heard an American lady say that she watched it like one who is going to die, but even that did not frighten me: I somehow felt that she had promised me to live.

All those long blue days when I sat beside her talking about Finmark and the sea, she must have known that I loved her. I sat with my hands idle on my knees and let the tide come up in me. It carried me so swiftly that, across the narrow space of deck between us, it must have swayed her, too, a little. I had no wish to disturb or distress her. If a little, a very little of it reached her, I was satisfied. If it drew her softly, but drew her, I wanted no more. Sometimes I could see that even the light pressure of my thoughts made her paler. One still evening, after a long talk, she whispered to me, "You must go and walk now, and—don't think about me." She had been held too long and too closely in my thoughts, and she begged me to release her for a little while. I went out into the bow and put her far away, at the skyline, with the faintest star, and thought of her gently across the water. When I went back to her, she was asleep.

But even in those first days I had my hours of misery. Why, for instance, should she have been born in Finmark, and why should Lars Ebbling have been her only door of escape? Why should she be silently taking leave of the world at the age when I was just beginning it, having had nothing, nothing of whatever is worth while?

She never talked about taking leave of things, and yet I sometimes felt that she was counting the sunsets. One yellow afternoon, when we were gliding between the shores of Spain and Africa, she spoke of her illness for the first time. I had got some magnolias at Gibraltar, and she wore a bunch of them in her girdle and the rest lay on her lap. She held the cool leaves against her cheek and fingered the white petals. "I can never," she remarked, "get enough of the flowers of the South. They make me breathless, just as they did at first. Because of them I should like to live a long while—almost forever."

I leaned forward and looked at her. "We could live almost forever if we had enough courage. It's of our lives that we die. If we had the courage to change it all, to run away to some blue coast like that over there, we could live on and on, until we were tired."

She smiled tolerantly and looked southward through half shut eyes. "I am afraid I should never have courage enough to go behind that mountain, at least. Look at it, it looks as if it hid horrible things."

A sea mist, blown in from the Atlantic, began to mask the impassive African coast, and above the fog, the gray mountain peak took on the angry red of the sunset. It burned sullen and threatening until the dark land drew the night about her and settled back into the sea. We watched it sink, while under us, slowly but ever increasing, we felt the throb of the Atlantic come and go, the thrill of the vast, untamed waters of that lugubrious and passionate sea. I drew Mrs. Ebbling's wraps about her and shut the magnolias under her cloak. When I left her, she slipped me one warm, white flower.

IV

From the Straits of Gibraltar we dropped into the abyss, and by morning we were rolling in the trough of a sea that drew us down and held us deep, shaking us gently back and forth until the timbers creaked, and then shooting us out on the crest of a swelling mountain. The water was bright and blue, but so cold that the breath of it penetrated one's bones, as if the chill of the deep under-fathoms of the sea were being loosed upon us. There were not more than a dozen people upon the deck that morning, and Mrs. Ebbling was sheltered behind the stern, muffled in a sea jacket, with drops of moisture upon her long lashes and on her hair. When a shower of icy spray beat back over the deck rail, she took it gleefully.

"After all," she insisted, "this is my own kind of water; the kind I was born in. This is first cousin to the Pole waters, and the sea we have left is only a kind of fairy tale. It's like the burnt-out volcanoes; its day is over. This is the real sea now, where the doings of the world go on."

"It is not our reality, at any rate," I answered.

"Oh, yes, it is! These are the waters that carry men to their work, and they will carry you to yours."

I sat down and watched her hair grow more alive and iridescent in the moisture. "You are pleased to take an attitude," I complained.

"No, I don't love realities any more than another, but I admit them, all the same."

"And who are you and I to define the realities?"

"Our minds define them clearly enough, yours and mine, everybody's. Those are the lines we never cross, though we flee from the equator to the Pole. I have never really got out of Finmark, of course. I shall live and die in a fishing town on the Arctic Ocean, and the blue seas and the pink islands are as much a dream as they ever were. All the same, I shall continue to dream them."

The Gulf Stream gave us warm blue days again, but pale, like sad memories. The water had faded, and the thin, tepid sunshine made something tighten about one's heart. The stars watched us coldly, and seemed always to be asking me what I was going to do. The advancing line on the chart, which at first had been mere foolishness, began to mean something, and the wind from the west brought disturbing fears and forebodings. I slept lightly, and all day I was restless and uncertain except when I was with Mrs. Ebbling. She quieted me as she did little Carin, and soothed me without saying anything, as she had done that evening at Naples when we watched the sunset. It seemed to me that every day her eyes grew more tender and her lips more calm. A kind of fortitude seemed to be gathering about her mouth, and I dreaded it. Yet when, in an involuntary glance, I put to her the question that tortured me, her eyes always met mine steadily, deep and gentle and full of reassurance. That I had my word at last, happened almost by accident.

On the second night out from shore there was the concert for the Sailors' Orphanage, and Mrs. Ebbling dressed and went down to dinner for the first time, and sat on her husband's right. I was not the only one who was glad to see her. Even the women were pleased. She wore a pale green gown, and she came up out of it regally white and gold. I was so proud that I blushed when any one spoke of her. After dinner she was standing by her deck-chair talking to her husband when people began to go below for the concert. She took up a long cloak and attempted to put it on. The wind blew the light thing about, and Ebbling chatted and smiled his public smile while she struggled with it. Suddenly his roving eye caught sight of the Chicago girl, who was having a similar difficulty with her draperies, and he pranced half the length of the deck to assist her. I had been watching from the rail, and when she was left alone I threw my cigar away and wrapped Mrs. Ebbling up roughly.

"Don't go down," I begged. "Stay up here. I want to talk to you."

She hesitated a moment and looked at me thoughtfully. Then, with a sigh, she sat down. Every one hurried down to the saloon, and we were absolutely alone at last, behind the shelter of the stern, with the thick darkness all about us and a warm east wind rushing over the sea. I was too sore and angry to think. I leaned toward her, holding the arm of her chair with both hands, and began anywhere.

"You remember those two blue coasts out of Gibraltar? It shall be either one you choose, if you will come with me. I have not much money, but we shall get on somehow. There has got to be an end of this. We are neither one of us cowards, and this is humiliating, intolerable."

She sat looking down at her hands, and I pulled her chair impatiently toward me.

"I felt," she said at last, "that you were going to say something like this. You are sorry for me, and I don't wish to be pitied. You think Ebbling neglects me, but you are mistaken. He has had his disappointments, too. He wants children and a gay, hospitable house, and he is tied to a sick woman who cannot get on with people. He has more to complain of than I have, and yet he bears with me. I am grateful to him, and there is no more to be said."

"Oh, isn't there?" I cried, "and I?"

She laid her hand entreatingly upon my arm. "Ah, you! you! Don't ask me to talk about that. You—;" Her fingers slipped down my coat sleeve to my hand and pressed it. I caught her two hands and held them, telling her I would never let them go.

"And you meant to leave me day after tomorrow, to say goodbye to me as you will to the other people on this boat? You meant to cut me adrift like this, with my heart on fire and all my life unspent in me?"

She sighed despondently. "I am willing to suffer—whatever I must suffer—to have had you," she answered simply. "I was ill—and so lonely— and it came so quickly and quietly. Ah, don't begrudge it to me! Do not leave me in bitterness. If I have been wrong, forgive me." She bowed her head and pressed my fingers entreatingly. A warm tear splashed on my hand. It occurred to me that she bore my anger as she bore little Carin's importunities, as she bore Ebbling. What a circle of pettiness she had about her! I fell back in my chair and my hands dropped at my side. I felt like a creature with its back broken. I asked her what she wished me to do.

"Don't ask me," she whispered. "There is nothing that we can do. I thought you knew that. You forget that—that I am too ill to begin my life over. Even if there were nothing else in the way, that would be enough. And that is what has made it all possible, our loving each other, I mean. If I were well, we couldn't have had even this much. Don't reproach me. Hasn't it been at all pleasant to you to find me waiting for you every morning, to feel me thinking of you when you went to sleep? Every night I have watched the sea for you, as if it were mine and I had made it, and I have listened to the water rushing by you, full of sleep and youth and hope. And everything you had done or said during the day came back to me, and when I went to sleep it was only to feel you more. You see there was never any one else; I have never thought of any one in the dark but you." She spoke pleadingly, and her voice had sunk so low that I could scarcely hear her.

"And yet you will do nothing," I groaned. "You will dare nothing. You will give me nothing."

"Don't say that. When I leave you day after tomorrow, I shall have given you all my life. I can't tell you how, but it is true. There is something in each of us that does not belong to the family or to society, not even to ourselves. Sometimes it is given in marriage, and sometimes it is given in love, but oftener it is never given at all. We have nothing to do with giving or withholding it. It is a wild thing that sings in us once and flies away and never comes back, and mine has flown to you. When one loves like that, it is enough somehow. The other things can go if they must. That is why I can live without you, and die without you."

I caught her hands and looked into her eyes that shone warm in the darkness. She shivered and whispered in a tone so different from any I ever heard from her before or afterward: "Do you grudge it to me? You are so young and strong, and you have everything before you. I shall have only a little while to want you in—and I could want you forever and not weary." I kissed her hair, her cheeks, her lips, until her head fell forward on my shoulder and she put my face away with her soft, trembling fingers. She took my hand and held it close to her, in both her own. We sat silent, and the moments came and went, bringing us closer and closer, and the wind and water rushed by us, obliterating our tomorrows and all our yesterdays.

The next day Mrs. Ebbling kept her cabin, and I sat stupidly by her chair until dark, with the rugged little girl to keep me company, and an occasional nod from the engineer.

I saw Mrs. Ebbling again only for a few moments, when we were coming into the New York harbor. She wore a street dress and a hat, and these alone would have made her seem far away from me. She was very pale, and looked down when she spoke to me, as if she had been guilty of a wrong toward me. I have never been able to remember that interview without heartache and shame, but then I was too desperate to care about anything. I stood like a wooden post and let her approach me, let her speak to me, let her leave me as if it were a hard thing to do, and held out a little package, timidly, and her gloved hand shook as if she were afraid of me.

"I want to give you something," she said. "You will not want it now, so I shall ask you to keep it until you hear from me. You gave me your address a long time ago, when you were making that drawing. Some day I shall write to you and ask you to open this. You must not come to tell me goodbye this morning, but I shall be watching you when you go ashore. Please don't forget that."

I took the little box mechanically and thanked her. I think my eyes must have filled, for she uttered an exclamation of pity, touched my sleeve quickly, and left me. It was one of those strange, low, musical exclamations which meant everything and nothing, like the one that had thrilled me that night at Naples, and it was the last sound I ever heard from her lips.

An hour later I went on shore, one of those who crowded over the gang-plank the moment it was lowered. But the next afternoon I wandered back to the docks and went on board the *Germania*. I asked for the engineer, and he came up in his shirt sleeves from the engine room. He was red and dishevelled, angry and voluble; his bright eye had a hard glint, and I did not once see his masterful smile. When he heard my inquiry he became profane. Mrs. Ebbling had sailed for Bremen on the *Hohenstauffen* that morning at eleven o'clock. She had decided to return by the northern route and pay a visit to her father in Finmark. She was in no condition to travel alone, he said. He evidently smarted under her extravagance. But who, he asked, with a blow of his fist on the rail, could stand between a woman and her whim? She had always been a wilful girl, and she had a doting father behind her. When she set her head with the wind, there was no holding her; she ought to have married the Arctic Ocean. I think Ebbling was still talking when I walked away.

I spent that winter in New York. My consular appointment hung fire (indeed, I did not pursue it with much enthusiasm), and I had a good many idle hours in which to think of Mrs. Ebbling. She had never mentioned the name of her father's village, and somehow I could never quite bring myself to go to the docks when Ebbling's boat was in and ask for news of her. More than once I made up my mind definitely to go to Finmark and take my chance at finding her; the shipping people would know where Ebbling came from. But I never went. I have often wondered why. When my resolve was made and my courage high, when I could almost feel myself approaching her, suddenly everything crumbled under me, and I fell back as I had done that night when I dropped her hands, after telling her, only a moment before, that I would never let them go.

In the twilight of a wet March day, when the gutters were running black outside and the Square was liquefying under crusts of dirty snow, the housekeeper brought me a damp letter which bore a blurred foreign postmark. It was from Niels Nannestad, who wrote that it was his sad duty to inform me that his daughter, Alexandra Ebbling, had died on the second day of February, in the twenty-sixth year of her age. Complying with her request, he inclosed a letter which she had written some days before her death.

I at last brought myself to break the seal of the second letter. It read thus:

MY FRIEND:

You may open now the little package I gave you. May I ask you to keep it? I gave it to you because there is no one else who would care about it in just that way. Ever since I left you I have been thinking what it would be like to live a lifetime caring and being cared for like that. It was not the life I was meant to live, and yet, in a way, I have been living it ever since I first knew you.

Of course you understand now why I could not go with you. I would have spoiled your life for you. Besides that, I was ill—and I was too proud to give you the shadow of myself. I had much to give you, if you had come earlier. As it was, I was ashamed. Vanity sometimes saves us when nothing else will, and mine saved you. Thank you for everything. I hold this to my heart, where I once held your hand.

ALEXANDRA

The dusk had thickened into night long before I got up from my chair and took the little box from its place in my desk drawer. I opened it and lifted out a thick coil, cut from where her hair grew thickest and brightest. It was tied firmly at one end, and when it fell over my arm it curled and clung about my sleeve like a living thing set free. How it gleamed, how it still gleams in the firelight! It was warm and softly scented under my lips, and stirred under my breath like seaweed in the tide. This, and a withered magnolia flower, and two pink sea shells; nothing more. And it was all twenty years ago!

POEMS

Emily Dickinson

I HAD NO TIME TO HATE

I had no time to hate, because
The grave would hinder me,
And life was not so ample I
Could finish enmity.

Nor had I time to love; but since
Some industry must be,
The little toil of love, I thought,
Was large enough for me.

THE CHARIOT

Because I could not stop for Death,
He kindly stopped for me;
The carriage held but just ourselves
And Immortality.

We slowly drove, he knew no haste,
And I had put away
My labor, and my leisure too,
For his civility.

We passed the school where children played,
Their lessons scarcely done;
We passed the fields of gazing grain,
We passed the setting sun.

We paused before a house that seemed
A swelling of the ground;
The roof was scarcely visible,
The cornice but a mound.

Since then 'tis centuries; but each
Feels shorter than the day
I first surmised the horses' heads
Were toward eternity.

HOPE IS THE THING WITH FEATHERS

Hope is the thing with feathers
That perches in the soul,
And sings the tune without the words,
And never stops at all,

And sweetest in the gale is heard;
And sore must be the storm
That could abash the little bird
That kept so many warm.

I've heard it in the chillest land,
And on the strangest sea;
Yet, never, in extremity,
It asked a crumb of me.

WILD NIGHTS! WILD NIGHTS!

Wild nights! Wild nights!
Were I with thee,
Wild nights should be
Our luxury!

Futile the winds
To a heart in port,—
Done with the compass,
Done with the chart.

Rowing in Eden!
Ah! the sea!
Might I but moor
To-night in thee!

The Voyage Out

Virginia Woolf

CHAPTER I

As the streets that lead from the Strand to the Embankment are very narrow, it is better not to walk down them arm-in-arm. If you persist, lawyers' clerks will have to make flying leaps into the mud; young lady typists will have to fidget behind you. In the streets of London where beauty goes unregarded, eccentricity must pay the penalty, and it is better not to be very tall, to wear a long blue cloak, or to beat the air with your left hand.

One afternoon in the beginning of October when the traffic was becoming brisk a tall man strode along the edge of the pavement with a lady on his arm. Angry glances struck upon their backs. The small, agitated figures—for in comparison with this couple most people looked small—decorated with fountain pens, and burdened with despatch-boxes, had appointments to keep, and drew a weekly salary, so that there was some reason for the unfriendly stare which was bestowed upon Mr. Ambrose's height and upon Mrs. Ambrose's cloak. But some enchantment had put both man and woman beyond the reach of malice and unpopularity. In his case one might guess from the moving lips that it was thought; and in hers from the eyes fixed stonily straight in front of her at a level above the eyes of most that it was sorrow. It was only by scorning all she met that she kept herself from tears, and the friction of people brushing past her was evidently painful. After watching the traffic on the Embankment for a minute or two with a stoical gaze she twitched her husband's sleeve, and they crossed between the swift discharge of motor cars. When they were safe on the further side, she gently withdrew her arm from his, allowing her mouth at the same time to relax, to tremble; then tears rolled down, and leaning her elbows on the balustrade, she shielded her face from the curious. Mr. Ambrose attempted consolation; he patted her shoulder; but she showed no signs of admitting him, and feeling it awkward to stand beside a grief that was greater than his, he crossed his arms behind him, and took a turn along the pavement.

The embankment juts out in angles here and there, like pulpits; instead of preachers, however, small boys occupy them, dangling string, dropping pebbles, or launching wads of paper for a cruise. With their sharp eye for eccentricity, they were inclined to think Mr. Ambrose awful; but the quickest witted cried "Bluebeard!" as he passed. In case they should proceed to tease his wife, Mr.

Ambrose flourished his stick at them, upon which they decided that he was grotesque merely, and four instead of one cried "Bluebeard!" in chorus.

Although Mrs. Ambrose stood quite still, much longer than is natural, the little boys let her be. Someone is always looking into the river near Waterloo Bridge; a couple will stand there talking for half an hour on a fine afternoon; most people, walking for pleasure, contemplate for three minutes; when, having compared the occasion with other occasions, or made some sentence, they pass on. Sometimes the flats and churches and hotels of Westminster are like the outlines of Constantinople in a mist; sometimes the river is an opulent purple, sometimes mud-coloured, sometimes sparkling blue like the sea. It is always worth while to look down and see what is happening. But this lady looked neither up nor down; the only thing she had seen, since she stood there, was a circular iridescent patch slowly floating past with a straw in the middle of it. The straw and the patch swam again and again behind the tremulous medium of a great welling tear, and the tear rose and fell and dropped into the river. Then there struck close upon her ears—

Lars Porsena of Clusium
By the nine Gods he swore—

and then more faintly, as if the speaker had passed her on his walk—

That the Great House of Tarquin
Should suffer wrong no more.

Yes, she knew she must go back to all that, but at present she must weep. Screening her face she sobbed more steadily than she had yet done, her shoulders rising and falling with great regularity. It was this figure that her husband saw when, having reached the polished Sphinx, having entangled himself with a man selling picture postcards, he turned; the stanza instantly stopped. He came up to her, laid his hand on her shoulder, and said, "Dearest." His voice was supplicating. But she shut her face away from him, as much as to say, "You can't possibly understand."

As he did not leave her, however, she had to wipe her eyes, and to raise them to the level of the factory chimneys on the other bank. She saw also the arches of Waterloo Bridge and the carts moving across them, like the line of animals in a shooting gallery. They were seen blankly, but to see anything was of course to end her weeping and begin to walk.

"I would rather walk," she said, her husband having hailed a cab already occupied by two city men.

The fixity of her mood was broken by the action of walking. The shooting motor cars, more like spiders in the moon than terrestrial objects, the thundering drays, the jingling hansoms, and little black broughams, made her think of the world she lived in. Somewhere up there above the pinnacles where the smoke rose in a pointed hill, her children were now asking for her, and getting a soothing reply. As for the mass of streets, squares, and public buildings which parted them, she only felt at this moment how little London had done to make her love it, although thirty of her forty years had been spent in a street. She knew how to read the people who were passing her; there were the rich who were running to and from each others' houses at this hour; there were the bigoted workers driving in a straight line to their offices; there were the poor who were unhappy and rightly malignant. Already, though there was sunlight in the haze, tattered old men and women were nodding off to sleep upon the seats. When one gave up seeing the beauty that clothed things, this was the skeleton beneath.

A fine rain now made her still more dismal; vans with the odd names of those engaged in odd industries—Sprules, Manufacturer of Saw-dust; Grabb, to whom no piece of waste paper comes amiss—fell flat as a bad joke; bold lovers, sheltered behind one cloak, seemed to her sordid, past their passion; the flower women, a contented company, whose talk is always worth hearing, were sodden hags; the red, yellow, and blue flowers, whose heads were pressed together, would not blaze. Moreover, her husband walking with a quick rhythmic stride, jerking his free hand occasionally, was either a Viking or a stricken Nelson; the sea-gulls had changed his note.

"Ridley, shall we drive? Shall we drive, Ridley?"

Mrs. Ambrose had to speak sharply; by this time he was far away.

The cab, by trotting steadily along the same road, soon withdrew them from the West End, and plunged them into London. It appeared that this was a great manufacturing place, where the people were engaged in making things, as though the West End, with its electric lamps, its vast plate-glass windows all shining yellow, its carefully-finished houses, and tiny live figures trotting on the pavement, or bowled along on wheels in the road, was the finished work. It appeared to her a very small bit of work for such an enormous factory to have made. For some reason it appeared to her as a small golden tassel on the edge of a vast black cloak.

Observing that they passed no other hansom cab, but only vans and waggons, and that not one of the thousand men and women she saw was either a gentleman or a lady, Mrs. Ambrose understood that after all it is the ordinary thing to be poor, and that London is the city of innumerable poor people. Startled by this discovery and seeing herself pacing a circle all the days of her life round Piccadilly Circus she was greatly relieved to pass a building put up by the London County Council for Night Schools.

"Lord, how gloomy it is!" her husband groaned. "Poor creatures!"

What with the misery for her children, the poor, and the rain, her mind was like a wound exposed to dry in the air.

At this point the cab stopped, for it was in danger of being crushed like an egg-shell. The wide Embankment which had had room for cannonballs and squadrons, had now shrunk to a cobbled lane steaming with smells of malt and oil and blocked by waggons. While her husband read the placards pasted on the brick announcing the hours at which certain ships would sail for Scotland, Mrs. Ambrose did her best to find information. From a world exclusively occupied in feeding waggons with sacks, half obliterated too in a fine yellow fog, they got neither help nor attention. It seemed a miracle when an old man approached, guessed their condition, and proposed to row them out to their ship in the little boat which he kept moored at the bottom of a flight of steps. With some hesitation they trusted themselves to him, took their places, and were soon waving up and down upon the water, London having shrunk to two lines of buildings on either side of them, square buildings and oblong buildings placed in rows like a child's avenue of bricks.

The river, which had a certain amount of troubled yellow light in it, ran with great force; bulky barges floated down swiftly escorted by tugs; police boats shot past everything; the wind went with the current. The open rowing-boat in which they sat bobbed and curtseyed across the line of traffic. In mid-stream the old man stayed his hands upon the oars, and as the water rushed past them, remarked that once he had taken many passengers across, where now he took scarcely any. He seemed to recall an age when his boat, moored among rushes, carried delicate feet across to lawns at Rotherhithe.

"They want bridges now," he said, indicating the monstrous outline of the Tower Bridge. Mournfully Helen regarded him, who was putting water between her and her children. Mournfully she gazed at the ship they were approaching; anchored in the middle of the stream they could dimly read her name—*Euphrosyne*.

Very dimly in the falling dusk they could see the lines of the rigging, the masts and the dark flag which the breeze blew out squarely behind.

As the little boat sidled up to the steamer, and the old man shipped his oars, he remarked once more pointing above, that ships all the world over flew that flag the day they sailed. In the minds of both the passengers the blue flag appeared a sinister token, and this the moment for presentiments, but nevertheless they rose, gathered their things together, and climbed on deck.

Down in the saloon of her father's ship, Miss Rachel Vinrace, aged twenty-four, stood waiting her uncle and aunt nervously. To begin with, though nearly related, she scarcely remembered them; to go on with, they were elderly people, and finally, as her father's daughter she must be in some sort prepared to entertain them. She looked forward to seeing them as civilised people generally look forward to the first sight of civilised people, as though they were of the nature of an approaching physical discomfort—a tight shoe or a draughty window. She was already unnaturally braced to receive them. As she occupied herself in laying forks severely straight by the side of knives, she heard a man's voice saying gloomily:

"On a dark night one would fall down these stairs head foremost," to which a woman's voice added, "And be killed."

As she spoke the last words the woman stood in the doorway. Tall, large-eyed, draped in purple shawls, Mrs. Ambrose was romantic and beautiful; not perhaps sympathetic, for her eyes looked straight and considered what they saw. Her face was much warmer than a Greek face; on the other hand it was much bolder than the face of the usual pretty Englishwoman.

"Oh, Rachel, how d'you do," she said, shaking hands.

"How are you, dear," said Mr. Ambrose, inclining his forehead to be kissed. His niece instinctively liked his thin angular body, and the big head with its sweeping features, and the acute, innocent eyes.

"Tell Mr. Pepper," Rachel bade the servant. Husband and wife then sat down on one side of the table, with their niece opposite to them.

"My father told me to begin," she explained. "He is very busy with the men... You know Mr. Pepper?"

A little man who was bent as some trees are by a gale on one side of them had slipped in. Nodding to Mr. Ambrose, he shook hands with Helen.

"Draughts," he said, erecting the collar of his coat.

"You are still rheumatic?" asked Helen. Her voice was low and seductive, though she spoke absently enough, the sight of town and river being still present to her mind.

"Once rheumatic, always rheumatic, I fear," he replied. "To some extent it depends on the weather, though not so much as people are apt to think."

"One does not die of it, at any rate," said Helen.

"As a general rule—no," said Mr. Pepper.

"Soup, Uncle Ridley?" asked Rachel.

"Thank you, dear," he said, and, as he held his plate out, sighed audibly, "Ah! she's not like her mother." Helen was just too late in thumping her tumbler on the table to prevent Rachel from hearing, and from blushing scarlet with embarrassment.

"The way servants treat flowers!" she said hastily. She drew a green vase with a crinkled lip towards her, and began pulling out the tight little chrysanthemums, which she laid on the table-cloth, arranging them fastidiously side by side.

There was a pause.

"You knew Jenkinson, didn't you, Ambrose?" asked Mr. Pepper across the table.

"Jenkinson of Peterhouse?"

"He's dead," said Mr. Pepper.

"Ah, dear!—I knew him—ages ago," said Ridley. "He was the hero of the punt accident, you remember? A queer card. Married a young woman out of a tobacconist's, and lived in the Fens—never heard what became of him."

"Drink—drugs," said Mr. Pepper with sinister conciseness. "He left a commentary. Hopeless muddle, I'm told."

"The man had really great abilities," said Ridley.

"His introduction to Jellaby holds its own still," went on Mr. Pepper, "which is surprising, seeing how text-books change."

"There was a theory about the planets, wasn't there?" asked Ridley.

"A screw loose somewhere, no doubt of it," said Mr. Pepper, shaking his head.

Now a tremor ran through the table, and a light outside swerved. At the same time an electric bell rang sharply again and again.

"We're off," said Ridley.

A slight but perceptible wave seemed to roll beneath the floor; then it sank; then another came, more perceptible. Lights slid right across the uncurtained window. The ship gave a loud melancholy moan.

"We're off!" said Mr. Pepper. Other ships, as sad as she, answered her outside on the river. The chuckling and hissing of water could be plainly heard, and the ship heaved so that the steward bringing plates had to balance himself as he drew the curtain. There was a pause.

"Jenkinson of Cats—d'you still keep up with him?" asked Ambrose.

"As much as one ever does," said Mr. Pepper. "We meet annually. This year he has had the misfortune to lose his wife, which made it painful, of course."

"Very painful," Ridley agreed.

"There's an unmarried daughter who keeps house for him, I believe, but it's never the same, not at his age."

Both gentlemen nodded sagely as they carved their apples.

"There was a book, wasn't there?" Ridley enquired.

"There *was* a book, but there never *will* be a book," said Mr. Pepper with such fierceness that both ladies looked up at him.

"There never will be a book, because someone else has written it for him," said Mr. Pepper with considerable acidity. "That's what comes of putting things off, and collecting fossils, and sticking Norman arches on one's pigsties."

"I confess I sympathise," said Ridley with a melancholy sigh. "I have a weakness for people who can't begin."

". . . The accumulations of a lifetime wasted," continued Mr. Pepper. "He had accumulations enough to fill a barn."

"It's a vice that some of us escape," said Ridley. "Our friend Miles has another work out today."

Mr. Pepper gave an acid little laugh. "According to my calculations," he said, "he has produced two volumes and a half annually, which, allowing for time spent in the cradle and so forth, shows a commendable industry."

"Yes, the old Master's saying of him has been pretty well realised," said Ridley.

"A way they had," said Mr. Pepper. "You know the Bruce collection?—not for publication, of course."

"I should suppose not," said Ridley significantly. "For a Divine he was—remarkably free."

"The Pump in Neville's Row, for example?" enquired Mr. Pepper.

"Precisely," said Ambrose.

Each of the ladies, being after the fashion of their sex, highly trained in promoting men's talk without listening to it, could think—about the education of children, about the use of fog sirens in an opera—without betraying herself. Only it struck Helen that Rachel was perhaps too still for a hostess, and that she might have done something with her hands.

"Perhaps—?" she said at length, upon which they rose and left, vaguely to the surprise of the gentlemen, who had either thought them attentive or had forgotten their presence.

"Ah, one could tell strange stories of the old days," they heard Ridley say, as he sank into his chair again. Glancing back, at the doorway, they saw Mr. Pepper as though he had suddenly loosened his clothes, and had become a vivacious and malicious old ape.

Winding veils round their heads, the women walked on deck. They were now moving steadily down the river, passing the dark shapes of ships at anchor, and London was a swarm of lights with a pale yellow canopy drooping above it. There were the lights of the great theatres, the lights of the long streets, lights that indicated huge squares of domestic comfort, lights that hung high in air. No darkness would ever settle upon those lamps, as no darkness had settled upon them for hundreds of years. It seemed dreadful that the town should blaze forever in the same spot; dreadful at least to people going away to adventure upon the sea, and beholding it as a circumscribed mound, eternally burnt, eternally scarred. From the deck of the ship the great city appeared a crouched and cowardly figure, a sedentary miser.

Leaning over the rail, side by side, Helen said, "Won't you be cold?" Rachel replied, "No . . . How beautiful!" she added a moment later. Very little was visible—a few masts, a shadow of land here, a line of brilliant windows there. They tried to make head against the wind.

"It blows—it blows!" gasped Rachel, the words rammed down her throat. Struggling by her side, Helen was suddenly overcome by the spirit of movement, and pushed along with her skirts wrapping themselves round her knees, and both arms to her hair. But slowly the intoxication of movement died down, and the wind became rough and chilly. They looked through a chink in the blind and saw that long cigars were being smoked in the dining-room; they saw Mr. Ambrose throw himself violently against the back of his chair, while Mr. Pepper crinkled his cheeks as though they had been cut in wood. The ghost of a roar of laughter came out to them, and was drowned at once in the wind. In the dry yellow-lighted room Mr. Pepper and Mr. Ambrose were oblivious of all tumult; they were in Cambridge, and it was probably about the year 1875.

"They're old friends," said Helen, smiling at the sight. "Now, is there a room for us to sit in?"

Rachel opened a door.

"It's more like a landing than a room," she said. Indeed it had nothing of the shut stationary character of a room on shore. A table was rooted in the middle, and seats were stuck to the sides. Happily the tropical suns had bleached the tapestries to a faded blue-green colour, and the mirror with its frame of shells, the work of the steward's love, when the time hung heavy in the southern seas, was quaint rather than ugly. Twisted shells with red lips like unicorn's horns ornamented the mantelpiece, which was draped by a pall of purple plush from which depended a certain number of balls. Two windows opened on to the deck, and the light beating through them when the ship was roasted on the Amazons had turned the prints on the opposite wall to a faint yellow colour, so that "The Coliseum" was scarcely to be distinguished from Queen Alexandra playing with her Spaniels. A pair of wicker armchairs by the fireside invited one to warm one's hands at a grate full of gilt shavings; a great lamp swung above the table—the kind of lamp which makes the light of civilisation across dark fields to one walking in the country.

"It's odd that every one should be an old friend of Mr. Pepper's," Rachel started nervously, for the situation was difficult, the room cold, and Helen curiously silent.

"I suppose you take him for granted?" said her aunt.

"He's like this," said Rachel, lighting on a fossilised fish in a basin, and displaying it.

"I expect you're too severe," Helen remarked.

Rachel immediately tried to qualify what she had said against her belief.

"I don't really know him," she said, and took refuge in facts, believing that elderly people really like them better than feelings. She produced what she knew of William Pepper. She told Helen that he always called on Sundays when they were at home; he knew about a great many things—about mathematics, history, Greek, zoology, economics, and the Icelandic Sagas. He had turned Persian poetry into English prose, and English prose into Greek iambics; he was an authority upon coins; and—one other thing—oh yes, she thought it was vehicular traffic.

He was here either to get things out of the sea, or to write upon the probable course of Odysseus, for Greek after all was his hobby.

"I've got all his pamphlets," she said. "Little pamphlets. Little yellow books." It did not appear that she had read them.

"Has he ever been in love?" asked Helen, who had chosen a seat.

This was unexpectedly to the point.

"His heart's a piece of old shoe leather," Rachel declared, dropping the fish. But when questioned she had to own that she had never asked him.

"I shall ask him," said Helen.

"The last time I saw you, you were buying a piano," she continued. "Do you remember—the piano, the room in the attic, and the great plants with the prickles?"

"Yes, and my aunts said the piano would come through the floor, but at their age one wouldn't mind being killed in the night?" she enquired.

"I heard from Aunt Bessie not long ago," Helen stated. "She is afraid that you will spoil your arms if you insist upon so much practising."

"The muscles of the forearm—and then one won't marry?"

"She didn't put it quite like that," replied Mrs. Ambrose.

"Oh, no—of course she wouldn't," said Rachel with a sigh.

Helen looked at her. Her face was weak rather than decided, saved from insipidity by the large enquiring eyes; denied beauty, now that she was sheltered indoors, by the lack of colour and definite outline. Moreover, a hesitation in speaking, or rather a tendency to use the wrong words, made her seem more than normally incompetent for her years. Mrs. Ambrose, who had been speaking much at random, now reflected that she certainly did not look forward to the intimacy of three or four weeks on board ship which was threatened. Women of her own age usually boring her, she supposed that girls would be worse. She glanced at Rachel again. Yes! how clear it was that she would be vacillating, emotional, and when you said something to her it would make no more lasting impression than the stroke of a stick upon water. There was nothing to take hold of in girls—nothing hard, permanent, satisfactory. Did Willoughby say three weeks, or did he say four? She tried to remember.

At this point, however, the door opened and a tall burly man entered the room, came forward and shook Helen's hand with an emotional kind of heartiness, Willoughby himself, Rachel's father, Helen's brother-in-law. As a great deal of flesh would have been needed to make a fat man of him, his frame being so large, he was not fat; his face was a large framework too, looking, by the smallness of the features and the glow in the hollow of the cheek, more fitted to withstand assaults of the weather than to express sentiments and emotions, or to respond to them in others.

"It is a great pleasure that you have come," he said, "for both of us."

Rachel murmured in obedience to her father's glance.

"We'll do our best to make you comfortable. And Ridley. We think it an honour to have charge of him. Pepper'll have someone to contradict him—which I daren't do. You find this child grown, don't you? A young woman, eh?"

Still holding Helen's hand he drew his arm round Rachel's shoulder, thus making them come uncomfortably close, but Helen forbore to look.

"You think she does us credit?" he asked.

"Oh yes," said Helen.

"Because we expect great things of her," he continued, squeezing his daughter's arm and releasing her. "But about you now." They sat down side by side on the little sofa. "Did you leave the children well? They'll be ready for school, I suppose. Do they take after you or Ambrose? They've got good heads on their shoulders, I'll be bound?"

At this Helen immediately brightened more than she had yet done, and explained that her son was six and her daughter ten. Everybody said that her boy was like her and her girl like Ridley. As for brains, they were quick brats, she thought, and modestly she ventured on a little story about her son—how left alone for a minute he had taken the pat of butter in his fingers, run across the room with it, and put it on the fire—merely for the fun of the thing, a feeling which she could understand.

"And you had to show the young rascal that these tricks wouldn't do, eh?"

"A child of six? I don't think they matter."

"I'm an old-fashioned father."

"Nonsense, Willoughby; Rachel knows better."

Much as Willoughby would doubtless have liked his daughter to praise him she did not; her eyes were unreflecting as water, her fingers still toying with the fossilised fish, her mind absent. The elder people went on to speak of arrangements that could be made for Ridley's comfort—a table placed where he couldn't help looking at the sea, far from boilers, at the same time sheltered from the view of people passing. Unless he made this a holiday, when his books were all packed, he would have no holiday whatever; for out at Santa Marina Helen knew, by experience, that he would work all day; his boxes, she said, were packed with books.

"Leave it to me—leave it to me!" said Willoughby, obviously intending to do much more than she asked of him. But Ridley and Mr. Pepper were heard fumbling at the door.

"How are you, Vinrace?" said Ridley, extending a limp hand as he came in, as though the meeting were melancholy to both, but on the whole more so to him.

Willoughby preserved his heartiness, tempered by respect. For the moment nothing was said.

"We looked in and saw you laughing," Helen remarked. "Mr. Pepper had just told a very good story."

"Pish. None of the stories were good," said her husband peevishly.

"Still a severe judge, Ridley?" enquired Mr. Vinrace.

"We bored you so that you left," said Ridley, speaking directly to his wife.

As this was quite true Helen did not attempt to deny it, and her next remark, "But didn't they improve after we'd gone?" was unfortunate, for her husband answered with a droop of his shoulders, "If possible they got worse."

The situation was now one of considerable discomfort for every one concerned, as was proved by a long interval of constraint and silence. Mr. Pepper, indeed, created a diversion of a kind by leaping on to his seat, both feet tucked under him, with the action of a spinster who detects a mouse, as the draught struck at his ankles. Drawn up there, sucking at his cigar, with his arms encircling his knees, he looked like the image of Buddha, and from this elevation began a discourse, addressed to nobody, for nobody had called for it, upon the unplumbed depths of ocean. He professed himself surprised to learn that although Mr. Vinrace possessed ten ships, regularly plying between London and Buenos Aires, not one of them was bidden to investigate the great white monsters of the lower waters.

"No, no," laughed Willoughby, "the monsters of the earth are too many for me!"

Rachel was heard to sigh, "Poor little goats!"

"If it weren't for the goats there'd be no music, my dear; music depends upon goats," said her father rather sharply, and Mr. Pepper went on to describe the white, hairless, blind monsters lying curled on the ridges of sand at the bottom of the sea, which would explode if you brought them to the surface, their sides bursting asunder and scattering entrails to the winds when released from pressure, with considerable detail and with such show of knowledge, that Ridley was disgusted, and begged him to stop.

From all this Helen drew her own conclusions, which were gloomy enough. Pepper was a bore; Rachel was an unlicked girl, no doubt prolific of confidences, the very first of which would be: "You see, I don't get on with my father." Willoughby, as usual, loved his business and built his Empire, and between them all she would be considerably bored. Being a woman of action, however, she rose, and said that for her part she was going to bed. At the door she glanced back instinctively at Rachel, expecting that as two of the same sex they would leave the room together. Rachel rose, looked vaguely into Helen's face, and remarked with her slight stammer, "I'm going out to t-t-triumph in the wind."

Mrs. Ambrose's worst suspicions were confirmed; she went down the passage lurching from side to side, and fending off the wall now with her right arm, now with her left; at each lurch she exclaimed emphatically, "Damn!"

CHAPTER II

Uncomfortable as the night, with its rocking movement, and salt smells, may have been, and in one case undoubtedly was, for Mr. Pepper had insufficient clothes upon his bed, the breakfast next morning wore a kind of beauty. The voyage had begun, and had begun happily with a soft blue sky, and a calm sea. The sense of untapped resources, things to say as yet unsaid, made the hour significant, so that in future years the entire journey perhaps would be represented by this one scene, with the sound of sirens hooting in the river the night before, somehow mixing in.

The table was cheerful with apples and bread and eggs. Helen handed Willoughby the butter, and as she did so cast her eye on him and reflected, "And she married you, and she was happy, I suppose."

She went off on a familiar train of thought, leading on to all kinds of well-known reflections, from the old wonder, why Theresa had married Willoughby?

"Of course, one sees all that," she thought, meaning that one sees that he is big and burly, and has a great booming voice, and a fist and a will of his own; "but—" here she slipped into a fine analysis of him which is best represented by one word, "sentimental," by which she meant that he was never simple and honest about his feelings. For example, he seldom spoke of the dead, but kept anniversaries with singular pomp. She suspected him of nameless atrocities with regard to his daughter, as indeed she had always suspected him of bullying his wife. Naturally she fell to comparing her own fortunes with the fortunes of her friend, for Willoughby's wife had been perhaps the one woman Helen called friend, and this comparison often made the staple of their talk. Ridley was a scholar, and Willoughby was a man of business. Ridley was bringing out the third volume of Pindar when Willoughby was launching his first ship. They built a new factory the very year the commentary on Aristotle—was it?—appeared at the University Press. "And Rachel," she looked at her, meaning, no doubt, to decide the argument, which was otherwise too evenly balanced, by declaring that Rachel was not comparable to her own children. "She really might be six years old," was all she said, however, this judgment referring to the smooth unmarked outline of the girl's face, and not condemning her otherwise, for if Rachel were ever to think, feel, laugh, or express herself, instead of dropping milk from a height as though to see what kind of drops it made, she might be interesting though never exactly pretty. She was like her mother, as the image in a pool on a still summer's day is like the vivid flushed face that hangs over it.

Meanwhile Helen herself was under examination, though not from either of her victims. Mr. Pepper considered her; and his meditations, carried on while he cut his toast into bars and neatly buttered them, took him through a considerable stretch of autobiography. One of his penetrating glances assured him that he was right last night in judging that Helen was beautiful. Blandly he passed her the jam. She was talking nonsense, but not worse nonsense than people usually do talk at breakfast, the cerebral circulation, as he knew to his cost, being apt to give trouble at that hour. He went on saying "No" to her, on principle, for he never yielded to a woman on account of her sex. And here, dropping his eyes to his plate, he became autobiographical. He had not married himself for the sufficient reason that he had never met a woman who commanded his respect. Condemned to pass the susceptible years of youth in a railway station in Bombay, he had seen only coloured women, military women, official women; and his ideal was a woman who could read Greek, if not Persian, was irreproachably fair in the face, and able to understand the small things he let fall while undressing. As it was he had contracted habits of which he was not in the least ashamed. Certain odd minutes every day went to learning things by heart; he never took a ticket without noting the number; he devoted January to Petronius, February to Catullus, March to the Etruscan vases perhaps; anyhow he had done good work in India, and there was nothing to regret in his life except the fundamental defects which no wise man regrets, when the present is still his. So concluding he looked up suddenly and smiled. Rachel caught his eye.

"And now you've chewed something thirty-seven times, I suppose?" she thought, but said politely aloud, "Are your legs troubling you today, Mr. Pepper?"

"My shoulder blades?" he asked, shifting them painfully. "Beauty has no effect upon uric acid that I'm aware of," he sighed, contemplating the round pane opposite, through which the sky and sea showed blue. At the same time he took a little parchment volume from his pocket and laid it on the table. As it was clear that he invited comment, Helen asked him the name of it. She got the name; but she got also a disquisition upon the proper method of making roads. Beginning with the Greeks, who had, he said, many difficulties to contend with, he continued with the Romans, passed to England and the right method, which speedily became the wrong method, and wound up with such a fury of denunciation directed against the road-makers of the present day in general, and the road-makers of Richmond Park in particular, where Mr. Pepper had the habit of cycling every morning before breakfast, that the spoons fairly jingled against the coffee cups, and the insides of at least four rolls mounted in a heap beside Mr. Pepper's plate.

"Pebbles!" he concluded, viciously dropping another bread pellet upon the heap. "The roads of England are mended with pebbles! 'With the first heavy rainfall,' I've told 'em, 'your road will be a swamp.' Again and again my words have proved true. But d'you suppose they listen to me when I tell 'em so, when I point out the consequences, the consequences to the public purse, when I recommend 'em to read Coryphaeus? Not a bit of it; they've other interests to attend to. No, Mrs. Ambrose, you will form no just opinion of the stupidity of mankind until you have sat upon a Borough Council!" The little man fixed her with a glance of ferocious energy.

"I have had servants," said Mrs. Ambrose, concentrating her gaze. "At this moment I have a nurse. She's a good woman as they go, but she's determined to make my children pray. So far, owing to great care on my part, they think of God as a kind of walrus; but now that my back's turned—Ridley," she demanded, swinging round upon her husband, "what shall we do if we find them saying the Lord's Prayer when we get home again?"

Ridley made the sound which is represented by "Tush." But Willoughby, whose discomfort as he listened was manifested by a slight movement rocking of his body, said awkwardly, "Oh, surely, Helen, a little religion hurts nobody."

"I would rather my children told lies," she replied, and while Willoughby was reflecting that his sister-in-law was even more eccentric than he remembered, pushed her chair back and swept upstairs. In a second they heard her calling back, "Oh, look! We're out at sea!"

They followed her on to the deck. All the smoke and the houses had disappeared, and the ship was out in a wide space of sea very fresh and clear though pale in the early light. They had left London sitting on its mud. A very thin line of shadow tapered on the horizon, scarcely thick enough to stand the burden of Paris, which nevertheless rested upon it. They were free of roads, free of mankind, and the same exhilaration at their freedom ran through them all. The ship was making her way steadily through small waves which slapped her and then fizzled like effervescing water, leaving a little border of bubbles and foam on either side. The colourless October sky above was thinly clouded as if by the trail of wood-fire smoke, and the air was wonderfully salt and brisk. Indeed it was too cold to stand still. Mrs. Ambrose drew her arm within her husband's, and as they moved off it could be seen from the way in which her sloping cheek turned up to his that she had something private to communicate. They went a few paces and Rachel saw them kiss.

Down she looked into the depth of the sea. While it was slightly disturbed on the surface by the passage of the *Euphrosyne*, beneath it was green and dim, and it grew dimmer and dimmer until the sand at the bottom was only a pale blur. One could scarcely see the black ribs of wrecked ships, or the spiral towers made by the burrowings of great eels, or the smooth green-sided monsters who came by flickering this way and that.

"And, Rachel, if anyone wants me, I'm busy till one," said her father, enforcing his words as he often did, when he spoke to his daughter, by a smart blow upon the shoulder.

"Until one," he repeated. "And you'll find yourself some employment, eh? Scales, French, a little German, eh? There's Mr. Pepper who knows more about separable verbs than any man in Europe, eh?" and he went off laughing. Rachel laughed, too, as indeed she had laughed ever since she could remember, without thinking it funny, but because she admired her father.

But just as she was turning with a view perhaps to finding some employment, she was intercepted by a woman who was so broad and so thick that to be intercepted by her was inevitable. The discreet tentative way in which she moved, together with her sober black dress, showed that she belonged to the lower orders; nevertheless she took up a rock-like position, looking about her to see that no gentry were near before she delivered her message, which had reference to the state of the sheets, and was of the utmost gravity.

"How ever we're to get through this voyage, Miss Rachel, I really can't tell," she began with a shake of her head. "There's only just sheets enough to go round, and the master's has a rotten place you could put your fingers through. And the counterpanes. Did you notice the counterpanes? I thought to myself a poor person would have been ashamed of them. The one I gave Mr. Pepper was hardly fit to cover a dog . . . No, Miss Rachel, they could *not* be mended; they're only fit for dust sheets. Why, if one sewed one's finger to the bone, one would have one's work undone the next time they went to the laundry."

Her voice in its indignation wavered as if tears were near.

There was nothing for it but to descend and inspect a large pile of linen heaped upon a table. Mrs. Chailey handled the sheets as if she knew each by name, character, and constitution. Some had yellow stains, others had places where the threads made long ladders; but to the ordinary eye they looked much as sheets usually do look, very chill, white, cold, and irreproachably clean.

Suddenly Mrs. Chailey, turning from the subject of sheets, dismissing them entirely, clenched her fists on the top of them, and proclaimed, "And you couldn't ask a living creature to sit where I sit!"

Mrs. Chailey was expected to sit in a cabin which was large enough, but too near the boilers, so that after five minutes she could hear her heart "go," she complained, putting her hand above it, which was a state of things that Mrs. Vinrace, Rachel's mother, would never have dreamt of inflicting—Mrs. Vinrace, who knew every sheet in her house, and expected of every one the best they could do, but no more.

It was the easiest thing in the world to grant another room, and the problem of sheets simultaneously and miraculously solved itself, the spots and ladders not being past cure after all, but—

"Lies! Lies! Lies!" exclaimed the mistress indignantly, as she ran up on to the deck. "What's the use of telling me lies?"

In her anger that a woman of fifty should behave like a child and come cringing to a girl because she wanted to sit where she had not leave to sit, she did not think of the particular case, and, unpacking her music, soon forgot all about the old woman and her sheets.

Mrs. Chailey folded her sheets, but her expression testified to flatness within. The world no longer cared about her, and a ship was not a home. When the lamps were lit yesterday, and the sailors went tumbling above her head, she had cried; she would cry this evening; she would cry tomorrow. It was not home. Meanwhile she arranged her ornaments in the room which she had won too easily. They were strange ornaments to bring on a sea voyage—china pugs, tea-sets in miniature, cups stamped floridly with the arms of the city of Bristol, hair-pin boxes crusted with shamrock, antelopes' heads in coloured plaster, together with a multitude of tiny photographs, representing downright workmen in their Sunday best, and women holding white babies. But there was one portrait in a gilt frame, for which a nail was needed, and before she sought it Mrs. Chailey put on her spectacles and read what was written on a slip of paper at the back:

"This picture of her mistress is given to Emma Chailey by Willoughby Vinrace in gratitude for thirty years of devoted service."

Tears obliterated the words and the head of the nail.

"So long as I can do something for your family," she was saying, as she hammered at it, when a voice called melodiously in the passage:

"Mrs. Chailey! Mrs. Chailey!"

Chailey instantly tidied her dress, composed her face, and opened the door.

"I'm in a fix," said Mrs. Ambrose, who was flushed and out of breath. "You know what gentlemen are. The chairs too high—the tables too low—there's six inches between the floor and the door. What I want's a hammer, an old quilt, and have you such a thing as a kitchen table? Anyhow, between us"—she now flung open the door of her husband's sitting room, and revealed Ridley pacing up and down, his forehead all wrinkled, and the collar of his coat turned up.

"It's as though they'd taken pains to torment me!" he cried, stopping dead.

"Did I come on this voyage in order to catch rheumatism and pneumonia? Really one might have credited Vinrace with more sense. My dear," Helen was on her knees under a table, "you are only making yourself untidy, and we had much better recognise the fact that we are condemned to six weeks of unspeakable misery. To come at all was the height of folly, but now that we are here I suppose that I can face it like a man. My diseases of course will be increased—I feel already worse than I did yesterday, but we've only ourselves to thank, and the children happily—"

"Move! Move! Move!" cried Helen, chasing him from corner to corner with a chair as though he were an errant hen. "Out of the way, Ridley, and in half an hour you'll find it ready."

She turned him out of the room, and they could hear him groaning and swearing as he went along the passage.

"I daresay he isn't very strong," said Mrs. Chailey, looking at Mrs. Ambrose compassionately, as she helped to shift and carry.

"It's books," sighed Helen, lifting an armful of sad volumes from the floor to the shelf. "Greek from morning to night. If ever Miss Rachel marries, Chailey, pray that she may marry a man who doesn't know his ABC."

The preliminary discomforts and harshnesses, which generally make the first days of a sea voyage so cheerless and trying to the temper, being somehow lived through, the succeeding days passed pleasantly enough. October was well advanced, but steadily burning with a warmth that made the early months of the summer appear very young and capricious. Great tracts of the earth lay now beneath the autumn sun, and the whole of England, from the bald moors to the Cornish rocks, was lit up from dawn to sunset, and showed in stretches of yellow, green, and purple. Under that illumination even the roofs of the great towns glittered. In thousands of small gardens, millions of dark-red flowers were blooming, until the old ladies who had tended them so carefully came down the paths with their scissors, snipped through their juicy stalks, and laid them upon cold stone ledges in the village church. Innumerable parties of picnickers coming home at sunset cried, "Was there ever such a day as this?" "It's you," the young men whispered; "Oh, it's you," the young women replied. All old people and many sick people were drawn, were it only for a foot or two, into the open air, and prognosticated pleasant things about the course of the world. As for the confidences and expressions of love that were heard not only in cornfields but in lamplit rooms, where the windows opened on the garden, and men with cigars kissed women with grey hairs, they were not to be counted. Some said that the sky was an emblem of the life they had; others that it was the promise of the life to come. Long-tailed birds clattered and screamed, and crossed from wood to wood, with golden eyes in their plumage.

But while all this went on by land, very few people thought about the sea. They took it for granted that the sea was calm; and there was no need, as there is in many houses when the creeper taps on the bedroom windows, for the couples to murmur before they kiss, "Think of the ships tonight," or "Thank Heaven, I'm not the man in the lighthouse!" For all they imagined, the ships when they vanished on the sky-line dissolved, like snow in water. The grown-up view, indeed, was not much clearer than the view of the little creatures in bathing drawers who were trotting in to the foam all along the coasts of England, and scooping up buckets full of water. They saw white sails or tufts of smoke pass across the horizon, and if you had said that these were waterspouts, or the petals of white sea flowers, they would have agreed.

The people in ships, however, took an equally singular view of England. Not only did it appear to them to be an island, and a very small island, but it was a shrinking island in which people were imprisoned. One figured them first swarming about like aimless ants, and almost pressing each other over the edge; and then, as the ship withdrew, one figured them making a vain clamour, which, being unheard, either ceased, or rose into a brawl. Finally, when the ship was out of sight of land, it became plain that the people of England were completely mute. The disease attacked other parts of the earth; Europe shrank, Asia shrank, Africa and America shrank, until it seemed doubtful whether the ship would ever run against any of those wrinkled little rocks again. But, on the other hand, an immense dignity had descended upon her; she was an inhabitant of the great world, which has so few inhabitants, travelling all day across an empty universe, with veils drawn before her and behind. She was more lonely than the caravan crossing the desert; she was infinitely more mysterious, moving by her own power and sustained by her own resources. The sea might give her death or some unexampled joy, and none would know of it. She was a bride going forth to her husband, a virgin unknown of men; in her vigor and purity she might be likened to all beautiful things, for as a ship she had a life of her own.

Indeed if they had not been blessed in their weather, one blue day being bowled up after another, smooth, round, and flawless. Mrs. Ambrose would have found it very dull. As it was, she had her embroidery frame set up on deck, with a little table by her side on which lay open a black volume of philosophy. She chose a thread from the vari-coloured tangle that lay in her lap, and sewed red into the bark of a tree, or yellow into the river torrent. She was working at a great design of a tropical river running through a tropical forest, where spotted deer would eventually browse upon masses of fruit, bananas, oranges, and giant pomegranates, while a troop of naked natives whirled darts into the air. Between the stitches she looked to one side and read a sentence about the Reality of Matter, or the Nature of Good. Round her men in blue jerseys knelt and scrubbed the boards, or leant over the rails and whistled, and not far off Mr. Pepper sat cutting up roots with a penknife. The rest were occupied in other parts of the ship: Ridley at his Greek—he had never found quarters more to his liking; Willoughby at his documents, for he used a voyage to work of arrears of business; and Rachel—Helen, between her sentences of philosophy, wondered sometimes what Rachel *did* do with herself? She meant vaguely to go and see. They had scarcely spoken two words to each other since that first evening; they were polite when they met, but there had been no confidence of any kind. Rachel seemed to get on very well with her father—much better, Helen thought, than she ought to— and was as ready to let Helen alone as Helen was to let her alone.

At that moment Rachel was sitting in her room doing absolutely nothing. When the ship was full this apartment bore some magnificent title and was the resort of elderly sea-sick ladies who left the deck to their youngsters. By virtue of the piano, and a mess of books on the floor, Rachel considered it her room, and there she would sit for hours playing very difficult music, reading a little German, or a little English when the mood took her, and doing—as at this moment—absolutely nothing.

The way she had been educated, joined to a fine natural indolence, was of course partly the reason of it, for she had been educated as the majority of well-to-do girls in the last part of the nineteenth century were educated. Kindly doctors and gentle old professors had taught her the rudiments of about ten different branches of knowledge, but they would as soon have forced her to go through one piece of drudgery thoroughly as they would have told her that her hands were dirty. The one hour or the two hours weekly passed very pleasantly, partly owing to the other pupils, partly to the fact that the window looked upon the back of a shop, where figures appeared against the red windows in winter, partly to the accidents that are bound to happen when more than two people are in the same room together. But there was no subject in the world which she knew accurately. Her mind was in the state of an intelligent man's in the beginning of the reign of Queen Elizabeth; she would believe practically anything she was told, invent reasons for anything she said. The shape of the earth, the history of the world, how trains worked, or money was invested, what laws were in force, which people wanted what, and why they wanted it, the most elementary idea of a system in modern life—none of this had been imparted to her by any of her professors or mistresses. But this system of education had one great advantage. It did not teach anything, but it put no obstacle in the way of any real talent that the pupil might chance to have. Rachel, being musical, was allowed to learn nothing but music; she became a fanatic about music. All the energies that might have gone into languages, science, or literature, that might have made her friends, or shown her the world, poured straight into music. Finding her teachers inadequate, she had practically taught herself. At the age of twenty-four she knew as much about music as most people do when they are thirty; and could play as well as nature allowed her to, which, as became daily more obvious, was a really generous allowance. If this one definite gift was surrounded by dreams and ideas of the most extravagant and foolish description, no one was any the wiser.

Her education being thus ordinary, her circumstances were no more out of the common. She was an only child and had never been bullied and laughed at by brothers and sisters. Her mother having died when she was eleven, two aunts, the sisters of her father, brought her up, and they lived for the sake of the air in a comfortable house in Richmond. She was of course brought up with excessive care, which as a child was for her health; as a girl and a young woman was for what it seems almost crude to call her morals. Until quite lately she had been completely ignorant that for women such things existed. She groped for knowledge in old books, and found it in repulsive chunks, but she did not naturally care for books and thus never troubled her head about the censorship which was exercised first by her aunts, later by her father. Friends might have told her things, but she had few of her own age—Richmond being an awkward place to reach—and, as it happened, the only girl she knew well was a religious zealot, who in the fervour of intimacy talked about God, and the best ways of taking up one's cross, a topic only fitfully interesting to one whose mind reached other stages at other times.

But lying in her chair, with one hand behind her head, the other grasping the knob on the arm, she was clearly following her thoughts intently. Her education left her abundant time for thinking. Her eyes were fixed so steadily upon a ball on the rail of the ship that she would have been startled and annoyed if anything had chanced to obscure it for a second. She had begun her meditations with a shout of laughter, caused by the following translation from *Tristan*:

> *In shrinking trepidation*
> *His shame he seems to hide*
> *While to the king his relation*
> *He brings the corpse-like Bride.*
> *Seems it so senseless what I say?*

She cried that it did, and threw down the book. Next she had picked up *Cowper's Letters*, the classic prescribed by her father which had bored her, so that one sentence chancing to say something about the smell of broom in his garden, she had thereupon seen the little hall at Richmond laden with

flowers on the day of her mother's funeral, smelling so strong that now any
flower-scent brought back the sickly horrible sensation; and so from one
scene she passed, half-hearing, half-seeing, to another. She saw her Aunt
Lucy arranging flowers in the drawing-room.

"Aunt Lucy," she volunteered, "I don't like the smell of broom; it reminds
me of funerals."

"Nonsense, Rachel," Aunt Lucy replied; "don't say such foolish things,
dear. I always think it a particularly cheerful plant."

Lying in the hot sun her mind was fixed upon the characters of her aunts,
their views, and the way they lived. Indeed this was a subject that lasted her
hundreds of morning walks round Richmond Park, and blotted out the trees
and the people and the deer. Why did they do the things they did, and what
did they feel, and what was it all about? Again she heard Aunt Lucy talking
to Aunt Eleanor. She had been that morning to take up the character of a
servant, "And, of course, at half-past ten in the morning one expects to find
the housemaid brushing the stairs." How odd! How unspeakably odd! But
she could not explain to herself why suddenly as her aunt spoke the whole
system in which they lived had appeared before her eyes as something quite
unfamiliar and inexplicable, and themselves as chairs or umbrellas dropped
about here and there without any reason. She could only say with her slight
stammer, "Are you f-f-fond of Aunt Eleanor, Aunt Lucy?" to which her aunt
replied, with her nervous hen-like twitter of a laugh, "My dear child, what
questions you do ask!"

"How fond? Very fond!" Rachel pursued.

"I can't say I've ever thought 'how,'" said Miss Vinrace. "If one cares one
doesn't think 'how,' Rachel," which was aimed at the niece who had never yet
"come" to her aunts as cordially as they wished.

"But you know I care for you, don't you, dear, because you're your mother's
daughter, if for no other reason, and there *are* plenty of other reasons"—and
she leant over and kissed her with some emotion, and the argument was spilt
irretrievably about the place like a bucket of milk.

By these means Rachel reached that stage in thinking, if thinking it
can be called, when the eyes are intent upon a ball or a knob and the lips
cease to move. Her efforts to come to an understanding had only hurt her
aunt's feelings, and the conclusion must be that it is better not to try. To
feel anything strongly was to create an abyss between oneself and others
who feel strongly perhaps but differently. It was far better to play the piano
and forget all the rest. The conclusion was very welcome. Let these odd
men and women—her aunts, the Hunts, Ridley, Helen, Mr. Pepper, and the
rest—be symbols—featureless but dignified, symbols of age, of youth, of
motherhood, of learning, and beautiful often as people upon the stage are

beautiful. It appeared that nobody ever said a thing they meant, or ever talked of a feeling they felt, but that was what music was for. Reality dwelling in what one saw and felt, but did not talk about, one could accept a system in which things went round and round quite satisfactorily to other people, without often troubling to think about it, except as something superficially strange. Absorbed by her music she accepted her lot very complacently, blazing into indignation perhaps once a fortnight, and subsiding as she subsided now. Inextricably mixed in dreamy confusion, her mind seemed to enter into communion, to be delightfully expanded and combined with the spirit of the whitish boards on deck, with the spirit of the sea, with the spirit of Beethoven Op. 112, even with the spirit of poor William Cowper there at Olney. Like a ball of thistledown it kissed the sea, rose, kissed it again, and thus rising and kissing passed finally out of sight. The rising and falling of the ball of thistledown was represented by the sudden droop forward of her own head, and when it passed out of sight she was asleep.

Ten minutes later Mrs. Ambrose opened the door and looked at her. It did not surprise her to find that this was the way in which Rachel passed her mornings. She glanced round the room at the piano, at the books, at the general mess. In the first place she considered Rachel aesthetically; lying unprotected she looked somehow like a victim dropped from the claws of a bird of prey, but considered as a woman, a young woman of twenty-four, the sight gave rise to reflections. Mrs. Ambrose stood thinking for at least two minutes. She then smiled, turned noiselessly away and went, lest the sleeper should waken, and there should be the awkwardness of speech between them.

CHAPTER III

Early next morning there was a sound as of chains being drawn roughly overhead; the steady heart of the *Euphrosyne* slowly ceased to beat; and Helen, poking her nose above deck, saw a stationary castle upon a stationary hill. They had dropped anchor in the mouth of the Tagus, and instead of cleaving new waves perpetually, the same waves kept returning and washing against the sides of the ship.

As soon as breakfast was done, Willoughby disappeared over the vessel's side, carrying a brown leather case, shouting over his shoulder that every one was to mind and behave themselves, for he would be kept in Lisbon doing business until five o'clock that afternoon.

At about that hour he reappeared, carrying his case, professing himself tired, bothered, hungry, thirsty, cold, and in immediate need of his tea. Rubbing his hands, he told them the adventures of the day: how he had come upon poor old Jackson combing his moustache before the glass in the office, little expecting his descent, had put him through such a morning's work as seldom came his way; then treated him to a lunch of champagne and ortolans; paid a call upon Mrs. Jackson, who was fatter than ever, poor woman, but asked kindly after Rachel—and O Lord, little Jackson had confessed to a confounded piece of weakness—well, well, no harm was done, he supposed, but what was the use of his giving orders if they were promptly disobeyed? He had said distinctly that he would take no passengers on this trip. Here he began searching in his pockets and eventually discovered a card, which he planked down on the table before Rachel. On it she read, "Mr. and Mrs. Richard Dalloway, 23 Browne Street, Mayfair."

"Mr. Richard Dalloway," continued Vinrace, "seems to be a gentleman who thinks that because he was once a member of Parliament, and his wife's the daughter of a peer, they can have what they like for the asking. They got round poor little Jackson anyhow. Said they must have passages—produced a letter from Lord Glenaway, asking me as a personal favour—overruled any objections Jackson made (I don't believe they came to much), and so there's nothing for it but to submit, I suppose."

But it was evident that for some reason or other Willoughby was quite pleased to submit, although he made a show of growling.

The truth was that Mr. and Mrs. Dalloway had found themselves stranded in Lisbon. They had been travelling on the Continent for some weeks, chiefly with a view to broadening Mr. Dalloway's mind. Unable for a season, by one of the accidents of political life, to serve his country in Parliament, Mr. Dalloway was doing the best he could to serve it out of Parliament. For that purpose the Latin countries did very well, although the East, of course, would have done better.

"Expect to hear of me next in Petersburg or Teheran," he had said, turning to wave farewell from the steps of the Travellers'. But a disease had broken out in the East, there was cholera in Russia, and he was heard of, not so romantically, in Lisbon. They had been through France; he had stopped at manufacturing centres where, producing letters of introduction, he had been shown over works, and noted facts in a pocket-book. In Spain he and Mrs. Dalloway had mounted mules, for they wished to understand how the peasants live. Are they ripe for rebellion, for example? Mrs. Dalloway had then insisted upon a day or two at Madrid with the pictures. Finally they arrived in Lisbon and spent six days which, in a journal privately issued afterwards, they described as of "unique interest." Richard had audiences with ministers, and foretold a crisis at no distant date, "the foundations of government being incurably corrupt. Yet how blame, etc."; while Clarissa inspected the royal stables, and took several snapshots showing men now exiled and windows now broken. Among other things she photographed Fielding's grave, and let loose a small bird which some ruffian had trapped, "because one hates to think of anything in a cage where English people lie buried," the diary stated. Their tour was thoroughly unconventional, and followed no meditated plan. The foreign correspondents of the *Times* decided their route as much as anything else. Mr. Dalloway wished to look at certain guns, and was of opinion that the African coast is far more unsettled than people at home were inclined to believe. For these reasons they wanted a slow inquisitive kind of ship, comfortable, for they were bad sailors, but not extravagant, which would stop for a day or two at this port and at that, taking in coal while the Dalloways saw things for themselves. Meanwhile they found themselves stranded in Lisbon, unable for the moment to lay hands upon the precise vessel they wanted. They heard of the *Euphrosyne*, but heard also that she was primarily a cargo boat, and only took passengers by special arrangement, her business being to carry dry goods to the Amazons, and rubber home again. "By special arrangement," however, were words of high encouragement to them, for they came of a class where almost everything was specially arranged, or could be if necessary. On this occasion all that Richard did was to write a note to Lord Glenaway, the head of the line which bears his title; to call on poor old Jackson; to represent to him how Mrs. Dalloway was so-and-so, and he had been something or other else, and what they wanted was such and such a thing. It was done. They parted with compliments and pleasure on both sides, and here, a week later, came the boat rowing up to the ship in the dusk with the Dalloways on board of it; in three minutes they were standing together on the deck of the *Euphrosyne*. Their arrival, of course, created some stir, and it was seen by several pairs of eyes that Mrs. Dalloway was a tall slight woman, her body wrapped in furs, her head in veils, while Mr. Dalloway appeared to be a middle-sized man of sturdy build, dressed like a sportsman on an autumnal moor. Many solid leather bags of a rich brown hue soon surrounded them, in addition to which Mr. Dalloway carried a despatch box, and his wife a dressing-case suggestive of a diamond necklace and bottles with silver tops.

"It's so like Whistler!" she exclaimed, with a wave towards the shore, as she shook Rachel by the hand, and Rachel had only time to look at the grey hills on one side of her before Willoughby introduced Mrs. Chailey, who took the lady to her cabin.

Momentary though it seemed, nevertheless the interruption was upsetting; every one was more or less put out by it, from Mr. Grice, the steward, to Ridley himself. A few minutes later Rachel passed the smoking-room, and found Helen moving armchairs. She was absorbed in her arrangements, and on seeing Rachel remarked confidentially:

"If one can give men a room to themselves where they will sit, it's all to the good. Armchairs are *the* important things—" She began wheeling them about. "Now, does it still look like a bar at a railway station?"

She whipped a plush cover off a table. The appearance of the place was marvellously improved.

Again, the arrival of the strangers made it obvious to Rachel, as the hour of dinner approached, that she must change her dress; and the ringing of the great bell found her sitting on the edge of her berth in such a position that the little glass above the washstand reflected her head and shoulders. In the glass she wore an expression of tense melancholy, for she had come to the depressing conclusion, since the arrival of the Dalloways, that her face was not the face she wanted, and in all probability never would be.

However, punctuality had been impressed on her, and whatever face she had, she must go in to dinner.

These few minutes had been used by Willoughby in sketching to the Dalloways the people they were to meet, and checking them upon his fingers.

"There's my brother-in-law, Ambrose, the scholar (I daresay you've heard his name), his wife, my old friend Pepper, a very quiet fellow, but knows everything, I'm told. And that's all. We're a very small party. I'm dropping them on the coast."

Mrs. Dalloway, with her head a little on one side, did her best to recollect Ambrose—was it a surname?—but failed. She was made slightly uneasy by what she had heard. She knew that scholars married anyone—girls they met in farms on reading parties; or little suburban women who said disagreeably, "Of course I know it's my husband you want; not *me*."

But Helen came in at that point, and Mrs. Dalloway saw with relief that though slightly eccentric in appearance, she was not untidy, held herself well, and her voice had restraint in it, which she held to be the sign of a lady. Mr. Pepper had not troubled to change his neat ugly suit.

"But after all," Clarissa thought to herself as she followed Vinrace in to dinner, "*everyone's* interesting really."

When seated at the table she had some need of that assurance, chiefly because of Ridley, who came in late, looked decidedly unkempt, and took to his soup in profound gloom.

An imperceptible signal passed between husband and wife, meaning that they grasped the situation and would stand by each other loyally. With scarcely a pause Mrs. Dalloway turned to Willoughby and began:

"What I find so tiresome about the sea is that there are no flowers in it. Imagine fields of hollyhocks and violets in mid-ocean! How divine!"

"But somewhat dangerous to navigation," boomed Richard, in the bass, like the bassoon to the flourish of his wife's violin. "Why, weeds can be bad enough, can't they, Vinrace? I remember crossing in the *Mauretania* once, and saying to the Captain—Richards—did you know him?—'Now tell me what perils you really dread most for your ship, Captain Richards?' expecting him to say icebergs, or derelicts, or fog, or something of that sort. Not a bit of it. I've always remembered his answer. '*Sedgius aquatici*,' he said, which I take to be a kind of duck-weed."

Mr. Pepper looked up sharply, and was about to put a question when Willoughby continued:

"They've an awful time of it—those captains! Three thousand souls on board!"

"Yes, indeed," said Clarissa. She turned to Helen with an air of profundity. "I'm convinced people are wrong when they say it's work that wears one; it's responsibility. That's why one pays one's cook more than one's housemaid, I suppose."

"According to that, one ought to pay one's nurse double; but one doesn't," said Helen.

"No; but think what a joy to have to do with babies, instead of saucepans!" said Mrs. Dalloway, looking with more interest at Helen, a probable mother.

"I'd much rather be a cook than a nurse," said Helen. "Nothing would induce me to take charge of children."

"Mothers always exaggerate," said Ridley. "A well-bred child is no responsibility. I've travelled all over Europe with mine. You just wrap 'em up warm and put 'em in the rack."

Helen laughed at that. Mrs. Dalloway exclaimed, looking at Ridley:

"How like a father! My husband's just the same. And then one talks of the equality of the sexes!"

"Does one?" said Mr. Pepper.

"Oh, some do!" cried Clarissa. "My husband had to pass an irate lady every afternoon last session who said nothing else, I imagine."

"She sat outside the house; it was very awkward," said Dalloway. "At last I plucked up courage and said to her, 'My good creature, you're only in the way where you are. You're hindering me, and you're doing no good to yourself.'"

"And then she caught him by the coat, and would have scratched his eyes out—" Mrs. Dalloway put in.

"Pooh—that's been exaggerated," said Richard. "No, I pity them, I confess. The discomfort of sitting on those steps must be awful."

"Serve them right," said Willoughby curtly.

"Oh, I'm entirely with you there," said Dalloway. "Nobody can condemn the utter folly and futility of such behaviour more than I do; and as for the whole agitation, well! may I be in my grave before a woman has the right to vote in England! That's all I say."

The solemnity of her husband's assertion made Clarissa grave.

"It's unthinkable," she said. "Don't tell me you're a suffragist?" she turned to Ridley.

"I don't care a fig one way or t'other," said Ambrose. "If any creature is so deluded as to think that a vote does him or her any good, let him have it. He'll soon learn better."

"You're not a politician, I see," she smiled.

"Goodness, no," said Ridley.

"I'm afraid your husband won't approve of me," said Dalloway aside, to Mrs. Ambrose. She suddenly recollected that he had been in Parliament.

"Don't you ever find it rather dull?" she asked, not knowing exactly what to say.

Richard spread his hands before him, as if inscriptions were to be read in the palms of them.

"If you ask me whether I ever find it rather dull," he said, "I am bound to say yes; on the other hand, if you ask me what career do you consider on the whole, taking the good with the bad, the most enjoyable and enviable, not to speak of its more serious side, of all careers, for a man, I am bound to say, 'The Politician's.'"

"The Bar or politics, I agree," said Willoughby. "You get more run for your money."

"All one's faculties have their play," said Richard. "I may be treading on dangerous ground; but what I feel about poets and artists in general is this: on your own lines, you can't be beaten—granted; but off your own lines— puff—one has to make allowances. Now, I shouldn't like to think that anyone had to make allowances for me."

"I don't quite agree, Richard," said Mrs. Dalloway. "Think of Shelley. I feel that there's almost everything one wants in 'Adonais.'"

"Read 'Adonais' by all means," Richard conceded. "But whenever I hear of Shelley I repeat to myself the words of Matthew Arnold, 'What a set! What a set!'"

This roused Ridley's attention. "Matthew Arnold? A detestable prig!" he snapped.

"A prig—granted," said Richard; "but, I think a man of the world. That's where my point comes in. We politicians doubtless seem to you" (he grasped somehow that Helen was the representative of the arts) "a gross commonplace set of people; but we see both sides; we may be clumsy, but we do our best to get a grasp of things. Now your artists *find* things in a mess, shrug their shoulders, turn aside to their visions—which I grant may be very beautiful—and *leave* things in a mess. Now that seems to me evading one's responsibilities. Besides, we aren't all born with the artistic faculty."

"It's dreadful," said Mrs. Dalloway, who, while her husband spoke, had been thinking. "When I'm with artists I feel so intensely the delights of shutting oneself up in a little world of one's own, with pictures and music and everything beautiful, and then I go out into the streets and the first child I meet with its poor, hungry, dirty little face makes me turn round and say, 'No, I *can't* shut myself up—I *won't* live in a world of my own. I should like to stop all the painting and writing and music until this kind of thing exists no longer.' Don't you feel," she wound up, addressing Helen, "that life's a perpetual conflict?" Helen considered for a moment. "No," she said. "I don't think I do."

There was a pause, which was decidedly uncomfortable. Mrs. Dalloway then gave a little shiver, and asked whether she might have her fur cloak brought to her. As she adjusted the soft brown fur about her neck a fresh topic struck her.

"I own," she said, "that I shall never forget the *Antigone*. I saw it at Cambridge years ago, and it's haunted me ever since. Don't you think it's quite the most modern thing you ever saw?" she asked Ridley. "It seemed to me I'd known twenty Clytemnestras. Old Lady Ditchling for one. I don't know a word of Greek, but I could listen to it forever—"

Here Mr. Pepper struck up:

πολλὰ τὰ δεινά, κοὐδὲν ἀν-
θρώπου δεινότερον πέλει.
τοῦτο καὶ πολιοῦ πέραν
πόντου χειμερίῳ νότῳ
χωρεῖ, περιβρυχίοισι
περῶν ὑπ' οἴδμασι

Mrs. Dalloway looked at him with compressed lips.

"I'd give ten years of my life to know Greek," she said, when he had done.

"I could teach you the alphabet in half an hour," said Ridley, "and you'd read Homer in a month. I should think it an honour to instruct you."

Helen, engaged with Mr. Dalloway and the habit, now fallen into decline, of quoting Greek in the House of Commons, noted, in the great commonplace book that lies open beside us as we talk, the fact that all men, even men like Ridley, really prefer women to be fashionable.

Clarissa exclaimed that she could think of nothing more delightful. For an instant she saw herself in her drawing-room in Browne Street with a Plato open on her knees—Plato in the original Greek. She could not help believing that a real scholar, if specially interested, could slip Greek into her head with scarcely any trouble.

Ridley engaged her to come tomorrow.

"If only your ship is going to treat us kindly!" she exclaimed, drawing Willoughby into play. For the sake of guests, and these were distinguished,

Willoughby was ready with a bow of his head to vouch for the good behaviour even of the waves.

"I'm dreadfully bad; and my husband's not very good," sighed Clarissa.

"I am never sick," Richard explained. "At least, I have only been actually sick once," he corrected himself. "That was crossing the Channel. But a choppy sea, I confess, or still worse, a swell, makes me distinctly uncomfortable. The great thing is never to miss a meal. You look at the food, and you say, 'I can't'; you take a mouthful, and Lord knows how you're going to swallow it; but persevere, and you often settle the attack for good. My wife's a coward."

They were pushing back their chairs. The ladies were hesitating at the doorway.

"I'd better show the way," said Helen, advancing.

Rachel followed. She had taken no part in the talk; no one had spoken to her; but she had listened to every word that was said. She had looked from Mrs. Dalloway to Mr. Dalloway, and from Mr. Dalloway back again. Clarissa, indeed, was a fascinating spectacle. She wore a white dress and a long glittering necklace. What with her clothes, and her arch delicate face, which showed exquisitely pink beneath hair turning grey, she was astonishingly like an eighteenth-century masterpiece—a Reynolds or a Romney. She made Helen and the others look coarse and slovenly beside her. Sitting lightly upright she seemed to be dealing with the world as she chose; the enormous solid globe spun round this way and that beneath her fingers. And her husband! Mr. Dalloway rolling that rich deliberate voice was even more impressive. He seemed to come from the humming oily centre of the machine where the polished rods are sliding, and the pistons thumping; he grasped things so firmly but so loosely; he made the others appear like old maids cheapening remnants. Rachel followed in the wake of the matrons, as if in a trance; a curious scent of violets came back from Mrs. Dalloway, mingling with the soft rustling of her skirts, and the tinkling of her chains. As she followed, Rachel thought with supreme self-abasement, taking in the whole course of her life and the lives of all her friends, "She said we lived in a world of our own. It's true. We're perfectly absurd."

"We sit in here," said Helen, opening the door of the saloon.

"You play?" said Mrs. Dalloway to Mrs. Ambrose, taking up the score of *Tristan* which lay on the table.

"My niece does," said Helen, laying her hand on Rachel's shoulder.

"Oh, how I envy you!" Clarissa addressed Rachel for the first time. "D'you remember this? Isn't it divine?" She played a bar or two with ringed fingers upon the page.

"And then Tristan goes like this, and Isolde—oh!—it's all too thrilling! Have you been to Bayreuth?"

"No, I haven't," said Rachel.

"Then that's still to come. I shall never forget my first *Parsifal*—a grilling August day, and those fat old German women, come in their stuffy high frocks, and then the dark theatre, and the music beginning, and one couldn't help sobbing. A kind man went and fetched me water, I remember; and I could only cry on his shoulder! It caught me here" (she touched her throat). "It's like nothing else in the world! But where's your piano?"

"It's in another room," Rachel explained.

"But you will play to us?" Clarissa entreated. "I can't imagine anything nicer than to sit out in the moonlight and listen to music—only that sounds too like a schoolgirl! You know," she said, turning to Helen, "I don't think music's altogether good for people—I'm afraid not."

"Too great a strain?" asked Helen.

"Too emotional, somehow," said Clarissa. "One notices it at once when a boy or girl takes up music as a profession. Sir William Broadley told me just the same thing. Don't you hate the kind of attitudes people go into over Wagner—like this—" She cast her eyes to the ceiling, clasped her hands, and assumed a look of intensity. "It really doesn't mean that they appreciate him; in fact, I always think it's the other way round. The people who really care about an art are always the least affected. D'you know Henry Philips, the painter?" she asked.

"I have seen him," said Helen.

"To look at, one might think he was a successful stockbroker, and not one of the greatest painters of the age. That's what I like."

"There are a great many successful stockbrokers, if you like looking at them," said Helen.

Rachel wished vehemently that her aunt would not be so perverse.

"When you see a musician with long hair, don't you know instinctively that he's bad?" Clarissa asked, turning to Rachel. "Watts and Joachim—they looked just like you and me."

"And how much nicer they'd have looked with curls!" said Helen. "The question is, are you going to aim at beauty or are you not?"

"Cleanliness!" said Clarissa, "I do want a man to look clean!"

"By cleanliness you really mean well-cut clothes," said Helen.

"There's something one knows a gentleman by," said Clarissa, "but one can't say what it is."

"Take my husband now, does he look like a gentleman?"

The question seemed to Clarissa in extraordinarily bad taste. "One of the things that can't be said," she would have put it. She could find no answer, but a laugh.

"Well, anyhow," she said, turning to Rachel, "I shall insist upon your playing to me tomorrow."

There was that in her manner that made Rachel love her.

Mrs. Dalloway hid a tiny yawn, a mere dilation of the nostrils.

"D'you know," she said, "I'm extraordinarily sleepy. It's the sea air. I think I shall escape."

A man's voice, which she took to be that of Mr. Pepper, strident in discussion, and advancing upon the saloon, gave her the alarm.

"Good-night—good-night!" she said. "Oh, I know my way—do pray for calm! Good-night!"

Her yawn must have been the image of a yawn. Instead of letting her mouth droop, dropping all her clothes in a bunch as though they depended on one string, and stretching her limbs to the utmost end of her berth, she merely changed her dress for a dressing-gown, with innumerable frills, and wrapping her feet in a rug, sat down with a writing-pad on her knee. Already this cramped little cabin was the dressing room of a lady of quality. There were bottles containing liquids; there were trays, boxes, brushes, pins. Evidently not an inch of her person lacked its proper instrument. The scent which had intoxicated Rachel pervaded the air. Thus established, Mrs. Dalloway began to write. A pen in her hands became a thing one caressed paper with, and she might have been stroking and tickling a kitten as she wrote:

Picture us, my dear, afloat in the very oddest ship you can imagine. It's not the ship, so much as the people. One does come across queer sorts as one travels. I must say I find it hugely amusing. There's the manager of the line—called Vinrace—a nice big Englishman, doesn't say much—you know the sort. As for the rest—they might have come trailing out of an old number of Punch. *They're like people playing croquet in the 'sixties. How long they've all been shut up in this ship I don't know—years and years I should say—but one feels as though one had boarded a little separate world, and they'd never been on shore, or done ordinary things in their lives. It's what I've always said about literary people—they're far the hardest of any to get on with. The worst of it is, these people—a man and his wife and a niece—might have been, one feels, just like everybody else, if they hadn't got swallowed up by Oxford or Cambridge or some such place, and been made cranks of. The man's really delightful (if he'd cut his nails), and the woman has quite a fine face, only she dresses, of course, in a potato sack, and wears her hair like a Liberty shopgirl's. They talk about art, and think us such poops for dressing in the evening. However, I can't help that; I'd rather die than come in to dinner without changing—wouldn't you? It matters ever so much more than the soup. (It's odd how things like that do matter so much more than what's generally supposed to matter. I'd rather have my head cut off than wear flannel next the skin.) Then there's a nice shy girl— poor thing—I wish one could rake her out before it's too late. She has quite nice*

*eyes and hair, only, of course, she'll get funny too. We ought to start a society
for broadening the minds of the young—much more useful than missionaries,
Hester! Oh, I'd forgotten there's a dreadful little thing called Pepper. He's just
like his name. He's indescribably insignificant, and rather queer in his temper,
poor dear. It's like sitting down to dinner with an ill-conditioned fox-terrier, only
one can't comb him out, and sprinkle him with powder, as one would one's dog.
It's a pity, sometimes, one can't treat people like dogs! The great comfort is that
we're away from newspapers, so that Richard will have a real holiday this time.
Spain wasn't a holiday . . .*

"You coward!" said Richard, almost filling the room with his sturdy figure.

"I did my duty at dinner!" cried Clarissa.

"You've let yourself in for the Greek alphabet, anyhow."

"Oh, my dear! Who *is* Ambrose?"

"I gather that he was a Cambridge don; lives in London now, and edits classics."

"Did you ever see such a set of cranks? The woman asked me if I thought her husband looked like a gentleman!"

"It was hard to keep the ball rolling at dinner, certainly," said Richard. "Why is it that the women, in that class, are so much queerer than the men?"

"They're not half bad-looking, really—only—they're so odd!"

They both laughed, thinking of the same things, so that there was no need to compare their impressions.

"I see I shall have quite a lot to say to Vinrace," said Richard. "He knows Sutton and all that set. He can tell me a good deal about the conditions of ship-building in the North."

"Oh, I'm glad. The men always *are* so much better than the women."

"One always has something to say to a man certainly," said Richard. "But I've no doubt you'll chatter away fast enough about the babies, Clarice."

"Has she got children? She doesn't look like it somehow."

"Two. A boy and girl."

A pang of envy shot through Mrs. Dalloway's heart.

"We *must* have a son, Dick," she said.

"Good Lord, what opportunities there are now for young men!" said Dalloway, for his talk had set him thinking. "I don't suppose there's been so good an opening since the days of Pitt."

"And it's yours!" said Clarissa.

"To be a leader of men," Richard soliloquised. "It's a fine career. My God—what a career!"

The chest slowly curved beneath his waistcoat.

"D'you know, Dick, I can't help thinking of England," said his wife meditatively, leaning her head against his chest. "Being on this ship seems to make it so much more vivid—what it really means to be English. One thinks of all we've done, and our navies, and the people in India and Africa, and how we've gone on century after century, sending out boys from little country villages—and of men like you, Dick, and it makes one feel as if one couldn't bear *not* to be English! Think of the light burning over the House, Dick! When I stood on deck just now I seemed to see it. It's what one means by London."

"It's the continuity," said Richard sententiously. A vision of English history, King following King, Prime Minister Prime Minister, and Law Law had come over him while his wife spoke. He ran his mind along the line of conservative policy, which went steadily from Lord Salisbury to Alfred, and gradually enclosed, as though it were a lasso that opened and caught things, enormous chunks of the habitable globe.

"It's taken a long time, but we've pretty nearly done it," he said; "it remains to consolidate."

"And these people don't see it!" Clarissa exclaimed.

"It takes all sorts to make a world," said her husband. "There would never be a government if there weren't an opposition."

"Dick, you're better than I am," said Clarissa. "You see round, where I only see *there*." She pressed a point on the back of his hand.

"That's my business, as I tried to explain at dinner."

"What I like about you, Dick," she continued, "is that you're always the same, and I'm a creature of moods."

"You're a pretty creature, anyhow," he said, gazing at her with deeper eyes.

"You think so, do you? Then kiss me."

He kissed her passionately, so that her half-written letter slid to the ground. Picking it up, he read it without asking leave.

"Where's your pen?" he said; and added in his little masculine hand:

> R.D. loquitur: *Clarice has omitted to tell you that she looked exceedingly pretty at dinner, and made a conquest by which she has bound herself to learn the Greek alphabet. I will take this occasion of adding that we are both enjoying ourselves in these outlandish parts, and only wish for the presence of our friends (yourself and John, to wit) to make the trip perfectly enjoyable as it promises to be instructive . . .*

Voices were heard at the end of the corridor. Mrs. Ambrose was speaking low; William Pepper was remarking in his definite and rather acid voice, "That is the type of lady with whom I find myself distinctly out of sympathy. She—"

But neither Richard nor Clarissa profited by the verdict, for directly it seemed likely that they would overhear, Richard crackled a sheet of paper.

"I often wonder," Clarissa mused in bed, over the little white volume of Pascal which went with her everywhere, "whether it is really good for a woman to live with a man who is morally her superior, as Richard is mine. It makes one so dependent. I suppose I feel for him what my mother and women of her generation felt for Christ. It just shows that one can't do without *something*." She then fell into a sleep, which was as usual extremely sound and refreshing, but visited by fantastic dreams of great Greek letters stalking round the room, when she woke up and laughed to herself, remembering where she was and that the Greek letters were real people, lying asleep not many yards away. Then, thinking of the black sea outside tossing beneath the moon, she shuddered, and thought of her husband and the others as companions on the voyage. The dreams were not confined to her indeed, but went from one brain to another. They all dreamt of each other that night, as was natural, considering how thin the partitions were between them, and how strangely they had been lifted off the earth to sit next each other in mid-ocean, and see every detail of each other's faces, and hear whatever they chanced to say.

CHAPTER IV

Next morning Clarissa was up before anyone else. She dressed, and was out on deck, breathing the fresh air of a calm morning, and, making the circuit of the ship for the second time, she ran straight into the lean person of Mr. Grice, the steward. She apologised, and at the same time asked him to enlighten her: what were those shiny brass stands for, half glass on the top? She had been wondering, and could not guess. When he had done explaining, she cried enthusiastically:

"I do think that to be a sailor must be the finest thing in the world!"

"And what d'you know about it?" said Mr. Grice, kindling in a strange manner. "Pardon me. What does any man or woman brought up in England know about the sea? They profess to know; but they don't."

The bitterness with which he spoke was ominous of what was to come. He led her off to his own quarters, and, sitting on the edge of a brass-bound table, looking uncommonly like a sea-gull, with her white tapering body and thin alert face, Mrs. Dalloway had to listen to the tirade of a fanatical man. Did she realise, to begin with, what a very small part of the world the land was? How peaceful, how beautiful, how benignant in comparison the sea? The deep waters could sustain Europe unaided if every earthly animal died of the plague tomorrow. Mr. Grice recalled dreadful sights which he had seen in the richest city of the world—men and women standing in line hour after hour to receive a mug of greasy soup. "And I thought of the good flesh down here waiting and asking to be caught. I'm not exactly a Protestant, and I'm not a Catholic, but I could almost pray for the days of popery to come again—because of the fasts."

As he talked he kept opening drawers and moving little glass jars. Here were the treasures which the great ocean had bestowed upon him—pale fish in greenish liquids, blobs of jelly with streaming tresses, fish with lights in their heads, they lived so deep.

"They have swum about among bones," Clarissa sighed.

"You're thinking of Shakespeare," said Mr. Grice, and taking down a copy from a shelf well lined with books, recited in an emphatic nasal voice:

"Full fathom five thy father lies,

"A grand fellow, Shakespeare," he said, replacing the volume.

Clarissa was so glad to hear him say so.

"Which is your favourite play? I wonder if it's the same as mine?"

"*Henry the Fifth*," said Mr. Grice.

"Joy!" cried Clarissa. "It is!"

Hamlet was what you might call too introspective for Mr. Grice, the sonnets too passionate; Henry the Fifth was to him the model of an English gentleman. But his favourite reading was Huxley, Herbert Spencer, and Henry George; while Emerson and Thomas Hardy he read for relaxation. He was giving Mrs. Dalloway his views upon the present state of England when the breakfast bell rung so imperiously that she had to tear herself away, promising to come back and be shown his sea-weeds.

The party, which had seemed so odd to her the night before, was already gathered round the table, still under the influence of sleep, and therefore uncommunicative, but her entrance sent a little flutter like a breath of air through them all.

"I've had the most interesting talk of my life!" she exclaimed, taking her seat beside Willoughby. "D'you realise that one of your men is a philosopher and a poet?"

"A very interesting fellow—that's what I always say," said Willoughby, distinguishing Mr. Grice. "Though Rachel finds him a bore."

"He's a bore when he talks about currents," said Rachel. Her eyes were full of sleep, but Mrs. Dalloway still seemed to her wonderful.

"I've never met a bore yet!" said Clarissa.

"And I should say the world was full of them!" exclaimed Helen. But her beauty, which was radiant in the morning light, took the contrariness from her words.

"I agree that it's the worst one can possibly say of anyone," said Clarissa.

"How much rather one would be a murderer than a bore!" she added, with her usual air of saying something profound. "One can fancy liking a murderer. It's the same with dogs. Some dogs are awful bores, poor dears."

It happened that Richard was sitting next to Rachel. She was curiously conscious of his presence and appearance—his well-cut clothes, his crackling shirt-front, his cuffs with blue rings round them, and the square-tipped, very clean fingers with the red stone on the little finger of the left hand.

"We had a dog who was a bore and knew it," he said, addressing her in cool, easy tones. "He was a Skye terrier, one of those long chaps, with little feet poking out from their hair like—like caterpillars—no, like sofas I should say. Well, we had another dog at the same time, a black brisk animal—a Schipperke, I think, you call them. You can't imagine a greater contrast. The Skye so slow and deliberate, looking up at you like some old gentleman in the club, as much as to say, 'You don't really mean it, do you?' and the Schipperke as quick as a knife. I liked the Skye best, I must confess. There was something pathetic about him."

The story seemed to have no climax.

"What happened to him?" Rachel asked.

"That's a very sad story," said Richard, lowering his voice and peeling an apple. "He followed my wife in the car one day and got run over by a brute of a cyclist."

"Was he killed?" asked Rachel.

But Clarissa at her end of the table had overheard.

"Don't talk of it!" she cried. "It's a thing I can't bear to think of to this day."

Surely the tears stood in her eyes?

"That's the painful thing about pets," said Mr. Dalloway; "they die. The first sorrow I can remember was for the death of a dormouse. I regret to say that I sat upon it. Still, that didn't make one any the less sorry. Here lies the duck that Samuel Johnson sat on, eh? I was big for my age."

"Then we had canaries," he continued, "a pair of ring-doves, a lemur, and at one time a martin."

"Did you live in the country?" Rachel asked him.

"We lived in the country for six months of the year. When I say 'we' I mean four sisters, a brother, and myself. There's nothing like coming of a large family. Sisters particularly are delightful."

"Dick, you were horribly spoilt!" cried Clarissa across the table.

"No, no. Appreciated," said Richard.

Rachel had other questions on the tip of her tongue; or rather one enormous question, which she did not in the least know how to put into words. The talk appeared too airy to admit of it.

"Please tell me—everything." That was what she wanted to say. He had drawn apart one little chink and showed astonishing treasures. It seemed to her incredible that a man like that should be willing to talk to her. He had sisters and pets, and once lived in the country. She stirred her tea round and round; the bubbles which swam and clustered in the cup seemed to her like the union of their minds.

The talk meanwhile raced past her, and when Richard suddenly stated in a jocular tone of voice, "I'm sure Miss Vinrace, now, has secret leanings towards Catholicism," she had no idea what to answer, and Helen could not help laughing at the start she gave.

However, breakfast was over and Mrs. Dalloway was rising. "I always think religion's like collecting beetles," she said, summing up the discussion as she went up the stairs with Helen. "One person has a passion for black beetles; another hasn't; it's no good arguing about it. What's *your* black beetle now?"

"I suppose it's my children," said Helen.

"Ah—that's different," Clarissa breathed. "Do tell me. You have a boy, haven't you? Isn't it detestable, leaving them?"

It was as though a blue shadow had fallen across a pool. Their eyes became deeper, and their voices more cordial. Instead of joining them as they began to pace the deck, Rachel was indignant with the prosperous matrons, who made her feel outside their world and motherless, and turning back, she left them abruptly. She slammed the door of her room, and pulled out her music. It was all old music—Bach and Beethoven, Mozart and Purcell—the pages yellow, the engraving rough to the finger. In three minutes she was deep in a very difficult, very classical fugue in A, and over her face came a queer remote impersonal expression of complete absorption and anxious satisfaction. Now she stumbled; now she faltered and had to play the same bar twice over; but an invisible line seemed to string the notes together, from which rose a shape, a building. She was so far absorbed in this work, for it was really difficult to find how all these sounds should stand together, and drew upon the whole of her faculties, that she never heard a knock at the door. It was burst impulsively open, and Mrs. Dalloway stood in the room leaving the door open, so that a strip of the white deck and of the blue sea appeared through the opening. The shape of the Bach fugue crashed to the ground.

"Don't let me interrupt," Clarissa implored. "I heard you playing, and I couldn't resist. I adore Bach!"

Rachel flushed and fumbled her fingers in her lap. She stood up awkwardly.

"It's too difficult," she said.

"But you were playing quite splendidly! I ought to have stayed outside."

"No," said Rachel.

She slid *Cowper's Letters* and *Wuthering Heights* out of the armchair, so that Clarissa was invited to sit there.

"What a dear little room!" she said, looking round. "Oh, *Cowper's Letters*! I've never read them. Are they nice?"

"Rather dull," said Rachel.

"He wrote awfully well, didn't he?" said Clarissa; "—if one likes that kind of thing—finished his sentences and all that. *Wuthering Heights*! Ah—that's more in my line. I really couldn't exist without the Brontës! Don't you love them? Still, on the whole, I'd rather live without them than without Jane Austen."

Lightly and at random though she spoke, her manner conveyed an extraordinary degree of sympathy and desire to befriend.

"Jane Austen? I don't like Jane Austen," said Rachel.

"You monster!" Clarissa exclaimed. "I can only just forgive you. Tell me why?"

"She's so—so—well, so like a tight plait," Rachel floundered.

"Ah—I see what you mean. But I don't agree. And you won't when you're older. At your age I only liked Shelley. I can remember sobbing over him in the garden.

> He has outsoared the shadow of our night,
> Envy and calumny and hate and pain—

you remember?

> Can touch him not and torture not again
> From the contagion of the world's slow stain.

How divine!—and yet what nonsense!" She looked lightly round the room. "I always think it's *living*, not dying, that counts. I really respect some snuffy old stockbroker who's gone on adding up column after column all his days, and trotting back to his villa at Brixton with some old pug dog he worships, and a dreary little wife sitting at the end of the table, and going off to Margate for a fortnight—I assure you I know heaps like that—well, they seem to me *really* nobler than poets whom every one worships, just because they're geniuses and die young. But I don't expect *you* to agree with me!"

She pressed Rachel's shoulder.

"Um-m-m—" she went on quoting—

> Unrest which men miscall delight—

"When you're my age you'll see that the world is *crammed* with delightful things. I think young people make such a mistake about that—not letting themselves be happy. I sometimes think that happiness is the only thing that counts. I don't know you well enough to say, but I should guess you might be a little inclined to—when one's young and attractive—I'm going to say it!—*every*thing's at one's feet." She glanced round as much as to say, "not only a few stuffy books and Bach."

"I long to ask questions," she continued. "You interest me so much. If I'm impertinent, you must just box my ears."

"And I—I want to ask questions," said Rachel with such earnestness that Mrs. Dalloway had to check her smile.

"D'you mind if we walk?" she said. "The air's so delicious."

She snuffed it like a racehorse as they shut the door and stood on deck.

"Isn't it good to be alive?" she exclaimed, and drew Rachel's arm within hers. "Look, look! How exquisite!"

The shores of Portugal were beginning to lose their substance; but the land was still the land, though at a great distance. They could distinguish the little towns that were sprinkled in the folds of the hills, and the smoke rising faintly. The towns appeared to be very small in comparison with the great purple mountains behind them.

"Honestly, though," said Clarissa, having looked, "I don't like views. They're too inhuman." They walked on.

"How odd it is!" she continued impulsively. "This time yesterday we'd never met. I was packing in a stuffy little room in the hotel. We know absolutely nothing about each other—and yet—I feel as if I *did* know you!"

"You have children—your husband was in Parliament?"

"You've never been to school, and you live—?"

"With my aunts at Richmond."

"Richmond?"

"You see, my aunts like the Park. They like the quiet."

"And you don't! I understand!" Clarissa laughed.

"I like walking in the Park alone; but not—with the dogs," she finished.

"No; and some people *are* dogs; aren't they?" said Clarissa, as if she had guessed a secret. "But not every one—oh no, not every one."

"Not every one," said Rachel, and stopped.

"I can quite imagine you walking alone," said Clarissa: "and thinking—in a little world of your own. But how you will enjoy it—some day!"

"I shall enjoy walking with a man—is that what you mean?" said Rachel, regarding Mrs. Dalloway with her large enquiring eyes.

"I wasn't thinking of a man particularly," said Clarissa. "But you will."

"No. I shall never marry," Rachel determined.

"I shouldn't be so sure of that," said Clarissa. Her sidelong glance told Rachel that she found her attractive although she was inexplicably amused.

"Why do people marry?" Rachel asked.

"That's what you're going to find out," Clarissa laughed.

Rachel followed her eyes and found that they rested for a second, on the robust figure of Richard Dalloway, who was engaged in striking a match on the sole of his boot; while Willoughby expounded something, which seemed to be of great interest to them both.

"There's nothing like it," she concluded. "Do tell me about the Ambroses. Or am I asking too many questions?"

"I find you easy to talk to," said Rachel.

The short sketch of the Ambroses was, however, somewhat perfunctory, and contained little but the fact that Mr. Ambrose was her uncle.

"Your mother's brother?"

When a name has dropped out of use, the lightest touch upon it tells. Mrs. Dalloway went on:

"Are you like your mother?"

"No; she was different," said Rachel.

She was overcome by an intense desire to tell Mrs. Dalloway things she had never told anyone—things she had not realised herself until this moment.

"I am lonely," she began. "I want—" She did not know what she wanted, so that she could not finish the sentence; but her lip quivered.

But it seemed that Mrs. Dalloway was able to understand without words.

"I know," she said, actually putting one arm round Rachel's shoulder. "When I was your age I wanted too. No one understood until I met Richard. He gave me all I wanted. He's man and woman as well." Her eyes rested upon Mr. Dalloway, leaning upon the rail, still talking. "Don't think I say that because I'm his wife—I see his faults more clearly than I see anyone else's. What one wants in the person one lives with is that they should keep one at one's best. I often wonder what I've done to be so happy!" she exclaimed, and a tear slid down her cheek. She wiped it away, squeezed Rachel's hand, and exclaimed:

"How good life is!" At that moment, standing out in the fresh breeze, with the sun upon the waves, and Mrs. Dalloway's hand upon her arm, it seemed indeed as if life which had been unnamed before was infinitely wonderful, and too good to be true.

Here Helen passed them, and seeing Rachel arm-in-arm with a comparative stranger, looking excited, was amused, but at the same time slightly irritated. But they were immediately joined by Richard, who had enjoyed a very interesting talk with Willoughby and was in a sociable mood.

"Observe my Panama," he said, touching the brim of his hat. "Are you aware, Miss Vinrace, how much can be done to induce fine weather by appropriate headdress? I have determined that it is a hot summer day; I warn you that nothing you can say will shake me. Therefore I am going to sit down. I advise you to follow my example." Three chairs in a row invited them to be seated.

Leaning back, Richard surveyed the waves.

"That's a very pretty blue," he said. "But there's a little too much of it. Variety is essential to a view. Thus, if you have hills you ought to have a river; if a river, hills. The best view in the world in my opinion is that from Boars Hill on a fine day—it must be a fine day, mark you—A rug?—Oh, thank you, my dear . . . in that case you have also the advantage of associations—the Past."

"D'you want to talk, Dick, or shall I read aloud?"

Clarissa had fetched a book with the rugs.

"*Persuasion*," announced Richard, examining the volume.

"That's for Miss Vinrace," said Clarissa. "She can't bear our beloved Jane."

"That—if I may say so—is because you have not read her," said Richard. "She is incomparably the greatest female writer we possess."

"She is the greatest," he continued, "and for this reason: she does not attempt to write like a man. Every other woman does; on that account, I don't read 'em."

"Produce your instances, Miss Vinrace," he went on, joining his finger-tips. "I'm ready to be converted."

He waited, while Rachel vainly tried to vindicate her sex from the slight he put upon it.

"I'm afraid he's right," said Clarissa. "He generally is—the wretch!"

"I brought *Persuasion*," she went on, "because I thought it was a little less threadbare than the others—though, Dick, it's no good *your* pretending to know Jane by heart, considering that she always sends you to sleep!"

"After the labours of legislation, I deserve sleep," said Richard.

"You're not to think about those guns," said Clarissa, seeing that his eye, passing over the waves, still sought the land meditatively, "or about navies, or empires, or anything." So saying she opened the book and began to read:

"'Sir Walter Elliott, of Kellynch Hall, in Somersetshire, was a man who, for his own amusement, never took up any book but the *Baronetage*'— don't you know Sir Walter?—'There he found occupation for an idle hour, and consolation in a distressed one.' She does write well, doesn't she? 'There—'" She read on in a light humorous voice. She was determined that Sir Walter should take her husband's mind off the guns of Britain, and divert him in an exquisite, quaint, sprightly, and slightly ridiculous world. After a time it appeared that the sun was sinking in that world, and the points becoming softer. Rachel looked up to see what caused the change. Richard's eyelids were closing and opening; opening and closing. A loud nasal breath announced that he no longer considered appearances, that he was sound asleep.

"Triumph!" Clarissa whispered at the end of a sentence. Suddenly she raised her hand in protest. A sailor hesitated; she gave the book to Rachel, and stepped lightly to take the message—"Mr. Grice wished to know if it was convenient," etc. She followed him. Ridley, who had prowled unheeded, started forward, stopped, and, with a gesture of disgust, strode off to his study. The sleeping politician was left in Rachel's charge. She read a sentence, and took a look at him. In sleep he looked like a coat hanging at the end of a bed; there were all the wrinkles, and the sleeves and trousers kept their shape though no longer filled out by legs and arms. You can then best judge the age and state of the coat. She looked him all over until it seemed to her that he must protest.

He was a man of forty perhaps; and here there were lines round his eyes, and there curious clefts in his cheeks. Slightly battered he appeared, but dogged and in the prime of life.

"Sisters and a dormouse and some canaries," Rachel murmured, never taking her eyes off him. "I wonder, I wonder" she ceased, her chin upon her hand, still looking at him. A bell chimed behind them, and Richard raised his head. Then he opened his eyes which wore for a second the queer look of a shortsighted person's whose spectacles are lost. It took him a moment to recover from the impropriety of having snored, and possibly grunted, before a young lady. To wake and find oneself left alone with one was also slightly disconcerting.

"I suppose I've been dozing," he said. "What's happened to everyone? Clarissa?"

"Mrs. Dalloway has gone to look at Mr. Grice's fish," Rachel replied.

"I might have guessed," said Richard. "It's a common occurrence. And how have you improved the shining hour? Have you become a convert?"

"I don't think I've read a line," said Rachel.

"That's what I always find. There are too many things to look at. I find nature very stimulating myself. My best ideas have come to me out of doors."

"When you were walking?"

"Walking—riding—yachting—I suppose the most momentous conversations of my life took place while perambulating the great court at Trinity. I was at both universities. It was a fad of my father's. He thought it broadening to the mind. I think I agree with him. I can remember—what an age ago it seems!—settling the basis of a future state with the present Secretary for India. We thought ourselves very wise. I'm not sure we weren't. We were happy, Miss Vinrace, and we were young—gifts which make for wisdom."

"Have you done what you said you'd do?" she asked.

"A searching question! I answer—Yes and No. If on the one hand I have not accomplished what I set out to accomplish—which of us does!—on the other I can fairly say this: I have not lowered my ideal."

He looked resolutely at a sea-gull, as though his ideal flew on the wings of the bird.

"But," said Rachel, "what *is* your ideal?"

"There you ask too much, Miss Vinrace," said Richard playfully.

She could only say that she wanted to know, and Richard was sufficiently amused to answer.

"Well, how shall I reply? In one word—Unity. Unity of aim, of dominion, of progress. The dispersion of the best ideas over the greatest area."

"The English?"

"I grant that the English seem, on the whole, whiter than most men, their records cleaner. But, good Lord, don't run away with the idea that I don't see the drawbacks—horrors—unmentionable things done in our very midst! I'm under no illusions. Few people, I suppose, have fewer illusions than I have. Have you ever been in a factory, Miss Vinrace!—No, I suppose not—I may say I hope not."

As for Rachel, she had scarcely walked through a poor street, and always under the escort of father, maid, or aunts.

"I was going to say that if you'd ever seen the kind of thing that's going on round you, you'd understand what it is that makes me and men like me politicians. You asked me a moment ago whether I'd done what I set out to do. Well, when I consider my life, there is one fact I admit that I'm proud of; owing to me some thousands of girls in Lancashire—and many thousands to come after them—can spend an hour every day in the open air which their mothers had to spend over their looms. I'm prouder of that, I own, than I should be of writing Keats and Shelley into the bargain!"

It became painful to Rachel to be one of those who write Keats and Shelley. She liked Richard Dalloway, and warmed as he warmed. He seemed to mean what he said.

"I know nothing!" she exclaimed.

"It's far better that you should know nothing," he said paternally, "and you wrong yourself, I'm sure. You play very nicely, I'm told, and I've no doubt you've read heaps of learned books."

Elderly banter would no longer check her.

"You talk of unity," she said. "You ought to make me understand."

"I never allow my wife to talk politics," he said seriously. "For this reason. It is impossible for human beings, constituted as they are, both to fight and to have ideals. If I have preserved mine, as I am thankful to say that in great measure I have, it is due to the fact that I have been able to come home to my wife in the evening and to find that she has spent her day in calling, music, play with the children, domestic duties—what you will; her illusions have not been destroyed. She gives me courage to go on. The strain of public life is very great," he added.

This made him appear a battered martyr, parting every day with some of the finest gold, in the service of mankind.

"I can't think," Rachel exclaimed, "how anyone does it!"

"Explain, Miss Vinrace," said Richard. "This is a matter I want to clear up."

His kindness was genuine, and she determined to take the chance he gave her, although to talk to a man of such worth and authority made her heart beat.

"It seems to me like this," she began, doing her best first to recollect and then to expose her shivering private visions.

"There's an old widow in her room, somewhere, let us suppose in the suburbs of Leeds."

Richard bent his head to show that he accepted the widow.

"In London you're spending your life, talking, writing things, getting bills through, missing what seems natural. The result of it all is that she goes to her cupboard and finds a little more tea, a few lumps of sugar, or a little less tea and a newspaper. Widows all over the country I admit do this. Still, there's the mind of the widow—the affections; those you leave untouched. But you waste you own."

"If the widow goes to her cupboard and finds it bare," Richard answered, "her spiritual outlook we may admit will be affected. If I may pick holes in your philosophy, Miss Vinrace, which has its merits, I would point out that a human being is not a set of compartments, but an organism. Imagination, Miss Vinrace; use your imagination; that's where you young Liberals fail. Conceive the world as a whole. Now for your second point; when you assert that in trying to set the house in order for the benefit of the young generation I am wasting my higher capabilities, I totally disagree with you. I can conceive no more exalted aim—to be the citizen of the Empire. Look at it in this way, Miss Vinrace; conceive the state as a complicated machine; we citizens are parts of that machine; some fulfil more important duties; others (perhaps I am one of them) serve only to connect some obscure parts of the mechanism, concealed from the public eye. Yet if the meanest screw fails in its task, the proper working of the whole is imperilled."

It was impossible to combine the image of a lean black widow, gazing out of her window, and longing for someone to talk to, with the image of a vast machine, such as one sees at South Kensington, thumping, thumping, thumping. The attempt at communication had been a failure.

"We don't seem to understand each other," she said.

"Shall I say something that will make you very angry?" he replied.

"It won't," said Rachel.

"Well, then; no woman has what I may call the political instinct. You have very great virtues; I am the first, I hope, to admit that; but I have never met a woman who even saw what is meant by statesmanship. I am going to make you still more angry. I hope that I never shall meet such a woman. Now, Miss Vinrace, are we enemies for life?"

Vanity, irritation, and a thrusting desire to be understood, urged her to make another attempt.

"Under the streets, in the sewers, in the wires, in the telephones, there is something alive; is that what you mean? In things like dust-carts, and men mending roads? You feel that all the time when you walk about London, and when you turn on a tap and the water comes?"

"Certainly," said Richard. "I understand you to mean that the whole of modern society is based upon cooperative effort. If only more people would realise that, Miss Vinrace, there would be fewer of your old widows in solitary lodgings!"

Rachel considered.

"Are you a Liberal or are you a Conservative?" she asked.

"I call myself a Conservative for convenience sake," said Richard, smiling. "But there is more in common between the two parties than people generally allow."

There was a pause, which did not come on Rachel's side from any lack of things to say; as usual she could not say them, and was further confused by the fact that the time for talking probably ran short. She was haunted by absurd jumbled ideas—how, if one went back far enough, everything perhaps was intelligible; everything was in common; for the mammoths who pastured in the fields of Richmond High Street had turned into paving stones and boxes full of ribbon, and her aunts.

"Did you say you lived in the country when you were a child?" she asked.

Crude as her manners seemed to him, Richard was flattered. There could be no doubt that her interest was genuine.

"I did," he smiled.

"And what happened?" she asked. "Or do I ask too many questions?"

"I'm flattered, I assure you. But—let me see—what happened? Well, riding, lessons, sisters. There was an enchanted rubbish heap, I remember, where all kinds of queer things happened. Odd, what things impress children! I can remember the look of the place to this day. It's a fallacy to think that children are happy. They're not; they're unhappy. I've never suffered so much as I did when I was a child."

"Why?" she asked.

"I didn't get on well with my father," said Richard shortly. "He was a very able man, but hard. Well—it makes one determined not to sin in that way oneself. Children never forget injustice. They forgive heaps of things grown-up people mind; but that sin is the unpardonable sin. Mind you—I daresay I was a difficult child to manage; but when I think what I was ready to give! No, I was more sinned against than sinning. And then I went to school, where I did very fairly well; and and then, as I say, my father sent me to both universities . . . D'you know, Miss Vinrace, you've made me think? How little, after all, one can tell anybody about one's life! Here I sit; there you sit; both, I doubt not, chock-full of the most interesting experiences, ideas, emotions; yet how communicate? I've told you what every second person you meet might tell you."

"I don't think so," she said. "It's the way of saying things, isn't it, not the things?"

"True," said Richard. "Perfectly true." He paused. "When I look back over my life—I'm forty-two—what are the great facts that stand out? What were the revelations, if I may call them so? The misery of the poor and—" (he hesitated and pitched over) "love!"

Upon that word he lowered his voice; it was a word that seemed to unveil the skies for Rachel.

"It's an odd thing to say to a young lady," he continued. "But have you any idea what—what I mean by that? No, of course not. I don't use the word in a conventional sense. I use it as young men use it. Girls are kept very ignorant, aren't they? Perhaps it's wise—perhaps—You *don't* know?"

He spoke as if he had lost consciousness of what he was saying.

"No; I don't," she said, scarcely speaking above her breath.

"Warships, Dick! Over there! Look!" Clarissa, released from Mr. Grice, appreciative of all his seaweeds, skimmed towards them, gesticulating.

She had sighted two sinister grey vessels, low in the water, and bald as bone, one closely following the other with the look of eyeless beasts seeking their prey. Consciousness returned to Richard instantly.

"By George!" he exclaimed, and stood shielding his eyes.

"Ours, Dick?" said Clarissa.

"The Mediterranean Fleet," he answered.

"The *Euphrosyne* was slowly dipping her flag. Richard raised his hat. Convulsively Clarissa squeezed Rachel's hand.

"Aren't you glad to be English!" she said.

The warships drew past, casting a curious effect of discipline and sadness upon the waters, and it was not until they were again invisible that people spoke to each other naturally. At lunch the talk was all of valour and death, and the magnificent qualities of British admirals. Clarissa quoted one poet, Willoughby quoted another. Life on board a man-of-war was splendid, so they agreed, and sailors, whenever one met them, were quite especially nice and simple.

This being so, no one liked it when Helen remarked that it seemed to her as wrong to keep sailors as to keep a Zoo, and that as for dying on a battle-field, surely it was time we ceased to praise courage—"or to write bad poetry about it," snarled Pepper.

But Helen was really wondering why Rachel, sitting silent, looked so queer and flushed.

CHAPTER V

She was not able to follow up her observations, however, or to come to any conclusion, for by one of those accidents which are liable to happen at sea, the whole course of their lives was now put out of order.

Even at tea the floor rose beneath their feet and pitched too low again, and at dinner the ship seemed to groan and strain as though a lash were descending. She who had been a broad-backed dray-horse, upon whose hind-quarters pierrots might waltz, became a colt in a field. The plates slanted away from the knives, and Mrs. Dalloway's face blanched for a second as she helped herself and saw the potatoes roll this way and that. Willoughby, of course, extolled the virtues of his ship, and quoted what had been said of her by experts and distinguished passengers, for he loved his own possessions. Still, dinner was uneasy, and directly the ladies were alone Clarissa owned that she would be better off in bed, and went, smiling bravely.

Next morning the storm was on them, and no politeness could ignore it. Mrs. Dalloway stayed in her room. Richard faced three meals, eating valiantly at each; but at the third, certain glazed asparagus swimming in oil finally conquered him.

"That beats me," he said, and withdrew.

"Now we are alone once more," remarked William Pepper, looking round the table; but no one was ready to engage him in talk, and the meal ended in silence.

On the following day they met—but as flying leaves meet in the air. Sick they were not; but the wind propelled them hastily into rooms, violently downstairs. They passed each other gasping on deck; they shouted across tables. They wore fur coats; and Helen was never seen without a bandanna on her head. For comfort they retreated to their cabins, where with tightly wedged feet they let the ship bounce and tumble. Their sensations were the sensations of potatoes in a sack on a galloping horse. The world outside was merely a violent grey tumult. For two days they had a perfect rest from their old emotions. Rachel had just enough consciousness to suppose herself a donkey on the summit of a moor in a hail-storm, with its coat blown into furrows; then she became a wizened tree, perpetually driven back by the salt Atlantic gale.

Helen, on the other hand, staggered to Mrs. Dalloway's door, knocked, could not be heard for the slamming of doors and the battering of wind, and entered.

There were basins, of course. Mrs. Dalloway lay half-raised on a pillow, and did not open her eyes. Then she murmured, "Oh, Dick, is that you?"

Helen shouted—for she was thrown against the washstand—"How are you?"

Clarissa opened one eye. It gave her an incredibly dissipated appearance. "Awful!" she gasped. Her lips were white inside.

Planting her feet wide, Helen contrived to pour champagne into a tumbler with a tooth-brush in it.

"Champagne," she said.

"There's a toothbrush in it," murmured Clarissa, and smiled; it might have been the contortion of one weeping. She drank.

"Disgusting," she whispered, indicating the basins. Relics of humour still played over her face like moonshine.

"Want more?" Helen shouted. Speech was again beyond Clarissa's reach. The wind laid the ship shivering on her side. Pale agonies crossed Mrs. Dalloway in waves. When the curtains flapped, grey lights puffed across her. Between the spasms of the storm, Helen made the curtain fast, shook the pillows, stretched the bed-clothes, and smoothed the hot nostrils and forehead with cold scent.

"You *are* good!" Clarissa gasped. "Horrid mess!"

She was trying to apologise for white underclothes fallen and scattered on the floor. For one second she opened a single eye, and saw that the room was tidy.

"That's nice," she gasped.

Helen left her; far, far away she knew that she felt a kind of liking for Mrs. Dalloway. She could not help respecting her spirit and her desire, even in the throes of sickness, for a tidy bedroom. Her petticoats, however, rose above her knees.

Quite suddenly the storm relaxed its grasp. It happened at tea; the expected paroxysm of the blast gave out just as it reached its climax and dwindled away, and the ship instead of taking the usual plunge went steadily. The monotonous order of plunging and rising, roaring and relaxing, was interfered with, and every one at table looked up and felt something loosen within them. The strain was slackened and human feelings began to peep again, as they do when daylight shows at the end of a tunnel.

"Try a turn with me," Ridley called across to Rachel.

"Foolish!" cried Helen, but they went stumbling up the ladder. Choked by the wind their spirits rose with a rush, for on the skirts of all the grey tumult was a misty spot of gold. Instantly the world dropped into shape; they were no longer atoms flying in the void, but people riding a triumphant ship on the back of the sea. Wind and space were banished; the world floated like an apple in a tub, and the mind of man, which had been unmoored also, once more attached itself to the old beliefs.

Having scrambled twice round the ship and received many sound cuffs from the wind, they saw a sailor's face positively shine golden. They looked, and beheld a complete yellow circle of sun; next minute it was traversed by sailing stands of cloud, and then completely hidden. By breakfast the next morning, however, the sky was swept clean, the waves, although steep, were blue, and after their view of the strange under-world, inhabited by phantoms, people began to live among tea-pots and loaves of bread with greater zest than ever.

Richard and Clarissa, however, still remained on the borderland. She did not attempt to sit up; her husband stood on his feet, contemplated his waistcoat and trousers, shook his head, and then lay down again. The inside of his brain was still rising and falling like the sea on the stage. At four o'clock he woke from sleep and saw the sunlight make a vivid angle across the red plush curtains and the grey tweed trousers. The ordinary world outside slid into his mind, and by the time he was dressed he was an English gentleman again.

He stood beside his wife. She pulled him down to her by the lapel of his coat, kissed him, and held him fast for a minute.

"Go and get a breath of air, Dick," she said. "You look quite washed out ... How nice you smell! ... And be polite to that woman. She was so kind to me."

Thereupon Mrs. Dalloway turned to the cool side of her pillow, terribly flattened but still invincible.

Richard found Helen talking to her brother-in-law, over two dishes of yellow cake and smooth bread and butter.

"You look very ill!" she exclaimed on seeing him. "Come and have some tea."

He remarked that the hands that moved about the cups were beautiful.

"I hear you've been very good to my wife," he said. "She's had an awful time of it. You came in and fed her with champagne. Were you among the saved yourself?"

"I? Oh, I haven't been sick for twenty years—sea-sick, I mean."

"There are three stages of convalescence, I always say," broke in the hearty voice of Willoughby. "The milk stage, the bread-and-butter stage, and the roast-beef stage. I should say you were at the bread-and-butter stage." He handed him the plate.

"Now, I should advise a hearty tea, then a brisk walk on deck; and by dinner-time you'll be clamouring for beef, eh?" He went off laughing, excusing himself on the score of business.

"What a splendid fellow he is!" said Richard. "Always keen on something."

"Yes," said Helen, "he's always been like that."

"This is a great undertaking of his," Richard continued. "It's a business that won't stop with ships, I should say. We shall see him in Parliament, or I'm much mistaken. He's the kind of man we want in Parliament—the man who has done things."

But Helen was not much interested in her brother-in-law.

"I expect your head's aching, isn't it?" she asked, pouring a fresh cup.

"Well, it is," said Richard. "It's humiliating to find what a slave one is to one's body in this world. D'you know, I can never work without a kettle on the hob. As often as not I don't drink tea, but I must feel that I can if I want to."

"That's very bad for you," said Helen.

"It shortens one's life; but I'm afraid, Mrs. Ambrose, we politicians must make up our minds to that at the outset. We've got to burn the candle at both ends, or—"

"You've cooked your goose!" said Helen brightly.

"We can't make you take us seriously, Mrs. Ambrose," he protested. "May I ask how you've spent your time? Reading—philosophy?" (He saw the black book.) "Metaphysics and fishing!" he exclaimed. "If I had to live again I believe I should devote myself to one or the other." He began turning the pages.

" 'Good, then, is indefinable,' " he read out. "How jolly to think that's going on still! 'So far as I know there is only one ethical writer, Professor Henry Sidgwick, who has clearly recognised and stated this fact.' That's just the kind of thing we used to talk about when we were boys. I can remember arguing until five in the morning with Duffy—now Secretary for India—pacing round and round those cloisters until we decided it was too late to go to bed, and we went for a ride instead. Whether we ever came to any conclusion— that's another matter. Still, it's the arguing that counts. It's things like that that stand out in life. Nothing's been quite so vivid since. It's the philosophers, it's the scholars," he continued, "they're the people who pass the torch, who keep the light burning by which we live. Being a politician doesn't necessarily blind one to that, Mrs. Ambrose."

"No. Why should it?" said Helen. "But can you remember if your wife takes sugar?"

She lifted the tray and went off with it to Mrs. Dalloway.

Richard twisted a muffler twice round his throat and struggled up on deck. His body, which had grown white and tender in a dark room, tingled all over in the fresh air. He felt himself a man undoubtedly in the prime of life. Pride glowed in his eye as he let the wind buffet him and stood firm. With his head slightly lowered he sheered round corners, strode uphill, and met the blast. There was a collision. For a second he could not see what the body was he had run into. "Sorry." "Sorry." It was Rachel who apologised. They both laughed, too much blown about to speak. She drove open the door of her room and stepped into its calm. In order to speak to her, it was necessary that Richard should follow. They stood in a whirlpool of wind; papers began flying round in circles, the door crashed to, and they tumbled, laughing, into chairs. Richard sat upon Bach.

"My word! What a tempest!" he exclaimed.

"Fine, isn't it?" said Rachel. Certainly the struggle and wind had given her a decision she lacked; red was in her cheeks, and her hair was down.

"Oh, what fun!" he cried. "What am I sitting on? Is this your room? How jolly!" "There—sit there," she commanded. Cowper slid once more.

"How jolly to meet again," said Richard. "It seems an age. *Cowper's Letters?* . . . Bach? . . . *Wuthering Heights?* . . . Is this where you meditate on the world, and then come out and pose poor politicians with questions? In the intervals of sea-sickness I've thought a lot of our talk. I assure you, you made me think."

"I made you think! But why?"

"What solitary icebergs we are, Miss Vinrace! How little we can communicate! There are lots of things I should like to tell you about—to hear your opinion of. Have you ever read Burke?"

"Burke?" she repeated. "Who was Burke?"

"No? Well, then I shall make a point of sending you a copy. *The Speech on the French Revolution—The American Rebellion?* Which shall it be, I wonder?" He noted something in his pocket-book. "And then you must write and tell me what you think of it. This reticence—this isolation—that's what's the matter with modern life! Now, tell me about yourself. What are your interests and occupations? I should imagine that you were a person with very strong interests. Of course you are! Good God! When I think of the age we live in, with its opportunities and possibilities, the mass of things to be done and enjoyed—why haven't we ten lives instead of one? But about yourself?"

"You see, I'm a woman," said Rachel.

"I know—I know," said Richard, throwing his head back, and drawing his fingers across his eyes.

"How strange to be a woman! A young and beautiful woman," he continued sententiously, "has the whole world at her feet. That's true, Miss Vinrace. You have an inestimable power—for good or for evil. What couldn't you do—" he broke off.

"What?" asked Rachel.

"You have beauty," he said. The ship lurched. Rachel fell slightly forward. Richard took her in his arms and kissed her. Holding her tight, he kissed her passionately, so that she felt the hardness of his body and the roughness of his cheek printed upon hers. She fell back in her chair, with tremendous beats of the heart, each of which sent black waves across her eyes. He clasped his forehead in his hands.

"You tempt me," he said. The tone of his voice was terrifying. He seemed choked in fright. They were both trembling. Rachel stood up and went. Her head was cold, her knees shaking, and the physical pain of the emotion was so great that she could only keep herself moving above the great leaps of her heart. She leant upon the rail of the ship, and gradually ceased to feel, for a chill of body and mind crept over her. Far out between the waves little black and white sea-birds were riding. Rising and falling with smooth and graceful movements in the hollows of the waves they seemed singularly detached and unconcerned.

"You're peaceful," she said. She became peaceful too, at the same time possessed with a strange exultation. Life seemed to hold infinite possibilities she had never guessed at. She leant upon the rail and looked over the troubled grey waters, where the sunlight was fitfully scattered upon the crests of the waves, until she was cold and absolutely calm again. Nevertheless something wonderful had happened.

At dinner, however, she did not feel exalted, but merely uncomfortable, as if she and Richard had seen something together which is hidden in ordinary life, so that they did not like to look at each other. Richard slid his eyes over her uneasily once, and never looked at her again. Formal platitudes were manufactured with effort, but Willoughby was kindled.

"Beef for Mr. Dalloway!" he shouted. "Come now—after that walk you're at the beef stage, Dalloway!"

Wonderful masculine stories followed about Bright and Disraeli and coalition governments, wonderful stories which made the people at the dinner-table seem featureless and small. After dinner, sitting alone with Rachel under the great swinging lamp, Helen was struck by her pallor. It once more occurred to her that there was something strange in the girl's behaviour.

"You look tired. Are you tired?" she asked.

"Not tired," said Rachel. "Oh, yes, I suppose I am tired."

Helen advised bed, and she went, not seeing Richard again. She must have been very tired for she fell asleep at once, but after an hour or two of dreamless sleep, she dreamt. She dreamt that she was walking down a long tunnel, which grew so narrow by degrees that she could touch the damp bricks on either side. At length the tunnel opened and became a vault; she found herself trapped in it, bricks meeting her wherever she turned, alone with a little deformed man who squatted on the floor gibbering, with long nails. His face was pitted and like the face of an animal. The wall behind him oozed with damp, which collected into drops and slid down. Still and cold as death she lay, not daring to move, until she broke the agony by tossing herself across the bed, and woke crying "Oh!"

Light showed her the familiar things: her clothes, fallen off the chair; the water jug gleaming white; but the horror did not go at once. She felt herself pursued, so that she got up and actually locked her door. A voice moaned for her; eyes desired her. All night long barbarian men harassed the ship; they came scuffling down the passages, and stopped to snuffle at her door. She could not sleep again.

CHAPTER VI

That's the tragedy of life—as I always say!" said Mrs. Dalloway. "Beginning things and having to end them. Still, I'm not going to let *this* end, if you're willing." It was the morning, the sea was calm, and the ship once again was anchored not far from another shore.

She was dressed in her long fur cloak, with the veils wound around her head, and once more the rich boxes stood on top of each other so that the scene of a few days back seemed to be repeated.

"D'you suppose we shall ever meet in London?" said Ridley ironically. "You'll have forgotten all about me by the time you step out there."

He pointed to the shore of the little bay, where they could now see the separate trees with moving branches.

"How horrid you are!" she laughed. "Rachel's coming to see me anyhow—the instant you get back," she said, pressing Rachel's arm. "Now—you've no excuse!"

With a silver pencil she wrote her name and address on the flyleaf of *Persuasion*, and gave the book to Rachel. Sailors were shouldering the luggage, and people were beginning to congregate. There were Captain Cobbold, Mr. Grice, Willoughby, Helen, and an obscure grateful man in a blue jersey.

"Oh, it's time," said Clarissa. "Well, good-bye. I *do* like you," she murmured as she kissed Rachel. People in the way made it unnecessary for Richard to shake Rachel by the hand; he managed to look at her very stiffly for a second before he followed his wife down the ship's side.

The boat separating from the vessel made off towards the land, and for some minutes Helen, Ridley, and Rachel leant over the rail, watching. Once Mrs. Dalloway turned and waved; but the boat steadily grew smaller and smaller until it ceased to rise and fall, and nothing could be seen save two resolute backs.

"Well, that's over," said Ridley after a long silence. "We shall never see *them* again," he added, turning to go to his books. A feeling of emptiness and melancholy came over them; they knew in their hearts that it was over, and that they had parted forever, and the knowledge filled them with far greater depression than the length of their acquaintance seemed to justify. Even as the boat pulled away they could feel other sights and sounds beginning to take the place of the Dalloways, and the feeling was so unpleasant that they tried to resist it. For so, too, would they be forgotten.

In much the same way as Mrs. Chailey downstairs was sweeping the withered rose-leaves off the dressing-table, so Helen was anxious to make things straight again after the visitors had gone. Rachel's obvious languor and listlessness made her an easy prey, and indeed Helen had devised a kind of trap. That something had happened she now felt pretty certain; moreover, she had come to think that they had been strangers long enough; she wished to know what the girl was like, partly of course because Rachel showed no disposition to be known. So, as they turned from the rail, she said:

"Come and talk to me instead of practising," and led the way to the sheltered side where the deck-chairs were stretched in the sun. Rachel followed her indifferently. Her mind was absorbed by Richard; by the extreme strangeness of what had happened, and by a thousand feelings of which she had not been conscious before. She made scarcely any attempt to listen to what Helen was saying, as Helen indulged in commonplaces to begin with. While Mrs. Ambrose arranged her embroidery, sucked her silk, and threaded her needle, she lay back gazing at the horizon.

"Did you like those people?" Helen asked her casually.

"Yes," she replied blankly.

"You talked to him, didn't you?"

She said nothing for a minute.

"He kissed me," she said without any change of tone.

Helen started, looked at her, but could not make out what she felt.

"M-m-m'yes," she said, after a pause. "I thought he was that kind of man."

"What kind of man?" said Rachel.

"Pompous and sentimental."

"I like him," said Rachel.

"So you really didn't mind?"

For the first time since Helen had known her Rachel's eyes lit up brightly.

"I did mind," she said vehemently. "I dreamt. I couldn't sleep."

"Tell me what happened," said Helen. She had to keep her lips from twitching as she listened to Rachel's story. It was poured out abruptly with great seriousness and no sense of humour.

"We talked about politics. He told me what he had done for the poor somewhere. I asked him all sorts of questions. He told me about his own life. The day before yesterday, after the storm, he came in to see me. It happened then, quite suddenly. He kissed me. I don't know why." As she spoke she grew flushed. "I was a good deal excited," she continued. "But I didn't mind till afterwards; when—" she paused, and saw the figure of the bloated little man again—"I became terrified."

From the look in her eyes it was evident she was again terrified. Helen was really at a loss what to say. From the little she knew of Rachel's upbringing she supposed that she had been kept entirely ignorant as to the relations of men with women. With a shyness which she felt with women and not with men she did not like to explain simply what these are. Therefore she took the other course and belittled the whole affair.

"Oh, well," she said, "He was a silly creature, and if I were you, I'd think no more about it."

"No," said Rachel, sitting bolt upright, "I shan't do that. I shall think about it all day and all night until I find out exactly what it does mean."

"Don't you ever read?" Helen asked tentatively.

"*Cowper's Letters*—that kind of thing. Father gets them for me or my Aunts."

Helen could hardly restrain herself from saying out loud what she thought of a man who brought up his daughter so that at the age of twenty-four she scarcely knew that men desired women and was terrified by a kiss. She had good reason to fear that Rachel had made herself incredibly ridiculous.

"You don't know many men?" she asked.

"Mr. Pepper," said Rachel ironically.

"So no one's ever wanted to marry you?"

"No," she answered ingenuously.

Helen reflected that as, from what she had said, Rachel certainly would think these things out, it might be as well to help her.

"You oughtn't to be frightened," she said. "It's the most natural thing in the world. Men will want to kiss you, just as they'll want to marry you. The pity is to get things out of proportion. It's like noticing the noises people make when they eat, or men spitting; or, in short, any small thing that gets on one's nerves."

Rachel seemed to be inattentive to these remarks.

"Tell me," she said suddenly, "what are those women in Piccadilly?"

"In Picadilly? They are prostituted," said Helen.

"It *is* terrifying—it *is* disgusting," Rachel asserted, as if she included Helen in the hatred.

"It is," said Helen. "But—"

"I did like him," Rachel mused, as if speaking to herself. "I wanted to talk to him; I wanted to know what he'd done. The women in Lancashire—"

It seemed to her as she recalled their talk that there was something lovable about Richard, good in their attempted friendship, and strangely piteous in the way they had parted.

The softening of her mood was apparent to Helen.

"You see," she said, "you must take things as they are; and if you want friendship with men you must run risks. Personally," she continued, breaking into a smile, "I think it's worth it; I don't mind being kissed; I'm rather jealous, I believe, that Mr. Dalloway kissed you and didn't kiss me. Though," she added, "he bored me considerably."

But Rachel did not return the smile or dismiss the whole affair, as Helen meant her to. Her mind was working very quickly, inconsistently and painfully. Helen's words hewed down great blocks which had stood there always, and the light which came in was cold. After sitting for a time with fixed eyes, she burst out:

"So that's why I can't walk alone!"

By this new light she saw her life for the first time a creeping hedged-in thing, driven cautiously between high walls, here turned aside, there plunged in darkness, made dull and crippled forever—her life that was the only chance she had—a thousand words and actions became plain to her.

"Because men are brutes! I hate men!" she exclaimed.

"I thought you said you liked him?" said Helen.

"I liked him, and I liked being kissed," she answered, as if that only added more difficulties to her problem.

Helen was surprised to see how genuine both shock and problem were, but she could think of no way of easing the difficulty except by going on talking. She wanted to make her niece talk, and so to understand why this rather dull, kindly, plausible politician had made so deep an impression on her, for surely at the age of twenty-four this was not natural.

"And did you like Mrs. Dalloway too?" she asked.

As she spoke she saw Rachel redden; for she remembered silly things she had said, and also, it occurred to her that she treated this exquisite woman rather badly, for Mrs. Dalloway had said that she loved her husband.

"She was quite nice, but a thimble-pated creature," Helen continued. "I never heard such nonsense! Chitter-chatter-chitter-chatter—fish and the Greek alphabet—never listened to a word anyone said—chock-full of idiotic theories about the way to bring up children—I'd far rather talk to him any day. He was pompous, but he did at least understand what was said to him."

The glamour insensibly faded a little both from Richard and Clarissa. They had not been so wonderful after all, then, in the eyes of a mature person.

"It's very difficult to know what people are like," Rachel remarked, and Helen saw with pleasure that she spoke more naturally. "I suppose I was taken in."

There was little doubt about that according to Helen, but she restrained herself and said aloud:

"One has to make experiments."

"And they *were* nice," said Rachel. "They were extraordinarily interesting." She tried to recall the image of the world as a live thing that Richard had given her, with drains like nerves, and bad houses like patches of diseased skin. She recalled his watch-words—Unity—Imagination, and saw again the bubbles meeting in her tea-cup as he spoke of sisters and canaries, boyhood and his father, her small world becoming wonderfully enlarged.

"But all people don't seem to you equally interesting, do they?" asked Mrs. Ambrose.

Rachel explained that most people had hitherto been symbols; but that when they talked to one they ceased to be symbols, and became—"I could listen to them forever!" she exclaimed. She then jumped up, disappeared downstairs for a minute, and came back with a fat red book.

"*Who's Who*," she said, laying it upon Helen's knee and turning the pages. "It gives short lives of people—for instance: 'Sir Roland Beal; born 1852; parents from Moffatt; educated at Rugby; passed first into R.E.; married 1878 the daughter of T. Fishwick; served in the Bechuanaland Expedition 1884–85 (honourably mentioned). Clubs: United Service, Naval and Military. Recreations: an enthusiastic curler.'"

Sitting on the deck at Helen's feet she went on turning the pages and reading biographies of bankers, writers, clergymen, sailors, surgeons, judges, professors, statesmen, editors, philanthropists, merchants, and actresses; what clubs they belonged to, where they lived, what games they played, and how many acres they owned.

She became absorbed in the book.

Helen meanwhile stitched at her embroidery and thought over the things they had said. Her conclusion was that she would very much like to show her niece, if it were possible, how to live, or as she put it, how to be a reasonable person. She thought that there must be something wrong in this confusion between politics and kissing politicians, and that an elder person ought to be able to help.

"I quite agree," she said, "that people are very interesting; only—" Rachel, putting her finger between the pages, looked up enquiringly.

"Only I think you ought to discriminate," she ended. "It's a pity to be intimate with people who are—well, rather second-rate, like the Dalloways, and to find it out later."

"But how does one know?" Rachel asked.

"I really can't tell you," replied Helen candidly, after a moment's thought. "You'll have to find out for yourself. But try and—Why don't you call me Helen?" she added. "'Aunt's' a horrid name. I never liked my Aunts."

"I should like to call you Helen," Rachel answered.

"D'you think me very unsympathetic?"

Rachel reviewed the points which Helen had certainly failed to understand; they arose chiefly from the difference of nearly twenty years in age between them, which made Mrs. Ambrose appear too humorous and cool in a matter of such moment.

"No," she said. "Some things you don't understand, of course."

"Of course," Helen agreed. "So now you can go ahead and be a person on your own account," she added.

The vision of her own personality, of herself as a real everlasting thing, different from anything else, unmergeable, like the sea or the wind, flashed into Rachel's mind, and she became profoundly excited at the thought of living.

"I can by m-m-myself," she stammered, "in spite of you, in spite of the Dalloways, and Mr. Pepper, and Father, and my Aunts, in spite of these?" She swept her hand across a whole page of statesmen and soldiers.

"In spite of them all," said Helen gravely. She then put down her needle, and explained a plan which had come into her head as they talked. Instead of wandering on down the Amazons until she reached some sulphurous tropical port, where one had to lie within doors all day beating off insects with a fan, the sensible thing to do surely was to spend the season with them in their villa by the seaside, where among other advantages Mrs. Ambrose herself would be at hand to—"After all, Rachel," she broke off, "it's silly to pretend that because there's twenty years' difference between us we therefore can't talk to each other like human beings."

"No; because we like each other," said Rachel.

"Yes," Mrs. Ambrose agreed.

That fact, together with other facts, had been made clear by their twenty minutes' talk, although how they had come to these conclusions they could not have said.

However they were come by, they were sufficiently serious to send Mrs. Ambrose a day or two later in search of her brother-in-law. She found him sitting in his room working, applying a stout blue pencil authoritatively to bundles of filmy paper. Papers lay to left and to right of him, there were great envelopes so gorged with papers that they spilt papers on to the table. Above him hung a photograph of a woman's head. The need of sitting absolutely still before a Cockney photographer had given her lips a queer little pucker, and her eyes for the same reason looked as though she thought the whole situation ridiculous. Nevertheless it was the head of an individual and interesting woman, who would no doubt have turned and laughed at Willoughby if she could have caught his eye; but when he looked up at her he sighed profoundly. In his mind this work of his, the great factories at Hull which showed like mountains at night, the ships that crossed the ocean punctually, the schemes for combining this and that and building up a solid mass of industry, was all an offering to her; he laid his success at her feet; and was always thinking how to educate his daughter so that Theresa might be glad. He was a very ambitious man; and although he had not been particularly kind to her while she lived, as Helen thought, he now believed that she watched him from Heaven, and inspired what was good in him.

Mrs. Ambrose apologised for the interruption, and asked whether she might speak to him about a plan of hers. Would he consent to leave his daughter with them when they landed, instead of taking her on up the Amazons?

"We would take great care of her," she added, "and we should really like it."

Willoughby looked very grave and carefully laid aside his papers.

"She's a good girl," he said at length. "There is a likeness?"—he nodded his head at the photograph of Theresa and sighed. Helen looked at Theresa pursing up her lips before the Cockney photographer. It suggested her in an absurd human way, and she felt an intense desire to share some joke.

"She's the only thing that's left to me," sighed Willoughby. "We go on year after year without talking about these things—" He broke off. "But it's better so. Only life's very hard."

Helen was sorry for him, and patted him on the shoulder, but she felt uncomfortable when her brother-in-law expressed his feelings, and took refuge in praising Rachel, and explaining why she thought her plan might be a good one.

"True," said Willoughby when she had done. "The social conditions are bound to be primitive. I should be out a good deal. I agreed because she wished it. And of course I have complete confidence in you . . . You see, Helen," he continued, becoming confidential, "I want to bring her up as her mother would have wished. I don't hold with these modern views—any more than you do, eh? She's a nice quiet girl, devoted to her music—a little less of *that* would do no harm. Still, it's kept her happy, and we lead a very quiet life at Richmond. I should like her to begin to see more people. I want to take her about with me when I get home. I've half a mind to rent a house in London, leaving my sisters at Richmond, and take her to see one or two people who'd be kind to her for my sake. I'm beginning to realise," he continued, stretching himself out, "that all this is tending to Parliament, Helen. It's the only way to get things done as one wants them done. I talked to Dalloway about it. In that case, of course, I should want Rachel to be able to take more part in things. A certain amount of entertaining would be necessary—dinners, an occasional evening party. One's constituents like to be fed, I believe. In all these ways Rachel could be of great help to me. So," he wound up, "I should be very glad, if we arrange this visit (which must be upon a business footing, mind), if you could see your way to helping my girl, bringing her out—she's a little shy now—making a woman of her, the kind of woman her mother would have liked her to be," he ended, jerking his head at the photograph.

Willoughby's selfishness, though consistent as Helen saw with real affection for his daughter, made her determined to have the girl to stay with her, even if she had to promise a complete course of instruction in the feminine graces. She could not help laughing at the notion of it—Rachel a Tory hostess!— and marvelling as she left him at the astonishing ignorance of a father.

Rachel, when consulted, showed less enthusiasm than Helen could have wished. One moment she was eager, the next doubtful. Visions of a great river, now blue, now yellow in the tropical sun and crossed by bright birds, now white in the moon, now deep in shade with moving trees and canoes sliding out from the tangled banks, beset her. Helen promised a river. Then she did not want to leave her father. That feeling seemed genuine too, but in the end Helen prevailed, although when she had won her case she was beset by doubts, and more than once regretted the impulse which had entangled her with the fortunes of another human being.

CHAPTER VII

From a distance the *Euphrosyne* looked very small. Glasses were turned upon her from the decks of great liners, and she was pronounced a tramp, a cargo-boat, or one of those wretched little passenger steamers where people rolled about among the cattle on deck. The insect-like figures of Dalloways, Ambroses, and Vinraces were also derided, both from the extreme smallness of their persons and the doubt which only strong glasses could dispel as to whether they were really live creatures or only lumps on the rigging. Mr. Pepper with all his learning had been mistaken for a cormorant, and then, as unjustly, transformed into a cow. At night, indeed, when the waltzes were swinging in the saloon, and gifted passengers reciting, the little ship—shrunk to a few beads of light out among the dark waves, and one high in air upon the mast-head—seemed something mysterious and impressive to heated partners resting from the dance. She became a ship passing in the night—an emblem of the loneliness of human life, an occasion for queer confidences and sudden appeals for sympathy.

On and on she went, by day and by night, following her path, until one morning broke and showed the land. Losing its shadow-like appearance it became first cleft and mountainous, next coloured grey and purple, next scattered with white blocks which gradually separated themselves, and then, as the progress of the ship acted upon the view like a field-glass of increasing power, became streets of houses. By nine o'clock the *Euphrosyne* had taken up her position in the middle of a great bay; she dropped her anchor; immediately, as if she were a recumbent giant requiring examination, small boats came swarming about her. She rang with cries; men jumped on to her; her deck was thumped by feet. The lonely little island was invaded from all quarters at once, and after four weeks of silence it was bewildering to hear human speech. Mrs. Ambrose alone heeded none of this stir. She was pale with suspense while the boat with mail bags was making towards them. Absorbed in her letters she did not notice that she had left the *Euphrosyne*, and felt no sadness when the ship lifted up her voice and bellowed thrice like a cow separated from its calf.

"The children are well!" she exclaimed. Mr. Pepper, who sat opposite with a great mound of bag and rug upon his knees, said, "Gratifying." Rachel, to whom the end of the voyage meant a complete change of perspective, was too much bewildered by the approach of the shore to realise what children were well or why it was gratifying. Helen went on reading.

Moving very slowly, and rearing absurdly high over each wave, the little boat was now approaching a white crescent of sand. Behind this was a deep green valley, with distinct hills on either side. On the slope of the right-hand hill white houses with brown roofs were settled, like nesting sea-birds, and at intervals cypresses striped the hill with black bars. Mountains whose sides were flushed with red, but whose crowns were bald, rose as a pinnacle, half-concealing another pinnacle behind it. The hour being still early, the whole view was exquisitely light and airy; the blues and greens of sky and tree were intense but not sultry. As they drew nearer and could distinguish details, the effect of the earth with its minute objects and colours and different forms of life was overwhelming after four weeks of the sea, and kept them silent.

"Three hundred years odd," said Mr. Pepper meditatively at length.

As nobody said, "What?" he merely extracted a bottle and swallowed a pill. The piece of information that died within him was to the effect that three hundred years ago five Elizabethan barques had anchored where the *Euphrosyne* now floated. Half-drawn up upon the beach lay an equal number of Spanish galleons, unmanned, for the country was still a virgin land behind a veil. Slipping across the water, the English sailors bore away bars of silver, bales of linen, timbers of cedar wood, golden crucifixes knobbed with emeralds. When the Spaniards came down from their drinking, a fight ensued, the two parties churning up the sand, and driving each other into the surf.

The Spaniards, bloated with fine living upon the fruits of the miraculous land, fell in heaps; but the hardy Englishmen, tawny with sea-voyaging, hairy for lack of razors, with muscles like wire, fangs greedy for flesh, and fingers itching for gold, despatched the wounded, drove the dying into the sea, and soon reduced the natives to a state of superstitious wonderment. Here a settlement was made; women were imported; children grew. All seemed to favour the expansion of the British Empire, and had there been men like Richard Dalloway in the time of Charles the First, the map would undoubtedly be red where it is now an odious green. But it must be supposed that the political mind of that age lacked imagination, and, merely for want of a few thousand pounds and a few thousand men, the spark died that should have been a conflagration. From the interior came Indians with subtle poisons, naked bodies, and painted idols; from the sea came vengeful Spaniards and rapacious Portuguese; exposed to all these enemies (though the climate proved wonderfully kind and the earth abundant) the English dwindled away and all but disappeared. Somewhere about the middle of the seventeenth century a single sloop watched its season and slipped out by night, bearing within it all that was left of the great British colony, a few men, a few women, and perhaps a dozen dusky children. English history then denies all knowledge of the place. Owing to one cause and another civilisation shifted its centre to a spot some four or five hundred miles to the south, and today Santa Marina is not much larger than it was three hundred years ago. In population it is a happy compromise, for Portuguese fathers wed Indian mothers, and their children intermarry with the Spanish. Although they get their ploughs from Manchester, they make their coats from their own sheep, their silk from their own worms, and their furniture from their own cedar trees, so that in arts and industries the place is still much where it was in Elizabethan days.

The reasons which had drawn the English across the sea to found a small colony within the last ten years are not so easily described, and will never perhaps be recorded in history books. Granted facility of travel, peace, good trade, and so on, there was besides a kind of dissatisfaction among the English with the older countries and the enormous accumulations of carved stone, stained glass, and rich brown painting which they offered to the tourist. The movement in search of something new was of course infinitely small, affecting only a handful of well-to-do people. It began by a few schoolmasters serving their passage out to South America as the pursers of tramp steamers. They returned in time for the summer term, when their stories of the splendours and hardships of life at sea, the humours of sea-captains, the wonders of night and dawn, and the marvels of the place delighted outsiders, and sometimes found their way into print. The country itself taxed all their powers of description, for they said it was much bigger than Italy, and really nobler than Greece. Again, they declared that the natives were strangely beautiful, very big in stature, dark, passionate, and quick to seize the knife. The place seemed new and full of new forms of beauty, in proof of which they showed handkerchiefs which the women had worn round their heads, and primitive carvings coloured bright greens and blues. Somehow or other, as fashions do, the fashion spread; an old monastery was quickly turned into a hotel, while a famous line of steamships altered its route for the convenience of passengers.

Oddly enough it happened that the least satisfactory of Helen Ambrose's brothers had been sent out years before to make his fortune, at any rate to keep clear of race-horses, in the very spot which had now become so popular. Often, leaning upon the column in the verandah, he had watched the English ships with English schoolmasters for pursers steaming into the bay. Having at length earned enough to take a holiday, and being sick of the place, he proposed to put his villa, on the slope of the mountain, at his sister's disposal. She, too, had been a little stirred by the talk of a new world, where there was always sun and never a fog, which went on around her, and the chance, when they were planning where to spend the winter out of England, seemed too good to be missed. For these reasons she determined to accept Willoughby's offer of free passages on his ship, to place the children with their grand-parents, and to do the thing thoroughly while she was about it.

Taking seats in a carriage drawn by long-tailed horses with pheasants' feathers erect between their ears, the Ambroses, Mr. Pepper, and Rachel rattled out of the harbour. The day increased in heat as they drove up the hill. The road passed through the town, where men seemed to be beating brass and crying "Water," where the passage was blocked by mules and cleared by whips and curses, where the women walked barefoot, their heads balancing baskets, and cripples hastily displayed mutilated members; it issued among steep green fields, not so green but that the earth showed through. Great trees now shaded all but the centre of the road, and a mountain stream, so shallow and so swift that it plaited itself into strands as it ran, raced along the edge. Higher they went, until Ridley and Rachel walked behind; next they turned along a lane scattered with stones, where Mr. Pepper raised his stick and silently indicated a shrub, bearing among sparse leaves a voluminous purple blossom; and at a rickety canter the last stage of the way was accomplished.

The villa was a roomy white house, which, as is the case with most continental houses, looked to an English eye frail, ramshackle, and absurdly frivolous, more like a pagoda in a tea-garden than a place where one slept. The garden called urgently for the services of gardener. Bushes waved their branches across the paths, and the blades of grass, with spaces of earth between them, could be counted. In the circular piece of ground in front of the verandah were two cracked vases, from which red flowers drooped, with a stone fountain between them, now parched in the sun. The circular garden led to a long garden, where the gardener's shears had scarcely been, unless now and then, when he cut a bough of blossom for his beloved. A few tall trees shaded it, and round bushes with wax-like flowers mobbed their heads together in a row. A garden smoothly laid with turf, divided by thick hedges, with raised beds of bright flowers, such as we keep within walls in England, would have been out of place upon the side of this bare hill. There was no ugliness to shut out, and the villa looked straight across the shoulder of a slope, ribbed with olive trees, to the sea.

The indecency of the whole place struck Mrs. Chailey forcibly. There were no blinds to shut out the sun, nor was there any furniture to speak of for the sun to spoil. Standing in the bare stone hall, and surveying a staircase of superb breadth, but cracked and carpetless, she further ventured the opinion that there were rats, as large as terriers at home, and that if one put one's foot down with any force one would come through the floor. As for hot water—at this point her investigations left her speechless.

"Poor creature!" she murmured to the sallow Spanish servant-girl who came out with the pigs and hens to receive them, "no wonder you hardly look like a human being!" Maria accepted the compliment with an exquisite Spanish grace. In Chailey's opinion they would have done better to stay on board an English ship, but none knew better than she that her duty commanded her to stay.

When they were settled in, and in train to find daily occupation, there was some speculation as to the reasons which induced Mr. Pepper to stay, taking up his lodging in the Ambroses' house. Efforts had been made for some days before landing to impress upon him the advantages of the Amazons.

"That great stream!" Helen would begin, gazing as if she saw a visionary cascade, "I've a good mind to go with you myself, Willoughby—only I can't. Think of the sunsets and the moonrises—I believe the colours are unimaginable."

"There are wild peacocks," Rachel hazarded.

"And marvellous creatures in the water," Helen asserted.

"One might discover a new reptile," Rachel continued.

"There's certain to be a revolution, I'm told," Helen urged.

The effect of these subterfuges was a little dashed by Ridley, who, after regarding Pepper for some moments, sighed aloud, "Poor fellow!" and inwardly speculated upon the unkindness of women.

He stayed, however, in apparent contentment for six days, playing with a microscope and a notebook in one of the many sparsely furnished sitting-rooms, but on the evening of the seventh day, as they sat at dinner, he appeared more restless than usual. The dinner-table was set between two long windows which were left uncurtained by Helen's orders. Darkness fell as sharply as a knife in this climate, and the town then sprang out in circles and lines of bright dots beneath them. Buildings which never showed by day showed by night, and the sea flowed right over the land judging by the moving lights of the steamers. The sight fulfilled the same purpose as an orchestra in a London restaurant, and silence had its setting. William Pepper observed it for some time; he put on his spectacles to contemplate the scene.

"I've identified the big block to the left," he observed, and pointed with his fork at a square formed by several rows of lights.

"One should infer that they can cook vegetables," he added.

"An hotel?" said Helen.

"Once a monastery," said Mr. Pepper.

Nothing more was said then, but, the day after, Mr. Pepper returned from a midday walk, and stood silently before Helen who was reading in the verandah.

"I've taken a room over there," he said.

"You're not going?" she exclaimed.

"On the whole—yes," he remarked. "No private cook *can* cook vegetables."

Knowing his dislike of questions, which she to some extent shared, Helen asked no more. Still, an uneasy suspicion lurked in her mind that William was hiding a wound. She flushed to think that her words, or her husband's, or Rachel's had penetrated and stung. She was half-moved to cry, "Stop, William; explain!" and would have returned to the subject at luncheon if William had not shown himself inscrutable and chill, lifting fragments of salad on the point of his fork, with the gesture of a man pronging seaweed, detecting gravel, suspecting germs.

"If you all die of typhoid I won't be responsible!" he snapped.

"If you die of dulness, neither will I," Helen echoed in her heart.

She reflected that she had never yet asked him whether he had been in love. They had got further and further from that subject instead of drawing nearer to it, and she could not help feeling it a relief when William Pepper, with all his knowledge, his microscope, his note-books, his genuine kindliness and good sense, but a certain dryness of soul, took his departure. Also she could not help feeling it sad that friendships should end thus, although in this case to have the room empty was something of a comfort, and she tried to console herself with the reflection that one never knows how far other people feel the things they might be supposed to feel.

CHAPTER VIII

The next few months passed away, as many years can pass away, without definite events, and yet, if suddenly disturbed, it would be seen that such months or years had a character unlike others. The three months which had passed had brought them to the beginning of March. The climate had kept its promise, and the change of season from winter to spring had made very little difference, so that Helen, who was sitting in the drawing-room with a pen in her hand, could keep the windows open though a great fire of logs burnt on one side of her. Below, the sea was still blue and the roofs still brown and white, though the day was fading rapidly. It was dusk in the room, which, large and empty at all times, now appeared larger and emptier than usual. Her own figure, as she sat writing with a pad on her knee, shared the general effect of size and lack of detail, for the flames which ran along the branches, suddenly devouring little green tufts, burnt intermittently and sent irregular illuminations across her face and the plaster walls. There were no pictures on the walls but here and there boughs laden with heavy-petalled flowers spread widely against them. Of the books fallen on the bare floor and heaped upon the large table, it was only possible in this light to trace the outline.

Mrs. Ambrose was writing a very long letter. Beginning "Dear Bernard," it went on to describe what had been happening in the Villa San Gervasio during the past three months, as, for instance, that they had had the British Consul to dinner, and had been taken over a Spanish man-of-war, and had seen a great many processions and religious festivals, which were so beautiful that Mrs. Ambrose couldn't conceive why, if people must have a religion, they didn't all become Roman Catholics. They had made several expeditions though none of any length. It was worth coming if only for the sake of the flowering trees which grew wild quite near the house, and the amazing colours of sea and earth. The earth, instead of being brown, was red, purple, green. "You won't believe me," she added, "there is no colour like it in England." She adopted, indeed, a condescending tone towards that poor island, which was now advancing chilly crocuses and nipped violets in nooks, in copses, in cosy corners, tended by rosy old gardeners in mufflers, who were always touching their hats and bobbing obsequiously. She went on to deride the islanders themselves. Rumours of London all in a ferment over a General Election had reached them even out here. "It seems incredible," she went on, "that people should care whether Asquith is in or Austen Chamberlin out, and while you scream yourselves hoarse about politics you let the only people who are trying for something good starve or simply laugh at them. When have you ever encouraged a living artist? Or bought his best work? Why are you all so ugly and so servile? Here the servants are human beings. They talk to one as if they were equals. As far as I can tell there are no aristocrats."

Perhaps it was the mention of aristocrats that reminded her of Richard Dalloway and Rachel, for she ran on with the same penful to describe her niece.

"It's an odd fate that has put me in charge of a girl," she wrote, "considering that I have never got on well with women, or had much to do with them. However, I must retract some of the things that I have said against them. If they were properly educated I don't see why they shouldn't be much the same as men—as satisfactory I mean; though, of course, very different. The question is, how should one educate them. The present method seems to me abominable. This girl, though twenty-four, had never heard that men desired women, and, until I explained it, did not know how children were born. Her ignorance upon other matters as important" (here Mrs. Ambrose's letter may not be quoted) . . . "was complete. It seems to me not merely foolish but criminal to bring people up like that. Let alone the suffering to them, it explains why women are what they are—the wonder is they're no worse. I have taken it upon myself to enlighten her, and now, though still a good deal prejudiced and liable to exaggerate, she is more or less a reasonable human being. Keeping them ignorant, of course, defeats its own object, and when they begin to understand they take it all much too seriously. My brother-in-law really deserved a catastrophe—which he won't get. I now pray for a young man to come to my help; someone, I mean, who would talk to her openly, and prove how absurd most of her ideas about life are. Unluckily such men seem almost as rare as the women. The English colony certainly doesn't provide one; artists, merchants, cultivated people—they are stupid, conventional, and flirtatious . . ." She ceased, and with her pen in her hand sat looking into the fire, making the logs into caves and mountains, for it had grown too dark to go on writing. Moreover, the house began to stir as the hour of dinner approached; she could hear the plates being chinked in the dining-room next door, and Chailey instructing the Spanish girl where to put things down in vigorous English. The bell rang; she rose, met Ridley and Rachel outside, and they all went in to dinner.

Three months had made but little difference in the appearance either of Ridley or Rachel; yet a keen observer might have thought that the girl was more definite and self-confident in her manner than before. Her skin was brown, her eyes certainly brighter, and she attended to what was said as though she might be going to contradict it. The meal began with the comfortable silence of people who are quite at their ease together. Then Ridley, leaning on his elbow and looking out of the window, observed that it was a lovely night.

"Yes," said Helen. She added, "The season's begun," looking at the lights beneath them. She asked Maria in Spanish whether the hotel was not filling up with visitors. Maria informed her with pride that there would come a time when it was positively difficult to buy eggs—the shopkeepers would not mind what prices they asked; they would get them, at any rate, from the English.

"That's an English steamer in the bay," said Rachel, looking at a triangle of lights below. "She came in early this morning."

"Then we may hope for some letters and send ours back," said Helen.

For some reason the mention of letters always made Ridley groan, and the rest of the meal passed in a brisk argument between husband and wife as to whether he was or was not wholly ignored by the entire civilised world.

"Considering the last batch," said Helen, "you deserve beating. You were asked to lecture, you were offered a degree, and some silly woman praised not only your books but your beauty—she said he was what Shelley would have been if Shelley had lived to fifty-five and grown a beard. Really, Ridley, I think you're the vainest man I know," she ended, rising from the table, "which I may tell you is saying a good deal."

Finding her letter lying before the fire she added a few lines to it, and then announced that she was going to take the letters now—Ridley must bring his—and Rachel?

"I hope you've written to your Aunts? It's high time."

The women put on cloaks and hats, and after inviting Ridley to come with them, which he emphatically refused to do, exclaiming that Rachel he expected to be a fool, but Helen surely knew better, they turned to go. He stood over the fire gazing into the depths of the looking-glass, and compressing his face into the likeness of a commander surveying a field of battle, or a martyr watching the flames lick his toes, rather than that of a secluded Professor.

Helen laid hold of his beard.

"Am I a fool?" she said.

"Let me go, Helen."

"Am I a fool?" she repeated.

"Vile woman!" he exclaimed, and kissed her.

"We'll leave you to your vanities," she called back as they went out of the door.

It was a beautiful evening, still light enough to see a long way down the road, though the stars were coming out. The pillar-box was let into a high yellow wall where the lane met the road, and having dropped the letters into it, Helen was for turning back.

"No, no," said Rachel, taking her by the wrist. "We're going to see life. You promised."

"Seeing life" was the phrase they used for their habit of strolling through the town after dark. The social life of Santa Marina was carried on almost entirely by lamp-light, which the warmth of the nights and the scents culled from flowers made pleasant enough. The young women, with their hair magnificently swept in coils, a red flower behind the ear, sat on the doorsteps, or issued out on to balconies, while the young men ranged up and down beneath, shouting up a greeting from time to time and stopping here and there to enter into amorous talk. At the open windows merchants could be seen making up the day's account, and older women lifting jars from shelf to shelf. The streets were full of people, men for the most part, who interchanged their views of the world as they walked, or gathered round the wine-tables at the street corner, where an old cripple was twanging his guitar strings, while a poor girl cried her passionate song in the gutter. The two Englishwomen excited some friendly curiosity, but no one molested them.

Helen sauntered on, observing the different people in their shabby clothes, who seemed so careless and so natural, with satisfaction.

"Just think of the Mall tonight!" she exclaimed at length. "It's the fifteenth of March. Perhaps there's a Court." She thought of the crowd waiting in the cold spring air to see the grand carriages go by. "It's very cold, if it's not raining," she said. "First there are men selling picture postcards; then there are wretched little shop-girls with round bandboxes; then there are bank clerks in tail coats; and then—any number of dressmakers. People from South Kensington drive up in a hired fly; officials have a pair of bays; earls, on the other hand, are allowed one footman to stand up behind; dukes have two, royal dukes—so I was told—have three; the king, I suppose, can have as many as he likes. And the people believe in it!"

Out here it seemed as though the people of England must be shaped in the body like the kings and queens, knights and pawns of the chessboard, so strange were their differences, so marked and so implicitly believed in.

They had to part in order to circumvent a crowd.

"They believe in God," said Rachel as they regained each other. She meant that the people in the crowd believed in Him; for she remembered the crosses with bleeding plaster figures that stood where foot-paths joined, and the inexplicable mystery of a service in a Roman Catholic church.

"We shall never understand!" she sighed.

They had walked some way and it was now night, but they could see a large iron gate a little way farther down the road on their left.

"Do you mean to go right up to the hotel?" Helen asked.

Rachel gave the gate a push; it swung open, and, seeing no one about and judging that nothing was private in this country, they walked straight on. An avenue of trees ran along the road, which was completely straight. The trees suddenly came to an end; the road turned a corner, and they found themselves confronted by a large square building. They had come out upon the broad terrace which ran round the hotel and were only a few feet distant from the windows. A row of long windows opened almost to the ground. They were all of them uncurtained, and all brilliantly lighted, so that they could see everything inside. Each window revealed a different section of the life of the hotel. They drew into one of the broad columns of shadow which separated the windows and gazed in. They found themselves just outside the dining-room. It was being swept; a waiter was eating a bunch of grapes with his leg across the corner of a table. Next door was the kitchen, where they were washing up; white cooks were dipping their arms into cauldrons, while the waiters made their meal voraciously off broken meats, sopping up the gravy with bits of crumb. Moving on, they became lost in a plantation of bushes, and then suddenly found themselves outside the drawing-room, where the ladies and gentlemen, having dined well, lay back in deep armchairs, occasionally speaking or turning over the pages of magazines. A thin woman was flourishing up and down the piano.

"What is a dahabeeyah, Charles?" the distinct voice of a widow, seated in an armchair by the window, asked her son.

It was the end of the piece, and his answer was lost in the general clearing of throats and tapping of knees.

"They're all old in this room," Rachel whispered.

Creeping on, they found that the next window revealed two men in shirt-sleeves playing billiards with two young ladies.

"He pinched my arm!" the plump young woman cried, as she missed her stroke.

"Now you two—no ragging," the young man with the red face reproved them, who was marking.

"Take care or we shall be seen," whispered Helen, plucking Rachel by the arm. Incautiously her head had risen to the middle of the window.

Turning the corner they came to the largest room in the hotel, which was supplied with four windows, and was called the Lounge, although it was really a hall. Hung with armour and native embroideries, furnished with divans and screens, which shut off convenient corners, the room was less formal than the others, and was evidently the haunt of youth. Signor Rodriguez, whom they knew to be the manager of the hotel, stood quite near them in the doorway surveying the scene—the gentlemen lounging in chairs, the couples leaning over coffee-cups, the game of cards in the centre under profuse clusters of electric light. He was congratulating himself upon the enterprise which had turned the refectory, a cold stone room with pots on trestles, into the most comfortable room in the house. The hotel was very full, and proved his wisdom in decreeing that no hotel can flourish without a lounge.

The people were scattered about in couples or parties of four, and either they were actually better acquainted, or the informal room made their manners easier. Through the open window came an uneven humming sound like that which rises from a flock of sheep pent within hurdles at dusk. The card-party occupied the centre of the foreground.

Helen and Rachel watched them play for some minutes without being able to distinguish a word. Helen was observing one of the men intently. He was a lean, somewhat cadaverous man of about her own age, whose profile was turned to them, and he was the partner of a highly-coloured girl, obviously English by birth.

Suddenly, in the strange way in which some words detach themselves from the rest, they heard him say quite distinctly:—

"All you want is practice, Miss Warrington; courage and practice—one's no good without the other."

"Hughling Elliot! Of course!" Helen exclaimed. She ducked her head immediately, for at the sound of his name he looked up. The game went on for a few minutes, and was then broken up by the approach of a wheeled chair, containing a voluminous old lady who paused by the table and said:—

"Better luck tonight, Susan?"

"All the luck's on our side," said a young man who until now had kept his back turned to the window. He appeared to be rather stout, and had a thick crop of hair.

"Luck, Mr. Hewet?" said his partner, a middle-aged lady with spectacles. "I assure you, Mrs. Paley, our success is due solely to our brilliant play."

"Unless I go to bed early I get practically no sleep at all," Mrs. Paley was heard to explain, as if to justify her seizure of Susan, who got up and proceeded to wheel the chair to the door.

"They'll get someone else to take my place," she said cheerfully. But she was wrong. No attempt was made to find another player, and after the young man had built three stories of a card-house, which fell down, the players strolled off in different directions.

Mr. Hewet turned his full face towards the window. They could see that he had large eyes obscured by glasses; his complexion was rosy, his lips clean-shaven; and, seen among ordinary people, it appeared to be an interesting face. He came straight towards them, but his eyes were fixed not upon the eavesdroppers but upon a spot where the curtain hung in folds.

"Asleep?" he said.

Helen and Rachel started to think that someone had been sitting near to them unobserved all the time. There were legs in the shadow. A melancholy voice issued from above them.

"Two women," it said.

A scuffling was heard on the gravel. The women had fled. They did not stop running until they felt certain that no eye could penetrate the darkness and the hotel was only a square shadow in the distance, with red holes regularly cut in it.

CHAPTER IX

An hour passed, and the downstairs rooms at the hotel grew dim and were almost deserted, while the little box-like squares above them were brilliantly irradiated. Some forty or fifty people were going to bed. The thump of jugs set down on the floor above could be heard and the clink of china, for there was not as thick a partition between the rooms as one might wish, so Miss Allan, the elderly lady who had been playing bridge, determined, giving the wall a smart rap with her knuckles. It was only matchboard, she decided, run up to make many little rooms of one large one. Her grey petticoats slipped to the ground, and, stooping, she folded her clothes with neat, if not loving fingers, screwed her hair into a plait, wound her father's great gold watch, and opened the complete works of Wordsworth. She was reading the "Prelude," partly because she always read the "Prelude" abroad, and partly because she was engaged in writing a short *Primer of English Literature— Beowulf to Swinburne*—which would have a paragraph on Wordsworth. She was deep in the fifth book, stopping indeed to pencil a note, when a pair of boots dropped, one after another, on the floor above her. She looked up and speculated. Whose boots were they, she wondered. She then became aware of a swishing sound next door—a woman, clearly, putting away her dress. It was succeeded by a gentle tapping sound, such as that which accompanies hair-dressing. It was very difficult to keep her attention fixed upon the "Prelude." Was it Susan Warrington tapping? She forced herself, however, to read to the end of the book, when she placed a mark between the pages, sighed contentedly, and then turned out the light.

Very different was the room through the wall, though as like in shape as one egg-box is like another. As Miss Allan read her book, Susan Warrington was brushing her hair. Ages have consecrated this hour, and the most majestic of all domestic actions, to talk of love between women; but Miss Warrington being alone could not talk; she could only look with extreme solicitude at her own face in the glass. She turned her head from side to side, tossing heavy locks now this way now that; and then withdrew a pace or two, and considered herself seriously.

"I'm nice-looking," she determined. "Not pretty—possibly," she drew herself up a little. "Yes—most people would say I was handsome."

She was really wondering what Arthur Venning would say she was. Her feeling about him was decidedly queer. She would not admit to herself that she was in love with him or that she wanted to marry him, yet she spent every minute when she was alone in wondering what he thought of her, and in comparing what they had done today with what they had done the day before.

"He didn't ask me to play, but he certainly followed me into the hall," she meditated, summing up the evening. She was thirty years of age, and owing to the number of her sisters and the seclusion of life in a country parsonage had as yet had no proposal of marriage. The hour of confidences was often a sad one, and she had been known to jump into bed, treating her hair unkindly, feeling herself overlooked by life in comparison with others. She was a big, well-made woman, the red lying upon her cheeks in patches that were too well defined, but her serious anxiety gave her a kind of beauty.

She was just about to pull back the bed-clothes when she exclaimed, "Oh, but I'm forgetting," and went to her writing-table. A brown volume lay there stamped with the figure of the year. She proceeded to write in the square ugly hand of a mature child, as she wrote daily year after year, keeping the diaries, though she seldom looked at them.

"A.M.—Talked to Mrs. H. Elliot about country neighbours. She knows the Manns; also the Selby-Carroways. How small the world is! Like her. Read a chapter of *Miss Appleby's Adventure* to Aunt E. P.M.—Played lawn-tennis with Mr. Perrott and Evelyn M. Don't *like* Mr. P. Have a feeling that he is not 'quite,' though clever certainly. Beat them. Day splendid, view wonderful. One gets used to no trees, though much too bare at first. Cards after dinner. Aunt E. cheerful, though twingy, she says. Mem.: *ask about damp sheets.*"

She knelt in prayer, and then lay down in bed, tucking the blankets comfortably about her, and in a few minutes her breathing showed that she was asleep. With its profoundly peaceful sighs and hesitations it resembled that of a cow standing up to its knees all night through in the long grass.

A glance into the next room revealed little more than a nose, prominent above the sheets. Growing accustomed to the darkness, for the windows were open and showed grey squares with splinters of starlight, one could distinguish a lean form, terribly like the body of a dead person, the body indeed of William Pepper, asleep too. Thirty-six, thirty-seven, thirty-eight— here were three Portuguese men of business, asleep presumably, since a snore came with the regularity of a great ticking clock. Thirty-nine was a corner room, at the end of the passage, but late though it was—"One" struck gently downstairs—a line of light under the door showed that someone was still awake.

"How late you are, Hugh!" a woman, lying in bed, said in a peevish but solicitous voice. Her husband was brushing his teeth, and for some moments did not answer.

"You should have gone to sleep," he replied. "I was talking to Thornbury."

"But you know that I never can sleep when I'm waiting for you," she said.

To that he made no answer, but only remarked, "Well then, we'll turn out the light." They were silent.

The faint but penetrating pulse of an electric bell could now be heard in the corridor. Old Mrs. Paley, having woken hungry but without her spectacles, was summoning her maid to find the biscuit-box. The maid having answered the bell, drearily respectful even at this hour though muffled in a mackintosh, the passage was left in silence. Downstairs all was empty and dark; but on the upper floor a light still burnt in the room where the boots had dropped so heavily above Miss Allan's head. Here was the gentleman who, a few hours previously, in the shade of the curtain, had seemed to consist entirely of legs. Deep in an armchair he was reading the third volume of Gibbon's *History of the Decline and Fall of Rome* by candle-light. As he read he knocked the ash automatically, now and again, from his cigarette and turned the page, while a whole procession of splendid sentences entered his capacious brow and went marching through his brain in order. It seemed likely that this process might continue for an hour or more, until the entire regiment had shifted its quarters, had not the door opened, and the young man, who was inclined to be stout, come in with large naked feet.

"Oh, Hirst, what I forgot to say was—"

"Two minutes," said Hirst, raising his finger.

He safely stowed away the last words of the paragraph.

"What was it you forgot to say?" he asked.

"D'you think you *do* make enough allowance for feelings?" asked Mr. Hewet. He had again forgotten what he had meant to say.

After intense contemplation of the immaculate Gibbon Mr. Hirst smiled at the question of his friend. He laid aside his book and considered.

"I should call yours a singularly untidy mind," he observed. "Feelings? Aren't they just what we do allow for? We put love up there, and all the rest somewhere down below." With his left hand he indicated the top of a pyramid, and with his right the base.

"But you didn't get out of bed to tell me that," he added severely.

"I got out of bed," said Hewet vaguely, "merely to talk I suppose."

"Meanwhile I shall undress," said Hirst. When naked of all but his shirt, and bent over the basin, Mr. Hirst no longer impressed one with the majesty of his intellect, but with the pathos of his young yet ugly body, for he stooped, and he was so thin that there were dark lines between the different bones of his neck and shoulders.

"Women interest me," said Hewet, who, sitting on the bed with his chin resting on his knees, paid no attention to the undressing of Mr. Hirst.

"They're so stupid," said Hirst. "You're sitting on my pyjamas."

"I suppose they *are* stupid?" Hewet wondered.

"There can't be two opinions about that, I imagine," said Hirst, hopping briskly across the room, "unless you're in love—that fat woman Warrington?" he enquired.

"Not one fat woman—all fat women," Hewet sighed.

"The women I saw tonight were not fat," said Hirst, who was taking advantage of Hewet's company to cut his toe-nails.

"Describe them," said Hewet.

"You know I can't describe things!" said Hirst. "They were much like other women, I should think. They always are."

"No; that's where we differ," said Hewet. "I say everything's different. No two people are in the least the same. Take you and me now."

"So I used to think once," said Hirst. "But now they're all types. Don't take us—take this hotel. You could draw circles round the whole lot of them, and they'd never stray outside."

("You can kill a hen by doing that"), Hewet murmured.

"Mr. Hughling Elliot, Mrs. Hughling Elliot, Miss Allan, Mr. and Mrs. Thornbury—one circle," Hirst continued. "Miss Warrington, Mr. Arthur Venning, Mr. Perrott, Evelyn M. another circle; then there are a whole lot of natives; finally ourselves."

"Are we all alone in our circle?" asked Hewet.

"Quite alone," said Hirst. "You try to get out, but you can't. You only make a mess of things by trying."

"I'm not a hen in a circle," said Hewet. "I'm a dove on a tree-top."

"I wonder if this is what they call an ingrowing toe-nail?" said Hirst, examining the big toe on his left foot.

"I flit from branch to branch," continued Hewet. "The world is profoundly pleasant." He lay back on the bed, upon his arms.

"I wonder if it's really nice to be as vague as you are?" asked Hirst, looking at him. "It's the lack of continuity—that's what's so odd bout you," he went on. "At the age of twenty-seven, which is nearly thirty, you seem to have drawn no conclusions. A party of old women excites you still as though you were three."

Hewet contemplated the angular young man who was neatly brushing the rims of his toe-nails into the fire-place in silence for a moment.

"I respect you, Hirst," he remarked.

"I envy you—some things," said Hirst. "One: your capacity for not thinking; two: people like you better than they like me. Women like you, I suppose."

"I wonder whether that isn't really what matters most?" said Hewet. Lying now flat on the bed he waved his hand in vague circles above him.

"Of course it is," said Hirst. "But that's not the difficulty. The difficulty is, isn't it, to find an appropriate object?"

"There are no female hens in your circle?" asked Hewet.

"Not the ghost of one," said Hirst.

Although they had known each other for three years Hirst had never yet heard the true story of Hewet's loves. In general conversation it was taken for granted that they were many, but in private the subject was allowed to lapse. The fact that he had money enough to do no work, and that he had left Cambridge after two terms owing to a difference with the authorities, and had then travelled and drifted, made his life strange at many points where his friends' lives were much of a piece.

"I don't see your circles—I don't see them," Hewet continued. "I see a thing like a teetotum spinning in and out—knocking into things—dashing from side to side—collecting numbers—more and more and more, till the whole place is thick with them. Round and round they go—out there, over the rim—out of sight."

His fingers showed that the waltzing teetotums had spun over the edge of the counterpane and fallen off the bed into infinity.

"Could you contemplate three weeks alone in this hotel?" asked Hirst, after a moment's pause.

Hewet proceeded to think.

"The truth of it is that one never is alone, and one never is in company," he concluded.

"Meaning?" said Hirst.

"Meaning? Oh, something about bubbles—auras—what d'you call 'em? You can't see my bubble; I can't see yours; all we see of each other is a speck, like the wick in the middle of that flame. The flame goes about with us everywhere; it's not ourselves exactly, but what we feel; the world is short, or people mainly; all kinds of people."

"A nice streaky bubble yours must be!" said Hirst.

"And supposing my bubble could run into someone else's bubble—"

"And they both burst?" put in Hirst.

"Then—then—then—" pondered Hewet, as if to himself, "it would be an e—nor—mous world," he said, stretching his arms to their full width, as though even so they could hardly clasp the billowy universe, for when he was with Hirst he always felt unusually sanguine and vague.

"I don't think you altogether as foolish as I used to, Hewet," said Hirst. "You don't know what you mean but you try to say it."

"But aren't you enjoying yourself here?" asked Hewet.

"On the whole—yes," said Hirst. "I like observing people. I like looking at things. This country is amazingly beautiful. Did you notice how the top of the mountain turned yellow tonight? Really we must take our lunch and spend the day out. You're getting disgustingly fat." He pointed at the calf of Hewet's bare leg.

"We'll get up an expedition," said Hewet energetically. "We'll ask the entire hotel. We'll hire donkeys and—"

"Oh, Lord!" said Hirst, "do shut it! I can see Miss Warrington and Miss Allan and Mrs. Elliot and the rest squatting on the stones and quacking, 'How jolly!'"

"We'll ask Venning and Perrott and Miss Murgatroyd—every one we can lay hands on," went on Hewet. "What's the name of the little old grasshopper with the eyeglasses? Pepper?—Pepper shall lead us."

"Thank God, you'll never get the donkeys," said Hirst.

"I must make a note of that," said Hewet, slowly dropping his feet to the floor. "Hirst escorts Miss Warrington; Pepper advances alone on a white ass; provisions equally distributed—or shall we hire a mule? The matrons—there's Mrs. Paley, by Jove!—share a carriage."

"That's where you'll go wrong," said Hirst. "Putting virgins among matrons."

"How long should you think that an expedition like that would take, Hirst?" asked Hewet.

"From twelve to sixteen hours I would say," said Hirst. "The time usually occupied by a first confinement."

"It will need considerable organisation," said Hewet. He was now padding softly round the room, and stopped to stir the books on the table. They lay heaped one upon another.

"We shall want some poets too," he remarked. "Not Gibbon; no; d'you happen to have *Modern Love* or *John Donne*? You see, I contemplate pauses when people get tired of looking at the view, and then it would be nice to read something rather difficult aloud."

"Mrs. Paley *will* enjoy herself," said Hirst.

"Mrs. Paley will enjoy it certainly," said Hewet. "It's one of the saddest things I know—the way elderly ladies cease to read poetry. And yet how appropriate this is:

> *I speak as one who plumbs*
> *Life's dim profound,*
> *One who at length can sound*
> *Clear views and certain.*
> *But—after love what comes?*
> *A scene that lours,*
> *A few sad vacant hours,*
> *And then, the Curtain.*

I daresay Mrs. Paley is the only one of us who can really understand that."

"We'll ask her," said Hirst. "Please, Hewet, if you must go to bed, draw my curtain. Few things distress me more than the moonlight."

Hewet retreated, pressing the poems of Thomas Hardy beneath his arm, and in their beds next door to each other both the young men were soon asleep.

Between the extinction of Hewet's candle and the rising of a dusky Spanish boy who was the first to survey the desolation of the hotel in the early morning, a few hours of silence intervened. One could almost hear a hundred people breathing deeply, and however wakeful and restless it would have been hard to escape sleep in the middle of so much sleep. Looking out of the windows, there was only darkness to be seen. All over the shadowed half of the world people lay prone, and a few flickering lights in empty streets marked the places where their cities were built. Red and yellow omnibuses were crowding each other in Piccadilly; sumptuous women were rocking at a standstill; but here in the darkness an owl flitted from tree to tree, and when the breeze lifted the branches the moon flashed as if it were a torch. Until all people should awake again the houseless animals were abroad, the tigers and the stags, and the elephants coming down in the darkness to drink at pools. The wind at night blowing over the hills and woods was purer and fresher than the wind by day, and the earth, robbed of detail, more mysterious than the earth coloured and divided by roads and fields. For six hours this profound beauty existed, and then as the east grew whiter and whiter the ground swam to the surface, the roads were revealed, the smoke rose and the people stirred, and the sun shone upon the windows of the hotel at Santa Marina until they were uncurtained, and the gong blaring all through the house gave notice of breakfast.

Directly breakfast was over, the ladies as usual circled vaguely, picking up papers and putting them down again, about the hall.

"And what are you going to do today?" asked Mrs. Elliot drifting up against Miss Warrington.

Mrs. Elliot, the wife of Hughling the Oxford Don, was a short woman, whose expression was habitually plaintive. Her eyes moved from thing to thing as though they never found anything sufficiently pleasant to rest upon for any length of time.

"I'm going to try to get Aunt Emma out into the town," said Susan. "She's not seen a thing yet."

"I call it so spirited of her at her age," said Mrs. Elliot, "coming all this way from her own fireside."

"Yes, we always tell her she'll die on board ship," Susan replied. "She was born on one," she added.

"In the old days," said Mrs. Elliot, "a great many people were. I always pity the poor women so! We've got a lot to complain of!" She shook her head. Her eyes wandered about the table, and she remarked irrelevantly, "The poor little Queen of Holland! Newspaper reporters practically, one may say, at her bedroom door!"

"Were you talking of the Queen of Holland?" said the pleasant voice of Miss Allan, who was searching for the thick pages of *The Times* among a litter of thin foreign sheets.

"I always envy anyone who lives in such an excessively flat country," she remarked.

"How very strange!" said Mrs. Elliot. "I find a flat country so depressing."

"I'm afraid you can't be very happy here then, Miss Allan," said Susan.

"On the contrary," said Miss Allan, "I am exceedingly fond of mountains." Perceiving *The Times* at some distance, she moved off to secure it.

"Well, I must find my husband," said Mrs. Elliot, fidgeting away.

"And I must go to my aunt," said Miss Warrington, and taking up the duties of the day they moved away.

Whether the flimsiness of foreign sheets and the coarseness of their type is any proof of frivolity and ignorance, there is no doubt that English people scarce consider news read there as news, any more than a programme bought from a man in the street inspires confidence in what it says. A very respectable elderly pair, having inspected the long tables of newspapers, did not think it worth their while to read more than the headlines.

"The debate on the fifteenth should have reached us by now," Mrs. Thornbury murmured. Mr. Thornbury, who was beautifully clean and had red rubbed into his handsome worn face like traces of paint on a weather-beaten wooden figure, looked over his glasses and saw that Miss Allan had *The Times*.

The couple therefore sat themselves down in armchairs and waited.

"Ah, there's Mr. Hewet," said Mrs. Thornbury. "Mr. Hewet," she continued, "do come and sit by us. I was telling my husband how much you reminded me of a dear old friend of mine—Mary Umpleby. She was a most delightful woman, I assure you. She grew roses. We used to stay with her in the old days."

"No young man likes to have it said that he resembles an elderly spinster," said Mr. Thornbury.

"On the contrary," said Mr. Hewet, "I always think it a compliment to remind people of someone else. But Miss Umpleby—why did she grow roses?"

"Ah, poor thing," said Mrs. Thornbury, "that's a long story. She had gone through dreadful sorrows. At one time I think she would have lost her senses if it hadn't been for her garden. The soil was very much against her—a blessing in disguise; she had to be up at dawn—out in all weathers. And then there are creatures that eat roses. But she triumphed. She always did. She was a brave soul." She sighed deeply but at the same time with resignation.

"I did not realise that I was monopolising the paper," said Miss Allan, coming up to them.

"We were so anxious to read about the debate," said Mrs. Thornbury, accepting it on behalf of her husband.

"One doesn't realise how interesting a debate can be until one has sons in the navy. My interests are equally balanced, though; I have sons in the army too; and one son who makes speeches at the Union—my baby!"

"Hirst would know him, I expect," said Hewet.

"Mr. Hirst has such an interesting face," said Mrs. Thornbury. "But I feel one ought to be very clever to talk to him. Well, William?" she enquired, for Mr. Thornbury grunted.

"They're making a mess of it," said Mr. Thornbury. He had reached the second column of the report, a spasmodic column, for the Irish members had been brawling three weeks ago at Westminster over a question of naval efficiency. After a disturbed paragraph or two, the column of print once more ran smoothly.

"You have read it?" Mrs. Thornbury asked Miss Allan.

"No, I am ashamed to say I have only read about the discoveries in Crete," said Miss Allan.

"Oh, but I would give so much to realise the ancient world!" cried Mrs. Thornbury. "Now that we old people are alone—we're on our second honeymoon—I am really going to put myself to school again. After all we are *founded* on the past, aren't we, Mr. Hewet? My soldier son says that there is still a great deal to be learnt from Hannibal. One ought to know so much more than one does. Somehow when I read the paper, I begin with the debates first, and, before I've done, the door always opens—we're a very large party at home—and so one never does think enough about the ancients and all they've done for us. But *you* begin at the beginning, Miss Allan."

"When I think of the Greeks I think of them as naked black men," said Miss Allan, "which is quite incorrect, I'm sure."

"And you, Mr. Hirst?" said Mrs. Thornbury, perceiving that the gaunt young man was near. "I'm sure you read everything."

"I confine myself to cricket and crime," said Hirst. "The worst of coming from the upper classes," he continued, "is that one's friends are never killed in railway accidents."

Mr. Thornbury threw down the paper, and emphatically dropped his eyeglasses. The sheets fell in the middle of the group, and were eyed by them all.

"It's not gone well?" asked his wife solicitously.

Hewet picked up one sheet and read, "A lady was walking yesterday in the streets of Westminster when she perceived a cat in the window of a deserted house. The famished animal—"

"I shall be out of it anyway," Mr. Thornbury interrupted peevishly.

"Cats are often forgotten," Miss Allan remarked.

"Remember, William, the Prime Minister has reserved his answer," said Mrs. Thornbury.

"At the age of eighty, Mr. Joshua Harris of Eeles Park, Brondesbury, has had a son," said Hirst.

". . . The famished animal, which had been noticed by workmen for some days, was rescued, but—by Jove! it bit the man's hand to pieces!"

"Wild with hunger, I suppose," commented Miss Allan.

"You're all neglecting the chief advantage of being abroad," said Mr. Hughling Elliot, who had joined the group. "You might read your news in French, which is equivalent to reading no news at all."

Mr. Elliot had a profound knowledge of Coptic, which he concealed as far as possible, and quoted French phrases so exquisitely that it was hard to believe that he could also speak the ordinary tongue. He had an immense respect for the French.

"Coming?" he asked the two young men. "We ought to start before it's really hot."

"I beg of you not to walk in the heat, Hugh," his wife pleaded, giving him an angular parcel enclosing half a chicken and some raisins.

"Hewet will be our barometer," said Mr. Elliot. "He will melt before I shall." Indeed, if so much as a drop had melted off his spare ribs, the bones would have lain bare. The ladies were left alone now, surrounding *The Times* which lay upon the floor. Miss Allan looked at her father's watch.

"Ten minutes to eleven," she observed.

"Work?" asked Mrs. Thornbury.

"Work," replied Miss Allan.

"What a fine creature she is!" murmured Mrs. Thornbury, as the square figure in its manly coat withdrew.

"And I'm sure she has a hard life," sighed Mrs. Elliot.

"Oh, it *is* a hard life," said Mrs. Thornbury. "Unmarried women—earning their livings—it's the hardest life of all."

"Yet she seems pretty cheerful," said Mrs. Elliot.

"It must be very interesting," said Mrs. Thornbury. "I envy her her knowledge."

"But that isn't what women want," said Mrs. Elliot.

"I'm afraid it's all a great many can hope to have," sighed Mrs. Thornbury.

"I believe that there are more of us than ever now. Sir Harley Lethbridge was telling me only the other day how difficult it is to find boys for the navy—partly because of their teeth, it is true. And I have heard young women talk quite openly of—"

"Dreadful, dreadful!" exclaimed Mrs. Elliot. "The crown, as one may call it, of a woman's life. I, who know what it is to be childless—" she sighed and ceased.

"But we must not be hard," said Mrs. Thornbury. "The conditions are so much changed since I was a young woman."

"Surely *maternity* does not change," said Mrs. Elliot.

"In some ways we can learn a great deal from the young," said Mrs. Thornbury. "I learn so much from my own daughters."

"I believe that Hughling really doesn't mind," said Mrs. Elliot. "But then he has his work."

"Women without children can do so much for the children of others," observed Mrs. Thornbury gently.

"I sketch a great deal," said Mrs. Elliot, "but that isn't really an occupation. It's so disconcerting to find girls just beginning doing better than one does oneself! And nature's difficult—very difficult!"

"Are there not institutions—clubs—that you could help?" asked Mrs. Thornbury.

"They are so exhausting," said Mrs. Elliot. "I look strong, because of my colour; but I'm not; the youngest of eleven never is."

"If the mother is careful before," said Mrs. Thornbury judicially, "there is no reason why the size of the family should make any difference. And there is no training like the training that brothers and sisters give each other. I am sure of that. I have seen it with my own children. My eldest boy Ralph, for instance—"

But Mrs. Elliot was inattentive to the elder lady's experience, and her eyes wandered about the hall.

"My mother had two miscarriages, I know," she said suddenly. "The first because she met one of those great dancing bears—they shouldn't be allowed; the other—it was a horrid story—our cook had a child and there was a dinner party. So I put my dyspepsia down to that."

"And a miscarriage is so much worse than a confinement," Mrs. Thornbury murmured absentmindedly, adjusting her spectacles and picking up *The Times*. Mrs. Elliot rose and fluttered away.

When she had heard what one of the million voices speaking in the paper had to say, and noticed that a cousin of hers had married a clergyman at Minehead—ignoring the drunken women, the golden animals of Crete, the movements of battalions, the dinners, the reforms, the fires, the indignant, the learned and benevolent, Mrs. Thornbury went upstairs to write a letter for the mail.

The paper lay directly beneath the clock, the two together seeming to represent stability in a changing world. Mr. Perrott passed through; Mr. Venning poised for a second on the edge of a table. Mrs. Paley was wheeled past. Susan followed. Mr. Venning strolled after her. Portuguese military families, their clothes suggesting late rising in untidy bedrooms, trailed across, attended by confidential nurses carrying noisy children. As midday drew on, and the sun beat straight upon the roof, an eddy of great flies droned in a circle; iced drinks were served under the palms; the long blinds were pulled down with a shriek, turning all the light yellow. The clock now had a silent hall to tick in, and an audience of four or five somnolent merchants. By degrees white figures with shady hats came in at the door, admitting a wedge of the hot summer day, and shutting it out again. After resting in the dimness for a minute, they went upstairs. Simultaneously, the clock wheezed one, and the gong sounded, beginning softly, working itself into a frenzy, and ceasing. There was a pause. Then all those who had gone upstairs came down; cripples came, planting both feet on the same step lest they should slip; prim little girls came, holding the nurse's finger; fat old men came still buttoning waistcoats. The gong had been sounded in the garden, and by degrees recumbent figures rose and strolled in to eat, since the time had come for them to feed again. There were pools and bars of shade in the garden even at midday, where two or three visitors could lie working or talking at their ease.

Owing to the heat of the day, luncheon was generally a silent meal, when people observed their neighbors and took stock of any new faces there might be, hazarding guesses as to who they were and what they did. Mrs. Paley, although well over seventy and crippled in the legs, enjoyed her food and the peculiarities of her fellow-beings. She was seated at a small table with Susan.

"I shouldn't like to say what *she* is!" she chuckled, surveying a tall woman dressed conspicuously in white, with paint in the hollows of her cheeks, who was always late, and always attended by a shabby female follower, at which remark Susan blushed, and wondered why her aunt said such things.

Lunch went on methodically, until each of the seven courses was left in fragments and the fruit was merely a toy, to be peeled and sliced as a child destroys a daisy, petal by petal. The food served as an extinguisher upon any faint flame of the human spirit that might survive the midday heat, but Susan sat in her room afterwards, turning over and over the delightful fact that Mr. Venning had come to her in the garden, and had sat there quite half an hour while she read aloud to her aunt. Men and women sought different corners where they could lie unobserved, and from two to four it might be said without exaggeration that the hotel was inhabited by bodies without souls. Disastrous would have been the result if a fire or a death had suddenly demanded something heroic of human nature, but tragedies come in the hungry hours. Towards four o'clock the human spirit again began to lick the body, as a flame licks a black promontory of coal. Mrs. Paley felt it unseemly to open her toothless jaw so widely, though there was no one near, and Mrs. Elliot surveyed her found flushed face anxiously in the looking-glass.

Half an hour later, having removed the traces of sleep, they met each other in the hall, and Mrs. Paley observed that she was going to have her tea.

"You like your tea too, don't you?" she said, and invited Mrs. Elliot, whose husband was still out, to join her at a special table which she had placed for her under a tree.

"A little silver goes a long way in this country," she chuckled.

She sent Susan back to fetch another cup.

"They have such excellent biscuits here," she said, contemplating a plateful. "Not sweet biscuits, which I don't like—dry biscuits . . . Have you been sketching?"

"Oh, I've done two or three little daubs," said Mrs. Elliot, speaking rather louder than usual. "But it's so difficult after Oxfordshire, where there are so many trees. The light's so strong here. Some people admire it, I know, but I find it very fatiguing."

"I really don't need cooking, Susan," said Mrs. Paley, when her niece returned. "I must trouble you to move me." Everything had to be moved. Finally the old lady was placed so that the light wavered over her, as though she were a fish in a net. Susan poured out tea, and was just remarking that they were having hot weather in Wiltshire too, when Mr. Venning asked whether he might join them.

"It's so nice to find a young man who doesn't despise tea," said Mrs. Paley, regaining her good humour. "One of my nephews the other day asked for a glass of sherry—at five o'clock! I told him he could get it at the public house round the corner, but not in my drawing room."

"I'd rather go without lunch than tea," said Mr. Venning. "That's not strictly true. I want both."

Mr. Venning was a dark young man, about thirty-two years of age, very slapdash and confident in his manner, although at this moment obviously a little excited. His friend Mr. Perrott was a barrister, and as Mr. Perrott refused to go anywhere without Mr. Venning it was necessary, when Mr. Perrott came to Santa Marina about a Company, for Mr. Venning to come too. He was a barrister also, but he loathed a profession which kept him indoors over books, and directly his widowed mother died he was going, so he confided to Susan, to take up flying seriously, and become partner in a large business for making aeroplanes. The talk rambled on. It dealt, of course, with the beauties and singularities of the place, the streets, the people, and the quantities of unowned yellow dogs.

"Don't you think it dreadfully cruel the way they treat dogs in this country?" asked Mrs. Paley.

"I'd have 'em all shot," said Mr. Venning.

"Oh, but the darling puppies," said Susan.

"Jolly little chaps," said Mr. Venning. "Look here, you've got nothing to eat." A great wedge of cake was handed Susan on the point of a trembling knife. Her hand trembled too as she took it.

"I have such a dear dog at home," said Mrs. Elliot.

"My parrot can't stand dogs," said Mrs. Paley, with the air of one making a confidence. "I always suspect that he (or she) was teased by a dog when I was abroad."

"You didn't get far this morning, Miss Warrington," said Mr. Venning.

"It was hot," she answered. Their conversation became private, owing to Mrs. Paley's deafness and the long sad history which Mrs. Elliot had embarked upon of a wire-haired terrier, white with just one black spot, belonging to an uncle of hers, which had committed suicide. "Animals do commit suicide," she sighed, as if she asserted a painful fact.

"Couldn't we explore the town this evening?" Mr. Venning suggested.

"My aunt—" Susan began.

"You deserve a holiday," he said. "You're always doing things for other people."

"But that's my life," she said, under cover of refilling the teapot.

"That's no one's life," he returned, "no young person's. You'll come?"

"I should like to come," she murmured.

At this moment Mrs. Elliot looked up and exclaimed, "Oh, Hugh! He's bringing someone," she added.

"He would like some tea," said Mrs. Paley. "Susan, run and get some cups—there are the two young men."

"We're thirsting for tea," said Mr. Elliot. "You know Mr. Ambrose, Hilda? We met on the hill."

"He dragged me in," said Ridley, "or I should have been ashamed. I'm dusty and dirty and disagreeable." He pointed to his boots which were white with dust, while a dejected flower drooping in his buttonhole, like an exhausted animal over a gate, added to the effect of length and untidiness. He was introduced to the others. Mr. Hewet and Mr. Hirst brought chairs, and tea began again, Susan pouring cascades of water from pot to pot, always cheerfully, and with the competence of long use.

"My wife's brother," Ridley explained to Hilda, whom he failed to remember, "has a house here, which he has lent us. I was sitting on a rock thinking of nothing at all when Elliot started up like a fairy in a pantomime."

"Our chicken got into the salt," Hewet said dolefully to Susan. "Nor is it true that bananas include moisture as well as sustenance."

Hirst was already drinking.

"We've been cursing you," said Ridley in answer to Mrs. Elliot's kind enquiries about his wife. "You tourists eat up all the eggs, Helen tells me. That's an eye-sore too"—he nodded his head at the hotel. "Disgusting luxury, I call it. We live with pigs in the drawing-room."

"The food is not at all what it ought to be, considering the price," said Mrs. Paley seriously. "But unless one goes to a hotel where is one to go to?"

"Stay at home," said Ridley. "I often wish I had! Everyone ought to stay at home. But, of course, they won't."

Mrs. Paley conceived a certain grudge against Ridley, who seemed to be criticising her habits after an acquaintance of five minutes.

"I believe in foreign travel myself," she stated, "if one knows one's native land, which I think I can honestly say I do. I should not allow anyone to travel until they had visited Kent and Dorsetshire—Kent for the hops, and Dorsetshire for its old stone cottages. There is nothing to compare with them here."

"Yes—I always think that some people like the flat and other people like the downs," said Mrs. Elliot rather vaguely.

Hirst, who had been eating and drinking without interruption, now lit a cigarette, and observed, "Oh, but we're all agreed by this time that nature's a mistake. She's either very ugly, appallingly uncomfortable, or absolutely terrifying. I don't know which alarms me most—a cow or a tree. I once met a cow in a field by night. The creature looked at me. I assure you it turned my hair grey. It's a disgrace that the animals should be allowed to go at large."

"And what did the cow think of *him*?" Venning mumbled to Susan, who immediately decided in her own mind that Mr. Hirst was a dreadful young man, and that although he had such an air of being clever he probably wasn't as clever as Arthur, in the ways that really matter.

"Wasn't it Wilde who discovered the fact that nature makes no allowance for hip-bones?" enquired Hughling Elliot. He knew by this time exactly what scholarships and distinction Hirst enjoyed, and had formed a very high opinion of his capacities.

But Hirst merely drew his lips together very tightly and made no reply.

Ridley conjectured that it was now permissible for him to take his leave.

Politeness required him to thank Mrs. Elliot for his tea, and to add, with a wave of his hand, "You must come up and see us."

The wave included both Hirst and Hewet, and Hewet answered, "I should like it immensely."

The party broke up, and Susan, who had never felt so happy in her life, was just about to start for her walk in the town with Arthur, when Mrs. Paley beckoned her back. She could not understand from the book how Double Demon patience is played; and suggested that if they sat down and worked it out together it would fill up the time nicely before dinner.

CHAPTER X

A mong the promises which Mrs. Ambrose had made her niece should she stay was a room cut off from the rest of the house, large, private—a room in which she could play, read, think, defy the world, a fortress as well as a sanctuary. Rooms, she knew, became more like worlds than rooms at the age of twenty-four. Her judgment was correct, and when she shut the door Rachel entered an enchanted place, where the poets sang and things fell into their right proportions. Some days after the vision of the hotel by night she was sitting alone, sunk in an armchair, reading a brightly-covered red volume lettered on the back *Works of Henrik Ibsen*. Music was open on the piano, and books of music rose in two jagged pillars on the floor; but for the moment music was deserted.

Far from looking bored or absent-minded, her eyes were concentrated almost sternly upon the page, and from her breathing, which was slow but repressed, it could be seen that her whole body was constrained by the working of her mind. At last she shut the book sharply, lay back, and drew a deep breath, expressive of the wonder which always marks the transition from the imaginary world to the real world.

"What I want to know," she said aloud, "is this: What is the truth? What's the truth of it all?" She was speaking partly as herself, and partly as the heroine of the play she had just read. The landscape outside, because she had seen nothing but print for the space of two hours, now appeared amazingly solid and clear, but although there were men on the hill washing the trunks of olive trees with a white liquid, for the moment she herself was the most vivid thing in it—an heroic statue in the middle of the foreground, dominating the view. Ibsen's plays always left her in that condition. She acted them for days at a time, greatly to Helen's amusement; and then it would be Meredith's turn and she became Diana of the Crossways. But Helen was aware that it was not all acting, and that some sort of change was taking place in the human being. When Rachel became tired of the rigidity of her pose on the back of the chair, she turned round, slid comfortably down into it, and gazed out over the furniture through the window opposite which opened on the garden. (Her mind wandered away from Nora, but she went on thinking of things that the book suggested to her, of women and life.)

During the three months she had been here she had made up considerably, as Helen meant she should, for time spent in interminable walks round sheltered gardens, and the household gossip of her aunts. But Mrs. Ambrose would have been the first to disclaim any influence, or indeed any belief that to influence was within her power. She saw her less shy, and less serious, which was all to the good, and the violent leaps and the interminable mazes which had led to that result were usually not even guessed at by her. Talk was the medicine she trusted to, talk about everything, talk that was free, unguarded, and as candid as a habit of talking with men made natural in her own case. Nor did she encourage those habits of unselfishness and amiability founded upon insincerity which are put at so high a value in mixed households of men and women. She desired that Rachel should think, and for this reason offered books and discouraged too entire a dependence upon Bach and Beethoven and Wagner. But when Mrs. Ambrose would have suggested Defoe, Maupassant, or some spacious chronicle of family life, Rachel chose modern books, books in shiny yellow covers, books with a great deal of gilding on the back, which were tokens in her aunt's eyes of harsh wrangling and disputes about facts which had no such importance as the moderns claimed for them. But she did not interfere. Rachel read what she chose, reading with the curious literalness of one to whom written sentences are unfamiliar, and handling words as though they were made of wood, separately of great importance, and possessed of shapes like tables or chairs. In this way she came to conclusions, which had to be remodelled according to the adventures of the day, and were indeed recast as liberally as anyone could desire, leaving always a small grain of belief behind them.

Ibsen was succeeded by a novel such as Mrs. Ambrose detested, whose purpose was to distribute the guilt of a woman's downfall upon the right shoulders; a purpose which was achieved, if the reader's discomfort were any proof of it. She threw the book down, looked out of the window, turned away from the window, and relapsed into an armchair.

The morning was hot, and the exercise of reading left her mind contracting and expanding like the main-spring of a clock, and the small noises of midday, which one can ascribe to no definite cause, in a regular rhythm. It was all very real, very big, very impersonal, and after a moment or two she began to raise her first finger and to let it fall on the arm of her chair so as to bring back to herself some consciousness of her own existence. She was next overcome by the unspeakable queerness of the fact that she should be sitting in an armchair, in the morning, in the middle of the world. Who were the people moving in the house—moving things from one place to another? And life, what was that? It was only a light passing over the surface and vanishing, as in time she would vanish, though the furniture in the room would remain. Her dissolution became so complete that she could not raise her finger any more, and sat perfectly still, listening and looking always at the same spot. It became stranger and stranger. She was overcome with awe that things should exist at all . . . She forgot that she had any fingers to raise . . . The things that existed were so immense and so desolate . . . She continued to be conscious of these vast masses of substance for a long stretch of time, the clock still ticking in the midst of the universal silence.

"Come in," she said mechanically, for a string in her brain seemed to be pulled by a persistent knocking at the door. With great slowness the door opened and a tall human being came towards her, holding out her arm and saying:

"What am I to say to this?"

The utter absurdity of a woman coming into a room with a piece of paper in her hand amazed Rachel.

"I don't know what to answer, or who Terence Hewet is," Helen continued, in the toneless voice of a ghost. She put a paper before Rachel on which were written the incredible words:

> Dear Mrs. Ambrose:
>
> I am getting up a picnic for next Friday, when we propose to start at eleven-thirty if the weather is fine, and to make the ascent of Monte Rosa. It will take some time, but the view should be magnificent. It would give me great pleasure if you and Miss Vinrace would consent to be of the party.
>
> Yours sincerely,
> Terence Hewet

Rachel read the words aloud to make herself believe in them. For the same reason she put her hand on Helen's shoulder.

"Books—books—books," said Helen, in her absent-minded way. "More new books—I wonder what you find in them . . ."

For the second time Rachel read the letter, but to herself. This time, instead of seeming vague as ghosts, each word was astonishingly prominent; they came out as the tops of mountains come through a mist. *Friday—eleven-thirty—Miss Vinrace.* The blood began to run in her veins; she felt her eyes brighten.

"We must go," she said, rather surprising Helen by her decision. "We must certainly go"—such was the relief of finding that things still happened, and indeed they appeared the brighter for the mist surrounding them.

"Monte Rosa—that's the mountain over there, isn't it?" said Helen; "but Hewet—who's he? One of the young men Ridley met, I suppose. Shall I say yes, then? It may be dreadfully dull."

She took the letter back and went, for the messenger was waiting for her answer.

The party which had been suggested a few nights ago in Mr. Hirst's bedroom had taken shape and was the source of great satisfaction to Mr. Hewet, who had seldom used his practical abilities, and was pleased to find them equal to the strain. His invitations had been universally accepted, which was the more encouraging as they had been issued against Hirst's advice to people who were very dull, not at all suited to each other, and sure not to come.

"Undoubtedly," he said, as he twirled and untwirled a note signed Helen Ambrose, "the gifts needed to make a great commander have been absurdly overrated. About half the intellectual effort which is needed to review a book of modern poetry has enabled me to get together seven or eight people, of opposite sexes, at the same spot at the same hour on the same day. What else is generalship, Hirst? What more did Wellington do on the field of Waterloo? It's like counting the number of pebbles of a path, tedious but not difficult."

He was sitting in his bedroom, one leg over the arm of the chair, and Hirst was writing a letter opposite. Hirst was quick to point out that all the difficulties remained.

"For instance, here are two women you've never seen. Suppose one of them suffers from mountain-sickness, as my sister does, and the other—"

"Oh, the women are for you," Hewet interrupted. "I asked them solely for your benefit. What you want, Hirst, you know, is the society of young women of your own age. You don't know how to get on with women, which is a great defect, considering that half the world consists of women."

Hirst groaned that he was quite aware of that.

But Hewet's complacency was a little chilled as he walked with Hirst to the place where a general meeting had been appointed. He wondered why on earth he had asked these people, and what one really expected to get from bunching human beings up together.

"Cows," he reflected, "draw together in a field; ships in a calm; and we're just the same when we've nothing else to do. But why do we do it?—is it to prevent ourselves from seeing to the bottom of things" (he stopped by a stream and began stirring it with his walking-stick and clouding the water with mud), "making cities and mountains and whole universes out of nothing, or do we really love each other, or do we, on the other hand, live in a state of perpetual uncertainty, knowing nothing, leaping from moment to moment as from world to world?—which is, on the whole, the view *I* incline to."

He jumped over the stream; Hirst went round and joined him, remarking that he had long ceased to look for the reason of any human action.

Half a mile further, they came to a group of plane trees and the salmon-pink farmhouse standing by the stream which had been chosen as meeting-place. It was a shady spot, lying conveniently just where the hill sprung out from the flat. Between the thin stems of the plane trees the young men could see little knots of donkeys pasturing, and a tall woman rubbing the nose of one of them, while another woman was kneeling by the stream lapping water out of her palms.

As they entered the shady place, Helen looked up and then held out her hand. "I must introduce myself," she said. "I am Mrs. Ambrose."

Having shaken hands, she said, "That's my niece."

Rachel approached awkwardly. She held out her hand, but withdrew it. "It's all wet," she said.

Scarcely had they spoken, when the first carriage drew up.

The donkeys were quickly jerked into attention, and the second carriage arrived. By degrees the grove filled with people—the Elliots, the Thornburys, Mr. Venning and Susan, Miss Allan, Evelyn Murgatroyd, and Mr. Perrott. Mr. Hirst acted the part of hoarse energetic sheep-dog. By means of a few words of caustic Latin he had the animals marshalled, and by inclining a sharp shoulder he lifted the ladies. "What Hewet fails to understand," he remarked, "is that we must break the back of the ascent before midday." He was assisting a young lady, by name Evelyn Murgatroyd, as he spoke. She rose light as a bubble to her seat. With a feather drooping from a broad-brimmed hat, in white from top to toe, she looked like a gallant lady of the time of Charles the First leading royalist troops into action.

"Ride with me," she commanded; and, as soon as Hirst had swung himself across a mule, the two started, leading the cavalcade.

"You're not to call me Miss Murgatroyd. I hate it," she said. "My name's Evelyn. What's yours?"

"St. John," he said.

"I like that," said Evelyn. "And what's your friend's name?"

"His initials being R. S. T., we call him Monk," said Hirst.

"Oh, you're all too clever," she said. "Which way? Pick me a branch. Let's canter."

She gave her donkey a sharp cut with a switch and started forward. The full and romantic career of Evelyn Murgatroyd is best hit off by her own words, "Call me Evelyn and I'll call you St. John." She said that on very slight provocation—her surname was enough—but although a great many young men had answered her already with considerable spirit she went on saying it and making choice of none. But her donkey stumbled to a jog-trot, and she had to ride in advance alone, for the path when it began to ascend one of the spines of the hill became narrow and scattered with stones. The cavalcade wound on like a jointed caterpillar, tufted with the white parasols of the ladies, and the panama hats of the gentlemen. At one point where the ground rose sharply, Evelyn M. jumped off, threw her reins to the native boy, and adjured St. John Hirst to dismount too. Their example was followed by those who felt the need of stretching.

"I don't see any need to get off," said Miss Allan to Mrs. Elliot just behind her, "considering the difficulty I had getting on."

"These little donkeys stand anything, *n'est-ce pas?*" Mrs. Elliot addressed the guide, who obligingly bowed his head.

"Flowers," said Helen, stooping to pick the lovely little bright flowers which grew separately here and there. "You pinch their leaves and then they smell," she said, laying one on Miss Allan's knee.

"Haven't we met before?" asked Miss Allan, looking at her.

"I was taking it for granted," Helen laughed, for in the confusion of meeting they had not been introduced.

"How sensible!" chirped Mrs. Elliot. "That's just what one would always like—only unfortunately it's not possible."

"Not possible?" said Helen. "Everything's possible. Who knows what mayn't happen before night-fall?" she continued, mocking the poor lady's timidity, who depended implicitly upon one thing following another that the mere glimpse of a world where dinner could be disregarded, or the table moved one inch from its accustomed place, filled her with fears for her own stability.

Higher and higher they went, becoming separated from the world. The world, when they turned to look back, flattened itself out, and was marked with squares of thin green and grey.

"Towns are very small," Rachel remarked, obscuring the whole of Santa Marina and its suburbs with one hand. The sea filled in all the angles of the coast smoothly, breaking in a white frill, and here and there ships were set firmly in the blue. The sea was stained with purple and green blots, and there was a glittering line upon the rim where it met the sky. The air was very clear and silent save for the sharp noise of grasshoppers and the hum of bees, which sounded loud in the ear as they shot past and vanished. The party halted and sat for a time in a quarry on the hillside.

"Amazingly clear," exclaimed St. John, identifying one cleft in the land after another.

Evelyn M. sat beside him, propping her chin on her hand. She surveyed the view with a certain look of triumph.

"D'you think Garibaldi was ever up here?" she asked Mr. Hirst. Oh, if she had been his bride! If, instead of a picnic party, this was a party of patriots, and she, red-shirted like the rest, had lain among grim men, flat on the turf, aiming her gun at the white turrets beneath them, screening her eyes to pierce through the smoke! So thinking, her foot stirred restlessly, and she exclaimed:

"I don't call this *life*, do you?"

"What do you call life?" said St. John.

"Fighting—revolution," she said, still gazing at the doomed city. "You only care for books, I know."

"You're quite wrong," said St. John.

"Explain," she urged, for there were no guns to be aimed at bodies, and she turned to another kind of warfare.

"What do I care for? People," he said.

"Well, I *am* surprised!" she exclaimed. "You look so awfully serious. Do let's be friends and tell each other what we're like. I hate being cautious, don't you?"

But St. John was decidedly cautious, as she could see by the sudden constriction of his lips, and had no intention of revealing his soul to a young lady. "The ass is eating my hat," he remarked, and stretched out for it instead of answering her. Evelyn blushed very slightly and then turned with some impetuosity upon Mr. Perrott, and when they mounted again it was Mr. Perrott who lifted her to her seat.

"When one has laid the eggs one eats the omelette," said Hughling Elliot, exquisitely in French, a hint to the rest of them that it was time to ride on again.

The midday sun which Hirst had foretold was beginning to beat down hotly. The higher they got the more of the sky appeared, until the mountain was only a small tent of earth against an enormous blue background. The English fell silent; the natives who walked beside the donkeys broke into queer wavering songs and tossed jokes from one to the other. The way grew very steep, and each rider kept his eyes fixed on the hobbling curved form of the rider and donkey directly in front of him. Rather more strain was being put upon their bodies than is quite legitimate in a party of pleasure, and Hewet overheard one or two slightly grumbling remarks.

"Expeditions in such heat are perhaps a little unwise," Mrs. Elliot murmured to Miss Allan.

But Miss Allan returned, "I always like to get to the top"; and it was true, although she was a big woman, stiff in the joints, and unused to donkey-riding, but as her holidays were few she made the most of them.

The vivacious white figure rode well in front; she had somehow possessed herself of a leafy branch and wore it round her hat like a garland. They went on for a few minutes in silence.

"The view will be wonderful," Hewet assured them, turning round in his saddle and smiling encouragement. Rachel caught his eye and smiled too. They struggled on for some time longer, nothing being heard but the clatter of hooves striving on the loose stones. Then they saw that Evelyn was off her ass, and that Mr. Perrott was standing in the attitude of a statesman in Parliament Square, stretching an arm of stone towards the view. A little to the left of them was a low ruined wall, the stump of an Elizabethan watchtower.

"I couldn't have stood it much longer," Mrs. Elliot confided to Mrs. Thornbury, but the excitement of being at the top in another moment and seeing the view prevented anyone from answering her. One after another they came out on the flat space at the top and stood overcome with wonder. Before them they beheld an immense space—grey sands running into forest, and forest merging in mountains, and mountains washed by air, the infinite distances of South America. A river ran across the plain, as flat as the land, and appearing quite as stationary. The effect of so much space was at first rather chilling. They felt themselves very small, and for some time no one said anything. Then Evelyn exclaimed, "Splendid!" She took hold of the hand that was next her; it chanced to be Miss Allan's hand.

"North—South—East—West," said Miss Allan, jerking her head slightly towards the points of the compass.

Hewet, who had gone a little in front, looked up at his guests as if to justify himself for having brought them. He observed how strangely the people standing in a row with their figures bent slightly forward and their clothes plastered by the wind to the shape of their bodies resembled naked statues. On their pedestal of earth they looked unfamiliar and noble, but in another moment they had broken their rank, and he had to see to the laying out of food. Hirst came to his help, and they handed packets of chicken and bread from one to another.

As St. John gave Helen her packet she looked him full in the face and said: "Do you remember—two women?"

He looked at her sharply.

"I do," he answered.

"So you're the two women!" Hewet exclaimed, looking from Helen to Rachel.

"Your lights tempted us," said Helen. "We watched you playing cards, but we never knew that we were being watched."

"It was like a thing in a play," Rachel added.

"And Hirst couldn't describe you," said Hewet.

It was certainly odd to have seen Helen and to find nothing to say about her.

Hughling Elliot put up his eyeglass and grasped the situation.

"I don't know of anything more dreadful," he said, pulling at the joint of a chicken's leg, "than being seen when one isn't conscious of it. One feels sure one has been caught doing something ridiculous—looking at one's tongue in a hansom, for instance."

Now the others ceased to look at the view, and drawing together sat down in a circle round the baskets.

"And yet those little looking-glasses in hansoms have a fascination of their own," said Mrs. Thornbury. "One's features look so different when one can only see a bit of them."

"There will soon be very few hansom cabs left," said Mrs. Elliot. "And four-wheeled cabs—I assure you even at Oxford it's almost impossible to get a four-wheeled cab."

"I wonder what happens to the horses," said Susan.

"Veal pie," said Arthur.

"It's high time that horses should become extinct anyhow," said Hirst. "They're distressingly ugly, besides being vicious."

But Susan, who had been brought up to understand that the horse is the noblest of God's creatures, could not agree, and Venning thought Hirst an unspeakable ass, but was too polite not to continue the conversation.

"When they see us falling out of aeroplanes they get some of their own back, I expect," he remarked.

"You fly?" said old Mr. Thornbury, putting on his spectacles to look at him.

"I hope to, some day," said Arthur.

Here flying was discussed at length, and Mrs. Thornbury delivered an opinion which was almost a speech to the effect that it would be quite necessary in time of war, and in England we were terribly behind-hand. "If I were a young fellow," she concluded, "I should certainly qualify." It was odd to look at the little elderly lady, in her grey coat and skirt, with a sandwich in her hand, her eyes lighting up with zeal as she imagined herself a young man in an aeroplane. For some reason, however, the talk did not run easily after this, and all they said was about drink and salt and the view. Suddenly Miss Allan, who was seated with her back to the ruined wall, put down her sandwich, picked something off her neck, and remarked, "I'm covered with little creatures." It was true, and the discovery was very welcome. The ants were pouring down a glacier of loose earth heaped between the stones of the ruin—large brown ants with polished bodies. She held out one on the back of her hand for Helen to look at.

"Suppose they sting?" said Helen.

"They will not sting, but they may infest the victuals," said Miss Allan, and measures were taken at once to divert the ants from their course. At Hewet's suggestion it was decided to adopt the methods of modern warfare against an invading army. The table-cloth represented the invaded country, and round it they built barricades of baskets, set up the wine bottles in a rampart, made fortifications of bread and dug fosses of salt. When an ant got through it was exposed to a fire of bread-crumbs, until Susan pronounced that that was cruel, and rewarded those brave spirits with spoil in the shape of tongue. Playing this game they lost their stiffness, and even became unusually daring, for Mr. Perrott, who was very shy, said, "Permit me," and removed an ant from Evelyn's neck.

"It would be no laughing matter really," said Mrs. Elliot confidentially to Mrs. Thornbury, "if an ant did get between the vest and the skin."

The noise grew suddenly more clamorous, for it was discovered that a long line of ants had found their way on to the table-cloth by a back entrance, and if success could be gauged by noise, Hewet had every reason to think his party a success. Nevertheless he became, for no reason at all, profoundly depressed.

"They are not satisfactory; they are ignoble," he thought, surveying his guests from a little distance, where he was gathering together the plates. He glanced at them all, stooping and swaying and gesticulating round the table-cloth. Amiable and modest, respectable in many ways, lovable even in their contentment and desire to be kind, how mediocre they all were, and capable of what insipid cruelty to one another! There was Mrs. Thornbury, sweet but trivial in her maternal egoism; Mrs. Elliot, perpetually complaining of her lot; her husband a mere pea in a pod; and Susan—she had no self, and counted neither one way nor the other; Venning was as honest and as brutal as a schoolboy; poor old Thornbury merely trod his round like a horse in a mill; and the less one examined into Evelyn's character the better, he suspected. Yet these were the people with money, and to them rather than to others was given the management of the world. Put among them someone more vital, who cared for life or for beauty, and what an agony, what a waste would they inflict on him if he tried to share with them and not to scourge!

"There's Hirst," he concluded, coming to the figure of his friend; with his usual little frown of concentration upon his forehead he was peeling the skin off a banana. "And he's as ugly as sin." For the ugliness of St. John Hirst, and the limitations that went with it, he made the rest in some way responsible. It was their fault that he had to live alone. Then he came to Helen, attracted to her by the sound of her laugh. She was laughing at Miss Allan. "You wear combinations in this heat?" she said in a voice which was meant to be private. He liked the look of her immensely, not so much her beauty, but her largeness and simplicity, which made her stand out from the rest like a great stone woman, and he passed on in a gentler mood. His eye fell upon Rachel. She was lying back rather behind the others resting on one elbow; she might have been thinking precisely the same thoughts as Hewet himself. Her eyes were fixed rather sadly but not intently upon the row of people opposite her. Hewet crawled up to her on his knees, with a piece of bread in his hand.

"What are you looking at?" he asked.

She was a little startled, but answered directly, "Human beings."

CHAPTER XI

One after another they rose and stretched themselves, and in a few minutes divided more or less into two separate parties. One of these parties was dominated by Hughling Elliot and Mrs. Thornbury, who, having both read the same books and considered the same questions, were now anxious to name the places beneath them and to hang upon them stores of information about navies and armies, political parties, natives and mineral products—all of which combined, they said, to prove that South America was the country of the future.

Evelyn M. listened with her bright blue eyes fixed upon the oracles.

"How it makes one long to be a man!" she exclaimed.

Mr. Perrott answered, surveying the plain, that a country with a future was a very fine thing.

"If I were you," said Evelyn, turning to him and drawing her glove vehemently through her fingers, "I'd raise a troop and conquer some great territory and make it splendid. You'd want women for that. I'd love to start life from the very beginning as it ought to be—nothing squalid—but great halls and gardens and splendid men and women. But you—you only like Law Courts!"

"And would you really be content without pretty frocks and sweets and all the things young ladies like?" asked Mr. Perrott, concealing a certain amount of pain beneath his ironical manner.

"I'm not a young lady," Evelyn flashed; she bit her underlip. "Just because I like splendid things you laugh at me. Why are there no men like Garibaldi now?" she demanded.

"Look here," said Mr. Perrott, "you don't give me a chance. You think we ought to begin things fresh. Good. But I don't see precisely—conquer a territory? They're all conquered already, aren't they?"

"It's not any territory in particular," Evelyn explained. "It's the idea, don't you see? We lead such tame lives. And I feel sure you've got splendid things in you."

Hewet saw the scars and hollows in Mr. Perrott's sagacious face relax pathetically. He could imagine the calculations which even then went on within his mind, as to whether he would be justified in asking a woman to marry him, considering that he made no more than five hundred a year at the Bar, owned no private means, and had an invalid sister to support. Mr. Perrott again knew that he was not "quite," as Susan stated in her diary; not quite a gentleman she meant, for he was the son of a grocer in Leeds, had started life with a basket on his back, and now, though practically indistinguishable from a born gentleman, showed his origin to keen eyes in an impeccable neatness of dress, lack of freedom in manner, extreme cleanliness of person, and a certain indescribable timidity and precision with his knife and fork which might be the relic of days when meat was rare, and the way of handling it by no means gingerly.

The two parties who were strolling about and losing their unity now came together, and joined each other in a long stare over the yellow and green patches of the heated landscape below. The hot air danced across it, making it impossible to see the roofs of a village on the plain distinctly. Even on the top of the mountain where a breeze played lightly, it was very hot, and the heat, the food, the immense space, and perhaps some less well-defined cause produced a comfortable drowsiness and a sense of happy relaxation in them. They did not say much, but felt no constraint in being silent.

"Suppose we go and see what's to be seen over there?" said Arthur to Susan, and the pair walked off together, their departure certainly sending some thrill of emotion through the rest.

"An odd lot, aren't they?" said Arthur. "I thought we should never get 'em all to the top. But I'm glad we came, by Jove! I wouldn't have missed this for something."

"I don't *like* Mr. Hirst," said Susan inconsequently. "I suppose he's very clever, but why should clever people be so—I expect he's awfully nice, really," she added, instinctively qualifying what might have seemed an unkind remark.

"Hirst? Oh, he's one of these learned chaps," said Arthur indifferently. "He don't look as if he enjoyed it. You should hear him talking to Elliot. It's as much as I can do to follow 'em at all . . . I was never good at my books."

With these sentences and the pauses that came between them they reached a little hillock, on the top of which grew several slim trees.

"D'you mind if we sit down here?" said Arthur, looking about him. "It's jolly in the shade—and the view—" They sat down, and looked straight ahead of them in silence for some time.

"But I do envy those clever chaps sometimes," Arthur remarked. "I don't suppose they ever . . ." He did not finish his sentence.

"I can't see why you should envy them," said Susan, with great sincerity.

"Odd things happen to one," said Arthur. "One goes along smoothly enough, one thing following another, and it's all very jolly and plain sailing, and you think you know all about it, and suddenly one doesn't know where one is a bit, and everything seems different from what it used to seem. Now today, coming up that path, riding behind you, I seemed to see everything as if—" he paused and plucked a piece of grass up by the roots. He scattered the little lumps of earth which were sticking to the roots—"As if it had a kind of meaning. You've made the difference to me," he jerked out, "I don't see why I shouldn't tell you. I've felt it ever since I knew you . . . It's because I love you."

Even while they had been saying commonplace things Susan had been conscious of the excitement of intimacy, which seemed not only to lay bare something in her, but in the trees and the sky, and the progress of his speech which seemed inevitable was positively painful to her, for no human being had ever come so close to her before.

She was struck motionless as his speech went on, and her heart gave great separate leaps at the last words. She sat with her fingers curled round a stone, looking straight in front of her down the mountain over the plain. So then, it had actually happened to her, a proposal of marriage.

Arthur looked round at her; his face was oddly twisted. She was drawing her breath with such difficulty that she could hardly answer.

"You might have known." He seized her in his arms; again and again and again they clasped each other, murmuring inarticulately.

"Well," sighed Arthur, sinking back on the ground, "that's the most wonderful thing that's ever happened to me." He looked as if he were trying to put things seen in a dream beside real things.

There was a long silence.

"It's the most perfect thing in the world," Susan stated, very gently and with great conviction. It was no longer merely a proposal of marriage, but of marriage with Arthur, with whom she was in love.

In the silence that followed, holding his hand tightly in hers, she prayed to God that she might make him a good wife.

"And what will Mr. Perrott say?" she asked at the end of it.

"Dear old fellow," said Arthur who, now that the first shock was over, was relaxing into an enormous sense of pleasure and contentment. "We must be very nice to him, Susan."

He told her how hard Perrott's life had been, and how absurdly devoted he was to Arthur himself. He went on to tell her about his mother, a widow lady, of strong character. In return Susan sketched the portraits of her own family—Edith in particular, her youngest sister, whom she loved better than anyone else, "except you, Arthur . . . Arthur," she continued, "what was it that you first liked me for?"

"It was a buckle you wore one night at sea," said Arthur, after due consideration. "I remember noticing—it's an absurd thing to notice!—that you didn't take peas, because I don't either."

From this they went on to compare their more serious tastes, or rather Susan ascertained what Arthur cared about, and professed herself very fond of the same thing. They would live in London, perhaps have a cottage in the country near Susan's family, for they would find it strange without her at first. Her mind, stunned to begin with, now flew to the various changes that her engagement would make—how delightful it would be to join the ranks of the married women—no longer to hang on to groups of girls much younger than herself—to escape the long solitude of an old maid's life. Now and then her amazing good fortune overcame her, and she turned to Arthur with an exclamation of love.

They lay in each other's arms and had no notion that they were observed. Yet two figures suddenly appeared among the trees above them. "Here's shade," began Hewet, when Rachel suddenly stopped dead. They saw a man and woman lying on the ground beneath them, rolling slightly this way and that as the embrace tightened and slackened. The man then sat upright and the woman, who now appeared to be Susan Warrington, lay back upon the ground, with her eyes shut and an absorbed look upon her face, as though she were not altogether conscious. Nor could you tell from her expression whether she was happy, or had suffered something. When Arthur again turned to her, butting her as a lamb butts a ewe, Hewet and Rachel retreated without a word. Hewet felt uncomfortably shy.

"I don't like that," said Rachel after a moment.

"I can remember not liking it either," said Hewet. "I can remember—" but he changed his mind and continued in an ordinary tone of voice, "Well, we may take it for granted that they're engaged. D'you think he'll ever fly, or will she put a stop to that?"

But Rachel was still agitated; she could not get away from the sight they had just seen. Instead of answering Hewet she persisted.

"Love's an odd thing, isn't it, making one's heart beat."

"It's so enormously important, you see," Hewet replied. "Their lives are now changed forever."

"And it makes one sorry for them too," Rachel continued, as though she were tracing the course of her feelings. "I don't know either of them, but I could almost burst into tears. That's silly, isn't it?"

"Just because they're in love," said Hewet. "Yes," he added after a moment's consideration, "there's something horribly pathetic about it, I agree."

And now, as they had walked some way from the grove of trees, and had come to a rounded hollow very tempting to the back, they proceeded to sit down, and the impression of the lovers lost some of its force, though a certain intensity of vision, which was probably the result of the sight, remained with them. As a day upon which any emotion has been repressed is different from other days, so this day was now different, merely because they had seen other people at a crisis of their lives.

"A great encampment of tents they might be," said Hewet, looking in front of him at the mountains. "Isn't it like a water-colour too—you know the way water-colours dry in ridges all across the paper—I've been wondering what they looked like."

His eyes became dreamy, as though he were matching things, and reminded Rachel in their colour of the green flesh of a snail. She sat beside him looking at the mountains too. When it became painful to look any longer, the great size of the view seeming to enlarge her eyes beyond their natural limit, she looked at the ground; it pleased her to scrutinise this inch of the soil of South America so minutely that she noticed every grain of earth and made it into a world where she was endowed with the supreme power. She bent a blade of grass, and set an insect on the utmost tassel of it, and wondered if the insect realised his strange adventure, and thought how strange it was that she should have bent that tassel rather than any other of the million tassels.

"You've never told me your name," said Hewet suddenly. "Miss Somebody Vinrace . . . I like to know people's Christian names."

"Rachel," she replied.

"Rachel," he repeated. "I have an aunt called Rachel, who put the life of Father Damien into verse. She is a religious fanatic—the result of the way she was brought up, down in Northamptonshire, never seeing a soul. Have you any aunts?"

"I live with them," said Rachel.

"And I wonder what they're doing now?" Hewet enquired.

"They are probably buying wool," Rachel determined. She tried to describe them. "They are small, rather pale women," she began, "very clean. We live in Richmond. They have an old dog, too, who will only eat the marrow out of bones . . . They are always going to church. They tidy their drawers a good deal." But here she was overcome by the difficulty of describing people.

"It's impossible to believe that it's all going on still!" she exclaimed.

The sun was behind them and two long shadows suddenly lay upon the ground in front of them, one waving because it was made by a skirt, and the other stationary, because thrown by a pair of legs in trousers.

"You look very comfortable!" said Helen's voice above them.

"Hirst," said Hewet, pointing at the scissorlike shadow; he then rolled round to look up at them.

"There's room for us all here," he said.

When Hirst had seated himself comfortably, he said:

"Did you congratulate the young couple?"

It appeared that, coming to the same spot a few minutes after Hewet and Rachel, Helen and Hirst had seen precisely the same thing.

"No, we didn't congratulate them," said Hewet. "They seemed very happy."

"Well," said Hirst, pursing up his lips, "so long as I needn't marry either of them—"

"We were very much moved," said Hewet.

"I thought you would be," said Hirst. "Which was it, Monk? The thought of the immortal passions, or the thought of new-born males to keep the Roman Catholics out? I assure you," he said to Helen, "he's capable of being moved by either."

Rachel was a good deal stung by his banter, which she felt to be directed equally against them both, but she could think of no repartee.

"Nothing moves Hirst," Hewet laughed; he did not seem to be stung at all. "Unless it were a transfinite number falling in love with a finite one—I suppose such things do happen, even in mathematics."

"On the contrary," said Hirst with a touch of annoyance, "I consider myself a person of very strong passions." It was clear from the way he spoke that he meant it seriously; he spoke of course for the benefit of the ladies.

"By the way, Hirst," said Hewet, after a pause, "I have a terrible confession to make. Your book—the poems of Wordsworth, which if you remember I took off your table just as we were starting, and certainly put in my pocket here—"

"Is lost," Hirst finished for him.

"I consider that there is still a chance," Hewet urged, slapping himself to right and left, "that I never did take it after all."

"No," said Hirst. "It is here." He pointed to his breast.

"Thank God," Hewet exclaimed. "I need no longer feel as though I'd murdered a child!"

"I should think you were always losing things," Helen remarked, looking at him meditatively.

"I don't lose things," said Hewet. "I mislay them. That was the reason why Hirst refused to share a cabin with me on the voyage out."

"You came out together?" Helen enquired.

"I propose that each member of this party now gives a short biographical sketch of himself or herself," said Hirst, sitting upright. "Miss Vinrace, you come first; begin."

Rachel stated that she was twenty-four years of age, the daughter of a ship-owner, that she had never been properly educated; played the piano, had no brothers or sisters, and lived at Richmond with aunts, her mother being dead.

"Next," said Hirst, having taken in these facts; he pointed at Hewet. "I am the son of an English gentleman. I am twenty-seven," Hewet began. "My father was a fox-hunting squire. He died when I was ten in the hunting field. I can remember his body coming home, on a shutter I suppose, just as I was going down to tea, and noticing that there was jam for tea, and wondering whether I should be allowed—"

"Yes; but keep to the facts," Hirst put in.

"I was educated at Winchester and Cambridge, which I had to leave after a time. I have done a good many things since—"

"Profession?"

"None—at least—"

"Tastes?"

"Literary. I'm writing a novel."

"Brothers and sisters?"

"Three sisters, no brother, and a mother."

"Is that all we're to hear about you?" said Helen. She stated that she was very old—forty last October, and her father had been a solicitor in the city who had gone bankrupt, for which reason she had never had much education—they lived in one place after another—but an elder brother used to lend her books.

"If I were to tell you everything—" she stopped and smiled. "It would take too long," she concluded. "I married when I was thirty, and I have two children. My husband is a scholar. And now—it's your turn," she nodded at Hirst.

"You've left out a great deal," he reproved her. "My name is St. John Alaric Hirst," he began in a jaunty tone of voice. "I'm twenty-four years old. I'm the son of the Reverend Sidney Hirst, vicar of Great Wappyng in Norfolk. Oh, I got scholarships everywhere—Westminster—King's. I'm now a fellow of King's. Don't it sound dreary? Parents both alive (alas). Two brothers and one sister. I'm a very distinguished young man," he added.

"One of the three, or is it five, most distinguished men in England," Hewet remarked.

"Quite correct," said Hirst.

"That's all very interesting," said Helen after a pause. "But of course we've left out the only questions that matter. For instance, are we Christians?"

"I am not," "I am not," both the young men replied.

"I am," Rachel stated.

"You believe in a personal God?" Hirst demanded, turning round and fixing her with his eyeglasses.

"I believe—I believe," Rachel stammered, "I believe there are things we don't know about, and the world might change in a minute and anything appear."

At this Helen laughed outright. "Nonsense," she said. "You're not a Christian. You've never thought what you are. And there are lots of other questions," she continued, "though perhaps we can't ask them yet." Although they had talked so freely they were all uncomfortably conscious that they really knew nothing about each other.

"The important questions," Hewet pondered, "the really interesting ones. I doubt that one ever does ask them."

Rachel, who was slow to accept the fact that only a very few things can be said even by people who know each other well, insisted on knowing what he meant.

"Whether we've ever been in love?" she enquired. "Is that the kind of question you mean?"

Again Helen laughed at her, benignantly strewing her with handfuls of the long tasselled grass, for she was so brave and so foolish.

"Oh, Rachel," she cried. "It's like having a puppy in the house having you with one—a puppy that brings one's underclothes down into the hall."

But again the sunny earth in front of them was crossed by fantastic wavering figures, the shadows of men and women.

"There they are!" exclaimed Mrs. Elliot. There was a touch of peevishness in her voice. "And we've had *such* a hunt to find you. Do you know what the time is?"

Mrs. Elliot and Mr. and Mrs. Thornbury now confronted them; Mrs. Elliot was holding out her watch, and playfully tapping it upon the face. Hewet was recalled to the fact that this was a party for which he was responsible, and he immediately led them back to the watch-tower, where they were to have tea before starting home again. A bright crimson scarf fluttered from the top of the wall, which Mr. Perrott and Evelyn were tying to a stone as the others came up. The heat had changed just so far that instead of sitting in the shadow they sat in the sun, which was still hot enough to paint their faces red and yellow, and to colour great sections of the earth beneath them.

"There's nothing half so nice as tea!" said Mrs. Thornbury, taking her cup.

"Nothing," said Helen. "Can't you remember as a child chopping up hay—" She spoke much more quickly than usual, and kept her eye fixed upon Mrs. Thornbury, "and pretending it was tea, and getting scolded by the nurses— why I can't imagine, except that nurses are such brutes, won't allow pepper instead of salt though there's no earthly harm in it. Weren't your nurses just the same?"

During this speech Susan came into the group, and sat down by Helen's side. A few minutes later Mr. Venning strolled up from the opposite direction. He was a little flushed, and in the mood to answer hilariously whatever was said to him.

"What have you been doing to that old chap's grave?" he asked, pointing to the red flag which floated from the top of the stones.

"We have tried to make him forget his misfortune in having died three hundred years ago," said Mr. Perrott.

"It would be awful—to be dead!" ejaculated Evelyn M.

"To be dead?" said Hewet. "I don't think it would be awful. It's quite easy to imagine. When you go to bed tonight fold your hands so—breathe slower and slower—" He lay back with his hands clasped upon his breast, and his eyes shut, "Now," he murmured in an even monotonous voice, "I shall never, never, never move again." His body, lying flat among them, did for a moment suggest death.

"This is a horrible exhibition, Mr. Hewet!" cried Mrs. Thornbury.

"More cake for us!" said Arthur.

"I assure you there's nothing horrible about it," said Hewet, sitting up and laying hands upon the cake.

"It's so natural," he repeated. "People with children should make them do that exercise every night . . . Not that I look forward to being dead."

"And when you allude to a grave," said Mr. Thornbury, who spoke almost for the first time, "have you any authority for calling that ruin a grave? I am quite with you in refusing to accept the common interpretation which declares it to be the remains of an Elizabethan watch-tower—any more than I believe that the circular mounds or barrows which we find on the top of our English downs were camps. The antiquaries call everything a camp. I am always asking them, Well then, where do you think our ancestors kept their cattle? Half the camps in England are merely the ancient pound or barton as we call it in my part of the world. The argument that no one would keep his cattle in such exposed and inaccessible spots has no weight at all, if you reflect that in those days a man's cattle were his capital, his stock-in-trade, his daughter's dowries. Without cattle he was a serf, another man's man . . ." His eyes slowly lost their intensity, and he muttered a few concluding words under his breath, looking curiously old and forlorn.

Hughling Elliot, who might have been expected to engage the old gentleman in argument, was absent at the moment. He now came up holding out a large square of cotton upon which a fine design was printed in pleasant bright colours that made his hand look pale.

"A bargain," he announced, laying it down on the cloth. "I've just bought it from the big man with the ear-rings. Fine, isn't it? It wouldn't suit every one, of course, but it's just the thing—isn't it, Hilda?—for Mrs. Raymond Parry."

"Mrs. Raymond Parry!" cried Helen and Mrs. Thornbury at the same moment.

They looked at each other as though a mist hitherto obscuring their faces had been blown away.

"Ah—you have been to those wonderful parties too?" Mrs. Elliot asked with interest.

Mrs. Parry's drawing-room, though thousands of miles away, behind a vast curve of water on a tiny piece of earth, came before their eyes. They who had had no solidity or anchorage before seemed to be attached to it somehow, and at once grown more substantial. Perhaps they had been in the drawing-room at the same moment; perhaps they had passed each other on the stairs; at any rate they knew some of the same people. They looked one another up and down with new interest. But they could do no more than look at each other, for there was no time to enjoy the fruits of the discovery. The donkeys were advancing, and it was advisable to begin the descent immediately, for the night fell so quickly that it would be dark before they were home again.

Accordingly, remounting in order, they filed off down the hillside. Scraps of talk came floating back from one to another. There were jokes to begin with, and laughter; some walked part of the way, and picked flowers, and sent stones bounding before them.

"Who writes the best Latin verse in your college, Hirst?" Mr. Elliot called back incongruously, and Mr. Hirst returned that he had no idea.

The dusk fell as suddenly as the natives had warned them, the hollows of the mountain on either side filling up with darkness and the path becoming so dim that it was surprising to hear the donkeys' hooves still striking on hard rock. Silence fell upon one, and then upon another, until they were all silent, their minds spilling out into the deep blue air. The way seemed shorter in the dark than in the day; and soon the lights of the town were seen on the flat far beneath them.

Suddenly someone cried, "Ah!"

In a moment the slow yellow drop rose again from the plain below; it rose, paused, opened like a flower, and fell in a shower of drops.

"Fireworks," they cried.

Another went up more quickly; and then another; they could almost hear it twist and roar.

"Some Saint's day, I suppose," said a voice. The rush and embrace of the rockets as they soared up into the air seemed like the fiery way in which lovers suddenly rose and united, leaving the crowd gazing up at them with strained white faces. But Susan and Arthur, riding down the hill, never said a word to each other, and kept accurately apart.

Then the fireworks became erratic, and soon they ceased altogether, and the rest of the journey was made almost in darkness, the mountain being a great shadow behind them, and bushes and trees little shadows which threw darkness across the road. Among the plane-trees they separated, bundling into carriages and driving off, without saying good-night, or saying it only in a half-muffled way.

It was so late that there was no time for normal conversation between their arrival at the hotel and their retirement to bed. But Hirst wandered into Hewet's room with a collar in his hand.

"Well, Hewet," he remarked, on the crest of a gigantic yawn, "that was a great success, I consider." He yawned. "But take care you're not landed with that young woman . . . I don't really like young women . . ."

Hewet was too much drugged by hours in the open air to make any reply. In fact every one of the party was sound asleep within ten minutes or so of each other, with the exception of Susan Warrington. She lay for a considerable time looking blankly at the wall opposite, her hands clasped above her heart, and her light burning by her side. All articulate thought had long ago deserted her; her heart seemed to have grown to the size of a sun, and to illuminate her entire body, shedding like the sun a steady tide of warmth.

"I'm happy, I'm happy, I'm happy," she repeated. "I love every one. I'm happy."

CHAPTER XII

When Susan's engagement had been approved at home, and made public to anyone who took an interest in it at the hotel—and by this time the society at the hotel was divided so as to point to invisible chalk-marks such as Mr. Hirst had described, the news was felt to justify some celebration—an expedition? That had been done already. A dance then. The advantage of a dance was that it abolished one of those long evenings which were apt to become tedious and lead to absurdly early hours in spite of bridge.

Two or three people standing under the erect body of the stuffed leopard in the hall very soon had the matter decided. Evelyn slid a pace or two this way and that, and pronounced that the floor was excellent. Signor Rodriguez informed them of an old Spaniard who fiddled at weddings—fiddled so as to make a tortoise waltz; and his daughter, although endowed with eyes as black as coal-scuttles, had the same power over the piano. If there were any so sick or so surly as to prefer sedentary occupations on the night in question to spinning and watching others spin, the drawing-room and billiard-room were theirs. Hewet made it his business to conciliate the outsiders as much as possible. To Hirst's theory of the invisible chalk-marks he would pay no attention whatever. He was treated to a snub or two, but, in reward, found obscure lonely gentlemen delighted to have this opportunity of talking to their kind, and the lady of doubtful character showed every symptom of confiding her case to him in the near future. Indeed it was made quite obvious to him that the two or three hours between dinner and bed contained an amount of unhappiness, which was really pitiable, so many people had not succeeded in making friends.

It was settled that the dance was to be on Friday, one week after the engagement, and at dinner Hewet declared himself satisfied.

"They're all coming!" he told Hirst. "Pepper!" he called, seeing William Pepper slip past in the wake of the soup with a pamphlet beneath his arm, "We're counting on you to open the ball."

"You will certainly put sleep out of the question," Pepper returned.

"You are to take the floor with Miss Allan," Hewet continued, consulting a sheet of pencilled notes.

Pepper stopped and began a discourse upon round dances, country dances, morris dances, and quadrilles, all of which are entirely superior to the bastard waltz and spurious polka which have ousted them most unjustly in contemporary popularity—when the waiters gently pushed him on to his table in the corner.

The dining-room at this moment had a certain fantastic resemblance to a farmyard scattered with grain on which bright pigeons kept descending. Almost all the ladies wore dresses which they had not yet displayed, and their hair rose in waves and scrolls so as to appear like carved wood in Gothic churches rather than hair. The dinner was shorter and less formal than usual, even the waiters seeming to be affected with the general excitement. Ten minutes before the clock struck nine the committee made a tour through the ballroom. The hall, when emptied of its furniture, brilliantly lit, adorned with flowers whose scent tinged the air, presented a wonderful appearance of ethereal gaiety.

"It's like a starlit sky on an absolutely cloudless night," Hewet murmured, looking about him, at the airy empty room.

"A heavenly floor, anyhow," Evelyn added, taking a run and sliding two or three feet along.

"What about those curtains?" asked Hirst. The crimson curtains were drawn across the long windows. "It's a perfect night outside."

"Yes, but curtains inspire confidence," Miss Allan decided. "When the ball is in full swing it will be time to draw them. We might even open the windows a little . . . If we do it now elderly people will imagine there are draughts."

Her wisdom had come to be recognised, and held in respect. Meanwhile as they stood talking, the musicians were unwrapping their instruments, and the violin was repeating again and again a note struck upon the piano. Everything was ready to begin.

After a few minutes' pause, the father, the daughter, and the son-in-law who played the horn flourished with one accord. Like the rats who followed the piper, heads instantly appeared in the doorway. There was another flourish; and then the trio dashed spontaneously into the triumphant swing of the waltz. It was as though the room were instantly flooded with water. After a moment's hesitation first one couple, then another, leapt into midstream, and went round and round in the eddies. The rhythmic swish of the dancers sounded like a swirling pool. By degrees the room grew perceptibly hotter. The smell of kid gloves mingled with the strong scent of flowers. The eddies seemed to circle faster and faster, until the music wrought itself into a crash, ceased, and the circles were smashed into little separate bits. The couples struck off in different directions, leaving a thin row of elderly people stuck fast to the walls, and here and there a piece of trimming or a handkerchief or a flower lay upon the floor. There was a pause, and then the music started again, the eddies whirled, the couples circled round in them, until there was a crash, and the circles were broken up into separate pieces.

When this had happened about five times, Hirst, who leant against a window-frame, like some singular gargoyle, perceived that Helen Ambrose and Rachel stood in the doorway. The crowd was such that they could not move, but he recognised them by a piece of Helen's shoulder and a glimpse of Rachel's head turning round. He made his way to them; they greeted him with relief.

"We are suffering the tortures of the damned," said Helen.

"This is my idea of hell," said Rachel.

Her eyes were bright and she looked bewildered.

Hewet and Miss Allan, who had been waltzing somewhat laboriously, paused and greeted the newcomers.

"This *is* nice," said Hewet. "But where is Mr. Ambrose?"

"Pindar," said Helen. "May a married woman who was forty in October dance? I can't stand still." She seemed to fade into Hewet, and they both dissolved in the crowd.

"We must follow suit," said Hirst to Rachel, and he took her resolutely by the elbow. Rachel, without being expert, danced well, because of a good ear for rhythm, but Hirst had no taste for music, and a few dancing lessons at Cambridge had only put him into possession of the anatomy of a waltz, without imparting any of its spirit. A single turn proved to them that their methods were incompatible; instead of fitting into each other their bones seemed to jut out in angles making smooth turning an impossibility, and cutting, moreover, into the circular progress of the other dancers.

"Shall we stop?" said Hirst. Rachel gathered from his expression that he was annoyed.

They staggered to seats in the corner, from which they had a view of the room. It was still surging, in waves of blue and yellow, striped by the black evening-clothes of the gentlemen.

"An amazing spectacle," Hirst remarked. "Do you dance much in London?" They were both breathing fast, and both a little excited, though each was determined not to show any excitement at all.

"Scarcely ever. Do you?"

"My people give a dance every Christmas."

"This isn't half a bad floor," Rachel said. Hirst did not attempt to answer her platitude. He sat quite silent, staring at the dancers. After three minutes the silence became so intolerable to Rachel that she was goaded to advance another commonplace about the beauty of the night. Hirst interrupted her ruthlessly.

"Was that all nonsense what you said the other day about being a Christian and having no education?" he asked.

"It was practically true," she replied. "But I also play the piano very well," she said, "better, I expect than anyone in this room. You are the most distinguished man in England, aren't you?" she asked shyly.

"One of the three," he corrected.

Helen whirling past here tossed a fan into Rachel's lap.

"She is very beautiful," Hirst remarked.

They were again silent. Rachel was wondering whether he thought her also nice-looking; St. John was considering the immense difficulty of talking to girls who had no experience of life. Rachel had obviously never thought or felt or seen anything, and she might be intelligent or she might be just like all the rest. But Hewet's taunt rankled in his mind—"you don't know how to get on with women," and he was determined to profit by this opportunity. Her evening-clothes bestowed on her just that degree of unreality and distinction which made it romantic to speak to her, and stirred a desire to talk, which irritated him because he did not know how to begin. He glanced at her, and she seemed to him very remote and inexplicable, very young and chaste. He drew a sigh, and began.

"About books now. What have you read? Just Shakespeare and the Bible?"

"I haven't read many classics," Rachel stated. She was slightly annoyed by his jaunty and rather unnatural manner, while his masculine acquirements induced her to take a very modest view of her own power.

"D'you mean to tell me you've reached the age of twenty-four without reading Gibbon?" he demanded.

"Yes, I have," she answered.

"Mon Dieu!" he exclaimed, throwing out his hands. "You must begin tomorrow. I shall send you my copy. What I want to know is—" he looked at her critically. "You see, the problem is, can one really talk to you? Have you got a mind, or are you like the rest of your sex? You seem to me absurdly young compared with men of your age."

Rachel looked at him but said nothing.

"About Gibbon," he continued. "D'you think you'll be able to appreciate him? He's the test, of course. It's awfully difficult to tell about women," he continued, "how much, I mean, is due to lack of training, and how much is native incapacity. I don't see myself why you shouldn't understand—only I suppose you've led an absurd life until now—you've just walked in a crocodile, I suppose, with your hair down your back."

The music was again beginning. Hirst's eye wandered about the room in search of Mrs. Ambrose. With the best will in the world he was conscious that they were not getting on well together.

"I'd like awfully to lend you books," he said, buttoning his gloves, and rising from his seat. "We shall meet again. I'm going to leave you now."

He got up and left her.

Rachel looked round. She felt herself surrounded, like a child at a party, by the faces of strangers all hostile to her, with hooked noses and sneering, indifferent eyes. She was by a window, she pushed it open with a jerk. She stepped out into the garden. Her eyes swam with tears of rage.

"Damn that man!" she exclaimed, having acquired some of Helen's words. "Damn his insolence!"

She stood in the middle of the pale square of light which the window she had opened threw upon the grass. The forms of great black trees rose massively in front of her. She stood still, looking at them, shivering slightly with anger and excitement. She heard the trampling and swinging of the dancers behind her, and the rhythmic sway of the waltz music.

"There are trees," she said aloud. Would the trees make up for St. John Hirst? She would be a Persian princess far from civilisation, riding her horse upon the mountains alone, and making her women sing to her in the evening, far from all this, from the strife and men and women—a form came out of the shadow; a little red light burnt high up in its blackness.

"Miss Vinrace, is it?" said Hewet, peering at her. "You were dancing with Hirst?"

"He's made me furious!" she cried vehemently. "No one's any right to be insolent!"

"Insolent?" Hewet repeated, taking his cigar from his mouth in surprise. "Hirst—insolent?"

"It's insolent to—" said Rachel, and stopped. She did not know exactly why she had been made so angry. With a great effort she pulled herself together.

"Oh, well," she added, the vision of Helen and her mockery before her,

"I dare say I'm a fool." She made as though she were going back into the ballroom, but Hewet stopped her.

"Please explain to me," he said. "I feel sure Hirst didn't mean to hurt you."

When Rachel tried to explain, she found it very difficult. She could not say that she found the vision of herself walking in a crocodile with her hair down her back peculiarly unjust and horrible, nor could she explain why Hirst's assumption of the superiority of his nature and experience had seemed to her not only galling but terrible—as if a gate had clanged in her face. Pacing up and down the terrace beside Hewet she said bitterly:

"It's no good; we should live separate; we cannot understand each other; we only bring out what's worst."

Hewet brushed aside her generalisation as to the natures of the two sexes, for such generalisations bored him and seemed to him generally untrue. But, knowing Hirst, he guessed fairly accurately what had happened, and, though secretly much amused, was determined that Rachel should not store the incident away in her mind to take its place in the view she had of life.

"Now you'll hate him," he said, "which is wrong. Poor old Hirst—he can't help his method. And really, Miss Vinrace, he was doing his best; he was paying you a compliment—he was trying—he was trying—" he could not finish for the laughter that overcame him.

Rachel veered round suddenly and laughed out too. She saw that there was something ridiculous about Hirst, and perhaps about herself.

"It's his way of making friends, I suppose," she laughed. "Well—I shall do my part. I shall begin—'Ugly in body, repulsive in mind as you are, Mr. Hirst—'"

"Hear, hear!" cried Hewet. "That's the way to treat him. You see, Miss Vinrace, you must make allowances for Hirst. He's lived all his life in front of a looking-glass, so to speak, in a beautiful panelled room, hung with Japanese prints and lovely old chairs and tables, just one splash of colour, you know, in the right place—between the windows I think it is—and there he sits hour after hour with his toes on the fender, talking about philosophy and God and his liver and his heart and the hearts of his friends. They're all broken. You can't expect him to be at his best in a ballroom. He wants a cosy, smoky, masculine place, where he can stretch his legs out, and only speak when he's got something to say. For myself, I find it rather dreary. But I do respect it. They're all so much in earnest. They do take the serious things very seriously."

The description of Hirst's way of life interested Rachel so much that she almost forgot her private grudge against him, and her respect revived.

"They are really very clever then?" she asked.

"Of course they are. So far as brains go I think it's true what he said the other day; they're the cleverest people in England. But—you ought to take him in hand," he added. "There's a great deal more in him than's ever been got at. He wants someone to laugh at him . . . The idea of Hirst telling you that you've had no experiences! Poor old Hirst!"

They had been pacing up and down the terrace while they talked, and now one by one the dark windows were uncurtained by an invisible hand, and panes of light fell regularly at equal intervals upon the grass. They stopped to look in at the drawing-room, and perceived Mr. Pepper writing alone at a table.

"There's Pepper writing to his aunt," said Hewet. "She must be a very remarkable old lady, eighty-five he tells me, and he takes her for walking tours in the New Forest . . . Pepper!" he cried, rapping on the window. "Go and do your duty. Miss Allan expects you."

When they came to the windows of the ballroom, the swing of the dancers and the lilt of the music was irresistible.

"Shall we?" said Hewet, and they clasped hands and swept off magnificently into the great swirling pool. Although this was only the second time they had met, the first time they had seen a man and woman kissing each other, and the second time Mr. Hewet had found that a young woman angry is very like a child. So that when they joined hands in the dance they felt more at their ease than is usual.

It was midnight and the dance was now at its height. Servants were peeping in at the windows; the garden was sprinkled with the white shapes of couples sitting out. Mrs. Thornbury and Mrs. Elliot sat side by side under a palm tree, holding fans, handkerchiefs, and brooches deposited in their laps by flushed maidens. Occasionally they exchanged comments.

"Miss Warrington *does* look happy," said Mrs. Elliot; they both smiled; they both sighed.

"He has a great deal of character," said Mrs. Thornbury, alluding to Arthur.

"And character is what one wants," said Mrs. Elliot. "Now that young man is *clever* enough," she added, nodding at Hirst, who came past with Miss Allan on his arm.

"He does not look strong," said Mrs. Thornbury. "His complexion is not good. Shall I tear it off?" she asked, for Rachel had stopped, conscious of a long strip trailing behind her.

"I hope you are enjoying yourselves?" Hewet asked the ladies.

"This is a very familiar position for me!" smiled Mrs. Thornbury. "I have brought out five daughters—and they all loved dancing! You love it too, Miss Vinrace?" she asked, looking at Rachel with maternal eyes. "I know I did when I was your age. How I used to beg my mother to let me stay—and now I sympathise with the poor mothers—but I sympathise with the daughters too!"

She smiled sympathetically, and at the same time rather keenly, at Rachel.

"They seem to find a great deal to say to each other," said Mrs. Elliot, looking significantly at the backs of the couple as they turned away. "Did you notice at the picnic? He was the only person who could make her utter."

"Her father is a very interesting man," said Mrs. Thornbury. "He has one of the largest shipping businesses in Hull. He made a very able reply, you remember, to Mr. Asquith at the last election. It is so interesting to find that a man of his experience is a strong Protectionist."

She would have liked to discuss politics, which interested her more than personalities, but Mrs. Elliot would only talk about the Empire in a less abstract form.

"I hear there are dreadful accounts from England about the rats," she said. "A sister-in-law, who lives at Norwich, tells me it has been quite unsafe to order poultry. The plague—you see. It attacks the rats, and through them other creatures."

"And the local authorities are not taking proper steps?" asked Mrs. Thornbury.

"That she does not say. But she describes the attitude of the educated people—who should know better—as callous in the extreme. Of course, my sister-in-law is one of those active modern women, who always takes things up, you know—the kind of woman one admires, though one does not feel, at least I do not feel—but then she has a constitution of iron."

Mrs. Elliot, brought back to the consideration of her own delicacy, here sighed.

"A very animated face," said Mrs. Thornbury, looking at Evelyn M. who had stopped near them to pin tight a scarlet flower at her breast. It would not stay, and, with a spirited gesture of impatience, she thrust it into her partner's button-hole. He was a tall melancholy youth, who received the gift as a knight might receive his lady's token.

"Very trying to the eyes," was Mrs. Eliot's next remark, after watching the yellow whirl in which so few of the whirlers had either name or character for her, for a few minutes. Bursting out of the crowd, Helen approached them, and took a vacant chair.

"May I sit by you?" she said, smiling and breathing fast. "I suppose I ought to be ashamed of myself," she went on, sitting down, "at my age."

Her beauty, now that she was flushed and animated, was more expansive than usual, and both the ladies felt the same desire to touch her.

"I *am* enjoying myself," she panted. "Movement—isn't it amazing?"

"I have always heard that nothing comes up to dancing if one is a good dancer," said Mrs. Thornbury, looking at her with a smile.

Helen swayed slightly as if she sat on wires.

"I could dance forever!" she said. "They ought to let themselves go more!" she exclaimed. "They ought to leap and swing. Look! How they mince!"

"Have you seen those wonderful Russian dancers?" began Mrs. Elliot. But Helen saw her partner coming and rose as the moon rises. She was half round the room before they took their eyes off her, for they could not help admiring her, although they thought it a little odd that a woman of her age should enjoy dancing.

Directly Helen was left alone for a minute she was joined by St. John Hirst, who had been watching for an opportunity.

"Should you mind sitting out with me?" he asked. "I'm quite incapable of dancing." He piloted Helen to a corner which was supplied with two armchairs, and thus enjoyed the advantage of semi-privacy. They sat down, and for a few minutes Helen was too much under the influence of dancing to speak.

"Astonishing!" she exclaimed at last. "What sort of shape can she think her body is?" This remark was called forth by a lady who came past them, waddling rather than walking, and leaning on the arm of a stout man with globular green eyes set in a fat white face. Some support was necessary, for she was very stout, and so compressed that the upper part of her body hung considerably in advance of her feet, which could only trip in tiny steps, owing to the tightness of the skirt round her ankles. The dress itself consisted of a small piece of shiny yellow satin, adorned here and there indiscriminately with round shields of blue and green beads made to imitate hues of a peacock's breast. On the summit of a frothy castle of hair a purple plume stood erect, while her short neck was encircled by a black velvet ribbon knobbed with gems, and golden bracelets were tightly wedged into the flesh of her fat gloved arms. She had the face of an impertinent but jolly little pig, mottled red under a dusting of powder.

St. John could not join in Helen's laughter.

"It makes me sick," he declared. "The whole thing makes me sick . . . Consider the minds of those people—their feelings. Don't you agree?"

"I always make a vow never to go to another party of any description," Helen replied, "and I always break it."

She leant back in her chair and looked laughingly at the young man. She could see that he was genuinely cross, if at the same time slightly excited.

"However," he said, resuming his jaunty tone, "I suppose one must just make up one's mind to it."

"To what?"

"There never will be more than five people in the world worth talking to."

Slowly the flush and sparkle in Helen's face died away, and she looked as quiet and as observant as usual.

"Five people?" she remarked. "I should say there were more than five."

"You've been very fortunate, then," said Hirst. "Or perhaps I've been very unfortunate." He became silent.

"Should you say I was a difficult kind of person to get on with?" he asked sharply.

"Most clever people are when they're young," Helen replied.

"And of course I am—immensely clever," said Hirst. "I'm infinitely cleverer than Hewet. It's quite possible," he continued in his curiously impersonal manner, "that I'm going to be one of the people who really matter. That's utterly different from being clever, though one can't expect one's family to see it," he added bitterly.

Helen thought herself justified in asking, "Do you find your family difficult to get on with?"

"Intolerable . . . They want me to be a peer and a privy councillor. I've come out here partly in order to settle the matter. It's got to be settled. Either I must go to the bar, or I must stay on in Cambridge. Of course, there are obvious drawbacks to each, but the arguments certainly do seem to me in favour of Cambridge. This kind of thing!" he waved his hand at the crowded ballroom. "Repulsive. I'm conscious of great powers of affection too. I'm not susceptible, of course, in the way Hewet is. I'm very fond of a few people. I think, for example, that there's something to be said for my mother, though she is in many ways so deplorable . . . At Cambridge, of course, I should inevitably become the most important man in the place, but there are other reasons why I dread Cambridge—" he ceased.

"Are you finding me a dreadful bore?" he asked. He changed curiously from a friend confiding in a friend to a conventional young man at a party.

"Not in the least," said Helen. "I like it very much."

"You can't think," he exclaimed, speaking almost with emotion, "what a difference it makes finding someone to talk to! Directly I saw you I felt you might possibly understand me. I'm very fond of Hewet, but he hasn't the remotest idea what I'm like. You're the only woman I've ever met who seems to have the faintest conception of what I mean when I say a thing."

The next dance was beginning; it was the Barcarolle out of Hoffman, which made Helen beat her toe in time to it; but she felt that after such a compliment it was impossible to get up and go, and, besides being amused, she was really flattered, and the honesty of his conceit attracted her. She suspected that he was not happy, and was sufficiently feminine to wish to receive confidences.

"I'm very old," she sighed.

"The odd thing is that I don't find you old at all," he replied. "I feel as though we were exactly the same age. Moreover—" here he hesitated, but took courage from a glance at her face, "I feel as if I could talk quite plainly to you as one does to a man—about the relations between the sexes, about . . . and . . ."

In spite of his certainty a slight redness came into his face as he spoke the last two words.

She reassured him at once by the laugh with which she exclaimed, "I should hope so!"

He looked at her with real cordiality, and the lines which were drawn about his nose and lips slackened for the first time.

"Thank God!" he exclaimed. "Now we can behave like civilised human beings."

Certainly a barrier which usually stands fast had fallen, and it was possible to speak of matters which are generally only alluded to between men and women when doctors are present, or the shadow of death. In five minutes he was telling her the history of his life. It was long, for it was full of extremely elaborate incidents, which led on to a discussion of the principles on which morality is founded, and thus to several very interesting matters, which even in this ballroom had to be discussed in a whisper, lest one of the pouter pigeon ladies or resplendent merchants should overhear them, and proceed to demand that they should leave the place. When they had come to an end, or, to speak more accurately, when Helen intimated by a slight slackening of her attention that they had sat there long enough, Hirst rose, exclaiming, "So there's no reason whatever for all this mystery!"

"None, except that we are English people," she answered. She took his arm and they crossed the ball-room, making their way with difficulty between the spinning couples, who were now perceptibly dishevelled, and certainly to a critical eye by no means lovely in their shapes. The excitement of undertaking a friendship and the length of their talk, made them hungry, and they went in search of food to the dining-room, which was now full of people eating at little separate tables. In the doorway they met Rachel, going up to dance again with Arthur Venning. She was flushed and looked very happy, and Helen was struck by the fact that in this mood she was certainly more attractive than the generality of young women. She had never noticed it so clearly before.

"Enjoying yourself?" she asked, as they stopped for a second.

"Miss Vinrace," Arthur answered for her, "has just made a confession; she'd no idea that dances could be so delightful."

"Yes!" Rachel exclaimed. "I've changed my view of life completely!"

"You don't say so!" Helen mocked. They passed on.

"That's typical of Rachel," she said. "She changes her view of life about every other day. D'you know, I believe you're just the person I want," she said, as they sat down, "to help me complete her education? She's been brought up practically in a nunnery. Her father's too absurd. I've been doing what I can—

but I'm too old, and I'm a woman. Why shouldn't you talk to her—explain things to her—talk to her, I mean, as you talk to me?"

"I have made one attempt already this evening," said St. John. "I rather doubt that it was successful. She seems to me so very young and inexperienced. I have promised to lend her Gibbon."

"It's not Gibbon exactly," Helen pondered. "It's the facts of life, I think—d'you see what I mean? What really goes on, what people feel, although they generally try to hide it? There's nothing to be frightened of. It's so much more beautiful than the pretences—always more interesting—always better, I should say, than *that* kind of thing."

She nodded her head at a table near them, where two girls and two young men were chaffing each other very loudly, and carrying on an arch insinuating dialogue, sprinkled with endearments, about, it seemed, a pair of stockings or a pair of legs. One of the girls was flirting a fan and pretending to be shocked, and the sight was very unpleasant, partly because it was obvious that the girls were secretly hostile to each other.

"In my old age, however," Helen sighed, "I'm coming to think that it doesn't much matter in the long run what one does: people always go their own way—nothing will ever influence them." She nodded her head at the supper party.

But St. John did not agree. He said that he thought one could really make a great deal of difference by one's point of view, books and so on, and added that few things at the present time mattered more than the enlightenment of women. He sometimes thought that almost everything was due to education.

In the ballroom, meanwhile, the dancers were being formed into squares for the lancers. Arthur and Rachel, Susan and Hewet, Miss Allan and Hughling Elliot found themselves together.

Miss Allan looked at her watch.

"Half-past one," she stated. "And I have to despatch Alexander Pope tomorrow."

"Pope!" snorted Mr. Elliot. "Who reads Pope, I should like to know? And as for reading about him—No, no, Miss Allan; be persuaded you will benefit the world much more by dancing than by writing." It was one of Mr. Elliot's affectations that nothing in the world could compare with the delights of dancing—nothing in the world was so tedious as literature. Thus he sought pathetically enough to ingratiate himself with the young, and to prove to them beyond a doubt that though married to a ninny of a wife, and rather pale and bent and careworn by his weight of learning, he was as much alive as the youngest of them all.

"It's a question of bread and butter," said Miss Allan calmly. "However, they seem to expect me." She took up her position and pointed a square black toe.

"Mr. Hewet, you bow to me." It was evident at once that Miss Allan was the only one of them who had a thoroughly sound knowledge of the figures of the dance.

After the lancers there was a waltz; after the waltz a polka; and then a terrible thing happened; the music, which had been sounding regularly with five-minute pauses, stopped suddenly. The lady with the great dark eyes began to swathe her violin in silk, and the gentleman placed his horn carefully in its case. They were surrounded by couples imploring them in English, in French, in Spanish, of one more dance, one only; it was still early. But the old man at the piano merely exhibited his watch and shook his head. He turned up the collar of his coat and produced a red silk muffler, which completely dashed his festive appearance. Strange as it seemed, the musicians were pale and heavy-eyed; they looked bored and prosaic, as if the summit of their desire was cold meat and beer, succeeded immediately by bed.

Rachel was one of those who had begged them to continue. When they refused she began turning over the sheets of dance music which lay upon the piano. The pieces were generally bound in coloured covers, with pictures on them of romantic scenes—gondoliers astride on the crescent of the moon, nuns peering through the bars of a convent window, or young women with their hair down pointing a gun at the stars. She remembered that the general effect of the music to which they had danced so gaily was one of passionate regret for dead love and the innocent years of youth; dreadful sorrows had always separated the dancers from their past happiness.

"No wonder they get sick of playing stuff like this," she remarked reading a bar or two; "they're really hymn tunes, played very fast, with bits out of Wagner and Beethoven."

"Do you play? Would you play? Anything, so long as we can dance to it!" From all sides her gift for playing the piano was insisted upon, and she had to consent. As very soon she had played the only pieces of dance music she could remember, she went on to play an air from a sonata by Mozart.

"But that's not a dance," said someone pausing by the piano.

"It is," she replied, emphatically nodding her head. "Invent the steps." Sure of her melody she marked the rhythm boldly so as to simplify the way. Helen caught the idea; seized Miss Allan by the arm, and whirled round the room, now curtseying, now spinning round, now tripping this way and that like a child skipping through a meadow.

"This is the dance for people who don't know how to dance!" she cried. The tune changed to a minuet; St. John hopped with incredible swiftness first on his left leg, then on his right; the tune flowed melodiously; Hewet, swaying his arms and holding out the tails of his coat, swam down the room in imitation of the voluptuous dreamy dance of an Indian maiden dancing before her Rajah. The tune marched; and Miss Allen advanced with skirts extended and bowed profoundly to the engaged pair. Once their feet fell in with the rhythm they showed a complete lack of self-consciousness. From Mozart Rachel passed without stopping to old English hunting songs, carols, and hymn tunes, for, as she had observed, any good tune, with a little management, became a tune one could dance to. By degrees every person in the room was tripping and turning in pairs or alone. Mr. Pepper executed an ingenious pointed step derived from figure-skating, for which he once held some local championship; while Mrs. Thornbury tried to recall an old country dance which she had seen danced by her father's tenants in Dorsetshire in the old days. As for Mr. and Mrs. Elliot, they gallopaded round and round the room with such impetuosity that the other dancers shivered at their approach. Some people were heard to criticise the performance as a romp; to others it was the most enjoyable part of the evening.

"Now for the great round dance!" Hewet shouted. Instantly a gigantic circle was formed, the dancers holding hands and shouting out, "D'you ken John Peel," as they swung faster and faster and faster, until the strain was too great, and one link of the chain—Mrs. Thornbury—gave way, and the rest went flying across the room in all directions, to land upon the floor or the chairs or in each other's arms as seemed most convenient.

Rising from these positions, breathless and unkempt, it struck them for the first time that the electric lights pricked the air very vainly, and instinctively a great many eyes turned to the windows. Yes—there was the dawn. While they had been dancing the night had passed, and it had come. Outside, the mountains showed very pure and remote; the dew was sparkling on the grass, and the sky was flushed with blue, save for the pale yellows and pinks in the East. The dancers came crowding to the windows, pushed them open, and here and there ventured a foot upon the grass.

"How silly the poor old lights look!" said Evelyn M. in a curiously subdued tone of voice. "And ourselves; it isn't becoming." It was true; the untidy hair, and the green and yellow gems, which had seemed so festive half an hour ago, now looked cheap and slovenly. The complexions of the elder ladies suffered terribly, and, as if conscious that a cold eye had been turned upon them, they began to say good-night and to make their way up to bed.

Rachel, though robbed of her audience, had gone on playing to herself. From John Peel she passed to Bach, who was at this time the subject of her intense enthusiasm, and one by one some of the younger dancers came in from the garden and sat upon the deserted gilt chairs round the piano, the room being now so clear that they turned out the lights. As they sat and listened, their nerves were quieted; the heat and soreness of their lips, the result of incessant talking and laughing, was smoothed away. They sat very still as if they saw a building with spaces and columns succeeding each other rising in the empty space. Then they began to see themselves and their lives, and the whole of human life advancing very nobly under the direction of the music. They felt themselves ennobled, and when Rachel stopped playing they desired nothing but sleep.

Susan rose. "I think this has been the happiest night of my life!" she exclaimed. "I do adore music," she said, as she thanked Rachel. "It just seems to say all the things one can't say oneself." She gave a nervous little laugh and looked from one to another with great benignity, as though she would like to say something but could not find the words in which to express it. "Every one's been so kind—so very kind," she said. Then she too went to bed.

The party having ended in the very abrupt way in which parties do end, Helen and Rachel stood by the door with their cloaks on, looking for a carriage.

"I suppose you realise that there are no carriages left?" said St. John, who had been out to look. "You must sleep here."

"Oh, no," said Helen; "we shall walk."

"May we come too?" Hewet asked. "We can't go to bed. Imagine lying among bolsters and looking at one's washstand on a morning like this—Is that where you live?" They had begun to walk down the avenue, and he turned and pointed at the white and green villa on the hillside, which seemed to have its eyes shut.

"That's not a light burning, is it?" Helen asked anxiously.

"It's the sun," said St. John. The upper windows had each a spot of gold on them.

"I was afraid it was my husband, still reading Greek," she said. "All this time he's been editing *Pindar*."

They passed through the town and turned up the steep road, which was perfectly clear, though still unbordered by shadows. Partly because they were tired, and partly because the early light subdued them, they scarcely spoke, but breathed in the delicious fresh air, which seemed to belong to a different state of life from the air at midday. When they came to the high yellow wall, where the lane turned off from the road, Helen was for dismissing the two young men.

"You've come far enough," she said. "Go back to bed."

But they seemed unwilling to move.

"Let's sit down a moment," said Hewet. He spread his coat on the ground. "Let's sit down and consider." They sat down and looked out over the bay; it was very still, the sea was rippling faintly, and lines of green and blue were beginning to stripe it. There were no sailing boats as yet, but a steamer was anchored in the bay, looking very ghostly in the mist; it gave one unearthly cry, and then all was silent.

Rachel occupied herself in collecting one grey stone after another and building them into a little cairn; she did it very quietly and carefully.

"And so you've changed your view of life, Rachel?" said Helen.

Rachel added another stone and yawned. "I don't remember," she said, "I feel like a fish at the bottom of the sea." She yawned again. None of these people possessed any power to frighten her out here in the dawn, and she felt perfectly familiar even with Mr. Hirst.

"My brain, on the contrary," said Hirst, "is in a condition of abnormal activity." He sat in his favourite position with his arms binding his legs together and his chin resting on the top of his knees. "I see through everything—absolutely everything. Life has no more mysteries for me." He spoke with conviction, but did not appear to wish for an answer. Near though they sat, and familiar though they felt, they seemed mere shadows to each other.

"And all those people down there going to sleep," Hewet began dreamily, "thinking such different things—Miss Warrington, I suppose, is now on her knees; the Elliots are a little startled, it's not often *they* get out of breath, and they want to get to sleep as quickly as possible; then there's the poor lean young man who danced all night with Evelyn; he's putting his flower in water and asking himself, 'Is this love?'—and poor old Perrott, I daresay, can't get to sleep at all, and is reading his favourite Greek book to console himself—and the others—no, Hirst," he wound up, "I don't find it simple at all."

"I have a key," said Hirst cryptically. His chin was still upon his knees and his eyes fixed in front of him.

A silence followed. Then Helen rose and bade them good-night. "But," she said, "remember that you've got to come and see us."

They waved good-night and parted, but the two young men did not go back to the hotel; they went for a walk, during which they scarcely spoke, and never mentioned the names of the two women, who were, to a considerable extent, the subject of their thoughts. They did not wish to share their impressions. They returned to the hotel in time for breakfast.

CHAPTER XIII

There were many rooms in the villa, but one room which possessed a character of its own because the door was always shut, and no sound of music or laughter issued from it. Every one in the house was vaguely conscious that something went on behind that door, and without in the least knowing what it was, were influenced in their own thoughts by the knowledge that if they passed it the door would be shut, and if they made a noise Mr. Ambrose inside would be disturbed. Certain acts therefore possessed merit, and others were bad, so that life became more harmonious and less disconnected than it would have been had Mr. Ambrose given up editing *Pindar*, and taken to a nomad existence, in and out of every room in the house. As it was, every one was conscious that by observing certain rules, such as punctuality and quiet, by cooking well, and performing other small duties, one ode after another was satisfactorily restored to the world, and they shared the continuity of the scholar's life. Unfortunately, as age puts one barrier between human beings, and learning another, and sex a third, Mr. Ambrose in his study was some thousand miles distant from the nearest human being, who in this household was inevitably a woman. He sat hour after hour among white-leaved books, alone like an idol in an empty church, still except for the passage of his hand from one side of the sheet to another, silent save for an occasional choke, which drove him to extend his pipe a moment in the air. As he worked his way further and further into the heart of the poet, his chair became more and more deeply encircled by books, which lay open on the floor, and could only be crossed by a careful process of stepping, so delicate that his visitors generally stopped and addressed him from the outskirts.

On the morning after the dance, however, Rachel came into her uncle's room and hailed him twice, "Uncle Ridley," before he paid her any attention.

At length he looked over his spectacles.

"Well?" he asked.

"I want a book," she replied. "Gibbon's *History of the Roman Empire*. May I have it?"

She watched the lines on her uncle's face gradually rearrange themselves at her question. It had been smooth as a mask before she spoke.

"Please say that again," said her uncle, either because he had not heard or because he had not understood.

She repeated the same words and reddened slightly as she did so.

"Gibbon! What on earth d'you want him for?" he enquired.

"Somebody advised me to read it," Rachel stammered.

"But I don't travel about with a miscellaneous collection of eighteenth-century historians!" her uncle exclaimed. "Gibbon! Ten big volumes at least."

Rachel said that she was sorry to interrupt, and was turning to go.

"Stop!" cried her uncle. He put down his pipe, placed his book on one side, and rose and led her slowly round the room, holding her by the arm. "Plato," he said, laying one finger on the first of a row of small dark books, "and Jorrocks next door, which is wrong. Sophocles, Swift. You don't care for German commentators, I presume. French, then. You read French? You should read Balzac. Then we come to Wordsworth and Coleridge, Pope, Johnson, Addison, Wordsworth, Shelley, Keats. One thing leads to another. Why is Marlowe here? Mrs. Chailey, I presume. But what's the use of reading if you don't read Greek? After all, if you read Greek, you need never read

anything else, pure waste of time—pure waste of time," thus speaking half
to himself, with quick movements of his hands; they had come round again
to the circle of books on the floor, and their progress was stopped.

"Well," he demanded, "which shall it be?"

"Balzac," said Rachel, "or have you *The Speech on the American Revolution*,
Uncle Ridley?"

"*The Speech on the American Revolution*?" he asked. He looked at her very
keenly again. "Another young man at the dance?"

"No. That was Mr. Dalloway," she confessed.

"Good Lord!" he flung back his head in recollection of Mr. Dalloway.

She chose for herself a volume at random, submitted it to her uncle, who,
seeing that it was *La Cousine Bette*, bade her throw it away if she found it too
horrible, and was about to leave him when he demanded whether she had
enjoyed her dance?

He then wanted to know what people did at dances, seeing that he had
only been to one thirty-five years ago, when nothing had seemed to him
more meaningless and idiotic. Did they enjoy turning round and round to
the screech of a fiddle? Did they talk, and say pretty things, and if so, why
didn't they do it, under reasonable conditions? As for himself—he sighed and
pointed at the signs of industry lying all about him, which, in spite of his sigh,
filled his face with such satisfaction that his niece thought good to leave. On
bestowing a kiss she was allowed to go, but not until she had bound herself
to learn at any rate the Greek alphabet, and to return her French novel when
done with, upon which something more suitable would be found for her.

As the rooms in which people live are apt to give off something of the
same shock as their faces when seen for the first time, Rachel walked very
slowly downstairs, lost in wonder at her uncle, and his books, and his neglect
of dances, and his queer, utterly inexplicable, but apparently satisfactory view
of life, when her eye was caught by a note with her name on it lying in the
hall. The address was written in a small strong hand unknown to her, and the
note, which had no beginning, ran:—

> I send the first volume of Gibbon as I promised. Personally I find little to be
> said for the moderns, but I'm going to send you Wedekind when I've done him.
> Donne? Have you read Webster and all that set? I envy you reading them for the
> first time. Completely exhausted after last night. And you?

The flourish of initials which she took to be St. J. A. H., wound up the
letter. She was very much flattered that Mr. Hirst should have remembered
her, and fulfilled his promise so quickly.

There was still an hour to luncheon, and with Gibbon in one hand, and

Balzac in the other she strolled out of the gate and down the little path of beaten mud between the olive trees on the slope of the hill. It was too hot for climbing hills, but along the valley there were trees and a grass path running by the river bed. In this land where the population was centred in the towns it was possible to lose sight of civilisation in a very short time, passing only an occasional farmhouse, where the women were handling red roots in the courtyard; or a little boy lying on his elbows on the hillside surrounded by a flock of black strong-smelling goats. Save for a thread of water at the bottom, the river was merely a deep channel of dry yellow stones. On the bank grew those trees which Helen had said it was worth the voyage out merely to see. April had burst their buds, and they bore large blossoms among their glossy green leaves with petals of a thick wax-like substance coloured an exquisite cream or pink or deep crimson. But filled with one of those unreasonable exultations which start generally from an unknown cause, and sweep whole countries and skies into their embrace, she walked without seeing. The night was encroaching upon the day. Her ears hummed with the tunes she had played the night before; she sang, and the singing made her walk faster and faster. She did not see distinctly where she was going, the trees and the landscape appearing only as masses of green and blue, with an occasional space of differently coloured sky. Faces of people she had seen last night came before her; she heard their voices; she stopped singing, and began saying things over again or saying things differently, or inventing things that might have been said. The constraint of being among strangers in a long silk dress made it unusually exciting to stride thus alone. Hewet, Hirst, Mr. Venning, Miss Allan, the music, the light, the dark trees in the garden, the dawn—as she walked they went surging round in her head, a tumultuous background from which the present moment, with its opportunity of doing exactly as she liked, sprung more wonderfully vivid even than the night before.

So she might have walked until she had lost all knowledge of her way, had it not been for the interruption of a tree, which, although it did not grow across her path, stopped her as effectively as if the branches had struck her in the face. It was an ordinary tree, but to her it appeared so strange that it might have been the only tree in the world. Dark was the trunk in the middle, and the branches sprang here and there, leaving jagged intervals of light between them as distinctly as if it had but that second risen from the ground. Having seen a sight that would last her for a lifetime, and for a lifetime would preserve that second, the tree once more sank into the ordinary ranks of trees, and she was able to seat herself in its shade and to pick the red flowers with the thin green leaves which were growing beneath it. She laid them side by side, flower to flower and stalk to stalk, caressing them for walking alone. Flowers and even pebbles in the earth had their own life and disposition, and brought back the feelings of a child to whom they were companions. Looking up, her eye was caught by the line of the mountains flying out energetically across the sky like the lash of a curling whip. She looked at the pale distant sky, and the high bare places on the mountain-tops lying exposed to the sun. When she sat down she had dropped her books on to the earth at her feet, and now she looked down on them lying there, so square in the grass, a tall stem bending over and tickling the smooth brown cover of Gibbon, while the mottled blue Balzac lay naked in the sun. With a feeling that to open and read would certainly be a surprising experience, she turned the historian's page and read that—

His generals, in the early part of his reign, attempted the reduction of Aethiopia and Arabia Felix. They marched near a thousand miles to the south of the tropic; but the heat of the climate soon repelled the invaders and protected the unwarlike natives of those sequestered regions . . . The northern countries of Europe scarcely deserved the expense and labour of conquest. The forests and morasses of Germany were filled with a hardy race of barbarians, who despised life when it was separated from freedom.

Never had any words been so vivid and so beautiful—Arabia Felix—Aethiopia. But those were not more noble than the others, hardy barbarians, forests, and morasses. They seemed to drive roads back to the very beginning of the world, on either side of which the populations of all times and countries stood in avenues, and by passing down them all knowledge would be hers, and the book of the world turned back to the very first page. Such was her excitement at the possibilities of knowledge now opening before her that she ceased to read, and a breeze turning the page, the covers of Gibbon gently ruffled and closed together. She then rose again and walked on. Slowly her mind became less confused and sought the origins of her exaltation, which were twofold and could be limited by an effort to the persons of Mr. Hirst and Mr. Hewet. Any clear analysis of them was impossible owing to the haze of wonder in which they were enveloped. She could not reason about them as about people whose feelings went by the same rule as her own did, and her mind dwelt on them with a kind of physical pleasure such as is caused by the contemplation of bright things hanging in the sun. From them all life seemed to radiate; the very words of books were steeped in radiance. She then became haunted by a suspicion which she was so reluctant to face that she welcomed a trip and stumble over the grass because thus her attention was dispersed, but in a second it had collected itself again. Unconsciously she had been walking faster and faster, her body trying to outrun her mind; but she was now on the summit of a little hillock of earth which rose above the river and displayed the valley. She was no longer able to juggle with several ideas, but must deal with the most persistent, and a kind of melancholy replaced her excitement. She sank down on to the earth clasping her knees together, and looking blankly in front of her. For some time she observed a great yellow butterfly, which was opening and closing its wings very slowly on a little flat stone.

"What is it to be in love?" she demanded, after a long silence; each word as it came into being seemed to shove itself out into an unknown sea. Hypnotised by the wings of the butterfly, and awed by the discovery of a terrible possibility in life, she sat for some time longer. When the butterfly flew away, she rose, and with her two books beneath her arm returned home again, much as a soldier prepared for battle.

CHAPTER XIV

The sun of that same day going down, dusk was saluted as usual at the hotel by an instantaneous sparkle of electric lights. The hours between dinner and bedtime were always difficult enough to kill, and the night after the dance they were further tarnished by the peevishness of dissipation. Certainly, in the opinion of Hirst and Hewet, who lay back in long armchairs in the middle of the hall, with their coffee-cups beside them, and their cigarettes in their hands, the evening was unusually dull, the women unusually badly dressed, the men unusually fatuous. Moreover, when the mail had been distributed half an hour ago there were no letters for either of the two young men. As every other person, practically, had received two or three plump letters from England, which they were now engaged in reading, this seemed hard, and prompted Hirst to make the caustic remark that the animals had been fed. Their silence, he said, reminded him of the silence in the lion-house when each beast holds a lump of raw meat in its paws. He went on, stimulated by this comparison, to liken some to hippopotamuses, some to canary birds, some to swine, some to parrots, and some to loathsome reptiles curled round the half-decayed bodies of sheep. The intermittent sounds— now a cough, now a horrible wheezing or throat-clearing, now a little patter of conversation—were just, he declared, what you hear if you stand in the lion-house when the bones are being mauled. But these comparisons did not rouse Hewet, who, after a careless glance round the room, fixed his eyes upon a thicket of native spears which were so ingeniously arranged as to run their points at you whichever way you approached them. He was clearly oblivious of his surroundings; whereupon Hirst, perceiving that Hewet's mind was a complete blank, fixed his attention more closely upon his fellow-creatures. He was too far from them, however, to hear what they were saying, but it pleased him to construct little theories about them from their gestures and appearance.

Mrs. Thornbury had received a great many letters. She was completely engrossed in them. When she had finished a page she handed it to her husband, or gave him the sense of what she was reading in a series of short quotations linked together by a sound at the back of her throat. "Evie writes that George has gone to Glasgow. 'He finds Mr. Chadbourne so nice to work with, and we hope to spend Christmas together, but I should not like to move Betty and Alfred any great distance (no, quite right), though it is difficult to imagine cold weather in this heat . . . Eleanor and Roger drove over in the new trap . . . Eleanor certainly looked more like herself than I've seen her since the winter. She has put Baby on three bottles now, which I'm sure is wise (I'm sure it is too), and so gets better nights . . . My hair still falls out. I find it on the pillow! But I am cheered by hearing from Tottie Hall Green . . . Muriel is in Torquay enjoying herself greatly at dances. She *is* going to show her black pug after all.' . . . A line from Herbert—so busy, poor fellow! Ah! Margaret says, 'Poor old Mrs. Fairbank died on the eighth, quite suddenly in the conservatory, only a maid in the house, who hadn't the presence of mind to lift her up, which they think might have saved her, but the doctor says it might have come at any moment, and one can only feel thankful that it was in the house and not in the street (I should think so!). The pigeons have increased terribly, just as the rabbits did five years ago . . .' " While she read her husband kept nodding his head very slightly, but very steadily in sign of approval.

Near by, Miss Allan was reading her letters too. They were not altogether pleasant, as could be seen from the slight rigidity which came over her large fine face as she finished reading them and replaced them neatly in their envelopes. The lines of care and responsibility on her face made her resemble an elderly man rather than a woman. The letters brought her news of the failure of last year's fruit crop in New Zealand, which was a serious matter, for Hubert, her only brother, made his living on a fruit farm, and if it failed again, of course, he would throw up his place, come back to England, and what were they to do with him this time? The journey out here, which meant the loss of a term's work, became an extravagance and not the just and wonderful holiday due to her after fifteen years of punctual lecturing and correcting essays upon English literature. Emily, her sister, who was a teacher also, wrote: "We ought to be prepared, though I have no doubt Hubert will be more reasonable this time." And then went on in her sensible way to say that she was enjoying a very jolly time in the Lakes. "They are looking exceedingly pretty just now. I have seldom seen the trees so forward at this time of year. We have taken our lunch out several days. Old Alice is as young as ever, and asks after every one affectionately. The days pass very quickly, and term will soon be here. Political prospects *not* good, I think privately, but do not like to damp Ellen's enthusiasm. Lloyd George has taken the Bill up, but so have many before now, and we are where we are; but trust to find myself mistaken. Anyhow, we have our work cut out for us . . . Surely Meredith lacks the *human* note one likes in W. W.?" she concluded, and went on to discuss some questions of English literature which Miss Allan had raised in her last letter.

At a little distance from Miss Allan, on a seat shaded and made semi-private by a thick clump of palm trees, Arthur and Susan were reading each other's letters. The big slashing manuscripts of hockey-playing young women in Wiltshire lay on Arthur's knee, while Susan deciphered tight little legal hands which rarely filled more than a page, and always conveyed the same impression of jocular and breezy goodwill.

"I do hope Mr. Hutchinson will like me, Arthur," she said, looking up.

"Who's your loving Flo?" asked Arthur.

"Flo Graves—the girl I told you about, who was engaged to that dreadful Mr. Vincent," said Susan. "Is Mr. Hutchinson married?" she asked.

Already her mind was busy with benevolent plans for her friends, or rather with one magnificent plan—which was simple too—they were all to get married—at once—directly she got back. Marriage, marriage that was the right thing, the only thing, the solution required by every one she knew, and a great part of her meditations was spent in tracing every instance of discomfort, loneliness, ill-health, unsatisfied ambition, restlessness, eccentricity, taking things up and dropping them again, public speaking, and philanthropic activity on the part of men and particularly on the part of women to the fact that they wanted to marry, were trying to marry, and had not succeeded in getting married. If, as she was bound to own, these symptoms sometimes persisted after marriage, she could only ascribe them to the unhappy law of nature which decreed that there was only one Arthur Venning, and only one Susan who could marry him. Her theory, of course, had the merit of being fully supported by her own case. She had been vaguely uncomfortable at home for two or three years now, and a voyage like this with her selfish old aunt, who paid her fare but treated her as servant and companion in one, was typical of the kind of thing people expected of her. Directly she became engaged, Mrs. Paley behaved with instinctive respect, positively protested when Susan as usual knelt down to lace her shoes, and appeared really grateful for an hour of Susan's company where she had been used to exact two or three as her right. She therefore foresaw a life of far greater comfort than she had been used to, and the change had already produced a great increase of warmth in her feelings towards other people.

It was close on twenty years now since Mrs. Paley had been able to lace her own shoes or even to see them, the disappearance of her feet having coincided more or less accurately with the death of her husband, a man of business, soon after which event Mrs. Paley began to grow stout. She was a selfish, independent old woman, possessed of a considerable income, which she spent upon the upkeep of a house that needed seven servants and a charwoman in Lancaster Gate, and another with a garden and carriage-horses in Surrey. Susan's engagement relieved her of the one great anxiety of her life—that her son Christopher should "entangle himself" with his cousin. Now that this familiar source of interest was removed, she felt a little low and inclined to see more in Susan than she used to. She had decided to give her a very handsome wedding present, a cheque for two hundred, two hundred and fifty, or possibly, conceivably—it depended upon the under-gardener and Huths' bill for doing up the drawing-room—three hundred pounds sterling.

She was thinking of this very question, revolving the figures, as she sat in her wheeled chair with a table spread with cards by her side. The Patience had somehow got into a muddle, and she did not like to call for Susan to help her, as Susan seemed to be busy with Arthur.

"She's every right to expect a handsome present from me, of course," she thought, looking vaguely at the leopard on its hind legs, "and I've no doubt she does! Money goes a long way with every one. The young are very selfish. If I were to die, nobody would miss me but Dakyns, and she'll be consoled by the will! However, I've got no reason to complain . . . I can still enjoy myself. I'm not a burden to anyone . . . I like a great many things a good deal, in spite of my legs."

Being slightly depressed, however, she went on to think of the only people she had known who had not seemed to her at all selfish or fond of money, who had seemed to her somehow rather finer than the general run; people she willingly acknowledged, who were finer than she was. There were only two of them. One was her brother, who had been drowned before her eyes, the other was a girl, her greatest friend, who had died in giving birth to her first child. These things had happened some fifty years ago.

"They ought not to have died," she thought. "However, they did—and we selfish old creatures go on." The tears came to her eyes; she felt a genuine regret for them, a kind of respect for their youth and beauty, and a kind of shame for herself; but the tears did not fall; and she opened one of those innumerable novels which she used to pronounce good or bad, or pretty middling, or really wonderful. "I can't think how people come to imagine such things," she would say, taking off her spectacles and looking up with the old faded eyes, that were becoming ringed with white.

Just behind the stuffed leopard Mr. Elliot was playing chess with Mr.

Pepper. He was being defeated, naturally, for Mr. Pepper scarcely took his eyes off the board, and Mr. Elliot kept leaning back in his chair and throwing out remarks to a gentleman who had only arrived the night before, a tall handsome man, with a head resembling the head of an intellectual ram. After a few remarks of a general nature had passed, they were discovering that they knew some of the same people, as indeed had been obvious from their appearance directly they saw each other.

"Ah yes, old Truefit," said Mr. Elliot. "He has a son at Oxford. I've often stayed with them. It's a lovely old Jacobean house. Some exquisite Greuzes— one or two Dutch pictures which the old boy kept in the cellars. Then there were stacks upon stacks of prints. Oh, the dirt in that house! He was a miser, you know. The boy married a daughter of Lord Pinwells. I know them too. The collecting mania tends to run in families. This chap collects buckles— men's shoe-buckles they must be, in use between the years 1580 and 1660; the dates mayn't be right, but fact's as I say. Your true collector always has some unaccountable fad of that kind. On other points he's as level-headed as a breeder of shorthorns, which is what he happens to be. Then the Pinwells, as you probably know, have their share of eccentricity too. Lady Maud, for instance—" he was interrupted here by the necessity of considering his move—"Lady Maud has a horror of cats and clergymen, and people with big front teeth. I've heard her shout across a table, 'Keep your mouth shut, Miss Smith; they're as yellow as carrots!' across a table, mind you. To me she's always been civility itself. She dabbles in literature, likes to collect a few of us in her drawing-room, but mention a clergyman, a bishop even, nay, the Archbishop himself, and she gobbles like a turkey-cock. I've been told it's a family feud—something to do with an ancestor in the reign of Charles the First. Yes," he continued, suffering check after check, "I always like to know something of the grandmothers of our fashionable young men. In my opinion they preserve all that we admire in the eighteenth century, with the advantage, in the majority of cases, that they are personally clean. Not that one would insult old Lady Barborough by calling her clean. How often d'you think, Hilda," he called out to his wife, "her ladyship takes a bath?"

"I should hardly like to say, Hugh," Mrs. Elliot tittered, "but wearing puce velvet, as she does even on the hottest August day, it somehow doesn't show."

"Pepper, you have me," said Mr. Elliot. "My chess is even worse than I remembered." He accepted his defeat with great equanimity, because he really wished to talk.

He drew his chair beside Mr. Wilfrid Flushing, the newcomer.

"Are these at all in your line?" he asked, pointing at a case in front of them, where highly polished crosses, jewels, and bits of embroidery, the work of the natives, were displayed to tempt visitors.

"Shams, all of them," said Mr. Flushing briefly. "This rug, now, isn't at all bad." He stopped and picked up a piece of the rug at their feet. "Not old, of course, but the design is quite in the right tradition. Alice, lend me your brooch. See the difference between the old work and the new."

A lady, who was reading with great concentration, unfastened her brooch and gave it to her husband without looking at him or acknowledging the tentative bow which Mr. Elliot was desirous of giving her. If she had listened, she might have been amused by the reference to old Lady Barborough, her great-aunt, but, oblivious of her surroundings, she went on reading.

The clock, which had been wheezing for some minutes like an old man preparing to cough, now struck nine. The sound slightly disturbed certain somnolent merchants, government officials, and men of independent means who were lying back in their chairs, chatting, smoking, ruminating about their affairs, with their eyes half shut; they raised their lids for an instant at the sound and then closed them again. They had the appearance of crocodiles so fully gorged by their last meal that the future of the world gives them no anxiety whatever. The only disturbance in the placid bright room was caused by a large moth which shot from light to light, whizzing over elaborate heads of hair, and causing several young women to raise their hands nervously and exclaim, "Someone ought to kill it!"

Absorbed in their own thoughts, Hewet and Hirst had not spoken for a long time.

When the clock struck, Hirst said:

"Ah, the creatures begin to stir . . ." He watched them raise themselves, look about them, and settle down again. "What I abhor most of all," he concluded, "is the female breast. Imagine being Venning and having to get into bed with Susan! But the really repulsive thing is that they feel nothing at all—about what I do when I have a hot bath. They're gross, they're absurd, they're utterly intolerable!"

So saying, and drawing no reply from Hewet, he proceeded to think about himself, about science, about Cambridge, about the Bar, about Helen and what she thought of him, until, being very tired, he was nodding off to sleep.

Suddenly Hewet woke him up.

"How d'you know what you feel, Hirst?"

"Are you in love?" asked Hirst. He put in his eyeglass.

"Don't be a fool," said Hewet.

"Well, I'll sit down and think about it," said Hirst. "One really ought to. If these people would only think about things, the world would be a far better place for us all to live in. Are you trying to think?"

That was exactly what Hewet had been doing for the last half-hour, but he did not find Hirst sympathetic at the moment.

"I shall go for a walk," he said.

"Remember we weren't in bed last night," said Hirst with a prodigious yawn.

Hewet rose and stretched himself.

"I want to go and get a breath of air," he said.

An unusual feeling had been bothering him all the evening and forbidding him to settle into any one train of thought. It was precisely as if he had been in the middle of a talk which interested him profoundly when someone came up and interrupted him. He could not finish the talk, and the longer he sat there the more he wanted to finish it. As the talk that had been interrupted was a talk with Rachel, he had to ask himself why he felt this, and why he wanted to go on talking to her. Hirst would merely say that he was in love with her. But he was not in love with her. Did love begin in that way, with the wish to go on talking? No. It always began in his case with definite physical sensations, and these were now absent, he did not even find her physically attractive. There was something, of course, unusual about her—she was young, inexperienced, and inquisitive, they had been more open with each other than was usually possible. He always found girls interesting to talk to, and surely these were good reasons why he should wish to go on talking to her; and last night, what with the crowd and the confusion, he had only been able to begin to talk to her. What was she doing now? Lying on a sofa and looking at the ceiling, perhaps. He could imagine her doing that, and Helen in an armchair, with her hands on the arm of it, so—looking ahead of her, with her great big eyes—oh no, they'd be talking, of course, about the dance. But suppose Rachel was going away in a day or two, suppose this was the end of her visit, and her father had arrived in one of the steamers anchored in the bay—it was intolerable to know so little. Therefore he exclaimed, "How d'you know what you feel, Hirst?" to stop himself from thinking.

But Hirst did not help him, and the other people with their aimless movements and their unknown lives were disturbing, so that he longed for the empty darkness. The first thing he looked for when he stepped out of the hall door was the light of the Ambroses' villa. When he had definitely decided that a certain light apart from the others higher up the hill was their light, he was considerably reassured. There seemed to be at once a little stability in all this incoherence. Without any definite plan in his head, he took the turning to the right and walked through the town and came to the wall by the meeting of the roads, where he stopped. The booming of the sea was audible. The dark-blue mass of the mountains rose against the paler blue of the sky. There was no moon, but myriads of stars, and lights were anchored up and down in the dark waves of earth all round him. He had meant to go back, but the single light of the Ambroses' villa had now become three separate lights, and he was tempted to go on. He might as well make sure that Rachel was still there. Walking fast, he soon stood by the iron gate of their garden, and pushed it open; the outline of the house suddenly appeared sharply before his eyes, and the thin column of the verandah cutting across the palely lit gravel of the terrace. He hesitated. At the back of the house someone was rattling cans. He approached the front; the light on the terrace showed him that the sitting-rooms were on that side. He stood as near the light as he could by the corner of the house, the leaves of a creeper brushing his face. After a moment he could hear a voice. The voice went on steadily; it was not talking, but from the continuity of the sound it was a voice reading aloud. He crept a little closer; he crumpled the leaves together so as to stop their rustling about his ears. It might be Rachel's voice. He left the shadow and stepped into the radius of the light, and then heard a sentence spoken quite distinctly.

"And there we lived from the year 1860 to 1895, the happiest years of my parents' lives, and there in 1862 my brother Maurice was born, to the delight of his parents, as he was destined to be the delight of all who knew him."

The voice quickened, and the tone became conclusive rising slightly in pitch, as if these words were at the end of the chapter. Hewet drew back again into the shadow. There was a long silence. He could just hear chairs being moved inside. He had almost decided to go back, when suddenly two figures appeared at the window, not six feet from him.

"It was Maurice Fielding, of course, that your mother was engaged to," said Helen's voice. She spoke reflectively, looking out into the dark garden, and thinking evidently as much of the look of the night as of what she was saying.

"Mother?" said Rachel. Hewet's heart leapt, and he noticed the fact. Her voice, though low, was full of surprise.

"You didn't know that?" said Helen.

"I never knew there'd been anyone else," said Rachel. She was clearly surprised, but all they said was said low and inexpressively, because they were speaking out into the cool dark night.

"More people were in love with her than with anyone I've ever known," Helen stated. "She had that power—she enjoyed things. She wasn't beautiful, but—I was thinking of her last night at the dance. She got on with every kind of person, and then she made it all so amazingly—funny."

It appeared that Helen was going back into the past, choosing her words deliberately, comparing Theresa with the people she had known since Theresa died.

"I don't know how she did it," she continued, and ceased, and there was a long pause, in which a little owl called first here, then there, as it moved from tree to tree in the garden.

"That's so like Aunt Lucy and Aunt Katie," said Rachel at last. "They always make out that she was very sad and very good."

"Then why, for goodness' sake, did they do nothing but criticize her when she was alive?" said Helen. Very gentle their voices sounded, as if they fell through the waves of the sea.

"If I were to die tomorrow . . ." she began.

The broken sentences had an extraordinary beauty and detachment in Hewet's ears, and a kind of mystery too, as though they were spoken by people in their sleep.

"No, Rachel," Helen's voice continued, "I'm not going to walk in the garden; it's damp—it's sure to be damp; besides, I see at least a dozen toads."

"Toads? Those are stones, Helen. Come out. It's nicer out. The flowers smell," Rachel replied.

Hewet drew still farther back. His heart was beating very quickly. Apparently Rachel tried to pull Helen out on to the terrace, and Helen resisted. There was a certain amount of scuffling, entreating, resisting, and laughter from both of them. Then a man's form appeared. Hewet could not hear what they were all saying. In a minute they had gone in; he could hear bolts grating then; there was dead silence, and all the lights went out.

He turned away, still crumpling and uncrumpling a handful of leaves which he had torn from the wall. An exquisite sense of pleasure and relief possessed him; it was all so solid and peaceful after the ball at the hotel, whether he was in love with them or not, and he was not in love with them; no, but it was good that they should be alive.

After standing still for a minute or two he turned and began to walk towards the gate. With the movement of his body, the excitement, the romance and the richness of life crowded into his brain. He shouted out a line of poetry, but the words escaped him, and he stumbled among lines and fragments of lines which had no meaning at all except for the beauty of the words. He shut the gate, and ran swinging from side to side down the hill, shouting any nonsense that came into his head. "Here am I," he cried rhythmically, as his feet pounded to the left and to the right, "plunging along, like an elephant in the jungle, stripping the branches as I go (he snatched at the twigs of a bush at the roadside), roaring innumerable words, lovely words about innumerable things, running downhill and talking nonsense aloud to myself about roads and leaves and lights and women coming out into the darkness— about women—about Rachel, about Rachel." He stopped and drew a deep breath. The night seemed immense and hospitable, and although so dark there seemed to be things moving down there in the harbour and movement out at sea. He gazed until the darkness numbed him, and then he walked on quickly, still murmuring to himself. "And I ought to be in bed, snoring and dreaming, dreaming, dreaming. Dreams and realities, dreams and realities, dreams and realities," he repeated all the way up the avenue, scarcely knowing what he said, until he reached the front door. Here he paused for a second, and collected himself before he opened the door.

His eyes were dazed, his hands very cold, and his brain excited and yet half asleep. Inside the door everything was as he had left it except that the hall was now empty. There were the chairs turning in towards each other where people had sat talking, and the empty glasses on little tables, and the newspapers scattered on the floor. As he shut the door he felt as if he were enclosed in a square box, and instantly shrivelled up. It was all very bright and very small. He stopped for a minute by the long table to find a paper which he had meant to read, but he was still too much under the influence of the dark and the fresh air to consider carefully which paper it was or where he had seen it.

As he fumbled vaguely among the papers he saw a figure cross the tail of his eye, coming downstairs. He heard the swishing sound of skirts, and to his great surprise, Evelyn M. came up to him, laid her hand on the table as if to prevent him from taking up a paper, and said:

"You're just the person I wanted to talk to." Her voice was a little unpleasant and metallic, her eyes were very bright, and she kept them fixed upon him.

"To talk to me?" he repeated. "But I'm half asleep."

"But I think you understand better than most people," she answered, and sat down on a little chair placed beside a big leather chair so that Hewet had to sit down beside her.

"Well?" he said. He yawned openly, and lit a cigarette. He could not believe that this was really happening to him. "What is it?"

"Are you really sympathetic, or is it just a pose?" she demanded.

"It's for you to say," he replied. "I'm interested, I think." He still felt numb all over and as if she was much too close to him.

"Anyone can be interested!" she cried impatiently. "Your friend Mr. Hirst's interested, I daresay however, I do believe in you. You look as if you'd got a nice sister, somehow." She paused, picking at some sequins on her knees, and then, as if she had made up her mind, she started off, "Anyhow, I'm going to ask your advice. D'you ever get into a state where you don't know your own mind? That's the state I'm in now. You see, last night at the dance Raymond Oliver—he's the tall dark boy who looks as if he had Indian blood in him, but he says he's not really—well, we were sitting out together, and he told me all about himself, how unhappy he is at home, and how he hates being out here. They've put him into some beastly mining business. He says it's beastly—I should like it, I know, but that's neither here nor there. And I felt awfully sorry for him, one couldn't help being sorry for him, and when he asked me to let him kiss me, I did. I don't see any harm in that, do you? And then this morning he said he'd thought I meant something more, and I wasn't the sort to let anyone kiss me. And we talked and talked. I daresay I was very silly, but one can't help liking people when one's sorry for them. I do like him most awfully—" She paused. "So I gave him half a promise, and then, you see, there's Alfred Perrott."

"Oh, Perrott," said Hewet.

"We got to know each other on that picnic the other day," she continued. "He seemed so lonely, especially as Arthur had gone off with Susan, and one couldn't help guessing what was in his mind. So we had quite a long talk when you were looking at the ruins, and he told me all about his life, and his struggles, and how fearfully hard it had been. D'you know, he was a boy in a grocer's shop and took parcels to people's houses in a basket? That interested me awfully, because I always say it doesn't matter how you're born if you've got the right stuff in you. And he told me about his sister who's paralysed, poor girl, and one can see she's a great trial, though he's evidently very devoted to her. I must say I do admire people like that! I don't expect you do because you're so clever. Well, last night we sat out in the garden together, and I couldn't help seeing what he wanted to say, and comforting him a little, and telling him I did care—I really do—only, then, there's Raymond Oliver. What I want you to tell me is, can one be in love with two people at once, or can't one?"

She became silent, and sat with her chin on her hands, looking very intent, as if she were facing a real problem which had to be discussed between them.

"I think it depends what sort of person you are," said Hewet. He looked at her. She was small and pretty, aged perhaps twenty-eight or twenty-nine, but though dashing and sharply cut, her features expressed nothing very clearly, except a great deal of spirit and good health.

"Who are you, what are you; you see, I know nothing about you," he continued.

"Well, I was coming to that," said Evelyn M. She continued to rest her chin on her hands and to look intently ahead of her. "I'm the daughter of a mother and no father, if that interests you," she said. "It's not a very nice thing to be. It's what often happens in the country. She was a farmer's daughter, and he was rather a swell—the young man up at the great house. He never made things straight—never married her—though he allowed us quite a lot of money. His people wouldn't let him. Poor father! I can't help liking him. Mother wasn't the sort of woman who could keep him straight, anyhow. He was killed in the war. I believe his men worshipped him. They say great big troopers broke down and cried over his body on the battlefield. I wish I'd known him. Mother had all the life crushed out of her. The world—" She clenched her fist. "Oh, people can be horrid to a woman like that!" She turned upon Hewet.

"Well," she said, "d'you want to know any more about me?"

"But you?" he asked, "Who looked after you?"

"I've looked after myself mostly," she laughed. "I've had splendid friends. I do like people! That's the trouble. What would you do if you liked two people, both of them tremendously, and you couldn't tell which most?"

"I should go on liking them—I should wait and see. Why not?"

"But one has to make up one's mind," said Evelyn. "Or are you one of the people who doesn't believe in marriages and all that? Look here—this isn't fair, I do all the telling, and you tell nothing. Perhaps you're the same as your friend"—she looked at him suspiciously; "perhaps you don't like me?"

"I don't know you," said Hewet.

"I know when I like a person directly I see them! I knew I liked you the very first night at dinner. Oh dear," she continued impatiently, "what a lot of bother would be saved if only people would say the things they think straight out! I'm made like that. I can't help it."

"But don't you find it leads to difficulties?" Hewet asked.

"That's men's fault," she answered. "They always drag it in—love, I mean."

"And so you've gone on having one proposal after another," said Hewet.

"I don't suppose I've had more proposals than most women," said Evelyn, but she spoke without conviction.

"Five, six, ten?" Hewet ventured.

Evelyn seemed to intimate that perhaps ten was the right figure, but that it really was not a high one.

"I believe you're thinking me a heartless flirt," she protested. "But I don't care if you are. I don't care what anyone thinks of me. Just because one's interested and likes to be friends with men, and talk to them as one talks to women, one's called a flirt."

"But Miss Murgatroyd—"

"I wish you'd call me Evelyn," she interrupted.

"After ten proposals do you honestly think that men are the same as women?"

"Honestly, honestly—how I hate that word! It's always used by prigs," cried Evelyn. "Honestly I think they ought to be. That's what's so disappointing. Every time one thinks it's not going to happen, and every time it does."

"The pursuit of Friendship," said Hewet. "The title of a comedy."

"You're horrid," she cried. "You don't care a bit really. You might be Mr. Hirst."

"Well," said Hewet, "let's consider. Let us consider—" He paused, because for the moment he could not remember what it was that they had to consider. He was far more interested in her than in her story, for as she went on speaking his numbness had disappeared, and he was conscious of a mixture of liking, pity, and distrust. "You've promised to marry both Oliver and Perrott?" he concluded.

"Not exactly promised," said Evelyn. "I can't make up my mind which I really like best. Oh how I detest modern life!" she flung off. "It must have been so much easier for the Elizabethans! I thought the other day on that mountain how I'd have liked to be one of those colonists, to cut down trees and make laws and all that, instead of fooling about with all these people who think one's just a pretty young lady. Though I'm not. I really might *do* something." She reflected in silence for a minute. Then she said:

"I'm afraid right down in my heart that Alfred Perrot *won't* do. He's not strong, is he?"

"Perhaps he couldn't cut down a tree," said Hewet. "Have you never cared for anybody?" he asked.

"I've cared for heaps of people, but not to marry them," she said. "I suppose I'm too fastidious. All my life I've wanted somebody I could look up to, somebody great and big and splendid. Most men are so small."

"What d'you mean by splendid?" Hewet asked. "People are—nothing more."

Evelyn was puzzled.

"We don't care for people because of their qualities," he tried to explain. "It's just them that we care for"—he struck a match—"just that," he said, pointing to the flames.

"I see what you mean," she said, "but I don't agree. I do know why I care for people, and I think I'm hardly ever wrong. I see at once what they've got in them. Now I think you must be rather splendid; but not Mr. Hirst."

Hewlet shook his head.

"He's not nearly so unselfish, or so sympathetic, or so big, or so understanding," Evelyn continued.

Hewet sat silent, smoking his cigarette.

"I should hate cutting down trees," he remarked.

"I'm not trying to flirt with you, though I suppose you think I am!" Evelyn shot out. "I'd never have come to you if I'd thought you'd merely think odious things of me!" The tears came into her eyes.

"Do you never flirt?" he asked.

"Of course I don't," she protested. "Haven't I told you? I want friendship; I want to care for someone greater and nobler than I am, and if they fall in love with me it isn't my fault; I don't want it; I positively hate it."

Hewet could see that there was very little use in going on with the conversation, for it was obvious that Evelyn did not wish to say anything in particular, but to impress upon him an image of herself, being, for some reason which she would not reveal, unhappy, or insecure. He was very tired, and a pale waiter kept walking ostentatiously into the middle of the room and looking at them meaningly.

"They want to shut up," he said. "My advice is that you should tell Oliver and Perrott tomorrow that you've made up your mind that you don't mean to marry either of them. I'm certain you don't. If you change your mind you can always tell them so. They're both sensible men; they'll understand. And then all this bother will be over." He got up.

But Evelyn did not move. She sat looking up at him with her bright eager eyes, in the depths of which he thought he detected some disappointment, or dissatisfaction.

"Good-night," he said.

"There are heaps of things I want to say to you still," she said. "And I'm going to, some time. I suppose you must go to bed now?"

"Yes," said Hewet. "I'm half asleep." He left her still sitting by herself in the empty hall.

"Why is it that they *won't* be honest?" he muttered to himself as he went upstairs. Why was it that relations between different people were so unsatisfactory, so fragmentary, so hazardous, and words so dangerous that the instinct to sympathise with another human being was an instinct to be examined carefully and probably crushed? What had Evelyn really wished to say to him? What was she feeling left alone in the empty hall? The mystery of life and the unreality even of one's own sensations overcame him as he walked down the corridor which led to his room. It was dimly lighted, but sufficiently for him to see a figure in a bright dressing-gown pass swiftly in front of him, the figure of a woman crossing from one room to another.

CHAPTER XV

Whether too slight or too vague the ties that bind people casually meeting in a hotel at midnight, they possess one advantage at least over the bonds which unite the elderly, who have lived together once and so must live forever. Slight they may be, but vivid and genuine, merely because the power to break them is within the grasp of each, and there is no reason for continuance except a true desire that continue they shall. When two people have been married for years they seem to become unconscious of each other's bodily presence so that they move as if alone, speak aloud things which they do not expect to be answered, and in general seem to experience all the comfort of solitude without its loneliness. The joint lives of Ridley and Helen had arrived at this stage of community, and it was often necessary for one or the other to recall with an effort whether a thing had been said or only thought, shared or dreamt in private. At four o'clock in the afternoon two or three days later Mrs. Ambrose was standing brushing her hair, while her husband was in the dressing-room which opened out of her room, and occasionally, through the cascade of water—he was washing his face—she caught exclamations, "So it goes on year after year; I wish, I wish, I wish I could make an end of it," to which she paid no attention.

"It's white? Or only brown?" Thus she herself murmured, examining a hair which gleamed suspiciously among the brown. She pulled it out and laid it on the dressing-table. She was criticising her own appearance, or rather approving of it, standing a little way back from the glass and looking at her own face with superb pride and melancholy, when her husband appeared in the doorway in his shirt sleeves, his face half obscured by a towel.

"You often tell me I don't notice things," he remarked.

"Tell me if this is a white hair, then?" she replied. She laid the hair on his hand.

"There's not a white hair on your head," he exclaimed.

"Ah, Ridley, I begin to doubt," she sighed; and bowed her head under his eyes so that he might judge, but the inspection produced only a kiss where the line of parting ran, and husband and wife then proceeded to move about the room, casually murmuring.

"What was that you were saying?" Helen remarked, after an interval of conversation which no third person could have understood.

"Rachel—you ought to keep an eye upon Rachel," he observed significantly, and Helen, though she went on brushing her hair, looked at him. His observations were apt to be true.

"Young gentlemen don't interest themselves in young women's education without a motive," he remarked.

"Oh, Hirst," said Helen.

"Hirst and Hewet, they're all the same to me—all covered with spots," he replied. "He advises her to read Gibbon. Did you know that?"

Helen did not know that, but she would not allow herself inferior to her husband in powers of observation. She merely said:

"Nothing would surprise me. Even that dreadful flying man we met at the dance—even Mr. Dalloway—even—"

"I advise you to be circumspect," said Ridley. "There's Willoughby, remember—Willoughby"; he pointed at a letter.

Helen looked with a sigh at an envelope which lay upon her dressing-table. Yes, there lay Willoughby, curt, inexpressive, perpetually jocular, robbing a whole continent of mystery, enquiring after his daughter's manners and morals—hoping she wasn't a bore, and bidding them pack her off to him on board the very next ship if she were—and then grateful and affectionate with suppressed emotion, and then half a page about his own triumphs over wretched little natives who went on strike and refused to load his ships, until he roared English oaths at them, "popping my head out of the window just as I was, in my shirt sleeves. The beggars had the sense to scatter."

"If Theresa married Willoughby," she remarked, turning the page with a hairpin, "one doesn't see what's to prevent Rachel—"

But Ridley was now off on grievances of his own connected with the washing of his shirts, which somehow led to the frequent visits of Hughling Elliot, who was a bore, a pedant, a dry stick of a man, and yet Ridley couldn't simply point at the door and tell him to go. The truth of it was, they saw too many people. And so on and so on, more conjugal talk pattering softly and unintelligibly, until they were both ready to go down to tea.

The first thing that caught Helen's eye as she came downstairs was a carriage at the door, filled with skirts and feathers nodding on the tops of hats. She had only time to gain the drawing-room before two names were oddly mispronounced by the Spanish maid, and Mrs. Thornbury came in slightly in advance of Mrs. Wilfrid Flushing.

"Mrs. Wilfrid Flushing," said Mrs. Thornbury, with a wave of her hand. "A friend of our common friend Mrs. Raymond Parry."

Mrs. Flushing shook hands energetically. She was a woman of forty perhaps, very well set up and erect, splendidly robust, though not as tall as the upright carriage of her body made her appear.

She looked Helen straight in the face and said, "You have a charmin' house."

She had a strongly marked face, her eyes looked straight at you, and though naturally she was imperious in her manner she was nervous at the same time. Mrs. Thornbury acted as interpreter, making things smooth all round by a series of charming commonplace remarks.

"I've taken it upon myself, Mr. Ambrose," she said, "to promise that you will be so kind as to give Mrs. Flushing the benefit of your experience. I'm sure no one here knows the country as well as you do. No one takes such wonderful long walks. No one, I'm sure, has your encyclopaedic knowledge upon every subject. Mr. Wilfrid Flushing is a collector. He has discovered really beautiful things already. I had no notion that the peasants were so artistic—though of course in the past—"

"Not old things—new things," interrupted Mrs. Flushing curtly. "That is, if he takes my advice."

The Ambroses had not lived for many years in London without knowing something of a good many people, by name at least, and Helen remembered hearing of the Flushings. Mr. Flushing was a man who kept an old furniture shop; he had always said he would not marry because most women have red cheeks, and would not take a house because most houses have narrow staircases, and would not eat meat because most animals bleed when they are killed; and then he had married an eccentric aristocratic lady, who certainly was not pale, who looked as if she ate meat, who had forced him to do all the things he most disliked—and this then was the lady. Helen looked at her with interest. They had moved out into the garden, where the tea was laid under a tree, and Mrs. Flushing was helping herself to cherry jam. She had a peculiar jerking movement of the body when she spoke, which caused the canary-coloured plume on her hat to jerk too. Her small but finely-cut and vigorous features, together with the deep red of lips and cheeks, pointed to many generations of well-trained and well-nourished ancestors behind her.

"Nothin' that's more than twenty years old interests me," she continued. "Mouldy old pictures, dirty old books, they stick 'em in museums when they're only fit for burnin'."

"I quite agree," Helen laughed. "But my husband spends his life in digging up manuscripts which nobody wants." She was amused by Ridley's expression of startled disapproval.

"There's a clever man in London called John who paints ever so much better than the old masters," Mrs. Flushing continued. "His pictures excite me—nothin' that's old excites me."

"But even his pictures will become old," Mrs. Thornbury intervened.

"Then I'll have 'em burnt, or I'll put it in my will," said Mrs. Flushing.

"And Mrs. Flushing lived in one of the most beautiful old houses in England—Chillingley," Mrs. Thornbury explained to the rest of them.

"If I'd my way I'd burn that tomorrow," Mrs. Flushing laughed. She had a laugh like the cry of a jay, at once startling and joyless.

"What does any sane person want with those great big houses?" she demanded. "If you go downstairs after dark you're covered with black beetles, and the electric lights always goin' out. What would you do if spiders came out of the tap when you turned on the hot water?" she demanded, fixing her eye on Helen.

Mrs. Ambrose shrugged her shoulders with a smile.

"This is what I like," said Mrs. Flushing. She jerked her head at the Villa. "A little house in a garden. I had one once in Ireland. One could lie in bed in the mornin' and pick roses outside the window with one's toes."

"And the gardeners, weren't they surprised?" Mrs. Thornbury enquired.

"There were no gardeners," Mrs. Flushing chuckled. "Nobody but me and an old woman without any teeth. You know the poor in Ireland lose their teeth after they're twenty. But you wouldn't expect a politician to understand that—Arthur Balfour wouldn't understand that."

Ridley sighed that he never expected anyone to understand anything, least of all politicians.

"However," he concluded, "there's one advantage I find in extreme old age—nothing matters a hang except one's food and one's digestion. All I ask is to be left alone to moulder away in solitude. It's obvious that the world's going as fast as it can to—the Nethermost Pit, and all I can do is to sit still and consume as much of my own smoke as possible." He groaned, and with a melancholy glance laid the jam on his bread, for he felt the atmosphere of this abrupt lady distinctly unsympathetic.

"I always contradict my husband when he says that," said Mrs. Thornbury sweetly. "You men! Where would you be if it weren't for the women!"

"Read the *Symposium*," said Ridley grimly.

"*Symposium?*" cried Mrs. Flushing. "That's Latin or Greek? Tell me, is there a good translation?"

"No," said Ridley. "You will have to learn Greek."

Mrs. Flushing cried, "Ah, ah, ah! I'd rather break stones in the road. I always envy the men who break stones and sit on those nice little heaps all day wearin' spectacles. I'd infinitely rather break stones than clean out poultry runs, or feed the cows, or—"

Here Rachel came up from the lower garden with a book in her hand.

"What's that book?" said Ridley, when she had shaken hands.

"It's Gibbon," said Rachel as she sat down.

"*The Decline and Fall of the Roman Empire?*" said Mrs. Thornbury. "A very wonderful book, I know. My dear father was always quoting it at us, with the result that we resolved never to read a line."

"Gibbon the historian?" enquired Mrs. Flushing. "I connect him with some of the happiest hours of my life. We used to lie in bed and read Gibbon—about the massacres of the Christians, I remember—when we were supposed to be asleep. It's no joke, I can tell you, readin' a great big book, in double columns, by a night-light, and the light that comes through a chink in the door. Then there were the moths—tiger moths, yellow moths, and horrid cockchafers. Louisa, my sister, would have the window open. I wanted it shut. We fought every night of our lives over that window. Have you ever seen a moth dyin' in a night-light?" she enquired.

Again there was an interruption. Hewet and Hirst appeared at the drawing-room window and came up to the tea-table.

Rachel's heart beat hard. She was conscious of an extraordinary intensity in everything, as though their presence stripped some cover off the surface of things; but the greetings were remarkably commonplace.

"Excuse me," said Hirst, rising from his chair directly he had sat down. He went into the drawing-room, and returned with a cushion which he placed carefully upon his seat.

"Rheumatism," he remarked, as he sat down for the second time.

"The result of the dance?" Helen enquired.

"Whenever I get at all run down I tend to be rheumatic," Hirst stated. He bent his wrist back sharply. "I hear little pieces of chalk grinding together!"

Rachel looked at him. She was amused, and yet she was respectful; if such a thing could be, the upper part of her face seemed to laugh, and the lower part to check its laughter.

Hewet picked up the book that lay on the ground.

"You like this?" he asked in an undertone.

"No, I don't like it," she replied. She had indeed been trying all the afternoon to read it, and for some reason the glory which she had perceived at first had faded, and, read as she would, she could not grasp the meaning with her mind.

"It goes round, round, round, like a roll of oil-cloth," she hazarded. Evidently she meant Hewet alone to hear her words, but Hirst demanded, "What d'you mean?"

She was instantly ashamed of her figure of speech, for she could not explain it in words of sober criticism.

"Surely it's the most perfect style, so far as style goes, that's ever been invented," he continued. "Every sentence is practically perfect, and the wit—"

"Ugly in body, repulsive in mind," she thought, instead of thinking about Gibbon's style. "Yes, but strong, searching, unyielding in mind." She looked at his big head, a disproportionate part of which was occupied by the forehead, and at the direct, severe eyes.

"I give you up in despair," he said. He meant it lightly, but she took it seriously, and believed that her value as a human being was lessened because she did not happen to admire the style of Gibbon. The others were talking now in a group about the native villages which Mrs. Flushing ought to visit.

"I despair too," she said impetuously. "How are you going to judge people merely by their minds?"

"You agree with my spinster Aunt, I expect," said St. John in his jaunty manner, which was always irritating because it made the person he talked to appear unduly clumsy and in earnest. "'Be good, sweet maid'—I thought Mr. Kingsley and my Aunt were now obsolete."

"One can be very nice without having read a book," she asserted. Very silly and simple her words sounded, and laid her open to derision.

"Did I ever deny it?" Hirst enquired, raising his eyebrows.

Most unexpectedly Mrs. Thornbury here intervened, either because it was her mission to keep things smooth or because she had long wished to speak to Mr. Hirst, feeling as she did that young men were her sons.

"I have lived all my life with people like your Aunt, Mr. Hirst," she said, leaning forward in her chair. Her brown squirrel-like eyes became even brighter than usual. "They have never heard of Gibbon. They only care for their pheasants and their peasants. They are great big men who look so fine on horseback, as people must have done, I think, in the days of the great wars. Say what you like against them—they are animal, they are unintellectual; they don't read themselves, and they don't want others to read, but they are some of the finest and the kindest human beings on the face of the earth! You would be surprised at some of the stories I could tell. You have never guessed, perhaps, at all the romances that go on in the heart of the country. There are the people, I feel, among whom Shakespeare will be born if he is ever born again. In those old houses, up among the Downs—"

"My Aunt," Hirst interrupted, "spends her life in East Lambeth among the degraded poor. I only quoted my Aunt because she is inclined to persecute people she calls 'intellectual,' which is what I suspect Miss Vinrace of doing. It's all the fashion now. If you're clever it's always taken for granted that you're completely without sympathy, understanding, affection—all the things that really matter. Oh, you Christians! You're the most conceited, patronising, hypocritical set of old humbugs in the kingdom! Of course," he continued, "I'm the first to allow your country gentlemen great merits. For one thing, they're probably quite frank about their passions, which we are not. My father, who is a clergyman in Norfolk, says that there is hardly a squire in the country who does not—"

"But about Gibbon?" Hewet interrupted. The look of nervous tension which had come over every face was relaxed by the interruption.

"You find him monotonous, I suppose. But you know—" He opened the book, and began searching for passages to read aloud, and in a little time he found a good one which he considered suitable. But there was nothing in the world that bored Ridley more than being read aloud to, and he was besides scrupulously fastidious as to the dress and behaviour of ladies. In the space of fifteen minutes he had decided against Mrs. Flushing on the ground that her orange plume did not suit her complexion, that she spoke too loud, that she crossed her legs, and finally, when he saw her accept a cigarette that Hewet offered her, he jumped up, exclaiming something about "bar parlours," and left them. Mrs. Flushing was evidently relieved by his departure. She puffed her cigarette, stuck her legs out, and examined Helen closely as to the character and reputation of their common friend Mrs. Raymond Parry. By a series of little strategems she drove her to define Mrs. Parry as somewhat elderly, by no means beautiful, very much made up—an insolent old harridan, in short, whose parties were amusing because one met odd people; but Helen herself always pitied poor Mr. Parry, who was understood to be shut up downstairs with cases full of gems, while his wife enjoyed herself in the drawing-room. "Not that I believe what people say against her—although she hints, of course—" Upon which Mrs. Flushing cried out with delight:

"She's my first cousin! Go on—go on!"

When Mrs. Flushing rose to go she was obviously delighted with her new acquaintances. She made three or four different plans for meeting or going on an expedition, or showing Helen the things they had bought, on her way to the carriage. She included them all in a vague but magnificent invitation.

As Helen returned to the garden again, Ridley's words of warning came into her head, and she hesitated a moment and looked at Rachel sitting between Hirst and Hewet. But she could draw no conclusions, for Hewet was still reading Gibbon aloud, and Rachel, for all the expression she had, might have been a shell, and his words water rubbing against her ears, as water rubs a shell on the edge of a rock.

Hewet's voice was very pleasant. When he reached the end of the period Hewet stopped, and no one volunteered any criticism.

"I do adore the aristocracy!" Hirst exclaimed after a moment's pause. "They're so amazingly unscrupulous. None of us would dare to behave as that woman behaves."

"What I like about them," said Helen as she sat down, "is that they're so well put together. Naked, Mrs. Flushing would be superb. Dressed as she dresses, it's absurd, of course."

"Yes," said Hirst. A shade of depression crossed his face. "I've never weighed more than ten stone in my life," he said, "which is ridiculous, considering my height, and I've actually gone down in weight since we came here. I daresay that accounts for the rheumatism." Again he jerked his wrist back sharply, so that Helen might hear the grinding of the chalk stones. She could not help smiling.

"It's no laughing matter for me, I assure you," he protested. "My mother's a chronic invalid, and I'm always expecting to be told that I've got heart disease myself. Rheumatism always goes to the heart in the end."

"For goodness' sake, Hirst," Hewet protested; "one might think you were an old cripple of eighty. If it comes to that, I had an aunt who died of cancer myself, but I put a bold face on it—" He rose and began tilting his chair backwards and forwards on its hind legs. "Is anyone here inclined for a walk?" he said. "There's a magnificent walk, up behind the house. You come out on to a cliff and look right down into the sea. The rocks are all red; you can see them through the water. The other day I saw a sight that fairly took my breath away—about twenty jelly-fish, semi-transparent, pink, with long streamers, floating on the top of the waves."

"Sure they weren't mermaids?" said Hirst. "It's much too hot to climb uphill." He looked at Helen, who showed no signs of moving.

"Yes, it's too hot," Helen decided.

There was a short silence.

"I'd like to come," said Rachel.

"But she might have said that anyhow," Helen thought to herself as Hewet and Rachel went away together, and Helen was left alone with St. John, to St. John's obvious satisfaction.

He may have been satisfied, but his usual difficulty in deciding that one subject was more deserving of notice than another prevented him from speaking for some time. He sat staring intently at the head of a dead match, while Helen considered—so it seemed from the expression of her eyes—something not closely connected with the present moment.

At last St. John exclaimed, "Damn! Damn everything! Damn everybody!" he added. "At Cambridge there are people to talk to."

"At Cambridge there are people to talk to," Helen echoed him, rhythmically and absent-mindedly. Then she woke up. "By the way, have you settled what you're going to do—is it to be Cambridge or the Bar?"

He pursed his lips, but made no immediate answer, for Helen was still slightly inattentive. She had been thinking about Rachel and which of the two young men she was likely to fall in love with, and now sitting opposite to Hirst she thought, "He's ugly. It's a pity they're so ugly."

She did not include Hewet in this criticism; she was thinking of the clever, honest, interesting young men she knew, of whom Hirst was a good example, and wondering whether it was necessary that thought and scholarship should thus maltreat their bodies, and should thus elevate their minds to a very high tower from which the human race appeared to them like rats and mice squirming on the flat.

"And the future?" she reflected, vaguely envisaging a race of men becoming more and more like Hirst, and a race of women becoming more and more like Rachel. "Oh no," she concluded, glancing at him, "one wouldn't marry you. Well, then, the future of the race is in the hands of Susan and Arthur; no—that's dreadful. Of farm labourers; no—not of the English at all, but of Russians and Chinese." This train of thought did not satisfy her, and was interrupted by St. John, who began again:

"I wish you knew Bennett. He's the greatest man in the world."

"Bennett?" she enquired. Becoming more at ease, St. John dropped the concentrated abruptness of his manner, and explained that Bennett was a man who lived in an old windmill six miles out of Cambridge. He lived the perfect life, according to St. John, very lonely, very simple, caring only for the truth of things, always ready to talk, and extraordinarily modest, though his mind was of the greatest.

"Don't you think," said St. John, when he had done describing him, "that kind of thing makes this kind of thing rather flimsy? Did you notice at tea how poor old Hewet had to change the conversation? How they were all ready to pounce upon me because they thought I was going to say something improper? It wasn't anything, really. If Bennett had been there he'd have said exactly what he meant to say, or he'd have got up and gone. But there's something rather bad for the character in that—I mean if one hasn't got Bennett's character. It's inclined to make one bitter. Should you say that I was bitter?"

Helen did not answer, and he continued:

"Of course I am, disgustingly bitter, and it's a beastly thing to be. But the worst of me is that I'm so envious. I envy every one. I can't endure people who do things better than I do—perfectly absurd things too—waiters balancing piles of plates—even Arthur, because Susan's in love with him. I want people to like me, and they don't. It's partly my appearance, I expect," he continued, "though it's an absolute lie to say I've Jewish blood in me—as a matter of fact we've been in Norfolk, Hirst of Hirstbourne Hall, for three centuries at least. It must be awfully soothing to be like you—every one liking one at once."

"I assure you they don't," Helen laughed.

"They do," said Hirst with conviction. "In the first place, you're the most beautiful woman I've ever seen; in the second, you have an exceptionally nice nature."

If Hirst had looked at her instead of looking intently at his teacup he would have seen Helen blush, partly with pleasure, partly with an impulse of affection towards the young man who had seemed, and would seem again, so ugly and so limited. She pitied him, for she suspected that he suffered, and she was interested in him, for many of the things he said seemed to her true; she admired the morality of youth, and yet she felt imprisoned. As if her instinct were to escape to something brightly coloured and impersonal, which she could hold in her hands, she went into the house and returned with her embroidery. But he was not interested in her embroidery; he did not even look at it.

"About Miss Vinrace," he began—"oh, look here, do let's be St. John and Helen, and Rachel and Terence—what's she like? Does she reason, does she feel, or is she merely a kind of footstool?"

"Oh no," said Helen, with great decision. From her observations at tea she was inclined to doubt whether Hirst was the person to educate Rachel. She had gradually come to be interested in her niece, and fond of her; she disliked some things about her very much, she was amused by others; but she felt her, on the whole, a live if unformed human being, experimental, and not always fortunate in her experiments, but with powers of some kind, and a capacity for feeling. Somewhere in the depths of her, too, she was bound to Rachel by the indestructible if inexplicable ties of sex. "She seems vague, but she's a will of her own," she said, as if in the interval she had run through her qualities.

The embroidery, which was a matter for thought, the design being difficult and the colours wanting consideration, brought lapses into the dialogue when she seemed to be engrossed in her skeins of silk, or, with head a little drawn back and eyes narrowed, considered the effect of the whole. Thus she merely said, "Um-m-m" to St. John's next remark, "I shall ask her to go for a walk with me."

Perhaps he resented this division of attention. He sat silent watching Helen closely.

"You're absolutely happy," he proclaimed at last.

"Yes?" Helen enquired, sticking in her needle.

"Marriage, I suppose," said St. John.

"Yes," said Helen, gently drawing her needle out.

"Children?" St. John enquired.

"Yes," said Helen, sticking her needle in again. "I don't know why I'm happy," she suddenly laughed, looking him full in the face. There was a considerable pause.

"There's an abyss between us," said St. John. His voice sounded as if it issued from the depths of a cavern in the rocks. "You're infinitely simpler than I am. Women always are, of course. That's the difficulty. One never knows how a woman gets there. Supposing all the time you're thinking, 'Oh, what a morbid young man!'"

Helen sat and looked at him with her needle in her hand. From her position she saw his head in front of the dark pyramid of a magnolia-tree. With one foot raised on the rung of a chair, and her elbow out in the attitude for sewing, her own figure possessed the sublimity of a woman's of the early world, spinning the thread of fate—the sublimity possessed by many women of the present day who fall into the attitude required by scrubbing or sewing. St. John looked at her.

"I suppose you've never paid any a compliment in the course of your life," he said irrelevantly.

"I spoil Ridley rather," Helen considered.

"I'm going to ask you point blank—do you like me?"

After a certain pause, she replied, "Yes, certainly."

"Thank God!" he exclaimed. "That's one mercy. You see," he continued with emotion, "I'd rather you liked me than anyone I've ever met."

"What about the five philosophers?" said Helen, with a laugh, stitching firmly and swiftly at her canvas. "I wish you'd describe them."

Hirst had no particular wish to describe them, but when he began to consider them he found himself soothed and strengthened. Far away to the other side of the world as they were, in smoky rooms, and grey medieval courts, they appeared remarkable figures, free-spoken men with whom one could be at ease; incomparably more subtle in emotion than the people here. They gave him, certainly, what no woman could give him, not Helen even. Warming at the thought of them, he went on to lay his case before Mrs. Ambrose. Should he stay on at Cambridge or should he go to the Bar? One day he thought one thing, another day another. Helen listened attentively. At last, without any preface, she pronounced her decision.

"Leave Cambridge and go to the Bar," she said. He pressed her for her reasons.

"I think you'd enjoy London more," she said. It did not seem a very subtle reason, but she appeared to think it sufficient. She looked at him against the background of flowering magnolia. There was something curious in the sight. Perhaps it was that the heavy wax-like flowers were so smooth and inarticulate, and his face—he had thrown his hat away, his hair was rumpled, he held his eyeglasses in his hand, so that a red mark appeared on either side of his nose—was so worried and garrulous. It was a beautiful bush, spreading very widely, and all the time she had sat there talking she had been noticing the patches of shade and the shape of the leaves, and the way the great white flowers sat in the midst of the green. She had noticed it half-consciously, nevertheless the pattern had become part of their talk. She laid down her sewing, and began to walk up and down the garden, and Hirst rose too and paced by her side. He was rather disturbed, uncomfortable, and full of thought. Neither of them spoke.

The sun was beginning to go down, and a change had come over the mountains, as if they were robbed of their earthly substance, and composed merely of intense blue mist. Long thin clouds of flamingo red, with edges like the edges of curled ostrich feathers, lay up and down the sky at different altitudes. The roofs of the town seemed to have sunk lower than usual; the cypresses appeared very black between the roofs, and the roofs themselves were brown and white. As usual in the evening, single cries and single bells became audible rising from beneath.

St. John stopped suddenly.

"Well, you must take the responsibility," he said. "I've made up my mind; I shall go to the Bar."

His words were very serious, almost emotional; they recalled Helen after a second's hesitation.

"I'm sure you're right," she said warmly, and shook the hand he held out. "You'll be a great man, I'm certain."

Then, as if to make him look at the scene, she swept her hand round the immense circumference of the view. From the sea, over the roofs of the town, across the crests of the mountains, over the river and the plain, and again across the crests of the mountains it swept until it reached the villa, the garden, the magnolia-tree, and the figures of Hirst and herself standing together, when it dropped to her side.

CHAPTER XVI

Hewet and Rachel had long ago reached the particular place on the edge of the cliff where, looking down into the sea, you might chance on jelly-fish and dolphins. Looking the other way, the vast expanse of land gave them a sensation which is given by no view, however extended, in England; the villages and the hills there having names, and the farthest horizon of hills as often as not dipping and showing a line of mist which is the sea; here the view was one of infinite sun-dried earth, earth pointed in pinnacles, heaped in vast barriers, earth widening and spreading away and away like the immense floor of the sea, earth chequered by day and by night, and partitioned into different lands, where famous cities were founded, and the races of men changed from dark savages to white civilised men, and back to dark savages again. Perhaps their English blood made this prospect uncomfortably impersonal and hostile to them, for having once turned their faces that way they next turned them to the sea, and for the rest of the time sat looking at the sea. The sea, though it was a thin and sparkling water here, which seemed incapable of surge or anger, eventually narrowed itself, clouded its pure tint with grey, and swirled through narrow channels and dashed in a shiver of broken waters against massive granite rocks. It was this sea that flowed up to the mouth of the Thames; and the Thames washed the roots of the city of London.

Hewet's thoughts had followed some such course as this, for the first thing he said as they stood on the edge of the cliff was—

"I'd like to be in England!"

Rachel lay down on her elbow, and parted the tall grasses which grew on the edge, so that she might have a clear view. The water was very calm; rocking up and down at the base of the cliff, and so clear that one could see the red of the stones at the bottom of it. So it had been at the birth of the world, and so it had remained ever since. Probably no human being had ever broken that water with boat or with body. Obeying some impulse, she determined to mar that eternity of peace, and threw the largest pebble she could find. It struck the water, and the ripples spread out and out. Hewet looked down too.

"It's wonderful," he said, as they widened and ceased. The freshness and the newness seemed to him wonderful. He threw a pebble next. There was scarcely any sound.

"But England," Rachel murmured in the absorbed tone of one whose eyes are concentrated upon some sight. "What d'you want with England?"

"My friends chiefly," he said, "and all the things one does."

He could look at Rachel without her noticing it. She was still absorbed in the water and the exquisitely pleasant sensations which a little depth of the sea washing over rocks suggests. He noticed that she was wearing a dress of deep blue colour, made of a soft thin cotton stuff, which clung to the shape of her body. It was a body with the angles and hollows of a young woman's body not yet developed, but in no way distorted, and thus interesting and even lovable. Raising his eyes Hewet observed her head; she had taken her hat off, and the face rested on her hand. As she looked down into the sea, her lips were slightly parted. The expression was one of childlike intentness, as if she were watching for a fish to swim past over the clear red rocks. Nevertheless her twenty-four years of life had given her a look of reserve. Her hand, which lay on the ground, the fingers curling slightly in, was well shaped and competent; the square-tipped and nervous fingers were the fingers of a musician. With something like anguish Hewet realised that, far from being unattractive, her body was very attractive to him. She looked up suddenly. Her eyes were full of eagerness and interest.

"You write novels?" she asked.

For the moment he could not think what he was saying. He was overcome with the desire to hold her in his arms.

"Oh yes," he said. "That is, I want to write them."

She would not take her large grey eyes off his face.

"Novels," she repeated. "Why do you write novels? You ought to write music. Music, you see"—she shifted her eyes, and became less desirable as her brain began to work, inflicting a certain change upon her face—"music goes straight for things. It says all there is to say at once. With writing it seems to me there's so much"—she paused for an expression, and rubbed her fingers in the earth—"scratching on the matchbox. Most of the time when I was reading Gibbon this afternoon I was horribly, oh infernally, damnably bored!" She gave a shake of laughter, looking at Hewet, who laughed too.

"*I* shan't lend you books," he remarked.

"Why is it," Rachel continued, "that I can laugh at Mr. Hirst to you, but not to his face? At tea I was completely overwhelmed, not by his ugliness—by his mind." She enclosed a circle in the air with her hands. She realised with a great sense of comfort how easily she could talk to Hewet, those thorns or ragged corners which tear the surface of some relationships being smoothed away.

"So I observed," said Hewet. "That's a thing that never ceases to amaze me." He had recovered his composure to such an extent that he could light and smoke a cigarette, and feeling her ease, became happy and easy himself.

"The respect that women, even well-educated, very able women, have for men," he went on. "I believe we must have the sort of power over you that we're said to have over horses. They see us three times as big as we are or they'd never obey us. For that very reason, I'm inclined to doubt that you'll ever do anything even when you have the vote." He looked at her reflectively. She appeared very smooth and sensitive and young. "It'll take at least six generations before you're sufficiently thick-skinned to go into law courts and business offices. Consider what a bully the ordinary man is," he continued, "the ordinary hard-working, rather ambitious solicitor or man of business with a family to bring up and a certain position to maintain. And then, of course, the daughters have to give way to the sons; the sons have to be educated; they have to bully and shove for their wives and families, and so it all comes over again. And meanwhile there are the women in the background . . . Do you really think that the vote will do you any good?"

"The vote?" Rachel repeated. She had to visualise it as a little bit of paper which she dropped into a box before she understood his question, and looking at each other they smiled at something absurd in the question.

"Not to me," she said. "But I play the piano . . . Are men really like that?" she asked, returning to the question that interested her. "I'm not afraid of you." She looked at him easily.

"Oh, I'm different," Hewet replied. "I've got between six and seven hundred a year of my own. And then no one takes a novelist seriously, thank heavens. There's no doubt it helps to make up for the drudgery of a profession if a man's taken very, very seriously by every one—if he gets appointments, and has offices and a title, and lots of letters after his name, and bits of ribbon and degrees. I don't grudge it 'em, though sometimes it comes over me—what an amazing concoction! What a miracle the masculine conception of life is—judges, civil servants, army, navy, Houses of Parliament, lord mayors—what a world we've made of it! Look at Hirst now. I assure you," he said, "not a day's passed since we came here without a discussion as to whether he's to stay on at Cambridge or to go to the Bar. It's his career—his sacred career. And if I've heard it twenty times, I'm sure his mother and sister have heard it five hundred times. Can't you imagine the family conclaves, and the sister told to run out and feed the rabbits because St. John must have the school-room to himself—'St. John's working,' 'St. John wants his tea brought to him.' Don't you know the kind of thing? No wonder that St. John thinks it a matter of considerable importance. It is too. He has to earn his living. But St. John's sister—" Hewet puffed in silence. "No one takes her seriously, poor dear. She feeds the rabbits."

"Yes," said Rachel. "I've fed rabbits for twenty-four years; it seems odd now." She looked meditative, and Hewet, who had been talking much at random and instinctively adopting the feminine point of view, saw that she would now talk about herself, which was what he wanted, for so they might come to know each other.

She looked back meditatively upon her past life.

"How do you spend your day?" he asked.

She meditated still. When she thought of their day it seemed to her it was cut into four pieces by their meals. These divisions were absolutely rigid, the contents of the day having to accommodate themselves within the four rigid bars. Looking back at her life, that was what she saw.

"Breakfast nine; luncheon one; tea five; dinner eight," she said.

"Well," said Hewet, "what d'you do in the morning?"

"I use to play the piano for hours and hours."

"And after luncheon?"

"Then I went shopping with one of my aunts. Or we went to see someone, or we took a message; or we did something that had to be done—the taps might be leaking. They visit the poor a good deal—old char-women with bad legs, women who want tickets for hospitals. Or I used to walk in the park by myself. And after tea people sometimes called; or in summer we sat in the garden or played croquet; in winter I read aloud, while they worked; after dinner I played the piano and they wrote letters. If father was at home we had friends of his to dinner, and about once a month we went up to the play. Every now and then we dined out; sometimes I went to a dance in London, but that was difficult because of getting back. The people we saw were old family friends, and relations, but we didn't see many people. There was the clergyman, Mr. Pepper, and the Hunts. Father generally wanted to be quiet when he came home, because he works very hard at Hull. Also my aunts aren't very strong. A house takes up a lot of time if you do it properly. Our servants were always bad, and so Aunt Lucy used to do a good deal in the kitchen, and Aunt Clara, I think, spent most of the morning dusting the drawing-room and going through the linen and silver. Then there were the dogs. They had to be exercised, besides being washed and brushed. Now Sandy's dead, but Aunt Clara has a very old cockatoo that came from India. Everything in our house," she exclaimed, "comes from somewhere! It's full of old furniture, not really old, Victorian, things mother's family had or father's family had, which they didn't like to get rid of, I suppose, though we've really no room for them. It's rather a nice house," she continued, "except that it's a little dingy— dull I should say." She called up before her eyes a vision of the drawing-room at home; it was a large oblong room, with a square window opening on the garden. Green plush chairs stood against the wall; there was a heavy carved book-case, with glass doors, and a general impression of faded sofa covers, large spaces of pale green, and baskets with pieces of wool-work dropping out of them. Photographs from old Italian masterpieces hung on the walls, and views of Venetian bridges and Swedish waterfalls which members of the family had seen years ago. There were also one or two portraits of fathers and grandmothers, and an engraving of John Stuart Mill, after the picture by Watts. It was a room without definite character, being neither typically and openly hideous, nor strenuously artistic, nor really comfortable. Rachel roused herself from the contemplation of this familiar picture.

"But this isn't very interesting for you," she said, looking up.

"Good Lord!" Hewet exclaimed. "I've never been so much interested in my life." She then realised that while she had been thinking of Richmond, his eyes had never left her face. The knowledge of this excited her.

"Go on, please go on," he urged. "Let's imagine it's a Wednesday. You're all at luncheon. You sit there, and Aunt Lucy there, and Aunt Clara here"; he arranged three pebbles on the grass between them.

"Aunt Clara carves the neck of lamb," Rachel continued. She fixed her gaze upon the pebbles. "There's a very ugly yellow china stand in front of me, called a dumb waiter, on which are three dishes, one for biscuits, one for butter, and one for cheese. There's a pot of ferns. Then there's Blanche the maid, who snuffles because of her nose. We talk—oh yes, it's Aunt Lucy's afternoon at Walworth, so we're rather quick over luncheon. She goes off. She has a purple bag, and a black notebook. Aunt Clara has what they call a G.F.S. meeting in the drawing-room on Wednesday, so I take the dogs out. I go up Richmond Hill, along the terrace, into the park. It's the 18th of April— the same day as it is here. It's spring in England. The ground is rather damp. However, I cross the road and get on to the grass and we walk along, and I sing as I always do when I'm alone, until we come to the open place where you can see the whole of London beneath you on a clear day. Hampstead Church spire there, Westminster Cathedral over there, and factory chimneys about here. There's generally a haze over the low parts of London; but it's often blue over the park when London's in a mist. It's the open place that the balloons cross going over to Hurlingham. They're pale yellow. Well, then, it smells very good, particularly if they happen to be burning wood in the keeper's lodge which is there. I could tell you now how to get from place to place, and exactly what trees you'd pass, and where you'd cross the roads. You see, I played there when I was small. Spring is good, but it's best in the autumn when the deer are barking; then it gets dusky, and I go back through the streets, and you can't see people properly; they come past very quick, you just see their faces and then they're gone—that's what I like—and no one knows in the least what you're doing—"

"But you have to be back for tea, I suppose?" Hewet checked her.

"Tea? Oh yes. Five o'clock. Then I say what I've done, and my aunts say what they've done, and perhaps someone comes in: Mrs. Hunt, let's suppose. She's an old lady with a lame leg. She has or she once had eight children; so we ask after them. They're all over the world; so we ask where they are, and sometimes they're ill, or they're stationed in a cholera district, or in some place where it only rains once in five months. Mrs. Hunt," she said with a smile, "had a son who was hugged to death by a bear."

Here she stopped and looked at Hewet to see whether he was amused by the same things that amused her. She was reassured. But she thought it necessary to apologise again; she had been talking too much.

"You can't conceive how it interests me," he said. Indeed, his cigarette had gone out, and he had to light another.

"Why does it interest you?" she asked.

"Partly because you're a woman," he replied. When he said this, Rachel, who had become oblivious of anything, and had reverted to a childlike state of interest and pleasure, lost her freedom and became self-conscious. She felt herself at once singular and under observation, as she felt with St. John Hirst. She was about to launch into an argument which would have made them both feel bitterly against each other, and to define sensations which had no such importance as words were bound to give them when Hewet led her thoughts in a different direction.

"I've often walked along the streets where people live all in a row, and one house is exactly like another house, and wondered what on earth the women were doing inside," he said. "Just consider: it's the beginning of the twentieth century, and until a few years ago no woman had ever come out by herself and said things at all. There it was going on in the background, for all those thousands of years, this curious silent unrepresented life. Of course we're always writing about women—abusing them, or jeering at them, or worshipping them; but it's never come from women themselves. I believe we still don't know in the least how they live, or what they feel, or what they do precisely. If one's a man, the only confidences one gets are from young women about their love affairs. But the lives of women of forty, of unmarried women, of working women, of women who keep shops and bring up children, of women like your aunts or Mrs. Thornbury or Miss

Allan—one knows nothing whatever about them. They won't tell you. Either they're afraid, or they've got a way of treating men. It's the man's view that's represented, you see. Think of a railway train: fifteen carriages for men who want to smoke. Doesn't it make your blood boil? If I were a woman I'd blow someone's brains out. Don't you laugh at us a great deal? Don't you think it all a great humbug? You, I mean—how does it all strike you?"

His determination to know, while it gave meaning to their talk, hampered her; he seemed to press further and further, and made it appear so important. She took some time to answer, and during that time she went over and over the course of her twenty-four years, lighting now on one point, now on another—on her aunts, her mother, her father, and at last her mind fixed upon her aunts and her father, and she tried to describe them as at this distance they appeared to her.

They were very much afraid of her father. He was a great dim force in the house, by means of which they held on to the great world which is represented every morning in the *Times*. But the real life of the house was something quite different from this. It went on independently of Mr. Vinrace, and tended to hide itself from him. He was good-humoured towards them, but contemptuous. She had always taken it for granted that his point of view was just, and founded upon an ideal scale of things where the life of one person was absolutely more important than the life of another, and that in that scale they were much less importance than he was. But did she really believe that? Hewet's words made her think. She always submitted to her father, just as they did, but it was her aunts who influenced her really; her aunts who built up the fine, closely woven substance of their life at home. They were less splendid but more natural than her father was. All her rages had been against them; it was their world with its four meals, its punctuality, and servants on the stairs at half-past ten, that she examined so closely and wanted so vehemently to smash to atoms. Following these thoughts she looked up and said:

"And there's a sort of beauty in it—there they are at Richmond at this very moment building things up. They're all wrong, perhaps, but there's a sort of beauty in it," she repeated. "It's so unconscious, so modest. And yet they feel things. They do mind if people die. Old spinsters are always doing things. I don't quite know what they do. Only that was what I felt when I lived with them. It was very real."

She reviewed their little journeys to and fro, to Walworth, to charwomen with bad legs, to meetings for this and that, their minute acts of charity and unselfishness which flowered punctually from a definite view of what they ought to do, their friendships, their tastes and habits; she saw all these things like grains of sand falling, falling through innumerable days, making an atmosphere and building up a solid mass, a background. Hewet observed her as she considered this.

"Were you happy?" he demanded.

Again she had become absorbed in something else, and he called her back to an unusually vivid consciousness of herself.

"I was both," she replied. "I was happy and I was miserable. You've no conception what it's like—to be a young woman." She looked straight at him. "There are terrors and agonies," she said, keeping her eye on him as if to detect the slightest hint of laughter.

"I can believe it," he said. He returned her look with perfect sincerity.

"Women one sees in the streets," she said.

"Prostitutes?"

"Men kissing one."

He nodded his head.

"You were never told?"

She shook her head.

"And then," she began and stopped. Here came in the great space of life into which no one had ever penetrated. All that she had been saying about her father and her aunts and walks in Richmond Park, and what they did from hour to hour, was merely on the surface. Hewet was watching her. Did he demand that she should describe that also? Why did he sit so near and keep his eye on her? Why did they not have done with this searching and agony? Why did they not kiss each other simply? She wished to kiss him. But all the time she went on spinning out words.

"A girl is more lonely than a boy. No one cares in the least what she does. Nothing's expected of her. Unless one's very pretty people don't listen to what you say . . . And that is what I like," she added energetically, as if the memory were very happy. "I like walking in Richmond Park and singing to myself and knowing it doesn't matter a damn to anybody. I like seeing things go on—as we saw you that night when you didn't see us—I love the freedom of it—it's like being the wind or the sea." She turned with a curious fling of her hands and looked at the sea. It was still very blue, dancing away as far as the eye could reach, but the light on it was yellower, and the clouds were turning flamingo red.

A feeling of intense depression crossed Hewet's mind as she spoke. It seemed plain that she would never care for one person rather than another; she was evidently quite indifferent to him; they seemed to come very near, and then they were as far apart as ever again; and her gesture as she turned away had been oddly beautiful.

"Nonsense," he said abruptly. "You like people. You like admiration. Your real grudge against Hirst is that he doesn't admire you."

She made no answer for some time. Then she said:

"That's probably true. Of course I like people—I like almost every one I've ever met."

She turned her back on the sea and regarded Hewet with friendly if critical eyes. He was good-looking in the sense that he had always had a sufficiency of beef to eat and fresh air to breathe. His head was big; the eyes were also large; though generally vague they could be forcible; and the lips were sensitive. One might account him a man of considerable passion and fitful energy, likely to be at the mercy of moods which had little relation to facts; at once tolerant and fastidious. The breadth of his forehead showed capacity for thought. The interest with which Rachel looked at him was heard in her voice.

"What novels do you write?" she asked.

"I want to write a novel about Silence," he said; "the things people don't say. But the difficulty is immense." He sighed. "However, you don't care," he continued. He looked at her almost severely. "Nobody cares. All you read a novel for is to see what sort of person the writer is, and, if you know him, which of his friends he's put in. As for the novel itself, the whole conception, the way one's seen the thing, felt about it, make it stand in relation to other things, not one in a million cares for that. And yet I sometimes wonder whether there's anything else in the whole world worth doing. These other people," he indicated the hotel, "are always wanting something they can't get. But there's an extraordinary satisfaction in writing, even in the attempt to write. What you said just now is true: one doesn't want to be things; one wants merely to be allowed to see them."

Some of the satisfaction of which he spoke came into his face as he gazed out to sea.

It was Rachel's turn now to feel depressed. As he talked of writing he had become suddenly impersonal. He might never care for anyone; all that desire to know her and get at her, which she had felt pressing on her almost painfully, had completely vanished.

"Are you a good writer?" she asked.

"Yes," he said. "I'm not first-rate, of course; I'm good second-rate; about as good as Thackeray, I should say."

Rachel was amazed. For one thing it amazed her to hear Thackeray called second-rate; and then she could not widen her point of view to believe that there could be great writers in existence at the present day, or if there were, that anyone she knew could be a great writer, and his self-confidence astounded her, and he became more and more remote.

"My other novel," Hewet continued, "is about a young man who is obsessed by an idea—the idea of being a gentleman. He manages to exist at Cambridge on a hundred pounds a year. He has a coat; it was once a very good coat. But the trousers—they're not so good. Well, he goes up to London, gets into good society, owing to an early-morning adventure on the banks of the Serpentine. He is led into telling lies—my idea, you see, is to show the gradual corruption of the soul—calls himself the son of some great landed proprietor in Devonshire. Meanwhile the coat becomes older and older, and he hardly dares to wear the trousers. Can't you imagine the wretched man, after some splendid evening of debauchery, contemplating these garments—hanging them over the end of the bed, arranging them now in full light, now in shade, and wondering whether they will survive him, or he will survive them? Thoughts of suicide cross his mind. He has a friend, too, a man who somehow subsists upon selling small birds, for which he sets traps in the fields near Uxbridge. They're scholars, both of them. I know one or two wretched starving creatures like that who quote Aristotle at you over a fried herring and a pint of porter. Fashionable life, too, I have to represent at some length, in order to show my hero under all circumstances. Lady Theo Bingham Bingley, whose bay mare he had the good fortune to stop, is the daughter of a very fine old Tory peer. I'm going to describe the kind of parties I once went to—the fashionable intellectuals, you know, who like to have the latest book on their tables. They give parties, river parties, parties where you play games. There's no difficulty in conceiving incidents; the difficulty is to put them into shape—not to get run away with, as Lady Theo was. It ended disastrously for her, poor woman, for the book, as I planned it, was going to end in profound and sordid respectability. Disowned by her father, she marries my hero, and they live in a snug little villa outside Croydon, in which town he is set up as a house agent. He never succeeds in becoming a real gentleman after all. That's the interesting part of it. Does it seem to you the kind of book you'd like to read?" he enquired; "or perhaps you'd like my Stuart tragedy better," he continued, without waiting for her to answer him. "My idea is that there's a certain quality of beauty in the past, which the ordinary historical novelist completely ruins by his absurd conventions. The moon becomes the Regent of the Skies. People clap spurs to their horses, and so on. I'm going to treat people as though they were exactly the same as we are. The advantage is that, detached from modern conditions, one can make them more intense and more abstract then people who live as we do."

Rachel had listened to all this with attention, but with a certain amount of bewilderment. They both sat thinking their own thoughts.

"I'm not like Hirst," said Hewet, after a pause; he spoke meditatively; "I don't see circles of chalk between people's feet. I sometimes wish I did. It seems to me so tremendously complicated and confused. One can't come to any decision at all; one's less and less capable of making judgments. D'you find that? And then one never knows what anyone feels. We're all in the dark.

We try to find out, but can you imagine anything more ludicrous than one person's opinion of another person? One goes along thinking one knows; but one really doesn't know."

As he said this he was leaning on his elbow arranging and rearranging in the grass the stones which had represented Rachel and her aunts at luncheon. He was speaking as much to himself as to Rachel. He was reasoning against the desire, which had returned with intensity, to take her in his arms; to have done with indirectness; to explain exactly what he felt. What he said was against his belief; all the things that were important about her he knew; he felt them in the air around them; but he said nothing; he went on arranging the stones.

"I like you; d'you like me?" Rachel suddenly observed.

"I like you immensely," Hewet replied, speaking with the relief of a person who is unexpectedly given an opportunity of saying what he wants to say. He stopped moving the pebbles.

"Mightn't we call each other Rachel and Terence?" he asked.

"Terence," Rachel repeated. "Terence—that's like the cry of an owl."

She looked up with a sudden rush of delight, and in looking at Terence with eyes widened by pleasure she was struck by the change that had come over the sky behind them. The substantial blue day had faded to a paler and more ethereal blue; the clouds were pink, far away and closely packed together; and the peace of evening had replaced the heat of the southern afternoon, in which they had started on their walk.

"It must be late!" she exclaimed.

It was nearly eight o'clock.

"But eight o'clock doesn't count here, does it?" Terence asked, as they got up and turned inland again. They began to walk rather quickly down the hill on a little path between the olive trees.

They felt more intimate because they shared the knowledge of what eight o'clock in Richmond meant. Terence walked in front, for there was not room for them side by side.

"What I want to do in writing novels is very much what you want to do when you play the piano, I expect," he began, turning and speaking over his shoulder. "We want to find out what's behind things, don't we?—Look at the lights down there," he continued, "scattered about anyhow. Things I feel come to me like lights . . . I want to combine them . . . Have you ever seen fireworks that make figures? . . . I want to make figures . . . Is that what you want to do?"

Now they were out on the road and could walk side by side.

"When I play the piano? Music is different . . . But I see what you mean." They tried to invent theories and to make their theories agree. As Hewet had no knowledge of music, Rachel took his stick and drew figures in the thin white dust to explain how Bach wrote his fugues.

"My musical gift was ruined," he explained, as they walked on after one of these demonstrations, "by the village organist at home, who had invented a system of notation which he tried to teach me, with the result that I never got to the tune-playing at all. My mother thought music wasn't manly for boys; she wanted me to kill rats and birds—that's the worst of living in the country. We live in Devonshire. It's the loveliest place in the world. Only— it's always difficult at home when one's grown up. I'd like you to know one of my sisters . . . Oh, here's your gate—" He pushed it open. They paused for a moment. She could not ask him to come in. She could not say that she hoped they would meet again; there was nothing to be said, and so without a word she went through the gate, and was soon invisible. Directly Hewet lost sight of her, he felt the old discomfort return, even more strongly than before. Their talk had been interrupted in the middle, just as he was beginning to say the things he wanted to say. After all, what had they been able to say? He ran his mind over the things they had said, the random, unnecessary things which had eddied round and round and used up all the time, and drawn them so close together and flung them so far apart, and left him in the end unsatisfied, ignorant still of what she felt and of what she was like. What was the use of talking, talking, merely talking?

CHAPTER XVII

It was now the height of the season, and every ship that came from England left a few people on the shores of Santa Marina who drove up to the hotel. The fact that the Ambroses had a house where one could escape momentarily from the slightly inhuman atmosphere of an hotel was a source of genuine pleasure not only to Hirst and Hewet, but to the Elliots, the Thornburys, the Flushings, Miss Allan, Evelyn M., together with other people whose identity was so little developed that the Ambroses did not discover that they possessed names. By degrees there was established a kind of correspondence between the two houses, the big and the small, so that at most hours of the day one house could guess what was going on in the other, and the words "the villa" and "the hotel" called up the idea of two separate systems of life. Acquaintances showed signs of developing into friends, for that one tie to Mrs. Parry's drawing-room had inevitably split into many other ties attached to different parts of England, and sometimes these alliances seemed cynically fragile, and sometimes painfully acute, lacking as they did the supporting background of organised English life. One night when the moon was round between the trees, Evelyn M. told Helen the story of her life, and claimed her everlasting friendship; or another occasion, merely because of a sigh, or a pause, or a word thoughtlessly dropped, poor Mrs. Elliot left the villa half in tears, vowing never again to meet the cold and scornful woman who had insulted her, and in truth, meet again they never did. It did not seem worth while to piece together so slight a friendship.

Hewet, indeed, might have found excellent material at this time up at the villa for some chapters in the novel which was to be called "Silence, or the Things People Don't Say." Helen and Rachel had become very silent. Having detected, as she thought, a secret, and judging that Rachel meant to keep it from her, Mrs. Ambrose respected it carefully, but from that cause, though unintentionally, a curious atmosphere of reserve grew up between them. Instead of sharing their views upon all subjects, and plunging after an idea wherever it might lead, they spoke chiefly in comment upon the people they saw, and the secret between them made itself felt in what they said even of Thornburys and Elliots. Always calm and unemotional in her judgments, Mrs. Ambrose was now inclined to be definitely pessimistic. She was not severe upon individuals so much as incredulous of the kindness of destiny, fate, what happens in the long run, and apt to insist that this was generally adverse to people in proportion as they deserved well. Even this theory she was ready to discard in favour of one which made chaos triumphant, things happening for no reason at all, and every one groping about in illusion and ignorance. With a certain pleasure she developed these views to her niece, taking a letter from home as her test: which gave good news, but might just as well have given bad. How did she know that at this very moment both her children were not lying dead, crushed by motor omnibuses? "It's happening to somebody: why shouldn't it happen to me?" she would argue, her face taking on the stoical expression of anticipated sorrow. However sincere these views may have been, they were undoubtedly called forth by the irrational state of her niece's mind. It was so fluctuating, and went so quickly from joy to despair, that it seemed necessary to confront it with some stable opinion which naturally became dark as well as stable. Perhaps Mrs. Ambrose had some idea that in leading the talk into these quarters she might discover what was in Rachel's mind, but it was difficult to judge, for sometimes she would agree with the gloomiest thing that was said, at other times she refused to listen, and rammed Helen's theories down her throat with laughter, chatter, ridicule of the wildest, and fierce bursts of anger even at what she called the "croaking of a raven in the mud."

"It's hard enough without that," she asserted.

"What's hard?" Helen demanded.

"Life," she replied, and then they both became silent.

Helen might draw her own conclusions as to why life was hard, as to why an hour later, perhaps, life was something so wonderful and vivid that the eyes of Rachel beholding it were positively exhilarating to a spectator. True to her creed, she did not attempt to interfere, although there were enough of those weak moments of depression to make it perfectly easy for a less scrupulous person to press through and know all, and perhaps Rachel was sorry that she did not choose. All these moods ran themselves into one general effect, which Helen compared to the sliding of a river, quick, quicker, quicker still, as it races to a waterfall. Her instinct was to cry out Stop! but even had there been any use in crying Stop! she would have refrained, thinking it best that things should take their way, the water racing because the earth was shaped to make it race.

It seemed that Rachel herself had no suspicion that she was watched, or that there was anything in her manner likely to draw attention to her. What had happened to her she did not know. Her mind was very much in the condition of the racing water to which Helen compared it. She wanted to see Terence; she was perpetually wishing to see him when he was not there; it was an agony to miss seeing him; agonies were strewn all about her day on account of him, but she never asked herself what this force driving through her life arose from. She thought of no result any more than a tree perpetually pressed downwards by the wind considers the result of being pressed downwards by the wind.

During the two or three weeks which had passed since their walk, half a dozen notes from him had accumulated in her drawer. She would read them, and spend the whole morning in a daze of happiness; the sunny land outside the window being no less capable of analysing its own colour and heat than she was of analysing hers. In these moods she found it impossible to read or play the piano, even to move being beyond her inclination. The time passed without her noticing it. When it was dark she was drawn to the window by the lights of the hotel. A light that went in and out was the light in Terence's window: there he sat, reading perhaps, or now he was walking up and down pulling out one book after another; and now he was seated in his chair again, and she tried to imagine what he was thinking about. The steady lights marked the rooms where Terence sat with people moving round him. Every one who stayed in the hotel had a peculiar romance and interest about them. They were not ordinary people. She would attribute wisdom to Mrs. Elliot, beauty to Susan Warrington, a splendid vitality to Evelyn M., because Terence spoke to them. As unreflecting and pervasive were the moods of depression. Her mind was as the landscape outside when dark beneath clouds and straitly lashed by wind and hail. Again she would sit passive in her chair exposed to pain, and Helen's fantastical or gloomy words were like so many darts goading her to cry out against the hardness of life. Best of all were the moods when for no reason again this stress of feeling slackened, and life went on as usual, only with a joy and colour in its events that was unknown before; they had a significance like that which she had seen in the tree: the nights were black bars separating her from the days; she would have liked to run all the days into one long continuity of sensation. Although these moods were directly or indirectly caused by the presence of Terence or the thought of him, she never said to herself that she was in love with him, or considered what was to happen if she continued to feel such things, so that Helen's image of the river sliding on to the waterfall had a great likeness to the facts, and the alarm which Helen sometimes felt was justified.

In her curious condition of unanalysed sensations she was incapable of making a plan which should have any effect upon her state of mind. She abandoned herself to the mercy of accidents, missing Terence one day, meeting him the next, receiving his letters always with a start of surprise. Any woman experienced in the progress of courtship would have come by certain opinions from all this which would have given her at least a theory to go upon; but no one had ever been in love with Rachel, and she had never been in love with anyone. Moreover, none of the books she read, from *Wuthering Heights* to *Man and Superman*, and the plays of Ibsen, suggested from their analysis of love that what their heroines felt was what she was feeling now. It seemed to her that her sensations had no name.

She met Terence frequently. When they did not meet, he was apt to send a note with a book or about a book, for he had not been able after all to neglect that approach to intimacy. But sometimes he did not come or did not write for several days at a time. Again when they met their meeting might be one of inspiriting joy or of harassing despair. Over all their partings hung the sense of interruption, leaving them both unsatisfied, though ignorant that the other shared the feeling.

If Rachel was ignorant of her own feelings, she was even more completely ignorant of his. At first he moved as a god; as she came to know him better he was still the centre of light, but combined with this beauty a wonderful power of making her daring and confident of herself. She was conscious of emotions and powers which she had never suspected in herself, and of a depth in the world hitherto unknown. When she thought of their relationship she saw rather than reasoned, representing her view of what Terence felt by a picture of him drawn across the room to stand by her side. This passage across the room amounted to a physical sensation, but what it meant she did not know.

Thus the time went on, wearing a calm, bright look upon its surface. Letters came from England, letters came from Willoughby, and the days accumulated their small events which shaped the year. Superficially, three odes of Pindar were mended, Helen covered about five inches of her embroidery, and St.

John completed the first two acts of a play. He and Rachel being now very good friends, he read them aloud to her, and she was so genuinely impressed by the skill of his rhythms and the variety of his adjectives, as well as by the fact that he was Terence's friend, that he began to wonder whether he was not intended for literature rather than for law. It was a time of profound thought and sudden revelations for more than one couple, and several single people.

A Sunday came, which no one in the villa with the exception of Rachel and the Spanish maid proposed to recognise. Rachel still went to church, because she had never, according to Helen, taken the trouble to think about it. Since they had celebrated the service at the hotel she went there expecting to get some pleasure from her passage across the garden and through the hall of the hotel, although it was very doubtful whether she would see Terence, or at any rate have the chance of speaking to him.

As the greater number of visitors at the hotel were English, there was almost as much difference between Sunday and Wednesday as there is in England, and Sunday appeared here as there, the mute black ghost or penitent spirit of the busy weekday. The English could not pale the sunshine, but they could in some miraculous way slow down the hours, dull the incidents, lengthen the meals, and make even the servants and page-boys wear a look of boredom and propriety. The best clothes which every one put on helped the general effect; it seemed that no lady could sit down without bending a clean starched petticoat, and no gentleman could breathe without a sudden crackle from a stiff shirt-front. As the hands of the clock neared eleven, on this particular Sunday, various people tended to draw together in the hall, clasping little red-leaved books in their hands. The clock marked a few minutes to the hour when a stout black figure passed through the hall with a preoccupied expression, as though he would rather not recognise salutations, although aware of them, and disappeared down the corridor which led from it.

"Mr. Bax," Mrs. Thornbury whispered.

The little group of people then began to move off in the same direction as the stout black figure. Looked at in an odd way by people who made no effort to join them, they moved with one exception slowly and consciously towards the stairs. Mrs. Flushing was the exception. She came running downstairs, strode across the hall, joined the procession much out of breath, demanding of Mrs. Thornbury in an agitated whisper, "Where, where?"

"We are all going," said Mrs. Thornbury gently, and soon they were descending the stairs two by two. Rachel was among the first to descend. She did not see that Terence and Hirst came in at the rear possessed of no black volume, but of one thin book bound in light-blue cloth, which St. John carried under his arm.

The chapel was the old chapel of the monks. It was a profound cool place where they had said Mass for hundreds of years, and done penance in the cold moonlight, and worshipped old brown pictures and carved saints which stood with upraised hands of blessing in the hollows in the walls. The transition from Catholic to Protestant worship had been bridged by a time of disuse, when there were no services, and the place was used for storing jars of oil, liqueur, and deck-chairs; the hotel flourishing, some religious body had taken the place in hand, and it was now fitted out with a number of glazed yellow benches, claret-coloured footstools; it had a small pulpit, and a brass eagle carrying the Bible on its back, while the piety of different women had supplied ugly squares of carpet, and long strips of embroidery heavily wrought with monograms in gold.

As the congregation entered they were met by mild sweet chords issuing from a harmonium, where Miss Willett, concealed from view by a baize curtain, struck emphatic chords with uncertain fingers. The sound spread through the chapel as the rings of water spread from a fallen stone. The twenty or twenty-five people who composed the congregation first bowed their heads and then sat up and looked about them. It was very quiet, and the light down here seemed paler than the light above. The usual bows and smiles were dispensed with, but they recognised each other. The Lord's Prayer was read over them. As the childlike battle of voices rose, the congregation, many of whom had only met on the staircase, felt themselves pathetically united and well-disposed towards each other. As if the prayer were a torch applied to fuel, a smoke seemed to rise automatically and fill the place with the ghosts of innumerable services on innumerable Sunday mornings at home. Susan Warrington in particular was conscious of the sweetest sense of sisterhood, as she covered her face with her hands and saw slips of bent backs through the chinks between her fingers. Her emotions rose calmly and evenly, approving of herself and of life at the same time. It was all so quiet and so good. But having created this peaceful atmosphere Mr. Bax suddenly turned the page and read a psalm. Though he read it with no change of voice the mood was broken.

"Be merciful unto me, O God," he read, "for man goeth about to devour me: he is daily fighting and troubling me . . . They daily mistake my words: all that they imagine is to do me evil. They hold all together and keep themselves close . . . Break their teeth, O God, in their mouths; smite the jaw-bones of the lions, O Lord: let them fall away like water that runneth apace; and when they shoot their arrows let them be rooted out."

Nothing in Susan's experience at all corresponded with this, and as she had no love of language she had long ceased to attend to such remarks, although she followed them with the same kind of mechanical respect with which she heard many of Lear's speeches read aloud. Her mind was still serene and really occupied with praise of her own nature and praise of God, that is of the solemn and satisfactory order of the world.

But it could be seen from a glance at their faces that most of the others, the men in particular, felt the inconvenience of the sudden intrusion of this old savage. They looked more secular and critical as then listened to the ravings of the old black man with a cloth round his loins cursing with vehement gesture by a camp-fire in the desert. After that there was a general sound of pages being turned as if they were in class, and then they read a little bit of the Old Testament about making a well, very much as school boys translate an easy passage from the *Anabasis* when they have shut up their French grammar. Then they returned to the New Testament and the sad and beautiful figure of Christ. While Christ spoke they made another effort to fit his interpretation of life upon the lives they lived, but as they were all very different, some practical, some ambitious, some stupid, some wild and experimental, some in love, and others long past any feeling except a feeling of comfort, they did very different things with the words of Christ.

From their faces it seemed that for the most part they made no effort at all, and, recumbent as it were, accepted the ideas the words gave as representing goodness, in the same way, no doubt, as one of those industrious needlewomen had accepted the bright ugly pattern on her mat as beauty.

Whatever the reason might be, for the first time in her life, instead of slipping at once into some curious pleasant cloud of emotion, too familiar to be considered, Rachel listened critically to what was being said. By the time they had swung in an irregular way from prayer to psalm, from psalm to history, from history to poetry, and Mr. Bax was giving out his text, she was in a state of acute discomfort. Such was the discomfort she felt when forced to sit through an unsatisfactory piece of music badly played. Tantalised, enraged by the clumsy insensitiveness of the conductor, who put the stress on the wrong places, and annoyed by the vast flock of the audience tamely praising and acquiescing without knowing or caring, so she was not tantalized and enraged, only here, with eyes half-shut and lips pursed together, the atmosphere of forced solemnity increased her anger. All round her were people pretending to feel what they did not feel, while somewhere above her floated the idea which they could none of them grasp, which they pretended to grasp, always escaping out of reach, a beautiful idea, an idea like a butterfly. One after another, vast and hard and cold, appeared to her the churches all over the world where this blundering effort and misunderstanding were perpetually going on, great buildings, filled with innumerable men and women, not seeing clearly, who finally gave up the effort to see, and relapsed tamely into praise and acquiescence, half-shutting their eyes and pursing up their lips. The thought had the same sort of physical discomfort as is caused by a film of mist always coming between the eyes and the printed page. She did her best to brush away the film and to conceive something to be worshipped as the service went on, but failed, always misled by the voice of Mr. Bax saying things which misrepresented the idea, and by the patter of baaing inexpressive human voices falling round her like damp leaves. The effort was tiring and dispiriting. She ceased to listen, and fixed her eyes on the face of a woman near her, a hospital nurse, whose expression of devout attention seemed to prove that she was at any rate receiving satisfaction. But looking at her carefully she came to the conclusion that the hospital nurse was only slavishly acquiescent, and that the look of satisfaction was produced by no splendid conception of God within her. How indeed, could she conceive anything far outside her own experience, a woman with a commonplace face like hers, a little round red face, upon which trivial duties and trivial spites had drawn lines, whose weak blue eyes saw without intensity or individuality, whose features were blurred, insensitive, and callous? She was adoring something shallow and smug, clinging to it, so the obstinate mouth witnessed, with the assiduity of a limpet; nothing would tear her from her demure belief in her own virtue and the virtues of her religion. She was a limpet, with the sensitive side of her stuck to a rock, forever dead to the rush of fresh and beautiful things past her. The face of this single worshipper became printed on Rachel's mind with an impression of keen horror, and she had it suddenly revealed to her what Helen meant and St. John meant when they proclaimed their hatred of Christianity. With the violence that now marked her feelings, she rejected all that she had implicitly believed.

Meanwhile Mr. Bax was half-way through the second lesson. She looked at him. He was a man of the world with supple lips and an agreeable manner, he was indeed a man of much kindliness and simplicity, though by no means clever, but she was not in the mood to give anyone credit for such qualities, and examined him as though he were an epitome of all the vices of his service.

Right at the back of the chapel Mrs. Flushing, Hirst, and Hewet sat in a row in a very different frame of mind. Hewet was staring at the roof with his legs stuck out in front of him, for as he had never tried to make the service fit any feeling or idea of his, he was able to enjoy the beauty of the language without hindrance. His mind was occupied first with accidental things, such as the women's hair in front of him, the light on the faces, then with the words which seemed to him magnificent, and then more vaguely with the characters of the other worshippers. But when he suddenly perceived Rachel, all these thoughts were driven out of his head, and he thought only of her. The psalms, the prayers, the Litany, and the sermon were all reduced to one chanting sound which paused, and then renewed itself, a little higher or a little lower. He stared alternately at Rachel and at the ceiling, but his expression was now produced not by what he saw but by something in his mind. He was almost as painfully disturbed by his thoughts as she was by hers.

Early in the service Mrs. Flushing had discovered that she had taken up a Bible instead of a prayer-book, and, as she was sitting next to Hirst, she stole a glance over his shoulder. He was reading steadily in the thin pale-blue volume. Unable to understand, she peered closer, upon which Hirst politely laid the book before her, pointing to the first line of a Greek poem and then to the translation opposite.

"What's that?" she whispered inquisitively.

"Sappho," he replied. "The one Swinburne did—the best thing that's ever been written."

Mrs. Flushing could not resist such an opportunity. She gulped down the Ode to Aphrodite during the Litany, keeping herself with difficulty from asking when Sappho lived, and what else she wrote worth reading, and contriving to come in punctually at the end with "the forgiveness of sins, the Resurrection of the body, and the life everlastin'. Amen."

Meanwhile Hirst took out an envelope and began scribbling on the back of it. When Mr. Bax mounted the pulpit he shut up Sappho with his envelope between the pages, settled his spectacles, and fixed his gaze intently upon the clergyman. Standing in the pulpit he looked very large and fat; the light coming through the greenish unstained window-glass made his face appear smooth and white like a very large egg.

He looked round at all the faces looking mildly up at him, although some of them were the faces of men and women old enough to be his grandparents, and gave out his text with weighty significance. The argument of the sermon was that visitors to this beautiful land, although they were on a holiday, owed a duty to the natives. It did not, in truth, differ very much from a leading article upon topics of general interest in the weekly newspapers. It rambled with a kind of amiable verbosity from one heading to another, suggesting that all human beings are very much the same under their skins, illustrating this by the resemblance of the games which little Spanish boys play to the games little boys in London streets play, observing that very small things do influence people, particularly natives; in fact, a very dear friend of Mr. Bax's had told him that the success of our rule in India, that vast country, largely depended upon the strict code of politeness which the English adopted towards the natives, which led to the remark that small things were not necessarily small, and that somehow to the virtue of sympathy, which was a virtue never more needed than today, when we lived in a time of experiment and upheaval—witness the aeroplane and wireless telegraph, and there were other problems which hardly presented themselves to our fathers, but which no man who called himself a man could leave unsettled. Here Mr. Bax became more definitely clerical, if it were possible, he seemed to speak with a certain innocent craftiness, as he pointed out that all this laid a special duty upon earnest Christians. What men were inclined to say now was, "Oh, that fellow— he's a parson." What we want them to say is, "He's a good fellow"—in other words, "He is my brother." He exhorted them to keep in touch with men of the modern type; they must sympathise with their multifarious interests in order to keep before their eyes that whatever discoveries were made there was one discovery which could not be superseded, which was indeed as much of a necessity to the most successful and most brilliant of them all as it had been to their fathers. The humblest could help; the least important things had an influence (here his manner became definitely priestly and his remarks seemed to be directed to women, for indeed Mr. Bax's congregations were mainly composed of women, and he was used to assigning them their duties in his innocent clerical campaigns). Leaving more definite instruction, he passed on, and his theme broadened into a peroration for which he drew a long breath and stood very upright—"As a drop of water, detached, alone, separate from others, falling from the cloud and entering the great ocean, alters, so scientists tell us, not only the immediate spot in the ocean where it falls, but all the myriad drops which together compose the great universe of waters, and by this means alters the configuration of the globe and the lives of millions of sea creatures, and finally the lives of the men and women who seek their living upon the shores—as all this is within the compass of a single drop of water, such as any rain shower sends in millions to lose themselves in the earth, to lose themselves we say, but we know very well that the fruits of the earth could not flourish without them—so is a marvel comparable to this within the reach of each one of us, who dropping a little word or a little deed into the great universe alters it; yea, it is a solemn thought, *alters* it, for good or for evil, not for one instant, or in one vicinity, but throughout the entire race, and for all eternity." Whipping round as though to avoid applause, he continued with the same breath, but in a different tone of voice—"And now to God the Father . . ."

He gave his blessing, and then, while the solemn chords again issued from the harmonium behind the curtain, the different people began scraping and fumbling and moving very awkwardly and consciously towards the door. Half-way upstairs, at a point where the light and sounds of the upper world conflicted with the dimness and the dying hymn-tune of the under, Rachel felt a hand drop upon her shoulder.

"Miss Vinrace," Mrs. Flushing whispered peremptorily, "stay to luncheon. It's such a dismal day. They don't even give one beef for luncheon. Please stay."

Here they came out into the hall, where once more the little band was greeted with curious respectful glances by the people who had not gone to church, although their clothing made it clear that they approved of Sunday to the very verge of going to church. Rachel felt unable to stand any more of this particular atmosphere, and was about to say she must go back, when Terence passed them, drawn along in talk with Evelyn M. Rachel thereupon contented herself with saying that the people looked very respectable, which negative remark Mrs. Flushing interpreted to mean that she would stay.

"English people abroad!" she returned with a vivid flash of malice. "Ain't they awful! But we won't stay here," she continued, plucking at Rachel's arm. "Come up to my room."

She bore her past Hewet and Evelyn and the Thornburys and the Elliots. Hewet stepped forward.

"Luncheon—" he began.

"Miss Vinrace has promised to lunch with me," said Mrs. Flushing, and began to pound energetically up the staircase, as though the middle classes of England were in pursuit. She did not stop until she had slammed her bedroom door behind them.

"Well, what did you think of it?" she demanded, panting slightly.

All the disgust and horror which Rachel had been accumulating burst forth beyond her control.

"I thought it the most loathsome exhibition I'd ever seen!" she broke out. "How can they—how dare they—what do you mean by it—Mr. Bax, hospital nurses, old men, prostitutes, disgusting—"

She hit off the points she remembered as fast as she could, but she was too indignant to stop to analyse her feelings. Mrs. Flushing watched her with keen gusto as she stood ejaculating with emphatic movements of her head and hands in the middle of the room.

"Go on, go on, do go on," she laughed, clapping her hands. "It's delightful to hear you!"

"But why do you go?" Rachel demanded.

"I've been every Sunday of my life ever since I can remember," Mrs. Flushing chuckled, as though that were a reason by itself.

Rachel turned abruptly to the window. She did not know what it was that had put her into such a passion; the sight of Terence in the hall had confused her thoughts, leaving her merely indignant. She looked straight at their own villa, half-way up the side of the mountain. The most familiar view seen framed through glass has a certain unfamiliar distinction, and she grew calm as she gazed. Then she remembered that she was in the presence of someone she did not know well, and she turned and looked at Mrs. Flushing. Mrs. Flushing was still sitting on the edge of the bed, looking up, with her lips parted, so that her strong white teeth showed in two rows.

"Tell me," she said, "which d'you like best, Mr. Hewet or Mr. Hirst?"

"Mr. Hewet," Rachel replied, but her voice did not sound natural.

"Which is the one who reads Greek in church?" Mrs. Flushing demanded.

It might have been either of them and while Mrs. Flushing proceeded to describe them both, and to say that both frightened her, but one frightened her more than the other, Rachel looked for a chair. The room, of course, was one of the largest and most luxurious in the hotel. There were a great many armchairs and settees covered in brown holland, but each of these was occupied by a large square piece of yellow cardboard, and all the pieces of cardboard were dotted or lined with spots or dashes of bright oil paint.

"But you're not to look at those," said Mrs. Flushing as she saw Rachel's eye wander. She jumped up, and turned as many as she could, face downwards, upon the floor. Rachel, however, managed to possess herself of one of them, and, with the vanity of an artist, Mrs. Flushing demanded anxiously, "Well, well?"

"It's a hill," Rachel replied. There could be no doubt that Mrs. Flushing had represented the vigorous and abrupt fling of the earth up into the air; you could almost see the clods flying as it whirled.

Rachel passed from one to another. They were all marked by something of the jerk and decision of their maker; they were all perfectly untrained onslaughts of the brush upon some half-realised idea suggested by hill or tree; and they were all in some way characteristic of Mrs. Flushing.

"I see things movin'," Mrs. Flushing explained. "So"—she swept her hand through a yard of the air. She then took up one of the cardboards which Rachel had laid aside, seated herself on a stool, and began to flourish a stump of charcoal. While she occupied herself in strokes which seemed to serve her as speech serves others, Rachel, who was very restless, looked about her.

"Open the wardrobe," said Mrs. Flushing after a pause, speaking indistinctly because of a paint-brush in her mouth, "and look at the things."

As Rachel hesitated, Mrs. Flushing came forward, still with a paint-brush in her mouth, flung open the wings of her wardrobe, and tossed a quantity of shawls, stuffs, cloaks, embroideries, on to the bed. Rachel began to finger them. Mrs. Flushing came up once more, and dropped a quantity of beads, brooches, earrings, bracelets, tassels, and combs among the draperies. Then she went back to her stool and began to paint in silence. The stuffs were coloured and dark and pale; they made a curious swarm of lines and colours upon the counterpane, with the reddish lumps of stone and peacocks' feathers and clear pale tortoise-shell combs lying among them.

"The women wore them hundreds of years ago, they wear 'em still," Mrs. Flushing remarked. "My husband rides about and finds 'em; they don't know what they're worth, so we get 'em cheap. And we shall sell 'em to smart women in London," she chuckled, as though the thought of these ladies and their absurd appearance amused her. After painting for some minutes, she suddenly laid down her brush and fixed her eyes upon Rachel.

"I tell you what I want to do," she said. "I want to go up there and see things for myself. It's silly stayin' here with a pack of old maids as though we were at the seaside in England. I want to go up the river and see the natives in their camps. It's only a matter of ten days under canvas. My husband's done it. One would lie out under the trees at night and be towed down the river by day, and if we saw anythin' nice we'd shout out and tell 'em to stop." She rose and began piercing the bed again and again with a long golden pin, as she watched to see what effect her suggestion had upon Rachel.

"We must make up a party," she went on. "Ten people could hire a launch. Now you'll come, and Mrs. Ambrose'll come, and will Mr. Hirst and t'other gentleman come? Where's a pencil?"

She became more and more determined and excited as she evolved her plan. She sat on the edge of the bed and wrote down a list of surnames, which she invariably spelt wrong. Rachel was enthusiastic, for indeed the idea was immeasurably delightful to her. She had always had a great desire to see the river, and the name of Terence threw a lustre over the prospect, which made it almost too good to come true. She did what she could to help Mrs. Flushing by suggesting names, helping her to spell them, and counting up the days of the week upon her fingers. As Mrs. Flushing wanted to know all she could tell her about the birth and pursuits of every person she suggested, and threw in wild stories of her own as to the temperaments and habits of artists, and people of the same name who used to come to Chillingley in the old days, but were doubtless not the same, though they too were very clever men interested in Egyptology, the business took some time.

At last Mrs. Flushing sought her diary for help, the method of reckoning dates on the fingers proving unsatisfactory. She opened and shut every drawer in her writing-table, and then cried furiously, "Yarmouth! Yarmouth! Drat the woman! She's always out of the way when she's wanted!"

At this moment the luncheon gong began to work itself into its midday frenzy. Mrs. Flushing rang her bell violently. The door was opened by a handsome maid who was almost as upright as her mistress.

"Oh, Yarmouth," said Mrs. Flushing, "just find my diary and see where ten days from now would bring us to, and ask the hall porter how many men 'ud be wanted to row eight people up the river for a week, and what it 'ud cost, and put it on a slip of paper and leave it on my dressing-table. Now—" she pointed at the door with a superb forefinger so that Rachel had to lead the way.

"Oh, and Yarmouth," Mrs. Flushing called back over her shoulder. "Put those things away and hang 'em in their right places, there's a good girl, or it fusses Mr. Flushin'."

To all of which Yarmouth merely replied, "Yes, ma'am."

As they entered the long dining-room it was obvious that the day was still Sunday, although the mood was slightly abating. The Flushings' table was set by the side in the window, so that Mrs. Flushing could scrutinise each figure as it entered, and her curiosity seemed to be intense.

"Old Mrs. Paley," she whispered as the wheeled chair slowly made its way through the door, Arthur pushing behind. "Thornburys" came next. "That nice woman," she nudged Rachel to look at Miss Allan. "What's her name?" The painted lady who always came in late, tripping into the room with a prepared smile as though she came out upon a stage, might well have quailed before Mrs. Flushing's stare, which expressed her steely hostility to the whole tribe of painted ladies. Next came the two young men whom Mrs. Flushing called collectively the Hirsts. They sat down opposite, across the gangway.

Mr. Flushing treated his wife with a mixture of admiration and indulgence, making up by the suavity and fluency of his speech for the abruptness of hers. While she darted and ejaculated he gave Rachel a sketch of the history of South American art. He would deal with one of his wife's exclamations, and then return as smoothly as ever to his theme. He knew very well how to make a luncheon pass agreeably, without being dull or intimate. He had formed the opinion, so he told Rachel, that wonderful treasures lay hid in the depths of the land; the things Rachel had seen were merely trifles picked up in the course of one short journey. He thought there might be giant gods hewn out of stone in the mountain-side; and colossal figures standing by themselves in the middle of vast green pasture lands, where none but natives had ever trod. Before the dawn of European art he believed that the primitive huntsmen and priests had built temples of massive stone slabs, had formed out of the dark rocks and the great cedar trees majestic figures of gods and of beasts, and symbols of the great forces, water, air, and forest among which they lived. There might be prehistoric towns, like those in Greece and Asia, standing in open places among the trees, filled with the works of this early race. Nobody had been there; scarcely anything was known. Thus talking and displaying the most picturesque of his theories, Rachel's attention was fixed upon him.

She did not see that Hewet kept looking at her across the gangway, between the figures of waiters hurrying past with plates. He was inattentive, and Hirst was finding him also very cross and disagreeable. They had touched upon all the usual topics—upon politics and literature, gossip and Christianity. They had quarrelled over the service, which was every bit as fine as Sappho, according to Hewet; so that Hirst's paganism was mere ostentation. Why go to church, he demanded, merely in order to read Sappho? Hirst observed that he had listened to every word of the sermon, as he could prove if Hewet would like a repetition of it; and he went to church in order to realise the nature of his Creator, which he had done very vividly that morning, thanks to Mr. Bax, who had inspired him to write three of the most superb lines in English literature, an invocation to the Deity.

"I wrote 'em on the back of the envelope of my aunt's last letter," he said, and pulled it from between the pages of Sappho.

"Well, let's hear them," said Hewet, slightly mollified by the prospect of a literary discussion.

"My dear Hewet, do you wish us both to be flung out of the hotel by an enraged mob of Thornburys and Elliots?" Hirst enquired. "The merest whisper would be sufficient to incriminate me forever. God!" he broke out, "what's the use of attempting to write when the world's peopled by such damned fools? Seriously, Hewet, I advise you to give up literature. What's the good of it? There's your audience."

He nodded his head at the tables where a very miscellaneous collection of Europeans were now engaged in eating, in some cases in gnawing, the stringy foreign fowls. Hewet looked, and grew more out of temper than ever. Hirst looked too. His eyes fell upon Rachel, and he bowed to her.

"I rather think Rachel's in love with me," he remarked, as his eyes returned to his plate. "That's the worst of friendships with young women—they tend to fall in love with one."

To that Hewet made no answer whatever, and sat singularly still. Hirst did not seem to mind getting no answer, for he returned to Mr. Bax again, quoting the peroration about the drop of water; and when Hewet scarcely replied to these remarks either, he merely pursed his lips, chose a fig, and relapsed quite contentedly into his own thoughts, of which he always had a very large supply. When luncheon was over they separated, taking their cups of coffee to different parts of the hall.

From his chair beneath the palm-tree Hewet saw Rachel come out of the dining-room with the Flushings; he saw them look round for chairs, and choose three in a corner where they could go on talking in private. Mr. Flushing was now in the full tide of his discourse. He produced a sheet of paper upon which he made drawings as he went on with his talk. He saw Rachel lean over and look, pointing to this and that with her finger. Hewet unkindly compared Mr. Flushing, who was extremely well dressed for a hot climate, and rather elaborate in his manner, to a very persuasive shop-keeper. Meanwhile, as he sat looking at them, he was entangled in the Thornburys and Miss Allan, who, after hovering about for a minute or two, settled in chairs round him, holding their cups in their hands. They wanted to know whether he could tell them anything about Mr. Bax. Mr. Thornbury as usual sat saying nothing, looking vaguely ahead of him, occasionally raising his eyeglasses, as if to put them on, but always thinking better of it at the last moment, and letting them fall again. After some discussion, the ladies put it beyond a doubt that Mr. Bax was not the son of Mr. William Bax. There was a pause. Then Mrs. Thornbury remarked that she was still in the habit of saying Queen instead of King in the National Anthem. There was another pause. Then Miss Allan observed reflectively that going to church abroad always made her feel as if she had been to a sailor's funeral.

There was then a very long pause, which threatened to be final, when, mercifully, a bird about the size of a magpie, but of a metallic blue colour, appeared on the section of the terrace that could be seen from where they sat. Mrs. Thornbury was led to enquire whether we should like it if all our rooks were blue—"What do *you* think, William?" she asked, touching her husband on the knee.

"If all our rooks were blue," he said—he raised his glasses; he actually placed them on his nose—"they would not live long in Wiltshire," he concluded; he dropped his glasses to his side again. The three elderly people now gazed meditatively at the bird, which was so obliging as to stay in the middle of the view for a considerable space of time, thus making it unnecessary for them to speak again. Hewet began to wonder whether he might not cross over to the Flushings' corner, when Hirst appeared from the background, slipped into a chair by Rachel's side, and began to talk to her with every appearance of familiarity. Hewet could stand it no longer. He rose, took his hat and dashed out of doors.

CHAPTER XVIII

Everything he saw was distasteful to him. He hated the blue and white, the intensity and definiteness, the hum and heat of the south; the landscape seemed to him as hard and as romantic as a cardboard background on the stage, and the mountain but a wooden screen against a sheet painted blue. He walked fast in spite of the heat of the sun.

Two roads led out of the town on the eastern side; one branched off towards the Ambroses' villa, the other struck into the country, eventually reaching a village on the plain, but many footpaths, which had been stamped in the earth when it was wet, led off from it, across great dry fields, to scattered farmhouses, and the villas of rich natives. Hewet stepped off the road on to one of these, in order to avoid the hardness and heat of the main road, the dust of which was always being raised in small clouds by carts and ramshackle flies which carried parties of festive peasants, or turkeys swelling unevenly like a bundle of air balls beneath a net, or the brass bedstead and black wooden boxes of some newly wedded pair.

The exercise indeed served to clear away the superficial irritations of the morning, but he remained miserable. It seemed proved beyond a doubt that Rachel was indifferent to him, for she had scarcely looked at him, and she had talked to Mr. Flushing with just the same interest with which she talked to him. Finally, Hirst's odious words flicked his mind like a whip, and he remembered that he had left her talking to Hirst. She was at this moment talking to him, and it might be true, as he said, that she was in love with him. He went over all the evidence for this supposition—her sudden interest in Hirst's writing, her way of quoting his opinions respectfully, or with only half a laugh; her very nickname for him, "the great Man," might have some serious meaning in it. Supposing that there were an understanding between them, what would it mean to him?

"Damn it all!" he demanded, "am I in love with her?" To that he could only return himself one answer. He certainly was in love with her, if he knew what love meant. Ever since he had first seen her he had been interested and attracted, more and more interested and attracted, until he was scarcely able to think of anything except Rachel. But just as he was sliding into one of the long feasts of meditation about them both, he checked himself by asking whether he wanted to marry her? That was the real problem, for these miseries and agonies could not be endured, and it was necessary that he should make up his mind. He instantly decided that he did not want to marry anyone. Partly because he was irritated by Rachel the idea of marriage irritated him. It immediately suggested the picture of two people sitting alone over the fire; the man was reading, the woman sewing. There was a second picture. He saw a man jump up, say good-night, leave the company and hasten away with the quiet secret look of one who is stealing to certain happiness. Both these pictures were very unpleasant, and even more so was a third picture, of husband and wife and friend; and the married people glancing at each other as though they were content to let something pass unquestioned, being themselves possessed of the deeper truth. Other pictures—he was walking very fast in his irritation, and they came before him without any conscious effort, like pictures on a sheet—succeeded these. Here were the worn husband and wife sitting with their children round them, very patient, tolerant, and wise. But that too, was an unpleasant picture. He tried all sorts of pictures, taking them from the lives of friends of his, for he knew many different married couples; but he saw them always, walled up in a warm firelit room. When, on the other hand, he began to think of unmarried people, he saw them active in an unlimited world; above all, standing on the same ground as the rest, without shelter or advantage. All the most individual and humane of his friends were bachelors and spinsters; indeed he was surprised to find that the women he most admired and knew best were unmarried women. Marriage seemed to be worse for them than it was for men. Leaving these general pictures he considered the people whom he had been observing lately at the hotel. He had often revolved these questions in his mind, as he watched Susan and Arthur, or Mr. and Mrs. Thornbury, or Mr. and Mrs. Elliot. He had observed how the shy happiness and surprise of the engaged couple had gradually been replaced by a comfortable, tolerant state of mind, as if they had already done with the adventure of intimacy and were taking up their parts. Susan used to pursue Arthur about with a sweater, because he had one day let slip that a brother of his had died of pneumonia. The sight amused him, but was not pleasant if you substituted Terence and Rachel for Arthur and Susan; and Arthur was far less eager to get you in a corner and talk about flying and the mechanics of aeroplanes. They would settle down. He then looked at the couples who had been married for several years. It was true that Mrs. Thornbury had a husband, and that for the most part she was wonderfully successful in bringing him into the conversation, but one could not imagine what they said to each other when they were alone. There was the same difficulty with regard to the Elliots, except that they probably bickered openly in private. They sometimes bickered in public, though these disagreements were painfully covered over by little insincerities on the part of the wife, who was afraid of public opinion, because she was much stupider than her husband, and had to make efforts to keep hold of him. There could be no doubt, he decided, that it would have been far better for the world if these couples had separated. Even the Ambroses, whom he admired and respected profoundly—in spite of all the love between them, was not their marriage too a compromise? She gave way to him; she spoilt him; she arranged things for him; she who was all truth to others was not true to her husband, was not true to her friends if they came in conflict with her husband. It was a strange and piteous flaw in her nature. Perhaps Rachel had been right, then, when she said that night in the garden, "We bring out what's worst in each other—we should live separate."

No, Rachel had been utterly wrong! Every argument seemed to be against undertaking the burden of marriage until he came to Rachel's argument, which was manifestly absurd. From having been the pursued, he turned and became the pursuer. Allowing the case against marriage to lapse, he began to consider the peculiarities of character which had led to her saying that. Had she meant it? Surely one ought to know the character of the person with whom one might spend all one's life; being a novelist, let him try to discover what sort of person she was. When he was with her he could not analyse her qualities, because he seemed to know them instinctively, but when he was away from her it sometimes seemed to him that he did not know her at all. She was young, but she was also old; she had little self-confidence, and yet she was a good judge of people. She was happy; but what made her happy? If they were alone and the excitement had worn off, and they had to deal with the ordinary facts of the day, what would happen? Casting his eye upon his own character, two things appeared to him: that he was very unpunctual, and that he disliked answering notes. As far as he knew Rachel was inclined to be punctual, but he could not remember that he had ever seen her with a pen in her hand. Let him next imagine a dinner-party, say at the Crooms, and Wilson, who had taken her down, talking about the state of the Liberal party. She would say—of course she was absolutely ignorant of politics. Nevertheless she was intelligent certainly, and honest too. Her temper was uncertain—that he had noticed—and she was not domestic, and she was not easy, and she was not quiet, or beautiful, except in some dresses in some lights. But the great gift she had was that she understood what was said to her; there had never been anyone like her for talking to. You could say anything—you could say everything, and yet she was never servile. Here he pulled himself up, for it seemed to him suddenly that he knew less about her than about anyone. All these thoughts had occurred to him many times already; often had he tried to argue and reason; and again he had reached the old state of doubt. He did not know her, and he did not know what she felt, or whether they could live together, or whether he wanted to marry her, and yet he was in love with her.

Supposing he went to her and said (he slackened his pace and began to speak aloud, as if he were speaking to Rachel):

"I worship you, but I loathe marriage, I hate its smugness, its safety, its compromise, and the thought of you interfering in my work, hindering me; what would you answer?"

He stopped, leant against the trunk of a tree, and gazed without seeing them at some stones scattered on the bank of the dry river-bed. He saw Rachel's face distinctly, the grey eyes, the hair, the mouth; the face that could look so many things—plain, vacant, almost insignificant, or wild, passionate, almost beautiful, yet in his eyes was always the same because of the extraordinary freedom with which she looked at him, and spoke as she felt. What would she answer? What did she feel? Did she love him, or did she feel nothing at all for him or for any other man, being, as she had said that afternoon, free, like the wind or the sea?

"Oh, you're free!" he exclaimed, in exultation at the thought of her, "and I'd keep you free. We'd be free together. We'd share everything together. No happiness would be like ours. No lives would compare with ours." He opened his arms wide as if to hold her and the world in one embrace.

No longer able to consider marriage, or to weigh coolly what her nature was, or how it would be if they lived together, he dropped to the ground and sat absorbed in the thought of her, and soon tormented by the desire to be in her presence again.

CHAPTER XIX

But Hewet need not have increased his torments by imagining that Hirst was still talking to Rachel. The party very soon broke up, the Flushings going in one direction, Hirst in another, and Rachel remaining in the hall, pulling the illustrated papers about, turning from one to another, her movements expressing the unformed restless desire in her mind. She did not know whether to go or to stay, though Mrs. Flushing had commanded her to appear at tea. The hall was empty, save for Miss Willett who was playing scales with her fingers upon a sheet of sacred music, and the Carters, an opulent couple who disliked the girl, because her shoe laces were untied, and she did not look sufficiently cheery, which by some indirect process of thought led them to think that she would not like them. Rachel certainly would not have liked them, if she had seen them, for the excellent reason that Mr. Carter waxed his moustache, and Mrs. Carter wore bracelets, and they were evidently the kind of people who would not like her; but she was too much absorbed by her own restlessness to think or to look.

She was turning over the slippery pages of an American magazine, when the hall door swung, a wedge of light fell upon the floor, and a small white figure upon whom the light seemed focussed, made straight across the room to her.

"What! You here?" Evelyn exclaimed. "Just caught a glimpse of you at lunch; but you wouldn't condescend to look at *me*."

It was part of Evelyn's character that in spite of many snubs which she received or imagined, she never gave up the pursuit of people she wanted to know, and in the long run generally succeeded in knowing them and even in making them like her.

She looked round her. "I hate this place. I hate these people," she said. "I wish you'd come up to my room with me. I do want to talk to you."

As Rachel had no wish to go or to stay, Evelyn took her by the wrist and drew her out of the hall and up the stairs. As they went upstairs two steps at a time, Evelyn, who still kept hold of Rachel's hand, ejaculated broken sentences about not caring a hang what people said. "Why should one, if one knows one's right? And let 'em all go to blazes! Them's my opinions!"

She was in a state of great excitement, and the muscles of her arms were twitching nervously. It was evident that she was only waiting for the door to shut to tell Rachel all about it. Indeed, directly they were inside her room, she sat on the end of the bed and said, "I suppose you think I'm mad?"

Rachel was not in the mood to think clearly about anyone's state of mind. She was however in the mood to say straight out whatever occurred to her without fear of the consequences.

"Somebody's proposed to you," she remarked.

"How on earth did you guess that?" Evelyn exclaimed, some pleasure mingling with her surprise. "Do as I look as if I'd just had a proposal?"

"You look as if you had them every day," Rachel replied.

"But I don't suppose I've had more than you've had," Evelyn laughed rather insincerely.

"I've never had one."

"But you will—lots—it's the easiest thing in the world—But that's not what's happened this afternoon exactly. It's—Oh, it's a muddle, a detestable, horrible, disgusting muddle!"

She went to the wash-stand and began sponging her cheeks with cold water; for they were burning hot. Still sponging them and trembling slightly she turned and explained in the high pitched voice of nervous excitement: "Alfred Perrott says I've promised to marry him, and I say I never did. Sinclair says he'll shoot himself if I don't marry him, and I say, 'Well, shoot yourself!' But of course he doesn't—they never do. And Sinclair got hold of me this afternoon and began bothering me to give an answer, and accusing me of flirting with Alfred Perrott, and told me I'd no heart, and was merely a Siren, oh, and quantities of pleasant things like that. So at last I said to him, 'Well, Sinclair, you've said enough now. You can just let me go.' And then he caught me and kissed me—the disgusting brute—I can still feel his nasty hairy face just there—as if he'd any right to, after what he'd said!"

She sponged a spot on her left cheek energetically.

"I've never met a man that was fit to compare with a woman!" she cried; "they've no dignity, they've no courage, they've nothing but their beastly passions and their brute strength! Would any woman have behaved like that— if a man had said he didn't want her? We've too much self-respect; we're infinitely finer than they are."

She walked about the room, dabbing her wet cheeks with a towel. Tears were now running down with the drops of cold water.

"It makes me angry," she explained, drying her eyes.

Rachel sat watching her. She did not think of Evelyn's position; she only thought that the world was full or people in torment.

"There's only one man here I really like," Evelyn continued; "Terence Hewet. One feels as if one could trust him."

At these words Rachel suffered an indescribable chill; her heart seemed to be pressed together by cold hands.

"Why?" she asked. "Why can you trust him?"

"I don't know," said Evelyn. "Don't you have feelings about people? Feelings you're absolutely certain are right? I had a long talk with Terence the other night. I felt we were really friends after that. There's something of a woman in him—" She paused as though she were thinking of very intimate things that Terence had told her, so at least Rachel interpreted her gaze.

She tried to force herself to say, "Has he proposed to you?" but the question was too tremendous, and in another moment Evelyn was saying that the finest men were like women, and women were nobler than men—for example, one couldn't imagine a woman like Lillah Harrison thinking a mean thing or having anything base about her.

"How I'd like you to know her!" she exclaimed.

She was becoming much calmer, and her cheeks were now quite dry. Her eyes had regained their usual expression of keen vitality, and she seemed to have forgotten Alfred and Sinclair and her emotion. "Lillah runs a home for inebriate women in the Deptford Road," she continued. "She started it, managed it, did everything off her own bat, and it's now the biggest of its kind in England. You can't think what those women are like—and their homes. But she goes among them at all hours of the day and night. I've often been with her . . . That's what's the matter with us . . . We don't *do* things. What do you *do*?" she demanded, looking at Rachel with a slightly ironical smile. Rachel had scarcely listened to any of this, and her expression was vacant and unhappy. She had conceived an equal dislike for Lillah Harrison and her work in the Deptford Road, and for Evelyn M. and her profusion of love affairs.

"I play," she said with an affection of stolid composure.

"That's about it!" Evelyn laughed. "We none of us do anything but play. And that's why women like Lillah Harrison, who's worth twenty of you and me, have to work themselves to the bone. But I'm tired of playing," she went on, lying flat on the bed, and raising her arms above her head. Thus stretched out, she looked more diminutive than ever.

"I'm going to do something. I've got a splendid idea. Look here, you must join. I'm sure you've got any amount of stuff in you, though you look—well, as if you'd lived all your life in a garden." She sat up, and began to explain with animation. "I belong to a club in London. It meets every Saturday, so it's called the Saturday Club. We're supposed to talk about art, but I'm sick of talking about art—what's the good of it? With all kinds of real things going on round one? It isn't as if they'd got anything to say about art, either. So what I'm going to tell 'em is that we've talked enough about art, and we'd better talk about life for a change. Questions that really matter to people's lives, the White Slave Traffic, Women Suffrage, the Insurance Bill, and so on. And when we've made up our mind what we want to do we could form ourselves into a society for doing it . . . I'm certain that if people like ourselves were to take things in hand instead of leaving it to policemen and magistrates, we could put a stop to—prostitution"—she lowered her voice at the ugly word—"in six months. My idea is that men and women ought to join in these matters. We ought to go into Piccadilly and stop one of these poor wretches and say: 'Now, look here, I'm no better than you are, and I don't pretend to be any better, but you're doing what you know to be beastly, and I won't have you doing beastly things, because we're all the same under our skins, and if you do a beastly thing it does matter to me.' That's what Mr. Bax was saying this morning, and it's true, though you clever people—you're clever too, aren't you?—don't believe it."

When Evelyn began talking—it was a fact she often regretted—her thoughts came so quickly that she never had any time to listen to other people's thoughts. She continued without more pause than was needed for taking breath.

"I don't see why the Saturday club people shouldn't do a really great work in that way," she went on. "Of course it would want organisation, someone to give their life to it, but I'm ready to do that. My notion's to think of the human beings first and let the abstract ideas take care of themselves. What's wrong with Lillah—if there is anything wrong—is that she thinks of Temperance first and the women afterwards. Now there's one thing I'll say to my credit," she continued; "I'm not intellectual or artistic or anything of that sort, but I'm jolly human." She slipped off the bed and sat on the floor, looking up at Rachel. She searched up into her face as if she were trying to read what kind of character was concealed behind the face. She put her hand on Rachel's knee.

"It *is* being human that counts, isn't it?" she continued. "Being real, whatever Mr. Hirst may say. Are you real?"

Rachel felt much as Terence had felt that Evelyn was too close to her, and that there was something exciting in this closeness, although it was also disagreeable. She was spared the need of finding an answer to the question, for Evelyn proceeded, "Do you *believe* in anything?"

In order to put an end to the scrutiny of these bright blue eyes, and to relieve her own physical restlessness, Rachel pushed back her chair and exclaimed, "In everything!" and began to finger different objects, the books on the table, the photographs, the freshly leaved plant with the stiff bristles, which stood in a large earthenware pot in the window.

"I believe in the bed, in the photographs, in the pot, in the balcony, in the sun, in Mrs. Flushing," she remarked, still speaking recklessly, with something at the back of her mind forcing her to say the things that one usually does not say. "But I don't believe in God, I don't believe in Mr. Bax, I don't believe in the hospital nurse. I don't believe—" She took up a photograph and, looking at it, did not finish her sentence.

"That's my mother," said Evelyn, who remained sitting on the floor binding her knees together with her arms, and watching Rachel curiously.

Rachel considered the portrait. "Well, I don't much believe in her," she remarked after a time in a low tone of voice.

Mrs. Murgatroyd looked indeed as if the life had been crushed out of her; she knelt on a chair, gazing piteously from behind the body of a Pomeranian dog which she clasped to her cheek, as if for protection.

"And that's my dad," said Evelyn, for there were two photographs in one frame. The second photograph represented a handsome soldier with high regular features and a heavy black moustache; his hand rested on the hilt of his sword; there was a decided likeness between him and Evelyn.

"And it's because of them," said Evelyn, "that I'm going to help the other women. You've heard about me, I suppose? They weren't married, you see; I'm not anybody in particular. I'm not a bit ashamed of it. They loved each other anyhow, and that's more than most people can say of their parents."

Rachel sat down on the bed, with the two pictures in her hands, and compared them—the man and the woman who had, so Evelyn said, loved each other. That fact interested her more than the campaign on behalf of unfortunate women which Evelyn was once more beginning to describe. She looked again from one to the other.

"What d'you think it's like," she asked, as Evelyn paused for a minute, "being in love?"

"Have you never been in love?" Evelyn asked. "Oh no—one's only got to look at you to see that," she added. She considered. "I really was in love once," she said. She fell into reflection, her eyes losing their bright vitality and approaching something like an expression of tenderness. "It was heavenly!—while it lasted. The worst of it is it don't last, not with me. That's the bother."

She went on to consider the difficulty with Alfred and Sinclair about which she had pretended to ask Rachel's advice. But she did not want advice; she wanted intimacy. When she looked at Rachel, who was still looking at the photographs on the bed, she could not help seeing that Rachel was not thinking about her. What was she thinking about, then? Evelyn was tormented by the little spark of life in her which was always trying to work through to other people, and was always being rebuffed. Falling silent she looked at her visitor, her shoes, her stockings, the combs in her hair, all the details of her dress in short, as though by seizing every detail she might get closer to the life within.

Rachel at last put down the photographs, walked to the window and remarked, "It's odd. People talk as much about love as they do about religion."

"I wish you'd sit down and talk," said Evelyn impatiently.

Instead Rachel opened the window, which was made in two long panes, and looked down into the garden below.

"That's where we got lost the first night," she said. "It must have been in those bushes."

"They kill hens down there," said Evelyn. "They cut their heads off with a knife—disgusting! But tell me—what—"

"I'd like to explore the hotel," Rachel interrupted. She drew her head in and looked at Evelyn, who still sat on the floor.

"It's just like other hotels," said Evelyn.

That might be, although every room and passage and chair in the place had a character of its own in Rachel's eyes; but she could not bring herself to stay in one place any longer. She moved slowly towards the door.

"What is it you want?" said Evelyn. "You make me feel as if you were always thinking of something you don't say . . . Do say it!"

But Rachel made no response to this invitation either. She stopped with her fingers on the handle of the door, as if she remembered that some sort of pronouncement was due from her.

"I suppose you'll marry one of them," she said, and then turned the handle and shut the door behind her. She walked slowly down the passage, running her hand along the wall beside her. She did not think which way she was going, and therefore walked down a passage which only led to a window and a balcony. She looked down at the kitchen premises, the wrong side of the hotel life, which was cut off from the right side by a maze of small bushes. The ground was bare, old tins were scattered about, and the bushes wore towels and aprons upon their heads to dry. Every now and then a waiter came out in a white apron and threw rubbish on to a heap. Two large women in cotton dresses were sitting on a bench with blood-smeared tin trays in front of them and yellow bodies across their knees. They were plucking the birds, and talking as they plucked. Suddenly a chicken came floundering, half flying, half running into the space, pursued by a third woman whose age could hardly be under eighty. Although wizened and unsteady on her legs she kept up the chase, egged on by the laughter of the others; her face was expressive of furious rage, and as she ran she swore in Spanish. Frightened by hand-clapping here, a napkin there, the bird ran this way and that in sharp angles, and finally fluttered straight at the old woman, who opened her scanty grey skirts to enclose it, dropped upon it in a bundle, and then holding it out cut its head off with an expression of vindictive energy and triumph combined. The blood and the ugly wriggling fascinated Rachel, so that although she knew that someone had come up behind and was standing beside her, she did not turn round until the old woman had settled down on the bench beside the others. Then she looked up sharply, because of the ugliness of what she had seen. It was Miss Allan who stood beside her.

"Not a pretty sight," said Miss Allan, "although I daresay it's really more humane than our method . . . I don't believe you've ever been in my room," she added, and turned away as if she meant Rachel to follow her. Rachel followed, for it seemed possible that each new person might remove the mystery which burdened her.

The bedrooms at the hotel were all on the same pattern, save that some were larger and some smaller; they had a floor of dark red tiles; they had a high bed, draped in mosquito curtains; they had each a writing-table and a dressing-table, and a couple of armchairs. But directly a box was unpacked the rooms became very different, so that Miss Allan's room was very unlike Evelyn's room. There were no variously coloured hatpins on her dressing-table; no scent-bottles; no narrow curved pairs of scissors; no great variety of shoes and boots; no silk petticoats lying on the chairs. The room was extremely neat. There seemed to be two pairs of everything. The writing-table, however, was piled with manuscript, and a table was drawn out to stand by the armchair on which were two separate heaps of dark library books, in which there were many slips of paper sticking out at different degrees of thickness. Miss Allan had asked Rachel to come in out of kindness, thinking that she was waiting about with nothing to do. Moreover, she liked young women, for she had taught many of them, and having received so much hospitality from the Ambroses she was glad to be able to repay a minute part of it. She looked about accordingly for something to show her. The room did not provide much entertainment. She touched her manuscript. "Age of Chaucer; Age of Elizabeth; Age of Dryden," she reflected; "I'm glad there aren't many more ages. I'm still in the middle of the eighteenth century. Won't you sit down, Miss Vinrace? The chair, though small, is firm . . . Euphues. The germ of the English novel," she continued, glancing at another page. "Is that the kind of thing that interests you?"

She looked at Rachel with great kindness and simplicity, as though she would do her utmost to provide anything she wished to have. This expression had a remarkable charm in a face otherwise much lined with care and thought.

"Oh no, it's music with you, isn't it?" she continued, recollecting, "and I generally find that they don't go together. Sometimes of course we have prodigies—" She was looking about her for something and now saw a jar on the mantelpiece which she reached down and gave to Rachel. "If you put your finger into this jar you may be able to extract a piece of preserved ginger. Are you a prodigy?"

But the ginger was deep and could not be reached.

"Don't bother," she said, as Miss Allan looked about for some other implement. "I daresay I shouldn't like preserved ginger."

"You've never tried?" enquired Miss Allan. "Then I consider that it is your duty to try now. Why, you may add a new pleasure to life, and as you are still young—" She wondered whether a button-hook would do. "I make it a rule to try everything," she said. "Don't you think it would be very annoying if you tasted ginger for the first time on your death-bed, and found you never liked anything so much? I should be so exceedingly annoyed that I think I should get well on that account alone."

She was now successful, and a lump of ginger emerged on the end of the button-hook. While she went to wipe the button-hook, Rachel bit the ginger and at once cried, "I must spit it out!"

"Are you sure you have really tasted it?" Miss Allan demanded.

For answer Rachel threw it out of the window.

"An experience anyhow," said Miss Allan calmly. "Let me see—I have nothing else to offer you, unless you would like to taste this." A small cupboard hung above her bed, and she took out of it a slim elegant jar filled with a bright green fluid.

"Crême de Menthe," she said. "Liqueur, you know. It looks as if I drank, doesn't it? As a matter of fact it goes to prove what an exceptionally abstemious person I am. I've had that jar for six-and-twenty years," she added, looking at it with pride, as she tipped it over, and from the height of the liquid it could be seen that the bottle was still untouched.

"Twenty-six years?" Rachel exclaimed.

Miss Allan was gratified, for she had meant Rachel to be surprised.

"When I went to Dresden six-and-twenty years ago," she said, "a certain friend of mine announced her intention of making me a present. She thought that in the event of shipwreck or accident a stimulant might be useful. However, as I had no occasion for it, I gave it back on my return. On the eve of any foreign journey the same bottle always makes its appearance, with the same note; on my return in safety it is always handed back. I consider it a kind of charm against accidents. Though I was once detained twenty-four hours by an accident to the train in front of me, I have never met with any accident myself. Yes," she continued, now addressing the bottle, "we have seen many climes and cupboards together, have we not? I intend one of these days to have a silver label made with an inscription. It is a gentleman, as you may observe, and his name is Oliver . . . I do not think I could forgive you, Miss Vinrace, if you broke my Oliver," she said, firmly taking the bottle out of Rachel's hands and replacing it in the cupboard.

Rachel was swinging the bottle by the neck. She was interested by Miss Allan to the point of forgetting the bottle.

"Well," she exclaimed, "I do think that odd; to have had a friend for twenty-six years, and a bottle, and—to have made all those journeys."

"Not at all; I call it the reverse of odd," Miss Allan replied. "I always consider myself the most ordinary person I know. It's rather distinguished to be as ordinary as I am. I forget—are you a prodigy, or did you say you were not a prodigy?"

She smiled at Rachel very kindly. She seemed to have known and experienced so much, as she moved cumbrously about the room, that surely there must be balm for all anguish in her words, could one induce her to have recourse to them. But Miss Allan, who was now locking the cupboard door, showed no signs of breaking the reticence which had snowed her under for years. An uncomfortable sensation kept Rachel silent; on the one hand, she wished to whirl high and strike a spark out of the cool pink flesh; on the other she perceived there was nothing to be done but to drift past each other in silence.

"I'm not a prodigy. I find it very difficult to say what I mean—" she observed at length.

"It's a matter of temperament, I believe," Miss Allan helped her. "There are some people who have no difficulty; for myself I find there are a great many things I simply cannot say. But then I consider myself very slow. One of my colleagues now, knows whether she likes you or not—let me see, how does she do it?—by the way you say good-morning at breakfast. It is sometimes a matter of years before I can make up my mind. But most young people seem to find it easy?"

"Oh no," said Rachel. "It's hard!"

Miss Allan looked at Rachel quietly, saying nothing; she suspected that there were difficulties of some kind. Then she put her hand to the back of her head, and discovered that one of the grey coils of hair had come loose.

"I must ask you to be so kind as to excuse me," she said, rising, "if I do my hair. I have never yet found a satisfactory type of hairpin. I must change my dress, too, for the matter of that; and I should be particularly glad of your assistance, because there is a tiresome set of hooks which I *can* fasten for myself, but it takes from ten to fifteen minutes; whereas with your help—"

She slipped off her coat and skirt and blouse, and stood doing her hair before the glass, a massive homely figure, her petticoat being so short that she stood on a pair of thick slate-grey legs.

"People say youth is pleasant; I myself find middle age far pleasanter," she remarked, removing hair pins and combs, and taking up her brush. When it fell loose her hair only came down to her neck.

"When one was young," she continued, "things could seem so very serious if one was made that way . . . And now my dress."

In a wonderfully short space of time her hair had been reformed in its usual loops. The upper half of her body now became dark green with black stripes on it; the skirt, however, needed hooking at various angles, and Rachel had to kneel on the floor, fitting the eyes to the hooks.

"Our Miss Johnson used to find life very unsatisfactory, I remember," Miss Allan continued. She turned her back to the light. "And then she took to breeding guinea-pigs for their spots, and became absorbed in that. I have just heard that the yellow guinea-pig has had a black baby. We had a bet of sixpence on about it. She will be very triumphant."

The skirt was fastened. She looked at herself in the glass with the curious stiffening of her face generally caused by looking in the glass.

"Am I in a fit state to encounter my fellow-beings?" she asked. "I forget which way it is—but they find black animals very rarely have coloured babies—it may be the other way round. I have had it so often explained to me that it is very stupid of me to have forgotten again."

She moved about the room acquiring small objects with quiet force, and fixing them about her—a locket, a watch and chain, a heavy gold bracelet, and the parti-coloured button of a suffrage society. Finally, completely equipped for Sunday tea, she stood before Rachel, and smiled at her kindly. She was not an impulsive woman, and her life had schooled her to restrain her tongue. At the same time, she was possessed of an amount of good-will towards others, and in particular towards the young, which often made her regret that speech was so difficult.

"Shall we descend?" she said.

She put one hand upon Rachel's shoulder, and stooping, picked up a pair of walking-shoes with the other, and placed them neatly side by side outside her door. As they walked down the passage they passed many pairs of boots and shoes, some black and some brown, all side by side, and all different, even to the way in which they lay together.

"I always think that people are so like their boots," said Miss Allan. "That is Mrs. Paley's—" but as she spoke the door opened, and Mrs. Paley rolled out in her chair, equipped also for tea.

She greeted Miss Allan and Rachel.

"I was just saying that people are so like their boots," said Miss Allan. Mrs. Paley did not hear. She repeated it more loudly still. Mrs. Paley did not hear. She repeated it a third time. Mrs. Paley heard, but she did not understand. She was apparently about to repeat it for the fourth time, when Rachel suddenly said something inarticulate, and disappeared down the corridor. This misunderstanding, which involved a complete block in the passage, seemed to her unbearable. She walked quickly and blindly in the opposite direction, and found herself at the end of a *cul de sac*. There was a window, and a table and a chair in the window, and upon the table stood a rusty inkstand, an ashtray, an old copy of a French newspaper, and a pen with a broken nib. Rachel sat down, as if to study the French newspaper, but a tear fell on the blurred French print, raising a soft blot. She lifted her head sharply, exclaiming aloud, "It's intolerable!" Looking out of the window with eyes that would have seen nothing even had they not been dazed by tears, she indulged herself at last in violent abuse of the entire day. It had been miserable from start to finish; first, the service in the chapel; then luncheon; then Evelyn; then Miss Allan; then old Mrs. Paley blocking up the passage. All day long she had been tantalized and put off. She had now reached one of those eminences, the result of some crisis, from which the world is finally displayed in its true proportions. She disliked the look of it immensely— churches, politicians, misfits, and huge impostures—men like Mr. Dalloway, men like Mr. Bax, Evelyn and her chatter, Mrs. Paley blocking up the passage. Meanwhile the steady beat of her own pulse represented the hot current of feeling that ran down beneath; beating, struggling, fretting. For the time, her own body was the source of all the life in the world, which tried to burst forth here—there—and was repressed now by Mr. Bax, now by Evelyn, now by the imposition of ponderous stupidity, the weight of the entire world. Thus tormented, she would twist her hands together, for all things were wrong, all people stupid. Vaguely seeing that there were people down in the garden beneath she represented them as aimless masses of matter, floating hither and thither, without aim except to impede her. What were they doing, those other people in the world?

"Nobody knows," she said. The force of her rage was beginning to spend itself, and the vision of the world which had been so vivid became dim.

"It's a dream," she murmured. She considered the rusty inkstand, the pen, the ash-tray, and the old French newspaper. These small and worthless objects seemed to her to represent human lives.

"We're asleep and dreaming," she repeated. But the possibility which now suggested itself that one of the shapes might be the shape of Terence roused her from her melancholy lethargy. She became as restless as she had been before she sat down. She was no longer able to see the world as a town laid out beneath her. It was covered instead by a haze of feverish red mist. She had returned to the state in which she had been all day. Thinking was no escape. Physical movement was the only refuge, in and out of rooms, in and out of people's minds, seeking she knew not what. Therefore she rose, pushed back the table, and went downstairs. She went out of the hall door, and, turning the corner of the hotel, found herself among the people whom she had seen from the window. But owing to the broad sunshine after shaded passages, and to the substance of living people after dreams, the group appeared with startling intensity, as though the dusty surface had been peeled off everything, leaving only the reality and the instant. It had the look of a vision printed on the dark at night. White and grey and purple figures were scattered on the green, round wicker tables, in the middle the flame of the tea-urn made the air waver like a faulty sheet of glass, a massive green tree stood over them as if it were a moving force held at rest. As she approached, she could hear Evelyn's voice repeating monotonously, "Here then—here—good doggie, come here"; for a moment nothing seemed to happen; it all stood still, and then she realised that one of the figures was Helen Ambrose; and the dust again began to settle.

The group indeed had come together in a miscellaneous way; one tea-table joining to another tea-table, and deck-chairs serving to connect two groups. But even at a distance it could be seen that Mrs. Flushing, upright and imperious, dominated the party. She was talking vehemently to Helen across the table.

"Ten days under canvas," she was saying. "No comforts. If you want comforts, don't come. But I may tell you, if you don't come you'll regret it all your life. You say yes?"

At this moment Mrs. Flushing caught sight of Rachel.

"Ah, there's your niece. She's promised. You're coming, aren't you?" Having adopted the plan, she pursued it with the energy of a child.

Rachel took her part with eagerness.

"Of course I'm coming. So are you, Helen. And Mr. Pepper too." As she sat she realised that she was surrounded by people she knew, but that Terence was not among them. From various angles people began saying what they thought of the proposed expedition. According to some it would be hot, but the nights would be cold; according to others, the difficulties would lie rather in getting a boat, and in speaking the language. Mrs. Flushing disposed of all objections, whether due to man or due to nature, by announcing that her husband would settle all that.

Meanwhile Mr. Flushing quietly explained to Helen that the expedition was really a simple matter; it took five days at the outside; and the place—a native village—was certainly well worth seeing before she returned to England. Helen murmured ambiguously, and did not commit herself to one answer rather than to another.

The tea-party, however, included too many different kinds of people for general conversation to flourish; and from Rachel's point of view possessed the great advantage that it was quite unnecessary for her to talk. Over there Susan and Arthur were explaining to Mrs. Paley that an expedition had been proposed; and Mrs. Paley having grasped the fact, gave the advice of an old traveller that they should take nice canned vegetables, fur cloaks, and insect powder. She leant over to Mrs. Flushing and whispered something which from the twinkle in her eyes probably had reference to bugs. Then Helen was reciting "Toll for the Brave" to St. John Hirst, in order apparently to win a sixpence which lay upon the table; while Mr. Hughling Elliot imposed silence upon his section of the audience by his fascinating anecdote of Lord Curzon and the undergraduate's bicycle. Mrs. Thornbury was trying to remember the name of a man who might have been another Garibaldi, and had written a book which they ought to read; and Mr. Thornbury recollected that he had a pair of binoculars at anybody's service. Miss Allan meanwhile murmured with the curious intimacy which a spinster often achieves with dogs, to the fox-terrier which Evelyn had at last induced to come over to them. Little particles of dust or blossom fell on the plates now and then when the branches sighed above. Rachel seemed to see and hear a little of everything, much as a river feels the twigs that fall into it and sees the sky above, but her eyes were too vague for Evelyn's liking. She came across, and sat on the ground at Rachel's feet.

"Well?" she asked suddenly. "What are you thinking about?"

"Miss Warrington," Rachel replied rashly, because she had to say something. She did indeed see Susan murmuring to Mrs. Elliot, while Arthur stared at her with complete confidence in his own love. Both Rachel and Evelyn then began to listen to what Susan was saying.

"There's the ordering and the dogs and the garden, and the children coming to be taught," her voice proceeded rhythmically as if checking the list, "and my tennis, and the village, and letters to write for father, and a thousand little things that don't sound much; but I never have a moment to myself, and when I got to bed, I'm so sleepy I'm off before my head touches the pillow. Besides I like to be a great deal with my Aunts—I'm a great bore, aren't I, Aunt Emma?" (she smiled at old Mrs. Paley, who with head slightly drooped was regarding the cake with speculative affection), "and father has to be very careful about chills in winter which means a great deal of running about, because he won't look after himself, any more than you will, Arthur! So it all mounts up!"

Her voice mounted too, in a mild ecstasy of satisfaction with her life and her own nature. Rachel suddenly took a violent dislike to Susan, ignoring all that was kindly, modest, and even pathetic about her. She appeared insincere and cruel; she saw her grown stout and prolific, the kind blue eyes now shallow and watery, the bloom of the cheeks congealed to a network of dry red canals.

Helen turned to her. "Did you go to church?" she asked. She had won her sixpence and seemed making ready to go.

"Yes," said Rachel. "For the last time," she added.

In preparing to put on her gloves, Helen dropped one.

"You're not going?" Evelyn asked, taking hold of one glove as if to keep them.

"It's high time we went," said Helen. "Don't you see how silent every one's getting—?"

A silence had fallen upon them all, caused partly by one of the accidents of talk, and partly because they saw someone approaching. Helen could not see who it was, but keeping her eyes fixed upon Rachel observed something which made her say to herself, "So it's Hewet." She drew on her gloves with a curious sense of the significance of the moment. Then she rose, for Mrs. Flushing had seen Hewet too, and was demanding information about rivers and boats which showed that the whole conversation would now come over again.

Rachel followed her, and they walked in silence down the avenue. In spite of what Helen had seen and understood, the feeling that was uppermost in her mind was now curiously perverse; if she went on this expedition, she would not be able to have a bath, the effort appeared to her to be great and disagreeable.

"It's so unpleasant, being cooped up with people one hardly knows," she remarked. "People who mind being seen naked."

"You don't mean to go?" Rachel asked.

The intensity with which this was spoken irritated Mrs. Ambrose.

"I don't mean to go, and I don't mean not to go," she replied. She became more and more casual and indifferent.

"After all, I daresay we've seen all there is to be seen; and there's the bother of getting there, and whatever they may say it's bound to be vilely uncomfortable."

For some time Rachel made no reply; but every sentence Helen spoke increased her bitterness. At last she broke out—

"Thank God, Helen, I'm not like you! I sometimes think you don't think or feel or care to do anything but exist! You're like Mr. Hirst. You see that things are bad, and you pride yourself on saying so. It's what you call being honest; as a matter of fact it's being lazy, being dull, being nothing. You don't help; you put an end to things."

Helen smiled as if she rather enjoyed the attack.

"Well?" she enquired.

"It seems to me bad—that's all," Rachel replied.

"Quite likely," said Helen.

At any other time Rachel would probably have been silenced by her Aunt's candour; but this afternoon she was not in the mood to be silenced by anyone. A quarrel would be welcome.

"You're only half alive," she continued.

"Is that because I didn't accept Mr. Flushing's invitation?" Helen asked, "or do you always think that?"

At the moment it appeared to Rachel that she had always seen the same faults in Helen, from the very first night on board the *Euphrosyne*, in spite of her beauty, in spite of her magnanimity and their love.

"Oh, it's only what's the matter with every one!" she exclaimed. "No one feels—no one does anything but hurt. I tell you, Helen, the world's bad. It's an agony, living, wanting—"

Here she tore a handful of leaves from a bush and crushed them to control herself.

"The lives of these people," she tried to explain, the aimlessness, the way they live. "One goes from one to another, and it's all the same. One never gets what one wants out of any of them."

Her emotional state and her confusion would have made her an easy prey if Helen had wished to argue or had wished to draw confidences. But instead of talking she fell into a profound silence as they walked on. Aimless, trivial, meaningless, oh no—what she had seen at tea made it impossible for her to believe that. The little jokes, the chatter, the inanities of the afternoon had shrivelled up before her eyes. Underneath the likings and spites, the comings together and partings, great things were happening—terrible things, because they were so great. Her sense of safety was shaken, as if beneath twigs and dead leaves she had seen the movement of a snake. It seemed to her that a moment's respite was allowed, a moment's make-believe, and then again the profound and reasonless law asserted itself, moulding them all to its liking, making and destroying.

She looked at Rachel walking beside her, still crushing the leaves in her fingers and absorbed in her own thoughts. She was in love, and she pitied her profoundly. But she roused herself from these thoughts and apologised. "I'm very sorry," she said, "but if I'm dull, it's my nature, and it can't be helped." If it was a natural defect, however, she found an easy remedy, for she went on to say that she thought Mr. Flushing's scheme a very good one, only needing a little consideration, which it appeared she had given it by the time they reached home. By that time they had settled that if anything more was said, they would accept the invitation.

CHAPTER XX

When considered in detail by Mr. Flushing and Mrs. Ambrose the expedition proved neither dangerous nor difficult. They found also that it was not even unusual. Every year at this season English people made parties which steamed a short way up the river, landed, and looked at the native village, bought a certain number of things from the natives, and returned again without damage done to mind or body. When it was discovered that six people really wished the same thing the arrangements were soon carried out.

Since the time of Elizabeth very few people had seen the river, and nothing has been done to change its appearance from what it was to the eyes of the Elizabethan voyagers. The time of Elizabeth was only distant from the present time by a moment of space compared with the ages which had passed since the water had run between those banks, and the green thickets swarmed there, and the small trees had grown to huge wrinkled trees in solitude. Changing only with the change of the sun and the clouds, the waving green mass had stood there for century after century, and the water had run between its banks ceaselessly, sometimes washing away earth and sometimes the branches of trees, while in other parts of the world one town had risen upon the ruins of another town, and the men in the towns had become more and more articulate and unlike each other. A few miles of this river were visible from the top of the mountain where some weeks before the party from the hotel had picnicked. Susan and Arthur had seen it as they kissed each other, and Terence and Rachel as they sat talking about Richmond, and Evelyn and Perrott as they strolled about, imagining that they were great captains sent to colonise the world. They had seen the broad blue mark across the sand where it flowed into the sea, and the green cloud of trees mass themselves about it farther up, and finally hide its waters altogether from sight. At intervals for the first twenty miles or so houses were scattered on the bank; by degrees the houses became huts, and, later still, there was neither hut nor house, but trees and grass, which were seen only by hunters, explorers, or merchants, marching or sailing, but making no settlement.

By leaving Santa Marina early in the morning, driving twenty miles and riding eight, the party, which was composed finally of six English people, reached the river-side as the night fell. They came cantering through the trees—Mr. and Mrs. Flushing, Helen Ambrose, Rachel, Terence, and St. John. The tired little horses then stopped automatically, and the English dismounted. Mrs. Flushing strode to the river-bank in high spirits. The day had been long and hot, but she had enjoyed the speed and the open air; she had left the hotel which she hated, and she found the company to her liking. The river was swirling past in the darkness; they could just distinguish the smooth moving surface of the water, and the air was full of the sound of it. They stood in an empty space in the midst of great tree-trunks, and out there a little green light moving slightly up and down showed them where the steamer lay in which they were to embark.

When they all stood upon its deck they found that it was a very small boat which throbbed gently beneath them for a few minutes, and then shoved smoothly through the water. They seemed to be driving into the heart of the night, for the trees closed in front of them, and they could hear all round them the rustling of leaves. The great darkness had the usual effect of taking away all desire for communication by making their words sound thin and small; and, after walking round the deck three or four times, they clustered together, yawning deeply, and looking at the same spot of deep gloom on the banks. Murmuring very low in the rhythmical tone of one oppressed by the air, Mrs. Flushing began to wonder where they were to sleep, for they could not sleep downstairs, they could not sleep in a doghole smelling of oil, they could not sleep on deck, they could not sleep—She yawned profoundly. It was as Helen had foreseen; the question of nakedness had risen already, although they were half asleep, and almost invisible to each other. With St. John's help she stretched an awning, and persuaded Mrs. Flushing that she could take off her clothes behind this, and that no one would notice if by chance some part of her which had been concealed for forty-five years was laid bare to the human eye. Mattresses were thrown down, rugs provided, and the three women lay near each other in the soft open air.

The gentlemen, having smoked a certain number of cigarettes, dropped the glowing ends into the river, and looked for a time at the ripples wrinkling the black water beneath them, undressed too, and lay down at the other end of the boat. They were very tired, and curtained from each other by the darkness. The light from one lantern fell upon a few ropes, a few planks of the deck, and the rail of the boat, but beyond that there was unbroken darkness, no light reached their faces, or the trees which were massed on the sides of the river.

Soon Wilfrid Flushing slept, and Hirst slept. Hewet alone lay awake looking straight up into the sky. The gentle motion and the black shapes that were drawn ceaselessly across his eyes had the effect of making it impossible for him to think. Rachel's presence so near him lulled thought asleep. Being so near him, only a few paces off at the other end of the boat, she made it as impossible for him to think about her as it would have been impossible to see her if she had stood quite close to him, her forehead against his forehead. In some strange way the boat became identified with himself, and just as it would have been useless for him to get up and steer the boat, so was it useless for him to struggle any longer with the irresistible force of his own feelings. He was drawn on and on away from all he knew, slipping over barriers and past landmarks into unknown waters as the boat glided over the smooth surface of the river. In profound peace, enveloped in deeper unconsciousness than had been his for many nights, he lay on deck watching the tree-tops change their position slightly against the sky, and arch themselves, and sink and tower huge, until he passed from seeing them into dreams where he lay beneath the shadow of the vast trees, looking up into the sky.

When they woke next morning they had gone a considerable way up the river; on the right was a high yellow bank of sand tufted with trees, on the left a swamp quivering with long reeds and tall bamboos on the top of which, swaying slightly, perched vivid green and yellow birds. The morning was hot and still. After breakfast they drew chairs together and sat in an irregular semicircle in the bow. An awning above their heads protected them from the heat of the sun, and the breeze which the boat made aired them softly. Mrs. Flushing was already dotting and striping her canvas, her head jerking this way and that with the action of a bird nervously picking up grain; the others had books or pieces of paper or embroidery on their knees, at which they looked fitfully and again looked at the river ahead. At one point Hewet read part of a poem aloud, but the number of moving things entirely vanquished his words. He ceased to read, and no one spoke. They moved on under the shelter of the trees. There was now a covey of red birds feeding on one of the little islets to the left, or again a blue-green parrot flew shrieking from tree to tree. As they moved on the country grew wilder and wilder. The trees and the undergrowth seemed to be strangling each other near the ground in a multitudinous wrestle; while here and there a splendid tree towered high above the swarm, shaking its thin green umbrellas lightly in the upper air. Hewet looked at his books again. The morning was peaceful as the night had been, only it was very strange because he could see it was light, and he could see Rachel and hear her voice and be near to her. He felt as if he were waiting, as if somehow he were stationary among things that passed over him and around him, voices, people's bodies, birds, only Rachel too was waiting with him. He looked at her sometimes as if she must know that they were waiting together, and being drawn on together, without being able to offer any resistance. Again he read from his book:

> *Whoever you are holding me now in your hand,*
> *Without one thing all will be useless.*

A bird gave a wild laugh, a monkey chuckled a malicious question, and, as fire fades in the hot sunshine, his words flickered and went out.

By degrees as the river narrowed, and the high sandbanks fell to level ground thickly grown with trees, the sounds of the forest could be heard. It echoed like a hall. There were sudden cries; and then long spaces of silence, such as there are in a cathedral when a boy's voice has ceased and the echo of it still seems to haunt about the remote places of the roof. Once Mr. Flushing rose and spoke to a sailor, and even announced that some time after luncheon the steamer would stop, and they could walk a little way through the forest.

"There are tracks all through the trees there," he explained. "We're no distance from civilisation yet."

He scrutinised his wife's painting. Too polite to praise it openly, he contented himself with cutting off one half of the picture with one hand, and giving a flourish in the air with the other.

"God!" Hirst exclaimed, staring straight ahead. "Don't you think it's amazingly beautiful?"

"Beautiful?" Helen enquired. It seemed a strange little word, and Hirst and herself both so small that she forgot to answer him.

Hewet felt that he must speak.

"That's where the Elizabethans got their style," he mused, staring into the profusion of leaves and blossoms and prodigious fruits.

"Shakespeare? I hate Shakespeare!" Mrs. Flushing exclaimed; and Wilfrid returned admiringly, "I believe you're the only person who dares to say that, Alice." But Mrs. Flushing went on painting. She did not appear to attach much value to her husband's compliment, and painted steadily, sometimes muttering a half-audible word or groan.

The morning was now very hot.

"Look at Hirst!" Mr. Flushing whispered. His sheet of paper had slipped on to the deck, his head lay back, and he drew a long snoring breath.

Terence picked up the sheet of paper and spread it out before Rachel. It was a continuation of the poem on God which he had begun in the chapel, and it was so indecent that Rachel did not understand half of it although she saw that it was indecent. Hewet began to fill in words where Hirst had left spaces, but he soon ceased; his pencil rolled on deck. Gradually they approached nearer and nearer to the bank on the right-hand side, so that the light which covered them became definitely green, falling through a shade of green leaves, and Mrs. Flushing set aside her sketch and stared ahead of her in silence. Hirst woke up; they were then called to luncheon, and while they ate it, the steamer came to a standstill a little way out from the bank. The boat which was towed behind them was brought to the side, and the ladies were helped into it.

For protection against boredom, Helen put a book of memoirs beneath her arm, and Mrs. Flushing her paint-box, and, thus equipped, they allowed themselves to be set on shore on the verge of the forest.

They had not strolled more than a few hundred yards along the track which ran parallel with the river before Helen professed to find it was unbearably hot. The river breeze had ceased, and a hot steamy atmosphere, thick with scents, came from the forest.

"I shall sit down here," she announced, pointing to the trunk of a tree which had fallen long ago and was now laced across and across by creepers and thong-like brambles. She seated herself, opened her parasol, and looked at the river which was barred by the stems of trees. She turned her back to the trees which disappeared in black shadow behind her.

"I quite agree," said Mrs. Flushing, and proceeded to undo her paint-box. Her husband strolled about to select an interesting point of view for her. Hirst cleared a space on the ground by Helen's side, and seated himself with great deliberation, as if he did not mean to move until he had talked to her for a long time. Terence and Rachel were left standing by themselves without occupation. Terence saw that the time had come as it was fated to come, but although he realised this he was completely calm and master of himself. He chose to stand for a few moments talking to Helen, and persuading her to leave her seat. Rachel joined him too in advising her to come with them.

"Of all the people I've ever met," he said, "you're the least adventurous. You might be sitting on green chairs in Hyde Park. Are you going to sit there the whole afternoon? Aren't you going to walk?"

"Oh, no," said Helen, "one's only got to use one's eye. There's everything here—everything," she repeated in a drowsy tone of voice. "What will you gain by walking?"

"You'll be hot and disagreeable by tea-time, we shall be cool and sweet," put in Hirst. Into his eyes as he looked up at them had come yellow and green reflections from the sky and the branches, robbing them of their intentness, and he seemed to think what he did not say. It was thus taken for granted by them both that Terence and Rachel proposed to walk into the woods together; with one look at each other they turned away.

"Good-bye!" cried Rachel.

"Good-by. Beware of snakes," Hirst replied. He settled himself still more comfortably under the shade of the fallen tree and Helen's figure. As they went, Mr. Flushing called after them, "We must start in an hour. Hewet, please remember that. An hour."

Whether made by man, or for some reason preserved by nature, there was a wide pathway striking through the forest at right angles to the river. It resembled a drive in an English forest, save that tropical bushes with their sword-like leaves grew at the side, and the ground was covered with an unmarked springy moss instead of grass, starred with little yellow flowers. As they passed into the depths of the forest the light grew dimmer, and the noises of the ordinary world were replaced by those creaking and sighing sounds which suggest to the traveller in a forest that he is walking at the bottom of the sea. The path narrowed and turned; it was hedged in by dense creepers which knotted tree to tree, and burst here and there into star-shaped crimson blossoms. The sighing and creaking up above were broken every now and then by the jarring cry of some startled animal. The atmosphere was close and the air came at them in languid puffs of scent. The vast green light was broken here and there by a round of pure yellow sunlight which fell through some gap in the immense umbrella of green above, and in these yellow spaces crimson and black butterflies were circling and settling. Terence and Rachel hardly spoke.

Not only did the silence weigh upon them, but they were both unable to frame any thoughts. There was something between them which had to be spoken of. One of them had to begin, but which of them was it to be? Then Hewet picked up a red fruit and threw it as high as he could. When it dropped, he would speak. They heard the flapping of great wings; they heard the fruit go pattering through the leaves and eventually fall with a thud. The silence was again profound.

"Does this frighten you?" Terence asked when the sound of the fruit falling had completely died away.

"No," she answered. "I like it."

She repeated "I like it." She was walking fast, and holding herself more erect than usual. There was another pause.

"You like being with me?" Terence asked.

"Yes, with you," she replied.

He was silent for a moment. Silence seemed to have fallen upon the world.

"That is what I have felt ever since I knew you," he replied. "We are happy together." He did not seem to be speaking, or she to be hearing.

"Very happy," she answered.

They continued to walk for some time in silence. Their steps unconsciously quickened.

"We love each other," Terence said.

"We love each other," she repeated.

The silence was then broken by their voices which joined in tones of strange unfamiliar sound which formed no words. Faster and faster they walked; simultaneously they stopped, clasped each other in their arms, then releasing themselves, dropped to the earth. They sat side by side. Sounds stood out from the background making a bridge across their silence; they heard the swish of the trees and some beast croaking in a remote world.

"We love each other," Terence repeated, searching into her face. Their faces were both very pale and quiet, and they said nothing. He was afraid to kiss her again. By degrees she drew close to him, and rested against him. In this position they sat for some time. She said "Terence" once; he answered "Rachel."

"Terrible—terrible," she murmured after another pause, but in saying this she was thinking as much of the persistent churning of the water as of her own feeling. On and on it went in the distance, the senseless and cruel churning of the water. She observed that the tears were running down Terence's cheeks.

The next movement was on his part. A very long time seemed to have passed. He took out his watch.

"Flushing said an hour. We've been gone more than half an hour."

"And it takes that to get back," said Rachel. She raised herself very slowly. When she was standing up she stretched her arms and drew a deep breath, half a sigh, half a yawn. She appeared to be very tired. Her cheeks were white. "Which way?" she asked.

"There," said Terence.

They began to walk back down the mossy path again. The sighing and creaking continued far overhead, and the jarring cries of animals. The butterflies were circling still in the patches of yellow sunlight. At first Terence was certain of his way, but as they walked he became doubtful. They had to stop to consider, and then to return and start once more, for although he was certain of the direction of the river he was not certain of striking the point where they had left the others. Rachel followed him, stopping where he stopped, turning where he turned, ignorant of the way, ignorant why he stopped or why he turned.

"I don't want to be late," he said, "because—" He put a flower into her hand and her fingers closed upon it quietly. "We're so late—so late—so horribly late," he repeated as if he were talking in his sleep. "Ah—this is right. We turn here."

They found themselves again in the broad path, like the drive in the English forest, where they had started when they left the others. They walked on in silence as people walking in their sleep, and were oddly conscious now and again of the mass of their bodies. Then Rachel exclaimed suddenly, "Helen!"

In the sunny space at the edge of the forest they saw Helen still sitting on the tree-trunk, her dress showing very white in the sun, with Hirst still propped on his elbow by her side. They stopped instinctively. At the sight of other people they could not go on. They stood hand in hand for a minute or two in silence. They could not bear to face other people.

"But we must go on," Rachel insisted at last, in the curious dull tone of voice in which they had both been speaking, and with a great effort they forced themselves to cover the short distance which lay between them and the pair sitting on the tree-trunk.

As they approached, Helen turned round and looked at them. She looked at them for some time without speaking, and when they were close to her she said quietly:

"Did you meet Mr. Flushing? He has gone to find you. He thought you must be lost, though I told him you weren't lost."

Hirst half turned round and threw his head back so that he looked at the branches crossing themselves in the air above him.

"Well, was it worth the effort?" he enquired dreamily.

Hewet sat down on the grass by his side and began to fan himself.

Rachel had balanced herself near Helen on the end of the tree trunk.

"Very hot," she said.

"You look exhausted anyhow," said Hirst.

"It's fearfully close in those trees," Helen remarked, picking up her book and shaking it free from the dried blades of grass which had fallen between the leaves. Then they were all silent, looking at the river swirling past in front of them between the trunks of the trees until Mr. Flushing interrupted them. He broke out of the trees a hundred yards to the left, exclaiming sharply:

"Ah, so you found the way after all. But it's late—much later than we arranged, Hewet."

He was slightly annoyed, and in his capacity as leader of the expedition, inclined to be dictatorial. He spoke quickly, using curiously sharp, meaningless words.

"Being late wouldn't matter normally, of course," he said, "but when it's a question of keeping the men up to time—"

He gathered them together and made them come down to the river-bank, where the boat was waiting to row them out to the steamer.

The heat of the day was going down, and over their cups of tea the Flushings tended to become communicative. It seemed to Terence as he listened to them talking, that existence now went on in two different layers. Here were the Flushings talking, talking somewhere high up in the air above him, and he and Rachel had dropped to the bottom of the world together. But with something of a child's directness, Mrs. Flushing had also the instinct which leads a child to suspect what its elders wish to keep hidden. She fixed Terence with her vivid blue eyes and addressed herself to him in particular. What would he do, she wanted to know, if the boat ran upon a rock and sank.

"Would you care for anythin' but savin' yourself? Should I? No, no," she laughed, "not one scrap—don't tell me. There's only two creatures the ordinary woman cares about," she continued, "her child and her dog; and I don't believe it's even two with men. One reads a lot about love—that's why poetry's so dull. But what happens in real life, he? It ain't love!" she cried.

Terence murmured something unintelligible. Mr. Flushing, however, had recovered his urbanity. He was smoking a cigarette, and he now answered his wife.

"You must always remember, Alice," he said, "that your upbringing was very unnatural—unusual, I should say. They had no mother," he explained, dropping something of the formality of his tone; "and a father—he was a very delightful man, I've no doubt, but he cared only for racehorses and Greek statues. Tell them about the bath, Alice."

"In the stable-yard," said Mrs. Flushing. "Covered with ice in winter. We had to get in; if we didn't, we were whipped. The strong ones lived—the others died. What you call survival of the fittest—a most excellent plan, I daresay, if you've thirteen children!"

"And all this going on in the heart of England, in the nineteenth century!" Mr. Flushing exclaimed, turning to Helen.

"I'd treat my children just the same if I had any," said Mrs. Flushing.

Every word sounded quite distinctly in Terence's ears; but what were they saying, and who were they talking to, and who were they, these fantastic people, detached somewhere high up in the air? Now that they had drunk their tea, they rose and leant over the bow of the boat. The sun was going down, and the water was dark and crimson. The river had widened again, and they were passing a little island set like a dark wedge in the middle of the stream. Two great white birds with red lights on them stood there on stilt-like legs, and the beach of the island was unmarked, save by the skeleton print of birds' feet. The branches of the trees on the bank looked more twisted and angular than ever, and the green of the leaves was lurid and splashed with gold. Then Hirst began to talk, leaning over the bow.

"It makes one awfully queer, don't you find?" he complained. "These trees get on one's nerves—it's all so crazy. God's undoubtedly mad. What sane person could have conceived a wilderness like this, and peopled it with apes and alligators? I should go mad if I lived here—raving mad."

Terence attempted to answer him, but Mrs. Ambrose replied instead. She bade him look at the way things massed themselves—look at the amazing colours, look at the shapes of the trees. She seemed to be protecting Terence from the approach of the others.

"Yes," said Mr. Flushing. "And in my opinion," he continued, "the absence of population to which Hirst objects is precisely the significant touch. You must admit, Hirst, that a little Italian town even would vulgarise the whole scene, would detract from the vastness—the sense of elemental grandeur." He swept his hands towards the forest, and paused for a moment, looking at the great green mass, which was now falling silent. "I own it makes us seem pretty small—us, not them." He nodded his head at a sailor who leant over the side spitting into the river. "And that, I think, is what my wife feels, the essential superiority of the peasant—" Under cover of Mr. Flushing's words, which continued now gently reasoning with St. John and persuading him, Terence drew Rachel to the side, pointing ostensibly to a great gnarled tree-trunk which had fallen and lay half in the water. He wished, at any rate, to be near her, but he found that he could say nothing. They could hear Mr. Flushing flowing on, now about his wife, now about art, now about the future of the country, little meaningless words floating high in air. As it was becoming cold he began to pace the deck with Hirst. Fragments of their talk came out distinctly as they passed—art, emotion, truth, reality.

"Is it true, or is it a dream?" Rachel murmured, when they had passed.

"It's true, it's true," he replied.

But the breeze freshened, and there was a general desire for movement. When the party rearranged themselves under cover of rugs and cloaks, Terence and Rachel were at opposite ends of the circle, and could not speak to each other. But as the dark descended, the words of the others seemed to curl up and vanish as the ashes of burnt paper, and left them sitting perfectly silent at the bottom of the world. Occasional starts of exquisite joy ran through them, and then they were peaceful again.

CHAPTER XXI

Thanks to Mr. Flushing's discipline, the right stages of the river were reached at the right hours, and when next morning after breakfast the chairs were again drawn out in a semicircle in the bow, the launch was within a few miles of the native camp which was the limit of the journey. Mr. Flushing, as he sat down, advised them to keep their eyes fixed on the left bank, where they would soon pass a clearing, and in that clearing, was a hut where Mackenzie, the famous explorer, had died of fever some ten years ago, almost within reach of civilisation—Mackenzie, he repeated, the man who went farther inland than anyone's been yet. Their eyes turned that way obediently. The eyes of Rachel saw nothing. Yellow and green shapes did, it is true, pass before them, but she only knew that one was large and another small; she did not know that they were trees. These directions to look here and there irritated her, as interruptions irritate a person absorbed in thought, although she was not thinking of anything. She was annoyed with all that was said, and with the aimless movements of people's bodies, because they seemed to interfere with her and to prevent her from speaking to Terence. Very soon Helen saw her staring moodily at a coil of rope, and making no effort to listen. Mr. Flushing and St. John were engaged in more or less continuous conversation about the future of the country from a political point of view, and the degree to which it had been explored; the others, with their legs stretched out, or chins poised on the hands, gazed in silence.

Mrs. Ambrose looked and listened obediently enough, but inwardly she was prey to an uneasy mood not readily to be ascribed to any one cause.

Looking on shore as Mr. Flushing bade her, she thought the country very beautiful, but also sultry and alarming. She did not like to feel herself the victim of unclassified emotions, and certainly as the launch slipped on and on, in the hot morning sun, she felt herself unreasonably moved. Whether the unfamiliarity of the forest was the cause of it, or something less definite, she could not determine. Her mind left the scene and occupied itself with anxieties for Ridley, for her children, for far-off things, such as old age and poverty and death. Hirst, too, was depressed. He had been looking forward to this expedition as to a holiday, for, once away from the hotel, surely wonderful things would happen, instead of which nothing happened, and here they were as uncomfortable, as restrained, as self-conscious as ever. That, of course, was what came of looking forward to anything; one was always disappointed. He blamed Wilfrid Flushing, who was so well dressed and so formal; he blamed Hewet and Rachel. Why didn't they talk? He looked at them sitting silent and self-absorbed, and the sight annoyed him. He supposed that they were engaged, or about to become engaged, but instead of being in the least romantic or exciting, that was as dull as everything else; it annoyed him, too, to think that they were in love. He drew close to Helen and began to tell her how uncomfortable his night had been, lying on the deck, sometimes too hot, sometimes too cold, and the stars so bright that he couldn't get to sleep. He had lain awake all night thinking, and when it was light enough to see, he had written twenty lines of his poem on God, and the awful thing was that he'd practically proved the fact that God did not exist. He did not see that he was teasing her, and he went on to wonder what would happen if God did exist— "an old gentleman in a beard and a long blue dressing gown, extremely testy and disagreeable as he's bound to be? Can you suggest a rhyme? God, rod, sod—all used; any others?"

Although he spoke much as usual, Helen could have seen, had she looked, that he was also impatient and disturbed. But she was not called upon to answer, for Mr. Flushing now exclaimed "There!" They looked at the hut on the bank, a desolate place with a large rent in the roof, and the ground round it yellow, scarred with fires and scattered with rusty open tins.

"Did they find his dead body there?" Mrs. Flushing exclaimed, leaning forward in her eagerness to see the spot where the explorer had died.

"They found his body and his skins and a notebook," her husband replied. But the boat had soon carried them on and left the place behind.

It was so hot that they scarcely moved, except now to change a foot, or, again, to strike a match. Their eyes, concentrated upon the bank, were full of the same green reflections, and their lips were slightly pressed together as though the sights they were passing gave rise to thoughts, save that Hirst's lips moved intermittently as half consciously he sought rhymes for God. Whatever the thoughts of the others, no one said anything for a considerable space. They had grown so accustomed to the wall of trees on either side that they looked up with a start when the light suddenly widened out and the trees came to an end.

"It almost reminds one of an English park," said Mr. Flushing.

Indeed no change could have been greater. On both banks of the river lay an open lawn-like space, grass covered and planted, for the gentleness and order of the place suggested human care, with graceful trees on the top of little mounds. As far as they could gaze, this lawn rose and sank with the undulating motion of an old English park. The change of scene naturally suggested a change of position, grateful to most of them. They rose and leant over the rail.

"It might be Arundel or Windsor," Mr. Flushing continued, "if you cut down that bush with the yellow flowers; and, by Jove, look!"

Rows of brown backs paused for a moment and then leapt with a motion as if they were springing over waves out of sight. For a moment no one of them could believe that they had really seen live animals in the open—a herd of wild deer, and the sight aroused a childlike excitement in them, dissipating their gloom.

"I've never in my life seen anything bigger than a hare!" Hirst exclaimed with genuine excitement. "What an ass I was not to bring my Kodak!"

Soon afterwards the launch came gradually to a standstill, and the captain explained to Mr. Flushing that it would be pleasant for the passengers if they now went for a stroll on shore; if they chose to return within an hour, he would take them on to the village; if they chose to walk—it was only a mile or two farther on—he would meet them at the landing-place.

The matter being settled, they were once more put on shore: the sailors, producing raisins and tobacco, leant upon the rail and watched the six English, whose coats and dresses looked so strange upon the green, wander off. A joke that was by no means proper set them all laughing, and then they turned round and lay at their ease upon the deck.

Directly they landed, Terence and Rachel drew together slightly in advance of the others.

"Thank God!" Terence exclaimed, drawing a long breath. "At last we're alone."

"And if we keep ahead we can talk," said Rachel.

Nevertheless, although their position some yards in advance of the others made it possible for them to say anything they chose, they were both silent.

"You love me?" Terence asked at length, breaking the silence painfully. To speak or to be silent was equally an effort, for when they were silent they were keenly conscious of each other's presence, and yet words were either too trivial or too large.

She murmured inarticulately, ending, "And you?"

"Yes, yes," he replied; but there were so many things to be said, and now that they were alone it seemed necessary to bring themselves still more near, and to surmount a barrier which had grown up since they had last spoken. It was difficult, frightening even, oddly embarrassing. At one moment he was clear-sighted, and, at the next, confused.

"Now I'm going to begin at the beginning," he said resolutely. "I'm going to tell you what I ought to have told you before. In the first place, I've never been in love with other women, but I've had other women. Then I've great faults. I'm very lazy, I'm moody—" He persisted, in spite of her exclamation, "You've got to know the worst of me. I'm lustful. I'm overcome by a sense of futility—incompetence. I ought never to have asked you to marry me, I expect. I'm a bit of a snob; I'm ambitious—"

"Oh, our faults!" she cried. "What do they matter?" Then she demanded, "Am I in love—is this being in love—are we to marry each other?"

Overcome by the charm of her voice and her presence, he exclaimed, "Oh, you're free, Rachel. To you, time will make no difference, or marriage or—"

The voices of the others behind them kept floating, now farther, now nearer, and Mrs. Flushing's laugh rose clearly by itself.

"Marriage?" Rachel repeated.

The shouts were renewed behind, warning them that they were bearing too far to the left. Improving their course, he continued, "Yes, marriage." The feeling that they could not be united until she knew all about him made him again endeavour to explain.

"All that's been bad in me, the things I've put up with—the second best—"

She murmured, considered her own life, but could not describe how it looked to her now.

"And the loneliness!" he continued. A vision of walking with her through the streets of London came before his eyes. "We will go for walks together," he said. The simplicity of the idea relieved them, and for the first time they laughed. They would have liked had they dared to take each other by the hand, but the consciousness of eyes fixed on them from behind had not yet deserted them.

"Books, people, sights—Mrs. Nutt, Greeley, Hutchinson," Hewet murmured.

With every word the mist which had enveloped them, making them seem unreal to each other, since the previous afternoon melted a little further, and their contact became more and more natural. Up through the sultry southern landscape they saw the world they knew appear clearer and more vividly than it had ever appeared before. As upon that occasion at the hotel when she had sat in the window, the world once more arranged itself beneath her gaze very vividly and in its true proportions. She glanced curiously at Terence from time to time, observing his grey coat and his purple tie; observing the man with whom she was to spend the rest of her life.

After one of these glances she murmured, "Yes, I'm in love. There's no doubt; I'm in love with you."

Nevertheless, they remained uncomfortably apart; drawn so close together, as she spoke, that there seemed no division between them, and the next moment separate and far away again. Feeling this painfully, she exclaimed, "It will be a fight."

But as she looked at him she perceived from the shape of his eyes, the lines about his mouth, and other peculiarities that he pleased her, and she added:

"Where I want to fight, you have compassion. You're finer than I am; you're much finer."

He returned her glance and smiled, perceiving, much as she had done, the very small individual things about her which made her delightful to him. She was his forever. This barrier being surmounted, innumerable delights lay before them both.

"I'm not finer," he answered. "I'm only older, lazier; a man, not a woman."

"A man," she repeated, and a curious sense of possession coming over her, it struck her that she might now touch him; she put out her hand and lightly touched his cheek. His fingers followed where hers had been, and the touch of his hand upon his face brought back the overpowering sense of unreality. This body of his was unreal; the whole world was unreal.

"What's happened?" he began. "Why did I ask you to marry me? How did it happen?"

"Did you ask me to marry you?" she wondered. They faded far away from each other, and neither of them could remember what had been said.

"We sat upon the ground," he recollected.

"We sat upon the ground," she confirmed him. The recollection of sitting upon the ground, such as it was, seemed to unite them again, and they walked on in silence, their minds sometimes working with difficulty and sometimes ceasing to work, their eyes alone perceiving the things round them. Now he would attempt again to tell her his faults, and why he loved her; and she would describe what she had felt at this time or at that time, and together they would interpret her feeling. So beautiful was the sound of their voices that by degrees they scarcely listened to the words they framed. Long silences came between their words, which were no longer silences of struggle and confusion but refreshing silences, in which trivial thoughts moved easily. They began to speak naturally of ordinary things, of the flowers and the trees, how they grew there so red, like garden flowers at home, and there bent and crooked like the arm of a twisted old man.

Very gently and quietly, almost as if it were the blood singing in her veins, or the water of the stream running over stones, Rachel became conscious of a new feeling within her. She wondered for a moment what it was, and then said to herself, with a little surprise at recognising in her own person so famous a thing:

"This is happiness, I suppose." And aloud to Terence she spoke, "This is happiness."

On the heels of her words he answered, "This is happiness," upon which they guessed that the feeling had sprung in both of them the same time. They began therefore to describe how this felt and that felt, how like it was and yet how different; for they were very different.

Voices crying behind them never reached through the waters in which they were now sunk. The repetition of Hewet's name in short, dissevered syllables was to them the crack of a dry branch or the laughter of a bird. The grasses and breezes sounding and murmuring all round them, they never noticed that the swishing of the grasses grew louder and louder, and did not cease with the lapse of the breeze. A hand dropped abrupt as iron on Rachel's shoulder; it might have been a bolt from heaven. She fell beneath it, and the grass whipped across her eyes and filled her mouth and ears. Through the waving stems she saw a figure, large and shapeless against the sky. Helen was upon her. Rolled this way and that, now seeing only forests of green, and now the high blue heaven; she was speechless and almost without sense. At last she lay still, all the grasses shaken round her and before her by her panting. Over her loomed two great heads, the heads of a man and woman, of Terence and Helen.

Both were flushed, both laughing, and the lips were moving; they came together and kissed in the air above her. Broken fragments of speech came down to her on the ground. She thought she heard them speak of love and then of marriage. Raising herself and sitting up, she too realised Helen's soft body, the strong and hospitable arms, and happiness swelling and breaking in one vast wave. When this fell away, and the grasses once more lay low, and the sky became horizontal, and the earth rolled out flat on each side, and the trees stood upright, she was the first to perceive a little row of human figures standing patiently in the distance. For the moment she could not remember who they were.

"Who are they?" she asked, and then recollected.

Falling into line behind Mr. Flushing, they were careful to leave at least three yards' distance between the toe of his boot and the rim of her skirt.

He led them across a stretch of green by the river-bank and then through a grove of trees, and bade them remark the signs of human habitation, the blackened grass, the charred tree-stumps, and there, through the trees, strange wooden nests, drawn together in an arch where the trees drew apart, the village which was the goal of their journey.

Stepping cautiously, they observed the women, who were squatting on the ground in triangular shapes, moving their hands, either plaiting straw or in kneading something in bowls. But when they had looked for a moment undiscovered, they were seen, and Mr. Flushing, advancing into the centre of the clearing, was engaged in talk with a lean majestic man, whose bones and hollows at once made the shapes of the Englishman's body appear ugly and unnatural. The women took no notice of the strangers, except that their hands paused for a moment and their long narrow eyes slid round and fixed upon them with the motionless inexpensive gaze of those removed from each other far far beyond the plunge of speech. Their hands moved again, but the stare continued. It followed them as they walked, as they peered into the huts where they could distinguish guns leaning in the corner, and bowls upon the floor, and stacks of rushes; in the dusk the solemn eyes of babies regarded them, and old women stared out too. As they sauntered about, the stare followed them, passing over their legs, their bodies, their heads, curiously not without hostility, like the crawl of a winter fly. As she drew apart her shawl and uncovered her breast to the lips of her baby, the eyes of a woman never left their faces, although they moved uneasily under her stare, and finally turned away, rather than stand there looking at her any longer. When sweetmeats were offered them, they put out great red hands to take them, and felt themselves treading cumbrously like tight-coated soldiers among these soft instinctive people. But soon the life of the village took no notice of them; they had become absorbed in it. The women's hands became busy again with the straw; their eyes dropped. If they moved, it was to fetch something from the hut, or to catch a straying child, or to cross the space with a jar balanced on their heads; if they spoke, it was to cry some harsh unintelligible cry. Voices rose when a child was beaten, and fell again; voices rose in song, which slid up a little way and down a little way, and settled again upon the same low and melancholy note. Seeking each other, Terence and Rachel drew together under a tree. Peaceful, and even beautiful at first, the sight of the women, who had given up looking at them, made them now feel very cold and melancholy.

"Well," Terence sighed at length, "it makes us seem insignificant, doesn't it?"

Rachel agreed. So it would go on forever and ever, she said, those women sitting under the trees, the trees and the river. They turned away and began to walk through the trees, leaning, without fear of discovery, upon each other's arms. They had not gone far before they began to assure each other once more that they were in love, were happy, were content; but why was it so painful being in love, why was there so much pain in happiness?

The sight of the village indeed affected them all curiously though all differently. St. John had left the others and was walking slowly down to the river, absorbed in his own thoughts, which were bitter and unhappy, for he felt himself alone; and Helen, standing by herself in the sunny space among the native women, was exposed to presentiments of disaster. The cries of the senseless beasts rang in her ears high and low in the air, as they ran from tree-trunk to tree-top. How small the little figures looked wandering through the trees! She became acutely conscious of the little limbs, the thin veins, the delicate flesh of men and women, which breaks so easily and lets the life escape compared with these great trees and deep waters. A falling branch, a foot that slips, and the earth has crushed them or the water drowned them. Thus thinking, she kept her eyes anxiously fixed upon the lovers, as if by doing so she could protect them from their fate. Turning, she found the Flushings by her side.

They were talking about the things they had bought and arguing whether they were really old, and whether there were not signs here and there of European influence. Helen was appealed to. She was made to look at a brooch, and then at a pair of ear-rings. But all the time she blamed them for having come on this expedition, for having ventured too far and exposed themselves. Then she roused herself and tried to talk, but in a few moments she caught herself seeing a picture of a boat upset on the river in England, at midday. It was morbid, she knew, to imagine such things; nevertheless she sought out the figures of the others between the trees, and whenever she saw them she kept her eyes fixed on them, so that she might be able to protect them from disaster.

But when the sun went down and the steamer turned and began to steam back towards civilisation, again her fears were calmed. In the semi-darkness the chairs on deck and the people sitting in them were angular shapes, the mouth being indicated by a tiny burning spot, and the arm by the same spot moving up or down as the cigar or cigarette was lifted to and from the lips. Words crossed the darkness, but, not knowing where they fell, seemed to lack energy and substance. Deep sights proceeded regularly, although with some attempt at suppression, from the large white mound which represented the person of Mrs. Flushing. The day had been long and very hot, and now that all the colours were blotted out the cool night air seemed to press soft fingers upon the eyelids, sealing them down. Some philosophical remark directed, apparently, at St. John Hirst missed its aim, and hung so long suspended in the air until it was engulfed by a yawn, that it was considered dead, and this gave the signal for stirring of legs and murmurs about sleep. The white mound moved, finally lengthened itself and disappeared, and after a few turns and paces St. John and Mr. Flushing withdrew, leaving the three chairs still occupied by three silent bodies. The light which came from a lamp high on the mast and a sky pale with stars left them with shapes but without features; but even in this darkness the withdrawal of the others made them feel each other very near, for they were all thinking of the same thing. For some time no one spoke, then Helen said with a sigh, "So you're both very happy?"

As if washed by the air her voice sounded more spiritual and softer than usual. Voices at a little distance answered her, "Yes."

Through the darkness she was looking at them both, and trying to distinguish him. What was there for her to say? Rachel had passed beyond her guardianship. A voice might reach her ears, but never again would it carry as far as it had carried twenty-four hours ago. Nevertheless, speech seemed to be due from her before she went to bed. She wished to speak, but she felt strangely old and depressed.

"D'you realise what you're doing?" she demanded. "She's young, you're both young; and marriage—" Here she ceased. They begged her, however, to continue, with such earnestness in their voices, as if they only craved advice, that she was led to add:

"Marriage! well, it's not easy."

"That's what we want to know," they answered, and she guessed that now they were looking at each other.

"It depends on both of you," she stated. Her face was turned towards Terence, and although he could hardly see her, he believed that her words really covered a genuine desire to know more about him. He raised himself from his semi-recumbent position and proceeded to tell her what she wanted to know. He spoke as lightly as he could in order to take away her depression.

"I'm twenty-seven, and I've about seven hundred a year," he began. "My temper is good on the whole, and health excellent, though Hirst detects a gouty tendency. Well, then, I think I'm very intelligent." He paused as if for confirmation.

Helen agreed.

"Though, unfortunately, rather lazy. I intend to allow Rachel to be a fool if she wants to, and—Do you find me on the whole satisfactory in other respects?" he asked shyly.

"Yes, I like what I know of you," Helen replied.

"But then—one knows so little."

"We shall live in London," he continued, "and—" With one voice they suddenly enquired whether she did not think them the happiest people that she had ever known.

"Hush," she checked them, "Mrs. Flushing, remember. She's behind us."

Then they fell silent, and Terence and Rachel felt instinctively that their happiness had made her sad, and, while they were anxious to go on talking about themselves, they did not like to.

"We've talked too much about ourselves," Terence said. "Tell us—"

"Yes, tell us—" Rachel echoed. They were both in the mood to believe that every one was capable of saying something very profound.

"What can I tell you?" Helen reflected, speaking more to herself in a rambling style than as a prophetess delivering a message. She forced herself to speak.

"After all, though I scold Rachel, I'm not much wiser myself. I'm older, of course, I'm half-way through, and you're just beginning. It's puzzling—sometimes, I think, disappointing; the great things aren't as great, perhaps, as one expects—but it's interesting—Oh, yes, you're certain to find it interesting—And so it goes on," they became conscious here of the procession of dark trees into which, as far as they could see, Helen was now looking, "and there are pleasures where one doesn't expect them (you must write to your father), and you'll be very happy, I've no doubt. But I must go to bed, and if you are sensible you will follow in ten minutes, and so," she rose and stood before them, almost featureless and very large, "Good-night." She passed behind the curtain.

After sitting in silence for the greater part of the ten minutes she allowed them, they rose and hung over the rail. Beneath them the smooth black water slipped away very fast and silently. The spark of a cigarette vanished behind them. "A beautiful voice," Terence murmured.

Rachel assented. Helen had a beautiful voice.

After a silence she asked, looking up into the sky, "Are we on the deck of a steamer on a river in South America? Am I Rachel, are you Terence?"

The great black world lay round them. As they were drawn smoothly along it seemed possessed of immense thickness and endurance. They could discern pointed tree-tops and blunt rounded tree-tops. Raising their eyes above the trees, they fixed them on the stars and the pale border of sky above the trees. The little points of frosty light infinitely far away drew their eyes and held them fixed, so that it seemed as if they stayed a long time and fell a great distance when once more they realised their hands grasping the rail and their separate bodies standing side by side.

"You'd forgotten completely about me," Terence reproached her, taking her arm and beginning to pace the deck, "and I never forget you."

"Oh, no," she whispered, she had not forgotten, only the stars—the night—the dark—

"You're like a bird half asleep in its nest, Rachel. You're asleep. You're talking in your sleep."

Half asleep, and murmuring broken words, they stood in the angle made by the bow of the boat. It slipped on down the river. Now a bell struck on the bridge, and they heard the lapping of water as it rippled away on either side, and once a bird startled in its sleep creaked, flew on to the next tree, and was silent again. The darkness poured down profusely, and left them with scarcely any feeling of life, except that they were standing there together in the darkness.

CHAPTER XXII

The darkness fell, but rose again, and as each day spread widely over the earth and parted them from the strange day in the forest when they had been forced to tell each other what they wanted, this wish of theirs was revealed to other people, and in the process became slightly strange to themselves. Apparently it was not anything unusual that had happened; it was that they had become engaged to marry each other. The world, which consisted for the most part of the hotel and the villa, expressed itself glad on the whole that two people should marry, and allowed them to see that they were not expected to take part in the work which has to be done in order that the world shall go on, but might absent themselves for a time. They were accordingly left alone until they felt the silence as if, playing in a vast church, the door had been shut on them. They were driven to walk alone, and sit alone, to visit secret places where the flowers had never been picked and the trees were solitary. In solitude they could express those beautiful but too vast desires which were so oddly uncomfortable to the ears of other men and women—desires for a world, such as their own world which contained two people seemed to them to be, where people knew each other intimately and thus judged each other by what was good, and never quarrelled, because that was waste of time.

They would talk of such questions among books, or out in the sun, or sitting in the shade of a tree undisturbed. They were no longer embarrassed, or half-choked with meaning which could not express itself; they were not afraid of each other, or, like travellers down a twisting river, dazzled with sudden beauties when the corner is turned; the unexpected happened, but even the ordinary was lovable, and in many ways preferable to the ecstatic and mysterious, for it was refreshingly solid, and called out effort, and effort under such circumstances was not effort but delight.

While Rachel played the piano, Terence sat near her, engaged, as far as the occasional writing of a word in pencil testified, in shaping the world as it appeared to him now that he and Rachel were going to be married. It was different certainly. The book called *Silence* would not now be the same book that it would have been. He would then put down his pencil and stare in front of him, and wonder in what respects the world was different—it had, perhaps, more solidity, more coherence, more importance, greater depth. Why, even the earth sometimes seemed to him very deep; not carved into hills and cities and fields, but heaped in great masses. He would look out of the window for ten minutes at a time; but no, he did not care for the earth swept of human beings. He liked human beings—he liked them, he suspected, better than Rachel did. There she was, swaying enthusiastically over her music, quite forgetful of him—but he liked that quality in her. He liked the impersonality which it produced in her. At last, having written down a series of little sentences, with notes of interrogation attached to them, he observed aloud, "Women—'under the heading Women I've written:

"'Not really vainer than men. Lack of self-confidence at the base of most serious faults. Dislike of own sex traditional, or founded on fact? Every woman not so much a rake at heart, as an optimist, because they don't think.' What do you say, Rachel?" He paused with his pencil in his hand and a sheet of paper on his knee.

Rachel said nothing. Up and up the steep spiral of a very late Beethoven sonata she climbed, like a person ascending a ruined staircase, energetically at first, then more laboriously advancing her feet with effort until she could go no higher and returned with a run to begin at the very bottom again.

"'Again, it's the fashion now to say that women are more practical and less idealistic than men, also that they have considerable organising ability but no sense of honour'—query, what is meant by masculine term, honour?—what corresponds to it in your sex? Eh?"

Attacking her staircase once more, Rachel again neglected this opportunity of revealing the secrets of her sex. She had, indeed, advanced so far in the pursuit of wisdom that she allowed these secrets to rest undisturbed; it seemed to be reserved for a later generation to discuss them philosophically.

Crashing down a final chord with her left hand, she exclaimed at last, swinging round upon him:

"No, Terence, it's no good; here am I, the best musician in South America, not to speak of Europe and Asia, and I can't play a note because of you in the room interrupting me every other second."

"You don't seem to realise that that's what I've been aiming at for the last half-hour," he remarked. "I've no objection to nice simple tunes—indeed, I find them very helpful to my literary composition, but that kind of thing is merely like an unfortunate old dog going round on its hind legs in the rain."

He began turning over the little sheets of note-paper which were scattered on the table, conveying the congratulations of their friends.

"'—all possible wishes for all possible happiness,'" he read; "correct, but not very vivid, are they?"

"They're sheer nonsense!" Rachel exclaimed. "Think of words compared

with sounds!" she continued. "Think of novels and plays and histories—"
Perched on the edge of the table, she stirred the red and yellow volumes
contemptuously. She seemed to herself to be in a position where she could
despise all human learning. Terence looked at them too.

"God, Rachel, you do read trash!" he exclaimed. "And you're behind the
times too, my dear. No one dreams of reading this kind of thing now—
antiquated problem plays, harrowing descriptions of life in the east end—oh,
no, we've exploded all that. Read poetry, Rachel, poetry, poetry, poetry!"

Picking up one of the books, he began to read aloud, his intention being to
satirise the short sharp bark of the writer's English; but she paid no attention,
and after an interval of meditation exclaimed:

"Does it ever seem to you, Terence, that the world is composed entirely
of vast blocks of matter, and that we're nothing but patches of light—" she
looked at the soft spots of sun wavering over the carpet and up the wall—
"like that?"

"No," said Terence, "I feel solid; immensely solid; the legs of my chair
might be rooted in the bowels of the earth. But at Cambridge, I can remember,
there were times when one fell into ridiculous states of semi-coma about five
o'clock in the morning. Hirst does now, I expect—oh, no, Hirst wouldn't."

Rachel continued, "The day your note came, asking us to go on the picnic,
I was sitting where you're sitting now, thinking that; I wonder if I could
think that again? I wonder if the world's changed? and if so, when it'll stop
changing, and which is the real world?"

"When I first saw you," he began, "I thought you were like a creature
who'd lived all its life among pearls and old bones. Your hands were wet,
d'you remember, and you never said a word until I gave you a bit of bread,
and then you said, 'Human Beings!'"

"And I thought you—a prig," she recollected. "No; that's not quite it.
There were the ants who stole the tongue, and I thought you and St. John
were like those ants—very big, very ugly, very energetic, with all your virtues
on your backs. However, when I talked to you I liked you—"

"You fell in love with me," he corrected her. "You were in love with me all
the time, only you didn't know it."

"No, I never fell in love with you," she asserted.

"Rachel—what a lie—didn't you sit here looking at my window—didn't
you wander about the hotel like an owl in the sun—?"

"No," she repeated, "I never fell in love, if falling in love is what people
say it is, and it's the world that tells the lies and I tell the truth. Oh, what
lies—what lies!"

She crumpled together a handful of letters from Evelyn M., from Mr.
Pepper, from Mrs. Thornbury and Miss Allan, and Susan Warrington. It was

strange, considering how very different these people were, that they used almost the same sentences when they wrote to congratulate her upon her engagement.

That any one of these people had ever felt what she felt, or could ever feel it, or had even the right to pretend for a single second that they were capable of feeling it, appalled her much as the church service had done, much as the face of the hospital nurse had done; and if they didn't feel a thing why did they go and pretend to? The simplicity and arrogance and hardness of her youth, now concentrated into a single spark as it was by her love of him, puzzled Terence; being engaged had not that effect on him; the world was different, but not in that way; he still wanted the things he had always wanted, and in particular he wanted the companionship of other people more than ever perhaps. He took the letters out of her hand, and protested:

"Of course they're absurd, Rachel; of course they say things just because other people say them, but even so, what a nice woman Miss Allan is; you can't deny that; and Mrs. Thornbury too; she's got too many children I grant you, but if half-a-dozen of them had gone to the bad instead of rising infallibly to the tops of their trees—hasn't she a kind of beauty—of elemental simplicity as Flushing would say? Isn't she rather like a large old tree murmuring in the moonlight, or a river going on and on and on? By the way, Ralph's been made governor of the Carroway Islands—the youngest governor in the service; very good, isn't it?"

But Rachel was at present unable to conceive that the vast majority of the affairs of the world went on unconnected by a single thread with her own destiny.

"I won't have eleven children," she asserted; "I won't have the eyes of an old woman. She looks at one up and down, up and down, as if one were a horse."

"We must have a son and we must have a daughter," said Terence, putting down the letters, "because, let alone the inestimable advantage of being our children, they'd be so well brought up." They went on to sketch an outline of the ideal education—how their daughter should be required from infancy to gaze at a large square of cardboard painted blue, to suggest thoughts of infinity, for women were grown too practical; and their son—he should be taught to laugh at great men, that is, at distinguished successful men, at men who wore ribands and rose to the tops of their trees. He should in no way resemble (Rachel added) St. John Hirst.

At this Terence professed the greatest admiration for St. John Hirst. Dwelling upon his good qualities he became seriously convinced of them; he had a mind like a torpedo, he declared, aimed at falsehood. Where should we all be without him and his like? Choked in weeds; Christians, bigots—why, Rachel herself, would be a slave with a fan to sing songs to men when they felt drowsy.

"But you'll never see it!" he exclaimed; "because with all your virtues you don't, and you never will, care with every fibre of your being for the pursuit of truth! You've no respect for facts, Rachel; you're essentially feminine."

She did not trouble to deny it, nor did she think good to produce the one unanswerable argument against the merits which Terence admired. St. John Hirst said that she was in love with him; she would never forgive that; but the argument was not one to appeal to a man.

"But I like him," she said, and she thought to herself that she also pitied him, as one pities those unfortunate people who are outside the warm mysterious globe full of changes and miracles in which we ourselves move about; she thought that it must be very dull to be St. John Hirst.

She summed up what she felt about him by saying that she would not kiss him supposing he wished it, which was not likely.

As if some apology were due to Hirst for the kiss which she then bestowed upon him, Terence protested:

"And compared with Hirst I'm a perfect Zany."

The clock here struck twelve instead of eleven.

"We're wasting the morning—I ought to be writing my book, and you ought to be answering these."

"We've only got twenty-one whole mornings left," said Rachel. "And my father'll be here in a day or two."

However, she drew a pen and paper towards her and began to write laboriously,

"My dear Evelyn—"

Terence, meanwhile, read a novel which someone else had written, a process which he found essential to the composition of his own. For a considerable time nothing was to be heard but the ticking of the clock and the fitful scratch of Rachel's pen, as she produced phrases which bore a considerable likeness to those which she had condemned. She was struck by it herself, for she stopped writing and looked up; looked at Terence deep in the armchair, looked at the different pieces of furniture, at her bed in the corner, at the window-pane which showed the branches of a tree filled in with sky, heard the clock ticking, and was amazed at the gulf which lay between all that and her sheet of paper. Would there ever be a time when the world was one and indivisible? Even with Terence himself—how far apart they could be, how little she knew what was passing in his brain now! She then finished her sentence, which was awkward and ugly, and stated that they were "both very happy, and going to be married in the autumn probably and hope to live in London, where we hope you will come and see us when we get back." Choosing "affectionately," after some further speculation, rather than sincerely, she signed the letter and was doggedly beginning on another when Terence remarked, quoting from his book:

"Listen to this, Rachel. 'It is probable that Hugh' (he's the hero, a literary man), 'had not realised at the time of his marriage, any more than the young man of parts and imagination usually does realise, the nature of the gulf which separates the needs and desires of the male from the needs and desires of the female . . . At first they had been very happy. The walking tour in Switzerland had been a time of jolly companionship and stimulating revelations for both of them. Betty had proved herself the ideal comrade . . . They had shouted *Love in the Valley* to each other across the snowy slopes of the Riffelhorn' (and so on, and so on—I'll skip the descriptions) . . . 'But in London, after the boy's birth, all was changed. Betty was an admirable mother; but it did not take her long to find out that motherhood, as that function is understood by the mother of the upper middle classes, did not absorb the whole of her energies. She was young and strong, with healthy limbs and a body and brain that called urgently for exercise . . .' (In short she began to give tea-parties.) . . . 'Coming in late from this singular talk with old Bob Murphy in his smoky, book-lined room, where the two men had each unloosened his soul to the other, with the sound of the traffic humming in his ears, and the foggy London sky slung tragically across his mind . . . he found women's hats dotted about among his papers. Women's wraps and absurd little feminine shoes and umbrellas were in the hall . . . Then the bills began to come in . . . He tried to speak frankly to her. He found her lying on the great polar-bear skin in their bedroom, half-undressed, for they were dining with the Greens in Wilton Crescent, the ruddy firelight making the diamonds wink and twinkle on her bare arms and in the delicious curve of her breast—a vision of adorable femininity. He forgave her all.' (Well, this goes from bad to worse, and finally about fifty pages later, Hugh takes a weekend ticket to Swanage and 'has it out with himself on the downs above Corfe' . . . Here there's fifteen pages or so which we'll skip. The conclusion is . . .) 'They were different. Perhaps, in the far future, when generations of men had struggled and failed as he must now struggle and fail, woman would be, indeed, what she now made a pretence of being—the friend and companion—not the enemy and parasite of man.'

"The end of it is, you see, Hugh went back to his wife, poor fellow. It was his duty, as a married man. Lord, Rachel," he concluded, "will it be like that when we're married?"

Instead of answering him she asked,

"Why don't people write about the things they do feel?"

"Ah, that's the difficulty!" he sighed, tossing the book away.

"Well, then, what will it be like when we're married? What are the things people do feel?"

She seemed doubtful.

"Sit on the floor and let me look at you," he commanded. Resting her chin on his knee, she looked straight at him.

He examined her curiously.

"You're not beautiful," he began, "but I like your face. I like the way your hair grows down in a point, and your eyes too—they never see anything. Your mouth's too big, and your cheeks would be better if they had more colour in them. But what I like about your face is that it makes one wonder what the devil you're thinking about—it makes me want to do that—" He clenched his fist and shook it so near her that she started back, "because now you look as if you'd blow my brains out. There are moments," he continued, "when, if we stood on a rock together, you'd throw me into the sea."

Hypnotised by the force of his eyes in hers, she repeated, "If we stood on a rock together—"

To be flung into the sea, to be washed hither and thither, and driven about the roots of the world—the idea was incoherently delightful. She sprang up, and began moving about the room, bending and thrusting aside the chairs and tables as if she were indeed striking through the waters. He watched her with pleasure; she seemed to be cleaving a passage for herself, and dealing triumphantly with the obstacles which would hinder their passage through life.

"It does seem possible!" he exclaimed, "though I've always thought it the most unlikely thing in the world—I shall be in love with you all my life, and our marriage will be the most exciting thing that's ever been done! We'll never have a moment's peace—" He caught her in his arms as she passed him, and they fought for mastery, imagining a rock, and the sea heaving beneath them. At last she was thrown to the floor, where she lay gasping, and crying for mercy.

"I'm a mermaid! I can swim," she cried, "so the game's up." Her dress was torn across, and peace being established, she fetched a needle and thread and began to mend the tear.

"And now," she said, "be quiet and tell me about the world; tell me about everything that's ever happened, and I'll tell you—let me see, what can I tell you?—I'll tell you about Miss Montgomerie and the river party. She was left, you see, with one foot in the boat, and the other on shore."

They had spent much time already in thus filling out for the other the course of their past lives, and the characters of their friends and relations, so that very soon Terence knew not only what Rachel's aunts might be expected to say upon every occasion, but also how their bedrooms were furnished, and what kind of bonnets they wore. He could sustain a conversation between Mrs. Hunt and Rachel, and carry on a tea-party including the Rev. William Johnson and Miss Macquoid, the Christian Scientists, with remarkable likeness to the truth. But he had known many more people, and was far more highly skilled in the art of narrative than Rachel was, whose experiences were, for the most part, of a curiously childlike and humorous kind, so that it generally fell to her lot to listen and ask questions.

He told her not only what had happened, but what he had thought and felt, and sketched for her portraits which fascinated her of what other men and women might be supposed to be thinking and feeling, so that she became very anxious to go back to England, which was full of people, where she could merely stand in the streets and look at them. According to him, too, there was an order, a pattern which made life reasonable, or if that word was foolish, made it of deep interest anyhow, for sometimes it seemed possible to understand why things happened as they did. Nor were people so solitary and uncommunicative as she believed. She should look for vanity—for vanity was a common quality—first in herself, and then in Helen, in Ridley, in St. John, they all had their share of it—and she would find it in ten people out of every twelve she met; and once linked together by one such tie she would find them not separate and formidable, but practically indistinguishable, and she would come to love them when she found that they were like herself.

If she denied this, she must defend her belief that human beings were as various as the beasts at the Zoo, which had stripes and manes, and horns and humps; and so, wrestling over the entire list of their acquaintances, and diverging into anecdote and theory and speculation, they came to know each other. The hours passed quickly, and seemed to them full to leaking-point. After a night's solitude they were always ready to begin again.

The virtues which Mrs. Ambrose had once believed to exist in free talk between men and women did in truth exist for both of them, although not quite in the measure she prescribed. Far more than upon the nature of sex they dwelt upon the nature of poetry, but it was true that talk which had no boundaries deepened and enlarged the strangely small bright view of a girl. In return for what he could tell her she brought him such curiosity and sensitiveness of perception, that he was led to doubt whether any gift bestowed by much reading and living was quite the equal of that for pleasure and pain. What would experience give her after all, except a kind of ridiculous formal balance, like that of a drilled dog in the street? He looked at her face and wondered how it would look in twenty years' time, when the eyes had dulled, and the forehead wore those little persistent wrinkles which seem to show that the middle-aged are facing something hard which the young do not see? What would the hard thing be for them, he wondered? Then his thoughts turned to their life in England.

The thought of England was delightful, for together they would see the old things freshly; it would be England in June, and there would be June nights in the country; and the nightingales singing in the lanes, into which they could steal when the room grew hot; and there would be English meadows gleaming with water and set with stolid cows, and clouds dipping low and trailing across the green hills. As he sat in the room with her, he wished very often to be back again in the thick of life, doing things with Rachel.

He crossed to the window and exclaimed, "Lord, how good it is to think of lanes, muddy lanes, with brambles and nettles, you know, and real grass fields, and farmyards with pigs and cows, and men walking beside carts with pitchforks—there's nothing to compare with that here—look at the stony red earth, and the bright blue sea, and the glaring white houses—how tired one gets of it! And the air, without a stain or a wrinkle. I'd give anything for a sea mist."

Rachel, too, had been thinking of the English country: the flat land rolling away to the sea, and the woods and the long straight roads, where one can walk for miles without seeing anyone, and the great church towers and the curious houses clustered in the valleys, and the birds, and the dusk, and the rain falling against the windows.

"But London, London's the place," Terence continued. They looked together at the carpet, as though London itself were to be seen there lying on the floor, with all its spires and pinnacles pricking through the smoke.

"On the whole, what I should like best at this moment," Terence pondered, "would be to find myself walking down Kingsway, by those big placards, you know, and turning into the Strand. Perhaps I might go and look over Waterloo Bridge for a moment. Then I'd go along the Strand past the shops with all the new books in them, and through the little archway into the Temple. I always like the quiet after the uproar. You hear your own footsteps suddenly quite loud. The Temple's very pleasant. I think I should go and see if I could find dear old Hodgkin—the man who writes books about Van Eyck, you know. When I left England he was very sad about his tame magpie. He suspected that a man had poisoned it. And then Russell lives on the next staircase. I think you'd like him. He's a passion for Handel. Well, Rachel," he concluded, dismissing the vision of London, "we shall be doing that together in six weeks' time, and it'll be the middle of June then—and June in London—my God! how pleasant it all is!"

"And we're certain to have it too," she said. "It isn't as if we were expecting a great deal—only to walk about and look at things."

"Only a thousand a year and perfect freedom," he replied. "How many people in London d'you think have that?"

"And now you've spoilt it," she complained. "Now we've got to think of the horrors." She looked grudgingly at the novel which had once caused her perhaps an hour's discomfort, so that she had never opened it again, but kept it on her table, and looked at it occasionally, as some medieval monk kept a skull, or a crucifix to remind him of the frailty of the body.

"Is it true, Terence," she demanded, "that women die with bugs crawling across their faces?"

"I think it's very probable," he said. "But you must admit, Rachel, that we so seldom think of anything but ourselves that an occasional twinge is really rather pleasant."

Accusing him of an affection of cynicism which was just as bad as sentimentality itself, she left her position by his side and knelt upon the window sill, twisting the curtain tassels between her fingers. A vague sense of dissatisfaction filled her.

"What's so detestable in this country," she exclaimed, "is the blue—always blue sky and blue sea. It's like a curtain—all the things one wants are on the other side of that. I want to know what's going on behind it. I hate these divisions, don't you, Terence? One person all in the dark about another person. Now I liked the Dalloways," she continued, "and they're gone. I shall never see them again. Just by going on a ship we cut ourselves off entirely from the rest of the world. I want to see England there—London there— all sorts of people—why shouldn't one? why should one be shut up all by oneself in a room?"

While she spoke thus half to herself and with increasing vagueness, because her eye was caught by a ship that had just come into the bay, she did not see that Terence had ceased to stare contentedly in front of him, and was looking at her keenly and with dissatisfaction. She seemed to be able to cut herself adrift from him, and to pass away to unknown places where she had no need of him. The thought roused his jealousy.

"I sometimes think you're not in love with me and never will be," he said energetically. She started and turned round at his words.

"I don't satisfy you in the way you satisfy me," he continued. "There's something I can't get hold of in you. You don't want me as I want you— you're always wanting something else."

He began pacing up and down the room.

"Perhaps I ask too much," he went on. "Perhaps it isn't really possible to have what I want. Men and women are too different. You can't understand— you don't understand—"

He came up to where she stood looking at him in silence.

It seemed to her now that what he was saying was perfectly true, and that she wanted many more things than the love of one human being—the sea, the sky. She turned again the looked at the distant blue, which was so smooth and serene where the sky met the sea; she could not possibly want only one human being.

"Or is it only this damnable engagement?" he continued. "Let's be married here, before we go back—or is it too great a risk? Are we sure we want to marry each other?"

They began pacing up and down the room, but although they came very near each other in their pacing, they took care not to touch each other. The hopelessness of their position overcame them both. They were impotent; they could never love each other sufficiently to overcome all these barriers, and they could never be satisfied with less. Realising this with intolerable keenness she stopped in front of him and exclaimed:

"Let's break it off, then."

The words did more to unite them than any amount of argument. As if they stood on the edge of a precipice they clung together. They knew that they could not separate; painful and terrible it might be, but they were joined forever. They lapsed into silence, and after a time crept together in silence. Merely to be so close soothed them, and sitting side by side the divisions disappeared, and it seemed as if the world were once more solid and entire, and as if, in some strange way, they had grown larger and stronger.

It was long before they moved, and when they moved it was with great reluctance. They stood together in front of the looking-glass, and with a brush tried to make themselves look as if they had been feeling nothing all the morning, neither pain nor happiness. But it chilled them to see themselves in the glass, for instead of being vast and indivisible they were really very small and separate, the size of the glass leaving a large space for the reflection of other things.

CHAPTER XXIII

But no brush was able to efface completely the expression of happiness, so that Mrs. Ambrose could not treat them when they came downstairs as if they had spent the morning in a way that could be discussed naturally. This being so, she joined in the world's conspiracy to consider them for the time incapacitated from the business of life, struck by their intensity of feeling into enmity against life, and almost succeeded in dismissing them from her thoughts.

She reflected that she had done all that it was necessary to do in practical matters. She had written a great many letters, and had obtained Willoughby's consent. She had dwelt so often upon Mr. Hewet's prospects, his profession, his birth, appearance, and temperament, that she had almost forgotten what he was really like. When she refreshed herself by a look at him, she used to wonder again what he was like, and then, concluding that they were happy at any rate, thought no more about it.

She might more profitably consider what would happen in three years' time, or what might have happened if Rachel had been left to explore the world under her father's guidance. The result, she was honest enough to own, might have been better—who knows? She did not disguise from herself that Terence had faults. She was inclined to think him too easy and tolerant, just as he was inclined to think her perhaps a trifle hard—no, it was rather that she was uncompromising. In some ways she found St. John preferable; but then, of course, he would never have suited Rachel. Her friendship with St. John was established, for although she fluctuated between irritation and interest in a way that did credit to the candour of her disposition, she liked his company on the whole. He took her outside this little world of love and emotion. He had a grasp of facts. Supposing, for instance, that England made a sudden move towards some unknown port on the coast of Morocco, St. John knew what was at the back of it, and to hear him engaged with her husband in argument about finance and the balance of power, gave her an odd sense of stability. She respected their arguments without always listening to them, much as she respected a solid brick wall, or one of those immense municipal buildings which, although they compose the greater part of our cities, have been built day after day and year after year by unknown hands. She liked to sit and listen, and even felt a little elated when the engaged couple, after showing their profound lack of interest, slipped from the room, and were seen pulling flowers to pieces in the garden. It was not that she was jealous of them, but she did undoubtedly envy them their great unknown future that lay before them. Slipping from one such thought to another, she was at the dining-room with fruit in her hands. Sometimes she stopped to straighten a candle stooping with the heat, or disturbed some too rigid arrangement of the chairs. She had reason to suspect that Chailey had been balancing herself on the top of a ladder with a wet duster during their absence, and the room had never been quite like itself since. Returning from the dining-room for the third time, she perceived that one of the armchairs was now occupied by St. John. He lay back in it, with his eyes half shut, looking, as he always did, curiously buttoned up in a neat grey suit and fenced against the exuberance of a foreign climate which might at any moment proceed to take liberties with him. Her eyes rested on him gently and then passed on over his head. Finally she took the chair opposite.

"I didn't want to come here," he said at last, "but I was positively driven to it . . . Evelyn M.," he groaned.

He sat up, and began to explain with mock solemnity how the detestable woman was set upon marrying him.

"She pursues me about the place. This morning she appeared in the smoking-room. All I could do was to seize my hat and fly. I didn't want to come, but I couldn't stay and face another meal with her."

"Well, we must make the best of it," Helen replied philosophically. It was very hot, and they were indifferent to any amount of silence, so that they lay back in their chairs waiting for something to happen. The bell rang for luncheon, but there was no sound of movement in the house. Was there any news? Helen asked; anything in the papers? St. John shook his head. O yes, he had a letter from home, a letter from his mother, describing the suicide of the parlour-maid. She was called Susan Jane, and she came into the kitchen one afternoon, and said that she wanted cook to keep her money for her; she had twenty pounds in gold. Then she went out to buy herself a hat. She came in at half-past five and said that she had taken poison. They had only just time to get her into bed and call a doctor before she died.

"Well?" Helen enquired.

"There'll have to be an inquest," said St. John.

Why had she done it? He shrugged his shoulders. Why do people kill themselves? Why do the lower orders do any of the things they do do? Nobody knows. They sat in silence.

"The bell's run fifteen minutes and they're not down," said Helen at length.

When they appeared, St. John explained why it had been necessary for him to come to luncheon. He imitated Evelyn's enthusiastic tone as she confronted him in the smoking-room. "She thinks there can be nothing *quite* so thrilling as mathematics, so I've lent her a large work in two volumes. It'll be interesting to see what she makes of it."

Rachel could now afford to laugh at him. She reminded him of Gibbon; she had the first volume somewhere still; if he were undertaking the education of Evelyn, that surely was the test; or she had heard that Burke, upon the American Rebellion—Evelyn ought to read them both simultaneously. When St. John had disposed of her argument and had satisfied his hunger, he proceeded to tell them that the hotel was seething with scandals, some of the most appalling kind, which had happened in their absence; he was indeed much given to the study of his kind.

"Evelyn M., for example—but that was told me in confidence."

"Nonsense!" Terence interposed.

"You've heard about poor Sinclair, too?"

"Oh, yes, I've heard about Sinclair. He's retired to his mine with a revolver. He writes to Evelyn daily that he's thinking of committing suicide. I've assured her that he's never been so happy in his life, and, on the whole, she's inclined to agree with me."

"But then she's entangled herself with Perrott," St. John continued; "and I have reason to think, from something I saw in the passage, that everything isn't as it should be between Arthur and Susan. There's a young female lately arrived from Manchester. A very good thing if it were broken off, in my opinion. Their married life is something too horrible to contemplate. Oh, and I distinctly heard old Mrs. Paley rapping out the most fearful oaths as I passed her bedroom door. It's supposed that she tortures her maid in private—it's practically certain she does. One can tell it from the look in her eyes."

"When you're eighty and the gout tweezes you, you'll be swearing like a trooper," Terence remarked. "You'll be very fat, very testy, very disagreeable. Can't you imagine him—bald as a coot, with a pair of sponge-bag trousers, a little spotted tie, and a corporation?"

After a pause Hirst remarked that the worst infamy had still to be told. He addressed himself to Helen.

"They've hoofed out the prostitute. One night while we were away that old numskull Thornbury was doddering about the passages very late. (Nobody seems to have asked him what *he* was up to.) He saw the Signora Lola Mendoza, as she calls herself, cross the passage in her nightgown. He communicated his suspicions next morning to Elliot, with the result that Rodriguez went to the woman and gave her twenty-four hours in which to clear out of the place. No one seems to have enquired into the truth of the story, or to have asked Thornbury and Elliot what business it was of theirs; they had it entirely their own way. I propose that we should all sign a Round Robin, go to Rodriguez in a body, and insist upon a full enquiry. Something's got to be done, don't you agree?"

Hewet remarked that there could be no doubt as to the lady's profession.

"Still," he added, "it's a great shame, poor woman; only I don't see what's to be done—"

"I quite agree with you, St. John," Helen burst out. "It's monstrous. The hypocritical smugness of the English makes my blood boil. A man who's made a fortune in trade as Mr. Thornbury has is bound to be twice as bad as any prostitute."

She respected St. John's morality, which she took far more seriously than anyone else did, and now entered into a discussion with him as to the steps that were to be taken to enforce their peculiar view of what was right. The argument led to some profoundly gloomy statements of a general nature. Who were they, after all—what authority had they—what power against the mass of superstition and ignorance? It was the English, of course; there must be something wrong in the English blood. Directly you met an English person, of the middle classes, you were conscious of an indefinable sensation of loathing; directly you saw the brown crescent of houses above Dover, the same thing came over you. But unfortunately St. John added, you couldn't trust these foreigners—

They were interrupted by sounds of strife at the further end of the table. Rachel appealed to her aunt.

"Terence says we must go to tea with Mrs. Thornbury because she's been so kind, but I don't see it; in fact, I'd rather have my right hand sawn in pieces—just imagine! the eyes of all those women!"

"Fiddlesticks, Rachel," Terence replied. "Who wants to look at you? You're consumed with vanity! You're a monster of conceit! Surely, Helen, you ought to have taught her by this time that she's a person of no conceivable importance whatever—not beautiful, or well dressed, or conspicuous for elegance or intellect, or deportment. A more ordinary sight than you are," he concluded, "except for the tear across your dress has never been seen. However, stay at home if you want to. I'm going."

She appealed again to her aunt. It wasn't the being looked at, she explained, but the things people were sure to say. The women in particular. She liked women, but where emotion was concerned they were as flies on a lump of sugar. They would be certain to ask her questions. Evelyn M. would say: "Are you in love? Is it nice being in love?" And Mrs. Thornbury—her eyes would go up and down, up and down—she shuddered at the thought of it. Indeed, the retirement of their life since their engagement had made her so sensitive, that she was not exaggerating her case.

She found an ally in Helen, who proceeded to expound her views of the human race, as she regarded with complacency the pyramid of variegated fruits in the centre of the table. It wasn't that they were cruel, or meant to hurt, or even stupid exactly; but she had always found that the ordinary person had so little emotion in his own life that the scent of it in the lives of others was like the scent of blood in the nostrils of a bloodhound. Warming to the theme, she continued:

"Directly anything happens—it may be a marriage, or a birth, or a death—on the whole they prefer it to be a death—every one wants to see you. They insist upon seeing you. They've got nothing to say; they don't care a rap for you; but you've got to go to lunch or to tea or to dinner, and if you don't you're damned. It's the smell of blood," she continued; "I don't blame 'em; only they shan't have mine if I know it!"

She looked about her as if she had called up a legion of human beings, all hostile and all disagreeable, who encircled the table, with mouths gaping for blood, and made it appear a little island of neutral country in the midst of the enemy's country.

Her words roused her husband, who had been muttering rhythmically to himself, surveying his guests and his food and his wife with eyes that were now melancholy and now fierce, according to the fortunes of the lady in his ballad. He cut Helen short with a protest. He hated even the semblance of cynicism in women. "Nonsense, nonsense," he remarked abruptly.

Terence and Rachel glanced at each other across the table, which meant that when they were married they would not behave like that. The entrance of Ridley into the conversation had a strange effect. It became at once more formal and more polite. It would have been impossible to talk quite easily of anything that came into their heads, and to say the word prostitute as simply as any other word. The talk now turned upon literature and politics, and Ridley told stories of the distinguished people he had known in his youth. Such talk was of the nature of an art, and the personalities and informalities of the young were silenced. As they rose to go, Helen stopped for a moment, leaning her elbows on the table.

"You've all been sitting here," she said, "for almost an hour, and you haven't noticed my figs, or my flowers, or the way the light comes through, or anything. I haven't been listening, because I've been looking at you. You looked very beautiful; I wish you'd go on sitting forever."

She led the way to the drawing-room, where she took up her embroidery, and began again to dissuade Terence from walking down to the hotel in this heat. But the more she dissuaded, the more he was determined to go. He became irritated and obstinate. There were moments when they almost disliked each other. He wanted other people; he wanted Rachel, to see them with him. He suspected that Mrs. Ambrose would now try to dissuade her from going. He was annoyed by all this space and shade and beauty, and Hirst, recumbent, drooping a magazine from his wrist.

"I'm going," he repeated. "Rachel needn't come unless she wants to."

"If you go, Hewet, I wish you'd make enquiries about the prostitute," said Hirst. "Look here," he added, "I'll walk half the way with you."

Greatly to their surprise he raised himself, looked at his watch, and remarked that, as it was now half an hour since luncheon, the gastric juices had had sufficient time to secrete; he was trying a system, he explained, which involved short spells of exercise interspaced by longer intervals of rest.

"I shall be back at four," he remarked to Helen, "when I shall lie down on the sofa and relax all my muscles completely."

"So you're going, Rachel?" Helen asked. "You won't stay with me?"

She smiled, but she might have been sad.

Was she sad, or was she really laughing? Rachel could not tell, and she felt for the moment very uncomfortable between Helen and Terence. Then she turned away, saying merely that she would go with Terence, on condition that he did all the talking.

A narrow border of shadow ran along the road, which was broad enough for two, but not broad enough for three. St. John therefore dropped a little behind the pair, and the distance between them increased by degrees. Walking with a view to digestion, and with one eye upon his watch, he looked from time to time at the pair in front of him. They seemed to be so happy, so intimate, although they were walking side by side much as other people walk. They turned slightly toward each other now and then, and said something which he thought must be something very private. They were really disputing about Helen's character, and Terence was trying to explain why it was that she annoyed him so much sometimes. But St. John thought that they were saying things which they did not want him to hear, and was led to think of his own isolation. These people were happy, and in some ways he despised them for being made happy so simply, and in other ways he envied them. He was much more remarkable than they were, but he was not happy. People never liked him; he doubted sometimes whether even Helen liked him. To be simple, to be able to say simply what one felt, without the terrific self-consciousness which possessed him, and showed him his own face and words perpetually in a mirror, that would be worth almost any other gift, for it made one happy. Happiness, happiness, what was happiness? He was never happy. He saw too clearly the little vices and deceits and flaws of life, and, seeing them, it seemed to him honest to take notice of them. That was the reason, no doubt, why people generally disliked him, and complained that he was heartless and bitter. Certainly they never told him the things he wanted to be told, that he was nice and kind, and that they liked him. But it was true that half the sharp things that he said about them were said because he was unhappy or hurt himself. But he admitted that he had very seldom told anyone that he cared for them, and when he had been demonstrative, he had generally regretted it afterwards. His feelings about Terence and Rachel were so complicated that he had never yet been able to bring himself to say that he was glad that they were going to be married. He saw their faults so clearly, and the inferior nature of a great deal of their feeling for each other, and he expected that their love would not last. He looked at them again, and, very strangely, for he was so used to thinking that he seldom saw anything, the look of them filled him with a simple emotion of affection in which there were some traces of pity also. What, after all, did people's faults matter in comparison with what was good in them? He resolved that he would now tell them what he felt. He quickened his pace and came up with them just as they reached the corner where the lane joined the main road. They stood still and began to laugh at him, and to ask him whether the gastric juices—but he stopped them and began to speak very quickly and stiffly.

"D'you remember the morning after the dance?" he demanded. "It was here we sat, and you talked nonsense, and Rachel made little heaps of stones. I, on the other hand, had the whole meaning of life revealed to me in a flash." He paused for a second, and drew his lips together in a tight little purse. "Love," he said. "It seems to me to explain everything. So, on the whole, I'm very glad that you two are going to be married." He then turned round abruptly, without looking at them, and walked back to the villa. He felt both exalted and ashamed of himself for having thus said what he felt. Probably they were laughing at him, probably they thought him a fool, and, after all, had he really said what he felt?

It was true that they laughed when he was gone; but the dispute about Helen which had become rather sharp, ceased, and they became peaceful and friendly.

CHAPTER XXIV

They reached the hotel rather early in the afternoon, so that most people were still lying down, or sitting speechless in their bedrooms, and Mrs. Thornbury, although she had asked them to tea, was nowhere to be seen. They sat down, therefore, in the shady hall, which was almost empty, and full of the light swishing sounds of air going to and fro in a large empty space. Yes, this armchair was the same armchair in which Rachel had sat that afternoon when Evelyn came up, and this was the magazine she had been looking at, and this the very picture, a picture of New York by lamplight. How odd it seemed—nothing had changed.

By degrees a certain number of people began to come down the stairs and to pass through the hall, and in this dim light their figures possessed a sort of grace and beauty, although they were all unknown people. Sometimes they went straight through and out into the garden by the swing door, sometimes they stopped for a few minutes and bent over the tables and began turning over the newspapers. Terence and Rachel sat watching them through their half-closed eyelids—the Johnsons, the Parkers, the Baileys, the Simmons', the Lees, the Morleys, the Campbells, the Gardiners. Some were dressed in white flannels and were carrying racquets under their arms, some were short, some tall, some were only children, and some perhaps were servants, but they all had their standing, their reason for following each other through the hall, their money, their position, whatever it might be. Terence soon gave up looking at them, for he was tired; and, closing his eyes, he fell half asleep in his chair. Rachel watched the people for some time longer; she was fascinated by the certainty and the grace of their movements, and by the inevitable way in which they seemed to follow each other, and loiter and pass on and disappear. But after a time her thoughts wandered, and she began to think of the dance, which had been held in this room, only then the room itself looked quite different. Glancing round, she could hardly believe that it was the same room. It had looked so bare and so bright and formal on that night when they came into it out of the darkness; it had been filled, too, with little red, excited faces, always moving, and people so brightly dressed and so animated that they did not seem in the least like real people, nor did you feel that you could talk to them. And now the room was dim and quiet, and beautiful silent people passed through it, to whom you could go and say anything you liked. She felt herself amazingly secure as she sat in her armchair, and able to review not only the night of the dance, but the entire past, tenderly and humorously, as if she had been turning in a fog for a long time, and could now see exactly where she had turned. For the methods by which she had reached her present position, seemed to her very strange, and the strangest thing about them was that she had not known where they were leading her. That was the strange thing, that one did not know where one was going, or what one wanted, and followed blindly, suffering so much in secret, always unprepared and amazed and knowing nothing; but one thing led to another and by degrees something had formed itself out of nothing, and so one reached at last this calm, this quiet, this certainty, and it was this process that people called living. Perhaps, then, every one really knew as she knew now where they were going; and things formed themselves into a pattern not only for her, but for them, and in that pattern lay satisfaction and meaning. When she looked back she could see that a meaning of some kind was apparent in the lives of her aunts, and in the brief visit of the Dalloways whom she would never see again, and in the life of her father.

The sound of Terence, breathing deep in his slumber, confirmed her in her calm. She was not sleepy although she did not see anything very distinctly, but although the figures passing through the hall became vaguer and vaguer, she believed that they all knew exactly where they were going, and the sense of their certainty filled her with comfort. For the moment she was as detached and disinterested as if she had no longer any lot in life, and she thought that she could now accept anything that came to her without being perplexed by the form in which it appeared. What was there to frighten or to perplex in the prospect of life? Why should this insight ever again desert her? The world was in truth so large, so hospitable, and after all it was so simple. "Love," St. John had said, "that seems to explain it all." Yes, but it was not the love of man for woman, of Terence for Rachel. Although they sat so close together, they had ceased to be little separate bodies; they had ceased to struggle and desire one another. There seemed to be peace between them. It might be love, but it was not the love of man for woman.

Through her half-closed eyelids she watched Terence lying back in his chair, and she smiled as she saw how big his mouth was, and his chin so small, and his nose curved like a switchback with a knob at the end. Naturally, looking like that he was lazy, and ambitious, and full of moods and faults. She remembered their quarrels, and in particular how they had been quarreling about Helen that very afternoon, and she thought how often they would quarrel in the thirty, or forty, or fifty years in which they would be living in the same house together, catching trains together, and getting annoyed because they were so different. But all this was superficial, and had nothing to do with the life that went on beneath the eyes and the mouth and the chin, for that life was independent of her, and independent of everything else. So too, although she was going to marry him and to live with him for thirty, or forty, or fifty years, and to quarrel, and to be so close to him, she was independent of him; she was independent of everything else. Nevertheless, as St. John said, it was love that made her understand this, for she had never felt this independence, this calm, and this certainty until she fell in love with him, and perhaps this too was love. She wanted nothing else.

For perhaps two minutes Miss Allan had been standing at a little distance looking at the couple lying back so peacefully in their armchairs. She could not make up her mind whether to disturb them or not, and then, seeming to recollect something, she came across the hall. The sound of her approach woke Terence, who sat up and rubbed his eyes. He heard Miss Allan talking to Rachel.

"Well," she was saying, "this is very nice. It is very nice indeed. Getting engaged seems to be quite the fashion. It cannot often happen that two couples who have never seen each other before meet in the same hotel and decide to get married." Then she paused and smiled, and seemed to have nothing more to say, so that Terence rose and asked her whether it was true that she had finished her book. Someone had said that she had really finished it. Her face lit up; she turned to him with a livelier expression than usual.

"Yes, I think I can fairly say I have finished it," she said. "That is, omitting Swinburne—Beowulf to Browning—I rather like the two B's myself. Beowulf to Browning," she repeated, "I think that is the kind of title which might catch one's eye on a railway book-stall."

She was indeed very proud that she had finished her book, for no one knew what an amount of determination had gone to the making of it. Also she thought that it was a good piece of work, and, considering what anxiety she had been in about her brother while she wrote it, she could not resist telling them a little more about it.

"I must confess," she continued, "that if I had known how many classics there are in English literature, and how verbose the best of them contrive to be, I should never have undertaken the work. They only allow one seventy thousand words, you see."

"Only seventy thousand words!" Terence exclaimed.

"Yes, and one has to say something about everybody," Miss Allan added. "That is what I find so difficult, saying something different about everybody." Then she thought that she had said enough about herself, and she asked whether they had come down to join the tennis tournament. "The young people are very keen about it. It begins again in half an hour."

Her gaze rested benevolently upon them both, and, after a momentary pause, she remarked, looking at Rachel as if she had remembered something that would serve to keep her distinct from other people.

"You're the remarkable person who doesn't like ginger." But the kindness of the smile in her rather worn and courageous face made them feel that although she would scarcely remember them as individuals, she had laid upon them the burden of the new generation.

"And in that I quite agree with her," said a voice behind; Mrs. Thornbury had overheard the last few words about not liking ginger. "It's associated in my mind with a horrid old aunt of ours (poor thing, she suffered dreadfully, so it isn't fair to call her horrid) who used to give it to us when we were small, and we never had the courage to tell her we didn't like it. We just had to put it out in the shrubbery—she had a big house near Bath."

They began moving slowly across the hall, when they were stopped by the impact of Evelyn, who dashed into them, as though in running downstairs to catch them her legs had got beyond her control.

"Well," she exclaimed, with her usual enthusiasm, seizing Rachel by the arm, "I call this splendid! I guessed it was going to happen from the very beginning! I saw you two were made for each other. Now you've just got to tell me all about it—when's it to be, where are you going to live—are you both tremendously happy?"

But the attention of the group was diverted to Mrs. Elliot, who was passing them with her eager but uncertain movement, carrying in her hands a plate and an empty hot-water bottle. She would have passed them, but Mrs. Thornbury went up and stopped her.

"Thank you, Hughling's better," she replied, in answer to Mrs. Thornbury's enquiry, "but he's not an easy patient. He wants to know what his temperature is, and if I tell him he gets anxious, and if I don't tell him he suspects. You know what men are when they're ill! And of course there are none of the proper appliances, and, though he seems very willing and anxious to help" (here she lowered her voice mysteriously), "one can't feel that Dr. Rodriguez is the same as a proper doctor. If you would come and see him, Mr. Hewet," she added, "I know it would cheer him up—lying there in bed all day—and the flies—But I must go and find Angelo—the food here—of course, with an invalid, one wants things particularly nice." And she hurried past them in search of the head waiter. The worry of nursing her husband had fixed a plaintive frown upon her forehead; she was pale and looked unhappy and more than usually inefficient, and her eyes wandered more vaguely than ever from point to point.

"Poor thing!" Mrs. Thornbury exclaimed. She told them that for some days Hughling Elliot had been ill, and the only doctor available was the brother of the proprietor, or so the proprietor said, whose right to the title of doctor was not above suspicion.

"I know how wretched it is to be ill in a hotel," Mrs. Thornbury remarked, once more leading the way with Rachel to the garden. "I spent six weeks on my honeymoon in having typhoid at Venice," she continued. "But even so, I look back upon them as some of the happiest weeks in my life. Ah, yes," she said, taking Rachel's arm, "you think yourself happy now, but it's nothing to the happiness that comes afterwards. And I assure you I could find it in my heart to envy you young people! You've a much better time than we had, I may tell you. When I look back upon it, I can hardly believe how things have changed. When we were engaged I wasn't allowed to go for walks with William alone—someone had always to be in the room with us—I really believe I had to show my parents all his letters!—though they were very fond of him too. Indeed, I may say they looked upon him as their own son. It amuses me," she continued, "to think how strict they were to us, when I see how they spoil their grand-children!"

The table was laid under the tree again, and taking her place before the teacups, Mrs. Thornbury beckoned and nodded until she had collected quite a number of people, Susan and Arthur and Mr. Pepper, who were strolling about, waiting for the tournament to begin. A murmuring tree, a river brimming in the moonlight, Terence's words came back to Rachel as she sat drinking the tea and listening to the words which flowed on so lightly, so kindly, and with such silvery smoothness. This long life and all these children had left her very smooth; they seemed to have rubbed away the marks of individuality, and to have left only what was old and maternal.

"And the things you young people are going to see!" Mrs. Thornbury continued. She included them all in her forecast, she included them all in her maternity, although the party comprised William Pepper and Miss Allan, both of whom might have been supposed to have seen a fair share of the panorama. "When I see how the world has changed in my lifetime," she went on, "I can set no limit to what may happen in the next fifty years. Ah, no,

Mr. Pepper, I don't agree with you in the least," she laughed, interrupting his gloomy remark about things going steadily from bad to worse. "I know I ought to feel that, but I don't, I'm afraid. They're going to be much better people than we were. Surely everything goes to prove that. All round me I see women, young women, women with household cares of every sort, going out and doing things that we should not have thought it possible to do."

Mr. Pepper thought her sentimental and irrational like all old women, but her manner of treating him as if he were a cross old baby baffled him and charmed him, and he could only reply to her with a curious grimace which was more a smile than a frown.

"And they remain women," Mrs. Thornbury added. "They give a great deal to their children."

As she said this she smiled slightly in the direction of Susan and Rachel. They did not like to be included in the same lot, but they both smiled a little self-consciously, and Arthur and Terence glanced at each other too. She made them feel that they were all in the same boat together, and they looked at the women they were going to marry and compared them. It was inexplicable how anyone could wish to marry Rachel, incredible that anyone should be ready to spend his life with Susan; but singular though the other's taste must be, they bore each other no ill-will on account of it; indeed, they liked each other rather the better for the eccentricity of their choice.

"I really must congratulate you," Susan remarked, as she leant across the table for the jam.

There seemed to be no foundation for St. John's gossip about Arthur and Susan. Sunburnt and vigorous they sat side by side, with their racquets across their knees, not saying much but smiling slightly all the time. Through the thin white clothes which they wore, it was possible to see the lines of their bodies and legs, the beautiful curves of their muscles, his leanness and her flesh, and it was natural to think of the firm-fleshed sturdy children that would be theirs. Their faces had too little shape in them to be beautiful, but they had clear eyes and an appearance of great health and power of endurance, for it seemed as if the blood would never cease to run in his veins, or to lie deeply and calmly in her cheeks. Their eyes at the present moment were brighter than usual, and wore the peculiar expression of pleasure and self-confidence which is seen in the eyes of athletes, for they had been playing tennis, and they were both first-rate at the game.

Evelyn had not spoken, but she had been looking from Susan to Rachel. Well—they had both made up their minds very easily, they had done in a very few weeks what it sometimes seemed to her that she would never be able to do. Although they were so different, she thought that she could see in each the same look of satisfaction and completion, the same calmness of manner, and the same slowness of movement. It was that slowness, that confidence, that content which she hated, she thought to herself. They moved so slowly because they were not single but double, and Susan was attached to Arthur, and Rachel to Terence, and for the sake of this one man they had renounced all other men, and movement, and the real things of life. Love was all very well, and those snug domestic houses, with the kitchen below and the nursery above, which were so secluded and self-contained, like little islands in the torrents of the world; but the real things were surely the things that happened, the causes, the wars, the ideals, which happened in the great world outside, and went so independently of these women, turning so quietly and beautifully towards the men. She looked at them sharply. Of course they were happy and content, but there must be better things than that. Surely one could get nearer to life, one could get more out of life, one could enjoy more and feel more than they would ever do. Rachel in particular looked so young—what could she know of life? She became restless, and getting up, crossed over to sit beside Rachel. She reminded her that she had promised to join her club.

"The bother is," she went on, "that I mayn't be able to start work seriously till October. I've just had a letter from a friend of mine whose brother is in business in Moscow. They want me to stay with them, and as they're in the thick of all the conspiracies and anarchists, I've a good mind to stop on my way home. It sounds too thrilling." She wanted to make Rachel see how thrilling it was. "My friend knows a girl of fifteen who's been sent to Siberia for life merely because they caught her addressing a letter to an anarchist. And the letter wasn't from her, either. I'd give all I have in the world to help on a revolution against the Russian government, and it's bound to come."

She looked from Rachel to Terence. They were both a little touched by the sight of her remembering how lately they had been listening to evil words about her, and Terence asked her what her scheme was, and she explained that she was going to found a club—a club for doing things, really doing them. She became very animated, as she talked on and on, for she professed herself certain that if once twenty people—no, ten would be enough if they were keen—set about doing things instead of talking about doing them, they could abolish almost every evil that exists. It was brains that were needed. If only people with brains—of course they would want a room, a nice room, in Bloomsbury preferably, where they could meet once a week . . .

As she talked Terence could see the traces of fading youth in her face, the lines that were being drawn by talk and excitement round her mouth and eyes, but he did not pity her; looking into those bright, rather hard, and very courageous eyes, he saw that she did not pity herself, or feel any desire to exchange her own life for the more refined and orderly lives of people like himself and St. John, although, as the years went by, the fight would become harder and harder. Perhaps, though, she would settle down; perhaps, after all, she would marry Perrott. While his mind was half occupied with what she was saying, he thought of her probable destiny, the light clouds of tobacco smoke serving to obscure his face from her eyes.

Terence smoked and Arthur smoked and Evelyn smoked, so that the air was full of the mist and fragrance of good tobacco. In the intervals when no one spoke, they heard far off the low murmur of the sea, as the waves quietly broke and spread the beach with a film of water, and withdrew to break again. The cool green light fell through the leaves of the tree, and there were soft crescents and diamonds of sunshine upon the plates and the tablecloth. Mrs. Thornbury, after watching them all for a time in silence, began to ask Rachel kindly questions—When did they all go back? Oh, they expected her father. She must want to see her father—there would be a great deal to tell him, and (she looked sympathetically at Terence) he would be so happy, she felt sure. Years ago, she continued, it might have been ten or twenty years ago, she remembered meeting Mr. Vinrace at a party, and, being so much struck by his face, which was so unlike the ordinary face one sees at a party, that she had asked who he was, and she was told that it was Mr. Vinrace, and she had always remembered the name—an uncommon name—and he had a lady with him, a very sweet-looking woman, but it was one of those dreadful London crushes, where you don't talk—you only look at each other—and although she had shaken hands with Mr. Vinrace, she didn't think they had said anything. She sighed very slightly, remembering the past.

Then she turned to Mr. Pepper, who had become very dependent on her, so that he always chose a seat near her, and attended to what she was saying, although he did not often make any remark of his own.

"You who know everything, Mr. Pepper," she said, "tell us how did those wonderful French ladies manage their salons? Did we ever do anything of the same kind in England, or do you think that there is some reason why we cannot do it in England?"

Mr. Pepper was pleased to explain very accurately why there has never been an English salon. There were three reasons, and they were very good ones, he said. As for himself, when he went to a party, as one was sometimes obliged to, from a wish not to give offence—his niece, for example, had been married the other day—he walked into the middle of the room, said "Ha! ha!" as loud as ever he could, considered that he had done his duty, and walked away again. Mrs. Thornbury protested. She was going to give a party directly she got back, and they were all to be invited, and she should set people to watch Mr. Pepper, and if she heard that he had been caught saying "Ha! ha!" she would—she would do something very dreadful indeed to him.

Arthur Venning suggested that what she must do was to rig up something in the nature of a surprise—a portrait, for example, of a nice old lady in a lace cap, concealing a bath of cold water, which at a signal could be sprung on Pepper's head; or they'd have a chair which shot him twenty feet high directly he sat on it.

Susan laughed. She had done her tea; she was feeling very well contented, partly because she had been playing tennis brilliantly, and then every one was so nice; she was beginning to find it so much easier to talk, and to hold her own even with quite clever people, for somehow clever people did not frighten her any more. Even Mr. Hirst, whom she had disliked when she first met him, really wasn't disagreeable; and, poor man, he always looked so ill; perhaps he was in love; perhaps he had been in love with Rachel—she really shouldn't wonder; or perhaps it was Evelyn—she was of course very attractive to men. Leaning forward, she went on with the conversation. She said that she thought that the reason why parties were so dull was mainly because gentlemen will not dress: even in London, she stated, it struck her very much how people don't think it necessary to dress in the evening, and of course if they don't dress in London they won't dress in the country. It was really quite a treat at Christmas-time when there were the Hunt balls, and the gentlemen wore nice red coats, but Arthur didn't care for dancing, so she supposed that they wouldn't go even to the ball in their little country town. She didn't think that people who were fond of one sport often care for another, although her father was an exception. But then he was an exception in every way—such a gardener, and he knew all about birds and animals, and of course he was simply adored by all the old women in the village, and at the same time what he really liked best was a book. You always knew where to find him if he were wanted; he would be in his study with a book. Very likely it would be an old, old book, some fusty old thing that no one else would dream of reading. She used to tell him that he would have made a first-rate old bookworm if only he hadn't had a family of six to support, and six children, she added, charmingly confident of universal sympathy, didn't leave one much time for being a bookworm.

Still talking about her father, of whom she was very proud, she rose, for Arthur upon looking at his watch found that it was time they went back again to the tennis court. The others did not move.

"They're very happy!" said Mrs. Thornbury, looking benignantly after them. Rachel agreed; they seemed to be so certain of themselves; they seemed to know exactly what they wanted.

"D'you think they *are* happy?" Evelyn murmured to Terence in an undertone, and she hoped that he would say that he did not think them happy; but, instead, he said that they must go too—go home, for they were always being late for meals, and Mrs. Ambrose, who was very stern and particular, didn't like that. Evelyn laid hold of Rachel's skirt and protested. Why should they go? It was still early, and she had so many things to say to them. "No," said Terence, "we must go, because we walk so slowly. We stop and look at things, and we talk."

"What d'you talk about?" Evelyn enquired, upon which he laughed and said that they talked about everything.

Mrs. Thornbury went with them to the gate, trailing very slowly and gracefully across the grass and the gravel, and talking all the time about flowers and birds. She told them that she had taken up the study of botany since her daughter married, and it was wonderful what a number of flowers there were which she had never seen, although she had lived in the country all her life and she was now seventy-two. It was a good thing to have some occupation which was quite independent of other people, she said, when one got old. But the odd thing was that one never felt old. She always felt that she was twenty-five, not a day more or a day less, but, of course, one couldn't expect other people to agree to that.

"It must be very wonderful to be twenty-five, and not merely to imagine that you're twenty-five," she said, looking from one to the other with her smooth, bright glance. "It must be very wonderful, very wonderful indeed." She stood talking to them at the gate for a long time; she seemed reluctant that they should go.

CHAPTER XXV

The afternoon was very hot, so hot that the breaking of the waves on the shore sounded like the repeated sigh of some exhausted creature, and even on the terrace under an awning the bricks were hot, and the air danced perpetually over the short dry grass. The red flowers in the stone basins were drooping with the heat, and the white blossoms which had been so smooth and thick only a few weeks ago were now dry, and their edges were curled and yellow. Only the stiff and hostile plants of the south, whose fleshy leaves seemed to be grown upon spines, still remained standing upright and defied the sun to beat them down. It was too hot to talk, and it was not easy to find any book that would withstand the power of the sun. Many books had been tried and then let fall, and now Terence was reading Milton aloud, because he said the words of Milton had substance and shape, so that it was not necessary to understand what he was saying; one could merely listen to his words; one could almost handle them.

There is a gentle nymph not far from hence,

he read,

> *That with moist curb sways the smooth Severn stream.*
> *Sabrina is her name, a virgin pure;*
> *Whilom she was the daughter of Locrine,*
> *That had the sceptre from his father Brute.*

The words, in spite of what Terence had said, seemed to be laden with meaning, and perhaps it was for this reason that it was painful to listen to them; they sounded strange; they meant different things from what they usually meant. Rachel at any rate could not keep her attention fixed upon them, but went off upon curious trains of thought suggested by words such as "curb" and "Locrine" and "Brute," which brought unpleasant sights before her eyes, independently of their meaning. Owing to the heat and the dancing air the garden too looked strange—the trees were either too near or too far, and her head almost certainly ached. She was not quite certain, and therefore she did not know, whether to tell Terence now, or to let him go on reading. She decided that she would wait until he came to the end of a stanza, and if by that time she had turned her head this way and that, and it ached in every position undoubtedly, she would say very calmly that her head ached.

> *Sabrina fair,*
> *Listen where thou art sitting*
> *Under the glassy, cool, translucent wave,*
> *In twisted braids of lilies knitting*
> *The loose train of thy amber dropping hair,*
> *Listen for dear honour's sake,*
> *Goddess of the silver lake,*
> *Listen and save!*

But her head ached; it ached whichever way she turned it.

She sat up and said as she had determined, "My head aches so that I shall go indoors." He was half-way through the next verse, but he dropped the book instantly.

"Your head aches?" he repeated.

For a few moments they sat looking at one another in silence, holding each other's hands. During this time his sense of dismay and catastrophe were almost physically painful; all round him he seemed to hear the shiver of broken glass which, as it fell to earth, left him sitting in the open air. But at the end of two minutes, noticing that she was not sharing his dismay, but was only rather more languid and heavy-eyed than usual, he recovered, fetched Helen, and asked her to tell him what they had better do, for Rachel had a headache.

Mrs. Ambrose was not discomposed, but advised that she should go to bed, and added that she must expect her head to ache if she sat up to all hours and went out in the heat, but a few hours in bed would cure it completely. Terence was unreasonably reassured by her words, as he had been unreasonably depressed the moment before. Helen's sense seemed to have much in common with the ruthless good sense of nature, which avenged rashness by a headache, and, like nature's good sense, might be depended upon.

Rachel went to bed; she lay in the dark, it seemed to her, for a very long time, but at length, waking from a transparent kind of sleep, she saw the windows white in front of her, and recollected that some time before she had gone to bed with a headache, and that Helen had said it would be gone when she woke. She supposed, therefore, that she was now quite well again. At the same time the wall of her room was painfully white, and curved slightly, instead of being straight and flat. Turning her eyes to the window, she was not reassured by what she saw there. The movement of the blind as it filled with air and blew slowly out, drawing the cord with a little trailing sound along the floor, seemed to her terrifying, as if it were the movement of an animal in the room. She shut her eyes, and the pulse in her head beat so strongly that each thump seemed to tread upon a nerve, piercing her forehead with a little stab of pain. It might not be the same headache, but she certainly had a headache. She turned from side to side, in the hope that the coolness of the sheets would cure her, and that when she next opened her eyes to look the room would be as usual. After a considerable number of vain experiments, she resolved to put the matter beyond a doubt. She got out of bed and stood upright, holding on to the brass ball at the end of the bedstead. Ice-cold at first, it soon became as hot as the palm of her hand, and as the pains in her head and body and the instability of the floor proved that it would be far more intolerable to stand and walk than to lie in bed, she got into bed again; but though the change was refreshing at first, the discomfort of bed was soon as great as the discomfort of standing up. She accepted the idea that she would have to stay in bed all day long, and as she laid her head on the pillow, relinquished the happiness of the day.

When Helen came in an hour or two later, suddenly stopped her cheerful words, looked startled for a second and then unnaturally calm, the fact that she was ill was put beyond a doubt. It was confirmed when the whole household knew of it, when the song that someone was singing in the garden stopped suddenly, and when Maria, as she brought water, slipped past the bed with averted eyes. There was all the morning to get through, and then all the afternoon, and at intervals she made an effort to cross over into the ordinary world, but she found that her heat and discomfort had put a gulf between her world and the ordinary world which she could not bridge. At one point the door opened, and Helen came in with a little dark man who had—it was the chief thing she noticed about him—very hairy hands. She was drowsy and intolerably hot, and as he seemed shy and obsequious she scarcely troubled to answer him, although she understood that he was a doctor. At another point the door opened and Terence came in very gently, smiling too steadily, as she realised, for it to be natural. He sat down and talked to her, stroking her hands until it became irksome to her to lie any more in the same position and she turned round, and when she looked up again Helen was beside her and Terence had gone. It did not matter; she would see him tomorrow when things would be ordinary again. Her chief occupation during the day was to try to remember how the lines went:

> Under the glassy, cool, translucent wave,
>   In twisted braids of lilies knitting
> The loose train of thy amber dropping hair;

and the effort worried her because the adjectives persisted in getting into the wrong places.

The second day did not differ very much from the first day, except that her bed had become very important, and the world outside, when she tried to think of it, appeared distinctly further off. The glassy, cool, translucent wave was almost visible before her, curling up at the end of the bed, and as it was refreshingly cool she tried to keep her mind fixed upon it. Helen was here, and Helen was there all day long; sometimes she said that it was lunchtime, and sometimes that it was teatime; but by the next day all landmarks were obliterated, and the outer world was so far away that the different sounds, such as the sounds of people moving overhead, could only be ascribed to their cause by a great effort of memory. The recollection of what she had felt, or of what she had been doing and thinking three days before, had faded entirely. On the other hand, every object in the room, and the bed itself, and her own body with its various limbs and their different sensations were more and more important each day. She was completely cut off, and unable to communicate with the rest of the world, isolated alone with her body.

Hours and hours would pass thus, without getting any further through the morning, or again a few minutes would lead from broad daylight to the depths of the night. One evening when the room appeared very dim, either because it was evening or because the blinds were drawn, Helen said to her, "Someone is going to sit here tonight. You won't mind?"

Opening her eyes, Rachel saw not only Helen but a nurse in spectacles, whose face vaguely recalled something that she had once seen. She had seen her in the chapel. "Nurse McInnis," said Helen, and the nurse smiled steadily as they all did, and said that she did not find many people who were frightened of her. After waiting for a moment they both disappeared, and having turned on her pillow Rachel woke to find herself in the midst of one of those interminable nights which do not end at twelve, but go on into the double figures—thirteen, fourteen, and so on until they reach the twenties, and then the thirties, and then the forties. She realised that there is nothing to prevent nights from doing this if they choose. At a great distance an elderly woman sat with her head bent down; Rachel raised herself slightly and saw with dismay that she was playing cards by the light of a candle which stood in the hollow of a newspaper. The sight had something inexplicably sinister about it, and she was terrified and cried out, upon which the woman laid down her cards and came across the room, shading the candle with her hands. Coming nearer and nearer across the great space of the room, she stood at last above Rachel's head and said, "Not asleep? Let me make you comfortable."

She put down the candle and began to arrange the bedclothes. It struck Rachel that a woman who sat playing cards in a cavern all night long would have very cold hands, and she shrunk from the touch of them.

"Why, there's a toe all the way down there!" the woman said, proceeding to tuck in the bedclothes. Rachel did not realise that the toe was hers.

"You must try and lie still," she proceeded, "because if you lie still you will be less hot, and if you toss about you will make yourself more hot, and we don't want you to be any hotter than you are." She stood looking down upon Rachel for an enormous length of time.

"And the quieter you lie the sooner you will be well," she repeated.

Rachel kept her eyes fixed upon the peaked shadow on the ceiling, and all her energy was concentrated upon the desire that this shadow should move. But the shadow and the woman seemed to be eternally fixed above her. She shut her eyes. When she opened them again several more hours had passed, but the night still lasted interminably. The woman was still playing cards, only she sat now in a tunnel under a river, and the light stood in a little archway in the wall above her. She cried "Terence!" and the peaked shadow again moved across the ceiling, as the woman with an enormous slow movement rose, and they both stood still above her.

"It's just as difficult to keep you in bed as it was to keep Mr. Forrest in bed," the woman said, "and he was such a tall gentleman."

In order to get rid of this terrible stationary sight Rachel again shut her eyes, and found herself walking through a tunnel under the Thames, where there were little deformed women sitting in archways playing cards, while the bricks of which the wall was made oozed with damp, which collected into drops and slid down the wall. But the little old women became Helen and Nurse McInnis after a time, standing in the window together whispering, whispering incessantly.

Meanwhile outside her room the sounds, the movements, and the lives of the other people in the house went on in the ordinary light of the sun, throughout the usual succession of hours. When, on the first day of her illness, it became clear that she would not be absolutely well, for her temperature was very high, until Friday, that day being Tuesday, Terence was filled with resentment, not against her, but against the force outside them which was separating them. He counted up the number of days that would almost certainly be spoilt for them. He realised, with an odd mixture of pleasure and annoyance, that, for the first time in his life, he was so dependent upon another person that his happiness was in her keeping. The days were completely wasted upon trifling, immaterial things, for after three weeks of such intimacy and intensity all the usual occupations were unbearably flat and beside the point. The least intolerable occupation was to talk to St. John about Rachel's illness, and to discuss every symptom and its meaning, and, when this subject was exhausted, to discuss illness of all kinds, and what caused them, and what cured them.

Twice every day he went in to sit with Rachel, and twice every day the same thing happened. On going into her room, which was not very dark, where the music was lying about as usual, and her books and letters, his spirits rose instantly. When he saw her he felt completely reassured. She did not look very ill. Sitting by her side he would tell her what he had been doing, using his natural voice to speak to her, only a few tones lower down than usual; but by the time he had sat there for five minutes he was plunged into the deepest gloom. She was not the same; he could not bring them back to their old relationship; but although he knew that it was foolish he could not prevent himself from endeavouring to bring her back, to make her remember, and when this failed he was in despair. He always concluded as he left her room that it was worse to see her than not to see her, but by degrees, as the day wore on, the desire to see her returned and became almost too great to be borne.

On Thursday morning when Terence went into her room he felt the usual increase of confidence. She turned round and made an effort to remember certain facts from the world that was so many millions of miles away.

"You have come up from the hotel?" she asked.

"No; I'm staying here for the present," he said. "We've just had luncheon," he continued, "and the mail has come in. There's a bundle of letters for you—letters from England."

Instead of saying, as he meant her to say, that she wished to see them, she said nothing for some time.

"You see, there they go, rolling off the edge of the hill," she said suddenly.

"Rolling, Rachel? What do you see rolling? There's nothing rolling."

"The old woman with the knife," she replied, not speaking to Terence in particular, and looking past him. As she appeared to be looking at a vase on the shelf opposite, he rose and took it down.

"Now they can't roll any more," he said cheerfully. Nevertheless she lay gazing at the same spot, and paid him no further attention although he spoke to her. He became so profoundly wretched that he could not endure to sit with her, but wandered about until he found St. John, who was reading *The Times* in the verandah. He laid it aside patiently, and heard all that Terence had to say about delirium. He was very patient with Terence. He treated him like a child.

By Friday it could not be denied that the illness was no longer an attack that would pass off in a day or two; it was a real illness that required a good deal of organisation, and engrossed the attention of at least five people, but there was no reason to be anxious. Instead of lasting five days it was going to last ten days. Rodriguez was understood to say that there were well-known varieties of this illness. Rodriguez appeared to think that they were treating the illness with undue anxiety. His visits were always marked by the same show of confidence, and in his interviews with Terence he always waved aside his anxious and minute questions with a kind of flourish which seemed to indicate that they were all taking it much too seriously. He seemed curiously unwilling to sit down.

"A high temperature," he said, looking furtively about the room, and appearing to be more interested in the furniture and in Helen's embroidery than in anything else. "In this climate you must expect a high temperature. You need not be alarmed by that. It is the pulse we go by" (he tapped his own hairy wrist), "and the pulse continues excellent."

Thereupon he bowed and slipped out. The interview was conducted laboriously upon both sides in French, and this, together with the fact that he was optimistic, and that Terence respected the medical profession from hearsay, made him less critical than he would have been had he encountered the doctor in any other capacity. Unconsciously he took Rodriguez' side against Helen, who seemed to have taken an unreasonable prejudice against him.

When Saturday came it was evident that the hours of the day must be more strictly organised than they had been. St. John offered his services; he said that he had nothing to do, and that he might as well spend the day at the villa if he could be of use. As if they were starting on a difficult expedition together, they parcelled out their duties between them, writing out an elaborate scheme of hours upon a large sheet of paper which was pinned to the drawing-room door. Their distance from the town, and the difficulty of procuring rare things with unknown names from the most unexpected places, made it necessary to think very carefully, and they found it unexpectedly difficult to do the simple but practical things that were required of them, as if they, being very tall, were asked to stoop down and arrange minute grains of sand in a pattern on the ground.

It was St. John's duty to fetch what was needed from the town, so that Terence would sit all through the long hot hours alone in the drawing-room, near the open door, listening for any movement upstairs, or call from Helen. He always forgot to pull down the blinds, so that he sat in bright sunshine, which worried him without his knowing what was the cause of it. The room was terribly stiff and uncomfortable. There were hats in the chairs, and medicine bottles among the books. He tried to read, but good books were too good, and bad books were too bad, and the only thing he could tolerate was the newspaper, which with its news of London, and the movements of real people who were giving dinner-parties and making speeches, seemed to give a little background of reality to what was otherwise mere nightmare. Then, just as his attention was fixed on the print, a soft call would come from Helen, or Mrs. Chailey would bring in something which was wanted upstairs, and he would run up very quietly in his socks, and put the jug on the little table which stood crowded with jugs and cups outside the bedroom door; or if he could catch Helen for a moment he would ask, "How is she?"

"Rather restless . . . On the whole, quieter, I think."

The answer would be one or the other.

As usual she seemed to reserve something which she did not say, and Terence was conscious that they disagreed, and, without saying it aloud, were arguing against each other. But she was too hurried and pre-occupied to talk.

The strain of listening and the effort of making practical arrangements and seeing that things worked smoothly, absorbed all Terence's power. Involved in this long dreary nightmare, he did not attempt to think what it amounted to. Rachel was ill; that was all; he must see that there was medicine and milk, and that things were ready when they were wanted. Thought had ceased; life itself had come to a standstill. Sunday was rather worse than Saturday had been, simply because the strain was a little greater every day, although nothing else had changed. The separate feelings of pleasure, interest, and pain, which combine to make up the ordinary day, were merged in one long-drawn sensation of sordid misery and profound boredom. He had never been so bored since he was shut up in the nursery alone as a child. The vision of Rachel as she was now, confused and heedless, had almost obliterated the vision of her as she had been once long ago; he could hardly believe that they had ever been happy, or engaged to be married, for what were feelings, what was there to be felt? Confusion covered every sight and person, and he seemed to see St. John, Ridley, and the stray people who came up now and then from the hotel to enquire, through a mist; the only people who were not hidden in this mist were Helen and Rodriguez, because they could tell him something definite about Rachel.

Nevertheless the day followed the usual forms. At certain hours they went into the dining-room, and when they sat round the table they talked about indifferent things. St. John usually made it his business to start the talk and to keep it from dying out.

"I've discovered the way to get Sancho past the white house," said St. John on Sunday at luncheon. "You crackle a piece of paper in his ear, then he bolts for about a hundred yards, but he goes on quite well after that."

"Yes, but he wants corn. You should see that he has corn."

"I don't think much of the stuff they give him; and Angelo seems a dirty little rascal."

There was then a long silence. Ridley murmured a few lines of poetry under his breath, and remarked, as if to conceal the fact that he had done so, "Very hot today."

"Two degrees higher than it was yesterday," said St. John. "I wonder where these nuts come from," he observed, taking a nut out of the plate, turning it over in his fingers, and looking at it curiously.

"London, I should think," said Terence, looking at the nut too.

"A competent man of business could make a fortune here in no time," St. John continued. "I suppose the heat does something funny to people's brains. Even the English go a little queer. Anyhow they're hopeless people to deal with. They kept me three-quarters of an hour waiting at the chemist's this morning, for no reason whatever."

There was another long pause. Then Ridley enquired, "Rodriguez seems satisfied?"

"Quite," said Terence with decision. "It's just got to run its course." Whereupon Ridley heaved a deep sigh. He was genuinely sorry for every one, but at the same time he missed Helen considerably, and was a little aggrieved by the constant presence of the two young men.

They moved back into the drawing-room.

"Look here, Hirst," said Terence, "there's nothing to be done for two hours." He consulted the sheet pinned to the door. "You go and lie down. I'll wait here. Chailey sits with Rachel while Helen has her luncheon."

It was asking a good deal of Hirst to tell him to go without waiting for a sight of Helen. These little glimpses of Helen were the only respites from strain and boredom, and very often they seemed to make up for the discomfort of the day, although she might not have anything to tell them. However, as they were on an expedition together, he had made up his mind to obey.

Helen was very late in coming down. She looked like a person who has been sitting for a long time in the dark. She was pale and thinner, and the expression of her eyes was harassed but determined. She ate her luncheon quickly, and seemed indifferent to what she was doing. She brushed aside Terence's enquiries, and at last, as if he had not spoken, she looked at him with a slight frown and said:

"We can't go on like this, Terence. Either you've got to find another doctor, or you must tell Rodriguez to stop coming, and I'll manage for myself. It's no use for him to say that Rachel's better; she's not better; she's worse."

Terence suffered a terrific shock, like that which he had suffered when Rachel said, "My head aches." He stilled it by reflecting that Helen was overwrought, and he was upheld in this opinion by his obstinate sense that she was opposed to him in the argument.

"Do you think she's in danger?" he asked.

"No one can go on being as ill as that day after day—" Helen replied. She looked at him, and spoke as if she felt some indignation with somebody.

"Very well, I'll talk to Rodriguez this afternoon," he replied.

Helen went upstairs at once.

Nothing now could assuage Terence's anxiety. He could not read, nor could he sit still, and his sense of security was shaken, in spite of the fact that he was determined that Helen was exaggerating, and that Rachel was not very ill. But he wanted a third person to confirm him in his belief.

Directly Rodriguez came down he demanded, "Well, how is she? Do you think her worse?"

"There is no reason for anxiety, I tell you—none," Rodriguez replied in his execrable French, smiling uneasily, and making little movements all the time as if to get away.

Hewet stood firmly between him and the door. He was determined to see for himself what kind of man he was. His confidence in the man vanished as he looked at him and saw his insignificance, his dirty appearance, his shiftiness, and his unintelligent, hairy face. It was strange that he had never seen this before.

"You won't object, of course, if we ask you to consult another doctor?" he continued.

At this the little man became openly incensed.

"Ah!" he cried. "You have not confidence in me? You object to my treatment? You wish me to give up the case?"

"Not at all," Terence replied, "but in serious illness of this kind—"

Rodriguez shrugged his shoulders.

"It is not serious, I assure you. You are overanxious. The young lady is not seriously ill, and I am a doctor. The lady of course is frightened," he sneered. "I understand that perfectly."

"The name and address of the doctor is—?" Terence continued.

"There is no other doctor," Rodriguez replied sullenly. "Every one has confidence in me. Look! I will show you."

He took out a packet of old letters and began turning them over as if in search of one that would confute Terence's suspicions. As he searched, he began to tell a story about an English lord who had trusted him—a great English lord, whose name he had, unfortunately, forgotten.

"There is no other doctor in the place," he concluded, still turning over the letters.

"Never mind," said Terence shortly. "I will make enquiries for myself." Rodriguez put the letters back in his pocket.

"Very well," he remarked. "I have no objection."

He lifted his eyebrows, shrugged his shoulders, as if to repeat that they took the illness much too seriously and that there was no other doctor, and slipped out, leaving behind him an impression that he was conscious that he was distrusted, and that his malice was aroused.

After this Terence could no longer stay downstairs. He went up, knocked at Rachel's door, and asked Helen whether he might see her for a few minutes. He had not seen her yesterday. She made no objection, and went and sat at a table in the window.

Terence sat down by the bedside. Rachel's face was changed. She looked as though she were entirely concentrated upon the effort of keeping alive. Her lips were drawn, and her cheeks were sunken and flushed, though without colour. Her eyes were not entirely shut, the lower half of the white part showing, not as if she saw, but as if they remained open because she was too much exhausted to close them. She opened them completely when he kissed her. But she only saw an old woman slicing a man's head off with a knife.

"There it falls!" she murmured. She then turned to Terence and asked him anxiously some question about a man with mules, which he could not understand. "Why doesn't he come? Why doesn't he come?" she repeated. He was appalled to think of the dirty little man downstairs in connection with illness like this, and turning instinctively to Helen, but she was doing something at a table in the window, and did not seem to realise how great the shock to him must be. He rose to go, for he could not endure to listen any longer; his heart beat quickly and painfully with anger and misery. As he passed Helen she asked him in the same weary, unnatural, but determined voice to fetch her more ice, and to have the jug outside filled with fresh milk.

When he had done these errands he went to find Hirst. Exhausted and very hot, St. John had fallen asleep on a bed, but Terence woke him without scruple.

"Helen thinks she's worse," he said. "There's no doubt she's frightfully ill. Rodriguez is useless. We must get another doctor."

"But there is no other doctor," said Hirst drowsily, sitting up and rubbing his eyes.

"Don't be a damned fool!" Terence exclaimed. "Of course there's another doctor, and, if there isn't, you've got to find one. It ought to have been done days ago. I'm going down to saddle the horse." He could not stay still in one place.

In less than ten minutes St. John was riding to the town in the scorching heat in search of a doctor, his orders being to find one and bring him back if he had to be fetched in a special train.

"We ought to have done it days ago," Hewet repeated angrily.

When he went back into the drawing-room he found that Mrs. Flushing was there, standing very erect in the middle of the room, having arrived, as people did in these days, by the kitchen or through the garden unannounced.

"She's better?" Mrs. Flushing enquired abruptly; they did not attempt to shake hands.

"No," said Terence. "If anything, they think she's worse."

Mrs. Flushing seemed to consider for a moment or two, looking straight at Terence all the time.

"Let me tell you," she said, speaking in nervous jerks, "it's always about the seventh day one begins to get anxious. I daresay you've been sittin' here worryin' by yourself. You think she's bad, but anyone comin' with a fresh eye would see she was better. Mr. Elliot's had fever; he's all right now," she threw out. "It wasn't anythin' she caught on the expedition. What's it matter—a few days' fever? My brother had fever for twenty-six days once. And in a week or two he was up and about. We gave him nothin' but milk and arrowroot—"

Here Mrs. Chailey came in with a message.

"I'm wanted upstairs," said Terence.

"You see—she'll be better," Mrs. Flushing jerked out as he left the room. Her anxiety to persuade Terence was very great, and when he left her without saying anything she felt dissatisfied and restless; she did not like to stay, but she could not bear to go. She wandered from room to room looking for someone to talk to, but all the rooms were empty.

Terence went upstairs, stood inside the door to take Helen's directions, looked over at Rachel, but did not attempt to speak to her. She appeared vaguely conscious of his presence, but it seemed to disturb her, and she turned, so that she lay with her back to him.

For six days indeed she had been oblivious of the world outside, because it needed all her attention to follow the hot, red, quick sights which passed incessantly before her eyes. She knew that it was of enormous importance that she should attend to these sights and grasp their meaning, but she was always being just too late to hear or see something which would explain it all. For this reason, the faces—Helen's face, the nurse's, Terence's, the doctor's—which occasionally forced themselves very close to her, were worrying because they distracted her attention and she might miss the clue. However, on the fourth afternoon she was suddenly unable to keep Helen's face distinct from the sights themselves; her lips widened as she bent down over the bed, and she began to gabble unintelligibly like the rest. The sights were all concerned in some plot, some adventure, some escape. The nature of what they were doing changed incessantly, although there was always a reason behind it, which she must endeavour to grasp. Now they were among trees and savages, now they were on the sea, now they were on the tops of high towers; now they jumped; now they flew. But just as the crisis was about to happen, something invariably slipped in her brain, so that the whole effort had to begin over again. The heat was suffocating. At last the faces went further away; she fell into a deep pool of sticky water, which eventually closed over her head. She saw nothing and heard nothing but a faint booming sound, which was the sound of the sea rolling over her head. While all her tormentors thought that she was dead, she was not dead, but curled up at the bottom of the sea. There she lay, sometimes seeing darkness, sometimes light, while every now and then someone turned her over at the bottom of the sea.

After St. John had spent some hours in the heat of the sun wrangling with evasive and very garrulous natives, he extracted the information that there was a doctor, a French doctor, who was at present away on a holiday in the hills. It was quite impossible, so they said, to find him. With his experience of the country, St. John thought it unlikely that a telegram would either be sent or received; but having reduced the distance of the hill town, in which he was staying, from a hundred miles to thirty miles, and having hired a carriage and horses, he started at once to fetch the doctor himself. He succeeded in finding him, and eventually forced the unwilling man to leave his young wife and return forthwith. They reached the villa at midday on Tuesday.

Terence came out to receive them, and St. John was struck by the fact that he had grown perceptibly thinner in the interval; he was white too; his eyes looked strange. But the curt speech and the sulky masterful manner of Dr. Lesage impressed them both favourably, although at the same time it was obvious that he was very much annoyed at the whole affair. Coming downstairs he gave his directions emphatically, but it never occurred to him to give an opinion either because of the presence of Rodriguez who was now obsequious as well as malicious, or because he took it for granted that they knew already what was to be known.

"Of course," he said with a shrug of his shoulders, when Terence asked him, "Is she very ill?"

They were both conscious of a certain sense of relief when Dr. Lesage was gone, leaving explicit directions, and promising another visit in a few hours' time; but, unfortunately, the rise of their spirits led them to talk more than usual, and in talking they quarrelled. They quarrelled about a road, the Portsmouth Road. St. John said that it is macadamised where it passes Hindhead, and Terence knew as well as he knew his own name that it is not macadamised at that point. In the course of the argument they said some very sharp things to each other, and the rest of the dinner was eaten in silence, save for an occasional half-stifled reflection from Ridley.

When it grew dark and the lamps were brought in, Terence felt unable to control his irritation any longer. St. John went to bed in a state of complete exhaustion, bidding Terence good-night with rather more affection than usual because of their quarrel, and Ridley retired to his books. Left alone, Terence walked up and down the room; he stood at the open window.

The lights were coming out one after another in the town beneath, and it was very peaceful and cool in the garden, so that he stepped out on to the terrace. As he stood there in the darkness, able only to see the shapes of trees through the fine grey light, he was overcome by a desire to escape, to have done with this suffering, to forget that Rachel was ill. He allowed himself to lapse into forgetfulness of everything. As if a wind that had been raging incessantly suddenly fell asleep, the fret and strain and anxiety which had been pressing on him passed away. He seemed to stand in an unvexed space of air, on a little island by himself; he was free and immune from pain. It did not matter whether Rachel was well or ill; it did not matter whether they were apart or together; nothing mattered—nothing mattered. The waves beat on the shore far away, and the soft wind passed through the branches of the trees, seeming to encircle him with peace and security, with dark and nothingness. Surely the world of strife and fret and anxiety was not the real world, but this was the real world, the world that lay beneath the superficial world, so that, whatever happened, one was secure. The quiet and peace seemed to lap his body in a fine cool sheet, soothing every nerve; his mind seemed once more to expand, and become natural.

But when he had stood thus for a time a noise in the house roused him; he turned instinctively and went into the drawing-room. The sight of the lamp-lit room brought back so abruptly all that he had forgotten that he stood for a moment unable to move. He remembered everything, the hour, the minute even, what point they had reached, and what was to come. He cursed himself for making believe for a minute that things were different from what they are. The night was now harder to face than ever.

Unable to stay in the empty drawing-room, he wandered out and sat on the stairs half-way up to Rachel's room. He longed for someone to talk to, but Hirst was asleep, and Ridley was asleep; there was no sound in Rachel's room. The only sound in the house was the sound of Chailey moving in the kitchen. At last there was a rustling on the stairs overhead, and Nurse McInnis came down fastening the links in her cuffs, in preparation for the night's watch. Terence rose and stopped her. He had scarcely spoken to her, but it was possible that she might confirm him in the belief which still persisted in his own mind that Rachel was not seriously ill. He told her in a whisper that Dr. Lesage had been and what he had said.

"Now, Nurse," he whispered, "please tell me your opinion. Do you consider that she is very seriously ill? Is she in any danger?"

"The doctor has said—" she began.

"Yes, but I want your opinion. You have had experience of many cases like this?"

"I could not tell you more than Dr. Lesage, Mr. Hewet," she replied cautiously, as though her words might be used against her. "The case is serious, but you may feel quite certain that we are doing all we can for Miss Vinrace." She spoke with some professional self-approbation. But she realised perhaps that she did not satisfy the young man, who still blocked her way, for she shifted her feet slightly upon the stair and looked out of the window where they could see the moon over the sea.

"If you ask me," she began in a curiously stealthy tone, "I never like May for my patients."

"May?" Terence repeated.

"It may be a fancy, but I don't like to see anybody fall ill in May," she continued. "Things seem to go wrong in May. Perhaps it's the moon. They say the moon affects the brain, don't they, Sir?"

He looked at her but he could not answer her; like all the others, when one looked at her she seemed to shrivel beneath one's eyes and become worthless, malicious, and untrustworthy.

She slipped past him and disappeared.

Though he went to his room he was unable even to take his clothes off. For a long time he paced up and down, and then leaning out of the window gazed at the earth which lay so dark against the paler blue of the sky. With a mixture of fear and loathing he looked at the slim black cypress trees which were still visible in the garden, and heard the unfamiliar creaking and grating sounds which show that the earth is still hot. All these sights and sounds appeared sinister and full of hostility and foreboding; together with the natives and the nurse and the doctor and the terrible force of the illness itself they seemed to be in conspiracy against him. They seemed to join together in their effort to extract the greatest possible amount of suffering from him. He could not get used to his pain, it was a revelation to him. He had never realised before that underneath every action, underneath the life of every day, pain lies, quiescent, but ready to devour; he seemed to be able to see suffering, as if it were a fire, curling up over the edges of all action, eating away the lives of men and women. He thought for the first time with understanding of words which had before seemed to him empty: the struggle of life; the hardness of life. Now he knew for himself that life is hard and full of suffering. He looked at the scattered lights in the town beneath, and thought of Arthur and Susan, or Evelyn and Perrott venturing out unwittingly, and by their happiness laying themselves open to suffering such as this. How did they dare to love each other, he wondered; how had he himself dared to live as he had lived, rapidly and carelessly, passing from one thing to another, loving Rachel as he had loved her? Never again would he feel secure; he would never believe in the stability of life, or forget what depths of pain lie beneath small happiness and feelings of content and safety. It seemed to him as he looked back that their happiness had never been so great as his pain was now. There had always been something imperfect in their happiness, something they had wanted and had not been able to get. It had been fragmentary and incomplete, because they were so young and had not known what they were doing.

The light of his candle flickered over the boughs of a tree outside the window, and as the branch swayed in the darkness there came before his mind a picture of all the world that lay outside his window; he thought of the immense river and the immense forest, the vast stretches of dry earth and the plains of the sea that encircled the earth; from the sea the sky rose steep and enormous, and the air washed profoundly between the sky and the sea. How vast and dark it must be tonight, lying exposed to the wind; and in all this great space it was curious to think how few the towns were, and how small little rings of light, or single glow-worms he figured them, scattered here and there, among the swelling uncultivated folds of the world. And in those towns were little men and women, tiny men and women. Oh, it was absurd, when one thought of it, to sit here in a little room suffering and caring. What did anything matter? Rachel, a tiny creature, lay ill beneath him, and here in his little room he suffered on her account. The nearness of their bodies in this vast universe, and the minuteness of their bodies, seemed to him absurd and laughable. Nothing mattered, he repeated; they had no power, no hope. He leant on the window-sill, thinking, until he almost forgot the time and the place. Nevertheless, although he was convinced that it was absurd and laughable, and that they were small and hopeless, he never lost the sense that these thoughts somehow formed part of a life which he and Rachel would live together.

Owing perhaps to the change of doctor, Rachel appeared to be rather better next day. Terribly pale and worn though Helen looked, there was a slight lifting of the cloud which had hung all these days in her eyes.

"She talked to me," she said voluntarily. "She asked me what day of the week it was, like herself."

Then suddenly, without any warning or any apparent reason, the tears formed in her eyes and rolled steadily down her cheeks. She cried with scarcely any attempt at movement of her features, and without any attempt to stop herself, as if she did not know that she was crying. In spite of the relief which her words gave him, Terence was dismayed by the sight; had everything given way? Were there no limits to the power of this illness? Would everything go down before it? Helen had always seemed to him strong and determined, and now she was like a child. He took her in his arms, and she clung to him like a child, crying softly and quietly upon his shoulder. Then she roused herself and wiped her tears away; it was silly to behave like that, she said; very silly, she repeated, when there could be no doubt that Rachel was better. She asked Terence to forgive her for her folly. She stopped at the door and came back and kissed him without saying anything.

On this day indeed Rachel was conscious of what went on round her. She had come to the surface of the dark, sticky pool, and a wave seemed to bear her up and down with it; she had ceased to have any will of her own; she lay on the top of the wave conscious of some pain, but chiefly of weakness. The wave was replaced by the side of a mountain. Her body became a drift of melting snow, above which her knees rose in huge peaked mountains of bare bone. It was true that she saw Helen and saw her room, but everything had become very pale and semi-transparent. Sometimes she could see through the wall in front of her. Sometimes when Helen went away she seemed to go so far that Rachel's eyes could hardly follow her. The room also had an odd power of expanding, and though she pushed her voice out as far as possible until sometimes it became a bird and flew away, she thought it doubtful whether it ever reached the person she was talking to. There were immense intervals or chasms, for things still had the power to appear visibly before her, between one moment and the next; it sometimes took an hour for Helen to raise her arm, pausing long between each jerky movement, and pour out medicine. Helen's form stooping to raise her in bed appeared of gigantic size, and came down upon her like the ceiling falling. But for long spaces of time she would merely lie conscious of her body floating on the top of the bed and her mind driven to some remote corner of her body, or escaped and gone flitting round the room. All sights were something of an effort, but the sight of Terence was the greatest effort, because he forced her to join mind to body in the desire to remember something. She did not wish to remember; it troubled her when people tried to disturb her loneliness; she wished to be alone. She wished for nothing else in the world.

Although she had cried, Terence observed Helen's greater hopefulness with something like triumph; in the argument between them she had made the first sign of admitting herself in the wrong. He waited for Dr. Lesage to come down that afternoon with considerable anxiety, but with the same certainty at the back of his mind that he would in time force them all to admit that they were in the wrong.

As usual, Dr. Lesage was sulky in his manner and very short in his answers. To Terence's demand, "She seems to be better?" he replied, looking at him in an odd way, "She has a chance of life."

The door shut and Terence walked across to the window. He leant his forehead against the pane.

"Rachel," he repeated to himself. "She has a chance of life. Rachel."

How could they say these things of Rachel? Had anyone yesterday seriously believed that Rachel was dying? They had been engaged for four weeks. A fortnight ago she had been perfectly well. What could fourteen days have done to bring her from that state to this? To realise what they meant by saying that she had a chance of life was beyond him, knowing as he did that they were engaged. He turned, still enveloped in the same dreary mist, and walked towards the door. Suddenly he saw it all. He saw the room and the garden, and the trees moving in the air, they could go on without her; she could die. For the first time since she fell ill he remembered exactly what she looked like and the way in which they cared for each other. The immense happiness of feeling her close to him mingled with a more intense anxiety than he had felt yet. He could not let her die; he could not live without her. But after a momentary struggle, the curtain fell again, and he saw nothing and felt nothing clearly. It was all going on—going on still, in the same way as before. Save for a physical pain when his heart beat, and the fact that his fingers were icy cold, he did not realise that he was anxious about anything. Within his mind he seemed to feel nothing about Rachel or about anyone or anything in the world. He went on giving orders, arranging with Mrs. Chailey, writing out lists, and every now and then he went upstairs and put something quietly on the table outside Rachel's door. That night Dr. Lesage seemed to be less sulky than usual. He stayed voluntarily for a few moments, and, addressing St. John and Terence equally, as if he did not remember which of them was engaged to the young lady, said, "I consider that her condition tonight is very grave."

Neither of them went to bed or suggested that the other should go to bed. They sat in the drawing-room playing picquet with the door open. St. John made up a bed upon the sofa, and when it was ready insisted that Terence should lie upon it. They began to quarrel as to who should lie on the sofa and who should lie upon a couple of chairs covered with rugs. St. John forced Terence at last to lie down upon the sofa.

"Don't be a fool, Terence," he said. "You'll only get ill if you don't sleep."

"Old fellow," he began, as Terence still refused, and stopped abruptly, fearing sentimentality; he found that he was on the verge of tears.

He began to say what he had long been wanting to say, that he was sorry for Terence, that he cared for him, that he cared for Rachel. Did she know how much he cared for her—had she said anything, asked perhaps? He was very anxious to say this, but he refrained, thinking that it was a selfish question after all, and what was the use of bothering Terence to talk about such things? He was already half asleep. But St. John could not sleep at once. If only, he thought to himself, as he lay in the darkness, something would happen—if only this strain would come to an end. He did not mind what happened, so long as the succession of these hard and dreary days was broken; he did not mind if she died. He felt himself disloyal in not minding it, but it seemed to him that he had no feelings left.

All night long there was no call or movement, except the opening and shutting of the bedroom door once. By degrees the light returned into the untidy room. At six the servants began to move; at seven they crept downstairs into the kitchen; and half an hour later the day began again.

Nevertheless it was not the same as the days that had gone before, although it would have been hard to say in what the difference consisted. Perhaps it was that they seemed to be waiting for something. There were certainly fewer things to be done than usual. People drifted through the drawing-room—Mr. Flushing, Mr. and Mrs. Thornbury. They spoke very apologetically in low tones, refusing to sit down, but remaining for a considerable time standing up, although the only thing they had to say was, "Is there anything we can do?" and there was nothing they could do.

Feeling oddly detached from it all, Terence remembered how Helen had said that whenever anything happened to you this was how people behaved. Was she right, or was she wrong? He was too little interested to frame an opinion of his own. He put things away in his mind, as if one of these days he would think about them, but not now. The mist of unreality had deepened and deepened until it had produced a feeling of numbness all over his body. Was it his body? Were those really his own hands?

This morning also for the first time Ridley found it impossible to sit alone in his room. He was very uncomfortable downstairs, and, as he did not know what was going on, constantly in the way; but he would not leave the drawing-room. Too restless to read, and having nothing to do, he began to pace up and down reciting poetry in an undertone. Occupied in various ways—now in undoing parcels, now in uncorking bottles, now in writing directions, the sound of Ridley's song and the beat of his pacing worked into the minds of Terence and St. John all the morning as a half comprehended refrain.

> They wrestled up, they wrestled down,
> They wrestled sore and still:
> The fiend who blinds the eyes of men,
> That night he had his will.
> Like stags full spent, among the bent
> They dropped awhile to rest—

"Oh, it's intolerable!" Hirst exclaimed, and then checked himself, as if it were a breach of their agreement. Again and again Terence would creep half-way up the stairs in case he might be able to glean news of Rachel. But the only news now was of a very fragmentary kind; she had drunk something; she had slept a little; she seemed quieter. In the same way, Dr. Lesage confined himself to talking about details, save once when he volunteered the information that he had just been called in to ascertain, by severing a vein in the wrist, that an old lady of eighty-five was really dead. She had a horror of being buried alive.

"It is a horror," he remarked, "that we generally find in the very old, and seldom in the young." They both expressed their interest in what he told them; it seemed to them very strange. Another strange thing about the day was that the luncheon was forgotten by all of them until it was late in the afternoon, and then Mrs. Chailey waited on them, and looked strange too, because she wore a stiff print dress, and her sleeves were rolled up above her elbows. She seemed as oblivious of her appearance, however, as if she had been called out of her bed by a midnight alarm of fire, and she had forgotten, too, her reserve and her composure; she talked to them quite familiarly as if she had nursed them and held them naked on her knee. She assured them over and over again that it was their duty to eat.

The afternoon, being thus shortened, passed more quickly than they expected. Once Mrs. Flushing opened the door, but on seeing them shut it again quickly; once Helen came down to fetch something, but she stopped as she left the room to look at a letter addressed to her. She stood for a moment turning it over, and the extraordinary and mournful beauty of her attitude struck Terence in the way things struck him now—as something to be put away in his mind and to be thought about afterwards. They scarcely spoke, the argument between them seeming to be suspended or forgotten.

Now that the afternoon sun had left the front of the house, Ridley paced up and down the terrace repeating stanzas of a long poem, in a subdued but suddenly sonorous voice. Fragments of the poem were wafted in at the open window as he passed and repassed.

> *Peor and Baalim*
> *Forsake their Temples dim,*
>   *With that twice batter'd God of Palestine*
> *And mooned Astaroth—*

The sound of these words were strangely discomforting to both the young men, but they had to be borne. As the evening drew on and the red light of the sunset glittered far away on the sea, the same sense of desperation attacked both Terence and St. John at the thought that the day was nearly over, and that another night was at hand. The appearance of one light after another in the town beneath them produced in Hirst a repetition of his terrible and disgusting desire to break down and sob. Then the lamps were brought in by Chailey. She explained that Maria, in opening a bottle, had been so foolish as to cut her arm badly, but she had bound it up; it was unfortunate when there was so much work to be done. Chailey herself limped because of the rheumatism in her feet, but it appeared to her mere waste of time to take any notice of the unruly flesh of servants. The evening went on. Dr. Lesage arrived unexpectedly, and stayed upstairs a very long time. He came down once and drank a cup of coffee.

"She is very ill," he said in answer to Ridley's question. All the annoyance had by this time left his manner, he was grave and formal, but at the same time it was full of consideration, which had not marked it before. He went upstairs again. The three men sat together in the drawing-room. Ridley was quite quiet now, and his attention seemed to be thoroughly awakened. Save for little half-voluntary movements and exclamations that were stifled at once, they waited in complete silence. It seemed as if they were at last brought together face to face with something definite.

It was nearly eleven o'clock when Dr. Lesage again appeared in the room. He approached them very slowly, and did not speak at once. He looked first at St. John and then at Terence, and said to Terence, "Mr. Hewet, I think you should go upstairs now."

Terence rose immediately, leaving the others seated with Dr. Lesage standing motionless between them.

Chailey was in the passage outside, repeating over and over again, "It's wicked—it's wicked."

Terence paid her no attention; he heard what she was saying, but it conveyed no meaning to his mind. All the way upstairs he kept saying to himself, "This has not happened to me. It is not possible that this has happened to me."

He looked curiously at his own hand on the banisters. The stairs were very steep, and it seemed to take him a long time to surmount them. Instead of feeling keenly, as he knew that he ought to feel, he felt nothing at all. When he opened the door he saw Helen sitting by the bedside. There were shaded lights on the table, and the room, though it seemed to be full of a great many things, was very tidy. There was a faint and not unpleasant smell of disinfectants. Helen rose and gave up her chair to him in silence. As they passed each other their eyes met in a peculiar level glance, he wondered at the extraordinary clearness of his eyes, and at the deep calm and sadness that dwelt in them. He sat down by the bedside, and a moment afterwards heard the door shut gently behind her. He was alone with Rachel, and a faint reflection of the sense of relief that they used to feel when they were left alone possessed him. He looked at her. He expected to find some terrible change in her, but there was none. She looked indeed very thin, and, as far as he could see, very tired, but she was the same as she had always been. Moreover, she saw him and knew him. She smiled at him and said, "Hullo, Terence."

The curtain which had been drawn between them for so long vanished immediately.

"Well, Rachel," he replied in his usual voice, upon which she opened her eyes quite widely and smiled with her familiar smile. He kissed her and took her hand.

"It's been wretched without you," he said.

She still looked at him and smiled, but soon a slight look of fatigue or perplexity came into her eyes and she shut them again.

"But when we're together we're perfectly happy," he said. He continued to hold her hand.

The light being dim, it was impossible to see any change in her face. An immense feeling of peace came over Terence, so that he had no wish to move or to speak. The terrible torture and unreality of the last days were over, and he had come out now into perfect certainty and peace. His mind began to work naturally again and with great ease. The longer he sat there the more profoundly was he conscious of the peace invading every corner of his soul. Once he held his breath and listened acutely; she was still breathing; he went on thinking for some time; they seemed to be thinking together; he seemed to be Rachel as well as himself; and then he listened again; no, she had ceased to breathe. So much the better—this was death. It was nothing; it was to cease to breathe. It was happiness, it was perfect happiness. They had now what they had always wanted to have, the union which had been impossible while they lived. Unconscious whether he thought the words or spoke them aloud, he said, "No two people have ever been so happy as we have been. No one has ever loved as we have loved."

It seemed to him that their complete union and happiness filled the room with rings eddying more and more widely. He had no wish in the world left unfulfilled. They possessed what could never be taken from them.

He was not conscious that anyone had come into the room, but later, moments later, or hours later perhaps, he felt an arm behind him. The arms were round him. He did not want to have arms round him, and the mysterious whispering voices annoyed him. He laid Rachel's hand, which was now cold, upon the counterpane, and rose from his chair, and walked across to the window. The windows were uncurtained, and showed the moon, and a long silver pathway upon the surface of the waves.

"Why," he said, in his ordinary tone of voice, "look at the moon. There's a halo round the moon. We shall have rain tomorrow."

The arms, whether they were the arms of man or of woman, were round him again; they were pushing him gently towards the door. He turned of his own accord and walked steadily in advance of the arms, conscious of a little amusement at the strange way in which people behaved merely because someone was dead. He would go if they wished it, but nothing they could do would disturb his happiness.

As he saw the passage outside the room, and the table with the cups and the plates, it suddenly came over him that here was a world in which he would never see Rachel again.

"Rachel! Rachel!" he shrieked, trying to rush back to her. But they prevented him, and pushed him down the passage and into a bedroom far from her room. Downstairs they could hear the thud of his feet on the floor, as he struggled to break free; and twice they heard him shout, "Rachel, Rachel!"

CHAPTER XXVI

For two or three hours longer the moon poured its light through the empty air. Unbroken by clouds it fell straightly, and lay almost like a chill white frost over the sea and the earth. During these hours the silence was not broken, and the only movement was caused by the movement of trees and branches which stirred slightly, and then the shadows that lay across the white spaces of the land moved too. In this profound silence one sound only was audible, the sound of a slight but continuous breathing which never ceased, although it never rose and never fell. It continued after the birds had begun to flutter from branch to branch, and could be heard behind the first thin notes of their voices. It continued all through the hours when the east whitened, and grew red, and a faint blue tinged the sky, but when the sun rose it ceased, and gave place to other sounds.

The first sounds that were heard were little inarticulate cries, the cries, it seemed, of children or of the very poor, of people who were very weak or in pain. But when the sun was above the horizon, the air which had been thin and pale grew every moment richer and warmer, and the sounds of life became bolder and more full of courage and authority. By degrees the smoke began to ascend in wavering breaths over the houses, and these slowly thickened, until they were as round and straight as columns, and instead of striking upon pale white blinds, the sun shone upon dark windows, beyond which there was depth and space.

The sun had been up for many hours, and the great dome of air was warmed through and glittering with thin gold threads of sunlight, before anyone moved in the hotel. White and massive it stood in the early light, half asleep with its blinds down.

At about half-past nine Miss Allan came very slowly into the hall, and walked very slowly to the table where the morning papers were laid, but she did not put out her hand to take one; she stood still, thinking, with her head a little sunk upon her shoulders. She looked curiously old, and from the way in which she stood, a little hunched together and very massive, you could see what she would be like when she was really old, how she would sit day after day in her chair looking placidly in front of her. Other people began to come into the room, and to pass her, but she did not speak to any of them or even look at them, and at last, as if it were necessary to do something, she sat down in a chair, and looked quietly and fixedly in front of her. She felt very old this morning, and useless too, as if her life had been a failure, as if it had been hard and laborious to no purpose. She did not want to go on living, and yet she knew that she would. She was so strong that she would live to be a very old woman. She would probably live to be eighty, and as she was now fifty, that left thirty years more for her to live. She turned her hands over and over in her lap and looked at them curiously; her old hands, that had done so much work for her. There did not seem to be much point in it all; one went on, of course one went on . . . She looked up to see Mrs. Thornbury standing beside her, with lines drawn upon her forehead, and her lips parted as if she were about to ask a question.

Miss Allan anticipated her.

"Yes," she said. "She died this morning, very early, about three o'clock."

Mrs. Thornbury made a little exclamation, drew her lips together, and the tears rose in her eyes. Through them she looked at the hall which was now laid with great breadths of sunlight, and at the careless, casual groups of people who were standing beside the solid armchairs and tables. They looked to her unreal, or as people look who remain unconscious that some great explosion is about to take place beside them. But there was no explosion, and they went on standing by the chairs and the tables. Mrs. Thornbury no longer saw them, but, penetrating through them as though they were without substance, she saw the house, the people in the house, the room, the bed in the room, and the figure of the dead lying still in the dark beneath the sheets. She could almost see the dead. She could almost hear the voices of the mourners.

"They expected it?" she asked at length.

Miss Allan could only shake her head.

"I know nothing," she replied, "except what Mrs. Flushing's maid told me. She died early this morning."

The two women looked at each other with a quiet significant gaze, and then, feeling oddly dazed, and seeking she did not know exactly what, Mrs. Thornbury went slowly upstairs and walked quietly along the passages, touching the wall with her fingers as if to guide herself. Housemaids were passing briskly from room to room, but Mrs. Thornbury avoided them; she hardly saw them; they seemed to her to be in another world. She did not even look up directly when Evelyn stopped her. It was evident that Evelyn had been lately in tears, and when she looked at Mrs. Thornbury she began to cry again. Together they drew into the hollow of a window, and stood there in silence. Broken words formed themselves at last among Evelyn's sobs. "It was wicked," she sobbed, "it was cruel—they were so happy."

Mrs. Thornbury patted her on the shoulder.

"It seems hard—very hard," she said. She paused and looked out over the slope of the hill at the Ambroses' villa; the windows were blazing in the sun, and she thought how the soul of the dead had passed from those windows. Something had passed from the world. It seemed to her strangely empty.

"And yet the older one grows," she continued, her eyes regaining more than their usual brightness, "the more certain one becomes that there is a reason. How could one go on if there were no reason?" she asked.

She asked the question of someone, but she did not ask it of Evelyn. Evelyn's sobs were becoming quieter. "There must be a reason," she said. "It can't only be an accident. For it was an accident—it need never have happened."

Mrs. Thornbury sighed deeply.

"But we must not let ourselves think of that," she added, "and let us hope that they don't either. Whatever they had done it might have been the same. These terrible illnesses—"

"There's no reason—I don't believe there's any reason at all!" Evelyn broke out, pulling the blind down and letting it fly back with a little snap.

"Why should these things happen? Why should people suffer? I honestly believe," she went on, lowering her voice slightly, "that Rachel's in Heaven, but Terence . . ."

"What's the good of it all?" she demanded.

Mrs. Thornbury shook her head slightly but made no reply, and pressing Evelyn's hand she went on down the passage. Impelled by a strong desire to hear something, although she did not know exactly what there was to hear, she was making her way to the Flushings' room. As she opened their door she felt that she had interrupted some argument between husband and wife. Mrs. Flushing was sitting with her back to the light, and Mr. Flushing was standing near her, arguing and trying to persuade her of something.

"Ah, here is Mrs. Thornbury," he began with some relief in his voice. "You have heard, of course. My wife feels that she was in some way responsible. She urged poor Miss Vinrace to come on the expedition. I'm sure you will agree with me that it is most unreasonable to feel that. We don't even know— in fact I think it most unlikely—that she caught her illness there. These diseases—Besides, she was set on going. She would have gone whether you asked her or not, Alice."

"Don't, Wilfrid," said Mrs. Flushing, neither moving nor taking her eyes off the spot on the floor upon which they rested. "What's the use of talking? What's the use—?" She ceased.

"I was coming to ask you," said Mrs. Thornbury, addressing Wilfrid, for it was useless to speak to his wife. "Is there anything you think that one could do? Has the father arrived? Could one go and see?"

The strongest wish in her being at this moment was to be able to do something for the unhappy people—to see them—to assure them—to help them. It was dreadful to be so far away from them. But Mr. Flushing shook his head; he did not think that now—later perhaps one might be able to help. Here Mrs. Flushing rose stiffly, turned her back to them, and walked to the dressing-room opposite. As she walked, they could see her breast slowly rise and slowly fall. But her grief was silent. She shut the door behind her.

When she was alone by herself she clenched her fists together, and began beating the back of a chair with them. She was like a wounded animal. She hated death; she was furious, outraged, indignant with death, as if it were a living creature. She refused to relinquish her friends to death. She would not submit to dark and nothingness. She began to pace up and down, clenching her hands, and making no attempt to stop the quick tears which raced down her cheeks. She sat still at last, but she did not submit. She looked stubborn and strong when she had ceased to cry.

In the next room, meanwhile, Wilfrid was talking to Mrs. Thornbury with greater freedom now that his wife was not sitting there.

"That's the worst of these places," he said. "People will behave as though they were in England, and they're not. I've no doubt myself that Miss Vinrace caught the infection up at the villa itself. She probably ran risks a dozen times a day that might have given her the illness. It's absurd to say she caught it with us."

If he had not been sincerely sorry for them he would have been annoyed. "Pepper tells me," he continued, "that he left the house because he thought them so careless. He says they never washed their vegetables properly. Poor people! It's a fearful price to pay. But it's only what I've seen over and over again—people seem to forget that these things happen, and then they do happen, and they're surprised."

Mrs. Thornbury agreed with him that they had been very careless, and that there was no reason whatever to think that she had caught the fever on the expedition; and after talking about other things for a short time, she left him and went sadly along the passage to her own room. There must be some reason why such things happen, she thought to herself, as she shut the door. Only at first it was not easy to understand what it was. It seemed so strange—so unbelievable. Why, only three weeks ago—only a fortnight ago, she had seen Rachel; when she shut her eyes she could almost see her now, the quiet, shy girl who was going to be married. She thought of all that she would have missed had she died at Rachel's age, the children, the married life, the unimaginable depths and miracles that seemed to her, as she looked back, to have lain about her, day after day, and year after year. The stunned feeling, which had been making it difficult for her to think, gradually gave way to a feeling of the opposite nature; she thought very quickly and very clearly, and, looking back over all her experiences, tried to fit them into a kind of order. There was undoubtedly much suffering, much struggling, but, on the whole, surely there was a balance of happiness—surely order did prevail. Nor were the deaths of young people really the saddest things in life—they were saved so much; they kept so much. The dead—she called to mind those who had died early, accidentally—were beautiful; she often dreamt of the dead. And in time Terence himself would come to feel—She got up and began to wander restlessly about the room.

For an old woman of her age she was very restless, and for one of her clear, quick mind she was unusually perplexed. She could not settle to anything, so that she was relieved when the door opened. She went up to her husband, took him in her arms, and kissed him with unusual intensity, and then as they sat down together she began to pat him and question him as if he were a baby, an old, tired, querulous baby. She did not tell him about Miss Vinrace's death, for that would only disturb him, and he was put out already. She tried to discover why he was uneasy. Politics again? What were those horrid people doing? She spent the whole morning in discussing politics with her husband, and by degrees she became deeply interested in what they were saying. But every now and then what she was saying seemed to her oddly empty of meaning.

At luncheon it was remarked by several people that the visitors at the hotel were beginning to leave; there were fewer every day. There were only forty people at luncheon, instead of the sixty that there had been. So old Mrs. Paley computed, gazing about her with her faded eyes, as she took her seat at her own table in the window. Her party generally consisted of Mr. Perrott as well as Arthur and Susan, and today Evelyn was lunching with them also.

She was unusually subdued. Having noticed that her eyes were red, and guessing the reason, the others took pains to keep up an elaborate conversation between themselves. She suffered it to go on for a few minutes, leaning both elbows on the table, and leaving her soup untouched, when she exclaimed suddenly, "I don't know how you feel, but I can simply think of nothing else!"

The gentlemen murmured sympathetically, and looked grave.

Susan replied, "Yes—isn't it perfectly awful? When you think what a nice girl she was—only just engaged, and this need never have happened—it seems too tragic." She looked at Arthur as though he might be able to help her with something more suitable.

"Hard lines," said Arthur briefly. "But it was a foolish thing to do—to go up that river." He shook his head. "They should have known better. You can't expect Englishwomen to stand roughing it as the natives do who've been acclimatised. I'd half a mind to warn them at tea that day when it was being discussed. But it's no good saying these sort of things—it only puts people's backs up—it never makes any difference."

Old Mrs. Paley, hitherto contented with her soup, here intimated, by raising one hand to her ear, that she wished to know what was being said.

"You heard, Aunt Emma, that poor Miss Vinrace has died of the fever," Susan informed her gently. She could not speak of death loudly or even in her usual voice, so that Mrs. Paley did not catch a word. Arthur came to the rescue.

"Miss Vinrace is dead," he said very distinctly.

Mrs. Paley merely bent a little towards him and asked, "Eh?"

"Miss Vinrace is dead," he repeated. It was only by stiffening all the muscles round his mouth that he could prevent himself from bursting into laughter, and forced himself to repeat for the third time, "Miss Vinrace . . . She's dead."

Let alone the difficulty of hearing the exact words, facts that were outside her daily experience took some time to reach Mrs. Paley's consciousness.

A weight seemed to rest upon her brain, impeding, though not damaging its action. She sat vague-eyed for at least a minute before she realised what Arthur meant.

"Dead?" she said vaguely. "Miss Vinrace dead? Dear me . . . that's very sad. But I don't at the moment remember which she was. We seem to have made so many new acquaintances here." She looked at Susan for help. "A tall dark girl, who just missed being handsome, with a high colour?"

"No," Susan interposed. "She was—" then she gave it up in despair. There was no use in explaining that Mrs. Paley was thinking of the wrong person.

"She ought not to have died," Mrs. Paley continued. "She looked so strong. But people will drink the water. I can never make out why. It seems such a simple thing to tell them to put a bottle of Seltzer water in your bedroom. That's all the precaution I've ever taken, and I've been in every part of the world, I may say—Italy a dozen times over . . . But young people always think they know better, and then they pay the penalty. Poor thing—I am very sorry for her." But the difficulty of peering into a dish of potatoes and helping herself engrossed her attention.

Arthur and Susan both secretly hoped that the subject was now disposed of, for there seemed to them something unpleasant in this discussion. But Evelyn was not ready to let it drop. Why would people never talk about the things that mattered?

"I don't believe you care a bit!" she said, turning savagely upon Mr. Perrott, who had sat all this time in silence.

"I? Oh, yes, I do," he answered awkwardly, but with obvious sincerity. Evelyn's questions made him too feel uncomfortable.

"It seems so inexplicable," Evelyn continued. "Death, I mean. Why should she be dead, and not you or I? It was only a fortnight ago that she was here with the rest of us. What d'you believe?" she demanded of Mr. Perrott. "D'you believe that things go on, that she's still somewhere—or d'you think it's simply a game—we crumble up to nothing when we die? I'm positive Rachel's not dead."

Mr. Perrott would have said almost anything that Evelyn wanted him to say, but to assert that he believed in the immortality of the soul was not in his power. He sat silent, more deeply wrinkled than usual, crumbling his bread.

Lest Evelyn should next ask him what he believed, Arthur, after making a pause equivalent to a full stop, started a completely different topic.

"Supposing," he said, "a man were to write and tell you that he wanted five pounds because he had known your grandfather, what would you do? It was this way. My grandfather—"

"Invented a stove," said Evelyn. "I know all about that. We had one in the conservatory to keep the plants warm."

"Didn't know I was so famous," said Arthur. "Well," he continued, determined at all costs to spin his story out at length, "the old chap, being about the second best inventor of his day, and a capable lawyer too, died, as they always do, without making a will. Now Fielding, his clerk, with how much justice I don't know, always claimed that he meant to do something for him. The poor old boy's come down in the world through trying inventions on his own account, lives in Penge over a tobacconist's shop. I've been to see him there. The question is—must I stump up or not? What does the abstract spirit of justice require, Perrott? Remember, I didn't benefit under my grandfather's will, and I've no way of testing the truth of the story."

"I don't know much about the abstract spirit of justice," said Susan, smiling complacently at the others, "but I'm certain of one thing—he'll get his five pounds!"

As Mr. Perrott proceeded to deliver an opinion, and Evelyn insisted that he was much too stingy, like all lawyers, thinking of the letter and not of the spirit, while Mrs. Paley required to be kept informed between the courses as to what they were all saying, the luncheon passed with no interval of silence, and Arthur congratulated himself upon the tact with which the discussion had been smoothed over.

As they left the room it happened that Mrs. Paley's wheeled chair ran into the Elliots, who were coming through the door, as she was going out. Brought thus to a standstill for a moment, Arthur and Susan congratulated Hughling Elliot upon his convalescence—he was down, cadaverous enough, for the first time—and Mr. Perrott took occasion to say a few words in private to Evelyn.

"Would there be any chance of seeing you this afternoon, about three-thirty say? I shall be in the garden, by the fountain."

The block dissolved before Evelyn answered. But as she left them in the hall, she looked at him brightly and said, "Half-past three, did you say? That'll suit me."

She ran upstairs with the feeling of spiritual exaltation and quickened life which the prospect of an emotional scene always aroused in her. That Mr. Perrott was again about to propose to her, she had no doubt, and she was aware that on this occasion she ought to be prepared with a definite answer, for she was going away in three days' time. But she could not bring her mind to bear upon the question. To come to a decision was very difficult to her, because she had a natural dislike of anything final and done with; she liked to go on and on—always on and on. She was leaving, and, therefore, she occupied herself in laying her clothes out side by side upon the bed. She observed that some were very shabby. She took the photograph of her father and mother, and, before she laid it away in her box, she held it for a minute in her hand. Rachel had looked at it. Suddenly the keen feeling of someone's personality, which things that they have owned or handled sometimes preserves, overcame her; she felt Rachel in the room with her; it was as if she were on a ship at sea, and the life of the day was as unreal as the land in the distance. But by degrees the feeling of Rachel's presence passed away, and she could no longer realise her, for she had scarcely known her. But this momentary sensation left her depressed and fatigued. What had she done with her life? What future was there before her? What was make-believe, and what was real? Were these proposals and intimacies and adventures real, or was the contentment which she had seen on the faces of Susan and Rachel more real than anything she had ever felt?

She made herself ready to go downstairs, absentmindedly, but her fingers were so well trained that they did the work of preparing her almost of their own accord. When she was actually on the way downstairs, the blood began to circle through her body of its own accord too, for her mind felt very dull.

Mr. Perrott was waiting for her. Indeed, he had gone straight into the garden after luncheon, and had been walking up and down the path for more than half an hour, in a state of acute suspense.

"I'm late as usual!" she exclaimed, as she caught sight of him. "Well, you must forgive me; I had to pack up . . . My word! It looks stormy! And that's a new steamer in the bay, isn't it?"

She looked at the bay, in which a steamer was just dropping anchor, the smoke still hanging about it, while a swift black shudder ran through the waves. "One's quite forgotten what rain looks like," she added.

But Mr. Perrott paid no attention to the steamer or to the weather.

"Miss Murgatroyd," he began with his usual formality, "I asked you to come here from a very selfish motive, I fear. I do not think you need to be assured once more of my feelings; but, as you are leaving so soon, I felt that I could not let you go without asking you to tell me—have I any reason to hope that you will ever come to care for me?"

He was very pale, and seemed unable to say any more.

The little gush of vitality which had come into Evelyn as she ran downstairs had left her, and she felt herself impotent. There was nothing for her to say; she felt nothing. Now that he was actually asking her, in his elderly gentle words, to marry him, she felt less for him than she had ever felt before.

"Let's sit down and talk it over," she said rather unsteadily.

Mr. Perrott followed her to a curved green seat under a tree. They looked at the fountain in front of them, which had long ceased to play. Evelyn kept looking at the fountain instead of thinking of what she was saying; the fountain without any water seemed to be the type of her own being.

"Of course I care for you," she began, rushing her words out in a hurry; "I should be a brute if I didn't. I think you're quite one of the nicest people

I've ever known, and one of the finest too. But I wish . . . I wish you didn't care for me in that way. Are you sure you do?" For the moment she honestly desired that he should say no.

"Quite sure," said Mr. Perrott.

"You see, I'm not as simple as most women," Evelyn continued. "I think I want more. I don't know exactly what I feel."

He sat by her, watching her and refraining from speech.

"I sometimes think I haven't got it in me to care very much for one person only. Someone else would make you a better wife. I can imagine you very happy with someone else."

"If you think that there is any chance that you will come to care for me, I am quite content to wait," said Mr. Perrott.

"Well—there's no hurry, is there?" said Evelyn. "Suppose I thought it over and wrote and told you when I get back? I'm going to Moscow; I'll write from Moscow."

But Mr. Perrott persisted.

"You cannot give me any kind of idea. I do not ask for a date . . . that would be most unreasonable." He paused, looking down at the gravel path.

As she did not immediately answer, he went on.

"I know very well that I am not—that I have not much to offer you either in myself or in my circumstances. And I forget; it cannot seem the miracle to you that it does to me. Until I met you I had gone on in my own quiet way— we are both very quiet people, my sister and I—quite content with my lot. My friendship with Arthur was the most important thing in my life. Now that I know you, all that has changed. You seem to put such a spirit into everything. Life seems to hold so many possibilities that I had never dreamt of."

"That's splendid!" Evelyn exclaimed, grasping his hand. "Now you'll go back and start all kinds of things and make a great name in the world; and we'll go on being friends, whatever happens . . . we'll be great friends, won't we?"

"Evelyn!" he moaned suddenly, and took her in his arms, and kissed her. She did not resent it, although it made little impression on her.

As she sat upright again, she said, "I never see why one shouldn't go on being friends—though some people do. And friendships do make a difference, don't they? They are the kind of things that matter in one's life?"

He looked at her with a bewildered expression as if he did not really understand what she was saying. With a considerable effort he collected himself, stood up, and said, "Now I think I have told you what I feel, and I will only add that I can wait as long as ever you wish."

Left alone, Evelyn walked up and down the path. What did matter than? What was the meaning of it all?

CHAPTER XXVII

All that evening the clouds gathered, until they closed entirely over the blue of the sky. They seemed to narrow the space between earth and heaven, so that there was no room for the air to move in freely; and the waves, too, lay flat, and yet rigid, as if they were restrained. The leaves on the bushes and trees in the garden hung closely together, and the feeling of pressure and restraint was increased by the short chirping sounds which came from birds and insects.

So strange were the lights and the silence that the busy hum of voices which usually filled the dining-room at meal times had distinct gaps in it, and during these silences the clatter of the knives upon plates became audible. The first roll of thunder and the first heavy drop striking the pane caused a little stir.

"It's coming!" was said simultaneously in many different languages.

There was then a profound silence, as if the thunder had withdrawn into itself. People had just begun to eat again, when a gust of cold air came through the open windows, lifting tablecloths and skirts, a light flashed, and was instantly followed by a clap of thunder right over the hotel. The rain swished with it, and immediately there were all those sounds of windows being shut and doors slamming violently which accompany a storm.

The room grew suddenly several degrees darker, for the wind seemed to be driving waves of darkness across the earth. No one attempted to eat for a time, but sat looking out at the garden, with their forks in the air. The flashes now came frequently, lighting up faces as if they were going to be photographed, surprising them in tense and unnatural expressions. The clap followed close and violently upon them. Several women half rose from their chairs and then sat down again, but dinner was continued uneasily with eyes upon the garden. The bushes outside were ruffled and whitened, and the wind pressed upon them so that they seemed to stoop to the ground. The waiters had to press dishes upon the diners' notice; and the diners had to draw the attention of waiters, for they were all absorbed in looking at the storm. As the thunder showed no signs of withdrawing, but seemed massed right overhead, while the lightning aimed straight at the garden every time, an uneasy gloom replaced the first excitement.

Finishing the meal very quickly, people congregated in the hall, where they felt more secure than in any other place because they could retreat far from the windows, and although they heard the thunder, they could not see anything. A little boy was carried away sobbing in the arms of his mother.

While the storm continued, no one seemed inclined to sit down, but they collected in little groups under the central skylight, where they stood in a yellow atmosphere, looking upwards. Now and again their faces became white, as the lightning flashed, and finally a terrific crash came, making the panes of the skylight lift at the joints.

"Ah!" several voices exclaimed at the same moment.

"Something struck," said a man's voice.

The rain rushed down. The rain seemed now to extinguish the lightning and the thunder, and the hall became almost dark.

After a minute or two, when nothing was heard but the rattle of water upon the glass, there was a perceptible slackening of the sound, and then the atmosphere became lighter.

"It's over," said another voice.

At a touch, all the electric lights were turned on, and revealed a crowd of people all standing, all looking with rather strained faces up at the skylight, but when they saw each other in the artificial light they turned at once and began to move away. For some minutes the rain continued to rattle upon the skylight, and the thunder gave another shake or two; but it was evident from the clearing of the darkness and the light drumming of the rain upon the roof, that the great confused ocean of air was travelling away from them, and passing high over head with its clouds and its rods of fire, out to sea. The building, which had seemed so small in the tumult of the storm, now became as square and spacious as usual.

As the storm drew away, the people in the hall of the hotel sat down; and with a comfortable sense of relief, began to tell each other stories about great storms, and produced in many cases their occupations for the evening. The chess-board was brought out, and Mr. Elliot, who wore a stock instead of a collar as a sign of convalescence, but was otherwise much as usual, challenged Mr. Pepper to a final contest. Round them gathered a group of ladies with pieces of needlework, or in default of needlework, with novels, to superintend the game, much as if they were in charge of two small boys playing marbles. Every now and then they looked at the board and made some encouraging remark to the gentlemen.

Mrs. Paley just round the corner had her cards arranged in long ladders before her, with Susan sitting near to sympathise but not to correct, and the merchants and the miscellaneous people who had never been discovered to possess names were stretched in their armchairs with their newspapers on their knees. The conversation in these circumstances was very gentle, fragmentary, and intermittent, but the room was full of the indescribable stir of life. Every now and then the moth, which was now grey of wing and shiny of thorax, whizzed over their heads, and hit the lamps with a thud.

A young woman put down her needlework and exclaimed, "Poor creature! it would be kinder to kill it." But nobody seemed disposed to rouse himself in order to kill the moth. They watched it dash from lamp to lamp, because they were comfortable, and had nothing to do.

On the sofa, beside the chess-players, Mrs. Elliot was imparting a new stitch in knitting to Mrs. Thornbury, so that their heads came very near together, and were only to be distinguished by the old lace cap which Mrs. Thornbury wore in the evening. Mrs. Elliot was an expert at knitting, and disclaimed a compliment to that effect with evident pride.

"I suppose we're all proud of something," she said, "and I'm proud of my knitting. I think things like that run in families. We all knit well. I had an uncle who knitted his own socks to the day of his death—and he did it better than any of his daughters, dear old gentleman. Now I wonder that you, Miss Allan, who use your eyes so much, don't take up knitting in the evenings. You'd find it such a relief, I should say—such a rest to the eyes—and the bazaars are so glad of things." Her voice dropped into the smooth half-conscious tone of the expert knitter; the words came gently one after another. "As much as I do I can always dispose of, which is a comfort, for then I feel that I am not wasting my time—"

Miss Allan, being thus addressed, shut her novel and observed the others placidly for a time. At last she said, "It is surely not natural to leave your wife because she happens to be in love with you. But that—as far as I can make out—is what the gentleman in my story does."

"Tut, tut, that doesn't sound good—no, that doesn't sound at all natural," murmured the knitters in their absorbed voices.

"Still, it's the kind of book people call very clever," Miss Allan added.

"*Maternity*—by Michael Jessop—I presume," Mr. Elliot put in, for he could never resist the temptation of talking while he played chess.

"D'you know," said Mrs. Elliot, after a moment, "I don't think people *do* write good novels now—not as good as they used to, anyhow."

No one took the trouble to agree with her or to disagree with her. Arthur Venning who was strolling about, sometimes looking at the game, sometimes reading a page of a magazine, looked at Miss Allan, who was half asleep, and said humorously, "A penny for your thoughts, Miss Allan."

The others looked up. They were glad that he had not spoken to them. But Miss Allan replied without any hesitation, "I was thinking of my imaginary uncle. Hasn't every one got an imaginary uncle?" she continued. "I have one—a most delightful old gentleman. He's always giving me things. Sometimes it's a gold watch; sometimes it's a carriage and pair; sometimes it's a beautiful little cottage in the New Forest; sometimes it's a ticket to the place I most want to see."

She set them all thinking vaguely of the things they wanted. Mrs. Elliot knew exactly what she wanted; she wanted a child; and the usual little pucker deepened on her brow.

"We're such lucky people," she said, looking at her husband. "We really have no wants." She was apt to say this, partly in order to convince herself, and partly in order to convince other people. But she was prevented from wondering how far she carried conviction by the entrance of Mr. and Mrs. Flushing, who came through the hall and stopped by the chess-board. Mrs. Flushing looked wilder than ever. A great strand of black hair looped down across her brow, her cheeks were whipped a dark blood red, and drops of rain made wet marks upon them.

Mr. Flushing explained that they had been on the roof watching the storm.

"It was a wonderful sight," he said. "The lightning went right out over the sea, and lit up the waves and the ships far away. You can't think how wonderful the mountains looked too, with the lights on them, and the great masses of shadow. It's all over now."

He slid down into a chair, becoming interested in the final struggle of the game.

"And you go back tomorrow?" said Mrs. Thornbury, looking at Mrs. Flushing.

"Yes," she replied.

"And indeed one is not sorry to go back," said Mrs. Elliot, assuming an air of mournful anxiety, "after all this illness."

"Are you afraid of dyin'?" Mrs. Flushing demanded scornfully.

"I think we are all afraid of that," said Mrs. Elliot with dignity.

"I suppose we're all cowards when it comes to the point," said Mrs. Flushing, rubbing her cheek against the back of the chair. "I'm sure I am."

"Not a bit of it!" said Mr. Flushing, turning round, for Mr. Pepper took a very long time to consider his move. "It's not cowardly to wish to live, Alice. It's the very reverse of cowardly. Personally, I'd like to go on for a hundred years—granted, of course, that I had the full use of my faculties. Think of all the things that are bound to happen!"

"That is what I feel," Mrs. Thornbury rejoined. "The changes, the improvements, the inventions—and beauty. D'you know I feel sometimes that I couldn't bear to die and cease to see beautiful things about me?"

"It would certainly be very dull to die before they have discovered whether there is life in Mars," Miss Allan added.

"Do you really believe there's life in Mars?" asked Mrs. Flushing, turning to her for the first time with keen interest. "Who tells you that? Someone who knows? D'you know a man called—?"

Here Mrs. Thornbury laid down her knitting, and a look of extreme solicitude came into her eyes.

"There is Mr. Hirst," she said quietly.

St. John had just come through the swing door. He was rather blown about by the wind, and his cheeks looked terribly pale, unshorn, and cavernous. After taking off his coat he was going to pass straight through the hall and up to his room, but he could not ignore the presence of so many people he knew, especially as Mrs. Thornbury rose and went up to him, holding out her hand. But the shock of the warm lamp-lit room, together with the sight of so many cheerful human beings sitting together at their ease, after the dark walk in the rain, and the long days of strain and horror, overcame him completely. He looked at Mrs. Thornbury and could not speak.

Every one was silent. Mr. Pepper's hand stayed upon his Knight. Mrs. Thornbury somehow moved him to a chair, sat herself beside him, and with tears in her own eyes said gently, "You have done everything for your friend."

Her action set them all talking again as if they had never stopped, and Mr. Pepper finished the move with his Knight.

"There was nothing to be done," said St. John. He spoke very slowly. "It seems impossible—"

He drew his hand across his eyes as if some dream came between him and the others and prevented him from seeing where he was.

"And that poor fellow," said Mrs. Thornbury, the tears falling again down her cheeks.

"Impossible," St. John repeated.

"Did he have the consolation of knowing—?" Mrs. Thornbury began very tentatively.

But St. John made no reply. He lay back in his chair, half-seeing the others, half-hearing what they said. He was terribly tired, and the light and warmth, the movements of the hands, and the soft communicative voices soothed him; they gave him a strange sense of quiet and relief. As he sat there, motionless, this feeling of relief became a feeling of profound happiness. Without any sense of disloyalty to Terence and Rachel he ceased to think about either of them. The movements and the voices seemed to draw together from different parts of the room, and to combine themselves into a pattern before his eyes; he was content to sit silently watching the pattern build itself up, looking at what he hardly saw.

The game was really a good one, and Mr. Pepper and Mr. Elliot were becoming more and more set upon the struggle. Mrs. Thornbury, seeing that St. John did not wish to talk, resumed her knitting.

"Lightning again!" Mrs. Flushing suddenly exclaimed. A yellow light flashed across the blue window, and for a second they saw the green trees outside. She strode to the door, pushed it open, and stood half out in the open air.

But the light was only the reflection of the storm which was over. The rain had ceased, the heavy clouds were blown away, and the air was thin and clear, although vapourish mists were being driven swiftly across the moon.

The sky was once more a deep and solemn blue, and the shape of the earth was visible at the bottom of the air, enormous, dark, and solid, rising into the tapering mass of the mountain, and pricked here and there on the slopes by the tiny lights of villas. The driving air, the drone of the trees, and the flashing light which now and again spread a broad illumination over the earth filled Mrs. Flushing with exultation. Her breasts rose and fell.

"Splendid! Splendid!" she muttered to herself. Then she turned back into the hall and exclaimed in a peremptory voice, "Come outside and see, Wilfrid; it's wonderful."

Some half-stirred; some rose; some dropped their balls of wool and began to stoop to look for them.

"To bed—to bed," said Miss Allan.

"It was the move with your Queen that gave it away, Pepper," exclaimed Mr. Elliot triumphantly, sweeping the pieces together and standing up. He had won the game.

"What? Pepper beaten at last? I congratulate you!" said Arthur Venning, who was wheeling old Mrs. Paley to bed.

All these voices sounded gratefully in St. John's ears as he lay half-asleep, and yet vividly conscious of everything around him. Across his eyes passed a procession of objects, black and indistinct, the figures of people picking up their books, their cards, their balls of wool, their work-baskets, and passing him one after another on their way to bed.

RENASCENCE

Edna St. Vincent Millay

All I could see from where I stood
Was three long mountains and a wood;
I turned and looked another way,
And saw three islands in a bay.
So with my eyes I traced the line
Of the horizon, thin and fine,
Straight around till I was come
Back to where I'd started from;
And all I saw from where I stood
Was three long mountains and a wood.
Over these things I could not see;
These were the things that bounded me;
And I could touch them with my hand,
Almost, I thought, from where I stand.
And all at once things seemed so small
My breath came short, and scarce at all.
But, sure, the sky is big, I said;
Miles and miles above my head;
So here upon my back I'll lie
And look my fill into the sky.
And so I looked, and, after all,
The sky was not so very tall.
The sky, I said, must somewhere stop,
And—sure enough!—I see the top!
The sky, I thought, is not so grand;
I 'most could touch it with my hand!
And reaching up my hand to try,
I screamed to feel it touch the sky.
I screamed, and—lo!—Infinity
Came down and settled over me;
Forced back my scream into my chest,
Bent back my arm upon my breast,
And, pressing of the Undefined
The definition on my mind,

Held up before my eyes a glass
Through which my shrinking sight did pass
Until it seemed I must behold
Immensity made manifold;
Whispered to me a word whose sound
Deafened the air for worlds around,
And brought unmuffled to my ears
The gossiping of friendly spheres,
The creaking of the tented sky,
The ticking of Eternity.
I saw and heard, and knew at last
The How and Why of all things, past,
And present, and forevermore.
The Universe, cleft to the core,
Lay open to my probing sense
That, sick'ning, I would fain pluck thence
But could not,—nay! But needs must suck
At the great wound, and could not pluck
My lips away till I had drawn
All venom out.—Ah, fearful pawn!
For my omniscience paid I toll
In infinite remorse of soul.
All sin was of my sinning, all
Atoning mine, and mine the gall
Of all regret. Mine was the weight
Of every brooded wrong, the hate
That stood behind each envious thrust,
Mine every greed, mine every lust.
And all the while for every grief,
Each suffering, I craved relief
With individual desire,—
Craved all in vain! And felt fierce fire
About a thousand people crawl;
Perished with each,—then mourned for all!
A man was starving in Capri;
He moved his eyes and looked at me;
I felt his gaze, I heard his moan,
And knew his hunger as my own.
I saw at sea a great fog bank
Between two ships that struck and sank;

A thousand screams the heavens smote;
And every scream tore through my throat.
No hurt I did not feel, no death
That was not mine; mine each last breath
That, crying, met an answering cry
From the compassion that was I.
All suffering mine, and mine its rod;
Mine, pity like the pity of God.
Ah, awful weight! Infinity
Pressed down upon the finite Me!
My anguished spirit, like a bird,
Beating against my lips I heard;
Yet lay the weight so close about
There was no room for it without.
And so beneath the weight lay I
And suffered death, but could not die.

Long had I lain thus, craving death,
When quietly the earth beneath
Gave way, and inch by inch, so great
At last had grown the crushing weight,
Into the earth I sank till I
Full six feet under ground did lie,
And sank no more,—there is no weight
Can follow here, however great.
From off my breast I felt it roll,
And as it went my tortured soul
Burst forth and fled in such a gust
That all about me swirled the dust.

Deep in the earth I rested now;
Cool is its hand upon the brow
And soft its breast beneath the head
Of one who is so gladly dead.
And all at once, and over all
The pitying rain began to fall;
I lay and heard each pattering hoof
Upon my lowly, thatched roof,
And seemed to love the sound far more
Than ever I had done before.

For rain it hath a friendly sound
To one who's six feet underground;
And scarce the friendly voice or face:
A grave is such a quiet place.

The rain, I said, is kind to come
And speak to me in my new home.
I would I were alive again
To kiss the fingers of the rain,
To drink into my eyes the shine
Of every slanting silver line,
To catch the freshened, fragrant breeze
From drenched and dripping apple-trees.
For soon the shower will be done,
And then the broad face of the sun
Will laugh above the rain-soaked earth
Until the world with answering mirth
Shakes joyously, and each round drop
Rolls, twinkling, from its grass-blade top.
How can I bear it; buried here,
While overhead the sky grows clear
And blue again after the storm?
O, multi-colored, multiform,
Beloved beauty over me,
That I shall never, never see
Again! Spring-silver, autumn-gold,
That I shall never more behold!
Sleeping your myriad magics through,
Close-sepulchred away from you!
O God, I cried, give me new birth,
And put me back upon the earth!
Upset each cloud's gigantic gourd
And let the heavy rain, down-poured
In one big torrent, set me free,
Washing my grave away from me!

I ceased; and through the breathless hush
That answered me, the far-off rush
Of herald wings came whispering
Like music down the vibrant string

Of my ascending prayer, and—crash!
Before the wild wind's whistling lash
The startled storm-clouds reared on high
And plunged in terror down the sky,
And the big rain in one black wave
Fell from the sky and struck my grave.
I know not how such things can be;
I only know there came to me
A fragrance such as never clings
To aught save happy living things;
A sound as of some joyous elf
Singing sweet songs to please himself,
And, through and over everything,
A sense of glad awakening.
The grass, a-tiptoe at my ear,
Whispering to me I could hear;
I felt the rain's cool finger-tips
Brushed tenderly across my lips,
Laid gently on my sealed sight,
And all at once the heavy night
Fell from my eyes and I could see,—
A drenched and dripping apple-tree,
A last long line of silver rain,
A sky grown clear and blue again.
And as I looked a quickening gust
Of wind blew up to me and thrust
Into my face a miracle
Of orchard-breath, and with the smell,—
I know not how such things can be!—
I breathed my soul back into me.
Ah! Up then from the ground sprang I
And hailed the earth with such a cry
As is not heard save from a man
Who has been dead, and lives again.
About the trees my arms I wound;
Like one gone mad I hugged the ground;
I raised my quivering arms on high;
I laughed and laughed into the sky,
Till at my throat a strangling sob
Caught fiercely, and a great heart-throb

Sent instant tears into my eyes;
O God, I cried, no dark disguise
Can e'er hereafter hide from me
Thy radiant identity!
Thou canst not move across the grass
But my quick eyes will see Thee pass,
Nor speak, however silently,
But my hushed voice will answer Thee.
I know the path that tells Thy way
Through the cool eve of every day;
God, I can push the grass apart
And lay my finger on Thy heart!

The world stands out on either side
No wider than the heart is wide;
Above the world is stretched the sky,—
No higher than the soul is high.
The heart can push the sea and land
Farther away on either hand;
The soul can split the sky in two,
And let the face of God shine through.
But East and West will pinch the heart
That can not keep them pushed apart;
And he whose soul is flat—the sky
Will cave in on him by and by.

XINGU

Edith Wharton

CHAPTER I

Mrs. Ballinger is one of the ladies who pursue Culture in bands, as though it were dangerous to meet alone. To this end she had founded the Lunch Club, an association composed of herself and several other indomitable huntresses of erudition. The Lunch Club, after three or four winters of lunching and debate, had acquired such local distinction that the entertainment of distinguished strangers became one of its accepted functions; in recognition of which it duly extended to the celebrated "Osric Dane," on the day of her arrival in Hillbridge, an invitation to be present at the next meeting.

The club was to meet at Mrs. Ballinger's. The other members, behind her back, were of one voice in deploring her unwillingness to cede her rights in favor of Mrs. Plinth, whose house made a more impressive setting for the entertainment of celebrities; while, as Mrs. Leveret observed, there was always the picture-gallery to fall back on.

Mrs. Plinth made no secret of sharing this view. She had always regarded it as one of her obligations to entertain the Lunch Club's distinguished guests. Mrs. Plinth was almost as proud of her obligations as she was of her picture-gallery; she was in fact fond of implying that the one possession implied the other, and that only a woman of her wealth could afford to live up to a standard as high as that which she had set herself. An all-round sense of duty, roughly adaptable to various ends, was, in her opinion, all that Providence exacted of the more humbly stationed; but the power which had predestined Mrs. Plinth to keep a footman clearly intended her to maintain an equally specialized staff of responsibilities. It was the more to be regretted that Mrs. Ballinger, whose obligations to society were bounded by the narrow scope of two parlour-maids, should have been so tenacious of the right to entertain Osric Dane.

The question of that lady's reception had for a month past profoundly moved the members of the Lunch Club. It was not that they felt themselves unequal to the task, but that their sense of the opportunity plunged them into the agreeable uncertainty of the lady who weighs the alternatives of a well-stocked wardrobe. If such subsidiary members as Mrs. Leveret were fluttered by the thought of exchanging ideas with the author of "The Wings of Death," no forebodings disturbed the conscious adequacy of Mrs. Plinth, Mrs. Ballinger and Miss Van Vluyck. "The Wings of Death" had, in fact, at Miss Van Vluyck's suggestion, been chosen as the subject of discussion at the last club meeting, and each member had thus been enabled to express her own opinion or to appropriate whatever sounded well in the comments of the others.

Mrs. Roby alone had abstained from profiting by the opportunity; but it was now openly recognised that, as a member of the Lunch Club, Mrs. Roby was a failure. "It all comes," as Miss Van Vluyck put it, "of accepting a woman on a man's estimation." Mrs. Roby, returning to Hillbridge from a prolonged sojourn in exotic lands—the other ladies no longer took the trouble to remember where—had been heralded by the distinguished biologist, Professor Foreland, as the most agreeable woman he had ever met; and the members of the Lunch Club, impressed by an encomium that carried the weight of a diploma, and rashly assuming that the Professor's social sympathies would follow the line of his professional bent, had seized the chance of annexing a biological member. Their disillusionment was complete. At Miss Van Vluyck's first off-hand mention of the pterodactyl Mrs. Roby had confusedly murmured: "I know so little about metres—" and after that painful betrayal of incompetence she had prudently withdrawn from farther participation in the mental gymnastics of the club.

"I suppose she flattered him," Miss Van Vluyck summed up—"or else it's the way she does her hair."

The dimensions of Miss Van Vluyck's dining-room having restricted the membership of the club to six, the nonconductiveness of one member was a serious obstacle to the exchange of ideas, and some wonder had already been expressed that Mrs. Roby should care to live, as it were, on the intellectual bounty of the others. This feeling was increased by the discovery that she had not yet read "The Wings of Death." She owned to having heard the name of Osric Dane; but that—incredible as it appeared—was the extent of her acquaintance with the celebrated novelist. The ladies could not conceal their surprise; but Mrs. Ballinger, whose pride in the club made her wish to put even Mrs. Roby in the best possible light, gently insinuated that, though she had not had time to acquaint herself with "The Wings of Death," she must at least be familiar with its equally remarkable predecessor, "The Supreme Instant."

Mrs. Roby wrinkled her sunny brows in a conscientious effort of memory, as a result of which she recalled that, oh, yes, she *had* seen the book at her brother's, when she was staying with him in Brazil, and had even carried it off to read one day on a boating party; but they had all got to shying things at each other in the boat, and the book had gone overboard, so she had never had the chance—

The picture evoked by this anecdote did not increase Mrs. Roby's credit with the club, and there was a painful pause, which was broken by Mrs. Plinth's remarking:

"I can understand that, with all your other pursuits, you should not find much time for reading; but I should have thought you might at least have *got up* 'The Wings of Death' before Osric Dane's arrival."

Mrs. Roby took this rebuke good-humouredly. She had meant, she owned, to glance through the book; but she had been so absorbed in a novel of Trollope's that—

"No one reads Trollope now," Mrs. Ballinger interrupted.

Mrs. Roby looked pained. "I'm only just beginning," she confessed.

"And does he interest you?" Mrs. Plinth enquired.

"He amuses me."

"Amusement," said Mrs. Plinth, "is hardly what I look for in my choice of books."

"Oh, certainly, 'The Wings of Death' is not amusing," ventured Mrs. Leveret, whose manner of putting forth an opinion was like that of an obliging salesman with a variety of other styles to submit if his first selection does not suit.

"Was it *meant* to be?" enquired Mrs. Plinth, who was fond of asking questions that she permitted no one but herself to answer. "Assuredly not."

"Assuredly not—that is what I was going to say," assented Mrs. Leveret, hastily rolling up her opinion and reaching for another. "It was meant to—to elevate."

Miss Van Vluyck adjusted her spectacles as though they were the black cap of condemnation. "I hardly see," she interposed, "how a book steeped in the bitterest pessimism can be said to elevate however much it may instruct."

"I meant, of course, to instruct," said Mrs. Leveret, flurried by the unexpected distinction between two terms which she had supposed to be synonymous. Mrs. Leveret's enjoyment of the Lunch Club was frequently marred by such surprises; and not knowing her own value to the other ladies as a mirror for their mental complacency she was sometimes troubled by a doubt of her worthiness to join in their debates. It was only the fact of having a dull sister who thought her clever that saved her, from a sense of hopeless inferiority.

"Do they get married in the end?" Mrs. Roby interposed.

"They—who?" the Lunch Club collectively exclaimed.

"Why, the girl and man. It's a novel, isn't it? I always think that's the one thing that matters. If they're parted it spoils my dinner."

Mrs. Plinth and Mrs. Ballinger exchanged scandalised glances, and the latter said: "I should hardly advise you to read 'The Wings of Death' in that spirit. For my part, when there are so many books one *has* to read; I wonder how anyone can find time for those that are merely amusing."

"The beautiful part of it," Laura Glyde murmured, "is surely just this—that no one can tell *how* 'The Wings of Death' ends. Osric Dane, overcome by the awful significance of her own meaning, has mercifully veiled it—perhaps even from herself—as Apelles, in representing the sacrifice of Iphigenia, veiled the face of Agamemnon."

"What's that? Is it poetry?" whispered Mrs. Leveret to Mrs. Plinth, who, disdaining a definite reply, said coldly: "You should look it up. I always make it a point to look things up." Her tone added—"though I might easily have it done for me by the footman."

"I was about to say," Miss Van Vluyck resumed, "that it must always be a question whether a book *can* instruct unless it elevates."

"Oh—" murmured Mrs. Leveret, now feeling herself hopelessly astray.

"I don't know," said Mrs. Ballinger, scenting in Miss Van Vluyck's tone a tendency to depreciate the coveted distinction of entertaining Osric Dane; "I don't know that such a question can seriously be raised as to a book which has attracted more attention among thoughtful people than any novel since 'Robert Elsmere.' "

"Oh, but don't you see," exclaimed Laura Glyde, "that it's just the dark hopelessness of it all—the wonderful tone-scheme of black on black—that makes it such an artistic achievement? It reminded me when I read it of Prince Rupert's *manière noire* . . . the book is etched, not painted, yet one feels the colour-values so intensely . . ."

"Who is *he*?" Mrs. Leveret whispered to her neighbour. "Someone she's met abroad?"

"The wonderful part of the book," Mrs. Bellinger conceded, "is that it may be looked at from so many points of view. I hear that as a study of determinism Professor Lupton ranks it with 'The Data of Ethics.'"

"I'm told that Osric Dane spent ten years in preparatory studies before beginning to write it," said Mrs. Plinth. "She looks up everything—verifies everything. It has always been my principle, as you know. Nothing would induce me, now, to put aside a book before I'd finished it, just because I can buy as many more as I want."

"And what do *you* think of 'The Wings of Death'?" Mrs. Roby abruptly asked her.

It was the kind of question that might be termed out of order, and the ladies glanced at each other as though disclaiming any share in such a breach of discipline. They all knew there was nothing Mrs. Plinth so much disliked as being asked her opinion of a book. Books were written to read; if one read them what more could be expected? To be questioned in detail regarding the contents of a volume seemed to her as great an outrage as being searched for smuggled laces at the Custom House. The club had always respected this idiosyncrasy of Mrs. Plinth's. Such opinions as she had were imposing and substantial: her mind, like her house, was furnished with monumental "pieces" that were not meant to be disarranged; and it was one of the unwritten rules of the Lunch Club that, within her own province, each member's habits of thought should be respected. The meeting therefore closed with an increased sense, on the part of the other ladies, of Mrs. Roby's hopeless unfitness to be one of them.

CHAPTER II

Mrs. Leveret, on the eventful day, arrived early at Mrs. Ballinger's, her volume of Appropriate Allusions in her pocket.

It always flustered Mrs. Leveret to be late at the Lunch Club: she liked to collect her thoughts and gather a hint, as the others assembled, of the turn the conversation was likely to take. Today, however, she felt herself completely at a loss; and even the familiar contact of Appropriate Allusions, which stuck into her as she sat down, failed to give her any reassurance. It was an admirable little volume, compiled to meet all the social emergencies; so that, whether on the occasion of Anniversaries, joyful or melancholy (as the classification ran), of Banquets, social or municipal, or of Baptisms, Church of England or sectarian, its student need never be at a loss for a pertinent reference. Mrs. Leveret, though she had for years devoutly conned its pages, valued it, however, rather for its moral support than for its practical services; for though in the privacy of her own room she commanded an army of quotations, these invariably deserted her at the critical moment, and the only phrase she retained—*Canst thou draw out leviathan with a hook?*—was one she had never yet found occasion to apply.

Today she felt that even the complete mastery of the volume would hardly have insured her self-possession; for she thought it probable that, even if she *did*, in some miraculous way, remember an Allusion, it would be only to find that Osric Dane used a different volume (Mrs. Leveret was convinced that literary people always carried them), and would consequently not recognise her quotations.

Mrs. Leveret's sense of being adrift was intensified by the appearance of Mrs. Ballinger's drawing-room. To a careless eye its aspect was unchanged; but those acquainted with Mrs. Ballinger's way of arranging her books would instantly have detected the marks of recent perturbation. Mrs. Ballinger's province, as a member of the Lunch Club, was the Book of the Day. On that, whatever it was, from a novel to a treatise on experimental psychology, she was confidently, authoritatively "up." What became of last year's books, or last week's even; what she did with the "subjects" she had previously professed with equal authority; no one had ever yet discovered. Her mind was an hotel where facts came and went like transient lodgers, without leaving their address behind, and frequently without paying for their board. It was Mrs. Ballinger's boast that she was "abreast with the Thought of the Day," and her pride that this advanced position should be expressed by the books on her table. These volumes, frequently renewed, and almost always damp from the press, bore names generally unfamiliar to Mrs. Leveret, and giving her, as she furtively scanned them, a disheartening glimpse of new fields of knowledge to be breathlessly traversed in Mrs. Ballinger's wake. But to-day a number of maturer-looking volumes were adroitly mingled with the *primeurs* of the press—Karl Marx jostled Professor Bergson, and the "Confessions of St. Augustine" lay beside the last work on "Mendelism"; so that even to Mrs. Leveret's fluttered perceptions it was clear that Mrs. Ballinger didn't in the least know what Osric Dane was likely to talk about, and had taken measures to be prepared for anything. Mrs. Leveret felt like a passenger on an ocean steamer who is told that there is no immediate danger, but that she had better put on her life-belt.

It was a relief to be roused from these forebodings by Miss Van Vluyck's arrival.

"Well, my dear," the new-comer briskly asked her hostess, "what subjects are we to discuss today?"

Mrs. Ballinger was furtively replacing a volume of Wordsworth by a copy of Verlaine. "I hardly know," she said, somewhat nervously. "Perhaps we had better leave that to circumstances."

"Circumstances?" said Miss Van Vluyck drily. "That means, I suppose, that Laura Glyde will take the floor as usual, and we shall be deluged with literature."

Philanthropy and statistics were Miss Van Vluyck's province, and she resented any tendency to divert their guest's attention from these topics.

Mrs. Plinth at this moment appeared.

"Literature?" she protested in a tone of remonstrance. "But this is perfectly unexpected. I understood we were to talk of Osric Dane's novel."

Mrs. Ballinger winced at the discrimination, but let it pass. "We can hardly make that our chief subject—at least not *too* intentionally," she suggested. "Of course we can let our talk *drift* in that direction; but we ought to have some other topic as an introduction, and that is what I wanted to consult you about. The fact is, we know so little of Osric Dane's tastes and interests that it is difficult to make any special preparation."

"It may be difficult," said Mrs. Plinth with decision, "but it is necessary. I know what that happy-go-lucky principle leads to. As I told one of my nieces the other day, there are certain emergencies for which a lady should always be prepared. It's in shocking taste to wear colours when one pays a visit of condolence, or a last year's dress when there are reports that one's husband is on the wrong side of the market; and so it is with conversation. All I ask is that I should know beforehand what is to be talked about; then I feel sure of being able to say the proper thing."

"I quite agree with you," Mrs. Ballinger assented; "but——"

And at that instant, heralded by the fluttered parlourmaid, Osric Dane appeared upon the threshold.

Mrs. Leveret told her sister afterward that she had known at a glance what was coming. She saw that Osric Dane was not going to meet them half way. That distinguished personage had indeed entered with an air of compulsion not calculated to promote the easy exercise of hospitality. She looked as though she were about to be photographed for a new edition of her books.

The desire to propitiate a divinity is generally in inverse ratio to its responsiveness, and the sense of discouragement produced by Osric Dane's entrance visibly increased the Lunch Club's eagerness to please her. Any lingering idea that she might consider herself under an obligation to her entertainers was at once dispelled by her manner: as Mrs. Leveret said afterward to her sister, she had a way of looking at you that made you feel as if there was something wrong with your hat. This evidence of greatness produced such an immediate impression on the ladies that a shudder of awe ran through them when Mrs. Roby, as their hostess led the great personage into the dining-room, turned back to whisper to the others: "What a brute she is!"

The hour about the table did not tend to revise this verdict. It was passed by Osric Dane in the silent deglutition of Mrs. Bollinger's menu, and by the members of the club in the emission of tentative platitudes which their guest seemed to swallow as perfunctorily as the successive courses of the luncheon.

Mrs. Ballinger's reluctance to fix a topic had thrown the club into a mental disarray which increased with the return to the drawing-room, where the actual business of discussion was to open. Each lady waited for the other to speak; and there was a general shock of disappointment when their hostess opened the conversation by the painfully commonplace enquiry. "Is this your first visit to Hillbridge?"

Even Mrs. Leveret was conscious that this was a bad beginning; and a vague impulse of deprecation made Miss Glyde interject: "It is a very small place indeed."

Mrs. Plinth bristled. "We have a great many representative people," she said, in the tone of one who speaks for her order.

Osric Dane turned to her. "What do they represent?" she asked.

Mrs. Plinth's constitutional dislike to being questioned was intensified by her sense of unpreparedness; and her reproachful glance passed the question on to Mrs. Ballinger.

"Why," said that lady, glancing in turn at the other members, "as a community I hope it is not too much to say that we stand for culture."

"For art—" Miss Glyde interjected.

"For art and literature," Mrs. Ballinger emended.

"And for sociology, I trust," snapped Miss Van Vluyck.

"We have a standard," said Mrs. Plinth, feeling herself suddenly secure on the vast expanse of a generalisation; and Mrs. Leveret, thinking there must be room for more than one on so broad a statement, took courage to murmur: "Oh, certainly; we have a standard."

"The object of our little club," Mrs. Ballinger continued, "is to concentrate the highest tendencies of Hillbridge—to centralise and focus its intellectual effort."

This was felt to be so happy that the ladies drew an almost audible breath of relief.

"We aspire," the President went on, "to be in touch with whatever is highest in art, literature and ethics."

Osric Dane again turned to her. "What ethics?" she asked.

A tremor of apprehension encircled the room. None of the ladies required any preparation to pronounce on a question of morals; but when they were called ethics it was different. The club, when fresh from the "Encyclopaedia Britannica," the "Reader's Handbook" or Smith's "Classical Dictionary," could deal confidently with any subject; but when taken unawares it had been known to define agnosticism as a heresy of the Early Church and Professor Froude as a distinguished histologist; and such minor members as Mrs. Leveret still secretly regarded ethics as something vaguely pagan.

Even to Mrs. Ballinger, Osric Dane's question was unsettling, and there was a general sense of gratitude when Laura Glyde leaned forward to say, with her most sympathetic accent: "You must excuse us, Mrs. Dane, for not being able, just at present, to talk of anything but 'The Wings of Death.'"

"Yes," said Miss Van Vluyck, with a sudden resolve to carry the war into the enemy's camp. "We are so anxious to know the exact purpose you had in mind in writing your wonderful book."

"You will find," Mrs. Plinth interposed, "that we are not superficial readers."

"We are eager to hear from you," Miss Van Vluyck continued, "if the pessimistic tendency of the book is an expression of your own convictions or—"

"Or merely," Miss Glyde thrust in, "a sombre background brushed in to throw your figures into more vivid relief. Are you not primarily plastic?"

"*I* have always maintained," Mrs. Ballinger interposed, "that you represent the purely objective method—"

Osric Dane helped herself critically to coffee. "How do you define objective?" she then enquired.

There was a flurried pause before Laura Glyde intensely murmured: "In reading you we don't define, we feel."

Otsric Dane smiled. "The cerebellum," she remarked, "is not infrequently the seat of the literary emotions." And she took a second lump of sugar.

The sting that this remark was vaguely felt to conceal was almost neutralised by the satisfaction of being addressed in such technical language.

"Ah, the cerebellum," said Miss Van Vluyck complacently. "The club took a course in psychology last winter."

"Which psychology?" asked Osric Dane.

There was an agonising pause, during which each member of the club secretly deplored the distressing inefficiency of the others. Only Mrs. Roby went on placidly sipping her chartreuse. At last Mrs. Ballinger said, with an attempt at a high tone: "Well, really, you know, it was last year that we took psychology, and this winter we have been so absorbed in—"

She broke off, nervously trying to recall some of the club's discussions; but her faculties seemed to be paralysed by the petrifying stare of Osric Dane. What *had* the club been absorbed in? Mrs. Ballinger, with a vague purpose of gaining time, repeated slowly: "We've been so intensely absorbed in—"

Mrs. Roby put down her liqueur glass and drew near the group with a smile.

"In Xingu?" she gently prompted.

A thrill ran through the other members. They exchanged confused glances, and then, with one accord, turned a gaze of mingled relief and interrogation on their rescuer. The expression of each denoted a different phase of the same emotion. Mrs. Plinth was the first to compose her features to an air of reassurance: after a moment's hasty adjustment her look almost implied that it was she who had given the word to Mrs. Ballinger.

"Xingu, of course!" exclaimed the latter with her accustomed promptness, while Miss Van Vluyck and Laura Glyde seemed to be plumbing the depths of memory, and Mrs. Leveret, feeling apprehensively for Appropriate Allusions, was somehow reassured by the uncomfortable pressure of its bulk against her person.

Osric Dane's change of countenance was no less striking than that of her entertainers. She too put down her coffee-cup, but with a look of distinct annoyance; she too wore, for a brief moment, what Mrs. Roby afterward described as the look of feeling for something in the back of her head; and before she could dissemble these momentary signs of weakness, Mrs. Roby, turning to her with a deferential smile, had said: "And we've been so hoping that to-day you would tell us just what you think of it."

Osric Dane received the homage of the smile as a matter of course; but the accompanying question obviously embarrassed her, and it became clear to her observers that she was not quick at shifting her facial scenery. It was as though her countenance had so long been set in an expression of unchallenged superiority that the muscles had stiffened, and refused to obey her orders.

"Xingu—" she said, as if seeking in her turn to gain time.

Mrs. Roby continued to press her. "Knowing how engrossing the subject is, you will understand how it happens that the club has let everything else go to the wall for the moment. Since we took up Xingu I might almost say—were it not for your books—that nothing else seems to us worth remembering."

Osric Dane's stern features were darkened rather than lit up by an uneasy smile. "I am glad to hear that you make one exception," she gave out between narrowed lips.

"Oh, of course," Mrs. Roby said prettily; "but as you have shown us that— so very naturally!—you don't care to talk of your own things, we really can't let you off from telling us exactly what you think about Xingu; especially," she added, with a still more persuasive smile, "as some people say that one of your last books was saturated with it."

It was an *it*, then—the assurance sped like fire through the parched minds of the other members. In their eagerness to gain the least little clue to Xingu they almost forgot the joy of assisting at the discomfiture of Mrs. Dane.

The latter reddened nervously under her antagonist's challenge. "May I ask," she faltered out, "to which of my books you refer?"

Mrs. Roby did not falter. "That's just what I want you to tell us; because, though I was present, I didn't actually take part."

"Present at what?" Mrs. Dane took her up; and for an instant the trembling members of the Lunch Club thought that the champion Providence had raised up for them had lost a point. But Mrs. Roby explained herself gaily: "At the discussion, of course. And so we're dreadfully anxious to know just how it was that you went into the Xingu."

There was a portentous pause, a silence so big with incalculable dangers that the members with one accord checked the words on their lips, like soldiers dropping their arms to watch a single combat between their leaders. Then Mrs. Dane gave expression to their inmost dread by saying sharply: "Ah—you say *the* Xingu, do you?"

Mrs. Roby smiled undauntedly. "It *is* a shade pedantic, isn't it? Personally, I always drop the article; but I don't know how the other members feel about it."

The other members looked as though they would willingly have dispensed with this appeal to their opinion, and Mrs. Roby, after a bright glance about the group, went on: "They probably think, as I do, that nothing really matters except the thing itself—except Xingu."

No immediate reply seemed to occur to Mrs. Dane, and Mrs. Ballinger gathered courage to say: "Surely everyone must feel that about Xingu."

Mrs. Plinth came to her support with a heavy murmur of assent, and Laura Glyde sighed out emotionally: "I have known cases where it has changed a whole life."

"It has done me worlds of good," Mrs. Leveret interjected, seeming to herself to remember that she had either taken it or read it the winter before.

"Of course," Mrs. Roby admitted, "the difficulty is that one must give up so much time to it. It's very long."

"I can't imagine," said Miss Van Vluyck, "grudging the time given to such a subject."

"And deep in places," Mrs. Roby pursued; (so then it was a book!) "And it isn't easy to skip."

"I never skip," said Mrs. Plinth dogmatically.

"Ah, it's dangerous to, in Xingu. Even at the start there are places where one can't. One must just wade through."

"I should hardly call it *wading*," said Mrs. Ballinger sarcastically.

Mrs. Roby sent her a look of interest. "Ah—you always found it went swimmingly?"

Mrs. Ballinger hesitated. "Of course there are difficult passages," she conceded.

"Yes; some are not at all clear—even," Mrs. Roby added, "if one is familiar with the original."

"As I suppose you are?" Osric Dane interposed, suddenly fixing her with a look of challenge.

Mrs. Roby met it by a deprecating gesture. "Oh, it's really not difficult up to a certain point; though some of the branches are very little known, and it's almost impossible to get at the source."

"Have you ever tried?" Mrs. Plinth enquired, still distrustful of Mrs. Roby's thoroughness.

Mrs. Roby was silent for a moment; then she replied with lowered lids: "No—but a friend of mine did; a very brilliant man; and he told me it was best for women—not to . . ."

A shudder ran around the room. Mrs. Leveret coughed so that the parlour-maid, who was handing the cigarettes, should not hear; Miss Van Vluyck's face took on a nauseated expression, and Mrs. Plinth looked as if she were passing someone she did not care to bow to. But the most remarkable result of Mrs. Roby's words was the effect they produced on the Lunch Club's distinguished guest. Osric Dane's impassive features suddenly softened to an expression of the warmest human sympathy, and edging her chair toward Mrs. Roby's she asked: "Did he really? And—did you find he was right?"

Mrs. Ballinger, in whom annoyance at Mrs. Roby's unwonted assumption of prominence was beginning to displace gratitude for the aid she had rendered, could not consent to her being allowed, by such dubious means, to monopolise the attention of their guest. If Osric Dane had not enough self-respect to resent Mrs. Roby's flippancy, at least the Lunch Club would do so in the person of its President.

Mrs. Ballinger laid her hand on Mrs. Roby's arm. "We must not forget," she said with a frigid amiability, "that absorbing as Xingu is to *us*, it may be less interesting to—"

"Oh, no, on the contrary, I assure you," Osric Dane intervened.

"—to others," Mrs. Ballinger finished firmly; "and we must not allow our little meeting to end without persuading Mrs. Dane to say a few words to us on a subject which, today, is much more present in all our thoughts. I refer, of course, to 'The Wings of Death.' "

The other members, animated by various degrees of the same sentiment, and encouraged by the humanised mien of their redoubtable guest, repeated after Mrs. Ballinger: "Oh, yes, you really *must* talk to us a little about your book."

Osric Dane's expression became as bored, though not as haughty, as when her work had been previously mentioned. But before she could respond to Mrs. Ballinger's request, Mrs. Roby had risen from her seat, and was pulling down her veil over her frivolous nose.

"I'm so sorry," she said, advancing toward her hostess with outstretched hand, "but before Mrs. Dane begins I think I'd better run away. Unluckily, as you know, I haven't read her books, so I should be at a terrible disadvantage among you all, and besides, I've an engagement to play bridge."

If Mrs. Roby had simply pleaded her ignorance of Osric Dane's works as a reason for withdrawing, the Lunch Club, in view of her recent prowess, might have approved such evidence of discretion; but to couple this excuse with the brazen announcement that she was foregoing the privilege for the purpose of joining a bridge-party was only one more instance of her deplorable lack of discrimination.

The ladies were disposed, however, to feel that her departure—now that she had performed the sole service she was ever likely to render them—would probably make for greater order and dignity in the impending discussion, besides relieving them of the sense of self-distrust which her presence always mysteriously produced. Mrs. Ballinger therefore restricted herself to a formal murmur of regret, and the other members were just grouping themselves comfortably about Osric Dane when the latter, to their dismay, started up from the sofa on which she had been seated.

"Oh wait—do wait, and I'll go with you!" she called out to Mrs. Roby; and, seizing the hands of the disconcerted members, she administered a series of farewell pressures with the mechanical haste of a railway-conductor punching tickets.

"I'm so sorry—I'd quite forgotten—" she flung back at them from the threshold; and as she joined Mrs. Roby, who had turned in surprise at her appeal, the other ladies had the mortification of hearing her say, in a voice which she did not take the pains to lower: "If you'll let me walk a little way with you, I should so like to ask you a few more questions about Xingu . . ."

CHAPTER III

The incident had been so rapid that the door closed on the departing pair before the other members had time to understand what was happening. Then a sense of the indignity put upon them by Osric Dane's unceremonious desertion began to contend with the confused feeling that they had been cheated out of their due without exactly knowing how or why.

There was a silence, during which Mrs. Ballinger, with a perfunctory hand, rearranged the skilfully grouped literature at which her distinguished guest had not so much as glanced; then Miss Van Vluyck tartly pronounced: "Well, I can't say that I consider Osric Dane's departure a great loss."

This confession crystallised the resentment of the other members, and Mrs. Leveret exclaimed: "I do believe she came on purpose to be nasty!"

It was Mrs. Plinth's private opinion that Osric Dane's attitude toward the Lunch Club might have been very different had it welcomed her in the majestic setting of the Plinth drawing-rooms; but not liking to reflect on the inadequacy of Mrs. Ballinger's establishment she sought a roundabout satisfaction in depreciating her lack of foresight.

"I said from the first that we ought to have had a subject ready. It's what always happens when you're unprepared. Now if we'd only got up Xingu—"

The slowness of Mrs. Plinth's mental processes was always allowed for by the club; but this instance of it was too much for Mrs. Ballinger's equanimity.

"Xingu!" she scoffed. "Why, it was the fact of our knowing so much more about it than she did—unprepared though we were—that made Osric Dane so furious. I should have thought that was plain enough to everybody!"

This retort impressed even Mrs. Plinth, and Laura Glyde, moved by an impulse of generosity, said: "Yes, we really ought to be grateful to Mrs. Roby for introducing the topic. It may have made Osric Dane furious, but at least it made her civil."

"I am glad we were able to show her," added Miss Van Vluyck, "that a broad and up-to-date culture is not confined to the great intellectual centres."

This increased the satisfaction of the other members, and they began to forget their wrath against Osric Dane in the pleasure of having contributed to her discomfiture.

Miss Van Vluyck thoughtfully rubbed her spectacles. "What surprised me most," she continued, "was that Fanny Roby should be so up on Xingu."

This remark threw a slight chill on the company, but Mrs. Ballinger said with an air of indulgent irony: "Mrs. Roby always has the knack of making a little go a long way; still, we certainly owe her a debt for happening to remember that she'd heard of Xingu." And this was felt by the other members to be a graceful way of cancelling once for all the club's obligation to Mrs. Roby.

Even Mrs. Leveret took courage to speed a timid shaft of irony. "I fancy Osric Dane hardly expected to take a lesson in Xingu at Hillbridge!"

Mrs. Ballinger smiled. "When she asked me what we represented—do you remember? I wish I'd simply said we represented Xingu!"

All the ladies laughed appreciatively at this sally, except Mrs. Plinth, who said, after a moment's deliberation: "I'm not sure it would have been wise to do so."

Mrs. Ballinger, who was already beginning to feel as if she had launched at Osric Dane the retort which had just occurred to her, turned ironically on Mrs. Plinth. "May I ask why?" she enquired.

Mrs. Plinth looked grave. "Surely," she said, "I understood from Mrs. Roby herself that the subject was one it was as well not to go into too deeply?"

Miss Van Vluyck rejoined with precision: "I think that applied only to an investigation of the origin of the—of the—" and suddenly she found that her usually accurate memory had failed her. "It's a part of the subject I never studied myself," she concluded.

"Nor I," said Mrs. Ballinger.

Laura Glyde bent toward them with widened eyes. "And yet it seems—doesn't it?—the part that is fullest of an esoteric fascination?"

"I don't know on what you base that," said Miss Van Vluyck argumentatively.

"Well, didn't you notice how intensely interested Osric Dane became as soon as she heard what the brilliant foreigner—he *was* a foreigner, wasn't he?—had told Mrs. Roby about the origin—the origin of the rite—or whatever you call it?"

Mrs. Plinth looked disapproving, and Mrs. Ballinger visibly wavered. Then she said: "It may not be desirable to touch on the—on that part of the subject in general conversation; but, from the importance it evidently has to a woman of Osric Dane's distinction, I feel as if we ought not to be afraid to discuss it among ourselves—without gloves—though with closed doors, if necessary."

"I'm quite of your opinion," Miss Van Vluyck came briskly to her support; "on condition, that is, that all grossness of language is avoided."

"Oh, I'm sure we shall understand without that," Mrs. Leveret tittered; and Laura Glyde added significantly: "I fancy we can read between the lines," while Mrs. Ballinger rose to assure herself that the doors were really closed.

Mrs. Plinth had not yet given her adhesion. "I hardly see," she began, "what benefit is to be derived from investigating such peculiar customs—"

But Mrs. Ballinger's patience had reached the extreme limit of tension. "This at least," she returned; "that we shall not be placed again in the humiliating position of finding ourselves less up on our own subjects than Fanny Roby!"

Even to Mrs. Plinth this argument was conclusive. She peered furtively about the room and lowered her commanding tones to ask: "Have you got a copy?"

"A—a copy?" stammered Mrs. Ballinger. She was aware that the other members were looking at her expectantly, and that this answer was inadequate, so she supported it by asking another question. "A copy of what?"

Her companions bent their expectant gaze on Mrs. Plinth, who, in turn, appeared less sure of herself than usual. "Why, of—of—the book," she explained.

"What book?" snapped Miss Van Vluyck, almost as sharply as Osric Dane.

Mrs. Ballinger looked at Laura Glyde, whose eyes were interrogatively fixed on Mrs. Leveret. The fact of being deferred to was so new to the latter that it filled her with an insane temerity. "Why, Xingu, of course!" she exclaimed.

A profound silence followed this challenge to the resources of Mrs. Ballinger's library, and the latter, after glancing nervously toward the Books of the Day, returned with dignity: "It's not a thing one cares to leave about."

"I should think *not!*" exclaimed Mrs. Plinth.

"It *is* a book, then?" said Miss Van Vluyck.

This again threw the company into disarray, and Mrs. Ballinger, with an impatient sigh, rejoined: "Why—there *is* a book—naturally . . ."

"Then why did Miss Glyde call it a religion?"

Laura Glyde started up. "A religion? I never—"

"Yes, you did," Miss Van Vluyck insisted; "you spoke of rites; and Mrs. Plinth said it was a custom."

Miss Glyde was evidently making a desperate effort to recall her statement; but accuracy of detail was not her strongest point. At length she began in a deep murmur: "Surely they used to do something of the kind at the Eleusinian mysteries—"

"Oh—" said Miss Van Vluyck, on the verge of disapproval; and Mrs. Plinth protested: "I understood there was to be no indelicacy!"

Mrs. Ballinger could not control her irritation. "Really, it is too bad that we should not be able to talk the matter over quietly among ourselves. Personally, I think that if one goes into Xingu at all—"

"Oh, so do I!" cried Miss Glyde.

"And I don't see how one can avoid doing so, if one wishes to keep up with the Thought of the Day—"

Mrs. Leveret uttered an exclamation of relief. "There—that's it!" she interposed.

"What's it?" the President took her up.

"Why—it's a—a Thought: I mean a philosophy."

This seemed to bring a certain relief to Mrs. Ballinger and Laura Glyde, but Miss Van Vluyck said: "Excuse me if I tell you that you're all mistaken. Xingu happens to be a language."

"A language!" the Lunch Club cried.

"Certainly. Don't you remember Fanny Roby's saying that there were several branches, and that some were hard to trace? What could that apply to but dialects?"

Mrs. Ballinger could no longer restrain a contemptuous laugh. "Really, if the Lunch Club has reached such a pass that it has to go to Fanny Roby for instruction on a subject like Xingu, it had almost better cease to exist!"

"It's really her fault for not being clearer," Laura Glyde put in.

"Oh, clearness and Fanny Roby!" Mrs. Ballinger shrugged. "I daresay we shall find she was mistaken on almost every point."

"Why not look it up?" said Mrs. Plinth.

As a rule this recurrent suggestion of Mrs. Plinth's was ignored in the heat of discussion, and only resorted to afterward in the privacy of each member's home. But on the present occasion the desire to ascribe their own confusion of thought to the vague and contradictory nature of Mrs. Roby's statements caused the members of the Lunch Club to utter a collective demand for a book of reference.

At this point the production of her treasured volume gave Mrs. Leveret, for a moment, the unusual experience of occupying the centre front; but she was not able to hold it long, for Appropriate Allusions contained no mention of Xingu.

"Oh, that's not the kind of thing we want!" exclaimed Miss Van Vluyck. She cast a disparaging glance over Mrs. Ballinger's assortment of literature, and added impatiently: "Haven't you any useful books?"

"Of course I have," replied Mrs. Ballinger indignantly; "I keep them in my husband's dressing-room."

From this region, after some difficulty and delay, the parlour-maid produced the W–Z volume of an Encyclopaedia and, in deference to the fact that the demand for it had come from Miss Van Vluyck, laid the ponderous tome before her.

There was a moment of painful suspense while Miss Van Vluyck rubbed her spectacles, adjusted them, and turned to Z; and a murmur of surprise when she said: "It isn't here."

"I suppose," said Mrs. Plinth, "it's not fit to be put in a book of reference."

"Oh, nonsense!" exclaimed Mrs. Ballinger. "Try X."

Miss Van Vluyck turned back through the volume, peering short-sightedly up and down the pages, till she came to a stop and remained motionless, like a dog on a point.

"Well, have you found it?" Mrs. Ballinger enquired after a considerable delay.

"Yes. I've found it," said Miss Van Vluyck in a queer voice.

Mrs. Plinth hastily interposed: "I beg you won't read it aloud if there's anything offensive."

Miss Van Vluyck, without answering, continued her silent scrutiny.

"Well, what *is* it?" exclaimed Laura Glyde excitedly.

"*Do* tell us!" urged Mrs. Leveret, feeling that she would have something awful to tell her sister.

Miss Van Vluyck pushed the volume aside and turned slowly toward the expectant group.

"It's a river."

"A *river?*"

"Yes: in Brazil. Isn't that where she's been living?"

"Who? Fanny Roby? Oh, but you must be mistaken. You've been reading the wrong thing," Mrs. Ballinger exclaimed, leaning over her to seize the volume.

"It's the only *Xingu* in the Encyclopaedia; and she has been living in Brazil," Miss Van Vluyck persisted.

"Yes: her brother has a consulship there," Mrs. Leveret interposed.

"But it's too ridiculous! I—we—why we *all* remember studying Xingu last year—or the year before last," Mrs. Ballinger stammered.

"I thought I did when *you* said so," Laura Glyde avowed.

"*I* said so?" cried Mrs. Ballinger.

"Yes. You said it had crowded everything else out of your mind."

"Well *you* said it had changed your whole life!"

"For that matter. Miss Van Vluyck said she had never grudged the time she'd given it."

Mrs. Plinth interposed: "I made it clear that I knew nothing whatever of the original."

Mrs. Ballinger broke off the dispute with a groan. "Oh, what does it all matter if she's been making fools of us? I believe Miss Van Vluyck's right— she was talking of the river all the while!"

"How could she? It's too preposterous," Miss Glyde exclaimed.

"Listen." Miss Van Vluyck had repossessed herself of the Encyclopaedia, and restored her spectacles to a nose reddened by excitement. "'The Xingu, one of the principal rivers of Brazil, rises on the plateau of Mato Grosso, and flows in a northerly direction for a length of no less than one thousand one hundred and eighteen miles, entering the Amazon near the mouth of the latter river. The upper course of the Xingu is auriferous and fed by numerous branches. Its source was first discovered in 1884 by the German explorer von den Steinen, after a difficult and dangerous expedition through a region inhabited by tribes still in the Stone Age of culture.'"

The ladies received this communication in a state of stupefied silence from which Mrs. Leveret was the first to rally. "She certainly *did* speak of its having branches."

The word seemed to snap the last thread of their incredulity. "And of its great length," gasped Mrs. Ballinger.

"She said it was awfully deep, and you couldn't skip—you just had to wade through," Miss Glyde added.

The idea worked its way more slowly through Mrs. Plinth's compact resistances. "How could there be anything improper about a river?" she enquired.

"Improper?"

"Why, what she said about the source—that it was corrupt?"

"Not corrupt, but hard to get at," Laura Glyde corrected. "Someone who'd been there had told her so. I daresay it was the explorer himself—doesn't it say the expedition was dangerous?"

" 'Difficult and dangerous,' " read Miss Van Vluyck.

Mrs. Ballinger pressed her hands to her throbbing temples. "There's nothing she said that wouldn't apply to a river—to this river!" She swung about excitedly to the other members. "Why, do you remember her telling us that she hadn't read 'The Supreme Instant' because she'd taken it on a boating party while she was staying with her brother, and someone had 'shied' it overboard—'shied' of course was her own expression."

The ladies breathlessly signified that the expression had not escaped them.

"Well—and then didn't she tell Osric Dane that one of her books was simply saturated with Xingu? Of course it was, if one of Mrs. Roby's rowdy friends had thrown it into the river!"

This surprising reconstruction of the scene in which they had just participated left the members of the Lunch Club inarticulate. At length, Mrs.

Plinth, after visibly labouring with the problem, said in a heavy tone: "Osric Dane was taken in too."

Mrs. Leveret took courage at this. "Perhaps that's what Mrs. Roby did it for. She said Osric Dane was a brute, and she may have wanted to give her a lesson."

Miss Van Vluyck frowned. "It was hardly worth while to do it at our expense."

"At least," said Miss Glyde with a touch of bitterness, "she succeeded in interesting her, which was more than we did."

"What chance had we?" rejoined Mrs. Ballinger.

"Mrs. Roby monopolised her from the first. And that, I've no doubt, was her purpose—to give Osric Dane a false impression of her own standing in the club. She would hesitate at nothing to attract attention: we all know how she took in poor Professor Foreland."

"She actually makes him give bridge-teas every Thursday," Mrs. Leveret piped up.

Laura Glyde struck her hands together. "Why, this is Thursday, and it's *there* she's gone, of course; and taken Osric with her!"

"And they're shrieking over us at this moment," said Mrs. Ballinger between her teeth.

This possibility seemed too preposterous to be admitted. "She would hardly dare," said Miss Van Vluyck, "confess the imposture to Osric Dane."

"I'm not so sure: I thought I saw her make a sign as she left. If she hadn't made a sign, why should Osric Dane have rushed out after her?"

"Well, you know, we'd all been telling her how wonderful Xingu was, and she said she wanted to find out more about it," Mrs. Leveret said, with a tardy impulse of justice to the absent.

This reminder, far from mitigating the wrath of the other members, gave it a stronger impetus.

"Yes—and that's exactly what they're both laughing over now," said Laura Glyde ironically.

Mrs. Plinth stood up and gathered her expensive furs about her monumental form. "I have no wish to criticise," she said; "but unless the Lunch Club can protect its members against the recurrence of such—such unbecoming scenes, I for one—"

"Oh, so do I!" agreed Miss Glyde, rising also.

Miss Van Vluyck closed the Encyclopaedia and proceeded to button herself into her jacket "My time is really too valuable—" she began.

"I fancy we are all of one mind," said Mrs. Ballinger, looking searchingly at Mrs. Leveret, who looked at the others.

"I always deprecate anything like a scandal—" Mrs. Plinth continued.

"She has been the cause of one today!" exclaimed Miss Glyde.

Mrs. Leveret moaned: "I don't see how she could!" and Miss Van Vluyck said, picking up her notebook: "Some women stop at nothing."

"—but if," Mrs. Plinth took up her argument impressively, "anything of the kind had happened in my house" (it never would have, her tone implied), "I should have felt that I owed it to myself either to ask for Mrs. Roby's resignation—or to offer mine."

"Oh, Mrs. Plinth—" gasped the Lunch Club.

"Fortunately for me," Mrs. Plinth continued with an awful magnanimity, "the matter was taken out of my hands by our President's decision that the right to entertain distinguished guests was a privilege vested in her office; and I think the other members will agree that, as she was alone in this opinion, she ought to be alone in deciding on the best way of effacing its—its really deplorable consequences."

A deep silence followed this outbreak of Mrs. Plinth's long-stored resentment.

"I don't see why *I* should be expected to ask her to resign—" Mrs. Ballinger at length began; but Laura Glyde turned back to remind her: "You know she made you say that you'd got on swimmingly in Xingu."

An ill-timed giggle escaped from Mrs. Leveret, and Mrs. Ballinger energetically continued "—but you needn't think for a moment that I'm afraid to!"

The door of the drawing-room closed on the retreating backs of the Lunch Club, and the President of that distinguished association, seating herself at her writing-table, and pushing away a copy of "The Wings of Death" to make room for her elbow, drew forth a sheet of the club's note-paper, on which she began to write: "My dear Mrs. Roby—"

PATTERNS

Amy Lowell

I walk down the garden-paths,
And all the daffodils
Are blowing, and the bright blue squills.
I walk down the patterned garden-paths
In my stiff, brocaded gown.
With my powdered hair and jewelled fan,
I too am a rare
Pattern. As I wander down
The garden-paths.

My dress is richly figured,
And the train
Makes a pink and silver stain
On the gravel, and the thrift
Of the borders.
Just a plate of current fashion,
Tripping by in high-heeled, ribboned shoes.
Not a softness anywhere about me,
Only whalebone and brocade.
And I sink on a seat in the shade
Of a lime-tree. For my passion
Wars against the stiff brocade.
The daffodils and squills
Flutter in the breeze
As they please.
And I weep;
For the lime-tree is in blossom
And one small flower has dropped upon
    my bosom.

And the plashing of waterdrops
In the marble fountain
Comes down the garden-paths.
The dripping never stops.
Underneath my stiffened gown

Is the softness of a woman bathing in a
    marble basin,
A basin in the midst of hedges grown
So thick, she cannot see her lover hiding,
But she guesses he is near,
And the sliding of the water
Seems the stroking of a dear
Hand upon her.
What is Summer in a fine brocaded gown!
I should like to see it lying in a heap upon
    the ground.
All the pink and silver crumpled up on the
    ground.

I would be the pink and silver as I ran along
    the paths,
And he would stumble after,
Bewildered by my laughter.
I should see the sun flashing from his sword-hilt
    and the buckles on his shoes.
I would choose
To lead him in a maze along the patterned paths,
A bright and laughing maze for my heavy-booted
    lover,
Till he caught me in the shade,
And the buttons of his waistcoat bruised my body
    as he clasped me,
Aching, melting, unafraid.
With the shadows of the leaves and the sundrops,
And the plopping of the waterdrops,
All about us in the open afternoon—
I am very like to swoon
With the weight of this brocade,
For the sun sifts through the shade.

Underneath the fallen blossom
In my bosom,
Is a letter I have hid.
It was brought to me this morning by a rider from
    the Duke.
"Madam, we regret to inform you that Lord Hartwell

Died in action Thursday se'nnight."
As I read it in the white, morning sunlight,
The letters squirmed like snakes.
"Any answer, Madam," said my footman.
"No," I told him.
"See that the messenger takes some refreshment.
No, no answer."
And I walked into the garden,
Up and down the patterned paths,
In my stiff, correct brocade.
The blue and yellow flowers stood up proudly in
    the sun,
Each one.
I stood upright too,
Held rigid to the pattern
By the stiffness of my gown.
Up and down I walked,
Up and down.

In a month he would have been my husband.
In a month, here, underneath this lime,
We would have broke the pattern;
He for me, and I for him,
He as Colonel, I as Lady,
On this shady seat.
He had a whim
That sunlight carried blessing.
And I answered, "It shall be as you have said."
Now he is dead.

In Summer and in Winter I shall walk
Up and down
The patterned garden-paths
In my stiff, brocaded gown.
The squills and daffodils
Will give place to pillared roses, and to asters, and
    to snow.
I shall go
Up and down,
In my gown.
Gorgeously arrayed,

Boned and stayed.
And the softness of my body will be guarded
 from embrace
By each button, hook, and lace.
For the man who should loose me is dead,
Fighting with the Duke in Flanders,
In a pattern called a war.
Christ! What are patterns for?

THE GARDEN PARTY

Katherine Mansfield

And after all the weather was ideal. They could not have had a more perfect day for a garden-party if they had ordered it. Windless, warm, the sky without a cloud. Only the blue was veiled with a haze of light gold, as it is sometimes in early summer. The gardener had been up since dawn, mowing the lawns and sweeping them, until the grass and the dark flat rosettes where the daisy plants had been seemed to shine. As for the roses, you could not help feeling they understood that roses are the only flowers that impress people at garden-parties; the only flowers that everybody is certain of knowing. Hundreds, yes, literally hundreds, had come out in a single night; the green bushes bowed down as though they had been visited by archangels.

Breakfast was not yet over before the men came to put up the marquee.

"Where do you want the marquee put, mother?"

"My dear child, it's no use asking me. I'm determined to leave everything to you children this year. Forget I am your mother. Treat me as an honoured guest."

But Meg could not possibly go and supervise the men. She had washed her hair before breakfast, and she sat drinking her coffee in a green turban, with a dark wet curl stamped on each cheek. Jose, the butterfly, always came down in a silk petticoat and a kimono jacket.

"You'll have to go, Laura; you're the artistic one."

Away Laura flew, still holding her piece of bread-and-butter. It's so delicious to have an excuse for eating out of doors, and besides, she loved having to arrange things; she always felt she could do it so much better than anybody else.

Four men in their shirt-sleeves stood grouped together on the garden path. They carried staves covered with rolls of canvas, and they had big tool-bags slung on their backs. They looked impressive. Laura wished now that she had not got the bread-and-butter, but there was nowhere to put it, and she couldn't possibly throw it away. She blushed and tried to look severe and even a little bit short-sighted as she came up to them.

"Good morning," she said, copying her mother's voice. But that sounded so fearfully affected that she was ashamed, and stammered like a little girl, "Oh—er—have you come—is it about the marquee?"

"That's right, miss," said the tallest of the men, a lanky, freckled fellow, and he shifted his tool-bag, knocked back his straw hat and smiled down at her. "That's about it."

His smile was so easy, so friendly that Laura recovered. What nice eyes he had, small, but such a dark blue! And now she looked at the others, they were smiling too. "Cheer up, we won't bite," their smile seemed to say. How very nice workmen were! And what a beautiful morning! She mustn't mention the morning; she must be business-like. The marquee.

"Well, what about the lily-lawn? Would that do?"

And she pointed to the lily-lawn with the hand that didn't hold the bread-and-butter. They turned, they stared in the direction. A little fat chap thrust out his under-lip, and the tall fellow frowned.

"I don't fancy it," said he. "Not conspicuous enough. You see, with a thing like a marquee," and he turned to Laura in his easy way, "you want to put it somewhere where it'll give you a bang slap in the eye, if you follow me."

Laura's upbringing made her wonder for a moment whether it was quite respectful of a workman to talk to her of bangs slap in the eye. But she did quite follow him.

"A corner of the tennis-court," she suggested. "But the band's going to be in one corner."

"H'm, going to have a band, are you?" said another of the workmen. He was pale. He had a haggard look as his dark eyes scanned the tennis-court. What was he thinking?

"Only a very small band," said Laura gently. Perhaps he wouldn't mind so much if the band was quite small. But the tall fellow interrupted.

"Look here, miss, that's the place. Against those trees. Over there. That'll do fine."

Against the karakas. Then the karaka-trees would be hidden. And they were so lovely, with their broad, gleaming leaves, and their clusters of yellow fruit. They were like trees you imagined growing on a desert island, proud, solitary, lifting their leaves and fruits to the sun in a kind of silent splendour. Must they be hidden by a marquee?

They must. Already the men had shouldered their staves and were making for the place. Only the tall fellow was left. He bent down, pinched a sprig of lavender, put his thumb and forefinger to his nose and snuffed up the smell. When Laura saw that gesture she forgot all about the karakas in her wonder at him caring for things like that—caring for the smell of lavender. How many men that she knew would have done such a thing? Oh, how extraordinarily nice workmen were, she thought. Why couldn't she have workmen for her friends rather than the silly boys she danced with and who came to Sunday night supper? She would get on much better with men like these.

It's all the fault, she decided, as the tall fellow drew something on the back of an envelope, something that was to be looped up or left to hang, of these absurd class distinctions. Well, for her part, she didn't feel them. Not a bit, not an atom . . . And now there came the chock-chock of wooden hammers. Someone whistled, someone sang out, "Are you right there, matey?" "Matey!" The friendliness of it, the—the—Just to prove how happy she was, just to show the tall fellow how at home she felt, and how she despised stupid conventions, Laura took a big bite of her bread-and-butter as she stared at the little drawing. She felt just like a work-girl.

"Laura, Laura, where are you? Telephone, Laura!" a voice cried from the house.

"Coming!" Away she skimmed, over the lawn, up the path, up the steps, across the veranda, and into the porch. In the hall her father and Laurie were brushing their hats ready to go to the office.

"I say, Laura," said Laurie very fast, "you might just give a squiz at my coat before this afternoon. See if it wants pressing."

"I will," said she. Suddenly she couldn't stop herself. She ran at Laurie and gave him a small, quick squeeze. "Oh, I do love parties, don't you?" gasped Laura.

"Ra-ther," said Laurie's warm, boyish voice, and he squeezed his sister too, and gave her a gentle push. "Dash off to the telephone, old girl."

The telephone. "Yes, yes; oh yes. Kitty? Good morning, dear. Come to lunch? Do, dear. Delighted of course. It will only be a very scratch meal— just the sandwich crusts and broken meringue-shells and what's left over. Yes, isn't it a perfect morning? Your white? Oh, I certainly should. One moment— hold the line. Mother's calling." And Laura sat back. "What, mother? Can't hear."

Mrs. Sheridan's voice floated down the stairs. "Tell her to wear that sweet hat she had on last Sunday."

"Mother says you're to wear that *sweet* hat you had on last Sunday. Good. One o'clock. Bye-bye."

Laura put back the receiver, flung her arms over her head, took a deep breath, stretched and let them fall. "Huh," she sighed, and the moment after the sigh she sat up quickly. She was still, listening. All the doors in the house seemed to be open. The house was alive with soft, quick steps and running voices. The green baize door that led to the kitchen regions swung open and shut with a muffled thud. And now there came a long, chuckling absurd sound. It was the heavy piano being moved on its stiff castors. But the air! If you stopped to notice, was the air always like this? Little faint winds were playing chase, in at the tops of the windows, out at the doors. And there were two tiny spots of sun, one on the inkpot, one on a silver photograph frame, playing too. Darling little spots. Especially the one on the inkpot lid. It was quite warm. A warm little silver star. She could have kissed it.

The front door bell pealed, and there sounded the rustle of Sadie's print skirt on the stairs. A man's voice murmured; Sadie answered, careless, "I'm sure I don't know. Wait. I'll ask Mrs Sheridan."

"What is it, Sadie?" Laura came into the hall.

"It's the florist, Miss Laura."

It was, indeed. There, just inside the door, stood a wide, shallow tray full of pots of pink lilies. No other kind. Nothing but lilies—canna lilies, big pink flowers, wide open, radiant, almost frighteningly alive on bright crimson stems.

"O-oh, Sadie!" said Laura, and the sound was like a little moan. She crouched down as if to warm herself at that blaze of lilies; she felt they were in her fingers, on her lips, growing in her breast.

"It's some mistake," she said faintly. "Nobody ever ordered so many. Sadie, go and find mother."

But at that moment Mrs. Sheridan joined them.

"It's quite right," she said calmly. "Yes, I ordered them. Aren't they lovely?" She pressed Laura's arm. "I was passing the shop yesterday, and I saw them in the window. And I suddenly thought for once in my life I shall have enough canna lilies. The garden-party will be a good excuse."

"But I thought you said you didn't mean to interfere," said Laura. Sadie had gone. The florist's man was still outside at his van. She put her arm round her mother's neck and gently, very gently, she bit her mother's ear.

"My darling child, you wouldn't like a logical mother, would you? Don't do that. Here's the man."

He carried more lilies still, another whole tray.

"Bank them up, just inside the door, on both sides of the porch, please," said Mrs. Sheridan. "Don't you agree, Laura?"

"Oh, I *do*, mother."

In the drawing-room Meg, Jose and good little Hans had at last succeeded in moving the piano.

"Now, if we put this chesterfield against the wall and move everything out of the room except the chairs, don't you think?"

"Quite."

"Hans, move these tables into the smoking-room, and bring a sweeper to take these marks off the carpet and—one moment, Hans—" Jose loved giving orders to the servants, and they loved obeying her. She always made them feel they were taking part in some drama. "Tell mother and Miss Laura to come here at once.

"Very good, Miss Jose."

She turned to Meg. "I want to hear what the piano sounds like, just in case I'm asked to sing this afternoon. Let's try over 'This life is Weary.'"

Pom! Ta-ta-ta *Tee*-ta! The piano burst out so passionately that Jose's face changed. She clasped her hands. She looked mournfully and enigmatically at her mother and Laura as they came in.

> This Life is *Wee*-ary,
> A Tear—a Sigh.
> A Love that *Chan*-ges,
> This Life is *Wee*-ary,
> A Tear—a Sigh.
> A Love that *Chan*-ges,
> And then . . . Good-bye!

But at the word "Good-bye," and although the piano sounded more desperate than ever, her face broke into a brilliant, dreadfully unsympathetic smile.

"Aren't I in good voice, mummy?" she beamed.

> This Life is *Wee*-ary,
> Hope comes to Die.
> A Dream—a *Wa*-kening.

But now Sadie interrupted them. "What is it, Sadie?"

"If you please, m'm, cook says have you got the flags for the sandwiches?"

"The flags for the sandwiches, Sadie?" echoed Mrs. Sheridan dreamily. And the children knew by her face that she hadn't got them. "Let me see." And she said to Sadie firmly, "Tell cook I'll let her have them in ten minutes."

Sadie went.

"Now, Laura," said her mother quickly, "come with me into the smoking-room. I've got the names somewhere on the back of an envelope. You'll have to write them out for me. Meg, go upstairs this minute and take that wet thing off your head. Jose, run and finish dressing this instant. Do you hear me, children, or shall I have to tell your father when he comes home to-night? And—and, Jose, pacify cook if you do go into the kitchen, will you? I'm terrified of her this morning."

The envelope was found at last behind the dining-room clock, though how it had got there Mrs. Sheridan could not imagine.

"One of you children must have stolen it out of my bag, because I remember vividly—cream cheese and lemon-curd. Have you done that?"

"Yes."

"Egg and—" Mrs. Sheridan held the envelope away from her. "It looks like mice. It can't be mice, can it?"

"Olive, pet," said Laura, looking over her shoulder.

"Yes, of course, olive. What a horrible combination it sounds. Egg and olive."

They were finished at last, and Laura took them off to the kitchen. She found Jose there pacifying the cook, who did not look at all terrifying.

"I have never seen such exquisite sandwiches," said Jose's rapturous voice. "How many kinds did you say there were, cook? Fifteen?"

"Fifteen, Miss Jose."

"Well, cook, I congratulate you."

Cook swept up crusts with the long sandwich knife, and smiled broadly.

"Godber's has come," announced Sadie, issuing out of the pantry. She had seen the man pass the window.

That meant the cream puffs had come. Godber's were famous for their cream puffs. Nobody ever thought of making them at home.

"Bring them in and put them on the table, my girl," ordered cook.

Sadie brought them in and went back to the door. Of course Laura and Jose were far too grown-up to really care about such things. All the same, they couldn't help agreeing that the puffs looked very attractive. Very. Cook began arranging them, shaking off the extra icing sugar.

"Don't they carry one back to all one's parties?" said Laura.

"I suppose they do," said practical Jose, who never liked to be carried back. "They look beautifully light and feathery, I must say."

"Have one each, my dears," said cook in her comfortable voice. "Yer ma won't know."

Oh, impossible. Fancy cream puffs so soon after breakfast. The very idea made one shudder. All the same, two minutes later Jose and Laura were licking their fingers with that absorbed inward look that only comes from whipped cream.

"Let's go into the garden, out by the back way," suggested Laura. "I want to see how the men are getting on with the marquee. They're such awfully nice men."

But the back door was blocked by cook, Sadie, Godber's man and Hans.

Something had happened.

"Tuk-tuk-tuk," clucked cook like an agitated hen. Sadie had her hand clapped to her cheek as though she had toothache. Hans's face was screwed up in the effort to understand. Only Godber's man seemed to be enjoying himself; it was his story.

"What's the matter? What's happened?"

"There's been a horrible accident," said Cook. "A man killed."

"A man killed! Where? How? When?"

But Godber's man wasn't going to have his story snatched from under his very nose.

"Know those little cottages just below here, miss?" Know them? Of course, she knew them. "Well, there's a young chap living there, name of Scott, a carter. His horse shied at a traction-engine, corner of Hawke Street this morning, and he was thrown out on the back of his head. Killed."

"Dead!" Laura stared at Godber's man.

"Dead when they picked him up," said Godber's man with relish. "They were taking the body home as I come up here." And he said to the cook, "He's left a wife and five little ones."

"Jose, come here." Laura caught hold of her sister's sleeve and dragged her through the kitchen to the other side of the green baize door. There she paused and leaned against it. "Jose!" she said, horrified, "however are we going to stop everything?"

"Stop everything, Laura!" cried Jose in astonishment. "What do you mean?"

"Stop the garden-party, of course." Why did Jose pretend?

But Jose was still more amazed. "Stop the garden-party? My dear Laura, don't be so absurd. Of course we can't do anything of the kind. Nobody expects us to. Don't be so extravagant."

"But we can't possibly have a garden-party with a man dead just outside the front gate."

That really was extravagant, for the little cottages were in a lane to themselves at the very bottom of a steep rise that led up to the house. A broad road ran between. True, they were far too near. They were the greatest possible eyesore, and they had no right to be in that neighbourhood at all. They were little mean dwellings painted a chocolate brown. In the garden patches there was nothing but cabbage stalks, sick hens and tomato cans. The very smoke coming out of their chimneys was poverty-stricken. Little rags and shreds of smoke, so unlike the great silvery plumes that uncurled from the Sheridans' chimneys. Washerwomen lived in the lane and sweeps and a cobbler, and a man whose house-front was studded all over with minute bird-cages. Children swarmed. When the Sheridans were little they were forbidden to set foot there because of the revolting language and of what they might catch. But since they were grown up, Laura and Laurie on their prowls sometimes walked through. It was disgusting and sordid. They came out with a shudder. But still one must go everywhere; one must see everything. So through they went.

"And just think of what the band would sound like to that poor woman," said Laura.

"Oh, Laura!" Jose began to be seriously annoyed. "If you're going to stop a band playing every time someone has an accident, you'll lead a very strenuous life. I'm every bit as sorry about it as you. I feel just as sympathetic." Her eyes hardened. She looked at her sister just as she used to when they were little and fighting together. "You won't bring a drunken workman back to life by being sentimental," she said softly.

"Drunk! Who said he was drunk?" Laura turned furiously on Jose. She said, just as they had used to say on those occasions, "I'm going straight up to tell mother."

"Do, dear," cooed Jose.

"Mother, can I come into your room?" Laura turned the big glass door-knob.

"Of course, child. Why, what's the matter? What's given you such a colour?" And Mrs. Sheridan turned round from her dressing-table. She was trying on a new hat.

"Mother, a man's been killed," began Laura.

"Not in the garden?" interrupted her mother.

"No, no!"

"Oh, what a fright you gave me!" Mrs. Sheridan sighed with relief, and took off the big hat and held it on her knees.

"But listen, mother," said Laura. Breathless, half-choking, she told the dreadful story. "Of course, we can't have our party, can we?" she pleaded. "The band and everybody arriving. They'd hear us, mother; they're nearly neighbours!"

To Laura's astonishment her mother behaved just like Jose; it was harder to bear because she seemed amused. She refused to take Laura seriously.

"But, my dear child, use your common sense. It's only by accident we've heard of it. If some one had died there normally—and I can't understand how they keep alive in those poky little holes—we should still be having our party, shouldn't we?"

Laura had to say "yes" to that, but she felt it was all wrong. She sat down on her mother's sofa and pinched the cushion frill.

"Mother, isn't it terribly heartless of us?" she asked.

"Darling!" Mrs. Sheridan got up and came over to her, carrying the hat. Before Laura could stop her she had popped it on. "My child!" said her mother, "the hat is yours. It's made for you. It's much too young for me. I have never seen you look such a picture. Look at yourself!" And she held up her hand-mirror.

"But, mother," Laura began again. She couldn't look at herself; she turned aside.

This time Mrs. Sheridan lost patience just as Jose had done.

"You are being very absurd, Laura," she said coldly. "People like that don't expect sacrifices from us. And it's not very sympathetic to spoil everybody's enjoyment as you're doing now."

"I don't understand," said Laura, and she walked quickly out of the room into her own bedroom. There, quite by chance, the first thing she saw was this charming girl in the mirror, in her black hat trimmed with gold daisies, and a long black velvet ribbon. Never had she imagined she could look like that. Is mother right? she thought. And now she hoped her mother was right. Am I being extravagant? Perhaps it was extravagant. Just for a moment she had another glimpse of that poor woman and those little children, and the body being carried into the house. But it all seemed blurred, unreal, like a picture in the newspaper. I'll remember it again after the party's over, she decided. And somehow that seemed quite the best plan . . .

Lunch was over by half-past one. By half-past two they were all ready for the fray. The green-coated band had arrived and was established in a corner of the tennis-court.

"My dear!" trilled Kitty Maitland, "aren't they too like frogs for words? You ought to have arranged them round the pond with the conductor in the middle on a leaf."

Laurie arrived and hailed them on his way to dress. At the sight of him Laura remembered the accident again. She wanted to tell him. If Laurie agreed with the others, then it was bound to be all right. And she followed him into the hall.

"Laurie!"

"Hallo!" He was half-way upstairs, but when he turned round and saw Laura he suddenly puffed out his cheeks and goggled his eyes at her. "My word, Laura! You do look stunning," said Laurie. "What an absolutely topping hat!"

Laura said faintly "Is it?" and smiled up at Laurie, and didn't tell him after all.

Soon after that people began coming in streams. The band struck up; the hired waiters ran from the house to the marquee. Wherever you looked there were couples strolling, bending to the flowers, greeting, moving on over the lawn. They were like bright birds that had alighted in the Sheridans' garden for this one afternoon, on their way to—where? Ah, what happiness it is to be with people who all are happy, to press hands, press cheeks, smile into eyes.

"Darling Laura, how well you look!"

"What a becoming hat, child!"

"Laura, you look quite Spanish. I've never seen you look so striking."

And Laura, glowing, answered softly, "Have you had tea? Won't you have an ice? The passion-fruit ices really are rather special." She ran to her father and begged him. "Daddy darling, can't the band have something to drink?"

And the perfect afternoon slowly ripened, slowly faded, slowly its petals closed.

"Never a more delightful garden-party . . ."

"The greatest success . . ."

"Quite the most . . ."

Laura helped her mother with the good-byes. They stood side by side in the porch till it was all over.

"All over, all over, thank heaven," said Mrs. Sheridan. "Round up the others, Laura. Let's go and have some fresh coffee. I'm exhausted. Yes, it's been very successful. But oh, these parties, these parties! Why will you children insist on giving parties!" And they all of them sat down in the deserted marquee.

"Have a sandwich, daddy dear. I wrote the flag."

"Thanks." Mr. Sheridan took a bite and the sandwich was gone. He took another. "I suppose you didn't hear of a beastly accident that happened to-day?" he said.

"My dear," said Mrs. Sheridan, holding up her hand, "we did. It nearly ruined the party. Laura insisted we should put it off."

"Oh, mother!" Laura didn't want to be teased about it.

"It was a horrible affair all the same," said Mr. Sheridan. "The chap was married too. Lived just below in the lane, and leaves a wife and half a dozen kiddies, so they say."

An awkward little silence fell. Mrs. Sheridan fidgeted with her cup. Really, it was very tactless of father . . .

Suddenly she looked up. There on the table were all those sandwiches, cakes, puffs, all uneaten, all going to be wasted. She had one of her brilliant ideas.

"I know," she said. "Let's make up a basket. Let's send that poor creature some of this perfectly good food. At any rate, it will be the greatest treat for the children. Don't you agree? And she's sure to have neighbours calling in and so on. What a point to have it all ready prepared. Laura!" She jumped up. "Get me the big basket out of the stairs cupboard."

"But, mother, do you really think it's a good idea?" said Laura.

Again, how curious, she seemed to be different from them all. To take scraps from their party. Would the poor woman really like that?

"Of course! What's the matter with you to-day? An hour or two ago you were insisting on us being sympathetic, and now—"

Oh well! Laura ran for the basket. It was filled, it was heaped by her mother.

"Take it yourself, darling," said she. "Run down just as you are. No, wait, take the arum lilies too. People of that class are so impressed by arum lilies."

"The stems will ruin her lace frock," said practical Jose.

So they would. Just in time. "Only the basket, then. And, Laura!"—her mother followed her out of the marquee—"don't on any account—"

"What mother?"

No, better not put such ideas into the child's head! "Nothing! Run along."

It was just growing dusky as Laura shut their garden gates. A big dog ran by like a shadow. The road gleamed white, and down below in the hollow the little cottages were in deep shade. How quiet it seemed after the afternoon. Here she was going down the hill to somewhere where a man lay dead, and she couldn't realize it. Why couldn't she? She stopped a minute. And it seemed to her that kisses, voices, tinkling spoons, laughter, the smell of crushed grass were somehow inside her. She had no room for anything else. How strange! She looked up at the pale sky, and all she thought was, "Yes, it was the most successful party."

Now the broad road was crossed. The lane began, smoky and dark. Women in shawls and men's tweed caps hurried by. Men hung over the palings; the children played in the doorways. A low hum came from the mean little cottages. In some of them there was a flicker of light, and a shadow, crab-like, moved across the window. Laura bent her head and hurried on. She wished now she had put on a coat. How her frock shone! And the big hat with the velvet streamer—if only it was another hat! Were the people looking at her? They must be. It was a mistake to have come; she knew all along it was a mistake. Should she go back even now?

No, too late. This was the house. It must be. A dark knot of people stood outside. Beside the gate an old, old woman with a crutch sat in a chair, watching. She had her feet on a newspaper. The voices stopped as Laura drew near. The group parted. It was as though she was expected, as though they had known she was coming here.

Laura was terribly nervous. Tossing the velvet ribbon over her shoulder, she said to a woman standing by, "Is this Mrs. Scott's house?" and the woman, smiling queerly, said, "It is, my lass."

Oh, to be away from this! She actually said, "Help me, God," as she walked up the tiny path and knocked. To be away from those staring eyes, or to be covered up in anything, one of those women's shawls even. I'll just leave the basket and go, she decided. I shan't even wait for it to be emptied.

Then the door opened. A little woman in black showed in the gloom.

Laura said, "Are you Mrs. Scott?" But to her horror the woman answered, "Walk in please, miss," and she was shut in the passage.

"No," said Laura, "I don't want to come in. I only want to leave this basket. Mother sent—"

The little woman in the gloomy passage seemed not to have heard her. "Step this way, please, miss," she said in an oily voice, and Laura followed her.

She found herself in a wretched little low kitchen, lighted by a smoky lamp. There was a woman sitting before the fire.

"Em," said the little creature who had let her in. "Em! It's a young lady."

She turned to Laura. She said meaningly, "I'm 'er sister, miss. You'll excuse 'er, won't you?"

"Oh, but of course!" said Laura. "Please, please don't disturb her. I—I only want to leave—"

But at that moment the woman at the fire turned round. Her face, puffed up, red, with swollen eyes and swollen lips, looked terrible. She seemed as though she couldn't understand why Laura was there. What did it mean? Why was this stranger standing in the kitchen with a basket? What was it all about? And the poor face puckered up again.

"All right, my dear," said the other. "I'll thenk the young lady."

And again she began, "You'll excuse her, miss, I'm sure," and her face, swollen too, tried an oily smile.

Laura only wanted to get out, to get away. She was back in the passage. The door opened. She walked straight through into the bedroom, where the dead man was lying.

"You'd like a look at 'im, wouldn't you?" said Em's sister, and she brushed past Laura over to the bed. "Don't be afraid, my lass,"—and now her voice sounded fond and sly, and fondly she drew down the sheet—"'e looks a picture. There's nothing to show. Come along, my dear."

Laura came.

There lay a young man, fast asleep—sleeping so soundly, so deeply, that he was far, far away from them both. Oh, so remote, so peaceful. He was dreaming. Never wake him up again. His head was sunk in the pillow, his eyes were closed; they were blind under the closed eyelids. He was given up to his dream. What did garden-parties and baskets and lace frocks matter to him? He was far from all those things. He was wonderful, beautiful. While they were laughing and while the band was playing, this marvel had come to the lane. Happy . . . happy . . . All is well, said that sleeping face. This is just as it should be. I am content.

But all the same you had to cry, and she couldn't go out of the room without saying something to him. Laura gave a loud childish sob.

"Forgive my hat," she said.

And this time she didn't wait for Em's sister. She found her way out of the door, down the path, past all those dark people. At the corner of the lane she met Laurie.

He stepped out of the shadow. "Is that you, Laura?"

"Yes."

"Mother was getting anxious. Was it all right?"

"Yes, quite. Oh, Laurie!" She took his arm, she pressed up against him.

"I say, you're not crying, are you?" asked her brother.

Laura shook her head. She was.

Laurie put his arm round her shoulder. "Don't cry," he said in his warm, loving voice. "Was it awful?"

"No," sobbed Laura. "It was simply marvellous. But Laurie—" She stopped, she looked at her brother. "Isn't life," she stammered, "isn't life—" But what life was she couldn't explain. No matter. He quite understood.

"*Isn't* it, darling?" said Laurie.

TENDER BUTTONS

Gertrude Stein

Objects

A CARAFE, THAT IS A BLIND GLASS.

A kind in glass and a cousin, a spectacle and nothing strange a single hurt color and an arrangement in a system to pointing. All this and not ordinary, not unordered in not resembling. The difference is spreading.

GLAZED GLITTER.

Nickel, what is nickel, it is originally rid of a cover.

The change in that is that red weakens an hour. The change has come. There is no search. But there is, there is that hope and that interpretation and sometime, surely any is unwelcome, sometime there is breath and there will be a sinecure and charming very charming is that clean and cleansing. Certainly glittering is handsome and convincing.

There is no gratitude in mercy and in medicine. There can be breakages in Japanese. That is no programme. That is no color chosen. It was chosen yesterday, that showed spitting and perhaps washing and polishing. It certainly showed no obligation and perhaps if borrowing is not natural there is some use in giving.

A SUBSTANCE IN A CUSHION.

The change of color is likely and a difference a very little difference is prepared. Sugar is not a vegetable.

Callous is something that hardening leaves behind what will be soft if there is a genuine interest in there being present as many girls as men. Does this change. It shows that dirt is clean when there is a volume.

A cushion has that cover. Supposing you do not like to change, supposing it is very clean that there is no change in appearance, supposing that there is regularity and a costume is that any the worse than an oyster and an exchange. Come to season that is there any extreme use in feather and cotton. Is there not much more joy in a table and more chairs and very likely roundness and a place to put them.

A circle of fine card board and a chance to see a tassel.

What is the use of a violent kind of delightfulness if there is no pleasure in not getting tired of it. The question does not come before there is a quotation. In any kind of place there is a top to covering and it is a pleasure at any rate there is some venturing in refusing to believe nonsense. It shows what use there is in a whole piece if one uses it and it is extreme and very likely the little things could be dearer but in any case there is a bargain and if there is the best thing to do is to take it away and wear it and then be reckless be reckless and resolved on returning gratitude.

Light blue and the same red with purple makes a change. It shows that there is no mistake. Any pink shows that and very likely it is reasonable. Very likely there should not be a finer fancy present. Some increase means a calamity and this is the best preparation for three and more being together. A little calm is so ordinary and in any case there is sweetness and some of that.

A seal and matches and a swan and ivy and a suit.

A closet, a closet does not connect under the bed. The band if it is white and black, the band has a green string. A sight a whole sight and a little groan grinding makes a trimming such a sweet singing trimming and a red thing not a round thing but a white thing, a red thing and a white thing.

The disgrace is not in carelessness nor even in sewing it comes out out of the way.

What is the sash like. The sash is not like anything mustard it is not like a same thing that has stripes, it is not even more hurt than that, it has a little top.

A BOX.

Out of kindness comes redness and out of rudeness comes rapid same question, out of an eye comes research, out of selection comes painful cattle. So then the order is that a white way of being round is something suggesting a pin and is it disappointing, it is not, it is so rudimentary to be analysed and see a fine substance strangely, it is so earnest to have a green point not to red but to point again.

A PIECE OF COFFEE.

More of double.

A place in no new table.

A single image is not splendor. Dirty is yellow. A sign of more in not mentioned. A piece of coffee is not a detainer. The resemblance to yellow is dirtier and distincter. The clean mixture is whiter and not coal color, never more coal color than altogether.

The sight of a reason, the same sight slighter, the sight of a simpler negative answer, the same sore sounder, the intention to wishing, the same splendor, the same furniture.

The time to show a message is when too late and later there is no hanging in a blight.

A not torn rose-wood color. If it is not dangerous then a pleasure and more than any other if it is cheap is not cheaper. The amusing side is that the sooner there are no fewer the more certain is the necessity dwindled. Supposing that the case contained rose-wood and a color. Supposing that there was no reason for a distress and more likely for a number, supposing that there was no astonishment, is it not necessary to mingle astonishment.

The settling of stationing cleaning is one way not to shatter scatter and scattering. The one way to use custom is to use soap and silk for cleaning. The one way to see cotton is to have a design concentrating the illusion and the illustration. The perfect way is to accustom the thing to have a lining and the shape of a ribbon and to be solid, quite solid in standing and to use heaviness in morning. It is light enough in that. It has that shape nicely. Very nicely may not be exaggerating. Very strongly may be sincerely fainting. May be strangely flattering. May not be strange in everything. May not be strange to.

DIRT AND NOT COPPER.

Dirt and not copper makes a color darker. It makes the shape so heavy and makes no melody harder.

It makes mercy and relaxation and even a strength to spread a table fuller. There are more places not empty. They see cover.

NOTHING ELEGANT.

A charm a single charm is doubtful. If the red is rose and there is a gate surrounding it, if inside is let in and there places change then certainly something is upright. It is earnest.

MILDRED'S UMBRELLA.

A cause and no curve, a cause and loud enough, a cause and extra a loud clash and an extra wagon, a sign of extra, a sac a small sac and an established color and cunning, a slender grey and no ribbon, this means a loss a great loss a restitution.

A METHOD OF A CLOAK.

A single climb to a line, a straight exchange to a cane, a desperate adventure and courage and a clock, all this which is a system, which has feeling, which has resignation and success, all makes an attractive black silver.

A RED STAMP.

If lilies are lily white if they exhaust noise and distance and even dust, if they dusty will dirt a surface that has no extreme grace, if they do this and it is not necessary it is not at all necessary if they do this they need a catalogue.

A BOX.

A large box is handily made of what is necessary to replace any substance. Suppose an example is necessary, the plainer it is made the more reason there is for some outward recognition that there is a result.

A box is made sometimes and them to see to see to it neatly and to have the holes stopped up makes it necessary to use paper.

A custom which is necessary when a box is used and taken is that a large part of the time there are three which have different connections. The one is on the table. The two are on the table. The three are on the table. The one, one is the same length as is shown by the cover being longer. The other is different there is more cover that shows it. The other is different and that makes the corners have the same shade the eight are in singular arrangement to make four necessary.

Lax, to have corners, to be lighter than some weight, to indicate a wedding journey, to last brown and not curious, to be wealthy, cigarettes are established by length and by doubling.

Left open, to be left pounded, to be left closed, to be circulating in summer and winter, and sick color that is grey that is not dusty and red shows, to be sure cigarettes do measure an empty length sooner than a choice in color.

Winged, to be winged means that white is yellow and pieces pieces that are brown are dust color if dust is washed off, then it is choice that is to say it is fitting cigarettes sooner than paper.

An increase why is an increase idle, why is silver cloister, why is the spark brighter, if it is brighter is there any result, hardly more than ever.

A PLATE.

An occasion for a plate, an occasional resource is in buying and how soon does washing enable a selection of the same thing neater. If the party is small a clever song is in order.

Plates and a dinner set of colored china. Pack together a string and enough with it to protect the centre, cause a considerable haste and gather more as it is cooling, collect more trembling and not any even trembling, cause a whole thing to be a church.

A sad size a size that is not sad is blue as every bit of blue is precocious. A kind of green a game in green and nothing flat nothing quite flat and more round, nothing a particular color strangely, nothing breaking the losing of no little piece.

A splendid address a really splendid address is not shown by giving a flower freely, it is not shown by a mark or by wetting.

Cut cut in white, cut in white so lately. Cut more than any other and show it. Show it in the stem and in starting and in evening coming complication.

A lamp is not the only sign of glass. The lamp and the cake are not the only sign of stone. The lamp and the cake and the cover are not the only necessity altogether.

A plan a hearty plan, a compressed disease and no coffee, not even a card or a change to incline each way, a plan that has that excess and that break is the one that shows filling.

A SELTZER BOTTLE.

Any neglect of many particles to a cracking, any neglect of this makes around it what is lead in color and certainly discolor in silver. The use of this is manifold. Supposing a certain time selected is assured, suppose it is even necessary, suppose no other extract is permitted and no more handling is needed, suppose the rest of the message is mixed with a very long slender needle and even if it could be any black border, supposing all this altogether made a dress and suppose it was actual, suppose the mean way to state it was occasional, if you suppose this in August and even more melodiously, if you suppose this even in the necessary incident of there certainly being no middle in summer and winter, suppose this and an elegant settlement a very elegant settlement is more than of consequence, it is not final and sufficient and substituted. This which was so kindly a present was constant.

A LONG DRESS.

What is the current that makes machinery, that makes it crackle, what is the current that presents a long line and a necessary waist. What is this current. What is the wind, what is it.

Where is the serene length, it is there and a dark place is not a dark place, only a white and red are black, only a yellow and green are blue, a pink is scarlet, a bow is every color. A line distinguishes it. A line just distinguishes it.

A RED HAT.

A dark grey, a very dark grey, a quite dark grey is monstrous ordinarily, it is so monstrous because there is no red in it. If red is in everything it is not necessary. Is that not an argument for any use of it and even so is there any place that is better, is there any place that has so much stretched out.

A BLUE COAT.

A blue coat is guided guided away, guided and guided away, that is the particular color that is used for that length and not any width not even more than a shadow.

A PIANO.

If the speed is open, if the color is careless, if the selection of a strong scent is not awkward, if the button holder is held by all the waving color and there is no color, not any color. If there is no dirt in a pin and there can be none scarcely, if there is not then the place is the same as up standing.

This is no dark custom and it even is not acted in any such a way that a restraint is not spread. That is spread, it shuts and it lifts and awkwardly not awkwardly the centre is in standing.

A CHAIR.

A widow in a wise veil and more garments shows that shadows are even. It addresses no more, it shadows the stage and learning. A regular arrangement, the severest and the most preserved is that which has the arrangement not more than always authorised.

A suitable establishment, well housed, practical, patient and staring, a suitable bedding, very suitable and not more particularly than complaining, anything suitable is so necessary.

A fact is that when the direction is just like that, no more, longer, sudden and at the same time not any sofa, the main action is that without a blaming there is no custody.

Practice measurement, practice the sign that means that really means a necessary betrayal, in showing that there is wearing.

Hope, what is a spectacle, a spectacle is the resemblance between the circular side place and nothing else, nothing else.

To choose it is ended, it is actual and more than that it has it certainly has the same treat, and a seat all that is practiced and more easily much more easily ordinarily.

Pick a barn, a whole barn, and bend more slender accents than have ever been necessary, shine in the darkness necessarily. Actually not aching, actually not aching, a stubborn bloom is so artificial and even more than that, it is a spectacle, it is a binding accident, it is animosity and accentuation.

If the chance to dirty diminishing is necessary, if it is why is there no complexion, why is there no rubbing, why is there no special protection.

A FRIGHTFUL RELEASE.

A bag which was left and not only taken but turned away was not found. The place was shown to be very like the last time. A piece was not exchanged, not a bit of it, a piece was left over. The rest was mismanaged.

A PURSE.

A purse was not green, it was not straw color, it was hardly seen and it had a use a long use and the chain, the chain was never missing, it was not misplaced, it showed that it was open, that is all that it showed.

A MOUNTED UMBRELLA.

What was the use of not leaving it there where it would hang what was the use if there was no chance of ever seeing it come there and show that it was handsome and right in the way it showed it. The lesson is to learn that it does show it, that it shows it and that nothing, that there is nothing, that there is no more to do about it and just so much more is there plenty of reason for making an exchange.

A CLOTH.

Enough cloth is plenty and more, more is almost enough for that and besides if there is no more spreading is there plenty of room for it. Any occasion shows the best way.

More.

An elegant use of foliage and grace and a little piece of white cloth and oil. Wondering so winningly in several kinds of oceans is the reason that makes red so regular and enthusiastic. The reason that there is more snips are the same shining very colored rid of no round color.

A new cup and saucer.

Enthusiastically hurting a clouded yellow bud and saucer, enthusiastically so is the bite in the ribbon.

Objects.

Within, within the cut and slender joint alone, with sudden equals and no more than three, two in the centre make two one side.

If the elbow is long and it is filled so then the best example is all together. The kind of show is made by squeezing.

Eye glasses.

A color in shaving, a saloon is well placed in the centre of an alley.

Cutlet.

A blind agitation is manly and uttermost.

Careless water.

No cup is broken in more places and mended, that is to say a plate is broken and mending does do that it shows that culture is Japanese. It shows the whole element of angels and orders. It does more to choosing and it does more to that ministering counting. It does, it does change in more water.

Supposing a single piece is a hair supposing more of them are orderly, does that show that strength, does that show that joint, does that show that balloon famously. Does it.

A PAPER.

A courteous occasion makes a paper show no such occasion and this makes readiness and eyesight and likeness and a stool.

A DRAWING.

The meaning of this is entirely and best to say the mark, best to say it best to show sudden places, best to make bitter, best to make the length tall and nothing broader, anything between the half.

WATER RAINING.

Water astonishing and difficult altogether makes a meadow and a stroke.

COLD CLIMATE.

A season in yellow sold extra strings makes lying places.

MALACHITE.

The sudden spoon is the same in no size. The sudden spoon is the wound in the decision.

AN UMBRELLA.

Coloring high means that the strange reason is in front not more in front behind. Not more in front in peace of the dot.

A PETTICOAT.

A light white, a disgrace, an ink spot, a rosy charm.

A WAIST.

A star glide, a single frantic sullenness, a single financial grass greediness.

Object that is in wood. Hold the pine, hold the dark, hold in the rush, make the bottom.

A piece of crystal. A change, in a change that is remarkable there is no reason to say that there was a time.

A woolen object gilded. A country climb is the best disgrace, a couple of practices any of them in order is so left.

A TIME TO EAT.

A pleasant simple habitual and tyrannical and authorised and educated and resumed and articulate separation. This is not tardy.

A LITTLE BIT OF A TUMBLER.

A shining indication of yellow consists in there having been more of the same color than could have been expected when all four were bought. This was the hope which made the six and seven have no use for any more places and this necessarily spread into nothing. Spread into nothing.

A FIRE.

What was the use of a whole time to send and not send if there was to be the kind of thing that made that come in. A letter was nicely sent.

A HANDKERCHIEF.

A winning of all the blessings, a sample not a sample because there is no worry.

RED ROSES.

A cool red rose and a pink cut pink, a collapse and a sold hole, a little less hot.

IN BETWEEN.

In between a place and candy is a narrow foot-path that shows more mounting than anything, so much really that a calling meaning a bolster measured a whole thing with that. A virgin a whole virgin is judged made and so between curves and outlines and real seasons and more out glasses and a perfectly unprecedented arrangement between old ladies and mild colds there is no satin wood shining.

COLORED HATS.

Colored hats are necessary to show that curls are worn by an addition of blank spaces, this makes the difference between single lines and broad stomachs, the least thing is lightening, the least thing means a little flower and a big delay a big delay that makes more nurses than little women really little women. So clean is a light that nearly all of it shows pearls and little ways. A large hat is tall and me and all custard whole.

A FEATHER.

A feather is trimmed, it is trimmed by the light and the bug and the post, it is trimmed by little leaning and by all sorts of mounted reserves and loud volumes. It is surely cohesive.

A BROWN.

A brown which is not liquid not more so is relaxed and yet there is a change, a news is pressing.

A LITTLE CALLED PAULINE.

A little called anything shows shudders.

Come and say what prints all day. A whole few watermelon. There is no pope.

No cut in pennies and little dressing and choose wide soles and little spats really little spices.

A little lace makes boils. This is not true.

Gracious of gracious and a stamp a blue green white bow a blue green lean, lean on the top.

If it is absurd then it is leadish and nearly set in where there is a tight head.

A peaceful life to arise her, noon and moon and moon. A letter a cold sleeve a blanket a shaving house and nearly the best and regular window.

Nearer in fairy sea, nearer and farther, show white has lime in sight, show a stitch of ten. Count, count more so that thicker and thicker is leaning.

I hope she has her cow. Bidding a wedding, widening received treading, little leading mention nothing.

Cough out cough out in the leather and really feather it is not for.

Please could, please could, jam it not plus more sit in when.

A SOUND.

Elephant beaten with candy and little pops and chews all bolts and reckless reckless rats, this is this.

A TABLE.

A table means does it not my dear it means a whole steadiness. Is it likely that a change.

A table means more than a glass even a looking glass is tall. A table means necessary places and a revision a revision of a little thing it means it does mean that there has been a stand, a stand where it did shake.

SHOES.

To be a wall with a damper a stream of pounding way and nearly enough choice makes a steady midnight. It is pus.

A shallow hole rose on red, a shallow hole in and in this makes ale less. It shows shine.

A DOG.

A little monkey goes like a donkey that means to say that means to say that more sighs last goes. Leave with it. A little monkey goes like a donkey.

A WHITE HUNTER.

A white hunter is nearly crazy.

A LEAVE.

In the middle of a tiny spot and nearly bare there is a nice thing to say that wrist is leading. Wrist is leading.

SUPPOSE AN EYES.

Suppose it is within a gate which open is open at the hour of closing summer that is to say it is so.

All the seats are needing blackening. A white dress is in sign. A soldier a real soldier has a worn lace a worn lace of different sizes that is to say if he can read, if he can read he is a size to show shutting up twenty-four.

Go red go red, laugh white.

Suppose a collapse in rubbed purr, in rubbed purr get.

Little sales ladies little sales ladies little saddles of mutton.

Little sales of leather and such beautiful beautiful, beautiful beautiful.

A SHAWL.

A shawl is a hat and hurt and a red balloon and an under coat and a sizer a sizer of talks.

A shawl is a wedding, a piece of wax a little build. A shawl.

Pick a ticket, pick it in strange steps and with hollows. There is hollow hollow belt, a belt is a shawl.

A plate that has a little bobble, all of them, any so.

Please a round it is ticket.

It was a mistake to state that a laugh and a lip and a laid climb and a depot and a cultivator and little choosing is a point it.

BOOK.

Book was there, it was there. Book was there. Stop it, stop it, it was a cleaner, a wet cleaner and it was not where it was wet, it was not high, it was directly placed back, not back again, back it was returned, it was needless, it put a bank, a bank when, a bank care.

Suppose a man a realistic expression of resolute reliability suggests pleasing itself white all white and no head does that mean soap. It does not so. It means kind wavers and little chance to beside beside rest. A plain.

Suppose ear rings, that is one way to breed, breed that. Oh chance to say, oh nice old pole. Next best and nearest a pillar. Chest not valuable, be papered.

Cover up cover up the two with a little piece of string and hope rose and green, green.

Please a plate, put a match to the seam and really then really then, really then it is a remark that joins many many lead games. It is a sister and sister and a flower and a flower and a dog and a colored sky a sky colored grey and nearly that nearly that let.

PEELED PENCIL, CHOKE.

Rub her coke.

IT WAS BLACK, BLACK TOOK.

Black ink best wheel bale brown.

Excellent not a hull house, not a pea soup, no bill no care, no precise no past pearl pearl goat.

THIS IS THE DRESS, AIDER.

Aider, why aider why whow, whow stop touch, aider whow, aider stop the muncher, muncher munchers.

A jack in kill her, a jack in, makes a meadowed king, makes a to let.

Food

ROASTBEEF; MUTTON; BREAKFAST; SUGAR; CRANBERRIES; MILK; EGGS; APPLE; TAILS; LUNCH; CUPS; RHUBARB; SINGLE; FISH; CAKE; CUSTARD; POTATOES; ASPARAGUS; BUTTER; END OF SUMMER; SAUSAGES; CELERY; VEAL; VEGETABLE; COOKING; CHICKEN; PASTRY; CREAM; CUCUMBER; DINNER; DINING; EATING; SALAD; SAUCE; SALMON; ORANGE; COCOA; AND CLEAR SOUP AND ORANGES AND OATMEAL; SALAD DRESSING AND AN ARTICHOKE; A CENTRE IN A TABLE.

ROASTBEEF.

In the inside there is sleeping, in the outside there is reddening, in the morning there is meaning, in the evening there is feeling. In the evening there is feeling. In feeling anything is resting, in feeling anything is mounting, in feeling there is resignation, in feeling there is recognition, in feeling there is recurrence and entirely mistaken there is pinching. All the standards have steamers and all the curtains have bed linen and all the yellow has discrimination and all the circle has circling. This makes sand.

Very well. Certainly the length is thinner and the rest, the round rest has a longer summer. To shine, why not shine, to shine, to station, to enlarge, to hurry the measure all this means nothing if there is singing, if there is singing then there is the resumption.

The change the dirt, not to change dirt means that there is no beefsteak and not to have that is no obstruction, it is so easy to exchange meaning, it is so easy to see the difference. The difference is that a plain resource is not entangled with thickness and it does not mean that thickness shows such cutting, it does mean that a meadow is useful and a cow absurd. It does not mean that there are tears, it does not mean that exudation is cumbersome, it means no more than a memory, a choice and a reëstablishment, it means more than any escape from a surrounding extra. All the time that there is use there is use and any time there is a surface there is a surface, and every time there is an exception there is an exception and every time there is a division there is a dividing. Any time there is a surface there is a surface and every time there is a suggestion there is a suggestion and every time there is silence there is silence and every time that is languid there is that there then and not oftener, not always, not particular, tender and changing and external and central and surrounded and singular and simple and the same and the surface and the circle and the shine and the succor and the white and the same and the better and the red and the same and the centre and the yellow and the tender and the better, and altogether.

Considering the circumstances there is no occasion for a reduction, considering that there is no pealing there is no occasion for an obligation, considering that there is no outrage there is no necessity for any reparation, considering that there is no particle sodden there is no occasion for deliberation. Considering everything and which way the turn is tending, considering everything why is there no restraint, considering everything what makes the place settle and the plate distinguish some specialties. The whole thing is not understood and this is not strange considering that there is no education, this is not strange because having that certainly does show the difference in cutting, it shows that when there is turning there is no distress.

In kind, in a control, in a period, in the alteration of pigeons, in kind cuts and thick and thin spaces, in kind ham and different colors, the length of leaning a strong thing outside not to make a sound but to suggest a crust, the principal taste is when there is a whole chance to be reasonable, this does not mean that there is overtaking, this means nothing precious, this means clearly that the chance to exercise is a social success. So then the sound is not obtrusive. Suppose it is obtrusive suppose it is. What is certainly the desertion is not a reduced description, a description is not a birthday.

Lovely snipe and tender turn, excellent vapor and slender butter, all the splinter and the trunk, all the poisonous darkening drunk, all the joy in weak success, all the joyful tenderness, all the section and the tea, all the stouter symmetry.

Around the size that is small, inside the stern that is the middle, besides the remains that are praying, inside the between that is turning, all the region is measuring and melting is exaggerating.

Rectangular ribbon does not mean that there is no eruption it means that if there is no place to hold there is no place to spread. Kindness is not earnest, it is not assiduous it is not revered.

Room to comb chickens and feathers and ripe purple, room to curve single plates and large sets and second silver, room to send everything away, room to save heat and distemper, room to search a light that is simpler, all room has no shadow.

There is no use there is no use at all in smell, in taste, in teeth, in toast, in anything, there is no use at all and the respect is mutual.

Why should that which is uneven, that which is resumed, that which is tolerable why should all this resemble a smell, a thing is there, it whistles, it is not narrower, why is there no obligation to stay away and yet courage, courage is everywhere and the best remains to stay.

If there could be that which is contained in that which is felt there would be a chair where there are chairs and there would be no more denial about a clatter. A clatter is not a smell. All this is good.

The Saturday evening which is Sunday is every week day. What choice is there when there is a difference. A regulation is not active. Thirstiness is not equal division.

Anyway, to be older and ageder is not a surfeit nor a suction, it is not dated and careful, it is not dirty. Any little thing is clean, rubbing is black. Why should ancient lambs be goats and young colts and never beef, why should they, they should because there is so much difference in age.

A sound, a whole sound is not separation, a whole sound is in an order.

Suppose there is a pigeon, suppose there is.

Looseness, why is there a shadow in a kitchen, there is a shadow in a kitchen because every little thing is bigger.

The time when there are four choices and there are four choices in a difference, the time when there are four choices there is a kind and there is a kind. There is a kind. There is a kind. Supposing there is a bone, there is a bone. Supposing there are bones. There are bones. When there are bones there is no supposing there are bones. There are bones and there is that consuming. The kindly way to feel separating is to have a space between. This shows a likeness.

Hope in gates, hope in spoons, hope in doors, hope in tables, no hope in daintiness and determination. Hope in dates.

Tin is not a can and a stove is hardly. Tin is not necessary and neither is a stretcher. Tin is never narrow and thick.

Color is in coal. Coal is outlasting roasting and a spoonful, a whole spoon that is full is not spilling. Coal any coal is copper.

Claiming nothing, not claiming anything, not a claim in everything, collecting claiming, all this makes a harmony, it even makes a succession.

Sincerely gracious one morning, sincerely graciously trembling, sincere in gracious eloping, all this makes a furnace and a blanket. All this shows quantity.

Like an eye, not so much more, not any searching, no compliments.

Please be the beef, please beef, pleasure is not wailing. Please beef, please be carved clear, please be a case of consideration.

Search a neglect. A sale, any greatness is a stall and there is no memory, there is no clear collection.

A satin sight, what is a trick, no trick is mountainous and the color, all the rush is in the blood.

Bargaining for a little, bargain for a touch, a liberty, an estrangement, a characteristic turkey.

Please spice, please no name, place a whole weight, sink into a standard rising, raise a circle, choose a right around, make the resonance accounted and gather green any collar.

To bury a slender chicken, to raise an old feather, to surround a garland and to bake a pole splinter, to suggest a repose and to settle simply, to surrender one another, to succeed saving simpler, to satisfy a singularity and not to be blinder, to sugar nothing darker and to read redder, to have the color better, to sort out dinner, to remain together, to surprise no sinner, to curve nothing sweeter, to continue thinner, to increase in resting recreation to design string not dimmer.

Cloudiness what is cloudiness, is it a lining, is it a roll, is it melting.

The sooner there is jerking, the sooner freshness is tender, the sooner the round it is not round the sooner it is withdrawn in cutting, the sooner the measure means service, the sooner there is chinking, the sooner there is sadder than salad, the sooner there is none do her, the sooner there is no choice, the sooner there is a gloom freer, the same sooner and more sooner, this is no error in hurry and in pressure and in opposition to consideration.

A recital, what is a recital, it is an organ and use does not strengthen valor, it soothes medicine.

A transfer, a large transfer, a little transfer, some transfer, clouds and tracks do transfer, a transfer is not neglected.

Pride, when is there perfect pretence, there is no more than yesterday and ordinary.

A sentence of a vagueness that is violence is authority and a mission and stumbling and also certainly also a prison. Calmness, calm is beside the plate and in way in. There is no turn in terror. There is no volume in sound.

There is coagulation in cold and there is none in prudence. Something is preserved and the evening is long and the colder spring has sudden shadows in a sun. All the stain is tender and lilacs really lilacs are disturbed. Why is the perfect reëstablishment practiced and prized, why is it composed. The result the pure result is juice and size and baking and exhibition and nonchalance and sacrifice and volume and a section in division and the surrounding recognition and horticulture and no murmur. This is a result. There is no superposition and circumstance, there is hardness and a reason and the rest and remainder. There is no delight and no mathematics.

MUTTON.

A letter which can wither, a learning which can suffer and an outrage which is simultaneous is principal.

Student, students are merciful and recognised they chew something.

Hate rests that is solid and sparse and all in a shape and largely very largely. Interleaved and successive and a sample of smell all this makes a certainty a shade.

Light curls very light curls have no more curliness than soup. This is not a subject.

Change a single stream of denting and change it hurriedly, what does it express, it expresses nausea. Like a very strange likeness and pink, like that and not more like that than the same resemblance and not more like that than no middle space in cutting.

An eye glass, what is an eye glass, it is water. A splendid specimen, what is it when it is little and tender so that there are parts. A centre can place and four are no more and two and two are not middle.

Melting and not minding, safety and powder, a particular recollection and a sincere solitude all this makes a shunning so thorough and so unrepeated and surely if there is anything left it is a bone. It is not solitary.

Any space is not quiet it is so likely to be shiny. Darkness very dark darkness is sectional. There is a way to see in onion and surely very surely rhubarb and a tomato, surely very surely there is that seeding. A little thing in is a little thing.

Mud and water were not present and not any more of either. Silk and stockings were not present and not any more of either. A receptacle and a symbol and no monster were present and no more. This made a piece show and was it a kindness, it can be asked was it a kindness to have it warmer, was it a kindness and does gliding mean more. Does it.

Does it dirty a ceiling. It does not. Is it dainty, it is if prices are sweet. Is it lamentable, it is not if there is no undertaker. Is it curious, it is not when there is youth. All this makes a line, it even makes makes no more. All this makes cherries. The reason that there is a suggestion in vanity is due to this that there is a burst of mixed music.

A temptation any temptation is an exclamation if there are misdeeds and little bones. It is not astonishing that bones mingle as they vary not at all and in any case why is a bone outstanding, it is so because the circumstance that does not make a cake and character is so easily churned and cherished.

Mouse and mountain and a quiver, a quaint statue and pain in an exterior and silence more silence louder shows salmon a mischief intender. A cake, a real salve made of mutton and liquor, a specially retained rinsing and an established cork and blazing, this which resignation influences and restrains, restrains more altogether. A sign is the specimen spoken.

A meal in mutton, mutton, why is lamb cheaper, it is cheaper because so little is more. Lecture, lecture and repeat instruction.

BREAKFAST.

A change, a final change includes potatoes. This is no authority for the abuse of cheese. What language can instruct any fellow.

A shining breakfast, a breakfast shining, no dispute, no practice, nothing, nothing at all.

A sudden slice changes the whole plate, it does so suddenly.

An imitation, more imitation, imitation succeed imitations.

Anything that is decent, anything that is present, a calm and a cook and more singularly still a shelter, all these show the need of clamor. What is the custom, the custom is in the centre.

What is a loving tongue and pepper and more fish than there is when tears many tears are necessary. The tongue and the salmon, there is not salmon when brown is a color, there is salmon when there is no meaning to an early morning being pleasanter. There is no salmon, there are no tea-cups, there are the same kind of mushes as are used as stomachers by the eating hopes that makes eggs delicious. Drink is likely to stir a certain respect for an egg cup and more water melon than was ever eaten yesterday. Beer is neglected and cocoanut is famous. Coffee all coffee and a sample of soup all soup these are the choice of a baker. A white cup means a wedding. A wet cup means a vacation. A strong cup means an especial regulation. A single cup means a capital arrangement between the drawer and the place that is open.

Price a price is not in language, it is not in custom, it is not in praise.

A colored loss, why is there no leisure. If the persecution is so outrageous that nothing is solemn is there any occasion for persuasion.

A grey turn to a top and bottom, a silent pocketful of much heating, all the pliable succession of surrendering makes an ingenious joy.

A breeze in a jar and even then silence, a special anticipation in a rack, a gurgle a whole gurgle and more cheese than almost anything, is this an astonishment, does this incline more than the original division between a tray and a talking arrangement and even then a calling into another room gently with some chicken in any way.

A bent way that is a way to declare that the best is all together, a bent way shows no result, it shows a slight restraint, it shows a necessity for retraction.

Suspect a single buttered flower, suspect it certainly, suspect it and then glide, does that not alter a counting.

A hurt mended stick, a hurt mended cup, a hurt mended article of exceptional relaxation and annoyance, a hurt mended, hurt and mended is so necessary that no mistake is intended.

What is more likely than a roast, nothing really and yet it is never disappointed singularly.

A steady cake, any steady cake is perfect and not plain, any steady cake has a mounting reason and more than that it has singular crusts. A season of more is a season that is instead. A season of many is not more a season than most.

Take no remedy lightly, take no urging intently, take no separation leniently, beware of no lake and no larder.

Burden the cracked wet soaking sack heavily, burden it so that it is an institution in fright and in climate and in the best plan that there can be.

An ordinary color, a color is that strange mixture which makes, which does make which does not make a ripe juice, which does not make a mat.

A work which is a winding a real winding of the cloaking of a relaxing rescue. This which is so cool is not dusting, it is not dirtying in smelling, it could use white water, it could use more extraordinarily and in no solitude altogether. This which is so not winsome and not widened and really not so dipped as dainty and really dainty, very dainty, ordinarily, dainty, a dainty, not in that dainty and dainty. If the time is determined, if it is determined and there is reunion there is reunion with that then outline, then there is in that a piercing shutter, all of a piercing shouter, all of a quite weather, all of a withered exterior, all of that in most violent likely.

An excuse is not dreariness, a single plate is not butter, a single weight is not excitement, a solitary crumbling is not only martial.

A mixed protection, very mixed with the same actual intentional unstrangeness and riding, a single action caused necessarily is not more a sign than a minister.

Seat a knife near a cage and very near a decision and more nearly a timely working cat and scissors. Do this temporarily and make no more mistake in standing. Spread it all and arrange the white place, does this show in the house, does it not show in the green that is not necessary for that color, does it not even show in the explanation and singularly not at all stationary.

SUGAR.

A violent luck and a whole sample and even then quiet.

Water is squeezing, water is almost squeezing on lard. Water, water is a mountain and it is selected and it is so practical that there is no use in money. A mind under is exact and so it is necessary to have a mouth and eye glasses.

A question of sudden rises and more time than awfulness is so easy and shady. There is precisely that noise.

A peck a small piece not privately overseen, not at all not a slice, not at all crestfallen and open, not at all mounting and chaining and evenly surpassing, all the bidding comes to tea.

A separation is not tightly in worsted and sauce, it is so kept well and sectionally.

Put it in the stew, put it to shame. A little slight shadow and a solid fine furnace.

The teasing is tender and trying and thoughtful.

The line which sets sprinkling to be a remedy is beside the best cold.

A puzzle, a monster puzzle, a heavy choking, a neglected Tuesday.

Wet crossing and a likeness, any likeness, a likeness has blisters, it has that and teeth, it has the staggering blindly and a little green, any little green is ordinary.

One, two and one, two, nine, second and five and that.

A blaze, a search in between, a cow, only any wet place, only this tune.

Cut a gas jet uglier and then pierce pierce in between the next and negligence. Choose the rate to pay and pet pet very much. A collection of all around, a signal poison, a lack of languor and more hurts at ease.

A white bird, a colored mine, a mixed orange, a dog.

Cuddling comes in continuing a change.

A piece of separate outstanding rushing is so blind with open delicacy.

A canoe is orderly. A period is solemn. A cow is accepted.

A nice old chain is widening, it is absent, it is laid by.

CRANBERRIES.

Could there not be a sudden date, could there not be in the present settlement of old age pensions, could there not be by a witness, could there be.

Count the chain, cut the grass, silence the noon and murder flies. See the basting undip the chart, see the way the kinds are best seen from the rest, from that and untidy.

Cut the whole space into twenty-four spaces and then and then is there a yellow color, there is but it is smelled, it is then put where it is and nothing stolen.

A remarkable degree of red means that, a remarkable exchange is made.

Climbing altogether in when there is a solid chance of soiling no more than a dirty thing, coloring all of it in steadying is jelly.

Just as it is suffering, just as it is succeeded, just as it is moist so is there no countering.

MILK.

A white egg and a colored pan and a cabbage showing settlement, a constant increase.

A cold in a nose, a single cold nose makes an excuse. Two are more necessary.

All the goods are stolen, all the blisters are in the cup.

Cooking, cooking is the recognition between sudden and nearly sudden very little and all large holes.

A real pint, one that is open and closed and in the middle is so bad.

Tender colds, seen eye holders, all work, the best of change, the meaning, the dark red, all this and bitten, really bitten.

Guessing again and golfing again and the best men, the very best men.

MILK.

Climb up in sight climb in the whole utter needles and a guess a whole guess is hanging. Hanging hanging.

EGGS.

Kind height, kind in the right stomach with a little sudden mill.

Cunning shawl, cunning shawl to be steady.

In white in white handkerchiefs with little dots in a white belt all shadows are singular they are singular and procured and relieved.

No that is not the cows shame and a precocious sound, it is a bite.

Cut up alone the paved way which is harm. Harm is old boat and a likely dash.

APPLE.

Apple plum, carpet steak, seed clam, colored wine, calm seen, cold cream, best shake, potato, potato and no no gold work with pet, a green seen is called bake and change sweet is bready, a little piece a little piece please.

A little piece please. Cane again to the presupposed and ready eucalyptus tree, count out sherry and ripe plates and little corners of a kind of ham. This is use.

TAILS.

Cold pails, cold with joy no joy.

A tiny seat that means meadows and a lapse of cuddles with cheese and nearly bats, all this went messed. The post placed a loud loose sprain. A rest is no better. It is better yet. All the time.

LUNCH.

Luck in loose plaster makes holy gauge and nearly that, nearly more states, more states come in town light kite, blight not white.

A little lunch is a break in skate a little lunch so slimy, a west end of a board line is that which shows a little beneath so that necessity is a silk under wear. That is best wet. It is so natural, and why is there flake, there is flake to explain exhaust.

A real cold hen is nervous is nervous with a towel with a spool with real beads. It is mostly an extra sole nearly all that shaved, shaved with an old mountain, more than that bees more than that dinner and a bunch of likes that is to say the hearts of onions aim less.

Cold coffee with a corn a corn yellow and green mass is a gem.

CUPS.

A single example of excellence is in the meat. A bent stick is surging and might all might is mental. A grand clothes is searching out a candle not that wheatly not that by more than an owl and a path. A ham is proud of cocoanut.

A cup is neglected by being all in size. It is a handle and meadows and sugar any sugar.

A cup is neglected by being full of size. It shows no shade, in come little wood cuts and blessing and nearly not that not with a wild bought in, not at all so polite, not nearly so behind.

Cups crane in. They need a pet oyster, they need it so hoary and nearly choice. The best slam is utter. Nearly be freeze.

Why is a cup a stir and a behave. Why is it so seen.

A cup is readily shaded, it has in between no sense that is to say music, memory, musical memory.

Peanuts blame, a half sand is holey and nearly.

RHUBARB.

Rhubarb is susan not susan not seat in bunch toys not wild and laughable not in little places not in neglect and vegetable not in fold coal age not please.

SINGLE FISH.

Single fish single fish single fish egg-plant single fish sight.

A sweet win and not less noisy than saddle and more ploughing and nearly well painted by little things so.

Please shade it a play. It is necessary and beside the large sort is puff.

Every way oakly, please prune it near. It is so found.

It is not the same.

CAKE.

Cake cast in went to be and needles wine needles are such.

This is today. A can experiment is that which makes a town, makes a town dirty, it is little please. We came back. Two bore, bore what, a mussed ash, ash when there is tin. This meant cake. It was a sign.

Another time there was extra a hat pin sought long and this dark made a display. The result was yellow. A caution, not a caution to be.

It is no use to cause a foolish number. A blanket stretch a cloud, a shame, all that bakery can tease, all that is beginning and yesterday yesterday we had it met. It means some change. No some day.

A little leaf upon a scene an ocean any where there, a bland and likely in the stream a recollection green land. Why white.

CUSTARD.

Custard is this. It has aches, aches when. Not to be. Not to be narrowly. This makes a whole little hill.

It is better than a little thing that has mellow real mellow. It is better than lakes whole lakes, it is better than seeding.

POTATOES.

Real potatoes cut in between.

POTATOES.

In the preparation of cheese, in the preparation of crackers, in the preparation of butter, in it.

ROAST POTATOES.

Roast potatoes for.

ASPARAGUS.

Asparagus in a lean in a lean to hot. This makes it art and it is wet wet weather wet weather wet.

BUTTER.

Boom in boom in, butter. Leave a grain and show it, show it. I spy.

It is a need it is a need that a flower a state flower. It is a need that a state rubber. It is a need that a state rubber is sweet and sight and a swelled stretch. It is a need. It is a need that state rubber.

Wood a supply. Clean little keep a strange, estrange on it.

Make a little white, no and not with pit, pit on in within.

END OF SUMMER.

Little eyelets that have hammer and a check with stripes between a lounge, in wit, in a rested development.

SAUSAGES.

Sausages in between a glass.

There is read butter. A loaf of it is managed. Wake a question. Eat an instant, answer.

A reason for bed is this, that a decline, any decline is poison, poison is a toe a toe extractor, this means a solemn change. Hanging.

No evil is wide, any extra in leaf is so strange and singular a red breast.

CELERY.

Celery tastes tastes where in curled lashes and little bits and mostly in remains. A green acre is so selfish and so pure and so enlivened.

VEAL.

Very well very well, washing is old, washing is washing.

Cold soup, cold soup clear and particular and a principal a principal question to put into.

VEGETABLE.

What is cut. What is cut by it. What is cut by it in.

It was a cress a crescent a cross and an unequal scream, it was upslanting, it was radiant and reasonable with little ins and red.

News. News capable of glees, cut in shoes, belike under pump of wide chalk, all this combing.

WAY LAY VEGETABLE.

Leaves in grass and mow potatoes, have a skip, hurry you up flutter.

Suppose it is ex a cake suppose it is new mercy and leave charlotte and nervous bed rows. Suppose it is meal. Suppose it is sam.

COOKING.

Alas, alas the pull alas the bell alas the coach in china, alas the little put in leaf alas the wedding butter meat, alas the receptacle, alas the back shape of mussle, mussle and soda.

CHICKEN.

Pheasant and chicken, chicken is a peculiar third.

CHICKEN.

Alas a dirty word, alas a dirty third alas a dirty third, alas a dirty bird.

CHICKEN.

Alas a doubt in case of more go to say what it is cress. What is it. Mean. Potato. Loaves.

CHICKEN.

Stick stick call then, stick stick sticking, sticking with a chicken. Sticking in a extra succession, sticking in.

CHAIN-BOATS.

Chain-boats are merry, are merry blew, blew west, carpet.

PASTRY.

Cutting shade, cool spades and little last beds, make violet, violet when.

CREAM.

In a plank, in a play sole, in a heated red left tree there is shut in specs with salt be where. This makes an eddy. Necessary.

CREAM.

Cream cut. Any where crumb. Left hop chambers.

CUCUMBER.

Not a razor less, not a razor, ridiculous pudding, red and relet put in, rest in a slender go in selecting, rest in, rest in in white widening.

DINNER.

Not a little fit, not a little fit sun sat in shed more mentally.
Let us why, let us why weight, let us why winter chess, let us why way.
Only a moon to soup her, only that in the sell never never be the cocups nice be, shatter it they lay.
Egg ear nuts, look a bout. Shoulder. Let it strange, sold in bell next herds.
It was a time when in the acres in late there was a wheel that shot a burst of land and needless are niggers and a sample sample set of old eaten butterflies with spoons, all of it to be are fled and measure make it, make it, yet all the one in that we see where shall not it set with a left and more so, yes there add when the longer not it shall the best in the way when all be with when shall not for there with see and chest how for another excellent and excellent and easy easy excellent and easy express e c, all to be nice all to be no so. All to be

no so no so. All to be not a white old chat churner. Not to be any example of an edible apple in.

DINING.

Dining is west.

EATING.

Eat ting, eating a grand old man said roof and never never re soluble burst, not a near ring not a bewildered neck, not really any such bay.

Is it so a noise to be is it a least remain to rest, is it a so old say to be, is it a leading are been. Is it so, is it so, is it so, is it so is it so is it so.

Eel us eel us with no no pea no pea cool, no pea cool cooler, no pea cooler with a land a land cost in, with a land cost in stretches.

Eating he heat eating he heat it eating, he heat it heat eating. He heat eating.

A little piece of pay of pay owls owls such as pie, bolsters.

Will leap beat, willie well all. The rest rest oxen occasion occasion to be so purred, so purred how.

It was a ham it was a square come well it was a square remain, a square remain not it a bundle, not it a bundle so is a grip, a grip to shed bay leave bay leave draught, bay leave draw cider in low, cider in low and george. George is a mass.

EATING.

It was a shame it was a shame to stare to stare and double and relieve relieve be cut up show as by the elevation of it and out out more in the steady where the come and on and the all the shed and that.

It was a garden and belows belows straight. It was a pea, a pea pour it in its not a succession, not it a simple, not it a so election, election with.

SALAD.

It is a winning cake.

SAUCE.

What is bay labored what is all be section, what is no much. Sauce sam in.

SALMON.

It was a peculiar bin a bin fond in beside.

ORANGE.

Why is a feel oyster an egg stir. Why is it orange centre.

A show at tick and loosen loosen it so to speak sat.

It was an extra leaker with a see spoon, it was an extra licker with a see spoon.

ORANGE.

A type oh oh new new not no not knealer knealer of old show beefsteak, neither neither.

ORANGES.

Build is all right.

ORANGE IN.

Go lack go lack use to her.

Cocoa and clear soup and oranges and oat-meal.

Whist bottom whist close, whist clothes, woodling.

Cocoa and clear soup and oranges and oat-meal.

Pain soup, suppose it is question, suppose it is butter, real is, real is only, only excreate, only excreate a no since.

A no, a no since, a no since when, a no since when since, a no since when since a no since when since, a no since, a no since when since, a no since, a no, a no since a no since, a no since, a no since.

SALAD DRESSING AND AN ARTICHOKE.

Please pale hot, please cover rose, please acre in the red stranger, please butter all the beef-steak with regular feel faces.

SALAD DRESSING AND AN ARTICHOKE.

It was please it was please carriage cup in an ice-cream, in an ice-cream it was too bended bended with scissors and all this time. A whole is inside a part, a part does go away, a hole is red leaf. No choice was where there was and a second and a second.

A CENTRE IN A TABLE.

It was a way a day, this made some sum. Suppose a cod liver a cod liver is an oil, suppose a cod liver oil is tunny, suppose a cod liver oil tunny is pressed suppose a cod liver oil tunny pressed is china and secret with a bestow a bestow reed, a reed to be a reed to be, in a reed to be.

Next to me next to a folder, next to a folder some waiter, next to a foldersome waiter and re letter and read her. Read her with her for less.

Rooms

Act so that there is no use in a centre. A wide action is not a width. A preparation is given to the ones preparing. They do not eat who mention silver and sweet. There was an occupation.

A whole centre and a border make hanging a way of dressing. This which is not why there is a voice is the remains of an offering. There was no rental.

So the tune which is there has a little piece to play, and the exercise is all there is of a fast. The tender and true that makes no width to hew is the time that there is question to adopt.

To begin the placing there is no wagon. There is no change lighter. It was done. And then the spreading, that was not accomplishing that needed standing and yet the time was not so difficult as they were not all in place. They had no change. They were not respected. They were that, they did it so much in the matter and this showed that that settlement was not condensed. It was spread there. Any change was in the ends of the centre. A heap was heavy. There was no change.

Burnt and behind and lifting a temporary stone and lifting more than a drawer.

The instance of there being more is an instance of more. The shadow is not shining in the way there is a black line. The truth has come. There is a disturbance. Trusting to a baker's boy meant that there would be very much exchanging and anyway what is the use of a covering to a door. There is a use, they are double.

If the centre has the place then there is distribution. That is natural. There is a contradiction and naturally returning there comes to be both sides and the centre. That can be seen from the description.

The author of all that is in there behind the door and that is entering in the morning. Explaining darkening and expecting relating is all of a piece. The stove is bigger. It was of a shape that made no audience bigger if the opening is assumed why should there not be kneeling. Any force which is bestowed on a floor shows rubbing. This is so nice and sweet and yet there comes the change, there comes the time to press more air. This does not mean the same as disappearance.

A little lingering lion and a Chinese chair, all the handsome cheese which is stone, all of it and a choice, a choice of a blotter. If it is difficult to do it one way there is no place of similar trouble. None. The whole arrangement is established. The end of which is that there is a suggestion, a suggestion that there can be a different whiteness to a wall. This was thought.

A page to a corner means that the shame is no greater when the table is longer. A glass is of any height, it is higher, it is simpler and if it were placed there would not be any doubt.

Something that is an erection is that which stands and feeds and silences a tin which is swelling. This makes no diversion that is to say what can please exaltation, that which is cooking.

A shine is that which when covered changes permission. An enclosure blends with the same that is to say there is blending. A blend is that which holds no mice and this is not because of a floor it is because of nothing, it is not in a vision.

A fact is that when the place was replaced all was left that was stored and all was retained that would not satisfy more than another. The question is this, is it possible to suggest more to replace that thing. This question and this perfect denial does make the time change all the time.

The sister was not a mister. Was this a surprise. It was. The conclusion came when there was no arrangement. All the time that there was a question there was a decision. Replacing a casual acquaintance with an ordinary daughter does not make a son.

It happened in a way that the time was perfect and there was a growth of a whole dividing time so that where formerly there was no mistake there was no mistake now. For instance before when there was a separation there was waiting, now when there is separation there is the division between intending and departing. This made no more mixture than there would be if there had been no change.

A little sign of an entrance is the one that made it alike. If it were smaller it was not alike and it was so much smaller that a table was bigger. A table was much bigger, very much bigger. Changing that made nothing bigger, it did not make anything bigger littler, it did not hinder wood from not being used as leather. And this was so charming. Harmony is so essential. Is there pleasure when there is a passage, there is when every room is open. Every room is open when there are not four, there were there and surely there were four, there were two together. There is no resemblance.

A single speed, the reception of table linen, all the wonder of six little spoons, there is no exercise.

The time came when there was a birthday. Every day was no excitement and a birthday was added, it was added on Monday, this made the memory clear, this which was a speech showed the chair in the middle where there was copper.

Alike and a snail, this means Chinamen, it does there is no doubt that to be right is more than perfect there is no doubt and glass is confusing it confuses the substance which was of a color. Then came the time for discrimination, it came then and it was never mentioned it was so triumphant, it showed the whole head that had a hole and should have a hole it showed the resemblance between silver.

Startling a starving husband is not disagreeable. The reason that nothing is hidden is that there is no suggestion of silence. No song is sad. A lesson is of consequence.

Blind and weak and organised and worried and betrothed and resumed and also asked to a fast and always asked to consider and never startled and not at all bloated, this which is no rarer than frequently is not so astonishing when hair brushing is added. There is quiet, there certainly is.

No eye-glasses are rotten, no window is useless and yet if air will not come in there is a speech ready, there always is and there is no dimness, not a bit of it.

All along the tendency to deplore the absence of more has not been authorised. It comes to mean that with burning there is that pleasant state of stupefication. Then there is a way of earning a living. Who is a man.

A silence is not indicated by any motion, less is indicated by a motion, more is not indicated it is enthralled. So sullen and so low, so much resignation, so much refusal and so much place for a lower and an upper, so much and yet more silence, why is not sleeping a feat why is it not and when is there some discharge when. There never is.

If comparing a piece that is a size that is recognised as not a size but a piece, comparing a piece with what is not recognised but what is used as it is held by holding, comparing these two comes to be repeated. Suppose they are put together, suppose that there is an interruption, supposing that beginning again they are not changed as to position, suppose all this and suppose that any five two of whom are not separating suppose that the five are not consumed. Is there an exchange, is there a resemblance to the sky which is admitted to be there and the stars which can be seen. Is there. That was a question. There was no certainty. Fitting a failing meant that any two were indifferent and yet they were all connecting that, they were all connecting that consideration. This did not determine rejoining a letter. This did not make letters smaller. It did.

The stamp that is not only torn but also fitting is not any symbol. It suggests nothing. A sack that has no opening suggests more and the loss is not commensurate. The season gliding and the torn hangings receiving mending all this shows an example, it shows the force of sacrifice and likeness and disaster and a reason.

The time when there is not the question is only seen when there is a shower. Any little thing is water.

There was a whole collection made. A damp cloth, an oyster, a single mirror, a manikin, a student, a silent star, a single spark, a little movement and the bed is made. This shows the disorder, it does, it shows more likeness than anything else, it shows the single mind that directs an apple. All the coats have a different shape, that does not mean that they differ in color, it means a union between use and exercise and a horse.

A plain hill, one is not that which is not white and red and green, a plain hill makes no sunshine, it shows that without a disturber. So the shape is there and the color and the outline and the miserable centre, it is not very likely that there is a centre, a hill is a hill and no hill is contained in a pink tender descender.

A can containing a curtain is a solid sentimental usage. The trouble in both eyes does not come from the same symmetrical carpet, it comes from there being no more disturbance than in little paper. This does show the teeth, it shows color.

A measure is that which put up so that it shows the length has a steel construction. Tidiness is not delicacy, it does not destroy the whole piece, certainly not it has been measured and nothing has been cut off and even if that has been lost there is a name, no name is signed and left over, not any space is fitted so that moving about is plentiful. Why is there so much resignation in a package, why is there rain, all the same the chance has come, there is no bell to ring.

A package and a filter and even a funnel, all this together makes a scene and supposing the question arises is hair curly, is it dark and dusty, supposing that question arises, is brushing necessary, is it, the whole special suddenness commences then, there is no delusion.

A cape is a cover, a cape is not a cover in summer, a cape is a cover and the regulation is that there is no such weather. A cape is not always a cover, a cape is not a cover when there is another, there is always something in that thing in establishing a disposition to put wetting where it will not do more harm. There is always that disposition and in a way there is some use in not mentioning changing and in establishing the temperature, there is some use in it as establishing all that lives dimmer freer and there is no dinner in the middle of anything. There is no such thing.

Why is a pale white not paler than blue, why is a connection made by a stove, why is the example which is mentioned not shown to be the same, why is there no adjustment between the place and the separate attention. Why is there a choice in gamboling. Why is there no necessary dull stable, why is there a single piece of any color, why is there that sensible silence. Why is there the resistance in a mixture, why is there no poster, why is there that in the window, why is there no suggester, why is there no window, why is there no oyster closer. Why is there a circular diminisher, why is there a bather, why is there no scraper, why is there a dinner, why is there a bell ringer, why is there a duster, why is there a section of a similar resemblance, why is there that scissor.

South, south which is a wind is not rain, does silence choke speech or does it not.

Lying in a conundrum, lying so makes the springs restless, lying so is a reduction, not lying so is arrangeable.

Releasing the oldest auction that is the pleasing some still renewing.

Giving it away, not giving it away, is there any difference. Giving it away. Not giving it away.

Almost very likely there is no seduction, almost very likely there is no stream, certainly very likely the height is penetrated, certainly certainly the target is cleaned. Come to sit, come to refuse, come to surround, come slowly and age is not lessening. The time which showed that was when there was no eclipse. All the time that resenting was removal all that time there was breadth. No breath is shadowed, no breath is paintaking and yet certainly what could be the use of paper, paper shows no disorder, it shows no desertion.

Why is there a difference between one window and another, why is there a difference, because the curtain is shorter. There is no distaste in beefsteak or in plums or in gallons of milk water, there is no defiance in original piling up over a roof, there is no daylight in the evening, there is none there empty.

A tribune, a tribune does not mean paper, it means nothing more than cake, it means more sugar, it shows the state of lengthening any nose. The last spice is that which shows the whole evening spent in that sleep, it shows so that walking is an alleviation, and yet this astonishes everybody the distance is so sprightly. In all the time there are three days, those are not passed uselessly. Any little thing is a change that is if nothing is wasted in that cellar. All the rest of the chairs are established.

A success, a success is alright when there are there rooms and no vacancies, a success is alright when there is a package, success is alright anyway and any curtain is wholesale. A curtain diminishes and an ample space shows varnish.

One taste one tack, one taste one bottle, one taste one fish, one taste one barometer. This shows no distinguishing sign when there is a store.

Any smile is stern and any coat is a sample. Is there any use in changing more doors than there are committees. This question is so often asked that squares show that they are blotters. It is so very agreeable to hear a voice and to see all the signs of that expression.

Cadences, real cadences, real cadences and a quiet color. Careful and curved, cake and sober, all accounts and mixture, a guess at anything is righteous, should there be a call there would be a voice.

A line in life, a single line and a stairway, a rigid cook, no cook and no equator, all the same there is higher than that another evasion. Did that mean shame, it meant memory. Looking into a place that was hanging and was visible looking into this place and seeing a chair did that mean relief, it did, it certainly did not cause constipation and yet there is a melody that has white for a tune when there is straw color. This shows no face.

Star-light, what is star-light, star-light is a little light that is not always mentioned with the sun, it is mentioned with the moon and the sun, it is mixed up with the rest of the time.

Why is the name changed The name is changed because in the little space there is a tree, in some space there are no trees, in every space there is a hint of more, all this causes the decision.

Why is there education, there is education because the two tables which are folding are not tied together with a ribbon, string is used and string being used there is a necessity for another one and another one not being used to hearing shows no ordinary use of any evening and yet there is no disgrace in looking, none at all. This came to separate when there was simple selection of an entire pre-occupation.

A curtain, a curtain which is fastened discloses mourning, this does not mean sparrows or elocution or even a whole preparation, it means that there are ears and very often much more altogether.

Climate, climate is not southern, a little glass, a bright winter, a strange supper an elastic tumbler, all this shows that the back is furnished and red which is red is a dark color. An example of this is fifteen years and a separation of regret.

China is not down when there are plates, lights are not ponderous and incalculable.

Currents, currents are not in the air and on the floor and in the door and behind it first. Currents do not show it plainer. This which is mastered has so thin a space to build it all that there is plenty of room and yet is it quarreling, it is not and the insistence is marked. A change is in a current and there is no habitable exercise.

A religion, almost a religion, any religion, a quintal in religion, a relying and a surface and a service in indecision and a creature and a question and a syllable in answer and more counting and no quarrel and a single scientific statement and no darkness and no question and an earned administration and a single set of sisters and an outline and no blisters and the section seeing yellow and the centre having spelling and no solitude and no quaintness and yet solid quite so solid and the single surface centred and the question in the placard and the singularity, is there a singularity, and the singularity, why is there a question and the singularity why is the surface outrageous, why is it beautiful why is it not when there is no doubt, why is anything vacant, why is not disturbing a centre no virtue, why is it when it is and why is it when it is and there is no doubt, there is no doubt that the singularity shows.

A climate, a single climate, all the time there is a single climate, any time there is a doubt, any time there is music that is to question more and more and there is no politeness, there is hardly any ordeal and certainly there is no tablecloth.

This is a sound and obligingness more obligingness leads to a harmony in hesitation.

A lake a single lake which is a pond and a little water any water which is an ant and no burning, not any burning, all this is sudden.

A canister that is the remains of furniture and a looking-glass and a bedroom and a larger size, all the stand is shouted and what is ancient is practical. Should the resemblance be so that any little cover is copied, should it be so that yards are measured, should it be so and there be a sin, should it be so then certainly a room is big enough when it is so empty and the corners are gathered together.

The change is mercenary that settles whitening the coloring and serving dishes where there is metal and making yellow any yellow every color in a shade which is expressed in a tray. This is a monster and awkward quite awkward and the little design which is flowered which is not strange and yet has visible writing, this is not shown all the time but at once, after that it rests where it is and where it is in place. No change is not needed. That does show design.

Excellent, more excellence is borrowing and slanting very slanting is light and secret and a recitation and emigration. Certainly shoals are shallow and nonsense more nonsense is sullen. Very little cake is water, very little cake has that escape.

Sugar any sugar, anger every anger, lover sermon lover, centre no distractor, all order is in a measure.

Left over to be a lamp light, left over in victory, left over in saving, all this and negligence and bent wood and more even much more is not so exact as a pen and a turtle and even, certainly, and even a piece of the same experience as more.

To consider a lecture, to consider it well is so anxious and so much a charity and really supposing there is grain and if a stubble every stubble is urgent, will there not be a chance of legality. The sound is sickened and the price is purchased and golden what is golden, a clergyman, a single tax, a currency and an inner chamber.

Checking an emigration, checking it by smiling and certainly by the same satisfactory stretch of hands that have more use for it than nothing, and mildly not mildly a correction, not mildly even a circumstance and a sweetness and a serenity. Powder, that has no color, if it did have would it be white.

A whole soldier any whole soldier has no more detail than any case of measles.

A bridge a very small bridge in a location and thunder, any thunder, this is the capture of reversible sizing and more indeed more can be cautious. This which makes monotony careless makes it likely that there is an exchange in principle and more than that, change in organization.

This cloud does change with the movements of the moon and the narrow the quite narrow suggestion of the building. It does and then when it is settled and no sounds differ then comes the moment when cheerfulness is so assured that there is an occasion.

A plain lap, any plain lap shows that sign, it shows that there is not so much extension as there would be if there were more choice in everything. And why complain of more, why complain of very much more. Why complain at all when it is all arranged that as there is no more opportunity and no more appeal and not even any more clinching that certainly now some time has come.

A window has another spelling, it has "f" all together, it lacks no more then and this is rain, this may even be something else, at any rate there is no dedication in splendor. There is a turn of the stranger.

Catholic to be turned is to venture on youth and a section of debate, it even means that no class where each one over fifty is regular is so stationary that there are invitations.

A curving example makes righteous finger-nails. This is the only object in secretion and speech.

To being the same four are no more than were taller. The rest had a big chair and a surveyance a cold accumulation of nausea, and even more than that, they had a disappointment.

Nothing aiming is a flower, if flowers are abundant then they are lilac, if they are not they are white in the centre.

Dance a clean dream and an extravagant turn up, secure the steady rights and translate more than translate the authority, show the choice and make no more mistakes than yesterday.

This means clearness, it means a regular notion of exercise, it means more than that, it means liking counting, it means more than that, it does not mean exchanging a line.

Why is there more craving than there is in a mountain. This does not seem strange to one, it does not seem strange to an echo and more surely is in there not being a habit. Why is there so much useless suffering. Why is there.

Any wet weather means an open window, what is attaching eating, anything that is violent and cooking and shows weather is the same in the end and why is there more use in something than in all that.

The cases are made and books, back books are used to secure tears and church. They are even used to exchange black slippers. They can not be mended with wax. They show no need of any such occasion.

A willow and no window, a wide place stranger, a wideness makes an active center.

The sight of no pussy cat is so different that a tobacco zone is white and cream.

A lilac, all a lilac and no mention of butter, not even bread and butter, no butter and no occasion, not even a silent resemblance, not more care than just enough haughty.

A safe weight is that which when it pleases is hanging. A safer weight is one more naughty in a spectacle. The best game is that which is shiny and scratching. Please a pease and a cracker and a wretched use of summer.

Surprise, the only surprise has no occasion. It is an ingredient and the section the whole section is one season.

A pecking which is petting and no worse than in the same morning is not the only way to be continuous often.

A light in the moon the only light is on Sunday. What was the sensible decision. The sensible decision was that notwithstanding many declarations and more music, not even notwithstanding the choice and a torch and a collection, notwithstanding the celebrating hat and a vacation and even more noise than cutting, notwithstanding Europe and Asia and being overbearing, not even notwithstanding an elephant and a strict occasion, not even withstanding more cultivation and some seasoning, not even with drowning and with the ocean being encircling, not even with more likeness and any cloud, not even with terrific sacrifice of pedestrianism and a special resolution, not even more likely to be pleasing. The care with which the rain is wrong and the green is wrong and the white is wrong, the care with which there is a chair and plenty of breathing. The care with which there is incredible justice and likeness, all this makes a magnificent asparagus, and also a fountain.

THE SHADOWY THIRD

Ellen Glasgow

When the call came I remember that I turned from the telephone in a romantic flutter. Though I had spoken only once to the great surgeon, Roland Maradick, I felt on that December afternoon that to speak to him only once—to watch him in the operating-room for a single hour—was an adventure which drained the colour and the excitement from the rest of life. After all these years of work on typhoid and pneumonia cases, I can still feel the delicious tremor of my young pulses; I can still see the winter sunshine slanting through the hospital windows over the white uniforms of the nurses.

"He didn't mention me by name. Can there be a mistake?" I stood, incredulous yet ecstatic, before the superintendent of the hospital.

"No, there isn't a mistake. I was talking to him before you came down." Miss Hemphill's strong face softened while she looked at me. She was a big, resolute woman, a distant Canadian relative of my mother's, and the kind of nurse I had discovered in the month since I had come up from Richmond, that Northern hospital boards, if not Northern patients, appear instinctively to select. From the first, in spite of her hardness, she had taken a liking—I hesitate to use the word "fancy" for a preference so impersonal—to her Virginia cousin. After all, it isn't every Southern nurse, just out of training, who can boast a kinswoman in the superintendent of a New York hospital.

"And he made you understand positively that he meant me?" The thing was so wonderful that I simply couldn't believe it.

"He asked particularly for the nurse who was with Miss Hudson last week when he operated. I think he didn't even remember that you had a name. When I asked if he meant Miss Randolph, he repeated that he wanted the nurse who had been with Miss Hudson. She was small, he said, and cheerful-looking. This, of course, might apply to one or two of the others, but none of these was with Miss Hudson."

"Then I suppose it is really true?" My pulses were tingling. "And I am to be there at six o'clock?"

"Not a minute later. The day nurse goes off duty at that hour, and Mrs. Maradick is never left by herself for an instant."

"It is her mind, isn't it? And that makes it all the stranger that he should select me, for I have had so few mental cases."

"So few cases of any kind," Miss Hemphill was smiling, and when she smiled I wondered if the other nurses would know her. "By the time you have gone through the treadmill in New York, Margaret, you will have lost a good many things besides your inexperience. I wonder how long you will keep your sympathy and your imagination? After all, wouldn't you have made a better novelist than a nurse?"

"I can't help putting myself into my cases. I suppose one ought not to?"

"It isn't a question of what one ought to do, but of what one must. When you are drained of every bit of sympathy and enthusiasm, and have got nothing in return for it, not even thanks, you will understand why I try to keep you from wasting yourself."

"But surely in a case like this—for Doctor Maradick?"

"Oh, well, of course—for Doctor Maradick." She must have seen that I implored her confidence, for, after a minute, she let fall carelessly a gleam of light on the situation: "It is a very sad case when you think what a charming man and a great surgeon Doctor Maradick is."

Above the starched collar of my uniform I felt the blood leap in bounds to my cheeks. "I have spoken to him only once," I murmured, "but he is charming, and so kind and handsome, isn't he?"

"His patients adore him."

"Oh, yes, I've seen that. Everyone hangs on his visits." Like the patients and the other nurses, I also had come by delightful, if imperceptible, degrees to hang on the daily visits of Doctor Maradick. He was, I suppose, born to be a hero to women. From my first day in his hospital, from the moment when I watched, through closed shutters, while he stepped out of his car, I have never doubted that he was assigned to the great part in the play. If I had been ignorant of his spell—of the charm he exercised over his hospital—I should have felt it in the waiting hush, like a drawn breath, which followed his ring at the door and preceded his imperious footstep on the stairs. My first impression of him, even after the terrible events of the next year, records a memory that is both careless and splendid. At that moment, when, gazing through the chinks in the shutters, I watched him, in his coat of dark fur, cross the pavement over the pale streaks of sunshine, I knew beyond any doubt—I knew with a sort of infallible prescience—that my fate was irretrievably bound up with his in the future. I knew this, I repeat, though Miss Hemphill would still insist that my foreknowledge was merely a sentimental gleaning from indiscriminate novels. But it wasn't only first love, impressionable as my kinswoman believed me to be. It wasn't only the way he looked. Even more than his appearance—more than the shining dark of his eyes, the silvery brown of his hair, the dusky glow in his face—even more than his charm and his magnificence, I think, the beauty and sympathy in his voice won my heart. It was a voice, I heard someone say afterwards, that ought always to speak poetry.

So you will see why—if you do not understand at the beginning, I can never hope to make you believe impossible things!—so you will see why I accepted the call when it came as an imperative summons. I couldn't have stayed away after he sent for me. However much I may have tried not to go, I know that in the end I must have gone. In those days, while I was still hoping to write novels, I used to talk a great deal about "destiny" (I have learned since then how silly all such talk is), and I suppose it was my "destiny" to be caught in the web of Roland Maradick's personality. But I am not the first nurse to grow love-sick about a doctor who never gave her a thought.

"I am glad you got the call, Margaret. It may mean a great deal to you. Only try not to be too emotional." I remember that Miss Hemphill was holding a bit of rose-geranium in her hand while she spoke—one of the patients had given it to her from a pot she kept in her room, and the scent of the flower is still in my nostrils—or my memory. Since then—oh, long since then—I have wondered if she also had been caught in the web.

"I wish I knew more about the case." I was pressing for light. "Have you ever seen Mrs. Maradick?"

"Oh, dear, yes. They have been married only a little over a year, and in the beginning she used to come sometimes to the hospital and wait outside while the doctor made his visits. She was a very sweet-looking woman then—not exactly pretty, but fair and slight, with the loveliest smile, I think, I have ever seen. In those first months she was so much in love that we used to laugh about it among ourselves. To see her face light up when the doctor came out of the hospital and crossed the pavement to his car, was as good as a play. We never tired of watching her—I wasn't superintendent then, so I had more time to look out of the window while I was on day duty. Once or twice she brought her little girl in to see one of the patients. The child was so much like her that you would have known them anywhere for mother and daughter."

I had heard that Mrs. Maradick was a widow, with one child, when she first met the doctor, and I asked now, still seeking an illumination I had not found, "There was a great deal of money, wasn't there?"

"A great fortune. If she hadn't been so attractive, people would have said, I suppose, that Doctor Maradick married her for her money. Only," she appeared to make an effort of memory, "I believe I've heard somehow that it was all left in trust away from Mrs. Maradick if she married again. I can't, to save my life, remember just how it was; but it was a queer will, I know, and Mrs. Maradick wasn't to come into the money unless the child didn't live to grow up. The pity of it—"

A young nurse came into the office to ask for something—the keys, I think, of the operating-room, and Miss Hemphill broke off inconclusively as she hurried out of the door. I was sorry that she left off just when she did.

Poor Mrs. Maradick! Perhaps I was too emotional, but even before I saw her I had begun to feel her pathos and her strangeness.

My preparations took only a few minutes. In those days I always kept a suitcase packed and ready for sudden calls; and it was not yet six o'clock when I turned from Tenth Street into Fifth Avenue, and stopped for a minute, before ascending the steps, to look at the house in which Doctor Maradick lived. A fine rain was falling, and I remember thinking, as I turned the corner, how depressing the weather must be for Mrs. Maradick. It was an old house, with damp-looking walls (though that may have been because of the rain) and a spindle-shaped iron railing which ran up the stone steps to the black door, where I noticed a dim flicker through the old-fashioned fanlight. Afterwards I discovered that Mrs. Maradick had been born in the house—her maiden name was Calloran—and that she had never wanted to live anywhere else. She was a woman—this I found out when I knew her better—of strong attachments to both persons and places; and though Doctor Maradick had tried to persuade her to move uptown after her marriage, she had clung, against his wishes, to the old house in lower Fifth Avenue. I dare say she was obstinate about it in spite of her gentleness and her passion for the doctor. Those sweet, soft women, especially when they have always been rich, are sometimes amazingly obstinate. I have nursed so many of them since—women with strong affections and weak intellects—that I have come to recognize the type as soon as I set eyes upon it.

My ring at the bell was answered after a little delay, and when I entered the house I saw that the hall was quite dark except for the waning glow from an open fire which burned in the library. When I gave my name, and added that I was the night nurse, the servant appeared to think my humble presence unworthy of illumination. He was an old negro butler, inherited perhaps from Mrs. Maradick's mother, who, I learned afterwards, was from South Carolina; and while he passed me on his way up the staircase, I heard him vaguely muttering that he "wa'n't gwinter tu'n on dem lights twel de chile had done playin'."

To the right of the hall, the soft glow drew me into the library, and crossing the threshold timidly, I stooped to dry my wet coat by the fire. As I bent there, meaning to start up at the first sound of a footstep, I thought how cosy the room was after the damp walls outside to which some bared creepers were clinging; and I was watching the strange shapes and patterns the firelight made on the old Persian rug, when the lamps of a slowly turning motor flashed on me through the white shades at the window. Still dazzled by the glare, I looked round in the dimness and saw a child's ball of red and blue rubber roll towards me out of the gloom of the adjoining room. A moment later, while I made a vain attempt to capture the toy as it spun past me, a little girl darted airily, with peculiar lightness and grace, through the doorway, and stopped quickly, as if in surprise at the sight of a stranger. She was a small child—so small and slight that her footsteps made no sound on the polished floor of the threshold; and I remember thinking while I looked at her that she had the gravest and sweetest face I had ever seen. She couldn't—I decided this afterwards—have been more than six or seven years old, yet she stood there with a curious prim dignity, like the dignity of an elderly person, and gazed up at me with enigmatical eyes. She was dressed in Scotch plaid, with a bit of red ribbon in her hair, which was cut in a fringe over her forehead and hung very straight to her shoulders. Charming as she was, from her uncurled brown hair to the white socks and black slippers on her little feet, I recall most vividly the singular look in her eyes, which appeared in the shifting light to be of an indeterminate colour. For the odd thing about this look was that it was not the look of childhood at all. It was the look of profound experience, of bitter knowledge.

"Have you come for your ball?" I asked; but while the friendly question was still on my lips, I heard the servant returning. In my confusion I made a second ineffectual grasp at the play-thing, which had rolled away from me into the dusk of the drawing-room. Then, as I raised my head, I saw that the child also had slipped from the room; and without looking after her I followed the old negro into the pleasant study above, where the great surgeon awaited me.

Ten years ago, before hard nursing had taken so much out of me, I blushed very easily, and I was aware at the moment when I crossed Doctor Maradick's study that my cheeks were the colour of peonies. Of course, I was a fool—no one knows this better than I do—but I had never been alone, even for an instant, with him before, and the man was more than a hero to me, he was—there isn't any reason now why I should blush over the confession—almost a god. At that age I was mad about the wonders of surgery, and Roland Maradick in the operating-room was magician enough to have turned an older and more sensible head than mine. Added to his great reputation and his marvelous skill, he was, I am sure of this, the most splendid-looking man, even at forty-five, that one could imagine. Had he been ungracious—had he been positively rude to me, I should still have adored him; but when he held out his hand, and greeted me in the charming way he had with women, I felt that I would have died for him. It is no wonder that a saying went about the hospital that every woman he operated on fell in love with him. As for the nurses—well, there wasn't a single one of them who had escaped his spell—not even Miss Hemphill, who could have been scarcely a day under fifty.

"I am glad you could come, Miss Randolph. You were with Miss Hudson last week when I operated?"

I bowed. To save my life I couldn't have spoken without blushing the redder.

"I noticed your bright face at the time. Brightness, I think, is what Mrs. Maradick needs. She finds her day nurse depressing." His eyes rested so kindly upon me that I have suspected since that he was not entirely unaware of my worship. It was a small thing, heaven knows, to flatter his vanity—a nurse just out of a training-school—but to some men no tribute is too insignificant to give pleasure.

"You will do your best, I am sure." He hesitated an instant—just long enough for me to perceive the anxiety beneath the genial smile on his face—and then added gravely, "We wish to avoid, if possible, having to send her away."

I could only murmur in response, and after a few carefully chosen words about his wife's illness, he rang the bell and directed the maid to take me upstairs to my room. Not until I was ascending the stairs to the third storey did it occur to me that he had really told me nothing. I was as perplexed about the nature of Mrs. Maradick's malady as I had been when I entered the house.

I found my room pleasant enough. It had been arranged—at Doctor Maradick's request, I think—that I was to sleep in the house, and after my austere little bed at the hospital, I was agreeably surprised by the cheerful look of the apartment into which the maid led me. The walls were papered in roses, and there were curtains of flowered chintz at the window, which looked down on a small formal garden at the rear of the house. This the maid told me, for it was too dark for me to distinguish more than a marble fountain and a fir-tree, which looked old, though I afterwards learned that it was replanted almost every season.

In ten minutes I had slipped into my uniform and was ready to go to my patient; but for some reason—to this day I have never found out what it was that turned her against me at the start—Mrs. Maradick refused to receive me. While I stood outside her door I heard the day nurse trying to persuade her to let me come in. It wasn't any use, however, and in the end I was obliged to go back to my room and wait until the poor lady got over her whim and consented to see me. That was long after dinner—it must have been nearer eleven than ten o'clock—and Miss Peterson was quite worn out by the time she came for me.

"I'm afraid you'll have a bad night," she said as we went downstairs together. That was her way, I soon saw, to expect the worst of everything and everybody.

"Does she often keep you up like this?"

"Oh, no, she is usually very considerate. I never knew a sweeter character. But she still has this hallucination—"

Here again, as in the scene with Doctor Maradick, I felt that the explanation had only deepened the mystery. Mrs. Maradick's hallucination, whatever form it assumed, was evidently a subject for evasion and subterfuge in the household. It was on the tip of my tongue to ask, "What is her hallucination?"—but before I could get the words past my lips we had reached Mrs. Maradick's door, and Miss Peterson motioned me to be silent. As the door opened a little way to admit me, I saw that Mrs. Maradick was already in bed, and that the lights were out except for a night-lamp burning on a candle-stand beside a book and a carafe of water.

"I won't go in with you," said Miss Peterson in a whisper; and I was on the point of stepping over the threshold when I saw the little girl, in the dress of Scotch plaid, slip by me from the dusk of the room into the electric light of the hall. She held a doll in her arms, and as she went by she dropped a doll's work-basket in the doorway. Miss Peterson must have picked up the toy, for when I turned in a minute to look for it I found that it was gone. I remember thinking that it was late for a child to be up—she looked delicate, too—but, after all, it was no business of mine, and four years in a hospital had taught me never to meddle in things that do not concern me. There is nothing a nurse learns quicker than not to try to put the world to rights in a day.

When I crossed the floor to the chair by Mrs. Maradick's bed, she turned over on her side and looked at me with the sweetest and saddest smile.

"You are the night nurse," she said in a gentle voice; and from the moment she spoke I knew that there was nothing hysterical or violent about her mania—or hallucination, as they called it. "They told me your name, but I have forgotten it."

"Randolph—Margaret Randolph." I liked her from the start, and I think she must have seen it.

"You look very young, Miss Randolph."

"I am twenty-two, but I suppose I don't look quite my age. People usually think I am younger."

For a minute she was silent, and while I settled myself in the chair by the bed, I thought how strikingly she resembled the little girl I had seen first in the afternoon, and then leaving her room a few moments before. They had the same small, heart-shaped faces, coloured ever so faintly; the same straight, soft hair, between brown and flaxen; and the same large, grave eyes, set very far apart under arched eyebrows. What surprised me most, however, was that they both looked at me with that enigmatical and vaguely wondering expression—only in Mrs. Maradick's face the vagueness seemed to change now and then to a definite fear—a flash, I had almost said, of startled horror.

I sat quite still in my chair, and until the time came for Mrs. Maradick to take her medicine not a word passed between us. Then, when I bent over her with the glass in my hand, she raised her head from the pillow and said in a whisper of suppressed intensity:

"You look kind. I wonder if you could have seen my little girl?"

As I slipped my arm under the pillow I tried to smile cheerfully down on her. "Yes, I've seen her twice. I'd know her anywhere by her likeness to you."

A glow shone in her eyes, and I thought how pretty she must have been before illness took the life and animation out of her features. "Then I know you're good." Her voice was so strained and low that I could barely hear it. "If you weren't good you couldn't have seen her."

I thought this queer enough, but all I answered was, "She looked delicate to be sitting up so late."

A quiver passed over her thin features, and for a minute I thought she was going to burst into tears. As she had taken the medicine, I put the glass back on the candle-stand, and bending over the bed, smoothed the straight brown hair, which was as fine and soft as spun silk, back from her forehead. There was something about her—I don't know what it was—that made you love her as soon as she looked at you.

"She always had that light and airy way, though she was never sick a day in her life," she answered calmly after a pause. Then, groping for my hand, she whispered passionately, "You must not tell him—you must not tell anyone that you have seen her!"

"I must not tell anyone?" Again I had the impression that had come to me first in Doctor Maradick's study, and afterwards with Miss Peterson on the staircase, that I was seeking a gleam of light in the midst of obscurity.

"Are you sure there isn't anyone listening—that there isn't anyone at the door?" she asked, pushing aside my arm and raising herself on the pillows.

"Quite, quite sure. They have put out the lights in the hall."

"And you will not tell him? Promise me that you will not tell him." The startled horror flashed from the vague wonder of her expression. "He doesn't like her to come back, because he killed her."

"Because he killed her!" Then it was that light burst on me in a blaze. So this was Mrs. Maradick's hallucination! She believed that her child was dead—the little girl I had seen with my own eyes leaving her room; and she believed that her husband—the great surgeon we worshipped in the hospital—had murdered her. No wonder they veiled the dreadful obsession in mystery! No wonder that even Miss Peterson had not dared to drag the horrid thing out into the light! It was the kind of hallucination one simply couldn't stand having to face.

"There is no use telling people things that nobody believes," she resumed slowly, still holding my hand in a grasp that would have hurt me if her fingers had not been so fragile. "Nobody believes that he killed her. Nobody believes that she comes back every day to the house. Nobody believes—and yet you saw her—"

"Yes, I saw her—but why should your husband have killed her?" I spoke soothingly, as one would speak to a person who was quite mad. Yet she was not mad, I could have sworn this while I looked at her.

For a moment she moaned inarticulately, as if the horror of her thoughts were too great to pass into speech. Then she flung out her thin, bare arm with a wild gesture.

"Because he never loved me!" she said. "He never loved me!"

"But he married you," I urged gently while I stroked her hair. "If he hadn't loved you, why should he have married you?"

"He wanted the money—my little girl's money. It all goes to him when I die."

"But he is rich himself. He must make a fortune from his profession."

"It isn't enough. He wanted millions." She had grown stern and tragic. "No, he never loved me. He loved someone else from the beginning—before I knew him."

It was quite useless, I saw, to reason with her. If she wasn't mad, she was in a state of terror and despondency so black that it had almost crossed the border-line into madness. I thought once that I would go upstairs and bring the child down from her nursery; but, after a moment's hesitation, I realized that Miss Peterson and Doctor Maradick must have long ago tried all these measures. Clearly, there was nothing to do except soothe and quiet her as much as I could; and this I did until she dropped into a light sleep which lasted well into the morning.

By seven o'clock I was worn out—not from work but from the strain on my sympathy—and I was glad, indeed, when one of the maids came in to bring me an early cup of coffee. Mrs. Maradick was still sleeping—it was a mixture of bromide and chloral I had given her—and she did not wake until Miss Peterson came on duty an hour or two later. Then, when I went downstairs, I found the dining-room deserted except for the old housekeeper, who was looking over the silver. Doctor Maradick, she explained to me presently, had his breakfast served in the morning-room on the other side of the house.

"And the little girl? Does she take her meals in the nursery?"

She threw me a startled glance. Was it, I questioned afterwards, one of distrust or apprehension?

"There isn't any little girl. Haven't you heard?"

"Heard? No. Why, I saw her only yesterday."

The look she gave me—I was sure of it now—was full of alarm.

"The little girl—she was the sweetest child I ever saw—died just two months ago of pneumonia."

"But she couldn't have died." I was a fool to let this out, but the shock had completely unnerved me. "I tell you I saw her yesterday."

The alarm in her face deepened. "That is Mrs. Maradick's trouble. She believes that she still sees her."

"But don't you see her?" I drove the question home bluntly.

"No." She set her lips tightly. "I never see anything." So I had been wrong, after all, and the explanation, when it came, only accentuated the terror. The child was dead—she had died of pneumonia two months ago—and yet I had seen her, with my own eyes, playing ball in the library; I had seen her slipping out of her mother's room, with her doll in her arms.

"Is there another child in the house? Could there be a child belonging to one of the servants?" A gleam had shot through the fog in which I was groping.

"No, there isn't any other. The doctors tried bringing one once, but it threw the poor lady into such a state she almost died of it. Besides, there wouldn't be any other child as quiet and sweet-looking as Dorothea. To see her skipping along in her dress of Scotch plaid used to make me think of a fairy, though they say that fairies wear nothing but white or green."

"Has anyone else seen her—the child, I mean—any of the servants?"

"Only old Gabriel, the coloured butler, who came with Mrs. Maradick's mother from South Carolina. I've heard that negroes often have a kind of second sight—though I don't know that that is just what you would call it. But they seem to believe in the supernatural by instinct, and Gabriel is so old and doty—he does no work except answer the door-bell and clean the silver—that nobody pays much attention to anything that he sees—"

"Is the child's nursery kept as it used to be?"

"Oh, no. The doctor had all the toys sent to the children's hospital. That was a great grief to Mrs. Maradick; but Doctor Brandon thought, and all the nurses agreed with him, that it was best for her not to be allowed to keep the room as it was when Dorothea was living."

"Dorothea? Was that the child's name?"

"Yes, it means the gift of God, doesn't it? She was named after the mother of Mrs. Maradick's first husband, Mr. Ballard. He was the grave, quiet kind—not the least like the doctor."

I wondered if the other dreadful obsession of Mrs. Maradick's had drifted down through the nurses or the servants to the housekeeper; but she said nothing about it, and since she was, I suspected, a garrulous person, I thought it wiser to assume that the gossip had not reached her.

A little later, when breakfast was over and I had not yet gone upstairs to my room, I had my first interview with Doctor Brandon, the famous alienist who was in charge of the case. I had never seen him before, but from the first moment that I looked at him I took his measure almost by intuition. He was, I suppose, honest enough—I have always granted him that, bitterly as I have felt towards him. It wasn't his fault that he lacked red blood in his brain, or that he had formed the habit, from long association with abnormal phenomena, of regarding all life as a disease. He was the sort of physician—every nurse will understand what I mean—who deals instinctively with groups instead of with individuals. He was long and solemn and very round in the face; and I hadn't talked to him ten minutes before I knew he had been educated in Germany, and that he had learned over there to treat every emotion as a pathological manifestation. I used to wonder what he got out of life—what anyone got out of life who had analyzed away everything except the bare structure.

When I reached my room at last, I was so tired that I could barely remember either the questions Doctor Brandon had asked or the directions he had given me. I fell asleep, I know, almost as soon as my head touched the pillow; and the maid who came to inquire if I wanted luncheon decided to let me finish my nap. In the afternoon, when she returned with a cup of tea, she found me still heavy and drowsy. Though I was used to night nursing, I felt as if I had danced from sunset to daybreak. It was fortunate, I reflected, while I drank my tea, that every case didn't wear on one's sympathies as acutely as Mrs. Maradick's hallucination had worn on mine.

Through the day I did not see Doctor Maradick; but at seven o'clock when I came up from my early dinner on my way to take the place of Miss Peterson, who had kept on duty an hour later than usual, he met me in the hall and asked me to come into his study. I thought him handsomer than ever in his evening clothes, with a white flower in his buttonhole. He was going to some public dinner, the housekeeper told me, but, then, he was always going somewhere. I believe he didn't dine at home a single evening that winter.

"Did Mrs. Maradick have a good night?" He had closed the door after us, and turning now with the question, he smiled kindly, as if he wished to put me at ease in the beginning.

"She slept very well after she took the medicine. I gave her that at eleven o'clock."

For a minute he regarded me silently, and I was aware that his personality—his charm—was focused upon me. It was almost as if I stood in the centre of converging rays of light, so vivid was my impression of him.

"Did she allude in any way to her—to her hallucination?" he asked.

How the warning reached me—what invisible waves of sense-perception transmitted the message—I have never known; but while I stood there, facing the splendour of the doctor's presence, every intuition cautioned me that the time had come when I must take sides in the household. While I stayed there I must stand either with Mrs. Maradick or against her.

"She talked quite rationally," I replied after a moment.

"What did she say?"

"She told me how she was feeling, that she missed her child, and that she walked a little every day about her room." His face changed—how I could not at first determine. "Have you seen Doctor Brandon?"

"He came this morning to give me his directions."

"He thought her less well today. He has advised me to send her to Rosedale."

I have never, even in secret, tried to account for Doctor Maradick. He may have been sincere. I tell only what I know—not what I believe or imagine—and the human is sometimes as inscrutable, as inexplicable, as the supernatural.

While he watched me I was conscious of an inner struggle, as if opposing angels warred somewhere in the depths of my being. When at last I made my decision, I was acting less from reason, I knew, than in obedience to the pressure of some secret current of thought. Heaven knows, even then, the man held me captive while I defied him.

"Doctor Maradick," I lifted my eyes for the first time frankly to his, "I believe that your wife is as sane as I am—or as you are."

He started. "Then she did not talk freely to you?"

"She may be mistaken, unstrung, piteously distressed in mind"—I brought this out with emphasis—"but she is not—I am willing to stake my future on it—a fit subject for an asylum. It would be foolish—it would be cruel to send her to Rosedale."

"Cruel, you say?" A troubled look crossed his face, and his voice grew very gentle. "You do not imagine that I could be cruel to her?"

"No, I do not think that." My voice also had softened.

"We will let things go on as they are. Perhaps Doctor Brandon may have some other suggestion to make." He drew out his watch and compared it with the clock—nervously, I observed, as if his action were a screen for his discomfiture or perplexity. "I must be going now. We will speak of this again in the morning."

But in the morning we did not speak of it, and during the month that I nursed Mrs. Maradick I was not called again into her husband's study. When I met him in the hall or on the staircase, which was seldom, he was as charming as ever; yet, in spite of his courtesy, I had a persistent feeling that he had taken my measure on that evening, and that he had no further use for me.

As the days went by Mrs. Maradick seemed to grow stronger. Never, after our first night together, had she mentioned the child to me; never had she alluded by so much as a word to her dreadful charge against her husband. She was like any woman recovering from a great sorrow, except that she was sweeter and gentler. It is no wonder that everyone who came near her loved her; for there was a mysterious loveliness about her like the mystery of light, not of darkness. She was, I have always thought, as much of an angel as it is possible for a woman to be on this earth. And yet, angelic as she was, there were times when it seemed to me that she both hated and feared her husband. Though he never entered her room while I was there, and I never heard his name on her lips until an hour before the end, still I could tell by the look of terror in her face whenever his step passed down the hall that her very soul shivered at his approach.

During the whole month I did not see the child again, though one night, when I came suddenly into Mrs. Maradick's room, I found a little garden, such as children make out of pebbles and bits of box, on the window-sill. I did not mention it to Mrs. Maradick, and a little later, as the maid lowered the shades, I noticed that the garden had vanished. Since then I have often wondered if the child were invisible only to the rest of us, and if her mother still saw her. But there was no way of finding out except by questioning, and Mrs. Maradick was so well and patient that I hadn't the heart to question. Things couldn't have been better with her than they were, and I was beginning to tell myself that she might soon go out for an airing, when the end came so suddenly.

It was a mild January day—the kind of day that brings the foretaste of spring in the middle of winter, and when I came downstairs in the afternoon, I stopped a minute by the window at the end of the hall to look down on the box maze in the garden. There was an old fountain, bearing two laughing boys in marble, in the centre of the gravelled walk, and the water, which had been turned on that morning for Mrs. Maradick's pleasure, sparkled now like silver as the sunlight splashed over it. I had never before felt the air quite so soft and springlike in January; and I thought, as I gazed down on the garden, that it would be a good idea for Mrs. Maradick to go out and bask for an hour or so in the sunshine. It seemed strange to me that she was never allowed to get any fresh air except the air that came through her windows.

When I went into her room, however, I found that she had no wish to go out. She was sitting, wrapped in shawls, by the open window, which looked down on the fountain; and as I entered she glanced up from a little book she was reading. A pot of daffodils stood on the window-sill—she was very fond of flowers and we tried always to keep some growing in her room.

"Do you know what I am reading, Miss Randolph?" she asked in her soft voice; and she read aloud a verse while I went over to the candle-stand to measure out a dose of medicine.

"'If thou hast two loaves of bread, sell one and buy daffodils, for bread nourisheth the body, but daffodils delight the soul.' That is very beautiful, don't you think so?"

I said "Yes," that it was beautiful; and then I asked her if she wouldn't go downstairs and walk about in the garden.

"He wouldn't like it," she answered; and it was the first time she had mentioned her husband to me since the night I came to her. "He doesn't want me to go out."

I tried to laugh her out of the idea; but it was no use, and after a few minutes I gave up and began talking of other things. Even then it did not occur to me that her fear of Doctor Maradick was anything but a fancy. I could see, of course, that she wasn't out of her head; but sane persons, I knew, sometimes have unaccountable prejudices, and I accepted her dislike as a mere whim or aversion. I did not understand then and—I may as well confess this before the end comes—I do not understand any better today. I am writing down the things I actually saw, and I repeat that I have never had the slightest twist in the direction of the miraculous.

The afternoon slipped away while we talked—she talked brightly when any subject came up that interested her—and it was the last hour of day—that grave, still hour when the movement of life seems to droop and falter for a few precious minutes—that brought us the thing I had dreaded silently since my first night in the house. I remember that I had risen to close the window, and was leaning out for a breath of the mild air, when there was the sound of steps, consciously softened, in the hall outside, and Doctor Brandon's usual knock fell on my ears. Then, before I could cross the room, the door opened, and the doctor entered with Miss Peterson. The day nurse, I knew, was a stupid woman; but she had never appeared to me so stupid, so armoured and encased in her professional manner, as she did at that moment.

"I am glad to see that you are taking the air." As Doctor Brandon came over to the window, I wondered maliciously what devil of contradictions had made him a distinguished specialist in nervous diseases.

"Who was the other doctor you brought this morning?" asked Mrs. Maradick gravely; and that was all I ever heard about the visit of the second alienist.

"Someone who is anxious to cure you." He dropped into a chair beside her and patted her hand with his long, pale fingers. "We are so anxious to cure you that we want to send you away to the country for a fortnight or so. Miss Peterson has come to help you to get ready, and I've kept my car waiting for you. There couldn't be a nicer day for a trip, could there?"

The moment had come at last. I knew at once what he meant, and so did Mrs. Maradick. A wave of colour flowed and ebbed in her thin cheeks, and I felt her body quiver when I moved from the window and put my arms on her shoulders. I was aware again, as I had been aware that evening in Doctor Maradick's study, of a current of thought that beat from the air around into my brain. Though it cost me my career as a nurse and my reputation for sanity, I knew that I must obey that invisible warning.

"You are going to take me to an asylum," said Mrs. Maradick.

He made some foolish denial or evasion; but before he had finished I turned from Mrs. Maradick and faced him impulsively. In a nurse this was flagrant rebellion, and I realized that the act wrecked my professional future. Yet I did not care—I did not hesitate. Something stronger than I was driving me on.

"Doctor Brandon," I said, "I beg you—I implore you to wait until to-morrow. There are things I must tell you."

A queer look came into his face, and I understood, even in my excitement, that he was mentally deciding in which group he should place me—to which class of morbid manifestations I must belong.

"Very well, very well, we will hear everything," he replied soothingly; but I saw him glance at Miss Peterson, and she went over to the wardrobe for Mrs. Maradick's fur coat and hat.

Suddenly, without warning, Mrs. Maradick threw the shawls away from her, and stood up. "If you send me away," she said, "I shall never come back. I shall never live to come back."

The grey of twilight was just beginning, and while she stood there, in the dusk of the room, her face shone out as pale and flower-like as the daffodils on the window-sill. "I cannot go away!" she cried in a sharper voice. "I cannot go away from my child!"

I saw her face clearly; I heard her voice; and then—the horror of the scene sweeps back over me!—I saw the door open slowly and the little girl run across the room to her mother. I saw the child lift her little arms, and I saw the mother stoop and gather her to her bosom. So closely locked were they in that passionate embrace that their forms seemed to mingle in the gloom that enveloped them.

"After this can you doubt?" I threw out the words almost savagely—and then, when I turned from the mother and child to Doctor Brandon and Miss Peterson, I knew breathlessly—oh, there was a shock in the discovery!—that they were blind to the child. Their blank faces revealed the consternation of ignorance, not of conviction. They had seen nothing except the vacant arms of the mother and the swift, erratic gesture with which she stooped to embrace some invisible presence. Only my vision—and I have asked myself since if the power of sympathy enabled me to penetrate the web of material fact and see the spiritual form of the child—only my vision was not blinded by the clay through which I looked.

"After this can you doubt?" Doctor Brandon had flung my words back to me. Was it his fault, poor man, if life had granted him only the eyes of flesh? Was it his fault if he could see only half of the thing there before him?

But they couldn't see, and since they couldn't see I realized that it was useless to tell them. Within an hour they took Mrs. Maradick to the asylum; and she went quietly, though when the time came for parting from me she showed some faint trace of feeling. I remember that at the last, while we stood on the pavement, she lifted her black veil, which she wore for the child, and said: "Stay with her, Miss Randolph, as long as you can. I shall never come back."

Then she got into the car and was driven off, while I stood looking after her with a sob in my throat. Dreadful as I felt it to be, I didn't, of course, realize the full horror of it, or I couldn't have stood there quietly on the pavement. I didn't realize it, indeed, until several months afterwards when word came that she had died in the asylum. I never knew what her illness was, though I vaguely recall that something was said about "heart failure"—a loose enough term. My own belief is that she died simply of the terror of life.

To my surprise Doctor Maradick asked me to stay on as his office nurse after his wife went to Rosedale; and when the news of her death came there was no suggestion of my leaving. I don't know to this day why he wanted me in the house. Perhaps he thought I should have less opportunity to gossip if I stayed under his roof; perhaps he still wished to test the power of his charm over me. His vanity was incredible in so great a man. I have seen him flush with pleasure when people turned to look at him in the street, and I know that he was not above playing on the sentimental weakness of his patients. But he was magnificent, heaven knows! Few men, I imagine, have been the objects of so many foolish infatuations.

The next summer Doctor Maradick went abroad for two months, and while he was away I took my vacation in Virginia. When we came back the work was heavier than ever—his reputation by this time was tremendous—and my days were so crowded with appointments, and hurried flittings to emergency cases, that I had scarcely a minute left in which to remember poor Mrs. Maradick. Since the afternoon when she went to the asylum the child had not been in the house; and at last I was beginning to persuade myself that the little figure had been an optical illusion—the effect of shifting lights in the gloom of the old rooms—not the apparition I had once believed it to be. It does not take long for a phantom to fade from the memory—especially when one leads the active and methodical life I was forced into that winter. Perhaps—who knows?—(I remember telling myself) the doctors may have been right, after all, and the poor lady may have actually been out of her mind. With this view of the past, my judgment of Doctor Maradick insensibly altered. It ended, I think, in my acquitting him altogether. And then, just as he stood clear and splendid in my verdict of him, the reversal came so precipitately that I grow breathless now whenever I try to live it over again. The violence of the next turn in affairs left me, I often fancy, with a perpetual dizziness of the imagination.

It was in May that we heard of Mrs. Maradick's death, and exactly a year later, on a mild and fragrant afternoon, when the daffodils were blooming in patches around the old fountain in the garden, the housekeeper came into the office, where I lingered over some accounts, to bring me news of the doctor's approaching marriage.

"It is no more than we might have expected," she concluded rationally. "The house must be lonely for him—he is such a sociable man. But I can't help feeling," she brought out slowly after a pause in which I felt a shiver pass over me, "I can't help feeling that it is hard for that other woman to have all the money poor Mrs. Maradick's first husband left her."

"There is a great deal of money, then?" I asked curiously.

"A great deal." She waved her hand, as if words were futile to express the sum. "Millions and millions!"

"They will give up this house, of course?"

"That's done already, my dear. There won't be a brick left of it by this time next year. It's to be pulled down and an apartment-house built on the ground."

Again the shiver passed over me. I couldn't bear to think of Mrs. Maradick's old home falling to pieces.

"You didn't tell me the name of the bride," I said. "Is she someone he met while he was in Europe?"

"Dear me, no! She is the very lady he was engaged to before he married Mrs. Maradick, only she threw him over, so people said, because he wasn't rich enough. Then she married some lord or prince from over the water; but there was a divorce, and now she has turned again to her old lover. He is rich enough now, I guess, even for her!"

It was all perfectly true, I suppose; it sounded as plausible as a story out of a newspaper; and yet while she told me I felt, or dreamed that I felt, a sinister, an impalpable hush in the air. I was nervous, no doubt; I was shaken by the suddenness with which the housekeeper had sprung her news on me; but as I sat there I had quite vividly an impression that the old house was listening—that there was a real, if invisible, presence somewhere in the room or the garden. Yet, when an instant afterwards I glanced through the long window which opened down to the brick terrace, I saw only the faint sunshine over the deserted garden, with its maze of box, its marble fountain, and its patches of daffodils.

The housekeeper had gone—one of the servants, I think, came for her—and I was sitting at my desk when the words of Mrs. Maradick on that last evening floated into my mind. The daffodils brought her back to me; for I thought, as I watched them growing, so still and golden in the sunshine, how she would have enjoyed them. Almost unconsciously I repeated the verse she had read to me:

"If thou hast two loaves of bread, sell one and buy daffodils"—and it was at this very instant, while the words were still on my lips, that I turned my eyes to the box maze, and saw the child skipping rope along the gravelled path to the fountain. Quite distinctly, as clear as day, I saw her come, with what children call the dancing step, between the low box borders to the place where the daffodils bloomed by the fountain. From her straight brown hair to her frock of Scotch plaid and her little feet, which twinkled in white socks and black slippers over the turning rope, she was as real to me as the ground on which she trod or the laughing marble boys under the splashing water. Starting up from my chair, I made a single step to the terrace. If I could only reach her—only speak to her—I felt that I might at last solve the mystery. But with the first flutter of my dress on the terrace, the airy little form melted into the quiet dusk of the maze. Not a breath stirred the daffodils, not a shadow passed over the sparkling flow of the water; yet, weak and shaken in every nerve, I sat down on the brick step of the terrace and burst into tears. I must have known that something terrible would happen before they pulled down Mrs. Maradick's home.

The doctor dined out that night. He was with the lady he was going to marry, the housekeeper told me; and it must have been almost midnight when I heard him come in and go upstairs to his room. I was downstairs because I had been unable to sleep, and the book I wanted to finish I had left that afternoon in the office. The book—I can't remember what it was—had seemed to me very exciting when I began it in the morning; but after the visit of the child I found the romantic novel as dull as a treatise on nursing. It was impossible for me to follow the lines, and I was on the point of giving up and going to bed, when Doctor Maradick opened the front door with his latch-key and went up the staircase. "There can't be a bit of truth in it," I thought over and over again as I listened to his even step ascending the stairs. "There can't be a bit of truth in it." And yet, though I assured myself that "there couldn't be a bit of truth in it," I shrank, with a creepy sensation, from going through the house to my room in the third storey. I was tired out after a hard day, and my nerves must have reacted morbidly to the silence and the darkness. For the first time in my life I knew what it was to be afraid of the unknown, of the unseen; and while I bent over my book, in the glare of the electric light, I became conscious presently that I was straining my senses for some sound in the spacious emptiness of the rooms overhead. The noise of a passing motor-car in the street jerked me back from the intense hush of expectancy; and I can recall the wave of relief that swept over me as I turned to my book again and tried to fix my distracted mind on its pages.

I was still sitting there when the telephone on my desk rang, with what seemed to my overwrought nerves a startling abruptness, and the voice of the superintendent told me hurriedly that Doctor Maradick was needed at the hospital. I had become so accustomed to these emergency calls in the night that I felt reassured when I had rung up the doctor in his room and had heard the hearty sound of his response. He had not yet undressed, he said, and would come down immediately while I ordered back his car, which must just have reached the garage.

"I'll be with you in five minutes!" he called as cheerfully as if I had summoned him to his wedding.

I heard him cross the floor of his room; and before he could reach the head of the staircase, I opened the door and went out into the hall in order that I might turn on the light and have his hat and coat waiting. The electric button was at the end of the hall, and as I moved towards it, guided by the glimmer that fell from the landing above, I lifted my eyes to the staircase, which climbed dimly, with its slender mahogany balustrade, as far as the third storey. Then it was, at the very moment when the doctor, humming gaily, began his quick descent of the steps, that I distinctly saw—I will swear to this on my deathbed—a child's skipping-rope lying loosely coiled, as if it had dropped from a careless little hand, in the bend of the staircase. With a spring I had reached the electric button, flooding the hall with light; but as I did so, while my arm was still outstretched behind me, I heard the humming voice change to a cry of surprise or terror, and the figure on the staircase tripped heavily and stumbled with groping hands into emptiness. The scream of warning died in my throat while I watched him pitch forward down the long flight of stairs to the floor at my feet. Even before I bent over him, before I wiped the blood from his brow and felt for his silent heart, I knew that he was dead.

Something—it may have been, as the world believes, a misstep in the dimness, or it may have been, as I am ready to bear witness, an invisible judgment—something had killed him at the very moment when he most wanted to live.

AFTERWARD

Edith Wharton

I

"Oh, there is one, of course, but you'll never know it."

The assertion, laughingly flung out six months earlier in a bright June garden, came back to Mary Boyne with a sharp perception of its latent significance as she stood, in the December dusk, waiting for the lamps to be brought into the library.

The words had been spoken by their friend Alida Stair, as they sat at tea on her lawn at Pangbourne, in reference to the very house of which the library in question was the central, the pivotal "feature." Mary Boyne and her husband, in quest of a country place in one of the southern or southwestern counties, had, on their arrival in England, carried their problem straight to Alida Stair, who had successfully solved it in her own case; but it was not until they had rejected, almost capriciously, several practical and judicious suggestions that she threw it out: "Well, there's Lyng, in Dorsetshire. It belongs to Hugo's cousins, and you can get it for a song."

The reasons she gave for its being obtainable on these terms—its remoteness from a station, its lack of electric light, hot-water pipes, and other vulgar necessities—were exactly those pleading in its favor with two romantic Americans perversely in search of the economic drawbacks which were associated, in their tradition, with unusual architectural felicities.

"I should never believe I was living in an old house unless I was thoroughly uncomfortable," Ned Boyne, the more extravagant of the two, had jocosely insisted; "the least hint of 'convenience' would make me think it had been bought out of an exhibition, with the pieces numbered, and set up again." And they had proceeded to enumerate, with humorous precision, their various suspicions and exactions, refusing to believe that the house their cousin recommended was *really* Tudor till they learned it had no heating system, or that the village church was literally in the grounds till she assured them of the deplorable uncertainty of the water-supply.

"It's too uncomfortable to be true!" Edward Boyne had continued to exult as the avowal of each disadvantage was successively wrung from her; but he had cut short his rhapsody to ask, with a sudden relapse to distrust: "And the ghost? You've been concealing from us the fact that there is no ghost!"

Mary, at the moment, had laughed with him, yet almost with her laugh, being possessed of several sets of independent perceptions, had noted a sudden flatness of tone in Alida's answering hilarity.

"Oh, Dorsetshire's full of ghosts, you know."

"Yes, yes; but that won't do. I don't want to have to drive ten miles to see somebody else's ghost. I want one of my own on the premises. *Is* there a ghost at Lyng?"

His rejoinder had made Alida laugh again, and it was then that she had flung back tantalizingly: "Oh, there is one, of course, but you'll never know it."

"Never know it?" Boyne pulled her up. "But what in the world constitutes a ghost except the fact of its being known for one?"

"I can't say. But that's the story."

"That there's a ghost, but that nobody knows it's a ghost?"

"Well—not till afterward, at any rate."

"Till afterward?"

"Not till long, long afterward."

"But if it's once been identified as an unearthly visitant, why hasn't its *signalement* been handed down in the family? How has it managed to preserve its incognito?"

Alida could only shake her head. "Don't ask me. But it has."

"And then suddenly—" Mary spoke up as if from some cavernous depth of divination—"suddenly, long afterward, one says to one's self, '*That was it?*'"

She was oddly startled at the sepulchral sound with which her question fell on the banter of the other two, and she saw the shadow of the same surprise flit across Alida's clear pupils. "I suppose so. One just has to wait."

"Oh, hang waiting!" Ned broke in. "Life's too short for a ghost who can only be enjoyed in retrospect. Can't we do better than that, Mary?"

But it turned out that in the event they were not destined to, for within three months of their conversation with Mrs. Stair they were established at Lyng, and the life they had yearned for to the point of planning it out in all its daily details had actually begun for them.

It was to sit, in the thick December dusk, by just such a wide-hooded fireplace, under just such black oak rafters, with the sense that beyond the mullioned panes the downs were darkening to a deeper solitude: it was for the ultimate indulgence in such sensations that Mary Boyne had endured for nearly fourteen years the soul-deadening ugliness of the Middle West, and that Boyne had ground on doggedly at his engineering till, with a suddenness that still made her blink, the prodigious windfall of the Blue Star Mine had put them at a stroke in possession of life and the leisure to taste it. They had never for a moment meant their new state to be one of idleness; but they meant to give themselves only to harmonious activities. She had her vision of painting and gardening (against a background of gray walls), he dreamed of the production of his long-planned book on the "Economic Basis of Culture"; and with such absorbing work ahead no existence could be too sequestered; they could not get far enough from the world, or plunge deep enough into the past.

Dorsetshire had attracted them from the first by a semblance of remoteness out of all proportion to its geographical position. But to the Boynes it was one of the ever-recurring wonders of the whole incredibly compressed island—a nest of counties, as they put it—that for the production of its effects so little of a given quality went so far: that so few miles made a distance, and so short a distance a difference.

"It's that," Ned had once enthusiastically explained, "that gives such depth to their effects, such relief to their least contrasts. They've been able to lay the butter so thick on every exquisite mouthful."

The butter had certainly been laid on thick at Lyng: the old gray house, hidden under a shoulder of the downs, had almost all the finer marks of commerce with a protracted past. The mere fact that it was neither large nor exceptional made it, to the Boynes, abound the more richly in its special sense—the sense of having been for centuries a deep, dim reservoir of life. The life had probably not been of the most vivid order: for long periods, no doubt, it had fallen as noiselessly into the past as the quiet drizzle of autumn fell, hour after hour, into the green fish-pond between the yews; but these back-waters of existence sometimes breed, in their sluggish depths, strange acuities of emotion, and Mary Boyne had felt from the first the occasional brush of an intenser memory.

The feeling had never been stronger than on the December afternoon when, waiting in the library for the belated lamps, she rose from her seat and stood among the shadows of the hearth. Her husband had gone off, after luncheon, for one of his long tramps on the downs. She had noticed of late that he preferred to be unaccompanied on these occasions; and, in the tried security of their personal relations, had been driven to conclude that his book was bothering him, and that he needed the afternoons to turn over in solitude the problems left from the morning's work. Certainly the book was not going as smoothly as she had imagined it would, and the lines of perplexity between his eyes had never been there in his engineering days. Then he had often looked fagged to the verge of illness, but the native demon of "worry" had never branded his brow. Yet the few pages he had so far read to her—the introduction, and a synopsis of the opening chapter—gave evidences of a firm possession of his subject, and a deepening confidence in his powers.

The fact threw her into deeper perplexity, since, now that he had done with "business" and its disturbing contingencies, the one other possible element of anxiety was eliminated. Unless it were his health, then? But physically he had gained since they had come to Dorsetshire, grown robuster, ruddier, and fresher-eyed. It was only within a week that she had felt in him the undefinable change that made her restless in his absence, and as tongue-tied in his presence as though it were *she* who had a secret to keep from him!

The thought that there was a secret somewhere between them struck her with a sudden smart rap of wonder, and she looked about her down the dim, long room.

"Can it be the house?" she mused.

The room itself might have been full of secrets. They seemed to be piling themselves up, as evening fell, like the layers and layers of velvet shadow dropping from the low ceiling, the dusky walls of books, the smoke-blurred sculpture of the hooded hearth.

"Why, of course—the house is haunted!" she reflected.

The ghost—Alida's imperceptible ghost—after figuring largely in the banter of their first month or two at Lyng, had been gradually discarded as too ineffectual for imaginative use. Mary had, indeed, as became the tenant of a haunted house, made the customary inquiries among her few rural neighbors, but, beyond a vague, "They do say so, Ma'am," the villagers had nothing to impart. The elusive specter had apparently never had sufficient identity for a legend to crystallize about it, and after a time the Boynes had laughingly set the matter down to their profit-and-loss account, agreeing that Lyng was one of the few houses good enough in itself to dispense with supernatural enhancements.

"And I suppose, poor, ineffectual demon, that's why it beats its beautiful wings in vain in the void," Mary had laughingly concluded.

"Or, rather," Ned answered, in the same strain, "why, amid so much that's ghostly, it can never affirm its separate existence as *the* ghost." And thereupon their invisible housemate had finally dropped out of their references, which were numerous enough to make them promptly unaware of the loss.

Now, as she stood on the hearth, the subject of their earlier curiosity revived in her with a new sense of its meaning—a sense gradually acquired through close daily contact with the scene of the lurking mystery. It was the house itself, of course, that possessed the ghost-seeing faculty, that communed visually but secretly with its own past; and if one could only get into close enough communion with the house, one might surprise its secret, and acquire the ghost-sight on one's own account. Perhaps, in his long solitary hours in this very room, where she never trespassed till the afternoon, her husband had acquired it already, and was silently carrying the dread weight of whatever it had revealed to him. Mary was too well-versed in the code of the spectral world not to know that one could not talk about the ghosts one saw: to do so was almost as great a breach of good-breeding as to name a lady in a club. But this explanation did not really satisfy her. "What, after all, except for the fun of the *frisson*," she reflected, "would he really care for any of their old ghosts?" And thence she was thrown back once more on the fundamental dilemma: the fact that one's greater or less susceptibility to spectral influences had no particular bearing on the case, since, when one *did* see a ghost at Lyng, one did not know it.

"Not till long afterward," Alida Stair had said. Well, supposing Ned *had* seen one when they first came, and had known only within the last week what had happened to him? More and more under the spell of the hour, she threw back her searching thoughts to the early days of their tenancy, but at first only to recall a gay confusion of unpacking, settling, arranging of books, and calling to each other from remote corners of the house as treasure after treasure of their habitation revealed itself to them. It was in this particular connection that she presently recalled a certain soft afternoon of the previous October, when, passing from the first rapturous flurry of exploration to a detailed inspection of the old house, she had pressed (like a novel heroine) a panel that opened at her touch, on a narrow flight of stairs leading to an unsuspected flat ledge of the roof—the roof which, from below, seemed to slope away on all sides too abruptly for any but practised feet to scale.

The view from this hidden coign was enchanting, and she had flown down to snatch Ned from his papers and give him the freedom of her discovery. She remembered still how, standing on the narrow ledge, he had passed his arm about her while their gaze flew to the long, tossed horizon-line of the downs, and then dropped contentedly back to trace the arabesque of yew hedges about the fish-pond, and the shadow of the cedar on the lawn.

"And now the other way," he had said, gently turning her about within his arm; and closely pressed to him, she had absorbed, like some long, satisfying draft, the picture of the gray-walled court, the squat lions on the gates, and the lime-avenue reaching up to the highroad under the downs.

It was just then, while they gazed and held each other, that she had felt his arm relax, and heard a sharp "Hullo!" that made her turn to glance at him.

Distinctly, yes, she now recalled she had seen, as she glanced, a shadow of anxiety, of perplexity, rather, fall across his face; and, following his eyes, had beheld the figure of a man—a man in loose, grayish clothes, as it appeared to her—who was sauntering down the lime-avenue to the court with the tentative gait of a stranger seeking his way. Her short-sighted eyes had given her but a blurred impression of slightness and grayness, with something foreign, or at least unlocal, in the cut of the figure or its garb; but her husband had apparently seen more—seen enough to make him push past her with a sharp "Wait!" and dash down the twisting stairs without pausing to give her a hand for the descent.

A slight tendency to dizziness obliged her, after a provisional clutch at the chimney against which they had been leaning, to follow him down more cautiously; and when she had reached the attic landing she paused again for a less definite reason, leaning over the oak banister to strain her eyes through the silence of the brown, sun-flecked depths below. She lingered there till, somewhere in those depths, she heard the closing of a door; then, mechanically impelled, she went down the shallow flights of steps till she reached the lower hall.

The front door stood open on the mild sunlight of the court, and hall and court were empty. The library door was open, too, and after listening in vain for any sound of voices within, she quickly crossed the threshold, and found her husband alone, vaguely fingering the papers on his desk.

He looked up, as if surprised at her precipitate entrance, but the shadow of anxiety had passed from his face, leaving it even, as she fancied, a little brighter and clearer than usual.

"What was it? Who was it?" she asked.

"Who?" he repeated, with the surprise still all on his side.

"The man we saw coming toward the house." Boyne shrugged his shoulders. "So I thought; but he must have got up steam in the interval. What do you say to our trying a scramble up Meldon Steep before sunset?"

That was all. At the time the occurrence had been less than nothing, had, indeed, been immediately obliterated by the magic of their first vision from Meldon Steep, a height which they had dreamed of climbing ever since they had first seen its bare spine heaving itself above the low roof of Lyng. Doubtless it was the mere fact of the other incident's having occurred on the very day of their ascent to Meldon that had kept it stored away in the unconscious fold of association from which it now emerged; for in itself it had no mark of the portentous. At the moment there could have been nothing more natural than that Ned should dash himself from the roof in the pursuit of dilatory tradesmen. It was the period when they were always on the watch for one or the other of the specialists employed about the place; always lying in wait for them, and dashing out at them with questions, reproaches, or reminders. And certainly in the distance the gray figure had looked like Peters.

Yet now, as she reviewed the rapid scene, she felt her husband's explanation of it to have been invalidated by the look of anxiety on his face. Why had the familiar appearance of Peters made him anxious? Why, above all, if it was of such prime necessity to confer with that authority on the subject of the stable-drains, had the failure to find him produced such a look of relief?

Mary could not say that any one of these considerations had occurred to her at the time, yet, from the promptness with which they now marshaled themselves at her summons, she had a sudden sense that they must all along have been there, waiting their hour.

II

Weary with her thoughts, she moved toward the window. The library was now completely dark, and she was surprised to see how much faint light the outer world still held.

As she peered out into it across the court, a figure shaped itself in the tapering perspective of bare lines: it looked a mere blot of deeper gray in the grayness, and for an instant, as it moved toward her, her heart thumped to the thought, "It's the ghost!"

She had time, in that long instant, to feel suddenly that the man of whom, two months earlier, she had a brief distant vision from the roof was now, at his predestined hour, about to reveal himself as not having been Peters; and her spirit sank under the impending fear of the disclosure. But almost with the next tick of the clock the ambiguous figure, gaining substance and character, showed itself even to her weak sight as her husband's; and she turned away to meet him, as he entered, with the confession of her folly.

"It's really too absurd," she laughed out from the threshold, "but I never can remember!"

"Remember what?" Boyne questioned as they drew together.

"That when one sees the Lyng ghost one never knows it."

Her hand was on his sleeve, and he kept it there, but with no response in his gesture or in the lines of his fagged, preoccupied face.

"Did you think you'd seen it?" he asked, after an appreciable interval.

"Why, I actually took *you* for it, my dear, in my mad determination to spot it!"

"Me—just now?" His arm dropped away, and he turned from her with a faint echo of her laugh. "Really, dearest, you'd better give it up, if that's the best you can do."

"Yes, I give it up—I give it up. Have *you*?" she asked, turning round on him abruptly.

The parlor-maid had entered with letters and a lamp, and the light struck up into Boyne's face as he bent above the tray she presented.

"Have you?" Mary perversely insisted, when the servant had disappeared on her errand of illumination.

"Have I what?" he rejoined absently, the light bringing out the sharp stamp of worry between his brows as he turned over the letters.

"I never tried," he said, tearing open the wrapper of a newspaper.

"Well, of course," Mary persisted, "the exasperating thing is that there's no use trying, since one can't be sure till so long afterward."

He was unfolding the paper as if he had hardly heard her; but after a pause, during which the sheets rustled spasmodically between his hands, he lifted his head to say abruptly, "Have you any idea how long?"

Mary had sunk into a low chair beside the fireplace. From her seat she looked up, startled, at her husband's profile, which was darkly projected against the circle of lamplight.

"No; none. Have you?" she retorted, repeating her former phrase with an added keenness of intention.

Boyne crumpled the paper into a bunch, and then inconsequently turned back with it toward the lamp.

"Lord, no! I only meant," he explained, with a faint tinge of impatience, "is there any legend, any tradition, as to that?"

"Not that I know of," she answered; but the impulse to add, "What makes you ask?" was checked by the reappearance of the parlor-maid with tea and a second lamp.

With the dispersal of shadows, and the repetition of the daily domestic office, Mary Boyne felt herself less oppressed by that sense of something mutely imminent which had darkened her solitary afternoon. For a few moments she gave herself silently to the details of her task, and when she looked up from it she was struck to the point of bewilderment by the change in her husband's face. He had seated himself near the farther lamp, and was absorbed in the perusal of his letters; but was it something he had found in them, or merely the shifting of her own point of view, that had restored his features to their normal aspect? The longer she looked, the more definitely the change affirmed itself. The lines of painful tension had vanished, and such traces of fatigue as lingered were of the kind easily attributable to steady mental effort. He glanced up, as if drawn by her gaze, and met her eyes with a smile.

"I'm dying for my tea, you know; and here's a letter for you," he said.

She took the letter he held out in exchange for the cup she proffered him, and, returning to her seat, broke the seal with the languid gesture of the reader whose interests are all inclosed in the circle of one cherished presence.

Her next conscious motion was that of starting to her feet, the letter falling to them as she rose, while she held out to her husband a long newspaper clipping.

"Ned! What's this? What does it mean?"

He had risen at the same instant, almost as if hearing her cry before she uttered it; and for a perceptible space of time he and she studied each other, like adversaries watching for an advantage, across the space between her chair and his desk.

"What's what? You fairly made me jump!" Boyne said at length, moving toward her with a sudden, half-exasperated laugh. The shadow of apprehension was on his face again, not now a look of fixed foreboding, but a shifting vigilance of lips and eyes that gave her the sense of his feeling himself invisibly surrounded.

Her hand shook so that she could hardly give him the clipping.

"This article—from the *Waukesha Sentinel*—that a man named Elwell has brought suit against you—that there was something wrong about the Blue Star Mine. I can't understand more than half."

They continued to face each other as she spoke, and to her astonishment, she saw that her words had the almost immediate effect of dissipating the strained watchfulness of his look.

"Oh, that!" He glanced down the printed slip, and then folded it with the gesture of one who handles something harmless and familiar. "What's the matter with you this afternoon, Mary? I thought you'd got bad news."

She stood before him with her undefinable terror subsiding slowly under the reassuring touch of his composure.

"You knew about this, then—it's all right?"

"Certainly I knew about it; and it's all right."

"But what is it? I don't understand. What does this man accuse you of?"

"Oh, pretty nearly every crime in the calendar." Boyne had tossed the clipping down, and thrown himself comfortably into an arm-chair near the fire. "Do you want to hear the story? It's not particularly interesting—just a squabble over interests in the Blue Star."

"But who is this Elwell? I don't know the name."

"Oh, he's a fellow I put into it—gave him a hand up. I told you all about him at the time."

"I daresay. I must have forgotten." Vainly she strained back among her memories. "But if you helped him, why does he make this return?"

"Oh, probably some shyster lawyer got hold of him and talked him over. It's all rather technical and complicated. I thought that kind of thing bored you."

His wife felt a sting of compunction. Theoretically, she deprecated the American wife's detachment from her husband's professional interests, but in practice she had always found it difficult to fix her attention on Boyne's report of the transactions in which his varied interests involved him. Besides, she had felt from the first that, in a community where the amenities of living could be obtained only at the cost of efforts as arduous as her husband's professional labors, such brief leisure as they could command should be used as an escape from immediate preoccupations, a flight to the life they always dreamed of living. Once or twice, now that this new life had actually drawn its magic circle about them, she had asked herself if she had done right; but hitherto such conjectures had been no more than the retrospective excursions of an active fancy. Now, for the first time, it startled her a little to find how little she knew of the material foundation on which her happiness was built.

She glanced again at her husband, and was reassured by the composure of his face; yet she felt the need of more definite grounds for her reassurance.

"But doesn't this suit worry you? Why have you never spoken to me about it?"

He answered both questions at once: "I didn't speak of it at first because it *did* worry me—annoyed me, rather. But it's all ancient history now. Your correspondent must have got hold of a back number of the *Sentinel.*"

She felt a quick thrill of relief. "You mean it's over? He's lost his case?"

There was a just perceptible delay in Boyne's reply. "The suit's been withdrawn—that's all."

But she persisted, as if to exonerate herself from the inward charge of being too easily put off. "Withdrawn because he saw he had no chance?"

"Oh, he had no chance," Boyne answered.

She was still struggling with a dimly felt perplexity at the back of her thoughts.

"How long ago was it withdrawn?"

He paused, as if with a slight return of his former uncertainty. "I've just had the news now; but I've been expecting it."

"Just now—in one of your letters?"

"Yes; in one of my letters."

She made no answer, and was aware only, after a short interval of waiting, that he had risen, and strolling across the room, had placed himself on the sofa at her side. She felt him, as he did so, pass an arm about her, she felt his hand seek hers and clasp it, and turning slowly, drawn by the warmth of his cheek, she met the smiling clearness of his eyes.

"It's all right—it's all right?" she questioned, through the flood of her dissolving doubts; and "I give you my word it never was righter!" he laughed back at her, holding her close.

III

One of the strangest things she was afterward to recall out of all the next day's incredible strangeness was the sudden and complete recovery of her sense of security.

It was in the air when she woke in her low-ceilinged, dusky room; it accompanied her down-stairs to the breakfast-table, flashed out at her from the fire, and re-duplicated itself brightly from the flanks of the urn and the sturdy flutings of the Georgian teapot. It was as if, in some roundabout way, all her diffused apprehensions of the previous day, with their moment of sharp concentration about the newspaper article,—as if this dim questioning of the future, and startled return upon the past,—had between them liquidated the arrears of some haunting moral obligation. If she had indeed been careless of her husband's affairs, it was, her new state seemed to prove, because her faith in him instinctively justified such carelessness; and his right to her faith had overwhelmingly affirmed itself in the very face of menace and suspicion. She had never seen him more untroubled, more naturally and unconsciously in possession of himself, than after the cross-examination to which she had subjected him: it was almost as if he had been aware of her lurking doubts, and had wanted the air cleared as much as she did.

It was as clear, thank Heaven! as the bright outer light that surprised her almost with a touch of summer when she issued from the house for her daily round of the gardens. She had left Boyne at his desk, indulging herself, as she passed the library door, by a last peep at his quiet face, where he bent, pipe in his mouth, above his papers, and now she had her own morning's task to perform. The task involved on such charmed winter days almost as much delighted loitering about the different quarters of her demesne as if spring were already at work on shrubs and borders. There were such inexhaustible possibilities still before her, such opportunities to bring out the latent graces of the old place, without a single irreverent touch of alteration, that the winter months were all too short to plan what spring and autumn executed. And her recovered sense of safety gave, on this particular morning, a peculiar zest to her progress through the sweet, still place. She went first to the kitchen-garden, where the espaliered pear-trees drew complicated patterns on the walls, and pigeons were fluttering and preening about the silvery-slated roof of their cot. There was something wrong about the piping of the hothouse, and she was expecting an authority from Dorchester, who was to drive out between trains and make a diagnosis of the boiler. But when she dipped into the damp heat of the greenhouses, among the spiced scents and waxy pinks and reds of old-fashioned exotics,—even the flora of Lyng was in the note!—she learned that the great man had not arrived, and the day being too rare to waste in an artificial atmosphere, she came out again and paced slowly along the springy turf of the bowling-green to the gardens behind the house. At their farther end rose a grass terrace, commanding, over the fish-pond and the yew hedges, a view of the long house-front, with its twisted chimney-stacks and the blue shadows of its roof angles, all drenched in the pale gold moisture of the air.

Seen thus, across the level tracery of the yews, under the suffused, mild light, it sent her, from its open windows and hospitably smoking chimneys, the look of some warm human presence, of a mind slowly ripened on a sunny wall of experience. She had never before had so deep a sense of her intimacy with it, such a conviction that its secrets were all beneficent, kept, as they said to children, "for one's good," so complete a trust in its power to gather up her life and Ned's into the harmonious pattern of the long, long story it sat there weaving in the sun.

She heard steps behind her, and turned, expecting to see the gardener, accompanied by the engineer from Dorchester. But only one figure was in sight, that of a youngish, slightly built man, who, for reasons she could not on the spot have specified, did not remotely resemble her preconceived notion of an authority on hot-house boilers. The new-comer, on seeing her, lifted his hat, and paused with the air of a gentleman—perhaps a traveler—desirous of having it immediately known that his intrusion is involuntary. The local fame of Lyng occasionally attracted the more intelligent sight-seer, and Mary half-expected to see the stranger dissemble a camera, or justify his presence by producing it. But he made no gesture of any sort, and after a moment she asked, in a tone responding to the courteous deprecation of his attitude: "Is there any one you wish to see?"

"I came to see Mr. Boyne," he replied. His intonation, rather than his accent, was faintly American, and Mary, at the familiar note, looked at him more closely. The brim of his soft felt hat cast a shade on his face, which, thus obscured, wore to her short-sighted gaze a look of seriousness, as of a person arriving "on business," and civilly but firmly aware of his rights.

Past experience had made Mary equally sensible to such claims; but she was jealous of her husband's morning hours, and doubtful of his having given any one the right to intrude on them.

"Have you an appointment with Mr. Boyne?" she asked.

He hesitated, as if unprepared for the question.

"Not exactly an appointment," he replied.

"Then I'm afraid, this being his working-time, that he can't receive you now. Will you give me a message, or come back later?"

The visitor, again lifting his hat, briefly replied that he would come back later, and walked away, as if to regain the front of the house. As his figure receded down the walk between the yew hedges, Mary saw him pause and look up an instant at the peaceful house-front bathed in faint winter sunshine; and it struck her, with a tardy touch of compunction, that it would have been more humane to ask if he had come from a distance, and to offer, in that case, to inquire if her husband could receive him. But as the thought occurred to her he passed out of sight behind a pyramidal yew, and at the same moment her attention was distracted by the approach of the gardener, attended by the bearded pepper-and-salt figure of the boiler-maker from Dorchester.

The encounter with this authority led to such far-reaching issues that they resulted in his finding it expedient to ignore his train, and beguiled Mary into spending the remainder of the morning in absorbed confabulation among the greenhouses. She was startled to find, when the colloquy ended, that it was nearly luncheon-time, and she half expected, as she hurried back to the house, to see her husband coming out to meet her. But she found no one in the court but an under-gardener raking the gravel, and the hall, when she entered it, was so silent that she guessed Boyne to be still at work behind the closed door of the library.

Not wishing to disturb him, she turned into the drawing-room, and there, at her writing-table, lost herself in renewed calculations of the outlay to which the morning's conference had committed her. The knowledge that she could permit herself such follies had not yet lost its novelty; and somehow, in contrast to the vague apprehensions of the previous days, it now seemed an element of her recovered security, of the sense that, as Ned had said, things in general had never been "righter."

She was still luxuriating in a lavish play of figures when the parlor-maid, from the threshold, roused her with a dubiously worded inquiry as to the expediency of serving luncheon. It was one of their jokes that Trimmle announced luncheon as if she were divulging a state secret, and Mary, intent upon her papers, merely murmured an absent-minded assent.

She felt Trimmle wavering expressively on the threshold as if in rebuke of such offhand acquiescence; then her retreating steps sounded down the passage, and Mary, pushing away her papers, crossed the hall, and went to the library door. It was still closed, and she wavered in her turn, disliking to disturb her husband, yet anxious that he should not exceed his normal measure of work. As she stood there, balancing her impulses, the esoteric Trimmle returned with the announcement of luncheon, and Mary, thus impelled, opened the door and went into the library.

Boyne was not at his desk, and she peered about her, expecting to discover him at the book-shelves, somewhere down the length of the room; but her call brought no response, and gradually it became clear to her that he was not in the library.

She turned back to the parlor-maid.

"Mr. Boyne must be up-stairs. Please tell him that luncheon is ready."

The parlor-maid appeared to hesitate between the obvious duty of obeying orders and an equally obvious conviction of the foolishness of the injunction laid upon her. The struggle resulted in her saying doubtfully, "If you please, Madam, Mr. Boyne's not up-stairs."

"Not in his room? Are you sure?"

"I'm sure, Madam."

Mary consulted the clock. "Where is he, then?"

"He's gone out," Trimmle announced, with the superior air of one who has respectfully waited for the question that a well-ordered mind would have first propounded.

Mary's previous conjecture had been right, then. Boyne must have gone to the gardens to meet her, and since she had missed him, it was clear that he had taken the shorter way by the south door, instead of going round to the court. She crossed the hall to the glass portal opening directly on the yew garden, but the parlor-maid, after another moment of inner conflict, decided to bring out recklessly, "Please, Madam, Mr. Boyne didn't go that way."

Mary turned back. "Where *did* he go? And when?"

"He went out of the front door, up the drive, Madam." It was a matter of principle with Trimmle never to answer more than one question at a time.

"Up the drive? At this hour?" Mary went to the door herself, and glanced across the court through the long tunnel of bare limes. But its perspective was as empty as when she had scanned it on entering the house.

"Did Mr. Boyne leave no message?" she asked.

Trimmle seemed to surrender herself to a last struggle with the forces of chaos.

"No, Madam. He just went out with the gentleman."

"The gentleman? What gentleman?" Mary wheeled about, as if to front this new factor.

"The gentleman who called, Madam," said Trimmle, resignedly.

"When did a gentleman call? Do explain yourself, Trimmle!"

Only the fact that Mary was very hungry, and that she wanted to consult her husband about the greenhouses, would have caused her to lay so unusual an injunction on her attendant; and even now she was detached enough to note in Trimmle's eye the dawning defiance of the respectful subordinate who has been pressed too hard.

"I couldn't exactly say the hour, Madam, because I didn't let the gentleman in," she replied, with the air of magnanimously ignoring the irregularity of her mistress's course.

"You didn't let him in?"

"No, Madam. When the bell rang I was dressing, and Agnes—"

"Go and ask Agnes, then," Mary interjected. Trimmle still wore her look of patient magnanimity. "Agnes would not know, Madam, for she had unfortunately burnt her hand in trying the wick of the new lamp from town—" Trimmle, as Mary was aware, had always been opposed to the new lamp—"and so Mrs. Dockett sent the kitchen-maid instead."

Mary looked again at the clock. "It's after two! Go and ask the kitchen-maid if Mr. Boyne left any word."

She went into luncheon without waiting, and Trimmle presently brought her there the kitchen-maid's statement that the gentleman had called about one o'clock, that Mr. Boyne had gone out with him without leaving any message. The kitchen-maid did not even know the caller's name, for he had written it on a slip of paper, which he had folded and handed to her, with the injunction to deliver it at once to Mr. Boyne.

Mary finished her luncheon, still wondering, and when it was over, and Trimmle had brought the coffee to the drawing-room, her wonder had deepened to a first faint tinge of disquietude. It was unlike Boyne to absent himself without explanation at so unwonted an hour, and the difficulty of identifying the visitor whose summons he had apparently obeyed made his disappearance the more unaccountable. Mary Boyne's experience as the wife of a busy engineer, subject to sudden calls and compelled to keep irregular hours, had trained her to the philosophic acceptance of surprises; but since Boyne's withdrawal from business he had adopted a Benedictine regularity of life. As if to make up for the dispersed and agitated years, with their "stand-up" lunches and dinners rattled down to the joltings of the dining-car, he cultivated the last refinements of punctuality and monotony, discouraging his wife's fancy for the unexpected; and declaring that to a delicate taste there were infinite gradations of pleasure in the fixed recurrences of habit.

Still, since no life can completely defend itself from the unforeseen, it was evident that all Boyne's precautions would sooner or later prove unavailable, and Mary concluded that he had cut short a tiresome visit by walking with his caller to the station, or at least accompanying him for part of the way.

This conclusion relieved her from farther preoccupation, and she went out herself to take up her conference with the gardener. Thence she walked to the village post-office, a mile or so away; and when she turned toward home, the early twilight was setting in.

She had taken a foot-path across the downs, and as Boyne, meanwhile, had probably returned from the station by the highroad, there was little likelihood of their meeting on the way. She felt sure, however, of his having reached the house before her; so sure that, when she entered it herself, without even pausing to inquire of Trimmle, she made directly for the library. But the library was still empty, and with an unwonted precision of visual memory she immediately observed that the papers on her husband's desk lay precisely as they had lain when she had gone in to call him to luncheon.

Then of a sudden she was seized by a vague dread of the unknown. She had closed the door behind her on entering, and as she stood alone in the long, silent, shadowy room, her dread seemed to take shape and sound, to be there audibly breathing and lurking among the shadows. Her short-sighted eyes strained through them, half-discerning an actual presence, something aloof, that watched and knew; and in the recoil from that intangible propinquity she threw herself suddenly on the bell-rope and gave it a desperate pull.

The long, quavering summons brought Trimmle in precipitately with a lamp, and Mary breathed again at this sobering reappearance of the usual.

"You may bring tea if Mr. Boyne is in," she said, to justify her ring.

"Very well, Madam. But Mr. Boyne is not in," said Trimmle, putting down the lamp.

"Not in? You mean he's come back and gone out again?"

"No, Madam. He's never been back."

The dread stirred again, and Mary knew that now it had her fast.

"Not since he went out with—the gentleman?"

"Not since he went out with the gentleman."

"But who was the gentleman?" Mary gasped out, with the sharp note of some one trying to be heard through a confusion of meaningless noises.

"That I couldn't say, Madam." Trimmle, standing there by the lamp, seemed suddenly to grow less round and rosy, as though eclipsed by the same creeping shade of apprehension.

"But the kitchen-maid knows—wasn't it the kitchen-maid who let him in?"

"She doesn't know either, Madam, for he wrote his name on a folded paper."

Mary, through her agitation, was aware that they were both designating the unknown visitor by a vague pronoun, instead of the conventional formula which, till then, had kept their allusions within the bounds of custom. And at the same moment her mind caught at the suggestion of the folded paper.

"But he must have a name! Where is the paper?"

She moved to the desk, and began to turn over the scattered documents that littered it. The first that caught her eye was an unfinished letter in her husband's hand, with his pen lying across it, as though dropped there at a sudden summons.

"My dear Parvis,"—who was Parvis?—"I have just received your letter announcing Elwell's death, and while I suppose there is now no farther risk of trouble, it might be safer—"

She tossed the sheet aside, and continued her search; but no folded paper was discoverable among the letters and pages of manuscript which had been swept together in a promiscuous heap, as if by a hurried or a startled gesture.

"But the kitchen-maid saw him. Send her here," she commanded, wondering at her dullness in not thinking sooner of so simple a solution.

Trimmle, at the behest, vanished in a flash, as if thankful to be out of the room, and when she reappeared, conducting the agitated underling, Mary had regained her self-possession, and had her questions pat.

The gentleman was a stranger, yes—that she understood. But what had he said? And, above all, what had he looked like? The first question was easily enough answered, for the disconcerting reason that he had said so little—had merely asked for Mr. Boyne, and, scribbling something on a bit of paper, had requested that it should at once be carried in to him.

"Then you don't know what he wrote? You're not sure it was his name?"

The kitchen-maid was not sure, but supposed it was, since he had written it in answer to her inquiry as to whom she should announce.

"And when you carried the paper in to Mr. Boyne, what did he say?"

The kitchen-maid did not think that Mr. Boyne had said anything, but she could not be sure, for just as she had handed him the paper and he was opening it, she had become aware that the visitor had followed her into the library, and she had slipped out, leaving the two gentlemen together.

"But then, if you left them in the library, how do you know that they went out of the house?"

This question plunged the witness into momentary inarticulateness, from which she was rescued by Trimmle, who, by means of ingenious circumlocutions, elicited the statement that before she could cross the hall to the back passage she had heard the gentlemen behind her, and had seen them go out of the front door together.

"Then, if you saw the gentleman twice, you must be able to tell me what he looked like."

But with this final challenge to her powers of expression it became clear that the limit of the kitchen-maid's endurance had been reached. The obligation of going to the front door to "show in" a visitor was in itself so subversive of the fundamental order of things that it had thrown her faculties into hopeless disarray, and she could only stammer out, after various panting efforts at evocation, "His hat, mum, was different-like, as you might say—"

"Different? How different?" Mary flashed out at her, her own mind, in the same instant, leaping back to an image left on it that morning, but temporarily lost under layers of subsequent impressions.

"His hat had a wide brim, you mean? and his face was pale—a youngish face?" Mary pressed her, with a white-lipped intensity of interrogation. But if the kitchen-maid found any adequate answer to this challenge, it was swept away for her listener down the rushing current of her own convictions. The stranger—the stranger in the garden! Why had Mary not thought of him before? She needed no one now to tell her that it was he who had called for her husband and gone away with him. But who was he, and why had Boyne obeyed his call?

IV

It leaped out at her suddenly, like a grin out of the dark, that they had often called England so little—"such a confoundedly hard place to get lost in."

A confoundedly hard place to get lost in! That had been her husband's phrase. And now, with the whole machinery of official investigation sweeping its flash-lights from shore to shore, and across the dividing straits; now, with Boyne's name blazing from the walls of every town and village, his portrait (how that wrung her!) hawked up and down the country like the image of a hunted criminal; now the little compact, populous island, so policed, surveyed, and administered, revealed itself as a Sphinx-like guardian of abysmal mysteries, staring back into his wife's anguished eyes as if with the malicious joy of knowing something they would never know!

In the fortnight since Boyne's disappearance there had been no word of him, no trace of his movements. Even the usual misleading reports that raise expectancy in tortured bosoms had been few and fleeting. No one but the bewildered kitchen-maid had seen him leave the house, and no one else had seen "the gentleman" who accompanied him. All inquiries in the neighborhood failed to elicit the memory of a stranger's presence that day in the neighborhood of Lyng. And no one had met Edward Boyne, either alone or in company, in any of the neighboring villages, or on the road across the downs, or at either of the local railway-stations. The sunny English noon had swallowed him as completely as if he had gone out into Cimmerian night.

Mary, while every external means of investigation was working at its highest pressure, had ransacked her husband's papers for any trace of antecedent complications, of entanglements or obligations unknown to her, that might throw a faint ray into the darkness. But if any such had existed in the background of Boyne's life, they had disappeared as completely as the slip of paper on which the visitor had written his name. There remained no possible thread of guidance except—if it were indeed an exception—the letter which Boyne had apparently been in the act of writing when he received his mysterious summons. That letter, read and reread by his wife, and submitted by her to the police, yielded little enough for conjecture to feed on.

"I have just heard of Elwell's death, and while I suppose there is now no farther risk of trouble, it might be safer—" That was all. The "risk of trouble" was easily explained by the newspaper clipping which had apprised Mary of the suit brought against her husband by one of his associates in the Blue Star enterprise. The only new information conveyed in the letter was the fact of its showing Boyne, when he wrote it, to be still apprehensive of the results of the suit, though he had assured his wife that it had been withdrawn, and though the letter itself declared that the plaintiff was dead. It took several weeks of exhaustive cabling to fix the identity of the "Parvis" to whom the fragmentary communication was addressed, but even after these inquiries had shown him to be a Waukesha lawyer, no new facts concerning the Elwell suit were elicited. He appeared to have had no direct concern in it, but to have been conversant with the facts merely as an acquaintance, and possible intermediary; and he declared himself unable to divine with what object Boyne intended to seek his assistance.

This negative information, sole fruit of the first fortnight's feverish search, was not increased by a jot during the slow weeks that followed. Mary knew that the investigations were still being carried on, but she had a vague sense of their gradually slackening, as the actual march of time seemed to slacken. It was as though the days, flying horror-struck from the shrouded image of the one inscrutable day, gained assurance as the distance lengthened, till at last they fell back into their normal gait. And so with the human imaginations at work on the dark event. No doubt it occupied them still, but week by week and hour by hour it grew less absorbing, took up less space, was slowly but inevitably crowded out of the foreground of consciousness by the new problems perpetually bubbling up from the vaporous caldron of human experience.

Even Mary Boyne's consciousness gradually felt the same lowering of velocity. It still swayed with the incessant oscillations of conjecture; but they were slower, more rhythmical in their beat. There were moments of overwhelming lassitude when, like the victim of some poison which leaves the brain clear, but holds the body motionless, she saw herself domesticated with the Horror, accepting its perpetual presence as one of the fixed conditions of life.

These moments lengthened into hours and days, till she passed into a phase of stolid acquiescence. She watched the familiar routine of life with the incurious eye of a savage on whom the meaningless processes of civilization make but the faintest impression. She had come to regard herself as part of the routine, a spoke of the wheel, revolving with its motion; she felt almost like the furniture of the room in which she sat, an insensate object to be dusted and pushed about with the chairs and tables. And this deepening apathy held her fast at Lyng, in spite of the urgent entreaties of friends and the usual medical recommendation of "change." Her friends supposed that her refusal to move was inspired by the belief that her husband would one day return to the spot from which he had vanished, and a beautiful legend grew up about this imaginary state of waiting. But in reality she had no such belief: the depths of anguish inclosing her were no longer lighted by flashes of hope. She was sure that Boyne would never come back, that he had gone out of her sight as completely as if Death itself had waited that day on the threshold. She had even renounced, one by one, the various theories as to his disappearance which had been advanced by the press, the police, and her own agonized imagination. In sheer lassitude her mind turned from these alternatives of horror, and sank back into the blank fact that he was gone.

No, she would never know what had become of him—no one would ever know. But the house knew; the library in which she spent her long, lonely evenings knew. For it was here that the last scene had been enacted, here that the stranger had come, and spoken the word which had caused Boyne to rise and follow him. The floor she trod had felt his tread; the books on the shelves had seen his face; and there were moments when the intense consciousness of the old, dusky walls seemed about to break out into some audible revelation of their secret. But the revelation never came, and she knew it would never come. Lyng was not one of the garrulous old houses that betray the secrets intrusted to them. Its very legend proved that it had always been the mute accomplice, the incorruptible custodian of the mysteries it had surprised. And Mary Boyne, sitting face to face with its portentous silence, felt the futility of seeking to break it by any human means.

V

"I don't say it wasn't straight, yet don't say it was straight. It was business."

Mary, at the words, lifted her head with a start, and looked intently at the speaker.

When, half an hour before, a card with "Mr. Parvis" on it had been brought up to her, she had been immediately aware that the name had been a part of her consciousness ever since she had read it at the head of Boyne's unfinished letter. In the library she had found awaiting her a small neutral-tinted man with a bald head and gold eye-glasses, and it sent a strange tremor through her to know that this was the person to whom her husband's last known thought had been directed.

Parvis, civilly, but without vain preamble,—in the manner of a man who has his watch in his hand,—had set forth the object of his visit. He had "run over" to England on business, and finding himself in the neighborhood of Dorchester, had not wished to leave it without paying his respects to Mrs. Boyne; without asking her, if the occasion offered, what she meant to do about Bob Elwell's family.

The words touched the spring of some obscure dread in Mary's bosom. Did her visitor, after all, know what Boyne had meant by his unfinished phrase? She asked for an elucidation of his question, and noticed at once that he seemed surprised at her continued ignorance of the subject. Was it possible that she really knew as little as she said?

"I know nothing—you must tell me," she faltered out; and her visitor thereupon proceeded to unfold his story. It threw, even to her confused perceptions, and imperfectly initiated vision, a lurid glare on the whole hazy episode of the Blue Star Mine. Her husband had made his money in that brilliant speculation at the cost of "getting ahead" of some one less alert to seize the chance; the victim of his ingenuity was young Robert Elwell, who had "put him on" to the Blue Star scheme.

Parvis, at Mary's first startled cry, had thrown her a sobering glance through his impartial glasses.

"Bob Elwell wasn't smart enough, that's all; if he had been, he might have turned round and served Boyne the same way. It's the kind of thing that happens every day in business. I guess it's what the scientists call the survival of the fittest," said Mr. Parvis, evidently pleased with the aptness of his analogy.

Mary felt a physical shrinking from the next question she tried to frame; it was as though the words on her lips had a taste that nauseated her.

"But then—you accuse my husband of doing something dishonorable?"

Mr. Parvis surveyed the question dispassionately. "Oh, no, I don't. I don't even say it wasn't straight." He glanced up and down the long lines of books, as if one of them might have supplied him with the definition he sought. "I don't say it wasn't straight, and yet I don't say it was straight. It was business." After all, no definition in his category could be more comprehensive than that.

Mary sat staring at him with a look of terror. He seemed to her like the indifferent, implacable emissary of some dark, formless power.

"But Mr. Elwell's lawyers apparently did not take your view, since I suppose the suit was withdrawn by their advice."

"Oh, yes, they knew he hadn't a leg to stand on, technically. It was when they advised him to withdraw the suit that he got desperate. You see, he'd borrowed most of the money he lost in the Blue Star, and he was up a tree. That's why he shot himself when they told him he had no show."

The horror was sweeping over Mary in great, deafening waves.

"He shot himself? He killed himself because of *that?*"

"Well, he didn't kill himself, exactly. He dragged on two months before he died." Parvis emitted the statement as unemotionally as a gramophone grinding out its "record."

"You mean that he tried to kill himself, and failed? And tried again?"

"Oh, he didn't have to try again," said Parvis, grimly.

They sat opposite each other in silence, he swinging his eye-glass thoughtfully about his finger, she, motionless, her arms stretched along her knees in an attitude of rigid tension.

"But if you knew all this," she began at length, hardly able to force her voice above a whisper, "how is it that when I wrote you at the time of my husband's disappearance you said you didn't understand his letter?"

Parvis received this without perceptible discomfiture. "Why, I didn't understand it—strictly speaking. And it wasn't the time to talk about it, if I had. The Elwell business was settled when the suit was withdrawn. Nothing I could have told you would have helped you to find your husband."

Mary continued to scrutinize him. "Then why are you telling me now?"

Still Parvis did not hesitate. "Well, to begin with, I supposed you knew more than you appear to—I mean about the circumstances of Elwell's death. And then people are talking of it now; the whole matter's been raked up again. And I thought, if you didn't know, you ought to."

She remained silent, and he continued: "You see, it's only come out lately what a bad state Elwell's affairs were in. His wife's a proud woman, and she fought on as long as she could, going out to work, and taking sewing at home, when she got too sick—something with the heart, I believe. But she had his bedridden mother to look after, and the children, and she broke down under it, and finally had to ask for help. That attracted attention to the case, and the papers took it up, and a subscription was started. Everybody out there liked Bob Elwell, and most of the prominent names in the place are down on the list, and people began to wonder why—"

Parvis broke off to fumble in an inner pocket. "Here," he continued, "here's an account of the whole thing from the *Sentinel*—a little sensational, of course. But I guess you'd better look it over."

He held out a newspaper to Mary, who unfolded it slowly, remembering, as she did so, the evening when, in that same room, the perusal of a clipping from the *Sentinel* had first shaken the depths of her security.

As she opened the paper, her eyes, shrinking from the glaring head-lines, "Widow of Boyne's Victim Forced to Appeal for Aid," ran down the column of text to two portraits inserted in it. The first was her husband's, taken from a photograph made the year they had come to England. It was the picture of him that she liked best, the one that stood on the writing-table up-stairs in her bedroom. As the eyes in the photograph met hers, she felt it would be impossible to read what was said of him, and closed her lids with the sharpness of the pain.

"I thought if you felt disposed to put your name down—" she heard Parvis continue.

She opened her eyes with an effort, and they fell on the other portrait. It was that of a youngish man, slightly built, in rough clothes, with features somewhat blurred by the shadow of a projecting hat-brim. Where had she seen that outline before? She stared at it confusedly, her heart hammering in her throat and ears. Then she gave a cry.

"This is the man—the man who came for my husband!"

She heard Parvis start to his feet, and was dimly aware that she had slipped backward into the corner of the sofa, and that he was bending above her in alarm. With an intense effort she straightened herself, and reached out for the paper, which she had dropped.

"It's the man! I should know him anywhere!" she cried in a voice that sounded in her own ears like a scream.

Parvis's voice seemed to come to her from far off, down endless, fog-muffled windings.

"Mrs. Boyne, you're not very well. Shall I call somebody? Shall I get a glass of water?"

"No, no, no!" She threw herself toward him, her hand frantically clenching the newspaper. "I tell you, it's the man! I know him! He spoke to me in the garden!"

Parvis took the journal from her, directing his glasses to the portrait. "It can't be, Mrs. Boyne. It's Robert Elwell."

"Robert Elwell?" Her white stare seemed to travel into space. "Then it was Robert Elwell who came for him."

"Came for Boyne? The day he went away?" Parvis's voice dropped as hers rose. He bent over, laying a fraternal hand on her, as if to coax her gently back into her seat. "Why, Elwell was dead! Don't you remember?"

Mary sat with her eyes fixed on the picture, unconscious of what he was saying.

"Don't you remember Boyne's unfinished letter to me—the one you found on his desk that day? It was written just after he'd heard of Elwell's death." She noticed an odd shake in Parvis's unemotional voice. "Surely you remember that!" he urged her.

Yes, she remembered: that was the profoundest horror of it. Elwell had died the day before her husband's disappearance; and this was Elwell's portrait; and it was the portrait of the man who had spoken to her in the garden. She lifted her head and looked slowly about the library. The library could have borne witness that it was also the portrait of the man who had come in that day to call Boyne from his unfinished letter. Through the misty surgings of her brain she heard the faint boom of half-forgotten words—words spoken by Alida Stair on the lawn at Pangbourne before Boyne and his wife had ever seen the house at Lyng, or had imagined that they might one day live there.

"This was the man who spoke to me," she repeated.

She looked again at Parvis. He was trying to conceal his disturbance under what he imagined to be an expression of indulgent commiseration; but the edges of his lips were blue. "He thinks me mad; but I'm not mad," she reflected; and suddenly there flashed upon her a way of justifying her strange affirmation.

She sat quiet, controlling the quiver of her lips, and waiting till she could trust her voice to keep its habitual level; then she said, looking straight at Parvis: "Will you answer me one question, please? When was it that Robert Elwell tried to kill himself?"

"When—when?" Parvis stammered.

"Yes; the date. Please try to remember."

She saw that he was growing still more afraid of her. "I have a reason," she insisted gently.

"Yes, yes. Only I can't remember. About two months before, I should say."

"I want the date," she repeated.

Parvis picked up the newspaper. "We might see here," he said, still humoring her. He ran his eyes down the page. "Here it is. Last October—the—"

She caught the words from him. "The 20th, wasn't it?" With a sharp look at her, he verified. "Yes, the 20th. Then you *did* know?"

"I know now." Her white stare continued to travel past him. "Sunday, the 20th—that was the day he came first."

Parvis's voice was almost inaudible. "Came *here* first?"

"Yes."

"You saw him twice, then?"

"Yes, twice." She breathed it at him with dilated eyes. "He came first on the 20th of October. I remember the date because it was the day we went up Meldon Steep for the first time." She felt a faint gasp of inward laughter at the thought that but for that she might have forgotten.

Parvis continued to scrutinize her, as if trying to intercept her gaze.

"We saw him from the roof," she went on. "He came down the lime-avenue toward the house. He was dressed just as he is in that picture. My husband saw him first. He was frightened, and ran down ahead of me; but there was no one there. He had vanished."

"Elwell had vanished?" Parvis faltered.

"Yes." Their two whispers seemed to grope for each other. "I couldn't think what had happened. I see now. He *tried* to come then; but he wasn't dead enough—he couldn't reach us. He had to wait for two months; and then he came back again—and Ned went with him."

She nodded at Parvis with the look of triumph of a child who has successfully worked out a difficult puzzle. But suddenly she lifted her hands with a desperate gesture, pressing them to her bursting temples.

"Oh, my God! I sent him to Ned—I told him where to go! I sent him to this room!" she screamed out.

She felt the walls of the room rush toward her, like inward falling ruins;

and she heard Parvis, a long way off, as if through the ruins, crying to her, and struggling to get at her. But she was numb to his touch, she did not know what he was saying. Through the tumult she heard but one clear note, the voice of Alida Stair, speaking on the lawn at Pangbourne.

"You won't know till afterward," it said. "You won't know till long, long afterward."

POEMS

Sara Teasdale

BARTER

Life has loveliness to sell,
    All beautiful and splendid things,
Blue waves whitened on a cliff,
    Soaring fire that sways and sings,
And children's faces looking up
Holding wonder like a cup.

Life has loveliness to sell,
    Music like a curve of gold,
Scent of pine trees in the rain,
    Eyes that love you, arms that hold,
And for your spirit's still delight,
Holy thoughts that star the night.

Spend all you have for loveliness,
    Buy it and never count the cost;
For one white singing hour of peace
    Count many a year of strife well lost,
And for a breath of ecstasy
Give all you have been, or could be.

THERE WILL COME SOFT RAINS

There will come soft rains and the smell of the ground,
And swallows circling with their shimmering sound;

And frogs in the pools singing at night,
And wild plum trees in tremulous white,

Robins will wear their feathery fire
Whistling their whims on a low fence-wire;

And not one will know of the war, not one
Will care at last when it is done.

Not one would mind, neither bird nor tree
If mankind perished utterly;

And Spring herself, when she woke at dawn,
Would scarcely know that we were gone.

WINTER STARS

I went out at night alone;
    The young blood flowing beyond the sea
Seemed to have drenched my spirit's wings—
    I bore my sorrow heavily.

But when I lifted up my head
    From shadows shaken on the snow,
I saw Orion in the east
    Burn steadily as long ago.

From windows in my father's house,
    Dreaming my dreams on winter nights,
I watched Orion as a girl
    Above another city's lights.

Years go, dreams go, and youth goes too,
    The world's heart breaks beneath its wars,
All things are changed, save in the east
    The faithful beauty of the stars.